BRAZIL

BRAZIL

Errol Lincoln Uys

Silver Spring Books

Cover designed by Hope Forstenzer
Original cover illustration by Yves Besnier

Maps by Palacios

Text designed and typeset by Syllables

Printed and bound by Cushing-Malloy, Inc

Reprinted with the permission of Simon & Schuster, from BRAZIL by Errol Lincoln Uys. Copyright © 1986 by Errol Lincoln Uys.

Published by Silver Spring Books

Library of Congress Card Number: 00-104182

ISBN: 0-916562-51-4

Editorial Sales Rights and Permissions Inquiries should be addressed to:
Silver Spring Books, 8 Gray's Farm Road, Weston, CT 06883
Email: dww@lb.com

Manufactured in the United States of America
1 3 5 7 9 10 8 6 4 2

Distributed by LPC Group
1-800-626-4330

For my wife, Janette,
with love and thanks

Contents

Author's Note
to the New Edition

"Why choose Brazil as your subject?" people ask me. I immigrated to America from South Africa in 1977. One of my first assignments was with James A. Michener, the renowned historical novelist, working for two years as assistant on his South African book, *The Covenant*. We spoke about countries with an epic history that would lend itself to a novel on a grand scale. One of the places I suggested was Brazil, which has captivated me since I was a boy. In childhood, eccentric foreigners like the English engineer-explorer-mystic, Percy Fawcett, whose Amazon exploits filled the pages of adventure magazines like *Wide World*, fired my imagination.

When I decided to write *Brazil*, my choice was more complex. My birthplace was South Africa, where laws kept the races apart, a striking contrast to the racial melting pot of Brazil. I wanted to know what made the critical difference in the development of the two countries.

And then, too, there was my new home, the United States, where I found an ignorance about Brazil at every level of society, from the apocryphal "They speak Spanish, don't they?" to stereotypes about Carnival, samba, the Amazon and the beaches. The more I read and studied, the stronger my desire to help dispel this shallow view.

It was critical to have first-hand experience of the country. In April 1981, I began my research in Portugal, before traveling to Brazil, where I covered 15,000 miles, almost exclusively by bus to get a feel for that vast land. My journey took me into the *sertão*, the arid backlands of the Northeast and to the *Casas Grandes* of coastal Pernambuco. I voyaged the Amazon from Belém to Manaus and rode by bus down to southernmost Rondonia. I followed the route of the *bandeirantes*, the Brazilian pathfinders, west of São Paulo and roamed the highlands of Minas Gerais.

The writing of *Brazil* took five years. Like my fictional hero, Amador Flôres da Silva, I knew periods of utter loneliness and fear; times when I felt the *caatinga* closing in on me but always, I broke through the barrier. I never lost the will to understand the Brazilian "thing."

The Cavalcantis of Santo Tomás and the da Silvas of Itatinga and most of the incidents involving these two families are fictional. Aruanã, Segge Proot, Black Peter, the Ferreiras, Antônio Paciência, Bruno Salgado — these, too, are imaginary characters. The towns of Rosário and Jurema in Pernambuco and Tiberica in São Paulo do not exist.

King Afonso I of the Kongo; Nobrega and Anchieta; Tomé de Sousa; Mem de Sá; Raposo Tavares; Johan Maurits of Nassau-Siegen; "Ganga Zumba" of Palmares; Marquis of Pombal; Bento Parente Maciel; "Tooth-Puller;" Emperor Pedro II; President Francisco Solano Lopez; Eliza Lynch; Joaquim Nabuco; Antônio Conselheiro — these are real characters and what is said of them relates to recorded history.

The enslavement and massacre of the Brazilian Indians; the path-finding and prospecting journeys of the bandeirantes; the Lisbon earthquake; the republican uprising at Minas Gerais; the Paraguayan War; the abolition of slavery; the rebellion at Canudos; the birth of Brasília — these principle Brazilian historical events are faithfully summarized within the context of the novel.

I could not have accomplished *Brazil* without the help of numerous Brazilians on that long journey, including: José Honôrio Rodrigues; Gilberto Freyre; Fernando Freyre; Antônio Fantinato Netto; Max Justo Guedes; Eduardo Matarazzo Suplicy; Luiz Hafers; Edson Nery da Fonseca; Aluysio Magalhães; Vladimir Murtinho; Roberto Motta; Oswaldo Lima Filho; José Antonio Gonçalves de Mello; Fernando Antonio Novaes; Carlos Rizzini; Anna Amelia Viêra Nascimento; Antonietta de Aguiar Nunes; Amalia Correa; Christina Mattos; Eduardo Borcacov. Plus countless Brazilians I met along the way, like "Black Jimi" Carvalho, who showed me a tough side of Recife I would never have seen without his guidance. People like the anonymous woman in the bus station at Brasília, who asked a few coins to buy oranges for her child — all she could hope for on a thirty-six-hour trip that lay ahead. I never forgot her or many others who showed me the face and soul of Brazil.

My thanks to Herman Gollob, who guided this massive project through those five years. I am grateful to David Wilk of Silver Spring Books, whose enthusiasm and faith has brought *Brazil* back into print.

Publication of the new edition coincides with the nation's celebration of the 500-year anniversary of the arrival of the Portuguese explorer, Pedro Álvares Cabral. — The original work ended at the inauguration of Brasília in 1960. I have added an "Afterword" that brings the story up to April 2000. Returning to the manuscript after fifteen years, I have also cast a fresh eye over the core of the book, editing sections to make the journey that much easier and more captivating for the reader-explorer of *Brazil*.

Errol Lincoln Uys
Cambridge, Massachusetts
April 2000
www.erroluys.com

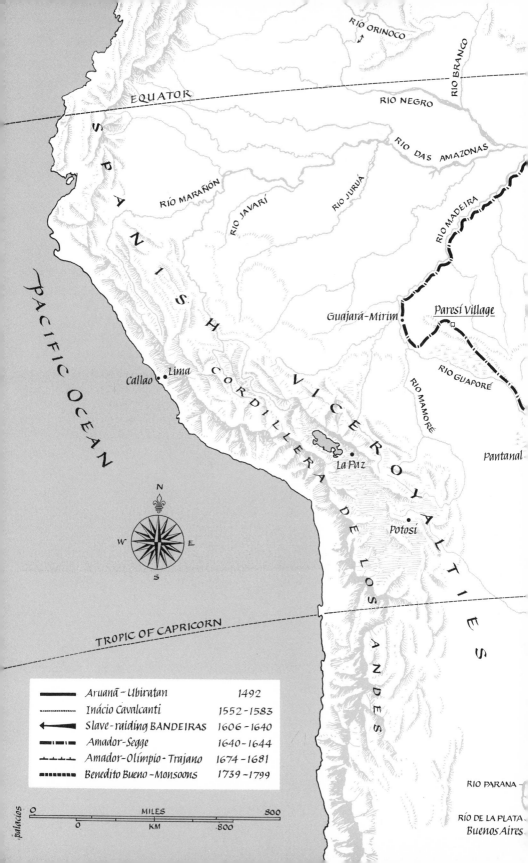

RÍO ORINOCO

RÍO BRANCO

EQUATOR

RÍO NEGRO

SPANISH

RÍO DAS AMAZONAS

RÍO MARAÑÓN

RÍO JURUÁ

RÍO JAVARÍ

RÍO MADEIRA

Guajará-Mirim

Paresí Village

CORDILLERA

PACIFIC OCEAN

Callao · Lima

RÍO GUAPORÉ

VICEROYALTIES

RÍO MAMORÉ

· La Paz

Pantanal

N

W   E

S

· Potosí

DE LOS ANDES

TROPIC OF CAPRICORN

	Aruanã – Ubiratan	1492
	Inácio Cavalcanti	1552–1583
←	Slave-raiding BANDEIRAS	1606–1640
	Amador–Segge	1640–1644
	Amador–Olímpio–Trajano	1674–1681
	Benedito Bueno–Monsoons	1739–1799

palacios

0	MILES	800
0	KM	800

RÍO PARANA

RÍO DE LA PLATA

Buenos Aires

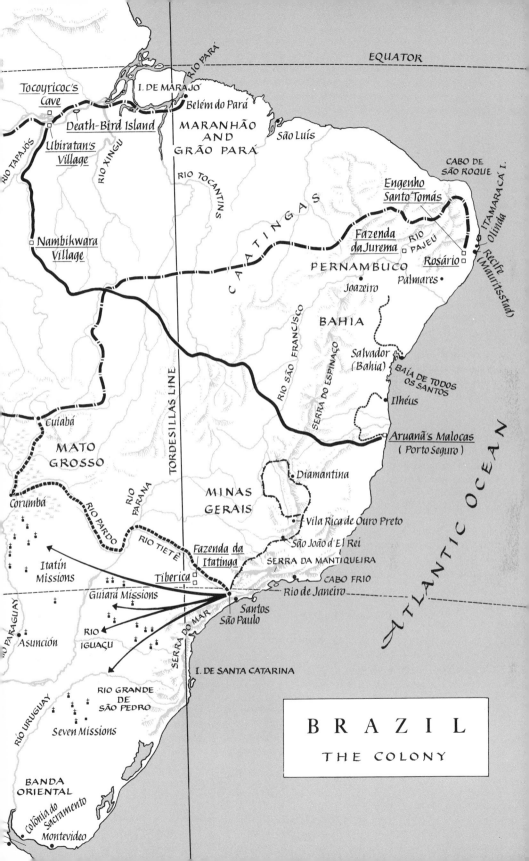

EQUATOR

RIO PARÁ

Tocoyricoc's Cave

I. DE MARAJÓ

Belém do Pará

Death-Bird Island

Ubiratan's Village

RIO TAPAJÓS

RIO XINGU

MARANHÃO AND GRÃO PARÁ

São Luís

RIO TOCANTINS

CABO DE SÃO ROQUE

ITAMARACÁ I.

Engenho Santo Tomás

Fazenda da Jurema

RIO PAJEÚ

PERNAMBUCO

Rosário

Olinda

Recife (Mauritsstad)

Nambikwara Village

C A A T I N G A S

Joazeiro

Palmares

BAHIA

RIO SÃO FRANCISCO

Salvador (Bahia)

BAÍA DE TODOS OS SANTOS

SERRA DO ESPINAÇO

Ilhéus

TORDESILLAS LINE

Cuiabá

MATO GROSSO

Aruanã's Malocas (Porto Seguro)

A T L A N T I C   O C E A N

Corumbá

RIO PARDO

RIO PARANÁ

Diamantina

MINAS GERAIS

Vila Rica de Ouro Preto

RIO TIETÊ

Fazenda da Itatinga

São João d'El Rei

RÍO PARAGUAY

Itatín Missions

Tiberica

SERRA DA MANTIQUEIRA

Guiara Missions

CABO FRIO

RIO IGUAÇU

Rio de Janeiro

Santos São Paulo

SERRA DO MAR

Asunción

I. DE SANTA CATARINA

RÍO URUGUAY

RIO GRANDE DE SÃO PEDRO

Seven Missions

BANDA ORIENTAL

Colônia do Sacramento

Montevideo

BRAZIL

THE COLONY

PROLOGUE

The Tupiniquin

I

May 1491

*T*he boy was sitting beside a branch of the river that marked the end of his people's place. These lesser waters struggled through the clan's fields, their way broken here and there by the trunks of fallen trees, until their stream was lost in this green island.

He was Aruanã, son of Pojucan, and stood taller than most boys of his age. His mother, Obapira, had counted the first four or five seasons following his birth but then stopped, for the next age that mattered would come when he was ready for manhood. Now he had reached this stage. His limbs were well formed, his shoulders sturdy and straight. His jet-black hair was shaved back in a half-moon above the temples, from ear to ear, and his eyebrows were plucked. His lower lip was bored through in the custom of his people, and in it he wore a plug of white bone as large as his thumb.

Aruanã dangled his feet in the cool water. No one ever came here, because it was too shallow for bathing and the fish were few and miserable, but such a place suited his thoughts this afternoon.

Could he not remember, two Great Rains past, when he would lie awake in the longhouse, listening to the sacred music from the clearing, rhythms that held back the sounds of the jungle, as the villagers sang the praises of his father, Pojucan, the Warrior, Pojucan, the Hunter? But Pojucan had stopped going to the celebrations and would hunt alone, often without success. And when Pojucan had become an outcast, so had his son, who was teased and taunted by his companions.

When they played the games of animals, Aruanã had to be the small rodent, Kanuatsin, who lived at the edge of the forest, and was forced to dash about, squeaking shrilly, until the others pounced upon him. At the river, they would lie in wait and ambush him when he went to swim: "Run, Aruanã, run to your sisters! Hurry to the fields of the women, for you'll never be a warrior!"

These torments had begun only after his father started to walk alone. Aruanã's early childhood had been happy: days of riding to the fields in the soft fiber sling at his mother's side, and playing in the sands while she worked with her digging stick, until he was able to stalk small birds and insects with the little bow and arrow made by Pojucan. Twice within the first five Great Rains of his life, the people had abandoned the village for the forest; but, to Aruanã, the migrations had been a tremendous adventure. Nor had he felt fear when his people prepared for war: As far back as he could remember, not a single enemy had got beyond the heavy stakes that protected his home. And hadn't he himself survived this long without being touched by the beings that dwelt in the depths of the forest and were known to devour children?

No sooner had this thought entered his mind than he detected a movement a little way downstream at the edge of the water. He sat absolutely still, his eyes riveted on the place where the undergrowth had been disturbed, listening intently for a sound.

Was it Caipora, stunted forest spirit, of whom his people spoke only in whispers? No one he knew had actually seen the tiny one-legged naked woman who hopped around in the shadows, and this was their good fortune, for her gaze brought the greatest misfortune to whoever looked into those fiery red eyes.

To his relief, it was not Caipora but the young otter, Ariranha, who peeked out at him, made some tentative gestures toward the water, and then dashed back into his hiding place. Aruanã did nothing that might alarm the little animal. After a while, there was a slight rustling sound as the otter poked his broad muzzle through the leaves and then took to the water.

Aruanã pictured the otter splashing upstream to his family and knew that he, too, must leave this place. The sun would be on the fields beyond, but its light was fading from the roof of the forest and it would soon be as night where he stood. He would want to think of himself as bold as Ariranha, but even a warrior like his father could fear this dark.

And what more does Pojucan fear? a voice within him asked. *What has he done to make his people see him worse than an enemy?*

It was true. Even those they took prisoner were more welcome in the clan, for as long as permitted by the elders. The sisters of his people would take the captives into their hammocks; they would be feasted and fed; songs would be sung about them. But, for Pojucan, there was only silence. And more than this, for Aruanã had observed that other men looked at his father as if he were invisible.

Aruanã emerged from the trees at the top of a gentle rise that sloped toward the village. An ugly tangle of scorched creeper and shrub marked where his people had slashed and burned the forest. Trees that had survived the flames stood black and stark against the sky; others lay uprooted and shattered in the ash. Farther down, beyond this uncleared land, were patchworks of plantings of *manioc*. In the language of his people, *mandi* meant bread and *oca* the house.

The village below was the largest his people had built, and had been enclosed by a double stockade of heavy posts lashed together with vines — two great circles that protected the five dwellings arranged around a central clearing. These *malocas* were no rude forest huts but the grand lodges of the five great families of the clan, and in each there lived more than a hundred men, women, and children. Two bowshots in length, or sixty paces, ten paces broad and of the same height, they were raised by an elaborate framework of beams and rafters held together with twigs and creepers and thatched with the fine fronds of the pindoba palm.

Aruanã passed through the stockade and was heading toward his maloca when a boy came up to him and announced: "Naurú has asked for the feathers of Macaw. We have been called to listen this night."

Aruanã was delighted: This meant that he would soon be taking his first step toward manhood.

Naurú, the *pagé* — prophet, seer, medicine man — had been keeping his eye on this group of boys for some time. Now he had given the word that the brilliant red and blue macaw feathers of his rattles needed replacing, his way of indicating that the boys must prepare for initiation.

෴

Tabajara, the elder of Aruanã's maloca, summoned his wives, and for two hours submitted himself to their attentions. There was Potira, little more than a child, with small, firm breasts and wide eyes; Sumá, who swam like a fish and had a magnificent body that brought great pleasure when he was alone with her; and Moema, "Old Mother," who had come first and never let the others forget this.

When Tabajara's body had to be painted, Old Mother would not let anyone else collect the colors from the fruit of the genipapo and the berry of the urucu tree — the one blue-black, the other an orangy red. Her fingers traced the most striking patterns on Tabajara's flesh. Sharp black strokes accented the permanently tattooed marks on his chest — as many stripes as the enemy he had slain. She filled in between the slashes with the red of the urucu. From his midriff down, she divided the marked part of his body into sections, painting half red, the other black, and repeated these designs on his back.

Of course, she could make life difficult, with her sharp tongue and interfering ways; still, he'd secretly allow that there was more in Old Mother than in the others.

He saw Aruanã enter the maloca and caught Old Mother's look as she followed the boy's progress toward the far end of the house.

"I see his unhappiness," Old Mother said. "It is not good that a boy must live with this."

"A boy must learn many things," Tabajara replied, "beginning with what he hears this night."

"This is the trouble of——"

"One who must not be named," he said quickly.

"It was not on my lips," she snapped at him.

"But in your thoughts?"

Her reply was to work the urucu dye onto his back with angry jabs.

Tabajara didn't want to discuss this problem with Old Mother. The boy's father had disgraced the clan, a dishonor that rested heaviest upon his maloca, since all under its roof were of the same blood. He saw Aruanã go to his hammock, and made a mental note to watch the boy closely for any sign of the weakness his father had shown.

Potira was on her knees, with Sumá, working on one of the few items Tabajara valued as a personal possession: a majestic cloak of brilliant scarlet made of hundreds of ibis feathers, selected with the greatest care for uniformity of size and color, linked together one by one with fiber string and attached to a cotton backing.

Tabajara also prized his other feather adornments: a high headdress of bright yellow and an ostrich bustle he'd wear on his rump.

Now only his face remained to be painted, but before Old Mother attended to this, she inspected him closely — and gave a little cry of triumph when she found a tiny hair at the edge of an eyelid. He gritted his teeth, great warrior that he was, when Old Mother plucked out the offending growth, gripping it with the edges of two small shells.

His face finally painted, Tabajara put the finishing touches to his appearance: He slipped a green stone, twice the size of the simple bone plug worn by Aruanã, into the hole in his lower lip, making it protrude in a way that brought murmurs of approval from his wives.

~

It was the first time the boys had seen the elders in full dress for their benefit alone. They sat in a semicircle on the ground between the malocas.

Tabajara was shorter than most men of the clan, but with his tall diadem he appeared as a giant before the boys.

"Sleep soundly this night, O Macaw, bird of the forest, wing of our ancestors," he said. "Sleep soundly, for those that will seek you are as worms of the dawn. How our enemies will rejoice when these poor things are sent against their villages."

His words were greeted with approving noises from the other elders, and the men, who stood around the clearing, echoed their feeling between gulps of fresh beer from the gourds passed among them.

Aruanã wanted the earth to take him when Tabajara, who had been pacing in front of them, stopped opposite him, the light from the log fires deepening the shades on his body and making his appearance as fearsome as anything Aruanã imagined among the spirits that filled the darkness.

"To your feet, boy!"

Aruanã scrambled up.

"Step closer to the fire so all may behold." When the boy was in the light, Tabajara went on: "Tell me, my child, why there is hope that you will find the feathers of Macaw."

Aruanã felt his heart pounding in his chest. "It is my wish to be a man of this tribe," he said, with firmness that surprised even him. "This is my first duty, to get the pagé's feathers, and I will not fail."

"Strong words, my child, but to find Macaw, you have to enter the forest alone. There will be no warriors to silence your whimpers. What if Caipora dances in your path? What if the one who seeks *tabak* is there?"

Tobacco Man, a specter like the woman who hopped on one leg, lay in wait for lone warriors and demanded the sacred herb, attacking them if they failed to supply it. "I cannot say what I will do."

The boy was honest, Tabajara thought. He was surprised that this son of the nameless one should answer so forthrightly and show so little fear in front of the elders. Many boys would be too frightened to utter a word.

Suddenly, all eyes turned as out of the shadows crept an ugly figure, mumbling incoherently. Among his people, Naurú was the only one with a physical defect — a bent back and twisted leg. Ordinarily among the Tupiniquin, deformed children were killed at birth, for their tortured bodies revealed the displeasure of the spirits. But Naurú's mother had disobeyed this dictate and hidden him in a secret place at the edge of the forest, until the passing of several Great Rains, and his survival was seen as miraculously intended by those same spirits who would have condemned him. The terrifyingly lonely time in a shelter his mother had scratched out of a riverbank had left him with a cold, solitary manner and a certain ignorance of those things boys of his age feared about the forest. He soon came to the attention of the former village pagé, who had led him to the secrets of that mystical world where ordinary men were interlopers.

When Naurú approached him, Aruanã's earlier bravado vanished under the icy stare of the keeper of the sacred rattles.

"I know this boy," Naurú said, not mumbling now but in a voice that all might hear. "He is from your maloca."

"There are three children in my house who seek your feathers," Tabajara replied. "Aruanã is one." Tabajara approached any confrontation with Naurú with extreme caution.

The village had no chief as such, the elders sharing in its leadership, but Tabajara's presence was generally acknowledged as the most imposing, especially when Tabajara led the warriors of the clan. Only one other man held a position of equal respect – Naurú.

"Why, when he stood up, did I feel something dark arise between us?"

"I cannot answer this," Tabajara said. He quickly saw that it had been a serious mistake to put the boy where he would attract attention.

"This is the child of a man who has brought dishonor to his people," Naurú continued.

Aruanã was trembling.

"Does Naurú wish this boy kept from the search for the feathers?" Tabajara asked.

"No, he must go," the pagé said immediately. "But I am curious, elder, why you still have the father in your maloca. It is bad for the village to be reminded of the shame he has brought. He may not be seen, but he is among us."

Tabajara knew that the death of the nameless one was being demanded. He saw the agony in the boy's face and wondered if, young as he was, he realized it.

"What you have said, Naurú, rests heavily with me. I will beseech the ancestors to help one who should have been more wakeful." Tabajara was determined that the matter be taken no further this night, and shifted his talk back to the boys. "Go — sit with the others!" he told Aruanã.

He saw Naurú scuttle away, pushing through the crowd toward the hut of the sacred rattles. Tabajara's opinion of the pagé wavered between dread of his powers and disgust at the manner in which he sometimes abused them. Naurú had had many opportunities to address this problem of Pojucan but had waited until tonight, when he could raise it before the village.

Until his last battle, few men could match Pojucan as warrior or hunter. He seemed destined to be the next leader of the maloca.

Two Great Rains past, the men of the clan had attacked their enemies' village. The battle raged for hours. Many on both sides were slain, until the clan's warriors were driven back into the forest, leaving the dead and those captured by the enemy, Pojucan among the latter.

Three sunrises after the clan had returned to the village, Pojucan came wandering back. He had escaped from the enemy, and it was this flight that damned him.

Prisoners were always killed but it was a glorious death that promised entry to Land of the Grandfather. To flee was to banish all hope of reaching this warriors' paradise and to become a man without a country — a nameless no-warrior.

Tabajara had found Pojucan's behavior inexplicable, and the memory of it troubled him greatly.

He accepted a gourd of beer passed to him and drank deeply.

The boys, not knowing what was expected of them, sat motionless as others began to drift away from the clearing, until Old Mother, bringing a fresh supply of beer, saw them and erupted with laughter:

"Aieee! What foolishness! Are you to sit until Macaw calls? Get up! Go to your hammocks and ask your fathers how you must hunt Macaw."

ℰᴐ

Aruanã's eyes adjusted to the smoky atmosphere inside the longhouse. Twenty families dwelt here, their hammocks slung on either side of a central walkway. Their disregard for possessions, other than the fine works of feather, was evident in the few items stored within this area — earthen pots, bows and arrows, clubs, stone axes, a digging stick. Each family kept a fire burning day and night, its glowing embers as much for cooking as for warding off malevolent spirits.

It made no difference where he went or what he did, Aruanã thought sadly: his father's trouble followed. He had heard Naurú; still he could not understand what Pojucan had done so terrible as to make him a no-warrior. How could one so fearless and brave be a man without honor?

When he approached his family's hammocks — hung the farthest distance from Tabajara's place since his father's return — he saw Pojucan making an arrow. Two were next to him on the hammock — arrows of a kind Aruanã would need for Macaw. Seeing this, he was suddenly happy. When had his father last taken an interest in anything that concerned him?

Pojucan greeted the boy, and continued working on the arrow. Unlike those used against men or in the hunt for meat, it ended in a small, round knob, not a point of bone or sharpened reed. Its snub-nosed head was designed to stun, not kill.

"A boy needs a swift arrow for Macaw," Pojucan said, "one that will fly true and fast."

"With such an arrow, I will be the first to shoot Macaw," Aruanã said eagerly. "I will find more feathers than all the rattles can wear."

"When I went on my first hunt, I was afraid of the forest."

"And so it is with me, Father. But this fear will not stop me."

"There is no need to go beyond the forest of our people. Many macaw live there."

"I remember the signs and will look for them." He was referring to the markers with which the clan defined its territory: a broken branch across the trail, a slash on a tree trunk. "You have been beyond these, Father, a longer journey than others. I will also remember this, for I am your son."

"There are things in the forest even the bravest warrior has no eyes or thoughts for."

"You led the hunt. You saw the trail as the animals do." Suddenly Aruanã implored, "Oh, Father, why has it changed?"

"It was a long time past," Pojucan said. "It was the other life."

Pojucan still did not know what had come over him when he was a prisoner. He should have danced before his captors, and mocked them, until they brought the slaughter club. Why had he, on the second night, looked up at the stars and thought that life held more than a death of honor?

"You must look for Macaw in the middle branches," he said abruptly. "There he makes his home."

But Aruanã did not want to lose this chance to hear his father. "I do not know this other life you speak of," he said.

"Think only of the sunrise and of what must be done for Naurú. It is your first hunt. Sleep, so you will have eyes for Macaw."

"My father is Pojucan, the Warrior. Pojucan, the Hunter. This I will always honor."

Pojucan, a deep ache in his heart, swung himself into his hammock and turned his back on his son.

Naurú was going to have him killed; of this he was sure. His death would come without ceremony, a group of warriors ambushing him in some quiet place in the forest or seizing him here in the maloca and dragging him beyond the stockade.

But why should he allow old bent-back Naurú to decide his life for him?

He was not so stupid as to seek an open confrontation with Naurú. He would be a twice-condemned man if he dared defy Naurú before the elders.

He dreaded Naurú, but there was something else, a fire within him that had begun as no more than the faint embers at the end of night in a maloca.

It was heresy, the denial of a glorious way of dying among the Tupiniquin, and he was the first man to think it.

☙

Aruanã lay awake for a long time, listening to the insects in the thatch, the creaking of hammock poles, the conversation of those still awake. He heard the cries from the jungle, so very close late at night.

Aruanã's people were Tupiniquin, one of the great tribes of the forest. The Tupiniquin lived beyond the farthest rivers, up to the lands of the Tupinambá. He had heard the names of other tribes as well, but he could not remember them all, and called them, mostly, The Enemy. Whenever there was a war, there would be prisoners, and they would always boast about their own villages, how much greater they were than the clan's. He never believed a word of this, but he listened to them, and learned about the tribes and lands they had come from.

Twice in his own lifetime the clan had moved its village.

The last move had led to a startling discovery for Aruanã.

One morning soon after the clan had raised its new malocas, the men left the village at sunrise and made for the river, where they boarded three dugouts.

"Where are we going, Father?" Aruanã was to ask this question again and again, but each time Pojucan only laughed and told him to wait.

They paddled downstream. After a bend, the river began to widen, and there was a low, rumbling noise.

"Father, what is it?" he asked uncertainly.

Before Pojucan could reply, the river was gone, and the earth itself was fast disappearing as they swept forward, onto the widest, bluest, most expansive stretch of water.

Behind him, Aruanã saw white sand backed by tall, graceful palms; behind the palms the earth rose, with patches of forest on the heights.

Between the white sand and the place where the water met the sky lay a line of foaming white. At sight of it, the men shouted from one canoe to the other, warnings to turn back. This was done, but the first craft to paddle toward the land was almost at the white sands when it was swamped.

The canoes of Pojucan and Tabajara raced toward the scene, but so close to shore had it occurred that by the time they got there, the warriors were already on the sands, laughing at their misfortune and delightedly pointing out that "Bluewater" had turned the urucu dye on their bodies a deep mahogany hue.

Aruanã fell asleep this night remembering a glorious day when he first saw Bluewater that flowed to the end of the earth.

❧

He awoke before anyone else in the maloca but did not rise from his hammock, and was lying there when he saw Aruanã stir. His son also did not get up immediately but sat in the net, clearly uncertain as to whether or not he should set out for the forest, since it was still dark outside. Pojucan did not let the boy see that he was awake. *Go now,* he willed the youngster. *When the fat and the lazy have wiped the sleep from their eyes, you will be across the river. Go now, my son!*

It pleased him that no sooner had his thoughts ended than Aruanã climbed out of the hammock. He watched the boy squat by one of the pots at the fire and throw back mouthfuls of manioc. Then Aruanã lifted the bark container with his arrows, slung it over his shoulder, and took up his bow. He paused briefly and looked back toward the hammocks. Then he made for the low opening at the end of the maloca, pushed aside the woven mat that covered it, and was gone.

Soon after Aruanã left, Pojucan swung out of his hammock: One man there was who was permitted to speak to a no-warrior, and Pojucan went to seek him at a neighboring maloca.

The man was at his hammock, and greeted Pojucan cheerfully enough. He was lean, with light, almost yellow skin and a sharp nose that had earned him the sobriquet Long Beak in the village. His real name was Ubiratan. Whether he was a prisoner of the village was moot. Some elders held that he had been captured by their canoes; others argued that this "capture" had occurred after the strange craft he'd ridden into the bay at the end of the clan's river had been destroyed in the white waters. As the prisoner theory had prevailed, no one paid much attention to Ubiratan's talking with no-warrior, particularly in the beginning, when he could not properly understand his dialect.

Ubiratan came from a people he called Tapajós, who had never made war with the Tupiniquin. Ubiratan was not clear about the distance between this place and his village, but he had been gone four Great Rains and the stars themselves had changed their place in the sky.

He regarded the Tupiniquin as a simple people compared with his own. The Tupiniquin thought themselves a great nation, but their malocas were buried in the forest, they had little trade with one another, and, what surprised him most, they had never talked of a great chief, one man who directed the affairs of all the tribes. At the head of his own Tapajós was such a person, a man of authority, whose word was obeyed throughout the land, who could call upon the warriors of every village, and whose name was honored wherever the Tapajós lived — and feared by tribes who dwelt farther along Mother of Rivers.

It was an order of this great chief that, indirectly, was the cause of Ubiratan's present misfortune. A skilled potter, he had been sent to the farthest village in the land to fetch the blue earth that Tapajós potters used for their finest vessels. The field of clay lay beyond the last Tapajós settlement, in a no-man's-land. Here a band of enemy warriors attacked Ubiratan and took him captive, dragging him to their canoes and riding the powerful currents to the very end of Mother of Rivers.

One day the headman of the village where he was held captive announced that he was taking two canoe parties on a long journey, and selected Ubiratan to join them. Instead of heading upriver, the boats went far beyond the largest island and down along the mainland. One disappeared in a storm; Ubiratan's was wrecked in a bay.

Separated from his companions, often near starvation, he struggled down the coast till he found a clan of fishermen whose canoes were like none he had ever seen.

These *jangadas* were built of six to eight balsa logs, roughly equal in size, laid side by side and lashed together with lianas. To catch the wind, a great woven mat was suspended from two mangrove wood poles erected upon the log platform in an A-position and supported with lianas. Within a short time, Ubiratan had mastered this wind-canoe and could send it rushing across the water as fast as the best of them, directing its course from the stern with the great paddle positioned there.

Ubiratan would sometimes take a *jangada* out by himself. The last time he did this, he was caught in a sudden squall and driven to the white waters, where the jangada was lost and the Tupiniquin captured him.

It was this man to whom Pojucan now turned for help. "You were in the clearing last night?" he asked.

"I heard Naurú," Ubiratan replied.

"I expect Tabajara to act, even before this sun has gone."

"You show no fear?"

"I am not afraid: I have lived two Great Rains since my last death and am ready to face this one."

"Ah, yes, it is so," Ubiratan said. "But *how* have you lived?"

Ubiratan had found it strange that a man could be an exile among his own people for the reason Pojucan was: To live to fight an enemy again must surely be more worthy than to be slain before the women and children of his village.

They walked beyond the village, heading toward the canoes, until they arrived at a place on the river where the mist was beginning to rise.

"My boy is already in the forest," Pojucan said. "Gone before any other. He will be first to get Macaw's feathers, the son of no-warrior." He laughed joylessly.

"Tell me, Ubiratan, is it so different for you? Wandering from the Tapajós, away from the sight of your people?"

"In my spirit it is the same, I agree."

"Must Ubiratan, son of the Tapajós, lost from his people, stay among the Tupiniquin, forever gone from Mother of Rivers?"

"What else?"

"You can return," Pojucan said directly.

"I remain only because I know how many lands lie between this place and the one I left."

"Only because of this?"

Ubiratan nodded. Until now, he had shown little emotion, but he could see what the Tupiniquin was leading up to, and a keener note rose in his voice: "It is a long and terrible journey, beyond even those stars that mean so much to you."

"But did you not make such a journey, my friend?"

Ubiratan had often thought of heading up along the white sands or into the forest, and there had been many opportunities, but not for a man alone.

"There is nothing for me here," Pojucan continued, "but dishonorable death. I will go with you, to your village."

Ubiratan leapt forward and embraced Pojucan, clasping him to his chest. "Oh, my friend! What I said about the dangers is true, but with two of us they can be overcome."

They agreed that there was no time to lose. They must go that night, when people were about in the clearing, make their separate ways to the small forest behind the clan's fields, and start from there.

❧

Aruanã was out of scale in the forest, dwarfed in this twilight world, where the simplest ferns and shrubs grew to a height twice his own and patches of light played through the latticed branches in the canopy far above, filtering through the lower trees and making strange shadows dance before his eyes.

Cautiously he slipped between writhing shapes of trees held in the grip of the strangler fig or hung with the tendrils of great lianas, vines too thick to encircle with both hands. It was a soggy, dripping world, mostly silent now that the waking chorus had stilled, but there were occasional cries from various levels above, parrots and toucans shattering the quiet with maniacal conversation as they took to wing, a cacophony of screeches and squawks that rose until, abruptly, they ceased. In the distance, a pack of howler monkeys started up.

The boy was nervous but also experienced a strange elation the deeper he walked into the forest. His life had begun in such a place: When his mother had felt the child, she had gone beyond the village to the trees, where she squatted on the damp cover to give birth.

Little happened in Aruanā's world that was not bound up with the jungle. The forest was mysterious and dangerous, and if its luxuriance and fecundity were not held back at the edge of the clearing, the trees and shrubs would invade the malocas.

In the forest were animals and plants that provided food, medicines, shelter, and weapons, more than man could ever need. But this paradise was also a land filled with a fantastic parade of evil.

Several times before crossing the river at dawn, Aruanā had inspected the dye smeared over his body. It was his only protection against Caipora, whom he feared most, and the others: The forest demons were unlikely to see a human who wore the red paint. And then, once on the other side, he had abruptly stopped, his heart beating furiously as he awaited a dreadful apparition. But there had been nothing, and he had walked on, a little bolder.

When a group of large brilliant blue butterflies flew in front of him, he dashed after them. Entering the forest where the fragrances were especially heavy, he paused and breathed deeply of the exotic perfume, examined strange insects, and plants growing high on the trees themselves, splashes of color flowering amid the dark green clouds of leaves.

Twice already he had caught a movement in the middle branches, where his father had told him to look for Macaw. The first time he'd watched in disgust as a turkey thrashed to the ground. The second time it had been a brilliantly feathered macaw, and he'd got a shot off into the trees but missed, and the arrow was lost. He stood there trying to attract Macaw by mimicking his call. Macaw screeched back, mocking him from very close, but he never saw him again.

He'd gone on, humiliated and reminded that there was much to learn before he could read the signs of the forest.

He wove through a thick stand of tall fern, hearing small animals scurry off at his approach.

I must take the finest feathers, he told himself. *They will see the great warrior I am to be. They will show our people there can be no dishonor in Pojucan.*

Aruanā moved quickly until he came to a tangled growth so dense he had difficulty getting through. He cried out as thorns pierced his flesh, but he was already too deep into the brush to backtrack and so decided to push ahead. It took longer than he expected, and as he struggled along, he saw through a rare break in the trees that the sun was near the middle of the sky.

He had finally got through this barrier and was moving quietly on the thick carpet of rotting vegetation when he found Macaw.

The bird was on a low limb of an enormous tree, facing the opposite direction. Without a sound, Aruanã fitted an arrow to his bow, took aim, and released the string. This time he did not miss, and the bird toppled off the branch. With a whoop of joy, he ran to collect Macaw, and saw that he had long and magnificently hued tail feathers.

"Forgive, O Macaw," he said as he plucked them, "that I leave you so weak. This night your glory will dress the rattles of our people." When he'd finished, he laid the bird to one side, carefully wrapping the feathers in two palm leaves to protect them on the journey back.

℘

When Aruanã reached the village, he was disappointed to discover that his father was not in the maloca. He greeted Obapira, but when her back was turned, he hid the palm leaves near his hammock. She was not to be the first to see his beautiful prize. He went in search of Pojucan, and was strutting through the clearing when he met two boys, sons of an elder in another maloca.

"We watched you," one said. "Your walk told much."

"What did you see in it?"

"The steps of one who is pleased," they both replied.

"I was alone in the forest where Caipora lives and have returned without harm."

One of the brothers said quietly, "We saw the palm leaves."

"You will see them again before this night has ended," Aruanã said. "Can you show the same?"

Their long faces said it all, but it was not every day that he could make those who had teased him squirm. "Did you find the feathers?"

"Macaw did not fly where we went in the forest," one said. But almost immediately his face brightened, and he added, "We found something else, far better than feathers." He looked at his brother, who nodded vigorously. "Come. Share with us!"

They had plundered a nest of bees, bringing back a honeycomb, which they had hidden near their maloca.

Before today, these boys would have led those who taunted him. Was he now experiencing the first result of success with Macaw?

They asked him to tell what he had seen deep in the forest, and then confessed that they had gone only to its edge. He was shocked that they'd admit such deceit at a time when they had been told to prove they were ready to be men. When he said as much, they looked genuinely scared, and begged him to tell no one.

He heard noises from the other side of the maloca: It was time for presentation of the feathers!

He should never have dallied this long, but they had kept pressing the sweet nectar upon him. He stood up, wiped his hands against the palm fronds of the maloca, noticing as he did that many people were already drifting toward the clearing. He ran to his house, grabbed the palm leaves in which he'd wrapped his feathers, and hurried outside.

Aruanã made his way to the front of the crowd gathered at the hut of the sacred rattles, where his age group had been ordered to sit. The boys who had shot Macaw were placed apart from the others. Aruanã saw only two with palm leaves before them, and ten boys who had often made his life a misery looking very gloomy.

Naurú was in his hut, the light from the fire within glowing dimly at the entrance. At several points in their lives, men entered that place to seek help or receive messages from the spirits, and they invariably faced such consultations with dread, never sure of the outcome.

Tonight, long before he showed himself, he had started chanting and shaking his rattles, louder and louder, the sounds mounting above those outside, the voice issuing from the small, twisted body remarkable in its power. A mantle of urubu feathers — only he was permitted the covering of the black vulture, bird of death — was slung over the hump on his back, and the sight of him in it was enough to make those closest jump back when he suddenly burst out of his hut. He halted a pace from the nearest group of men, turned his eye upon them, and moaned hideously, all the time shaking three rattles. From his neck hung a long chain made of hundreds of teeth drawn from the jaws of enemy warriors.

Naurú moved with a sort of hop toward the larger group of boys. He danced up and down before them with such ferocity that several began to whimper. Next he turned to those with feathers, stalking round them rather than dancing, circling several times, muttering and shaking the rattles when he paused opposite a boy, looking him over thoroughly before placing a rattle on the ground in front of him.

Aruanã was last to fall under his scrutiny.

He was enormously relieved when Naurú put a rattle down and backed away, but he grew worried again when the pagé went directly into his hut, the abrupt departure seeming to Aruanã to have something to do with him.

Naurú returned quickly, however, with a supply of *tabak* and lit the dry herb with an ember from the fire. He sat on the ground between the boys, and sucked at one end of the roll of smoldering leaves, filling his lungs.

The elders had elected Tabajara to speak, and he now stepped forward, his feather adornments more resplendent than on the previous night.

"O Great Pagé, Voice of the Spirits of our people, I ask to be heard."

Naurú puffed at the tabak and insolently blew smoke in the elder's direction before announcing, "They will listen."

"Believe, O Naurú, when our people were told that the sacred rattles had lost their feathers, every warrior wanted to take their bows."

A chorus of agreement greeted this statement, and Tabajara waited until it had died down. Naurú continued to sit, puffing away at the roll of tabak, looking on disinterestedly.

"But Naurú saw another way. . . ."

"It was the wisdom from Voice of the Spirits. It told of others to find feathers for the rattles. First we did not hear."

"You question Voice of the Spirits?"

"Never."

"Then, why were your thoughts weak?"

"They were not weak but small. As small as the thoughts of those Naurú appointed to find Macaw."

"There was a reason."

"We saw the wisdom of it."

"But not at first?"

"Not when boys were called to do the work of men. We feared the anger of the ancestors, O Great Pagé."

"Was it not they who asked, when they saw it was time for these boys to begin the work of men?"

"This was what we came to understand."

It was a ritual, this banter between elder and pagé, similar for every age group that approached initiation. To impress the boys, it sometimes went further, with Naurú seizing the opportunity to make a fool of the elder chosen to speak. But Tabajara was adept at meeting Naurú's provocations. He now lashed out at the boys without feathers: "I do not see one feather of Macaw! What kind of men will you be?"

None dared a response.

"I have seen such men," Tabajara told them. "Even the smallest girl in the malocas laughs. . . .

"They are the men who hang in their hammocks when the hunt is called, the men who hide when the enemy is near, the men who run from the fire in the sky. Look around you. Do you see such men?" Several shook their heads. "You will not find them among the Tupiniquin. Tell them, O Great Pagé, where the men without the spirit of men are."

Naurú was on his feet, a little unsteady from the effects of the tabak, which he had been inhaling furiously. He moved to the boys, so close that spittle dribbled from his lip hole onto the nearest one.

"They are taken into the forest," Naurú said. "Such men cannot hide their fear from the shadows. See Caipora with them, Caipora with her one leg, leaping as high as the trees. 'Dance, coward! Dance!' she demands. 'Dance for Caipora!' And Jurupari, he with the teeth of Jaguar and claws of Hawk. How Jurupari hungers for such miserable things! See the fire in his eye glow. Hear his stomach growl."

Naurú now launched into a grisly cautionary tale replete with inhuman beasts and demons, monstrous figures of that other world where cowards — and young boys who didn't bring feathers — might be tormented.

When Naurú had finished, Tabajara walked over to the boys with the feathers, motioning the one farthest from Aruanã to rise.

"O Voice of the Spirits, here is a true son of Tupiniquin, a boy who will be a man among us!"

Aruanã grew excited as he waited his turn, but he felt a deep sadness also: This night of all nights he wanted his father here — to see him praised in this way.

The two boys had presented their feathers, and now Aruanã was called. He stood up quickly and went to the elder and Naurú.

"Son of my maloca, Tabajara is happy that you have feathers. Your eye is good, your arrow true, your path that of a warrior-to-be. Let us hear where Macaw was found."

"Farther than I have been with our hunters."

"I saw you leave the maloca before the sun woke. Those who came back with nothing were still in their hammocks. Tell me, boy, were you not afraid of the darkness?"

"I left when hunters leave."

Tabajara smiled. He was pleased with the boy's answers. Last night he had had doubts about this son of no-warrior. It was good to see that he'd been wrong.

Naurú was not pleased. Here was bad blood, this son of a man who had denied a way of the ancestors. But he had found Macaw, and it was difficult to speak against him.

"Yes, boy, you were lucky this day."

"And swift, too," Tabajara hastened to add.

"Let the boy show his feathers!" he ordered.

Aruanã carefully removed the bindings around the palm leaves. His hands shook, such was his excitement, for he knew that the eyes of every man and boy present were upon him; and, he knew too that the feathers of the others were nothing against those he had brought.

He unrolled the leaves with a flourish, his eyes bright with anticipation.

Aruanã gasped in horror. The dazzling feathers of Macaw had become the worst pluckings from the wing of Heron!

"My feathers! Where are the feathers of Macaw?"

The men of the clan first greeted this incredible scene with silence. Eyes turned to Naurú and all willed that he act quickly to appease those offended.

To the surprise of all, the pagé began to cackle, and danced a wobbly jig before the boy, slapping his sides. He laughed until tears streamed from his eyes, and when others saw this, they began to laugh, too. The brothers who had lured Aruanã to their honeycomb, and other boys who had been in on the scheme to change the feathers, laughed as loudly as the adults standing behind them. As Naurú's mirth increased, so did everyone's, all but Tabajara.

The elder was furious. The boy had made a fool of him, in front of every man of the village. He grabbed Aruanã by the arm. "My anger, boy, is as nothing to the furies of our ancestors at your foolishness."

"O my father, it was not like this! Some of the boys tricked me. They took the feathers that I brought."

"Quiet, boy! Do you not see that Naurú will speak?"

The pagé had stopped laughing and was advancing toward him, with terrifying malice. "We heard that this boy went deep into the forest."

"I did this, O Great Pagé, and I found Macaw."

"Silence! If it is not a lie, why did Macaw's feathers get changed to the pluckings of a Heron?"

Tabajara watched him quizzically. What was in Naurú's mind?

"What do you say, elder?" Naurú asked.

"I saw feathers of Heron," Tabajara said. "But the boy said the others changed his feathers."

The men groaned, and several cried out, "O Great Pagé, we beseech you: Hear what wrongs the spirits of our village. Hear this night, or heavy is the fear in our malocas."

Naurú picked up the sacred rattles and began to shake them, letting the rattles tremble and moaning as if he was in great pain. Suddenly, he stopped. "It is Gray Wing," he announced. "The ancestor's name Gray Wing."

The crowd whispered the name, though no one knew this "Gray Wing."

Naurú's voice was entirely different from his normal tone. "We see Gray Wing gone to fight the enemy. Tupiniquin make war at sunrise when Cariri lie in their hammocks. Long is the battle. Gray Wing is a prisoner." He paused. Then:

"On the second night, Gray Wing shows the enemy no courage in Tupiniquin. He runs from their village."

Several cried out: "This is no-warrior. Here is his son — come to the ancestors with white feathers."

Aruanã tried to flee, but Tabajara stopped him.

"When we met last, I warned about this man," Naurú said, now in his normal voice.

"We heard, O Great Pagé," the men answered.

"What has come of my warning?"

The elder shoved Aruanã aside. "We have met to know how it will be done," he said.

"Now is the time!" a man called out.

"Find Gray Wing," another said. "Kill him!"

"No!" Aruanã screamed. "He is not Gray Wing. He is Pojucan, my father! Pojucan, warrior of the Tupiniquin!"

The few who took notice of this outburst jeered at the boy.

"You have heard," Naurú said, addressing Tabajara. "Let no-warrior be taken. Let him be silenced!" He turned abruptly, picked up the rattle near Aruanã, and disappeared into his hut.

The meeting broke up. A group of men went to Tabajara, for, as elder of the maloca, it was his duty to lead them to no-warrior. Others began to drift toward the opening in the stockade.

Aruanã was forgotten, in front of the pagé's hut.

O Father, he wept, *can it be? Can the one Aruanã has loved be a warrior without honor?*

Aruanã ran toward the main clearing, where a group was gathered outside his maloca, and he now saw one of them approach him.

"We must go quickly," the man said. "Your father waits."

"They will kill him," Aruanã said. He recognized the man as the Tapajós prisoner. "I cannot bear to watch."

"They will not find him."

"He will be in his hammock."

"Your father is gone from the village, and I am to join him," Ubiratan said.

"Where is my father?"

Ubiratan motioned for Aruanã to follow him to the side of the stockade far-thest from the opening. There he helped the boy over the long poles and then hauled himself up.

In the small forest where the boy had seen the otter, Ariranha, father and son met. The Tupiniquin told Aruanã that they were to journey to the lands of the Tapajós, but that nothing would prevent the boy from remaining in the village.

"I hear my father," Aruanã said simply.

II

June 1491 – April 1497

*T*hus did Pojucan and Aruanã of the Tupiniquin and Ubiratan of the Tapajós begin a journey across half a continent.

The two men carried their bows and arrows and clubs, stone-headed axes, a few sharp cutting tools, a small supply of manioc, and their most powerful charms — the teeth of a jaguar and a shell necklace.

They had struck inland that first night, following the big river upstream, a direction Ubiratan felt must eventually lead to a waterway that flowed into Mother of Rivers.

In the days that followed, they crossed many rivers and forests. They picked their way up escarpments; climbed out of valleys to cross mountains that gave way to more forests and streams. Some days food and game were plentiful; others they would find nothing, not even water.

They moved with quiet deliberation, ever watchful of dangers: insects, reptiles, hostile tribes. Before nightfall, if they had been on the move, they would seek a place to rest, and occasionally made a crude lean-to shelter, like the ones abandoned by the nomads, whose traces they found: no more than palm fronds resting against a branch, good for a night, maybe a week or two, never more. Sometimes, though, their terror got the better of them — the tracks of men, the distant rooting of a big herd of peccaries that could rush a frail shelter, ripping and slashing at anything in its path — and then they slept in the trees.

Pojucan was nominally the leader, but it was Ubiratan who guided the way. He would study the heavens, using the most brilliant stars as his guide to determine their position. He knew that the Great Rain would soon be upon them: When it was over, he believed they would be near the lands of the Shavante, who lived below the Tapajós.

One night, three new moons after the start of their journey, Aruanã lay listening to the men. He was stretched out close to the fire, and would often be asleep long before them, but this night he stayed alert, for he was curious about Ubiratan's talk of a great pagé among the Tapajós.

"You fear Naurú," the boy heard Ubiratan say, "who is known in only one village of the Tupiniquin. But the pagé Tocoyricoc is known to the farthest place where Tapajós live, and even farther."

"'Tocoyricoc'?" Pojucan said, with difficulty. "It is a strange name."

"'He-Who-Sees-Well.' It is his own word. He came to the Tapajós before I was born — from a land where the sun sleeps. His wisdom is more than any our elders show. He was very old when I left, but he may still live."

Ubiratan had more to say about this Tocoyricoc, who had lived in malocas built of stone, in villages that clung to mountains closer to the sun than any in these parts.

"Even before he went to live in a cave near our village," Ubiratan said, "he would go to the forest alone. He fears no spirits between the trees, because he does not believe they are there."

"Aieee! Now I see a fool. All know there are spirits. Unless. . . It has been known to the Tupiniquin — the evil that hides in the shape of a man."

"I have heard no one whose words hold less evil." Ubiratan looked at his hands. "He taught me the potters' work, but I was too foolish to see all he could show."

"But where is the land of the sleeping sun?" Pojucan asked.

Ubiratan couldn't say.

☙

The forest had now begun to give way to a higher country of tall grasses with patches of stunted vegetation and fewer stands of trees, those remaining galleried on the flanks of rivers or huddled at the edge of a lake.

The weather, too, was changing as the end of the long dry season approached. The heat was oppressive; a roll of thunder would occasionally promise relief, but it would pass, and the winds that brought the rain would die.

Late one morning the trio was crossing an expanse of open grassland, heading toward a clump of forest where they planned to take shelter from the heat, when they spotted an abandoned manioc field and rushed toward the precious crop, unaware that they were being watched from the trees.

There were thirty-three men, women, and children in this band, a people called Nambikwara, who spent the entire dry season roaming this high savanna in search of food. They had planted this manioc on an earlier migration, and would have feasted off it, however meager a supply remained, for through several sunrises they had eaten nothing but grubs and grasshoppers and a few rodents that had fallen to the sticks of their women.

Their leader, who went by the name Hare, was a scrawny individual with black eyes and pinched features and, at five feet one, tallest of the family, for all were interrelated. There were hundreds of groups like his dispersed over the grasslands. When the rains came, three or four of these would band together in the semblance of a village. There they'd wait out the winter.

Hare had his best hunters at his side. They spoke in whispers as they crouched behind the thornbushes at the foot of the trees.

"Let us kill them," said a squat, fat man known to the others as Toad.

"He is right," agreed Rock, so named after an angry young tapir had failed to knock him down. "They are three, we seven. It is easy." His bow, a foot longer than he, and his curare-tipped arrows lay ready.

"No," said Hare. "To take them with our arrows, we must walk beyond the trees. Surprise will be lost."

"Does it matter?" Rock asked.

"You talk of seven, but two are old and one still a boy."

"Our children cry for this manioc."

"Then let them who dig for it bring it to us."

⇛

Aruanã carried the manioc to the place beneath the trees where the men sat scraping the tubers. Next they would have to rasp them against a spiky palm and squeeze out a poisonous juice between strips of soft bark, and they sent Aruanã in search of these items.

Hare and four of his hunters, with their bows at the ready and their little bodies quivering with excitement, caught him in a small glade, surrounding him so that escape was impossible. He stood there, wide-eyed with fright, offering no resistance as they took away his bow and arrows and whooped about him, jabbering loudly.

Hare tied a vine around the boy's neck and handed the other end to Toad. "Take the little thief to camp," he said.

Encouraged by the capture of the boy, Hare and the others set off to find the two remaining manioc thieves. But on the way they ran into a drove of peccaries. Fifty of these bloodthirsty pigs, which could tear a man to pieces in minutes, suddenly burst from the undergrowth. Rock shot off an arrow and dropped one of the front runners. The rest of the pigs halted momentarily but then, squealing and grunting, charged the group of hunters, scattering them and sending them racing for the nearest trees.

Rock, closest to the herd, tripped over a fallen branch and three of the bristly backed beasts trotted toward him, almost leisurely, until one was close enough for the attack and rushed at the man. Rock shrieked as the peccary's jutting white tusks gashed his rump. Gasping with pain, he managed to pull himself onto the low branch of a tree.

The Nambikwara sat in the branches, not daring to move an inch from their perches. The tightly packed dark shapes below hurried from one tree to the next, butting and rooting at the base.

"They will hold us in the trees until dark," Rock said. "I hurt. Oh, how I hurt!"

"We must wait," Hare said.

"And the men with the manioc?" Rock howled.

Pojucan and Ubiratan had heard the noise, grabbed their weapons, and hurried toward the commotion, fearing that Aruanã had fallen among the pigs. They crept through the forest, to where the grinding of teeth and wicked grunts were loudest, and there they saw the peccaries and the men in the trees above.

So occupied were the beasts with shaking their enemy out of the trees, they didn't heed the new arrivals until arrows flew into their midst, killing two more and sending the rest bumping and crashing into one another as they hurried away.

The Nambikwara stayed where they were, for they had dropped their weapons in their flight and now feared that the men they'd been on their way to attack might be a worse threat than a herd of angered pigs. But Pojucan and Ubiratan stepped toward them, lowered their bows, and indicated their friendship.

The little hunters stood huddled together, chattering animatedly, unable to make themselves understood to their rescuers. Now they also began to worry about what would happen when these men learned that they had seized the boy. Rock grew quite frantic when reminding Hare about this and Hare, himself deeply troubled, tried to calm him. "They show no anger," he said. "They help us."

"And when they see we have the boy?"

Hare immediately determined to make peace with these men.

It was more difficult than he had expected, and took many signs and gestures to indicate that they had "met" the boy and had sent him to their camp with one of their hunters. Hare did his best to assure them that the boy would be unharmed and waiting at their shelters.

When at last he understood, Pojucan, furious, grabbed Hare about the neck and shook him. "This is my son," he growled. "If there is pain, you die."

Hare motioned that they should all return to his camp, where they would be reunited with the boy.

"We have to go with them," Pojucan said to Ubiratan.

"I have no fear," the other said contemptuously. "They are children."

While Pojucan took Hare to collect the manioc and their belongings, Ubiratan made the boy-hunters prepare two pigs for carrying to the Nambikwara camp.

The party set out with Pojucan and Ubiratan at the rear, ready with their bows should one attempt flight. Rock walked painfully, holding a bunch of leaves to his torn flesh with one hand, as he struggled to help a boy-hunter carry a peccary.

At the Nambikwara camp, Aruanã had spent one of the most confusing afternoons of his life.

Dragged through the forest by Toad, he had grown more apprehensive with each step that took him away from Pojucan and Ubiratan. The gallery forest followed a river course, and the Nambikwara encampment was along its bank, opposite a small cataract, where the water flowed weakly at this end of the dry season.

Aruanã saw seven lean-to shelters erected wherever a bush or tree offered support for a row of leafy branches or palm fronds. Tall baskets of plaited bamboo for transporting goods lay near the shelters. Aruanã saw a few calabashes, some crude blackened pots, the scattered remains of animals — bits of fur, teeth, claws — and some dried plants and roots. The men, Toad included, wore no more than a tuft of straw dangling from a belt above their genitals, the women nothing but a few strands of shell beads.

The hunters' wives and the old men were lolling in the sand, some preparing the forest fruits they'd gathered that morning, but most reclining lazily in the shade while the group's children played at the river's edge.

At the approach of Aruanã and Toad, all had rushed to examine the newcomer, jabbering at the same time, touching his body, dancing round him with unbridled joy, as if welcoming back a lost son. Most enthusiastic were the young women, only three in this family — small, graceful, elegant creatures with velvety beige skins. Two reached for the vine around Aruanã's neck, pulled it away from Toad, and, giggling, led him to a pool below the cataract where they plunged into the water, splashing and playing and crying happily when the "prisoner" began to join in.

When the water game had ended, the prettiest girl grabbed his arm and pulled him out of the pool, laughing merrily as she took him back to the shelters. When they passed Toad, the man said something and pointed to Aruanã's penis, and this provoked shrieks of laughter from the bystanders, but the girl hanging onto his arm only smiled sweetly.

She was slightly shorter than Aruanã, slender, with firm, round breasts, smooth skin, delicate features, and clean black hair, long and shiny.

She had led him to a place between the shelters and indicated that he should sit, and soon most of the people were on the ground around them or standing within earshot.

Toad told how they'd captured him, and reported that the others had gone to fetch the manioc.

When finally the file of hunters began to emerge from the trees, Aruanã leapt to his feet, and grew wide-eyed when he saw the two figures bringing up the rear. They were greeted even more enthusiastically than he had been, the little people dancing between the pigs and the tall strangers.

Hare called for silence and made a welcoming speech, telling his people that these great hunters were his guests, for as long as they wished. He ignored the fact that they'd been marched back to the shelters as virtual prisoners.

Aruanã ran to Pojucan and wanted to embrace him but instead said quietly, "My father, I saw much."

Pojucan looked at him expectantly.

"I was a prisoner, and I was waiting for the dark."

"And then?"

"I would have run into the forest."

"But this is not the way of a Tupiniquin," Pojucan said, almost gruffly.

"I wanted to be where Ubiratan and you sat — not here in the shelter of these people."

Pojucan smiled. "They have treated you well?" he asked.

"Oh, yes," he said brightly.

"It is good," Pojucan said.

The Nambikwara knew that they were at the end of this year's trek, and already were thinking about the journey to their wintering ground. The pigs and manioc provided the grandest finale they'd ever known to a "happy" season, and they feasted and sang and danced for hours.

When they'd all gorged themselves until their bellies were swollen and their faces shining with grease, Hare and Rock and Toad lapsed into a nostalgic recounting of how wonderful a season it had been.

One couple, though, was seen to sit slightly apart from the rest. The woman had a child at breast, and Hare, who was also medicine man, had decreed that until the baby was weaned they must not partake of a variety of forbidden foods, and that the man was not to hunt. But the worst prohibition was that they were forbidden to have sex. Sex, above all, was the Nambikwara's delight. Making love was good, they said — and they did so with gusto whenever the opportunity arose.

Now, as they lay around the fire after the feast, couples snuggled together, whispered, and caressed each other gently. One of the young hunters helped his wife to her feet and led her to the darkness beyond the shelters. These two were still young and modest; later they might think nothing of making love right there at the fireside.

Morning Flower, the young girl who had taken such an interest in Aruanã, sat by him all night; she shared her bowl of manioc with him.

When the speeches were over, and Pojucan lay dozing on the ground, Morning Flower held out her hand and Aruanã took it in his own. They lay like that for a time, this moonless night, until all around them slept. Then, with a finger to her lips, she bade him follow her.

Morning Flower led him to the sands by the pool below the cataract, where, in the gentlest way a Nambikwara woman knew, she made love to him.

ぐひ

The first rains came soon after the two men and the boy had decided to accompany the Nambikwara to their winter grounds.

The rains were heralded by a terrifying show of force. Great winds roared through the forests and swept down the *cerrado*, the vast plain, churning up dust clouds where the earth was bared. The skies opened first with jagged gashes of lightning that often cracked against a forest giant or sent fires racing through the brush. Then the rains erupted — short, violent storms that burst over the land, filling the forest canopy and streaming down the trees beneath. Whatever was weak, whatever was rotten crashed to the ground, huge trunks tearing away from the lianas that supported them and exploding on the forest floor. On the open cerrado, sheets of water fell upon parched earth and a thousand runnels gone in the dry season came to life, uniting in flash floods that carried all before them.

This prelude to the long wet season was erratic, driving away the dry mists and oppressive heat, then abruptly breaking off and leaving a cloudless blue sky. Gradually the storms would give way to a gentle, steady rain, till the lower banks of rivers disappeared and still the waters continued to rise, inundating vast areas of forest and drenching the dry cerrado.

The travelers walked in single file, the women carrying bamboo baskets as heavy and tall as themselves, balancing them on their backs and holding them in place with a strap that went round their foreheads. The Nambikwara men walked up front with their bows and arrows. Mud-splattered and shivering, they stumbled through the storm till they could go no farther, then huddled in little groups of misery between the grasses.

To get to the forest where they could winter, they had to cross a finger of territory where their enemies, the Shavante, hunted. Powerful and ferocious, the Shavante also spent part of the year on trek, and their hunting season closed with the coming of the Nambikwara — a final and deadly pursuit they followed as keenly as the chase of game.

A full moon had passed when, after a particularly violent rainstorm, they had first warning of the Shavante. Toward noon, as they were climbing the muddy slope of a long, flat-topped hill, Pojucan broke away from the others. He'd spotted something on the ground a distance to the left and below them. Hare and Ubiratan came up as he was examining the bones of a tapir.

"Many have eaten," Ubiratan said, noting their size.

Hare moved about excitedly, poking through the wet ashes of these hunters' fires, scratching in the undergrowth near the camp. "Shavante!" he announced. He indicated the remains of their sapling shelters, circular and hutlike He paced out an area where the grass had recently been flattened by Shavante mats.

They camped that night in a valley behind the same long hill, keeping their fires low, though these could still be seen from afar, for the grassy depression was open and treeless. They were tense and nervous, awaiting the worst hour — just before dawn, when the Shavante were known to attack.

ↀ

The Shavante attack did not come the next dawn but three mornings later, on the beaches of a gravely river the Nambikwara and the Shavante called Yellow Water. At the end of every dry season, hundreds of turtles would swim to these sands to lay thousands of eggs. The eggs and the hatchlings were voraciously sought by a multitude of hunters on wing and foot.

When the Nambikwara had seen the tamped-down earth at Yellow Water, the women dropped their baskets and ran to it, falling to their knees and scattering the sands in their haste to uncover the treasure. The men splashed into the stream and in no time had captured ten fine turtles.

Several young Shavante warriors, advance party of a group much larger than the Nambikwara, reached the river late afternoon and saw the enemy tending fires they had built for their feast. They watched angrily from across the water and then slipped away, back to the rest of their party. While the Nambikwara ate and sang and filled their bellies to bursting with turtle meat and eggs, the Shavante took up their war clubs.

They approached before dawn, when their enemy lay heavy with sleep, and the slaughter would have been terrible had Aruanã not been awake to warn of their advance. He and Morning Flower had chosen a spot away from the others, at a beach farther upstream. The night had turned bitterly cold and he awoke; but, since Morning Flower still slept peacefully beside him, he stayed where he was, dozing fitfully.

Aruanã saw the figures moving along the opposite bank. He shook the girl awake. "Shavante!"

In what little of her language he knew, he told her to stay while he went to warn the others.

He cut away from the riverbank, hunched over as he ran through the tall grass and dodged between the bushes, until he judged he was behind the Nambikwara encampment.

A thick growth of spiky plants barred his way, but he did not notice the thorns that raked his flesh when he plunged in. Blood came, and he began to feel pain, but by then he was through the tangle of brush.

The camp lay straight ahead, and nothing stirred among the dark shapes around the fires. Through every night since Pojucan had found the tapir bones, they had mounted a guard. But this night's limitless fare of rich food, and the heady beer the women had made from the buriti palm, had been too much.

Aruanã burst among the prone figures. "Shavante!" he cried. "Shavante coming!"

Almost as one person, everyone came alert.

Aruanã bounded over to where Pojucan and Ubiratan were reaching for their bows. "I saw them at the river," he said. "Many, many of them."

For a while, there was panic. The women and children shrieked and cried as though the Shavante were already swinging their war clubs in their midst. Hare ordered the women to take the children and flee beyond the thornbushes and keep running. If their men were victorious, it might take a day before they caught up with them. If they weren't, they'd at least have a chance of evading this enemy and falling in with another Nambikwara band.

The first Shavante cry pierced the predawn. The opposite bank was densely grown, giving good cover almost to the edge of the water. But it also gave the Nambikwara an advantage: It was slightly lower than where they were encamped.

Although there were but thirteen Nambikwara and twenty-nine Shavante, the small numbers did not lessen the ferocity of the battle. There were brilliant archers on both sides, and arrow after arrow flew across the water, falling thickest among the outnumbered Nambikwara, four of whom were instantly felled — two killed outright. Pojucan turned to Aruanã, who was fighting like the rest, and told him to collect dry grass. The boy crawled into the bush beyond reach of the Shavante arrows and did as he was told. Pojucan quickly bound tufts of grass to the ends of three long arrows and then made his way to the embers of their fires.

The flaming missiles worked splendidly, firing the bush where the Shavante hid.

Rock understood the Tupiniquin's frantic signals: He shouted for his men to stop shooting and to be ready when the Shavante entered the river.

As the fire spread, some Shavante, instead of backing off, plunged into the water and splashed toward the encampment. Three went down immediately, but five kept coming, yelling and shouting and waving their war clubs. Another was shot as he reached the riverbank; but four made it into the midst of the Nambikwara.

The melee that followed was short and brutal. The Nambikwara jabbed at the Shavante with their long arrows, threw stones and earth, wielded branches collected for the fire. Pojucan and Ubiratan leapt into the fight with their stone-headed axes, both going for the same Shavante and felling him like a tree.

One managed to flee along the riverbank. The Nambikwara trapped the other, beat him to the ground and slaughtered him like an animal. Seeing the eight stalwarts defeated, the main body of the Shavante, who had gone a little way upstream to escape the flames, gave up the chase and drifted off, to bitter taunts from across the water.

Hare, reveling in the moment, strutted up and down in full view of the departing enemy, proclaiming himself "warrior-of-warriors," "smasher-of-Shavante." But he did not forget the boy, and when they had seen the last of the enemy, he turned to his men and reminded them that it had been Aruanã of the Tupiniquin who had roused them from the sleep of the dead.

Aruanã was not there to hear this. He was racing to find Morning Flower.

The girl was exactly where he had left her, her delicate body broken under the blows from the Shavante, who had fled this way from the scene of battle.

❧

It was only a small blue-clay pot with a narrow opening and a wavy design, but it excited Ubiratan more than anything on their journey thus far.

They were passing the Great Rain with the Nambikwara at a village near a river that Ubiratan now knew must lead to Mother of Rivers.

He examined the pot with care, tracing his fingers over the pattern, tapping its sides, and gauging the thickness and quality of the material. The owner refused to part with it, which was understandable, since it was the only one of its kind in the village. Where had he got it? Ubiratan wanted to know. From men who had come down the next river, the Nambikwara said, tall men like Ubiratan and his friend. The owner of the pot accepted it as a fine object — his people made nothing like this — but could not comprehend the warrior's joy at the sight of it. Ubiratan explained that it was the work of his people, the Tapajós.

It rained day after day. Their winter houses were poor branch-and-thatch affairs, and the little hunters shivered in misery, ranting against this forced interruption to their wanderings.

They hunted and fished, and were much amused when Ubiratan showed how to collect the fish with the pulpy fibers of timbó. He beat the water with lengths of this green liana, and the fish began to leap to the surface, where they thrashed around frantically until they turned their bellies to the sky. But, after a few expeditions, the Nambikwara lost interest and returned to sit around their fires, trading stories about the last real hunt.

They showed as little interest in the canoe that the two men and the boy made. The Nambikwara had never looked to the waters as a means of passage: Able to roam the cerrado at will, they could see little advantage in confining themselves to the direction of one or another stream. As with the timbó at first they observed with curiosity as Pojucan and Ubiratan selected a tree, felled it, and went to work hollowing out the trunk section with fire and stone axes and scrapers. Soon they lost interest and drifted away.

Aruanã, even more than his two companions, was eager to resume the journey. The memory of Morning Flower remained bitterly painful, and he was overwhelmed by all the emotions unleashed at her loss. To be away from Hare, Rock, Toad — from all that reminded him of her — would help end the pain.

So he was jubilant when the rains finally let up and he found himself sitting in the canoe, hollering and waving at a great group of Nambikwara, as Pojucan and Ubiratan paddled the craft.

The canoe was just twenty feet, with a four-foot beam, and heavily stocked with provisions. Aruanã sat in the bow, posted as lookout by Ubiratan, who, having lived in sight of Mother of Rivers and as much at home upon water as on land, was more skilled in its navigation than the Tupiniquin. They quickly moved into mid-channel, where the current was most rapid, and within moments were drawn into the wildness of this serpentine stream winding through the forest.

Small beaches, some sandy, others muddy or pebble-strewn, lay in the hook of the river's inner turns. Opposite, the waters had eroded the banks, which rose perpendicularly, often to a height several times that of a tall man. The rise of water during the Great Rain and the gradual ebbing that had commenced were clearly marked at levels along the clayey soil and the tenacious vegetation that clung to it.

The effect of the wet season was most evident in the sight of many toppled trees, their precarious hold at the river's edge finally undermined, their roots upturned like so many beseeching fingers. In places the river lost its form and the canoe was carried onto what appeared to be a vast lake.

At this early hour, the small beaches were thickly populated. Files of white cranes stood stiffly, eyeing the small craft as it rode past; sometimes they merely broke rank and withdrew a few steps — elsewhere, a nervous sentinel would signal all to wing. Beautiful pink and white spoonbills skimmed the water for insects, flights of parakeets squawked among the trees, black urubus perched solemnly, patiently awaiting a repast to come drifting down the river.

Alligators lay angled in the mud, their ridged backs motionless, some offering throaty grunts. In the trees behind them, monkeys kept up a busy chatter. A potbellied monkey bared his fangs at the passersby.

On this first day, the travelers began a routine that would rarely vary. They would set out before dawn and paddle till the sun stood high above and the heat was unbearable. Then they'd draw toward the bank and tie their craft to a limb or run it onto one of the beaches. After they'd bathed, they'd sometimes explore the forest but preferred to slumber till afternoon. They did travel at night, when there was the suspicion of a village ahead, gliding rapidly along the silvery way that more often than not bypassed the habitation of river people.

Their passage was relatively easy except in those places where the river roared over a cataract and their small craft was shot through a narrow channel between the rocks. Then they had to use every skill to prevent the hollowed log from capsizing. And, where the rocky bed shelved, there were barriers — great slabs of granite worn smooth by the action of water and sand. They were forced to portage, dragging and shoving the canoe through the undergrowth.

They passed through two new moons, two men and a boy voyaging into the heart of a great continent, as much in harmony with this wilderness as the animals that sought the riverbanks, leaving scant trace of their presence as they moved from one bend of the stream to the next. But their innate suspicion of the evil that stalked humans in such mysterious places often made them fearful.

Ubiratan awoke one morning and refused to leave the beach where they had slept. "Three sunrises must pass," he declared.

Aruanã, stowing the supplies they'd removed from the canoe for the night, stopped his work. Pojucan had just emerged from the river, where he had bathed, and was drying off at the fire. He made no comment but waited for Ubiratan to explain his statement.

"I dreamt that there was evil," Ubiratan said. "I looked into the face of one who waited. I saw the tail of a serpent. His hand reached for me. Long, sharp claws fixed around my arm. He brought his hideous face to mine, eyes that glowed red. The stench of death was upon his body."

Pojucan saw that the horrible being bore a striking resemblance to a fiend that tormented the Tupiniquin. "This is Jurupari," he said, "who has brought misery to our malocas."

"How were three sunrises shown?" Pojucan asked.

"Waking Bird called three times."

For three days and nights they stayed on the beach. The nights were exhausting, for there could be no rest with the threat of Jurupari upon them. They used all the urucu dye they had, covering one another's bodies and praying that their gleaming red skin would work its magic.

So they waited, and when the three sunrises had passed, they continued onward. They were still frightened, but that day passed without incident, and they felt free of the threat of Jurupari.

Six sunrises later, they were in the middle of the river, when a sudden squall burst upon them. A furious wind swept upriver, making the waters boil, and tore along the margins of forest, snapping branches like twigs and felling blackened, hollowed-out ancient trees. Behind the wind came a belt of rain, such a downpour that those in the canoe could scarcely see one another.

The current flowed powerfully, and with this and the pelting rain, they struggled in vain to steer for the nearest bank.

Then, at the height of the storm, the men and the boy heard a horrendous noise.

They had actually seen the enormous mahogany tree riding just below the surface earlier that afternoon. Now they only heard the impact as it bore down upon them, driving into the canoe with such force that the craft splintered and sank immediately.

The storm raged on, but the men and the boy were good swimmers and remained within sight of one another. While the wind and rain continued, they saw little chance of reaching the bank, but as they struggled to get beyond the grip of the current, they saw a floating island, a piece of jungle torn loose by the raging waters and held together by a massive web of roots deeply interwoven beneath its surface.

All three reached the island at the same time, shouting encouragement to one another as they grabbed for a hold among the slimy roots. Finally, they clawed up the side, and collapsed in exhausted silence.

It was only then they noticed that the storm was passing, as swiftly as it had come. With the wind gone, the island remained in midstream, almost imperceptibly moving with the current.

They were able to see, in the last light, that the island appeared to be some forty paces at its broadest point and at least five times this distance in length. Beyond the tangle of its old wood on their right was a thick stand of cane. Where they'd climbed on, there were smaller shrubs, grasses, and patches of bamboo. They began to explore this section of the island, looking for fire sticks and branches they might burn once they had a flame.

The two sticks, one hard, one soft, were easily found, but the harder one needed sharpening at one end and the softer required a notch to take the point. Without their stone tools and scrapers, this was difficult to accomplish. Pojucan impatiently fell to his knees and began tearing up the earth in search of a stone, which he eventually found. Holding one firmly on the ground with his foot, Pojucan twirled the drill stick rapidly between his hands. The wood was damp and it took some time before the friction produced sparks and the sparks ignited the sawdust bored out by the drill. Adding the driest twigs they could find, they soon had a blazing fire.

As for food and drink, a brief search yielded only some bitter berries, and although they were surrounded by water, it was not easy to reach. To drink, they had to go down like animals, with one holding onto another to prevent him from slipping into the river. Their conversation at the fire was limited.

"It is as I once spoke — 'a long and terrible journey,' Ubiratan said. "We have come far, but cannot know how many moons must lie between this place and my village."

"It will not be made without a canoe," Pojucan said. After a pause, he added, "There is the village of the river people who welcomed us. We must go back."

"When we are off this land that moves, we will see," Ubiratan replied.

Pojucan stood up, saying that he was going to look for more wood, and walked off to the trees, clumped in the center of the island.

With each step he took, his curiosity about this mysterious place grew. The undergrowth was thick with ferns and mosses flourishing in the damp river mists, but it was not difficult to penetrate, and Pojucan pressed on to find what lay ahead, where this great "earth canoe" parted the waters. Once or twice he thought he heard a low growl, but he dismissed it, for such a sound seemed impossible here.

The jaguars rested between the canes, their cold yellow eyes unblinking as they peered into the darkness.

The male's big paws were stretched in front of him, his haunches raised high. He measured over eight feet from his muzzle to the root of his tail and weighed nearly three hundred pounds. The female, though fully grown, was smaller than her partner. She twitched her tail rapidly and opened her massive jaws as if to growl but only began a fast, throaty panting.

There was a natural clearing between the cluster of trees and the canebrake, and Pojucan boldly walked into this opening. He saw no reason for caution, since he'd encountered no living things in this deserted place except insects.

But suddenly he froze, leaning ever so slightly in the direction of the canes, straining his ears as he tried to identify the noise. Perhaps it was Capybara, the giant rodent who infested such places, and he waited for its clicking sound.

The male jaguar crept forward, his heavy body low to the ground and passing noiselessly between a gap in the canes. With a deep, guttural roar, the jaguar burst out of the reeds and leapt toward Pojucan. Pojucan fell back, fighting hopelessly as the claws ripped through his flesh. He screamed, loud and piteously.

His cries died quickly, for the jaguar scrambled on top of him and sank his teeth into Pojucan's throat. The female, snarling and growling alongside them, saw the sudden gush of blood and came forward.

The kill was over, and the male, his muzzle stained with Pojucan's blood, backed off a little way. He watched his mate licking at the deep furrows across the man's chest with her horny, rasping tongue. He uttered a long, low, tremorous growl. Afterward he pawed his face a few times, then suddenly stood motionless, a heavy forepaw slightly above the ground, his head cocked to one side. He kept this stance briefly before he started to pad swiftly and stealthily toward the trees. Clearly the female was reluctant to leave the body, but within seconds she was loping after him.

Ubiratan and the boy heard Pojucan's piercing, agonized screams, and there could be no equal to the terror that came to them in the quiet. Neither moved nor spoke in the dreadful silence following the attack. They stayed by the fire, their eyes occasionally meeting, the helplessness each saw in the other's eyes only adding to their fear.

The jaguars had come out of the wood and were standing a distance apart, but they didn't move when the spot of light flared up. The male gave a deep, hoarse growl. He heard the female grunt, and he answered her with a series of night-rending roars.

"Go!" Ubiratan urged in a deep whisper. "That way! Now!" The boy hesitated. "Get away!"

Aruanã first crawled, with frantic, panicky movements, unmindful of the warm urine that spurted as he lost control. Then he scrambled up, running forward, when suddenly he had the sensation of falling, with roots and branches jabbing and scratching him, until he hit the water and went under.

Before Ubiratan made to follow the boy, he grabbed a flaming brand and hurled it in the direction of the jaguars. It landed near the female, who scrambled off, snarling. The male bolted, too, but swung in a semicircle that brought him close to the man.

Ubiratan anticipated the charge, and when the jaguar exploded out of the dark, he struck at him with a burning log. It caught the huge beast on the side of the face, just below the glowing yellow eye, and he rushed past Ubiratan, howling with rage, and disappeared into the night. Ubiratan cried then, in agony, for the fiery wood had seared the flesh of his hands.

He stumbled after Aruanã, plunging on until he reached the land's edge, where he slid rather than fell down the slope toward the river, crying out as his wounded hands were grazed by the brush.

Ubiratan was forced to spend the rest of the night clinging to the slope, with Aruanã supporting him when the pain in his hands became too much to bear and he slipped toward unconsciousness. Somehow the boy, exhausted and terrified as he was, managed to hold him up, knowing that if Ubiratan fell into the water with those bloody hands, his bones would be picked clean by the greedy piranha.

Dawn came and still they waited, but when the sun had burned the mist off the river, they saw that the floating island had moved closer to the riverbank.

Caught in the roots near them was part of a tree trunk, which Aruanã pried loose. They used this to get to shore.

On gaining the mainland, Aruanã cast his eyes slowly along the isle of terror.

"Pojucan," Ubiratan heard him say. Then, again and yet again, louder each time, as if addressing the spirit gods themselves: "Pojucan! Pojucan!"

It was the boy's only way of honoring one who had been nameless among his own people.

ℰↃ

The young warrior was one of the finest specimens of his race. When he walked through the village, other men took quiet note and the women's pleasure went undisguised. He was loose-limbed and solidly muscled, with a broad chest. There was about him the easy grace of the jaguar, which he was famed for hunting. He had a strong face with dark, piercing eyes and a general look of authority. In battle, he was recognized as brave; in the forest, as resourceful and cunning.

The people of the village admired and respected him, but they could never get close enough to know him properly. Several girls thought they had, but they were wrong. Two old women, aunts of the chief, tended the fire at his place, and he appeared perfectly satisfied with this arrangement. If any felt his behavior strange, they kept their opinions to themselves, for this young man was the favorite of their chief, who called him Little Brother.

The chief, whose hands still bore ugly scars, was Ubiratan. "Little Brother" was Aruanã of the Tupiniquin, and five Great Rains had passed since the night the jaguars slew Pojucan.

That nightmare had continued long through the journey. Fever had gripped Ubiratan. The boy knew the plants used at his maloca for such sickness, but he had been unable to find them now.

When Ubiratan had recovered sufficiently, they set out on foot, keeping to the riverbank. Two full moons passed before they finally staggered back into the clearing where they had been greeted with friendship.

They built a new canoe and equipped it, and this time they succeeded in reaching the end of the river. They had passed an entire season upon its waters, for when they got to the mouth, the Great Rains had already come.

The river that they were leaving was itself enormous and flowed like a dark and dangerous serpent, but Aruanã had seen its waters swallowed by the yellowish flood of Mother of Rivers.

It took three sunrises to travel between the first Tapajós malocas they encountered and the place where Ubiratan's family lived: The waterfront settlements were so numerous that several were passed in a single morning's voyaging, and more people dwelt opposite, on the islands in Mother of Rivers.

On the last morning of their passage, six war canoes rode out to greet them, the warriors in body paint and finest feathers. They chanted a song of welcome, for word of the arrivals had been passed from the first malocas where they'd rested. When the travelers and their grand escort beached below the Tapajós village, Great Chief had stood on the sands with his elders and headmen, making no effort to conceal his joy at the return of a favorite son he'd mourned for so long.

"Why did you never tell us your father is Great Chief of these people?" Aruanã asked Ubiratan one day.

"It has no meaning for Tupiniquin," the Tapajós said.

After two Great Rains, Ubiratan's father had died in battle, and "He-Who-Returns," as Ubiratan's people called him, became Great Chief.

With Pojucan dead, Ubiratan had accepted responsibility for the boy and saw him through all the rites of manhood, which were not demanding for one who had passed from childhood to maturity in the dramatic circumstances of their journey. Ubiratan had placed him under the finest warriors and hunters, and bade them teach the young man all they knew.

Aruanã should have felt a contentment greater than that of most men, for now he was indeed a man in every sense. But, with the passing of each Great Rain, an emptiness he'd experienced the night his father was killed — a sense of the great distance between this place and the village he remembered as his own — always returned. *I am Tupiniquin,* he often reminded himself, *of the maloca of Tabajara, whose voice is most often heard in the clearing.*

He could fight and hunt with Ubiratan's men, and make love with their daughters, but something was missing. When he looked at the stars, as his father had done, he dreamt of his own people and felt a longing such as Ubiratan had known at the Tupiniquin village. He did not forget the dishonor of Pojucan or his own torment over the stolen feathers of Macaw, but there was something else, stronger, too vague to define, calling him to the side of the ancestors. *I am Tupiniquin.*

Such a notion might not have taken hold so profoundly had he not fallen under the spell of the mysterious old man of whom Ubiratan had spoken on their journey. Aruanã did not meet Tocoyricoc until more than two Great Rains had passed and he stood with the mature young men. Only then did Ubiratan take him to the ancient one, whom many Tapajós saw as a messenger of the spirits.

Tocoyricoc was bent with age, and after each meeting, Aruanã had gone away believing that it would be their last, but the old man still lived. No one knew exactly how old he was or where he had come from, except that it was a place where the sun set and the mountains stood in the clouds. Some said that he had reached the Tapajós at a time when Ubiratan's great-grandfather was Great Chief, but no one could be sure of this.

Tocoyricoc's body was short and emaciated, his face deeply lined and his head bald, but his eyes were alert, as was his mind. He and Aruanã spent so much time together that there were Tapajós elders who voiced a concern about one who was not of their people standing so close to He-Who-Sees-Well.

The old man rarely left the cave in which he dwelt, high on the side of a hill, three days' journey from the main Tapajós village.

When Aruanã first saw the entrance to the cave, he had been disappointed. He had not known what to expect, but surely it should have been more than a dark hole in the earth. While Ubiratan sought an audience for him, Aruanã stood watching those who served the old man: four maidens. Their families accepted it as a great honor that they should be taken for two Great Rains to attend to the wants of He-Who-Sees-Well. They slept in a hut below the hill — little girls, Aruanã noted, who could not have known men. They kept glancing in his direction, exchanging words and giggling, while they sat preparing the manioc.

Once he was admitted to Tocoyricoc's place alone, and his eyes adjusted to the gloom, Aruanã found the cavern large, with a high ceiling, thickly clustered with sleeping bats, and a broad gallery, at the end of which was a natural raised platform only a step up but wide enough to provide the main living space for the sole occupant of these shadows.

It was chilly and damp. The only light came from a fire to one side of the platform, its smoke curling against the blackened rock behind it.

Aruanã saw familiar items — sacred rattles, flutes, gourds, piles of herbs and roots- — and unknown things, too. But none of these intrigued him as much as a large square of material, stretched out against the rock wall next to the old man, depicting a strange-looking figure.

Aruanã had never seen such a man — or was it the spirit of a man? — captured in such a fashion: a fat little warrior, a yellow stick in his hand, with big ears and square eyes and the oddest headdress he'd ever seen, guarded by smaller warriors in rows about him.

"What is it, Old Father?" Aruanã asked — later, when it was proper to do so. He had already answered questions about the journey and his past.

"It is the past," Tocoyricoc replied.

The past? Aruanã was truly puzzled. How could something that clung to a rock be the past? "I have never seen such a person," he said, and added, "captured in a hammock!"

Tocoyricoc's terribly thin body trembled with laughter. "This is no man," he said, when he quieted. "It is no more than the scratching in the sand."

"There is no color in the sand," Aruanã said.

Tocoyricoc patiently tried to explain how he had woven the panel with soft palm fibers that had been dyed in different colors. His young listener continued to be baffled, until Tocoyricoc likened the weaving process to the making of a hammock, and then it became a little clearer.

"I have never seen such a warrior," Aruanã said.

"Nor has any man in this forest."

"But there are such men?"

"Of power and wisdom."

"More power than Great Chief?"

"They cannot be compared to each other."

"Are you one of those on the wall?"

Tocoyricoc either didn't want to answer him or lost track of the exchange, for he asked, "Great Chief has said that you come from where the sun rises. How is this?"

"At the very edge of the earth, Old Father."

"Your people?"

"I am Tupiniquin."

"And where are you from, Old Father?" Aruanã asked, directly.

"From the past," Tocoyricoc muttered, but, noting the question in the boy's eyes, he added: "I was on a journey across the seasons, from the great mountains into the forest, along rivers that took us from our villages."

"Where were you going?"

"We were looking," came the vague response.

"What were you seeking?" Aruanã asked.

"To learn of things beyond our world."

In their meetings to come, the old man would return to the same theme. He would sit there on the first stool Aruanã had ever seen, his body bent toward the young man as he spoke. Occasionally he'd lose track of what he was saying, and Aruanã would have to wait while he searched his memory.

Among the objects in Tocoyricoc's cave was something even more magical to Aruanã than the little warrior — "the lines that remembered." They appeared to be a bunch of bowstrings of different colors and lengths knotted together untidily. Tocoyricoc used a word from his own language to describe them: *quipu*.

When Aruanã first saw the old man consult it, he'd picked out a red cord. "First knot," he said, "is battle of Black Valley, where a young Tocoyricoc fought. Two and one knots is the age he had, this is his place among the warriors, these, the number of enemy killed."

"What magic is this?"

"It is a way of remembering," he said. "To show what is past."

With the quipu, the old man could count the Great Rains of his past and see the events that lay between the years. Every color stood for a specific thing or event; every knot he made was a mark on his memory. Black he used for time, red for war, white for peace, green for the journeys in the forest, and so on. Thinner strings and threads radiated from the main cords; lesser colors were for lesser events. It was a perfect record of all he had seen and endured.

He had lived in a land where the mountains stood in the clouds and the air was thin to any who had not taken it with their first breath.

"This was the land where Master — one you would call Great Chief — arose. Son of the Sun. He came to change our world when I was your age. Before He-Who-Transforms, we were a miserable people — living as those who see nothing but the forest." His voice shook with emotion as he told Aruanã about this great sky-being. He showed the young man his own golden earplugs —"tears of the sun"— and said that they were pitiful things compared with what adorned the Master. He was chief of all chiefs, supreme ruler of the quarters of earth. "When the Master led us, the ground trembled before our enemies. I marched with our warriors till not a voice was heard against the Master. When the enemies' malocas were burned and those who resisted slain, the Master forgave the rest for standing against him. He welcomed them as our own people."

When peace came, Tocoyricoc said, they had begun to transform the land according to the thoughts of the Master. They built great malocas of stone, and temples. The idea of a temple meant nothing to Aruanã until Tocoyricoc compared it with the huts where sacred rattles and flutes were kept.

"You seek feathers of Macaw and other birds for their beauty, is it not so?" he said. "You cry with pleasure when Ubiratan wears the adornments of Great Chief! All this will not compare with the beauty of this sacred maloca, guarded by women who serve those with words for the Master. They are called Virgins of the Sun."

Here was something unimaginable to the Tupiniquin: the notion that women were capable of anything beyond carrying the seed of man and raising manioc.

"The Virgins of the Sun — they have known men?"

"It is forbidden, but it happens. Yet, if a boy child comes from this mating, it is killed. It is forbidden for a boy to breathe in the maloca of the Master. Girls can be kept but not seen until they are grown and show themselves as Virgins of the Sun."

Aruanã heard many strange and wondrous stories in the cave: of canoes that sailed far upon Bluewater like that near his old village; of holes in the earth where men worked in darkness seeking the silvery light of the moon, and of rivers and lakes that flowed with tears of the sun; of great bowstrings tied between mountains so that men could cross from one height to another.

"These things you have told," he one day remarked to Tocoyricoc, "make me wonder why you did not return."

"I was alone."

"Others walked from the mountains with you."

"There was death in the high places and on the rivers. Arrows killed some in the forest; sickness took others."

"I came with my father and Ubiratan. There was a reason for the journey. You said you were 'looking.' I have not understood this."

"We came to see for the Master. We looked for tears of the sun, light of the moon—many things for the Master, but we came too far . . . .I waited for the next Great Rain, and then the next, until the past was lost."

Aruanã said quietly, "I wish to see the wonders you have told."

The old man's sudden anger was surprising. He rose unsteadily from his stool, moving his head from side to side, advancing on his feeble legs to where Aruanã sat. "No!" he shrieked. "Seek your own people! Find them! Find your maloca before you lie old and dying like Tocoyricoc."

It was an appeal that struck Aruanã's heart. The distance between this place and the Tupiniquin malocas grew wider with each season. There were nights when he would lie in his hammock and think of Tocoyricoc and shudder: He could see an old man waiting for death, and the old man was himself. He might be Little Brother and he walked with Great Chief, but Tocoyricoc was right: Sooner or later, Aruanã was going to have to speak to Ubiratan.

One evening, after the fifth Great Rain, he found himself alone with the Tapajós chief outside Tocoyricoc's cave. The young girls had been sent back to the village, the food pots lay shattered, the fires before the hut were extinguished.

Tocoyricoc had called for Ubiratan and Aruanã, and had warned that no others should approach.

Up on his platform, the old man already seemed no more than a pile of thin bones. "I will make the journey," he said, in a tiny voice, "before the sun is strongest." He had a rattle in his hand and shook it feebly. "I have been with the ancestors, Great Chief."

Tocoyricoc was in pain, and was short-winded as he struggled with precise instructions about how his body should be handled after death. He knew that the fire he asked for was totally different from the usual Tapajós burial practice, but he warned of hideous punishments if he was disobeyed.

"I do not want to sleep with the ancestors of the Tapajós," he said. "I must return to my own people. I have asked this, and your grandfathers grant my wish."

"You have been heard," Ubiratan assured him.

The old man was suddenly exhausted, his eyelids drooping, but he raised a trembling hand and beckoned Aruanã forward.

"Old Father," the young man said, "it will be as you have shown."

"The past must disappear," Tocoyricoc said. "All but this." He fumbled with something about his neck. With difficulty, he removed the stone and held it for Aruanã to take.

It was a green jade amulet in the shape of a small animal of a kind Aruanã had never seen.

"Carry it, Tupiniquin," he said. "Carry it . . . to your people."

"I am grateful, Old Father. It will go with me."

"Your people, Tupiniquin . . . Do not let them out of your thoughts."

෴

When Ubiratan and Aruanã entered the cave at dawn, it was deserted. They searched its darkest recesses hastily, and then fled into the open.

Neither said a word, but their thoughts were the same: How could they have been so thoughtless as to consider Tocoyricoc a mere human like themselves?

They were still standing in front of the cave, shivering with fright in the chill morning, when the sun rose. The noises of the forest were all about them, but they heard a human cry that drew their eyes upward toward the hill directly above.

Tocoyricoc had somehow reached the summit, and now he raised his arms to greet his beloved Son of the Sun, hailing the Master with all the voice he had left.

He stood once more facing the flaming sphere in the east and then started down. He was halfway along the slope when the men below heard a small cry, and he toppled forward, falling a distance before his body lodged against some boulders.

Ubiratan and Aruanã laid Tocoyricoc outside the mouth of the cave. They placed all his belongings about him, and made a fire in accord with the old man's wishes.

Aruanã watched as the flames raced along the colorful cords that remembered. "Now there is no past," he said.

They waited until everything that would burn had been consumed and then carried what was left to the waters of Mother of Rivers. To a people who took infinite care in preparing their dead, sealing their remains in large clay pots where they would be safe from evil, this seemed a poor and dangerous way to seek Land of the Grandfather, but it was as Tocoyricoc had requested.

"You will return?" Ubiratan asked.

Aruanã did not respond.

"It is a long and terrible journey," he said, remembering a day when he had stood with this young warrior's father. "But it is possible," he added.

III

March 1499 – April 1500

On a fine morning two Great Rains later, a group of boys were at play in the shallows of the river near their village when a warrior stepped out of the forest and stood watching from the opposite bank. They fled toward their malocas, yelling a warning, and their fathers rushed for their weapons, but there was no enemy horde, only the tall stranger now walking with purpose toward the stockade.

Two elders stood at the head of a knot of men jamming the narrow opening between the wooden stakes as all fought for a glimpse of the arrival. The older of the village leaders turned his head and growled at the warriors behind, demanding silence.

The elder began to move forward, his war club ready. To his astonishment, he heard the stranger call his name: "Tabajara! O my father, Tabajara! Great man of my maloca!"

Aruanã, the Tupiniquin, had found his people.

The village had never before experienced anything like the return of Aruanã. How to deal with one who fled from the enemy, like Pojucan, presented no problem: A coward must be nameless till the day he died. But Aruanã had come back with no such burden. The women lamented for days to show a joy they shared with Obapira, Aruanã's mother, still alive, who'd once shaved every hair of her head in mourning for this son. The men were more cautious, some thinking of spirits that walked with the body of man, and some remembering the time they stole feathers of Macaw and made this brave-looking warrior weep with feathers of Heron.

Strangely enough, it was Naurú — dreadful, bent-backed Naurú, become even more hideous with age — who spoke for Aruanã, son of a man he'd condemned to death. But, then, it wasn't really strange, since Naurú, who communed with Voice of the Spirits, could always divine what was good for Naurú.

The village was told that the sacred rattles would be heard, and that night the men were summoned to the clearing, where Naurú waited, grim-looking in his urubu cloak, already moaning with the powers that were upon him.

Aruanã had crossed half a continent and had braved the worst dangers, yet, standing again in that dark circle around the pagé, he was at once wary. He looked magnificent, for Old Mother had insisted on painting his body, ignoring the protests of Obapira, who was trying — with little success — to find a place in her son's eyes. And in his lip and cheek holes he had smooth green stones carried from the lands of the Tapajós, and around his neck the jade amulet given him by Tocoyricoc.

Now the men in the clearing began to dance around the pagé, stamping their feet in such a way that the seedpods tied around their calves shook in unison. From many mouths came the cries: "Now speak, O Voice of the Spirits." Naurú shuffled around in the middle of the circle, puffing at a roll of tabak and blowing smoke toward some of the dancers. Faster and faster they moved, leaping and shouting, dipping their heads toward the pagé. "Let us hear! Let us hear!"

Finally, Naurú intoned, "The spirits will speak!" and shook his rattle. The circle of dancers slowed and stopped. Naurú stood motionless, waiting for complete silence, and then he was heard, in a low, monotonous voice unlike his own.

"Aieee! It is Macachera!" came the response. "Macachera, who sees our steps."

This Macachera walked with travelers; depending on his mood, he could either clear the path ahead of danger or riddle it with sickness and fear.

"There is one who has made a journey."

All eyes turned to Aruanã. "It is so. Let us hear!"

"Macachera has seen all."

"It is good! Let Macachera talk in this clearing."

"Let the enemy tremble in the sight of this Tupiniquin! He has seen the waters of Mother of Rivers. His eyes have witnessed, his ears have heard more than any other man in his maloca. Such a man is among us, and it gives the ancestors joy. Let him know this! Let him be heard in the clearing."

When he'd finished, he did his peculiar little dance, dragging his crooked leg behind him and jerking his body along until he stood before Aruaná.

"The feathers were white!"

He waited but got no response from Aruanã.

"It was so because no-warrior was among us," Naurú said.

There were exclamations of surprise from the circle of men, most of whom remembered that awful time when one who had fled the Cariri darkened the village. It was his son who had now returned but with honor, as had been shown. Why was he who spoke with Voice of the Spirits bringing back the nameless one?

Naurú held the sacred rattle motionless before him. "Let the anger of the ancestors be remembered. Naurú heard their wishes. They were not obeyed."

Tabajara, the elder who had been responsible for the failure to execute Pojucan, took this reminder badly.

"No-warrior has been gone many Great Rains," the pagé said. "I stand before you, as it has always been. The spirits see this."

"We, too, see Naurú!" several cried.

"Then see this!" Naurú cried out, and he rushed to the spot in the clearing where he'd stamped his foot. Kneeling, he scratched in the sand till he found what he sought: the claws of the jaguar.

He picked these out of the dirt and staggered up, dragging himself over to where Aruanã stood.

"Now speak his name so all may hear!" Naurú ordered.

"It was Pojucan."

"Po-ju-can," the pagé said, drawing out the name. "With these claws, Naurú found Pojucan. Where the earth is upon the waters — Naurú and Macachera, who led him to that place!"

Naurú displayed the claws, and Aruaná took a step backward, but the pagé said, "It is past. The ancestors have been obeyed."

Aruanã was trembling, and so was every man who'd witnessed this performance, for they were reminded, once again, that if Naurú went against them, there was no way of escaping his wrath — even if it meant that he must take the form of the jaguar and run to the farthest place beyond the forest.

သ

After his return, when the first battle cry came and the warriors of this Tupiniquin village hurled themselves against a Cariri stockade, Aruanã was at the front of the onslaught. Never was there a more ferocious warrior. He ran in among the enemy when his arrows were shot and then battered them with his war club until their blood lay upon his body bright as urucu paint. But it was the final triumph, after this war party returned with Cariri prisoners, that made Aruanã, son of Pojucan, a man among men of the Tupiniquin.

Three sunrises after they'd left the Cariri village in flames, they returned to the clearing with three prisoners: two of them handsomely plump, who looked as though they might be brothers, and a third, who was taller than the others and had already occasioned amusement among the Tupiniquin, for he had the largest buttocks they'd ever seen.

Tabajara stood to one side with the rest of the men as Old Mother, throbbing with delight, inspected the capture. When she jabbed her fingers at a Cariri chest, the other women slapped their thighs and yelled with pleasure.

The two prisoners who looked alike glowered back at the women, but Big Buttocks became enraged. This increased the tirade, until they were breathless and Old Mother ordered: "Let them be prepared!"

"Prepare me well, women!" Big Buttocks declared. "When I stand before those who live beyond the sun, let them see a true warrior!"

He was given a few solid kicks for this insolence, and then a mountain of a woman seized him about the neck so that he could scarcely breathe, while others went to work shaving his head with shell scrapers. This accomplished, they slapped dollops of a sticky gum on his flesh, spread it with scrapers, and then bedecked him with an ugly assortment of gray feathers. The same was swiftly done with the other Cariri.

Old Mother expressed approval. She then addressed Tabajara: "We have passed many moons without seeing Cariri beasts."

Tabajara consulted with the elders of two other malocas.

Aruanã overheard their talk but paid no attention. He was looking at a lovely young woman named Juriti — "Dove" — who had just approached Old Mother with three lengths of cotton cord. Juriti's eyes were on Aruanã, too, and when she smiled, he smiled back.

"We have waited long," Old Mother repeated. She stomped about impatiently, her big feet stirring up puffs of dust. "Tell the number of beads!" she snapped.

"It is decided," Tabajara said. "There will be one."

Old Mother was aghast. "One?" Far better than she could possibly have hoped for.

"See, Cariri," she crowed, "our ancestors won't wait!" She took a cord from Juriti, threaded a single shell bead onto it, and went to Big Buttocks, who laughed as she tied the thin cotton strand around his neck.

When it was done, it signaled a new round of joyous hysteria among the women, who knew that one shell indicated that the Cariri beasts would be chased into the clearing within the time of one new moon.

⇛

"Yware-pemme!" Old Mother cried. "Bring Yware-pemme!"

She was sitting on a rough mat of fresh palm leaves inside Tabajara's maloca. Since the arrival of the Cariri prisoners, she had conducted preparations for the coming feast, and nothing deserved more attention than Yware-pemme.

Responding to her command, four girls led by Juriti entered the longhouse and came dancing slowly toward her, singing as they brought Yware-pemme. Similar to a weapon of war, with a broad, flattish head like that of a great serpent, it was twice the size of anything that a man would want to carry to battle: wielded by a strong warrior, it could crack the hardest skull in a single blow.

Juriti and the girls laid the weapon on the ground before Old Mother, who bent forward to stroke it with affection.

"Sing, O redwood of death. Let the ancestors witness the blow," crooned Old Mother. She lifted her eyes to the others. "Where are the feathers?" she asked. "Where is the gum? Bring. Bring all!"

Old Mother now supervised the making of delicate feather flowers, and she was quick to reject the slightest imperfection. Some women were working on long strands of threaded shells, and here, too, Old Mother demanded that sizes and shades be in perfect order.

Others smeared Yware-pemme's great head with gum and sprinkled it with a fine gray powder of ash and eggshells, chanting a song in remembrance of all its good works, calling out names of Tupiniquin warriors killed in battle against the Cariri or the Tupinambá — warriors who already knew the peace brought by Yware-pemme's revenge.

With a small stick, Old Mother traced a pattern on Yware-pemme's sticky head, similar to the markings on a warrior's face.

With Old Mother walking ahead, the women filed out of the maloca into the sunny clearing, dancing in a long, wavy line behind Yware-pemme as they headed toward a pole set up opposite Naurú's hut.

"It is ready!" Old Mother called out.

"We have seen," Naurú said from within, but did not immediately show his face.

The women stood the slaughter club against the pole and entwined both with the long strands of shells. Naurú emerged from his hut the moment they were finished. He shuffled around the pole, commenting on the flowers and the shells and, to the relief of the women, agreeing that they were excellent.

"Who will go first?" Old Mother asked.

"Big Buttocks," said the pagé without hesitation.

The objects of all these preparations — Big Buttocks and his compatriots — had been allowed the freedom of the village, and Big Buttocks had proven himself so tireless in composing ever-worse insults against his captors that he had earned the admiration of all.

After the women had displayed the slaughter club, there remained one task: opposite the stake against which the club rested — far enough so that Naurú would not be disturbed — they erected a crude shelter. This done, each group returned to its maloca.

Tonight, the men — the captives included — would drink until they began to fall down in the clearing. When the beer and the talk and the insults were concluded, the Cariri would be walked or carried to the rough hut. The women would have no part of this, for they must be ready before dawn.

Next morning, Aruanã lay in his hammock. To think that he'd wanted to match the elders in quaffing gourd after gourd of beer! He shifted position, the hammock lurched, and the maloca swung around him.

"Stand, on your feet!" Old Mother hissed at Tabajara, at Aruanã, at any who would hear.

"Be gone — to your own work," Tabajara said good-naturedly, and waved her away, but as he did, he lost balance and fell out of the hammock. Old Mother laughed heartily. Tabajara laughed, too, and more joined in.

It was, Old Mother thought as she took her leave, a good start to this great day.

At the clearing, the men watched Old Mother lead the first of many dances that would be performed before sunset.

Naurú stood on the opposite side of the clearing, a motionless gray figure come to observe the rousing of the Cariri. It had been a long and exhausting night for the pagé. While others slept or drank till they were senseless, he'd been busy with his rattles and herbs, preparing the ground for the feast.

The men needed no more than a covering of crimson to ward off the bad spirits who might come to spy on the village ceremonies. When it was done, their women hurried back to the Cariri, who had to be dressed for the kill. As happened on the first day, they were smeared with gum and bedecked with drab-colored feathers.

When they were satisfied with their work, the women cleared away the shelter where the captives had spent their last night, and then led the Cariri to the "spirit guides": men who rejoiced in the pagé's attention, for this singling out was an honor. It fell to them to show these beasts to those who could not be seen.

The women placed three big earthenware pots on the ground before the spirit guides and then went to stand at a distance. Ignoring the insults of the captives, two guides danced to the first pot and, dipping into it, began to extract a long, whitened cord. As intended, its appearance elicited cries of surprise from the women, though they themselves had spent weeks plaiting this thick rope from palm fiber.

The other spirit guides now grabbed Big Buttocks and held him, while those with the rope tied it round his waist, leaving two long ends by which he could be led. When the brothers had been dealt with similarly, the women fled the scene, shouting a warning to all that the guides were prepared.

The spirit guides paraded their charges around the deserted clearing, pausing outside each maloca to address dead warriors who waited for revenge. At the entrance to the stockade, the prisoners were lined up in front of the stakes where the skulls of earlier enemies dangled. Here, they were told, they would come to guard this village!

When the guides marched back to the clearing and announced that their work of "showing" the Cariri was done, the women again poured into the open. To reclaim the captives, they must fight for them, not with the spirit guides, who now drifted away, but alone — Tupiniquin women against Cariri warriors.

"Fight, Cariri!" the cry went up.

Big Buttocks stood back to back with the other prisoners, surrounded by a seething crowd of women and children, with Old Mother thumping along in front, her great breasts flopping against her body. The Cariri had been provided with weapons — stones and broken pots scattered on the ground. Big Buttocks was first to hurl a piece of pottery at Old Mother: "May your sons' bones whiten our clearings, old woman!"

The potsherd bounced off her shoulder into the crowd behind. She let out a furious sound, taken up by others.

More pottery and stones flew, the brothers sharing the rage of Big Buttocks and trying to match his flow of missiles and curses. The women merely leapt and laughed and shrieked when a missile hit home.

At a signal from Old Mother, they closed in and grabbed the ends of the white cords, as they dragged the men off to the far end of the clearing.

"See, Cariri, this is the place."

The Cariri only sneered contemptuously at being shown the spot where they would die.

A group of girls including Juriti came dancing across the clearing with Yware-pemme, and an opening was quickly made for them through the crowd. Many hands reached to touch the slaughter club, its delicate feather flowers still intact, and a great murmur of satisfaction ran through the ranks of agitated females. The girls paraded the club before the prisoners.

Big Buttocks laughed at it. "A sapling!" he called it. "A little stick for a Tupiniquin child."

But one of the brothers regarded the weapon with a look of horror that did not go unnoticed.

"Run, Caririi!" a woman shouted. "We will not stop you. Run — show your ancestors a coward!"

The young man stood his ground, and the girls with Yware-pemme moved on.

Old Mother began giving instructions for the fires that must be prepared. The strongest women came forward and drove hefty forked stakes into the ground. These would support the crosspieces upon which thinner timbers would rest to make the *boucan*, a wide grill for the meat to be served this day.

On the ground before the hut of the sacred rattles, another ceremony had almost ended. The young men, among them Aruanã, were waiting for word from the elders and Naurú, who were huddled together out of earshot. Finally, the pagé and Tabajara rose and walked over to them.

"You have decided?" one asked.

Tabajara spoke: "Let it be him!" He indicated toward Aruanã.

"Yware-pemme!" Aruanã cried with joy.

Immediately remembering where he was, he lowered his voice to a whisper. "The honor is too great for one so miserable," he said. "I cannot hold Yware-pemme. Let another be shown."

Juriti and the girls, waiting for this moment, came forward and handed the great club to Tabajara. No sooner had he taken it than the girls fled, for the innocent games played with Yware-pemme were at an end.

Tabajara again addressed Aruanã: "We hear your words, but it is the wise men of the malocas who have spoken."

"All better men than one who stands before you."

"They have known Yware-pemme."

"All were men who wasted little blood in the clearing."

"Then, may it be so with you, Aruanã, warrior of Tupiniquin!" Having said this, Tabajara held the great club with its head faced downward and swung it slowly, letting it pass between the young man's legs.

When one was thus indicated, he must no longer protest the choice, and Aruanã seized Yware-pemme. He must now select his attendants.

He chose eight young men, who took him to a place behind the malocas. His body was dusted with ash to dull the bright urucu; streaks of deep genipapo dye marked his forehead; the green stones he wore in his lip and cheek holes were replaced with common white bone; dull feathers similar to those of the captives were gummed from his waist downward. When his attendants had made him as ugly as possible, they covered themselves with ashes. They stripped the club of its feather flowers, and when this was done, they went to the place of slaughter with Aruanã leading them.

Big Buttocks roared at his executioner, inviting him to hurry, for his pleasure would be brief.

"You will die, Tupiniquin, when my people march. You will fall with all in your maloca. Slay me, now! Bring the hatred of my brothers — many brothers, Tupiniquin, with many arrows!"

It was as he mockingly demanded. Rushing at him from behind, Aruanã swung the great club. Big Buttocks made a move to avoid the blow, but he was too slow. He shuddered and went down. His fellow Cariri watched bleakly as Ywate-pemme smashed against his head — horrible, crunching blows — until he lay still.

"Your brothers, Cariri," Aruanã said, with surprising calmness, "this is what will come to your brothers."

Old Mother and her cohorts rushed forward to take possession of the body. They lifted Big Buttocks and, singing as they went, carried the body to the boucan.

She was holding a short piece of wood, sharpened at one end. She handed it to the women, who knelt by the body, and watched as it was driven deep between those great rounds of flesh. Always the first step, the bung would stop the rich juices from flowing.

Ywate-pemme struck again and again, and quickly there were three groups of women at work in the clearing.

The men avoided these preparations, turning instead to the gourds of beer set out for them. The first to drink was the executioner. As head of his maloca, it was Tabajara's privilege to serve the beer to Aruanã.

The young man drank and returned the gourd to the elder. "I give thanks, my father."

"For what?"

"There is no memory of no-warrior."

"A young warrior with three names," he said, "has no need for what is past." He paused for a moment, then continued: "Aruanã's hammock hangs next to Tabajara's, and Tabajara will soon be an old man."

Aruanã looked down humbly. First there were the three names of his victims to add to his own. And now Tabajara was suggesting that a time would come when Aruanã would lead the maloca.

"If it is shown by our ancestors," he said quietly, "it may happen."

Naurú approached them, with his awkward gait. "He must be taken away now," he said, "before the fire dances."

Aruanã looked past the pagé to the women. Those not busy with the bodies danced about the others, singing of revenge. Mothers rushed their children to where the Cariri lay, beckoning them to wet their little hands in the blood.

He saw Juriti standing on a small mound: her blood-stained arms were raised, her head tilted back, as she sang to the sky — a song that Aruanã could not hear but that those near her were following with obvious pleasure. He stood up reluctantly, indicating that he was ready to leave a celebration that had scarcely begun,

Tabajara and Naurú hastily led him to the maloca, where he stripped off the feathers on his legs and climbed into his hammock. Naurú gave him a small bow and arrows, similar to those placed with newborns, chanted some words over him, and then hurried away with Tabajara.

A man found glory in wielding Ywate-pemme — but at a price. For three sunrises he must leave his hammock only when absolutely necessary, for in this period he was in terrible danger from those he'd slain. Sickness, madness, sudden death — any could find him if he was caught by the ghosts of the Cariri. After the third sunrise, the names of the Cariri could be called and he would be free.

In the clearing, the bodies of the Cariri were scalded and skinned.

Big Buttocks's arms were cut off close to the shoulder, and his legs above the knee. Four women seized these limbs and danced them around the clearing, calling out:

"Awake! Awake, fallen Tupiniquin! Here is your death avenged. See the legs that marched against you. See the hands that held the bow."

The enemy were being dismembered with bamboo knife and stone ax. The trunks were split, the intestines removed and set aside; these would go with other parts of the viscera into a great broth, which all would sip, taking the strength of the enemy. Naurú made a silent appearance before each body to claim the thumbs and genitals. These would be prepared in the hut of the sacred rattles, the former in a concoction that would make arrows fly true, the latter for fertility in man and plant. When the limbs of the Cariri lay on the grill, Old Mother took her clay pot to the boucan and sat there, intent on catching the fat that dripped down the supports.

The butchers caroused and sometimes squabbled over the joints; the men danced in the clearing and sang with joy at having seen the suffering of the Cariri. So it would go, they warned, with any who dared gnaw the bones of Tupiniquin.

೭౨

There were other battles, and more prisoners slaughtered. By rallying a group of warriors and preventing the enemy from crossing the river near the village, Aruanã had demonstrated his unquestioned qualities of leadership. So there was great joy in the village when Juriti delivered his son and he took to his hammock for the lying-in period.

To bring a new child to the village made the greatest demands upon a father: a woman held the seed and matured it, but it could grow only with the spirit of man, and if any evil affected him, it would also touch the child.

During the five sunrises of his confinement, he must neither hunt nor take any meat, for the strength that would come to him could weaken the baby. His voice could not be heard above a whisper, and the names of enemy he'd slain must not be called in his presence. He must remain in his hammock as much as possible till the threats to his newborn had passed.

Four sunrises before, he had heard Juriti cry out in the maloca.

"I must go," she whispered afterward, and he had jumped out of his hammock to help her rise.

"You are worried?"

"So many would take this happiness."

"My little dove," he said, "I have strength for this first child."

"When I am alone, I will see the courage in your face." She clenched her teeth as a pain came. "It will be a boy child," she said, and smiled. "As his father, with the ways of a great Tupiniquin." But the smile faded and again she showed concern. "O Aruanã, go well. May the ancestors watch over you."

"I am prepared," he said. "Go — and bring the child."

She reached for some fresh wood for the fire and waited till it burned. She looked again at the manioc and fruits she had been gathering these past days, and hoped that they would be enough to satisfy her husband's hunger. She watched him climb back into his hammock before she left, heading for the edge of the forest.

There was a small glade just beyond the river, and she could hear the stream from the place where she waited to give birth. It was tranquil and comforting, reminding her that her people were not far off. The child moved in the early afternoon, and she tried to stifle her cries as the pain increased, but it was not possible. When the baby breathed on the soft mat of leaves where she had squatted, she looked around furtively lest an evil be attracted to this place.

She cut the cord with a shell, as Old Mother had instructed, and cleaned the baby. She was very weak when finally she got to her feet and walked slowly, clutching the tiny body to her own. She paused at the river's edge to bathe Aruanã's son, and knew great joy at the sight of the sturdy infant.

The news reached Aruanã long before she returned to the maloca, and he lay back, pleased but exhausted.

Juriti brought his son; he heard the strong cry and saw the robust little body and was enormously relieved that his efforts thus far had succeeded. Encouraged, he faced his confinement.

The sunrises passed quickly, for his friends came to the maloca to visit the new father and congratulate him on the son he had made. When her work in the fields was done, Juriti hurried back to his side, and did all she could to help him through this difficult period. Naurú, too, came to chant over the child, and on the last occasion, he asked for the umbilical cord, which Aruanã had received from Juriti. At the first new moon, Naurú would conceal pieces of this in the village, a guarantee of many children for the son of Aruanã.

The fifth sunrise came and the vigil was over but for one ritual: Aruanã must go alone to the sands at Bluewater that flowed to the end of the earth and find the tiny white shells for his son's first necklace. When the baby wore these, his lip could be pierced and his chosen name heard for the first time.

On this beach where he walked for the shells, Aruanã felt contentment at being alone.

One man, alone, at the edge of his world, his bare feet making an impression along great curves of sand. Beyond the palm groves rose the tattered fringe of the forest, which pressed so deeply upon his soul, perhaps because he had reached so far into its depths. Above was the sky, which he had come to share with the distant Tapajós, with the Nambikwara, and with those whom Tocoyricoc remembered.

He walked with his head bowed, and felt a twinge of excitement every time he found a shell. He didn't hesitate to toss away any that showed the slightest blemish, for the shells were for his son.

"My son!" he cried. "My son!" He leapt then, great bounds of joy. "Son of Aruanã!" he shouted. "Son of Tupiniquin!"

And then, at the height of his happiness, came a premonition.

Aruanã stopped in his tracks. He glanced first toward the palm grove, then looked out over Bluewater that flowed to the end of the earth. Every instinct, so finely tuned, alerted him that something was wrong.

His hand tightened around his club. He took a few steps, only to pause once more and search the land, his eyes scanning the waters at the very edge of the sands, where spirit creatures were said to rush out of the surf to assault man.

But there was no threat at the waterline, and he lifted his gaze. For a long moment he stared at it unknowingly — the very thing that was occasioning his disquiet — and then he recognized what had crept into his vision and had caused him to pause:

Tiny puffs of cloud had fallen to the end of the earth. Four . . . five . . . six were bunched together just above the horizon. Otherwise the sky was perfectly clear.

He made a hesitant progress toward the water, squinting into the distance at the strange clouds. But even as he did so and perplexed as he was, he began to see that his first impression had been wrong. Very quickly now the swiftest clouds lifted above the water. There was a flash of understanding: Here were great canoes coming from the end of the earth.

Aruanã watched as they came closer. The sun was gone behind the trees, and he found it difficult to discern the craft, but he stood rooted a while longer before he realized that he must hasten to the village and tell what he had seen. This made him gaze at the horizon again, to be absolutely certain, for it was a fantastic discovery for a man who had gone to seek no more than shells. They were there, darkening images now, these canoes that had come from the end of the earth.

Book One

The Portuguese

IV

March – April 1526

*S*tanding with the ship's master on the poop deck above *São Gabriel's* sterncastle, His Excellency Gomes de Pina was about to be violently ill.

Gomes de Pina held his frilly sleeve near his face as he observed a group of sailors below. They were keeping a protective half-circle at the ship's firebox, where a grisly meal was being prepared. Any who lurked close to these *marinheiros* were warned off with threatening glances and oaths.

Sixty-four days beyond the bar of Lisbon's Tagus, the marinheiros had seen one in three who had shipped out on the *São Gabriel's* in late March of this year 1526 die from scurvy or the bloody flux. What remained of the provisions was rotten or fermented and, besides, would last no longer than a week. These men, old hands at long voyages, had hunted in the hold, in the dank forecastle, wherever they might corner or spike rodents. Skinned and spread on the firebox grill, the rats were to be their sustenance.

"*Ratazana?*" His Excellency said querulously.

"Ratazana," the master of *São Gabriel* confirmed, with thinly disguised amusement.

The master was of medium height, sturdily built, with a discernible strength in his movements and intelligence in his face, burnt mahogany by the sun. He had green eyes that were brooding and melancholy, and a prematurely gray beard in this, his thirty-sixth year. His full name was Nicolau Gonçalves Cavalcanti. He was descended on his father's side from a long line of Florentine merchants who had settled

in Lisbon. His mother's family, the Gonçalves, brought the blood of old Portugal —
of Iberian and Celt, of seafaring Phoenician and the Roman of Lusitania province, of
Swabian and Visigoth, and of the sensuous and inquiring Moor, who ruled in the
peninsula for six centuries.

Cavalcanti noticed that the sight of rats cooking over a firebox was not the only
cause of Gomes de Pina's discomfort. As a *fidalgo*, a noble at the court of Lisbon,
Gomes de Pina would simply never consider any alteration of his appearance. Thus,
even in the intense heat of the tropics, every day he emerged from his cramped quarters draped with slashed doublet, thick breeches, and silken mantle and labored up
the steps to the poop, where he posted himself in sweltering authority. Today, as always, beads of sweat stood out on His Excellency's forehead, and his breathing was
labored.

"Sixty-four days out of Lisbon," the fidalgo said, "forty days west of Cabo
Verde, and still no Terra de Santa Cruz. Could it be the fault of this Guinea pilot?"

"I find nothing wrong with João Fernandes's reckoning," said Cavalcanti.
"There are signs of land." Just two days before, they had sighted bottle weed and
asses' tails, and a flight of birds had crossed their bow.

"Master, signs there are, but where is Santa Cruz?"

Cavalcanti did not reply immediately. He was thinking of Gomes de Pina's use
of the old name — Land of the Holy Cross — given to the territory by Pedro Álvares
Cabral when he discovered it for Portugal in 1500. On the Lisbon waterfront, to men
who knew better, it was *Terra do Papagaio* (Land of Parrots) or Terra do Brasil, named for
the brazilwood taken from its wild shores.

"The pilot can't be blamed for a slow ship," Cavalcanti finally said.

João Fernandes was in fact an excellent pilot. Like other navigators of his time,
he depended mainly on compass, half-hour glass, and a simple knotted line and
floating wood chip to track the ship's course. He had quadrant and astrolobe, tables
and charts; of latitude he could be reasonably sure, but determining longitude was
beyond his instruments. More important was Fernandes's special feel for the way of a
ship in the ocean, and his conviction that a pilot who erred but ten leagues in a thousand was no pilot at all.

Gomes de Pina fell to bemoaning that a fidalgo so eager as he to be of service
should be made to do the king's business in this battered old vessel. A terror among
Arab and Swahili dhowsmen from Malindi to the Malabar coast more than a quarter
of a century before, *São Gabriel* was a tired ship now, riding behind the two other
vessels —lateen-rigged caravels — that made up the squadron commanded by
Gomes de Pina.

What distinguished *São Gabriel* from those rakish caravels was her size — 120
tons against fifty or so; her broad, square sails spreading above a wide beam; her towering castles fore and aft. Low amidships, her beam a third of her length, she had a
round, bulging appearance. Her fore and main masts each carried two square sails
and topsails, and the mizzen bore a lateen rig; her sharply angled bowsprit was fitted
with a single sail. She had tremendous floating power and carried more canvas, but
had neither the caravel's speed nor its handiness in working to windward. She could
compensate for this with her greater armament of lombards, culverins, and falconets,

twenty guns in all. The weathered scars on her hull and bulwarks were signs of her fighting past. She was a tough old lady of the East, but the strains of her long voyages were telling: the crew had rarely let off pumping since clearing the bar of the Tagus.

As captain general with full command, Gomes de Pina had orders to guard the coast against pirates from Dieppe and Honfleur who came to steal brazilwood and burn Portuguese ships. The Portuguese king, João III, demanded an end to this wanton plunder of his New World estate by these Norman corsair/merchantmen.

The Normans raided with quiet approval of the admiral at the court of Francis I, who himself had always treated the protests of Lisbon with contempt and had argued that His Holiness the Pope had erred in 1494 when he promoted the Treaty of Tordesilhas, by which the unknown non-Christian world was divided between Portugal and Spain. Terra do Brasil had fallen in that half of the world to be protected by the Portuguese monarch. "Show me the clause in Adam's will that excluded me from the New World!" Francis had demanded.

All this had been told to Cavalcanti by Gomes de Pina, who had heard it at court. Squadrons had sailed before them, and there had been some success, but the coastline of Terra do Brasil was vast, with an infinite number of bays and hiding places, and for every Norman sunk, three others returned safely to the quays of Dieppe, where the brazilwood was rasped to a powder for dyeing the fabrics of Flanders.

One of the marinheiros at *São Gabriel's* firebox could wait no longer. As the captain general and Cavalcanti watched, he drew his long knife and speared a sizzling rat, dancing off with it to the edge of the main hatch, where he began to devour it greedily.

The captain general turned his back on the scene and walked with Cavalcanti to the opposite end of the deck. "I see that you're not disturbed by men eating vermin," he said. "But I don't expect you would be — not with the experience you've had."

"There has been worse," Cavalcanti acknowledged. "At Goa we ate rats — fat rats, thin rats — and when there were no rats, we boiled the leather from our buskins and off our trunks. And all the time we thanked the Virgin for such mercies!"

℘

That was sixteen years ago, Cavalcanti remembered. He'd been a young officer on *Frol da Rosa*, flagship of Afonso de Albuquerque, captain general and governor of Estado da India, Portugal's State of India.

He saw himself at the first triumph in 1510, when *Frol da Rosa* led twenty men-of-war against the Muslims holding the island of Goa, between the rivers Mandavi and Zuari, a key position on the Malabar coast. Sofala, Aden, Ormuz, Malacca — all were strategic points on the trade routes across the Indian Ocean, but none was so commanding as Goa. Let the Infidel hold the others, Albuquerque said, and the Indies could be conquered from Goa.

Albuquerque's name was already a byword for terror among the petty kings and sultans along the coast of India: O Terrível (The Terrible), they called him. The first battle for Goa was short. The Turkish mercenaries serving its Muslim rulers fled, leaving the Hindu islanders to welcome the Portuguese. But Ishmael Adil Shah, sultan of Bijapur and ruler of Goa, away at the time of the attack, returned with his war elephants and thousands of men and drove Albuquerque's men back to their ships moored in the Mandavi.

What could men like these aboard *São Gabriel* know of a time like that long monsoon in Goa? Cavalcanti wondered. For three months the ships had been trapped by the southwest winds, unable to clear the sand bars at the mouth of the Mandavi.

There were murderous raids ashore, against the gun emplacements of Adil Shah, and desperate actions to combat fire rafts launched downriver to scorch the beleaguered fleet. Impressed by the valor of his enemy, Adil Shah offered peace.

"Tell him," Albuquerque had said, "that Goa is the property of the king of Portugal."

For eighty-four days the ships held out; on the eighty-fifth day, the monsoon over, they could finally weigh anchor. But it was not long before Albuquerque was back, this time in a great armada with 1,700 fighting men. By ten o'clock on the feast day of St. Catherine, the garrison at Goa had fallen.

For three days and nights the fighting had raged in the city. By dawn on the fourth day, when O Terrível decreed a halt, they had slain six thousand disbelievers, men, women, and children, for Portugal — and for Christ.

One aftermath of the massacre, Cavalcanti remembered with special clarity:

"Spare the widows and daughters," Albuquerque had directed. "Those of fair skin and noble grace."

When the sacking of Goa was ended, several hundred of its loveliest treasures stood before Albuquerque. These he offered to two hundred of his most valiant fighting men. "Choose well," he told them, "for these daughters of mine are to mother the young in our king's great State of India."

What had it all come to? Cavalcanti asked himself. That men like Gomes de Pina should lead the king's ships? It was ridiculous that Gomes de Pina should want to consider himself in the same rank as Albuquerque. How different was this captain general from O Terrível: this one soft and vain; and Albuquerque — an iron will and a spirit given to dreams and visions.

Cavalcanti remembered Albuquerque after Ormuz, ill and exhausted with dysentery, afflicted with the hiccups, begging the men around him not to put his goods up for auction, for he did not wish his ragged breeches to be seen.

Even as Albuquerque lay dying, he had understood that many were coming to threaten all of his good works. As soon as their ships rounded Africa's stormy Cape, even the meanest marinheiros wanted to be captains and commanders, and dreamt of Moorish princesses on soft cushions. Many who had been placed in charge by the king summoned their brothers and uncles and nephews and cousins, and sought only to plunder the Indies and fill their own pockets.

Cavalcanti had been one of the few who refused to condone the corruption that came to flourish in the Portuguese enclaves. He stayed on in Goa for three years after Albuquerque's death. In 1518, he was ordered home to Lisbon by an official who was angered by Cavalcanti's open condemnation of bribes he had accepted from a Malay captain.

Because of his honesty, Cavalcanti had returned to Portugal with nothing but the king's allotment — the bonus of pepper he might sell for his own profit. Even his own father, a merchant by trade, made no effort to hide his disappointment in his son:

"You're a fool, Nicolau. Men go to the East to get rich. What can you show for ten years?"

"Nothing," Cavalcanti had to admit.

In February 1526, a month before it sailed, he joined this present squadron. Since Goa, he'd sailed in royal merchant vessels to the Low Countries and Bristol, and to the Hanse ports, along those ancient routes that had first awakened Lisbon to the great possibilities of trade. Goa had been but one climax in a long, exhausting endeavor, launched by the little barchas and caravels that had finally broken their dependence on those northern ports and turned south, sailing through the fog of terror on legend's Green Sea of Darkness to creep down the bulge of Africa, seeking gold and slaves and "grains of paradise," the pepper of Guinea.

Cavalcanti looked down and saw the men at *São Gabriel's* firebox taking their rats from the grill. They settled on the deck near him, ignoring the appeals from others who begged a portion of this nauseous repast. For men without rats, there would be a handful of salted fish, weevil-riddled biscuit, and a cup of evil-smelling water. Except for Gomes de Pina: At Lisbon, he'd loaded his private supplies of meats, preserves, and dried fruits, and his pages guarded these delicacies with their lives. Rarely did he share his table with the master and his officers, and then in so grudging a manner as to leave a foul taste in the mouths of those he fed.

Observing the comforts of a man like Gomes de Pina, Cavalcanti was coming to think that his father had been right: He should have sought more than honor and glory for Christendom in the East.

"It is not souls," the merchant Cavalcanti had often liked to remind him, "but wealth and power that drives men to *As Conquistas*."

As an example, his father often recounted the success of the greatest of all merchants, the *infante* Henry. When, after a humiliating fight with the Infidels at Tangier, the prince had realized that the Moor could not be beat at Portugal's door, he'd sent his corsairs and factors to the enemy's supply sites in Africa.

"Why send legions to die in North Africa when a fortune in slaves and gold and ivory could be carried to his counting houses without a struggle? There were dreamers and thinkers around Henry, with grand ideas about the reconquest of the holy places. He listened to them, just as he heard the words of those who read his stars, but the language he liked best was that of captains who sailed home with laden ships, and of merchants like your grandfather, who owed the *infante* half of all profits made with his license."

From a friend of his father's, an old Jew named Isaac Cardoso, Cavalcanti had learned just how grand such profits were even before he himself went to the East. It was a simple lesson, never forgotten.

He could see the two of them now, sitting on a bench outside his father's countinghouse, in the time the first great fleet sent to India, that of Pedro Álvares Cabral, had returned. Isaac was holding a stick of cinnamon in one hand, a sharp knife in the other. He cut off a small piece. "This," he said, "goes to the man who took it to Calicut." He cut off another. "This is for the Arab whose dhow will carry it to Jidda on the Red Sea; this, for the captain of the foist that will land it at Suez.

"Here are the dues to be paid at Suez, and this for the caravan master bound for Cairo. Now the boatman of the Nile wants his piece, and here is payment for the camel carrier to Alexandria." The little pile of cuttings grew. "Alexandria's Moor demands this for moving cargo in his port; here is Venice's price for the cost of her galley and the profits of her merchant. And these are the bribes to be passed out along the way."

Isaac had whittled the cinnamon until a small fragment lay in the palm of his hand. "From this must come the profit of the palace and merchants of Portugal," he said. Then he took up a second cinnamon stick, the same length as the original, and cut off slightly more than a third of it. "This is what it cost for Cabral to bring this cinnamon home," he said. "The rest is for our king."

Even more impressed by Isaac's vivid illustration were Cavalcanti's brothers: One older, one younger than he, they had gone into the countinghouse, while he had chosen this life at sea. And it hadn't been the excitement at the Cavalcanti warehouses, where captains and traders from many realms visited, but rather the atmosphere at quiet Sintra, beyond Lisbon, that inspired him to pursue this course.

Through his marriage to Inez Gonçalves, Cavalcanti's father had come to possess lands on those serene vales before the Serra de Sintra. Here, between jagged rocks of antiquity crowned with fallen battlement of Moor and the distant, azure expanse of the Atlantic, here was past and future, and whether Nicolau climbed through the thick woods to the lee of the old Infidel redoubt or stood on the windy headland at Cabo da Roça, he felt an intimacy with both.

Ten years of his life had been spent in the East, and when he'd returned to Portugal, there were great churches and palaces he'd not seen before, royal warehouses bursting at the seams, merchants and bankers of many nations thronging the praças, all clamoring for a share of this splendid wealth. One who had aided this reality could have pride in the result, but there'd been other sights less inspiring: rotten ships and decimated crews crawling up the Tagus; shipyards where fewer and fewer replacements lay on the slips; hordes of adventurers and exiles flocking to the realm; families who came to count one, two, three sons sacrificed on some distant shore.

He'd spoken of this to Gomes de Pina, but the fidalgo showed little concern: If there were fewer sons to till the soil of Portugal, he'd said, then bring in more *peças*, "pieces," of Africa — the slaves. "Nothing must restrain the work of empire," was his pompous pronouncement. "Nothing must restrain a people destined for greatness!"

Their sailing, sixty-four days before, had borne little resemblance to the departure of royal fleets in the past. But Gomes de Pina, so full of his noble antecedents, seemed unaware of any diminished glory. He had ordered that his vessels tarry in the river while he held a holy vigil in the new church of the Jeronymites, built at nearby Belém in gratitude to God for the passage to India. He'd assembled his family and hangers-on and proceeded to prayerful office — in the manner of great navigators like Vasco da Gama and Pedro Álvares Cabral, who had knelt in the humble chapel that had stood on the ground now occupied by the majestic limestone monastery.

When his lonely appeal was over, Gomes de Pina had led his entourage to the water's edge, where a boat waited to carry him to the ships. They were anchored close to the Tower of St. Vincent, a great bulwark that rose on a group of rocks in the Tagus.

Standing upright, his bearded jaw jutting forward, the fidalgo had allowed himself to be rowed past the fortress, oblivious to the fact that the guardsmen didn't give this departing hero a second glance.

And now here he was, far across the Atlantic, watching as men he commanded gnawed the bones of rodents.

"Disgusting," Gomes de Pina said as the marinheiros disposed of the last tidbits. "Have they no respect for themselves?"

"They respect the dead," Cavalcanti said pointedly.

The captain general turned away in silence.

☙

Two days later, under a pale, tropical moon, *São Gabriel* sailed with a fair breeze, her bow lifting and dipping gently in the easy sea; the caravels rode ahead, off to port, their canvas silvered, the cresset fires dancing at their sterns.

From the steerage, a ship's boy sang out:

> *"Four glasses be gone,*
> *And now a fifth floweth,*
> *God's will be done,*
> *His fair way we knoweth."*

There was a pause, and then the same lad cried, "Forecastle! Forecastle! Look sharp, up there!"

A grunted reply from near the bowsprit signaled that the man remained alert as they passed into the third hour of the 11-to-3 watch.

On the quarterdeck, Nicolau Cavalcanti smiled at the exaggerated challenge in the boy's voice: Brito Correia, not quite five feet tall, was the youngest and cheekiest of the ship's boys. A mulatto waif from Santarém, he'd given his age as thirteen, but Cavalcanti suspected him of being a year or two younger.

The master walked over to the dimly lit binnacle box and checked their heading. He leaned toward the open hatchway above the steerage. "Steady as she is, helmsman," he said.

Cavalcanti looked at the caravels in the distance, his eyes searching the vast expanse of moonlit sea.

Was it a night like this, in the year of Our Lord Jesus Christ 1492, when Cristovão Colombo first saw Ilha San Salvador? *O Santa Maria!* The scheming Genoese adventurer sailing for Castile and Aragon! O Portugal, robbed by Spanish dogs and the traitors who sail in their ships!

Cavalcanti's personal loathing for the Spaniards reflected age-old rivalries between Portugal and her Iberian neighbor. Columbus had turned to Ferdinand and Isabella for royal patronage only after being rejected by João II of Portugal, who had not been impressed by the plans of the inexperienced and impecunious Genoese. The triumphant return of Admiral Columbus with news that the "Indies" could be reached by sailing west had alarmed the Portuguese, who were seeking a passage around Africa for the same purpose and had been granted exclusive right to explore and conquer the Indies by Pope Nicolas V in 1454.

The Catholic monarchs took the dispute that arose after Columbus's discovery to Rome, where Pope Alexander VI issued a series of bulls embodied in the Treaty of Tordesilhas: Portuguese and Spanish discoveries were to be separated by a demarcation line running north and south, 370 leagues west of the Cape Verde Islands. The Portuguese were granted all lands and continents discovered or to be discovered for 180 degrees east of this line; the Spaniards enjoyed the same privilege for 180 degrees to the west. When Columbus was on his third voyage in 1498, the Portuguese navigator Vasco da Gama reached India via the Cape of Good Hope; two years later, Pedro Álvares Cabral, commander of the second Indies fleet, veered far to the west, making an unexpected landfall at Terra de Santa Cruz on April 22, 1500.

Cavalcanti knew little of Terra do Brasil. No gold, silver, or spices were to be found there; it was just a vast terra incognita, which provided little else but logs and feathers and slaves hardly worth reckoning: small batches of timid men who weakened almost from the outset and, if they survived the crossing, died soon after landing.

Cavalcanti had once seen a group of these natives in Lisbon's Rossio Square, brought there by a captain in one of the first fleets to sail with the king's license to collect brazilwood. There'd been eight or nine, and they drew an enormous crowd.

They had coppery skin and muscular builds, if slighter than those of the Guinea slaves. Their owner had directed them to paint themselves in the fashion they used for war. And he revealed to the onlookers that he himself had devised the little skirts of canvas they wore, since, in their own lands, they went as naked as Adam himself. All had headdresses of parrot feathers. They went barefoot, and around their ankles hung seedpods that rattled as they moved. But nothing had intrigued Cavalcanti as much as their faces: lodged in openings bored into their cheeks and lower lips were colorful stones, and pieces of bone protruded from their noses.

"Dance, Tupinambá!" the captain had ordered, first in Portuguese, then, to the amusement of all, in the tongue of the savages. "Dance! Great warriors you are!"

Cavalcanti was aware that a few wild, crazy men from Portugal dwelt in Terra do Brasil. Some lived there without choice, for it was either exile to Brazil or the gibbet hook. But others had gone freely to the logwood camps along the coast as woodsmen and laborers for those who held the king's contract to collect dyewood. It was in the interests of such men that Gomes de Pina sailed.

Cavalcanti was standing at the port side of the quarterdeck, his arm resting on the swivel gun mounted there. He thought of the squadron's mission — to patrol Brazil's shores for two years — and wondered whether *São Gabriel* could survive this order. Ahead, toward the horizon, he could see the caravels *Nossa Senhora da Consolação* and *São Bento*, plunging and throwing spray as they coursed ahead. With every square of canvas and her bonnets latched in place, *São Gabriel* would still have hard work to keep up with them.

Suddenly, Cavalcanti saw the flash from one of the *Consolação* port guns.

Almost simultaneously the lookout in *São Gabriel's* bow sang out "Land! Land!" though he could have seen nothing, but *Consolação's* signal was clear. "Land! Land!" the lookout called again, directing his cry into the heart of the ship.

The caravels hove to, waiting for the slower ship. Aboard *São Gabriel*, as she closed the distance between them, her men raised their voices in a tremendous rendering of the Gloria.

Pilot Fernandes could be well satisfied with this landfall. A morning's sail to the south would bring them to Porto Seguro, the secure haven Admiral Pedro Álvares Cabral had sought after the first sighting of Brazil.

Just before sunrise the offshore breeze freshened, and on *São Gabriel* and the other ships, spritsail, topsails, and mizzen were unfurled, a bonnet was latched to the foot of the main, and the yard, slung low during the night, was hoisted up. Rope-scarred hands hauled and made fast halyards and bowlines. With the wind on the starboard quarter, the ships held a southwest heading, sailing farther offshore but never losing the line of white and shaded green broken here and there by a rise of low cliff that stood golden in the early sun. Soon they caught sight of the mountain Cabral had called Pascoal, for the Easter week that had preceded his landfall.

At last they stood in toward that wide, beautiful bay. Near the beach they saw the great cross raised by Cabral. But off to the left were piles of logs. As the ships drew nearer, tiny figures could be seen, too, moving along the white sands.

São Gabriel hove to, the caravels drifting within hailing distance. Pilot Fernandes had a rough chart for these waters, but he was a cautious man and would not put his trust in it alone. Low waves broke over a jagged reef before the southern end of the bay, and this obstruction was marked on the chart, but the description, in the hand of an earlier navigator, was crude enough to make Fernandes wary of other, hidden dangers. Two boats, from *São Gabriel* and *Consolação*, were to go in first, taking soundings.

Cavalcanti gave orders to lower *São Gabriel's* longboat stowed in the waist, a task the crew hated — the craft was cumbersome and the space to work her free was limited. Men cursed as they struggled with block and tackle, hands were grazed and torn and muscles strained, tempers flared in the noon heat before the weighty boat was swung out over the bulwarks.

"I want the ten best men, armed and ready. Those men on shore may be Norman thieves," Cavalcanti said. "We'll take Fernandes across to *Consolação's* boat; then we'll go ashore."

Gomes de Pina frowned. "Norman thieves? Here? In Porto Seguro?"

"It's possible."

"But they've been on the beach since we arrived," the fidalgo said.

"That means nothing."

"In *Lisbon*," he said testily, "they reported a factory at the Bay of All Saints, at Cabo Frio, Pernambuco, and here."

Factory, Cavalcanti thought derisively. Goa, Malacca — those were factories, formidable trading posts established by Portugal's merchants. What manner of factory was this, a pile of logs and a group of castaways? "With respect, my Captain General," he said, "something about that group is not in order."

"Could it be" — Gomes de Pina paused, looking out across the water — "that they are alone? No savages out there, Master — only the men with the logs. Is this what appears strange to you?"

Cavalcanti glanced at the fidalgo with something close to admiration. It was a good observation, and coming from one who'd sunk so low in his eyes during the voyage, it surprised him. Where were the Tupiniquin? Ever since Cabral's day, they'd been known to dance on the beaches when the great ships came in, greedy for the little bells and beads they expected.

"Carry on, Master Cavalcanti," he heard the fidalgo say. "If those are the thieves of Dieppe, you'll know what to do."

Cavalcanti sat in the stern when they rowed across to *Consolação's* boat, sweating beneath his leather cuirass.

"Those palms," Cavalcanti said, indicating a place to the lee of the brazilwood logs. "Make for the beach there."

He almost hoped they were Dieppe pirates. With the aid of their sponsor, Jean d'Ango, wealthiest merchant of that port, the pirates had been attacking Portugal's ships for years, intercepting fleets from the Indies, raiding to the very mouth of the Tagus. On a trading voyage before this squadron, he'd seen the great house this d'Ango was building on the quay at Dieppe with exotic woods stolen from Brazil — a palace paid for with the blood of Lisbon marinheiros.

The closer they approached, the more suspicious Cavalcanti became: by now those men should be running to meet the boat, wading into the water to greet their brothers from home.

"Oars! Oars!" Cavalcanti cried, scanning the beach, from the mouth of a river that lay to the south, up to the logs, and along the sweep of the bay to where Cabral's great cross stood.

Any doubt about the identity of the men ashore vanished when he saw a puff of smoke.

Two guns concealed near the logs opened fire, hurling their iron balls at the longboat, now within their range. One fell short with a harmless burst of spray; the second reached the boat. By a hairsbreadth, it missed an arquebusier crouched forward, struck the rower behind him, and tore off a strip of the port gunwale, almost upsetting the craft with its blow. A man screamed pitifully — not the front oarsman, who was dead with half his face gone, but another, who had sat to port and was pierced by jagged splinters.

The water sloshing about his feet red with the blood of his men, Cavalcanti commanded: "Row! For the love of God, keep rowing!" The men, frozen in the moment of attack, moved their oars.

Cavalcanti saw that it was better to make for the shore than to pull back toward the ships: The Normans had time to reload and fire only once more before the boat beached.

He glanced at the ships, and observed men swarming over *São Gabriel's* deck: They were getting out the sweeps to maneuver her where her guns could blast those on the shore. But the Normans would be able to get off a second shot at the longboat before the *São Gabriel* could open fire.

Some corsairs had started to run toward that part of the beach picked out by Cavalcanti. Behind them, their gunners had worked swiftly and again the cannon roared, but this time the shots whistled over the boat.

The longboat's arquebusiers now fired at the men on the beach. Before they could reload, the keel skidded on the bottom and the boat jerked to a halt.

Cavalcanti caught his balance. Then he leapt into the chest-high water with his sword drawn. "Portugal!" he cried. "For the love of God and São Tiago!"

Most of his men were behind him, their lances and swords at the ready. But the arquebusiers dallied, and paid with their lives.

One pirate who ran to meet the Portuguese hurled a sputtering grenade into the longboat. It exploded at the feet of the arquebusiers, killing both and blasting a hole in the bottom of the craft.

Cavalcanti was slashing and stabbing his way through the Normans. Man for man, they were now evenly matched, eight to eight, but Cavalcanti had been careful to choose only men with experience. Those who stood with him had bloodied their swords on some African or Indian shore and proved too much for their foes from Dieppe.

The struggle was short and brutal. Within minutes, four of the Normans lay dead in the water. Three backed off, begging for quarter, but were slain.

"To the guns!" Cavalcanti ordered, and started off down the beach, but he hadn't gone far when he stopped in his tracks: the cannon in *São Gabriel* and *Consolação* opened up, bombarding the area around the log piles.

At the height of the barrage, a fire started between the logs; when it reached the Normans' magazine, a series of dull explosions followed. When the ships' guns ceased firing, a deathly silence fell on the shore.

Cavalcanti and his men advanced slowly, until they reached the battered and deserted camp. A great pile of logs blazed, and several shelters were also on fire. The master sent three men to search for the fugitive gunners.

Leaving the marinheiros near the burning camp, Cavalcanti waded a short way into the water, where he washed his sword blade clean.

He was puzzled by the absence of inhabitants. He gazed toward the nearest stand of palm and deeper into the trees, but he saw no sign of other men. He walked along the beach, his breathing gradually became calmer, and the only noise was the sound of his boots crunching the small white shells at the water's edge.

He moved in the direction of the river mouth at the end of the bay; nearing it, he realized just how far he had come from his party, and made to turn back.

At that moment the Tupiniquin began to emerge from the trees near the river. For the second time this afternoon, Cavalcanti's sword rasped out of its scabbard, but the Tupiniquin showed no belligerence as they approached.

It was the man who led them out of the trees who commanded his attention.

He was a brown-bearded giant, brutish-faced, and carried a long staff. He wore a doublet made from animal skin, ragged breeches, a long patchwork cloak. On his head was a faded blue-velvet cap; his feet were covered with rough leather, bound with thin vines.

He moved deliberately, and then, a few paces from Cavalcanti, he said in perfectly good Portuguese, "Be thankful, my friend, for Affonso Ribeiro. Thank your Holy Mother this night for this poor old *degredado*. Without him, the Normans would have taken you!"

✌

Gomes de Pina was enjoying every moment of the feast. The plentiful food and fresh fruits pleased him, but most especially he relished the Tupiniquin women, who served him and danced before him.

One plump, comely maiden gave the fidalgo all her attention. She was the daughter of the elder of a maloca — a princess of these people, according to Affonso Ribeiro.

"They're so young and pretty, so very, very innocent. I see paradise, Master, in the days before sin," the fidalgo said. He determined that as soon as he could depart this celebration, he would lead the girl to his cabin in *São Gabriel*.

Gomes de Pina and his captains and officers sat on palm-leaf mats in the clearing between the Tupiniquin malocas. To the left of them, the elders of the clan were sitting together on the ground, engaged in a lively conversation about these "Long Hairs."

Affonso Ribeiro, self-proclaimed degredado, "outcast," moved between the two groups like a great sultan. He had shed his tattered garments and wore a billowing skirtlike creation wrapped around his midriff; when he was alone with the Tupiniquin, alone with his three wives and sixteen children, he went naked.

What he'd told Nicolau Cavalcanti on the beach a week before this feast day was true: The master of *São Gabriel* and his men did have Affonso Ribeiro to thank for their lives; without his presence, the Tupiniquin would most likely have fought at the side of the Normans.

The corsairs of Dieppe differed from the Portuguese in their method of gathering brazilwood: Instead of setting up factories, they sent men to befriend and live with the natives. As friends, they warned the natives against the Portuguese, who they said would enslave and murder them.

The Normans the squadron found on the beach had come ashore a month before, and Ribeiro had been there to greet them.

"Who was I, forgotten subject of Dom Manuel, to deny them?" he'd said to Gomes de Pina. That Manuel was dead and King João III sat on the throne mattered little to a man who only remembered a Portugal from which he'd been exiled twenty-six years before.

"They could take as many trees as the Tupiniquin would cut," he said, "but I wasn't having them near this village, and my family agreed." There were many in the malocas, not only his wives and children, whom he regarded as "family." "When you landed, the Normans stood alone."

Gomes de Pina showed little gratitude, for he could not overlook the fact that Affonso Ribeiro was a degredado: Such men banished for their crimes at home were considered eminently suitable emissaries to unknown lands. They were dumped ashore to dwell among the natives and learn their customs and language. If they lived to be successful in this enterprise, the king would consider a pardon — after twenty years.

When Cabral's fleet had sailed for India after its New World landfall at Terra do Brasil, Affonso Ribeiro, a stealer of goats, who hailed from Cabral's native town of Belmonte, had been left behind. To his great good fortune, the Tupiniquin had been kind to him, especially one young, much respected warrior, who, when Ribeiro learned their language, told him that no man deserved to live without a name or people of his own. Ribeiro's third wife, Salpina, was a daughter of that same warrior, Aruanã, today elder of his maloca.

Toward midafternoon, Gomes de Pina could no longer contain his excitement at the prospect of playing with his little princess, and he signaled to his officers that he wished to return to the flagship. Except for Nicolau Cavalcanti, who stayed with Ribeiro, the Portuguese started back through the forest, intoxicated with the heady manioc brew, laughing as the giggling girls led them on.

The reason Cavalcanti hadn't gone off with the fidalgo was that the girl he desired was a daughter of Affonso Ribeiro. In most ways, she behaved as did the others offered to the village's guests, without guile, joyful in her eagerness to please. But there was something else that entranced Cavalcanti, something that reminded him of the loveliest, high-born roses of Portugal: the ever-so-slightly aloof manner she would assume playfully on occasion, pouting her lips. And rather than follow Gomes de Pina and the others, he was content to savor this alluring combination, with its subtle hint of the familiar and open eroticism of the strange and savage.

Such delight aside, Cavalcanti could not ignore the other realities: He saw the whitened skulls at the entrance to the stockade, heard soft tunes from flutes made of the bones of men. He caught the glances of their two pagés, filled with disapproval and suspicion. He'd remarked on this to Ribeiro, but the degredado, had only laughed. "Once there was a devil," he said, "who would have made you tremble." He slapped his side with amusement. "These two wizards — they're always together in the sacred hut, two men who know no women and love each other as much as the spirits they dance with."

It was obvious to Cavalcanti that the warrior Aruanã was the most powerful of the elders. He sat opposite him now, with Ribeiro.

"He has a question," Ribeiro said, then paused to hear it before translating. "How is it, he wants to know, that you come so far to fetch wood? Have you none in your own country?"

"We have forests," Cavalcanti said, "but not with the wood we seek in these lands. We need this wood for dyeing."

Aruanã nodded; this he already knew from Ribeiro. "But why do you want so much?" he asked.

Cavalcanti thought of the king, João III, and endeavored to explain: "In our country, there is a man, a chief among us, who has great riches." He had seen possessions the Tupiniquin had acquired in their contact with visiting ships. "He has axes, knives, looking glasses, and beads, more than enough for every man in this tribe and all the clans of these shores. The wood we collect is for him."

"But, tell me, does this man not die?"

"Certainly," Cavalcanti said. "Like all."

Aruanã again consulted with the elders, before continuing: "If this man dies, who has these things he leaves behind?"

"His children, his brothers and sisters."

Now Aruanã laughed. "This man must be a fool, and so, too, all who endure so much for him."

Translating, Ribeiro did not conceal his amusement at the insult, but Cavalcanti was angered: Such words from a Moor and the Infidel would speak no more.

"We also have the family of our malocas," Aruanã said, "and we love our children, but we know that as this earth supports us, it will in like manner support them."

Cavalcanti looked away to where Ribeiro's daughter sat with other girls, a distance from the men.

Ribeiro read the desire in his expression and shook Cavalcanti's shoulder with one of his great paws. "You like this forest child of Affonso Ribeiro?"

"She's lovely," Cavalcanti murmured.

"Then, Jandaia is yours, my friend, for as long as you want."

The meaning of this exchange, though conducted in Portuguese, was clear enough to Aruanã: Ever since the Long Hairs first landed in this bay, like the little Nambikwara ever hungry for love, they were never so happy as when enjoying the gifts of woman. This he had no difficulty comprehending; but there were many other things about the Long Hairs that continued to puzzle him even now, so many years after looking into their hairy faces, there at the white sands where he'd gone to find shells for First Child's necklace.

He would never forget their reception — his and Tabajara's — aboard Cabral's ship. He could recall walking slowly past men who stood with shiny coverings on their chests and long pointed arrows. He heard a strange babble of words, and saw that some pointed to his headdress, while others showed interest in his penis. He'd shrunk back when they put their hands out to touch his skin, not in fear but because of the smell they exuded, a stench offensive to a man accustomed to bathing three or more times a day.

The man Ribeiro later identified as Cabral sat in a chair far more impressive than the stool Aruanã had seen Tocoyricoc of the Tapajós sit upon.

Aruanã remembered his surprise:

"I have seen this!" he'd cried

"What?" Tabajara had asked.

Aruanã had taken a step forward and was pointing to Cabral's necklace. "These are tears of the sun," he said. "The same as I saw with Tocoyricoc."

Aruanã's pointing brought Cabral instantly to his feet; clearly he was excited. The interpreter addressed them in several tongues, but Aruanã only continued to point again and again to the neck chain and then to the land, trying to show that tears of the sun were a "long, long journey away."

They'd been fed after that. Aruanã took some food offered to him, but the taste was awful and he spat it all out; the same with a sour red drink. Then a jar had been set before them, but never had he sipped such foul water.

The next day they'd gone back to their people, and in the clearing they'd declared that the Long Hairs were no enemy of the Tupiniquin.

The Portuguese had been taken to the sweetest drinking water. The fields were dug for manioc, and the women sent to gather fruits and nuts. Bows and arrows and feathers, and birds themselves — macaw was Long Hairs' favorite — were exchanged for little bells and bracelets, and beads of many colors.

When the Long Hairs eventually sailed away, they'd left behind this man Ribeiro, whom the Tupiniquin came to call Ticuanga, because though he'd been soft as manioc dough when they first knew him, like *ticuanga* cakes, he'd hardened in the sun.

They had first puzzled over this "gift" of Cabral's. Why should the men in their great canoes hand over their prisoner? That Ticuanga had been a captive, they had no doubt, and the Tupiniquin had not known what to do with him. For his part, Ribeiro lived like a man without a past, becoming a great jovial warrior who loved and fought like the best of the clan.

Aruanã was still thinking of Ribeiro when he saw him rise at the approach of a group of young men dancing across the clearing. Ribeiro joined them, stamping his feet with theirs. Faster and faster he danced to the rhythm of the rattles they shook, until he could no longer keep up with them and collapsed on the ground next to Cavalcanti.

The master turned to him now. "Senhor," he said pointedly, "you've been away from Lisbon for twenty-six years. Surely the new king would pardon you for a mistake you made as a child. Don't you wish to return to the land of your birth?"

"Me? Affonso Ribeiro? Herder of goats? Go back to Portugal? Never! Here is my land! Here is my family!"

Quick as Ribeiro's avowal was, Cavalcanti sensed a false note in it, which only further piqued his curiosity as to why Ribeiro so emphatically chose these simple savages above his own people and why the Tupiniquin had accepted him.

Several began to contribute to a story then, translated by Ribeiro, about a long journey made by Aruanã. Cavalcanti paid little attention to the narrative, for he knew that the minds of these people were filled with fantasies and lies: Where, for example, was the empire of Africa's legendary Prester John, with his golden chariots and bejeweled palaces? How many years had Portuguese marinheiros believed the Africans who spoke of a wondrous kingdom in the interior — until the Portuguese reached Ethiopia! Black Christians they found, yes, but no more wealth than in a single Indies ship of Dom João III.

Ribeiro, who'd consumed great quantities of beer, announced that he was headed for his hammock. "And, you, Master — isn't it time for rest?" he asked, with mock earnestness, looking in the direction of his daughter. He called to his daughter, in Tupi: "Come swiftly, Jandaia, my child, here to his side. Show him — show Master Cavalcanti what his Lisbon women never can know!"

Jandaia laughed at her father's remarks, and skipped toward them.

Cavalcanti had known the soft, conquered females in the heat after battle — gentle Hindi maids who'd waited upon him at Goa. But never had a daughter been placed in his hands by the man she called her father.

Ribeiro gave him a great thump on the back and then headed off, still chuckling as he thumped toward his maloca.

Cavalcanti glanced round the clearing, wondering where he could take Jandaia, when he realized she was already moving forward and beckoning that he follow her. She led him beyond the stockade and across the fields to the forest.

She had brought him to a low waterfall on a stream that branched from the main river flowing past the village. Between towering trees, the water broke over a shelf of rock into a pool, where jewel-colored birds darted among the mosses and ferns. He began to remove his armor and weapons, and she tiptoed to the water.

"*Maravilhosa*," he breathed.

He leaned against a tree to watch her, but quickly drew away to brush some ugly wormlike insects off his arm. He wanted her to come out of the water; but, ignoring his call, she splashed her breasts and went on playing. After a while, she motioned him to join her.

Never!

Jandaia remained insistent, and swam almost to his feet, her fine body moving easily through the water. "Come, Portuguese," she called.

He could wait no longer. He threw off the rest of his clothes and plunged into the pool, shouting an oath when the chilly water covered his body.

He chased Jandaia around the pool. He held her to him, cool and wet in his arms, and he felt a fire within himself. They sat together, against the rock shelf that broke the stream, and laughed as the water danced off their bodies.

They made love beside that pool. First he felt a rage, a fury to possess this innocence. Then she'd begun a lingering advance, and he moved with her, slowly, toward a soaring moment when he cried out with pleasure.

❧

The squadron carried two priests, Aloysius Barreto and Miguel da Costa. Padre Aloysius was a jovial, ruddy-faced man in his fifties, who knew his unruly flock and was reasonable in dealing with them. Padre Miguel, hawkish-looking and fiery, a much younger man, was possessed with a knowledge of evil about him, unrelenting in his chastisement of transgressors sailing with the Order of Christ, and, consequently, heartily disliked.

On this second Sunday of their stay at Porto Seguro, the fidalgo ordered that every man attend a Mass and a sermon at the foot of Cabral's towering cross on the beach. An altar had been set up in front of it, with the little wooden saints each ship carried placed near it, and the men were gathered here as Padre Aloysius intoned the Mass, accompanied by his assistant, whose voice was as grating as his manner.

A distance away, in the shade of some palms, stood Affonso Ribeiro with Aruanã and the Tupiniquin elders.

Aruanã was remembering the day Cabral held the first devotions at this cross: As the pagés of the Long Hairs had gone about their sacred work, the Tupiniquin had followed their actions, kneeling when they knelt, standing with their hands uplifted, and breathing not a word when they were silent. There were no rattles with feathers, no Voice of the Spirits, but the Tupiniquin knew that Monan, who had made First Man, was in the sky with Sun, and it was good to chant to His happiness.

Aruanã's wife, Juriti, had been the only woman at the cross and was frightened. Her heart raced when one of the brown robes made his way toward her, and, trembling, she pressed against Aruanã. "Do not fear," was his calm response, though the pagé's behavior startled him, too.

The man had smiled gently and held out a small piece of cloth to Juriti, which she had hesitantly accepted, but, the moment he turned away, dropped to the ground.

When the singing and chanting had stopped, a Long Hair appeared carrying many little tin crosses, and it was he who showed the Tupiniquin, how to kneel and put their lips to the little cross, then raise their hands to the sky.

"It is for Monan," Tabajara had said, pointing to that part of the sky where the sun slept. "It is the way they talk with spirit of Monan — with all who dwell in Land of the Grandfather."

Others had agreed with this explanation. But one asked: "What of Naurú and the sacred rattles?"

"We hear our ancestors; they hear those of their people," Tabajara replied calmly.

"But who hears more words?" the same warrior persisted.

Aruanã had offered an answer: "In our clearing, Voice of the Spirits talks to Tupiniquin. Others hear the same at their malocas. There is no difference."

But, after the first Long Hairs, other men had come, and again and again they had told him he was wrong: Their Monan, they said, spoke with a voice that had more power.

Padre Miguel would surely have told Aruanã the same were he able to converse in Tupi, but, not knowing the language, he had to content himself with berating the marinheiros and their captains for their ungodliness. "My brothers, my brothers," he began, "why are you so weak?"

The men sat uncomfortably, the hot morning sun upon their backs, their faces blank.

"You sport before this bestial and barbarous people, without thought of sin. Yet know that these savages are simple and innocent, and we can stamp upon them any belief we should wish them to have. Let us accept them as children, who must be taught obedience to the cross."

When the service ended, Ribeiro and the Tupiniquin were rowed to *São Gabriel* to be entertained by the captain general. Gomes de Pina had ordered a banquet of his good ham and rice and delicacies from his private stores.

Wine, too, was passed to the Tupiniquin, and they downed great quantities. In the years since Aruanã first spat the dark liquid onto the deck of Cabral's ship, his people had become accustomed to it: Stronger than their beer, it was more like the tabak they puffed at their ceremonies, for to take much of this drink was to want to dance, to leap, to sing!

And this is what they did, Tupiniquin and Portuguese, in *São Gabriel* that sunny afternoon. While Gomes de Pina and his officers remained at the table observing with dignified amusement, the Tupiniquin danced beside members of the crew.

Cavalcanti, therefore, found it puzzling that amid such jollity Affonso Ribeiro should be miserable.

It was not until the celebration was over that the master of *São Gabriel* could be alone with Ribeiro and learn what was bothering him. Eager to see Jandaia, Cavalcanti had arranged to return to their village.

When they were put ashore, Aruanã stumbled along the beach He did not get far before he called a halt and sought the shade of the palms with the elders.

The other two continued on, Ribeiro taking a shortcut that led up the steep slope of a red-earth rise behind the beach. They climbed to the top of the hill, and there, amid a tangle of growth, stood the ruin of a small church. Ribeiro wanted to go on, but Cavalcanti stopped. He'd seen another church, also ruined, away from this place, where two Franciscans had settled a decade before: One had been drowned in a stream the Tupiniquin still called River of Brown Robe; the other, Ribeiro told him, had returned to Portugal. But this ruin was clearly much older, and could have no connection with the other.

"Who built this church?" he asked.

"Franciscans," Ribeiro said.

Cavalcanti turned his back to the mud walls and faced out to sea. The great bay with *São Gabriel* and the caravels lay directly below; to the north was another inlet, and a little to the south, the river that led to the Tupiniquin village.

"How can that be?" Cavalcanti asked. "Their buildings are near the place where the Normans camped."

"Those were different Franciscans and came years ago," Ribeiro said.

"You forgot them?"

"I did not forget."

"But you said nothing when you showed the other church."

"What was there to say? Another pile of ruins, same as the first."

"Those earlier friars," Cavalcanti asked, "when were they here?"

"They came in Noronha's ships," Ribeiro said. Fernando de Noronha had been first to get a contract from Dom Manuel to collect brazilwood, in 1502. "They built this church," he added. "Their mission — it wasn't a success."

Cavalcanti detected a flatness in Affonso Ribeiro's tone.

"Why did they fail?"

Ribeiro gazed into the ruin, then back at Cavalcanti. "They were good men, but they didn't understand the Tupiniquin." He laughed weakly. "They loved every creature but the one they loved most was the one who truly hated them.

" 'Brother Naurú,' they called him. 'Brother Naurú' they said, 'we are all God's creatures. Open your heart and you will find the paradise we speak of.' "

"Naurú?" Cavalcanti said. "Who was Naurú?"

"The devil himself," he spat. "Voice of the Spirits, with control over life and death. Men like the elder Aruanã controlled the village, in peace and war, but Naurú was the true ruler — a prince of fear."

"*You* feared him?"

"Yes, Master, I feared Naurú," Ribeiro said. "These two sodomites who share the sacred hut today — they awe the Tupiniquin with their rattles and ceremonies, but men still speak of Naurú as if he were alive."

"The Franciscans," Cavalcanti said. "What about them?"

"How Naurú raged against them. Since Cabral's day, he had wanted to turn the Tupiniquin against those they call Long Hairs, because in the ten days Cabral was here, Naurú was ignored. Warriors paid no attention to the rattle of a mad priest who saw only darkness in men who'd come out of the sunrise.

"When the Franciscans came, his fury reached new heights. He dragged his wasted body from maloca to maloca preaching against the brown robes, warning of miseries they would bring to the Tupiniquin, and when his awful prediction was shown correct, he rejoiced at the suffering of his own people."

"But you, Ribeiro, you're Portuguese," Cavalcanti said. "How was it that this Naurú's hatred didn't fall upon you? Today you live as a prince among these savages. What made it so, Ribeiro?"

"Naurú was a clever and cunning scoundrel. Didn't he know a miserable degredado when he saw one — a man without a people or a country? What could such a man do that would interfere with the work of Naurú?" The sun had just slipped behind some trees in the distance. "It's late. Let us go, Master," he said. "Let us take you to my Jandaia."

But Cavalcanti had a feeling Ribeiro's tale was far from finished. "What were these 'miseries' the Franciscans brought?" he asked.

Ribeiro let out a deep sigh, as of resignation. "Father Gaspar had a cough, and he gave his sickness to the Tupiniquin. When people lay groaning with fever in the malocas, Voice of the Spirits called from the clearing. Here was evil, Naurú announced, concealed in the bodies of the brown robes. Brothers of the dark, they had worked their beads to cast a spell over the Tupiniquin."

"The clan accepted this?"

"It did."

"And the Franciscans, Friar Gaspar and the other — what did they do?"

"Nothing," he replied, shrugging. "The savages heard Naurú, and the cries of their children, and they forbade the priests entry to the stockade."

"So they went away, like the one from the other church?"

Ribeiro did not reply.

It was quiet: that brief, uncertain time between day and the sudden onrush of night in the tropics, the open sky ablaze with the color of a sun no longer seen, the forest behind, darkening and still.

Now there came from deep within Affonso Ribeiro a howl of anguish, a piteous and terrible cry:

"Meu Deus!"

The thick shoulders trembled and shook; the big hands flew to the side of his head.

"Oh, Master," Ribeiro cried, "I was only a boy. How could a boy fight all the evil in Naurú?

"They were killed. The friars were killed — struck down, there in the clearing."

"You were with them?"

"What was there for a boy to do?" was Ribeiro's reply.

Cavalcanti had no desire to probe further into the martyrdom of the two friars.

But Ribeiro continued with his confession: "They made me come here, Master, and fetch the friars to take them where the Tupiniquin were calling for them."

Cavalcanti stared hard at the degredado. "And they went to their deaths?"

"Yes."

Now Cavalcanti understood why Ribeiro was so bound to these Tupiniquin: By leading the friars to their execution, he had shown the Tupiniquin that he was as ready to serve as those who waited to tear the limbs from the Franciscans. He had proved no love for his own and was honored for this treachery. After this, what choice did he have but to live with them, with no thought for the clean, pure soil of his homeland?

Momentarily, Cavalcanti felt an urge to go for his sword and mete out justice, right where Ribeiro stood with his back to the church he'd helped destroy, but he contained his rage. "Let's leave this place," he said gruffly, and they moved off, taking the same route along which Ribeiro had once led the friars.

Cavalcanti's assumption was essentially correct: Ribeiro's complicity in the murder of the friars had made him a brother of the Tupiniquin.

But there remained unspoken the darkest part of the degredado's confession.

Affonso Ribeiro could not summon the courage to tell a fellow Portuguese that it had been he, Ticuanga of the Tupiniquin, who had raised Yware-pemme above the scraped skulls. And that his chest still bore the marks of one who had slain his enemy.

V

<center>~~~>•<~~~</center>

June — September 1526

*H*is men called him, simply, Le Tigre (The Tiger) and that was enough. Before he got his own ship, he'd sailed with Jean Fleury, prowling the coasts of Africa and Brazil, standing away to the far reaches of the Atlantic, watching, waiting for the fat, laden vessels of Lisbon and Cadiz. He was with Fleury when they seized the first treasure sent by Cortes from Mexico — gold, silver, emeralds the size of a man's fist; he'd come within a raven's cry off the great cliffs of Cape St. Vincent, there to take the galleons of d'Avila; he'd watched without emotion when — her dyewood and parrots carried over to Fleury's ship — the Portuguese merchantman *Bom Jesus*, sails ripped, castles blown away, sank with all hands.

Le Tigre — Gautier de Saint Julien — was now half-owner of the carrack *Croissant*; the other share was held by Jean d'Ango, Dieppe's merchant marauder, always happy to invest in an enterprise to reduce the wealth of his Portuguese or Spanish competitors.

That the Portuguese regarded men like Fleury and himself as robbers, a pestilence sweeping the high seas, Le Tigre knew. This delighted him enormously, but not for one moment did he believe it: He sailed not as a pirate but as a good Norman, out for no more than a fair share of the spoils from America and the East.

"This small people," he said contemptuously of his Portuguese rivals, "the world is not large enough to satisfy their greed. They set foot on a piece of land and it is a 'conquest.'"

If, however, they insisted on keeping their possessions, then let them do so, he'd told Jean d'Ango. Only they must be prepared to pay a tax — the booty extracted by the men from Dieppe!

To collect his first dues, Le Tigre had sailed *Croissant* to Brazil in January 1526, moving down the coast to beyond the high headland of Cabo Frio and to Guanabara Bay, with its peaks and towers and pinnacles of aged rock standing sentinel behind the most serene haven on earth.

Le Tigre had avoided the Portuguese brazilwood factories and stood out to sea, waiting to pick up a homebound logger. But he'd had no success, and finally sought to cut his own trees. He knew that there were no Portuguese at Porto Seguro save a rascal abandoned there by Cabral. He'd taken *Croissant* to the bay where this man and his Tupiniquin were waiting on the beach.

While his men and the Tupiniquin readied the brazilwood, Le Tigre would sail as far north as Pernambuco, continuing his search for a Portuguese prize. He didn't know how long he'd be away, maybe two months, perhaps longer, and two of *Croissant's* guns were placed ashore for defense.

Leaving Porto Seguro, they'd made a stormy passage to Bahia de Todos os Santos (Bay of All Saints), which Le Tigre — his patience exhausted — had dared enter. They crossed the bar at night, hugging the shore of an island opposite the mainland, and rode deeper into the bay: Dawn came, and off to starboard, near the brazilwood factory, they espied two caravels.

The wind was right, every man in *Croissant* ready, and Le Tigre in his most dangerous mood: Their guns blasted three great shots through the side of the first ship, starting a fire that raced through her.

Le Tigre closed with the second ship, and his men swarmed over her bulwarks and into her rigging, making short work of the feeble resistance they encountered. Before the small shore battery could do serious damage, they were beyond range, the captured caravel under sail with them, survivors of her crew tossed overboard.

Le Tigre was satisfied: Months of patient cruising had been handsomely rewarded. *Croissant*, newest ship out of Dieppe, had been bloodied; before long, every Portuguese in these waters must hear her name with dread — a name they'd remember for its mocking reminder of the crescent of the enemy Turk.

But what pleasure Le Tigre derived was shattered when he learned of what had happened at Porto Seguro.

He'd been coasting along the shore, heading back toward the bay, and was two days' sail away, when his lookouts saw the column of smoke from a fire set on a lonely beach. They stood in to investigate, and there they found three of *Croissant's* men, who had fled from their guns when they saw how hopeless it was to resist the Portuguese. They'd made it to this distant beach, where, with faint hope and much prayer, they waited to signal *Croissant*.

Le Tigre's face did not show his anger. His expression remained cold and pitiless as he sat with his officers planning the destruction of the ships and men at Porto Seguro. He was in no great hurry: If he didn't trap the squadron at its secure anchorage, he'd hunt it down from one end of this coast to the other, ship by ship.

☙

Le Tigre chose a perfect night for his attack. Low clouds drifted to obscure a weak four-day-old moon; a gusty breeze troubling the bay set up enough noise across the water and in the rigging to confuse the men on watch and conceal the rattle of oars in oarlocks and the splash and drip of their blades.

More than the elements were propitious for Le Tigre's revenge. After a fortnight of romancing in the tropics, Gomes de Pina had finally come round to his sense of duty and ordered that preparations be made to sail within the week. The first task the men undertook was to careen the ships, and they'd begun that morning with *Consolação*. She now lay heeled over in shallow water, held secure by lines rigged from her mainmast to the trunks of the nearest trees. Most of her crew slept aboard *São Gabriel*; a few were ashore, bedded down near her useless guns and equipment.

Cavalcanti had gone to his bunk on *São Gabriel* immediately after Padre Miguel conducted the night's prayers. The padre had sailed over with Padre Aloysius in *São Bento*, but he had become so concerned with the laxities he was witnessing that he'd moved himself to the flagship to begin rehabilitating the morals of the marinheiros, under the eye of the erring fidalgo.

Other than Gomes de Pina, housed on the deck above, Cavalcanti was the only man to have a cabin. It was on the starboard side of the steerage, with a bunk and just enough space for a sea chest. Almost the moment he lay down he began to doze off, thinking of Jandaia and her people. It was not her innocence alone but that of *all* the Tupiniquin that charmed him. He'd begun to understand why the warrior Aruanã had seen no value in gathering dyewood: The Tupiniquin lived without money, property, and trade. They had no king, no church, but shared an easy and harmonious life, provided by nature with a plenitude of their needs. They were open and generous and gave freely of whatever they had.

A cry woke Cavalcanti — the shriek of a man surprised in the moment before death.

It was followed by the dull thud of footsteps on deck and the unmistakable sound of a boat grinding against the side of *São Gabriel*.

Cavalcanti swung off the bunk, and tore his sword out of its scabbard. He threw open the door of his cabin and stepped into the dark steerage.

Pilot Fernandes was there, fighting with three men.

Cavalcanti rushed to his aid.

"Normans!" Fernandes cried out.

The French were swarming amidships, and more were climbing over the bulwarks. How, in the name of God, had they got here? Cavalcanti wondered.

There were sixty men on *São Gabriel* at the time she was boarded, her crew augmented by men from *Consolação*. Within the first five minutes of the attack, twenty men lay dead; a group near the blasted forecastle were begging for quarter and getting none. Serious resistance to the Normans came only from the steerage, where Cavalcanti and Fernandes were fighting alongside others who had bedded down there.

The quarterdeck was a slaughterhouse. Le Tigre had stormed it with a body of his *matelots*, hacking at the dark shapes that stirred against the bulwarks and rushing to meet the few who were able to stagger to the fight.

And then Gomes de Pina appeared.

He stood on the quarterdeck, which was slippery with blood, bellowing his rage against the pirates. Though he had never before raised his sword in battle, he now used it with bravado, dispatching two Normans in quick succession. A third drew a line of blood along the fidalgo's cheek, then swung his blade with such force that it broke Gomes de Pina's sword at the hilt. The Norman drew back for the kill. For a split second the captain general looked at the useless weapon in his hand before hurling himself at his attacker. Pierced by the enemy's sword, he collapsed in the scuppers, and died quickly.

It seemed that *São Gabriel* was lost. But then a miracle occurred.

When the struggle first spilled over *São Gabriel's* decks, Brito Correia, the orphan from Santarém's slums, had been terror-struck. He leapt to the shrouds and climbed the ratlines as swiftly as he could. And there he clung, shivering with fear as he saw the *Consolação* ablaze.

From his post in the shrouds, he witnessed Gomes de Pina's desperate struggle, and at the moment the captain general was slain, the boy's fear vanished, to be replaced by a consuming mania for revenge. He was too short to carry a man's sword, but he wore a dagger at his side and drew it now, holding it between his teeth as he climbed higher into the rigging to get a better position. He watched the men fighting below, and chose the most ferocious combatant he saw: Le Tigre.

Brito let go of the shrouds, and light as he was, he slammed into the Norman like a cannonball. He knocked him off balance, and drove his knife into the side of Le Tigre's chest as they went down.

One of Le Tigre's men saw what had happened and swung his sword at Brito so violently that it bit a hole an inch deep in the railing in front of him; before he could take a second swipe, the boy had catapulted himself out of the way, leaping blindly through the hatch to the steerage.

Le Tigre was alive, and feebly ordered his men to fight on. But an officer on the quarterdeck realized they had made a mistake with *São Gabriel:* They'd boarded her with twenty-five men expecting no more than forty, but she'd obviously held most of the careened ship's crew. They still might take her, but with Le Tigre wounded, the officer wasn't prepared to chance it. Making certain Le Tigre was aided, he ordered a retreat.

Almost as suddenly as it had begun, this skirmish was over. Marinheiros ran to fight the fire in the forecastle; others worked their way over the decks with sword and pike, ruthlessly silencing wounded Normans who cried out in pain, while sparing a few who appeared most likely to survive-to be hanged at dawn.

But the battle had not ended. "Clear away those guns!" Cavalcanti ordered, at the starboard side. "Is there a gunner to speak?" A man answered. "Stand ready, then! Mind your powder with that fire behind!" Cavalcanti then leapt for the companionway to the quarterdeck. At the same time, Padre Miguel began shouting that the captain general was dead.

For the priest, the struggle had been a nightmare: He'd fled into Gomes de Pina's cabin, where he huddled in a corner, moaning his most fervent prayers; opposite him, equally stricken, was the little princess, Itariri, wondering what demon had come to beset the ship. She was also outside now, wailing as she knelt beside the body of the fidalgo.

Cavalcanti didn't pause to consider that he was now in command of *São Gabriel*. He saw *Consolação* burning; he saw the pirate boats in the water near *São Bento*, and those that held the survivors from the boarding party making for the beach. He swung over to the port railing and searched for the Norman's ship in the dim moonlight, but he detected nothing.

He hastened back to the waist and was heartened by Fernandes's cry that the forecastle fire could be contained.

"Ready!" the starboard gunner shouted.

Cavalcanti was pleased to see that others had been ordered to the two starboard swivel guns. It was still dark, but the conflagration of *Consolação* illumined part of the bay.

"Fire at the boats!" Cavalcanti ordered.

São Gabriel's four starboard cannon flashed and roared, and sent their balls whistling toward the small craft. Black spouts of water burst near the boats, but it was impossible to see whether the shots had caused damage.

As *São Gabriel's* cannon were being reloaded for a second round, suddenly the guns of *São Bento* opened up against her.

"Oh, dear God!" Cavalcanti cried at this certain confirmation that *São Bento* had fallen to the Normans. But swiftly his despair turned to resolution: He must unleash all the fury *São Gabriel* could muster against the men across the water and their ill-gotten prize. There were not men enough in *São Gabriel* to think of boarding and retaking the caravel.

He made a dangerous decision then — to set *São Gabriel's* main and fore sails — mindful of the fact that the wind was in their favor and could move them to a better point of attack.

He gave orders, and men broke away from the gun and fire parties to cut the anchor cables or hurry into the rigging. Fernandes himself took the helm. All the while, the gunner and those with him kept up a cannonade though they were not in effective range.

São Bento, too, was now being maneuvered with her sweeps, but no attempt was made to shake out her canvas.

Shots from *São Bento* struck *São Gabriel* toward the stern, reducing her mizzenmast to a jagged stump. The spar crashed down with a tangle of lines and stays; railings and topside planking were torn away and splintering wood blasted across the deck, lacerating those who lay wounded.

When the axes bit through the third anchor cable at the stern and she was free, *São Gabriel* moved forward slowly and began to close with *São Bento*. Small shot from *São Bento* tore into *São Gabriel's* rigging, snapping lines and ripping holes in the foresail but inflicting no serious damage.

When less than two hundred yards separated the two ships, *São Gabriel* belched a broadside of smoke and iron. One of the shots blasted through *São Bento's* planking, low at the waterline, deep into her hold, where it smashed aside the lamps that hung there and threw a line of fire toward her powder magazine. The deck of the caravel erupted in flame as an explosion tore out her heart, toppling her mainmast and silencing all but a single swivel gun on her poop, which stopped firing moments later.

The men aboard *São Gabriel* could take no satisfaction from the destruction of *São Bento*. No one said it, but all knew that their countrymen — her commander, marinheiros, the cheerful, ruddy-faced Padre Aloysius — must surely have perished. Not far off to the right, *Consolação* still glowed in the dark.

Cavalcanti moved to Fernandes's side. "Take her out," he said. "Away from this infernal place!"

℘

Cavalcanti laid a course for the Portuguese factory at Pernambuco, to the north, from whence they would proceed to Lisbon. But the southeast trade winds forced a change of plans. For a week *São Gabriel* fought contrary seas, taking so much water that the pumps were never unmanned. Finally Cavalcanti gave up, and turned the ship south to Cabo Frio. There, too, was a logwood factory, but the loggers received the *São Gabriel* coldly. They had hoped to welcome a squadron that would protect the coast against Norman pirates, not a single, broken ship with men worse off than they.

The crew repaired *São Gabriel* as best they could, and provisioned her with what little the loggers would give.

Pilot Fernandes saw that it might be weeks, even months before they could make passage to the north, and suggested that they sail with the southeast wind toward Africa. It would add hundreds of leagues to their journey but might offer a safer route, considering the state of *São Gabriel* and her depleted crew. The master included, there were thirty men, three boys, the priest, and the little princess.

They sailed for two weeks with fair weather and then were struck by a storm. Two marinheiros were lost in the black, blind tempest. The sky remained a threatening gray for most of the morning, but toward noon a weak sun broke through the clouds, and even this slight warmth and their first cooked meal in three days cheered the men, and they worked more keenly at repairing cracked yards, replacing rigging, patching sails.

For the next five days, *São Gabriel* was a quiet ship but for the ceaseless noise of pumps that were having little effect on the flooded hold. The ship rode so dangerously low that her crew feared she might yet founder before they reached land.

And then, early on the sixth day, there was a cry from aloft. Each man sought confirmation of the landfall and, when he had it, remained silent, his relief too great to be shared.

São Gabriel stood in toward the wide mouth of a river, passing a rufous-colored hillock on its northern bank. Fernandes, whom Gomes de Pina had mockingly spoken of as a "Guinea pilot," knew where they were, for he had guided ships from this Guinea coast to the Cape of Good Hope itself. Now he ordered the leadsman to call the marks, and took the helm.

Several miles upstream lay the port of Mpinda, visited by the Portuguese since 1482, when the navigator Diogo Cao discovered it. The river was the "Nzere," a word the Portuguese pronounced Zaire. This stretch of water and vast provinces to the south lay in the kingdom of the Bakongo people.

As *São Gabriel* moved slowly through the brown water, the crew suddenly began to cheer: Raised on the bank of the river was a marble pillar, symbol of their king's right in this sanctuary.

ా

Cavalcanti watched two boats approach *São Gabriel's* anchorage at Mpinda. They were filled with men-at-arms, and in the lead craft, standing up forward, were two men Cavalcanti could tell bore the self-enamored look of petty officials swollen with the authority they claimed thousands of miles from Lisbon.

Port Superintendent Sancho de Sousa came aboard in the manner of a grand admiral, letting his armed escort precede him and line up on deck before presenting himself and his customs officer.

Sousa was a short, nervous man with thin hair and steel-gray eyes. "You are the captain?" he asked, after Cavalcanti had greeted him.

"The master," Cavalcanti said. "The captain general, Gomes de Pina, is dead."

Sousa shifted a cold, suspicious look from Cavalcanti to Fernandes and then to the marinheiros near them.

"What you see, senhor," Cavalcanti said, "is all that remains of a squadron the king sent to Terra do Brasil."

The superintendent raised an eyebrow. "Santa Cruz?"

"The Normans attacked us at Porto Seguro. We lost two caravels, all the men in them, and our captain general."

"When?"

"A month ago. We've also had a terrible passage to your port; there was a storm such as few live to tell of."

Sousa murmured an aside to the customs official and then asked Cavalcanti, "Why did you come here?"

With a laugh, the master said, "Senhor, if our promised landfall was the shores of hell, we'd have accepted it!"

"Attacked by Normans, beaten across the Atlantic — terrible, terrible," Sousa said. Then he added, "What proof, Master?"

"Proof? Of what, senhor? Come now, you can see the men and the ship, both broken. What further proof do you seek?"

The superintendent replied with another question: "Where is the rest of the crew?"

"Dead!" Cavalcanti said harshly. "They died fighting Norman pirates for their king."

"Too often, Master, we have heard the same tale from pirates and mutineers."

Behind him, Cavalcanti heard Fernandes say, "Ask *him*, senhor, if we are thieves or mutineers." The pilot was pointing to Padre Miguel, who was standing on the quarterdeck.

Sousa observed the priest and, directly behind him, the Tupiniquin girl. "And this woman? What will she say?" he retorted.

"Our captain general is dead," Cavalcanti repeated stonily. "I am in command. I am taking this ship back to Lisbon."

The superintendent nodded his head rapidly. "Tomorrow, Master, we will return," he said. "Until then, no decision."

"We cannot land?"

"Tomorrow."

"Then, the senhor superintendent would be good enough to remove himself and his escort," Cavalcanti said. "*Now.*"

⟡

They were back the next morning, two boats again. Another man, not the customs official, accompanied the superintendent.

The newcomer introduced himself only as Lourenço Velloso of Mpinda, giving no indication of his position ashore but politely asking Cavalcanti to repeat his story.

Velloso was six feet, several inches taller than the average Portuguese, with long, silky black hair, light brown eyes, and a graceful body. He was the most prosperous slave trader in Mpinda.

When Cavalcanti had finished speaking, Velloso turned to Sousa. "A reasonable report," he said, with authority. "Would they have stayed the night if they were liars?"

"True, true," the superintendent said quickly. "I sought your opinion, senhor."

"Then you have it. Let them land or you'll be answering to Lisbon for refusing to aid a ship of the king."

"Never . . . I never intended this," Sousa said, with alarm. He looked appealingly at Velloso. "Tell them what dangers our ships face between my port and Lisbon. Even you have lost cargoes to pirates."

Rather than elaborate on his own misfortunes, Velloso began to inquire about Cavalcanti's needs. Later that day, when they'd finally gone ashore, Velloso took Cavalcanti to meet the local native chief, who responded to the crew's plight by sending cattle and a bounty of provender to the port. By week's end, *São Gabriel* had been careened and the full extent of damage to her hull revealed. Velloso again offered help by organizing a party of natives to lead her men to the timbers they needed for repairs.

Cavalcanti quickly realized that Velloso's aid was not given gratuitously. "A near-empty ship bound for Lisbon," the slave trader commented casually. "Why not carry a cargo of slaves when she sails? That way you'll not return to Lisbon a beggar," he added suggestively.

Cavalcanti had flashed him an angry look: He needed no reminder of the disreputable homecoming that awaited him. But he promised to consider Velloso's suggestion.

To help him make up his mind, the slaver offered an inducement: Five blacks were to be his alone — in exchange for the Tupiniquin girl.

"What would you want with the savage?"

"Ah, Captain, I've heard men praise the talents of such creatures. I wouldn't take her for myself," Velloso said. "A gift, Captain, for the royal household. Such a plump and exotic bird would give pleasure to the ManiKongo."

From Velloso, who'd lived here nine years, Cavalcanti heard much of this ManiKongo (Lord of the Kongo) and his royal city of Mbanza, in the interior. Cavalcanti had some idea of the place, gained from the talk on Lisbon's waterfront, but still found aspects of Velloso's descriptions difficult to accept. Who would acknowledge, for instance, that there was a black chief who called himself Affonso I, son of King João da Silva, (John of the Woods) and Queen Eleanor; who ruled his lands not with chiefs and elders but with nobles he addressed as his *duques, marquezes, viscondes*, and *baroes?*

According to the slaver, Affonso I, as a young man, had been banished from the capital by his father, who'd had second thoughts about the Portuguese. Affonso had gone into exile, taking with him those who had accepted the Christian faith. When King João da Silva died, Affonso returned to fight, and win, a war against a pagan relative. From the time of that victory, the Portuguese, who'd helped him, were his brothers, and Christ, Savior of his people. That all should know this, he had sent his own son, Henrique, to Lisbon and Rome, where the worldly Leo X had authorized the young man's elevation as bishop of Utica.

Three weeks after their arrival, Velloso announced that he was to journey to the capital, and invited Cavalcanti, Fernandes, and Padre Miguel to accompany him. Cavalcanti declined, saying that he could not leave *São Gabriel*.

"Why not, Captain? It's a month, perhaps more, before your men finish the work. Travel with us. You have my promise that we'll return before your ship is ready."

"God knows, the report we take to Lisbon is bleak enough," Cavalcanti said. "Our Brazil lies undefended. We dare not allow a single day to be lost."

"It isn't far," the slaver said. "Five, six days at most. Come, Captain" — he laughed — "your feet need not touch the ground! I, personally, will select for you the finest wooden horse in Mpinda!"

A "wooden horse" was a hefty log to the middle of which was strapped a hide saddle. Two slaves would shoulder this burden, where the pathway permitted, along one hundred miles between the port and the capital.

Cavalcanti gave in. "Hear me, Senhor Velloso: I'll hold you responsible if *São Gabriel's* departure is delayed for a single day!"

Two days later, they left for Mbanza, the capital, and had gone only a few leagues when Cavalcanti created a small scene:

"By all the saints, let me walk!" With great awkwardness, he abandoned his wooden horse and stood next to it.

"You'll regret it, Captain," Velloso said. "It can be a tiring journey. This way, you'll travel like a prince."

"Prince be damned! I'll not have my insides jolted apart. Send this infernal thing away."

"As you wish," Velloso said.

They continued their journey, with Padre Miguel the only member of Cavalcanti's party to remain in the saddle of a wooden horse. Also on foot from the start were little Brito Correia and Itariri. The little princess wandered the footpath, a cloth of rich purple around her waist, a faraway expression on her face. She had not the slightest idea where she was.

Their route lay to the southeast through lands that became increasingly populated as they neared the capital, the hillsides and valleys dotted with neat villages of straw huts. Droves of children ran down to the path, darting between the travelers, shouting greetings. Their parents observed from a distance, remaining at their fields or wherever they stood.

The third morning, the forest began to thin and the landscape became varied, with fields of green and gold grasses taller than any man, and lush, fertile soils and rivers crossed by sturdy branch-and-vine bridges. At each crossing, the small caravan had to halt and pay a toll to the representative of the local headman. It was just after passing one of these streams that Cavalcanti and his party got their first real glimpse of what lay ahead.

Six warriors, powerfully built, their shoulders oiled and glistening in the sun, came running along the path, shouting and waving their weapons as they neared the travelers.

Instinctively, Cavalcanti went for his sword.

"No!" Velloso barked. "They mean no harm."

Before Velloso could answer, the warriors drew abreast of them, still crying out their alarm.

"Move!" the slaver urged. "Quickly! Get off the road!"

The slaves shouldering Velloso's wooden horse needed no such command and were already swinging into the grass beside the track. The others did as they'd been told and stood near Velloso, who motioned Cavalcanti to keep still and wait.

Within minutes, there came the sound of a great multitude approaching, and it grew louder, until a thick file of warriors stomped into sight. Between their front and rear ranks, four slaves carried a litter in which a large man reclined amid cushions and drapes. Attendants kept pace on either side, one cooling the passenger with a palm-leaf fan.

"Who is he?" Cavalcanti asked, when the litter had passed.

"Chief of a western province," Velloso said. "He's less important than he appears to be. When Affonso comes this way, it's not only six runners who go before him: Every step must be swept so clean that you could eat your food off this path. God protect the villager who leaves a single pebble, a blade of grass on the ground. God help those whose eyes aren't averted when the king's litter comes."

On the morning of the sixth day, after crossing a wide valley that lay before a steep ridge, they reached the capital. There had been one more river to pass and then they were scaling the last, precipitous height before a grand plateau above the wet, steamy low country they'd traversed. For two centuries the kings of the Bakongo had ruled their empire from this lofty hideaway.

Cavalcanti's first impression of Mbanza, palace and place of justice of the ManiKongo, was one of confusion. He was taken aback by the sight of a wall, like those in Portugal, raised before this city in the heart of Africa. Parts of this defense were still under construction, a labor guided by stonemasons from Lisbon. Within the wall were thousands of people, their straw huts stretching as far as the eye could see. Most of the inhabitants were like those encountered in villages along the way, but some warriors carried swords of iron and pikes, and wore cloaks and tunics. Stone structures — small, solid houses — stood between the clusters of huts, and many more were in the process of being raised.

Velloso led the party along straight tree-lined roads toward the southern end of the city. "There," he said, "is where our people live." Before they reached the Portuguese quarter, he stopped to indicate a walled enclosure in the distance: "That is the court of their king."

"This king," Cavalcanti said, "whom none may look upon — is he ever seen?"

"Yes, Captain," the slaver replied. "Remember, you're Portuguese, the subject of his brother, João the Third. A day or two, Captain and I'll arrange a meeting." He now looked at the Tupiniquin girl. "He'll want to see you," he said to Cavalcanti. "Such a fine gift you've carried to these shores!"

Almost one hundred Portuguese lived at the capital. Besides Dom Carlos Machado, Lisbon's ambassador to the Bakongo, who greeted Velloso with great familiarity, and other officials of João III, who also showed the slaver respect, there were masons and carpenters, farmers and traders, some of whom had been here longer than Lourenço Velloso and had filled households with their children from Bakongo women. There were also some Portuguese ladies, not the orphans and whores Cavalcanti knew to be transported to the empire's outposts but women chosen for service at Mbanza as teachers of cooking and sewing.

The morning after their arrival, Padre Miguel went to inspect a new church being built near the royal enclosure. The priest who headed the mission to the Bakongo, Padre Antônio Andrade, an older man, lean and energetic, took him there.

"We have no problem with the minds and hearts of these pagans," Padre Antônio told his visitor, "but, oh, my son, the awful climate! Up here we do God's work in comfort, but in the forest and marshes, no white man can long endure the terrible fevers."

What was it, Padre Miguel asked his guide, that had made these blacks so receptive to His word?

"Their king," Padre Antônio replied without hesitation. "Affonso knows the Prophets and the Gospel of Our Lord Jesus Christ and all the lives of the saints. He is very assiduous in the exercise of his faith, and punishes with rigor those who worship idols, and has them burned along with the idols."

Cavalcanti and Fernandes presented themselves to Ambassador Dom Machado. The ambassador showed cursory interest in them. He was impatient to attend to two little black girls who stood waiting for his consideration: A settler who had chanced on them while on a hunting expedition had brought the girls in the night before. He was offering them for sale to the ambassador, whose private dealings in such merchandise nearly rivaled those of Velloso.

"There's scarcely one who's not involved," Velloso said afterward. They had left Dom Machado's house and were on their way to the capital's marketplace. "They're sent out as carpenters and stonecutters and even teachers; they amuse themselves with their skills, but soon they swear that nothing will keep them from making a fortune through slaving. Even the fathers, glorying in their conversion of so many heathen, see others as forest cattle herded to be sold on their behalf."

Mbanza's marketplace was filled with exotic wares to be seen, touched, and sniffed, amid the hum and bustle of an immense throng of merchants and their customers.

Cavalcanti stopped when he saw a group of lean, half-naked men with vaguely slanted eyes and yellowish skins. He remarked to Velloso that they were like men from the East.

"Not east but south," the slaver said. "They are Khoi-Khoi, who bring copper and ostriches to the kingdom. They live near the *Cape*." — The Cape of Good Hope, at the tip of Africa.

Velloso pointed out others who'd come from afar: Swahili merchants, most redoubtable of all wanderers, who had long traveled the width of Africa carrying the merchandise of the Moor. That trade had dwindled after the Portuguese seized the East Coast traffic, but small parties still ventured across the interior with the gold dust of the Monomotapa of Great Zimbabwe.

Two commodities predominated at the market: the Bakongo's palm manufactures and the anvil.

When Cavalcanti first saw the cloths woven from palm fibers, he had to reach out and touch those marvelous fabrics to assure himself that they were not the finest silk of the East.

As much as the softness and hues of the palm cloth impressed the visitors, so did the work of the Bakongo blacksmiths. More astonishing than the everyday items, such as tools and spearheads hammered out with great force, were the ornaments and musical instruments wrought in the same hard metal.

"Now, Captain," Velloso said, when they reached a part of the market fenced off with a stockade, "let me show you the real wealth of this kingdom."

He led them through the entrance, acknowledging the greetings of the men who stood there.

"Here, Cavalcanti, are riches enough to build a castle in Sintra!"

More than three hundred men, women, and children lay on the ground. Many turned to look in their direction, but some showed no interest at all and continued to doze in the sun.

"Where do they all come from?" Cavalcanti asked.

"Here, there . . . who knows? The men who capture them bring them here or to Mpinda, to sell to Lourenço Velloso and others. Affonso's slave commissioners must approve all peças as not being subjects of his kingdom.

"There will never be enough," Velloso added. "Today, Spain wants peças for her colonies in the New World. Tomorrow? Who knows what the demand will be for territories yet to be discovered? The Bakongo don't understand this commerce. They've always had slaves but treat them like family. Some come and go as they please; others are less free — serfs of their owners — but none were ever sold . . . until we taught the Bakongo, how much profit they can earn."

Their visit to King Affonso took place two days later. Four trumpeters stood at the entrance to the royal enclosure, with long, beautifully carved ivory instruments. Next to the musicians were royal guardsmen — tall, athletic soldiers with white tunics and black buffalo-hide shields, carrying the same weapons as the Portuguese and standing as smartly as men who might protect João III in Lisbon.

The visitors passed through the outer wall into the enclosure and faced yet another wall: In the space between these two barriers were housed the king's councilors and his bodyguard. A trumpeter blew short blasts and two pages came to meet them.

"They are dwarfs," Brito Correia said.

"Not dwarfs," Velloso corrected. "They are the little people from the forest. They never grow taller."

The Pygmies beckoned for the party to follow them through the last barrier before the royal palace. This was an intricate maze, a network of narrow passages between walls of latticed twigs.

"When we reach the end," Velloso said, "we must go down on our knees." His words were greeted with mutterings from Cavalcanti and Padre Miguel. He stilled them. "No stranger approaches the ManiKongo in any other manner."

They followed the Pygmies along the labyrinth's elaborate twists and turns as if working through the core of a great beehive. At one place, a Pygmy barred the way down an offshoot, and Fernandes asked where it led. "Follow it," the slaver said, "if you wish to meet the sacred crocodiles."

Itariri was awed by this strange maloca. She had been confined in the house of a Portuguese, and visited by a parade of the curious and the amused, who'd peered and poked at her and spoken words unintelligible to her. This trip through the maze was no less strange, but she followed the example of the others when it ended, falling to her knees the moment she stepped out of it.

Affonso I, Lord of the Kongo, sat upon a throne inlaid with gold and ivory and draped with leopard skins. He was dressed in the fashion of a Portuguese noble, with scarlet tabard, pale silk robe, satin cloak with embroidered coat of arms, and velvet slippers. As concessions to his tribal heritage, he wore a small cap of palm cloth, a necklace of iron, and over his left shoulder the insignia of kingship: a zebra tail.

Immediately to the right of him stood his son Henrique, with the white linen alb, chasuble, and other vestments of a bishop of the Church of Rome. Beyond the bishop and to the left of the king stood his senior councilors and the provincial. These, too, were dressed as fidalgos.

Elsewhere in the palace square were ranks of the royal bodyguard: Unlike their counterparts at the entrance, these retained their traditional appearance, their oiled bodies and the feathers and animal skins they wore a striking contrast to the sophisticated garb of their sovereign and his officials. There were women, too, dressed as Portuguese *donas*, with veils over their faces and velvet caps and cloth gowns. Their gold and jewels were such as few ladies of Lisbon possessed.

Several stone buildings faced the heart of the enclosure, but the royal palace itself was made up of several large huts of reeds and grass. Only their golden round tops were seen, for none but the king and his immediate family and their servants were allowed in the area, which was screened off with painted cloth panels and mats that swayed gently in the breeze.

Ambassador Machado approached the throne and spoke to the king in a low voice. Then he turned to the party on their knees: "His Highness Affonso the First, Lord of the Kongo, greets you and will hear from the one who comes from Santa Cruz."

Cavalcanti shuffled forward.

"Your Majesty, we thank you for the welcome given us by your people," Cavalcanti said.

"It is what we would hope for from our own friends," the king said.

He listened intently, with few interjections, to what Cavalcanti had to tell of Brazil. Some things he already knew, for other homebound ships had passed this way: In the royal gardens were plants from that land, including manioc, which had so amazed Affonso with its fertility that he had distributed cuttings to his farthest provinces.

When it was time to present Itariri to Affonso, there was excitement in the ranks of dukes and nobles. Never had they seen one of the people from Brazil. Velloso made the presentation:

"A gift, Your Highness, for the royal household."

"Rise, girl," Affonso commanded.

Velloso pushed her to her feet. "She does not know our language, Highness," he said, "but she's of noble birth — a princess, Highness, among her people."

Affonso climbed off his throne. "She is one of those who devour humans?" he asked Cavalcanti.

"True, my lord."

"A bestial practice," the king said. "There are pagans beyond our lands who do the same."

The girl was trembling.

"She is a pleasing sight," Affonso said. "Let her be taken to the women's place."

Affonso now gave his attention to the slaver, who moved near the edge of the carpet. "Were I to receive other gifts with such ease, it would be pleasing," the king said.

"I understand His Highness."

"Yes, Velloso, you say this: You Portuguese always understand the words of ManiKongo," he said. "If we are good friends, where is the ship I have asked for?"

Velloso looked from the king to Dom Machado.

"My lord," the ambassador began, "it is difficult — "

"*Difficult!*" Affonso snorted. "That is all I ever hear! That is all I've heard from those they sent before you: 'difficult'! A ship! One small caravel for your biggest friend in Africa is all I ask." He now looked at Cavalcanti: "Perhaps, Captain, I should seek this favor from your Norman enemies? Perhaps the men from Dieppe, who drove you to these shores, would be willing to find a ship for me?"

Cavalcanti said nothing.

"My lord," Dom Machado started again, "we wait for new word from Lisbon. Our king is aware of your need."

"And so, too, the thieves on São Thomé?"

The ambassador had no answer.

The clique of officials and traders at São Thomé Island, to the northwest of the kingdom, were virtually in control of the slave and other trade that flowed from Mpinda. Even Lourenço Velloso had to pay a bribe in slaves to them. Their operators were active in the kingdom itself, encouraging the kidnapping of Bakongo.

Affonso I had become obsessed with the idea of having a ship of his own so that his students and his emissaries might travel to Lisbon and Rome without interference from the Portuguese on São Thomé.

"I thank you for your gift," the ManiKongo said abruptly, and turned and stepped up to the platform before his throne. "You, Captain," he said to Cavalcanti over his shoulder, "tell Lisbon how sad they make their brother Affonso."

Clearly the audience was over.

Three days later, Cavalcanti and Velloso led their party from the capital, their journey to the port slowed by sixty slaves they were taking with them to the coast, part of the shipment Velloso planned to send to Lisbon with *São Gabriel*. The night before they reached Mpinda, they camped outside a village at which they'd stopped on their way up to Mbanza. Six burly warriors Velloso had hired in the capital guarded the slaves — men he had to watch as closely as the captives to prevent them from damaging his property. At the slightest provocation, they would beat a slave with brutal ferocity.

"What will you do when you get back to Lisbon?" the trader asked Cavalcanti, as they lay near the camp fire. Velloso had made his final check of the slaves, who were settled on the ground a hundred paces away.

"Make my report," Cavalcanti said. "Then I'll seek a way to return."

"To Brazil?"

"Yes, to Brazil, my friend — to chase the Norman dogs who destroyed the squadron."

"Why concern yourself with such a place?" Velloso asked, stifling a yawn.

"Brazil is a vast and fertile land — so vast you can't imagine. The scum from Dieppe must not be allowed a foothold there."

"Lisbon does not respond kindly to news of defeat," Velloso reminded him. "Even Cabral — knight, admiral, *discoverer* of Brazil — found it so."

True enough, Cavalcanti thought, with a shudder. Cabral, even before he'd reached Porto Seguro, had lost one ship, her crew disappeared off Cape Verde. Then, after Brazil, four of his vessels had been destroyed in a hurricane off the Cape of Good Hope. Of his thirteen ships, seven returned to Lisbon. There was praise for the admiral's New World discovery, but never again was Cabral given an important command.

At Mpinda, they found that work on *São Gabriel* had progressed slowly. Cavalcanti and Fernandes took charge of the refitting, but a further two weeks passed before the last of her new planks had been hewn and fixed into place.

While master and pilot guided these labors, Padre Miguel busied himself with the cargo of slaves, including five who were Cavalcanti's. Two days before they were to be taken aboard, Superintendent Sancho de Sousa sent his customs officials to brand the captives, marking their breasts with a red-hot iron. When this was done, Padre Miguel had the slaves assembled and, through an interpreter, informed them that they were to be baptized.

"You will taste the salt of our faith," he told them. "Your souls, servants, will be free."

The slaves stared at him blankly, but when it was time to make them Christians, they rushed forward eagerly, hoping that this black robe's ceremony would liberate more than their pagan hearts. They were disappointed.

On the morning *São Gabriel* was to sail, young Brito Correia sought permission to speak with Cavalcanti: "Please, Master, there's no one at Santarém. Dom Velloso, he's a good man."

The slaver was aboard, come to see his property safely stowed in the forecastle, a dark, uncomplaining group, silent but for the noise of the shackles that bound them together. Velloso had taken an instant liking to the orphan, and on their journey to the ManiKongo's capital, Brito had rarely been out of his sight. After their return from Mbanza, Velloso had gone to a southern province to set up a new source of slaves; Cavalcanti had let the boy accompany him, and it struck him how alike were the bastard of the Berber woman and the young mulatto from Santarém, almost like father and son.

Velloso and the boy left soon afterward. Cavalcanti gave the order for *São Gabriel's* anchors to be taken in. He stood alone on the quarterdeck as the crew maneuvered the ship into midstream with her long sweeps, so that she was set to run down to the mouth of the Zaire.

Cavalcanti thought gloomily of the humiliation of having to report a grievous loss to the men at Lisbon. He recalled, too, his own father's disappointment when he'd returned empty-handed from the Indies. Now he was going home under an even darker cloud.

VI

October 1534 – April 1546

*I*n the domed Sala das Armas of Sintra palace on a day in October 1534, the fidalgo Dom Duarte Coelho Pereira sat listening to the Keeper of Records, Belchior da Silveira, read part of a petition taken from the royal archives. Dom Duarte's features were strong and determined; his bright eyes, firm jaw, the deep lines marking his forehead — all were indicative of the drive of a man who, when made a fidalgo for services to his king, chose nothing less than the red, rampant lion to surmount his crest.

Dom Duarte and the Keeper of Records, a small, rotund man, stern-faced and with wisps of gray hair, were the only occupants of the hall. Dom Belchior's reputation went beyond his zeal for paperwork: He had a remarkable memory for people and events connected with the volumes he had guarded for the past two decades, so wide a knowledge that some of the very men whose escutcheons were displayed in this armorial chamber dreaded the diminutive record keeper's recollections.

The petition Dom Belchior was reading had been submitted to the Crown eight years ago by Master Nicolau Cavalcanti, who had reported on the ill-fated squadron of Captain General Gomes de Pina. Dom Belchior reached the concluding paragraphs of Cavalcanti's observations, which were addressed to King João III himself:

> "It seems to me, senhor, that much profit can be made by this land
> of Santa Cruz, but it will require permanent settlement, as in the realms
> of Your Highness in Africa and India. The Norman pirates freely harass

your logwood factories and ships because they see little evidence of your possession of Santa Cruz. The factories with your license have few men and are miserably defended; along the length of this coast there is not one settlement worthy of the name.

"At Porto Seguro, we saw that this is not a land of dyewood and parrots alone but is so vast, so fertile, so well watered that it could support many of your subjects in enterprises such as exist at Your Highness' islands of Madeira and the Azores. I have seen the fields of the Tupiniquin, who cultivate this land in the most primitive manner but receive Nature's bounty in abundance.

"Senhor, men and their families should be sent to make this land their home. Let them respect the trees and products that are your property, but encourage them to plant the crops of the Azores and São Thomé, sugarcane especially, my lord, and there will surely be great profit for Your Highness."

At the time Cavalcanti wrote this petition, it had been noted and forgotten. The court had been more concerned with the loss of the squadron and the fidalgo who led it to defeat.

When Dom Belchior stopped reading, Dom Duarte asked, "What do you know about this Nicolau Cavalcanti?"

"He is the son of the Lisbon merchant João Cavalcanti. Before he sailed with Gomes de Pina, he served with Dom Afonso de Albuquerque."

"I can't recall a Nicolau Cavalcanti in India," Dom Duarte said.

"He was at Goa and Ormuz."

"The name means nothing to me."

Dom Belchior stroked the end of his nose. If Cavalcanti had achieved anything of special note in the East, Dom Duarte Coelho would surely have remembered him.

Dom Belchior was aware that Coelho had gone from one success to another in the Indies. Little known when he first sailed out as a junior officer in 1509, he had been with Afonso de Albuquerque at Malacca's capture in 1511, and for the next eighteen years had continued to serve with honor. Twice ambassador to Siam, he had also voyaged to China, India, Java, and Indochina, and had captained ships of the king in victorious engagements against Chinese and Malay fleets.

Greatest among his triumphs, he counted his marriage into one of Portugal's most honored families; his wife, Dona Brites, was the niece of Jorge de Albuquerque, captain of Malacca during two periods Dom Duarte served in that city. And Jorge was a cousin of O Terrível himself.

Allying himself to such a powerful group was a coup indeed for an illegitimate son of respectable but not high birth. There were fidalgos at court, however, who called Dom Duarte a soldier of fortune. This he greatly resented, and energetically sought every chance to improve his standing.

A month ago, in September 1534, King João had given Coelho his most magnificent opportunity yet to rise above those who mocked his more common and obscure roots: He was among a group of nobles to whom the king had granted vast landholdings in Terra do Brasil.

A start at colonization had been made in 1531 on an island within a bay south of Porto Seguro and Cabo Frio, and the results at São Vicente had been promising — so much so that now, in 1534, João had announced a plan to divide his New World possession into captaincies, to be donated to nobles at his court, both the deserving and those he simply wished out of the way.

A year ago a Portuguese flotilla had inflicted a defeat on the French corsairs: Twenty-one Normans, the notorious Tigre included, had been executed at the log-wood factory of Pernambuco. Dom Duarte had been especially pleased by this news, for the lands he hoped to be granted — and in fact received — were at Pernambuco.

"You may take sixty leagues, Dom Duarte," the king had decreed, "from this river that encircles the island of Tamaraca — which river I want you to name Santa Cruz — to the river São Francisco, south of the Cabo de São Agostinho. At each point, you will set a marker with my coat of arms, and your land will extend to the west from those pillars as far as it can go." Here João had been vague: Dom Duarte's grant would run to the imaginary line between Portuguese and Spanish territory established by the Treaty of Tordesilhas, but just how much land existed out there was unknown.

Ten of the sixty leagues were to be the personal property of Dom Duarte and his heirs: Over the rest, he was to exercise powers not unlike those of a feudal lord.

João's irrevocable grant and charter went into the smallest detail: There would be no royal levy on soapmaking in the colony, no tax on a grain of salt; one in twenty fish caught by the settlers — except those on a pole — were to be Dom Duarte's.

Dom Duarte was forbidden the exploitation of brazilwood, forever the king's monopoly.

João's reward to Dom Duarte for all the services he had rendered in the East was given at a price, namely that Dom Duarte himself pay the cost of launching the colony. He had indeed amassed a fortune in the Indies, but there was enormous risk involved: Ruin could come easily — the wreck of a ship or two, even before they reached the new land, could be disastrous.

Such gloomy thoughts quickly vanished as he reconsidered the report just read to him by Dom Belchior. "I don't know this Cavalcanti," Dom Duarte repeated, "but it's obvious he's not fooled by parrots and logs; he sees the one thing that will bring a profit from Brazil."

"Which is?"

"Sugar! Sugar will be the treasure of our New World! I would very much like to meet Master Nicolau Cavalcanti. Is it known where he lives at present?"

"You'll most likely find him here, a few leagues beyond Sintra, at his father's estate. He wanted to return to Terra do Brasil to fight the pirates, but his requests were rejected."

"He no longer goes to sea?"

"I can't say, but he's often seen in Sintra."

"Good, good," said Dom Duarte. "I'll go to him."

Dom Duarte left soon afterward, with directions to the Cavalcanti lands from Dom Belchior.

&

João Cavalcanti found it difficult to conceal his disappointment in his son, even though he realized the importance of Dom Duarte Coelho Pereira's visit.

Nicolau was working in the fields and had been summoned. His father and Dom Duarte were sitting at a long oak-beamed table in a low-roofed room that served as living and eating quarters. It was the oldest part of the farmhouse, with rough limed walls.

"Does he speak much of Brazil?" Dom Duarte asked.

"Which one, senhor?"

Dom Duarte frowned. "I don't understand."

"The Brazil where he fought, again, for his king, or the one that belongs to the officials in Lisbon? You've read his report?" Dom Duarte nodded. "He brought the *São Gabriel* back, did he not? He fought off the Normans and faced death in the great storms of the Atlantic. Was he thanked? Far better had he listened to his father and followed my other sons into the countinghouse."

"Never, senhor!" a voice said strongly.

Their backs to the doorway, they had not seen Nicolau standing there. João Cavalcanti introduced the two men and then politely excused himself, saying that he had work to do.

"Let us walk, too," Dom Duarte said, when the old man had left.

They stepped into the courtyard. The Cavalcanti house had been added to over the years and formed a U-shape, with a chapel and the living quarters to the right, a storeroom between, and a long barn to the left. Casually, Dom Duarte remarked, "This is a home a man can be proud of."

Cavalcanti only nodded glumly. Cavalcanti no longer sailed in the king's nor anyone else's ships but halfheartedly led his father's laborers and slaves, a lonely dour man whose future seemed utterly hopeless.

Dom Duarte saw a person of character and strength, but one gripped by a profound melancholy. The brooding green eyes, the furrowed forehead said as much as if he'd openly revealed his bitterness to his visitor. His hair, like his beard, was almost all gray. Dom Duarte told Cavalcanti how he'd come to read Nicolau's report to João III.

"That was written eight years ago, senhor," Nicolau said.

"What you wrote remains as true as it was then. Sugar, Cavalcanti, is the future of Brazil. And Pernambuco, where my colony is to be established, will have the finest fields along that coast."

"But tell me, senhor, how long before others carry to Brazil the corruption and rot with which they infected Estado do India?"

"There have been changes at Goa and Malacca."

"For whom?" Cavalcanti said. "For the thieves who squandered Dom Afonso's legacy? No, senhor, no one can deny how bad it was, and is. Didn't they send Vasco da Gama himself to restore order? Three months, senhor, and he was dead — dead of a broken heart, I would say, at the sight of his great discoveries so misused."

"True," Dom Duarte said. "But Brazil can't be the same, senhor. If a man wants a profit, he'll have to earn it with the sweat of his labor. There are no markets, no traders, no great sultans to lead as milch cows. It's a place, Cavalcanti, for an honest man."

"Pray God it stays that way."

"You made several appeals to return, I understand."

"Then you must also know they were rejected by Lisbon."

"Your father tells me you have a wife and two strong sons. I need such families, Nicolau Cavalcanti, to build my colony."

"I'm satisfied, senhor, on my father's lands. Even the sea is no longer a home to me. When the king's men said no, I went to my brothers. 'For the love of God,' I begged them, 'get me a ship before my soul dies on these rocks.' They did, a command as captain. On my first voyage from Lisbon to Genoa, a storm broke that little barcha's back on a shore of Corsica. Such a man, Dom Duarte, can be of no help to you."

Dom Duarte ignored this gloomy recitation. "I'm prepared to give everything I have to this venture," he said. "I've fought from Malacca to Cochin, Cavalcanti, and what is there to show for it? Wealth? Yes. Honor? 'Dom Duarte,' they call me, 'lion of the East.' But what comes after, when I'm gone? A small memory of me in some corner of the world? At Santa Cruz, Cavalcanti, it's my wish that the name Duarte Coelho be remembered from one end of that land to the other!"

Pedro, the younger of Cavalcanti's sons, was at the open cow stall of the long barn to their left, paying more attention to the two men than to the animals.

"How old is he?" Dom Duarte asked.

"Fourteen, senhor."

"What a year for a young man! You and I, Cavalcanti, with our dreams of the East — what we were planning at his age! Today, Cavalcanti, there is a New World — for boys such as your sons."

"It's a wild, beautiful place that will take *real* men to conquer," Cavalcanti said, with mounting enthusiasm.

Dom Duarte sensed that he had Cavalcanti on the verge of accepting, and now he went into detail about the king's grant, and the opportunities for settlers who'd accompany him to Pernambuco: lands as far as the eye could see; riches from future harvests of sugar; honor in bringing Portuguese civilization and the faith to the tropics of Brazil.

"Think, Cavalcanti, of what a move to Pernambuco can mean to your family," Dom Duarte urged before he left. "What I'm offering is not a fort or a factory, where you must be confined for years, or a small field in Sintra. I'm offering paradise, Cavalcanti, waiting there for men who truly deserve it."

❧

Days passed in which Nicolau said little to his father or his family about Dom Duarte's visit. He wandered off alone through the woods, to the very edge of the land, where the blue-gray Atlantic rolled against the rocks.

He walked with the image of a nymph before him, her coppery body full but lithe as she danced. But he saw, too, the horror of battle in that secure haven, and he also looked beyond the flames of the squadron and into the forest, and there, too, he sensed a darkness. But the troubling images did not linger.

It was a week before he spoke to his family about Brazil, and by then his mind was made up. His wife, Helena, intuitively knew this, and whatever his plans might hold, she would not oppose them; she had married Nicolau the year after his return from India, and had always been aware of the restlessness that long campaign bred in him.

Helena was a quiet woman, who had lived with the older Cavalcantis since her marriage. She'd often hoped that Nicolau would seek a place of their own, but he never had, and she'd not complained. Her family came from nearby Collares and she sometimes visited them, but most often she never ventured farther than her father-in-law's courtyard.

It was thus remarkable that when her husband spoke of moving to another world entirely, she showed no alarm.

When Nicolau came to tell his father of his decision, his brothers were there too.

"Santa Cruz? What is there?" old Cavalcanti asked. "Wood you must ask the king to cut? Birds? Monkeys? Wild men?"

"Dom Duarte, senhor," Cavalcanti said respectfully, "believes there is sufficient to stake his fortune on."

"Then he's a wealthy fool."

"He goes not to trade but to found a colony."

"A settlement? Where have the Portuguese ever made a settlement? We're traders, merchants, shippers — this you should know better than most men."

"Madeira prospers," Nicolau said in a level voice.

The old man rapped his knuckles against the table. "Madeira, Azores — islands at the door of Lisbon. Brazil lies at the other side of the world. To fetch dyewood is one thing, certainly, but to move there — you'll live like savages and you'll be forgotten."

"Dom Duarte and the other donatários sail at the behest of the king."

"Will King João remember them when their sails are over the horizon?"

Nicolau ignored the question. "In Brazil, I saw how green and fertile the land is," he said. "Sugarcane, senhor, will make Pernambuco prosperous."

"So this is your decision, Nicolau. But what of the boys? Henriques and Pedro — what is there in such a wild place? What can they find with savages and monkeys as their tutors?"

Now Nicolau smiled. "Pedro, surely plenty," he said. The fourteen-year-old was a mischievous terror with no love for lessons. His brother, a year older, was quieter and reserved. "Henriques will find more than in these parts."

Hours passed as the men sat talking at the long table, with jars of wine from the vineyards of Helena's family. The boys stormed into the room and were told what they'd suspected since Pedro overheard the talk between Dom Duarte and his father earlier.

The sons of Nicolau's two brothers were with them. Felipe's oldest, Inácio, a soft-tempered and sickly child, was greatly excited by the news. "Oh, senhor," he addressed Nicolau, "you'll go to live among the heathen?"

Nicolau laughed kindly. "In their very lands," he said.

This son, the family knew, was born to be a priest: the pale Inácio lived in awe of the dark-robed men who guided him.

"But Padre Miguel tells us that they are an ugly and savage race, for whom there may be no salvation," the boy ventured.

Cavalcanti started. "Padre Miguel?"

"Yes, senhor, in Lisbon, where I take my lessons."

"Your padre, Inácio — he's been to Brazil?"

"Oh, yes, senhor, he's gone among the Tupiniquin and has preached to them, but he says they have hearts of stone."

"That he would," Nicolau said quietly: The Brazil Padre Miguel remembered was not the promised land to which Nicolau was to return.

ඏ

They came bursting into the small square, shrieking and yelling at the top of their voices, their chests smeared with red urucu dye, and heads crowned with feather diadems. Bare feet splattered the mud. Ahead were those they pursued, who cried that they were Normans. This failed to appease their adversaries, who loosed a barrage of missiles.

A group of warriors observed this battle with amusement, and began to laugh, as the children of the Portuguese pelted one another with manioc flour and rotten eggs.

Nicolau Cavalcanti was not surprised that the leader of the attack on the "Normans" should be his son Pedro. Almost a year had passed since their coming ashore in Brazil in March 1535, and Pedro had shown nothing but delight in his new home. Henriques remained reserved and thoughtful about his true feelings about the move.

Tomorrow was the start of Lent, and the little community was in a carnival mood. Colonists stood near the clearing or sat on benches at a prudent distance from their reveling youngsters. Less than one hundred souls had come to the captaincy of Pernambuco. Dom Duarte Coelho Pereira, ever ambitious, preferred to call his colony Nova Lusitania, after the name the Roman invaders gave to their conquest above the Tagus River.

Dom Duarte had done as his king commanded: Upon landing, he had erected a stone pillar fifty paces beyond an early Portuguese logwood camp on the south bank of a river he promptly named Santa Cruz. Opposite was a green island called Itamaracá; Dom Duarte had gazed at it enviously, but the marker placed it beyond his captaincy.

Near the pillar, a start had been made at a settlement also called Santa Cruz, but soon the settlers had moved inland to this more elevated position, and named it Villa do Cosmos, for the saint. Shortly, however, they were seduced by the cadences of the native word *Iguarassu* (Big River) and had begun to use it for both "stream" and "village."

The houses of the settlers stood within a sturdy mud-and-stone-wall stockade. Some of the dwellings, like those of Dom Duarte and Cavalcanti, were made of clay and stone; the rest, of palm fronds. At one end of the square was a long, squat, crumbling mud structure — their equivalent of the *câmara,* where Dom Duarte and his officials conducted their business. The building of which they were inordinately proud was their church, which had been recently built on the highest ground of the village.

Beyond the settlement were fields of manioc and sugar, nothing like the great sweep of canes envisaged in King João's charter, but at least a beginning. To be ready for the crop, Dom Duarte's brother-in-law, Jerónimo Albuquerque, was building the first cane press. He called it an *engenho,* a mill, and it was good for Dom Duarte to report to King João with such a grand term, but the engenho was really a very simple machine that could be worked by two men.

To comprehend the magnitude of the colonists' task was to see the labor expended to gain the crude blocks of dark, unrefined sugar. It was to stand alone at the edge of that green barrier and make the first cut in the first trunk, its upper branches lost in the tangle above; to hear the first crack and then the explosion as the tree broke away and fell; to hack with long-bladed knives at the first thicket and to kindle the first flame that would rise to a wall of fire sweeping all before it.

To comprehend the enormity of the task was to walk through the ruin of charred and blackened timbers smoking and hissing, glowing red within, and to breathe the scorched earth; to take such fields and, with hands grained by ash and scarred by splintered wood, to begin, inch by inch, turning over the red soil and laying cuttings of cane.

As the children fought the mock battle in the square, Nicolau and several colonists stood listening to Dom Duarte discuss the vicissitudes facing them, not only the problems involved in growing cane, but also difficulties with the natives.

Among the warriors invited to the carnival was the one-eyed chief Tabira, whose people, the Tobajara, lived in nearby villages. Tabira's missing eye was a reminder of this man's bravery: Leading a charge against an enemy stockade, Tabira had been struck in the eye by an arrow, and without slowing his pace, he had pulled out the shaft and gone back to the fight.

Tabira's people were similar to Aruanã's Tupiniquin, far to the south — with one exception: They had never practiced cannibalism. When Dom Duarte and his colonists landed, Tabira and his people, splendidly dressed in their body paints and feather adornments, greeted them joyfully. Dom Duarte was delighted, until he learned the reason for this welcome: Tabira desperately needed a Portuguese alliance against his old enemies, the Potiguara and the Caeté.

Of all the Tupi tribes, the Potiguara (Shrimp Eaters) were the most powerful, their big, settled villages extending over hundreds of miles north of the Portuguese settlement. Their chiefs had allied themselves with French loggers, who lived among them and knew the reason for the Potiguara's strength: Unlike other tribal leaders, the Potiguara chiefs permitted no dissension among the clans of their nation, thereby ensuring unity within them.

The third tribe in the area, the Caeté, enemies of both Tabira's people and the Potiguara, were a smaller but brutal and warlike band, who, as with the Tupiniquin at their malocas, raided to capture prisoners for ritual slaughter in their clearings. Recently these Caeté, who so rejoiced at the suffering of their victims, had themselves come up against a new and terrifying enemy: Portuguese slavers, who crept ashore at night, to villages south of Dom Duarte's settlement, and carried off entire malocas of men, women, and children.

"I'll hang those thieves if I catch them," Dom Duarte told the colonists standing with him. "They're worse than the Normans."

"They could have come from any one of the captaincies," his brother-in-law, Jerónimo, pointed out.

"Certainly. They wouldn't do this in their own colony," Dom Duarte said, "and risk setting their own Tupi against them. They come here, where we only want peace, and disturb our Caeté."

Dom Duarte's anger over slavers stealing his Caeté reflected his fear that the Caeté would be stirred up against the Pernambucan colonists. He did not oppose the enslavement of the savages. Tabira's warriors had recently herded twenty Potiguara to the settlement. In the past, the Tobajara had seen no value in taking Potiguara prisoners and had slaughtered them on the battlefield; they were now given a handful of trinkets for each healthy Potiguara delivered to the colonists.

As allies of the Portuguese, the Tobajara were spared slavery and encouraged to labor freely in the cane fields for payment of cloth and other rewards; but this arrangement was faring poorly, for now Dom João's brazilwood gatherers were competing with the colonists for Tobajara labor.

"When we arrived, the Tobajara did all we asked," Dom Duarte said. "They labored happily for a looking glass or worthless knife. Today?" He shook his head. "How does the king expect me to build an honest and orderly community when the men who come to cut his logs spoil the savages? They pay the Tobajara more than any colonist can match. Besides, the most stupid savage sees it's better to fell and haul timber for a short season than to work in our fields."

"With the guns and lances they get from the loggers, they're better able to fight the Potiguara and bring their captives to us," Cavalcanti remarked. He, too, saw no contradiction in enslaving the Potiguara while protesting the theft of the Caeté.

"True, Nicolau, but will they ever bring enough?"

"A man needs six slaves to live decently," Cavalcanti said. "One to fish for him, one to hunt for him, and the rest in his fields."

"Six?" Jerónimo interjected. "What will you accomplish with six? They sit around their huts like grandfathers and talk and drink, and send their women to the fields. No, senhor, not six — perhaps sixty and you may begin to make something of your lands!"

Dom Duarte turned again to Cavalcanti. "This man you wish to bring here — he would know how to handle our problem."

"Since Cabral's day, senhor, he's lived with these people. He knows them better than any man."

"But will he be willing to move?"

"I believe so," Cavalcanti said, "considering your irresistible offer."

Cavalcanti was sailing south on the next ship to Porto Seguro. He planned to fetch Affonso Ribeiro and his family and settle them at Pernambuco. That ugly business with the Franciscan friars — Ribeiro's confession of responsibility for their slaughter — no longer troubled Cavalcanti: More important now was the value a man of Ribeiro's experience could have in dealing with the Potiguara and the Caeté. Ribeiro was to be offered lands in the captaincy and Dom Duarte would write to the king and seek a full pardon for one who had stolen a goat so many years ago.

The carnival was a brave little affair, not without moments of nostalgia and melancholy: There would be something glimpsed in the turn of a dancer or heard in a voice that drew the observer away to a town or village in "old" Lusitania.

Though the colonists had moved once already, Dom Duarte had not been happy with this choice of Iguarassu as his main base. Hidden in the forest, it was a poor site for the capital of Nova Lusitania. A few weeks before, he had seen his "Lisbon": on the coast twenty-five miles to the south, there were seven hills, from any one of which he could look far inland, and which could be admirably defended seaward. Here, too, were rivers along which his planters could establish cane fields; opposite the coastline, a little farther south, was a long reef that formed a magnificent natural harbor.

There was at this time an old romance of chivalry and knighthood with its heroine, Olinda, a name meaning "beautiful." Dom Duarte found this a perfect description for those seven hills facing the sea: Olinda.

❧

Cavalcanti traveled to Porto Seguro and found Affonso Ribeiro willing to go to Pernambuco with his wives — including Aruanã's daughter, Salpina — and twenty children and relatives, a tribe in itself.

The Tupiniquin clan had moved its malocas to the north of the bay since Cavalcanti first came here with Gomes de Pina's squadron; when the master entered the new clearing, Ribeiro had recognized him immediately, and Jandaia, too, had come to meet him, standing back shyly as her father and Cavalcanti exchanged greetings.

Ribeiro saw Cavalcanti looking at his daughter. "All these years, Master, and you did not forget her?"

Cavalcanti said only: "Jandaia." She was as he'd remembered her, the smooth, copper-toned body, long black hair, that playful pout and slightly hesitant manner. She bent her head coyly when he mouthed her name.

Ribeiro told him that Jandaia had two children, a boy and a girl, by a warrior who had taken her after Cavalcanti's departure. This man had died in a Cariri raid.

The trip to fetch Ribeiro occupied two months. Dom Duarte granted the degredado a small landholding just beyond the stockade at Iguarassu, where Ribeiro erected a maloca of the kind his little tribe had known with the Tupiniquin. He laughed at the tight hovels the settlers built and told them that the airy palm structures were much more livable, but they rejected his "savage" tastes: They had come to build a civilization, not to lose it.

❧

Two months after the arrival of Affonso Ribeiro, Nicolau Cavalcanti made another journey in August 1536. With Ribeiro and three Potiguara slaves, he took his sons up a river that flowed near Olinda. Like Dom Duarte, who had moved to Olinda, Cavalcanti had concluded that Iguarassu and the lands about it were not the best choice for permanent settlement. Olinda was a far superior site, but the donatary and his family held absolute power over those seven hills: to give up his lands at Iguarassu and move close by would be like living just beyond the walls of a fort or factory. Thus, whenever he could, Cavalcanti made small probes into the forest, searching for he knew not precisely what but certain that he'd recognize it when he saw it.

Just before noon, the party came to a branch of the river. Cavalcanti, without the slightest hesitation, directed the two canoes along the smaller flow.

As they followed the stream, the forest became less dense, especially to one side, where the trees started up a range of hills. After an hour's travel, Cavalcanti called a halt and they pulled up on a narrow beach before a steep incline. They would stay here overnight, but before darkness, he wanted to stand on top of this hill.

The climb was difficult. In some places they had to pull themselves up by clinging to the roots of trees and vines that brushed the ground, but Cavalcanti moved with haste, keen to see what would be revealed from the summit. He was not disappointed.

The boys, Pedro and Henriques, were first to the top, and Pedro shouted excitedly, "Hurry, Father, hurry! All Brazil lies before us!"

Cavalcanti saw that the hill lay at one end of a long ridge curving to the northwest; the river they'd been following meandered lazily along the base of these heights. Far to the south was another series of hills, similar to this; about four leagues separated these two chains and between them lay the valley, as long as it was broad, the canopy of a lush and ancient forest undulating above low, gentle rises. Another river tumbled into the valley through a gorge in the heights to the south; the rivers met in a small lake. Near the lake, a line of smoke curled upward from a group of malocas.

His heart leapt with excitement as he envisioned fields of cane in the lowlands between the small rises and rolling up their sides — leagues of land to be cleared with fire and ax, season by season, for a valiant harvest!

Affonso Ribeiro had been last to reach the top of the hill, huffing and complaining as he dragged himself up. Like the Tupiniquin he'd lived with for so many years, Ribeiro did not take easily to unnecessary exertion. He leaned against the trunk of a fallen tree as Cavalcanti and his sons paced from one part of the heights to another seeking the best vantage points.

"Isn't it a glorious sight!" Cavalcanti exclaimed afterward.

"Good lands, senhor," Ribeiro agreed, "but far from Olinda."

"Far? A day by river?"

"Two, maybe three days if you pass through the forest. In Brazil, senhor, this can be far."

Cavalcanti knew what he meant. "But Tabira's clans are our friends," he said.

"Today, yes," Ribeiro said. "Tomorrow?" He shrugged his shoulders.

"I don't build to run back to Lisbon," Cavalcanti said. "If I take these lands, I take them for my sons, and *their* sons. This, Ribeiro, is what was promised me at Sintra."

Cavalcanti could think of nothing else on the passage back.

When they returned to Olinda, Dom Duarte listened to Nicolau's report but agreed with Affonso Ribeiro that it was dangerous to move so far from the main settlements.

"But Tabira's people stand between us and the Potiguara and Caeté," Cavalcanti argued.

"Settle your valley later, Nicolau," Dom Duarte counseled. "For now, stay with the others, along the rivers near Olinda. Here is fine land for everyone."

"I do not want a *roça* senhor," Cavalcanti said, referring to small grants used mostly for food crops. "I came for the same reason you did: to grow cane, and cane needs endless land."

"Certainly, Nicolau, and you'll have all you need, but if you strand yourself in the wilderness, will you survive to grow anything at all?"

Cavalcanti was persistent in the weeks that followed, and finally persuaded Dom Duarte to accept his petition for the valley and to record it in the colony's land register. Accordingly, Cavalcanti received, at no cost but the taxes that would become due to the king, an estate of some twelve square leagues, almost 75,000 acres — to a man from Portugal, a kingdom in itself. The deed stipulated that Cavalcanti must inhabit and cultivate his lands within eight years. Nearer Olinda, a shorter time limit was given, but Dom Duarte did not believe that Cavalcanti would soon move so far into the hinterland.

Cavalcanti continued to work his lands at Iguarassu, and quietly prepared for the conquest, as he thought of it, of his valley.

Many times he would describe the high ridges, the tumbling stream and crystal lake, and the broad, forested valley. And always Helena would listen attentively but without his enthusiasm: This untamed land remained as distant and fearsome as when she had first heard Nicolau tell of his wish to move here.

She spent her days in the stockaded village, in the clay-and-stone hut Nicolau had built, as rude a place as those inhabited by the peasants at her father's vineyards in Portugal. It contained one large room with a corner partitioned off for the adults. Their sons' hammocks were in the open section, which served the family as living quarters. With low, uneven rafters crawling with insects, and small holes for windows, it remained dark and depressing no matter how hard she worked at making it a home. When it rained, the clay floor loosened and became damp, until one side of the room was as muddy as the open ground.

Helena did not complain to Nicolau, but often she had to fight her tears when she sat with the other women. There was one thing, however, that did lift their spirits: the unflagging faith of Dona Brites, wife of Dom Duarte. She never failed to show concern toward the women who had joined her husband's colony.

One subject alone Helena would not discuss with Dona Brites or anyone else: her husband's relationship with the woman Jandaia.

Helena knew that Nicolau was making love to Ribeiro's daughter: When he came to their bed after he had been with Jandaia, it was with a passion Helena had not felt in him before. She was not jealous of the girl: He could make love with as many forest women as he desired, but he would never forsake his Portuguese wife, the mother of his heirs — of this Helena was as confident as were other women whose men did the same.

She wasn't jealous; still, it gave her pleasure to tell him on his return from the Iguarassu fields one evening, "We're to have a child."

He was overjoyed. Pedro, their youngest, was now sixteen; since his birth, there had been two other babies, but both had died. The infant who would come so late was a blessing in their new land, he told Helena, embracing her affectionately. Soon it would be no secret, he thought as he felt her against him, that not only his wife but also his wild mistress, Jandaia, was expecting his child.

A few days later, the settlement witnessed a furious activity at the Cavalcanti house.

It began when Nicolau paced out a square of ground adjoining his habitation. He then drove his Potiguara slaves to prepare the small patch for the floor of a room. Then he directed the raising of walls that would abut against the existing dwelling.

He explained the purpose of this new room to his wife thus: "It's wrong for you to work so hard," he said, quite genuinely. "With a child . . ."

Helena sat in her dark clothes, her small hands folded in her lap.

"The daughter of Ribeiro is a strong woman," he went on. "She'll be at your side, and will help you. This girl will refuse nothing you ask, my Dona Cavalcanti!"

Helena smiled, and taking it as a sign of her gratitude, Cavalcanti clapped his hands together.

"Good," he said. "I'll fetch her." And he hurried away, filled with the joy of having the two women in his life so close to him.

Not a single colonist objected to Cavalcanti's domestic arrangements. It was rare to find a Nova Lusitania man, married or single, who did not take at least one native mistress.

The priests did object weakly, and some of the colonists responded by presenting their concubines: "We lead them," they said, "not to temptation but to the faith." They were sincere in their affirmation. "Teach them, Father," they urged, "to be good Christians."

To fetch Jandaia, Cavalcanti had only to walk a short distance beyond the stockade to the clearing where Affonso Ribeiro had built his maloca.

Ribeiro had got his pardon from the king and been given lands near Iguarassu. For a time he'd had his sons work in the fields, but these were eventually abandoned: The Ribeiro clan now grew patches of manioc and other foods cultivated by their women and girls.

The day Cavalcanti came to fetch Jandaia, Ribeiro was sprawled as usual in the shade of a brazilwood tree. Around him were his sons, several men who worked with the loggers, and two degredados recently banished to Pernambuco.

These exiles, Rodrigues Bueno and Paulo da Costa, both from Coimbra, hadn't met until they boarded the ship transporting them to Brazil. Bueno was a large, scar-faced tough, who had been exiled for common theft. Da Costa was only twenty-two, a slight man with a pronounced stoop. He had come from a decent family but was a gambler, and to meet his losses, he had debased the king's coinage by rasping silver specie and accumulating the filings. Thrown together on the voyage out, the pair had become firm friends dedicated to profiting from their punishment.

Ribeiro knew about Cavalcanti's arrangement with his daughter and noisily welcomed it: He saw good prospects in having a tie with a man who dreamt of great valleys of cane.

"Oh, Master, what a fine house I've seen you build," he said with mock earnestness. "Nothing like this straw palace of mine."

Those on the ground laughed.

"Where is she?" Cavalcanti asked directly.

"Why, Master, are you always in such a hurry? You Portuguese," he said, as if he were not the same, "you seek a fast and rich conquest as you had in India. This is the land of Brazil. *Brazil*, Master, makes its own time." He swung away and grabbed a jar of liquor.

Cavalcanti remained silent.

"You want your valley, Master? In time you'll have it, with all the sugarcane you can grow!"

"If I ever find men to work it," Cavalcanti said.

Ribeiro looked at one of his sons, Mathias, reputedly the laziest creature at the settlement, his young face already showing the signs of excessive drinking. "Miserable dog!" he growled at the boy. "Will you work for Senhor Cavalcanti?"

The young man groaned loudly, and appeared to crawl deeper into the dirt.

"My Tupiniquin!" Ribeiro said, and laughed at him. "Same as the others, he won't work, because what need is there for work? You Portuguese know *nothing!*" he said, and now he grew serious. "These people would rather die than work in your fields. It's for women to turn the soil, not men. Men are warriors."

"It will change," Cavalcanti said, with quiet conviction.

"*Never.*"

"I'll work that valley, Ribeiro," Cavalcanti persisted, in the same level tone of voice. "If it takes ten of these to do the work of one honest man, then there'll be ten, and as many times ten as I need."

"It may have to be," Ribeiro said.

Strangely, it was Mathias who showed interest in Cavalcanti's remarks. Lazy as he was, Ribeiro's son was coming to the unhappy conclusion that to live with his father's people, he needed an income, and Bueno and da Costa had suggested a means of gaining one: They must go north along the coast to collect Potiguara slaves for men like Cavalcanti. It was dangerous and the reward was not great — a Potiguara now had the same value as a sheep from Portugal — but it was better than hauling logs or toiling in a field from dawn to dark.

Ribeiro's women came drifting in from the fields, Jandaia in front with the youngest of Ribeiro's wives, Salpina. These two began to speak animatedly when they saw Cavalcanti.

Cavalcanti had by now a good knowledge of Tupi, but not adequate enough to follow this rapid exchange.

"The children," Ribeiro explained. "This one" — he indicated Salpina — "seeks to know who will care for them."

Cavalcanti showed indifference: The warrior's boy and girl were not his concern.

Ribeiro spoke harshly to his wife, then turned to Cavalcanti. "They'll stay here, Master. What difference one or two at my maloca?"

☙

Season followed season, and for six years the fertile lands in Cavalcanti's valley lay untouched.

Cavalcanti had passed into his fifties and it required tremendous faith to keep alive the hopes he had for this valley, but whenever he doubted they'd be realized, he had only to look at his youngest child, Tomás, and his spirits would soar.

Tomás was now a vivacious, intelligent five-year-old, with his father's green eyes and dark complexion. He was much like his brothers at this age, yet there was something of untamed Brazil in him, something difficult to define, a sense of belonging to this land that set him apart. His brother Pedro had come to accept Brazil as his home, but Nicolau's older son, Henriques, had returned to Portugal with others who had no vision of wide and prosperous valleys. It was difficult to condemn their faint-heartedness: Iguarassu remained a small, depressing outpost with the same cluster of squalid buildings, a mill that crushed a still-profitless harvest of cane, and an ever-widening tract of graves in the woods.

The presence of Tomás had made Henriques's departure less painful for his parents — and, for Nicolau, there were also two sons Jandaia bore him. This wild, boisterous trio of little boys filled his house and noisily compensated for the disappointment he felt in a Nova Lusitania that was failing to live up to its glorious name.

Helena had always treated Jandaia with kindness, more like a zealous younger sister than a slave. Once the two had been able to converse, Helena led Jandaia to the church and instructed her husband's mistress in the manners of a good Christian. There was little dissension between them, and then only when Affonso Ribeiro was involved: Helena forbade him near her house.

Nicolau, too, had come to regret bringing Ribeiro's wild and unruly family to the colony. Most often when there was trouble, it started at Ribeiro's maloca.

Dom Duarte sent appeal after appeal to the king, begging him to stop shipping criminals to Pernambuco. "If God and nature cannot reform these men, how can I, my lord?"

But the degredados kept coming. The big Bueno and stooped da Costa who'd consorted with Mathias Ribeiro were typical specimens, and what they finally did threatened to bring all Dom Duarte's efforts to ruin.

Mathias and the two criminals attacked Potiguara villages and brought back scores of men and boys. Dom Duarte approved, because they were campaigning beyond the settlement. A recent raid had gone badly. The rigors of their march had been terrible, and they had been fortunate to escape with their own lives. But soon they were headed out on another expedition, and returned after only three weeks with more captives than ever before.

That next morning, the settlers in both towns awoke to find that all Tabira's people had gone, except for a few drunks and the women who had taken up with the Portuguese. Not one who wandered freely in and out of the towns or worked at the fields appeared that day.

Only at the end of a week was contact made with a local chief, through his daughter, Green Bow, whom Dom Duarte's brother-in-law had taken as wife. She was sent to her father's village and returned with a report for Dom Duarte:

"They ask why you enslave their people."

"It's a lie!" the donatário said. "We've never troubled the villages of our friends."

"Then, why do people from the malocas of Tabira's uncle sit in the pens at Iguarassu?"

Dom Duarte acted swiftly, knowing what the enmity of Tabira's people could mean to his settlements. Behind the colony lay a wall of hostile Potiguara and Caeté; if the alliance with Tabira was broken, the Portuguese could be swept into the sea.

Dom Duarte ordered the arrest of Mathias Ribeiro, Bueno, and da Costa, released their captives, and invited the local chiefs to witness his justice.

The inquiry was rapid but proper, with evidence being given by some of the former prisoners. The sentence of Dom Duarte and his magistrates was without appeal: "Hang them!"

When it was Mathias's turn for the hanging hook, he had to be dragged across the clearing. Crying for mercy, he ignored the priests who begged that he claim this last chance for forgiveness, though he did try to cling to their robes at the foot of the gibbet.

Tabira's people had been set free, but the time they spent in the pens with the Potiguara taught them that what they had feared for years was true: Slavery could afflict their own just as it had taken their enemies.

Dom Duarte had hoped that his swift justice would reassure Tabira's people about his honest intentions, but in fact it accomplished the opposite, and those who had worked for the Portuguese drifted away.

"I didn't come to found a colony of poor peasants," Dom Duarte told his leading settlers. "We try, God alone knows . . . we try to work with these people to make something of this place. How hopeless it is! Give them an ax or a knife or a piece of cloth and they stop laboring. They care nothing for possessions."

"Slaves," a colonist said. "Only as such do they learn the value of honest work."

"These natives will never do the work we expect of them," said Cavalcanti. Today he had fifteen slaves but had become convinced that what Affonso Ribeiro once said was correct: Take the savages away from their trees and they wilted like weak plants.

"We must persist with them," he added, "but surely we must also look elsewhere."

"Must my sons work the soil?" a planter asked.

"No. Nor will mine," Cavalcanti said.

"Then, who?"

"The slaves of Africa."

There were negative murmurs from the group. Bringing blacks to Brazil had been discussed many times but dismissed as too costly. A Potiguara could still be had for the value of a sheep; a black slave might demand a small flock, so expensive would it be to transport him across the Atlantic.

But Cavalcanti raised arguments in favor of importing the blacks: "One will be worth ten Potiguara," he said. "Remember the fields of Portugal and Madeira — of any place where slaves toil. . . . I've traveled in the kingdom of the ManiKongo. I've seen an infinite supply of peças, and men who know how to prepare them for the journey."

Cavalcanti won his argument and Dom Duarte wrote to King João asking for slaves, and a little over two years later, in February 1545, a caravel from Mpinda, at the mouth of the river Zaire, rode in to shelter behind the long reef opposite Olinda.

Cavalcanti stood in front of the group of planters on the shore anxiously watching the ship's boat draw in to the beach. Suddenly the young man in the prow called out to him:

"Cavalcanti! Oh, Master Cavalcanti!"

The man leapt from the boat and splashed through the surf toward Cavalcanti.

"Brito!" Cavalcanti cried. "Brito Correia!"

"The same!" came the response, and the little hero from the *São Gabriel* stood smartly before his former commander, broader in the chest, perhaps a foot taller, but unmistakably the same Brito Correia who'd hurled himself at Le Tigre with a knife.

For a moment they hesitated, and then embraced, the rank that had once separated them now forgotten.

Lourenço Velloso was dead and the orphan from Santarém had inherited all he'd owned, which was substantial. Brito had prospered: the sixty slaves in the ship, the king's fifth already paid, were his property.

Cavalcanti bought six: Three were grown men and three older boys. The most imposing, tall and muscular, bore a Christian name: Sebastião. Correia suggested that he should be head slave.

Cavalcanti addressed his slave, but the man made no response.

"Sebastião! Sebastião!" Brito chided him. "Where is your Portuguese — your lovely Portuguese?"

Still the man refused to speak, and was led off by Pedro Cavalcanti.

"They fear nothing but the whip," Correia advised.

But Cavalcanti wasn't listening. There was joy in his heart at the sight of that file of slaves moving along the beach. Now God in His mercy would allow him to move to the valley.

☙

On March 12, 1546, a year after the arrival of the slaves, Nicolau Cavalcanti gave thanks for that blessing. He knelt in a stockade they had built upon the rise overlooking the small lake, with twenty-four souls around him as he prayed. Eight he considered his immediate family: Helena and Tomás, and Pedro, now married to Maria, a settler's daughter, and their son; Jandaia, too, with Nicolau's two bastards.

Sebastião and the five other Bakongo knelt near the ten native slaves, half of whom were Potiguara. The two groups had little friendship for each other; it had been inevitable that the Bakongo would become overseers of the Potiguara, whom they found primitive and simple, with no heart for plantation work.

Engenho Santo Tomás, Cavalcanti called his lands. Fields had been planted with cane behind the rise with the stockade. The mill was being built alongside the stream that tumbled through the gorge.

The malocas Cavalcanti had seen the day he discovered this valley were at the far end of the rise. Cavalcanti had handled the natives kindly, arriving with many gifts and promising more if they helped him work these lands that were now his. As happened in most first contacts between the Portuguese and the people of Brazil, there was delight and happiness in the malocas; the natives were honored to have these strangers near their clearing. They saw the Potiguara driven to the fields by the black men, and they laughed at them.

The move had placed the Cavalcantis at the farthest limit of settlement. Dom Duarte still considered it too dangerous, but he did not object strongly, for he was pleased to see his colony expanding. If Cavalcanti gained a hold on his valley, others would be encouraged to settle the open leagues between Engenho Santo Tomás and Olinda.

But this day, even as the Cavalcantis gave thanks to God, as Nicolau's hope soared with his first year's accomplishments, humble as they were, another force was building — a force that would bring anguish and sorrow to the colony.

At Iguarassu, under the brazilwood tree where he held court, Affonso Ribeiro was giving a speech:

"Oh, senhores, I ask you, what need is there for work in paradise? Why this great labor when the land can provide a free bounty?"

The "senhores" — as dissolute a group of layabouts and criminals as Dom Duarte had ever railed against — shouted encouragement. Ribeiro's children and grandchildren ran among them, a mob of half-castes of all ages, who took care to stay beyond their father's reach.

There were others, too, who heard him, though they understood little of what he said. These men from nearby malocas found it good to visit with Ticuanga of the Tupiniquin. Here were no priests to give them ugly glances, no planters beseeching them to work their fields, but men like themselves, who loved to talk and sing and dance, away from the hot sun.

"Ah, the good Dom Duarte . . . " Ribeiro said. "Dom Duarte who labors hardest for this land." Bitterness came into his voice. "Dom Duarte, who hangs the sons of others to save himself . . .

"Dom Duarte loves to tell the king that he is the shepherd of his colony. Others claimed the same long before Dom Duarte: shepherds, they called themselves, come to lead this people to heaven. They told the people the great canoes were taking them to the lands of their ancestors. This I saw with my own eyes: how the naked savages wept with joy to be carried off into slavery.

"I tell you, senhores, from one end of this land to the other, the people know that the Portuguese will enslave them. I know this, senhores, for I, Ticuanga of the Tupiniquin, am a warrior with my people!" He swayed, unsteady with the effect of the wine, and moved toward the natives. "I stand here — a warrior among these, too!"

Suddenly Ribeiro broke away and stumbled toward his maloca. When he returned he held a rattle, and shook it as he swayed before the warriors, his big feet pounding the earth.

"Dance, Muraci! Dance, Piragybe!" he called out.

These two came forward, and they chanted and danced with Affonso Ribeiro.

The drinking session had started early, and went on into the night, the riffraff of the settlement and their native friends carousing until little liquor remained. One jar was jealously guarded by a degredado named Martim Pinto, who was sitting on the ground when a young warrior made a dive for the liquor.

"Thief!" Pinto yelled. "Son of a bitch!" He grabbed the warrior's ankle and threw him to the ground.

Warriors who saw the incident rushed to their comrade, and the clearing filled with the shouts of angry men.

A dagger in his hand, Pinto leapt at the young native. There were screams, and then sudden silence among all involved in the melee. The fighting stopped as abruptly as it had begun.

Affonso Ribeiro, who'd taken no part in the fight, came out of the darkness.

"Aieee! Pinto! You've killed the son of a chief!"

❧

Three days later, in the clearing at the malocas of the chief whose son had been slain, the father swore to avenge the young man's death. He had ordered that the victim's head be severed and his skull peeled.

"This is my son," he lamented, holding up the bare skull to his people. "Let any who deny that evil has come behold these silent lips and sightless eyes."

He passed the skull to six warriors, and ordered them to travel through the forest with a message:

"We welcomed the Portuguese as brothers. We sang and danced and rejoiced when our women went to lie with them. We laughed at the few among us who saw no good in this. We laughed at the enemy we drove to the fields of the Long Hairs. Here is the son of our chief — we ask you where is his laughter?"

From maloca to maloca they sped, often addressing clans for whom they'd once known only enmity. Word reached the Potiguara in the north, where the elders spoke with the French loggers who lived at their malocas. The Normans reminded their hosts of the fate of Le Tigre and twenty other corsairs captured by the Portuguese at Pernambuco in 1533: nine men had been hanged; the rest were buried up to their shoulders on a beach and used as targets for arquebus practice.

"If such be their cruelty toward Christians," the Normans told the elders, "how will it go with the Potiguara?"

The Potiguaras' answer was to march to destroy the settlement at Itamaracá, opposite Iguarassu.

When the skull finally reached the Caeté, ancient foes of the Tupi tribes around Olinda and Iguarassu, old differences were set aside. Their warriors took up their clubs and bows and marched north. The route for one group, forty strong, lay through the valley of Engenho Santo Tomás.

❧

Toward late afternoon on March 27, 1546, Nicolau Cavalcanti noticed smoke above the trees in the direction of the mill, where Pedro was working with the Bakongo, Sebastião, and three native slaves.

The engenho, distant as it was from Olinda and Iguarassu, knew nothing of the killing at Ribeiro's drinking party.

When the dark plume of smoke grew thicker, and the time for Pedro's return came and passed, a fear seized Cavalcanti.

Five Bakongo and seven natives had already returned to the stockade from the cane fields. Cavalcanti posted most along the timbered redoubt. He warned Helena and the other women to be alert. Then he took two Bakongo and set out down toward the mill.

When he walked into the small clearing, Nicolau Cavalcanti was filled with a horror he'd never known before.

"*Meu filho, meu filho!* O Mother of Mercy, my son!" he cried.

Pedro and three native slaves had been caught in the open, Pedro with his sword and two others with axes, their only means of self-defense. Pedro's body was punctured in a dozen places by arrows, his loins blood-splattered where knives had hacked at his private parts.

Cavalcanti gave a low, animal sound and slowly rocked from side to side. Without taking his eyes off his son's body, he backed off a few paces.

The Bakongo, Sebastião, had been at the water digging away at the riverbank. He'd seen the Caeté rushing out of the trees and had fled to the opposite side of the stream. He now emerged from his hiding place and crossed the river. He babbled a report, but Cavalcanti looked at him blindly.

Cavalcanti was trembling as he glanced toward the trees looking for those who had committed this atrocity, but there were none. With a cracking noise and a crash, a rafter in the burning mill broke and fell into the heart of the fire.

Cavalcanti began to gather the bits of rag that remained of Pedro's garments. He now recognized the slave Sebastião, but when Sebastião sought to carry Pedro's body, Cavalcanti shook his head. The two Bakongo who had accompanied Cavalcanti stood glancing nervously toward the trees.

Gently Nicolau lifted his son and moved off into the forest, the three Bakongo just a few paces ahead of him, beating a path through the jungle with their hands. At last they came to the edge of the clearing on the low rise.

The stockade was quiet, its entrance sealed with timbers and thornbush. When Nicolau could pass through, Helena came forward, her hands held up to her face, her mouth soundlessly forming words. Then, suddenly, a piteous cry, and she fell to her knees at Nicolau's feet. "Pedro! O sweet Jesus, my Pedro!" she sobbed, looking up at the mutilated body.

Nicolau wanted to move off, but Helena clung to his legs, until he made a furious movement to free himself. "For God's sake, mother," he said firmly, "the savages who did this may be upon us at any time." Forcefully he pushed her back, and walked to Pedro's hut. Inside, he placed his son's body on the ground and covered it. When he stepped outside, Maria was waiting there with Helena.

"Oh, Nicolau," his wife said weakly, "senhor—"

He put an arm around her thin shoulders and embraced her fiercely. "Little mother, the savages will pay for this sorrow. He tried to still her trembling. "Pray for our son," he said, and when he felt her stiffen, he released her and left.

Sebastião came running toward him with important news: One of the Potiguara slaves had tried to flee the stockade but had been captured.

"Where is he?" Cavalcanti demanded.

Sebastião indicated a direction with a motion of his head.

Cavalcanti hastened over to the Potiguara, a young man of fine physique whom Cavalcanti had bought at Olinda just three months ago. He was sitting with his head bowed toward the ground, his arms tied behind him and fixed to a post. At Cavalcanti's approach, he looked up in terror.

Cavalcanti said nothing but drew his sword and clasped it with both hands. The Potiguara made a frantic attempt to scramble away, jerking his bonds so wildly that the stake was loosened and pulled askew.

Cavalcanti swung his blade and decapitated the man.

The six remaining native slaves, four of whom were from Potiguara malocas, witnessed the execution.

Cavalcanti ordered a Potiguara who had been his slave for four years to step forward. The native had been given the name José.

"Are there others who want to run to the savages?"

"No, senhor!" José was staring at the corpse. "We do not want to run away." A priest at Olinda had baptized José. "We are Christians. This one was a savage."

"Put the head on the stockade," Cavalcanti ordered José. "Let the beasts in the forest see what awaits them."

"Yes, senhor!" And José, reciting one of the few Christian appeals he knew, added, "Jesus Christ be praised!"

With Cavalcanti in the stockade were his six Bakongo and six native slaves; four men from the malocas at the opposite end of the hill; Helena, Maria, and Jandaia, and Tomás and the other children.

Cavalcanti summoned one of the natives from the neighboring malocas and asked him to find out if his people would come to the defense of the stockade. The man declared that it was useless to risk crossing through the forest for nothing. His people would know what had happened at the mill and would have fled deep into the trees.

Cavalcanti accepted this as true. He made a thorough check of their meager defenses and had Sebastião, who'd been trained in the use of the falconet, load and fire the guns several times into the forest. Cavalcanti searched the encircling line of trees but detected nothing that suggested the savages were out there.

Guards were posted that night and through the next day, but no attack came. Cavalcanti did not relax his vigilance, but their water supply needed replenishing, and on the second morning, he sent one of the Bakongo and a Potiguara to the stream. Within minutes the black slave came dashing back to the stockade: The savages were nearby in the forest and had slain the other man; the Bakongo escaped only because he'd been trailing behind.

Cavalcanti had been hoping for a sign that it was safe to venture beyond the valley to fetch a priest for Pedro's burial, but the slaying of the man sent for water showed that the savages were lying in wait. During the funeral, Cavalcanti stood with Helena and Maria, a widow at eighteen. With every clod of earth thrown over Pedro's crude coffin, Nicolau's anger rose. He concentrated his gaze not on the burial site but on Tomás, who bore a look of understanding far beyond his nine years. Cavalcanti had lost two sons — one who had left Brazil, and one who would remain in its earth forever. *He would not lose this one!*

A week after the funeral, a group of natives broke out of the cover of the trees from the direction of the malocas and came streaming toward the stockade.

Cavalcanti made ready to fire one of the falconets, but then he recognized some of the natives who dwelt at Engenho Santo Tomás's malocas.

There were nine men, with a group of women and children. They reported that many from the malocas were hiding in the forest, but the same group who'd raided the mill had slaughtered others. They identified the enemy as Caeté, more ferocious than the Potiguara.

Cavalcanti realized that these newcomers would rapidly exhaust the food and water in the stockade, but he welcomed them anyway, for they almost doubled his small force.

He slept early that night, leaving Helena and Jandaia on guard at one falconet, Sebastião and another Bakongo at the other. He'd gone to rest long before midnight so that he'd be awake in the predawn hours, when the danger of assault by the Caeté was strongest.

The Caeté had sent spies to watch the stockade day and night. This dark evening, they decided to attack. Two advance groups, each with eight warriors, crept to the edge of the trees opposite the falconet positions.

The two women heard a noise behind the stockade and their hands tightened around their pikes. Helena wondered whether she should rouse her husband, but then she saw the figure of Sebastião and the other Bakongo standing calmly at the other gun.

Moments later the first group of Caeté moved swiftly and silently until they reached the stockade. Two made it to the top of the barricade, where Helena and Jandaia were posted, but when they tried to climb onto the platform, the women drove their pikes at them, Helena striking with such force that she plunged the sharp blade through one warrior's chest. Immediately she grabbed a firebrand and touched off the falconet, spewing a hail of small shot across the clearing in front of the stockade.

Sebastião fired, too, and now Cavalcanti himself was awake and running toward the women and helped Helena complete the reloading of the falconet. He saw that at points all along the stockade his men were shooting arrows into the dark; four Bakongo slaves fired the wheellocks, yelling the war cries of their people as the muskets roared. The instant the falconet was ready, Cavalcanti touched off another shot.

But Helena's first burst, and that of Sebastião, had been enough to send the attackers streaking back for cover, all except three, who scaled the stockade at a weakly defended place. Cavalcanti caught sight of them dashing across the clearing toward the buildings. He leapt off the platform, ten feet above the ground, hit the dirt with a thud that briefly winded him, then immediately started racing toward the warriors, screaming an alert to the others.

One of the Caeté stopped and hurled a club in Cavalcanti's direction, but it went hissing past his head. Cavalcanti slashed out with his sword, lacerating the man's chest and sending him reeling to the ground.

He caught the second one near the entrance to the hut with the children. This Caeté shouted at him mockingly and kept him at bay with his club, dancing from one spot to another. Cavalcanti lunged at him with his sword, but the warrior swung his club and landed a terrific blow on Cavalcanti's shoulder. Cavalcanti staggered back, struggled to regain his balance, and then attacked again, ignoring the pain in his shoulders and arm. He slashed the Caeté's wrist, and the man lost his grip on the club. But then a child screamed from within the hut.

A chilling fear seized Cavalcanti. His momentary hesitation gave the Caeté an opening to leap away from him and start racing across the stockade, but Cavalcanti's concern now was elsewhere. He burst into the dark hut. "Tomás!" he screamed. "Tomás!"

But his son was safe. The Potiguara slave José stood with a hatchet in his hand above a Caeté, who lay dying. Cavalcanti dropped his weapon and reached for Tomás, sweeping him off the ground with such violence that the child gave a cry of alarm. Cavalcanti clutched him to his chest. "Mother of Mercy be thanked," he said.

There were no further assaults that night. Toward dawn, Cavalcanti, back at the falconet platform, heard shots in the distance. He dared not leave the stockade to locate the source of the firing, but it was not long before a strong body of Portuguese came marching out of the forest, led by none other than Affonso Ribeiro himself.

Cavalcanti's joy at seeing the old degredado and his companions was unrestrained. He leapt up and down on the platform like a wild man, waving wildly, shouting his relief at the top of his voice. Then he tore down to meet them, working frantically alongside his slaves to remove the timbers and branches that blocked the entrance to the stockade.

"Ribeiro! Old comrade!" he cried joyously. "We weren't forgotten!"

"Dom Duarte feared for the safety of Engenho Santo Tomás. I, Affonso Ribeiro, volunteered to lead these men to the valley."

"God's thanks for that!"

Cavalcanti learned from his countrymen that what had happened at Engenho Santo Tomás was no isolated incident: Throughout the colony, the natives had risen against the Portuguese, even clans allied with the Tobajara. Settlers at other outlying holdings had been murdered, and both Iguarassu and Olinda besieged. Marinheiros had been able to land from a ship opposite Olinda and aid the defenders of the capital, but Iguarassu remained under siege.

Cavalcanti led his people out of the stockade within the hour, heading through the forested valley toward the tributary of the main river that led to Olinda. They moved below the ridge, from where Cavalcanti had first gazed upon this lovely valley. When he glanced back, he saw smoke enveloping his stockade. "We'll return, Tomás," he promised. "These lands, my son, everything you see from this ridge to those far hills, are Cavalcanti lands — *forever!* Your brother Pedro made it so."

BOOK TWO

The Jesuit

VII

March – July 1550

*T*here were no witnesses, this damp March morning in 1550, to the divine passion of Padre Inácio Cavalcanti. Those who could have observed the priest bent upon his knees — the men guiding him to Engenho Santo Tomás — were still asleep. This was not the first time Padre Inácio had been in the forest, but he was with strangers, far from those who had shared his first year in Brazil. He experienced a lone communion with this great wilderness such as he had not known before.

His spirit soared with the promise he beheld in everything around him. With fervent whispers, he recited the Paternoster, the Avé, the Credo.

Between prayers, his eyes moved slowly along the trunk of a monumental mahogany tree, up to where it branched out beneath the forest canopy, then returned to the mosaic of plants near him, and he reached toward a broad leaf, moving his long, slender fingers across its dewy surface. He watched a hump-backed beetle laboring up an exposed root of a jacaranda, before he was distracted by a pattern of small yellow butterflies dancing between the leaves of a spiky plant. He had a tremendous desire to rise and walk deep into the forest, to stride fearlessly between the trees and be at one with the fowl and beast and all things in this riotous garden of the Lord.

He closed his eyes, and envisioned himself passing into an enchanted glade. Here, shafts of brilliant light burst through the roof of the forest to lay a golden path for a host of His faithful martyrs. He saw himself crossing a dark barrier into that glade, a choir of angels offering triumphant welcome from the green boughs above.

There were tears on his cheeks. "O sweet saints," he begged, "open these eyes, this heart, this soul in this rich vineyard. Let this miserable body suffer every agony our Savior knew with those five terrible wounds."

Inácio Cavalcanti was now a man of thirty. He was tall, with a spare, bony frame and small, rounded shoulders. His features were delicate, a thin, pale face with soft, searching blue eyes beneath short, curly dark hair. Unlike most of his contemporaries, he was beardless. What he lacked in robustness, he made up for in spirituality and enthusiasm.

It was fifteen years since he had stood before his uncle Nicolau, telling him about his teacher Padre Miguel. Through all that time Inácio had continued to meet the expectations of his family, who accepted that the delicate, studious child in their midst was filled with awe and love for the Almighty.

Padre Miguel had inspired the youthful Inácio with his tales of savage souls in perdition, but it was not to him that Inácio owed his summons to Terra de Santa Cruz.

For Inácio, the journey had begun with his introduction to a man whom he'd come to regard with no less veneration than he accorded the saints.

In June 1540 Padre Francis Xavier had arrived in Lisbon with a fellow priest, Simon Rodrigues de Azevedo. They were both members of a new order marshaled to do battle for Christ and His Church: the Company of Jesus, as yet a small body of men formed by a warrior/apostle named Ignatius Loyola. Loyola, wounded in battle against the French at the little town of Najera, had laid down his sword to engage in the greater struggle for men's souls.

Francis Xavier and Rodrigues had been designated as missioners to the Indies. In Lisbon, they had learned that they would have to wait eight months for the next fleet sailing to Goa. Rodrigues, once a page to a cardinal at Lisbon's court, was well received by Dom João III. The king, entering middle age, was becoming increasingly concerned with the special duty demanded of a Most Catholic Majesty — the saving of his subject's souls. He was distressed when the two Jesuits informed him that his opulent and worldly Lisbon was as wicked and profane a locality as any they expected to encounter in some heathen land. While they waited for a ship, they announced, they would devote themselves to purging the capital.

At that time, Inácio had gone as far as he could in his religious studies in Lisbon and was planning to enter Sainte-Barbe in Paris, the same college Loyola, Xavier, and the other founders of the Company of Jesus had attended. But, before he'd set out on this course, he found himself in Lisbon's great Rossio Square, listening to Francis Xavier and Rodrigues.

The two priests stood at the top of the plaza, before the austere building that housed the Inquisition, reviling the vices and venality of Lisbon's citizens.

Francis Xavier's exhortations about the need for renewal, for simplicity and goodwill, touched Inácio Cavalcanti and hundreds more and sent them shuffling through the hot, narrow streets of Lisbon begging others to join their penitent processions.

Inácio had been at the forefront of a great throng, praying and singing aloud as they moved across Rossio. Days of self-inflicted punishment and fasting had left him weak and fatigued, and he stumbled and fell, striking his head on the stony ground. When he opened his eyes, he saw Francis Xavier on his knees next to him.

"Such sweet agony brings us closer to His side," the Jesuit had said. "But, brother in Christ, save your strength — for the great battles ahead!"

Here now in the forest, as he knelt and offered himself once more to Christ, Inácio felt again the power of Xavier's rallying cry: *the great battles ahead!* How eager he was to raise the sword of faith in the conflict between God and the devil. How he longed to embrace these savage souls with Christ's love and salvation!

A year had passed since his landing in Terra de Santa Cruz, and thus far the harvest was small. But he was patient: The great time of reaping lay ahead, when these erring children, so long denied their Father, would be led from the darkness they had endured since Creation.

In Lisbon, Inácio had never strayed far from Xavier's side. When the time came for Xavier's departure — Simon Rodrigues, sickly and hesitant, was urged by João III to remain in Lisbon — Inácio had wept openly. "Follow Simon," Xavier had consoled him. "Obey his instructions and the Lord will surely indicate His will for you."

Inácio had entered the old monastery of São Antonio, given to Rodrigues by João III for the first Jesuit house in Portugal. Perceiving the young man's grace and devotion, Rodrigues had ordered him to Coimbra University — which João III had also donated to the Jesuits — to commence the studies he would have followed at Paris. "Arm yourself, Inácio," Rodrigues had said, "to win the minds and hearts of others."

Shortly before his departure for Coimbra, Inácio had visited Padre Miguel, who lay dying with consumption in a wretched airless hovel in the hilly Alfama, Lisbon's oldest district. He had spoken of his enthusiasm for the mission of Francis Xavier and the new Company of Jesus and, above all, of his intense yearning for that brightest of all crowns: martyrdom in His service.

And Padre Miguel had shuddered when he heard this. "Inácio! Inácio!" he cried. "May you be saved my failures!"

"Failures?"

"Twice I was called to labor in His wild vineyards," Padre Miguel said, "and twice I denied Him." He stirred beneath the fetid, vermin-infested rags. "Once in Santa Cruz and once in Africa."

Padre Miguel had died a month after Inácio's visit. Inácio had already left for Coimbra, where he was to share a small dormitory with nine others, all seeking the Jesuit bonds of poverty, chastity, and obedience.

One day soon after his arrival, Inácio had been alone in the dormitory, his back to the door, when he heard someone enter. He turned to see a young man, of medium height but slender like himself, standing in the doorway.

"M-Manoel da Nó-Nóbrega," the newcomer volunteered, flinching with the effort it took to utter the words.

Inácio introduced himself and indicated a vacant cot. Nóbrega nodded his thanks but said no more as he placed a small bundle of belongings on the bed. Then, ignoring Inácio, he fell to his knees and began to pray.

"The Stammerer," others called this son of a chief magistrate; but Inácio found that, miraculously, when Nóbrega was in full communion with the Lord, his impediment disappeared.

That first night, while others in the dormitory were asleep, Nóbrega had gone across to Inácio. "Why do we rest?" he'd asked, "when there is a world of sinners beyond?"

And the two of them had crept out of the college into the streets of Coimbra. It was past 2:00 A.M. and the city slept soundly, but this did not deter Nóbrega from furiously ringing the bell he carried with him, nor the two young men from yelling at the top of their voices, "Hell awaits those in mortal sin!"

Through the next four years, during which they were both admitted to the Company of Jesus and became priests, Inácio and Nóbrega had labored unceasingly, roaming the countryside for months, fighting for people possessed by spirits, seeking out fallen women, begging those at the gallows to confess.

Late in 1548 Simon Rodrigues, who had become head of the Jesuit province of Portugal, summoned them to Lisbon. Inácio was elated: Never, during the seven years since Francis Xavier's departure, had he lost hope of joining the mission in the East. News about Xavier had come irregularly in letters to Lisbon and Rome. Goa, Ceylon, Cochin, Malacca — one after the other, those "Infidel" shores had been touched by this warrior of God.

From Rodrigues, now a powerful figure at court, Inácio learned that Xavier was planning to enter the kingdom of Cipangu to raise His holy banner among the warlords of the Rising Sun. But Inácio wouldn't be joining that mission, as he'd hoped. "You are not needed in the East, Inácio," Rodrigues said. "Instead, you will go with Father Nóbrega and four others to convert the pagans in our king's province of Santa Cruz."

With the exception of Pernambuco and São Vicente, João III's captaincies had failed; the French were again threatening Portugal's possessions and, worse, those planning the new incursions were Protestants. Dom João was sending Tomé de Sousa with one thousand settlers and soldiers, four hundred degredados included, to re-plant his colony of Brazil. Sousa would be the colony's first governor general.

Inácio, Nóbrega, and the four other Jesuits had sailed in February 1549 with Sousa's fleet. After a voyage of two months, they'd landed at Bahia de Todos os Santos, the Bay of All Saints, four hundred miles south of Pernambuco. Sousa had immediately set about building a town, which he named São Salvador. Within this past year, Nóbrega and his fellow Jesuits had completed a dormitory and chapel and begun work among the docile Tupinambá, who lived just beyond the walls rising around the new town. Already the brightest little savages were taking lessons in reading and writing alongside the colonists' children. Nóbrega had started to look further afield: He knew of Inácio's uncle in Pernambuco and ordered Inácio to travel there. "Report to us, Father Inácio, on the souls that wait to be saved in Nova Lusitania," were his parting words.

Inácio had landed at Olinda and immediately set out for Engenho Santo Tomás.

"Lord," he now prayed, just before rising from his knees in the forest, "we have come to bring the yoke of faith to these people. May they wear it joyously!"

Then he stood up and walked over to where his guides, two half-breeds and two Tobajara, lay dozing.

"Awake! Awake, my sons!" he cried happily. "Let us be on our way!"

"There's no hurry, Padre," one of the half-breeds said. "We're in the Cavalcantis' valley."

"My son, we *must* hurry. There is so little time."

The half-breed, offspring of a Portuguese logger and a Potiguara woman, proceeded to stretch.

"Do you know our Lord?" Inácio suddenly asked.

"Yes, Padre."

Inácio looked from this guide to the others. The two Tobajara were not unlike the Tupinambá he'd encountered at São Salvador: smallish, bronze-skinned men, with broad, hairless faces, dark eyes, and flattened noses. These guides did not paint their bodies with dye in the accepted fashion, and had become accustomed to concealing their nakedness with breeches, which they wore uncomfortably.

What fascinated Inácio about these and other savages was the way they wore their hair.

That narrow band from temple to temple, with the crown so clean-shaven: Could this be the tonsure, that sign of monkish dedication? And if so, how had these simple heathen come to learn about this symbol of His crown of thorns?

The fathers had considered the journeys of all the Apostles and concluded that if one of them had come here, it must have been St. Thomas. He had reached India, where he had ended his life. Was it not possible that his roving mission had led him first to these shores?

The guide who said he knew the Lord stood up and stepped close to Inácio. Smiling, he said, "Oh, yes, Padre, we know the Lord, and we know His padres at Olinda." He laughed, then added: "Almost as well as our mothers and sisters know them."

"God be praised!" Inácio said.

ↄ

"Oh, no, Padre, *this* is as far as we go," the guide said. As if to underline the words, he moved to a toppled tree trunk and sat upon it. "There is Senhor Cavalcanti's engenho," he said, gesturing in its direction with his head. "You can reach it without us."

They were at the bottom of the long, low hill upon which Nicolau Cavalcanti had built his first stockade, within sight of the stout timbers of a newer defense raised to replace the one destroyed by the Caeté, who had burned Engenho Santo Tomás four years before.

Sickly gray patches scarred the terrain. Clusters of poor plants burst from the ash-covered earth. Isolated palms with untidy crowns appeared to have resisted the devastation and clung dismally to the slope.

"But surely there can be no harm in coming up with me to Senhor Cavalcanti's door?" Inácio asked.

"The senhor, Padre, is an angry man. He is much feared – it's better to wait for the padre to call." He made no attempt to explain himself, but added, "We have friends at the malocas, Padre" — he broke into a wide grin — "and all the comforts men need!"

Inácio did not press him further but bade farewell to the four of them and trudged up the slope. His sandaled feet quickly were covered with ash and dust that puffed up as he walked.

The sun beat down on Inácio's back, leaving him hot and uncomfortable beneath his thick black cassock, and when finally he stood opposite the entrance to Engenho Santo Tomás, he was out of breath and soaked with perspiration. He paused just beyond the opening in the timbered wall and said a brief prayer.

He had seen some of the plantations closer to Olinda but had not gone beyond their stockades, and he did not know quite what to expect within the enclosure: some houses, perhaps, a barn, a sugar press, other necessities for so remote and harsh a life. The first thing he noticed about his uncle's engenho was the filth that littered the area. The stench of feces was overpowering. A variety of animals — sheep, pigs, goats, calves — paraded across the plaza unchecked. Dogs, too, bestirred themselves at Inácio's approach and came skulking out of the shade to yap at his heels. Swarms of noisy black flies hung in the air before him, and any attempt to wave them away was futile.

There were, as he'd expected, several buildings within the stockade. A sugar press stood beneath a palm-thatched roof at one side of the plaza, oxen straining against the great arms that turned the rollers into which men fed the cane stalks. Near these workers, other blacks and natives of Santa Cruz labored at the molasses cauldrons.

The main house was a squarish two-story building set back from the entrance, its rough gray walls of stone and clay with small, unequal-sized windows, shutterless and resembling gunports. This grim building and the enclosing stockade, along which Inácio observed platforms with falconet guns, were stark evidence of a perilous existence in these backlands. Inácio was not frightened — his spirit and enthusiasm were too great for that — but he felt a certain sensible wariness, heightened by the knowledge that this place was the scene of his cousin Pedro's savage murder.

He was almost at the doorway of the big house when there emerged from the dark interior a figure he recognized with difficulty as Nicolau Cavalcanti. The man who stood before him was not the man he remembered from Sintra. The features, of course, were essentially the same — the dark, weathered face more furrowed and the hair and beard silver — but gone was the intelligent, thoughtful visage and the sad, brooding expression of one who lived with a burden of memories.

Nicolau's face now was hard and cruel; there was a fierce look in his eyes that prompted Inácio to recall the half-breed's words. His uncle stood without boots or slippers, his bare feet grimy, his toenails long and filthy. He was dressed more like a beggar than a plantation lord. He wore thin, dusty cotton breeches held in place with a length of frayed rope, and a roughly cut leather jerkin that hung loosely from his shoulders, unlaced, so that his hairy chest was exposed. But, his wild and neglected appearance aside, Nicolau looked remarkably fit for a man in his sixties.

"So, Padre, what is it this time? What does the church seek now from Senhor Cavalcanti?"

"It is me, Inácio — Inácio Cavalcanti — your nephew!" he blurted out.

Nicolau leaned forward to peer at him. "Felipe's son," he said to himself as he searched Inácio's face, "A boy given to God," he said. Then: "Little mother! Little mother! Come look! Come see what we have here!" He grinned now, revealing a mouth of stained, broken teeth. "Here in Brazil, in Nova Lusitania — Felipe's son!" And in a gruff voice, he asked Inácio, "What in the name of God sent you to this place?"

A small, bent woman in black slowly crept out of the doorway, narrowing her eyes against the sun. "Padre," she murmured. "Padre."

"It's Inácio, little mother," Nicolau said. "Felipe's son, Inácio."

She nodded as if she knew, but nothing in her expression indicated she recognized her brother-in-law's child.

"Aunt Helena," Inácio greeted her, but couldn't go on. *Holy Mother*, he thought, *what pain I see in every line of this lined, weary face.*

"You've come from Olinda?" Nicolau asked.

"Directly," Inácio said. "I landed there from São Salvador, where we've been this past year, with Governor Tomé de Sousa — myself and five others of His Company."

"With Sousa?" To Nicolau, who knew nothing of the Jesuits, "His Company" had simply meant the company of colonists.

"Yes, and hundreds more sent by His Majesty to plant afresh his New World colony."

Nicolau's face hardened for a moment. Then he said, "Son of my brother, come; you've had a long journey. There's meat and manioc and beans — let us feed you!"

Nicolau indicated that they should enter the great block of a house, but before they could move, Helena reached out and placed a hand on Inácio's arm:

"My child — what of my Henriques?"

"Henriques is in good health, working with my father in the countinghouse. He is married." He stopped. "This you must know?"

But her expression told otherwise, and then Nicolau spoke:

"The last we heard of that coward, my son," he said, "was years ago. He ran away; he had no stomach for this conquest. So, he's married, is he? Good. Maybe there's man enough in him to satisfy one woman!"

"He is happy, Uncle, to be back in Portugal." And then Inácio remembered. "Dear Pedro," he said, "I pray for him."

"Yes, nephew, pray for my Pedro's rest — and all damnation for his blackhearted killers."

He swung away then and entered the house, the other two following him.

The interior consisted of one huge room, as filthy as the open ground of the stockade, low-ceilinged with a rough-hewn ladder that led to similar quarters above. Inácio was introduced to Pedro's widow, Maria, and was told that her child and Tomás, Nicolau's thirteen-year-old son, were out playing. Several other women and children were about, and grew silent at Inácio's entrance, but now they ignored him and resumed their conversations. Nicolau made no attempt to explain who they were or what function they served in his establishment. Several little half-breed children rubbed up against Inácio's cassock and tugged at the rosary that hung from his belt. Nicolau shouted at them in the language of the natives and they leapt away.

Nicolau led Inácio to a thick-beamed table and benches that occupied one section of the room. Here, too, were hammocks, where Nicolau, Helena, and Tomás slept, and again, Inácio was distressed to observe that everyone in the house lived openly and shamelessly without privacy.

A chaotic assortment of items cluttered the room: weapons and powder, heaps of manioc and beans, jars of wine and water, broken and rusted implements, lengths of chain to bind slaves; and from the uneven rafters hung strips of drying meat and bundles of roots and herbs. Chickens nested atop piles of goods and pecked their way across the hard mud floor. Pet birds flew beneath the rafters, where two small monkeys dangled, screeching and baring their teeth at Inácio. Flies, slower and fatter than those outside, swarmed everywhere. And permeating the atmosphere was the stench of rotting meat and sweat.

Bowls of powdery manioc, chunks of stringy, burnt meat, and beans swirling in fat were brought by two of the women occupants. Nicolau attacked his food voraciously, between mouthfuls telling Inácio of the early years at Iguarassu. At one point, when Inácio expressed joy at being able to teach the Gospel in these glorious woodlands, this "garden of the Lord," Nicolau gave his *own* vision of the forest — a hostile giant that had to be razed with fire and ax relentlessly to make this country fit for Christian. "They must either destroy it or be destroyed by it!" he said.

Inácio was even more disheartened by his uncle's attitude toward the savages: Nicolau recalled the massacre of Pedro, recounting every horrid detail of the butchery. "A thousand times since then," he said, "I've closed my eyes and beheld my ravaged son. A thousand times I've vowed revenge against those who slew him." His countenance became remarkably placid. "My dear nephew, such sweet revenge I've had."

"Uncle Nicolau, vengeance is God's alone," Inácio said quietly,

"Is it, *Padre* Inácio?" Nicolau retorted. "Then, God gave me these hands — this will — to act on His behalf. Pagans came to murder Pedro and destroy the labor of our first year. They sought to destroy every settlement of Christians in Nova Lusitania. But we drove them away from Iguarassu and Olinda and out of our lands, and we pursued them and their allies and slew what we caught. But they're still out there, living like animals in the forest, for they breed like vermin."

He took some wine, and added in a calmer tone, "We capture them if there's opportunity, and bring them to hunt and fish for us and to work in our fields. They're without human reason, cruel, vindictive, dishonest; they have strength for their barbarous pastimes, but here in our fields they're as weak as fish out of water."

"Perhaps we need to be patient with them. They are still wild children, not men with understanding."

"Yes," he said. "We do the savages a priceless service by dragging them out of the forest. We teach them to till, to sow, to reap, and to work for their upkeep — things unknown to them before the Portuguese arrived."

Nicolau rose from the table. "Get some rest, nephew," he said. "In a land of pagans, the weary Christian, Padre, needs his rest. This you will learn." He went over to the woman in the white robe, who laughed and swung out of the hammock to follow Nicolau into the sunlight.

"O Lord, take note of him," Inácio prayed quietly for his uncle. "Remove the thorns that bind his heart, and free his spirit in this lovely land."

&

The woman in the white robe was Jandaia, Affonso Ribeiro's daughter. By this her forty-first year, she had a mature, graceful appeal that made her as attractive as ever to Nicolau. That childish pout was gone, but the slight aloofness remained. The constancy of Nicolau's affection for her made Jandaia self-confident. Nicolau slept with others in the big room, but these were women he used without tenderness, and no one held the place of Jandaia.

When she'd followed him out of the house, he led her to the cane field near the stockade. They'd been here before, lying between the rows of sugarcane, and he would make love with a furious, demanding passion.

But this time she found him quiet, almost hesitant. When she cast off her robe, he did not immediately unclothe himself but stood there, his eyes upon her body, a withdrawn, distant expression on his face. She went down on her knees before him, and he loosened the rope at his waist, so that his breeches fell about his ankles. She caressed him, and he ran his hands through her hair, but he did not respond to her soft kisses. She looked up at his face and saw that he'd closed his eyes, as he often did when she touched him. But the troubled look had not disappeared.

"Is something wrong?" she asked.

He shook his head, and resting a hand on her shoulder, he lowered himself to the ground, gently pushing her down next to him. She welcomed this, pulling him toward her. Kicking off the breeches at his ankles, he began to make love to her with sharp, hurried motions, pressing her fiercely to the earth, his rough leather jerkin scratching and chafing her skin. He uttered none of his usual impassioned appeals but breathed loud and hard, his rasps and grunts mounting until he had his release. Then he rolled away, rustling and snapping dry leaves and stalks, and lay on his back.

"What is troubling you?" she now asked him again. She had no sooner put the question than she realized what it must be. Before he could reply, she said, "The one that flew in like the urubu, so scrawny and black, the padre — you do not like him?"

Nicolau was amused by her description of Inácio.

"Yes, Jandaia — such a bird, indeed. Black and hungry for the souls of men."

"So, Padre Urubu is hungry." She laughed gaily. "Then let him be fed — at my father's malocas. Let him find Affonso Ribeiro and he'll not want for devils."

"Inácio is honest — too honest for Terra do Brasil. But don't think him a fool."

She was hurt by his rebuke and looked at him apologetically. She did not forget that after the Caeté and their allies who'd besieged Iguarassu and Olinda were driven off, and the full facts of what had happened at Ribeiro's maloca became known, Dom Duarte had demanded that her father and all his tribe, every person related to him, be banished from Pernambuco. It had been Jandaia who had begged him to intercede on her father's behalf, pleading that she, too, would be exiled. And Nicolau had heard her and gone to Dom Duarte, saying that he, personally, would take responsibility for Affonso Ribeiro. He wanted none of the riffraff and drunken friends, but the immediate family could move to Engenho Santo Tomás. They were still here.

" I fear for this little padre," Nicolau said afterward. "Men like Affonso Ribeiro —and Nicolau Cavalcanti — are going to break his innocent heart."

❧

Inácio lay in a hammock Helena had ordered her house slaves to hang for him in a storeroom next to the big room.

Inácio could not sleep. He was deeply troubled by what he'd seen and heard at Engenho Santo Tomás.

This afternoon Nicolau had got back to the stockade, alone, at the same time his slaves began returning from the clearings. Inácio was watching them file through the entrance, and Nicolau approached him:

"Observe my peças — strong, healthy black sons of the soil — and then observe, nephew, those they drive ahead of them — soft, rheumy-eyed lambs! How, I ask you, are we to conquer this land with such servants?"

There were, Inácio saw when all had entered, ten Africans and some fifty natives, who did indeed appear miserable, walking dispiritedly, showing neither exhaustion at the end of a day's toil nor relief that rest was soon to come. Small men mostly — some almost womanish in the delicacy of their frames when compared with the more robust blacks — they displayed a marked resignation and docility.

"Where do the natives come from?" Inácio had asked.

"These are Caeté, Potiguara, a few unfriendly Tobajara. Some I took myself, in the wars after they rose up against us. Some I paid for: A cask of the cheapest wine, a rusty pike, a piece of cloth, and a savage will deliver his brother. Some were with the cord." He saw Inácio's frown. "That one there," he said, indicating a man at the back of the group, "he has me to thank that he enjoys this day. He was bound with the white cord of his enemy, being led to their place of slaughter, when I rescued him. You'd think that such a man would show gratitude, wouldn't you?

"The creature wails at me and calls me a thief. I stole from him the prospect of a glorious death, he tells the others. With such, nephew Inácio, your task is going to be hard."

While he'd been talking, a pack of young boys moved boisterously to where the two men stood, offering noisy greetings in both Portuguese and Tupi.

Nicolau calmed them. "Tomás," he said, and one had stepped forward. "Tomás —this is your uncle Felipe's son."

"He's a *padre?*" the boy said bluntly.

"Yes, little savage," Nicolau said, " and he'll be wanting your respect."

The boy looked into the pale, anxious face above him and, in an uncertain tone, bade Inácio a proper welcome. When they'd exchanged greetings, Tomás asked his father, "The padre is from Olinda?"

"No," Nicolau said, "from Portugal and the Bahia."

"Oh, yes?" the boy said, and then darted away to join his friends.

"He's been a great solace to Helena," Nicolau said quietly, "and, since Pedro's death, to me. A late child, Padre, given us by the Lord in this wilderness. Tomás knows nothing of Lisbon, nor of any land but this. He knows nothing of counting-houses and fancy fidalgos, and this is the way I wish it to remain. Let him grow up to be a little wild, a little like these savages, and he'll know better than any how to conquer Brazil."

"But surely the boy should be sent to Portugal for an education?"

"What will it profit him, here in this forest?"

During the early part of the evening, Inácio had sat with Nicolau and Helena and had more opportunity to observe their son. He'd found him ill-mannered, ill-educated, and every bit as wild as his father was hoping he'd become. He spoke Tupi, the language of his playmates, more fluently than Portuguese, and the only Latin he could recite was in the few prayers he knew. His scantily clad body had been burnt so dark and coppery by the sun that he appeared as a brother to the half-breeds with whom he played. Nicolau indulged the child, protesting neither his invasions of the big room nor his interruptions of their conversation, and Inácio unhappily saw that the child was in many ways, from his eating habits to his quick temper, a small replica of the lord of this valley.

Nicolau had sat talking until it became dark, giving Inácio a rambling account of his experiences since settling at Pernambuco with Dom Duarte Coelho.

"We've had peace — sometimes almost a year between troubles," he said, "but then the savages perform some treachery against a Christian and they have to be punished. Engenho Santo Tomás lies farthest from Olinda; none can safely venture beyond my valley, for the backlands are infested with these pagans. We're so few, they of limitless number. My wild Tomás will be an old man and still we'll not have cleared this barbarous race from the forests!"

It was this grim prophecy of Nicolau's that had kept Inácio awake in his hammock.

He'd begun to doze when he heard a dull, repetitive thudding that seemed to keep pace with the beat of his heart. Now, as he listened, he recognized the sounds as the rhythms of drums, and there was also the melodious note from a stringed instrument.

He climbed out of his hammock. The music was coming from the slave quarters across the stockade, a low and haunting refrain of the men of Africa, echoing in this valley of Santa Cruz.

As he stood listening, Inácio pondered his acceptance of the bondage of these peças. Since the days of Prince Henry, blacks had been shipped to Portugal to labor for Christian men. They were rescued from their ignorance and their brute natural laws and offered Christ's priceless redemption. What greater reward, even with their bondage, could these men expect?

Inácio returned to his hammock. He was awakened before dawn by the cry of a man in terrible pain.

He hurried out into the clearing before the big house. The slaves were assembled in front of an upright triangle formed by three stout posts. A native was bound to this contraption, his arms and legs spread-eagled.

Standing to one side was Nicolau, with Tomás and the gang of young boys. Sebastião, the overseer of the slaves, was in charge of the flogging, and directed two other Africans, who wielded thick tapir-hide whips.

Their victim was a young Caeté, no more than a boy, who howled and begged for mercy.

Inácio hurried over to his uncle. "For mercy's sake, Nicolau Cavalcanti, put an end to this savagery!"

"This little Caeté tried to run away last night, nephew Inácio. What savagery is there in teaching him to know his place among Christians?"

"You will teach him *nothing*."

Before Inácio arrived on the scene, the Caeté had already been given eighty lashes, and when these last twenty had been administered, Sebastião ordered a halt. He stepped forward with a bowl of salt mixed with the juice of limes. Then, as Sebastião poured the bitter, burning mixture over the Caété's raw flesh, the native screamed once, a long, withering cry, and then was silent.

The two Africans untied and unshackled the Caeté, and Inácio rushed over to him. It was obvious that the boy was dying.

Kneeling beneath that ghastly triangle, Padre Inácio Cavalcanti gave the young heathen his first and final anointing, and claimed his first pagan soul for Christ in Santa Cruz.

Two days later, Inácio called his guides from the malocas and prepared to leave Engenho Santo Tomás. He said he would return to the valley before departing Pernambuco, but was now eager to undertake the circuit of the colony which Padre Nóbrega had requested.

Nicolau welcomed Inácio's departure. "Visit others, and come and tell me whether you find it so different with them," he said.

❧

During his travels to the plantations between Nicolau's valley and Olinda, and up to the settlement of Iguarassu, Inácio met with kindness and generosity from his hosts. They greeted his arrival with open delight, grew devout and prayerful in his presence, and surprised him with their gentility. The prosperity of these landowners was still meager by Lisbon standards, but several had taken him to a vantage point above their estates, and indicating the cane fields reaching into the great valleys below, they declared that the culture and opulence of Pernambuco would yet rival anything known in Portugal. And he believed them.

But these kind and openhearted men were, like Nicolau, stained with immorality, and cheerfully revealed their numerous transgressions with the pagan girls. They did not understand that the young man who heard their loud boasting was not like the lascivious priests of Olinda, who kept concubines, but was deeply shocked by their sin and dismayed at the sight of the bastard progeny paraded before him.

It was Olinda, the capital, however, that truly scandalized Inácio. Those seven lovely hills were infested with a breed of godless, vice-ridden men. Inácio walked the narrow, stony lanes that wound along the hillsides and became aware of a great number of foreigners in the town — Italians, Galicians, Canary Islanders. Foulmouthed drunkards and riffraff with no respect for his cassock offered him the most depraved suggestions. He trembled at the sight of half-naked women, both native and half-breed, lewdly disporting themselves in public.

And he found priests who, to his sorrow, had been swept into the devil's embrace.

Angry and fearful at what he'd beheld, he called upon the donatário himself, Dom Duarte Coelho Pereira, in the white limestone bastion he'd erected upon one of Olinda's hills.

"Oh, Padre Inácio," Dom Duarte had welcomed him warmly, "How wonderful to have a true servant of God with us."

To Inácio's great surprise, the man who stood at the head of this cesspool of iniquity was a devout Christian. And even more so was his wife, Dona Brites, who, after the introductions, said directly, "Padre Inácio, are you come with your Jesuit brothers to save the souls of these wicked people?"

"Our mission is with Governor Tomé de Sousa at São Salvador," he'd replied. "From the Bahia, we will go to seek the pagans of Santa Cruz."

"Look just beyond the windows of this tower," she said, referring to part of the redoubt built by Dom Duarte at the time of the siege of Olinda, "and you'll find sinners enough." She glanced at her husband, who nodded his approval. "And you'll see the monastery we started for the brothers of St. Francis, who have not come. It will be for you, Padre Inácio, and those of your order who come to Nova Lusitania."

Inácio sensed a strength in Dona Brites, a large and imposing woman. But her husband seemed less formidable. Much was said in Lisbon about Dom Duarte, who had accomplished more than any other man who'd been donated a captaincy in Santa Cruz, but here, with gray hair and age-worn face and a tremor upon his limbs, it was obvious that the efforts to launch his colony had exhausted him.

"Why, Padre, do they want my lands?" Dom Duarte asked abruptly.

"Forgive me, senhor, I do not understand."

"King João promised me that sixty leagues of Brazil would be mine and my heirs to rule forever. What we've gained has been conquered from the forest and the savages, inch by inch. This year, for the first time, we've begun to show a profit. Now the king sends Dom Tomé de Sousa to take what was deeded to me."

"I cannot comment on such matters, senhor."

"I can!" the donatário declared. "He — Dom Tomé de Sousa, that knighted bastard — sent you to spy out these lands of mine!"

"Oh, no, Dom Duarte, it was Padre Nóbrega who sent me."

Dom Duarte looked at the Jesuit disbelievingly. "Tell Dom Tomé de Sousa and his agents that I'll not have them here," he said. "This is Nova Lusitania, captaincy of Dom Duarte and his planters, and we'll have no intruders and reformers. Sinners there may be, but Our Savior and Light has sustained us all these years and will continue to do so —*without* the intervention of Dom Tomé de Sousa."

Padre Inácio came to see, in the weeks that followed, that Dom Duarte was a good and deeply religious man albeit old and infirm and unable to govern effectively. Inácio would surely tell Padre Nóbrega and Governor Tomé that if Pernambuco's pagans were to be reached, the men setting them such evil and unholy examples must be dealt with first, and that this captaincy must be placed under Governor Tomé's jurisdiction.

He dared not mention these feelings to Dom Duarte, but he did urge that the donatary act immediately against those most openly in sin. "Order the men with wives in Portugal to send for them, senhor — or to return to their sides. And make these priests go out into the streets and drive those who live in concubinage to the altar."

"I always urged the bachelors, Padre, to marry these girls. I warned them of the damnations they would face, for all the good it did. Try to understand, Padre: They don't see savages; they see the Moorish princesses of their most lustful dreams. They can't live without them."

"But, Dom Duarte, how they will die," Inácio said.

"Ask your uncle how it is. You've visited him, no?"

"Yes, before my journey through your territories."

"And you've seen how he lives?"

Inácio looked at him bleakly. "Yes."

"Nicolau has been one of the pillars of our community. I thank God for such men. Without them we'd be the same as those ruined and desolate captaincies below us."

Inácio was not certain how to react to this praise for his uncle. "I will tell him you said this, Dom Duarte," he said simply. "I return to Engenho Santo Tomás within the week."

When he'd left them, Dona Brites said to her husband, "Perhaps it would have been better for the padre if you'd spoken openly about his 'righteous' uncle."

❧

"Rain! Rain! Rain!" grouched Inácio's traveling companion on the journey back to Engenho Santo Tomás, vexed at the downpour — now a fierce torrent, now a soft, drenching mist that soaked through the dense cover — which had plagued them almost ceaselessly since they'd left Olinda two days ago. Accompanying them were the half-breed guides Inácio had employed previously, and also the two Tobajara.

"Oh, lovely rain!" Inácio said, ignoring his companion's exasperation. He raised his face so that the huge drops of water splashed upon it. "Glorious rain! A blessing upon His paradise!"

He was Jacob de Noronha, commonly known as Parrot Man or, simply, Papagaio. With his large head, short neck, strongly hooked nose, and squat torso, he did bear more than a passing resemblance to a parrot. But he owed his nickname to the large parrot family that shared his lodgings at Olinda.

He had a fine house of four rooms, every one open to his raucous flock. He'd gone to great trouble to get his macaws, devoting to his search the energy and enthusiasm other men gave to hunting down slaves. He'd negotiated first with friendly natives at Olinda, who passed on his request to a tribe in the interior.

Not a few colonists thought Papagaio slightly crazy; still, they respected him. Some accepted his eccentricity with the privately voiced acknowledgment that Jacob was a Jew and therefore understandably given to such exotic pleasures. Whatever the case, they remained beholden to him, for Jacob was also a millwright and a money-lender.

Of five engenhos operating in the colony at that time, three — the Cavalcantis' included — had been raised under his direction. Other plantations owed their existence to his financial support, but he was more a sugar merchant than a moneylender, advancing loans only against sugar crops that were certain to come downriver to Olinda.

Jacob had fled Lisbon and the Inquisition in 1536. He went first to the isle of São Thomé and then, a decade ago, had come to Brazil. He had found Dom Duarte tolerant of his background. Catholic though he was, the donatário was also practical: In Pernambuco, he said, it was trees, not men, that should be destroyed by fire. With nations of pagans surrounding them, what value was there in persecuting one little Jew, who had come to help build Nova Lusitania? He had welcomed Jacob, and other Hebrews, who would bring their skills to Olinda.

Most were nominally Cristãos Novos — "New Christians" — who survived the burnings and floggings in Portugal by accepting baptism; but, in Pernambuco, they were able to reaffirm (though not too openly) their ancient obediences. A few had acquired plantations, but most, like Papagaio, preferred Olinda.

Papagaio, rarely visited Nicolau Cavalcanti, but he was eager now to see, firsthand, the prospects for that mill's next harvest. Cavalcanti had been borrowing heavily from Jacob to develop his plantation: more slaves, more and more clearings, plans for a bigger mill. Only 150 acres, a tiny fraction of the 75,000 acres owned by Cavalcanti, had been planted with cane; 100 acres more were to be cleared this season.

Cavalcanti's nephew had pleasantly surprised Papagaio. When the tall, slender man with the sober face came to his house, Papagaio wondered if he was there to question his "faith." But, as it turned out, Inácio had heard that Papagaio was bound for Cavalcanti's valley, and wanted only his companionship on the trip.

⁊

With the incessant rain slowing their progress, it took three days to reach the valley. Inácio had been away from Engenho Santo Tomás for three months. Now he sat again at the dinner table in the big room of the blockhouse. Outside, it was cool and wet, but here a sticky dampness clung to everything. Inácio had difficulty breathing the muggy air and felt acutely uncomfortable beneath his perspiration-soaked cassock.

Three Portuguese who worked for Nicolau and had been away at the time of Inácio's first visit were also present. One from Madeira was a sugar master; the other two also had experience with cane. They sat at one end of the table, keeping to themselves, and as soon as they'd eaten, they took leave of Senhor Cavalcanti and his guests and returned to their labors.

Inácio noticed that Jacob, who sat next to him, ate sparingly, almost like a bird, and seemed unconcerned by Nicolau's vulgar manners, the mongrels that groveled at their feet for some morsel to be tossed to them, and the flies that swarmed above the table.

From the conversation between Nicolau and Papagaio, it seemed to Inácio that nothing on this earth concerned them but sugar. He listened to them talk of its cultivation, of the clayey, fat soils that were best suited to it, and of the seasonal cycle to be observed. After the rains, from June onward, the forests must be cleared and the cuttings planted. And between the cuttings, there had to be the weeding: five times a year for new fields, three for older — every foot of ground between the rows of cane to be freed of the wild growth that spread so furiously. And there were rats and worms and plant diseases to be combated without rest, save on the days of the saints, when the slaves were free. For their labor, the slaves received a daily gourd of manioc and sun-dried meat and a ration of sugar syrup, the same given to cows and horses.

Inácio listened quietly as the two men spoke of the milling process, and what methods would extract the most juice from the cane, and whether it was time for Nicolau to consider returning to the site where Pedro had been killed to construct a larger, water-driven crusher. The press turned by the oxen had been erected within the stockade as a precaution against the savages, but with the reputation its owner had earned as a fighter and enslaver of his enemies, Engenho Santo Tomás seemed safe from further incursions.

Sugar! To Nicolau and Papagaio, it was the sweetest harvest on earth. They grew excited even at the mention of heaps of *baggase*, the cane trash, for, as they explained, the more left behind when the three iron-plated rollers had done their work, the greater the flow of juice along the wooden troughs to the first cauldron, where a sugar master must know the exact temperature to prevent the juice from being ruined by overboiling Inácio learned that the juice had to be boiled again and treated with lime to bring to the surface a fine scum, to be ladled off the purified syrup, after which the juice was boiled a third time, amid sickly sweet vapors, and stirred until thick and treacly. From this came both the blocks of rough sugar and, when filtered in clay pots, quality white crystals.

Sugar! As they spoke of mighty harvests of cane, of high-wheeled carts lumbering in from the fields from dawn to dusk, Inácio could not banish from his mind the picture of the Caeté who'd been flogged to death. *O Lord,* he cried silently, *how many more will be crucified to make these harvests!*

Papagaio grew most attentive when they considered the present crop, figuring how many arrobas — measures of 32 pounds — the mill would produce the next season. Cavalcanti reckoned on getting 2,000 arrobas of sugar from his lands — some 30 tons to be sent downriver to Olinda. Papagaio saw that this would require about 60 of the 1,100-pound chests in which sugar was packed for shipping to Lisbon, the best part of a shipload. He smiled contentedly, for there'd be a handsome profit for him, too. Then he suggested how Cavalcanti might even increase this output:

"Build the new mill, Nicolau, not for Engenho Santo Tomás alone but for others. You're one man, with one son; you'll never cultivate every acre of your estate. There are others, without the means to own a plantation; allow them into your valley to plant cane. They'll have to bring every stalk they grow to your mill. And you take two out of every three stalks as compensation for the favors you show them."

"This valley is mine," Nicolau said icily. "No other man will hold the smallest part of it."

"Who said they should be landowners? They would be your tenants. Already other plantation owners near Olinda do this: Ten, twenty acres they provide to a good man and his family. As long as the tenant clears it and brings his canes to the mill, good. If not, he goes. He has no rights to the land — only to the profit of his labor. The men at your malocas — the old scoundrel Ribeiro and others — what do they do to earn your hospitality?"

"Nothing! And I thank God for that."

In response to Nicolau's vehement remark, Papagaio said quietly, "It needn't be so."

"Forget Ribeiro," Nicolau said. "That useless dog has no value to me. But what you suggest may be worth considering. It's a big valley. There's land enough for many. If others come, and live by *my* law" — he seemed amused by this — "why *shouldn't* they grow cane for me!"

Suddenly Nicolau gave his full attention to his nephew, who was still listening intently: "So now you've seen, you've traveled these lands and met the men upon them. Tell me, Inácio, what did you find?"

Inácio stirred uncomfortably. Nicolau picked at something between his teeth with the long nail of his little finger. "Well, nephew, I'm waiting to hear," he said.

Inácio began hesitantly. "This wonderful land . . . this inviting garden that our Lord has placed upon this far shore . . . these cool, fresh groves that show the greatness of the Creator — the wonders of His work are everywhere. But, my dear uncle . . . this is also a sad land." He stopped, expecting some response, but neither of the men spoke.

Nicolau stopped picking his teeth and rested his chin on his hand. Papagaio stared down at the table, looking somewhat embarrassed.

"It is a sad land," Inácio went on, "because men are making it so. They defile Santa Cruz with their sin. How will we ever accomplish the greatest of all works in this land, the conversion of its pagans, if our own people turn away from the Lord?"

"Dom Duarte is a God-fearing man," Nicolau said, "but even he will tell you that these heathen will not be pacified by preaching but by the sword. Go to them as you must, but carry a staff and a rod of iron, for only with these will you bring them to their knees!"

❦

The next morning, Inácio was sitting alone on a bench outside the storeroom. Nicolau and Papagaio had gone to inspect the cane fields and the newest clearings. They'd taken Tomás and his playmates with them. Seeing the boy again, Inácio had determined to speak once more with his uncle about his education. He would urge Nicolau to send Tomás to his own father's house in Lisbon, and he knew that he would have Helena's support for such a suggestion, since she'd spoken to him after Nicolau and Papagaio had left for the fields. "Padre Inácio," she'd said, "must my child grow up no better than one of these savages? Please — make his father understand that he may lose Tomás, as surely as he lost Henriques, if he lets him go wild, without the graces of a good Christian."

As he sat outside the storeroom, Inácio saw a young woman come to the entrance of the stockade. From this distance, he didn't get a clear glimpse of her; she hesitated a few moments and then came directly to him.

She was part Portuguese, part native. She had a round, open face with mysterious, slightly elongated hazel eyes. Her nose was small and slightly flattened, her light copper skin smooth and without blemish. She was small but finely proportioned. Her hair was a rich chestnut brown, thick and flowing and reaching to the small of her back.

She wore a loose-fitting yellow garment, and from a thin cord around her neck there hung a pendant of tiny feathers. There was a childlike quality about her, a freshness, enhanced by her delicate features.

Inácio stood up as the girl neared him, and stepped forward to meet her. She hesitated, then nodded her head in greeting, though she kept her eyes downcast. Then she looked up at him and said, in Portuguese, "He asks for you."

"Who, child?"

"At the malocas — Affonso Ribeiro."

"The old man?"

She nodded, and glanced toward the big house, where Helena had come to stand in the doorway.

"I'll come immediately," he said.

"He asks all night. He has the sickness. Others, too."

"What sickness?"

She shook her head, indicating that she didn't know.

"You are his child?"

Her eyes widened. "No. I am Unauá, daughter of Jandaia. My mother is at the big house."

He looked at the girl, and was suddenly reminded of the handsome woman in the white robe. There was a similarity between them, in the shape of the face and the nose and in their confident, independent bearing.

Helena was making her way toward them, walking barefoot across the wet ground, and Inácio went to meet her, the girl following him. "She calls me to Affonso Ribeiro, who lies sick," he said.

"An evil and sinful man, Padre Inácio," she said. "Go to him. If anyone needs God's forgiveness, it's the degredado."

"This child lives with him?" he asked.

"At his maloca, yes, but she's innocent, Padre. She's the daughter of a woman of my house."

"The one in the white robe?"

"Yes. Jandaia."

"She does not live with her mother?"

Helena shook her head. "There's a brother, too — children from a Tupiniquin warrior now dead. They're cared for by one of Ribeiro's wives, also a Tupiniquin. Go to him and you'll see her — a pure savage, Padre."

"But why doesn't the mother raise them?"

"She has other children," Helena said, and then lowered her eyes, her gaze falling somewhere near the cross on his rosary. "Go to the maloca," she said flatly. Then she turned and walked off; without looking back, she swept over the threshold into the darkness of the big house.

Even before reaching the clearing of the malocas with Unauá, Inácio got an impression of neglect and impoverishment. The surrounding fields were badly in need of tending; scarcely any effort had been made to check the undergrowth. Native women were probing the earth with their digging sticks for manioc tubers, but, judging from the small pile they'd recovered, they were finding few plants under the dense mat of weeds.

As for the malocas themselves, the five once lofty palm-front structures were shot through with rotting thatch. The stockade of the engenho was strewn with filth, but the clearing was worse: Small, naked children squealed as they dragged themselves about in the quagmire in front of their parents and elders, who seemed totally oblivious to the dirt and stench around them.

As they approached Ribeiro's maloca, a woman and a young man came out to greet them.

"This is Salpina," Unauá said quietly, "favorite woman of Ribeiro." A strong note of pride came into her voice: "And my brother, Guaraci."

Salpina wore no clothes, but her body was lightly tinctured with urucu dye and she bore herself with un-self-conscious dignity, in contrast to the women who squatted near them or straggled about the clearing. Unauá's brother had a magnificent full-chested physique, with muscular arms and legs, and moved with the athletic grace of an animal in the wild.

Salpina was studying Inácio closely, with a firm gaze. "He is waiting within," she said.

The moment Inácio entered the maloca, its dark, dingy interior assailed him with such an overpowering fetor that he wanted to back out. He forced this weakness aside, and as his eyes adjusted to the dimness, he found that many lay in their hammocks; when he moved toward them, some groaned and cried out, but most lay still, their eyes closed, apparently too feeble to move.

Hemorrhagic dysentery was raging through these malocas, afflicting half the people who dwelt here. This debilitating sickness was aggravated by an outbreak of influenza, an alien illness to which the natives had no resistance. Some were attempting to combat the maladies with concoctions of herbs and plants and the broth of boiled parrots, but the majority lay ravaged and exhausted in their hammocks, amid their own filth, waiting for death.

As Inácio walked slowly between the hammocks, a sudden anger possessed him. Surely Nicolau, his uncle, master of these lands and these malocas, must be aware of this hideous epidemic, this horrible suffering. Yet he had said nothing.

Salpina had gone on ahead of him and was standing beside the hammock of Affonso Ribeiro.

Inácio looked down and saw a big man lying on his back. A stale, dry odor rose from the man's body, and great folds of loose flesh rolled against the netting of the hammock. Vermin crawled through the matted hair of Ribeiro's chest. Reflected in his eyes, shadowed and sunken though remarkably bright with fever, was naked fear.

"Thanks to our Mother, Padre," Ribeiro said, in a voice stronger than Inácio expected, "thanks that you came."

"As soon as the child called me," Inácio said.

There was a gurgling, phlegmy sound from the hammock, and Inácio realized that Ribeiro was trying to laugh. When the sounds ceased, Ribeiro went on: "They all came for Affonso Ribeiro: the king's soldiers, the Normans, Gomes de Pina,

Nicolau Cavalcanti, Dom Duarte Coelho. Now you, Padre . . .Who comes next? Who comes to fetch Affonso Ribeiro?"

"Fear not," Inácio said, understanding all too well what this man on the verge of death was asking.

"They must go back," Ribeiro said vaguely. "This is no place for them. Take them, Padre, to their own people."

Inácio was briefly puzzled; then he realized that Ribeiro was referring to Salpina and to Unauá and Guaraci.

"Salpina is a Tupiniquin, the daughter of the elder Aruanã," Ribeiro said moments later. "She's been at my hammock these many years, but has never forgotten the malocas of her father. They must leave this valley, Padre." With a tremendous effort, he turned his head so that he could look at Salpina as he continued: "She hated Pernambuco from the day we arrived. Her only joy — her only love — was these two. The girl is nineteen, Padre, the boy a year younger. *They must go back!*" he said.

"Where?"

"Your uncle knows Aruanã."

"My uncle would not object?"

Ribeiro ignored the question. "Take them away from this place — or surely they will be ruined like the others you see." He was seized by another spasm of coughing that left his voice weak. "When your uncle came to this valley, he said, 'This is Engenho Santo Tomás; there is nothing else.' Soon the people at these malocas saw that their past was gone. Work, work, work, Nicolau Cavalcanti told them, as every planter does — work and you'll be redeemed from your savagery. Work, work, work and you'll come to behold a real paradise in this Terra do Brasil!" Ribeiro tried to raise his head. "I told them — Nicolau Cavalcanti, every one of them — that the natives would rather die than work at their cane fields. I, Ticuanga of the Tupiniquin, saw this."

And here Affonso Ribeiro began to ramble, recalling feasts and fights with the Tupiniquin, when he lived at Aruanã's malocas. Salpina and the two young people, Unauá and Guaraci, stood near the hammock: Several times Ribeiro spoke briefly to them, telling them that this black robe would help them to return to the Tupiniquin. Finally he fell silent, except for his labored breathing.

And Inácio asked the question that had been nagging at him from the start: "The woman at the stockade — Jandaia — is she your daughter?" Ribeiro, in his delirium, had boasted of so many children and concubines that Inácio was not sure of the exact relationship of the girl or her brother to Ribeiro.

"Yes," Ribeiro said, following it with a weak laugh. "The one I gave to Senhor Cavalcanti."

Inácio did not grasp the implication of what Ribeiro had said. "Unauá and the boy would leave the place of their mother?"

"Mother? She's been no mother to them — not since she moved to Senhor Cavalcanti's house."

"Merciful Jesus," Inácio said quietly. "I did not see."

"What was there to see, Padre? Your uncle is no different from the others. He's not a bad man. Since the days at Porto Seguro, his life has been tied to this land. And this land, Padre, is the conqueror of men and their souls."

Inácio saw that he had been blind to the sins of Nicolau Cavalcanti because he had not wanted to recognize them.

And now Ribeiro was saying, "I, too, have sinned, Padre." Then he ordered Salpina, Unauá, and Guaraci away from the hammock.

"When did you last talk with a priest?" Inácio asked gently.

Affonso Ribeiro began to tremble violently and made a strong effort to control his limbs. His eyes filled with terror and he cried, "O sinner, sinner, Padre — see what I became! Ticuanga! Prince of the Tupiniquin! Ticuanga . . ." Ribeiro's voice trailed off, only to rise again, with one desperate appeal: "Absolve me! O dear God!"

An hour passed before Inácio had heard Affonso Ribeiro's full confession. Then he left the degredado's side and hurried away from the malocas. Unauá had been waiting to escort him back to the stockade, but he indicated that he'd make his way alone.

It was about half a mile to the stockade, and he soon came to the edge of the trees. There he fell to his knees and sobbed openly, cries torn from the very depths of his slender frame.

For hours, Inácio begged that the penances of this great sinner be heard. And only when it began to grow dark did he finally rise to make his way to the stockade.

৩

Inácio stood at the end of the bench in the big room, his bony frame gaunt and diminished in the wavering light from the tallow wick.

Inácio remembered entering this damp building only moments ago and looking at the women in the room with new eyes, wondering who were servants and who the harlots of Nicolau Cavalcanti. He'd seen their young, some at Nicolau's feet, a group somewhat older sitting with Tomás, and this living evidence of Nicolau's lust shocked him afresh. Slowly he had approached the bench, where Nicolau and Jacob de Noronha were sitting alone.

Staring at some point beyond Inácio, his hands clasped together on top of the table, Nicolau Cavalcanti began to speak:

"'And Sarah gave Hagar to Abraham to be his concubine, and when she was alone and pregnant, the Lord heard her cry of distress. You will have a son, He told her, and you shall call him Ishmael. Go back to your mistress and be her slave.'"

Nicolau spoke in the direction of Papagaio, who sat leaning back as far as he could, obviously unwilling to have any part in this exchange. "Lord, how I fear for this priest," Nicolau said, as if Inácio were not present. "How I wish he could be spared the ache of discovery."

"May I be spared *nothing*," Inácio said with force. "May every agony be mine! May I vomit up all the corruption brought to this land!"

Nicolau continued to speak as if his nephew were not there. "There were men, friend Papagaio, who sought a nirvana in the East. Sailors, soldiers, all with their visions of heaven's gate open to them if they smote the Infidel. We sailed out to the East as soldiers of Christ's Order and we were corrupted by greed, by every vice known to men. What, I ask, makes this nephew of mine think that it should be so different here — that veterans of the Indies should come to be angels on these shores?"

"We are all sinners," Inácio said. "But, Uncle . . . that glorious Easter, when Admiral Cabral discovered Santa Cruz — what have we done with this holy promise?"

Nicolau turned angrily on him. "For God's sake, *Padre*, open your eyes — and truly see this Santa Cruz you've come to!"

"I do see it, Uncle," Inácio said calmly. "There at your malocas, I see the people you crucify so that cane may flourish upon these lands. I see them worn and wasting upon lands that once were their people's —"

"*Their lands?*" Nicolau exploded. "*Their lands?* Take care, Padre. You may see only sinners among us, but we're Christians, and we may beg a return to His grace. You weep for pagans."

"I weep for His children who lie dying even as you speak."

"They die as they live — like beasts."

From the hammocks came the sound of a woman quietly weeping. Papagaio rose and walked to where Helena lay to comfort her.

Nicolau gestured fiercely at Inácio. "Go! Go to your pagans! Speak meekly when they cry out for the limbs of their enemies. Embrace them when they raise their bloodstained hands to mock you. Go!"

Plunging into the night, Inácio made his way out of the stockade and strode fearlessly through the trees, back to the malocas.

He stayed there four days, and was with Affonso Ribeiro when he died on the second night.

Ribeiro was buried the next morning, just beyond the clearing. Inácio saw that Salpina showed no interest in the service; but it pleased him that the girl Unauá followed the ritual with curiosity and that her brother, Guaraci, too, seemed interested.

All those days he was in the malocas, Inácio labored without food or rest, passing from one hammock to the next. He washed every wasted, soiled body with his own hands.

On the fourth day, a messenger came to tell him that Papagaio was returning to Olinda. It pained him to leave the many who lay so desperately ill, but he could not stay: Nóbrega had expected him back from Pernambuco a month ago.

He left the malocas the next morning with the guides who'd accompanied him and Papagaio from Olinda. And with Salpina, Unauá, and Guaraci: Honoring his solemn promise to Affonso Ribeiro, he planned to take the trio by sea to the Bahia. Once there, he would seek a way to return them to their malocas at Porto Seguro.

Salpina strode irritably ahead of him, clutching resentfully at the robe Inácio had persuaded her to wear. Unauá had on the same yellow garment she'd worn the day Inácio met her. Her brother, Guaraci, marched ahead of the group wearing only a ragged pair of breeches, a definite eagerness in his step. His mother might be Jandaia, daughter of Affonso Ribeiro, but the woman who had raised him as her own was Salpina — Salpina, daughter of Aruanã of the Tupiniquin, with whom his father had been a warrior.

Nicolau Cavalcanti was not at the stockade. He had gone off alone earlier that morning, no one knew where. Tomás, whom Inácio had wanted to see, was also away, playing with the sons of Jandaia. But Helena was there, and she asked that Inácio hear her confession.

Afterward they walked together into the clearing. Papagaio and the rest of the party bound for Olinda were waiting near the opening in the stockade. Inácio glanced toward the ugly main house and noticed Jandaia in the doorway.

"She has no sorrow at losing this son and daughter. For years she's shown them no love," Helena said. "Only toward the others. . . ."

Inácio's expression grew pained, as he looked at Helena in her humble black dress and bare feet.

"Padre, do not judge him by this alone. My Nicolau has given fifteen years of his life to the conquest of this wilderness." She turned her head to look at Jandaia. "I've shared those years, and I understand. . . ." Inácio was going to say something, but she stopped him. "I understand — and I forgive him," she said.

VIII

January 1552 – December 1553

On January 6, 1552, sixteen months after his return from Pernambuco, Padre Inácio Cavalcanti was present with a company of men gathered on the heights of a bluff overlooking the Bahia de Todos os Santos to witness a demonstration of justice as conceived by Governor Tomé de Sousa.

The soldiers who formed an escort for the governor carried themselves as if on parade for King João, their helmets and breastplates glittering in the sun, their pikes held uniformly upright. The bareheaded gunners stood at ease by the two cannon and the smoldering fire buckets; they wore leather cuirasses, light breeches, and clean, dark buskins.

Governor Tomé, his chief officers, and the town council of São Salvador placed themselves one hundred feet behind the cannon. Their escort moved off to the left and dressed in strict order, for the governor demanded the most punctilious observance of any ceremony. Padre Nóbrega, attached to the governor's party, was accompanied by four white-robed choirboys — two the sons of colonists, the others young Tupinambá — who carried aloft a shining gilded cross.

Inácio stood with a fellow Jesuit priest and two lay brothers, to the right of the cannon and the governor's party. He noticed that Governor Tomé wore a dark velvet cap, and a black cape with the simplest ornamentation. But this somber apparel belied the inner exuberance of João III's appointee. In less than three years, Governor Tomé had raised the settlement at the Bahia de Todos os Santos from the desperate retreat of a handful of men surviving a failed captaincy to a secure, thriving base. He had moved the town from its poorly defensible site to these commanding heights overlooking the great bay.

Governor Tomé had a keen sense of concern for all who served with him. He might be called a "knighted bastard" by men such as Dom Duarte Coelho, who resented his presence (he was indeed the bastard of a court fidalgo), but he was also a man of boundless energy, sworn to bring order and progress to this lawless colony.

Governor Tomé was aware that beyond the Bahia — where several clans lived peacefully with the Portuguese — in the forests of the hinterland were thousands of savage Tupinambá. "So many savages that they would never lack," the governor reported to Lisbon, "even if we were to cut them up in slaughterhouses." He did not balk at punishing those who dared interfere with his plans, and he took such action not for his sake alone but for the glory that should be promised King João in this land. "The Pious," as the king now was called, had made it clear that this time he would tolerate no nonsense from his native subjects.

"If the Tupinambá around the Bahia trouble you, Tomé de Sousa," Dom João had said, "punish them until they cry for mercy. After they have come to beg you for peace, it would be a good idea if you took a few of the chiefs responsible back to their clearings and hanged them in front of their malocas."

During the past fourteen months, Inácio had been present at several meetings between Governor Tomé and Padre Nóbrega. He had found the governor attentive to every suggestion made by the Jesuits, for whom he showed great love and whom he considered comrades in his struggle to reestablish João III's colony.

"By all means, Padre Inácio," Governor Tomé had told him at the most recent of these meetings, "show the natives a Christian's gentle mercy and forgiveness, always where possible, but let them know, too, the most divine justice."

It was for just such an exhibition of justice that the governor had ordered this day's gathering. He spoke briefly:

"Our Most Catholic Majesty has commanded me to do everything possible to win the friendship of those tribes friendly to us and to secure their aid against our enemies. But I am not to trust them blindly, the king said in his wisdom, as if he had witnessed the crime which brings us here this day."

Two old men, both Tupinambá were presented to Governor Tomé. They were uncles of a chief who'd earned the governor's wrath as a result of the murder of four degredados who had wandered off into the forest seeking to contact and trade with one of the native clans, and had been slain and eaten by men from the malocas of the two uncles.

Governor Tomé had sent out a punitive expedition, but it had captured only these two old men, who'd dallied at their hammocks while the rest of the clan fled to a valley far beyond the Bahia.

An aide now instructed the prisoners, through an interpreter, to go on their knees before Governor Tomé, and each was forced to kiss the governor's shiny boots.

The two uncles were ordered to rise, and now Padre Nóbrega and the boys carrying the cross made their way to the Tupinambá. A hush fell over the crowd as Nóbrega prayed: "May God have mercy upon you! May the Lord's mercy be with you this day."

Inácio noticed that the Tupinambá observed Padre Nóbrega and the cross held aloft before them almost worshipfully, and he added his own quiet prayers to those of his superior.

Then, after a long glance at Governor Tomé, signifying that this work was done, Nóbrega led his reverent escort away.

The colonists jostled one another for the best positions from which to view the proceedings, and several of the pikemen with the governor's escort were sent to restore order.

The gunners stood ready. Soldiers bound the condemned men to the cannon. The Tupinambá were secured to the squat nine-foot guns, arms and legs roped along the barrel, chest and midriff pressed against the muzzle. One began to shriek for mercy, calling upon his ancestors to witness that there was but one true lord of this land — Governor Tomé. But the other was silent, a curiously placid expression on his face.

"Fire!" the chief gunner shouted.

Padre Inácio's eyes were firmly shut when the guns roared almost simultaneously. The earth trembled beneath his feet as the Tupinambá were torn apart and blasted into the air.

~

Inácio was aware that Governor Tomé had been perfectly correct in demanding a just punishment for the heinous crime of the Tupinambá. The two uncles had admitted to feasting upon the degredados, and they'd earned the condemnation of decent men. But it had been a horrible way for them to die.

The roar of the guns, the torn flesh flying before them, an awful silence that had followed — all seemed to show the distance separating the natives and the Portuguese, and Inácio felt anew the urgency of the Jesuit mission to this land: Only in Christ could the savage and the Christian be brothers.

Whenever Inácio contemplated the promise of this unity, his thoughts went to the wonderful example of the girl Unauá, who, along with Salpina and Guaraci, were part of the small group of natives the Jesuits at the bay had thus far assembled for conversion.

Unauá had proved to be a dear, worshipful convert. Padre Nóbrega had baptized her six months ago, along with thirty-two others, including Guaraci, who had been given the name Cristovão, honoring that patron of wanderers. Inácio had chosen "Catarina" for Unauá, remembering the sainted virgin of Siena, woman of conciliation and peace.

Salpina, he learned from Unauá, had laughed when she was told of this new name: "My father, Aruanã, great elder of the Tupiniquin, was given three names for the Cariri he slew. What did you do, girl, to earn this honor?"

"I took the Lord," Unauá had replied.

"You slew him?"

"Oh, no!" Unauá had replied, aghast.

Three months ago the joy Inácio had experienced at the conversion of Unauá and her brother was marred when Guaraci disappeared — an occurrence Inácio strongly suspected Salpina to have abetted.

"He has gone, Padre," Unauá reported to him one morning the previous November. "He went with the sunrise."

"I promised that I would take you back to Porto Seguro, and I will. Guaraci knew this."

Unauá nodded. But at that time more than a year had passed since their arrival at the Bahia; her brother, grown weary of waiting, had set out to walk to Porto Seguro, six hundred miles south.

"But it is an impossible journey for a boy" — he saw her shake her head — "a *man* alone," he said. "Did Salpina not tell him this?"

"She warned him of the danger. But he said that he would ask the Lord's protection . . . and that if he waited, he'd grow old in this place, the servant of the Portuguese. In his heart, Padre, he is Tupiniquin," she added softly.

"And you, my child? What are you in your heart?"

"It is not the same as with my brother."

"No, it is not. Your heart is filled with knowledge of our Father and His love."

With Unauá's help, Inácio had made himself fluent in the Tupi language. There were significant regional variations in the Tupi language, but the fathers were also finding it possible to master a *lingua geral* as clear to a Tupinambá as it would be to a Tupiniquin or a Tobajara of Olinda.

On his return from Pernambuco, Inácio had reported in detail the conditions in that captaincy to Padre Nóbrega, who had been so alarmed at the extent of the iniquities revealed that he had gone to Pernambuco to see for himself. That brief trip the previous year, coupled with what both Nóbrega and Inácio witnessed at the Bahia, especially with regard to relations between the degredados and the native women, had convinced the two Jesuits that the natives of Santa Cruz must be kept apart from the colonists to prevent them from being enslaved and from succumbing to evil influences.

But they differed on how this could be achieved. Padre Nóbrega was convinced that the Jesuits should establish great *aldeias* — villages — beyond São Salvador, but not so far as to isolate the natives from the proper benefits of civilization, and that the scattered clans should be moved to these aldeias. "How else will so few fathers tend the huge flock waiting to be brought in?" he had pointed out.

But Inácio remembered the malocas at Engenho Santo Tomás, and he'd argued that the natives should be left in their villages, far beyond reach of the Portuguese, who wished only to enslave their men and degrade their women. The Jesuits should go to them.

The day after the execution of the two uncles, Padre Nóbrega agreed to give Inácio the opportunity to go as missioner to the natives. "Perhaps your way is right, f-f-friend. Perhaps we must t-t-take the Lord's solace to these children at their m-m-malocas."

Inácio was overjoyed. He reminded Nóbrega of the Tupiniquin he had brought from Pernambuco: "Salpina is the daughter of a chief. Let me return with her to her father's village at Porto Seguro. Catarina, too — our cherished convert . . . surely her example will soften their hearts."

On a February morning, four weeks later, Governor Tomé de Sousa, who endorsed Inácio's plan for a mission to the Tupiniquin, climbed down the steep hill to bid farewell to Inácio and Padre Nóbrega. They were sailing together, Inácio to Porto Seguro, Nóbrega farther south to make his first tour of the southern captaincy of São Vicente. The father general in Rome, Ignatius Loyola, had recently sent word that Nóbrega was elevated to vice- provincial of Santa Cruz, indicating that the Company of Jesus might soon recognize the captaincies as a full province. In anticipation of this, Nóbrega wanted to acquaint himself with the farthest outposts of this battlefield for Christ.

Governor Tomé was accompanied by a slightly stooped, elderly colonist known to the Tupinambá as Caramuru, "Fish Man," who had been waiting on this shore when the governor's fleet first sailed into the Bahia in March 1549.

Caramuru's real name was Diogo Alvares. The sole survivor of the wreck of an Indies ship off the shoals north of the Bahia in 1510, he had been found between the rocks by the Tupinambá. Caramuru had lived among the savages for more than two decades before the arrival of Dom Francisco Coutinho, one of Dom João's donatários. Dom Francisco had failed in his attempt to settle these lands granted him by the king, and had lost his life under a slaughter club. The Tupinambá had spared Caramuru because, not only was he their friend, but also because his wife, Paraguaçu, "Big River," was the daughter of their most powerful chief.

As Governor Tomé stood with the Jesuits waiting to sail, he looked at them fondly. "My dear Nóbrega," he said, "my dear soldiers of Christ, though your company is small, your faith is great! With a hundred such spirits in the ranks of my men, how we could tame this land!"

"In His time, G-Governor Tomé, the work you've b-b-begun will be completed."

"The work I've begun," the governor repeated. "Two years, Padre, almost three, and we're less than ten leagues from the beach where we landed."

Caramuru responded to this: "A league in Brazil, Governor, is ten leagues in Portugal. This, Governor Tomé, is no small advance!"

"Yes, Caramuru, but the forests behind the bay and the savages living there keep us clinging to these shores as if we were crabs scuttling from one beachhead to the next."

"But, Governor, since you've come, what claws we've grown!" said Caramuru. "Never again will we lose our hold on this captaincy!"

The governor accepted Caramuru's praise without comment. He looked at the two Jesuits: "I shall pray for your mission, Vice-Provincial. Your labors for the souls of these heathen will surely earn heaven's reward. 'But what products do *you* bring, Dom Tomé' he will ask. 'What products do *you* send to fill my warehouses?'" the governor said despondently. "The brazilwood is exhausted in these parts. What value are the cane and cotton that we struggle to plant? Why, Padre, are all the riches of this New World heaped upon the Spaniard? Jewels, gold, mountains of silver are his, wherever he treads."

"Surely there are other tr-treasures for us yet to b-be discovered," Nóbrega said. "This land, G-Governor Tomé, s-so vast and fertile, can be a paradise f-flowing with milk and h-honey."

"That's what Dom Duarte believes at Olinda."

"It is true, Governor Tomé," Inácio commented. "I have seen the great cane fields in his captaincy."

"But cane isn't all that flourishes in the fields of Dom Duarte."

The governor's meaning was clear: Nóbrega and Inácio had both given him their accounts of the iniquities of Nova Lusitania, with their recommendation that the king be petitioned to loosen Dom Duarte's hold on Pernambuco. And even more pressing was the need to separate Olinda's clergy from their savage harlots and sinful ways. What was required was a bishop, Nóbrega had said, who would shepherd these priests and any others — soldiers or colonists — guilty of equal weakness. Governor Tomé had responded by petitioning the king not only for a bishop but also for orphan girls, whose Christian innocence might be just the antidote for the spells cast upon the unsuspecting settlers by the native women.

The two Jesuits did not respond to Governor Tomé's comment about Dom Duarte. Suddenly, he sighed: "I am so weary — so *very* weary."

"Oh, Tomé, He s-sees all you do in th-this land. He will b-bring you the rest you deserve."

Governor Tomé stepped up to Padre Nóbrega and embraced him. "Go with God, my good friend." Then he moved to Inácio: "You know my great hopes for the Tupiniquin. They've always been friendly toward the Portuguese. If they could be made to understand how much is our capacity to love them, they'll march with us against the Tupinambá, and help us bring them to their knees." He placed a hand on Inácio's shoulder. "Show them the love they can expect from us."

୧୨

They heard the noise when they were still half a mile from the malocas — the voices of men and women, accompanied by the rattle of a hundred gourds and the piping of bone flutes.

Salpina had a jubilant expression on her face. Unauá moved lightly in front of Salpina, glancing uncertainly from side to side into the forest, a slight frown on her brow. In the lead was João Cardim, a settler from Porto Seguro, weighted down with a double-layered cuirass, festooned with so many weapons that he had to struggle through the brush. He had been appealing to Inácio to turn back: It was dangerous, he said, to disturb the Tupiniquin at their pleasures.

It had been two weeks since Inácio landed at Porto Seguro, after a pleasant, uneventful voyage from the Bahia. Padre Nóbrega had spent the first seven days with him in the tiny village on the heights above the white sands that fronted the bay, then left for São Vicente with the brigantine. It was with great excitement that Inácio had prepared for this last leg of his journey to Aruanã's malocas, which lay a day's march from the Portuguese settlement at Porto Seguro.

As the malocas came into sight, Cardim began to walk slowly, and Inácio snapped at him to hurry.

"They'll not go away, Padre," Cardim said. The singing of women, the harsh, excited cries of men, all could be plainly heard. "It's best that we approach with the greatest caution."

"But, why? We have the daughter of an elder with us!"

"You can be sure of nothing with these savages, Padre," he said. "As treacherous as serpents."

"They have harmed you, Cardim?"

"No, Padre."

"Move on," Inácio said sternly.

Suddenly, Salpina gave a cry of joy and broke away from them, her heavy buttocks swaying from side to side as she ran toward the malocas. Unauá stayed close to Inácio, who glanced at her quickly, failing to notice her apprehension. "Come!" he cried excitedly, and hastened after Salpina, his hand flying to his wide four-cornered hat.

Salpina had disappeared around the edge of the maloca. Inácio followed, taking great strides with his long legs, one hand clutching his hat, the other his cassock. At first, he saw only a vast gathering of men, women, and children, their naked bodies streaming with crimson and black paint, and adorned with feather diadems. Clouds of red dust hung above circles of men dancing to the sound of rattles in their hands and strings of dry pods attached to their ankles.

As he walked deeper into the crowd, he realized that many were horribly drunk; they reeked from beer and palm wine and from the fumes of tabak. A group of ululating women, old and ugly matrons, their arms wet with red dye, came out to meet him, slapping their bare feet in the dirt, cackling as they danced around.

And then the throng of Tupiniquin before him suddenly broke, revealing the Place of Slaughter.

"O merciful God!" he cried, his eyes widening with horror.

The bloodstained matrons who'd leapt before and behind him, those who had the honor of preparing the grill, had finished with the first of two Cariri felled this day by the slaughter club, Yware-pemme. They had dismembered the prisoner's body and the meat was on the boucan, its flames licking up from where the fat dripped. There were platters of intestines, the victim's head, and other rejected portions piled in readiness near a great earthenware pot, a dark liquid steaming within this cauldron.

Inácio could not immediately distinguish which was worse, the sight of the dead or the living. Small children, their hands and faces stained with blood, played near the fires; warriors, bodies glistening with sweat, waited with wild, famished expressions; young maidens sat naked, totally exposed without thought of shame; seven elders perched on the ground in a neat row, motionless as carrion birds.

The second victim lay face down. A deep wound on his head bore testimony to the manner in which he'd been slain, and a thick stake had been pounded up his anus.

Inácio suddenly was filled with a violent rage. He paced back and forth before the elders, pointing his finger at them accusingly: "The devil has come to this place!" he cried. "The devil is here!"

Two of the seven peered up uncomprehendingly; the others glanced at one another with equal puzzlement. The crowd around the boucan began to stir uneasily at the sight of this attack on the elders.

Seeing their discomfort, Inácio flew toward them, waving his arms wildly. "Go! Go!" he shouted. "Away from this accursed place!" A small boy got in his way, and with one movement Inácio swept him up and carried him to the nearest group of women. "Take this child away!" he demanded. "Take them all beyond this horror!" An alarmed girl grabbed the infant and fled. Other women now began to disperse, but not the grandmothers, who stood glaring at Inácio.

Inácio returned to the elders, and as he did, he noticed how still it had become. Two men were standing near the patriarchs. Both were old, one more advanced in years than the other. At that moment, Salpina dashed past the grill toward the pair of old men.

"O Aruanã, father of mine! Here is Salpina, the daughter of Juriti," she said, running up to the elder of the two.

He was seventy-one years old, his frame shrunken with age, his flesh loose. Still, he radiated the power of the great warrior he had been, with a determined lift of his jaw and an unwavering gaze for this intrusive black robe. The many slashes on his chest and thighs were heavily accented with dark paint; a great cloak of ibis feathers flowed to his ankles.

This daughter, wife of Ticuanga, Cabral's Long Hair, had been gone from the malocas for seventeen years. "It is Salpina," he said simply, looking at her briefly, and then returned his icy glare to the black robe.

"There, Padre, is Aruanã, greatest of all Tupiniquin!"

Inácio did not respond to Salpina. Aruanã and all the elders were looking at him.

He stepped to where the second Cariri lay; he bent down and picked up the body.

A low, angry murmur came from the onlookers, who were spread out in a great circle. Cardim stood nearby, his arquebus held ready to fire.

Two of the elders had risen to speak with the old man standing next to Aruanã. The man had a feminine appearance — a small, flat nose, a face remarkably unlined for his years. He was Pium, "The Gnat," surviving partner of the two homosexual pagés Affonso Ribeiro had known. Through the years of loneliness since his mate's death, he'd grown to be no insignificant annoyance to those who stood in his way.

"Poor, grieving soul," Inácio now said, carrying the corpse of the Cariri warrior. "He must be buried in God's good earth, not left as carrion for the devil!"

"Mother of Mercy!" It was Cardim who cried out. "Padre Inácio, leave the body! You'll have us all killed!"

But Inácio started to walk away, slowly at first.

Aruanã, Pium, and the elders jabbered among themselves in alarm, but no one made a move to stop Inácio. Pium, his thoughts confused by tabak and liquor, did no more than utter the names of a string of forest demons waiting to receive the black-robed thief.

Inácio walked past Cardim without a word. Cardim hesitated momentarily, then backed off slowly, his arquebus directed toward the middle of the group of elders. Inácio was far down the clearing before Cardim swung round and hurried after him.

They buried the Cariri in the forest beyond the malocas, hacking a shallow grave with Cardim's knives. Inácio fell to his knees and began to pray.

Cardim was convinced that they were not alone. He peered into the shadowed breaks between the trees, perceiving nothing but still apprehensive. "We must leave. *Now*, Padre, while there is still time. They are here. *Everywhere*."

"Go? Oh, no, *this* is my mission. It is where I remain." Inácio had risen from the graveside as they spoke, and faced Cardim with a glowing, almost ecstatic expression on his face. "I thank you for guiding me here. Go now, back to your family. I will not leave my Tupiniquin."

"Oh, damn yourself, then! Throw your Christian life to these savages!" Cardim marched away swiftly, not once looking behind him.

He remained with the Cariri for an hour, praying softly, and then he began his return to the malocas. But he stopped in the forest just before he reached the longhouses. The sounds of the awful celebrations were rising again, and he sat down, resting his back against a tree trunk, the dampness of the forest floor slowly penetrating his limbs. It grew dark, and he remained there, until his chin dropped on his chest and he slept.

He awoke before dawn, the forest gray and quiet around him. When he looked up, he saw the girl Unauá sitting close to him. "My child, what are you doing here?"

"I waited with you, Padre," she said simply.

&

The Tupiniquin began to emerge from their longhouses, and were greeted by an astonishing sight: The black robe who'd stolen the Cariri had come back.

He was on his knees at the ashes of the boucan, weeping and chanting in Tupi.

When word of the black robe's return spread, more people tumbled from their hammocks to see this strange Long Hair with the mighty courage to return to the Place of Slaughter, where he had so offended their ancestors.

For more than three hours the black robe kept at his vigil, with neither food nor water. The elders led by Aruanã, came out to observe, and sat in the same position they had assumed at the feast the previous afternoon. Pium, standing alone, watched impassively from the entrance to his hut.

&

Over the next three months, a truce prevailed between Padre Inácio Cavalcanti and the Tupiniquin. They were curious enough to want to continue their observation of the priest who, as the days passed, demonstrated an unwavering friendship toward them; and Inácio, having witnessed the depths of their depravity, had the good sense to bide his time.

As resident priest of a permanent mission, it was Inácio's duty to keep the vice-provincial at the Bahia informed of his progress. This he did in regular letters written in fine Latin in the privacy of his small hut. He would send a Tupiniquin to Porto Seguro with each letter, not knowing when the next ship bound for São Salvador was due to arrive.

"Oh, Padre Nóbrega, their hearts are stone," he lamented in his first letter. "I see that I must first content myself with the smallest pebbles, a handful of which I may take at one time and grind with no effort, until they are as fine and pure as the white sands upon these beaches."

He was referring to the children, the boys who were not yet called to seek feathers of Macaw, and the girls who were too young to work in the fields with their mothers. Inácio made quick progress with these youngsters. A week after his arrival at the malocas, the supplies for his mission were brought up from Porto Seguro, among them a quantity of the best Pernambucan sugar. For the little ones who attended his classes on the ground in front of his hut, there was always a spoonful of sugar, which he poured into their hands. They would squirm and giggle with delight as the grains trickled into their palms, and hurry off to lick up the sweet reward.

But it was not sugar alone that brought him his early converts. In the beginning, he had addressed his young charges in the gravest manner, almost in tears with his eagerness to fill them with the love of Jesus. But they were so easily distracted. And then Inácio had an inspiration: He considered the ways of the native pagé. . . .

One morning, to the delight of his audience, Padre Inácio forsook his solemn approach. As he told the story of David and Goliath, he pretended first to be Goliath, nine feet tall and clad in bronze; then the little shepherd David protecting his father's flocks against the lion and the bear, taking up his crook, five stones, and a catapult. He roared Goliath's challenges and pounded the ground. The little Tupiniquin cheered him and begged to hear more.

Gradually Inácio drew certain youngsters into the plays, giving them short parts to play, and sometimes he'd employ them all in grand, noisy marches around the clearing. Before the end of the third month, Padre Inácio was able to inform Nóbrega: "Sixty-two have been baptized. Dear friend, how I wish you could see the happiness of these little souls brought out of the desert!"

The rest of the village accepted him with a mixture of curiosity and suspicion, but were not unfriendly. After Inácio's return from the forest, Aruanã and the elders had agreed that he could stay at the malocas for an unspecified time. No one had mentioned the slain Cariri or the boucan. As for the pagé and the priest, Pium and Inácio maintained a cautious distance. Each considered the other a malevolent and forceful competitor, and neither was ready yet for a showdown that could result in a loss of face before the elders and the warriors.

Inácio had built a ten-by-twelve-foot mud-and-thatch hut that served as habitation, study, chapel, and infirmary. It was often hot and airless by day, damp and crawling with insects at night. The furnishings were simple: a table and stool he'd made himself, two chests containing his supplies and few personal belongings; one small, unframed canvas of St. Paul, given to him by his father, Felipe, before he'd left Lisbon; a crucifix; and a statue of St. Stephen the martyr. Inácio could not adapt to sleeping in a hammock — his long, angular body hung at the most wretched angles — and he slept instead on a cot of thin branches layered with dry palm fronds.

Later, adjoining the hut, he built a roomy open-sided shelter — his "church" — where he set up a simple altar of mud and stone, always draped with fine cloths when in use, and his "*colégio,*" where his converts gathered.

His meals came from several sources. Often the women of one of the eight longhouses would send him a bowl of manioc or beans. If there'd been a hunt, he would be offered a cut of the meat. And, always, there was Unauá to see that his meals were prepared and that his hut and church were kept clean.

Unauá lived with Salpina in Aruanã's maloca, but there were many days and nights, too, when she was away from her hammock. Her absences had delighted the entire longhouse until someone espied her asleep one night just outside the door of Padre Inácio's hut; they realized then that this black robe's words about a marriage to the Church were true.

For all his loving acceptance of the Jesuit vows of poverty, chastity, and obedience, Inácio was beset by periods of gnawing loneliness, in which he yearned for company different from these simple Tupiniquin. He was often invited to sit with the elders or to eat with the men of one maloca. But he'd come away from these meetings exhausted, for as the men sipped their beer and puffed their tabak, Inácio carefully weighed every word he offered, every song he delivered, for its effect in softening their hearts.

It was different, though, when he was with Unauá. She had accepted Christ, and when he spoke with her, it was to further her knowledge of the mysteries of the faith. But there were also times when she'd want to know about his own, personal life, and she would listen just as attentively to all that he said.

She knew how much he loved the forest and the things that grew there, and sometimes she would go alone beyond the malocas and return with a gift for him: a small bunch of fresh herbs or a pale mauve orchid, which she would secretly leave on the table in his room. When he entered, her gift would be waiting for him, and he would experience a deep contentment in knowing so faithful and loving a child.

✧

Toward the end of June 1552 the small group of settlers at Porto Seguro sent a messenger to invite Padre Inácio to their celebrations for the feast day of St. John the Baptist; their priest was away at the Bahia and they wished Padre Inácio to preside over the day's pastoral observances. This he did, in a small whitewashed church on the hill overlooking the bay — a neat little building on the site where the Franciscans Diogo and Gaspar had established their ill-fated mission. The settlers crowded the Masses he held, and most were eager to make their confessions. There was to be feasting and dancing and a great bonfire and fireworks.

It was an occasion when even the sternest plantation owner looked sympathetically upon his slaves and farm workers and ordered that they, too, celebrate the saint. The Africans were grateful for this rest, and showed thanks by bringing to the feast little dainties they'd made of sugar, cashew nuts, and manioc, and of corn and coconut, sweet combinations of what they remembered from Africa and what they found in the New World. The natives of Santa Cruz were less enthusiastic, puzzled especially by the appearance of their owners, many of whom, taken by the spirit of St. John's asceticism and simplicity, donned their oldest clothes to appear as poorly as their bonded servants.

The settler Cardim was often at Inácio's side.

"Oh, senhores, Daniel himself had no greater challenge in the lions' den!" Cardim said in the presence of several planters, though directing his words at the justice of the peace, Vasco Barbosa, corpulent and rumpled, who, with the dignity of his office in mind, had avoided donning rags but still appeared untidy. "Oh, senhores, it was a miracle!" Cardim continued. "To see how the padre stole the meat those barbarians were ready to devour."

"It is only what God — and our king — demands of us in Santa Cruz," Inácio said. "That we wean these people from their abominable past."

Barbosa, his fingers sticky from one of the slave confections, said, "God be praised, Padre, for the faith and the courage of His servants!" He popped the delicacy into his mouth and continued: "But I see little hope — may He prove me wrong! — little chance for the enlightenment of these savages."

"Come to the malocas, Senhor Barbosa and see the progress made there over these past months. I tell you, senhor, the Tupiniquin are more eager than many of our own people to hear the word of the Lord."

"I've heard of your company of children," Barbosa said. "A delight! There, Padre, you may have an answer. But what of their parents, always a threat to our settlements? Must *we* live in fear of the Tupiniquin, the Tupinambá, the Cariri, for a whole generation?"

"A generation and more, if need be — until we bring these nations into His church."

"Children!" Barbosa said suddenly. "The way I see it, Padre, they are *all* children. They must be brought in from the forest and tamed on the lands of the colonists." He looked for — and received — nods of approval from the group standing with him. "When they're obedient and submissive, like good children," he continued, "then, Padre, raise them as men, fit to be rewarded with Christianity!"

"From what I've seen, Justice of the Peace," Inácio said, using the title for the first time, "our laws themselves do not spare the natives long enough for them to collect that reward."

"We intend them no harm, Padre, but it's difficult to make them understand our simplest demands."

"No harm, Barbosa, except to be whipped to death and blown to pieces at the mouths of our cannon?"

A flush came to Barbosa's face. "We rule in Africa and India, Padre," he said, "because we permit no contempt for our laws and our way of life — or the Holy Cross. Why, then, should the knights of Portugal accept abuse from savages? The natives are ungrateful, cruel, and lazy. They abandon themselves to their vices — this you've witnessed."

"They are *also*," Padre Inácio said sternly, "the children of God."

"You mustn't think too harshly of us, Padre, for being more than a little troubled, especially after trying so honestly to work with them. As da Silva here knows, Padre, what wonderful liars these Tupiniquin make!"

Domingos da Silva was the holder of lands southwest of the bay, in that area once occupied by the malocas of Aruanã and his people. From Setubal, south of Lisbon, famed for its salt pans, da Silva had first visited Porto Seguro twenty years before as a brazilwood logger, later returning to settle permanently in the captaincy. He was short and stocky with small, piggish eyes beneath coarse, bushy eyebrows, an almost toothless grin, and a foul temper matched only by those of his three sons, Marcos's being the worst. Dubbed "The Silent," Marcos had throttled to death and then personally quartered a savage who had tried to incite others to flee the da Silva plantation.

"Yes! The greatest liars!" da Silva agreed with Barbosa. He had four remaining upper teeth, grouped together in front, and a habit of drawing his lip back and exposing them when he spoke. "I have a slave who claims to know the padre from Pernambuco, there in Dom Duarte Coelho's lands." He gave a small, wet laugh.

"I have traveled through the captaincy."

"Most assuredly," da Silva said, "but this one tells a fantastic story of being with the padre. . . ."

"Da Silva, *where* did you get him?"

The planter merely shrugged. "A vagabond," he said. "Starving when my Marcos found him. We fed him; we nursed him with the milk of kindness, Padre, until he was well. And now? Now he wants nothing but to run from our lands."

"I do not think he lies to you."

Da Silva gave him an angry look and then frowned at the justice of the peace. These two were good friends: The law always supported the da Silvas, and was ready to oblige with permits for the detention and enslavement of any pestiferous natives. Such permits had become necessary with the administration of Governor Tomé de Sousa, who was eager to promote orderly dealings with the savages.

"You have an explanation, Padre?" asked the justice of the peace.

"His name?" Inácio asked. "What is his name?"

Da Silva thought for a moment before replying: "Guaraci."

"I thought so."

"You know this savage, then?" da Silva asked.

"Yes, I know him," Inácio said, with restraint. "He is a grandson of the degredado Affonso Ribeiro."

Da Silva laughed, baring his teeth. "And so," he said, chuckling, "and so it is with every little *caboclo* in Porto Seguro!"

Inácio ignored da Silva's use of the word for "copper-colored," which denoted the crossbreed of white and native Brazilian. "I took Guaraci and his sister away from Olinda after Ribeiro died. I promised to return them to these Tupiniquin, from whose malocas their father had come."

"Then it can't be him," the justice of the peace said.

"*It is.* I was a year at the Bahia. Longer. Guaraci could not wait, and set out to walk to Porto Seguro."

Da Silva seemed to find this highly amusing. "Go see this one who calls himself Guaraci now, Padre. He walks nowhere."

Inácio said, "I'll fetch him in the morning."

The other men in the group were very quiet, looking from the priest to the planter, expecting da Silva to react angrily to the Jesuit's words. Instead, da Silva laughed so hard that his sides shook and he had to clasp his belly.

"Padre, it would be most unwise," the settler Cardim cautioned later. "Da Silva respects nothing and no one."

Despite the warning, the next morning Inácio hastened to the da Silva lands, accompanied by three Tupiniquin who had acted as his guides to Porto Seguro. They traveled by canoe for three hours, making slow headway up a river that flowed into the bay. They found a landing Cardim had described to Inácio, and beached the canoe.

Within an hour they were in sight of the da Silva stockade, similar to that of Nicolau Cavalcanti, positioned on the hill that sloped toward the place where the Tupiniquin malocas had stood when Aruanã was a boy.

Inácio was half a mile from the da Silva stronghold when he saw Domingos da Silva and a younger man, later identified as Marcos, riding down the rise toward him, the son keeping just behind the father. They did not rein in their mounts until they were twenty yards from him.

"So! You've come, Padre" — Domingos da Silva glanced at his son — "to fetch the little wanderer."

Marcos da Silva, darker and stockier than his father, reached for a whip hanging from the side of his saddle. Fourteen feet of finely plaited tapir hide, it was the kind used to drive the oxen hauling high-wheeled carts of cane, but Marcos preferred to save it for the backs of men who disobeyed him.

"Let's have no trouble, senhor," Inácio said. "There has been a mistake. Guaraci was walking to reach his people and was lost and starving."

"Yes, Padre, Yes — and here he found rest and shelter," the older da Silva said. "Now, Padre, isn't it right that he pay for this hospitality?"

Inácio fought to stay calm. "I am here — at the Tupiniquin malocas — for the cause of peace between them and our people," he said. "I take His message of love and compassion. How, Senhor da Silva, am I to make the Tupiniquin accept this if they see that we show neither?"

Marcos da Silva had uncoiled the whip as Inácio spoke and was flicking it with small movements.

"The boy Guaraci is my charge," Inácio said firmly. "Give him to me, senhor, or you'll answer to the governor himself."

"The governor?" Domingos da Silva grinned across at his son. "Why would His Excellency de Sousa vex himself with one little native when all Brazil is now his care?"

Inácio suddenly tired of this fruitless exchange, and started to walk off in the direction of the stockade.

Da Silva said in a hard voice, "God may save you from the jaws of the Tupiniquin, Cavalcanti — here, you're on my lands."

Inácio continued walking.

Then Marcos da Silva swore at him, and the whip cracked, snapping up dust in front of Inácio. "Priest! Go back!"

Inácio kept moving forward.

Marcos struck out again. The end of the whip, sharp and thin as a quill, slashed Inácio's right cheek.

Inácio's head jerked back, and his broad hat fell off. The whip had drawn a long, thin line that had begun to bleed. Inácio's eyes blazed; his mouth opened but he said nothing, and after the briefest of pauses, he started to walk again. But his eyes were on the whip.

When Marcos started to raise it again, Inácio stamped on it with his sandaled foot and suddenly grabbed the tapir hide. As he pulled it, Marcos, whose feet were out of the stirrups, lost his balance and tumbled to the ground. He mouthed a string of oaths as he scrambled to his feet. Then he drew a short, curved dagger.

The older da Silva drove his horse forward at his son. "Marcos! Get away!"

The young man was forced to leap aside, but immediately he started to creep back toward Inácio.

"He's a priest!" Domingos da Silva screamed. "Go — before you're eternally damned!" Using a section of the reins as a flail, he struck repeatedly at his son until finally Marcos ran off, dashing past the three Tupiniquin, who had watched the confrontation in absolute silence.

Da Silva turned upon Inácio. "Take your precious Tupiniquin!" he said in a high-pitched, shaking voice. He gave a tight, nervous laugh. "Why should I cry over one young savage when the good Lord provides us so abundantly?"

Inácio glared up at the planter, his right eye twitching above the deep cut on his cheek. "Take me to him," he said.

Guaraci was confined in stocks outside da Silva's slave quarters, lying naked upon his back, his legs pulled apart and thrust through two of six holes in the boards. Two slaves occupied the other openings. When Guaraci was released, he was too weak to get to his feet.

"Oh, Cristovão," Inácio gasped, using his baptismal name, "what have they done to you?" He was aghast at Guaraci's emaciated body and the ridges raised on the flesh of his back and buttocks.

The padre and the Tupiniquin carried him to the canoe they'd paddled upstream. Guaraci tried to say something, but his words caught deep in his throat. He opened his mouth wider and his tongue, Inácio saw, was raw and blistered — from the embers Marcos da Silva had pressed against it to punish Guaraci for his lies.

℘

When Guaraci was able to speak, he was invited to tell his story before the men of the clan.

When the others banged their beer gourds on the ground or signaled their impatience by whistling through their lip holes, Aruanã supported the young man, hissing for silence. "Who is there able to remember, on one night alone," he challenged, "everything witnessed on a journey where the stars change their place in the sky?"

Padre Inácio, seated on the ground near the elders, would also on occasion move to calm those impatient with Guaraci, and the men acknowledging his gestures would be silent for a while.

Inácio's relationship with the clan had changed since his return from Porto Seguro five weeks ago. The Tupiniquin had seen Guaraci and had listened to the reports of the three warriors who had been with the black robe. The elders had approached the priest's hut to get a closer look at the wound that marked his face — a rough, purplish scar that curved down from the side of his right eye almost to the corner of his mouth. They'd been impressed with this evidence of the priest's eagerness for their friendship. "He talks of love for the Tupiniquin and shows it is true," Aruanã said.

Great as Inácio's joy had been at a growing acceptance of him by the elders and men, his annoyance with Pium had been greater. The pagé had been summoning more and more men and women to the hut of the sacred rattles, there to examine their consciences and expel the evils he found possessing them. And he energetically harried into his presence those who appeared too friendly to the priest: a woman lingering too long with her child at the priest's house of chants, or the parents of a boy too eager to don the white robe offered by the father.

This night Pium stood back in the shadows, devoting most of his attention to Padre Inácio. He knew that many of the warriors were pointing to the mark on the priest's face and declaring that he must be the same as this "Jesus" he was always praising, for he had been willing to be whipped and to suffer for the Tupiniquin. To Pium's distress, the warriors also were beginning to show an interest in knowing more of this spirit, Jesus.

Inácio was aware of this, too, and it filled him with hope as he sat at the fires of the Tupiniquin.

Guaraci had managed, if haltingly, to cover the details of his journey from the Bahia, telling how he'd crossed the territory of the Tupinambá and evaded bands of Cariri, only to fall into the hands of the da Silvas.

When he came to the events of his rescue, his face grew animated as he described how he had been taken out of the stocks and carried to the canoe. Then the young man cried, "*He* saved me!"

Many warriors turned their heads toward Padre Inácio, and praises were shouted for him.

"He saved me!" Guaraci said again. "I prayed and prayed to Him, the Lord, and God sent Padre Inácio. When this tongue could not move, and I saw those men would kill me, perhaps, I said, if I ask the God whose Son died for me, He would hear me. 'Help me, free me!' I begged Him." Guaraci fell silent, and then stepped near to where Inácio sat. "And He did. Without the summons of smoke or the rattles but from within Guaraci, He heard. He sent Padre Inácio."

One ancient Tupiniquin was confused: "This black robe," he asked, raising a hand toward Inácio, "is Son of God?"

"No! No!" Inácio cried, pushing himself up to stand next to Guaraci. "No, I am but one of His servants on earth, an ordinary man seeking to share what I know of His love for all men." He placed a hand on Guaraci's shoulder. "This son of a Tupiniquin warrior has found Him and the strength of His power."

Pium gave a long, chilling cackle. "The black robe boasts of a power greater than any we know, and claims that this boy has been given this strength. Why is it that one who has not honored Voice of the Spirits with feathers of Macaw, who has fought no battles and brought no enemy to the clearing — why does such a creature have this power?" Inácio was about to interrupt, but Pium raced on: "How can it be so when the noblest ancestors of the Tupiniquin were not offered what this boy claims to have?"

Inácio addressed the question: "Know God, accept Him, and He may also hear your appeal for the ancestors. They are gone from the clearing, but their spirit lives. If you open your hearts to the Lord, He will see them, too."

"In Land of the Grandfather," Pium said, "our bravest warriors find all the honor and glory promised."

"Yes! Yes, Pium. The ancestors are there — all their souls together."

Pium stood with a look of satisfaction on his face.

"But, beyond Land of the Grandfather is a greater paradise," Inácio went on enthusiastically, "where God waits to welcome them."

"There is *nothing* beyond Land of the Grandfather," the pagé declared.

"No, Pium, there is more." He could see, from many expressions around him, that he had planted a powerful idea — a seed of doubt that could grow, for whom among them would risk denying the forefathers a passage toward greater glory? "You have seen the things brought by the Portuguese, the great canoes and powerful weapons, the marvelous tools of iron. See, too, my friends, the God we know, the Great Spirit of love and peace among men."

Pium shifted agitatedly before the elders, hopping from one spot to another and waving his tiny hands in the air. "Don't be deceived by the utterances of a Long Hair, a people who slash open the backs and burn the tongues of others."

Guaraci called out, "Padre Inácio is not the same!"

"You know nothing, boy." Pium turned back toward the elders and glared at them. "If you listen to his lies, the long rest of our ancestors will be broken. O, Tupiniquin, hear Pium: Follow this black robe's chants and Voice of the Spirits will not hear you!" Abruptly he turned on his heel and walked off, continuing to shout out dire predictions.

Before Inácio could say anything, Aruanã spoke: "Pium is right. My father, Pojucan, denied the ancestors' ways and he was killed."

"Tupiniquin, deny God who rules all men and you will surely be taken by the master of death," Inácio said, in a suddenly aggressive voice. "But then, I see you already know this great slayer of souls, one we call the devil. He is Jurupari! O my friends, Jurupari waits for every man, woman, and child who fails to receive the Holy Spirit. This we Portuguese have always known — that God, in His mercy, shows us how we may be saved from the devil, Jurupari. O Tupiniquin, let me lead you to this great salvation!"

Then, intentionally, he left as dramatically as had the pagé. "Come," he called to Guaraci, "there is work to be done!" And he prayed aloud: "O Jesus Christ, my Lord, be with us. Guide us against the legions of Jurupari."

The elders were thrown into confusion. The black robe not only accepted Jurupari, forest demon; he showed no fear of him. Nor did he quarrel with Tupiniquin belief in Land of the Grandfather. But he firmly rejected the "power" of the sacred rattles. As they watched the black robe leave, Aruanã said aloud, "O Voice of the Spirits protect him. Save him, for he is our friend."

When the children gathered for their lessons the next day, it was Unauá and Guaraci who led them in their singing and prayers, not Padre Inácio. "My dear friends," he'd told the two of them early that morning, "I must stay in my hut. I do battle with Jurupari."

Again the elders put their heads together, and Pium sat with them, fueling their fears about the consequences of offending Jurupari.

All that day and into the next, Padre Inácio remained in his hut. The elders finally grew so concerned about the dangers of provoking the demon Jurupari that they crossed the clearing to the hut, wearing their strongest charms, their bodies black and crimson with dye, and carrying their clubs.

Unauá and Guaraci sat on the ground just beyond the entrance, and greeted the elders respectfully, if apprehensively.

Aruanã walked ahead. He pulled back the mat that hung at the doorway and gave a small cry. "*Who did this?*"

Guaraci was on his feet and beside the elder immediately. "Nobody. It is his desire."

"His desire?" Aruanã said. "He welcomes this?"

Inácio lay on the floor of the small hut, his legs and arms bound tightly with cords, his body twisted in the most grotesque position. The ground was strewn with small thorned branches. He wore a simple loincloth and his exposed flesh was torn and bloody.

He looked up at Aruanã, and spoke in a dry, weak voice: "I seek to understand the suffering of God's son, Jesus, who fought man's greatest battle against evil. I beseech the dear Lord for His mercy and forgiveness — for the skulls broken, the flesh corrupted. I struggle against Jurupari, who vomits with pleasure at these evils."

Aruanã began to back away. "Please, Father, stop this," he begged, "this terrible . . ." He did not know what to call it.

"Never," Inácio said. "If my poor penance can move one heart —"

But Aruanã did not hear him, for he'd already fled.

The clearing was soon in tumult at the news of what had befallen Padre Inácio. Rattles sounded from within Pium's hut, but no one dared go near him. And then, when the Tupiniquin were approaching a state of panic, Padre Inácio staggered into daylight. Guaraci and some of the converts now carried a Cross of heavy timbers to Inácio and helped him lift it to his shoulders. He first collapsed beneath its weight; then slowly, he forced himself up until he managed to support the burden.

As Inácio began to drag the Cross along the clearing, Unauá came from the direction of a maloca, leading the children and the few older converts, all singing the hymns Inácio had taught them. They formed a procession behind him as he labored forward.

The Tupiniquin stood back, silent and awed, as the procession wound its way through the clearing, and noticed that many of their children were weeping. Again and again the weak, bleeding black robe stumbled and had to be helped to his feet by Guaraci, but the Tupiniquin saw that beyond his pain and exhaustion, there was a radiance — the same look as with a warrior of warriors when the enemy lay dead at his feet.

⌘

Seven months after his great procession of penance, Inácio wrote a report on his labors through the year he had been at the malocas to his superior at the Bahia in March 1553:

Oh, Padre Nóbrega, I feel so weak and helpless when I see the daily miracles our Lord works among these Tupiniquin. After I offered my penance, they pressed me continuously with questions: "What does it matter to a dead man whether you eat him or not?" "You see us naked as Adam, when the Lord sent him out of Paradise — what, Padre, was our sin?" "Why do we need God's Word when our ancestors lived well without it?" These people have been filled with so many lies and superstitions that they have the greatest difficulty accepting the simplest truth.

The senior elder, Aruanã, a proud savage of even disposition, will sit for hours hearing about Jesus, Mother Mary, and the wondrous powers of God, but when he begins to discuss them, it is with such confusion and misunderstanding that I beg the Lord to clear this man's mind.

Apart from the elders, so rooted in evil, more come each day to beg for the cleansing water of baptism, truly fearing the sorrows of damnation, which I am assiduously keeping before their minds.

Some I have baptized and married on the same day, for they are loving and faithful toward each other, and most have only one wife. Again, it is my intractable friends, the elders, who take up to four women. They will not abandon this practice, nor can I encourage them to forsake these great straw halls, where all are thrown together, for separate little dwellings where individual families may live in privacy.

But the children who remain Christ's fierce little angels wholly compensate for the constant anguish I feel at my failure in uprooting such practices. Some have grown so worshipful that they will come to me with sorrowful tales of the iniquities and transgressions of their parents. "Please, Padre, ask Jesus to forgive them," they plead, so fearful are they of the tyranny of the devil. And it was the children who did most to discredit their great sorcerer, Pium.

Pium, with his retinue of demons and dark spirits, I told the converts, was nothing but a superstitious old man who had taught their fathers to believe in his diabolical arts and lies, invocations against our Lord's goodness and truth. When I felt the moment right, I encouraged my little army to crusade against this master of evil.

Pium was crossing the clearing when six small boys danced up to him, telling him that as children of the Lord Jesus they rightly feared their fathers, who were great warriors and hunters, and their grandfathers, if those still lived, but, since Pium neither warred nor hunted, what did they have to fear from him? Following him all the way to his hut — dogging his heels, noisy little hounds snapping at the tail of Lucifer — they kept up a steady chorus: "Tell us! Tell us, Pium, what we must fear from you. We fear Jurupari, but Jesus gave His life to save us from him! Tell us, Pium — will you hurt and suffer for us? Tell us, Pium, that you are an old man and nothing more!"

And, the Lord be praised, the pagé cried that this he was — a tired old man, who wanted to be left alone.

He is still here, at his hut, and he is approached by the older ones and the grandmothers, but the Voices with which he terrified the clan are silent, his pagan festivals neglected — all thanks to the Redeemer, who leads us to the light in this vast forest of souls!

ↀↄ

Padre Nóbrega had wanted to send him an assistant, but such were the demands upon the small group of Jesuits in Santa Cruz that this had not been possible, and Inácio labored on alone with the Tupiniquin. The report to Nóbrega had marked the high point of Inácio's mission to the Tupiniquin. Five months later a ship carrying Nóbrega's pleased response to his fellow missioner's progress reached Porto Seguro and a messenger brought the dispatch. But whatever joy Inácio might have had in his superior's satisfaction was crushed by other news in the correspondence.

Tomé de Sousa, great supporter of the Company of Jesus, exhausted by his exertions in this vast land, had begged King João to be relieved of his governorship. He had been replaced by Dom Duarte da Costa, whom Nóbrega cautiously described as a man of honor and determination, who had served the king in his chambers — a hint at the fact that da Costa had had no experience in civil or military matters. And with Dom da Costa's fleet had come the first bishop of Brazil, Pedro Fernandes Sardinha, former vicar-general of India, a man who had just celebrated his sixtieth birthday at the Bahia. Nóbrega wrote: "Of fixed ideas and strong will, Bishop Sardinha desires to raise all the splendors of a great See in this colony. He expresses some pleasure with our work and offers prayers for our converts, but he shows the deepest concern for the souls of those from Europe."

Inácio found these guarded remarks of his friend disturbing; but another item in Nóbrega's letter brought him the most profound sadness. Francis Xavier had died the previous December, on an island in the Bay of Canton, where he'd been readying himself for a great march into China.

He was sitting at the table in his hut, his head in his hands, his eyes closed, and he did not immediately sense her presence.

Then he looked up and saw Unauá framed in the doorway, the light from beyond enhancing the rich chestnut color of her hair. Her cheeks were shadowed; there was a softness in her hazel eyes and in her round, open face. But there was also the faintest hint of excitement in her presence, revealed in a slight parting of her lips and in the nervous manner in which she placed an index finger on her chin.

"The saddest news from Padre Nóbrega," he said. "He writes that one of our most beloved Apostles, Francis Xavier, has died."

"He will be with Jesus."

"Oh, yes, my child," he said. He still called her a child, even though she was now almost twenty years old.

"Then, there should be great joy."

"Yes, but we will miss his wonderful example — especially those of us who do not have his mighty courage."

"*You* have courage."

"I am a weak man, so unworthy." He turned his head away from her, and the light fell upon his cheek, illuminating the long scar.

"I cannot bear to see you so sad," she said. "You have given my brother and me such precious gifts," she said, and moved to the side of the table. "Oh, Padre Inácio, please do not be so sad." She reached a hand toward him.

He looked at her then, and saw the tears in her eyes. "I thank our Lord every day for your support. Child, you are a blessing in this strange place."

"Padre Inácio, I have such love for Jesus and the Holy Father and Mother." In the quietest voice, she added: "There is the same for you."

He dared say her name. "Oh, Unauá."

"Padre Inácio, you are such a good man. How can it be wrong for you to take Unauá?"

He looked at her and saw all the longing and affection in her.

"Dear, sweet child, I have made a choice that I must live by."

"I know," she said quickly. "You wear the robe of the church."

"I gave my vow to serve Him alone, with soul and body."

Inácio had never been with a woman. There had been daughters of family friends, and one he'd loved and remembered with affection. But when he'd sworn his vow of chastity, he'd been a virgin. So filled had he been with his mission that he'd seldom had to do more than pray for constant strength against all temptations of the flesh. Now this lovely girl was offering him a most precious gift, and he felt a thrill at the tremendous strength and the grace God gave him to resist the temptation.

Unauá withdrew her hand from his. "I understand," she said quietly. She moved to the doorway, and looked back at him. "But I am sorry," she said, and hastened away.

The next day, when Padre Inácio returned to his shabby hut from classes with the children, there was a single mauve orchid on the table, a perfect bloom taken from the heart of the forest.

❧

Padre Inácio remembered that orchid two months later, in October 1553, when he was far away from the malocas, in the forest, where he had gone to perform the Spiritual Exercises devised by the Jesuit Father-General Ignatius Loyola for the self-examination and grace of his followers. Guaraci and two converts accompanied him, but, at his request, they kept to themselves and did not disturb his solitude. The place where they rested was four days' journey from the malocas, and to reach it, they had passed the villages of clans who greeted them with friendship, for the reputation of the Long Hair who bled for the Tupiniquin had spread.

Inácio had purposely come this way, almost within reach of Ilheus, the captaincy north of Porto Seguro, to explore the extent of his mission. He planned to appeal to Nóbrega again for assistance, but until someone came, he hoped to be able to travel from clan to clan, sharing his ministry with them. Just how demanding this would be was shown in the number of villages encountered along their route: nine

Tupiniquin settlements with sixty- four malocas, more than three thousand souls by Inácio's estimate. Had they chosen another direction, his escorts said, they might have found the same, up to the forests held by the enemy Tupinambá.

After passing the ninth group of malocas, Inácio had begun to look for a suitable site for contemplation. They were in hilly country, the forest less humid than at the coast, the vegetation thinning out in places. Still, there was a wild luxuriance, especially along the rivers that scored the land. They had crossed a small stream and were progressing along the side of a hill when, higher up, Inácio discerned a burst of mauve. He halted his escort and walked up to admire the orchids; they were clustered along the branches of a tree that in itself took Inácio's attention, for it was no ordinary denizen of the forest.

All day Inácio would stay on the hill, leaving the others before dawn and usually not returning until dark. He meditated upon the heinousness of sin, upon death, judgment. In the last days of his solitude, he walked around that orchid-bedecked tree, conversing in a whisper with Jesus, the Blessed Virgin, the Saints, sharing all the gladness of Resurrection. He felt refreshed and renewed, with a deepened consciousness of his mission and enormous spirit to pursue it.

On the march back to the malocas, they spent the last night of their journey with a clan whose village was the first beyond the Tupiniquin settlement near Porto Seguro. The elders received Padre Inácio with courtesy; they had a temporary shelter built for him to occupy that night. The women who erected it in the clearing joked about its being similar in detail to the sanctuary given a prisoner for his last sleep before meeting Yware-pemme.

Despite their hospitality, Inácio sensed an aloofness among his hosts. The elders showed little interest in his journey, and moved off by themselves as soon as they judged it proper. He sought out Guaraci, but the young man could offer no explanation. And then, in the morning, when they were ready to leave, they discovered that the two Tupiniquin converts were gone.

"What have you done with them?" Padre Inácio asked.

"Nothing, Father," an elder said. "They left by themselves."

"But we travel together."

The elder looked unconcerned. "Perhaps they move faster," he suggested.

"Come," Inácio said to Guaraci, who stood next to him, "we will go after them." He thanked the clan's leaders. "I promise to return soon," he said. "I wish nothing more, friends, than to share the great joy being discovered by the Tupiniquin at the maloca of Aruanã and the other longhouses. Every day more people come to know Jesus and His love."

೧೨

At first baffled over the disappearance of the warriors, Inácio decided that the Tupiniquin, who'd been away from their wives and families for a month, had simply been impatient to get back to them. The two were among his staunchest converts, accepting baptism and marriage, too.

As they marched through the woods, Inácio would occasionally burst into a hymn, and if Guaraci knew the words, he'd join in, sharing a delight at being so close to home. The young man contrasted this happy pilgrimage with the terrors of his own journey from the Bahia to Porto Seguro: The God he had found was indeed a mighty power.

They were moving through a part of the forest where the canopy was thin, when Inácio abruptly stopped singing and called to Guaraci to halt.

"What is it?"

"I don't know," Inácio said. He glanced deep into a grove of tall palms. "Something . . ."

Guaraci followed his gaze. "I see nothing."

"Wait." Inácio walked a few paces off the trail, continuing to search between the palms. It was odd for so many trees of a similar species to be grouped together. He moved his head slowly, scanning the palm grove from one end to the other. Suddenly, he gave a cry. "There!"

Guaraci had dropped a bundle of supplies and was holding his bow ready.

"A woman," Inácio said. "A little old woman hopping between those palms." He squinted against the sunlight. "No! Two women," he announced. "Poor souls — have they lost their way?"

One old woman, seen clearly now by both Inácio and Guaraci as she dashed from palm to palm, began to wail loudly, her lament immediately taken up by the second woman, and then by a third, whose cry changed to a maniacal shrieking, a string of unintelligible howlings. The closer the men approached, the farther back the trio sped.

"Stay!" Inácio shouted. "We'll not harm you!" He was running, out of breath. "What's wrong?" he gasped. "Why do they flee?"

"Cariri?" Guaraci said.

Inácio did not answer but kept pursuing the women. Their cries suddenly ceased.

"Cariri," Guaraci said again, "leading us into a trap?"

Inácio continued forward but at a slower pace.

"Please, Padre, go no farther," Guaraci appealed. "If these are Tupiniquin from our malocas, why would they run from Padre Inácio, whom they know to be their friend?"

Inácio laughed. "Guaraci, since when are the mothers, who feast at the devil's banquet, the friends of Padre Inácio?"

"But why would they flee?"

Inácio stood for some minutes, staring into the forest ahead. If they advanced, they might still flush the old women out of their hiding place. But perhaps Guaraci was correct, and this was a trap to lure them into a band of murderous Cariri. "Let us go," he said.

⋘

Two hours later, at the malocas, Padre Inácio discovered that the old mothers had not gone to the palm grove to seek the devil but to escape the hounds of hell.

Inácio was standing in the clearing of Aruanā's village, upon the spot where the Tupiniquin had once slaughtered their prisoners. He clasped the iron crucifix at the end of his rosary with such desperation that his knuckles were white.

The double stockade had been torn down at several places and all eight malocas had been destroyed by fire. Not a building had been spared. The clearing was strewn with smashed pots, rattles, scattered rainbows of feathers, discarded bows and clubs, and piles of food, which were now being raided by vultures.

Inácio began to walk leadenly toward the malocas. Guaraci kept near him, and as Inácio entered the heart of this desolation, the youth heard him begin to moan quietly, before he cried out "Guaraci! Where are they? *Where are all our dear souls?*"

Without replying, Guaraci cautiously stepped into the ruin of the first maloca they reached, climbing between the fallen beams, kicking up clouds of ashy dust as he trod where once he, Salpina, and Unaúa had hung their hammocks.

"Unaúa . . . the children . . . the Lord's children . . . where?" Inácio asked again, as in a daze.

They continued walking from the ruins of one maloca to the next, until they'd completed a circuit of the clearing. They stopped at the devastated hut of the sacred rattles, which reeked pungently of Pium's herbs and brews. Bones, too, both human and animal, were scattered among the ashes.

Beside his ruined chapel and school, Inácio wept convulsively.

A wild, frantic energy seized him then; he hurled himself into the ruin, tearing at gray fronds of palm, and forcing a passage to the altar. The Cross, blessed by Nóbrega himself, had been thrown to the ground, torn from the top of its humble base. He grabbed it out of the cinders and tenderly pressed his wet cheek against it.

Stumbling out of the ruin, he screamed across the clearing to Guaraci: "Who has done this dreadful thing? The Cariri, beasts of Satan?"

"Not the Cariri."

"*Who*, then?"

"*They* did it, Padre," Guaraci said, pointing to something on the ground not far from the ruined chapel. "Long Hairs who carry that."

Still holding the altar Cross, Inácio moved across to the object and picked it up: an iron shackle. "Christians! Children of God!" Inácio wept aloud. "They cannot be taken. Unaúa . . . the others . . . No! No! They cannot take His little ones! O God, hear me!"

Then he was quiet for a long time, standing there with the Cross in one hand, the shackle in the other, his eyes sweeping over every detail of the village. And he realized that there was nothing for him to do here, amid the scavenger birds and debris of a proud Tupiniquin community.

⁓

Driven by great sorrow and anger, Padre Inácio plunged back into the forest with Guaraci, and by early morning, his eyes bloodshot, his gaunt frame trembling with fatigue, he stood before the justice of the peace of Porto Seguro, Vasco Barbosa, and flung on the table before him the iron shackle found at the malocas.

"There, Barbosa, is all the evidence you need of a ghastly crime against the Tupiniquin. The malocas are destroyed, the people. God's own little house is ruined, defiled. Nothing remains, Barbosa — nothing!"

Barbosa leaned forward, his great belly pressed against the side of the table, his eyes on a cut the shackle had gouged in the wood.

"Padre Inácio, I know —"

"You know? You *knew* of this outrage?"

"After it was done," Barbosa said. With a fingernail, he investigated the scratch on the table. "Slavers, Padre — they came ashore south of here and attacked and carried off the Tupiniquin two weeks ago."

"Why here?" Inácio fairly shouted. "*Here*, where so many were coming to accept our Lord?"

"They came from the south," Barbosa repeated. "Two ships, it is believed, with close to a hundred men, well armed, well prepared. It happens all the time, Padre — you know this, all along the coast — but in this case it was at the invitation of Marcos da Silva that the slavers raided the malocas. They took the Tupiniquin before dawn, when they were still in their hammocks, asleep. Da Silva left Porto Seguro with the slavers."

"Every soul swept away," Inácio murmured, more to himself. "The smallest children among them."

"No, not all."

Inácio started. "There are survivors?"

"A hundred slavers, Padre, cannot herd seven times their number," he said, as if he was discussing the theft of cattle.

Inácio leaned across the table. "Where, Barbosa — where?"

Barbosa drew back. "The forest," he replied. "You'd go after them? You'd search for them?"

"It is my mission."

"I beg you to leave this ruin, Padre. Go back to the Bahia, to Manoel da Nóbrega. There's nothing here but suffering and failure." He rose from his chair and moved around the table to Inácio's side. "My failure."

"I do not understand."

The justice of the peace now looked worried, his big, round face miserable. "I only did what I believed to be just, Padre."

"What are you trying to tell me?"

"Your Christians — those who fled into the forest. A group caught four of the slavers and brought them to me. 'These attacked our malocas,' they said to me. 'Punish them, Portuguese!'

"Dear Lord, I did what I thought was just, Padre. The men they'd caught were savages, like themselves, not Tupiniquin but some other tribe consorting with the raiders."

"What did you do?" Inácio asked sharply.

"I asked these Tupiniquin if they were Christians, and they said they'd been taught by Padre Inácio. 'There is the law of the king with the Portuguese.' Oh, such obedient subjects, coming out of the forest to me. I was dealing with a matter between savages, as I saw it. I told them to punish their captives themselves."

"You *gave* them the captives?" Inácio was aghast.

Barbosa's big chest heaved. "We had a report about the punishment," he said.

"Senhor, tell it to me."

"Yes, yes. There, in the forest, your converts met others hiding in the trees. Together they crushed the skulls and roasted the flesh."

﷯

Inácio returned to the forest with Guaraci to search for the survivors of his mission. They traveled back to the ruins of the malocas and on to the palm grove where they had seen the old women; then to the village where the two Tupiniquin warriors had left them. They remained in that village for five days; it became obvious that the clan knew of the slavers' attack but were either unwilling or unable to offer more than a suggestion that the survivors had gone "toward the lands where the sun sleeps."

Inácio realized there was nothing left but to return to Porto Seguro — in such a way, however, that would carry them to the west. Their progress became slower, Inácio growing more fatigued each day. Occasionally Guaraci had to take the padre by the hand and lead him on, for he seemed almost to be blind.

Inácio's condition frightened the young man. Often the priest was delirious. He spoke of whips and shackles; he raved against every kind of sin, and then fell to repeating the Commandments, over and over, in a frenzied voice. Sometimes he would stand very still and silent, staring with a wild, fixed gaze into the darkness between the trees, and this Guaraci would find most disturbing, for there was nothing to see.

Then, one morning, Guaraci could not wake Inácio, and for that day and the next he sat with him. Inácio lay drenched with sweat and shivering; he slept for hours, until the tremors that shook his body began to subside. On the third morning, Guaraci was roused from his own sleep by Inácio's voice: "Thank you, Lord. Thank you."

Guaraci took him some water.

"The fever has left me. It is not time, Guaraci," Inácio said weakly as he took the gourd.

At that precise moment the Tupiniquin came out of the trees, about twenty of them, with clubs and bows, their bodies streaked with urucu and genipapo. Inácio tried to rise but was too weak.

Guaraci recognized several of the men. "Oh, my brothers, we have sought you through many sunrises."

The warriors did not respond; they stood in a half-circle, most of them with sullen expressions. One who'd been in the rear of the group pressed to the front and went to stand near Inácio, holding his club in his right hand, resting its head against his left palm.

"João," Inácio called him. "João."

The man, a convert Padre Inácio had baptized, said nothing.

Guaraci stepped closer to the warriors. "You see me — Guaraci, brother of Unauá; why do you not speak?"

Still no one answered.

Guaraci glanced back at Inácio, and the convert standing above him. "Padre — *you* speak to them."

"Oh, my Tupiniquin, I have come back," Inácio said. "I will share this terrible time with you. Help me, Guaraci!" he cried out, and the young man went to him. Inácio stood with his arm around Guaraci's shoulder. "Oh, friends, Tupiniquin, I feel your sorrow. I want to help you."

The half-circle of warriors opened up to make a passage for the elder Aruanã, stooping slightly, his tooth necklace swinging free of his chest. "Let him stand alone," he said to Guaraci, who obeyed his command.

Inácio tottered for a moment, but he remained on his feet.

"These men ask that the black robe's skull be broken," Aruanã said.

"So be it!" Inácio responded vehemently.

"You are not afraid?"

"No, Aruanã. I die happily for our Lord."

The warriors uttered cries of pleasure in praise of the prisoner who mocked his enemies.

"No!" It was Guaraci. "He is not the enemy. This is Padre Inácio, who has always loved you."

"Yes, Guaraci, he loves us, as his Jesus loves us," Aruanã said. Looking up at Inácio, he said, "We will not kill him."

The warriors had not ceased their acclamation of Inácio's willingness to die; now they began to mutter against Aruanã's decision.

He silenced them, very calmly. "You must live, Padre Inácio, for that is what Pium advises. 'Let him live,' says Pium, 'and he'll not see Land of the Grandfather but will fight Jurupari until his last breath.' "

"Merciful God," Inácio moaned. "They understand! Take me back, Aruanã — to your people. Please take me back."

"No, Padre. There is no wish to anger Voice of the Spirits as we did in our clearing. Pium warned us against your Jesus and he was right." Aruanã looked at him sadly. "Even this boy's sister, Unauá, your Jesus did not save. The Long Hair who cut your face took her."

Inácio collapsed then, crumpling to the ground.

Aruanã bent toward him. "Where is the *power?*" he asked.

Inácio could not speak.

The old warrior stepped back. "Take him to his people," he ordered Guaraci.

Guaraci looked from Inácio to Aruanã. "My father, I cannot do this. My place is here — with the Tupiniquin."

"Guaraci?" Inácio called out, just above a whisper.

Aruanã studied the boy thoughtfully. "Escort him to Porto Seguro," he said. "Then return — to your people."

Guaraci showed Aruanã an expression of enormous gratitude. "I will, my father," he said fervently.

✧

Guaraci accompanied the four warriors who carried Inácio back to the coast. There was a ship in the bay, bound for the north.

The padre made repeated requests to Guaraci to return with him to the Bahia. And always Guaraci refused, telling him he could not leave his family, the Tupiniquin.

"But you are of the family of Jesus," Padre Inácio reminded him.

"No. I am Tupiniquin," he said.

IX

June 1559 – September 1583

"*B*ehold! He comes! The Protector! Guardian of our lives and safety — he comes!"

"Give thanks to the Lord!"

"Praise be Jesus Christ!"

A throng of white-robed children — Tupinambá and Caeté — lined the processional route along which the governor-general of Brazil, Dom Mem de Sá, was entering the mission village of St. Peter and St. Paul, six miles beyond São Salvador. It was June 29, 1559, the feast day of the two Saints.

Dom Mem de Sá, one of Portugal's most respected judges, had been chosen governor-general by King João III to replace the ineffectual Dom Duarte da Costa, Tomé de Sousa's successor. Dom Duarte da Costa's tenure had been marked by conflict between the governor and the church over differing views on how the natives could be pacified and the governor's indulgent attitude toward the lax morals of many colonists.

Governor Mem de Sá clearly enjoyed the full approval of the Jesuit missioners and their charges: As the procession entered the aldeia, some children held palm fronds to form an archway above His Excellency and his party; others tossed handfuls of petals at Mem de Sá. The governor acknowledged this homage by nodding his head gravely, with something approaching a smile on his severe face.

Medium in height, slightly plump and stiff-limbed, Mem de Sá was not given to great displays of emotion. Months before, when he learned that the savages had slaughtered his son, Fernão, twenty years old, he'd reacted by withdrawing to his quarters to pray for the child he'd personally ordered into battle. At the time he was named governor in 1556, he was already fifty-nine years old, a widower, a member of the king's council, and chief justice of the court of appeals. João III had given him dictatorial powers and made him answerable to no one but his king. But then João III had died before the new governor left to take up his post, and was succeeded by Dom Sebastião, then only an infant of two. The child's grandmother, however, the regent Catarina, had upheld João's decision.

Even before landing at the Bahia, Mem de Sá had been shown a portent of how demanding his association with Terra do Brasil would be. His fleet was becalmed off the Guinea coast, where forty-two of the 336 aboard died of heat and starvation, and it took an incredible eight months to reach São Salvador. When at last he arrived, three days after Christmas 1557, he found Brazil everything he'd been led to expect: hot, vice-ridden, and offering every possible offense to a great lawgiver.

Upon taking office, Mem de Sá had immediately gone into retreat to perform the Spiritual Exercises of Ignatius Loyola. Through those eight days of preparation, he had sought the opinions of Manoel da Nóbrega and his fellow Jesuits on every aspect of life in Brazil, and there'd been little to please him in what they had to report.

Now, eighteen months later, he could begin to see progress, and it was with special pleasure that he had come to visit his Jesuit friends at this aldeia, which the fathers had planned in every detail with his support and encouragement. Four smaller missions had been amalgamated here, bringing together some eight hundred natives of all ages. At the head of this enterprise, Nóbrega had placed Padre Inácio Cavalcanti, whom Mem de Sá knew to have suffered a terrible defeat with his first attempt to convert the savages at Porto Seguro. Padre Inácio had repeatedly asked the governor to prosecute a slaver most responsible for the destruction of the Tupiniquin village, Marcos da Silva, but da Silva had fled the captaincies, west beyond the Tordesilhas Line to the provinces of the vast Spanish viceroyalty of Peru.

Behind the lines of children stood their parents, and they were a joy to the fathers: Not one was naked, not one adorned with ornaments of superstition, not one streaked with dyes.

Of all present, Padre Inácio Cavalcanti was perhaps most deeply moved by the events of this day. He stood at the doorway to the church. Near him were Padre Nóbrega and five other Jesuits, watching quietly as the governor's party progressed toward them. The children were to be baptized this morning, and the governor was to be a godfather — protector of their faith.

Much had been achieved here with the inspiration of Padre Nóbrega and the force of Governor de Sá: this fine church at the top of the plaza; dormitories for boys and girls; a colégio, where the children were instructed; and rows of neat houses built around a rectangle, each corner of which was marked by a Cross — to keep those brought down from the forest ever mindful of His presence in this aldeia.

Inácio looked beyond the cluster of white-robed children and upward, to where a flock of storks was parading against the open sky above the mission fields. Peripherally, he saw Padre Nóbrega looking at him.

When Padre Nóbrega, Provincial of all Santa Cruz, first learned of Inácio's failure with the Tupiniquin, he had wept with his friend and then insisted upon washing his feet, as a gesture of tender care. Inácio, following his return from Porto Seguro, had stayed two years at the colégio in São Salvador, performing whatever duty was asked of him; then he'd been sent to one of the four missions now joined here at the aldeia of St. Peter and St. Paul. It was difficult now for Inácio to recall the years of Dom Duarte da Costa — dark, dangerous years in which all had so nearly been lost. Da Costa, aloof, unmoved by the holy call to lead the natives to Christ, and ever ready to listen to those crying for more slaves. The wealthiest planters maintained private armies ready to march into the backlands in search of rebellious natives. If along the way they stumbled upon innocent malocas and enslaved their inhabitants, who was there to raise a cry? The Jesuit fathers would protest, but they were few and hard pressed to protect their own settlements against interference from these planters' militia and roving bands of pagans.

Dom da Costa felt a strong antipathy toward priests in his territory, as a result of his hatred of Bishop Pedro Fernandes Sardinha, first prelate of Brazil.

Bishop Sardinha had been grieved by the transgressions rampant among the colonists, and nothing vexed him so much as their sexual depravity. The chief offenders in his eyes were Dom Alvaro da Costa and a following of young men who, when not slaughtering and subjugating the natives, spent their nights whoring and drinking and gambling.

"A libertine!" Bishop Sardinha had stormed from the pulpit. "Dom Alvaro da Costa, the son of our governor, outranks all in this colony with his lewdness and licentiousness."

Dom da Costa had reacted to this slander against his son by drumming up charges of sedition against colonists close to the bishop. The prelate threatened the da Costas with excommunication. Finally, King João himself had been forced to intervene: "Dear Bishop, come home," he said. "We must discuss these problems."

Bishop Sardinha had sailed for Lisbon, vowing to rid Brazil of Dom da Costa and his libertines. Between the Bahia and Pernambuco, the ship was wrecked, but the bishop and one hundred of the passengers and crew managed to reach the shore, where the Caeté were waiting. The prelate's fellow survivors begged the savages not to eat this great man of God, but that had only increased the appetite of the Caeté; they slew all but three of the shipwrecked, who escaped to report that the first bishop of Brazil had been devoured by the pagans.

Dom Duarte da Costa was remorseful. He decreed that the Caeté be seized and enslaved for life. The planters' militia raged up the coast, wiping out village after village and driving the Caeté to the plantations and slave markets. And converts from this tribe were removed from the Jesuits' care.

What darkness had come to Santa Cruz, Inácio thought, remembering those days. Anarchy reigned among the colonists and natives around the Bahia and far beyond. And without fear of eviction, heretics had flocked to these shores: Frenchmen, who had audaciously returned to Santa Cruz not as squatters stealing brazilwood but as settlers. A colony that existed to this day had been planted upon an island in Guanabara Bay. A strong force of heretics manned the fortifications of this

Huguenot redoubt, which was flanked by granite buttresses that rolled up behind the shoreline and projected between great woods. The French made alliances with any natives who could be incited against the Portuguese. They'd had considerable success, for a group of degredados who'd been there long before — calling the place Rio de Janeiro, after the river they'd mistakenly believed must flow into so vast a bay, and the month they'd arrived — had so mistreated the natives that, prompted by the French, the savages had rebelled and slaughtered most of their tormentors.

Inácio focused his gaze on the governor. What a wondrous working of the Lord, when all seemed abandoned in His vineyard, to send Mem de Sá, with the wisdom of a Solomon and the arm of a Joshua! In so vast a territory, there were many places where Mem de Sá's authority could not reach, but where it did, he'd begun rigorously to apply the law. Among the colonists, his officers and soldiers had rounded up the gamblers, the vagabonds, the sellers of harlots, the degredados who'd failed to reform themselves, and put them in chains; they enforced the laws prohibiting illicit enslavement and cruelty toward the natives. Word was sent to the clans themselves: Break the peace, disturb the industry of the planters, and we shall bring you by force to the Jesuit villages and teach you how to distinguish between good and evil.

"Compel them to come in!" the Gospel of St. Luke urged, and it had become the rallying cry of the Jesuits.

Compel them . . . Inácio glanced at José de Anchieta, a young brother standing with the group. Brother José was eager to comply with this shibboleth. Anchieta was often sickly. But his zeal was militant and inspiring, and his craving for the harvest of souls insatiable. Inácio was convinced he'd been wrong in hoping to convert the Tupiniquin at their malocas. Nóbrega and Anchieta, who had contemplated an aldeia such as this, had had the true vision. And how they'd clung to it through those dark years with Dom Duarte da Costa!

Yet Inácio realized today that da Costa's very lack of support had in a way promoted the cause of the Jesuits. At the Bahia, both temporal and secular authority had been against them; and Nóbrega had realized that in the north, too, as long as the family of Dom Duarte Coelho Pereira dominated Pernambuco, there would be scant enthusiasm for the Company and its servants because they supported the removal of the donatário's powers. This had spurred Padre Nóbrega's interest in developing a great Jesuit establishment in the south of the colony.

After leaving Inácio at Porto Seguro to work with the Tupiniquin, Padre Nóbrega had gone on to tour the captaincy of São Vicente, the most southerly settlement. Thirty miles beyond São Vicente's small port of Santos, above precipitous heights sweeping up more than two thousand feet, Nóbrega came upon a great plain the local natives called Piratininga, which he saw as a gateway into the heartland of Santa Cruz. There'd been a settlement there, Santo André, headed by a João Ramalho, another castaway who'd made himself king by taking as wife the daughter of a local clan leader — many daughters, in fact, for the progeny of old Ramalho were as numerous as those of a biblical patriarch. Ramalho's bastards and the other half-breeds living beyond those mighty crags were known as *mamelucos*.

Nóbrega had returned to Tomé de Sousa, seeking permission to open those lands to Christ's mission. Governor Tomé had denied his request: There were too few

Jesuits for so far-flung a venture; worse, the opening of those lands could draw the colonists away from the coast, and if the few thousand Portuguese in Brazil were dispersed into the interior, that vast terra incognita, they could be lost as effectively as if they'd been swept into the sea.

In the time of Governor da Costa, Padre Nóbrega, Anchieta, and others had gone back to Piratininga. Nine miles from the mameluco settlement, on January 25, 1554, they had established the aldeia of São Paulo de Piratininga. And Nóbrega had immediately looked even farther south, toward the Spanish settlement of Asunción, in the province of Paraguay. Between that town and São Paulo were great numbers of natives related to the Tupi tribes of the littoral. Two fathers had been designated to contact them, and had set out — only to be slain by savages roused against them by a disgruntled Spaniard upset by their insistence that he marry the concubine with whom he lived.

"Inácio."

"Oh!" he cried, jolted away from his thoughts.

José Anchieta was smiling up at him. "The governor," the little hunchback said quietly.

Mem de Sá had been greeted by Padre Nóbrega and was moving with him toward the other Jesuits. The governor's fine apparel was sober, in keeping with his temperament; the only extravagant touch was the heavily jeweled hilt of his long sword, a weapon he was known to use with greater enthusiasm than might be expected of a judge of final appeal.

"Padre Inácio, what wonderful work you've done here," he said, after greeting Anchieta and Inácio.

"It is only what the Lord seeks to accomplish," Inácio said.

"Most surely, but . . . His servants help."

"So, too, our governor," Inácio said.

"Your uncle's son — young Tomás — is in São Salvador, with men from Pernambuco," Mem de Sá said. "We may need you, Padre Inácio. For the Tupiniquin." He began to turn away, joining Padre Nóbrega once again. "We will talk later," he said.

The governor and his party entered the church, and Inácio and Anchieta stayed outside to supervise the children, who were beginning to press forward eagerly.

"The trouble at Ilheus and Porto Seguro," Anchieta said, attempting to explain Mem da Sá's words.

"Yes, I've heard — two settlers murdered."

"Our old general will not wait for more."

"I fear he won't."

"*They* should fear — the Tupiniquin. If they but knew the lessons taught the Tupinambá in these lands."

The lessons Anchieta spoke of had been raids led by Mem de Sá against the Bahia Tupinambá, not successfully pacified since the day of Tomé de Sousa, when they had eaten the degredados. One especially arrogant elder, Bloated Toad, had mocked the new governor as the creature of a king who was a baby: He, Bloated Toad, was a man and would do as he'd always done, and to prove it, he'd sent his warriors to seize a plump enemy, who was slain by him and eaten in the middle of his clearing. "Come and judge me!" Bloated Toad dared Mem de Sá. "Judge me or sit with the cowards at São Salvador." Mem de Sá had attacked at night, burning down the malocas and taking the most prized captive of all: Bloated Toad.

Bloated Toad's defiance had, however, encouraged the murder of three Christian natives by men from another clan, and this crime had launched Mem de Sá on a campaign that had not ended until more than one hundred malocas had been destroyed, their occupants killed, dispersed into the forest, or driven to this and two similar aldeias. Engaged in subjugating these Tupinambá, the governor had received an appeal for help from Espirito Santo, a captaincy threatened by savages, south of Porto Seguro. He'd sent his son, Fernão, with a force that had conquered the rebellious clans, but Fernão had been killed.

Inácio pitied any tribe that provoked the wrath of Mem de Sá, but he did not disapprove of the governor's actions. The governor protected the natives who'd accepted Christianity, but those who persistently refused his kind advances he put down with a sword of fire.

When Mem de Sá, his officers, and São Salvador's councilmen and clerks had taken their places in the church, a simple, high-walled, whitewashed building, Inácio and Anchieta shepherded the boys and girls inside. Then, as many parents and friends as the church could hold were allowed to enter. The dignitaries sat on benches to the left of the altar; the children to the right, by the font.

The solemnity began with brother Anchieta's reciting of the Forty-second Psalm, which he rendered beautifully in the Tupi language.

"Praise Him! Praise Him!" several children called out.

Padre Nóbrega then proceeded with the Mass and the baptism of these converts, assisted by Inácio and another ordained Jesuit. The first child to receive the Sacrament was led forward by Anchieta; a boy of nine, he'd been carried to the aldeia after the defeat of Bloated Toad. Nothing was known about his parents.

Governor Mem de Sá was at the font, to be with his godchild "Peter," as the boy would be called. "Come child, to be born again," he said quietly, trying to comfort the nervous Tupinambá. "This lovely holy water will wash away the sin of First Father."

The boy's eyes moved to the hilt of Governor de Sá's sword.

Then Padre Nóbrega began talking, slowly and calmly, his speech impediment unnoticeable: "Child, what dost thou ask of the Church of God?"

The boy was hesitant, shifting his big brown eyes to gaze at Padre Inácio, who had been his instructor.

"Faith," the boy said.

"And how will faith reward you, child?"

"I will live forever," the boy said, in a small voice.

"If you are born again without the sin of First Father, will you keep the Commandments and love the Lord Jesus with all your heart and soul and thoughts . . . and treat your enemies as your friends?"

The boy nodded, and clasped his hands together. When Padre Nóbrega offered him the salt he'd been taught was symbolic of wisdom and of protection from evil, he thrust out his tongue eagerly to taste it. He repeated the vows Padre Inácio had taught him, renouncing the devil Jurupari and all his spirits, and he listened as the governor, most powerful man among the Portuguese, pledged to make a Christian hero out of him. Finally, a lighted candle was placed in his hand: His faith must burn as brightly and steadily as its flame. He smiled happily as Brother Anchieta led him back to the other children.

After this initial ceremony, the remaining eighty-three children were baptized in groups. Then came the next solemnity:

Governor Mem de Sá commanded, "Let Arm of Iron, who is also called Paulo, step forward."

A murmur rose among the crowd, and heads twisted round toward the doorway. Several people cried greetings to the man, who'd been waiting at the back of the church. The crowd parted to let him through and he walked slowly between them, nodding in recognition of those who were his friends. He had been an honored warrior at the malocas of Bloated Toad.

The fathers considered Arm of Iron a remarkable man. Among Bloated Toad's people, he had exchanged his wooden club for a double-bladed battle-ax taken from a slain Portuguese; his deadly skill with this weapon had earned him the name Arm of Iron. But Governor de Sá's soldiers had driven him to the aldeia, a beaten savage, fearing for his life. He refused food and lay in his hammock — waiting for death, other Tupinambá said. The fathers had set a watch over him, but one night at the end of his first week with them, when his guards slept, he had left his hammock; and the next morning, when the fathers went for early Mass, there, asleep before the altar, was Arm of Iron.

"I have spoken with your God — the God of Governor Mem de Sá," he'd announced, when he awakened and saw the black-robed men around him. "He wants me, too."

Now Paulo greeted the governors: "Judge of my people, I bow my head to you as one who makes peace. I am happy to be here."

"Arm of Iron," said Mem de Sá, purposely using the Tupinambá name, "you have witnessed the happiness of these children accepted into the house of His Divine Majesty."

Arm of Iron looked at the children. "They march with the Great Spirit in their hearts."

"And Arm of Iron? With whom does he march?"

"With Jesus. Obedient to His command."

"God be praised," the governor said. "You are washed clean, your past corruption cleansed and forgiven."

"I wish no more, my Lord-Governor," Paulo said.

"Here, in this aldeia, Arm of Iron will be my bailiff — one who sees that my laws are obeyed."

Two aides to the governor stepped up, their arms laden with garments, which Mem de Sá then presented to Arm of Iron.

"These will reflect the dignity of the office you have been given," the governor said, and helped Arm of Iron don a green doublet. Next, Mem de Sá took a brown cloak from one of his aides and draped it around the Tupinambá's shoulders; then he gave him a hat trimmed with yellow taffeta. There was also a linen shirt and brown breeches, but these the aides simply held aloft to exhibit to the crowd.

Mem de Sá accepted a staff from one of his aides, a length of burnished bronze inlaid with cheap jewels. "Here is the symbol of my authority, by which all will know you as the bailiff of this aldeia." Mem de Sá raised the staff high enough so that those in the back could see. "He who carries this speaks with the voice of the governor; you must obey him."

"We will! We will!" roared the crowd.

"When he tells you to carry out the wishes of the fathers, heed him. When he tells you to perform the labor that makes better Christians of you, obey."

"We will!"

The governor then kissed the staff of office and handed it to Paulo. "Go with God, my servant," Mem de Sá said.

The governor went to sit on the bench with his officers and officials, Paulo moved to one side, and Padre Inácio now led the mission choir in their hymns.

Mem de Sá sat with his eyes closed in great pleasure: There was nothing so soothing to him as the angelic voices of the young converts, and often on Sundays he would come to the mission church in preference to the São Salvador cathedral.

After the singing, the church was cleared of all but the governor's party and the Jesuits; they stood to one side as ten natives and three black slaves — two from south of the river Zaire, one from the Guinea coast — made preparations for them to dine. The slaves were among nine blacks owned by the Jesuits at the Bahia. In the time of Tomé de Sousa, Padre Nóbrega had written to King João, asking for slaves "to work our garden and supply our table, for otherwise we would starve, there being no concept of labor among the natives."

The padres continued to distinguish between the blacks, hundreds of whom were coming every month to the anchorages of the Bahia and Pernambuco, and the natives. The Africans had always been slaves and had both the constitution and the discipline for industrious toil; the Tupinambá, Tupiniquin, and all the other tribes of Brazil had neither.

But thousands of natives, taken legally or illegally, did slave on the plantations, for a peça from Africa still was much more expensive than a forest savage. Although Governor de Sá was not unsympathetic to the need for labor in the cane fields, he reminded his colonists that Lisbon's Board of Conscience and Order clearly defined those who could be taken: natives who sold themselves or their children into slavery for reasons of dire need; natives who practiced cannibalism; natives rescued or ransomed from "places of slaughter"; and, certainly, natives who took up arms against the Portuguese.

The Jesuits were making every effort to instill in the natives a sense of discipline, obedience, and industry. When this was accomplished, the natives would be hired out from the aldeias to work on the plantations. But that day still seemed far off.

During the meal in the church building, the governor spoke to Inácio, who sat opposite him, and again referred to the Tupiniquin of Porto Seguro, and the neighboring captaincy of Ilheus. "The murders they have committed prove how little they respect the Portuguese," he said. "And how little they fear the savior you so lovingly offered them."

"There are many thousands, Governor. In four days' journey north of Porto Seguro, I counted more than sixty malocas."

"And I have the Tupinambá!" Mem de Sá pronounced, with unusual excitement. "Those subdued around this bay wait happily for a place in an aldeia. Punish the Tupiniquin and they will join us, too, as many as our ships can hold. I want you to come with us, Padre Inácio — with the fleet that sails for Porto Seguro. Padre Nóbrega has no objection."

"Then I will go," Inácio said.

"Let the Tupiniquin see God's messenger whom they mocked," the governor added, with passion.

✑

Two weeks later, in mid-July 1559, in the lee of the heights of São Salvador, marinheiros were just beginning to take in the anchors of Governor Mem de Sá's flagship, *Nossa Senhora dos Remédios*. Already six vessels of the coastal fleet, with supplies for a long campaign and their decks crowded with Tupinambá warriors now in the service of His Majesty Dom Sebastião, were over the horizon bound for Porto Seguro and nearby Ilheus, which was under siege by savages.

Padre Inácio, his slender arms folded across his chest, leaned against a bulkhead in the flagship's cabin as the governor and his military commander, Vasco Rodrigues de Caldas, reprimanded the young man who was the cause of this delay: Tomás Cavalcanti.

Inácio had seen his cousin for the first time just before this confrontation, when the men sent to find him returned with Tomás and four other Pernambucans in the ship's boat. Tomás bore a strong resemblance to Nicolau; he was sturdily built and of medium height, with green-flecked eyes and sunburnt features. But there was a special arrogance about him, immediately apparent in his manner when he'd come aboard *Nossa Senhora dos Remédios*: Totally unabashed at having delayed the governor, and obviously unafraid of the consequences, he'd swung over the bulwarks, joking with his escort, and swaggered over to Mem de Sá's cabin.

"They said you'd be here," he'd greeted Inácio on the quarterdeck. "Certainly, I told them, a fine presence; it's good for our governor to see a saint among the Cavalcantis."

Before Inácio could respond, Tomás had entered the cabin, and Inácio had followed. Standing before Mem de Sá and de Caldas, Tomás lost some of his bravado, but his steady gaze and easy stance showed him to be far less intimidated than a young man might be in this situation.

"Capitão Cavalcanti," Mem de Sá said bitingly, though Tomás held no official rank as leader of thirty men from Pernambuco, "we would have sailed hours ago."

"Forgive me, Excellency . . . it was unavoidable."

Mem de Sá glared at him. "*Unavoidable*, was it? Detaining the governor and the commander of this expedition — this you could not avoid?"

"My men have had a hard journey, Excellency, a long campaign through the backlands. Terrible."

"My campaign has not begun. Delayed these hours because of *you*."

"Yes, Excellency, and I regret it. But we walked every league from Olinda to the Bahia."

Tomás Cavalcanti had marched down the coast in pursuit of runaway slaves, wandering into the backlands until he'd led his men so far south that they'd come on to São Salvador, from where they'd wanted to ship back to Olinda. But Governor de Sá had interviewed them and had declared that they were to serve with him for a period: "A fine opportunity to remind them and those who sent them south that they are part of His Majesty's empire," he'd confided to de Caldas.

"Surely, Cavalcanti, and you will return," Mem de Sá was now saying to Tomás, "*when* you have helped me pacify the Tupiniquin."

"A great honor" — Tomás smiled at Rodrigues de Caldas — "to march with you, my lord and knight."

De Caldas, a big, muscular man with a remorseless look about him, observed Tomás sourly. A veteran of the wars against the Tupinambá and the bloody punishment of the Caeté to the north, de Caldas was not impressed by this son of a wealthy Pernambucan planter, for whom the governor showed such patience. De Caldas did not expect much of this cocky *mazombo* — the term for those born of Portuguese parents in Brazil, totally lacking the refinements and traditions of old Portugal.

"If you value this commission so much," the governor snapped, "why weren't you aboard last night, with the rest of the men?"

Tomás turned to look at Inácio, and when he did not reply immediately, de Caldas said coldly, "We are waiting, Senhor Cavalcanti, to hear what detained you."

"Oh, no, Commander, it wasn't what you think!" he said. Then, to the governor: "Oh, Excellency, how I thank fate for leading me here."

Mem de Sá's stern expression began to relax.

"Governor de Sá, you've given me the victor's prize, even before I raised my sword once for you."

Now the governor smiled openly. "Tomás Cavalcanti, which one?" he asked, to the complete bafflement of Inácio and de Caldas.

"Theresa Dias!" Tomás cried. "All night I sat outside the window of Dom Almeida's house waiting for but one glimpse of her."

"And this was granted?"

"Yes, Governor — at dawn, with the soft light upon that loveliest of faces. Oh, forgive me, Excellency, but for such a sight, a man must risk much."

De Caldas had a look of incredulity on his face: He had sent his men to the dens of whores and thieves to fetch this rascal, certainly not to the house of Dom Almeida, a most respected councilman of São Salvador.

Mem de Sá noticed his commander's impatience and grew stern again. "This is no excuse to delay the fleet. Tomás Cavalcanti, take care that you follow your duty, not your heart!" From his tone, it was clear to the others that the governor had no intention of going beyond this mild rebuke. Theresa Dias, the king's "daughter," was a plump but fair-countenanced girl, one of a group of orphans sent to the Bahia at royal expense. Abandoned on the doorstep of a convent in Coimbra, Theresa had been raised by the nuns and was of sound morals and firm conviction. Mem de Sá had placed her under the protection of Dom Almeida, until such time as a suitor the governor approved came forward to beg his permission to marry her.

Mem de Sá spoke to Inácio. "I introduced your cousin, Padre, to one of the orphan girls the king has sent. It seems Tomás has an interest in the child."

Tomás smiled at Inácio. "Oh, Padre, what a rose she is! What a flower for any man who deserves her!"

Commander Rodrigues de Caldas made a low, angry noise, nodded at the governor, and left the cabin.

☙

Two weeks later, on July 30, 1559, Padre Inácio stood with Governor de Sá, Commander de Caldas, and a group of officers on a hill twenty miles south of the settlement of Ilheus. It was 4:00 A.M., but the sky was aglow, for along the opposite hills and in the valleys between, the forest burned.

A solid wall of fire extended for a mile along those hills, and fanned by a stiff breeze, it was burning deep into the lands beyond, pouring rivers of flame along the valleys to scorch the earth where the first Tupiniquin to face Governor de Sá's force had once hunted and fished.

Blasts of hot air reached the hill where Inácio stood. The light from the fire storm brought an eerie color to the men gathered there, spectators to the furies they'd set in action by firing the forest at the malocas they'd attacked four hours ago.

Only the morning before, they'd reached an anchorage convenient to the town of Ilheus, where planters from the captaincy's five engenhos had taken refuge with the settlers. Since the murder of two colonists by the Tupiniquin, these families, less than one hundred people, had not ventured out of the town, and had been reduced to surviving on oranges and a handful of manioc daily. The landing of Mem de Sá, with Portuguese soldiers and a thousand Tupinambá from the Bahia, had itself been sufficient to send the Tupiniquin besieging Ilheus fleeing into the forest.

The governor immediately marched his men to Tupiniquin malocas twenty miles beyond Ilheus, where the settlers said they would find the murderers of the two planters.

They'd sighted the village on a hill opposite the one on which the governor and his officers were now standing, and, close to midnight, had stormed through the five malocas they found, slaying every man, woman, and child they caught.

For Inácio, the memory of the devastation brought to the malocas of his own Tupiniquin had been inescapable. But what was happening this night was different, he'd told himself: These Tupiniquin had brought upon themselves a divine justice for their long and stubborn refusal to abandon their pagan ways. *God help them!* Inácio had prayed. *Through their suffering and scourging, may they be compelled to accept His Word and brought to an understanding of justice and salvation!*

☙

But these Tupiniquin were not ready for salvation. When dawn came on July 30, some who had been able to flee into the forest during the attack followed the trails of blood that led back to their village, and beheld their smoldering malocas and the blackened, scorched bodies of their families.

"Hear us, O Voice of the Spirits, this day of our sorrow!" the sole surviving elder cried out in the presence of seven warriors who'd returned to the blasted clearing.

"O ancestors, who rest in Land of the Grandfather, see your children this day!"

The elder had little to offer beyond these anguished appeals as he stumbled through the ruin. Then he stopped and examined the faces of the men with him, and detected the thirst he himself felt for the blood of the Portuguese.

"Must we lie in our hammocks like the old and the sick and wait for death?" many asked, and the answer was obvious: From every maloca within two days' march of Ilheus, the Tupiniquin rose to drive the Long Hairs into the Bluewater from whence they had come.

Governor de Sá and his troops were waiting for them, warned by Tupinambá scouts patrolling the forest, and hundreds were slain in ambushes on the approach to the settlement. But a second Tupiniquin advance was working its way through a low, wooded range that lay adjacent to the shore. Here were the warriors from sixteen villages, some twelve hundred men and boys in all, confident that their force would march over the huts and houses of the Long Hairs at Ilheus.

They were trapped between those hills and the sea — driven onto the long stretches of beach to make their stand against the Portuguese and the Tupinambá. The battle raged from dawn till dusk. The ranks of the Tupiniquin were decimated by cannon fire from two ships maneuvering offshore, and their enemies on land stormed down the hills to finish off those who remained, pressing them farther and farther back, until Tupiniquin stood up to their shoulders in the surf laboring to swing their clubs against the men who waded after them with sword and pike.

Not one of the twelve hundred Tupiniquin survived. When Mem de Sá came to inspect the scene of battle toward sunset, he walked the beach for a distance of a mile, moving very slowly, for hundreds of Tupiniquin lay along his path, their blood mingling with the water that foamed up to the white sand.

By rising against the Portuguese, these Tupiniquin had given His Excellency, Governor Mem de Sá, just cause to exterminate their nation.

*

Through the first swift weeks of the campaign against the Tupiniquin, Inácio had sought to be friendly toward his cousin, and Tomás had been responsive to his inquiries about Engenho Santo Tomás and its people. But even when he spoke about them, Tomás Cavalcanti frightened Inácio, for the padre had rarely heard expressed such hatred and contempt for the natives.

The ill-mannered youth he'd first met at Nicolau's stockade was twenty-two now, as harsh-tempered and abrasive as his father. Indeed, Tomás's reports had revealed Nicolau to be as unforgiving as Inácio had known him, and as fully abandoned to the harlots of his house. More so, Inácio reasoned, for Helena was dead. "Taken by illness this past year, cousin," Tomás had told him. "As surely a victim of this land as if slain by the savages." Clearly Tomás had been reluctant to talk about his mother, and, after accepting Inácio's condolences, had changed the subject to the engenho itself

The valley now had ten times the plantings Inácio had seen a decade before, an enormous water-driven mill financed by the Jew Papagaio, and two shiploads of sugar readied for Lisbon every season. Nicolau had leased lands to impoverished settlers, who produced cane for his engenho. And there was a new enterprise, too, with a herd of cattle introduced on grounds west of the valley. However, Inácio was not to think this exceptional, Tomás told him, for others knew such prosperity in Nova Lusitania. Olinda was no more a hovel clinging to those steep hills but a city as noble as São Salvador, with seven hundred households and, in the lands beyond, eighteen mills similar to that of Senhor Cavalcanti.

Tomás spoke almost reverently of Dona Brites, widow of Dom Duarte Coelho, who had died so sadly. When it became clear that João III had indeed wanted Dom Duarte to return rights and privileges to all lands except the ten leagues of coast granted him as his personal property, the donatário had sailed to Lisbon to appeal to his king. But João had received his old warrior coldly, ignoring all he'd done for Nova Lusitania, and Dom Duarte had collapsed and died within three days. Dona Brites, whom Inácio remembered as a severe, devout woman, had taken control of the captaincy, keeping the representatives of king and governor-generals at a distance that assured the donatário's family continued control of Pernambuco.

With obvious irritation, Tomás complained to Inácio that even as they marched here, against the Tupiniquin, the savages of Pernambuco, the Caeté and the Potiguara were sure to be attacking outlying engenhos and committing outrages against the Christians — even to within a league of Olinda. And without an adequate force to crush them, the colonists were faced with new problems:

Through their toil and industry, the settlers had acquired no less than four thousand slaves from the Kongo kingdom and the lands of the Guinea coast; Engenho Santo Tomás alone had more than one hundred. At first, these precious imports had been fearful of the forest savages, filled with a horror of their flesh-eating and brutal disposition. But when they'd seen how handily their masters slew Caeté and Potiguara, they began to lose their dread, and dozens of slaves had run from the plantations into the woods, where, though blessed as Christians before departing Africa, they now consorted with the heathens. Ten of Nicolau's slaves had fled in this manner, along with others from neighboring engenhos, and this was the reason Tomás had led thirty Pernambucans south. They had caught eight runaways, who were now part of Mem de Sá's expeditionary force.

"Drawn into the forest by the savages, our peças become the worst outlaws and murderers," Tomás explained. "I thanked God, when Governor de Sá invited me to join his campaign. Be swift my sword, I prayed — be swift, for there's no difference between a Caeté or a Tupiniquin beast."

☙

This morning, Rodrigues de Caldas was just finishing his address to the campaign leaders. Mem de Sá's force, he announced, was being split into three columns: One would march down the coast, along the hills that lay toward the sea; a second would make its way to Porto Seguro through the valleys behind the coastal range; the third, led by Tomás Cavalcanti, was to head inland in a southwesterly direction.

The objective of each column was the same: to seek out and destroy the villages of the Tupiniquin. Already not a single maloca remained within a day's march from Ilheus. Governor de Sá's initial conquests of the clan to which the colonists' murderers had belonged, and the Tupiniquin horde cut down on the beach, had been followed by a more orderly plan.

"Let us show them full Christian charity," the governor had said. "The Tupiniquin have only to abandon their forest hovels and move to aldeias they will build near our own settlements. There they will enjoy my protection and the guidance of the Company of Jesus."

The clans who accepted this promise without argument were to be given an opportunity to collect their possessions, and they were then to be led to the coast. The stockades and malocas were to be destroyed.

"If they refuse our offers, then force them out," the governor said. "Force them out and drive them to their new home, where they may gradually be brought to accept our honest and good intentions."

When the group around de Caldas started to break up and move off, Tomás remained talking with the commander. Inácio was surprised to note their shared enthusiasm, very different from their relationship that day in Mem de Sá's cabin. But then he had learned why soon enough.

De Caldas had mellowed toward Tomás for two reasons: After the first engagements with the Tupiniquin, he recognized that the planter's son, whom he'd first regarded with contempt, was a ferocious and fearless fighter. Few of his own seasoned soldiers of the king could match Tomás Cavalcanti's skill and daring against the savages, his canny appreciation of their tactics and treacheries. Second, de Caldas had discovered that Tomás had been telling the truth about his romantic vigil at the house where Mem de Sá's orphan ward was lodged. The commander's men assured him that Tomás had indeed been waiting to see the king's "daughter," Theresa Dias, and been begging Dom Almeida to protect the girl until he returned from the south.

As the other officers headed off to join their columns, de Caldas and Tomás approached Inácio. Because he'd journeyed through that part of the forest before, he was to accompany Tomás's column, with its eighty soldiers and colonists and four hundred Tupinamba.

Tomás hailed him enthusiastically: "Padre Inácio, we march to bring back to His pasture those who strayed from the field you prepared for them."

"A lovely solace, Tomás, if my lost Tupiniquin are found and returned to grace."

"I promise you, my cousin Inácio, no native who can be taken for Christ will be overlooked."

Tomás Cavalcanti kept his promise.

For three weeks the column pushed through the valleys and forests, first due west and then south, until it was following the direction Inácio had taken with Guaraci and the two converts at the time of his retreat. Tupinambá scouts ranged ahead of the main body, locating thirty Tupiniquin stockades — 140 malocas with nearly ten thousand people.

The Portuguese (actually, their ranks included Spaniards, a German, a Scot, and three Genoese, whose avowed Catholicism met the main criteria for serving or settling in Brazil) moved slowly, laden with weapons and baggage. In addition to swords and daggers, pikes and crossbows and hand axes, there were forty arquebuses, with enough power and shot to keep them supplied for months, and two falconet cannon.

In the first days beyond the encampment at Ilheus, two Tupiniquin villages joined the column peacefully, their elders persuaded by Padre Inácio that this was how they would be spared the punishments reported by warriors fleeing from the coast. The families at these malocas rolled up their hammocks, put aside their treasured feathers and dyepots, and obediently stood aside as the soldiers and Tupinambá tore down their stockade, burned their houses, and pulled up the manioc and other plants in their fields.

But, at other stockades, Tupiniquin chose flight, aware of the superior force gathered against them. When Tomás Cavalcanti's men reached the villages abandoned by these Tupiniquin, there was nothing for them to do but indulge in a destructive rage, unsatisfied until the malocas and tracts of forest around them were in flames.

At other villages the Tupiniquin simply refused to move: Nothing could persuade them to leave their homes. To Padre Inácio's pleas and the arguments of others, they responded by showing that their fields were still productive, the thatch on their houses new, the clay of the great pots their women fashioned for beer as fresh as the brew they held. Their people had slain no Long Hairs — why should they move?

They watched as their clearing filled with Portuguese and Tupinambá. Their people were forced out of the malocas. Then they were chased beyond the clearing to join other Tupiniquin waiting at the column's stopping place, and here they were told how foolish they'd been to reject the peace offered by the new lords of the forest. But nothing that was said made sense to them, for as they waited to move, they saw the smoke rising from their malocas, and the Tupinambá leaping with joy at the sight.

Among the last clans encountered in those first three weeks, the column began to meet fierce resistance. As tales of devastation and atrocities spread through the forest with intensifying horror, warriors took up their clubs and bows and arrows, and strode out as a body to meet the invaders.

On the twenty-second day of the column's march from Ilheus, it was attacked by one hundred warriors from malocas that Tupinambá scouts had reported to be an hour's march ahead of the column. Shouting their war cries from afar, they leaped noisily through the underbrush, running in closed ranks into a wall of fire and steel. The Tupinambá, who cut off all avenues of retreat, caught those not slain by the soldiers.

The expedition's casualties were light: two Portuguese killed, four wounded, and thirty Tupinambá lost. Immediately, Tomás Cavalcanti ordered an offensive against the malocas of the Tupiniquin attackers.

At the village, the few defenders were quickly subdued, and, as before on this campaign, the Portuguese experienced a bitter disappointment that there was no plunder. Their anger at such deprivation drove them to take the only prizes available: wives, daughters, and sons of warriors they had slain.

One man among the Portuguese refused these spoils: their captain, Tomás Cavalcanti. He stood alone near the entrance to the stockade, allowing his men their pleasures but making no attempt to participate.

A Tupiniquin girl did rush up to Tomás, begging him to save her from his men. He'd laughed, seizing her by her hair and shouting the name of the most brutal soldiers he could see in the clearing, one of the German mercenaries. But the man didn't hear him, and growing impatient with the girl screeching at his feet, Tomás stepped back, drew his sword, and killed her. He wiped the blade against her legs and replaced the weapon in its scabbard. Then he turned away and returned to the column's encampment.

Inácio had remained with the column, among the Tupiniquin already taken from other malocas and those too sick or wounded to participate in the storming of the stockade. Here, too, were the eight slaves from Pernambuco who had been recaptured by Tomás. They were now all exhausted by fever. Inácio had done all he could for them —three were Christians from the kingdom of the Kongo — but they were too sick even to show interest in his concern.

When the column reassembled the next morning, thirty-six Tupiniquin from the conquered stockade were added — a group of women, children, and the aged, all who remained of a community of three hundred.

Two days later, an old man who had been an elder at the destroyed village approached Inácio. "I remember you," he said.

To Inácio, he appeared no different from any other old native: small-framed, his face wrinkled, dry, and dusty, his shoulders straight, his gestures lively.

After studying him carefully, Inácio said, "I do not know you."

The man pointed to the scar on the black robe's face. "You came to our malocas seeking the Tupiniquin whose village had been attacked by the slavers. I remember you," he said again.

At first, Inácio was shocked. "Guaraci? The elder Aruanã? They were at your malocas?"

The Tupiniquin shook his head.

"Where, then?"

"I remember you" was all the old man would say, and nothing Inácio said or offered — food, liquor, tabak — could induce him to reveal more.

Only now did Inácio realize that it had been from the last malocas destroyed by the column that he had set out with Guaraci, three days to the west, to the place where Aruanã and his warriors had found them.

"Tomás, I beg you to march in that direction," he appealed to his cousin.

Tomás was reluctant: "Three days to the west — exhausting for men who've marched and fought so hard these past weeks."

"Aruanã's people were brought so close to His side; their children were converted."

"And they were lost?"

"As the lamb of the shepherd."

Inácio argued so strongly that Tomás finally relented. "Very well, Padre, let us find your strayed flock and bring them to safety."

ᴄ⁄ɔ

The six Tupinambá scouts for the column were found at a shaded rock pool where one had stopped to drink. This warrior floated face down in the shallows; the others were on the ground beside the water, their bodies riddled with arrows.

Tomás Cavalcanti walked between the naked corpses. "Bring the padre," he ordered, and Inácio was fetched. "Could it be, cousin, we seek not lambs but wolves?"

There were more than fifteen hundred people, conquerors and captives, in the column, and when it broke up for the night. Inácio spent much time with the eight ailing black slaves, two of whom he did not expect to survive the night. He'd bled them, but to no avail. Tomás and the Pernambucans who'd caught these runaways showed no sympathy but only cursed them for the trouble they'd caused.

Before dawn, there was a second attack against the column, a swift strike that killed thirty-four Tupiniquin captives who'd rested a distance from the main body. When the alarm was sounded, Tomás and others raced to the scene, but the attackers were gone.

Tomás sent Tupinambá to scout the forest in every direction and locate the source of these assaults. One group was back before noon: Two hours to the west was a stockade, they reported, where the warriors of several villages were assembled. Without delay, Tomás led his men against this stronghold. Inácio asked to accompany them, for he was certain he'd find Aruanã and those of his people not taken by the slavers; but he was told he'd be sent for as soon as the clearing had been captured.

The raiding party came straggling back between sunset and late into the evening, and all told of a miserable defeat: Four times they had stormed this Tupiniquin stockade, and on each occasion they had been stopped by a rain of arrows from the defenders. Tomás Cavalcanti was slightly wounded by an arrow that pierced his right forearm. Eight Portuguese were dead or missing, twice that number injured. It was not known how many Tupinambá were lost, for they hadn't stopped at the flight of arrows but had rushed on to the enemy's stockade, so many felled that a broad clearing outside the village was filled with their bodies.

Tomás sat on the ground, his back against a tree trunk, as soldier after soldier urged that they abandon this dangerous diversion and head for the coast.

"Oh, Capitão, we've achieved more than Governor de Sá expected of us," said one accepted by all as second-in-command, a middle-aged veteran of the Guinea-coast forts. "We've cleared the forest of thirty pagan villages and taken enough natives to the coast to employ the fathers of Jesus for years to come. Let's go, Tomás!"

"Eight Christians struck down by these pagans and all you can say is that our work is ended?"

None of the soldiers responded.

"Take heart, my men," Tomás continued. "Even the most cowardly among you will accept the plan I have to lure those Tupiniquin from their redoubt."

When Inácio learned of the stratagem, he was filled with disgust.

The eight sick slaves were to be carried to a place in the woods, bound together, and left near a stream from which these Tupiniquin fetched their water. When the eight offerings were sighted, Tomás was confident, a sizable force would be sent to collect them. And his men would be waiting.

Inácio had protested. "You cannot sacrifice them so heartlessly."

"They condemned themselves, cousin, by fleeing their rightful owners. They'll die before we reach the coast: Let them at least be of some use for all the trouble they've caused."

Before dawn, the slaves were in place, roped together on the ground near the stream. As Tomás had hoped, some Tupiniquin spotted them at sunrise. Sixty warriors rushed upon the blacks, smashing them with their clubs.

They were engaged in this slaughter when the arquebuses roared from the trees beyond, blasting their fiery shot into the throng of warriors and finishing off, too, the blacks who'd provided the lure. Within a quarter of an hour, forty-five Tupiniquin lay dead with the slaves; others tried to retreat to their stockade, but there the column had launched a new attack.

They had brought up the two small cannon carried from the coast, positioned them just beyond the broad clearing in front of the stockade entrance, and fired repetitive rounds through the wooden defense. The cannonballs were hand-sized and not solid but of a new design, containing gunpowder to explode upon impact. The Portuguese roared with pleasure as these innovative projectiles landed among the Tupiniquin.

Some of the best warriors among the defenders had been caught in the ambush with the slaves, and those remaining in the stockade quickly fell back as the balls burst among their ranks. Immediately their barrage of arrows lessened, and the attackers began to storm across the open ground. The Tupinambá raced to tear aside the branches and other obstacles placed at the entrance to the village.

Tomás Cavalcanti had led his men at the ambush, and he now led the fight being waged at the nine malocas, crying that none who resisted be spared or allowed escape.

Back at the column's encampment, Padre Inácio had waited until a messenger came to report that the ambush had succeeded and the malocas were being stormed. He hurried off then to the scene of battle, with the Tupinambá who'd brought the news.

Inácio had known what to expect, but the sight of the bound, broken corpses left him sick at heart. He weaved among the bodies of the slain Tupiniquin. Then, with an agonized cry, he dropped to his knees:

"Guaraci! My dear Guaraci!"

The Tupiniquin's chest had been punctured by shot, the side of his face split by the clubs wielded against him.

"Cristovão," Inácio cried then over the body of the painted warrior who had been received into Christ's presence with his sister, Unauá. He prayed silently, remaining for a long time at Guaraci's side.

The discovery of Guaraci confirmed that these were Inácio's Tupiniquin, and Inácio dreaded what he would find at the malocas. When he reached the stockade, the main conflict was over. The Portuguese and Tupinambá were rounding up the women and children, and disarmed Tupiniquin were held back by the victors; but for every one who stood captive, three or four others lay dying or wounded on the ground.

Inácio walked to the farthest maloca, where Tomás, a group of soldiers, and some Tupinambá were still meeting resistance. Wherever he looked was evidence of slaughter: warriors beheaded and mutilated, pinned to the ground with lances; others battered and broken by the clubs of many Tupinambá.

Tomás, sword in hand, his clothes splattered with blood, greeted his cousin jubilantly: "Let us thank the Lord — all the Saints, Inácio — for this great victory."

Inácio's face was deathly pale. "Tomás, so many have been killed," he said. "Their treachery is not to be denied, but so many put to the sword?"

"I warned you that this is not your battle. You wanted to convert them with love, Padre, and you failed. See them now, lambs who stand meekly, broken by the hammer of war."

"These people welcomed your father to Santa Cruz; they were there, Tomás, on the beach when Nicolau Cavalcanti came ashore."

"I know this," he said, and his expression hardened. "Today, cousin, I feel only joy in this clearing of my father's whore. Don't look so stricken, Padre: You know it's true that the bitch he took came from these people."

"But this was the sin of your father."

"And this sweet and bloody scourging is mine, Padre, for all the sorrow and sufferings borne by my sainted mother, Helena, whom you yourself have wept for — Helena, holy Christian, mocked by the forest harlot and her bastards, my *half-brothers!*"

At that moment an arquebus was fired into the side of the opposite maloca, from which volleys of arrows were being discharged at any who tried to approach.

After the blast from the arquebus, two more gunners stood ready with their weapons, but they held their fire when a short, stooped Tupiniquin stepped into the daylight.

Inácio gave a cry of recognition. "Pium," he said. "It is their sorcerer, Pium."

Pium appeared much older, his smooth skin lined now, his light frame bonier. He called out in a strident voice, "You returned, black robe; you came back to destroy us. Many Great Rains you waited, and now you come with soldiers and Tupinambá."

"No, Pium. This war you brought upon yourselves. You denied the love and peace of Jesus Christ."

The pagé looked at Inácio grimly, his small eyes narrowing. "Peace? Where we hunted, there are trails of our warrior's blood. Where our people rejoiced with the ancestors, the urubu waits to sing. In every field of the Tupiniquin, there *is* peace — for those who lie with eyes upon Land of the Grandfather."

"Where are the elders?"

Pium gestured toward the maloca. "One waits there."

"Aruanã?" Inácio asked hopefully.

Pium nodded. "Aruanã remembers you. He remembers that day you carried the Cross through our clearing. 'Let them behold,' Aruanã says, 'these sorrows of the Tupiniquin — how much greater they are than those the Son of Long Hair's God suffered.'"

There was a flash of steel as Tomás Cavalcanti lunged forward. "Blasphemer!" he howled, and drove his sword into Pium's side.

As Tomás stood over the pagé, Inácio started forward in the direction of the maloca.

"Padre!" a soldier cried. "Padre, stop!"

Tomás looked away from Pium's body and saw the cassocked figure hastening toward the longhouse. "For love of God, Inácio, come back!" he shouted. Then he ordered the two arquebusiers to fire into the maloca.

The shot from one of the guns went wide, hitting Inácio in the shoulder and knocking him down. Tomás dashed to his side and dragged him back as arrows launched from the maloca fell around them. He pushed Inácio roughly toward the line of his men. "Get him to safety before he endangers others!"

When two soldiers had taken Inácio away, Tomás called for Tupinambá bowmen and ordered them to shoot flaming arrows into the palm fronds of the maloca. "Stand ready," he warned. "They'll not endure the heat for long."

The Tupinambá warriors agreed, stamping their feet impatiently. "Come! Come, Tupiniquin! We wait for our enemy!"

Fanned by a breeze, the blaze tore through the dry fronds and raced down the maloca's gently curved sides. A few ran out of the low entrance but were shot down as they cleared the opening, and others did not follow.

Suddenly, Inácio returned, breaking through the front rank of those who stood watching the fire. He raised his good arm, gesturing for those behind the fire to escape.

One Tupiniquin did break through the burning wall, the flames engulfing him as he staggered and collapsed six feet away from Inácio.

Tomás was at his cousin's side. "The fires of hell," he declared, "come to earth to consume this pagan."

Inácio remained silent, gazing upon that face so hideously disfigured and yet recognizable to him. He could hear the roar of the blazing maloca but no longer the howling of those trapped within.

Inácio reached down toward the figure on the ground and snapped off the charred cord the man had worn around his neck. Attached to the cord was a green stone.

He turned toward Tomás. "Here," he said, thrusting the stone at him. "Take this. It was his treasure — the only spoil you'll find this day."

Inácio walked away slowly, leaving Tomás to admire the jade amulet taken from the body of Aruanã, the Tupiniquin.

✁

By 1562, three years after the conquest of the Tupiniquin clans of Porto Seguro and Ilheus, the results of Governor Mem de Sá's great harvest of souls — and of slaves — were everywhere in evidence. The colonists at the Bahia had acquired more than ten thousand natives ordered into bondage for taking up arms against the governor's militia.

Except for Pernambuco, where the family of Dom Duarte Coelho still ruled, the donatários of the other captaincies were no longer lord proprietors of their territories. But their families still held their hereditary allotments extending over hundreds of square miles. By 1562, a harvest of two thousand tons a year was reaching the merchants of Lisbon and the refineries of the Dutch, the sugar masters of Europe.

What made this output all the more remarkable was the small number of colonists responsible for it. From Pernambuco, in the northeast, to the farthest outposts at Santos, in the south, and São Paulo, on the plateau beyond, there were less than three thousand settlers, mainly Portuguese, though Spaniards, Genoese, and other foreign adherents of the faith were also permitted entry to the colony. Most plantations and engenhos were found near the Bahia and Olinda; the far north, above Pernambuco, remained unconquered, and the granite massifs rising behind the ocean all along the southern littoral provided a barrier to the hinterland.

Governor Mem de Sá was scrupulous in observing the laws regarding belligerent natives, taking great care that his officials enslave only those who'd rebelled against the authority of the future king of Portugal, Sebastião, now eight years old. Thousands of natives had accepted Mem de Sá's peace, and since they represented a triumph of persuasion and diplomacy, he treated them with utmost consideration.

The aldeia of St. Peter and St. Paul was still led by Padre Inácio, and by 1562 was home to more than two thousand natives. But this was only one aldeia, and in the region of the Bahia alone, there were now eleven Jesuit settlements with a total population of thirty thousand.

What joy, then, to find that this compulsion had worked to move the most reluctant heathens. At the aldeia of St. Peter and St. Paul, with its imposing church, college, and dormitories — here, at last, was a victory in the great battle for souls to which Inácio had been rallied as a young man.

Another Jesuit, Padre Agostinho Correia, two lay brothers, and a council of native elders assisted him. Among the elders was the convert Paulo — Arm of Iron, Mem de Sá's "bailiff" — who remained most dedicated to every discipline of the fathers.

Nine hundred at the aldeia had already been converted, and such progress had led Inácio to believe that in a year or two every soul in the village would be given the hope of salvation. This advancement had not come without the greatest exertion by Padre Inácio, Padre Agostinho, and a group of converts, whom they appointed as teachers.

Lapses among his flock were saddening to Inácio: There were bouts of drinking that led to fights and murders; adulteries exposed by women who'd formerly have given no thought to the sin of their spouses.

Always, Inácio returned to the children, with whom there was full hope of salvation. He was never so happy as at the end of day, when the boys and girls walked in white-robed procession through the streets of the aldeia reciting their Aves.

And then, toward the end of 1562, there occurred an event that was to have a profound effect on the aldeia of St. Peter and St. Paul: the departure from Lisbon of a one-hundred-ton caravel bound for Brazil.

São Felipe made a good passage of forty-seven days, with a cargo of supplies for the captaincy of Ilheus, which had begun to prosper since Mem de Sá's annihilation of the savages. In the first week of December, *São Felipe* rode off that same shore where the twelve hundred Tupiniquin had perished.

When *São Felipe* had been safely anchored, her captain and officers went ashore to arrange for the landing of her cargo. The settlers, who were always delighted to see a ship from Portugal bringing comforts and necessities denied them in the colony, gave them a rousing welcome

On this voyage, *São Felipe* carried something else, too, brought across the Atlantic by her marinheiros to these lands of Ilheus and soon to reach the Bahia and far beyond: the plague.

ᴄⱽᴢ

Padre Inácio was alone in the aldeia church, his dark shape just distinguishable in the moonlight that shone weakly through the windows high upon the wall behind the altar, and he did not hear Paulo enter. Inácio had been praying at length, though he would have been unable to say with any certainty how long he'd knelt here; he'd lost the proper sense of time through days and nights and weeks of witnessing the suffering of the natives of the aldeia.

Paulo moved so that he stood just behind the priest, off to the right. In the years since his appointment as bailiff, Paulo had filled his position with dignity and respect. While other men, most of them older than he, had been named elders by the Jesuits, and met regularly with the fathers and brothers, at such gatherings it was usually Paulo who had most to say about the welfare of the aldeia's natives in those areas that did not concern their faith.

Paulo went down on his knees; he did not pray but asked aloud, "Padre Inácio, why does the Lord God persecute us?"

Without turning, Inácio asked gently, "Paulo, why are you not at rest?"

"I am afraid, Father. Could it happen, I ask myself, that tomorrow Arm of Iron must wake to begin his dying?"

Inácio kept his eyes upon the outline of the altar. "Your faith is strong, Paulo."

"So many who believed are dead."

"But the souls of those who truly gave themselves to Him are unharmed and perfect."

"Even the smallest child freshly anointed?"

"Oh, Paulo, see them at His feet."

The children had been the first to come down with the sickness that brought chills and fever and delirium, attacked the intestines, the liver and lungs, and brought a bloody froth of spittle to the lips. For the worst afflicted, death came in two or three days. Nothing that had been tried, neither bloodletting nor infusions of the juice of limes and oranges, had helped. Week after week the epidemic raged, claiming first one hundred, then two hundred. Ultimately, so many were anointed for burial and carried to the great holes dug in the fields beyond the aldeia that Inácio lost track of the number. And after a month, just when it had seemed that the worst of the epidemic was over, there came a second pestilence, more horrible than the first.

A virulent pox attacked the bodies of the children, corrupting the flesh with a rash that started on their face and forearms and spread to the rest of the body. By the third day, blisters began to form and then enlarged to putrescent sores.

What had happened with the children was repeated with their parents, until almost the entire aldeia had been stricken with the deadly infection. Little could be done for the victims except scrape off the contaminated flesh and bathe them, but for the majority these ministrations only delayed the end.

"We never knew these illnesses before. When we lived at our malocas, our people did not suffer this way."

Remaining on his knees, Inácio twisted around to face Paulo. "It is true that the sickness was brought by the Portuguese, but it is God's will whether it attacks a man or not."

Inácio weighed his words carefully, for the epidemic was provoking the most awful doubt among the natives. Why did so many die immediately after they were anointed? they asked. Wherever the cross was and many natives were gathered, the sickness raged: Were the fathers of Jesus in league with the other Portuguese to kill all the clans?

Paulo had been a strong support through these terrible months, but lately even he had begun to show fear for his health and had begun to express doubts and ask probing questions.

"For every Portuguese, Padre, a hundred of our people are taken. Is there so much wickedness with us? Even among those who follow Jesus?"

Inácio shook his head. "So many questions, Paulo. What can be more important than to ask His mercy for all — His forgiveness for our sins?"

"I will pray, Father," Paulo said.

Inácio rose and left quietly. He slept restlessly till after dawn, and awoke unrefreshed. After morning mass, Inácio took leave of Padre Agostinho and set out for São Salvador, where he was expected at a meeting of fathers from the aldeias.

His old comrade Padre Manoel da Nóbrega was away in the south, working with José de Anchieta at São Paulo and Rio de Janeiro. Governor Mem de Sá had attacked the French Huguenot settlement at Guanabara Bay, driving the inhabitants from their island redoubt, forcing the survivors to the mainland, and then launching a campaign to expel them from Brazil.

At São Paulo, Nóbrega and Anchieta had welcomed this initiative, for the natives befriended by the French interlopers disturbed the peace in the lands between Guanabara Bay and the plains of Piratininga and were delaying an advance into the wilds beyond the São Paulo aldeia. This Jesuit village had been attacked the previous year by natives in league with the half-breed mamelucos, the tribe of the castaway João Ramalho, who had grown resentful of the Jesuits' repeated calls for order and civilization at Piratininga. But the Jesuits, led by the fierce hunchback Anchieta, had beaten off the assault with the help of their converts.

Padre Nóbrega had stepped down as Provincial to free himself for this mission in the south, and though Inácio was acquainted with the new Provincial, Luis de Gra, from his days at Coimbra, they did not enjoy the friendship Inácio and Nóbrega had shared.

Inácio was a lonely figure at the Jesuit colégio, a handsome two-story building raised on a vantage point overlooking the bay. His very appearance evoked sympathy from the scholarly and cultured fathers who devoted themselves to the teaching of the colonists' children and the spiritual welfare of the capital. They saw a tall, haggard man of indeterminate age. There were moments when Inácio seemed much older than his forty-four years; his expression was anguished and worn, and his back and shoulders sloped in a manner that suggested great weariness. When he arrived, his cassock was tattered and patched with dyed strips of canvas and his feet were bare. Such poverty moved several fathers at the colégio to offer him a new robe and sandals, which he accepted graciously.

At the colégio, he learned that in three months the epidemic had taken hold from Porto Seguro and Ilheus to the Bahia, and outbreaks were reported far beyond these regions, at Olinda and in the interior of Pernambuco. The extent of the calamity could be gauged from what was happening around the Bahia: Two-thirds of all the aldeia natives were dead, and among the ten thousand survivors, it was feared that the same percentage would yet succumb.

The same fatalities were to be found among the enslaved natives and the blacks, among whom the toll was so great that the cane fields, and their owners, faced ruin.

The desolation did not end there: From the reports of two fathers who had journeyed inland, the horrors of plague and pox were raging at the malocas of natives not yet contacted by the Portuguese. Many were fleeing toward the colony's settlements; crushed as they were by the diseases, they had faced yet another torment — famine.

"If you could see the poor things," said a father reporting on the condition of these refugees, "seeking a bowl of manioc. They arrive at a plantation begging the owner to take their children as slaves in exchange for a single meal. If they have no children, then they offer themselves, weak as they may be, and if they are refused, they do not give up but remove the shackles from slaves who have died and bind themselves with these, thinking to impress the master with this show of willing bondage."

These new forms of slavery, with men surrendering their liberty for a bowl of manioc, disgusted the fathers, and it was resolved that to fight this evil the fathers at São Salvador would seek the support of Governor de Sá. Inácio and the others, now apprised of the full threat to their missions, were to return to their aldeias.

※

One morning six weeks after his return from São Salvador, Inácio was conducting a burial service for nine natives who'd died during the night, when he noticed a young girl among those standing at the graveside. At the conclusion of the services, the girl hurried to his side.

"What is it, child?"

She stood with her eyes downcast. "Father, I must confess."

Seeing the urgent appeal in her eyes, he nodded and gestured for her to follow him to the church.

"No, Father, I have not sinned. There are men who speak words I fear, and my father is with them and I fear for him, for surely the anger of the Lord will not spare him."

"And what is their sin?"

"In the evenings, they . . . they pray with Paulo. They talk of the sickness when they are together at his house, and ask for protection against it. They burn pepper and roots of the forest, and there is talk of evil."

Exercising great control, Inácio calmly told the girl to keep silent about this and sent her on her way.

※

He waited till night, with Padre Agostinho and the two lay brothers. When most in the aldeia slept, they crept toward the house of Paulo, Inácio walking ahead of the others with a thick staff of wood as hard as iron.

When they were close enough to hear the proceedings from within the house, they paused: The sounds that reached them were not the chants and rattles they'd expected but a murmur of prayer and the low, faithfully voiced appeal of hymns, not to a pagan deity, but to the Lord Himself.

Inácio motioned his trio of companions to remain where they were; then he pressed forward, bending low as he made for a window. Apparently the girl had been confused, misinterpreting a fervent appeal by these converts, who perhaps believed that the pungent smoke of pepper warded off infection.

"O Lord Jesus, Son of God," he heard Paulo intone, "hear their cries in these sorrowful days. Lord Jesus, my friend, guide them through this long darkness."

'Jesus, Jesus," others cried.

"Holy Spirit," said one, "may he lead us to what has been lost."

"Where is Paulo, Arm of Iron, whom all in the aldeia followed?"

This question puzzled Inácio, for Paulo himself had asked it.

"There is the body but not the soul," a man said.

"Paulo rests. Paulo rests" another chanted.

Inácio hastily drew himself up to look through the window. In the light from several lamps, he saw the convert Paulo, wearing a long green robe in the style of a cassock and upon his head a red cap. A woman, whom Inácio recognized as Paulo's wife, stood near him, supporting a Cross.

"Holy Spirit who rules, Father, Son, Holy Mother," Paulo was saying, "your servant from heaven . . ."

"Saint! Saint!" several cried. "Saint of Heaven! Holy traveler without rest!"

"God alone will save our people," Paulo continued, "with His Son who died so that all may live. As the dawn rises, so did He, and His light is everywhere in the forest. O Tupinambá, where the fields are neglected and dying, where the boots of our persecutors tramp, the fruits of the earth will grow again. An abundance wherever our wives take their digging sticks. There will be happiness, for the Lord promises all these fruits for the sick and the slain, who will be born again. They will rise, wherever they were killed by the Portuguese, and in all the places where they have been afflicted by the plague of the Portuguese."

"Tell us, saint of Heaven," a native said, "what He has said about our enemies."

"When it is time, they will be turned into beasts, with eyes for nothing but the forest . . . and fear for the Tupinambá who hunt them."

"This has been promised, Santo António?"

"This is how it was revealed to me."

Inácio could bear no more. He burst through the entrance, pushing those in his way aside with his staff, and stormed toward Paulo. "Blasphemy!" he cried. "False witness! Satan!"

"I speak only the truth, as it was revealed to António, Saint of Heaven."

Inácio raised the staff threateningly.

"No!" several in the room cried. *"No!"*

But Inácio struck out, enraged, wielding the staff with both hands. "Satan! You damn every soul in Santa Cruz with your lies! Your pestilence has stained these shores, this forest, ever since you were cast from His heavenly temple!" His raving ended when several in the room seized him and dragged him down.

"O Santo António," one asked, "what must we do with him?"

Paulo stood looking down at the crumpled figure of Inácio and shaking his head. "Forgive him," he said finally.

For Paulo, who so impressed the Jesuits when they found him before the altar after Mem de Sá's forces had driven him to the aldeia, there had been another glorious encounter with God. How often he'd listened to Padre Inácio tell of St. Anthony, who had gone into the wilderness to do battle with the hosts of evil. When Paulo had witnessed so many dying at the aldeia, he'd gone alone to the forest to perform a retreat, and there he'd had a vision in which it was revealed to him that he was Santo António; and his wife, Mother of God. His mission on earth was to lead the Tupinambá away from this aldeia to lands where the past could be reborn. There they would wait for a day when every Long Hair was transformed into a lowly beast.

Padre Agostinho and the lay brothers had rushed up at the sound of Inácio's shouts, but they had been denied entrance to the house. They now saw the green-robed Paulo leave with his wife and twelve men, some of whom they recognized as their most devout converts.

❧

In July 1583 the office of the Jesuit Provincial at São Salvador sent Rafael Arroyo, a lay brother attached to the colégio, to assist Padre Inácio Cavalcanti at St. Peter and St. Paul's aldeia. Arroyo was only slightly over five feet tall, with a long nose, tiny dark eyes, olive skin, and oily black hair. The son of a sword maker in Toledo, he had recently arrived at the Bahia. He himself was an armorer by trade, and when he was twenty-five he had gone to Lisbon, where he'd worked in the royal armory alongside other craftsmen invited from Italy and Germany. The armorers had been welcomed by King Sebastião, then a flaxen-haired, large-limbed twenty-year-old filled with a sense of grand destiny, his spirit moved by fanatic fervor for the glories of the past.

In 1578, Dom Sebastião assembled sixteen thousand men and set out to conquer Morocco. At Alcacer-Quibir, south of Tangiers, the force was destroyed and Dom Sebastião himself slain. Less than fifty escaped, among them Rafael Arroyo, who had sworn that if God allowed him to live, never again would he put his hand to the creation of weapons of war.

The rout at Alcacer-Quibir had not ended in the sands of North Africa. Dom Sebastião had died a bachelor, and the heir to the Portuguese throne was his aged great-uncle, Cardinal Henriques. Eighteen months after his succession, Henriques died. This marked the end of the Aviz dynasty, so triumphant in the days of Manoel the Fortunate. Manoel's daughter Isabel had married Charles V, father of Philip II of Spain, who now claimed and won the throne of Portugal.

Not only had the Portuguese lost the independence of their homeland and empire; they had gained new enemies — the English and the Dutch — with whom their new king, Philip II, had long quarreled.

Thus it was that Rafael Arroyo, the Toledo armorer who'd become a servant of peace, found himself among the Portuguese at the Bahia, since the possessions of Spain and Portugal were now united under Philip's crown.

When Brother Rafael was told to move to the aldeia beyond São Salvador, he was not entirely pleased, for he'd been employed in the decoration of the church of the Ajuda. Brother Rafael had turned his talent for embossing and enameling breast-plates and gauntlets to the patterning of gold and silver leaf and had found it greatly rewarding — and comforting — to work alone at the altar in the church. But he obediently accepted the orders of the fathers at the colégio, and left at once for the aldeia of St. Peter and St. Paul.

Upon his arrival, he was distressed by the disorder he encountered. The church was in need of repair, its limed walls crumbling in many places. Although the great square was open and clean, the huts that flanked it were as shabby as the church.

The natives of the aldeia greeted him cheerfully enough, especially the chil-dren who ran to meet him, but they seemed to lack an enthusiasm he expected to find in a community of new converts. The children kept him company as he walked across the square, and directed him toward the house of Padre Inácio.

Brother Rafael was almost at the door of the small abode when its occupant came out to greet him, walking slowly with a staff in his hand. The black robe hung loosely about the father.

"Welcome. Welcome, dear friend, to our village."

"I am grateful to serve here, Padre Inácio."

"Wonderful, my son," he said. "There is so much to do for Him, always — and so little time for the work. How long have you been in Santa Cruz?"

"Seven months, Padre."

"Seven months," Inácio said, wistfully. "Manoel da Nóbrega was setting the stones for our church at the Bahia in the first seven months, after we came with Gov-ernor Tomé."

They toured the aldeia then, and Padre Inácio kept referring to a time before the plague when the village held not the 170 natives of today but two thousand souls — and Jesus seemed assured the triumph that should make this His land of promise. Suddenly he grew tearful and, seizing Brother Rafael's arm, cried, "Oh, Brother Rafael, I beg of you, serve Him as a true soldier! Serve Him without the weakness and unworthiness I have shown in His cause!"

In the days that followed, Brother Rafael would often find Padre Inácio's con-versation straying to thoughts of the past. He would talk of Nóbrega, who had died in 1570, and of other fathers he'd known at this aldeia and elsewhere. He told of his uncle Nicolau, who had lived to the grand age of eighty-four, twenty years more than he himself had seen, and of Tomás Cavalcanti, whom he had accompanied on a cam-paign against the Tupiniquin and whom he now called "one of the butchers." He had not seen Tomás in all this time, but he knew him to be married to the orphan Theresa Dias and to have fathered a large family, who were prospering at Engenho Santo Tomás. Most of all, Padre Inácio spoke of the natives, with whom he'd labored so hard.

Brother Rafael was deeply moved by Padre Inácio's unquenchable faith. Inácio told him of the many expeditions into the forest and beyond to search for natives —

a cycle repeated again and again, for often the plague had returned and the converts had died in great numbers, or they had drifted away, lured to the plantations as slaves, or simply wandered back to their malocas. Yet, true apostle that this lonely man was, he had not given up hope but had continued to reach out to find new corn for God's mill.

One afternoon two months after his arrival, when Rafael was at work in the aldeia's smithy, Padre Inácio came to him in a state of excitement. "Prepare yourself to travel, Brother," he said. "There are souls waiting for us to rescue. Ten days' journey and we'll find the malocas of a clan who seek to be led to this aldeia."

They departed the next morning, heading toward the northwest, journeying with eight of the aldeia converts. Inácio had found a tremendous energy, striding forward vigorously with his staff and constantly urging the others to hurry their pace, as if he feared that the malocas they sought might be snatched from them.

On the seventh day of their journey, their route took them out of the forest into open country, where the luxuriant vegetation quickly began to give way to an arid cover of spiky bushes and stunted plants. The humid forest floor was replaced by a way strewn with stones and crossed by the dusty beds of streams. Clumps of bush, stick-dry and dead; spiny cactus bent into grotesque shapes; gnarled branches of stripped trees — *caatinga*, "the white forest," the natives called this ash-gray landscape.

For two days they traveled through this region in the backlands of the Bahia captaincy before they decided they were lost. They decided to split into two groups, one with Padre Inácio to head north, the other west with Rafael Arroyo. If they did not find the malocas in two days, they were to return to this place, recognizable from a trio of rounded granite hills. If one of the parties did locate the missing clan, it was to send back a messenger.

Brother Rafael and his group found two small villages, but neither was the one they were seeking. They returned to the rendezvous, and so too, late the next day, did a native who'd been with Inácio. Rafael was jubilant as he saw the man approach from the north, for his lone arrival suggested that the malocas had been found.

But the Tupinambá cried out in fear: "Come quickly. He is ill!"

They broke camp immediately and marched through the night, but it was past noon two days later before they reached him.

It was ferociously hot. Inácio lay in the shade of a tree, on a bed of leaves and twigs. He was burning with fever. There'd been three natives to watch over him, but he was alone now.

"Padre Inácio, it is I — Rafael."

Inácio trembled with chills. He first moved his lips silently and tried to make a gesture with his head. Then his eyes, bright and watery, seemed to widen in recognition of the figure above him and he smiled. "Oh, Rafael . . . a wonder of wonders: In this stony desert where I am stricken — such a glorious vision — my tired eyes opened and my worthless spirit was brought to rejoice in the presence of our Mother of God and her favored Saint. The sweetest reward — to behold Santo António and the Holy Mother." And then, his face radiant with a final and tremendous joy for the marvelous vision of Our Lady and her Saint, Padre Inácio Cavalcanti died.

The three men who'd been with Inácio now came crawling out of the bushes. "We were frightened they would harm us," one said.

Brother Rafael frowned. "Who?"

The Tupinambá who'd spoken was a convert who'd been at the aldeia since childhood and was one of the few who survived the plague of 1563. His name was Peter, and he still recalled the day when Governor Mem de Sá had welcomed him at the font.

"They left an hour ago," Peter said. "We hid in the bushes for fear they would kill us," he repeated.

"Who were these people?" Brother Rafael asked again.

Peter's voice filled with alarm. "The devil came out of this stony earth to torment our beloved father." And then he explained: "Twenty years ago, at the time of the plague, a convert, Paulo, fled the aldeia. He called himself Santo António, and his wife, Mother of God." He stopped and began to sob.

"Go on, Peter," Rafael said gently.

"Santo António and others who roam the caatinga found us here. He saw that the padre was dying and he spoke to him. 'I am Santo António,' he said. His wife stood with him. 'This is Mother of God.'" Peter stopped again, gazing at Inácio.

"What happened then?"

"Oh, Brother Rafael! Santo António took the padre's hands in his own and told him that God had led him to this place — to summon Padre Inácio. The padre believed him. Paulo prayed with Padre Inácio and then told his followers that they must leave, for God wanted to be alone with Padre Inácio."

A scowl returned to Brother Rafael's face. Then he looked at Inácio's expression. "But, dear Lord, how happy he looks."

BOOK THREE

The
Bandeirantes

X

August 1628 – August 1639

"*I*shmael Pinheiro, you're a fat, lazy fool, but not half as foolish as I, Amador Flôres da Silva, who put my trust in you. 'Sleep soundly, Amador,' I told myself, 'for the bold Pinheiro will watch over you. The devils of the forest themselves will dance away from Ishmael Pinheiro.' What stupidity!"

Pinheiro was sitting on the ground, his legs stretched out in front of him. He said nothing but raised a balled fist to wipe his tears with his broad knuckles.

It was August 17, 1628, deep in a forest some 150 miles southwest of São Paulo de Piratininga, in the direction of the Spanish colony of Paraguay. Close by sat six men, a rearguard patrol with an army in which the boys' fathers served. Left behind at São Paulo, Amador and Ishmael had run away to join the force: Ishmael had fallen asleep on guard the night before and awoken to find the soldiers in their midst. The patrol leader had shown them no sympathy: "You want to be heroes?" he'd jeered. "Good. Be heroes. Show us how brave you are, when you face your fathers!"

Amador Flôres da Silva was a grandson of the renegade slaver Marcos da Silva and Unauá, the girl from the Tupiniquin. After the slavers had destroyed the malocas of Aruanã at Porto Seguro and the hopes of Padre Inácio, Unauá, had been taken captive. Seduced by Marcos da Silva, she had come to bear his children and to be a devoted wife to this man who had brutalized her people.

Amador was short and thickset. He had a large head, with raven-black, coarse hair and the beginnings of a beard; a small, fleshy mouth; hard brown eyes, alert and dark; and a face scarred by the pox, which he'd survived two years before, when one of the recurring epidemics had struck the São Paulo region. He wore a short coat, shirt, knee-length breeches, and a kerchief of green Manchester cotton angled across his brow and knotted at the back of his head. And he carried a bow and arrows and a long knife.

Indicating the patrol with a gesture of his head, Amador asked, "What if these had been Carijó, Ishmael?" He did not wait for a response. "Such a royal banquet you'd have made for them — down to the last morsel of your tiny brain."

"Please, Amador, please," he blubbered. "I'm sorry."

"You'll be sorrier, my friend, when you stand before your father," Amador said.

Now Ishmael smiled weakly. "At least it's not Bernardo da Silva to whom I must answer."

It was Amador's turn to look miserable. His father, Bernardo, was a wrathful man, with a heavy beard, a lined and ravaged countenance, and the same hard, secretive eyes as Amador's.

"Mother of mercy," Amador moaned, "when old Bernardo da Silva sees me carried out of the forest like a savage for ransom, what will he say? When I begged him to let me come on this war, he laughed. 'War is for men, Amador Flôres,' he said, and sent me back to the cows."

"Oh, Amador, you are a man." Ishmael looked up with open admiration for his friend. "You've led us through the forest, never losing your way."

Amador and Ishmael had left São Paulo ten days before, quickly picking up the trail of the army and following it through lands that lay southwest of the Piratininga heights. From the people of his grandmother, Amador had developed a bold and acute sense of the wilds.

Of course he was a man, Amador thought, and his father knew it, too. This very month he had turned fourteen. But Bernardo da Silva had deferred to the wishes of his third wife, Rosa Flôres, who insisted that her son stay home to tend the cows and pigs.

Amador had watched the 120 men from his father's lands, free laborers and slaves, march off to São Paulo, thirty miles away, to join the *bandeira* of Captain-Major Antônio Raposo Tavares, whom his father served as a lieutenant. The bandeiras of medieval Portugal had been small raiding parties sniping at the Moors; at São Paulo, a bandeira was an organized force that, regardless of size, set out for an expedition into the backlands. The army to which Bernardo da Silva had contributed his private militia consisted of three thousand men.

Shortly after the departure of the bandeira, Amador's mother had sent him to the Pinheiro house for salt. Ishmael's father, Nuno Fernandes, belonged to a small community of New Christians — Jews compelled to accept Catholicism. The Inquisition had not been established in Brazil, but occasionally Visitors were sent to examine the faith of the colonists and to investigate reports that Brazil was a haven for Jewish exiles and lax New Christians. The belief that there were significant numbers of crypto Jews was exaggerated, but Portugal had always been more tolerant of Jews than had Spain, and groups had come to the colony, particularly those with expertise in the sugar industry. At São Paulo, Nuno Fernandes observed his Catholic vows while secretly meeting with others to celebrate the old religion. He was a prosperous trader and an *armador*, a supplier to the bandeiras. He had departed with the army, as had all but twenty-five of those men of São Paulo capable of bearing arms, and left fat Ishmael to guard his velvets and satins, spices and salt.

Ishmael was also fourteen, an unlikely warrior in appearance, but he could read and had been greatly influenced by a book about the Crusaders he'd found at the colégio of the Jesuits, to which his father dutifully had sent him. When Amador had gone to fetch the salt, Ishmael had spoken to him of the brave knights of Christendom.

He'd listened to Ishmael until he could no longer contain his enthusiasm. "Let's join our fathers on their expedition — for Christ and Dom Sebastião!"

To mention a king of Portugal who died over three decades before either of them had been born was perfectly natural. The memory of Sebastião, who had fallen with the flower of Portugal's knighthood in battle against the Moor at Alcacer-Quibir in 1578, was kept alive even at São Paulo, one of the farthest outposts of the empire. "Our king died that day, and with him the pride of Portugal, mother of us all," Amador had heard from his father. "Our birthright and independence passed to the Spaniard, who has always coveted our conquests."

Amador had grown up with the knowledge of two special enemies: the untamed savage of the forest, and the Spanish masters of Brazil, toward whom his father and a man such as Captain-Major Raposo Tavares showed a passionate loathing. Hatred of the wild and bloodthirsty savage was easily understood, but the enmity toward the Spanish had been more difficult for Amador to comprehend. One in five of those who lived at São Paulo was Spanish, and there seemed no difference between them and the Portuguese.

But his father had explained that mainly the São Paulo Spanish came to the highlands to escape the authorities at the coast, as others had been doing even since before São Paulo had been established. No, the Spaniards to be despised were not these refugees and renegades but the power-hungry in Madrid. They had seized control of Portugal and all her possessions after the death of Dom Sebastião.

Philip II of Spain, son of the emperor Charles V and Isabella of Portugal, had taken the Portuguese crown in 1581. His son, the pious and pompous Philip III, had succeeded him, and now there was Philip IV, horseman, hunter, lover of art and letters, who, when not engaged in these pastimes, involved his country — and Portugal — in a vicious and exhausting conflict with England, France, and Holland.

Just four years ago São Paulo had been readied for defense against a Dutch invasion. Bernardo da Silva and others had scoffed at the idea of an army scaling the pinnacles and crags to the heights of Piratininga, on which their town stood, but they'd been vigilant all the same, for the Dutch had triumphed elsewhere in Brazil, seizing the capital, São Salvador, in May 1624. But, in April 1625, Madrid, already angered by Dutch attacks at sea on her treasure ships from the New World, had sent the greatest fleet ever to cross the equator — 52 ships with 12,500 men and 1,185 guns — and expelled the heretics from the Bahia.

Holland still actively sought a way to seize control of Brazil and the three hundred sugar mills now operating from Pernambuco to the south. Before the invasion of the Bahia, the Dutch West India Company had been established to achieve this conquest, and its nineteen directors — the Heeren XIX — continued to assure the stockholders that they would yet win a handsome profit from the Portuguese sugar-cane plantations in the region of Olinda and São Salvador.

Now, in the forest, the leader of the patrol that had surprised the boys announced that they were to resume their march to the main body of soldiers. "Come, my little captains, ready yourselves," he said, and gave a tremendous guffaw.

~

The Paulista force to which the fathers of Amador and Ishmael were attached consisted of sixty-nine Portuguese and Spaniards, nine hundred mamelucos and the rest natives from pacified clans, some free, some enslaved. All delighted that their conquerors and masters were employing them as warriors and not sending them to grovel in the fields. This three-thousand-man army, making its way through forest and swamp, over mountains and along deep valleys southwest of São Paulo, went forward beneath both the silken banners of the cross and the colorful devices of its own commanders. Its ranks, with half-naked savages and mamelucos clad in rags, gave the impression of a rabble horde storming through the countryside, but this was a well-organized military expedition headed by experienced commanders and officers who maintained severe discipline.

The army was penetrating deep into Paraguay, a province of the Spanish viceroyalty of Peru, west of the Tordesilhas Line. With one monarch now ruling both nations, the journeys of the Paulistas beyond the territory of Brazil could go relatively unchallenged.

Ostensibly, the army was marching with permission to pacify wild Carijó, long considered a threat to São Paulo. But the real objective was to find natives for sale to the coastal plantations, conquest and disease having decimated the tribes near settlements such as Olinda and those at the Bahia.

The Paulistas had been slave-raiding in these lands since long before Amador's birth, leading thousands of Carijó back to São Paulo. Eighteen years ago, however, Jesuits from Asunción had moved into this "province of Guairá," which they named for a famous chief of the area. Finding the "Guarani," as they called the Carijó, a people who already accepted the notion of a single Father/God and were willing converts to Christianity, they established twelve villages, or "reductions," which the Guarani clans were encouraged to inhabit. The earliest reductions now had a population of six thousand, and the ones that followed, too, had prospered beyond anything the Jesuits had accomplished at their aldeias in Brazil.

Year after year the black robes extended their sanctuaries, and as they prospered, the reductions, with their fabulous horde of natives, had become a temptation to the Paulistas. There was also the added incentive of striking a blow at the domain of the Spaniard.

Amador had often seen his father march off with raiding parties, sometimes staying away from the da Silva settlement for a year and almost always returning with a valuable share of captives. Though they kept a herd of cattle and grew fields of food crops, the da Silvas had been slavers since the days of Marcos. Amador had known neither his grandfather Marcos nor his grandmother Unauá.

Amador was the youngest of sixteen surviving sons and daughters of Bernardo, who'd fathered twenty-two children by Maria and Josefa, who were Portuguese and whom he'd outlived, and Rosa Flôres, Amador's mother — Spanish Rosa, brought from beyond the Rio Plata and Bernardo's bride these past sixteen years. Four of the sixteen, the issue not of these wives but of native women, Bernardo had freely acknowledged, counting them along with his church-blessed progeny.

Of Bernardo da Silva's children — the oldest a grandfather of fifty-four — most remained at or near the settlement of São Paulo.

Sixty-one years separated Amador and his father; but age had not diminished Bernardo's vigor. During the arduous journeys with the bandeiras, he kept up with the captains and officers, who accepted the old campaigner as a comrade.

Bernardo held the Jesuit fathers in contempt and had passed on to all his children, this rancorous disdain. Amador came to see, too, that the da Silvas were not alone in their animosity toward the Company of Jesus. Even the good priest Anselmo, a frequent visitor to their house, who'd taught him his prayers and catechism, despaired of the black robes: "They are wrong in their protests to Madrid and their accusations of slavery against God-fearing men," he had told Amador. "Our people bring the savages to the markets of São Paulo and elsewhere, where they may be taken into service with Christian families, who raise them to civilization."

Padre Anselmo was always ready to serve as chaplain and confessor to the men of the bandeiras, and was this day with the army ahead of the patrol taking Amador and Ishmael Pinheiro to their fathers.

The main body of the army was camped for the night on open ground rising beyond a broad, shallow river. This was the site of a Guarani village destroyed by a bandeira earlier. From every direction, the forest was reclaiming the clearing, but this secondary growth had not hidden the evidence of ruin.

Amador saw his father even before crossing the shallow river. The officers of the bandeira were gathered on a broad sandbank that sloped gently toward the water's edge. Several turned in the direction of the patrol as it emerged from the forest, and Amador recognized the short, stumpy figure in their midst.

"He would be greeting me as a hero had you not slept," Amador said to Ishmael Pinheiro. "Now look how I'm to be received — wet and wretched at his feet!"

"My father is there, too," Ishmael said. The elder Pinheiro, though no officer, stood with the group of commanders. As an armador, he would usually not accompany the force but would wait at São Paulo to receive his "profit" — the slaves who would be sold to cover his outlay and bring a reward for the risk he took in financing the expedition. But this raid was so promising that Pinheiro had been eager to join the bandeira.

The patrol leader encouraged the runaways into the water: "Come, come, my little captains — make the crossing."

The river was sixty paces wide at this point, slow-moving and seemingly easy to ford; stepping into it, Amador found himself in water up to his knees, and the farther he progressed, the stronger the current. Ishmael walked just ahead of him, upstream, stepping warily along the sandy bottom. Suddenly the sand beneath their feet gave way, and both lost their balance as the river bottom shelved. Ishmael gave a cry as he plunged into the depression, the water swirling up to his neck. Amador pumped his short legs furiously, trying to stay afloat, as Ishmael, panicking, clutched him violently. Both shouted unintelligibly as the swift current swept them along the deep channel.

Then, abruptly, they were freed from the current. Amador struggled to his feet. Fifteen paces of dark, slimy mud lay between them and the edge of the sandbank. Amador started through this quagmire, and just as he was about to reach the group of officers, his foot caught on a hidden branch and he was flung back into the mud.

"Amador Flôres da Silva!" a young officer shouted. "Is this how you greet your officers? On your belly before us, as the peças of Africa honor their kings? Or have you no strength to face Tenente Bernardo?"

Amador remained sprawled out before them, but he raised his head as he looked for his father. Lieutenant Bernardo da Silva was standing at the side of Captain-Major Raposo Tavares.

Bernardo da Silva's upper body was encased in a sleeveless leather jacket quilted and padded with cotton twill thick enough to withstand an arrow. Below the waist he wore coarse cotton breeches and boots that extended above the knee. On his head was a well-worn hat of French design with a broad brim turned up at both sides and a plume of feathers attached. On the belt that secured the quilted carapace was a good-sized pouch, a powder horn and ramrod for his musket, and a sword, knives, and small battle-ax.

Amador looked away, searching for Padre Anselmo, but there was no sign of the priest.

"Pray God he meets the enemy before he does himself harm," a voice nearby suddenly roared.

"Forgive me, Father," Amador cried. "I was wrong to leave the cows — and Dona Rosa." Hastily he clambered to his feet, ignoring a stinging, grazed knee but clasping a muddy hand to his buttocks. He stood silently, grimly awaiting the next word from his father or another of these men, who were even more formidable than he'd imagined in his dreams of fighting alongside them.

"Where are my cows, Amador Flôres?"

"The peças' sons have my orders," Amador replied earnestly.

"He gives the little peças his *orders*," Bernardo da Silva said, and laughed loudly. "*My* command he disobeys."

"Oh, Father, how could I stay with the cows and pigs — and the women — while other young men marched to this great war?"

At this moment, Ishmael Pinheiro, who'd been dragged from the mud by two of his father's native slaves, began to howl. The older Pinheiro was caning him as he tried to crawl away.

Amador looked fearfully at his father. "We would have joined the bandeira at the first battle," he said. "We wanted to raid the Carijó with you."

"What must I do with you, Amador Flôres?"

"Anything, senhor — *Dom Bernardo* — whatever you wish. I was thinking only of the honor there would be in fighting for the force of my father."

Before, Amador had addressed his father in this exalted manner, as "Dom Bernardo," and seen how it appeased the patriarch. Although a mameluco, Bernardo, unlike his brothers, had always wanted to be counted with the *homens bons*, the "good men" of São Paulo, who were mostly Portuguese.

"Captain-Major Raposo Tavares!" Bernardo now called out. "It would seem we have one more man for our ranks."

"Yes, Bernardo! Let him march with us, but one thing . . ."

"What is it, Captain-Major?"

"Your little soldier, Tenente, will have a brief war . . . if he shows his buttocks to the greedy savage."

Amador straightened his back and thrust out his chest. "I will ready myself — to serve Dom Bernardo and the captain-major."

Bernardo da Silva raised a hand as if to strike his son. "Be off with you, before you howl as loudly as your fat friend!" But there was a twinkle in his eye as he said to the captain-major: "It's time he did the work of men, this last-born pup of Bernardo da Silva."

☙

The late winter's night was settling over the camp, sudden and chill, when Amador was ready to report back to his father. He'd washed at the river, and a slave woman, one of a dozen blacks accompanying the army, had stitched his breeches. Blacks were rare at São Paulo, since there were no great plantations requiring their labor; but the da Silvas had kept four slaves from Loanda, which had replaced Mpinda as the main port for slaves from the decaying kingdom of the Kongo and the lands of 'Ngola south of it.

The woman who'd sewn Amador's breeches had been brought along to serve Bernardo, and was with the 120 people, mamelucos and natives, who belonged to Bernardo's private militia. The Paulista army was led by a field master, Manuel Preto, a veteran of these slave raids, and was divided into four companies, each with its captain-major. Bernardo was lieutenant of an advance group, consisting mostly of his own force. Three-quarters of his natives were Tupiniquin from the São Paulo region, some who served him as slaves, others attached to his party because their malocas were on lands claimed by da Silva or adjacent to his holdings.

Amador was making his way back to the sands at the river, passing the fires of natives and mamelucos, when he heard his name called. He stopped walking and waited until the cry came again; then he crossed to a clump of ferns.

Ishmael Pinheiro was lurking there, and he appeared miserable and defeated. "My father says I'm to be an armador and must learn to profit by war, not to fight. He's ordering three slaves to carry me back."

Amador looked closely at his friend. "Pray they're strong, Ishmael Pinheiro. The journey's long."

"You'll stay?" Ishmael asked

"Oh, yes, I'm welcome. These great men see how foolish it was to leave me with the cows."

"Go, Amador — before you see me cry a second time today."

Amador left Ishmael and went to report to Bernardo da Silva, whom he found sitting at a fire with the captain-major and other officers of the bandeira. The captain-major was telling of a recent entry into an unknown part of the backlands.

Helping himself to food, Amador took a seat near the fire. He saw his father heap a tin plate with meat and manioc and then begin a ceremony that accompanied every meal:

Bernardo da Silva set his plate on the ground in front of him and removed an item secured to his belt — a large silver spoon.

Bernardo had evidence enough — his lands and the slaves he owned and the fine wives he'd wed — to prove himself a "good man," but this spoon was important to him, and he never went without it on campaign. Many of the honorable men in his midst were content to eat with their fingers and toss lumps of manioc into their mouths as the savages did at their malocas. Bernardo would not say a word against their manners, but he would sit in their presence using his silver spoon with great pleasure and dignity, as he did now, listening to the captain-major.

Antônio Raposo Tavares was thirty years old. He had come to São Paulo ten years ago from the plains of Alemtejo, in central Portugal, where he spent his youth among the wheat fields and olive groves. Raposo Tavares was a tall, handsome, bearded man, powerfully built, decisive and confident. A born leader who devoutly believed he was destined to make great discoveries in Brazil, he was passionately eager for adventure.

The thought of Alemtejo, with its ancient citadels wrested from Roman, Goth, and Moor, now lying within the realm of Spain galled Raposo Tavares, who loathed the authority of Castile. This was not his first incursion into Paraguay, but never had he come with such a force into the provinces of his enemy.

At the fireside, Amador heard the captain-major and his father talking about the Spaniards, and one in particular: the new governor of Asunción, Don Luis de Céspedes, who'd passed through São Paulo some months before on his way to take up his post.

"If only every highborn Hidalgo could be brought to marry a good woman of our land. Don Luis sits in Asunción, but his heart? Oh, how his heart longs for the beautiful Victoria . . . and for her sugar plantation." He laughed, for it greatly amused the Paulistas that the impecunious Spaniard sent to protect their favorite raiding grounds had been smitten by the wealthy niece of the governor of Rio de Janeiro. Don Luis had been engaged to Victoria and had then set out for his new post, passing through São Paulo, where he'd found the Paulistas preparing for this great bandeira. He'd made a weak protest against the planned incursion into his colony, to which the Paulistas had replied that their only purpose would be to subdue savages who might destroy the peace Don Luis desired, now that life had so much to offer him.

"Don Luis is as old a campaigner as the one you see before you," Bernardo added, "and now that he has the love and lands and wealth of Victoria, he wants no more."

"Ah, but he does intend for his wife to be cared for with a share of the best captives from our expedition," said Raposo Tavares.

Bernardo grinned at this reminder. "It's nothing," he said, "a small token for a governor who'll ignore our passage through the province of the Jesuits."

The captain-major was a frequent visitor to the da Silva lands beyond São Paulo. When this army had been raised, Bernardo da Silva had immediately volunteered to put his militia under Raposo Tavares's command: "The man has the *sertão* in his heart," he'd explained to his family. "He may come from the plains of Alemtejo, but it's upon our *sertão* that he seeks his horizon."

This word — "sertão" — arose frequently in the conversation drifting back from the men at the fireside. "Backlands"; "wild country"; "the unknown forest"; "hill, valley, river hidden by the mist of Creation"; "place of thorn and desert"; "brutal land without end" — sertão was all these and more. It started not beyond the next rise or across the river ahead but deep within the soul.

The men of São Paulo, with their fusion of races, were born to answer the call of the sertão. From the amalgam of Iberian and Moor, African and Tupi, there emerged a breed of men singularly equipped to challenge the sertão: bold and brutal, cheerful and ingenious, brave discoverers and shrewd traders, fearless and rapacious and visionary wanderers of river and desert and forest. Always they carried the hope of a mountain of emeralds reflected in the heavens, a summit piled with rocks of gold in the shape of the crown, the spear and the nails of Christ.

Year after year the da Silvas and their countrymen had pressed deeper and deeper into the sertão; emerald mountains and lakes of gold still eluded them, but they remained believing and patient, and had not been entirely unrewarded, for there was the native horde pulled from their malocas in the sertão and driven to São Paulo.

São Paulo: a squalid blot upon the highlands above the Serra do Mar, where the Jesuits had founded it seven decades ago. Its officials were weak and corrupt, and men such as Bernardo da Silva viewed the settlement with suspicion.

The da Silvas kept mostly to their holding thirty miles away from São Paulo in hills rolling toward the Anhembi, or, as they called it, "*The* River," to denote its uniqueness, for it flowed neither east nor south down the Serra do Mar to the sea but instead to the west, a great artery into the heart of the sertão.

Several times a year, however, when there was a religious festival, the da Silvas dutifully tramped to São Paulo. The clan camped around Bernardo's town property near the *câmara*, the meeting place of the judges and officials of the town.

The colégio of the Jesuit fathers stood upon a good vantage point above the Piratininga plain. Here, too, were the Franciscans and Benedictines, their churches raised with care. But most of São Paulo was a slum of mud-and-wattle hovels planted along dirt-strewn streets, which were loose and stony in summer and thick with mud and filth in the rainy season.

In all, 2,300 people lived in the town and the lands beyond it. The majority were mamelucos and natives, and all knew a sense of isolation engendered by the mist-covered crags of the Serra do Mar that had to be descended to reach the coast; but, more than that, they felt a gnawing loneliness in this remote settlement that fostered an independent and arrogant cast of mind and made them turn not back toward the coast but to the promise of the vast sertão.

When Amador had finished eating, he remained seated where he was, keenly attentive to the words of the men near him.

"You're an old man, Bernardo, who has come this way many times," Captain-Major Raposo Tavares was saying. "Small wars, Tenente, to what this bandeira can achieve. We have the men, the muskets, the power to seize more Carijó than any previous bandeira."

Amador heard his father make a noise of approval, and saw him gesture with his silver spoon toward the south: "The fathers of the Company of Jesus labor faithfully to reduce the savages to submission."

"And such success they've had! Twelve great villages filled," Raposo Tavares said. "Think how glorious it will be to return with so vast a treasure snatched from the Spaniard — thousands of Carijó."

Amador was aware that the Paulista army was marching to the area of the reductions, but he had no idea of the number of slaves that might be taken from the black robes.

"Ten thousand Carijó, Bernardo," Raposo Tavares said. "More than you've seen in your long life."

૨ઝ

Six weeks later, in mid-October 1628, Amador was able to prove to his father and Captain-Major Raposo Tavares that he was as good a campaigner as any man who marched with them.

Penetrating deep into the Jesuit province, the four companies of the Paulista force had separated in order to cover as much ground as possible. The twelve Jesuit reductions lay between two great rivers, the Paranapanema, to the north, and the Iguazú, to the south, an area encompassing some 250 miles. The Paulistas concentrated on four southernmost settlements — Jesús Maria, San Miguel, Concepción, and San Antonio. Captain-Major Raposo Tavares and six hundred men were within a day's march of the reduction of San Antonio, where the Jesuit fathers had assembled four thousand natives.

Raposo Tavares and his company had been halted at a river, beyond which lay a small natural plain. The Paulistas (mainly the native warriors) raised a stockade around the camp, similar to those protecting the malocas, a great circle of tall poles implanted in the earth and lashed together with vines. Within the stockade, thatched palm-leaf shelters had been built: The natives and mamelucos had erected longhouses, where scores were able to hang their hammocks; the officers were quartered in smaller huts, the captain-major sharing his headquarters with five of his officers, Tenente da Silva included. Near Raposo Tavares's hut was the bandeira's chapel, in front of which a carefully hewn Cross had been planted.

In the stockade, too, an area had been cordoned off with wooden stakes as tall and strong as those that formed the outer defense works. This was the pen for prisoners taken in the surrounding countryside. At this point, only seventy Carijó were herded together in the enclosure. Most were wild savages, though seventeen of them claimed to be Christians who had been traveling from one Jesuit village to another when captured by Paulistas.

Patrols sent to spy out the San Antonio reduction had confirmed the presence of a vast congregation, but Captain-Major Raposo Tavares had not yet made a move against the Jesuit village: He was seeking that precise moment when he could be sure not one of the reduction's natives would escape the bandeira.

Ishmael Pinheiro's father, true to his word, had sent his son back to São Paulo. But Amador had quickly found new companions. Two boys, both with fathers attached to Bernardo da Silva's militia, were often with him — the mameluco Valentim Ramalho, and Abeguar, son of a Tupiniquin slave.

Valentim Ramalho's family belonged to a great clan of mamelucos related to João Ramalho, the castaway who had settled the high plateau long before the Jesuits Nóbrega and Anchieta arrived to establish São Paulo de Piratininga, and who had married the daughter of the most influential Tupiniquin elder in the region. Valentim's father had land of his own adjoining the da Silva holding, but he'd made no attempt to develop his property, electing instead to serve his neighbor Bernardo da Silva as captain of his militia.

Valentim was seventeen, with black eyes, a flat nose, and sallow complexion, as beardless as the people of his native mother. But he was only three and a half feet tall. His diminutive stature, however, had not prevented him from gaining notoriety two years before, when he bedded first the widow of a Spanish Gypsy who'd been settled at São Paulo, then the Gypsy's daughter, and then, to add injury to insult, a pair of Tupiniquin prostitutes who'd been bequeathed to the widow and happened to be her livelihood.

Amador had known Valentim and his four brothers and two sisters since childhood. One sister, Maria, a full-chested, big-limbed fifteen-year-old, had alarmed Amador with the passion she showed for him. Whereas her brother Valentim was abnormally short, Maria was almost inhumanly ugly. Her small, dark eyes, one of which wandered to the left, were set close to the bridge of a flat nose with huge nostrils. Her thin lips contrasted dismally with the fatness of her cheeks, and she had big ears that stuck out from the sides of her head. On her chin grew two moles, from which sprouted spiky tufts of hair.

A year after Valentim's episode with the widow, Maria had managed to lead Amador to a place in the woods behind their house. A coarse young girl, Maria Ramalho knew enough, mainly from the slave girls of her house, to mock Amador with talk of what small, lusty boys of São Paulo did with sheep and goats and other beasts, and before he could finish denying this, she'd wrestled him to the ground and was readying herself for him.

Knowing of Valentim's reputation as a lover, Amador had been proud of losing his virginity to Ramalho's sister, and there'd been other occasions since, when she'd stolen away from her house to make love to him.

Amador, who dreamed of chivalrous knights and fair ladies, was perturbed by Maria's grotesque homeliness, but he was also unable to resist her, and whenever there'd been an opportunity, he'd eagerly surrendered to her clammy embrace and the soft, inviting comfort of her enormous breasts.

Amador's second close companion, Abeguar, was the fourteen-year-old son of a Tupiniquin who, driven from his maloca sixty miles north of São Paulo fifteen years before, was undisputed leader of the native warriors — the slaves and the group from the malocas — on Bernardo da Silva's lands. Abeguar was slightly taller than Amador, and carried his lean, athletic body proudly. He wore nothing above the waist. A small ivory crucifix and a feather ornament fashioned by his father hung from the ends of two leather thongs around his neck.

One morning soon after work on the stockade and slave pen had ended, Amador, Valentim, and Abeguar left the camp. An unsuccessful raiding party returning the night before had reported a valley two hours to the east filled with game. With Bernardo da Silva's permission, Amador was leading his two companions on a hunt.

They each had bows, quivers made of soft bark and filled with iron-tipped arrows, and several knives, including a *facão* — the Spanish machete, the heavy eighteen-inch blade of which was excellent for hacking away undergrowth.

It was an easy descent down a wooded hill to the valley floor, and they quickly saw the accuracy of the patrol's report. The trio glimpsed deer, too far for a successful shot, and troubled a giant anteater probing for termites at the rotting base of a dead palm. Valentim grew excited and unsheathed his broad knife, clasping the weapon in both hands. The anteater rose up and made threatening gestures with its sickle-shaped claws, but when Valentim stepped closer and the others began to laugh at the sight of him ready to confront so forbidding an adversary, the anteater lifted its bushy tail and hurried away.

"Fools! Why did you alarm it?" Valentim complained.

"Oh, Valentim, such a creature wasn't worthy of your attention," Amador said, and, unstoppering a calabash flask of *cachaça*, a raw-sugarcane brandy, passed it to Valentim. "Drink."

Valentim grabbed the calabash, gulped the fiery cachaça, and, his eyes watering, gave a noisy burst of satisfaction. "One more!" he cried, but Amador demanded the flask back.

To the adults of the bandeira, casks of cachaça transported on the backs of slaves from São Paulo were as important as barrels of gunpowder. To three young braves, it was yet another introduction to the coveted pleasures of their warrior elders.

Amador sealed the calabash and they moved off. Abeguar took the lead, and they had not gone far when the Tupiniquin stopped in his tracks and urgently indicated that they should be quiet and remain where they were. He then took off alone, hurrying into the trees to his left, not making a sound as he darted away through the undergrowth.

Abeguar was gone less than fifteen minutes. He returned from the opposite direction in which he'd left, having circled around the place to which his attention had been drawn. "Seven Carijó. Five young, the same as us, and two older hunters," he reported.

"I saw nothing ahead in the trees," Amador said.

"There was nothing to see," the young Tupiniquin replied.

"But, how then — "

"The tapir!" Valentim said, suddenly remembering a sound he'd heard just before Abeguar urged them to be silent.

Abeguar nodded. "The killing was almost done. I heard the beast's cry."

Valentim beamed, and rocked from side to side, so great was his pleasure at having recognized this sound.

Amador studied him quietly, a serious look on his face. Then he said, "What would our fathers do if we were to bring them these animals?"

Now Valentim's delight reached such new heights that he began to tremble. "Oh, yes!" He shook his long knife. "Why don't we hunt these Carijó?"

"There are seven," Abeguar reminded them.

"We must have a plan," Amador said.

"They'll be a long time with the tapir," Abeguar said. "They're using stones to butcher it."

"We may fail if we try to rush them, even if there's surprise," Amador said.

Valentim had been eyeing the flask of cachaça Amador carried. "Wine!" he said suddenly. "Some wine for this problem."

Amador placed his hand on the calabash but did not pass it to Valentim. He merely nodded his head, as if agreeing with what Valentim had said. Then, quickly, he explained: "We'll go to them as friends. We'll offer to help with the butchering. Once among them, we can wait for the right moment to take away their weapons."

Abeguar agreed and so did Valentim, who repeated his demand for cachaça.

"We must save it," Amador said. "For the Carijó."

Immediately they set off toward their prey. The ground beneath their feet became loose and swampy, amid tall, straight trees that shot up from the valley floor. They hadn't gone far before the trees thinned out, the high brush providing cover as they crept forward. They first saw the Carijó crowded around the tapir, which lay on its back, its great white belly exposed.

The trio approached cautiously. When they were almost upon the savages, Amador whispered to Valentim, "Keep a distance behind us."

"What difference will that make?"

"Better they first see only two of us."

Amador and Abeguar showed themselves, crying out words of friendship, and created immediate panic among the Carijó. Some waved their hand axes; others ran to take up their bows. But when they heard the strangers speak Tupi, a language intelligible to them, their fear was replaced by intense curiosity.

"Friends!" Amador called out. "We are friends, come to hunt in this valley from the hills beyond."

Valentim, unable to contain his excitement, stepped into the open beside his friends. He was greeted with shrieks from the Carijó. Two leapt away to hide in the brush, but the rest remained, petrified with fear at the sight of Valentim.

"Aieee!" Amador exclaimed. "A little demon! This is what the Carijó think you are — a tiny demon to bewitch the innocent!"

Valentim was furious. He puffed out his chest, clenched his chubby hands into fists, and waved them angrily at the Carijó.

"*Calma! Calma*, Valentim," Amador exhorted him. "Do exactly as I say."

"Valentim is a man," Ramalho retorted. "A man — not the imp of Infidels!"

"The Gypsy widow and all at São Paulo know this," Amador said. "But, my friend, listen to me, *now*."

Valentim quieted down.

"Good. Now, sit . . . there, where you are. Good." He turned to Abeguar. "I want you to tell them that we've ordered this demon to keep away from them."

Abeguar told the Carijó that the tiny creature was indeed a fierce denizen of the forest whom they'd found wandering, lost, through the trees, and they had succored him with a wonderful drink they carried, and this had so placated him that he'd put himself at their service.

Valentim quickly began to realize the value of this deception and whole-heartedly entered into his role. Amador took the calabash of cachaça, sipped from it, and then offered it to the Carijó.

One of the older warriors stepped closer and Amador passed him the drink, saying, "A brew so powerful it will pacify the fiends of the forest."

The man cried out with delight at the strength of the cachaça and then called the others to taste it. To those hiding in the brush, he shouted that it was safe to return, for the strangers were their friends and possessed a marvelous power against evil spirits.

They were not accustomed to strong liquor, and there was enough cachaça in the calabash to make them drunk.

Amador offered to assist in butchering the tapir, and climbed down to the muddy depression. As he worked, he learned that the Carijós' malocas were one-hour's walk toward the east. They had lived peacefully in this valley since the days of their great-grandfathers and had never ventured beyond it.

Valentim remained seated on the soft earth, chuckling quietly to himself as he pretended to await the orders of his supposed masters.

Abeguar had slipped away; he returned with a bundle of thin vines — for the tapir meat, he said.

Very calmly Amador continued to hack away at the tapir, gratefully accepting the Carijós' repeated promises of a share of the meat. Two Carijó boys stood close to him; they'd drunk the least cachaça, being more interested in the magic of the long knife. As he worked, Amador saw first one, then the other of the older warriors lie down on the marshy ground, from where they drowsily observed his progress. He glanced at Abeguar; he looked back to where Valentim sat and saw that he had his attention.

"Now!" he cried. "Seize the beasts!"

Amador knocked one of the boys senseless with a blow to the side of his head, and leapt at the other. The Carijó tried to run, but he slipped on the bloody tapir meat at his feet and lay there, shaking and begging for mercy.

At the signal, Abeguar had jumped to the side of the two drunk warriors, ready to stun them with a stone ax he'd picked up. But Valentim the Demon rushed to his aid with mocking shrieks and laughter, taunting the Carijó and so terrifying them that Abeguar had only to bind them with the lianas he'd fetched.

The three remaining Carijó boys were so frightened they simply collapsed. "We are your prisoners," they cried. "Meat for your people!"

"No! No! Carijó, we do not eat the flesh of men," Amador assured them. "We take you to our people, who will offer you a good life."

The boys hurried their captives out of the valley and through the woods be-yond at such a rapid pace that they entered the stockade before sunset. The Carijó had given them no trouble. Four of them carried poles slung with great bloody strips of tapir. The two older warriors, groggy with cachaça, and the remaining youth had their hands bound and were also secured by liana "collars," to which vines were attached.

Would he ever forget this moment of glory? Amador wondered, as he walked ahead of the little column entering the stockade. From every direction men roused themselves and streamed forward, pressing close to the Carijó and their captors.

Amador did not stop until he was standing in front of his father and Captain-Major Raposo Tavares, who'd both stepped out of the officers' hut.

Bernardo da Silva looked from Amador to the Carijó, a smile spreading across his heavily lined face. He laughed then, joyously. "My friends," he called out, "this is *my son*, Amador Flôres! I send him for a little meat from the forest and he brings me seven live Carijó!"

There were wild cheers from the crowd in honor of the old patriarch for having fathered such a son.

Then Captain-Major Raposo Tavares, after asking for and receiving the boys' report on their adventure, said, "Tonight, my brave soldiers, you shall eat your tapir in the company of your officers."

Raposo Tavares next ordered that the Carijó be moved to the prisoners' pen, where they would be kept until they were docile enough to roam the stockade. Men came forward and dragged away the Carijó.

"The young ones are the best," Bernardo da Silva said to his son. "Just as it is with birds — taken captive when young, they are easier to tame."

"Father, I thank you for not making me go home," Amador said.

"You're a son of the sertão, Amador Flôres; there's no other home for you."

He never forgot those words of his father, nor something else Bernardo da Silva said later that same night, after the meal with the officers. They were alone at the fire, Bernardo smoking a roll of tabak, when Amador asked him: "Why has no man found Paraupava?"

"Paraupava" was the Tupi word for a low-lying great lake, but to the men who had been venturing from São Paulo for three decades in search of fabulous riches, it was an enchanted lake filled with gold, amid hills studded with emeralds.

It was said to be somewhere in the sertão above São Paulo, and should have been found after all these years, for allegedly the great rivers of Brazil flowed into it. Amador saw Brazil as an enormous island separated from the Spanish colonies by the waters of the Rios Plata, Paraná, and Paraguay in the south, and the Rio Orellano in the north. The Orellano, named for the Spaniard who'd first descended it in 1542, was said by the few at São Paulo to have seen it to be a river so vast as to resemble an inland sea. According to popular legend, Francisco de Orellano had seen the warrior women, the Amazons, on its banks; consequently, it was also called Rio das Amazonas.

"Perhaps there is no Paraupava," Bernardo da Silva finally said, and then re-cited the names of men he'd known, some dead, some still living — Domingos Grou, Antônio de Macedo, João Pereira de Sousa, Belchior Carneiro, among others — who had spent years in search of the enchanted lake, without success. "They found no gold or emeralds. Nothing. Nothing but endless sertão."

"But, Father, when a boy like Silvio Pizarro speaks, no matter how foolish he sounds, I wonder why it's so. — Why does the Spaniard have Potosi and the gold of Peru and we have nothing?"

Silvio Pizarro was one of four Spanish boys with the bandeira. Earlier in the day, he had tried to belittle the capture of the Carijó. "Seven Carijó! Not even seven hundred will equal what I, Silvio Pizarro, will find at the enchanted lake — gold, silver, emeralds, enough for the ransom of the king of Spain."

"You must expect to hear such things from a Spaniard," Bernardo da Silva said, referring to the boastful fantasies of Silvio Pizarro. "When the Spaniards came to São Paulo, after the time of Dom Sebastião, they brought their legend of El Dorado with them. 'Foolish Portuguese,' they said, 'why aren't you seeking El Dorado?'"

El Dorado — "The Gilded Man" — was believed to rule over a city hidden in the forest. Once a year this potentate would cover himself in gold dust and be immersed in a lake. His subjects would also make offerings of gold to these sacred waters.

"Yes, there's a little gold," he said, "and some silver, and emeralds, too, for these have been found in the rivers and hills near São Paulo, but El Dorado? All those men who've gone north — those who came back, the ones not lost forever, said nothing of El Dorado."

Amador had heard of a man who had ventured into those lands and, some said, made a great discovery. Amador now spoke his name softly: "Marcos de Azeredo?"

"The King of Emeralds!" Bernardo said derisively. "The year you were born, my son, he went into the sertão and came back with some green stones. Old Azeredo was no fool. 'Make me a knight of Christ's Order,' he said to the governor's men. 'Grant me a fine pension, and I'll tell you where I found them.' All this he was promised, and they continued to ask him to lead them to his mountain of emeralds, and always he had an excuse. This day his wife was ill, the next his lands needed tending — always an excuse, until even God tired of listening and took Marcos de Azeredo away."

"There was no emerald mountain?"

"From whom do all who seek such fortunes get their vision of El Dorado?" Amador had no answer.

Bernardo da Silva got up slowly. "Come, let me show you," he said, and immediately thumped off across the clearing.

"*There*, Amador Flôres, are the keepers of the secrets of El Dorado."

He was pointing at the pen that held the Carijó prisoners.

"It is from savages such as these that men hear of cities of gold and mountains of emeralds. Would you accept word of El Dorado from the Carijó you caught?"

"I would not, Father . . . But men *have* found gold and emeralds, and there's the Spaniard's silver . . ."

"A few drams from a stream, Azeredo's handful of stones. Not worth a man risking his life for," his father said. "Never forget this, my son: What you see before you — slaves to be sold — has always been a safer treasure."

It was to have been no more than a reconnaissance of the reduction of San Antonio, but, as it turned out, Tenente Bernardo da Silva's march into those lands in late October 1628 was a disaster.

He left the stockade with 140 men and headed southwest toward San Antonio. He planned a circular route that would take his company around the reduction lands and also carry it to several outlying malocas reported by earlier patrols that had been too small to invade them.

Amador was with the company, marching up front with his father. Bernardo da Silva had readily agreed to his son's request to accompany him. In the two weeks since the capture of the Carijó, Amador had found a change in the old man. It was almost as if Bernardo da Silva was seeing him for the first time.

On the second morning of their march, two miles from the reduction of San Antonio, Bernardo da Silva's force began to swarm out of the forest into a clearing abounding in manioc and beans, which they intended to steal as provision for their march. But hundreds of Carijó came pouring out of the trees.

Da Silva roared orders for the men with muskets to maintain a line at the forest's edge. He could see that his force was heavily outnumbered and would need an avenue of retreat. "Bugler!" he commanded a young mameluco. "Your eye on me! Every moment! If I go down, by God, blow the retreat!"

Then, to his son, he cried, "So, Amador Flôres, you're a man, are you?" He drew his sword. "Stay at my side!"

It was hopeless. At least twenty of the reduction natives were armed with muskets, and their fire was deadly. The bulk of the attackers wielded clubs, and beyond the main body of assailants, archers sniped at the ambushed Paulistas.

As Amador rushed into battle against the seething mobs of Carijó and heard the screams of the mortally wounded, he realized for the first time that he might die this morning, and he was terrified. He concentrated his attention on his father, whose rallying cries to his troops tore the air. This drove him on: He knew that if he weakened and ran away, the old warrior would surely kill him for his cowardice.

Then, suddenly, they were in the midst of a pack of Carijó. Bernardo da Silva never ceased cursing as he swung his two-handed sword, slashing at chests and arms. But, for every Carijó who fell, there were ten more to take his place. Without an order from Tenente da Silva, the Paulistas soon began to back off, fighting their way toward the trees, where their musketeers stood reloading as fast as they could.

Most of the Carijó remained at the site of the ambush, now littered with the bodies of dead and dying Paulistas. Exultant, the Carijó screamed insults and taunts at the retreating slavers.

Forty paces separated the last group of Paulistas from the line of musketeers, who were carefully directing their fire against the flanks of the savages.

At that very moment, Amador saw his father stumble and almost fall. They had just beaten off the last group of Carijó, and there were no enemy between them and the musketeers. "Father!" he cried, and leapt to his side.

The old man thrust out an arm and grabbed at Amador's shoulder for support. "Nothing!" he growled.

Amador saw a red patch blossoming below his father's right shoulder, where a ball had pierced the great cotton-armored jacket he wore. Two mamelucos near them quickly came to help the tenente to the safety of the trees. There Amador watched as others helped remove the jacket. The ball had passed through his father's shoulder.

An old Tupiniquin dressed the tenente's wound and bound it with strips of cloth. Bernardo trusted this man, who had accumulated a knowledge of the medicines of the forest as pagé at his clan's malocas.

Bernardo learned that one Portuguese and forty mamelucos and native soldiers were slain, almost one-third of the company. The Carijó showed no indication of returning to the attack; some held a position at the opposite end of the clearing, and others were beginning to drift away.

Within the hour, the tenente announced that he was ready to leave. He was helped to his feet, and Amador brought him the sword that Bernardo had dropped when wounded and that Amador had retrieved from the battlefield.

"How many Carijó, Amador Flôres?" Bernardo da Silva asked him.

"Three, I think."

"Enough for a boy who has just become a man." He smiled, but he was noticeably weak from the pain of the wound in his shoulder. "Today we go back to the stockade in defeat," he said to those around him. "Let those Carijó dogs return to their holy masters and boast of their victory. Let them sing their Aves and Hallelujahs. But it won't be long before we come this way again."

                                        ❧

When Bernardo da Silva's battered detachment had returned to the stockade, the officers of Raposo Tavares's company wanted to march immediately against San Antonio, but the captain-major had called for restraint. "The Jesuits will expect us to strike back. They'll be waiting with their Carijó. There are four thousand natives at San Antonio. If they are armed and prepared, we'll need the other companies."

This had been greeted with a murmur of disappointment, and one or two officers had openly begged the captain-major to lead an attack. But Raposo Tavares was adamant, proposing instead that he take a small band of men and visit San Antonio. "I have a question for the padres: By what right do they send their Christian savages on bloody missions against a Christian force?"

Bernardo da Silva, lying on an oxhide in the officers' hut, overheard Raposo Tavares, who'd been standing just beyond the entrance. When the captain-major stepped back inside, da Silva asked, "What have we to fear from the black robes? Savages with muskets caught us unaware. If we'd been prepared, they wouldn't have beaten us." He turned on his side as he spoke, grimacing with pain as he twisted his wounded shoulder. "Muskets," he repeated, "which the law forbids them. Surely the governor of Asunción wouldn't permit them to have muskets?"

Raposo Tavares shook his head. "Don Luis would do nothing that might jeopardize those who could provide him with slaves for Dona Victoria's lands. The Jesuits gave them those weapons. They're ambitious men, these black robes. Isn't it said that if they succeed here, they'll extend their control over every savage between this colony and the Rio das Amazonas? A vast Jesuit province open only to those who serve and obey them."

"What king — even a Philip of Castile — would permit this?"

"But, my friend . . . Madrid is far from Brazil, and at Madrid there are Jesuits who sing sweetly at court. Suppose they promise Don Philip that Rome will bestow the greatest honor upon anyone who supports their holy conquest of Brazil? We'll have a vast empire of savages, led by the Jesuits, and we can forget the bandeiras."

"If only I were fit enough to go with you to San Antonio."

"I go in peace — to judge how serious a threat they really are. God knows, there's reason enough to punish them for the attack on your company. But I'm in no hurry: When the time is right, I'll remove those savages the black robes shamelessly prefer above true Christians."

Bernardo slowly turned and lay on his back, probing his beard. "Captain-Major, take my son with you," he said. "Amador Flôres fought at my side on that bloody field. It will be good for him to see the camp of the enemy of his father and his grandfather."

In this way, Amador came to accompany the captain-major and the dozen men who went to the reduction of San Antonio four days later. Amador knew the aldeias beyond São Paulo, but compared with this great settlement, they were insignificant.

São Paulo itself did not have a population as large as that which existed behind the twenty-foot-high palisade surrounding this Jesuit town. The Carijó lived in houses ninety feet long, partitioned into separate family quarters. Walking with the Paulistas toward the reduction square, Amador counted nine rows of houses on either side of the main thoroughfare. Straight lanes ran between the rows. Facing the open side of the mission square was the church, flanked by a cemetery on the right, a school and "widows' house" on the left.

Wherever he looked, Amador saw Carijó, the men in shirts and short, loose breeches and white ponchos, the women in ankle-length cotton gowns. He saw a multitude of children, the girls dressed the same as their mothers, the boys bare-chested and wearing the simplest breeches.

Padre Pedro Mola was waiting for them at the entrance to the church. He was a small man with piercing eyes beneath thin brows that angled sharply upward, close-cropped hair, and a firm mouth. He greeted Captain-Major Raposo Tavares politely, commenting that it had been two months since he'd seen another Portuguese or Spaniard.

Raposo Tavares quietly stated that only a few days ago a group of Christians had been on their way to visit him but were hardly welcomed graciously. "These were the men, Padre Mola, whom the savages you shelter murdered," he added.

The Jesuit crossed his arms over his chest and looked toward a group of Carijó —the appointed officials of the reduction, former chiefs and elders of the Guarani — standing ten paces away. "These men remember past years, Captain-Major, when the bandeiras came. They are Christians now, not slaves."

"Christians?" Raposo Tavares said.

"Every Guarani here has been received into the Lord's protection."

"*Christans?*" Raposo Tavares persisted.

"The Lord has granted our company a merciful entry into these lands, where a multitude wait to be saved."

"And what, Padre Mola, does the Lord grant my men? The promise that they'll be cut down by savages in white breeches?"

"A fear arose in this land, Captain-Major, when your bandeira began its march. Thousands have been led away in the past. That is why your men were attacked."

"When have we ever enslaved your *Christians*, Padre? We come in peace to your town. Where are the chains, Padre, the bonds and fetters? We intend no harm to your children."

Padre Mola uncrossed his arms. "And what do you intend for the Guarani who live in the forest?"

"As God sees me, Padre, He knows that I hold it a sacred duty to make war on those pagans. They are sent to the plantations in Brazil. They are tamed and improved by the experience."

"Is it not preferable that these simple creatures of the land gain this knowledge through love and understanding, not in bondage to others?"

"God has ordered us to combat the pagan."

"You believe this?"

"I do."

"Do you not consider this judgment too harsh, Raposo Tavares?"

"No harsher than dispatching savages armed with muskets to combat a Christian force."

"Twenty old pieces is all we have. Twenty old muskets, Captain-Major. What defense is that against your bandeira? Padre Rafael warned me that when there were no more natives of Brazil left to enslave, the supply would be sought in this province. He saw what happened at the Bahia, where all were taken for the cane fields."

"Padre Rafael?"

"My old assistant, God bless his memory. He died two months ago. Forty-five years Rafael Arroyo labored in this vineyard, first at the Bahia, then Rio de Janeiro, and finally here. He knew much happiness at San Antonio, in his last days, at the sight of so many Guarani obedient to our Lord."

"Padre Mola, don't you see that we are subjects of the same king, bound to obey the same laws?"

"Forgive me, Captain-Major, but this is not true. It is well known that there are men from São Paulo who defy the decrees of His Royal Majesty."

Raposo Tavares declared, with conviction: "No company leaves São Paulo de Piratininga without His Majesty's license to capture wild Carijó, who are a threat to the peace."

"It was not what the law of 1609 intended."

"That law, Padre, is void."

"Would the king have decreed that every native of Brazil was free had it not been just and proper?"

"The decree was a mistake. It would have ruined the Christians of Brazil, who need slaves to work their lands. Had their protests against those laws been ignored, all Brazil would have been returned to the wilderness. Even in the two years it took to have those laws revoked, our people lived in fear of seeing the labor of generations lost."

Padre Mola pondered a response to this but changed the subject abruptly. "What do you seek at San Antonio, Captain-Major?" he asked, folding his arms again.

Raposo Tavares looked at his men, and beyond them to the group of reduction officials, who'd been silently observing the conversation. "Padre Mola, I've heard no denial of the outrage against my company. Do you think it right that so many who follow a Christian command should be killed?"

Padre Mola sighed. "They were raiding our gardens."

"Ah, yes, Padre — stealing a few manioc roots."

"What do you *want* of us, Captain-Major?"

"Today, Padre Mola, some food for my party. Tomorrow?" He shrugged. "I've no license to make war on *Christians*, even if they murdered my men."

This was of no consolation to Padre Mola, who knew that the men of the bandeiras had little concern for the legality of their actions. "You are welcome at my table, Captain-Major," he said bleakly.

At dinner that evening, Raposo Tavares made an agreement with Padre Mola guaranteeing that no Carijós who carried a written pass from the padre attesting that they were residents of the reduction would be arrested by the patrols of the bandeira.

Upon returning from San Antonio, Raposo Tavares ordered his men to keep away from the lands of that reduction and to honor the pact he'd made with Padre Mola.

"We're far beyond the Line of Tordesilhas, in Spanish territory," he explained to his officers. "We're subject to the same king, but many highly placed officials in Madrid and Lisbon call us brigands, a threat to Spain's great colonies to the west. As long as we violate no laws, their arguments for additional militia at Asunción and Buenos Aires go unheard. But, if we destroy the reductions and thereafter the Spanish towns beyond without provocation, His Majesty Philip will surely send an army to scourge us."

"Isn't the attack on Tenente da Silva's company provocation enough?" an officer asked.

"Twenty muskets against a company of Paulistas? They will be heroes at court. No, we must wait, Paulistas. Until none can deny our right to those so beloved of the Jesuits at San Antonio!"

On January 19, 1629, Carijó spies attached to the bandeira brought a report that infuriated one of Raposo Tavares's officers, Simão Alvares. On a previous bandeira, Alvares had captured a Carijó chief, Tatabrana, leading him and his people from their malocas to São Paulo. The spies reported that Tatabrana was presently at San Antonio, having escaped from Alvares's lands at São Paulo with ten other slaves. Padre Mola had given them all refuge.

"Demand they be handed over!" Raposo Tavares said, and immediately dispatched Alvares and a body of men to the reduction.

Alvares reported back that Padre Mola refused to let them go. "They're Christians now, Padre Mola says, and may not be held in captivity. Tatabrana will be the servant of none but the Lord."

The captain-major's blue-green eyes flashed with excitement. "I hear you, Simão Alvares," he said. "You tell me of a place where runaway slaves are sheltered, where laws that honor an owner's right are defied. What further provocation do we need? Officers, friends: Prepare yourselves!"

☙

A week later, as the bandeira made ready to leave, Tenente Bernardo da Silva lay on the oxhide in the corner of the dark hut. At first, the wound seemed to heal. But recently, he'd gone on a raid and that effort had exhausted him; the wound was festering.

Today he rested, miserable and complaining, in the presence of his son and Raposo Tavares, who had already sent off the advance guard of the force — Bernardo's command, now led by the father of Valentim Ramalho. Also at da Silva's side was Padre Anselmo, priest of the Paulistas, having journeyed from the Paulista camps located near the reductions of San Miguel, Jesús Maria, and Concepción. The commanders of the Paulista companies in those areas had learned about Raposo Tavares's impending attack on San Antonio and decided to initiate similar advances: If runaway slaves could find haven at San Antonio, then most certainly they were seeking sanctuary in the other towns as well.

With Amador's help, Bernardo da Silva had moved to an upright position, his back resting against a worn leather chest that held all his possessions. The light from the doorway illuminated his drawn and haggard face, the fleshy lips dry and cracked, his beard matted and unkempt.

"How I've prayed, Padre Anselmo, for strength to make this march," he said.

"Rest, dear old friend," Padre Anselmo said. "Our Lord is aware of your yearnings."

"But, Padre, there's never been the equal of this campaign. More Carijó slaves than I've seen in all my voyages."

"And they'll be brought to the stockade, Bernardo," said Raposo Tavares. "Your weary eyes will behold them — in bondage."

"I thank you, my Captain-Major. A lovely promise. But I lie here a prisoner of this darkness while sons of my friends are rallied against that horde."

"Bernardo, *your* son, who has served us so loyally, will be there," Raposo Tavares said.

I, Amador Flôres, he said to himself, *am invited to fight by the side of the bravest of men, Raposo Tavares, noble conqueror of the sertão!*

But Amador was brought rudely back to reality by the last few words of his father's remarks to Raposo Tavares, which exploded in his head:

"And he'll stay with me."

Amador was too confused to speak.

"It's your father's wish," Raposo Tavares said.

"I don't understand." Amador looked at Bernardo da Silva.

Padre Anselmo placed a hand on the young man's shoulder. "You must obey him, Amador."

"Forgive me, Padre, but I wasn't listening. I — "

Bernardo da Silva repeated his request. "It's a great honor to be asked by the captain-major himself, Amador, but he has more than enough men to clear the reduction. You'll stay with me."

Amador's eyes filled with tears. "Father?" he said. "Father?"

Padre Anselmo tightened his hold on Amador's shoulder. "Your father needs you at his side, my son."

Amador fought back his tears and looked imploringly at his father.

"I'm proud of your leaving the cows and the women at our house," Bernardo said. "Here, among my friends, you've shown yourself a true son of Tenente da Silva. There will be other times — many times when you carry on the conquest."

Despite his overwhelming disappointment, Amador was moved by something urgent and appealing in his father's voice. "Oh, Captain-Major, Your Honor," he said weakly, "I thank you, but I must stay with my father."

"Amador Flôres . . . may God grant me a son as obedient as you." Raposo Tavares looked down at the ailing tenente. "Take heart, Bernardo — this young man will yet honor the name of da Silva."

Raposo Tavares bade them farewell then, and Padre Anselmo left, too, to visit another company to the south, near the reduction of Concepción. Amador asked his father's permission to watch the departure of the main body of soldiers.

Walking among the groups of mamelucos and native warriors, Amador again felt terrible pangs of disappointment. He was stirred by this body of armed men, ready with their muskets and machetes, quivers tight with arrows; men who stood burdened by weights of iron chain and shackles and great lengths of cord for the multitude of slaves promised from this venture.

Amador was standing near the entrance to the stockade, watching the last of the departing company, when he heard a familiar voice:

"All the fine young men tend the cattle and the Carijó, while others march off to glory."

Amador turned, to find Valentim Ramalho standing with his hands on his hips, staring up at him. "A simple conquest — twenty muskets against the hundred our men carry," he said.

"That may be so, but it will be a conquest we won't see," Valentim replied.

Amador began to walk away, and Valentim hurried along next to him, continuing to bemoan this exclusion from the fighting force, when a black slave of Bernardo da Silva's hurried toward them. "Amador Flôres, your father calls for you," she said.

He returned to the small, dark hut, not knowing what to expect, and discovered Bernardo da Silva on his feet, leaning against one of the thick poles that supported the roof beams. His strained expression revealed the intense effort it had taken for him to rise. His left hand clutched the bandaged wound in his right shoulder.

"Don't stand there, my son. Help me with my garments."

"But, Father, you're to rest."

"Rest? Upon my back, when all I hear is the roll of drums? No, Amador Flôres. We go to San Antonio, where four thousand Carijó wait to be carried away!"

"Oh, Tenente!" he cried. "I'm to march in this campaign?"

"Yes, yes, Amador Flôres — *if* you hurry and help me prepare."

Amador needed no further urging. He went to the chest, took out the quilted war jacket, and helped his father into it. The old man groaned with pain as they pulled the garment over his right shoulder. "*Meu Deus!*" he exclaimed, much to Amador's distress. "Belt, pouch, powder flask, my knives — the rest, Amador Flôres." Amador fetched the broad leather belt and saw Bernardo's hands trembling as he reached for it. "*Meu Deus!*" his father repeated. "Help me!" Amador passed the belt around his father's waist and fastened its large brass clasps, "Pouch," Bernardo demanded, and when Amador brought it, the old man fingered its contents: replacement items for his matchlock musket — a few screws, a spare flash-guard support; small tin containers for powder charges; cotton wadding; seven silver reis; a small box of alum for sickness; a black-beaded rosary.

Bernardo felt the outside of the pouch. "My spoon?" Amador found it next to the leather chest, and as he handed it to his father, it slipped from Bernardo's fingers. "Let me do it, Father," he said, and taking the pouch, he secured the silver spoon in the loops at its side, as he'd seen his father do so many times. He attached the pouch to the broad belt. "Good. Good," Bernardo said.

When Amador had helped his father on with his stockings and tall boots, Bernardo attached his weapons, one by one, to his belt. Last was his broad-brimmed hat, which Amador found behind a deerskin hanging from a rafter and passed to his father. "Now fetch your own equipment," Bernardo said. "I'll wait beyond the hut."

Amador dashed out of the hut to the shelter where he hung his hammock, quickly collected the items he needed — his machete, knife, bow and arrows — and a leather jerkin given him by one of the mamelucos who served his father. As he was leaving the shelter, he ran into Valentim and Abeguar.

"Where are you going?" Valentim asked.

"My father's improved," he said. "I'm going with him to join the campaign."

"If you go, Amador Flôres, *we'll* do the same."

"My father asked me, alone."

"The tenente wouldn't object," Valentim said, not bothering to explain why. He turned to Abeguar. "You'll come?"

The young Tupiniquin nodded. "There are plenty of others to guard these miserable Carijó."

"No," Amador said. "You can't disobey your orders."

"Tenente da Silva can change the orders," Valentim said.

Amador saw his father coming out of the doorway of his hut. "I must go," he said. "We'll get our weapons. Wait for us!"

Amador hurried to his father, and just as they were about to set off, Valentim and Abeguar came running toward them

"What is this?" Bernardo da Silva asked.

Amador said. "They want to come with us."

"They have their posts."

The pair had reached their side, and Valentim immediately cried, "Oh, Tenente da Silva, *please*, we wish to march with Amador."

To their complete surprise, the old man did not object. "Come, then, my young men, but don't cry to me if your fathers take a whip to you!" To Abeguar, who stood quietly, he said, "Let us see, Tupiniquin, if you're as brave as your father." Then, to Amador: "You, da Silva, since you've already visited this Jesuit camp, will lead the way."

They trooped out of the stockade soon afterward, delaying awhile to add to the supplies. Amador marched ahead, his friends behind, and old Bernardo took up the rear. They had gone about two hundred paces when Bernardo uttered a string of terrible oaths; the boys swung around and saw the tenente sprawled on the ground. Amador hurried to him.

"Meu Deus," his father groaned. "Oh, dear God!"

"Your wound, Father — you fell on it?"

Bernardo started to rise, extending a hand to Amador, who grasped it and helped him to his feet. Valentim had picked up the tenente's musket.

"Mother of mercy," the old man growled, "such darkness."

"What's wrong, Father?" Amador asked, still clutching his arm.

"I didn't want to be a burden to the captain-major," Bernardo said, "but only to go along to share the fight. And, dear God, to be denied this final glory, this last sweet conquest . . ." He stopped suddenly. "Amador?"

"Yes, Father?"

"We *must* go on."

"It's a long way," Amador said, uncertainly.

"You'll help me. We must go on," Bernardo repeated. Then, suddenly, he gave an anguished cry.

"Oh, my son, your old father's eyes . . . So little sight remains to me, Amador."

Amador tightened his hold on his father's arm. "Your sight?"

"These past weeks it's worsened," Bernardo said. "Everything's become clouded, distorted."

"We'll return to the stockade," Amador said quietly.

"No! You'll help me, Amador Flôres. You'll lead me to this final conquest. I'll not be denied this march! I have sight enough to see the ruin of San Antonio, sight enough to look upon that multitude of slaves we'll remove. We'll keep behind the army until they enter the reduction. Raposo Tavares must not be troubled with an invalid. Then, my son, during the attack you'll be my eyes."

Thus they continued onward, Abeguar in the lead, Amador walking with his father, who kept a hand on his shoulder, and Valentim taking up the rear, carrying the tenente's musket.

They marched this way, for the next two days. Then Abeguar, after scouting ahead, reported that he'd sighted the entire force camped in the forest, two hours away. Bernardo ordered Abeguar to continue observing the bandeira and to return as soon as it began the final stage of its advance toward San Antonio.

❧

The attack on San Antonio came two days later, on January 30, 1629, and the da Silvas, father and son, were there.

When the bandeira broke camp, Abeguar had run through the forest to summon the others. They left immediately, an hour after dawn. Bernardo da Silva encouraged the young men forward with impatience and enthusiasm:

"Onward! Onward! Amador!" he cried, at the merest slackening of the pace.

Finally, they breasted a hill overlooking San Antonio, and the young men saw that the attack had already begun. Bernardo could not distinguish the figures of men still streaming toward the opening in the high palisade, but he did identify a cloud of gray smoke over a section of the reduction houses and heard the distant crack of musket shot. They rushed down the hill.

They entered the reduction with the last groups of Paulistas. An officer cried out greetings to Tenente da Silva, but, in the haste to join the fight, no one paid serious attention to the sudden arrival of Bernardo and his three cohorts.

Inside the reduction, panic and chaos prevailed.

Three days earlier, reduction natives had reported to Padre Pedro Mola the advance of Raposo Tavares's bandeira. The priest realized that it would be futile to commit the people of San Antonio, with their twenty muskets and primitive hunting weapons, to a pitched battle against the company of Paulistas. His Guarani had won that fight in the manioc fields, but they had faced only a single detachment of Paulistas, and surprise had been in their favor. Despite the odds against them, some of the elders in the reduction had urged a proper defense.

"Raposo Tavares is a determined man, but I cannot believe that he is entirely in the hands of the devil," Padre Mola had argued. "After all, he has honored the agreement we made: Not one of our people who carries a pass from me has been molested. When he comes, we will make certain that our church and square are filled with a worshipful host. Surely this bandit will realize that the Lord God will damn his soul eternally if his men harm these children of Jesus."

But, with each passing hour, the imminent threat from the bandeira made the padre increasingly apprehensive, and he had suddenly decided to strengthen his people for whatever ordeal they might have to face by granting them the blessing of the Lord. For seven hours, Padre Mola required the great congregation of Guarani to shuffle past him, one by one, and he gave each his blessing and baptized those not yet offered to the Lord. Before he was finished, his voice became a cracked whisper and others had to lift his arm for the Benediction.

At dawn on January 30, after a sleepless night, Padre Mola had dressed with care. He conducted two Masses, with the church filled to capacity. The Guarani also crowded together on the square in front of the church, groups falling on their knees to pray for deliverance from the evil they knew to be gathered in the forests beyond.

After the services, Padre Mola had stepped into the square, heading toward the main pathway that led from the reduction entrance. He remained at the edge of the square, his arms folded.

When lookouts had come running to warn that the Paulistas were approaching, Padre Mola acknowledged them but stayed where he was, slowly rocking back and forth, his rosary trembling in his hands. Nor did he move when the first Paulistas burst into the reduction. All but two of the elders and Tatabrana, the runaway slave, stood near him.

Ever since the sighting of the Paulistas, Tatabrana had warned that his former master and those with whom he marched would journey across these lands for no other reason than to enslave the men, women, and children of San Antonio. However, Padre Mola had prevailed with his promise of Christ's blessing.

But Tatabrana had been carried away by slavers once before, and when the Paulistas tore through the entrance, he and the two elders and seventeen Guarani, armed with the muskets of San Antonio, were standing in the lane between the first two blocks of houses.

From where he stood, Padre Mola could not see Tatabrana and his men at the far end of the main thoroughfare. He'd started to move slowly toward the Paulistas who were entering the reduction. When these troops passed the first row of houses, Tatabrana's tiny force opened fire on the front-runners.

"Oh, dear God, all is lost!" Padre Mola called out, and started to run. "Stop! Stop! Stop!"

Tatabrana's small group, after firing its first volley, backed off in order to gain time to reload. The first salvos had felled a few Paulistas, but the rest of the attackers continued to charge the musketeers. Tatabrana and six others stood firm, wielding their muskets against the first raiders to reach them. Within minutes they were overwhelmed.

Captain-Major Raposo Tavares had entered the reduction with a second wave of Paulistas, and found Padre Mola, so splendidly attired in his vestments, dashing along the main pathway.

"Men of São Paulo, it is God's preserve you violate!" Padre Mola cried out when he saw the captain-major and his officers. "For the love of God, stop!"

"Stand aside, Padre Mola," Raposo Tavares commanded. "We wish you no harm." His sword was drawn and held loosely at his side.

"You will be damned for this, Raposo Tavares."

'Jesuit, stand back!"

Raposo Tavares motioned the mamelucos and Tupiniquin forward, and they swarmed toward the main square, taking up their war cries against the Carijó.

When Amador and Bernardo da Silva entered the reduction, the last of Tatabrana's defenders had been chased to Padre Mola's own quarters near the church, where they had sought a final refuge. One was stabbed to death in the doorway as he tried to prevent the Paulistas from entering; the attackers rushed inside, seized the men who'd fought with Tatabrana, and dragged them out, along with the women and children who were hiding there. The raiders danced away gleefully with the priest's clothes. Others had great sport running down and wringing the necks of the padre's seven chickens.

The most rewarding task, of course, was the rounding up of the Carijó.

Some five hundred Paulistas were inside the reduction. Half of them were occupied with the Carijó in the square — those who had already been assembled when the Paulistas arrived, and others who had been turned out of the church. The rest of the raiding force, working in smaller groups, were systematically flushing out the occupants of the houses and driving them down the lanes toward the main thoroughfare.

Soon after entering, Bernardo da Silva and his youthful aides found themselves with a group of Paulistas clearing out the houses next to the main pathway.

"Amador, tell me everything you see," the tenente ordered, above the hysterical cries of the Carijó.

"Father, the savages are so helpless; our men pull them from their houses without the slightest difficulty. They're assembled at the square."

"Strong, well-bodied men?"

"The finest, Father."

"How many?"

"In their great plaza? Hundreds."

"Take me there."

It was difficult to move along the congested main thoroughfare. Carijó were being pushed toward the square. Everywhere Paulistas moved among them, cursing and mocking them for their quick submission.

Bernardo da Silva heard and felt the great crowd milling around them. "What a triumph, Amador!"

At some point, Amador and his father had become separated from Valentim and Abeguar; he didn't stop for them but hurried instead to guide his father to the main square.

"Faster, Amador!" Bernardo da Silva implored. "Our captain-major must see that his old tenente has come to savor the joy of this day."

Amador's excitement surpassed that of his father's. He could see the full extent of the prize the Paulista raiders had won this day: whole families with mothers and fathers clutching their young; Carijó of his age, miserable and apprehensive; old men chattering with astonishment; men of fighting age, who'd undoubtedly been at the battle in the manioc field, now completely broken by the superior Paulista force.

One hundred yards from the square, the crowd of raiders and their captives was impenetrable. Bernardo bellowed for a path to be opened, but his commands were ignored, and they were forced to swing down a lane to the left and make a circuitous approach to the square.

At last they reached the blocks of houses nearest the church and school. Bernardo da Silva stumbled and fell

Amador dropped to his father's side. "Father, what is it? What's wrong?" He started to help his father to his feet, but Bernardo da Silva gestured him away feebly.

"Oh, sweet Jesus." He placed a hand on his father's shoulder. "Father," he said softly, "I'll find the priest. Rest while I go for him."

Ten minutes later he found the Jesuit wandering toward the square along the main pathway. Padre Mola's vestments were in disarray, his chasuble pulled askew. He went agitatedly from one group of his Guarani to another, trying to calm them.

"My father lies mortally ill!" Amador cried. "You must come to him!"

Mola frowned at Amador, as if trying to remember where he'd seen him before.

"Hurry — please," Amador begged.

When they reached Bernardo da Silva, Raposo Tavares was with him, called to his side by one of the mamelucos.

"Dear old comrade," Amador heard the captain-major say, "you should've taken the rest you deserved instead of coming on this campaign." He stepped aside to let Padre Mola approach Bernardo da Silva.

"Mameluco," Padre Mola said to the old man on the ground, "I am the priest of those you came to steal from God. Make your peace with the Lord, mameluco, for it seems you have little time."

Bernardo da Silva's face twisted into an expression of such loathing that Padre Mola drew back.

"There is little time," the priest said.

A deep, animal-like cry came from Bernardo da Silva and he made a desperate effort to raise himself.

"No, Father — *no!*" Amador shouted, to no avail.

Forcing his shoulders off the ground, his eyes bulging, his entire head trembling with exertion and rage, the old man grabbed viciously at the outer vestments of the priest. Again came the terrible scream, but abruptly it was cut short. Bernardo da Silva fell back, his head striking the ground. He was dead.

Amador stepped closer to his father. "His confession?" he said, his voice quavering with alarm.

Padre Mola, kneeling, had started to pray over the mameluco. He stopped, and turned to look up at this son of a slave raider. "God would not allow it," the priest said.

ভა

Five days later, Amador stood at the front of a large group of men gathered in a semicircle in the Paulista stockade. Opposite them, Raposo Tavares and two officers were conducting a ceremony that Amador was witnessing for the first time:

Near the captain-major was Tenente Bernardo da Silva's leather chest, open and emptied of its contents. One of the men with Raposo Tavares was sorting these and arranging them neatly on the ground

"Observe with care, Amador Flôres, so that you may report to the widow da Silva that all was properly done," Raposo Tavares said.

The captain-major and his assistants then proceeded to auction off Bernardo da Silva's belongings, the purchasers affixing their signature or mark to a brief bill of sale, agreeing to pay the widow da Silva when they returned to São Paulo. When a Paulista of some means died on campaign, it was a bandeira custom to protect the interests of his widow and heirs by conducting such auctions; months might pass before the company returned to São Paulo, and the dead man's belongings could otherwise be lost or stolen.

Reserved for Amador were his father's silver spoon, musket, and war jacket. Everything else was sold — everything, that is, but the most valuable possessions: sixty-four Tupi slaves, part of his private militia, who'd survived the battle in the manioc fields. Raposo Tavares himself promised the safe return of the slaves to the lands of the widow Rosa Flôres. And he also undertook to protect the da Silva family's share of the Carijó taken on this raid.

It had been five days since they'd buried the tenente on a hillside overlooking San Antonio, with Padre Mola ordered to perform the last rites. Padre Mola had abandoned the reduction and left for Asunción with a few aged natives released to him. The remaining Carijó — almost four thousand — had been driven by the bandeira to an area just beyond this Paulista stockade.

When the company marched off, it left the stockade ablaze as a precaution against its possible occupation by wild Carijó, who would be a threat to future bandeiras. Reports from the three other companies of the army that had left São Paulo the previous August told of successes at San Miguel and Jesús Maria, where a total of 2,800 natives had been captured. At Concepción, the Paulistas had met resistance; the reduction priest and his natives had prevented the invaders from entering the stockade, and had survived on dogs, cats, rats, and mice until a relief force arrived from distant reductions and drove off the São Paulo raiders.

The companies rendezvoused three days after Raposo Tavares's column had started its march. Accompanying the slaves from the other reductions were two Jesuit fathers who had asked permission to join their natives on their march to São Paulo. Raposo Tavares was reluctant to grant this request. "They'll cry to our governor when we reach civilization. They'll have weeks to rehearse their lies against our men." But the other commanders were not concerned about this possibility, and suggested that it was a good thing to have the Jesuits along: "They'll keep these pagans cheerful for their presentation to the slave buyers."

On the forty-day march from the stockade to São Paulo, the column crossed mountains and valleys, and pushed through swamps and patches of noxious lowland. Hundreds sickened: weak from hunger, dozens succumbed from fevers and bloody dysenteries and were left dead in the forest. In those forty days, one out of every seven of the youngest children died.

On April 7, 1629, the bandeira reached the heights of Piratininga and São Paulo.

Amador marched at the side of Captain-Major Raposo Tavares. Around his head he wore a red kerchief, which an officer had given him. And in his hands he held Tenente Bernardo's musket.

The company's trumpets sounded as the advance group headed for the square in front of the câmara, where the few elderly councilmen who had not accompanied the bandeira stood waiting.

Amador's happiness at this victorious homecoming increased when he saw Ishmael Pinheiro move out of the crowd coming to welcome the Paulistas.

"Is it truly you?" asked the chubby-faced Ishmael excitedly.

"Oh, yes, my friend, and with such glorious company," Amador replied. "I'll never return to the cattle and pigs."

Ishmael laughed. "With so many Carijó to herd, you won't need to go back to your poor father's fields."

"No. And he wouldn't want me to. 'You're a son of the sertão, Amador Flôres,' he said to me. 'There's no other home for you.'"

☙

For ten years — from the raid in 1628 until 1638 — Amador da Silva marched with bandeiras that destroyed the remaining eight reductions in the province of Guiará and forced the fathers and the remnant of their great congregations to flee south in the direction of Buenos Aires. The Paulista depredations in Guiará went beyond the ruin of the reductions: Two towns founded by Spanish colonists in the area were attacked and looted.

The Jesuits established new missions between the Rio Uruguay and the Atlantic Ocean, six hundred miles from São Paulo. They also built six reductions in Itatin province, an area above Asunción and west of Guiará.

The Paulistas had destroyed the Itatin missions from 1633 to 1635, driving thousands of natives to São Paulo. Then they had returned their attention to the south, capturing 25,000 slaves in their first major campaign. But the long-suffering Jesuits were beginning to fight back. In 1637, Amador was with a bandeira that had been harassed by the Jesuits and their musketeers for ten days on its march back to São Paulo.

During this ten-year period, when not with the bandeiras, Amador was engaged in a lucrative venture with his friend Ishmael Pinheiro; Ishmael, trader and armador, had assumed the enterprises of his father, who died in 1634,

Amador and Ishmael participated in a flourishing contraband trade between Brazil and the Spanish colonies. Though united under one crown, Madrid and Lisbon had continued to administer their territories separately, the Spaniards maintaining a monopoly on trade with their vast viceroyalty of Peru which extended from the Pacific coast, across the Andes, to the Atlantic. Goods smuggled from São Paulo to the eastern provinces of Paraguay and Rio de La Plata cost as little as one-third of the price of the legal imports, a contraband traffic so extensive that the holds of half of the two hundred ships sailing annually to Brazil were filled with this forbidden merchandise. And it was not only the breach of their trading monopoly that angered the Spaniards; the smugglers were paid in silver from the mines of Potosi, treasure-house in the heart of Peru.

こ

While Amador and Ishmael and their fellow Paulistas were harassing the Spaniard, purloining his silver and smashing his missions and boasting of the "liberation of Guiará," elsewhere in Brazil, colonists were experiencing a decade of disaster.

That same year Amador had been with the bandeira of Raposo Tavares at San Antonio, a Dutch armada had reached Pernambuco, landing troops on a beach just north of Olinda — then a prosperous city with eight thousand settlers — and seizing the capital by the next evening. Another settlement had sprung up – Recife, named for a long, rocky reef that formed a natural harbor — and a fortnight after the conquest of Olinda, the Portuguese abandoned this small port town.

After losing Olinda and Recife, the captain-major of Pernambuco, Mathias de Albuquerque, a descendant of the first donatário, Duarte Coelho Pereira, launched a guerrilla war, keeping the Dutch penned into an area within a few miles of the two towns and harrying them until reinforcements for the Pernambucans arrived eighteen months later.

But at the end of 1634, to the north of Pernambuco, the Dutch commanders dispersed a combined force of Portuguese soldiers and Neapolitan mercenaries sent by Madrid and led by Giovanni Vicenzo San Felice, count of Bagnuoli. In March 1635 Bagnuoli and his men were in the south of the captaincy when again they were

defeated, and fled in the direction of the Bahia. Three months later Mathias de Albuquerque, who'd been carrying on this fight for six years, also abandoned the captaincy.

A relief force had returned to the south of the captaincy, and enjoyed no little
success until its commander, Rojas y Borgia, a former governor of Panama, and his
second-in-command were killed. Their replacement was none other than Bagnuoli,
who attempted to renew the guerrilla war.

Then, on January 23, 1637, there arrived in Recife the West India Company's
appointee for the governorship of the conquests: thirty-three-year-old Johan
Maurits, count of Nassau-Siegen. Maurits moved swiftly to end resistance to the
Dutch, opening battle against Bagnuoli, and driving him south, once again across
the broad Rio São Francisco, which Maurits considered a natural boundary for the
territories won by the Dutch.

In April 1638 Johan Maurits had appeared at the Bahia itself with 3,600
troops in thirty ships. For more than a month the Dutch tried to breach the count of
Bagnuoli's formidable defense works, and failed. After losing 237 men, they gave up
the siege and sailed north.

The defeat at the Bahia had not depressed Maurits. When the ships of his retreating force hove to behind the reef at Recife, he had reminded his commanders:
"Pernambuco and five captaincies to the north and south of it have been won from
the Portuguese — more than enough, gentlemen, for the foundation of New Holland."

ۍ

On June 29, 1638, the feast day of St. Peter and St. Paul, a group of seven
Paulistas stood outside the câmara as a religious procession passed the municipal
building, one of the few two-storied structures in town. The main floor was reserved
for council meetings, and there was also a jail, from the barred windows of which
prisoners were appealing in vain to the men in front of the câmara for release on this
holy day. But the men were listening raptly instead to Captain-Major Raposo Tavares
denounce the fathers of the Company of Jesus:

"How humbly and piously they walk today with those of St. Francis and St.
Benedict. But when they return to their house, they'll weep with indignation. They'll
fall on their knees and beg the Lord, God of us all, to afflict us with a thousand miseries."

Amador and Ishmael Pinheiro — the latter prosperously attired and grown
even fatter — were standing with the group, all of whom nodded in agreement with
the words of the man who had led so many raids against the Jesuit reductions.

Amador was twenty-four. He had more than fulfilled Bernardo da Silva's prediction that this last son of his would be forever bound to the sertão. Amador had
long ago lost his father's silver spoon, and with it, a serious desire to be the equal of
the sons of Portugal. He cared nothing for caste and privilege; rather, he saw himself
as a mameluco, enjoying the freedom of the sertão, where the only decrees were the
natural laws of survival.

His appearance had changed little since boyhood: He was still short and thickset and bore the scars of the pox he'd had as a child. The relentless voyaging into the

sertão, hardening him physically and spiritually, had wrought a change: Let him move silently between the trees, with the tall bow he often favored over a musket, and here was a warrior, a hunter of man and beast.

When the procession had passed them, Raposo Tavares continued: "The Jesuits tell our governor that I'm a bandit who's stolen sixty thousand Carijó from their protection. 'Tavares and the men of São Paulo must be scourged by savages bearing muskets,' they plead at the council of Madrid. Sixty thousand Carijó!" Raposo Tavares snorted. "With that horde of natives, I'd be even wealthier than Correia de Sá, with his great lands and his weighhouse!"

Salvador Correia de Sá e Benavides was the governor of Rio de Janeiro. His grandfather had been a nephew of the great lawgiver Mem de Sá, who'd led the slaughter of the coastal Tupiniquin and Tupinambá three-quarters of a century before. Though subordinate to the governor-general of Brazil at the Bahia, Correia de Sá exercised broad powers over the lower group of captaincies, including São Vicente, in which São Paulo was located. Correia de Sá had obtained a twenty-year monopoly on the weighing and warehousing of every grain of sugar produced in his captaincy.

"Our governor must surely know that I'm not a rich man — only one, as God sees me, who's consumed with love for the land of my father, dear Portugal," Raposo Tavares continued.

"Your love of Portugal wouldn't impress him," Ishmael Pinheiro said.

The meaning of Ishmael's remark was clear to everyone present. Correia de Sá's mother was Spanish, a daughter of the governor of Cadiz, where Correia de Sá was born. His father, Martim, had been governor of Rio de Janeiro before him, and as a young man, Correia de Sá had spent seven years in the Spanish colonies to the west of São Paulo. He had married a wealthy Creole heiress from the viceroyalty of Peru and gained firsthand knowledge of the vast Spanish holdings. The Paulistas had hoped for support and sympathy from Correia de Sá; but he favored the Jesuits and, too, was said to share their opinion that the Paulistas were a bandit rabble.

Then Amador spoke up:

"Why do the Jesuits go to Madrid to plead for muskets? Their savages are armed well enough already." He was thinking of the bandeira of 1637 in which the black robes and their musketeers had chased him for ten days.

"The Jesuits will tell Madrid what Madrid wants to hear," Raposo Tavares replied to Amador's question. "The lands south of São Paulo must be held for Spain. Every league won from the savages by the men of São Paulo, must become the property of Castile. They'll not ask for a few muskets more but for enough weapons to arm regiments of Carijó to protect the realm of His Spanish Majesty."

"Our governor supports the black robes at a time when half of Brazil, every captaincy from Maranhão, in the north, to the boundary of the Bahia, is already lost to the Dutch?"

A man who'd been quiet until now broke into the discussion: "Dom Correia's support for the Company of Jesus is personal, senhores. He's an honest and devout man." He was José Maria de Novais. He had accompanied many slave-raiding bandeiras and, at one time or another, had fought alongside every man here; today he was less active as slaver, owning a thousand cattle and the best wheat fields in the district, and was a member of the câmara of São Paulo. "It would be wrong to question his loyalty to the colony and Portugal," José Maria continued. "Every day he prays for deliverance from the heretic in the north."

"And while he meditates, the guns of the Dutch grow louder?" Raposo Tavares said.

"You speak boldly, Captain-Major, but what do you know of Dutch guns?" asked José Maria. "In this struggle, my friend, what have the men of São Paulo done to help Portugal? Show me a soldier of São Paulo who stood with our colonists of Pernambuco against the invader. Where were we this past April when the Dutch threatened the Bahia? Others have fought the great battles of this land."

"And lost," Raposo Tavares said.

"Yes, Captain-Major, a terrible loss, through treason and treachery, but Correia de Sá believes we can win back our lands from the Dutch," José Maria said.

José Maria was forty, the same age as Raposo Tavares, but he appeared older than the captain-major, who had been little changed by this decade of slave-raiding. Raposo Tavares was tall and straight-backed, his manner eager, confident, almost youthful. José Maria was of medium build, his shoulders slightly stooped, his neatly trimmed beard and his hair flecked with gray.

"Without aid from Lisbon and Madrid, the Dutch won't be expelled," Raposo Tavares said.

"Certainly, but if help does come, we must join the struggle. For ten years we've turned our backs on the other captaincies, wandering into the sertão and worrying about the Spaniard. Isn't it time we changed this?"

Raposo Tavares scowled. "Do you speak for yourself, José Maria, or Dom Correia de Sá?"

"Both." José Maria had recently returned from Rio de Janeiro.

"He told you to raise this issue?"

"He did."

"What does Dom Correia de Sá expect of us?"

"A fleet will come from Portugal next year. He wants a Paulista company ready to embark with it for Pernambuco."

"Ah, yes, we're the king's servants," Ishmael Pinheiro said quietly. "This we know, José Maria, but what reward will the king offer for the expense of raising such a company?"

"A full and free pardon for any accused by the Jesuits."

Some of the men laughed, but José Maria silenced them: "There's word in Rio de Janeiro that the leaders of the bandeiras are to be transported to Lisbon in chains."

"It's true," Raposo Tavares said. "The Jesuits plead for our excommunication. But tell me, José Maria, since you speak for the governor: With his fondness for the Company of Jesus, how can it be that he'd consider pardoning a man they say has enslaved sixty thousand Carijó?"

"Dom Correia believes that if you raise a company to fight the Dutch, many others will follow your example."

Amador laughed at this notion.

"Your father knew these black robes well," the captain-major said to him, "and so did your grandfather Marcos. Both could have told you how unforgiving these soldiers of the Lord can be. A pardon from the governor may be a salvation we can't dismiss."

℘

Raposo Tavares accepted Governor Correia de Sá's offer of clemency and raised a company of Paulistas for an army that would fight the Dutch at Pernambuco — only 150 men, many of whom, such as Amador, had volunteered out of personal loyalty to the captain-major. The armada dispatched from Spain to assist the colonists arrived at the Bahia in January 1639. Sickness and poor leadership had plagued the expedition; three thousand men had died from disease before reaching Brazil, and months were devoted to rebuilding the force.

On August 5, 1639, the Paulistas received orders to proceed down the Serra do Mar to Santos for embarkation in a vessel that would take them to the armada at the Bahia. A week later, on the eve of the contingent's departure from São Paulo, Amador invited his old comrade Valentim Ramalho and his father and the trader Ishmael Pinheiro to the da Silva house for a farewell *festa*.

Also gathered in the lofty central room of the homestead were Amador's mother, Rosa Flôres, and his half-brothers, Braz and Domingos, and their families. Braz, a son of Tenente Bernardo's first wife, was a man in his sixties; Domingos was twelve years younger. They lived here with their families, never participating in the bandeiras.

The da Silva homestead, some thirty miles northwest of São Paulo, was a one-storied whitewashed building made of tightly packed clay, its rammed earth walls two feet thick and eighteen feet high. In the front were two large rooms, with tall framed windows, on either side of a spacious verandah. Braz and Domingos and their wives occupied these rooms.

From the verandah, a heavy oak door, nine feet high, opened into the central room, where the da Silvas and their guests were gathered. Four rooms led off this open area — one for Rosa Flôres, another for the young boys of the house, a third for the girls, and the fourth a work area where the women and their slaves spent the days combing wool and cotton, spinning, weaving, and sewing.

There was no kitchen; the slaves prepared the meals beyond the back verandah at open fires and a clay oven.

One particularly distinctive feature of the house was its roof, made with half-round reddish tiles like those seen in Portugal and designed like a pagoda, with sloping sides that curved gracefully and came to a point in the center of the house, twenty-four feet above the floor.

When the party assembled to bid farewell to Amador had finished eating, the men stayed at the table and the women moved to a corner of the room where they sat or stood near a hammock in which the widow Rosa Flôres reclined. Two of them were native girls, the concubines of Amador. And here, too, was Maria Ramalho, who'd been invited by Rosa Flôres.

Maria was twenty-seven years old now and still unmarried, her ugly features having deterred the few prospects her father had lured to his house. Her ardor for

Amador remained strong, and she persistently offered appeals for a miracle that would open his eyes to the love she had for him.

As Amador sat at the table with the other men, he could sense that Maria Ramalho's gaze was upon him.

Amador had inherited a portion of his father's lands and slaves and had added to this with the profits of his own raids and smuggling, but he had no desire to settle down, especially with Maria Ramalho. He was now the father of two daughters and a son. Amador slept with the Carijó and the Tupiniquin when he was home, but showed little affection for his children.

It was not that he was incapable of love. Toward his mother, he was openly adoring. He worshipped Rosa Flôres. Only one discordant note marred the relationship between Amador and his mother: Rosa Flôres's support for Maria Ramalho.

"She loves you with all her heart," his mother had said many times, "And Maria is promised a good dowry."

Maria's father, Vasco Ramalho, who'd once led Bernardo da Silva's own militia, still lived with his family on lands adjoining the da Silva holding, but he no longer marched with the bandeiras. Three years before, he had located gold in a river northeast of São Paulo. His find had made him rich but had soon petered out, as had been the case with every gold strike in these parts. After a year of prospecting elsewhere, Vasco had given up and returned to his lands.

Amador's thoughts were interrupted by a familiar cry: "Cachaça! Oh, my friends, more wine!"

Valentim Ramalho had climbed up on the seat and was waving an empty gourd.

Amador called to a slave, who went for more liquor.

"Cachaça!" Valentim shouted. "We must toast our hero!"

Ishmael Pinheiro challenged this remark: "A hero? Oh, Amador, what will you gain from this foolish venture?"

Before Amador could respond, Valentim said, "Isn't his name listed with that of the captain-major and others whom the Jesuits want transported in chains to Lisbon?"

"Always — The Jesuits," Ishmael said. "They claim to be founders of São Paulo de Piratininga, but your own ancestors, Valentim— João Ramalho and his great family — were here before Nóbrega and Anchieta. And the Ramalho's will be here — long after these troublesome priests have been silenced."

"Many, many Ramalhos," Amador interjected, provoking laughter from all, Valentim's the loudest.

Shortly before the attack on San Antonio, Valentim had rhapsodied about the sexual delights he was enjoying with two Carijó girls; and every night on the long march of the slave column, he'd made love to both. Upon returning to São Paulo, he asked his father to claim these two Carijó girls as part of his share of captives, and Vasco Ramalho had arranged this gift for his small but hugely amorous son. In ten years the two Carijó had produced twelve children. To that brood were added four more from local girls.

When the tumult subsided, Amador asked Ishmael: "Why is it foolish to march with Raposo Tavares?"

"The time isn't right."

"But there's a great fleet at the Bahia, and more ships preparing to sail from Rio de Janeiro with reinforcements."

"And in whose cause? For the king of Spain, Amador — not for Portugal."

"Raposo Tavares believes that a change will come."

"Yes, Amador, and so do many others. If they're from Lisbon they talk of dissent against Spain. Talk, talk, talk. For years there's been nothing but talk. So it will always be. The Portugal that once was is no longer. Our great empire of India is in ruin, the triumphs of Afonso de Albuquerque lost. Our old conquests of Africa are threatened by these same Dutch, our Brazil broken —"

"By Portuguese Jews in Amsterdam," Braz da Silva suddenly interrupted. Braz was typical of many who saw the Jews as the cause of all the troubles that had beset Portugal. That Ishmael Pinheiro was the son of a New Christian, and a known sympathizer with Jews, did not deter him. "The Jews gave Pernambuco to the Dutch. They were ready to open the gates of Salvador."

"Always — the Jesuits," Ishmael said, repeating his earlier words and adding: "And the Jew. Yes, Braz, and it was also the Jew, with his gold and commerce, who opened the trade of the East when the conquest was made. The Jew who built the mills and sold the sugar of Pernambuco."

Braz, whose pale brown features were boorish and vacant, was stymied by this retort.

"At Madrid, the Holy Office is told that São Paulo is home to a nest of Israelites, who hide from the flames of Redemption," Ishmael said.

"There are some." Braz looked at Valentim and Amador, and found no support in their neutral expressions.

"There are a few," Ishmael said, and was silent. Already he'd said more than he should have. Although there was no Holy Office in Brazil, the Visitor had occasionally been sent from Lisbon to examine the faith of the colonists. These roving Inquisitors had not troubled Ishmael, but he'd been reminded of his Jewish descent in other ways. He had expressed interest in election to the câmara, but was informed that such a position was barred to him. He was married by that time to the daughter of an Old Christian family from Santos, but this failed to influence the electors. Even his children would be barred from holding any office under the Crown or from membership in the Portuguese military Orders of Christ: Aviz and Santiago. He had seriously considered leaving São Paulo for Pernambuco, where the Dutch imposed no restrictions against Jews. But then Vasco Ramalho, whose prospecting expeditions he'd financed, had found gold, and Ishmael stayed.

Valentim attempted to change the conversation to a less controversial subject, and began to speak enthusiastically about "the bed," only the third to be seen at São Paulo, carried in sections over the Serra do Mar for a justice of the peace and his wife, and a source of great envy to Valentim. But the atmosphere had been irremediably tainted, and Braz and Domingos left the table.

Soon afterwards, Amador and Ishmael went outside, leaving Valentim and his father. A taciturn, simple-minded man, the elder Ramalho had taken no part in the conversation, only occasionally nodding or shaking his head; he and Valentim went on drinking cachaça.

Amador and Ishmael strolled slowly, until they were on a small rise some distance opposite the house.

"Forget this ridiculous bandeira, Amador," he said, "these one hundred fifty men who go to challenge the mighty Dutch Company. Instead, go into the sertão and find gold."

"Gold? Why gold, Ishmael, when there's a mountain of emeralds for any man brave enough to believe it exists?"

"I'm serious, friend. I've seen enough evidence of gold to convince me."

"So has every other man who searched for it these past hundred years. The only gold of value, Ishmael, comes from the mine of the province of Guiará — Carijó, my friend, easy to collect, easy to sell."

"The days of the great bandeiras are past."

"The Jesuits make a noise, but the new reductions hold more Carijó than were ever assembled in those places we attacked."

"And they're also more distant and defensible," Ishmael said. "As armador, I see less and less chance for profit with Carijó. Better that I give my money to those who look for gold."

"These vagabonds seeking El Dorado are hopeless dreamers. They'll ruin you."

They were walking back in the direction of the house. On the verandah was a high-backed wooden bench, and they could see a lone figure seated upon it, her head turned toward them.

"She haunts me — a shadow forever hovering in the background. She's won the affection of my mother, so that she may visit whenever Vasco permits it."

"In a few days you'll be marching down the Serra do Mar with Raposo Tavares; you'll be saved."

"Will I?" he asked, glancing at the motionless figure on the bench.

XI

———◈◆◈———

January 1640 – September 1640

On January 17, 1640, the *Hopewell*, a three-hundred-ton English merchant-man, one of several foreign vessels chartered by Lisbon agents for the expedition against the Dutch at Pernambuco and now part of the fleet that had left the Bahia two months earlier, was drifting with a light wind, about fifty leagues north of Recife.

A three-masted flute, the *Hopewell* was a handy little trader that could be crewed by a dozen men and was lightly armed: eight pieces on the main deck, two swivel guns at the quarterdeck railings. In recent years the *Hopewell* had been transporting settlers and supplies to the new North American colonies.

Will Tuttle captained the Hopewell's mixed crew of English, Danes, and Portuguese. From an old Yorkshire family of sheep farmers, Tuttle was a big, ruddy-faced man in his late forties, with a heavy build and a slow, deliberative manner. His only previous action had been a brief exchange of cannon fire with a barque belonging to Chesapeake Bay fur traders, who had established themselves on an island in the bay before the Maryland Territory had been granted to Lord Baltimore's family.

It would have given Will Tuttle no small satisfaction to witness the defeat of the Dutch, those fervent adherents of the heresy, but as the *Hopewell* drifted north of Recife, Tuttle had begun to accept that such an outcome was remote. On each of the five days since January 12, the armada had engaged the Dutch fleet in a series of uninspired fights, and the *Hopewell* had yet to fire more than a practice round.

Since daybreak, Captain Tuttle had been on the poop deck in an attempt to escape the stench from the lower decks: The ship was crammed with three hundred soldiers, twice the number she was meant to hold.

It was now past noon. Earlier, two Dutch warships had engaged the fifty-four-gun galleon *São José*, one of the stoutest ships of the armada. The *Hopewell* and other transports had orders to maintain position seaward, away from the first line of fighting ships. When the distant boom of the battery guns had fallen silent, and the Hollanders had turned away, a cloud of smoke hung above the *São José*, still afloat but listing and crippled by the bombardment.

Such defeats had not been anticipated when the armada sailed from the Bahia in November with five thousand men in thirty great galleons and fifty-six smaller vessels, from armed merchantmen like the *Hopewell* to swift yachts. Yet even Will Tuttle had had misgivings, not about the armada's fighting potential, which was formidable, but about its leader, the Conde da Torre, Dom Fernão de Mascarenhas. On the voyage out from Lisbon fourteen months ago the count had led the men and ships into the Cape Verde Islands, where more than half of the five thousand recruits were left behind, dead or dying from disease. Upon reaching Brazil, the count had had to spend a year at the Bahia refitting the armada.

During his months at the Bahia, Captain Tuttle kept a journal, in which he noted his impressions of the bay and the city of Salvador, which he found so much more sophisticated than the English colonies, where many lived in bark wigwams or cellars dug out of the earth:

> From our Anchorage, there is first to be sene a longe and handsome Street, with cellars and the warehouses of merchants, craftsmen and artisans. The City of Salvador is walled, haveing fifteen hundred houses of stone and mortar, exceeding good with tiled roof and limed walls, and situate along hilly, cobbled streets, the same as the quarters of Lisbone. The palace of the Governor, cathedral, churches of Franciscans, Benedictines, and Fathers of the Company of Jesus are well built, with marbled floors, gilded ornaments. There is a great Infirmarie for sicke men . . .
>
> The Senhores de Ingenios have fiftie great Mills for the Sugar-Canes. In theire houses, they have much silver plate and gold, and treasures of the Orient and Occident; theire women favor onelie silks and the gold thread of Lyons, and have an extravagance of jewels about their person. The women are rarely sene, the Senhors confineing them to their houses in the manner of indolent Moorish princesses. Beyonde this delight in Riches and Apparells, aspects of the lives of the Portugalls are as mean as those sene with our people at Maryland.
>
> They grow nothing but Canes, Cottons and Tobaccos, and so long as these Fields prosper, they are as content with the same table as their slaves — a sloppe of the ordinary foode of this Countrey, that is called Mandioca.

Will Tuttle had put the journal aside when the *Hopewell* was ordered to Rio de Janeiro with four other ships to fetch recruits and supplies from the southern captaincies. From there he'd sailed on to Santos to take aboard the contingent raised by Captain-Major Raposo Tavares at São Paulo.

Returning to the Bahia, the *Hopewell* had rejoined the fleet, and the armada of eighty-six vessels had finally got under way the previous November. But contrary weather had driven the ships past Recife; retracing their course, they were met on January 12, 1640, by a Dutch squadron with less than half the number of their sail. On the five days since then, those desultory fights between their ships had seen a large and useless expenditure of powder and shot: The Dutch had sunk one galleon and ten small vessels; the armada had destroyed one enemy warship and disabled another.

Having witnessed the latest indecisive fight, Captain Tuttle was despondent as he stood on the *Hopewell's* poop deck: He realized that unless they could break the Dutch sea defense, they would be unable to land their troops near Recife. Puffing absently on his pipe and gazing out over the water, he observed a skiff making its way from the galleons to the *Hopewell*. Tuttle moved down to the 'tween-deck bulwark to hear what the messengers from the flagship had to say.

Since he spoke little Portuguese, standing next to him, ready to interpret, was a marinheiro who had once served with the English East India Company.

After a quick exchange with an officer in the skiff, the marinheiro turned to Tuttle. "The battle is over," he said. "Finish. The count is to return to the Bahia."

"Pedro, ask him what battle he —" Tuttle broke off, noticing the sad, bewildered faces of those below, and changed his mind: "No — ask only what our orders are, Pedro."

These came swiftly: The galleons were off the shoals of a dangerous cape — Cabo de São Roque, five degrees south of the Equator — and had no alternative but to stand out to sea and head for the West Indies or Spain, since there was no chance of their weathering this cape or returning to the Bahia through waters securely held by the Dutch; the *Hopewell*, a chartered vessel, was free to make her way home or wherever she pleased.

"Amazing!" Will Tuttle exclaimed. He pointed toward his crowded decks. "And what am I to do with this cargo of highlanders?" He knew little about the Paulistas other than that they were mostly wild half-breeds who lived on the heights above the Serra do Mar. "Carry them across the Atlantic?"

This provoked a lively discussion between the marinheiro Pedro and the officers.

"The troops will be landed. Their commanders have volunteered to march back to Salvador through the sertão," Pedro said. He saw the captain's incredulous expression. "These mamelucos don't know anyplace but Brazil; if they're taken away in our ship, they'll never get home."

"But, Pedro, if they're set ashore, what chance will they have?" Tuttle asked. "Four hundred leagues lie between these lands and Salvador, with savages and Dutch all along the way."

"Oh, Capitão, don't worry about such men," Pedro said. "If anyone can survive this march, it will be these mongrels of the sertão."

"May the Almighty, in His mercy, help them," Tuttle murmured.

&

Ishmael Pinheiro had warned him that this would be a foolish venture. To have come so far, imprisoned in the stinking bowels of a ship, and to have failed so miserably! How he had hated the sea, the waves rolling on and on with dreary monotony, the horizon rising and falling with such nauseous regularity, the world shrunk to a rough square of deck, groaning and creaking, and contested by other men and the vermin that alone thrived in such dark confines.

It was not only the conditions in the *Hopewell* that had embittered Amador Flôres da Silva. Six weeks had passed since they were put ashore by the armada. The Conde da Torre had fled in a swift yacht back to the Bahia, and with him, the count of Bagnuoli, of whom much had been heard at São Paulo before this misadventure; once again the Italian, master of the retreat, had run from the Dutch.

Amador recalled the grand design of this campaign: a swift landing near Recife, a junction with forces marching north from Salvador, a quick ravaging of the countryside, and then the siege of the Dutch. Instead, thirteen hundred seasick and dispirited men had been dumped ashore at the mouth of a river!

Raposo Tavares had claimed they would perform a glorious service for Portugal, but for six weeks now they had marched without thought of glory or honor. The captain-major himself was not with the column, having remained in one of the ships that returned to the Bahia. Day after day, a hungry, tired rabble with little hope of relief, they passed through lands garrisoned by the Hollanders and their native allies, merciless clans of "Tapuya," the Tupi word for savages whose language differed from Tupi, generally taken to mean "The Enemy." There had been short, bloody encounters with Dutch and Tapuya, no quarter given by either side.

They marched over charred fields set afire by the invaders; stood in defiled churches, the holy images cast down and shattered. Portuguese settlers who had remained in these captaincies reported how Tapuya, incited by the Dutch, had overrun engenhos, massacring entire settlements. And they told of black slaves encouraged to desert to the Dutch, who then armed them for mischief and murder against their former masters.

"We're ruined. Ruined!" these planters cried when they recalled how Olinda, loveliest town of Pernambuco, had been destroyed, the very stones of its temples carried off to build the houses of the heretics in their new town of Mauritsstad, opposite Recife.

Such reports encouraged the column's commanders to detach small patrols from the main body and send them raiding deep within the enemy-held lands. At the beginning of the seventh week of the march, Amador was with a patrol in the district behind Recife. The Dutch had spared most of the engenhos here, for these valleys held the richest cane fields of Pernambuco.

The twenty raiders with the patrol, led by a regular officer from the Spanish garrison at the Bahia, were mostly Paulistas, the mamelucos having proved themselves the best troops for this bush warfare.

On the third day after leaving the column, the patrol was ten leagues from the coast, moving along the bank of a river, when it came to an open, sandy beach. The sergeant called a halt; it was afternoon, and the patrol, which had been on a forced march, would rest the night. Tomorrow it would be in an area thickly infested with the Dutch.

While the others settled around the beach, Amador was sent to a ridge behind the river from which he could spy out the lands through which they were passing.

A full hour passed before he stood at the top of the ridge, shielding his eyes from the sun as he gazed over the valley. To the north, near the gray-blue smudge of a small lake, he saw an engenho with as many buildings as existed in a good-sized village, and vast cane fields.

A house that stood on a gentle rise near the lake dominated the settlement. Off to the right of the house was a chapel, and several smaller buildings close by.

The low hill with the big house and chapel sloped gently toward a river that flowed from the hills opposite the ridge where Amador stood. Near that river were the mill, and warehouse.

Amador wondered whether the family who owned this valley lived here or had been taken by the Dutch — surely one of the great engenhos of Pernambuco. He'd report it to the sergeant: If a Dutchman held it, as he suspected, then they'd burn it to the ground.

He was easing his way down the slope when he was suddenly startled by the report of a musket shot. He stopped. The buildings at the other end of the valley were barely discernible, as peaceful-looking in the distance as when he'd first beheld them.

Then the sound of muskets increased — furious, repeated volleys rising from the trees directly below.

Suddenly, the musket firing ceased. Within minutes he detected smoke, and he perceived a dull glow in the direction of the beach.

A few hundred paces from the river, the flames were clearly visible. Only as he broke out of the trees did he think to draw his machete; but his hand froze on the weapon's tapir-bone hilt and he made a low, agonized noise at the scene before him.

The bodies of the nineteen men of the patrol were strewn across the beach. Amador was transfixed by this horror, unable to flee. He did not perceive that on the dark river beyond, there drifted a canoe with Dutch soldiers; the last to leave the sands, they had been responsible for severing the heads of the Spanish sergeant and the mamelucos.

Two musket shots roared out of the dark, followed by another two. Amador's head jerked up, an amazed expression on his face, as a ball plowed along his side. Two more shots struck him and he toppled to the right, falling beside the headless corpse of his sergeant.

ↄ⊃

How long had he been confined to bed in this room, Amador wondered? A month? Two months? A square, high chamber with a chest against the opposite wall and one chair. By now he was familiar with every detail of the room: the patterns above, with the smooth-hewn beams and frames, and the exposed underside of the roof tiles; the uneven surfaces of the white walls, one bearing a black crucifix; the high window, with lines of light between the shutters coming and going.

He had no recollection of being brought here. His memory of events before being shot by the Dutch had also been confused with nightmares in which he saw the beheaded sergeant. He would lie with his eyes upon the crucifix, puzzling over the circumstances that had spared him.

He had been grievously wounded: His head was bandaged; there was a hole in his side, and pain when he moved his left leg.

After a time with only a vague awareness of his surroundings, there had been increasing periods in which he was lucid, still too weak to converse but recognizing people who tended him. He would listen to footfalls on the wooden floor in the house, and to sounds rising to the shuttered window — a church bell, the creak and rattle of carts, horses, dogs, voices. Voices, most mercifully, speaking Portuguese.

This morning, after a slave woman brought him his food, he'd dropped off to sleep, but now he was awake again. He'd heard the steps of someone approaching the room and sat up. The door opened to admit the owner of the house.

"Ah, Amador Flôres, they tell me that you may soon be well enough to rise."

"Only through the mercy of God, Senhor Fernão, and the kindness of your house," he said slowly.

Amador was in the grand house on the plantation he had seen from the ridge overlooking the valley — Engenho Santo Tomás, the property of Fernão Theodosio Cavalcanti, of an old and illustrious Pernambucan family. Nicolau Cavalcanti, the founder of this estate, had come to the captaincy with the first donatário, Duarte Coelho Pereira, and had passed these lands to his son, Tomás Cavalcanti. Fernão was the grandson of Tomás.

The shutters on the window were kept closed against "unhealthful airs." The light was poor, but Fernão Cavalcanti's features were clear enough to Amador. He was fifty but looked younger. He had a long, noble, unlined face, with pensive brow and melancholy green eyes, clipped beard and mustache, and dark brown hair. He was elegantly dressed in the Dutch Cavalier style. His hair was long, falling to his shoulders. He wore a large, square-cut linen collar edged with Flanders lace, a high-waisted doublet silver-threaded and trimmed with lace, loose breeches tied at the knee with ribbon sashes, white stockings, and fawn leather boots.

From the black slave, Celestina, who brought his food, Amador had learned that Cavalcanti was wedded to Dona Domitila Guedes, daughter of another wealthy planter. Dona Domitila, a slow, plump woman, had visited Amador twice to assure him that Padre Gregório Bonifácio, who lived at the engenho, was praying for him. The priest had also been to see him — a fat, elderly man who'd asked him questions about São Paulo and then dozed off in the chair while Amador responded.

Celestina had told him that there were six Cavalcanti children: two sons, Felipe and Alvaro, both in their twenties, and four daughters, two married and two — Joana and Beatriz — still in the house. Beatriz, a twelve-year-old, had spied on him several times, flying from the room as soon as he acknowledged her. Joana he had not seen, but the slave had hinted at a wild, free spirit.

"Donzela Joana — that one has a mind of her own," Celestina had said. "Will there ever be a man to tame Joana!"

Now, as on the two previous occasions when Fernão Cavalcanti had been to see him, Amador sensed an aloofness toward him, but he expected this from the master of such a grand estate. Amador had given Celestina and the priest some details of his own background, and it was clear that they had conveyed this to the senhor.

"The men you marched with are now beyond Pernambuco, into the captaincy of the Bahia."

"God saved that force, senhor, for the time it must return to drive the Dutch from these lands."

"It may be so."

"It must be so, senhor. God will never forgive the Portuguese if we allow these pirates and fishermen to spoil Brazil."

"You come late to this battle, Amador Flôres. There are many to tell us what we should do, and who accuse us of favoring the heretics. We fought the Hollanders for five years after they took Olinda and Recife — long, bloody campaigns, with all our captaincy contested.

"At São Paulo, senhor, we've heard about the shameful retreats of Bagnuoli."

"You've heard that he was a coward, whose purpose was to hasten the Dutch conquest?"

"This and more has been said, senhor."

"Dear God — was ever a man so slandered."

"Our own expedition was deserted by him!"

"Was he a coward because he asked the Hollanders for fair conditions of war? And got an agreement to end the slaughter of prisoners? And pleaded that women and children be spared? A coward because he refused to waste men's lives in campaigns he saw they couldn't win? Bagnuoli has dined in my house, Amador Flôres. He is a great soldier, who did as much for the Portuguese and Pernambuco as any man who fought here."

"But the Dutch conquered the captaincy."

Cavalcanti's boots squeaked as he shifted position irritably. "Was Bagnuoli to stop them with the miserable relief sent from Spain and Portugal? When a thousand Dutch guns blockaded the coast, and no supplies could be landed?"

Amador had no answer. While Fernão Cavalcanti had been defending Bagnuoli, Amador found himself wondering about the senhor's role during the backlands war. From that ridge overlooking Engenho Santo Tomás, he'd seen no evidence of war in the valley; not the slightest devastation. And here Cavalcanti stood, so fashionable and prosperous. But he wasn't about to pursue this potentially sensitive point. In this grand house, he was a common soldier given refuge by the lord of the plantation. Even this bed he rested in — four carved posts, brocaded canopy — made him acutely conscious of his inferior position.

Cavalcanti said no more about Bagnuoli but remarked: "There are Portuguese who would follow an endless holy war in Pernambuco."

"I understand them, senhor. Who but the Infidel would have dealt so barbarously with my patrol — the Infidel and the Hollander?"

"Only a few Hollanders are as brutal as Jan Vlok, captain of the men who attacked your patrol."

"You know the devil?"

"Vlok has a reputation. Even the governor, Count Maurits, despises the man for his cruelties. We're weary of Vlok and others who make a sport of suffering. These men have brought years of sorrow to the colony." Cavalcanti saw that Amador wanted to speak, but he gestured for silence. "Jan Vlok and his company still hunt the stragglers of your column, but you needn't worry. When you're well enough, I'll arrange a passage to the Bahia."

Cavalcanti stepped toward the door.

"Senhor Cavalcanti . . ."

"Yes?"

"Do you accept the Dutch in this valley — in all Pernambuco — forever?"

Cavalcanti moved back to the bed. "You speak very freely, da Silva."

"No offense, senhor. God knows, I owe you my life."

"I visited that beach, Amador Flôres. I saw what Jan Vlok did. I understand your anger. But in this valley, working with Count Maurits is the only way I know to save what the Cavalcantis have held for a hundred years. I make no bargains with Vlok and his butchers, but I will listen to reasonable men. If they are Dutch, as it happens Maurits is, so be it." He turned away then, and without another word, walked out of the room.

Amador lay thinking about what Cavalcanti had said: *Sweet Jesus, was the blood of my comrades shed so that the senhores of these valleys may prosper with the Hollanders?*

He would have risen there and then and left Fernão Cavalcanti's house, but he was overcome with exhaustion and soon fell asleep.

೮೨

And then, the next morning, Amador abandoned any notion of leaving Engenho Santo Tomás.

He heard someone approaching the room and expected the slave Celestina, bringing a bowl of food. When the door opened, it was an angel who had appeared at his bedside as he lay racked with fever.

"So, Amador Flôres, you're better — recovered enough at least to anger my father?"

"Senhorita Joana?"

"My father doesn't like it to be thought that he favors Dutch rule over that of Lisbon." She held out a bowl of food to him. "Here," she said. "Old Celestina is sick — perplexed, says Padre Bonifácio, by the wizards of 'Ngola, who dance in her mind."

As he took the bowl, Amador looked into Joana's face and was awed by its strength, beauty, and sweetness. Her skin was ivory; her eyes soft and dark and intelligent beneath dark eyebrows; her lips full and red. Her black hair fell in loose ringlets on either side of her face and, at the back, was plaited into a knot worn high on the crown.

Her gown was less sumptuous than her father's clothing, black with silver thread, tight at the waist and accenting her shapely figure. And now there was a lively sparkle in her eyes.

"Tell me . . ."

"Yes?"

"My father says the men of São Paulo are Gypsies, wanderers — Moors of the sertão, he also calls them. Are you such a man, Amador Flôres?"

"If the senhor says so."

"Before the Cavalcantis came to this valley, it was wild, my father says — as it must still be at São Paulo, I imagine?"

"It is, senhorita, with many, many Carijó," he said. "All my life, I've marched with the bandeiras of Captain-Major Raposo Tavares. Oh, Senhorita Joana, if Raposo Tavares had led our column in Pernambuco, the Hollanders wouldn't have driven off our army."

"But they always have," she said. "Since I was a girl, the age of my sister Beatriz, the Hollanders have beaten our soldiers. My father fought at Recife and in the south, but it did no good. When the Hollanders were ready, they marched across the land.

"Ask the others if Joana was ready — with musket and powder. Our dear Padre Bonifácio trembled at the sight. But I was ready, if ever they attacked Santo Tomás."

"You, Senhorita Joana, with a musket?"

"You don't know Joana Cavalcanti!" With a toss of her head, she danced out of the room, laughing as she went.

"*Senhorita* Joana," he whispered aloud.

A senhor de engenho's daughter was supposed to be untouchable, a captive of the big house, until the senhor de engenho found a man *he* was willing to accept as her husband. The donzela must do nothing but squat upon cushions and carpets, in the Moorish fashion, with the little dona's slaves cooing and gossiping around her, feeding her sweet confections and titillating tales from which she'd learn all she needed to know to satisfy the husband chosen by her father.

But Senhorita Joana was altogether different. Her coming alone to the bedside of a strange man was in itself revealing. What lovely, defiant talk. A girl with powder and a musket! Laughing at the Hollanders!

Amador lay listening to sounds from the rooms beyond, imagining that Senhorita Joana made them. But, after a time, his thoughts grew more realistic: A "Gypsy" of the sertão: what place was there for such a man with Senhorita Joana?

☙

Joana Cavalcanti was a rebel. Her sister Beatriz followed the customs of the big house, as had Fernão Cavalcanti's other daughters before their marriages, but not Joana. She was now nineteen, but even as a child she had revealed her free spirit.

While the other Cavalcanti girls played behind screens and shutters, Joana crept out of the house to the stables, swearing the slaves there to secrecy as she taught herself to ride, discovering on horseback the beauty of the valley of Santo Tomás, which had so delighted Nicolau Cavalcanti when he'd first seen it. Her sisters grew plump and obedient, with no ambition beyond a comfortable marriage, but not Joana.

"I won't marry without love," Joana had said to Fernão Cavalcanti, after rejecting several well-born Portuguese who'd had his permission to visit the house. "I won't be the plaything of a man who needs no more than a lazy queen with a brood of children."

Her father had expressed shock at such talk, and, sympathizing with Dona Domitila's concerns for this "heaven-sent flower of virginity," vowed to persist with his search for a husband for Joana, but secretly Fernão admired his unusual daughter.

When he saw Joana tearing across the engenho on one of her Arabian horses, her black hair streaming behind; when he heard her conversing on topics of no concern to women — the harvest, the mill, the sharp dealings of the sugar merchants at Recife; when he saw her as defiant as a man toward the Dutch — then Cavalcanti became open-minded, and realized that the Lord had given him a rare and exceptional daughter.

It came as no surprise to Senhor Cavalcanti that his daughter should befriend the mameluco. When Amador was able to get out of bed — two months after he'd been carried to the engenho from the river — they moved him out of the big house to the quarters of the Portuguese mill workers. Although his wounds were healing, he remained weak; a ball that had struck his leg left him with a permanent limp.

On many days, Cavalcanti had seen Amador resting in the shade of trees near the chapel: Sometimes Padre Bonifácio was with him; sometimes, Joana.

A senhor de engenho's daughter in the company of such a common man! Many fathers would order the overseer of the engenho to apply his thickest tapir-hide whip to the fellow. But Fernão Cavalcanti knew that such a response would be futile where Joana was concerned; and he would never question the innocence of her interest in da Silva, though he had to wonder what she saw in him. He soon found out.

At dinner one evening Dona Domitila, sorely vexed by her daughter's friendship toward the "half-breed savage," openly objected to the association.

"Mother, Amador Flôres is a fine teacher," Joana said. "No one knows the sertão as he does. He's made so many journeys, not a secret in the forest is hidden from him." Responding to Fernão Cavalcanti's contentious look, she added, "The Paulistas, Father, are different from the Pernambucans."

"How so, my child?"

"We're bound to our houses and plantations," she said. "We have no interest in what lies in the next valley — unless it's to be opened for more cane fields. Amador tells of the bandeiras that set out in every direction from São Paulo. They're as bold and brave as the settlers who came from Lisbon with nothing. The mamelucos, Father, are like Nicolau Cavalcanti and Grandfather Tomás: They still seek a country."

Fernão Cavalcanti noticed that Dona Domitila, who had initiated this conversation, was concerning herself now with Beatriz, who was biting her nails. Dona Domitila took Joana's words seriously only when her daughter referred to Dona Brites, widow of the first donatário, Dom Duarte Coelho. Dona Brites had led the colony after Dom Duarte's death, and Joana loved the idea that a lady governor had ruled Pernambuco for five years.

After a pause, Fernão responded to his daughter: "They search the sertão, but they find nothing except Carijó, who they take from the Jesuits, and a handful of gold. And they'll do nothing for Portugal and her captaincies."

Joana looked down at the dinner table. "For the smallest reward, Father, Amador Flôres and other Paulistas left their homes to fight for us. By the river, his friends . . ."

"Your nails, Beatriz," Dona Domitila said. "If you don't stop eating them, they'll lodge in your lungs, child; you'll get a canker that may kill you . . ."

ꬉ

The attack at the river had taken place at the beginning of March 1640. It was now July, and Amador's wounds had healed enough for him to begin the journey back to São Paulo. But he had made no effort to leave, nor had he pressed Senhor Cavalcanti to arrange for his departure.

Joana Cavalcanti was the source of his inertia . . . Oh, sweet Jesus, to find favor in the eyes of this lady. Paulistas were reviled as "mongrels," "outlaws," "slavers" by the Pernambucans, who also feared them, but Senhorita Joana understood how hard life was above those wild crags at Piratininga and with the long wanderings of the bandeiras.

Sweet Jesus, what torment! The image of Maria was constantly before him. If he saw the senhorita in his dreams, the big one would appear, too, demanding his return. And what of the two savage girls at São Paulo who were so ready to leap on their backs for him? In their pagan way, they were the most faithful of lovers.

Amador found himself plagued by other questions, too, which he had never considered before. Marcos da Silva, Tenente Bernardo, and now himself — what had they achieved with the great whore of the wilderness? After a lifetime in the sertão, what did they have that could match this grand engenho?

When he'd been able to walk with a stick, he'd investigated Fernão Cavalcanti's property, with its two hundred black slaves. Cavalcanti's slaves worked great tracts of cane, but other plantings were managed by families not unlike his own mamelucos, half-breeds with the blood of the natives.

He discovered that many families were related, claiming a common ancestor, Affonso Ribeiro, who had come to the valley of Santo Tomás with the first senhor de engenho, Nicolau Cavalcanti. There was at this time another Ribeiro with the name Affonso, a lumbering, potbellied braggart whose breath was always burning with cachaça and who occupied a group of dilapidated, mud-walled houses with three women and a multitude of children. By the tenants' standards, Ribeiro was prosperous, for he owned eight black slaves to tend his canes for the engenho.

This Affonso Ribeiro had been greatly taken with the "Tenente Paulista," as he called Amador, and had gathered his relatives at a celebration for him. Late at night, drunk and swaying on his feet, his breeches sagging, Affonso Ribeiro had made a speech about the "war," in which he associated himself with heroes, Tenente Paulista included, who sought to expel the Dutch.

Ribeiro told Amador that during the guerrilla war, he had served with two units, the first commanded by Felipe Camarão, a Potiguara chief, and the other by Henrique Dias, a free black. Loyal to the Portuguese, these commanders had accepted recruits such as Ribeiro, but the bulk of their forces were their own people, natives and blacks, and they had troubled the Dutch more than had the armies of General Bagnuoli.

"I was there, Tenente Paulista, when Henrique Dias lost his hand," Ribeiro said. "Oh, the brave man — with a sword in the hand that remained, howling like a wild black dog, for the Hollanders to come to him. And Dom Camarão — he deserves to be made a fidalgo for his services — Dom Camarão saw Affonso Ribeiro chop up three Hollanders, one after the other, with my machete."

"Will we ever get rid of the Dutch?" Amador had asked.

"Oh, yes, *amigo*," Ribeiro had said drunkenly. "They *must* go. Even Count Maurits, who seeks to be our friend."

"The senhor de engenho doesn't feel strongly about this?" Amador had queried.

"Why should he? What has he lost?"

"Nothing," Amador had responded.

After that night, when Ribeiro came to the mill he would seek out Amador, inviting him to return to his house, but Amador always had an excuse — his wounds, his fatigue.

Ribeiro had been sympathetic: "Ah, Tenente Paulista, may your strength return. The senhor says we have to work with the Hollanders, but you — you, Tenente Paulista — know better than this."

But this morning, as he sat in the shade of the trees by the church, Amador was preparing to meet a Dutchman, at the specific request of Joana Cavalcanti.

"But, Senhorita Joana, you know how I hate them," he'd said when she asked this of him the day before.

"*My* Dutchman is different. Secundus Proot isn't interested in war and killing, Amador. He's an artist — a painter."

He'd not heard the name clearly. "'Segge?'" he said.

"'Secundus Proot,'" she said. "He's been to the engenho before, Amador — to draw pictures of the house, the mill, the slaves."

"What do I want with this man?" he'd asked. "Other Hollanders come to see your father. I watch them, senhorita. I see the sergeant and my patrol. 'Damn the souls of the Dutch,' I say. 'Curse them!'"

"I know how you feel, Amador," she'd said. "You'll realize that he's not like those butchers. Secundus Proot would never kill a man. He's kind and gentle, Amador, and he loves the sertão."

Amador found himself powerless to refuse Senhorita Joana. And he also believed that his antagonism toward the Hollanders was lessening.

He had come to believe Senhor Fernão's statement that he worked with the Dutch not because he supported these heretics but primarily to save Engenho Santo Tomás. Months at the engenho had shown Amador that Cavalcanti and his family remained first and foremost Portuguese — in fact, more Portuguese than those from the old country itself. Not one of them had been to Lisbon, but it was *their* city, and Portugal *their* country, and their melancholy at being so far from the homeland was profound. "Better a beggar with the shield of the king than the richest planter in Brazil," the nobles of Pernambuco believed.

Amador was pondering this obsession with nobility when Joana Cavalcanti emerged from the house with her Dutch painter. Amador rose and started toward them, dragging his left leg.

Secundus Proot was one of the strangest-looking men Amador had ever seen. Proot's oval face was a bright pink and dominated by a wide red nose. His straw-colored hair was shoulder length. He had an upturned mustache, a yellow beard, and his eyes beneath his thin brows were a soft blue. He was a foot taller than Amador, with a heavy but muscular physique. His hands were freckled.

Amador had borrowed a red-velvet jacket from a mill worker to appear dignified in front of the Hollander. He need not have bothered, for "Segge's" attire was plain: buff leather jacket, square linen collar with only a touch of lace, black breeches, and shabby boots. The one elaborate touch was a large pearl in the lobe of Proot's right ear.

After Joana's introductions, the Hollander described in Tupi-Guarani his delight in this valley of Santo Tomás, hoping to lessen Amador's blatant hostility toward him. Amador was surprised at Segge's ability with the dialect, and interrupted Proot to ask how he'd come to learn it.

"From the Tobajara and other natives at Recife," Proot said. "I made this my first task."

"What need was there?"

"So that I could learn more about them and their customs. There's so much to learn, from so many different people."

"Secundus wants to paint portraits of everyone. You, too, Amador," Joana said.

"*Me?*"

She laughed merrily. "You would make a fine subject."

How lovely she was today! She wore an emerald green gown, which perfectly complemented her ivory skin and black hair.

"A marvelous subject," Proot said. "Man of the bandeira, in the sertão, with his armor."

"Oh, Senhorita Joana, tell him about the mameluco, please — before the man makes a fool of himself."

"Secundus Proot paints what he sees around him, Amador — the engenho, slaves, scenes of the forest. Why not a man of the bandeiras? Secundus is not a decorator of churches."

"Oh, we know this, senhorita: The Dutch only tear down churches."

"No, Amador, that wasn't his doing."

Proot brought the subject back to art: "I'd be grateful, Amador Flôres, for the opportunity to paint you here at the engenho. I don't believe I'll be allowed to visit you at São Paulo."

"No, senhor, that you won't — not in a thousand years."

Proot remained unruffled and agreeable. "I've heard it said that twelve soldiers could block an entire army's ascent up the Serra do Mar."

"*Exatamente!* And I would be one of the twelve!"

Joana intervened: "If the two of you must have a war, fight it when the portrait is finished. I do want to see how a famous artist draws the man of the sertão."

"You would truly wish to see it, senhorita?"

"Oh, yes, Amador, I want Secundus to make a very grand painting of you."

"Then I'll do it, senhorita."

"Oh, I knew you would, Amador Flôres!" she said.

Amador turned to Proot, and was irritated to see him smiling at Joana. "Is this all you do? Paint?" he asked.

"It's my work, yes."

"Work? What work in painting?"

"When I draw you, Amador Flôres, you'll understand."

"Me understand what a Hollander does? It's not possible."

"Secundus knows about your patrol," Joana interjected.

"What Hollander wouldn't? Tell me, Segge — at Recife, did they celebrate the killings?"

"I don't rejoice in death," Proot said quietly.

Amador was silent.

"*Please*, both of you, you're my friends. Let Secundus get on with his painting, Amador."

It was arranged that Amador would meet Proot the next morning. He told no one about the portrait, and in the morning he waited until the sugar master and the other Portuguese had gone before creeping out furtively with his weapons and equipment rolled up in his jacket.

Joana Cavalcanti was waiting with Proot on the verandah of the big house. To Amador's disappointment, she excused herself. "Secundus doesn't want me glancing over his shoulder," she said.

An hour later, Amador found himself seated on a bench outside Proot's room, which had a door opening onto the verandah. He had wanted to keep this meeting secret, but here he was, on display for anyone who walked past the house. He held one of the senhor de engenho's muskets, and Joana had also loaned him a wide-brimmed hat with a plume of ostrich feathers.

Proot was perched on a stool opposite him, making preliminary sketches with pen and ink.

"We don't sit on benches," Amador announced, after the artist had settled him down.

Proot did not respond but continued to draw furiously. Then, after a time: "What did you say?"

"With the bandeiras, we don't carry benches; we march!"

"Yes," Proot said, "you march."

"It would be wrong to have me sitting this way — an old man on a bench."

"Yes," Proot said, "it would be."

Damn Dutchman, Amador thought. *If he wants to exhibit his foolishness, then let him.* He watched Proot silently, following the rapid movements of his pen.

Finally, Proot said, "These are rough drawings. I'll use them to plan the painting."

"Yes?"

But Proot gave no further explanation, and Amador asked, "Why have you come here?"

"The Cavalcantis invited me."

"No, not to this valley. To Pernambuco. You're not a soldier, not a sugar merchant. Why do you come here to paint? Can't you do this in Holland?"

"Here the Lord has planted a second Eden. That's why Count Maurits has brought artists and scientists to this New World. Here in this second Eden, Amador, I, too, am given another chance."

"To do what?"

Proot looked at him keenly. "To draw and paint in such a way . . . even Master van Rijn will acknowledge the work of Secundus Proot."

"*Master?*"

"My teacher."

"You went to school — for painting?"

"For seven years."

"*Seven years?*"

"Rembrandt van Rijn did not think it enough," he said.

"This master — he paints, too?"

"Rembrandt's work is among the best in Holland. He's young, ambitious; his paintings are marvelous."

"And yours, Segge?"

"In time, others will see them," Proot said vaguely, and returned to his sketching, a deeply pensive look on his face.

It was a month before Secundus Proot completed his *Bandeirante*, a name suggested by Fernão Cavalcanti. Amador had been called to pose many times. During those sessions, their conversations had grown friendlier, though a gulf still remained between them.

At last, Amador was invited to Proot's quarters to view the finished painting.

Four feet by three, it depicted a stocky Amador in the middle ground, standing boldly in his padded jacket, festooned with weapons and crowned with the ostrich-plumed hat, and firing his musket. In the background, several Paulistas were discharging their weapons, others reloading. In the right-hand corner was a dying savage on the ground. In the trees, also to the right, was another native, taking aim with bow and arrow. The encounter was set deep in the forest, with Amador standing between two great tree trunks covered with vines and ferns.

"Oh, Segge!" Amador exclaimed. "What a fine painting we have painted!"

&

On a night in September 1640, planters from neighboring engenhos and a group of Dutchmen were gathered in the big house of Engenho Santo Tomás. Senhor Cavalcanti was holding a festa, and the senhor's orchestra played the most pleasant tunes with viol and lute. Cavalcanti took pride in his musicians: eleven slave boys who had been taught their Italian madrigals and old pastorales of Portugal by Padre Gregório Bonifácio.

Those attending this night's festa included no less a personage than the governor of New Holland, Johan Maurits, count of Nassau-Siegen. Maurits had arrived from Recife that morning with an escort of pikers and musketeers; during the day, Cavalcanti had taken him on a tour of the engenho, during which he expressed interest in almost everything he saw. And indeed, the governor's curiosity, his stream of questions put by an interpreter to Cavalcanti and his sons, Felipe and Alvaro, was not an expression of mere politeness. Since its settlement more than a century before, Pernambuco had had no more enthusiastic leader. In his first letter to Amsterdam, after landing at Recife in January 1637, the governor described his post as "the most beautiful country on earth."

The Heeren XIX had made a wise choice in appointing him governor. As a young man, Johan Maurits witnessed the first flowering of the Golden Age of the Netherlands. The nation brought together in the seven United Provinces, of which Holland was the richest, was beginning its climb toward dazzling brilliance in commerce.

By this year 1640, the directors of the East and West India companies had advanced far toward their goal of establishing a trading empire around the world. Their activities extended from the Hudson River and this conquest in Pernambuco, in the Americas, to the Guinea coast of Africa, and from there to the great emporium of Batavia in Java, then on to Siam and Formosa, and to Japan, where Iyeyasu, first shogun of the Tokugawa regime, had given the Dutch a license to trade in 1605.

Maurits, a Calvanist and a hero of wars still raging in Germany between Protestant armies and the princes of the Catholic League, was a liberal and a humanist. When effective resistance by the Portuguese in Pernambuco had collapsed, his first moves were to offer loans to colonists to rebuild engenhos and buy slaves, and to promise no interference with Portuguese customs and religion.

The orthodox dominies from Holland complained about concessions to the "Romish Papists," and also disapproved of the governor's friendliness toward Jews. But Maurits had proceeded unwaveringly. "God has appointed us custodians of Canaan," he said. "Dare we drag the old and bloody arguments of Europe to His fairest land?" He did make one exception: Since the Jesuits had a notorious reputation in Protestant Europe as militants and plotters, Maurits ordered their expulsion from Pernambuco and other areas of Dutch Brazil.

Opposite Recife, on an island formed by two rivers, the governor was building a new capital, Mauritsstad, a well-fortified town with broad avenues and two canals, as the Dutch had known in Amsterdam, with gabled homes and warehouses facing the water. A bridge two hundred paces long was planned to connect Recife with Mauritsstad.

Capable soldier and fine administrator, Maurits also showed himself to be a visionary. He assembled a group of forty-six scientists, scholars, writers, and artists from all over Europe and solemnly declared their assignment: "to reveal to the world the wonders of paradise."

Fernão Cavalcanti and like-minded Portuguese could not deny that Johan Maurits's artists and scientists, and his new capital, gave formidable proof of his love for Brazil.

Cavalcanti had fought with the regiments of Bagnuoli against Maurits, and had been influenced by the Italian's pragmatic attitude toward defeat: Since the regular army had been beaten soundly by the Dutch, Cavalcanti considered it futile to think of expelling the Hollanders with bands of outlaws sniping at their patrols from the bush.

Cavalcanti served with a planters' council organized by Maurits for consultations between the Portuguese and the Dutch. Still, he maintained a cautious, dignified attitude toward the Dutch. He would be a gracious, genial host to Governor Maurits, whose nobility and learning he greatly admired, but any suggestion that he was a traitor angered him. His first and main concern had been to save Engenho

Santo Tomás. "Besides," he told his detractors, "you cry for restoration to Portugal, after sixty years of Spanish captivity. What difference is there between the rule of Madrid and that of Amsterdam?" A huge difference, he knew: The Spaniards were hopeless merchants who knew nothing about marketing sugar. Before Portugal had been dragged into conflict with the Netherlands because of the union with Spain, the Hollanders had distributed Pernambucan sugar throughout Europe.

Cavalcanti considered his dealings with the Dutch mere expediency; his heart burned with secret longing for the restoration of Portugal, not only in Pernambuco but also at Lisbon. Reports reaching Recife told of a nationalist movement at Lisbon, with a strong pretender to the Portuguese throne in Dom João, duke of Bragança.

This day of the festa, while touring the engenho, Maurits had spoken of the Lisbon nationalists. "Think of it, Senhor Fernão: Holland and Portugal free and independent, with a truce between us. There would be a Golden Age for Pernambuco, without such hopeless Spanish adventures as the conde da Torre's."

"It may be so, Governor Maurits," Cavalcanti had responded guardedly.

Had the conde da Torre's armada succeeded, Cavalcanti and the men of his engenho would have marched to join it. But it had failed, and Cavalcanti had been thankful for concealing his intentions from the Dutch. Others had not been so prudent and had been imprisoned or expelled from the colony.

The threat of the armada had almost destroyed relations between Maurits and the planters, particularly when the column with which Amador had marched through the sertão, with its patrols breaking off to attack Dutch outposts. (Amazingly, most of the soldiers had survived the twelve-hundred-mile march.) As a reprisal, Maurits had sent a force by sea to the Bahia. In a surprise attack, twenty-seven mills had been destroyed. It had seemed as if a protracted war was inevitable.

However, Fernão Cavalcanti and planters who served on Maurits's council, the vicar-general, and several Catholic priests had been summoned to a secret meeting with the governor.

"Friends," he had called them, "when I came to Pernambuco nearly four years ago, it was a ruin. The next cane harvest will be the colony's best. Will you help me save it?"

The vicar-general pointed out that this was a strange request from one who had ordered the destruction of twenty-seven mills at the Bahia.

"I did not send an armada, with eighty-six ships and with orders to give no quarter," said Maurits. "'Every Dutch man, woman, and child to be handed over to the cannibals,'" he quoted, from a captured dispatch.

Then Maurits had made a proposal: "We can save the harvest, and the lives of our people, if we negotiate a truce."

Again the vicar-general reminded him of the twenty-seven ruined mills, saying that his countrymen at Salvador would not forgive that injury.

"That I understand," the governor agreed, and had turned to Fernão Cavalcanti and the other planters: "It is you who must initiate this truce."

"Impossible!" several objected, Cavalcanti included. "Already they condemn us as traitors for refusing to leave our lands."

"It *is* possible," Maurits had responded. "You, reverend padres, must petition me for an end to hostilities without quarter — for an end to the destruction of the engenhos. I will send your petition to the governor at the Bahia, suggesting that we negotiate on the basis of its contents."

∵

In celebration of Maurits's visit, Senhor Fernão declared a holiday for all at the engenho, and the slaves, free laborers, and tenants had their own festa at the slave quarters.

But it was not a happy night for Amador. Early in the evening, he stood outside the big house with a group of mill workers and slaves, who had come for a glimpse of the senhor and his guests. They kept a respectful distance and remained quiet, not wanting to be denied the grand sight through the open doors and windows of the saloon.

The long table, with Governor Maurits at its head, was covered with a white linen cloth. The men at the table wore squares of the same material tied around their necks to protect their lace collars. On the table was a startling array of silver bowls and dishes, and gold and silver candle-holders ornamented with birds and fruit. There were silver spoons and knives for each guest, and new implements, forks, an Italian device of great interest to the group outside.

Joana Cavalcanti, radiant and beautiful in a rich mauve gown, sat next to the painter, talking with him and laughing vivaciously at his conversation.

Amador thought of the many times he'd seen that pair together in the three months since Senhorita Joana introduced him to Segge, as he'd continued to call Proot.

Amador had come to like the big blond Dutchman. Moody when there was a problem with his painting, Proot for the most part had a placid, amiable nature, and it was not difficult after a time to accept Senhorita Joana's opinion that Segge was different from typical Dutchmen, who cut off the heads of their enemies.

Segge did not affect fancy airs. In the company of the Ribeiros, the artist had got as drunk as the rest. And Amador had been moved by Segge's passion for Brazil. On a night with a full moon, when the two of them had been at the lake below the hill, drinking cane brandy and smoking tabak, Segge had grown rhapsodic: "Why should I return to that gray, foggy land when I have found paradise? Amador, how I envy you."

Of all they talked about, the sertão and the savages interested Segge most. He would listen to anything Amador said about the natives."

When Amador spoke of the far-distant Carijó and Tupiniquin, Segge also began to understand the vastness of Brazil.

"We say that with New Holland we have an empire in the tropics. But it's only a small margin of land along the coast."

"You shouldn't feel so bad, my friend," Amador had said. "After a century and a half, we ourselves have yet to discover Brazil. We've been called crabs, clinging to the white sands, always looking to Europe."

"But you were *born* here. You're a son of São Paulo — of Brazil."

"I'm Portuguese," Amador said, adamantly.

"You're no more Portuguese than I am."

"You're wrong," Amador protested. "When we had a king at Lisbon, even the lowest-born mameluco was proud to be his subject. We will be free of Madrid one day. Free, and restored to Portugal, our mother."

Amador had been reminded of his own delay at Engenho Santo Tomás. Six months had passed and both he and the senhor had continued to be vague about plans for his departure. Fernão Cavalcanti was preoccupied with truce arrangements with the Hollanders, and Amador had done no more than ask Padre Bonifácio to write to Amador's family in São Paulo, telling them that he was alive.

Although Amador still limped, his wounds had healed, and he regularly went hunting in the valleys behind the engenho, accompanied by three natives of Fernão Cavalcanti's, the remaining descendants of the clan whose malocas had once stood on the hill. Sometimes Fernão Cavalcanti himself would join them.

He had become friendly with Segge, he had hunted with Senhor Fernão, and he had a secret passion for Joana Cavalcanti, but for all this, he was still a mameluco.

Watching her now at the sumptuous banquet table, delighting in a world totally different from his own, he knew he would always stand outside — *outside*, with the slaves and the workers . . . and the dogs of Fernão Cavalcanti.

As the senhor's orchestra began to play, Amador fled down the hill, and farther, until he heard another sound, music from the *senzala* — the slave quarters. "Yes!" he cried aloud. "Yes! Here is where you belong, mameluco!"

At the big house, the slave boys delivered their madrigals and pastorales, while here the drums of Africa reverberated.

Amador gave himself to the wild, lusty atmosphere, laughing and drinking with Affonso Ribeiro and the others, and when, later, a young slave girl approached him, he did not hesitate. He hurried the girl behind a row of slave quarters, and several times she cried out, for he used her brutally. Afterward, when she sat up next to him, she uttered a sudden, frightened giggle.

"What is it?" he asked.

"Oh, mameluco, my mother said. . . ."

"What?"

"You'll beat me?"

"No."

She looked down nervously at the ground between her naked legs. "A foolish man, with wild dreams for the senhorita.'"

"Who is your mother?"

"The slave Celestina."

"She's right. It was a sickness."

The girl looked at him dumbly, and he did not explain.

☙

Early the next morning when Governor Maurits and his party left Santo Tomás, a groggy red-eyed Amador watched their departure. He studied Maurits as the count rode past him, finding it hard to accept that this small, delicate-looking man with his daintily-trimmed mustache and a triangular tuft of hair on his chin was lord of half of Brazil. *Nossa Senhora!* Why hadn't Maurits attempted to climb the

Serra do Mar to São Paulo? What a welcome the Paulistas would've given the heretic! *Never!*

After Maurits and his escort had gone, Amador crept back to his hammock in the quarters he shared with the Portuguese millworkers. The Portuguese dragged themselves off to the engenho and he found himself alone.

Go now, Amador Flôres, he told himself as he lay in the hammock. *Go now, damn you — or stay forever lost. Lost, with Affonso Ribeiro and his people, a prisoner of this valley. Forget the lovely senhorita. Sweet Jesus, what madness — the senhorita and you, mameluco!*

His thoughts moved from his own lustfulness to that of Senhor Fernão Cavalcanti. The slave girls were the senhor's favorites — for a quick, sweet bite. But he also enjoyed another, more dignified passion: Dona Carlotta da Lago — "Dona Carlotta of the Lake" to all but Cavalcanti, who did not jest about his mulatta.

Carlotta, daughter of a Portuguese and a slave, lived in a house the senhor provided, overlooking the small lake, and maintained herself as a "lady," with the fine clothes and jewelry Cavalcanti had given her. She had her own slaves, and did little but gossip with her friends. Cavalcanti had been sleeping with her since her seventeenth birthday; she was thirty-five now, and plump, but still very much the temptress of Senhor Fernão.

The three children from this union stayed with Carlotta's parents, who were tenants in the valley. Like other bastards fathered by men of the Cavalcanti clan, they were openly acknowledged. There were senhores de engenho who grew so fond of their little bastards that they bequeathed them portions of their land and fortune and honored them with their name. This had not yet happened with any of the illegitimate issue of the Cavalcantis, most of whom had merged with the other half-breeds on the plantation, unimproved by the circumstances of their birth.

Dona Domitila's attitude toward Fernão's infidelity was unchanged from that of the first dona of Engenho Santo Tomás, Helena, the wife of Nicolau. Dona Domitila prayed for her husband, begging the Lord's forgiveness. She would achieve nothing by openly challenging Fernão Cavalcanti's behavior with the mulatta — nothing but the scorn of a man denied what he accepted as his simplest right.

Segge Proot had been most disapproving. "It's shameful, Amador. Cavalcanti is damned without hope. He'll burn in hell." Proot rarely expounded such harsh Calvinism, but Cavalcanti's wickedness was apparently too much for him.

Amador lay in the hammock now, thinking how miserable life must be for a Dutchman. He knew little of the heresies of the Dutch, but he imagined a wrathful, merciless God, deaf to the appeals of a confessed sinner. Amador's surprise was very great when, at this particular moment, a visitor appeared: Padre Gregório Bonifácio.

"So! Da Silva! Are you quite rested, *senhor?*"

"Just one more hour, Padre."

Bonifácio reached across and gave the hammock a vigorous shake. "Out! The senhor wants you!" he said. "Maybe he is tired, too — of lazy mamelucos."

Amador could not tell whether the priest was serious. "I'm to go?"

"Is it not time?"

"More than enough. I've been thinking this myself."

"I don't know what the senhor wants. He just sent me to fetch you." Bonifácio shook the hammock again. "Now, Amador!"

He swung out of the net, straightening his clothes as he tramped behind Bonifácio, whose gait was slowed by his enormous belly.

The priest had come to the engenho from Coimbra, in Portugal, thirty-six years ago, accepting the post from Tomás Cavalcanti. Bald now, his face dry and wrinkled, Bonifácio had enjoyed a long, lazy ministry with the Cavalcantis and the people of their valley.

He led Amador toward his messy, disorganized rooms at the side of the church, where he spent most of his time.

Opening the door to his rooms, Padre Bonifácio said, "Wait here, Amador, while I fetch the senhor."

Padre Bonifácio returned in ten minutes with Fernão Cavalcanti, who greeted Amador and asked the priest to leave them. This request puzzled Amador: Why should the senhor need privacy if he simply wanted to tell Amador that he must now leave the valley and go home? Even before Padre Bonifácio had gone, Amador spoke up, declaring that he, too, had realized it was time for him to return to São Paulo.

"That's not why I called you," Cavalcanti said.

Earlier this morning, when Governor Maurits left, the senhor had been formally dressed; now he wore his shirt and breeches. He looked tired, his eyes sad.

"What, then, senhor?"

"You do not approve of me," Cavalcanti said. "You think I sell myself to the Hollanders — that I collaborate." He ignored Amador's gestures of protest. "What choice is there, when you have nothing to fight them with? It's very different at São Paulo, where there are no Hollanders. Jesuits trouble you, yes, but not Hollanders." He shook his head. "But I didn't come to talk of this," he said. "There's a service you can do for me . . . a valuable service, Amador."

"Yes?"

"I want you to take the painter to the sertão."

"Segge?"

"Proot thinks our savages are the most divine creations. He wants to draw them at their malocas."

"Segge has talked about this," he said. "But isn't it to be arranged by the Dutch?"

"When?" Cavalcanti said. "This month? The next? A year from now? There are others — officials, scholars, better painters — they all want to travel their new land."

"Better painters, senhor? Segge's a fine artist, not so?"

"Other artists with Governor Maurits are more accomplished: Eckhout, Post —"

"I don't believe it."

"You like this Hollander?"

Amador shrugged his shoulders in reply.

"Take him to the sertão and let him draw; perhaps his work will improve. For you, Amador Flôres, a new musket, as much lead and powder as you want, supplies, slaves for part of the way. When you return, payment in silver."

"But you don't even like Segge's paintings," Amador protested.

"A journey of six months — to the Tapuya in the sertão," Cavalcanti went on. "Perhaps longer, I don't know; it's for you to decide. When you get back, I promise a passage in the first ship to the south."

"You ask me to take Segge hundreds of leagues into the sertão to draw pretty pictures of flesh eaters?"

"That is what the Hollander wants, more than anything else. Will you take him?"

"You've been good to me, senhor. All these months at the engenho . . ."

"Do me this favor, Amador Flôres, and it's I who will be forever grateful. Take him away, Amador — far from my house, my lands. Take Proot out of my sight."

Now Amador thought he understood. "He has angered the senhor?"

Cavalcanti paused for a time, as if gathering his thoughts. Finally he said, "Senhorita Joana has been very friendly toward you."

Amador began to feel a vague sense of alarm because of his secret feelings for the senhor's daughter.

"I have four daughters, two of whom are married to the best men to be found in the captaincy. Not yet spoken for are my child Beatriz, the image of her mother, and Joana — free, wild Joana."

Amador was embarrassed by such personal talk from the senhor about his daughters. But, as he listened, he'd begun to puzzle over something else: Immediately after Amador had asked a question about Segge, the senhor started to talk about Joana. Why?

"If Joana needed your help, you would give it?" he heard Cavalcanti say.

"Certainly, senhor," Amador replied guardedly.

"Then, take Proot from Engenho Santo Tomás . . . to the sertão. If he's never seen here again, I'll not care."

Suddenly Amador saw what Cavalcanti had been trying to say.

"Oh, senhor! He and the sweet senhorita? No, senhor! I won't take him to the sertão. I'll cut his throat here!"

Cavalcanti took a step toward him. "I do *not* want him killed."

"But hasn't he hurt the senhorita?"

"No. He's done nothing. It's Joana. She tells Dona Domitila she's in love with him. She loves the heretic and wants to marry him. *My* Joana."

"Senhorita Joana . . . and Segge?" Amador said, as if confirming this for himself. Should he weep or laugh? "Why don't you order him to take his things and get out of the valley, senhor?"

"Amador Flôres, you're young. You don't know what it's like with daughters. If Joana saw me drive him away, she'd never forgive me."

"Segge — Proot — has spoken to you?"

"He hasn't been to see me, and I don't want to wait until he does. Just tell me you'll take him away, Amador — six months, a year, whatever."

"And Proot?"

"Oh, yes, he wants to leave immediately. I said I would ask you."

"Isn't it strange, senhor, that a man who has the senhorita's love would be willing to leave your lands?"

"I'm thankful for it. I thank God for anything that will save my Joana from this disastrous romance. Take the Hollander and his paint pots, then, and let Joana recover, Amador Flôres, and before you return, I'll have found a man for her."

"Yes, Senhor Cavalcanti, may you find this man," Amador said.

XII

—————◆◦◆—————

November 1640 – September 1644

*I*n late November 1640, after an overland journey of four weeks from Engenho Santo Tomás, Amador and Segge reached the malocas of Nhandui, a powerful Tapuya chief, who was honored by the Hollanders as "King Jan de Wij." The malocas were two hundred miles north of Recife, five days' march inland from the coast. After the Dutch had consolidated their hold on Pernambuco, they had struck at captaincies to the north, and Nhandui's warriors had helped them to defeat the Portuguese.

The success of this alliance was due largely to one man, Jakob Rabbe, a German Jew, who'd been sent by the Dutch as envoy to Nhandui. Known as "Captain Jakob" to the Tapuya, Rabbe had arrived five years ago, with trumpets, halberds, goblets, and mirrors, but it was not these lavish gifts alone that had led to Rabbe's acceptance by the tribe. Captain Jakob had married a Tapuya woman and proved himself as accomplished as any warrior, and as ready to massacre Portuguese. On one occasion, Rabbe's troop herded seventy-two colonists into a plantation chapel, and slaughtered all but three who hid in the roof beams.

Captain Jakob was waiting in the clearing to greet Amador and Segge when they reached the Tapuya stockade. Secundus Proot he welcomed joyously, in Dutch. "I see savages and Portuguese all the time. But months pass, Heer Proot, between visits of civilized men."

To Amador, immediately afterward, Captain Jakob spoke in Tupi. He was a small man, with sensitive, weathered features that belied his violent nature; but his threatening tone had been undisguised. "You carry a passport from Count Maurits. I will tell my Tapuya, Portuguese, that they must respect this paper."

Amador could find nothing to like about Captain Jakob and his warriors. The natives were similar in appearance to the Tupi: small in stature, dark eyes, skin varying in shades from yellowish tan to bronze and most often streaked with dyes. They wore their hair longer than a Tupi's, almost to their shoulders at the back, and cut level across the front.

Segge immediately settled down to sketch and paint the natives. Once, his painting was influenced by what Amador had to say.

Segge had posed a Tapuya girl at the edge of a pretty pool. He sketched her with a bunch of leaves covering her genitals.

"I don't see a savage," Amador said bluntly.

They were in their hut. The canvas with the girl was well advanced and stood on an easel. Segge was busy with sketches for a painting of Chief Nhandui, and seemed not to hear Amador's comment.

"The bandeira is true to life," Amador added. "People can see how it is to march against the Carijó in the forest. But this . . ."

Segge stood up and moved to Amador's side at the easel.

"Nothing savage here, Segge."

"Bah! Anyone can see she is Tapuya — a princess of the wilds!"

Amador laughed. "Princess? Ah, Segge, how eagerly you accept the Jew captain's word. To Rabbe, the worst of these brutes is King Jan. I suppose he tells you this savage is a maid of honor?"

Segge cupped his chin in his hand, the tip of his index finger touching his nose. "What more does it need?"

"You're painting a cannibal — a flesh-eating, bone-grinding mother of pagans. Show this."

One morning four weeks after their arrival, Amador saw that Segge had made some changes in the painting of the Tapuya girl: One hand, resting on her knee, grasped a severed human hand. Segge had given her a basket, which she carried on her back, and protruding from the basket was a human foot.

"Bravo!" Amador exclaimed. "Exactly! A savage for the world to see!"

A few days after Segge had finished this painting, a group of boys who belonged to the Hut of the Bachelors had reached the end of a five-year initiation period. With the rise of the moon and the soft moan of sacred flutes, they were to take their place as young men in a new hut, and girls given to be their wives would be brought to their side.

Throughout the day, Amador and Segge witnessed preparations for this final phase of initiation. At dawn the boys made a circuit of the village, announcing their preparedness for their new status. Then they appeared before Chief Nhandui and the mature men, who gave permission for the bachelors' hut to be torn down. When this was done, the chief invited the initiates to take a brand from the elders' fire. The boys carried this smoldering branch to a site chosen as the new meeting place of "Green Palm," the name given their age group, and made a fire.

Jakob Rabbe explained that a Tapuya man moved through life with his age group. He entered it as a child, between the years five to twelve. From twelve to seventeen, he was a bachelor, for whom sexual relations with girls was taboo; these were years for learning the rites of man. When his age group completed its final initiation ceremony, they would be marriageable young men. Thereafter, every five years they would move up in the community, always part of the same group, until they were mature men.

"Wonderful!" Segge enthused. "Each season of life well defined as it is in nature."

Rabbe had been with these Tapuya for five years, but he confessed that he had made little progress comprehending their ways: "They have ancestral clans, family ties, noble lineages, factions linked to ancient rites. The families and clans I understand; but what is the meaning of *this* division?"

Rabbe asked the question as the most important of the day's ceremonies was about to begin: make-the-logs-run.

"Perhaps they don't know themselves," Rabbe continued. "The village is divided into two factions. Each will race with one of their team carrying the log for a distance before passing it to another. Some say the division of the village represents the strong and the weak; some, the sun and the moon; still others, life and death."

"Perhaps it's a secret they reveal to none but their own." Segge laughed.

"I have run in the race, Heer Proot. Why should they hide its meaning from me?"

The initiates were close by, having their heads shorn. Their bald crowns were then painted with urucu dye. While this was being done, Chief Nhandui and the village pagés addressed them, all exhorting them to carry their log swiftly to the finishing point.

Days before, the ground for the run had been prepared, a straight, wide path that started at a point six miles from the village. At noon the boys and a group of young men assembled here. At a signal from the elders, the boys raced off, one carrying the log for as long as he could keep a rapid pace; as soon as he slackened, he passed the log to another boy, a maneuver requiring great care, for it was a grievous dishonor if the buriti palm fell.

The initiates were given a few minutes' advantage before their competitors set out after them with the second log. But the race was not confined to these two groups alone; though not attempting to relay the logs, others sped over the course beside the competing runners.

Segge stood at the halfway point and cheered with the Tapuya lining the route as the logs approached their position. He started to move back to let the runners pass, but found it impossible to get out of their way, and was swept into the race.

The Tapuya were delighted to see the big blond Dutchman thumping along. When he began to drop behind the main crowd of men and boys, a few spectators stepped in to run with him, laughing and indicating that he should keep up with them. He did his best, his jacket flapping behind him.

The young men in scarlet dye were first to reach the village, and they carried the buriti palm to the meeting hut of mature men. The boys were not far behind, and carried their log to the hut of the winning group.

When Segge pounded into the clearing, crimson-faced and drenched with sweat, Amador stood there, his hands on his hips. "So, Hollander!" he called out, grinning. "What's it like to be a savage?"

The afternoon passed swiftly. The Green Palm group went off to prepare a shelter of leaves and branches next to the place where they had made their fire that morning. Other Tapuya erected a new bachelors' hut for boys of the tribe's youngest group, who would occupy these quarters for the next five years, a meeting place to be used for ceremonies and the lessons the boys would hear from their elders.

Toward dusk, the young men who had carried the first log into the village began to move from one hut to the next, singing that the Green Palm group were ready to receive their brides. The huts this happy choir approached were smaller than the malocas of the Tupiniquin or Tupinambá, circular and flimsily constructed, reflecting the Tapuya's frequent seasonal migrations, though Nhandui's tribe had become more sedentary since its alliance with the Dutch.

When these men finished their singing, an older warrior group — men in the prime of life — moved to the leafy shelter the initiates had built. Thirty girls to be given as brides this night were waiting with their mothers, just beyond the openings of their huts. When the warrior group was in position outside the shelter, the mothers led the girls toward them. Chief Nhandui, the elders, and the pagés watched from a distance but had no role in the ceremony.

The first mother to reach the warriors handed them a gift of a small cake of manioc and was given permission to pass into the boys' shelter with her daughter. After a few minutes, they stepped out together. This ceremony was performed quietly, until the last two betrothed were taken into the shelter. They were girls of three and four. And their screams reached far into the clearing.

"Beloved Lord, what's happening?" Segge asked.

"They're being married," Rabbe said unconcernedly.

"But those are children. Surely — "

"What happens in there cannot harm them."

"The screams . . ."

"The hut is strange to them; it is dark and unfamiliar."

"What happens . . . with these unions?"

"The young men lie with their backs to the entrance." He stopped, gazing toward the shelter.

"Yes?"

"In that hut, Heer Proot, the boys lie quietly, their eyes closed. The mothers make their daughters lie down behind the boys for a brief time. The boys must not move or gaze upon them. The mothers take their daughters away. That is all."

"Nothing more?"

"When the girls are old enough, the boys will sleep with them."

"Will there be a celebration tonight?" Segge asked.

"No. Not until the girl is ready to have babies. Then they feast with the bones of the dead."

Segge stared at Rabbe.

"It is their religion, Heer Proot. Have I not explained this?"

"No, Jakob, but I've seen the burial urns in their houses."

"For the bones of the dead, yes. The flesh, Heer Proot, they eat."

"Beloved Jesus!"

"When an infant dies, the parents devour it. With an older child or an adult, all the family expects a portion of the body. The skull and bones are preserved, ground to a powder for a holy cup at their feasts."

"Amador Flôres is correct: They're the worst of barbarians."

"With them, it is an act of love."

"You can't believe this." Segge had an expression of horror on his face. "Rabbe, you haven't . . ."

"I am a member of the tribe, Heer Proot. They are my people."

"You're a civilized man, Jakob Rabbe. Such behavior — "

"It revolts them," Rabbe interrupted.

"What?"

"The knowledge that civilized men inter their dead in the earth, where the remains are corrupted."

"No more, Rabbe — I wish to hear no more."

"They never take prisoners, as the cannibal Tupi do. They do not eat their enemies — only those closest to them."

☙

Later, Segge wandered toward the hut he shared with Amador. When he reached the hut, he found that Amador was inside with a native. "We have a visitor," Segge heard him say, as he entered. "Ibira."

Rabbe had told him much already about this Tupinambá. Ibira, "The Wanderer," was a great storyteller. He could hold his audience spellbound with tales of the deadly beak of the *tucano-yúa* bird; the water serpent *boia-asú*; Rudá, cloud warrior, whose mission was to give man longings for home when he was absent and cause him to return to his tribe.

Rudá's powers had not worked for Ibira. He was from a clan that had originally lived at the Bahia. During the previous century's reprisals and massacres by the Portuguese, these Tupinambá had abandoned their stockade and fled west, traveling until they came to the headwaters of the Tapajós.

Ibira was with an advance party that went upriver. They were captured, first by a Tapajós clan, later by Portuguese slavers who were beginning to work their way up the Rio das Amazonas from a settlement established on a tributary below its mouth in 1616 — Belém do Pará, the Bethlehem of the Rio Pará.

Inside the hut, a strong smell of freshly brewed palm wine and the heavy fumes of tabak suggested that Amador and Ibira had been together for a long time.

Segge sat down opposite them, settling his big frame into his hammock, his legs dangling over the sides of the net. "I'll drink, too."

"Captain Jakob told me you came from the Rio das Amazonas," Segge said.

"Yes, my Chief. Far beyond, too."

"A teller of stories."

"The best there is at this village." Ibira was chewing a wad of tabak, and dark juice issued from the empty plug-hole below his lip, drooling down his chin.

They sat drinking and Segge questioned Ibira in depth about his people. Amador showed little interest in the Tupinambá's story. But he began to listen attentively when Ibira mentioned a tribe of warrior women:

"When the rivers are low, men enter their territory in canoes. They are not contacted until they are deep in the lands of the warrior women. Then the women appear on the riverbank and order the men to beach their canoes."

"Are these men Tapajós?" Amador asked.

"They are from the forest below the Tapajós villages," he said, after a long pause.

"Have you seen them?" Amador asked.

"The Tapajós know them."

"Let him continue," Segge said.

"The men show that they come peacefully. The warrior women lay down their spears and clubs and run to the canoes. Each takes the first hammock she finds and carries it to her house. The man to whom it belongs will be her lover."

Segge had heard about the warrior women. Stories had been brought to Europe by Spanish explorers who had descended the great river. In 1542, when Francisco de Orellana, a kinsman of the Pizarros, traveled down the Mother of Rivers, his men were repeatedly told of a tribe of fair-skinned warrior women who ruled a territory in the forest. They lived in stone houses dedicated to the Sun, where men were forbidden except when the women sought to become pregnant. When the women were with child, the lovers would be expelled from their realm. Orellana and his conquistadors recognized the female warriors of Greek legend, the Amazons, and reported on the "River of the Amazons" when they returned to Spain.

Ibira described a capital of broad avenues, houses of stone, and five temples, filled with jewels, dedicated to the worship of the Sun. Virgins were the custodians of these temples.

Questioned further, Ibira said that when the warrior women went into battle, they wore a jaguar skin angled over one breast, making it easier to draw their bows. Their arrows were tipped with poison; their javelins, golden-hilted with iron shafts and blades that could pierce brass armor. Tribes near their territories were their vassals and owed them service and tribute, the latter to be paid in gold.

The two men interrupted Ibira to ask where the Amazons' territory lay. "Below the lands of the Tapajós, in the direction my father's people traveled," the Tupinambá replied.

"He means south," Amador said. "But you don't truly know, do you, Tupinambá — no more than any other savage with such a story."

"It is not my story alone. It is known to many men."

"Yes, we heard the same from the Tupiniquin and the Carijó at São Paulo. Wonderful lies about mountains of emeralds and Paraupava — the lake of gold."

"There is a lake."

"You've seen it?"

Ibira said nothing.

"Then, how can you say this?"

"The Tapajós and all the people at Mother of Rivers know that it exists."

Amador picked up the flask of cachaça. "More drink, Tupinambá. More drink and you may remember where these things are." He turned to Segge, who was picking paint off the handle of a long brush. "Do you believe these fantastic lies?"

Before Segge could reply, Ibira said, "There is a lake close to the lands of the warrior women, where the boys made with warrior women are sent. Once a year they, too, hold a ceremony. One boy is chosen to be Son of the Sun. When the Great Rains end and the Sun is strongest, this Spirit Man is covered with gold dust. He is taken to the lake and bathes in it. Every man of those lands must also offer gold to the water."

"The man the Spaniards call 'El Dorado,'" Segge observed.

"No such man exists," said Amador. "Many have searched for him. All have failed." He took Ibira's gourd. "Drink more cachaça, Ibira! Indeed, you're the best storyteller! Lies, all of it. But, Ibira, your stories are the best!"

Segge tapped Amador's shoulder with the end of his paint brush. "How do you know he lies?" Segge turned the brush round and round in his fingers. "Imagine for a moment, Amador, that you're a Spaniard. You've landed with Pizarro. A native tells of a fabulous highland empire with stone highways and gold and silver treasures. Would you believe him, conquistador?"

"Mmm . . . yes," Amador said, unsurely.

"But you wouldn't know it was there, Amador — the city, the mines, the treasures. You'd be listening to a story like the one we've just heard."

"Then, I *wouldn't* believe it."

"But you'd be wrong, my friend! Pizarro found Cuzco, capital of the Incaic Empire, exactly as the natives described it."

"True."

"Then, why deny what Ibira says?"

At last Amador got the point. "If Pizarro and others hadn't believed, if they hadn't accepted the word of the savages, they might never have found Cuzco."

"*Precisely*, Amador."

They kept talking until dawn. Amador climbed into his hammock then; before he dropped off, he said wearily, "Had I been a conquistador, I might not have believed . . ."

Segge lay in his hammock with his eyes closed. Dreamily, he imagined himself back in Amsterdam at the salons of the Magnificat, the group of the city's richest families.

"*Imagine*," they will say, "*Rembrandt van Rijn wanted to banish him to obscurity — Secundus Proot, artist, voyager, discoverer of the Queen of the Amazons!*"

ᘉ

There is no forgiveness in the caatinga, the white forest. When the rains fail and the earth cracks in the riverbeds, the parched northeaster roars between thickets of scrub, cactus, and leafless, misshapen trees. The wind blasts eroded hills, howls between rocky outcrops, swirls through dust-filled depressions. The northeaster passes, and there is a profound silence. Nothing moves in the airless furnace.

The green forest to the west is fecund, alive, its canopied plants seeking light. The white forest clings to the earth, its strangulated growth shrinking from the sun.

There is a metamorphosis when it rains. Turbulent rushes of water feed the clotted earth; the tangle of gnarled, stunted trees is transformed into a low, flowered forest; succulent grasses thrive magically in the thin soil. But always the great droughts return; the rains fail and the rivers disappear. This gray monotony of tinder-dry vegetation is deceptive, for it hides the true nature of the caatinga: a creeping desert.

In February 1641, twelve days after departing the village of Chief Nhandui, Amador and Segge were lost in the white forest.

It was six days since a Tapuya escort had abandoned them to flee back to the village. They had been left with three natives: Two had been prisoners of the Tapuya; the third was the storyteller Ibira, who had inspired this journey.

Ever since that first talk of Amazons and gold, Segge and Amador had repeatedly plied the Tupinambá with questions, their excitement mounting until they determined to find the fabled lands. Captain Rabbe said they were madmen to contemplate such a journey. " Go beyond the village into the caatinga and you'll wish you'd never heard of Ibira. It has not rained in those lands for three years."

After the Tapuya had fled, Amador led his party in a southwesterly direction. Their route was based on what they had heard from Ibira. According to every report, Ibira. said, the Amazons and the lake of gold were in the forest between the headwaters of the river of the Tapajós and the Rio das Amazonas.

Amador accepted this theory for several reasons: Bandeiras had pushed north from São Paulo into the backlands behind the Bahia and toward Belém do Pará, but the results of those expeditions had been inconclusive. The notion that Brazil was a vast island formed by the waters of the Paraguay, the Rio das Amazonas and their tributaries was not yet disproved. Amador knew that no Paulistas had ventured as far west as Ibira's Tupinambá had migrated. If the savages accomplished this journey, he believed, so could he. And if those warrior women were there, he would find them, just as Pizarro had found Cuzco.

It was a dream Amador and Segge shared with many men of their time. Even so experienced an explorer as Sir Walter Raleigh had been a believer in El Dorado. In 1617, already under sentence of death, he had been released for an expedition to the north coast of South America and up the Orinoco to find the gold of El Dorado. He failed, and on his return to England was walked to the chopping block.

Amador breathed the burning air, felt the sting of scratched and bleeding hands where they'd come up against walls of thorn.

For a time, the caatinga had been getting denser.

"Far enough!" Amador cried suddenly. Without turning toward the others strung out behind, he went to sit down.

They had been moving since dawn. It was midday and the sun was at its zenith. Later they'd march for a few hours before dark. The night would be chilling in contrast to the furnace of the day, but they did not dare wander the caatinga after sunset.

They sat listening to the three natives move around in the brush, cracking and snapping dry plants as they worked their way through the undergrowth. They did not talk, because in the six days since the Tapuya ran off, they had said everything there was to be said about their predicament. After the Tapuya had gone, they made good progress for three days through patchy caatinga and over several riverbeds.

Then they came to this thick scrub. They had expected to pass through it in a morning. Three days now and still no significant break. They were not at all sure that they weren't moving in a circle.

Burdened with the loads the Tapuya had left, they were making no more than ten to fifteen miles a day. They had food, but had drunk the last of their water the night before entering this choked caatinga.

Amador and Segge heard the others coming toward them. Ibira was at their side first, his arms cradling roots and cacti lopped off with a machete. He dropped these at their feet and Segge grunted appreciation. Both men grabbed for the roots and cut them with their knives; then they gnawed and sucked at the tuberous growths, their only source of moisture.

"Three days now . . . it must soon end," Segge said, flinging a root away.

"It must end, yes, but where?"

"If we turned east, we could reach Pernambuco and the coast," Segge suggested.

Amador wiped the sweat from his forehead with the back of his hand, streaking the dust on his skin. Despite the ferocious heat, he wore his father's war jacket from force of habit. "We're not defeated," he said. "Give it two days. If we don't break out of this, we'll go east." He lay back and closed his eyes. "To go east, we have to come back this way — every step."

Segge swore in Dutch. He stretched out his big frame, snapping and crushing the dry plants.

They came to places where the scrub forest thinned. At the first of such openings, they cheered and quickened their pace. But half an hour through the break and the stunted trees began to multiply.

The second afternoon, they did not stop as darkness approached. Amador chopped and slashed at dry branches with frenzied movements; when the tangle of thorn and cacti became impenetrable, he swung to the left or right, making probes to find a way ahead. But at last he gave up.

"It's useless," he said, moving back to Segge. "We'll turn back in the morning."

"God knows, we tried," Segge said.

First one, then the other of the natives who had been prisoners of the Tapuya came to stand near them. But not Ibira.

"Where is he?" Amador asked.

The two natives, both Tobajara from coastal Pernambuco, did not reply.

"*Ibira! Ibira!*" Amador shouted. Silence. He turned to the Tobajara. "Where's Ibira?"

"He was behind," said one.

"How far back?"

The native looked at him uncomprehendingly.

"When did you last see him? Where?"

"He walked behind us. We did not see him."

"Jesus!" Amador unslung his musket and prepared to load it. "Yours, too," he said to Segge. "If he's lucky, he'll hear our shots."

"And if he doesn't?"

"He won't have a hope."

"How did he fall that far behind?"

"How would I know!" Amador said testily. "Load."

They fired two shots and waited.

The natives set about preparing a place for the night and cut back bushes to clear a spot for a fire. Most of the birds and animals had fled the drought-stricken caatinga, but on previous nights the party had heard weird caterwauling close by their halting ground. And Amador had identified the bloodcurdling sounds as the screams of a puma.

After fifteen minutes they fired their muskets again, and later another round, but Ibira did not come. His disappearance cast a depression over them. Even Amador — not given to sympathy for Carijó, as he thought of most savages — was concerned. "Better that he'd never escaped the slavers than to be alone and lost and left to die in this desert!"

"Perhaps we'll find him when we turn back."

"Perhaps," Amador said unconvincingly.

That night the hours passed slowly. Neither Amador nor Segge wanted to dwell on the fact that this brief, bitter journey had cut short their dream of finding El Dorado and the Amazons. They must pray this night for nothing more than the good fortune to survive the return.

In the middle of the night, the four men were visited by a horror such as only the caatinga could deliver.

The long drought had affected every plant and creature, and had thrown all into a titanic struggle for survival. Not far from where the men rested was a knobby hill of granite boulders, its deep crevices infested by a colony of vampire bats. There were hundreds of them, with rufous brown fur and pointed ears. They had razor-edged incisors and V-notched lower lips on which to rest their grooved tongues.

When there was water in the caatinga, the vampires had no difficulty locating prey; the brush was home to deer, rhea and numerous other birds, and rodents — the giant capybara, the agouti, cavy, and coypu. But few animals or birds remained now in the caatinga, and the vampires' nocturnal forays had become desperate, ranging over a wider and wider area.

On this particular night, dense flights of vampires set out as usual. Several packs broke away from the main body, and one of these, a group of three, found the four men.

All three bats settled on the natives, who were naked. The first vampire to attack selected a Tobajara's big toe; it drank greedily, its back and ears shivering. When it could take no more, it pulled away and plopped onto the ground a few feet from the native.

Amador awoke slowly. As both he and Segge slept in their clothes, they had not been immediately inviting targets. When Amador opened his eyes, he saw a bat on the ground eighteen inches from his face. "*Vampiro!*" he screamed.

At that moment, the main swarm found them. "*Vampiro! Vampiro!*" Amador shouted.

Segge leapt to his feet, waving his arms, kicking, cursing. The two Tobajara, who had slept through the vampires' painless assault, scrambled up, slapping at bats that brushed against their bodies; especially vulnerable, the naked men fled into the caatinga.

Vampires became entangled in Segge's long locks. He gave a hoarse shout of pain as he tore out handfuls of his hair to rid himself of the hideous creatures.

Amador pulled the stopper out of his powder flask with his teeth while continuing to dance around and swipe at the bats with his other hand. He shook out a handful of powder and, with a warning to Segge, tossed it into the glowing embers. They jumped back as it flared up violently.

Vampires caught in the powder flash dropped into the fire. The rest broke off into the black night beyond the glare. Amador threw more powder into the fire, and here and there, small, dark bodies rose and swooped away. The two men stood motionless for a few minutes, until they saw that the pestilent visitation was over.

"Were you bitten?" Amador asked anxiously.

Segge rubbed his neck. He plunged his fingers into his hair and scratched violently in a fitful reaction to the touch of the vampires. "I don't think so," he said.

Amador did not think it necessary to say anything about the consequences of a vampire bite. *Furia* — "The Fury" — some Portuguese called it.

The Tobajara returned, both with unmistakable evidence of the vampires' attack. They began to moan that the night raiders had been evil spirits sent by their enemies.

Amador silenced them, but not for long. Soon they were screaming with pain as Amador, with a lancet given him by Segge, cut deeply around the flesh at the Tobajaras' toe and neck wounds.

Ibira had not been forgotten. Before they started to break camp, they again fired their muskets to attract his attention, but to no avail.

The swarm of bats had intensified their loathing for the caatinga, and they felt less reluctant to turn back.

Then, Ibira returned. He made a noisy approach and they heard him call out their names before they saw him. The Tobajara joined them in shouting wildly in response.

Soon Ibira pushed his way through a thick patch of scrub. As he came toward them, he appeared none the worse for his night in the caatinga.

Ibira had no sooner begun to work his way through the brush toward them when, from the direction he'd come, warriors stepped through the caatinga — twenty men with clubs and bows, their bodies streaked with war paint.

"We're done for!" Segge cried.

Amador whipped out his machete. He stood with his stumpy figure bent slightly forward, his dark eyes narrowed and defiant. The Tobajara faced the warriors with quiet resignation.

But Ibira quickly cried out, "They are not enemies; they are friends! Tupinambá! From *beyond* the caatinga." He excitedly pointed west. "*There!* Three hours march, the caatinga ends."

Amador did not relax his belligerent stance. "You saw this?"

"Yes. I found these men there." He shook his head. "They found me," he corrected.

"Where?"

The storyteller called out the names of two Tupinambá, who stepped forward. "These are the sons of Ipojuca, who leads the clan." And again he said, "You will see the caatinga end before the sun is in the middle of the sky."

Segge turned to Amador. "Do you believe him?"

"He must be telling the truth, else he wouldn't be alive." He lowered his machete and began to sheathe it. "But ready your musket all the same."

Segge looked at him quizzically.

"Your first lesson, Segge Proot: You must never trust wild savages. Look at them watching us." He jerked his head toward the sons of the chief. "Never think you know what's in their minds, because you'll be grievously wrong."

☙

Thus it came about that they joined forces with the Tupinambá Ipojuca.

The caatinga did not end as abruptly as Ibira said it would, though the dense scrub did thin out on a gray, dusty, rocky plain dotted with the same withered trees, palms, and cacti. The plain was incomparably easier to traverse, and within a day they found a muddy depression where they were able to fill their leather water pouches. Two weeks later they came to the living cerrado, high savanna with gallery forests, where game was plentiful. The slow-moving column rested to recover from the caatinga.

Ipojuca's Tupinambá were a typical remnant of the coastal tribes. Settled at the Bahia in the days of Ipojuca's great-grandfather, after a clash with the colonists the clan had moved 120 miles inland.

Eighteen months ago, Portuguese had come with the announcement that the river valley and lands to the south and north of it had been granted to them by the governor. For a year, Tupinambá and Portuguese had coexisted. Then some warriors stole a cow and feasted on it; in reprisal, the Portuguese burned their fields. "The next time you go near our cows, we will burn your malocas," the colonists warned them. Ipojuca led his people away from those lands.

Six months' migration from the lands behind the Bahia, through the caatinga had brought Ipojuca and his clan to the place where the warriors had led Ibira.

When the Tupinambá and the five newcomers reached the cerrado, the natives built sturdy shelters and threw a barrier of thorn and branches around their encampment. The men occupied themselves with daily hunts; the women planted manioc cuttings.

Ipojuca held different attitudes toward the men who had joined his column. He ignored the Tobajara: As prisoners who had left the Tapuya clearing, they were dishonored men. Ibira, a Tupinambá, he welcomed as a brother.

The mameluco Amador he despised. Such men were recognized as the scourge of the Tupinambá.

Ipojuca knew not what to make of the big Long Hair with the pearl in the lobe of his right ear and thick, drooping, straw-colored whiskers. "Yellow Beard," he'd called him. Ipojuca had heard of the Dutch. It was good to know that they were enemies of the Portuguese.

More intriguing to Ipojuca was Yellow Beard's work. He watched, as Ibira sat quietly while Yellow Beard fiddled with his sticks of color. A pagé of the clan, Ipojuca felt it his duty to observe Ibira closely for two weeks after Yellow Beard had made his image.

Although he'd noted no ill effect on Ibira, the elder stoutly refused to sit for Yellow Beard.

"Why not, Ipojuca?" Yellow Beard asked. "It can't harm you."

Ipojuca did not change his mind, and cautioned the other elders of the clan: "Yellow Beard shows friendship, but what if the image he makes is seen by Jurupari or another demon? What will happen to you under that evil gaze?"

Not one elder posed for Yellow Beard.

დ

They sat outside a shelter built by the Tabojara, Amador on the ground with his stiff leg stretched in front of him, Segge hunched over a sketch of two girls who were rasping manioc tubers nearby.

It was July 1641, four months since the Tupinambá column had halted. For weeks Segge had been complaining about this protracted delay, but Amador was not impatient. "El Dorado's lake and the Amazons have lain hidden for centuries," Amador said. "What difference will a few months make?"

Accustomed to the long campaigns of the bandeiras, Amador accepted the leisurely migration. "We are better off crossing this sertão with a strong body of warriors," he said. "These lands are infested with Tapuya."

Amador had two additional reasons for staying with the column: Yari and Yara, the girls scraping the manioc. Their long black hair brushed their shoulders, and their firm, bronze-skinned breasts shook as they worked. They were sisters, Yari seventeen and Yara eighteen, so similar in appearance they could be twins. They were both fleshy, with round stomachs and broad hips, wide mouths, and the darkest eyes.

Their father, Jupi, the elder of least influence, had offered them to Segge as a gesture of friendship. He also hoped that their association with Yellow Beard might enhance his own status at the men's meeting place.

Segge had been delighted when the girls were brought to him. He immediately sat them down side by side and sketched them. That night they were waiting beside his hammock. Segge had shooed them away.

"What is wrong with Yellow Beard?" Jupi had asked Amador the next morning.

"He has an angry God."

"Ah! He is the same as black robes who will not take a woman?"

It was as good as any explanation. "Yes," Amador said.

Suddenly, as he and Jupi were talking, there was a commotion at the entrance between the thorn-and-branch barrier around the shelters. A group of warriors had returned from the morning's hunt.

"Capybara!" the lead man shouted. "Capybara!"

The hunters had killed three rodents, each weighing more than one hundred pounds. When the trophies were carried into the clearing, the hunters were greeted with cheers from the women, who hastened toward the place where the capybara were to be butchered. Word was passed around that there'd be a feast to mark the splendid hunt. They had every intention of marching to the west, but saw no need to hurry when so many nights could be spent in celebration.

Two hours after the return of the hunters, Amador and Segge sauntered over to where the capybara were being butchered. Some men were skinning the third beast; women attended the other carcasses. Their hands and forearms were bloodstained, and they all appeared to be talking at the same time.

Segge laughed. "The grandmothers are in charge," he observed.

"They are the most experienced," Amador said.

"Surely, for they're old and there have been many hunts."

"The grandmothers do the honors when they roast men." Amador watched them with disgust. "With every step they take beyond our lands, they fall back to barbarity."

☙

The truth of Amador's words became shockingly evident two weeks later.

The Tupinambá had watched Segge draw the Tobajara at the shelters, on the cerrado, beside a river near the encampment. The suspicious Tupinambá said nothing to the Tobajara. But many times Ipojuca commented: "Who can say what will happen?"

Then the first Tobajara fell ill. He took to his hammock and was irritable and restless; he complained continuously of a dry throat.

Amador and Segge thought it no more than a bad humor with the savage, until Segge entered the shelter late one morning and found that the Tobajara was having difficulty breathing. He fetched Amador. They stood next to the man as he sighed and sobbed, struggling for air.

"He has a fever," Segge said.

"His toe," Amador said, pointing. Segge noticed that the scar left after Amador had cut away the flesh around the vampire's bite was now red and inflamed. "He has The Fury," Amador said.

The Tobajara did not live. The rabies had been dormant for months. Now within two days the Tobajara was seized with violent choking paroxysms. The sounds from his heaving chest were not unlike a dog's bark; foam flecked his lips; his jaws snapped at the air. On the third night, maniacal and raving and entangled in his hammock, he choked to death.

The second Tobajara had watched his friend with apprehension. Five days after the first Tobajara's death, he, too, was stricken. He was bled repeatedly, but developed the same symptoms. On the second evening of his seizures, the Tobajara staggered outside. A dozen paces into the clearing he fell dead, but not from rabies. An arrow, shot by a Tupinambá at the order of Ipojuca, had pierced his heart.

Amador and Segge buried the Tobajara alongside the other victim, beyond the brush barrier. They returned to their shelter and stayed there. It grew late as they lay talking. Even Amador now agreed that they should continue their journey. Neither Yari nor Yara had been near the shelter since the Tobajara took ill.

"Where is Ibira?" Segge asked, before he slept.

"With his savage friends."

"They are quiet."

"The death of the Tobajara unsettles them."

It had done more than that. At the men's meeting place, Ipojuca sat with the clan's sacred rattles and moaned an appeal to Voice of the Spirits, a melancholic incantation that begged forgiveness for the elder and pagé Ipojuca. He had promised the ancestors to lead his people to safety, but instead had invited a hideous evil into their midst.

His warriors listened as Ipojuca sought guidance against the devil that had taken the Tobajara. When at last Ipojuca raised his head, the warriors saw that his expression was no longer remorseful; this was the face Ipojuca assumed when he was ready to command.

"What has been learned, Ipojuca?" the elders asked.

"I see the white cords," he said, and every man there understood his meaning.

It was becoming light when forty warriors crept toward the hut of Amador and Segge. The women and children were posted in the gloom of their huts; they had been warned of severe punishment if they strayed into the clearing before the men's work was done. Six warriors led by Ipojuca slipped into the hut; others stood beyond the entrance; a group moved behind the shelter, where the branches and fronds were weak.

Amador woke the instant the Tupinambá entered the hut. "Segge!" he screamed. "Segge! They've come to murder us!"

Amador leapt from the hammock, and struck out with his fists as he tried to fight toward a machete on the opposite wall.

The warriors behind the shelter burst through the fronds. A dozen hands reached for Segge as he lay in his hammock. He was hoisted aloft and rushed into the clearing.

It took seven men to hold Amador down. They bound his arms and legs with thick white cords. Ipojuca tied a fiber rope around Amador's neck. "See, Portuguese," he said, "now you are my cow!" With a vicious jerk of the cord, he pulled Amador out of the hut.

Ibira had been present when Ipojuca called for the capture of Amador and Segge. He could have warned them, but he hadn't. "I am Tupinambá," he said to those around him. "I stand with Ipojuca."

In the clearing, the Tupinambá women and children streamed from the shelters and danced around the prisoners.

An old woman wobbled up to Segge and made as if she would take a great bite out of his arm. "See! See, Yellow Beard, how we take our enemy!"

Segge began to sing, a shaky rendering of the Twenty-third Psalm, in Dutch.

The harridan shrieked with delight: "See how he weeps! Yellow Beard, who casts spells — he weeps!"

Ipojuca stood in front of the warriors, who watched with approval as the old woman led the tormenting of the men. The grandmother was well qualified, having witnessed slayings as a young girl when the Tupinambá had taken many prisoners.

Amador screamed and cursed and tried to get to his feet. The cord around his neck was yanked, throwing him to one side, where he lay mouthing oaths against the Tupinambá, who jeered at him.

The grandmother leapt back to Segge's side. She grabbed his shirt and began to tug at it. This was a signal for the mob of women. They fell upon the prisoners and stripped them of every stitch of clothing.

The women prodded and pinched Segge's pink body, and passed endless remarks on the differences they observed between the two men. Amador had a worse time of it: They punched and kicked him, and beat him about the shoulders with sticks.

Ipojuca finally ordered them to stop, and Segge and Amador were left alone for hours. They lay on the ground with a group of warriors close by.

It was past noon when the women started in on them again. Four warriors restrained Amador as the women shaved his head, his beard, his eyebrows. Segge offered no resistance. One grandmother snatched the pearl Segge wore in his right earlobe, popped it into her mouth, and swallowed it.

They were then pulled to their feet and led toward the men's meeting place.

A great fire blazed at the meeting place. Ipojuca stood near it with the elders. "No!" Segge screamed. "No!"

As Segge watched, the Tupinambá proceeded to burn his sketches, paper, crayons, drawing pens. Everything taken from the hut was thrown into the flames.

◦

Women were readying Yware-pemme, anointing the slaughter club with gum and crushed eggshell and preparing a feather garland for its long shaft. Others had gone to the cerrado to fetch stout poles for the boucan, where the flesh of the prisoners would be grilled.

These preparations were in progress when Ibira addressed Ipojuca and the warriors with the suggestion that the slaying of the Portuguese and Yellow Beard be postponed.

He began with a question: "When their skulls are split and their meat roasted, what use will they be to you?"

"We will be free of the spell he cast over the Tobajara," Ipojuca said. He was seated on the ground and raised an arm to indicate Segge, who stood close by. Then he pointed at Amador and jabbed the air angrily. "He is our enemy on earth. His death will please the ancestors."

"I agree," Ibira said.

"If you agree, storyteller, why do you question my decision?"

"There is a different way," Ibira said. "Let them live for a while. They can be of more —"

His words were drowned out by an uproar from the warriors. One stepped up to Ibira: "Why do you speak for them, storyteller?" Ibira did not reply. "Why does he speak?" the warrior asked his cohorts. None answered. "Does he speak because he wants to join them when Yware-pemme sings?"

"No!" Ibira said. "I am Tupinambá!"

The warrior eyed him suspiciously. "But one who lived with the Tapuya. They are our enemies. Have you become our enemy, too?"

Ipojuca intervened: "Let us hear him."

"It is true that I lived with the Tapuya — and the Dutch, too," Ibira said. "With both, I saw that there is a better way to use your enemy."

The warriors shifted restlessly. Ipojuca quieted them with a wave of his hand. "Speak, storyteller."

"I was a young man when we came through these lands. We fought Tapuya in bloody battles where many Tupinambá were killed. With the Dutch, I saw Portuguese prisoners kept alive. The Dutch gained much more by this than if they had slaughtered the men."

"How?" Ipojuca and several elders asked simultaneously.

"They gave them to the Cariri and other enemies. 'Here is meat,' they said. 'Meat from friends.' So learn from the Dutch. Let these two live. Let them grow fat like the cows of the Portuguese. Lead them along your route. If there is an enemy who threatens you, offer him this meat."

Segge groaned loudly and made an open plea to the Lord. Amador was quiet as Ipojuca got to his feet and stalked around them. "Cows," the pagé said, several times. The idea clearly appealed to him.

In September 1641, the Tupinambá continued their migration, wandering slowly toward the west until the rainy season stopped the column in January 1642. They halted again for four months. Though striking west, they drifted farther and farther south. One year after leaving the camp in the cerrado, where Amador and Segge had so nearly come under the blows of Yware-pemme, the Tupinambá reached the northern edge of a great marsh in the heart of the continent.

There had been clashes with pesky bands of Nambikwara hunters and a serious ambush by warriors of a Shavante village, whose fields they had raided for manioc. Thus far the Tupinambá had given a good account of themselves, and it had not been necessary to offer the two men as security for a safe passage. Instead, they pampered them, now anticipating a feast with Yellow Beard and the Portuguese when the clan ended its migration.

However, there had been some critical days in the first week of May 1642 when a disturbing event again raised the possibility of an immediate dispatch of Yellow Beard and the Portuguese. The storyteller Ibira was murdered.

After Ipojuca had accepted Ibira's proposal to spare the lives of the two men, the storyteller's prestige soared, and he was held in the same esteem as the senior elders. This led to a bitter rivalry between Ibira and Jupi. After a night of drinking during which the two had argued, Ibira was found with his skull crushed by blows from a club.

His death was never fully explained. Ipojuca and other elders strongly suspected that Jupi and another elder were responsible. Ipojuca had been aware of Jupi's jealousy toward Ibira at the meeting place, but had no proof of his guilt.

When the column resumed their march, however, they found evidence of Tapuya in the vicinity of the camp — ashes of a fire, the remains of a curassow bird. Ipojuca, not wanting to create dissension in the clan by condemning two of their elders, accepted this as proof enough that Ibira had been slain by Tapuya.

The dream of finding El Dorado and the Amazons had died for Amador and Segge the day they stood naked before the Tupinambá. They rarely spoke of their original quest, and then with bitterness at what had become of it.

Segge more than Amador had spoken of flight, but escape was impossible. Everything they owned had been stolen — weapons, clothes, trade goods, supplies.

Amador mostly paraded around as naked as his captors, but Segge had not lost his modesty. He had made himself baggy deerskin breeches and a coarse jerkin cut from peccary hides.

They had bows and arrows and an accumulation of possessions — hammocks, gourds, baskets, bone fishhooks, some colorful feathers — but whenever Segge spoke of fleeing, Amador argued against it: "We'll succeed only in throwing ourselves into the arms of other savages, who won't accept that prisoners should be preserved for the enemy . . . Every day offers hope, Segge. These Tupinambá sing of a land without Portuguese. But the storyteller Ibira knew otherwise. He was a young man when our slavers were at the Rio das Amazonas. Twenty years ago, Segge, and already they were chasing natives out of those forests. Perhaps this savage band marches to where our men stand ready to receive them. Then, my friend . . . we run!"

Slave raiders had been working their way up the Rio das Amazonas ever since the foundation — on December 3, 1616, the day of St. Francis Xavier, whose image was raised to commemorate the event — of the settlement of Nossa Senhora do Belém, on the Rio Pará, below the estuary of the Rio das Amazonas.

With the establishment of Belém, the French, who had made several attempts to settle in the area, allying themselves with the Tupinambá as they had done elsewhere, were finally expelled from the north. But for three years the local Tupinambá continued the war against the Portuguese, because they feared that they would be enslaved. In 1619, they were defeated, and one victor of this campaign, Bento Maciel Parente, marched overland from Pernambuco to effect the triumph.

On one occasion, upon the word of an old woman that the subjugated Tupinambá near Belém were fomenting an uprising, Bento Maciel seized twenty-four chiefs. These Tupinambá were taken to the river, where cords were attached to their hands and feet. Then each man was suspended between two canoes. At a signal, the paddlers pulled with all their might in opposite directions, and the bodies of the condemned chiefs were torn apart.

By 1637, Bento Maciel had been rewarded for his services to the Crown with the Order of Christ. He was made a fidalgo and the lord donatário of lands on the north bank of the Rio das Amazonas. The following year, he rounded off his triumphs with his appointment as governor of Pará's sister captaincy to the south, Maranhão, these two territories being regarded as a separate state from Brazil because of their remoteness from the Bahia.

The prospect of meeting the likes of Bento Maciel Parente had not encouraged Segge, nor had he been optimistic of even reaching those northern lands. "The Rio das Amazonas lies far above us, Amador. We're marching south. What hope is there?"

"As long as they're moving, we have a chance," Amador had assured him. "Perhaps the Lord will lead these heathen into the arms of His servants . . ."

When they reached the marshes in September 1642, they were more than twelve hundred miles from the Atlantic coast and some fifteen degrees below the equator. On a straight line through the forest eight hundred miles to the north lay the Rio das Amazonas. São Paulo de Piratininga was a similar distance, directly southeast. Amador and Segge had no way of knowing this, though even without such knowledge, Segge had little faith in Amador's belief of rescue by slavers or priests.

The two men experienced the blackest depressions, their minds flooded with images of being butchered by their captors. But it was a tradition among the Tupi tribes that a prisoner not immediately felled by Yware-pemme be treated with the utmost kindness. The day of his execution, he would be taunted and tormented all the way to the "place of slaughter," but until then, he had to be cared for. Because they were rare prizes, Yellow Beard and the Portuguese were honored guests.

The best food, the freshest beer, sweet wild fruits — nothing was too good for the cows Ipojuca wanted fattened. And the Tupinambá also gave their daughters to condemned men. Amador demonstrated that he was more than willing to oblige. Yari lived with him as his wife; Yara was there, too, but showed that it was Yellow Beard she wanted to comfort. Amador did not confine his attentions to Yari; he regularly led four other women to the bushes. So lustily did he perform that he earned a nickname among the Tupinambá: "Big Penis."

Despite his protests about Amador's behavior and his own puritanical attitude toward the Tupinambá women, in the third month of their captivity, Segge had amazed Amador by announcing:

"My friend, I am in love."

Amador first thought of Joana Cavalcanti. Under threat of death, Segge had gone to his memory of the senhorita to fill his heart with love and longing.

Then Amador saw the look on Segge's face as the girl Yara came toward them. "*This* one?" he asked.

"A sweet girl," Segge said, "so natural and loving."

"By the blessed Saints, Segge Proot, your eyes have been opened!"

"I feel the purest love for her."

"Dear Jesus! Who can understand a Dutchman?"

"She's a fine young woman, Amador," Segge said, almost defensively.

"Truly, my friend. The daughter of fine savages, too. What on earth would she know of Christian love?"

Yara, who was nineteen now, came up to them, swinging her hips.

Amador clapped a hand on Segge's shoulder. "Love her, Segge — love your small savage!"

A few mornings later, a smiling Yara told Yari that Yellow Beard had led her to the grass. Yari promptly spread the good news among the women. The grandmothers were pleased. "Now Yellow Beard will not be sad when he sees Yware-pemme," they said.

ᴄʌᴐ

At the marsh the rains had not yet come, but the water level was high, flooded by the previous wet season. The Tupinambá were halted on the edge of a damp, grassy bog when their scouts returned to announce that they had seen villages to the north and south, but that the route directly across the marsh was clear.

On September 7, 1642, the Tupinambá moved off, picking their way along dry land between the marsh inlets. Soon they were in a gloomy, insect-infested jungle, muddy and watery and choked with beds of floating plants. The two hundred people were strung out over half a mile.

Late on the fourth afternoon since entering the marsh, after a forced march of ten hours, slogging through spongy land, they again reached firmer ground. Within four days they were at a valley with clear, tumbling streams and a forest where game and wild fruits abounded. The crossing of the marsh had exhausted the Tupinambá; if the scouting parties reported positively, this would be a good place to pass the approaching Great Rains, the elders decided. The scouts did not begin their long-ranging patrols immediately, but opted for a few days' rest at the halting place.

One aspect of Tupinambá life Segge had come to adopt was their daily bathing. Like other Europeans, Segge had regarded this as hazardous to one's health. But the long, hot marches changed his attitude, and when Yara came into his life, he found pleasure in frolicking in the water with her.

Mid-morning this day, he called her away from her place with the women of the elder Jupi's shelter and led her to a river a mile from the encampment.

After bathing, they made love, Segge performing in his customary hasty, anxious fashion. When it ended, Yara got up and went to sit on a small rock at the edge of the river. Occasionally, she would cup her hand beneath the surface and pour the cool water over her body.

Segge lay on his stomach opposite Yara, his hands propping up his chin. Segge studied Yara fondly, admiring her fine breasts and full figure. "What are you thinking of?" he asked, seeing her pensive expression.

She smiled at him. "I am thinking that the sun is shining."

What else are you thinking, my Eve? he wanted to ask, but he did not wish to spoil the moment.

He dozed, resting his head on his folded arms. When he opened his eyes, Yara was in the water, near the opposite bank, a vertical incline some twenty feet high. He got up and started across to her. He started to swim, with strong, even strokes. Yara was balancing on a submerged rock, and he playfully swept her into an embrace. She tried to squirm away, but he held her tightly and planted kisses on her lips and cheeks.

Suddenly he felt her go limp in his arms and saw a look of fright on her face.

"What — "

She did not answer.

He followed her gaze to the red earth of the riverbank.

An old man and a small girl stood grinning down at them.

ᔫ

The venerable native on the bank was taller than the average Tupinambá and handsomely adorned with a feather headdress. The small girl, whom Segge reckoned to be about five, wore an apron of blue and gray feathers that hung to her knees.

Segge felt Yara trembling. He smiled back at the man and shouted a greeting in Tupi-Guarani. The man gestured that he did not understand, but indicated that they should climb the bank.

"Let us flee!" Yara shrieked, tugging at Segge's arm.

"A very old man and a child? They can't harm us."

"Please! We must leave!"

"We're going to them," Segge said firmly, and grabbed Yara's arm.

She started to cry, but resisted only weakly as he pulled her off the rock. The riverbed sloped upward toward the bank. Segge could walk here, making, it easier for him to lead the reluctant Yara. Repeatedly, he assured her there was no need to be frightened.

At the top of the bank, Segge wondered if he had been terribly mistaken.

Between the trees stood a large group of warriors bearing long spears and bows.

Yara began to moan.

The old man gave an order to the warriors. Instantly, they melted away into the undergrowth.

Segge was overjoyed. "See? They're friendly."

Yara continued to moan loudly, and pressed close to Segge, who tried to comfort her by placing a hand on her shoulder. She sank to her knees opposite the child, who ignored her and stared at Segge with astonishment.

The old man proceeded to inspect Segge, and clucked with pleasure when he stroked his beard. Segge saw that beneath his feather diadem the man had more hair than a Tupinambá, though his upper lip and chin were as beardless. His cheeks were unscarred, only his lower lip and earlobes perforated. His face was painted with a black pattern on red urucu, which covered the rest of his body, and his shoulders and chest were powdered an ash gray color. He wore a straw sheath on his penis.

What impressed Segge most was a dark green object that hung from a leather thong around the man's neck. Segge considered the stone similar to jasper. But it was its shape that most fascinated Segge — that of a Maltese cross.

The elder was delighted at Segge's interest in the stone. He pointed to the cross. "Paresí," he said, and gestured toward the northwest.

Segge took this to mean that his name was Paresí. He grinned. "Segge," he said.

The man had difficulty trying to repeat the name. He gave up and again pointed north. He touched Segge's arm, indicating that he should accompany him.

Segge hesitated. What if he found himself among worse savages than the Tupinambá? He would be alone, without Amador at his side. On the other hand, already he was under sentence of death, with little real hope of escape. And nothing suggested that the old man's friendliness was anything but genuine. The elder had sent his warriors away and seemed happy to show Segge his cross. Had Almighty God, in His mercy, led him to a tame race of natives who would spare his life?

Segge indicated to the old man that he would follow him. If, by God's mercy, he was saved, he would find a way of returning for Amador. He looked at Yara, still whimpering at his feet. He could not send her to Amador, for she would alert the Tupinambá.

Segge became aware, then, of his nakedness. He pointed across the river to where his jerkin and breeches lay on the opposite bank, and touched his body. The old man laughed and tapped his penis sheath; he was an arm's length from Segge and put out his fingers to gently stroke Segge's skin. As he did so, it dawned on Segge that he was the first white man the old native had ever seen.

"Yara," he said. She looked up at him. "I'll fetch my clothes." She grabbed hold of his leg. "You'll stay," he demanded, and shook himself free. "The old man is not our enemy."

"They will kill us."

He left her lying on the ground, quickly retrieved his clothes, and returned. Before he put on the breeches and jerkin, the old man examined them, and then again when Segge was dressed.

They set off, Segge gently forcing Yara through the trees.

They marched out of the valley and through two others. By mid-afternoon they came to open savanna and soon, to Segge's astonishment, they reached a road, a straight path five yards broad and stripped of all undergrowth. A few miles farther, they were in sight of a very large village. On the outskirts, Segge saw extensive fields of manioc, maize, beans, and other crops. To reach them, they crossed a river by way of a simple but well-constructed wood-and-vine bridge.

At the fields, Segge stopped. The old man was at his side. Segge pointed excitedly, his expression one of pure delight: From the river to the crops, the natives had cut a broad, straight canal that ran for hundreds of yards.

Segge estimated that there were at least thirty malocas in the community; from those near them, it appeared that about forty people dwelled at each. The women were more attractive than the Tupinambá, with more delicate features, and all wore colorful feather aprons similar to the one Segge had seen on the child.

When they reached the center of the village, the old man issued orders. Low stools, each carved from a single piece of wood, were brought. The elder indicated that Segge should be seated in front of a small, circular hut, and then sat next to him. Two warriors came toward them with a man whom Segge immediately saw was different from these people — shorter, more round-faced, similar to a Tupinambá.

"I am Pitua, a prisoner of these Paresí," he said, in Tupi.

Segge's heart fell. *Dear God*, he thought, *they're the same.*

But there followed a long exchange in which Segge learned that the old man was Kaimari, the great chief of this Paresí clan. The clan occupied eighteen villages similar to this one, lying between these lands and a range of mountains a week's walk to the north. There were four Paresí chiefdoms, two of whom were Kaimari's allies and one with whom he quarreled.

To Segge's undisguised relief, he learned that the Paresí were not flesh eaters. Pitua, the interpreter, came from Tupi-speaking cannibals in the forests north of the border mountains, a tribe who had raided into Kaimari's lands. Pitua, a prisoner for five years, had a Paresí woman and children and worked in their fields.

Kaimari now wanted to know about the big blond, and delivered a string of questions through the interpreter. Segge was impressed by the chief's grasp of his answers. Kaimari was vague when it came to concepts of time and distance, his world being essentially confined to the limits of the Paresí chiefdoms; but he accepted that there were different men "a long way away," and showed no special surprise when Segge spoke of the ocean that separated Holland from this continent. There were great waters here, too, Kaimari said, and with a stick he scratched several lines on the ground; they all led up to one especially broad line — Mother of Rivers, great waters such as Segge had mentioned.

"We call it Rio das Amazonas," Segge said, thrilled that the Paresí should know of its existence.

"Why do you travel this way?" Kaimari asked.

Segge tried to explain the search for the warrior women and El Dorado. When neither made sense to Kaimari, Segge told him that the Tupinambá had taken him and a friend who journeyed with him captive.

"It was their hope to slay and eat us," Segge said.

Pitua did not translate these words, and seemed apprehensive.

"Why don't you tell him what I said?" Segge asked.

"The Paresí hate men who eat flesh. If I tell him what you said, it will remind him that I was one of those men." Nevertheless, at Kaimari's insistence, Pitua nervously relayed Segge's words.

The elders and pagés attending Kaimari became agitated at this report of cannibals so close to their lands. For a time, Kaimari did not speak to Segge but consulted with the Paresí.

"They are asking if they will have to make war on the Tupinambá," Pitua said.

Segge, the man who once said he did not rejoice in the death of men, experienced an uncommon pleasure at the notion of the Tupinambá column being torn to shreds.

He was surprised then when the interpreter told him that Kaimari had no argument with the Tupinambá. "He says that if they pass peacefully through his lands, he will not fight them."

"Kaimari is wise," Segge said. "But if they go, they'll take my friend, and they'll eat him as surely as they would eat Paresí if they had them."

After discussing Segge's concern with the elders, Kaimari spoke to the interpreter.

"Tonight they will decide if anything can be done to help your friend," Pitua said. "Now, Kaimari says, you must eat with him. He has had enough talk."

After a meal of deer meat, maize cakes, sweet potatoes, and a winelike liquor, Segge was taken to a small hut where he was to spend the night. A place for honored guests, the interpreter told him. Yara would sleep with his family, the man said. Segge did not question these arrangements, and very soon after climbing into a hammock, he fell into a deep sleep.

He awoke to see Kaimari on his small stool a few feet from the hammock. Elders stood silently in the shadows behind him, all looking expectantly in Segge's direction. The interpreter was with them. Segge swung out of the hammock and gave a cheerful greeting

"You are to fetch your friend," Pitua said.

"Thank Kaimari!" Segge said.

"Kaimari wants no war," Pitua said. "Go to the Tupinambá. Demand the prisoner. If they refuse to release him, kill them. Otherwise, Kaimari says the Tupinambá may pass through his chiefdom in peace. Then they are in the lands of Ixipi, who is also Paresí. Ixipi will give them war, as he gives to all his neighbors."

"Tell Kaimari I am pleased that it was he and not Ixipi who stood on the riverbank with his grandchild."

Pitua conveyed this to the old chief, who burst into laughter.

"What's wrong?" Segge asked.

Pitua was also amused. "She is not his grandchild."

"No?"

"She is his new wife. She will be a child only until he can have her as a woman."

Segge pictured the small, wide-eyed girl in the blue and gray feather apron. "Then tell him, interpreter, that I hope for many seasons in which he will enjoy this little flower."

When this was translated, the old man said, "I will wait for your return. Go now and fetch your friend."

Before he left, Segge went in search of Yara. He found her huddled in a corner of the interpreter's hut. She lay in a fetal position, her face in her hands.

"Yara," he said, "it's me."

"Oh, *please* . . . I want to go away." She took her hands from her face but did not raise herself.

Segge thought of the previous morning at the river, the water trickling down her skin. *I am thinking that the sun is shining.*

"My Yara," he said quietly, and with a sense of anguish. "It's better that you return to your people."

℘

Amador was convinced Segge had been captured and slain by savages. When search parties had failed to find him and the girl the previous afternoon, Amador felt total despair and passed hours reciting prayers Padre Anselmo had taught him in childhood. Early this morning, Amador had personally led another search along the river. They had found no trace of the couple.

He was now alone in a world of heathens. He could foresee nothing except a bloody death at their hands in this his twenty-eighth year.

Ipojuca was even more distressed than Amador. "Jupi wails about a daughter he has lost," he told the Portuguese. "It is much worse for me."

"Why?"

"I am pagé. I promised that Yware-pemme would rejoice with Yellow Beard. Now Yellow Beard is gone."

"Savage!" Amador screamed. "May you burn in eternal hell!"

Ipojuca's black eyes sparkled. "You will not be lost like Yellow Beard," he said. "I will see that you are protected because I, Ipojuca, have never eaten a Portuguese."

Amador stormed away, the Tupinambá's words burning in his ears. The encampment was on open ground that sloped toward a gallery forest bordering a stream. A mile away, this water flowed into the river where Segge and Yara had bathed. Amador was heading for the trees when he came to an abrupt halt.

Emerging alone from the trees was Segge Proot.

"*Meu Deus!*" Amador cried.

Amador flung his arms around Segge and held him in a wild embrace. "Segge! Oh, Segge Proot, my comrade!" Amador's dark eyes were filled with tears.

"Friendly savages . . . ," Segge said breathlessly, when Amador released him.

"You returned?" Amador looked dumbfounded. "Fool! Oh, Lord, *why?*"

"To fetch you, of course."

"You came back for *me?*"

"I'm not alone," Segge said, directing Amador's eyes to the forest behind him. "More than one hundred warriors wait back there," Segge said. "And behind *you*, Amador, the Tupinambá approach."

Amador turned, to see Ipojuca and half his warriors hurrying toward them, several armed with clubs.

"The cow!" they cried. "Yellow Beard, the cow, is back!"

"We run?" Amador queried. It seemed as if he would leap away.

"No," Segge said. "There's no need."

"So! The prisoner is back!" Ipojuca said. "Where did you wander, Yellow Beard?"

Segge did not respond. He was watching Jupi pushing toward him.

"My daughter — what have you done with Yara?" the elder cried.

Ipojuca ignored Jupi's frenzy. "Yellow Beard was lost and now he stands again with the Portuguese. The ancestors wanted this. The ancestors guided Yellow Beard back."

Segge addressed Jupi: "Yara is safe. She'll return to you."

Ipojuca looked at Segge with open admiration. "You have honor, Yellow Beard. There are no-warriors who flee Yware-pemme; you who do not know these things came back. This is the way of a Tupinambá who seeks Land of the Grandfather."

"That is not the truth, Ipojuca," Segge said.

"What do you mean, Yellow Beard?"

Segge raised his right arm high in the air and waved it. "Here's the truth!"

At his signal, the Paresí stepped out of the trees.

Ipojuca looked rapidly along the Paresí phalanx; then he swung around to search the area of the encampment, and was dismayed to see a group of Paresí warriors there, too.

Two Tupinambá *bravos* sprinted toward the Paresí ranks, yelling curses and brandishing their clubs as they ran. A crescendo of jeers and insults rose from the Paresí phalanx, until the two Tupinambá slammed against the wall of warriors.

The men closest to the assailants fell upon them, jabbing and slashing with their long spears. In less than a minute, the Paresí stepped back from the bodies and gave a triumphant whoop; then they began to taunt other Tupinambá to come forward.

"They're friendly?" Amador queried, when this brief clash was over.

"Toward us, yes," Segge said. "They abhor flesh eaters."

Ipojuca had watched the slaughter of his men impassively. Now he asked, "They will kill my people?"

"Return our possessions, our muskets, and our powder, let us leave unmolested," Segge said, "and no harm will come to you. But you must immediately march away from the lands of these Paresí."

Ipojuca looked puzzled. "Why don't they kill us?"

"Their chief doesn't want to fight. But be quick with your decision, Tupinambá."

Hurriedly, Ipojuca consulted with his warriors. "We will accept what Yellow Beard says. Were we Tupinambá ready for battle, not one of these 'women-who-will-not-fight' would live," he concluded imperiously. He issued orders for the muskets and other possessions to be fetched.

Segge signaled to two Paresí who were holding Jupi's daughter. When they released Yara, Segge watched resignedly as she broke into a run and fled directly to the shelters.

Ipojuca began to chuckle.

"Why do you laugh, Tupinambá?" Amador demanded angrily.

"I was remembering the storyteller," Ipojuca said. He looked at the Paresí. "'Keep the cows,' Ibira advised us, 'a gift for the enemy.'" He glanced at Jupi. "Was he not the wisest of storytellers?"

☙

Amador and Segge spent ten months, from September 1642 until July 1643, with the Paresí. Here, as Segge said, they were gods come down from Olympus. The simplest things they showed the Paresí left them in awe. It was understandable that they'd be grateful when Segge built sluices to control the flow of water to the Paresí fields; when Amador demonstrated how an anthill could be hollowed out to make an oven. But even an ordinary slipknot could send the Paresí into raptures.

Kaimari and his pagés put endless questions to the men, including requests that they tell about their God. Amador and Segge spoke of an all-powerful God, His Son, and the Holy Mother. Kaimari and the pagés were moved by stories of Jesus Christ, but they found the concept of an unseen, omnipotent God unacceptable. They told the two men that the most powerful spirit the Paresí knew revealed itself to man.

Amador and Segge saw this god of the Paresí on a hunt in a forest north of the border range — in lands of the Tupi-speaking cannibals.

On the second day of the hunt, thunder rolled above the forest canopy and lightning sent jagged fingers of fire probing among the trees. A storm exploded, rain hissing down through the forest levels, a sheet of water that splattered noisily onto the soft humus. The torrent lasted twenty minutes, and just when it ended, the four Paresí hunters were brought face to face with their deity:

A thirty-two-foot anaconda, olive green with large black spots, was coiled around the low branches of a tree next to a stream, its body twisted in a series of huge S's.

Amador reached for his musket, but the Paresí issued stern warnings against disturbing the Great Spirit. Even to hunt in its area was forbidden. They must leave immediately, the Paresí said.

They sped away through the trees until they considered they were at a safe distance from the anaconda. They rested for a day, and here Segge borrowed a stone axe, and on a boulder in the middle of the river, carved:

SECUNDUS PROOT — 1643

The report of the anaconda caused excitement back at Kaimari's village: A year could pass in which no one saw the Great Spirit. The Paresí feasted to mark the event. A bamboo trumpet of such length it required two men to carry it represented the anaconda. This serpent symbol was taken from the sacred house of Paresí warriors, and each man vied for the opportunity to pay homage to the anaconda by dancing at the trumpet's summons and bringing it an offering of meat. During these events the village women hid themselves, fearing punishment for gazing upon the trumpet.

Amador and Segge attended the rites, and witnessed an attack on a girl who strayed into the men's hut when they were eating the meat brought to propitiate their serpent god. The girl was raped by every man there and then strangled.

Kaimari was unmoved by their horror at her death. "It is forbidden for women to visit the men's sacred place," he said, through the interpreter Pitua. "She knew the penalty. To allow a woman to witness these ceremonies is dangerous."

"So dangerous they must be *killed?*" Segge asked.

"Yes, they must die." Pitua delivered the responses in a quavering voice.

"But why?" Segge asked. "*Why*, Kaimari?"

Kaimari's response startled them. "Men were nothing when women were warriors. Men were worms of the earth."

"Who were the warrior women, Kaimari?" Amador asked eagerly.

"In the beginning, a race of women ruled earth. A man's only use was to lie with them. The girls born to these women were trained as ferocious warriors. The boys? No one knows what happened to the boys."

"These warrior women — where are they now?" Segge asked.

Kaimari laughed. "There are no warrior women," he said. "There are only women who must hide at the huts when the men celebrate."

"What happened to the warrior women?" Segge asked.

"They were defeated. With the help of the great anaconda, men stole the secrets of women and became warriors. This is why it is important that women never witness our ceremonies. If they did, men could lose the power our forefathers stole for us."

This was Kaimari's last word on the subject, but Amador and Segge had more to say to each other, for it reawakened their interest in the Amazons.

Segge was popular with the village children. Parents were amused at the sight of the heavy-limbed Dutchman, his yellow locks flying as he bounded past with children in pursuit. Segge would often halt abruptly and hurl and object whizzing over their heads to the far side of the clearing. — This object, a crudely fashioned black ball, had fascinated Segge since he first saw it. When he asked where it came from, a group of children led him to the forest and showed him a large tree, the sap of which was bled to make the ball. Collected in gourds, the milky liquid formed a doughy mass; this was rolled out, and layers were spread over a round clay core.

Life among these people was so pleasant that Amador and Segge gave little thought to departing. But in July 1643 they finally decided to move on. Kaimari himself provided the incentive.

They had often inquired about the jasper object that Kaimari wore around his neck.

"Who gave them to the Paresí?" Segge asked Kaimari.

"Paresí elders, men of position and honor, have always worn them," Kaimari said.

"From whom did they get them?" Segge repeated.

"From our fathers and grandfathers," Kaimari said, offering no further explanation.

Then, in July 1643, Kaimari announced that he was sending men to fetch jasper. They would walk to a place below "Love-Me-River," one of the arms of Mother of Rivers, Kaimari said. There they would trade with the Mojo tribe for green stones.

"We would have a strong escort," Amador said. "When they've done their trading, they can take us to this Love-Me-River." He smiled saying the name. "From there we can go by canoe to the Rio das Amazonas. We'll find missions, traders —"

"Slavers?" Segge added.

"We'll be back with civilized Christians," Amador said.

They left the village in mid-July. Kaimari accompanied them for part of the way, leading them south to avoid the lands of Ixipi, who was again threatening war. They skirted Ixipi's territory; when they turned southwest, Kaimari bade them farewell.

The parting was as simple as the first meeting between Segge and Kaimari. Kaimari stood surveying them both.

"It was good," he said. That was all. He turned away, walked to his escort, and immediately set off for his village.

Amador and Segge were left with thirty Paresí and the interpreter, Pitua. They traveled for three weeks through a mixed region of swamp, savanna, and forest to reach the Mojo, the tribe from whom the Paresí obtained the green stones; for the trade, the Paresí carried fine feathers and an assortment of herbs and roots from their medicine men.

Amador and Segge were left behind with ten Paresí, while the rest of the party went to the Mojos. The traders accomplished their mission in ten days, the pagé carrying back a bag of the prized stones. Amador and Segge examined these, and identified the same quartz as seen with Kaimari's insignia of office. "Worthless," Amador said to Segge. "No more valuable than bits of broken glass."

The ten warriors who stayed with them had built two canoes, using fire and stone-ax to hew and shape the thirty-foot craft from tree trunks. These were launched the day after the traders' return. The Paresí agreed to accompany them to Love-Me-River, but there they would leave them.

On the afternoon of August 23, 1643, two days after beginning their voyage, they heard the roar of a fall. The poor boating skills of the Paresí made Amador and Segge apprehensive, but Pitua, who'd come this way before, laughed.

"Guajara Mirim," he said. "'Little Falls.'"

The canoes were moving with a strong current, some twenty yards from the left bank. The river was almost a mile wide, its flow north broken in several places by rocky, wooded isles.

Amador and Segge were in the second canoe. They saw the first craft turn away from the bank and head for a large island just above Guajara Mirim. The roar of the falls was growing ever louder. The paddlers in the second canoe began to follow the other craft. Pitua said something about spending the night on the island.

Neither of the men paid attention to him. Both leapt up simultaneously and began shouting at the top of their lungs.

On the west bank of the river stood the first white men Amador and Segge had encountered in two and a half years.

❧

Amador ordered the Paresí to pull over to the left bank, but they continued to head toward the island. "There are many flesh eaters in that forest. The Paresí refuse to land there," Pitua said. Segge, too, argued with them, but the paddlers were adamant. Amador and Segge deposited them on the island and headed back toward the west bank with Pitua, who made them promise they'd return him to the island before nightfall.

Even before the canoe ground to a stop on the gravelly shore, Amador jumped from the craft, splashing toward the men. There were eight of them, including a Jesuit. "Thank God, senhores, for a miraculous meeting!"

The leader, a small, wiry man, stood flanked by two sturdy musketeers. His thin, pale features reflected no pleasure whatsoever. In Spanish, he asked, "Where do you come from?"

Amador's ebullience began to diminish. "Senhor?"

The Jesuit came forward. "I am Juan Baptista Osorio. I speak Portuguese. Where do you come from?"

Amador laughed. Segge had come to stand next to him. "'Where do you come from,' he asks. For two and a half years, Padre, we've walked the sertão — from Dutch Pernambuco across the great sertão to this river."

The priest frowned as he translated this for the Spanish commander and the six men gathered near him. The commander's grave demeanor did not change. He spoke rapidly to Juan Baptista, who addressed Amador:

"You say that you have been away two and a half years?"

"Longer," Amador said. "We departed in the year of our Lord 1640 — the month of October. First we went to the Tapuya of Pernambuco." He indicated Segge. "My companion is a Hollander — Segge Proot. The Hollanders sent him to paint the Tapuya."

While the Jesuit relayed this to the commander, Segge asked Amador: "We're in Peru?"

"Who knows *where* we are."

"This is Don Hernando Ramirez de Ribera," the priest said. "He commands our expedition."

"Are we in Peru?" Amador asked.

The priest pondered this momentarily. He did not give a direct answer: "We have come from Pueblo Nuevo de Nuestro Señora de la Paz to this river the natives call Mamoré." They had been traveling for three months searching for gold. This Juan Baptista did not reveal to the two men. He looked intently at Segge. "A Dutch heretic?"

"I've told you already — a Hollander and a painter."

"And you — mameluco — who are you?" the priest asked.

"Amador Flôres da Silva, Padre — of São Paulo de Piratininga."

"Paulista," Juan Baptista said.

Amador nodded. He looked from the priest to the others and began to feel uneasy.

"What did he say?" Segge asked.

"This suspiciousness . . . I can understand how he might feel about a heretic enemy. But me? He knows I'm a subject of the same king — His Majesty Philip the Fourth."

Juan Baptista turned toward them. "I speak the lingua geral. I heard your words," he said. "You are wrong."

"Wrong about what?"

"His Majesty Philip is no longer king of Portugal — not since December 1640," Juan Baptista announced. "The Portuguese have a new king. The pretender João of Bragança is now Dom João the Fourth of Portugal. There is war between our countries."

"War?"

"The armies of King Philip were fighting in Flanders, Italy, and Catalonia . . . and the Portuguese rebelled," Juan Baptista continued. "Loyal garrisons of Spain have resisted."

"In the captaincies of Brazil?" Amador asked.

"At the Bahia and Rio de Janeiro, João the Fourth was acclaimed without opposition."

"At São Paulo?"

The priest smiled thinly. "The Paulistas wanted their own king."

"Dom João the Fourth."

Juan Baptista shook his head. "The Paulistas sought to crown one of their own."

"*Impossible*. They're the most loyal subjects of Lisbon," Amador replied hotly.

"Still, they called upon one — Amador Bueno — to serve as their liege."

"Bueno?" Amador knew this man: The son of a colonist from Seville, he was a slave raider. Amador roared with laughter. "Bueno a king? Never, Padre, would the Paulistas support such stupidity."

"It was so. Bueno himself rejected the rabble's scepter. He refused to be a party to one more dishonor and defeat."

Amador looked darkly at the priest. "What defeat?"

Juan Baptista raised a hand, indicating that Amador should wait for his answer, and spoke with Don Hernando.

"If Spain and Portugal are at war," Segge remarked, "we — Hollanders and Portuguese — must be allies. What a change of fortune!"

"Padre?" Amador said, impatient to have the Jesuit continue.

But first the priest put a question of Don Hernando's: "What is your purpose in these lands . . . of Spain?"

"The purpose? The purpose?" He nodded. "We sought Paraupava," he said, using the Tupi-Guarani word for the fabled lake of gold.

The Jesuit reported this to Don Hernando, and there was laughter from the Spaniards.

"And have you found it?"

Amador plucked at his deerskin breeches. "Had we discovered Paraupava — El Dorado — would we be standing before you as beggars? No, Padre, we found nothing but our Lord's mercy, for we were delivered from the Tupinambá. Only by heaven's power did we escape from the cannibals."

Segge spoke to the Jesuit for the first time, in the lingua geral. "Padre, what do you know of Pernambuco?"

"It is the same," the priest replied immediately. "In control of the Dutch. His people" — he glanced at Amador — "not content with the ruin of the holy alliance with Castile, have signed a ten-year truce with the Hollanders. To the eternal shame of Portugal."

"I fought the Dutch with the conde da Torre's armada," Amador said irritably. "There were other Paulistas, too. We didn't campaign for everlasting shame!"

" It is not what we know," said Juan Baptista. "of those we fought in the war of Guiará." His tone was unemotional. "The Paulistas have been defeated, da Silva. The fathers of Paraguay and their Guarani, strengthened with musket and cannon, defeated the bandeiras at Mbororé two years ago."

Amador knew the Rio Mbororé; it flowed into the Rio Uruguay.

"The victory came, da Silva, *after* your Paulistas had expelled the fathers of the Company from São Paulo." He noticed Amador's surprise at his words. "Our holy Father Urban has proclaimed the liberty of the natives and has prohibited their enslavement upon pain of excommunication. When the brief was read at São Paulo, your Paulistas drove the fathers from the captaincy."

"Please, Padre, this isn't São Paulo de Piratininga," Amador said. "We felt such joy at the sight of fellow Christians."

"Indeed, your appearance is that of men who have had much to endure."

Juan Baptista turned to Don Hernando, and after they had spoken, the mood of the Spaniards seemed to mellow slightly. Amador and Segge were offered food and wine and were plied with questions about their journey; they answered forthrightly, and Don Hernando showed genuine sympathy at their captivity with the Tupinambá. "The heathen of lands we crossed are no better," he said. "Juan Baptista, who seeks new subjects for his Company's reductions, finds them cowed and docile. But as God sees us, every day of our journey we pray for preservation."

Perhaps if the leader of the Spaniards had not been Don Hernando, an intimate of the viceroy at Lima, the encounter might have gone differently. But, what Amador and Segge couldn't have guessed, Don Hernando was perturbed by the presence of the mameluco and the Hollander so close to Spanish settlements. They could be spies, advance scouts of a large force, he'd said in an early aside to Juan Baptista. Don Hernando considered the Dutch quite capable of such an outrageous expedition: He knew that early in 1643 a flotilla from Pernambuco had rounded the stormy tip of the continent to occupy southern Chile, from which they had yet to be dislodged.

So they sat together in the jungle — Spaniard, Portuguese, Hollander with the roar of Guajara Mirim close by, old animosities preventing them from enjoying the drama of the situation: Here they were, the first colonists, venturing out from east and west, to meet in the heart of the South American continent.

There was a point in the conversation when Amador came close to recognition of the importance of this fact. "You have marched down the cordillera," he said. "We came from Pernambuco. We met at this river. There is no island of Brazil."

"That is correct — nothing but these dominions of our majesty, Don Philip," Don Hernando responded.

When it began to grow dark, the group heard a noise at the river's edge. Pitua was impatiently slapping the water with a paddle.

Amador stood up. "We must return him to the Paresí," he said, indicating the anxious Tupi.

While they had been drinking the Spaniards' wine, Amador explained that they planned to go up Love-Me-River to the Rio das Amazonas. However, since they now knew that La Paz could be reached, they would consider a march to that settlement. Their concern was no longer to find El Dorado but simply to return to their people, and this they could do via Peru.

"So, gentlemen . . . we'll go back to our savages," Amador added. "They sit with all our possessions. In the morning, we'll return."

Don Hernando and Juan Baptista conferred briefly before the priest spoke: "Considering that Portuguese are not welcome in Spain's territories, and heretical Hollanders even less so, it is best that you do not return to our camp but go your own way, Paulista, to lands where you belong. Don Hernando graciously declines to interfere with you or the heretic."

"We thank Don Hernando," Amador said, formally. "We're leaving," he said to Segge.

Within minutes Amador and Segge were off, pulling strongly across to the island. Well before they were out of musket range, Amador yelled at the top of his lungs — a triumphant "Long Live Dom João the Fourth! Long live our king and lord!" — at the Spaniards on the riverbank.

☙

They came the hour before dawn: twenty-four warriors of a Tupi clan in this forest, led by one Sabá, renowned for his ferocity. A mist rising from the foaming waters of Guajara Mirim covered the island where Amador and Segge and the Paresí slept, and it drifted across the water to the camp of the Spaniards. Sabá led his war party through the damp gray curtain. Not one of the eight Spaniards stirred as the Tupi notched arrows to their bows; not one man was able to reach for his weapon before he lay dying in the dirt.

After the slaughter, Sabá and his men grew restive. They lived in isolation beyond Guajara Mirim and had never heard of Long Hairs. What manner of creatures had they slain?

The bravest stepped up to the victims and hastily snatched for trophies: Don Hernando's one boot, a tin plate. Another warrior tried to pull loose a sword belt, but the Spaniard's eyes fell open, his head jerked violently, and the Tupi fled.

☙

Amador sat next to a dead Spaniard, trying on his boots. Segge, grim-faced, moved silently through the camp.

Amador and Segge ordered the Paresí to dig a single grave, and then proceeded to strip the camp of every useful item. Besides weapons and apparel, they found everything for a well-equipped expedition, including many lengths of cloth, fishhooks, beads, and other trinkets.

When the canoes had been loaded and the Spaniards interred with a stone cairn above the grave, Amador and Segge stood at opposite sides of the pile of rocks and offered prayers for Don Hernando Ramirez de Ribera and his men.

At the canoes, Amador spoke: "Spanish, Portuguese, Hollander — the sertão knows no distinction. The strong survive. The weak die."

☙

The canoe kept to the middle of the channel, rapidly gaining speed as it approached the crest of Guajara Mirim. Then it plunged into the downward rush of water. The channel swung to the left bank, and very soon the canoe was thrust into slower waters.

The jubilation at passing these falls was short-lived. Two hours later, with the roar of water ahead, Amador and Segge began to understand why the Tupi interpreter had laughed at the anxiety they had shown on the approach to Guajara Mirim.

"Guajara Assú!" Pitua now shouted. "'*Big* Falls!'"

Immense, water-worn boulders rose out of the river, the main stream of water boiling through a gap between them. Smaller streams shot through the rocks elsewhere, but not one suggested a navigable way over the falls.

After a restless night, they were up before dawn, ready to attack the problem of passing Guajara Assú.

This took three days to accomplish. On the first, the canoes were off-loaded and the goods carried through the jungle. They erred in thinking that a detour in a semicircle would offer a speedier trip than to head directly along the riverbank. Traversing the interior meant having to slash openings foot by foot. Swarms of sand flies and mosquitoes rose in incessant attack; ants with fiery stings and spiders as large as the palm of a man's hand assailed them. A Paresí was bitten by a six-foot fer-de-lance and died. By the second day, they had all the contents of the canoes at a landing place below the falls. Early the third morning, they began the haulage of the craft.

They collected long lianas and plaited smaller vines into strong cords, and, taking the canoes above the head of the falls, began to walk them through the rock-strewn river. Segge and ten Paresí were maneuvering the canoes in the water. Amador was with Paresí on the bank; they hung onto the ends of lianas attached to the canoes and worked their way along at the edge of the jungle.

Twice they reached a place where it was impossible to go forward and had to retreat, shoving the canoes back upstream until they were able to turn their bows toward an alternative gap between the rocks.

After five hours, they were safely at the bottom of Guajara Assú with both canoes and able to move the craft freely through the water as those ashore hauled on the lianas.

The next morning they carefully restowed the cargo, pushed off into midstream — the river was three-quarters of a mile wide at this point — and paddled at a steady speed for three hours. Then the current began to slacken, and there was a now-familiar roar in the distance.

Amador questioned Pitua more closely about this river: just how many falls were there? he wanted to know.

Pitua held up both hands, his fingers outstretched.

There proved to be *twice* that number. They passed twenty falls between Guajara Mirim and the last barrier before the unimpeded flow of Love-Me-River.

By day they had to endure a sun so hot that water hissed when splashed onto rocks by men struggling with the canoes. When the sun wasn't baking them, they were drenched by violent squalls. The mists rising from the water made the nights damp and chilly.

Two months after the August 23 sighting of the Spaniards, the canoes were finally below what Pitua promised were the last falls. The river was several hundred yards wide here, broken into numerous channels by the rock shelf; ahead lay blue-gray water that ran wide and fast.

ᗧᗣ

Love-Me-River finally lived up to its name. For five days they had an easy run down long bends of water that swung to the northeast. From six hundred to a thousand yards wide, occasionally a mile from bank to bank, the river often divided into multiple channels passing narrow islands, some of them five miles long.

Amador and Segge had tried to persuade the Paresí to stay with them, offering them generous gifts of the Spaniards' goods. But the Paresí could not be induced to go beyond the last falls. Pitua had also refused: "I want to see my sons."

"What do you know of the river tribes?" Amador asked, sensing more in Pitua's reluctance than a simple desire to return to Kaimari's village.

"Muras," Pitua said. "'Fish People' And Mundurucu." His expression was not happy. "Tupi-speaking . . . 'Head People.' Very dangerous."

"We'll keep the muskets ready," Amador said to Segge. They transferred their belongings to one canoe, abandoning the other craft.

As they drifted along, the mantle of forest was unbroken, with the crowns of silk cottons towering above terraces of myrtle, laurel, rosewood, acacia. A mesh of lianas and creepers hung motionless above reeds, ferns, and broad-leafed plants flourishing between cushions of moss and lichen on the forest floor. There were bursts of color: a tree splattered with red blooms or festooned with silvery leaves; a subtle shade of mauve orchids or a flaming spray of gold. But green was dominant — from the most delicate hint of yellow green to a vivid emerald verdure.

They saw flights of birds of brilliant plumage: scarlet macaws, snowy white egrets, iridescent hummingbirds, yellow and green parrots, gaudy tanagers, brown hawks, gray-black urubu — singing, piping, chirping, clucking, screaming as they exploded and swooped and hopped among the trees.

Their intention to shelter on islands at night was thwarted when, at the end of the fifth day's run, they found themselves on an open stretch of water. High banks to the east offered no landing place, and the western shore was choked with jungle. They paddled up a side stream into the quiet gloom of the forest and came to a small opening.

Amador was ill at ease in this sanctuary, for often what Segge saw as exotic, Amador regarded as menacing. His experience in the sertão had taught him that such solitude could be deceptive. But they were not disturbed here, and the next morning they decided to hunt in the area. When they were ready to set out, Segge picked up his musket, but Amador cautioned him against using it save in a life-threatening situation. Instead, Amador took a long bow and a dozen arrows, silent weapons that would not attract Fish People or Head People.

As they penetrated the woods behind the stream, Segge recognized in Amador the bandeirante he'd painted . . . and also something else: a hunter-killer, moving with the instincts and skill of his distant ancestors. Amador spoke of the natives as beasts and expressed pride in being Portuguese. But Segge saw clearly in this forest that Amador Flôres da Silva was no Portuguese but a true citizen of this New World, raw and savage.

A colony of potbellied spider monkeys fretted in the branches above them, chattering defiantly and baring their teeth in mocking grins. Coming downriver, Amador and Segge had seen monkeys of every description: capuchins, their hairstyle similar to the capuche of the Franciscan; the uakari, another monk of the forest, much larger but with bald pate, lean and bony face, and pink, hairless cheeks; saki, boasting a splendid hood of hair; and the tiny squirrel monkeys, often one hundred together at the edge of the river and invariably bolting at the approach of the canoe.

They had seen many other animals of the forest and river — tapir, caiman, peccary, capybara, jaguar — but, above all, this green world was the kingdom of the insect. The ant, the bug, the fly, in their most prolific forms, dominated every level of the jungle, their possession recorded by a persistent sibilance that rose from the decaying loam into the canopy above.

The day's hunt ended in success when Amador shot a huge red-haired monkey, known for the resonant howls with which it greeted the beginning and end of each day. They carried it back to camp, roasted it, and found its meat tough and poor. They ate the white heart of palm and forest fruits collected by Amador. They dozed fitfully, taking turns to keep the fire going. Toward midnight both were violently ill, especially Amador. The next day, Segge continued to complain of stomach cramps and by afternoon lay groaning in the bottom of the canoe. Amador paddled on listlessly, grateful for a current that helped the canoe along.

In this condition, they came upon a settlement of three families of Muras — the Fish People.

The Muras were eager to trade and offer hospitality in return for iron fishhooks. Amador and Segge were the first white men these families had encountered, but the Muras showed less curiosity than Kaimari's people. Mura watermen occasionally had brought reports of men like these seen along the Rio das Amazonas — mixed accounts that praised the fishhooks but raised disturbing questions about strangers who, said the Mura informants, fished not for *pirarucu* or *piraíba* but for as many men as their canoes would hold.

There was no need to fear these strangers, the Muras quickly saw: The day after arriving at their shelters, both men were incapacitated by violent fevers, which would afflict first one, then the other, with chills, delirium and soaring temperatures.

The Muras offered concoctions of roots and herbs and infusions of honey, and these brought a temporary respite, but always the fever returned. After two weeks, the Muras stopped ministering to the two men and left them alone in a small domed shelter near the water's edge. Bowls of food and water would be taken to them, but beyond this the Muras lost interest. Their pagé attributed the affliction to a malevolent watersprite against whose power no remedy was effective.

Amador and Segge inspected each other's bodies to make certain they were not suffering a long-delayed attack of The Fury. They saw that their feet were infested with minute worms that bored into the skin. Only by digging deeply into the flesh could they expel the worms, a treatment that left festering sores.

To add to their despair, the rains were approaching, heralded by storms that thrashed and shook their frail shelter. Worse, there was a perceptible rise in Love-Me-River. A few weeks more and the coming flood would trap them here for months.

On the thirtieth day, they both rose and made a valiant attempt to prepare the canoe, which was drawn up near their shelter. The Muras sat watching them but offered no assistance. "Urubu!" Amador scolded weakly. "They're waiting for us to die so that they can steal our goods." Segge's blue eyes danced in their yellow sockets. "Does it matter?" he asked. They worked slowly, but exhaustion caught up with them. Amador went down on his knees at the side of the canoe. "It's hopeless," he said. "We can't even get to the water. How can we expect to go downriver?" That night both suffered fresh bouts of fever, the strength they'd summoned earlier dissipated as they tossed and trembled and moaned with discomfort.

Amador woke late on the morning of the thirty-second day. Both men had scarcely moved in the forty-six hours since the attempt to ready the canoe. Segge's eyes were already open, his gaze fixed on the fronds above; he turned his head slowly, a frown on his face as he looked at Amador. Amador did not speak, but he was also clearly puzzled by something.

Motioning Segge to remain where he was, he climbed out of the hammock.

He paused when his feet touched the ground and then stepped shakily toward the low exit. He clutched at fronds as he bent his fever-racked body to pass through the opening.

The Muras were gone.

A plume of smoke rose from a fire in front of one of their huts, a hundred yards away. But there was not a Mura in sight.

Amador took a step back toward the opening. "They've left us," he said bleakly. "They're gone."

A groan came from within the hut.

Amador walked unevenly toward their canoe, cursing the Muras as he limped along. "They stole our goods," he muttered.

But the canoe and its contents were exactly as they'd left them two days ago. Amador looked toward a muddy beach where the Muras kept their own craft. It was deserted. Segge had got up and was hanging onto the fronds at the entrance to the shelter.

"Every one of them . . . Muras . . . canoes, everything — gone," Amador said. "But they took nothing of ours."

Amador began to cross to the other huts. He'd covered sixty paces when he felt a terrible dizziness. He forced himself on toward the hut where the fire smoldered. A parrot popped out of a shelter and wobbled across the ground. Amador looked at the bird, a green blur; his nausea rose overwhelmingly.

"Amador!"

He heard Segge call his name. His legs shook and he started to faint. But he never struck the ground. The moment he began to fall, he glimpsed urucu-stained arms reaching for him. Then he lost consciousness.

&

When they spoke afterward of the events of that morning and their experiences through the ensuing rainy season, they could only conclude that their preservation had been miraculous. Above all, Amador remembered what he'd once said to Segge: "Never think you know what's in their minds, because you'll be grievously wrong."

The men who'd streamed out of the hut were Mundurucu, mortal enemies of the Fish People.

When Amador had come to minutes later, he found Segge and himself surrounded by the red-painted warriors. Neither offered the feeblest resistance; both cried out that their hour had finally come. They had escaped the Tupinambá and the Spaniards' fate and innumerable other dangers, but now their luck had run out.

Yet they were wrong, for the Tupi-speaking Mundurucu escorted them to their village on a tributary of Love-Me-River, and not once on that two-day journey did the savages show animosity. On the contrary, they treated the two men with respect and admiration and evinced the gravest concern at their emaciated condition, a plight the Mundurucu blamed entirely on the Fish People, whom they vociferously promised would be chastised for their neglect of these honored guests.

At the Mundurucu village, Amador and Segge recovered with the help of medicine men who sent assistants on a search for the bark of a tree that flourished far to the west. The pagés prepared a bitter drink with this bark and served it to their patients. Within days they began to feel better, their temperatures dropped, and their appetites improved.

Amador and Segge grew stronger, but not strong enough to continue their journey. The warm, moisture-laden air masses from the north swept the forest, and the rainy season closed in. Small streams rose steadily until they broke their banks and spilled into the forest. The great rivers were swollen foot by foot, their flood roaring north to join that of the Rio das Amazonas.

Segge and Amador observed that the Mundurucu shared many aspects of life with the Tupinambá and the Paresí: cultivation of manioc and maize; body paints and feather adornments; mode of warfare and weapons; fear of forest spirits. And, like the Paresí men, the Mundurucu were fond of ceremonies, speechmaking, and dancing, and kept sacred trumpets their women were forbidden to see. However, they took their precautions against the opposite sex a step further: At no time were Amador and Segge permitted to sleep overnight in the company of women. They had to hang their hammocks in a men's house, where all Mundurucu males above adolescence lived. The men went to the women's dwellings to visit their children and have sex with their wives, but it was taboo to stay longer than necessary.

In their first days at the village, Amador and Segge had plied the Mundurucu with gifts of cloth, fishhooks, and beads. They seen little of the village, and had been unaware of ceremonies held on their behalf: When the rituals had ended, Mundurucu elders danced into the men's house to offer their guests reciprocal presents.

The grateful Mundurucu gave Amador and Segge each a shrunken head.

The skulls and brains were carefully removed, the skin gently daubed with urucu, the lips sealed with fiber strands. The head was filled with sand and left until it dried and shrank to the size of a man's fist. Then it was ready to be worn around the neck of the warrior who had taken it: a medallion of honor.

The presentation was made with profuse apologies that these were the heads of old enemies and not Fish People, whose evil had afflicted the guests. However, the Mundurucu assured them that these symbolic trophies would be exchanged for the real thing when the waters fell and "Reed Rat," as this Mundurucu clan was known, could pursue the hated Muras.

Why their own heads were not taken to dangle against the chests of Mundurucu greatly perplexed Amador and Segge. They could only surmise that their hosts spared them because of their shared loathing of the Fish People. Thus, from December 1643 till May 1644, though they were constantly on the alert, the Mundurucu never treated them with anything but the greatest kindness and respect. And when the rains began to let up and they spoke of leaving, this was accepted without question, and warriors offered to guide them to "river-at-the-top-of-the-earth."

They took this to be a Mundurucu description for the Rio das Amazonas, but the elders explained that Love-Me-River was "river-at-the-bottom-of-the-earth" and that far above lay river-at-the-top.

Gradually, Amador and Segge came to understand that the world of the Mundurucu was contained between two rivers that were tributaries of the Rio das Amazonas, river-at-the-top being the one farther east.

"What is special about river-at-the-top?" Segge asked the elders.

"Other Mundurucu live there."

"Is it far?"

"Very, very far," the elder said. "Near where the Tapajós live."

"Tapajós? Did you hear, Amador? Tapajós! The river people the storyteller Ibira spoke of! Where he said we would find the Amazons. El Dorado!"

♧

It took the three canoes that carried Amador and Segge and their Mundurucu guides three and a half weeks to travel from the Reed Rat's village to the mouth of Love-Me-River.

They hugged the left bank or the right, avoiding the midstream current, where dislodged trunks, flanked by numerous smaller branches, plunged through the short waves.

With debris stuck fast near one bank, often the canoes had been forced to cross Love-Me-River, lookouts posted in bow and stern as the brown-silted river swirled around the canoes and projectiles raced alongside. They were buffeted by free-floating logs; huge sawyers slammed into the rear of their canoes until they gained the calms. Even here the river was deep and active enough for a slower-moving log to cause serious damage. But the Mundurucu were excellent canoeists, and late afternoon of July 24,1644, they approached the mouth of Love-Me-River.

A green island divided the mouth into two channels. The rains had swollen Love-Me-River to forty feet above low water. When the explorer Pedro Teixeira, the first man to ascend the Amazon, passed this way five years before, he had seen that the torrent from the south carried hundreds of trees torn from its banks. He had named the tributary Rio Madeira ("River of Wood").

The Mundurucu now called out excitedly as they passed along the east bank of Love-Me-River, with the island to the left. Amador and Segge shared a thrill at knowing that they had reached the Rio das Amazonas. But only when they saw the waters of Love-Me-River rolling into those of the Rio das Amazonas did they realize the immensity of the river. The opposite bank was but a blur in the distance.

"Dear God, what a stream!" Segge exclaimed. "The river sea!"

There was a monotony to the voyage downriver, and this heightened the sense of limitlessness. Days on end, the line of trees on the opposite bank remained unchanged: enormous gnarled roots exposed by the torrent; stricken trees leaning precariously toward the water for the final assault that would hurl them downriver.

It was not excessively hot, as long as fair breezes wafted across the water, but when these died, the humidity rose to a stifling degree. This airlessness, the repetitive rhythms of the paddles, and a general lassitude added to the monotony and sense of infinity.

But what spectacular surprises to break that sameness!

To come to an island in the Rio das Amazonas a few days after leaving the mouth of Love-Me-River and discover it to be so large as to suggest a circumference of at least one hundred miles, and to learn that it was home to thousands of people, the Tupinambara, descendants of a great exodus from Pernambuco.

To see the Rio das Amazonas split into a dozen serpentine channels — each itself a good-sized river — coursing between low, half-flooded lands for miles until they abandoned these small diversions and were again united. A shock, then, to find the river shrinking to one mile and its bank rising to a bluff sixty feet above them, the only narrows encountered on its main course and through which the compressed flow of water poured at an astonishing rate.

The constant green and gray and blue was also relieved by the dance of sun and moon on the equator. Daybreak and a faint blush in the gray would presage the rim of orange sun behind the trees. The surface of the river would be painted in a way no mortal artist would emulate, passing through a spectrum of shades, from soft pinks and mauves to a fiery blaze that turned the waters of the Rio das Amazonas into molten gold. At sunset the flaming ball would sink, sometimes seen hovering full circle at the very edge of earth, where there was a gap in the foliage. After the briefest pause, a small, yellowish moon would rise above the horizon and climb swiftly, the constellations growing pale the higher it rose.

Where the canoes hugged the bank, the variety of birds was clearly noticeable, but opposite, there was nothing but a silent green belt; and far ahead, a full flight of flamingos or herons was no more than a smudge of pink or white between water and sky.

One species of bird, however, appeared in flocks of hundreds, sometimes crouching together on the limbs of a single tree, motionless, waiting: urubu. The vultures circled above, forever searching the flood for rotten carcasses; they floated on the surface, riding the current as they surveyed slimy mudflats, hoping to detect a stench that would lead them to their meal.

All along the passage from the mouth of the Rio Madeira to the Rio Tapajós, the voyagers found evidence of death and suffering among the river tribes, not from the natural hazards of this wild and dangerous kingdom, but from the depredations of Portuguese and Spaniard.

Every infamy that had occurred in lands to the south during the previous century was being reenacted here now. Bloody encounters between Portuguese and French (and Dutch and English); the frustrations of Jesuits and priests, who sought to establish aldeias among the river nations; the annihilation of clans who resisted; and, above all, the systematic capture of tens of thousands of natives, for whom the Mother of Rivers became the hell of waters along which they rode to perpetual slavery.

Ꮟ᷎

At a major village of the Tapajós nation on the south bank of the Rio das Amazonas, Segge Proot's second Eden offered a perfect vision of hell.

After a five-week voyage from the Rio Madeira, the Mundurucu had brought them to this settlement just beyond the mouth of the Rio Tapajós, where Amador and Segge sighted a small sailing vessel at anchor. The Mundurucu refused to go ashore here, and leaving them with one canoe and their possessions, they had immediately turned back to journey down the Tapajós to other Mundurucu.

Amador and Segge landed at a muddy beach where ninety canoes were drawn up. They carried a force of 120 Portuguese and half-breeds and six hundred native auxiliaries, mostly Tupinambá.

The commander introduced himself: "I am Bento Maciel Parente. Who are you?"

"Bento Maciel?" Amador asked, recalling the old soldier who'd gained such a fierce reputation in these lands.

"The son," the commander explained.

"Amador Flôres da Silva . . . of São Paulo."

Now Bento Maciel showed surprise: "São Paulo de Piratininga?"

"It's a long story," Amador began.

"I've no time for it," Bento Maciel said brusquely. His eyes swung to Segge. "You?"

"Secundus Proot," Segge said tonelessly, recalling what he'd heard of this vicious family back at Recife.

"Hollander?"

"Yes, senhor."

Bento Maciel turned back to Amador: "Why are you with this enemy?"

"He's not an enemy, Capitão. He's a comrade from the sertão." Hastily, Amador blurted out some facts of their journey.

Bento Maciel was astonished by Amador's account, but suddenly interjected: "Later we can talk; now my army is engaged." He started to walk away from them up the sloping riverbank to the sixteen malocas of these Tapajós natives. Amador and Segge followed him.

Two malocas burned, the flames and smoke a backdrop to the spectacle in the clearing.

Tapajós were being run down by their attackers, hurled to the earth, and dragged off by an arm or a leg and herded into a square formed by their Tupinambá

captors. To one side of this human square, ten Tapajós — seized after offering resistance were being mutilated by two swordsmen in bronze breastplates, who lopped off
a nose, ears, lower arm, continuing until the Tapajós who provided their sport keeled
over and died.

Babies who tottered into the path of the conquerors were impaled on the
points of spears. With a Portuguese marching up front, six Tupinambá braves carried
aloft a Tapajós pagé. They hurled the screaming elder into the flames.

Even as these atrocities were being carried out, a squad of Tupinambá supervised by half-breed slavers were hauling rough-cut timbers to an area near the beach.
They were raising an enclosure where the chief of this clan and his savage dignitaries
would be segregated until the flotilla left for Belém.

"Why go to the trouble?" Amador asked. "Keep them with the rest."

"That will not do," said Bento Maciel. "Already they've given us no end of
difficulty."

"In what way?"

"We came for a peaceful trade. We brought lengths of cloth to exchange for
heathen held prisoner by these Tapajós. But the chief sent his prisoners to another
village. The pagan will not accept this lawful commerce —"

"*Lawful?* Dear Jesus in heaven, what's *lawful* about this carnage?" Segge cried out.

"Hold your tongue, Hollander!" Bento Maciel's eyes radiated hate. "Our dear
father, Bento Maciel Parente, patriot of our king, was murdered by your people."

"I know nothing of this."

"You know *nothing*, Hollander. Three years ago our king, Dom João, so thankful to God to be rid of the Spaniards, made a pact for ten years' peace with the Dutch.
Friends, our king wanted; traitors he got! In Europe, the Hollanders spoke of peace;
here, they sent a force to take Maranhão and carry away its governor, my father. They
let him die, the hero. Seventy-five years old and left to rot in a dungeon of
Pernambuco!"

This was partly true. In 1641, before formal ratification of the ten-year truce
between the Dutch and the Portuguese, Count Maurits sent a force from Recife to
seize São Luis, the capital of Maranhão captaincy. But, when the defenders begged
Bento Maciel to resist the invasion, he had handed over the keys of his fort without
firing a shot. Taken prisoner and delivered to Count Maurits, the old butcher of
Belém so disgusted the Dutch prince that he had him banished to a remote fortress,
where he ended his life.

Amador now attempted to intervene between young Bento Maciel and Segge.
"There is justification for this war," he said.

"*War?*" Segge shook his head. "This is *war?*"

"Come, Hollander!" Bento Maciel snapped,

Segge hesitated.

"You ask for justification?" Bento Maciel began to walk along the side of the
clearing. Amador followed.

Segge walked behind them. They came to a landing place where the Tapajós
kept their canoes.

"*There* is our justification."

An enormous Cross lay flat in the mud.

"They were offered the Lord's protection," said Bento Maciel. "They rejected Him."

An advance party of Bento Maciel's force had brought this Cross to the Tapajós. "Always keep it pointing to heaven," the slavers advised, "that our Lord Jesus may see His children." Then they'd left, to take the same message to other natives. By accident or design — it was never determined which — the Crosses fell. And the raiders were legally able to act against pagans who neglected the symbol of their salvation.

"Merciful God . . . is there no forgiveness?" Segge murmured.

The slaver gave a long, disapproving look. "Come, Paulista," he said to Amador. "I have men to command."

☙

By nightfall, the Tapajós had been pacified. The women and children were confined in the remaining malocas. Bento Maciel had earlier addressed the Tapajós and informed them that those who remained docile would be favorably treated: He held up a length of coarse cotton cloth and promised that for a month of steady work at Belém they could possess such a strip of material. He also held up shackles and he promised, too, that if the Tapajós gave the slightest cause, he would throw them in chains. The chief of these Tapajós, Tabaliba, and nineteen elders got no such assurances and were already incarcerated at the enclosure.

Amador had spent the afternoon in the commander's company. From him, he had learned startling news: The Dutch had recalled Johan Maurits, and the count had left Recife the previous May. It was now August 1644, and Bento Maciel believed it possible that the Portuguese of Pernambuco could already be in revolt. With Count Maurits's departure, most of the Dutch garrison had also been withdrawn, Holland seeing no need to maintain a major force in the colony when a treaty of peace existed between Portugal and herself. "What they don't realize is that the treaty means nothing to planters who owe the Dutch Company a fortune," said Bento Maciel. "They'll support any uprising that throws the Hollanders — and their huge debts — into the Atlantic."

Bento Maciel listened to Amador's story of the journey across the sertão and accepted his explanation of how he'd come to undertake this exploration with a Hollander. "We'll take him to Belém, as you wish. We'll put him on a vessel to Europe or wherever he wants to go," he said. "But I warn you, da Silva — keep the Hollander from me! You've been too long in the sertão. You forget the nature of this enemy."

"Capitão Bento Maciel, I'll never forget my comrades beheaded by the Dutch."

"Good! Then remember, too, that your painter friend is one of them."

"Proot and I have seen and suffered much together."

"That I can understand, but now you're almost back in civilization — Portuguese civilization, da Silva, where many more have suffered by the actions of this heretic's countrymen."

Not long after this conversation, Amador found Segge at their canoe. All along the bank, the fires of slavers and Tupinambá burned brightly in the pitch-black moonless night. Segge was leaning against the prow of the canoe, which had been dragged a short distance up the muddy beach.

Neither spoke immediately. Since leaving Engenho Santo Tomás in October 1640, three years and ten months ago, there had been occasions when dissensions threatened their camaraderie, and always the conflict had passed when they continued their march. But now both men sensed a rift opening between them as wide as the river just beyond.

Segge's first words were directed at the cause of this breach. "What crimes have they committed to warrant this brutal treatment?"

"They defiled the Cross. They denied their prisoners the freedom Bento Maciel came prepared to bargain for. They're chastised for their wars against the Portuguese, their cannibalism. They won't change. They were savages before the Portuguese came, and savages they'll remain."

"And their souls?"

"Their souls?" Amador glared at his friend.

"What I've witnessed today — is this how the Portuguese maintain their souls for Christ?"

Amador gave the canoe a violent kick. "Jesus Christ knows Portuguese, Paulistas — *He* knows how we've suffered in this pagan land!" He lurched forward and seized Segge by the shoulder, almost knocking him into the canoe. "What do *you* know, Hollander? What do you know about Brazil — even your splendid count, who's been sent away from Recife, what —"

"Johan Maurits . . . *gone?*" Segge jerked loose from Amador's grasp.

"Yes, Segge Proot — sent back to Amsterdam where he belongs. He came to discover Brazil, to show the Portuguese how to tame this heathen hell with love and kindness . . . and *painters*. They've called him back. A failure."

"This can't be true," Segge exclaimed. "Maurits of Nassau loved this land as if it were his own. He wanted friendship between Hollander and Portuguese — to build a prosperous colony."

"Which his armies stole from us."

"I promise you this, Amador" — Segge's tone became deeply melancholic — "there will be Portuguese colonists who'll pray for the return of Count Maurits."

"Certainly — every collaborator and traitor."

What happened the next afternoon made the split between them irrevocable.

Segge was walking slowly along the beach when he saw a commotion at the enclosure in which the Tapajós chief and elders were penned. Fifty yards from it, he caught sight of something inside the pen that made him break into a run.

"No! No! Not them!" His shouts tore the air. "Mundurucu! Men who guided us on the river!"

A Tupinambá squad probing upriver for villages of potential slaves had captured the eight Mundurucu.

Segge argued with a slaver at the pen. "We brought them here. They served us faithfully for months. Their people saved us when we were dying of fever."

"I see savages, Hollander — as fit for Belém as any Tapajós!"

Segge stormed up to the village clearing, where Bento Maciel and his notary sat at a makeshift table making an inventory of the captives. Amador stood near them.

"Our Mundurucu" — Segge looked across at Amador — "they've thrown our Mundurucu in with the Tapajós!"

Amador glanced at Bento Maciel.

"Amador, for God's sake!" Segge cried. "The Mundurucu who guided us — these men have imprisoned them!"

"All eight, *Hollander*," said Bento Maciel. "Swept up by my Tupinambá!"

"They can't be taken as slaves."

"By whose authority?"

"For the love of God, Amador — *tell him!*"

"They're savages, Segge. What does it matter?"

"*Amador?*"

Amador looked at him quizzically.

Segge turned again to Bento Maciel: "Those Mundurucu saved my life, and *his*."

Bento Maciel looked at Amador. "I hear no objection from you, Paulista."

"Oh, no, Capitão," Amador said, without hesitation.

"*Damn you!*" Segge shouted. "*Damn you all!*"

Bento Maciel's hand flew to the hilt of his sword.

"Leave him be, Capitão!" Amador yelled. Then, to Segge: "Go! Go before he kills you!"

Segge hesitated for just a moment. Then, cursing under his breath, he turned away and trudged toward the trees.

Segge wandered back toward the enclosure. The temporary stockade of tree limbs and brush was poorly constructed, nowhere more than six feet high and intended more for segregating these men from the village than for preventing their escape. A man with distinctly Moorish features was in charge of twenty Tupinambá who guarded the prisoners. Segge ignored "The Turk," as he thought of him, and peered over the top of the enclosure.

The Mundurucu sat together. He hailed them, but when he tried to engage them in talk, they ignored him.

Beloved Jesus! he said to himself. *The Mundurucu think I'm one of these men. They think I'm responsible for their capture!*

కు

At midnight, Segge eased a canoe down the beach and into the water. He pushed it thirty feet offshore and lowered a stone anchor to hold it until he returned. Then he set out for the enclosure carrying a machete and a twelve-inch tapered dagger, the property of the late Don Hernando Ramirez de Ribera.

The Turk and his Tupinambá were at a fire up on the bank — all fast asleep. Segge slipped into the small stockade. The Mundurucu he roused first; then he woke the Tapajós chief, Tabaliba, and the elders nearest him. These men wore shackles, but ropes, not chain, were passed through the rings of the restraints. Segge hacked through the bonds with the dagger and indicated that the prisoners were to leave the enclosure at the side facing the water; to make a passage through the loosely packed brush and branches was no problem.

Segge told the captives to head for the Tapajós canoes, four hundred yards below the enclosure. Then he slipped out and hastened to his canoe.

He padded off silently, not daring to look back, for he now expected to be apprehended. He passed between other canoes and Bento Maciel's vessel. When he reached a point opposite the mud beach with the Cross, the Tapajós and Mundurucu were waiting for him in their canoes.

The chief, Tabaliba, and two Tapajós transferred to Segge's craft.

"Where are we going?" Segge asked.

'To a friend of my people," said Tabaliba. "There is a cave. Three days' walk through the forest."

This mention of a cave led Segge to believe that the desperate man was taking them to a sorcerer. He shook his head. "No, Tabaliba . . . no," he said. "No pagé has power to combat the evil of the Portuguese."

"You have helped us, have you not? We have another friend at the cave."

"A Hollander?"

Tabaliba said simply. "He will help us."

છ

He sat on a natural raised platform a foot up, deep in the cavern. The smoke from several lit tapers rose to the high ceiling, and the light cast long shadows across the floor of the broad gallery. A fire to one side of the platform provided warmth in the chilly, damp atmosphere. Opposite the man, Segge Proot sat with his legs crossed on a pile of animal skins and listened intently to this ally of the Tapajós.

High on the side of a mountain, three days' journey beyond the north bank of the Rio das Amazonas, this had been the cave of Tocoyricoc, but its present occupant was very different from that venerable exile from the realm of the Inca.

The man on the platform was only forty-four. He had strong shoulders, a full chest, and heavily muscled limbs. His hair was flaxen and thick, his beard the same. Many years in the tropics had burnt his face a deep brown. Beneath his wiry eyebrows danced the liveliest green eyes Segge had ever seen.

His name was Abel O'Brien. He was a son, not of provinces of the Inca, where the mountains stood high in the clouds, but of County Clare in Ireland, and of low meadows beyond the Shannon.

Yet, different as he was from old Tocoyricoc, when Abel O'Brien told Segge his story, he, too, spoke of lakes of gold and Virgins of the Sun.

"We saw gold and silver and jewels enough to ransom the Great Mogul! And oh, the wenches — nubile nymphs with skin as soft as the touch of silk. We saw it all, Secundus Proot, my cousin Bernard and I, beneath the stars on our voyage to this southern land in our Lord's year 1620. Bernard was just seventeen and I a man of twenty, but didn't we dream the dreams of kings? And if we asked our captain, Roger North, of these wonders, he'd say, 'Aye, aye, aye, my lads, the Amazones are there! The Amazones and grand El Dorado, to whom the Spaniard seeks exclusive recourse!' Who were we to challenge the promise of this man who'd marched with Raleigh into the Guianas just three years before in quest of that fabulous kingdom?"

Abel O'Brien had already explained to Segge that between 1610 and 1634, English and Irish parties had made persistent attempts to gain a foothold on the northern banks of the lower Rio das Amazonas, the 1620 expedition having been led by Captain Roger North, an officer who'd served with Sir Walter Raleigh. Four years later, Abel O'Brien's cousin Bernard O'Brien settled a group of colonists 250 miles upriver at a place called Pataui, "Coconut Grove." For a decade, the O'Brien's and their compatriots, rarely more than two hundred in number, with thousands of native allies and sometimes in alliance with the Dutch, confronted the Portuguese. Nominally, Spain, by right of the Tordesilhas Treaty, had claim to the entire Amazon basin. But the union of the two crowns between 1580 and 1640 gave the Portuguese free rein to occupy the lands around the river sea.

When approaching this settlement beyond the Rio das Amazonas, Segge had been instantly impressed: At the foot of the steep hill was a stockade built in a semi-circle to cordon off an area below the cave; upon entering the palisade, Segge saw that behind it, earthworks provided additional fortification. Within the stockade were more than a dozen habitations, most of native construction, though three nearest the cavern were of wattle and daub. The entrance of the Tapajós chief caused excitement among the natives who dwelt here; many of the eighty residents were from Tabaliba's village, including a daughter of the chief — one of Abel O'Brien's seven concubines.

When the lord of this forest hideaway approached him, Segge had glanced apprehensively at Tabaliba, but the chief was busily relating the disaster at his village. Segge's misgiving was caused by the appearance of the man. He wore the uniform of a knight of Spain: green breeches with crimson slashes, skirted doublet of the same color, burnished breastplate and tasset, with silk sash and fine-worked leather belt crossed over his chest from shoulder to waist, where a ceremonial sword hung at his left side. On his head he wore a feather-bedecked hat with the brim turned up on one side. His boots were of the same soft leather as the sword belt and reached to above his knees.

Segge, in his confusion, had called out a salutation in Dutch, and to his great joy, received a greeting in his own language.

"I don't speak it fluently," Abel O'Brien said, after the introductions, "just enough to get along with others who fight the Portuguese!"

O'Brien also spoke Tupi-Guarani, so he and Segge had been able to converse freely. Abel O'Brien had taken Segge up a winding path to the cavern. There was a level fenced-in area in front of the opening; passing through a sturdy gate, Segge was surprised by the order he found. To one side stood wooden storage bins for manioc and grain; next to them was a well-equipped forge, beside which lay a pile of iron spearheads and implements. On the opposite side were several water casks, placed at different levels. The uppermost cask was fed by a channel made from split and hollowed tree limbs; the water trickling into the top tank came from a spring beyond the small enclosure, the overflow from this cask filling the barrels below. Four parrots and a red macaw offered a raucous greeting as the men moved through this area.

A similar orderliness prevailed in the big cave. The stony base was swept clean; arranged neatly against the walls were chests and a collection of swords, muskets, and powder. When Segge asked how this small arsenal had been obtained, O'Brien smacked his fancy breastplate. "The Portuguese aren't the only men who make conquests," he said, and indicated that Segge should move to the platform.

Two of Abel O'Brien's women had entered. Both extremely young, they giggled as they approached the men with bowls of food and fruit and a tall silver jug with a drink served in crystal goblets! The liquid was thin and refreshing, with a fruity taste. Segge had nodded with satisfaction as he sipped it. "What is it?" he asked. "A wine?"

O'Brien laughed. "Drink as much as you desire and you'll not suffer for it. This is unfermented juice of the passion fruit and other products of the forest."

"I expected cachaça."

"Not here, my friend. Nor do I eat the flesh of beasts."

"For what reason?"

"Meat I lost the taste for — as prisoner of the cannibals. Cachaça?" He put an arm around the nearest of the two girls. "What need have I for cachaça or tabak?" He smiled broadly. "Can you not see? I am Abel . . . alive . . . in this second Eden."

Segge sighed heavily.

"This distresses you?"

Segge had then told O'Brien some of his experiences. Later, when they'd eaten and the girls had been sent away, O'Brien removed his Spanish armor, settled himself comfortably on a pile of hides, the top one a jaguar pelt, placed a bowl of fruit between them, and launched into the story of his own and Bernard's search for El Dorado, and the attempt to establish English colonies and plantations along the Amazon . . .

"Four years after we came, Bernard sailed home, not in defeat, but with the hope of returning with ships of pilgrims for this paradise. He was away when the old dog Maciel Bento Parente attacked."

O'Brien's hand went to his doublet and he withdrew a crucifix inlaid with mother-of-pearl, which he wore at his breast. "It was hers," he said. "My Rebecca . . . Rebecca Goodheart. Oh, my love!" O'Brien's voice cracked. "When I first saw Rebecca, she was a child, only thirteen years old and sailing with her father in Roger North's ship. I was a man of twenty, and wise to the world. All these years, Secundus Proot, and I can still see her on the deck of that ship, gazing out across the water with such tremendous hope toward this New World.

"When Parente attacked, Rebecca and the women and children were placed for their safety aboard the only ship in the vicinity. One hundred and twenty-five souls, Secundus. The ship was driven aground by the dog Parente, and one hundred and twenty-five souls put to the sword and torn to pieces.

"Five of us escaped to the side of your countrymen," O'Brien went on. "The Dutch had forts up the Rio das Amazonas and we joined them for three years. We were few men, even with the natives who stood with us, and we suffered many reverses. But then in 1629 Bernard came back. He persuaded a shipload of English and Irish Papists and other dissidents who had fled persecution in England to come to the Amazon. Some of had wanted to go to the settlements in North America, but Bernard promised to lead them to paradise, here, at the Amazon!

"But just when we'd begun to rebuild, we were again attacked by a force of Portuguese and natives — not Bento Maciel Parente but others equally vicious and unforgiving. That was the end. The Dutch offered help, but Bernard wouldn't accept it. Instead, he surrendered to the Portuguese, who swore by the Cross of Christ that we would be unmolested. We were taken to Belém, where some of our party began to doubt this holy Portuguese oath and fled —"

"You were one of them?"

"I stayed with Bernard," he said. "And how God punished me for believing the Portuguese who had killed my Rebecca. We were banished from Belém and sent in chains to the malocas of cannibals. Separated from Bernard, I was placed with flesh eaters at a village on the Rio Pará. 'You tell us you love the savages, Irishman,' the Portuguese said. 'Make friends with them so that we may have peace in our land!'" O'Brien laughed. "They expected me to be devoured, but I did exactly as the administrator ordered: I made friends. They spared me, for I led them in battles against their enemies. God forgive me, I delivered the cannibals more victims than they'd ever known."

"I was held by the Tupinambá," Segge said quietly. "I know to what lengths a man will be driven."

After a year with the cannibals, O'Brien added, he had left them and come upriver to the Tapajós led by Tabaliba. These natives he had aided, too, in clashes against their enemies, until he tired of the conflicts and moved to this cave, where he began his settlement ten years ago. His cousin Bernard who had been allowed to return to Belém, had left Brazil, having abandoned hope for his colony.

"You've never wanted to return to Ireland?"

"I swore that I would never leave until my work is done."

"What work?" Segge asked.

"Here a Spaniard, there a Portuguese — my work," O'Brien said, looking intently at the stack of muskets. "Never many, for we are not a large force, just myself and thirty warriors below. But, by the grace of God, we've been given success." He smiled broadly. "The Portuguese would call me a pirate — Bloody Abel O'Brien of the Rio das Amazonas! That's *if* they ever identified me and my wild gallants! We take every precaution, *Master* Proot. We leave no survivors; and if we did, they'd simply report another attack by savages raiding out of the forest, for we disguise ourselves as such."

They were outside now. Abel O'Brien paced slowly back and forth.

"*Bento Maciel Parente.*" He drew out the name with menacing emphasis. "The *son.* I have been thinking, Secundus, that it is time for me to end my work."

The Irishman was quiet for a while. Then he raised his face to the starlit heavens. "Yes, by God, I see it is time! We'll sail against the slavers, Secundus."

Segge was taken aback. "There are hundreds of them! They have a ship with guns!"

"So I've heard. But we, too, can bring a force such as has never been seen before on the Rio das Amazonas, if we act swiftly and send Tabaliba and the elders to every village downriver. Wherever there's a native who has felt or feared the sorrow inflicted by these Portuguese, he will be called to war. We'll ride them down in the

Rio das Amazonas, young Bento Maciel Parente and every dog who runs with him. We'll ride them down, Secundus, and liberate those they take to ruin at Belém!"

"Do you really think it can be done?" Segge asked, excitement growing in his chest.

"You've told me you are an artist."

"I was before . . ."

"Then fight alongside me, my friend, and I'll promise you a scene of glory — such a scene, *painter* Proot, as you could never imagine!"

☙

"Death-Bird Island," the natives called the mile-and-a-half-long kidney-shaped island sixty miles downriver from the Tapajós village raided by Bento Maciel Parente and his slavers. The island lay between two bends of the Rio das Amazonas, which was four miles wide at this point.

Death-Bird Island merited its name. It was thickly wooded, and the branches above a steep bank opposite the channel were heavy with urubu.

On this day, September 7, 1644, the single-masted, shallow-draft flagship of Bento Maciel Parente's slave flotilla approached the south bend. Built at Belém, she had been constructed with her river missions in mind. She was sixty feet long with ample beam and flush deck. She had no cabin but a thatched shelter toward the stern. Her mast was stepped close forward and she had a long bowsprit; two gaff-rigged sails and topsail could be raised, and a spread of canvas could be unfurled between mast and bowsprit. She was maneuverable, with fourteen pairs of oars to navigate her when there was no wind. And she was deadly: She mounted eight brass cannon and four swivel guns. She was called *Nossa Senhora do Desterro*, and shared this name with Fort Desterro, situated one hundred miles farther down the Rio das Amazonas and the last outpost beyond Belém.

To keep pace with her fleet this day, the *Desterro* was lightly rigged with only a foresail hoisted. Around her and half a mile astern of the vessel rode eighty canoes bearing slavers and the six hundred Tupinambá auxiliaries, and 736 men, women, and children seized from the village of Tabaliba and other settlements attacked by the force. The canoes were from twenty to thirty-six feet long, some of bark, others of single-tree construction. Many were crowded with as many as thirty people. The larger craft had eight oarsmen who stood up front with a bowman setting the beat as they paddled, an energetic stroke to keep up with the *Desterro*.

Amador sat on the deck under the thatched shelter with Bento Maciel and his officers. Three of the officers were Portuguese-born; one was from Lebanon (Segge Proot's "Turk"); four were half-breeds — two the sons of black women, and two mamelucos.

While boarding the *Desterro*, Amador was reminded of the *Hopewell*, which had carried him to Pernambuco. He had dreaded a repetition of that foul passage, but he needn't have worried: The smooth-flowing river and light breezes and the airy shelter on deck made life aboard the *Desterro* quite tolerable.

When the flight of Segge Proot and the natives from the enclosure had been discovered, Amador had raged the loudest, and offered to search for the fugitives.

"I brought the Hollander to your camp, Capitão Bento Maciel," he had cried. "Let me be the one who seeks redress!"

Bento Maciel had been furious at the loss of Tabaliba and the others, but his anger did not equal Amador's.

"A musket, Capitão! A machete! The Hollander must be captured!"

"*Calma*, Paulista . . . *calma!* We have hundreds of slaves. Why hazard a force in the forest for only twenty-eight savages and a heretic?"

"It's a matter of honor," Amador replied stoutly.

"Leave the Hollander to the savages. He will never survive this sertão."

As the *Desterro* sailed downriver, Amador's experiences during the years passed in the sertão with Segge Proot were uppermost in his thoughts. And he remembered, too, Senhor Fernão Cavalcanti's request that he take Proot away from Engenho Santo Tomás for six months. *If nothing else, I honored my arrangement with Senhor Fernão. I saved the senhorita from the worst temptation.*

The *Desterro* entered the south bend. Her helmsman held her on course for the middle of the channel between Death-Bird Island and the riverbank. A light breeze filled the big foresail.

In addition to the men at the shelter, the ship carried a crew of twenty. Two were up forward, one sitting astride the bowsprit looking out for tree trunks and similar hazards. Two men stood in the stern with the helmsman, one observing the progress of the eighty canoes spread out around and behind them, the other keeping an eye on two fishing lines he'd cast out over the railing.

Without warning, a barrage of musket fire was unleashed against the *Desterro* from both sides of the channel. To the right, assailants rose from a trench behind an earth mound camouflaged with branches and debris; to the left, they were concealed in the brush. Before the fusillade ended, archers with long bows loosed a storm of arrows to follow the hail of lead.

The instant the attack was launched, at the far end of the channel, a barrier constructed of 520 feet of lianas — expertly joined and nowhere less than ten inches thick — rose six feet out of the water.

"The guns!" Bento Maciel roared. "Man the guns!"

He dropped to his knees and crawled along the deck. Two crew were already tugging at a hatch that covered the area where gunpowder and shot were stored. Kegs of powder and weapons were also kept in the bow, where decking from bulwark to bulwark formed a low forecastle, no more than a crawl space into which men now scrambled frantically to supply the ship's guns.

Two swivel guns were situated amidships to port and starboard, and two at the stern. But only two of these four guns could be manned; the first shore volleys had knocked out almost a quarter of the *Desterro's* officers and crew.

The helmsman screamed and doubled up with pain as he was hit by an arrow that tore into his left arm, but he did not let go of the tiller.

On both banks, hundreds of warriors boldly showed themselves with taunts and bravado, as the forty muskets and two hundred bows kept up a furious assault against the slavers. In the canoe fleet, shocked Tupinambá began to rally and grabbed their bows, but the counterattack was initially weak and disorganized. Worst off at this moment were the hundreds of unarmed prisoners caught in the midst of this battle: Some huddled in the bottom of the canoes; others leapt or were thrown overboard, bewildered and terrified. Few thought to attack their guards.

And now those in the *Desterro* showed why the Portuguese men-of-war had such a fearsome reputation. It was true that the great Lusitanian Empire was virtually in ruin, smashed by the new power of the Hollander and the growing harassment by Englishmen. But it was equally true that wherever Portuguese were still called to fight, there rose all the power and glory that older generations had known with *As Conquistas!*

Within five minutes, gun ports had been banged open, charges rammed home and round shot fed into the barrels. With a thunderclap and burst of smoke, they hurled their first projectiles toward the shore. The swivel guns were ready, too. A musket ball grooved the scalp of the mameluco who stood beside the gun on the stern and killed him instantly. But The Turk — a blood-soaked kerchief around his neck — leapt up quickly to the gun and sent a hail of small shot in the direction of Death-Bird Island.

Swiftly the *Desterro* was converted to a fighting ship. But even as belching fire and acrid smoke signaled the *Desterro's* response, her men became aware of the full extent of the trap set for them.

Eight hundred yards ahead, where the mighty liana barrier blocked the slavers' passage, war canoes that had hidden behind the northern end of the island rode into view. The paddlers ducked as the canoes slipped beneath the liana cable; then they took up their stroke, dozens of craft moving toward the *Desterro*.

But this squadron did not represent the main threat. To the south, 150 canoes swept around the island. The *Desterro* and every craft that rode with Bento Maciel Parente's flotilla were bottled into the channel.

Abel O'Brien stood boldly in the prow of one of the lead craft, the spray flying up around him as the canoe raced through the water. "Faster, my Tapajós! Faster, my gallants!"

Segge was exultant as the canoe in which he was standing rushed to battle. Never before had he found himself in such a situation. *Today, Secundus Proot,* he told himself, *you're not an artist — you're a warrior come to deliver the wrath of God to those who richly deserve it!*

He had equipped himself from Abel O'Brien's ample resources. He wore a heavy leather jerkin, a bright orange sash, and blue breeches. Two bone-handled pistols, long knife, and war ax were thrust into his belt. Two loaded muskets lay at the feet of one of Abel O'Brien's warriors, who sat ready to reload for Segge.

Segge's appearance bore one comical aspect: Perched on his head was a rusty iron helmet. Segge had paraded around the cave in this headgear to Abel O'Brien's vast amusement. "Rather this than a musket ball in the brain," was Segge's defense.

A mile had separated this main force of attackers from the *Desterro* when they entered the channel, but the gap was swiftly narrowing. In accord with a plan of Abel O'Brien's, half the craft now swung off to the right to engage the slavers' canoes, and the rest of the force kept behind the seven lead canoes bearing toward the ship.

The *Desterro* was being maneuvered with oars, in an attempt to turn her so that she would offer less of a target to the land-based attackers. It was also hoped that by coming around, the *Desterro* might raise sail and attempt to blast a passage between the canoes surging up the channel.

But Bento Maciel Parente and his officers were aware that more than likely they would have to battle it out in the middle of the waterway. To improve their chances, they had signaled the canoes carrying the main corps of raiders, men with knowledge of the ordnance aboard, and succeeded in taking twenty of their comrades onto the *Desterro's* deck. Four of the cannon and three swivel guns were now in action.

"The Hollander!" Amador screamed the moment he distinguished the tall, big-bodied figure. "Proot! Oh, God! It's *Proot!*"

The *Desterro's* bulwarks were low and offered little enough protection from the missiles streaking across the water. But such was his anger that Amador leapt up from the gun where he'd been assisting Bento Maciel and dashed toward the stern. Ignoring the arrows that hissed past him, he almost knocked down The Turk at the swivel gun. "The Hollander — he's mine!"

He took up position there, with The Turk and another raider. When the swivel gun was readied, Amador blasted away at the approaching canoes — with no effect, for they were still out of range.

The *Desterro* finally had been turned, and she could now hurl her shot at the canoes closing in from the north. So tightly arrayed were the canoes — against Abel O'Brien's directive — that the first two exploding balls effectively destroyed five craft. The slavers cheered, for it was a critical blow, slowing the advance from that direction.

The squadron rushing up from the south closed the gap to five hundred yards. The *Desterro's* port guns fired. Her first shots fell harmlessly into the water between the canoes, which were spread out, as Abel O'Brien had cautioned. They raced forward, grabbing every precious moment as the men in the ship made ready to reload.

With the second round, two canoes were hit, the explosions immediately followed by the shrill screams of dying men and the cries of terror-stricken survivors flung into the bloody waters.

Abel O'Brien was within hailing distance of Segge's canoe. *"Secundus! Secundus! Now! Be ready!"*

The gap separating them from the *Desterro* was now 350 feet. O'Brien and Segge barked orders to the men in their craft. Each canoe carried smoldering fire buckets and hand grenades, which Abel O'Brien had made at his cave.

Then Segge saw Amador at the stern of the ship. The instant he recognized him, there was a puff of smoke as the swivel gun fired, and the hail of shot struck several men in an adjacent canoe. A small cry escaped Segge's lips. Calmly, then, he raised the two pistols he'd drawn and fired off both in Amador's direction. He saw Amador waving his fist at him. Instantly Segge called for a musket and fired that, too, but missed his target.

The *Desterro's* guns roared. Tabaliba's canoe was torn into pieces by the blast and every man in her killed or mortally wounded.

Then Abel O'Brien had been about to hurl his first grenade toward the *Desterro*, when a sharp-eyed musketeer on his belly near the bowsprit fired at him. The ball caught him in the shoulder. He lost his balance and fell out of the canoe. But the grenade flew from his hand and dropped back into the craft. Several explosions followed; within seconds, nothing was seen of men or canoe.

Segge was three canoe lengths behind and he saw it all.

"*Paddle!*" he screamed at his crew, who had hesitated momentarily. "*Faster! Faster!*"

About fifty yards separated his canoe from the *Desterro*. Segge glanced to the stern and saw Amador and The Turk bringing the swivel gun to bear.

Suddenly the canoe lurched sideways. In their frenzied haste, the paddlers had not seen a submerged log. But that violent swing to the left, which almost swamped the craft and made Segge fight desperately to keep his foothold, saved them from the shot fired by Amador and The Turk.

Then the nine-pounders fired.

Swung off course, the canoe lay directly in the line of fire of the third port gun. There was a roar and a flash and an earsplitting explosion as the grenades in the canoe ignited.

Secundus Proot, the artist with his dream of a second Eden, died instantly.

"Fool! Fool! God-forsaken heretic fool!" Amador screamed.

The *Desterro* now began a systematic bombardment of the enemy canoes. When the channel had been cleared, Bento Maciel turned his attention to the shore, both the beach and the high bank of Death-Bird Island. He put a party of musketeers and Tupinambá on the island with orders to spare no one.

On Death-Bird Island, the urubu, which had taken flight at the first burst of musket fire, now began to circle back to their territory. And into the channel streamed piranha.

Men who lived to tell of this day would never forget the horror. The blood attracted thousands of the deep-bellied fish, their triangular-shaped teeth snapping at those who thrashed about frantically to escape this ultimate enemy. The piranha feasted and the mighty Rio das Amazonas became a river of blood.

Late in the afternoon, two days after the battle, the *Desterro* was anchored four miles downstream. The slavers had lost twenty Portuguese and half-breed raiders, 175 Tupinambá, and two hundred slaves. They had no idea of the casualties among their attackers, though they spoke confidently of having exterminated the majority. Where they had failed, they suspected the piranha had succeeded.

But there was one man who had miraculously escaped the piranha and had been found half drowned and washed up on the shore. And now he knelt on a beach opposite the *Desterro*.

"Your father was a hound of hell! You are the same!" he said.

Bento Maciel Parente accepted this insult calmly. "Is that all you have to say?"

"That . . . and every curse upon your soul!"

Bento Maciel nodded to The Turk, who stood next to the prisoner.

"Mercy! Mercy, my beloved Lord! *Mercy!*" the man on his knees called out.

Then The Turk swung his ax and chopped off the head of Abel O'Brien.

❧

That night after the execution, Amador and Bento Maciel were seated in the stern of the *Desterro*.

"Will you take a ship from Belém to Santos?" Bento Maciel asked.

"No. My family is at São Paulo. I will return there. But first I'll go to Pernambuco."

"Whatever for?"

"There's a bag of silver waiting for me. A reward for rendering a service for Senhor Cavalcanti."

XIII

September 1644 – November 1692

When Amador reached Belém do Pará with Bento Maciel Parente in late September 1644, the tale of his mighty journey through the wilderness excited the local planters, who prevailed upon him to stay for a time: "You sought El Dorado, Amador Flôres, and from what you say, you found it! A hoard of savages for the fields of Belém!"

Amador had no intention of voyaging back to the lands he and Segge Proot had traveled, but two planters convinced him to lead a slave hunt to the Rio Xingu, a tributary of the Amazon, less than three hundred miles away. The expedition was not a success: Half of the fifty Tupinambá with him perished from sickness and attack by savages; the survivors returned to Belém with eighty-seven captives, a paltry number compared with thousands sold at the riverside pens at Belém.

Amador had agreed to the expedition because of reports reaching Belém from Pernambuco: Since Johan Maurits's departure in May 1644, a group of Portuguese settlers had been in a state of incipient rebellion. Maurits had governed for seven years with tact and tolerance, but many Portuguese had been embittered by his seizure of the capital of Maranhão captaincy and the settlement of Loanda in Africa, in the interim between the signing of the ten-year truce between the Netherlands and Portugal and its ratification at Recife. The capture of Loanda had been a particular blow to planters at the Bahia and Rio de Janeiro, for their supply of slaves from that port had dried up.

By 1643 the Dutch garrison at São Luis do Maranhão had been put to the sword by the local Portuguese. This heartened the Pernambucans, especially those who owed thousands of florins to the Dutch Company. Besides, despite Maurits's efforts at quelling religious hatred, most Portuguese resented the heretics and Hebrews in their midst. Many Jews were conscious of this ill will and had sailed away with the count's fleet; others were talking of migrating to Dutch possessions in the Caribbean or to the Dutch settlement of New Amsterdam in North America.

In May 1645, Amador at last resolved to leave Belém. The news of the emerging uprising in Pernambuco made him consider taking ship directly for Santos, but the prospect of the bag of silver awaiting him at the Engenho Santo Tomás was too alluring. Besides, if he did tangle with the Dutch again, so be it, for twice now he had suffered the treachery of these heretics, with Proot and with those who had silenced his comrades at Engenho Santo Tomás.

Amador took passage with a small trader that put him ashore at a secluded bay of Paraíba, a captaincy north of Pernambuco; from there, he made his way to the engenho through the backlands.

In early June, Amador finally trudged up the hill toward the house of Senhor Fernão Cavalcanti. It was four and a half years since he'd left this valley with Secundus Proot. With the exception of a row of outbuildings near the quarters he'd shared with the Portuguese mill workers, there were no conspicuous changes. But, ever since entering the Cavalcanti lands this morning, Amador had experienced a sense of foreboding, which intensified the nearer he got to the heart of the settlement. Now as he limped toward the house, his gaze roved from the chapel to the main dwelling.

There was not a soul in sight.

He stopped abruptly at a movement near the slave quarters, but continued walking when he saw a dog creep back into the shadows. He drew level with the chapel and noticed that its doors were closed, as were the shutters of Padre Gregório Bonifácio's rooms next to the small church. He kept walking, past the trees where Senhorita Joana had often found him.

"Stranger!"

Amador froze.

"The musket — drop it!"

He obeyed the command.

"The pistol! Your other weapons!" The orders came from the direction of the chapel, behind him.

He threw the pistol next to the musket. As he began to unsheathe his machete, he turned sideways and saw the chapel doors ajar, a musket barrel protruding between them.

"Senhorita? Senhorita Joana?"

The musket was still trained on him.

"Amador Flôres, senhorita . . . Amador Flôres da Silva." He held his machete loosely at his side. Momentarily he looked up at the second story of the big house, where he saw two more guns aimed at him. He returned his attention to the chapel just as one of the doors was pulled back.

" Oh, Senhorita Joana!" He made a move toward her.

"Stay!" She held the musket menacingly. Joana Cavalcanti was dressed in a plain black cotton gown and men's boots, and a pistol was thrust into a dark sash around her waist.

Again he identified himself, and added: "Five years ago I went into the sertão with Segge Proot . . ."

She stood ten feet from him, her brow furrowed, her lips pursed.

"Have I changed that much, senhorita?"

"The mameluco from São Paulo . . . Amador Flôres," she said, almost to herself, "Mother of mercy, it's you."

"Yes, Senhorita Joana, Amador Flôres, returned from . . ." He could not find words to describe it all. "Returned," he added simply. Joana stared at him silently.

"Where's the senhor?" Amador asked.

"He's gone away for a time," she replied evasively.

"Your brothers — Alvaro and Felipe?"

"Felipe is with his father. The Dutch killed Alvaro. He was ambushed with seven others."

Amador offered his condolences and then told her that the heretic Segge Proot was dead. Joana frowned and lowered her eyes at the news but said nothing, and Amador did not elaborate beyond relating that Proot had fallen in with a river pirate and his savage levies, who'd launched a hopeless raid against a force of Christians.

That evening Amador sat at the long table in the big house, and remembered how once he'd stood outside with the dogs and slaves of Fernão Cavalcanti. Joana sat opposite Amador, next to the bibulous Gregório Bonifácio. Here, too, were Dona Domitila, Beatriz — pregnant with the child of a husband Senhor Fernão had found for her — the wives of Fernão's sons, Alvaro and Felipe, and two aunts.

Sitting to the right of Amador was one other male: Jorge Cavalcanti, the elder brother of Senhor Fernão. Tomás Cavalcanti's son Lourenco had had three sons — Jorge, Fernão, and Francisco — and the same number of daughters. Francisco had died before Amador's first sojourn, a victim of the measles; Jorge had been away in Europe in 1640. He was now fifty-eight, three years Fernão's senior, with the same medium build, narrow, aristocratic face, and green eyes. But he looked much older than his age and was overbearingly pompous. Jorge had been twice widowed. Now he was married again — to Joana Cavalcanti.

Amador had been openly shocked when the senhorita introduced him to her husband. Jorge, in the lavish attire of a Spanish grandee, beribboned and hung with lace, had peered down his long nose at Amador, showing displeasure at Joana's announcement that the mameluco was an acquaintance of hers.

It was not the consanguineous union of uncle and niece that troubled Amador — such marriages were rarer than those between first cousins but not unheard of, given a chronic shortage of good Christian women in Brazil — but the thought of vibrant, lovely Joana wedded to this fop, whose style in clothing bespoke his political sentiments. While acknowledging the right of the Braganças in Lisbon, Jorge Cavalcanti expressed a longing for Madrid, where he had spent a decade as adviser to the court of Philip IV.

During dinner — a frugal meal by comparison with the last banquet Amador had witnessed here — Amador started to tell the Cavalcantis about his journey. They listened for a while, but were confused and disbelieving of the extent of his wanderings, and he was moved to give up his narrative. Instead, he himself listened attentively as Jorge Cavalcanti and Padre Bonifácio spoke of events in Pernambuco. Amador realized that only when they had assured themselves he was not here as an agent of the Dutch were they prepared to tell him what had happened to Fernão Cavalcanti.

Fernão had maintained friendly relations with Johan Maurits to the very day the count departed Brazil, and was one of many Portuguese who gathered to bid farewell to the governor.

A month after Count Maurits's departure in May 1644, a curse had descended upon the valley of Santo Tomás. The engenho lay in one of six administrative districts created by the Hollanders in Pernambuco. A soldier whose contract with the Dutch West India Company had expired was appointed district bailiff — Captain Jan Vlok, the man responsible for the massacre of Amador's comrades five years ago. Vlok and the ruffians who served him terrorized the Portuguese under their jurisdiction. They demanded bribes to ensure the safe passage of sugar chests to Recife; they encouraged slaves to run away, then caught them and sold them in other parts of the colony; they seized livestock and raided the sugarhouses of planters unable to meet summonses for debt. Complaints to the High Council at Recife by Fernão Cavalcanti and others went unheeded, for Jan Vlok had bought support there with a share of his loot. Six months ago, Fernão Cavalcanti had contacted other aggrieved planters.

Many of them had served together on Johan Maurits's councils; now they plotted to destroy what the count had built in Pernambuco. Their task seemed impossible. The Dutch garrison had been cut by two-thirds, but earlier years of hopeless resistance made most planters reluctant to take the field again. The recapture of São Luis do Maranhão had been exceptional, they argued — a small contingent of Hollanders beleaguered by every settler in Maranhão and weeks away from Recife. Even if all Pernambucans could be rallied, what use such insurrection without arms? After the abortive expedition of the conde da Torre five years ago, the engenhos' weapons had been confiscated, all but a few muskets licensed for personal protection. And in whose name would this rebellion be launched? Secret emissaries from Lisbon had emphasized the king's desire for peace with the Dutch. Spain, not the Netherlands, was João IV's enemy, the emissaries said. If the planters of Pernambuco rose, they would do so on their own.

João Fernandes Vieira, the son of a mulatta prostitute and a Portuguese, was a ringleader of the planned uprising. He had fought the Dutch in the first guerrilla war fifteen years ago; during the rule of Count Maurits, he had laid down his arms and prospered, coming to own five engenhos and serving as a town councilor at Mauritsstad, a hunter of runaway slaves, and captain of a Dutch militia corps. But he owed his benefactors more than 300,000 florins, making him one of the biggest debtors in the colony; when Maurits left, João Fernandes decided to rid himself of this crippling financial burden. Still, his primary motive was the holy restoration of the land.

Toward the end of 1644, messengers from João Fernandes approached a new governor-general at the Bahia, Antônio Telles da Silva. Publicly, Antônio Telles said that an insurrection in Pernambuco was unthinkable: Any colonist of his who contributed to such disorder would be prosecuted; and henceforth the Bahia authorities would return to Pernambuco any planter fleeing New Holland to escape his debts to the Dutch.

Privately, Antônio Telles sent word to João Fernandes Vieira: "Your password is 'sugar' — a call for the sweet victory we'll have!" And in a secret communiqué, he said: "I have dispatched word by sea to the Hollanders at Recife that Henrique Dias, the black devil, is a fugitive heading through the sertão toward Pernambuco. I have sent the regiment of Dom Felipe Camarão in pursuit."

Henrique Dias and Camarão, who had been knighted for his previous services to Pernambuco, had led the black and native volunteers in the first guerrilla war. This ruse to send them racing to the side of men like João Fernandes and Fernão Cavalcanti had been as inspiring to the conspirators as other assurances by Antônio Telles: He planned to dispatch a corps of forty veteran officers and soldiers overland to train the colonists; to send others by sea to reach Pernambuco as soon as an insurrection was under way.

Encouraged by this support, João Fernandes Viera and his fellow patriots had planned an uprising for Midsummer Day, June 24, 1645. But the first convoy of arms from the Bahia had been ambushed after crossing the Rio São Francisco: Fernão's son Alvaro had died in this clash.

Then, four days before Amador's arrival, on May 30, another disaster: An informer in Recife sent word to João Fernandes, the Cavalcantis, and their confidants that the High Council had been told of the rebellion planned for June 24, in an anonymous letter sent by three planters who'd signed themselves "The Truth."

And now, after these events had been related to Amador at the dinner table, Jorge Cavalcanti decried this treacherous correspondence but evinced no faith in the conspiracy. "Their cause is hopeless," he said. "They think they see the power of the Hollanders reduced here. But I, Jorge Cavalcanti, have seen the strength of this enemy in Europe. Even Spain with all her might could not suppress these heretics. And where is the ocean their admirals do not rule? Go to the river Tagus at Lisbon and see the hulks rotting there; then come and tell me how Portugal can supply men and munitions to sustain an insurrection in this colony."

Amador looked across at Joana Cavalcanti. "Where's the senhor?" Amador again asked her.

Jorge Cavalcanti responded: "*Fugitivo!*" He shook his head despairingly. "A noble senhor de engenho and his son hiding in the forest with slaves. I pleaded with my brother. There is a proper time for such action, I advised him."

Amador laughed loudly. "Yes, yes, Senhor Cavalcanti."

"You think my advice amusing?"

"Sixty years, senhor — for sixty years Portugal endured the Spanish captivity. Do you propose the same delay for these patriots?"

"Have you not seen the engenho?" Padre Bonifácio muttered. "Everything Cavalcanti men have worked for . . . everything threatened with ruin . . . every peça gone."

"Where are the slaves, Padre?"

Joana said, "Some slaves ran away. Thirty remain with my father. Most were removed from the engenho."

"By whom?"

"Jan Vlok. Eighty peças were seized to be sold for the interest on my father's debt. He borrowed money from Holland to build a new mill at the river. The interest — three percent a month."

"And to think it was the *Spaniard* we considered possessed by greed." Amador noticed Jorge Cavalcanti's acute displeasure at this remark, and paused for a moment. Then he asked, "What will Senhor Fernão do?"

"What *can* he do?" Jorge Cavalcanti responded. "The Dutch are offering two thousand florins for his capture; more for João Fernandes. Perhaps they'll flee across the São Francisco to the Bahia."

"*No!*"

Jorge Cavalcanti's eyes shifted nervously to Joana.

"My father promised he will not leave without us."

"Perhaps he'll have no choice," Jorge replied.

Why, Amador wondered, had the senhorita been given in marriage to this despicable man?

"Fernão Cavalcanti will never abandon Santo Tomás. He will *not* run away," Joana said.

Soon afterward, Amador was shown to a room along a passage that led from the main reception area; but he found he was unable to sleep. Two hours of restlessness and Amador arose and padded down the passage toward the front door. He was crossing the main reception area when he suddenly stopped: Joana Cavalcanti was sitting at the table in the dining room. He stepped silently toward her.

"Amador?"

"Yes, senhora Joana."

Joana was staring at the far wall, which remained darkly shadowed. "A fine painting, isn't it, Amador?"

"He stopped painting," Amador said. "The savages broke his spirit."

Joana Cavalcanti turned to him. "Please, Amador Flôres, tell me — everything."

"*Now*, senhora?"

"Now, Amador. Tell me what happened to you," she said, and in a whisper, "and to Secundus. Sit here, next to me. Talk."

It was difficult. Joana sat with her head lowered, her hands in her lap, waiting for his story. He began to speak slowly, omitting little from the time they left the engenho until they reached the Rio das Amazonas.

"Oh, Secundus . . . Secundus." She whispered the name. "He didn't understand, Amador."

"No, senhora, he didn't. Proot never should have gone to the sertão," he added. "It's not a place for painters."

"But that's what my father wanted, wasn't it, Amador?"

"I don't understand, senhora."

"You do, Amador," she said. "Fernão Cavalcanti ordered you to take him away from me."

"But, senhora —"

"It's true, Amador. Would Padre Gregório lie to me?"

"The padre?"

"He told me all he overheard when my father summoned you to the padre's quarters. The padre was in the chapel beyond the door."

"I was to take Segge only to the Tapuya of Jakob Rabbe. Segge himself wanted to go there to paint the savages. I swear it. To go farther was Proot's decision — *our* decision, senhora."

"I loved him deeply, Amador. Three years ago, when you hadn't returned, already I knew Secundus was gone forever."

"Senhor Jorge . . ." He stopped, not knowing what it was he wanted to ask or say.

"It wasn't your fault. You obeyed my father." She pushed her chair back and started to get up. "I'm going to bed. What will you do?"

"Me, senhora?" he asked uncertainly.

"You came to my father for a reward."

He also stood up. He bowed his head in shame. "Why did Bonifácio tell you all this?"

"He lay filled with cachaça."

"I'm sorry."

She stepped close to him. "Not as sorry as Fernão Cavalcanti — when I gave myself to that miserable pig upstairs. He hates him, Amador. But how could he refuse? His brother come back from Madrid to claim his portion of this estate — Jorge Cavalcanti, whose name was never mentioned in this house after he'd gone to serve the king of Spain." In a quiet voice she concluded, "The senhor had Masses said for your soul, Amador Flôres. For my Secundus, whom he sent away . . . for him, my father prays every day."

❦

"*This* is the army of patriots?"

"Oh, yes, Tenente Paulista, here is our governor of liberty, João Fernandes Vieira, with Senhor Fernão and all who stand with them."

"Then Jorge Cavalcanti is correct and the task is hopeless," Amador said.

Affonso Ribeiro, the bawdy, boastful tenant who had befriended Amador during his first stay at Engenho Santo Tomás, shook his head. "Oh, no, Tenente Paulista, this time we will defeat the Dutch."

A day's hard travel west of the engenho had brought them to the hiding place of those forced to flee when the conspiracy had been betrayed to the High Council at Recife. Ribeiro had been sent to the engenho with a message that the women were to remain there until Fernão Cavalcanti could arrange safe passage to the Bahia. Amador had marched back into the woods with him.

The rebel camp was on the top of a sparsely wooded hill on the Borborema plateau. Here and there, a strip of canvas spread between the branches of trees provided shelter for some of the governor of liberty's men, but most sat in the open.

There were twenty Portuguese, twice that many mamelucos and mulattos, fifteen natives, and one hundred slaves who were clearly enjoying this relief from daily servitude. A third of the men were armed with rusty muskets retrieved from caches at João Fernandes's engenhos; most had primitive bows and arrows and clubs.

Amador would have approached Cavalcanti quietly, but Affonso Ribeiro sped toward one of the canvas shelters: "Senhor Fernão! Oh, senhor, a miracle! The Paulista da Silva — he's come back!"

Cavalcanti stepped into the sunlight, his eyes narrowing against the glare. "Amador da Silva?"

"Yes, yes, senhor," said Ribeiro. "Returned from the dead."

"Senhor Fernão," Amador greeted Cavalcanti, who was studying da Silva's lined face with the same puzzlement Joana had shown.

Cavalcanti was slimmer, his hair grayer. "Dear God in heaven," he mouthed, just above a whisper. "We gave you up for dead three years ago . . . How is it possible?"

"A great mercy, senhor — all the providence of our Protector."

Cavalcanti lowered his voice: "The Hollander . . ."

"Dead, senhor. Killed at the Rio das Amazonas."

"Tell the senhor of the battle with the heretics and savages!" Ribeiro interjected. Amador had described to Ribeiro the engagement at Death-Bird Island.

But Amador was silent.

Cavalcanti shook his head in disbelief. "You survived! You came back. You must tell me all Amador Flôres."

A man who'd been watching them from the canvas shelter started toward them. Ruggedly built, he wore cotton breeches and leather jerkin similar to Fernão Cavalcanti's plain dress. His thin, upturned mustache and narrow, pointed beard were carefully groomed.

"João Fernandes Vieira, our governador," Cavalcanti announced. He introduced Amador and explained their relationship.

João Fernandes listened quietly. When Cavalcanti finished speaking, he asked, "What brings you to our camp, Amador Flôres?"

"Senhor Fernão has told you how the heretics massacred my comrades five years ago. Let me fight with you, Governador. I've been away from São Paulo so long, a few months will make no difference."

"A few months?" With a sweep of his hand, João Fernandes indicated the men near them. "We won't conquer the Hollanders in a few months."

"All Pernambuco will rise."

"I pray to God that they do," João Fernandes said. "Without support, I command no army but a bandit group in these backlands." He nodded. "You're welcome, Paulista." Then he walked away to a group of Portuguese, part of a contingent of forty soldiers and officers sent from the Bahia to train the rebels.

When Affonso Ribeiro had reported on his trip to the engenho, he left the two men alone together.

"How did Proot die?" Cavalcanti asked.

"There was a battle in which he took the side of the savages."

"What does it matter?" Cavalcanti said, to himself. "I'm responsible . . . But how could I permit the marriage of my daughter and a heretic?"

"You had no choice, senhor."

"Then, why — *why*, Amador Flôres — have I lost Joana's love and respect? Why did the Lord send Jorge Cavalcanti back to Engenho Santo Tomás?"

Amador couldn't bear the look of pain in Cavalcanti's eyes and glanced away. "These are questions I can't answer, senhor."

ぐ

On June 13, 1645, João Fernandes Viera ordered his men to break camp. Most of the 180 insurgents were to penetrate the valleys behind Recife to begin a campaign of terror against the Dutch, but Fernão Cavalcanti, Amador, Affonso Ribeiro, and seven others were being sent on a secret mission in the south of the captaincy.

"I'd go myself," João Fernandes said, "but I must organize the men in the field so that we're ready when Dias and Camarão arrive." For four weeks now, three hundred men with Henrique Dias and the pursuing force of Dom Felipe Camarão had been advancing through the sertão north of the Bahia; these corps were expected to join the governador's contingent in a fortnight, a rendezvous that would signal a full-scale rebellion.

Amador was present when João Fernandes discussed Fernão Cavalcanti's mission to the south.

"They've proved themselves in battle with the Hollanders," João Fernandes said. "Offer them freedom; promise anything that will get them to fight the Dutch with us."

The governador was referring to runaway black slaves who were in hiding at a place the Portuguese knew as Palmares, 140 miles southwest of Recife in the foothills of the Serra do Barriga. The first blacks had fled to the area fifteen years ago; the Hollanders had sent several expeditions to destroy the slave stronghold, and all of them had failed.

Two of João Fernandes's own slaves, who knew blacks living at Palmares, were to march with Cavalcanti and approach the runaways for a safe conduct for the rest of the party.

"A safe conduct?" Amador had queried. "To a hideout of fugitive peças? Surely, Governador, we need no more than the formality of a loaded musket?"

"No one enters the lands of Ganga Zumba without permission," João Fernandes said. "The name means 'Lord of the Devil.' I led a Dutch patrol to Palmares two years ago. A full army and we may have had a chance." He looked at Fernão Cavalcanti. "Convince Ganga Zumba to join us and we'll sweep the Hollanders into the sea, not within months but in weeks."

ぐ

Ten days later, on an unusually bright, sunny morning in late June, Nhungaza, a tall, stately African in a white cotton robe, stood beside a beaten clay area used for ceremonies and dances of his village. Greatly admired by his fellows, Nhungaza was a visitor this day, for he now lived at the capital of the kingdom where he commanded the Royal Regiment.

Nhungaza also was greatly feared. As representative of lord of the kingdom, the captain of the royal regiment was empowered to punish anyone who displeased him. The previous day Nhungaza had ordered the execution of two villagers for defying a decree against leaving the kingdom.

This morning Nhungaza was attending the ceremonial ground for a happier occasion. He was here to select men who would be taken to join the royal regiment. The candidates were to be presented to Nhungaza in pairs, and he would call on them to demonstrate their ability in mock combat.

At a signal from the first two warrior candidates, a group of musicians set up a rhythm with berimbau, bowlike stringed instruments with resonant half-gourds at the lower end. Wielding short sticks, the contestants leapt toward each other, seeking to gain points by the ingenuity with which they avoided the opponent's blows and kicks. This ritual was performed with cartwheels, somersaults, and lightning-quick evasive tactics.

As the sparring intensified, the rhythm of the berimbau increased, and so, too, the excitement of the spectators. Almost all 280 people of the village were present. The headman and his elders had cotton robes similar to Nhungaza's; other men wore loinskins of monkey fur. The women had cloth skirts; boys and girls, aprons of bark cloth. Both sexes of all ages wore necklaces with small pouches of charms, copper bracelets, beads, armbands of fur or shells.

One of fourteen smaller settlements of the kingdom and its northeastern border outpost, the village was a day's march from the capital, which was called Shoko — "Monkey," in the language of its founders, a name celebrating the Shoko clan of the ruling dynasty. Nhungaza's village had much in common with Shoko. Each family occupied a dome-shaped hut of thin branches thatched with long grass. There was a hut for young girls, whose activities were strictly controlled by their parents and who had special duties in the village: carriers of water, collectors of kindling for cooking fires, harvesters of wild fruits. Boys of marriageable age also lived away from home, in bachelors' quarters.

An area was set aside for potters and weavers, and there were huts for artisans who carved in wood and made articles from bark string and vines. The two village blacksmiths, whose clay furnace stood near a low stonewalled meeting place, enjoyed the most prestige. The furnace and men's enclosure were mostly off-limits to women; only those past childbearing age could witness the smelting of iron, and women required the headman's permission to attend the meeting place.

There were two village witch doctors, a man who practiced divination and a female herbalist, who occupied huts beyond the clay furnace.

Nhungaza had been at the village for three days. His first exchange with the headman, after their greetings, had been heated. Nhungaza ordered the man to accompany him to the edge of the settlement, where, with the iron staff of office of the captain of the royal regiment, he pointed to a section of the village stockade.

"Is this how you protect your people?" Nhungaza had demanded.

The headman stood speechless as he stared at a gaping hole in the pole-and-thorn barrier.

Nhungaza prodded the headman's chest with his staff. "Perhaps, old man, you must march back with us to Shoko. We will find work for you in the fields with the slaves."

"*Hau*, Nhungaza! Please! The wall will be repaired!"

Nhungaza said quietly, "Old Father, I am a son of your village. I have no wish to see you disgraced at the capital. *This* is not the earth of our ancestors. Here we are without protection from the old chiefs. A broken stockade . . ."

At mention of the ancestors, the headman's countenance brightened. "We have a gift for Nganga Dzimba we Bahwe," he said.

"What is it?" the captain of the royal regiment asked. "Nganga Dzimba we Bahwe" ("High Priest at the Place of Stones") was one of the titles of lord of the kingdom.

"Come, my son," the headman said. "Let me show you."

The headman led his visitor to a hut where the village's musical instruments were stored — the berimbau, rattles, whistles, and three sacred drums.

"Here is the gift of our village," said the headman. He stood back to await Nhungaza's reaction.

A large black bird with bright yellow plumage on its cheeks and throat was confined in a wooden cage. Its most distinctive feature was a huge bill, which curved downward and was nine inches long and three inches high at the base.

Nhungaza examined the bird closely. "Who trapped it?"

The headman gave the names of two men.

"Nganga Dzimba we Bahwe will be pleased," Nhungaza said.

"And our village will be protected?"

Nhungaza had straightened up. "Not if your stockade is broken."

The headman showed renewed alarm at this admonition by the captain of the royal regiment, who was standing with him in the sacred hut, not in Africa as the village and customs of its people suggested but one hundred forty miles southwest of Recife.

❧

When Nganga Dzimba we Bahwe was nineteen, a Franciscan had baptized him with the name João. This ceremony at the port of Loanda on the west coast of Africa was followed by a secondary observance: A branding iron pressed against João's right breast seared a small crown into the flesh. This mark was proof of the anointing of João and the payment of taxes due to the royal coffers for the export of this peça to Brazil. In the lands of his people, the Karanga, a nation of southeast Africa, João had been known as Nayamunyaka, the son of the high priest, the Nganga, at Dzimba we Bahwe — Zimbabwe in the kingdom of the Mwene-Mutapa.

After a thirty-five-day voyage to Pernambuco, João arrived at Olinda's slave market, where he received a second name, recorded in the register of transactions: "10 May 1620, João Angola, sold by Heitor dos Santos to José Borges de Menezes of Engenho Formosa, fifty-five milreis."

For ten years João Angola served his master, Menezes, but when the Dutch invaded Pernambuco in 1630, João and forty slaves from Engenho Formosa ran into the sertão. As a fugitive, João Angola received another set of names from the Portuguese, a corruption of "Nganga Dzimba we Bahwe": "Ganga Zumba."

By 1645, Ganga Zumba had achieved notoriety, for in the fifteen years since his flight, he had evaded recapture by Dutch or Portuguese in the sertão of the Serra do Barriga.

Nhungaza was with João Angola and João's mother when they were caught by slavers at the Zambesi River, ten days' march from the east coast of Africa. Nhungaza had also been sold to the owner of Engenho Formosa and had shared João Angola's experiences in the sertão.

Not only had Ganga Zumba remained free these past fifteen years; he had attracted fourteen thousand runaway slaves to his refuge. His capital, Shoko, was home to six thousand people, their huts lying along three avenues, each of which was a mile long. Three hours' walk from Shoko was a second city, with five thousand inhabitants, 'Ngola Jango ("Little Angola"). The royal enclosure of lord of the kingdom, his family, and councilors was equidistant from Shoko and 'Ngola Jango and lay in the foothills of the Serra do Barriga. Three miles from the cities, it was known as Place of Stones. At the time of their capture in 1619, only a few hundred slaves had been shipped from Mozambique Island and Sofala to Brazil. The majority of 250,000 slaves transported to the captaincies by the first quarter of the seventeenth century had come from the kingdom of the Kongo, Angola, and the Guinea coast. Their unique background helped João Angola and Nhungaza to remain aloof from the petty rivalries among 'Ngola, Kongo, Jaga, and other Bantu-speaking slaves.

At Pernambuco, Nhungaza was a regular visitor to the royal enclosure behind the cities of Shoko and 'Ngola Jango. When Nayamunyaka took him on a circuit of a high earth embankment thrown up around the royal huts and pointed agitatedly to piles of rough-hewn stone brought from the hills beyond, Nhungaza was sympathetic. He knew that Nayamunyaka envisaged walls and towers such as existed at Great Zimbabwe, but that ten years of sporadic effort had produced no more than forty feet of loose foundation. Still, the site was called Dzimba we Bahwe ("Place of Stones").

Within the earth embankment, Nayamunyaka had had more success in creating a court similar to what both men had known among the Karanga. Here the royal huts stood on raised platforms; they had well-packed clay floors, solid daub walls, and thatched roofs. Nayamunyaka and his three wives occupied four huts; another hut stood sixty feet from these and was the home of Great Mother.

Just beyond the royal enclosure was a stockade with the huts of the officials of the kingdom: captain of the household guard, keeper of the royal relics, chief diviner, master of ceremonies, drummer of the king.

When Nayamunyaka first stood among the boulders on the hill in Pernambuco, he saw a group of toucans in the trees below the rocks. They had immense bills similar to those of the sacred hornbills at Great Zimbabwe, and their presence had stirred a tremendous hope in Nayamunyaka. He decreed that anyone harming a toucan would be put to death.

℀

The two contestants now wheeling and dancing toward each other at Nhungaza's village were the same young men who had trapped the bird as a gift for the Nganga. After observing them for fifteen minutes, the captain raised his iron staff and brought it down sharply. The rhythms of the berimbau died away. The two men stopped their sparring and turned to face Nhungaza, their ebony skin glistening with sweat, their chests heaving.

Nhungaza stepped up to one and touched his shoulder with the staff. The young man smiled broadly at this sign of acceptance as candidate for the royal regiment. His opponent bowed his head with disappointment, but then Nhungaza moved over to him and touched his shoulder. The villagers cheered this rare selection of both candidates.

This excitement was short-lived. Nhungaza was standing opposite the second candidate when two men burst through the entrance to the stockade and ran toward the ceremonial ground.

"Portuguese!" they shouted. "Three! Others . . . one hour's march from the village!"

A panicky outcry rose from the crowd. Nhungaza shook his staff of office. "Silence!" he ordered. He turned to the warriors who'd come with the alarm. "How many march with them?"

"Seven," one man said.

"No more?"

The man shook his head.

Nhungaza spoke loudly for all to hear: "These Portuguese have been given permission to pass through our lands to see Nganga Dzimba we Bahwe."

"For what purpose?" the headman asked.

"They come to seek our help."

The headman slapped his thigh with merriment. "Is it not a memorable day when Portuguese come to us for help?"

c/o

As Nhungaza, captain of the royal regiment, led Amador and Fernão Cavalcanti along a main thoroughfare of Shoko, he kept turning to glance at the two men, curious at their reaction to the capital.

Fernão Cavalcanti's astonishment grew as they advanced down a mile-long street of grass huts; a few times, he expressed dismay at the extent of the fugitive stronghold, potentially as threatening to Pernambuco as the Dutch occupation.

Amador spoke breathlessly: "I didn't believe the governador. A hundred, perhaps two hundred peças, I thought. I never expected a city with *thousands*. Senhor Fernão, how in heaven's name was this allowed?"

"The Hollanders were occupied with destroying Portuguese engenhos and ignored the peril. They encouraged peças to desert the plantations and promised them their freedom if they took up arms against us. Most ran away to join others in these hills. Ganga Zumba rules them all. Planters have sent militia to capture runaways. When the Dutch finally woke to the danger, they dispatched squadrons. But not one peça has been taken from these lands."

Amador observed that many half-breeds and natives had joined the nation of fugitives. Yet Nhungaza had told them that a few miles distant was another city occupied by men from 'Ngola and led by one of their tribe, who was married to a daughter of Ganga Zumba.

Halfway along the thoroughfare, the party reached a plaza where a daily market was in progress. Food vendors offered a great variety of fresh produce, wild fruits and herbs, cakes of maize and manioc, sweetmeats and other edibles. There was a fish market, the catch coming from a lake close by the capital. Beyond the food vendors, other traders displayed their wares on grass mats: beads, shells, basketware, pottery, expertly forged farm implements.

Fernão Cavalcanti looked at five blacks squatting on the ground. "Why are they tied up?" he asked Nhungaza.

"They wait to be sold," Nhungaza said, in good Portuguese.

"Sold? But aren't these men runaways from the engenhos?"

Nhungaza shook his head. "They were captured by a force from Shoko. They're slaves."

"They're slaves who deserted their owners," Cavalcanti persisted.

"I told you, senhor, they were seized by my warriors."

"*Where?*"

Nhungaza ignored the question. "Nganga Dzimba we Bahwe has decreed that men forcibly seized by us are to remain slaves to work in the royal plantations."

A look of incredulity came to Cavalcanti's face.

"Most slaves we take remain with us, senhor. They have a better life than what they knew at the engenhos."

"It makes no sense, this trade by peças."

"We kept slaves in Africa," Nhungaza said. "The Nganga makes a distinction between these captives and slaves who voluntarily flee their engenhos. All runaways are free men when they reach our lands. There is one prohibition: A man who becomes the subject of the Nganga may never return to the Portuguese. If a deserter is caught, he is put to death."

Amador gestured at the five prisoners. "If these peças attempt to run away, will they be killed?"

"Why should we punish a man who seeks the freedom we have?"

Nhungaza led Amador and Cavalcanti to a compound with several huts behind a wall of reeds.

"You will stay here until the Nganga calls for you," he announced.

"And when may that be?" Fernão Cavalcanti asked irritably.

"When the Nganga is ready."

"Our mission is urgent."

"So, Senhor Cavalcanti, was the visit of men who came three weeks ago."

"Who?"

"The Hollanders, Blaer and Vlok. They wanted the help of my royal regiment."

"Did you offer it?"

"Would you be here if I had?"

Cavalcanti flushed with anger but said nothing.

The fourth morning after their arrival, Nhungaza sent a messenger to tell Amador and Cavalcanti to ready themselves for an audience with Nganga Dzimba we Bahwe.

"Prepare myself?" Fernão Cavalcanti said. "For a peça?" But, remembering João Fernandes's insistence on an alliance with Ganga Zumba, he dressed in a costly doublet with paned sleeves, clean breeches and silk stockings, a long gray cloak draped over his right arm, and a broad-brimmed hat with white feathers.

When Nhungaza and six warriors arrived to escort them to the royal enclosure, Amador and Affonso Ribeiro stood ready with their muskets. "You cannot take weapons into the royal enclosure," Nhungaza told them.

"Your escort is armed," Cavalcanti protested.

"Visitors do not appear before the Nganga bearing weapons," Nhungaza repeated.

Cavalcanti looked at Amador, who said, "The governador sent us to appeal to this king. We have no choice, senhor."

With Nhungaza walking up front, they came to a stockade a mile from the royal enclosure. Nhungaza halted the escort. "Let me show you the soldiers of our kingdom," he said to the visitors.

Beyond the entrance to the stockade were rows of small domed huts similar to those at Shoko and built in three great circles around a central parade ground — fifty huts to a row, six men to a hut, almost one thousand warriors.

At Nhungaza's approach, some men went down on their knees, some stood rigidly with bowed heads.

"First we teach obedience," Nhungaza said, as he signaled a group of young men to rise from their knees. "Obedience to the Nganga, to the royal household — to me."

"And if they disobey?"

"Death, senhor."

"They chose this regimen above life at our engenhos?"

"They live as we did in the lands of our fathers. Few disobey." Nhungaza turned away from them and spoke with one of his warriors.

"What will become of this kingdom if they continue to thrive here?" Amador asked Cavalcanti.

"These are peças. Where peças do not listen to reason, there are ways of persuading them."

Nhungaza rejoined them. "I wanted you to see my regiments. When Nganga Dzimba we Bahwe speaks, you will know that he has the power to enforce his words."

ოჴ

Fernão Cavalcanti sat uncomfortably on a grass mat, with Amador and Affonso Ribeiro behind him. To their left were court officials, including chief diviner, chief magistrate, and captain of the household guard; to the right, the drummer of the king stood behind three sacred instruments. A group of headmen from five outlying villages sat beyond the drummer, their loincloths and simple adornments reflecting their lower status. The court officials were richly dressed in colorful robes; two wore doublets and breeches and feathered hats. Standing farther back were the guards, who had adopted bright feather diadems similar to those of the natives of

Brazil. The guards had bands of light monkey fur around their upper arms and ankles. Nhungaza was on his knees, in front of the trio he had brought to the Nganga, who had yet to step out of his hut.

The three men had grumbled when Nhungaza told them that they were not to stand or speak in the presence of the Nganga unless ordered to do so. They would not have to "touch the earth," but were warned that an insult or displeasing word or deed before the high priest and lord of the kingdom would bring immediate expulsion from the enclosure.

The Nganga's hut was on a raised platform of stone and clay, fifty yards in front of the visitors. It was much larger than the habitations at Shoko, one hundred feet in circumference, with smooth circular clay wall and conical thatched roof. Three smaller huts of similar design stood close by, the abodes of the Nganga's wives, Nhungaza said, and off to the right, a lone hut where Great Mother lived.

Soon after they were seated, Great Mother emerged from her residence in a gaudy gown of mauve and green. All within the enclosure bent their backs and pressed their noses to the dirt as the Nganga's mother was led to a low chair outside the hut. Two virgins attended Great Mother, one holding a plaited grass parasol to shield her from the sun, the other fanning the venerable woman with a wild-banana leaf.

Then the Nganga Dzimba we Bahwe came out of his hut.

Again the Nganga's subjects touched the earth with their noses, then raised themselves and began to rub their palms together. The chief drummer beat the drums slowly. The Nganga moved forward on jaguar skins thrown over the ground from the entrance of his hut down three steps from the raised platform toward a high-backed chair twenty feet away from Cavalcanti and the others.

The Nganga was small, almost frail, with a narrow face and tiny eyes. He wore the simplest cotton robe, the same as Nhungaza's. He had a low crown of yellow and black feathers that had been shed by the toucans at his hill of worship. An inch-wide collar of beaten brass and a long iron staff were his symbols of kingship.

He stopped and smiled at the group of visiting headmen. Everyone in the enclosure smiled. He continued toward his chair and sat down. The drums fell quiet. The court stopped rubbing their palms, resumed their sitting positions, and waited for the day's business to begin.

Nhungaza rose to his feet to describe the arrival of the Portuguese and the purpose of their mission. The Nganga already knew the information Nhungaza was offering him; this formal introduction was for the benefit of the royal court. When Nhungaza completed his address, the Nganga spoke with him in Karanga; then Nhungaza turned to Cavalcanti:

"The Nganga wishes to hear from you," he said. "You may stand to speak with him — in Portuguese."

Fernão Cavalcanti got to his feet. Momentarily, he did not know what to say.

The Nganga smiled faintly. "It is difficult, is it not, for a senhor de engenho — lord of a great valley of Pernambuco — to stand before João Angola?"

Cavalcanti frowned.

"My master called me this — 'João Angola, the peça.' I am Nayamunyaka! Nayamunyaka of the royal house of the Mwene-Mutapa, 'The Great Pillager,' whom the Portuguese know as 'Monomotapa.'"

These acclamations made the Nganga's subjects rub their palms vigorously; the visiting headmen increased their adulation by pressing their noses to the dirt.

The Nganga tapped his staff to signal an end to the praise-giving.

"Let us hear, Senhor Cavalcanti, of your mission to us."

"You are a nephew of the great Monomotapa? One of his royal household?"

"All this, senhor, until one night when I was stolen from the land of my ancestors." He gestured with his staff toward the chief magistrate. "This man is from the kingdom of the ManiKongo, the great grandson of a prince the Portuguese honored with the title 'Duke of Nsundi.'" He pointed to another official. "This councilor was a chief of the 'Ngola. . . . But, senhor, of what concern is our past to one who buys peças as he would buy an ox?"

"We buy a peça's labor, not his flesh . . . not his body or his soul."

Nayamunyaka leaned forward. "You have come to us peças to ask for our help."

"We march for the cause of true liberty in Pernambuco," Cavalcanti said. "I have been told that you sent Blaer and Vlok away. God be praised, Ganga Zumba, for the wisdom given you in refusing the heretics. I have seen your regiments: Bring them to battle with us and we will have a glorious conquest."

"And when the war is over and the Hollanders have been defeated, who will help us when the senhores de engenhos demand their peças?"

"Our Governador João Fernandes promises the freedom of every man who fights for us."

"But the war will end, senhor, and the fields of cane will lie untended. Who will work those lands?"

"There will be other peças."

"Stolen from their lands and carried across the sea to Brazil?"

Cavalcanti looked at him sourly. "I have seen the slaves you keep here."

"We treat them as family. We do not whip them; we do not shackle them." He stroked the brass ring he wore around his neck. "We do not choke them with iron collars."

Cavalcanti admitted that there had been abuses. "March with us and you will be heroes. When the war is over, we will appeal to Dom João on your behalf to grant you these fields and plantations as free subjects."

"I, the Nganga, need no land grant from Dom João! You can talk for hours, Senhor Cavalcanti, and we will listen, but already my councilors and I have decided."

"You have?"

"We will not fight for the Hollanders."

Cavalcanti looked at him keenly. "Yes."

"And we will not fight for the Portuguese."

"You must! You *must* help us!"

"We are not *peças* who *must* obey the senhor de engenho."

"Refuse us today, Ganga Zumba, and you condemn every person here!"

Nhungaza stepped toward Cavalcanti, but Nayamunyaka ordered him to halt. "Leave now, senhor," he said to Cavalcanti, "before you anger my people."

"As God is my witness, you will come to regret this!" Nayamunyaka shook his head. "Seven years, senhor — "

"For what?" Cavalcanti interrupted.

"Seven years is how long a peça can expect to live when he comes to Pernambuco. Seven years, and most die from hard labor, from sickness . . . some because they are sad." He stood up. "We have lived for fifteen years in these hills — two lives for a peça. It would be madness, Senhor Cavalcanti, to march back to lands where we would long ago have been dead."

Then Nganga Dzimba we Bahwe turned away; holding his small shoulders stiffly, his back straight, he began to walk to the hut of Great Mother.

"Leave the enclosure!" Nhungaza ordered.

Amador and Ribeiro followed Cavalcanti as he started toward the opening in the earth embankment.

"There is one thing to thank God for."

"Senhor?"

"Blaer and Vlok failed to enlist them."

&

It was near the end of July 1645, seven weeks since João Fernandes Vieira had left his hideout in the woods. Rebels had killed some Hollanders at engenhos and outposts in valleys behind Recife, and one squad reported the bludgeoning of three Jews, but nothing suggested the start of a victorious advance. And worse, from the north came reports that Jakob Rabbe and his Tapuya had massacred dozens of Christians.

João Fernandes's headquarters had been established on a hill thirty miles west of Recife, the slopes and surrounding lands overgrown with a tangle of thorny reeds — *tabocas*, hence the name, Monte das Tabocas. The governador, disappointed by the failure of Cavalcanti's mission to Ganga Zumba, confessed, on their return four weeks ago, that he'd not been optimistic. "The Lord of the Devil possesses the peça horde. We will not liberate them until Christ the Redeemer again rules Pernambuco."

The governador's animosity toward the Dutch was motivated to a large extent by religious zeal. Thus, when he learned that a great apostate lurked in the woods near Monte das Tabocas, João Fernandes immediately dispatched Amador with six men to capture him.

Amador and his squad had no difficulty apprehending the offender: He was Manuel de Moraes, a Jesuit turncoat who had gone over to the Dutch a decade ago, throwing off his cassock and embracing Protestantism. He had sailed to Holland, where he had married twice. Two years ago, he'd fled back to Pernambuco, abandoning his second wife and children. Amador found de Moraes engaged in his newest occupation: brazilwood logger.

Immediately Manuel de Moraes was ushered into João Fernandes's presence, de Moraes cried out: "My confession! I am guilty of lust, Governador — I will offer every penance, every suffering, for *my* liberation!"

"Manuel de Moraes, you are in the presence of Christians," the governador said. "Your sad appeal moves us."

"João Fernandes, I *know* these heretics," de Moraes said. "Give me hope to redeem myself at your camp. Make me serve in whatever way you deem fit for so great a sinner."

"Then, pray to our Lord for forgiveness, Manuel de Moraes, and pray, too, for our victory upon this hill of thorns, where I will fight the first battle in this war!"

De Moraes sank to his knees and began to pray fervently, his fingers locked together, his knuckles white.

João Fernandes studied him sympathetically. "My friends, a sinner is brought down in our camp. Surely a miraculous portent for the next triumph our Lord will witness at this battle site?"

Amador quietly slipped out of the tent. He had not believed a word the Jesuit-turned-logger uttered.

⁊

Monte das Tabocas rose two hundred feet above ground level and offered a good vantage point in all directions. To the west and south of the hill flowed the Tapicura River; on the eastern side lay an old track used by brazilwood loggers. Thickets of tabocas encircled the hill at different levels and grew on the lands surrounding it. A gallery forest edged the Tapicura River; beyond this lay half a mile of open, level ground, then the first tangle of tabocas, which formed a natural barrier near the foot of the hill. A Dutch advance was anticipated from the direction of the river. With no cannon and limited powder for their muskets, the insurgents could only delay a crossing by the enemy. Their intention was to do this for as long as possible, then fall back with the Hollanders, pursuing them into the tabocas, where ambuscades would be waiting.

The contingents of Henrique Dias and Felipe Camarão had failed to make the rendezvous, having been trapped in the caatinga, which was drought-stricken despite the heavy rains at the coast. Runners reported that a third of the men with Dias and Camarão were dead and the survivors would not reach Pernambuco for another week. João Fernandes had convinced only a handful of planters to join the insurgents; most awaited the outcome of the first clash between the governador's ragtag army and the Dutch. Still, there were one thousand soldiers at Monte das Tabocas, representing every group in the captaincy — Portuguese, native, mameluco, mulatto, and slave, the latter in the majority.

Once the Dutch had accepted that a full revolt was imminent, they concentrated their forces near Recife; vastly superior to the patriots in experience and armament, they were under the command of Colonel Hendrik Haus. On August 2, 1645, a column of four hundred Dutch soldiers and mercenaries and three hundred natives and slaves, with Colonel Haus and his two bloodthirsty adjutants, Blaer and Vlok, located João Fernandes's camp at Monte das Tabocas.

⁊

At daybreak, August 3, the Pernambucans were in position at the trees beside the Tapicura River and in the first thickets of tabocas. The patriots had been cheered to see a cloudless sky, but found little else to encourage them. Scouts had reported every Dutchman and most of their natives armed with muskets, and the Hollanders' wagons loaded high with munitions and supplies. The rebels had some two hundred pieces, with less than ten rounds per man.

No sooner had it become light than the Hollanders started firing across the river, sustaining their fusillade for forty minutes, until the early-morning air lay heavy with smoke. The men concealed between the trees began to fall back. With ensigns aloft, drumbeat and trumpet blast, the Dutch force began to ford the river.

Amador, the Cavalcantis, and 120 men were hidden in the tabocas, one of three ambuscades, the others off to the left and right of their position. They heard the rattle of musketry at the river and saw their comrades beginning to retreat across the half-mile of level ground between the trees and the reed thickets.

Amador crouched next to Affonso Ribeiro, who was resting on his side, his belly heaving as he breathed.

"If only Dias and Camarão were here," Ribeiro said. "How the heretic blood would flow at that river!"

Amador turned his head in Ribeiro's direction. If gunpowder was in short supply at the camp, fiery cachaça wasn't: Ribeiro was pale and shaky this morning.

Amador looked at Fernão and Felipe Cavalcanti, a dozen feet away. During the weeks since their return from Ganga Zumba, Fernão had made one trip to Santo Tomás. The High Council at Recife had decreed that the wives and children of suspected insurgents must leave their homes. Some had gone into hiding in the forest, where they were suffering dreadful privations, but Fernão Cavalcanti had told his family to ignore the order, and the Hollanders had made no move to enforce it.

The patriots from the positions opposite the river were falling back step by step. Unable to expose their ambuscades, those hidden in the tabocas watched helplessly as men were shot down by a Dutch battalion that was advancing out of the trees. When the enemy officers saw the Pernambucans retreat in three directions into the tabocas, they ordered their troops to follow.

"Fire!" commanded Fernão Cavalcanti. Forty muskets roared alongside an eighty-yard passage cut through the tabocas, and twenty Hollanders were killed or wounded by the volley.

"Portugal! For Dom João! For our Lady of Victories!" Cavalcanti shouted.

His cries were taken up by half his men, who burst out of cover to fall upon the Dutch.

Ribeiro flung down his musket and took his machete from its scabbard. "Better a blade for the blood of the heretic!" he bellowed, and charged through the thicket.

A trumpet sounded: A second Dutch battalion was advancing beyond the trees and hurrying to support those ambushed in the tabocas.

Amador and other musketeers moved to direct their fire at the men on the open ground.

"Vlok!" a rebel shouted, indicating an officer in the enemy's front line. "The devil Vlok himself!"

Amador had just fired. His mouth fell open at the sight of the Hollander identified as Jan Vlok: tall, big-limbed, blond hair, ruddy complexion, orange sash, Vlok bore a striking likeness to Segge Proot. Amador started to reload, but he had no opportunity to fire at Vlok, for the Pernambucans fighting within the tabocas were calling for help.

"Senhor! Senhor!" Affonso Ribeiro shouted a warning to Cavalcanti, whose back was to a Hollander bearing down on him. Cavalcanti swung around with a clash of steel as his sword met his attacker's weapon. Another Hollander leapt toward him. "Fernão Cavalcanti!" the man cried. "A thousand florins for the head of this rebel!"

Wielding his machete with both hands, Ribeiro fought his way toward Cavalcanti. A Hollander's sword ripped through his leather jerkin. "Three sons, heretic! You killed three lovely boys!" With a mighty swipe, Ribeiro's machete cut deep into the man's side. "Portugal! Oh, Portu —" The words died as the point of another Hollander's sword punctured his throat.

Ribeiro's intervention saved the senhor de engenho's life; Felipe Cavalcanti and others had leapt to Fernão's side as more enemy pressed into the passage. The main body of the ambuscade was already abandoning these tabocas to make a new stand at reeds just below the foot of Monte das Tabocas. The Cavalcantis and Amador — with those men who'd fired their last rounds at the Hollanders on the open ground — reached this rearguard position fifteen minutes later.

Amador despairingly took his issue of powder and lead, enough for only three rounds.

Governador João Fernandes and his chief of staff, Antônio Dias Cardoso, who'd come secretly from the Bahia to train the rebel army, had observed the first engagements from the summit of the hill. After driving the men of the ambuscades out of the tabocas, the Hollanders had been pulled back to the open ground, where reinforcements were coming up to fill their ranks. The governador sent orders for the rebels to retake the outer tabocas.

Padre Manuel de Moraes, in a borrowed cassock, accompanied the officer sent down the hill to organize the counterattack. Wherever the fight was thickest, de Moraes was there, not with exhortations alone, but swinging an ax and felling heretics with all the energy he had recently devoted to brazilwood logging.

But the rebel counterattack was repulsed, and again they were driven to the reeds at the foot of the hill. Here they resisted briefly before being forced farther up the slope toward the third and last barrier of tabocas below João Fernandes's headquarters.

It was 1:00 P.M., six hours since the Dutch had crossed the river; both sides were exhausted and there was a lull in the battle. The Hollanders had lost ninety men in the ambushes, twice that many wounded, and another forty lay on the open ground beyond the trees. The patriots counted one hundred — one-tenth of their force — dead or out of action. However, at the governador's tent, Cavalcanti, Cardoso, and other rebel leaders realized their situation was desperate: They had six small barrels of powder, their last reserve.

The officers were therefore more than a little surprised to hear the governador say, in a voice filled with optimism, "Gentlemen, we must attack."

"Attack!" Cardoso looked stunned. "Twice already we've been thrown back to this hill."

João Fernandes addressed Cavalcanti: "Fernão, I own fifty peças here. They've remained loyal and obedient since I took the field. As God is my witness, I'll give every peça who storms the enemy lines his freedom. Fernão, you have thirty men from Santo Tomás. Will you promise the same?"

"What difference will it make? Peças with sticks and knives against the best troops of Europe?"

Nevertheless, it was decided to order the slaves to charge the Hollanders, and the owners of twenty-two other slaves also agreed to liberate them for this service.

"My slaves . . . will you fight for Pernambuco today?" João Fernandes exhorted them. "Will you fight for the good Jesus and the liberties all men cherish?"

"Yes, our Father, we will fight," said a huge, bare-chested 'Ngola.

"Every slave here will be freed."

The slaves greeted this indifferently.

"Do you understand my offer?"

The 'Ngola spoke again: "We hear your words, our Father. We will fight."

João Fernandes seemed disappointed. "I solemnly swear, peças, you will be freed."

The big African nodded.

"What is your name?"

"Moses Pequeno," the 'Ngola replied.

"Then lead these men, Little Moses. Chase the Dutch out of the tabocas and you will be liberated."

The slaves carried clubs and hardwood spears, hoes and scythes, but as they readied themselves for the charge, men came forward with offers of machetes, knives, a few swords. De Moraes moved among the slaves and told them to take courage from the sight of a mighty sinner whom the Lord had preserved in battle against these heretics. The governador presented the slaves with a silk banner and an old drum, which was handed to a Hottentot.

At 3:00 P.M., an hour after the slaves had been assembled, they began to descend the hill.

"Play the drum!" Moses Pequeno ordered.

The Hottentot thumped out a monotonous beat.

"Death to the Hollanders! Death to our masters' enemy!" Moses Pequeno cried.

"Death to the Hollanders!" The chant was taken up through their ranks as the 102 slaves passed the last line of Pernambucan defenders on Monte das Tabocas. Then Moses Pequeno gave a bloodcurdling yell, broke from the upper thicket of tabocas, and ran toward the enemy.

The Dutch musketeers had seen the slaves climbing down the hill. Their volleys brought down twenty Africans, but the others did not stop their charge. They tore into the Hollanders' ranks, with clubs rising and falling, spears and blades jabbing and slashing. So swift and so savage was the assault that it broke the enemy's advance positions and sent the survivors fleeing back to the third thicket of tabocas. The slaves split into three squads and stormed into the openings between the next reed barrier, where two bloody contests had already been fought this day.

The slaves' unexpected success brought a general advance by the rest of the rebel force. Within half an hour, the ground lost between the foot of the hill and the third thicket was won back. There the Pernambucans were halted, and the Dutch regrouped on the level ground beyond. But it was growing dark, with the sky clouding over, and the Hollanders' fourth assault was ill-prepared. The rebels inflicted heavy casualties upon the enemy flanks and forced them to retreat all the way back to the trees from where they had begun their advance that morning.

A blustery storm broke over the hill of thorns, the prelude to a night of wet and muddy misery for the men entrenched there. The last powder was distributed to the sentry posts. Scouts were sent to reconnoiter the Dutch positions: They reported the passage of men in both directions across the river.

Before sunrise, Amador and Felipe Cavalcanti were sent out with another party of scouts. They worked their way through the tabocas in a westerly direction until they reached a place where they could cross the Tapicura River and not be seen by Dutch lookouts. They headed along the opposite bank toward the enemy camp. First they saw a group of men struggling with a wagon bogged down in the mud; they crept closer, reaching the trees where the enemy had retreated the previous evening. Half an hour passed before they were convinced that they were not mistaken: The forest was deserted. The Dutch army had withdrawn!

Soon they were running across the open ground shouting wildly, "Victory! Victory, patriots! The Dutch have gone . . . fled back to Recife!"

The report was rushed up the hill to the governador, who immediately came down from his camp with Fernão Cavalcanti and Cardoso. Just beyond the last thicket of tabocas, João Fernandes halted beside the body of one of his soldiers:

"You are free, Moses Pequeno — free with the good Jesus, who gave us this triumph!"

The governador turned to the drummer and four of thirty-nine slaves who had survived the decisive charge. The Hottentot stood wet and bedraggled, with a weary look on his face.

The governador seized him in a fierce embrace. He kept his hand on the tall Hottentot's shoulder. "From this day on, you are a free man!" he announced.

છ৩

The Dutch had withdrawn to an engenho three miles from Recife, with more than half of the seven hundred soldiers and their native levies killed or wounded. Replacements arriving from Recife and Mauritsstad were few in number, for the towns anticipated an assault by the rebels. At Mauritsstad the guns of forts built by Count Maurits had been sited to defend the settlement from attack by sea. To open a field of fire inland, the High Councilors ordered houses and other structures to be torn down, the count's gardens cleared, and many stately old palms uprooted. Within a week the defenders had destroyed Mauritsstad, the splendid capital of New Holland.

Jan Vlok wanted revenge. For ten days after the battle of Monte das Tabocas, he fumed and fretted at the engenho where Colonel Haus had his headquarters.

Vlok sought out Johan Blaer, who had the same reputation for cruelty, and together they bemoaned the inactivity forced upon them by Haus, whose concern was to avert a siege of Recife. Haus's scouts reported that a force sent by sea from the

Bahia had landed in the south of the colony. The governor-general of Brazil, Antônio Telles da Silva, still issued proclamations in support of the truce between Holland and Portugal, claiming, further, that these regiments were to aid the Dutch in suppressing the rebellion. But Haus's spies confirmed a joyous meeting between André Vidal de Negreiros, commander of the Bahia troops, and João Fernandes. After their harrowing march through the caatinga, the contingents of Henrique Dias and Dom Felipe Camarão had also met up with the insurgents. Haus doubted that the Dutch land forces could withstand these combined units; only at sea did the Hollanders still have superiority, with their coastal fleet already dispatched to destroy the vessels that had transported the troops from the Bahia.

Then, on August 14, Captain Jan Vlok proposed a mission conceived by Blaer and himself:

"Colonel, give me twenty men and I'll strike a blow against João Fernandes and the leaders of this rebellion," he told Haus. "Let Johan Blaer ride to the plantations with a similar corps and the damage will be twofold."

Haus had commanded Count Maurits's guard and had shared the governor's disdain for this vicious man, but, with few experienced officers, he'd been forced to accept Vlok's commission. "What is your plan, Captain?"

"The High Councilors have ordered that women leave the engenhos, yet most maintain their houses as sanctuaries for rebels."

Haus looked sternly at Vlok. "We are Hollanders, not savages. I don't make war on women and children."

"If the slightest harm came to them, Colonel, they'd be of no value," Vlok said. "Let me go to the engenhos and carry the women safely to Recife. The enemy will hesitate to storm a city where their wives and daughters are held hostage."

"Bring them in," Haus said quietly. "Unharmed."

Vlok and Blaer left camp the next morning, Blaer heading north and Vlok west by canoe along a river near Haus's headquarters, the Capibaribe, a tributary of which led to Engenho Santo Tomás.

When the Dutch detachment marched up to the Cavalcanti house, they were met outside by Jorge and Padre Gregório Bonifácio.

"My brother is not at the engenho," Jorge Cavalcanti said. He was sweating profusely under layers of cotton and silk.

"We do not seek Fernão Cavalcanti, though God grant that he were here."

Some of Vlok's soldiers were moving past Jorge and the priest, into the house.

"No rebels hide here. Only women and children."

"What do you want from us?" Bonifácio asked weakly.

"The women and children — by order of the High Council."

"Women?" Jorge drew himself up. "No, Vlok. No! They have no part in this uprising."

"The wives and daughters of criminals. Yes, Senhor Jorge, your brother will hang at the end of a Dutch rope."

"My wife is innocent," Jorge said abruptly.

Vlok gave Jorge a studied look, from his well-groomed hair to his wide-topped spurred boots. "What good fortune Jorge Cavalcanti, to have found your brother's lovely daughter waiting for you."

"I warn you, Vlok." Jorge moved his hand tremulously to the hilt of his long sword. "Do not speak this way. You . . ." Jorge tried to hold his shoulders stiffly, but he could not control the quake that spread along his limbs. His lip quivered. "Vlok . . . heretic!"

Vlok's face turned a deep red. He mumbled an incoherent oath and lunged to grab Cavalcanti's coat and shove him backward. Jorge fell on a patch of sticky mud.

Vlok was standing with his hands on his hips, his laughter rising, when Dona Domitila and Joana came out of the house. Joana left Domitila's side and began to cross toward Vlok and her husband.

"Make haste, Joana Cavalcanti! Your Spanish lord needs you!"

A sergeant came up to report to Vlok that the house and outbuildings had been searched. Six slaves were being driven out of the main building. "Fire it, Captain?" the soldier asked.

Vlok gazed admiringly at the Cavalcantis' house. "No. Preserve it for a new owner." The pleasure he showed as he surveyed the big house indicated whom he saw as future master of Engenho Santo Tomás. "But burn *that* to the ground," he said, indicating the chapel.

Bonifácio ran toward the small building, gesticulating frantically at a soldier who was about to lop off with his machete the arms of an image of Santo Tomás, the patron and protector of the Cavalcantis' valley. "No!" the priest cried out, arms upraised. He swayed toward the man, but lost his balance and fell. A native levy stepped up and clubbed him senseless.

Bonifácio was alone when he regained consciousness. He dragged himself ten feet across the ground to the armless statue of Santo Tomás and pressed it to his chest.

◦⁄◦

Gregório Bonifácio was holding the statue of Santo Tomás sixteen hours later, in the early morning of August 16, 1645, when he rode into the camp of João Fernandes. He was so exhausted, he had to be lifted out of his saddle.

Witnesses to Fernão Cavalcanti's anger could not say with certainty what upset the senhor more: the desecrated image or the report that his family was being held hostage.

João Fernandes and the colonel from the Bahia, André Vidal de Negreiros, had not planned an immediate assault upon Haus's camp, but word of the vandalism against the statue of *Santo Tomás* spread and a clamor rose for the blood of the heretics. The governador agreed that Fernão Cavalcanti should lead the vanguard. A march of twelve hours would take the rebel army, now with eighteen hundred men, to within striking distance of the Hollanders' camp.

Amador was with Fernão Cavalcanti and Felipe and the sixty men who set off three hours in advance of the main force. Just after nightfall, they saw the glow of flames from an engenho below the south bank of the Capibaribe. They halted a mile from the buildings and sent scouts to investigate. The men returned forty minutes later with a sentinel from an enemy patrol that was raiding the engenho. The captive, a French Huguenot mercenary, was taken to Fernão Cavalcanti, who questioned him about the size of their squad and the main camp across the Capibaribe. The Frenchman told them that thirty men were at this engenho. At Haus's headquarters, there were 270 Dutch soldiers and more than two hundred natives. The force was divided into two regiments, one of which would march to Recife the next morning with the women from the engenhos, the other to be led by Vlok and Blaer into the valleys to destroy Portuguese properties. The soldier described siege preparations at Recife and Mauritsstad, then swore he'd told all he knew.

"I believe him," Cavalcanti said. The Frenchman showed relief. Cavalcanti nodded at a mulatto corporal. "Kill him," he said.

"Capitão! For God's sake, spare me! Mercy!"

Cavalcanti walked away. The Frenchman tried to follow him but was held back. Before he was killed, his executioners hacked off both his arms. "For the little *Santo Tomás* of Senhor Fernão," they said.

At midnight the main force reached this engenho. The governador gave orders for the men to rest until dawn, but at 3:00 A.M. he changed his mind. "How can we halt while Portuguese women remain in the hands of the heretics?" he asked Fernão Cavalcanti. "There must be no rest, Fernão — not until the last Hollander is returned to his cold and watery hell!"

☙

The Dutch were taken by surprise, and the rebels advanced to within a musket shot of the engenho where Haus and his men were billeted. Blowing a silver whistle, the Potiguara chief Dom Felipe Camarão led one hundred men on the first sweep along the edge of the campground. The natives tore into the enemy's ranks and scattered them, the Hollanders running to cover in the engenho buildings, from where they began a steady exchange of fire with the patriots.

Haus and his officers were in the main residence of this old and substantial plantation, the property of a widow, Dona Ana Paes. The dwelling, mill, slave quarters, and outbuildings were sited similarly to those at Santo Tomás; the big house was also double-storied but was built upon stilts. Access to the first floor was by two narrow stairways, one at the front and the other at the back of the house; its elevated position made the house eminently defensible, but the Hollanders inside had devised an additional stratagem.

"Mother of mercies!" Amador cried, from his position atop an outcrop of rock, 150 yards from the front of the house: The shutters on many windows had been flung back. Dona Domitila, Joana, and eighteen other women stood at the open windows.

"Cowards!" he shouted. "Heretic sons of heretic bitches! Vlok! Jan Vlok! Do you hear me? I, Amador Flôres da Silva, will see you dead!"

"Forget words! Lead! Powder! To the other buildings!"

The exhortation came from Manuel de Moraes. Already this morning he had excited the men by passing through their ranks with the *Santo Tomás* and inviting them to touch it. Many swore that clear water was issuing from the splintered stumps, and felt cool upon their brows when they made the sign of the Cross.

As the rebels started to exchange shots with the Hollanders holed up in the mill and outbuildings, Amador left his post and scrambled toward the governador's tent, two hundred yards behind the front positions. There he found Fernão and Felipe Cavalcanti.

"I beg that they be unharmed, João Fernandes, but I'll never agree to end the battle," Fernão was saying.

"My mother, my wife, my sisters," his son said. "How I cherish them, João Fernandes. But what my father says is right: We can't consider them above the conquest of heretics!"

"Friends, we dare not risk the lives of these brave women," João Fernandes said. "We must call off the battle. With the women freed, I will give my word: the Hollanders can march to Recife."

"To secure themselves there until a fleet comes from Europe?" Fernão said. "Never, my Commander. Never!"

"Fernão, we cannot storm the house," João Fernandes repeated.

"There's a woodpile just beyond," Cavalcanti said. He was looking in the direction of the stack of timber as he spoke. "Send men to carry those logs across and build a fire under their *fort*."

"The women, Fernão. You can't do this."

"Already I've sacrificed a son, Governador. If you refuse to give this order, I will."

Amador stepped closer. "Give me ten men. I'll take the wood across." He looked at Cavalcanti. "Five years ago, senhor, your family saved my life. May God help me this day, I'll return dearest Joana, the dona, all of them."

Cavalcanti clasped Amador's shoulders and nodded gravely.

Amador chose ten men: four mamelucos, three natives from Camarão's regiment, and three slaves.

They reached the logs without incident. Here Amador decided they would charge across the fifty yards to the house together, allowing the Dutch the opportunity for only one fusillade.

The Hollanders had spotted the activity at the woodpile, and when Amador and his men raced into the open, several of them staggering with their heavy loads of timber, they came under rapid musket fire.

"Run!" Amador screamed. "Run!" He reached the space below the house with six others. A mameluco shot in the stomach crawled in, moaning with pain, from the open ground beyond.

As they piled the wood beneath the supporting beams, they heard the sound of the Hollanders' feet on the boards above. They worked swiftly, two men using axes to split a log for kindling. Sparks flew when Amador scraped a flintstone, but he couldn't get the fire started. Someone had the idea to hack strips off the dry beams above, and soon flames rose, the logs hissing and smoking.

Fernão Cavalcanti and João Fernandes had moved to a position opposite the house and watched as the smoke began to rise between boards on the first-floor verandah. The hostages remained at the windows.

A group of Hollanders and natives from an outbuilding to the right of the house attempted to reach the rebels in the space below the dwelling; caught in crossfire, six who survived fled back to shelter.

Fifteen minutes passed. A musket cracked sporadically, but most men had stopped shooting and were watching the blaze grow. João Fernandes became desperate. He saw several of his men glancing in his direction.

"Your orders, Governador," a man cried out. "To advance!"

João Fernandes looked at Cavalcanti. "Fernão? They won't stand idly by . . ."

"*Nor I!*"— Cavalcanti declared. He jumped up then, in full view of the enemy.

"Get down, Fernão! Come back!" Fernandes shouted.

But Cavalcanti was already walking toward the house, and moved forward resolutely, looking neither left nor right, where he knew Hollanders in the outbuildings had muskets trained on him. He kept his head up, his eyes on the windows.

Cavalcanti stopped twenty feet from the verandah. "Hendrik Haus!" he called out. "It's Fernão Cavalcanti!"

Amador and his men waited for a response. There was none.

"Surrender, Haus! *Now!* Refuse . . . let one woman or child be hurt . . . and I promise you, at sundown not a single Hollander will be alive here. No quarter will be given."

Hendrik Haus stepped onto the verandah. He held his heavy ivory-butted pistol with its barrel pointed toward his chest. In this way, the Dutch colonel indicated the surrender of his regiments.

Cheers came from the patriots in sight of the house, cries of "Victory!" and "Portugal!"

Amador stood up and started to move into the open.

"*Hollanders!*" one of the natives with his squad shouted.

Amador swung around. Through the smoke that swirled below the beams, he saw a Dutch soldier on the sharply angled steps at the back of the house. "Vlok! Jan Vlok! You know me, heretic!"

The huge blond Hollander wielded a long, heavy-bladed sword. "No, bastard, I do not!"

"Nineteen men at Santo Tomás. Five years ago, Vlok."

Vlok sneered. "I remember."

"Nineteen beheaded, Vlok. I was left for dead."

"Nineteen?" The Hollander laughed. "Twenty! *Your* turn, Portuguese!" And he leapt to the attack.

Amador was not as expert a swordsman as Vlok, and his machete was a poor match for Vlok's long blade, but he was possessed by a driving fury. For five minutes he kept Vlok constantly on the defensive as he slashed at him with the machete.

But suddenly Vlok forced Amador backward with a series of vigorous thrusts, until they were at the fire. "Burn!" the Hollander shouted. "Burn, Papist dog!"

The machete flashed through the air and struck the sword with an impact that almost jarred it from Vlok's grip. Vlok stepped back, startled.

"Now, Vlok . . . *come!*"

Vlok's movements became erratic. Amador parried the frantic thrusts. Vlok was unnerved, his face growing rigid with anger. Amador swung the machete again, with a violent upward motion. The blow tore Vlok's sword from his grasp and flung it beyond his reach.

"Quarter!" Vlok shouted. "Quarter!"

"Yes, Vlok — quarter!" Amador said, and immediately drove his sharp blade between the Hollander's ribs. Vlok sank slowly to the ground, all the time begging for mercy. When he was down, Amador placed a foot on his chest; then he drew the machete across Jan Vlok's throat.

e⌒⌐

Three hours later, Amador stood on the front verandah of Dona Ana's house. The boards near him were scorched and an acrid smell rose from the charred beams below, but the fire had been extinguished before it had spread out of control. On the open ground in front of the house, 240 Dutch prisoners were under guard. From a room behind him, Amador heard the voices of the rebel leaders and Dutch officers as they argued about terms of surrender.

Despite objections by João Fernandes and Cavalcanti, Johan Blaer and others guilty of persecuting the Pernambucans were to be spared. Colonel de Negreiros pleaded that this war be conducted with fairness and humanity, and he guaranteed that Dutch prisoners would be safely escorted to Salvador. Hendrik Haus did not forget the natives who served him and asked the same conditions for them. In this instance, de Negreiros agreed with the Pernambucan patriots: The two hundred savages were guilty of treason, for they were the subjects of Dom João IV and had sided with the king's enemies.

Camarão's men waded into the prisoners with a ferocity that did not abate until every one of the two hundred traitors was dead, and most had been beheaded. They whooped with pleasure when they were given a grand salute by the governador, who doffed his plumed hat to them.

When Fernandes led his officers back into the house, Amador sat down on the verandah and rested his back against a wall. His eyes were closed. He realized that if he had had a mission in this war, the death of Jan Vlok had brought it to a close. He opened his eyes then and looked at the Dutch prisoners, silent and filled with terror as they undoubtedly envisaged a fate similar to that of their native Auxiliaries. But Amador knew that they were to be marched south, and here he was on the verandah waiting to volunteer to lead this heretic horde through the sertão. Dear Jesus! He would get them to the Bahia and there his long journey would end! Then nothing would prevent his returning to São Paulo.

He saw Jorge Cavalcanti, dirty and disheveled, step out of the front door. Hand on hip, he paused several times to survey the captives. Amador watched him slowly wander to where the two hundred natives lay. Shaking his head from side to side, he walked deep in among the bodies, treading gingerly between the heads and trunks of those who'd been decapitated.

"*Senhor!*" Amador screamed.

As Jorge stepped between the natives, one rose up with his last strength and stabbed Cavalcanti three times, mortally wounding him.

Amador thumped along the verandah to the front door, where he halted to yell out to Fernão Cavalcanti. Then he hastened to the side of Jorge.

One of Camarão's warriors had seized the assassin and was beheading him.

Jorge was not yet dead. He opened his eyes, but only to glimpse his avenger as he raised the severed head. Jorge gave an awful cry, made several gasping noises, and then was still.

Amador saw Joana at a window, in the same black gown she had worn the day he returned to Engenho Santo Tomás. *Dear Jesus, so young . . . the widow Cavalcanti. And before this, Segge Proot.* As he thought of Joana and Segge, he felt a pang of sorrow, but it passed quickly.

⁑

Amador's offer to escort the Dutch prisoners to the Bahia was accepted. On the forty-day march to Salvador, a vengeful Pernambucan murdered Captain Johan Blaer. At the Bahia, Amador took passage for Santos and on November 22, 1645 — six years after departing with Raposo Tavares's contingent — he climbed the precipitous path between the crags of the Serra do Mar up to São Paulo de Piratininga.

It was dark when Amador reached the house of Ishmael Pinheiro. Tears of joy streamed down Pinheiro's pockmarked cheeks when he recognized the companion of his youth and seized him in a tremendous embrace.

"Ishmael! My journey has ended! My friend, how many times was I reminded what a foolish venture you said it would be!"

"Tomorrow you'll rest with your family," Ishmael responded "But your journey will never end, Amador. You are a man of the sertão. It will call."

The next day, Amador was reunited with his family, his joy greatest at finding Rosa Flôres in good health. His half-brothers, Braz and Domingos, lazy, feckless, and disinterested as ever, had given him up for dead, but Rosa Flôres had not lost hope that he would return.

"The Lord strengthened my faith," his mother said, "but if I grew sad and worried, I had support. Maria. Maria Ramalho. If ever there was a word of doubt, she silenced it. Oh, Amador, she *knew* you would come back."

"Six *years?* Maria waited six years for . . . for nothing. Oh, Mother, I'm worn out, exhausted. I drag my leg like an old man. But I wouldn't take the Ramalho woman had I been gone sixty years and she'd waited all that time."

"Fetch Senhorita Maria," his mother ordered a Carijó slave.

Rosa Flôres had not been the first to mention Maria. The night before, Ishmael Pinheiro had informed Amador of the following events: Valentim Ramalho had died, a victim of a virulent syphilis. Valentim's father, Vasco, had involved himself in a feud between two family clans, and ended up in a ditch with his throat slit from ear to ear. Leaving Maria to bury the victim and care for Valentim's widows and seventeen children, two surviving sons had quickly gone about squandering their personal inheritance.

"Maria is a wealthy woman, Amador." Observing the look of distaste on his friend's face, he'd added, "Ugly, yes, and as round as Pinheiro, but with many bags of silver. She came to me five years ago and asked that I sell her quince marmalade. Today we send it to Rio de Janeiro, the Bahia, even to Lisbon."

Maria was thirty-two that November of Amador's return. At Dona Rosa's summons, she came riding upon a gray gelding to the da Silva house. Maria Ramalho was as hideous as Amador remembered her, with her wandering glance, oversize nostrils and tufted moles, and huge body, beneath which the gelding plodded with eyes bulging and flanks quivering.

Slaves helped Maria dismount. She stood there in a brown sacklike garment that had three uneven holes for her head and arms. A huge smile distorted her round, fleshy face. "Amador Flôres, the Lord sent you back to me!"

❧

On a day in May 1672 — twenty-seven years later — Amador was alone in Ishmael Pinheiro's storeroom, redolent with exotic aromas and the clean, fresh smell of bolts of cotton and canvas. Ishmael had stepped outside to inspect a load of hides.

A letter lay on a wooden chest in front of Amador. He could make out some of the inscribed words, but Ishmael had read the letter to him several times.

It was from the infante Dom Pedro, prince regent of Portugal, to his "wise, far-seeing, and discreet subject" Amador Flôres da Silva — Senhor Amador Flôres da Silva, homem bom of São Paulo de Piratininga, capitão of militia, conqueror of the sertão.

Amador was fifty-eight years old. He still had a good physique, though when he walked, it was with an exaggerated slouch, from his limp. He had lost two fingers of his left hand when a musket exploded; his hair and untrimmed beard were silver gray; his dark, secretive eyes smoldered beneath a deeply furrowed brow.

"Senhor Amador Flôres da Silva, homem bom," the prince regent had addressed him, and this was true, for Amador was now a citizen of quality among the Paulistas. Yet his appearance as he sat studying his prince's letter was more suggestive of a vagabond than a royal favorite: frayed black shortcoat and patched breeches, soiled shirt, loose stockings, and cowhide footwear.

At São Paulo, some petty nobles of Portugal and a pretentious clique of royal officials took pains with their appearance to distinguish themselves from the rabble they saw around them. But the Paulistas did not judge a man by his boots and breeches. Nothing could be more injurious to the pride of a homem bom than the suggestion of servility — to behold a colonist reduced by circumstances to daily toil in his fields.

By the grace of God and with a will to endure the sertão, Amador had never known this shame. Nine times since his return from Pernambuco, he had left São Paulo with bandeiras to pursue his march of glory. On four occasions there had been savages exterminated and the sertão pacified for Christian settlement.

Three bandeiras undertaken during the past five years had been supported by Ishmael Pinheiro to search for emeralds and silver. Gold, too, though Ishmael had lost confidence in a major strike.

Four months ago Ishmael had suggested that Amador offer his services to Lisbon and had drafted a letter to the prince regent. Only today there had been a reply, in which Dom Pedro stated: "It would be to the good of the kingdom, Senhor Amador Flôres, and all its subjects if you were to discover the emeralds of Marcos de Azeredo and the silver deposits in the vicinity."

Amador remembered his father's warning that the natives had misled De Azeredo, and he did not dismiss the experience of his abortive search for El Dorado.

But prospectors had drifted back to São Paulo with small finds of good emeralds and silver.

"What they show or talk about openly isn't important," Ishmael had often observed. "What matters is what they conceal from the Crown."

As a Jew who lived under the guise of a New Christian, Ishmael was scrupulous in dealing with royal officials and had always delivered the fifth of any finds by his bandeiras. Most Paulista prospectors joked about a royal *fiftieth* given to the Crown.

Ishmael, being obese and slow, loathed even the shortest journey, but he marched with the bandeiras in spirit, for he saw their wanderings as a continuation of the voyages of Portugal's great discoverers: Those captains had found their treasure in the halls of the sultans and maharajahs, and Ishmael was convinced that these voyages across the sertão would have an equally splendid and glittering outcome.

"The Carijó were a treasure for our fathers. Today that mine is worked out," he said. "We have to find silver and emeralds, even some gold. If we don't, São Paulo is ruined. *All* Brazil is ruined!"

At first, Amador had challenged Ishmael's statement: "But we're rid of our greatest enemies, Spain and Holland. How can you say that ruin is inevitable?"

"The cost of our triumph, my friend. The *cost!* I'm not a great conqueror but a *merchant* and I tell you it will take a mountain of silver to pay Portugal's debts!"

There was a reason for Ishmael's pessimism: The wars against the Dutch in northeast Brazil and the Spanish in Europe had exhausted the treasury. At Pernambuco in April 1648, the patriots had defeated five thousand Hollanders and their native troops at the Guararapes, a series of hillocks outside Recife. The next year had seen a second defeat at the same Guararapes. Despite these victories, five years passed before Recife was occupied in January 1654 by the Portuguese commander-in-chief Francisco Barreto and the patriot leaders João Fernandes Vieira and Fernão Cavalcanti.

Amador had sponsored a festa to mark the collapse of New Holland, but few Paulistas had shared his enthusiasm. Before the fall of Recife, they had experienced a setback. In 1648, a force sent from Rio de Janeiro had re-conquered from the Dutch the port of Loanda in Angola; the export of slaves from those lands to the Bahia and Rio de Janeiro was restored and the planters had lost interest in Carijó, whom they regarded as unproductive workers. This was the final blow to the Paulistas' lucrative slave trade.

The Portuguese at Lisbon had greeted the Pernambucan victory cautiously, for they feared Dutch retaliatory attacks on the homeland and further devastation of their dwindling Asian outposts by the East India Company. To appease the Netherlanders, they had agreed to pay four million cruzados for Dutch losses in New Holland and to grant the Hollanders liberal trading rights in all their possessions.

"With what can we pay these debts? Parrots? Monkeys? Dyewood? Even before our grandfathers' day, Europe tired of those treasures. Cotton? Tabak? Others grow better cotton and tabak," Ishmael said. "Well, then, it must be sugar . . . There was a time when I could swear this came from Brazil. Not today. English, French . . . Dutch chased out of Pernambuco — all grow canes on the islands of the Antilles. Today our senhores de engenho are no longer the great lords of sugar."

Amador heard a noise behind him.

"It is Trajano, Father."

Amador snatched up the letter and waved it in the air. "Ishmael has told you?"

"A commission from Lisbon."

"A letter to Amador Flôres da Silva of São Paulo! A commission to find emeralds and silver. The prince of Portugal himself has written to your father to ask his help."

Trajano da Silva, Amador's son by a Tupiniquin woman, had been eight when Amador marched off to Pernambuco. Amador had returned, to find the boy on the verge of manhood and bearing a marked resemblance to himself — stumpy, thickset build; dark, secretive eyes; small, fleshy mouth. But the resemblance had gone far beyond physical appearance.

Trajano had been seventeen when he marched with a bandeira in 1648, an exploration that Amador had been asked to accompany but that he'd declined to join despite the appeals of its leader, Captain-Major Antônio Raposo Tavares.

Raposo Tavares had explained that his bandeira was not a slave-raiding party but a mission to investigate ways to launch a future invasion against the Spanish viceroyalty of Peru. Amador had stuck by his words to Ishmael — only once does a man tempt Fate with such a journey — but when his son asked to accompany Raposo Tavares, Amador had agreed: "Go to the sertão, Trajano. March with the captain-major, as I did at your age!"

In May 1648, Raposo Tavares had set out, leading a company of men to the foothills of the Andes; from there to the headwaters of the Rio Madeira; and then along the route Amador and Segge had taken to Belém do Pará, a journey of 9,000 miles over three years. When Amador and Trajano saw the old bandeirante for the last time, before his death in October 1658, Raposo Tavares had raised himself from his cot. He looked out a window, his blue eyes sparkling and alive, and cried: "We have seen Brazil!"

Raposo Tavares had repeatedly predicted that every league of sertão his last bandeira crossed would one day be the domain of Portugal.

In Ishmael's store, Trajano appreciated how much a commission from the infante meant to his father. "It will be your greatest bandeira!" Trajano said. "By God's grace we'll soon find the emeralds, the silver. We'll return to São Paulo. You'll go to Santos, Father, and sail to Lisbon to present the jewels to the infante Pedro!"

"Whatever the reward, Trajano, you'll share it!" How he loved Trajano! He had many surviving children, but not one was the equal of this young man who had shared his successes and tribulations these many years.

Ishmael Pinheiro, finished with inspecting the load of hides, joined them, and for a while Amador continued to talk animatedly about the royal letter.

When Amador's excitement abated, Ishmael asked, "When will you leave?"

"Today, were it possible, but we must prepare for this search as never before. I won't return without the infante's emeralds."

"Yours, too, Amador," Ishmael reminded him. "One in five for Dom Pedro, the rest for those who find them. They'll be needed, for thousands of cruzados will go toward equipping such a bandeira."

"Everything I possess — *everything*, Ishmael — for this quest."

Ishmael studied his friend thoughtfully. He understood the mamelucos. They despised their native heritage, which put them on a level with the savages they enslaved and exterminated. For a prince of Portugal to offer them honors was the ultimate liberation.

Trajano laughed, and both men looked at him. "What will the dona say?" he asked.

Ishmael eased himself off a crate he had been sitting on. "Go to Maria, Amador Flôres, and promise her an emerald fit for the queen she is!"

∾

Amador stood in an open doorway on the front porch of the da Silva house; he was bareheaded, his hands holding the worn brim of his hat, as he peered into the chapel. It was many years since Rosa Flôres had moved Braz da Silva out of this room and made it a place of worship. They were dead now, Braz and Domingos, and Rosa Flôres too, who had lived for three years after Amador's return from Pernambuco. In this chapel, Rosa Flôres had watched contentedly as Maria Ramalho and her son were married in January 1647.

Maria was kneeling with her back toward Amador; her loose black dress fell in big folds around her; her head was covered with a dark shawl. Maria was fifty-nine and had grown larger over the years. Motionless in the light from a votive candle, she seemed to occupy a good portion of the small chapel.

Good Jesus, what strength there was in her huge presence. What tenacity and patience! For years he had fled from Maria Ramalho and made himself deaf to Dona Rosa, who knew what a worthy wife Maria would make. His alarm at finding Maria waiting for him upon his return from the north could not have been greater.

He had been polite to the mad, ugly thing so as not to ruin his mother's happiness at his homecoming. But that day when she'd come riding up on her gray gelding, Maria had given him his first understanding of the depth of her devotion to him.

He had seen her talking with Dona Rosa in the front room, and when she left, fifteen minutes later his mother called him and sent him to the back porch.

Maria was out there, alone.

"What do you want?" he'd asked curtly.

"Oh, Amador . . ."

Then Maria beckoned to a boy who stood beyond Amador's view at the back of the house. When he stepped onto the porch, she smiled at him. To Amador, she said, "Your son, Amador — from the Tupiniquin."

Trajano's mother had died with an attack of measles two months after Amador marched off to join the conde da Torre's armada. Maria had asked, and been granted, Dona Rosa's permission to care for the boy. And so lovingly had she done this that Trajano came to give Maria every regard and affection a son could offer a mother.

It had been Trajano more than anyone else who had opened Amador's eyes to Maria's goodness.

When Valentim died, Maria had assumed responsibility for his native women and a wild bunch of mameluco bastards he had bred with them. The making of quince marmalade provided an income and, as Ishmael had indicated, enough profit for Maria to have set aside close to a thousand Portuguese crowns.

Amador had kept his Carijó women and enjoyed sex with many others, but Maria had been installed as his wife and as patroness of his progeny. Maria had given him seven children, four of whom survived: three girls and a boy, Olímpio, their firstborn and now twenty-four years old. In addition, there were Trajano and seven acknowledged bastard sons and daughters, and also attached to the household were a group of Ramalhos from Valentim's couplings.

Maria had slaves to assist her with this small tribe, and the house was one of the best at Piratininga, but her life was relentlessly harsh and without any of the comforts lavished on a dona of Pernambuco. Yet, at the same time, Maria enjoyed far greater independence than a senhor de engenho's wife could ever know.

On nine occasions since their marriage, Amador had been away with bandeiras, sometimes for as long as two years. When he was absent, Maria controlled his house and lands — after compensation to Vasco's wastrel sons, the smaller Ramalho property had been incorporated with the da Silva holding — and Maria took responsibility for everything from the management of slaves to preparations for sowing and harvest. Except for salt and gunpowder, the settlement was self-sufficient; wheat, corn, manioc, tapioca, sugar, castor oil, cotton-seed oil — all the community's needs were produced here. Flourhouse, millhouse, sugarhouse — a primitive mill with one cauldron for *rapadura*, hard brown sugar, for their own use — manioc presses and roasting ovens; Maria saw that these functioned smoothly. She kept the women and girls occupied at combing wool and cotton, spinning, weaving, and sewing in a large, airy room in the house. She supervised the Carijó in the quince orchards and directed every stage of the marmalade production.

In the chapel, Maria had finished praying and slowly got to her feet. To her left was a door that led to their bedroom. Maria exited through it now. Amador followed, and found her sitting on the edge of their bed.

"Maria! Maria!" He spoke so fervently that she looked up with alarm, her head at an angle, for she was now blind in the eye that had been afflicted since birth. Amador took out the royal letter and waved it in the air. "The prince regent has replied. The infante asks me to lead a bandeira for Marcos de Azeredo's emeralds. I'm to be a captain-major . . . governador . . . more if I succeed!"

Amador unfolded the letter and handed it to her. "Everything is written here" — the lines on his face deepened as he smiled — "in royal Portuguese!" Most Paulistas spoke the lingua geral, the language of the backlands, and could neither read nor write.

Maria's eye roved across the letter, not a word of which she could decipher.

"Here," Amador said, and indicated the bottom of the letter. "Dom Pedro's signature."

Maria's expression was almost reverential as she put out a stubby finger and touched the royal mark. "Amador . . . my husband . . . I'm proud of you."

"The infante acknowledges a most trusted subject. He knows this soldier will not rest until Marcos de Azeredo's secret is uncovered . . . until we lift our eyes to the slopes of silver Sabarabuçu."

"What wonderful news," she said now. "God be thanked that it was you the prince chose!"

Amador knew that similar prizes and honors were offered to any Paulista who volunteered to organize a prospecting bandeira, but he did not qualify Maria's interpretation. Earlier treasure hunters had failed, said Amador, because they had been hasty and unmethodical and had often abandoned their search in favor of capturing slaves. Before he left São Paulo, he would send men in advance of his main party to establish camps and plant crops.

After his conversation with Maria in the bedroom, Amador returned to the porch, where Trajano joined him. They sat together on a high-backed wooden bench and talked about their plans until the Carijó and Tupi slaves began to drift toward the open area opposite the porch for evening prayers. Here, too, Amador would administer justice for the eighty-five Carijó and Tupi and three 'Ngola peças, and would issue work orders and attend to their grievances and disputes.

The house had doubled in size since Tenente Bernardo's day, without losing its admirable features, its whitewashed rammed-earth walls and pagoda-style roof. Trajano and his third wife occupied a room off the porch opposite the chapel. Trajano had eleven children, all but two from previous wives who had died from illness. Beyond the front porch was the *sala*, twenty feet square, where visitors were entertained, and behind this was the *sala intima*; the da Silva women spent most of their time here and in the workroom next to it. There were twelve rooms in all, including separate sleeping quarters for boys and girls, and storage areas for tools and prospecting equipment, as well as for provisions.

The da Silva lands now covered sixteen square miles below the south bank of the Anhembi. The soil was fertile, but, apart from the quince trees, cultivation was limited to food crops for the settlement, the clearings the same as the natives had maintained at their malocas. Cattle and pigs were occasionally driven the thirty miles to São Paulo, but the bandeiras always took precedence over these settled activities. When Amador marched off, all but ten of his eighty-five slaves would accompany him.

One of the first slaves to near the porch greeted Amador and Trajano with a customary "I beseech your blessing!" To which Amador replied, "Jesus Christ bless you forever!" Then Amador beckoned the Tupi to step closer to them.

"We march again, old man," he told him. "I'm going to lead a bandeira into the mountains."

"Oh, the Lord is good!" Abeguar said. "Jesus heard my prayer, Master." The Tupiniquin who had been with Amador and Valentim the day they captured the Carijó hunters so long ago was in his sixties, but he had the energy and spirit of a much younger man and was untiring on the long marches through the sertão.

When the slaves had been assembled, and Amador heard their evening prayer, they stood looking expectantly at him, for word of his remark to Abeguar had been passed among their ranks.

"The prince of Portugal, my Carijó, asks me to lead a bandeira to find emeralds and the mountain of Sabarabuçu," Amador said, and then told them about the next expedition on which they would accompany him. The slaves cheered wildly and cried out praises for a master who was a great captain of the sertão. As the assembly was breaking up, a rider came into view along a track that led up to the house. Amador smiled at Trajano. "The slaves greet my news so cheerfully. What will this one say?"

Approaching them on a mule was Olímpio Ramalho da Silva. He had earned his name at birth, for he was a particularly large infant. Today, he was a big man with a powerful physique. His face was long and unattractive, with a broken nose, darting hazel eyes, and bushy brows. He had a slow, deliberate manner that accompanied a stubborn temperament. "*Macho,*" he'd been called by Amador, not to denote vigorous manliness but for the word's alternative meaning: "mule."

It wasn't only obstinacy but also a genuine interest in these beasts that earned Olímpio this nickname. In Olímpio's thirteenth year, he had been sent to keep an eye on a muleteer transporting Maria's quince preserve to São Paulo. On this trip, the old Andalusian, then the only mule driver at São Paulo, had got drunk on cachaça. They had been on a broad, safe track at the edge of a small ravine, the muleteer singing a merry ballad as he thrashed his mount, when suddenly the mule had stopped dead in its tracks and toppled onto its side. The mule driver had been flung thirty feet into the ravine; Olímpio hurried down to him, but the Andalusian's neck was broken. Looking up, Olímpio saw that the mule had got to its feet and was gazing contentedly into the ravine, a sight that had left the boy with a healthy respect for the beast.

At São Paulo, Ishmael and Olímpio had taken the mule driver's body to his widow. Olímpio had offered to buy the mules. "With what?" Ishmael asked. "Oh, senhor, the son of Maria Ramalho will pay his debts," the boy insisted. Impressed, Ishmael had guaranteed payment to the widow, and Olímpio had returned home with seven mules and two asses.

Today, Olímpio had one hundred mules and maintained two packs with muleteers to transport goods between Santos and São Paulo. Maria supported this steady employment, but Amador found it a bitter disappointment that Olímpio chose to waste his time with the stubborn and cantankerous creatures when he could be marching with his father's bandeiras. Not once had Olímpio accompanied an expedition into the sertão.

So Amador was now surprised to see Olímpio dismount and hurry toward them, calling out excitedly, "Oh, senhor! I've heard . . . I saw Senhor Ishmael when I halted at São Paulo. He says you have a letter from the prince regent. May I see it?"

"*Read* it," Amador said. He handed the letter to Olímpio.

"A bandeira! For de Azeredo's emeralds . . . silver . . . gold. A grand expedition!" Olímpio said.

"It's all written there."

Olímpio was the only member of the da Silva family who could read and write Portuguese, and he knew some Latin, too. He had Maria to thank for these accomplishments. During three of Amador's long absences with the bandeiras, Maria had sent Olímpio to the Jesuit colégio. The black robes had returned to São Paulo in 1653, after a thirteen-year exile following their expulsion by the Paulistas; there had no longer been slaving expeditions for them to protest, but most Paulistas did not forgive them their past interference.

When Amador learned that Olímpio, had been to the colégio, he took a whip to Maria and forced her to flee his lands. She had gone to Ishmael for help, for though he shared the Paulistas' disapproval of Jesuit action against the bandeiras, he had faith in the Jesuit teachers: When the Company was banished from São Paulo, he sent his three sons — Mathias, Marco, and João —to the colégio at Santos. Old friend that he was, Ishmael managed to calm Amador enough to permit Olímpio to recite some Portuguese and Latin, and Amador had conceded that this knowledge was a fine thing for a da Silva.

Finished reading, Olímpio raised his long face and looked eagerly at his father: "This bandeira, Father — I will march with you."

"You always stayed behind with your mules and asses when we marched."

"Senhor Ishmael says that if there's a man to find these treasures, it will be Amador Flôres da Silva."

"And you believe him?"

"Oh, yes, Father, I believe!"

Amador smiled broadly. "Bring your mules and asses, Olímpio Ramalho. By God's grace, there'll be silver and emeralds, enough to spare you a lifetime with those stupid beasts!"

ɔ

The bandeira straggled in single file along a stony incline to the top of a pass over the Mantiqueira Mountains, an aged volcanic formation on the uplands above the Serra do Mar. With slate blue peaks rising more than eight thousand feet, the Mantiqueira started near São Paulo, ran east along the valley of the Rio Paraiba for some two hundred miles, and then curved to the north; beyond this range lay the highlands of Brazil.

There were fifty Paulistas with the column: Portuguese, both European and Brazilian-born; mamelucos and mulattos; three Spaniards; three Genoese. They were accompanied by 220 natives, mostly Carijó and Tupi, and seven black slaves. The bandeira had left São Paulo five weeks ago and had followed the valley of the Rio Paraiba to the small settlement of Taubaté, some one hundred miles northeast of São Paulo. There they had waited ten days for guides from an advance party that had set up headquarters in the highlands. From Taubaté, the bandeira had traveled for nine days before crossing the Paraiba to the foothills of the Mantiqueira.

Amador had been with the first group to reach the summit of the pass. He now stood alone on a rocky prominence and gazed back along the ridge, where the men and animals of his bandeira were strung out for a mile below him. He wore a quilted leather jacket and thick breeches, but still he shivered as gusts of icy wind stung his face. He could see tier upon tier of mountain, hill, hillock, and rise; slopes jagged and gashed with ravines; deep wooded valleys; streams cascading down shelves of granite and quartz; the distant horizon wavy with pinnacles and rocky summits.

It was July 11, 1674, a month before Amador's sixtieth birthday. It had taken two years to raise ten thousand cruzados to finance the bandeira, half from Amador's own resources — the major part of this from Maria's quince preserve profits — and the balance by loans, including three thousand cruzados from Ishmael Pinheiro. The bandeira's royal patronage had brought an offer of one thousand cruzados from the governor-general at the Bahia, but he had sent only 150 crowns. Amador did not complain, for the governor had given him the rank of captain-major and had reiterated the prince regent's promise of the highest honors.

The previous July, Amador had dispatched an advance party, the size of the column he now led, to set up headquarters and supply camps in the mountains. This company was headed by Capitão Paulo Cordeiro de Matos, a Paulista who had served with Amador on raids against savages in the sertão beyond Piratininga.

How truly infinite the world of the sertão, Amador thought. These damp, blue-gray heights; the low, dry hell of the caatinga; fertile valleys of Pernambuco; lonely grasslands of the north; rivers surging through forests without end.

Now as his gaze traveled over the rolling sea of hills, his heart leapt with the vision that this highland kingdom held at least one eminence gleaming with silver . . . that in a deeply cleft ravine or upon the shores of a lakelet there would be a cluster of green fire!

Abeguar, who was captain of the Carijó and Tupi, reached the end of a long slope. He greeted Amador, who acknowledged him with a wave of his hand. Abeguar had been manumitted this past June at the celebrations for St. John.

Far behind the slaves, Olímpio Ramalho took up the rear of the column, with forty mules and their drivers. Amador's prejudice against his son's pack animals had lessened when he saw their sure-footedness and the great burdens they were capable of carrying. But the large, lumbering Olímpio remained a disappointment. "When I was twenty-four I had conquered Guiará with Raposo Tavares," Amador had said to him a few nights ago. "Not mules, Olímpio Ramalho, but tens of thousands of Carijó to be driven overland. I'm pleased that you march with my bandeira. But I worry, Olímpio Ramalho, for you've so much to learn about the sertão."

"Certainly, my Captain-Major," Olímpio had responded good-naturedly, "but who is my teacher? Am I not a man with the company of Dom Amador Flôres, who is to be governor of Sabarabuçu?"

Amador laughed quietly to himself, and joined Trajano and others who were giving orders for the slaves to make camp.

Over the next twelve days, the bandeira descended the Mantiqueira in a northeasterly direction and crossed a plateau with knoblike hills, rifts, and wooded valleys, a trek that took them into the heart of the highlands.

The ranges beyond the Mantiqueira lay mostly in a north-south direction, with the predominant Espinhaço, ("The Spine"), a belt of scarps and mountains from thirty to 150 miles wide. The highlands separated the headwaters of the lower Rio São Francisco, which flowed north to Pernambuco and turned east to the sea, the Paraná-Paraguay-Plata system of the south, and the smaller Rio Doce streams, which tumbled east of the highlands to the Atlantic.

The previous century bandeiras had reached the western slopes of The Spine and the headwaters of the São Francisco, thus gaining access to the backlands of Bahia captaincy and Pernambuco. The valleys of the Rio Doce and rivers that emptied into the Atlantic below Porto Seguro, had provided a route to the highlands for Marcos de Azeredo. De Azeredo died before he could reveal where he had got his collection of imperfect gems, and for fifty years his find had inspired others to seek a mine of emeralds in these mountains.

Adventurers had also searched for Paraupava, the legendary lake of gold, between these ranges. Few Paulistas now believed in Paraupava, though since Tenente Bernardo's day there had been some proof that not all pagan stories were false. Men had returned to São Paulo from the sertão with strings of ears from slain savages — trophies taken for confirmation of their kills and for the nuggets of gold embedded in the lobes. No source of this gold had been located, for the clans whose warriors had been mutilated fled at the approach of Paulistas.

୧ଦ

On July 29, 1674, Amador's column reached the headquarters established by Capitão Paulo Cordeiro de Matos at Sumiduoro, below a southern spur of The Spine. During the year Cordeiro de Matos had been here with twenty-six Paulistas and 160 natives, the camp had grown to be a permanent settlement. The stockade stood beside the Rio das Velhas, which fed into the São Francisco; behind the ten-foot palisade were two rows of wattle-and-daub huts and three palm-front malocas. Tracts of forest close by had been burned and cleared for manioc, maize, and other crops.

Cordeiro de Matos, a mulatto originally from the Cape Verde Islands, had been at São Paulo for the past twenty-four years. He was forty-two, an energetic man with a quick temper and a mighty sadism toward slaves who offended him. The son of a slave woman, Cordeiro de Matos had visions of glory equal to those of his commander.

Amador allowed his men only two days rest and then ordered that they equip and provision themselves for the first march into the surrounding mountains. He divided the bandeira into three companies with Cordeiro de Matos, Trajano, and himself in command. Each party would take a different route, two to explore along the western flanks of The Spine, and Amador's group toward the east and the basin of the Rio Doce.

The night before Amador set out, he was sitting with Cordeiro de Matos and Trajano when Olímpio approached them. He was barefoot, and wore shirt and breeches, with a blanket thrown over his shoulders. He had been away from the stockade searching without success for seven mules that had wandered off, and had not been told whose search party he was to accompany.

"Senhor." Olímpio saw Trajano nudge Amador, who looked up at him. "You haven't told me whose company I'm to march with."

Amador tugged at the end of his beard as he bent his head and frowned at Trajano. "Which company is his, he asks."

Trajano began to grin; Cordeiro de Matos sat quietly, not wanting to interfere between Amador and his son.

"You can best serve the bandeira by staying at this camp."

"I came to help you find emeralds and silver."

"And so you shall, Olímpio Ramalho. You'll help me, my son, by obeying my command. I leave you as master of the camp. Guard it with your life, camp master! Keep everything ready for the heroes who'll return with the prince's emeralds!"

∐

Long afterward, Olímpio Ramalho remembered that night in July 1674 and the wild optimism of the leaders of the bandeira.

How brightly that fire had burned in the camp! They had saluted one another, the knights-errant of the high serra, and had declared that they stood at the very gates of Paradise.

Who, then, were these three men he now beheld at the camp this August day four years later? Dear God in heaven, were these the giants whose hopes had soared as high as the mountains?

Captain-Major Amador Flôres da Silva wandered from hut to hut, his exhortations endless and repetitive, summoning men to march back into the hills with a dream of another range, another valley, a new direction with fresh possibilities. His eyes were dark-rimmed and sunken, his hair and matted beard silver. He was bareheaded, his war jacket stained and shabby, his breeches ragged.

Trajano was also as unkempt as a mameluco beggar in the alleys of São Paulo — no boots, shirtless, torn breeches. He was moody and sullen and rarely spoke with anyone. Capitão Cordeiro de Matos, the third visionary, was close to open rebellion: He avoided the other two and kept company with Paulistas of like mind, who were ready to flee back to São Paulo.

In the four years since July 1674, when Amador marched off on his first exploration for emeralds and silver, he had led a company of men into the mountains seven times, and on one occasion had been away for six months. Savages of these highlands had killed Paulistas and natives; they had been struck down by sickness and exhaustion; they had deserted into the forest. One-third of the original bandeira were now dead or missing.

There had been finds of green stones, but every sample carried to Procópio Almeida, a goldsmith recommended to the bandeira by Ishmael Pinheiro, had been rejected as worthless.

After four years of failure, few were as disheartened as Cordeiro de Matos, who urged Amador to at least return to São Paulo not entirely empty-handed. But Amador adamantly refused to convert the prospecting bandeira into a slave-raiding party, even though he'd spent every cruzado he had and had also doubled his indebtedness to Ishmael Pinheiro.

∐

On August 6, 1678, Amador proposed another probe into the hills. The Paulistas around Cordeiro de Matos appeared to heed his call, and midmorning this day were assembled in the clearing of the stockade. In addition to Amador and his sons, seventy-six Paulistas had been in the ranks of the bandeira four years ago; forty-one remained, and twenty-nine of those stood with Cordeiro de Matos. Of 380 natives, 92 had died or fled; 164 of the survivors were slaves of the twenty-nine Paulistas ready to march.

Amador was on a bench outside a hut he occupied with Trajano and Olímpio. Now Cordeiro de Matos left his men and walked across to Amador.

"The men won't go north . . . I asked them to make one last search for the emeralds."

Amador's face grew taut. "Don't lie, Capitão Cordeiro de Matos," he said in a controlled voice. "This was your wish."

"Face the truth: We've failed. A thousand hills . . . a thousand valleys . . . every crack and crevice investigated. There are no riches in these hills." He swept his hand in a wide arc toward the shabby huts and malocas. "Look at me, Amador Flôres. Look at yourself. Haven't we suffered enough? Shouldn't there have been one small reward for all this effort?"

"Reward? You abandon the quest, Cordeiro de Matos, and ask for a reward?" He began to limp furiously toward the Paulistas and natives a hundred feet away. "He asks a reward!" he shouted. "The captain — your master — says your company deserves its prizes and honors. This company" — he glanced contemptuously along their ranks — "of cowards!"

When Amador's sons and Procópio Almeida saw Amador charging toward the Paulistas, they, too, hurried in that direction. Trajano and Olímpio drew their machetes.

Cordeiro de Matos also crossed the clearing. "Remind him, Almeida!" he shouted. "The pile of stones and pebbles at your hut. Worthless!"

Procópio Almeida shook his head and was silent.

Amador raised his left arm and pointed with the three fingers on his hand. "*There*, Cordeiro de Matos . . . in heaven is our Lord. He sees me abandoned by half my company."

Cordeiro de Matos motioned to his column and they began to move toward the opening in the stockade.

"*Go!*" Amador yelled. "Tell your sons at São Paulo how brave you were, heroes of the high serra!" Again and again he stabbed his three fingers at the sky. "But the Lord won't abandon me! He will yet lead us to a treasure of His creation!"

Very quickly, Cordeiro de Matos and his column were gone. Late that afternoon Trajano wanted to talk with Amador about the route they would take, but he couldn't find him. At a slave maloca, he was told that Amador had gone hunting with Abeguar. Sundown came, and night, which followed like a shot in these heights, closed around the stockade. After waiting for three hours, Trajano and Olímpio went to search for their father.

With six slaves, they headed in the direction of a valley four miles west of the camp, where Amador had often tracked peccary. Along their route were four malocas of Tupi-speaking natives, with whom they were at peace. As they neared this village, they heard the sounds of rattles and chants rising into the night; Trajano told them to approach cautiously, but these Tupi were engrossed in their ritual and ignored the group as it crossed toward the men's place.

Trajano stopped abruptly, one hundred feet from the circle of Tupi.

"Dear God!" Olímpio seized Trajano's arm.

Within this heathen circle, stripped to his ragged breeches and painted with red dye, Amador Flôres hopped with awkward, jerking steps and raised his voice to the chants of the savages.

"Father!" Olímpio cried out, and made as if to rush forward, but Trajano held him back. His long face was filled with an expression of utmost horror; his big frame shook. "Father! Come away from this place! For the love of Jesus and your soul, senhor, hurry away."

Amador smiled dementedly. "Quiet, Olímpio Ramalho," he said, his voice low and filled with menace. "Be silent lest you rouse the demons that haunt this assembly."

A terror rose within Olímpio at his father's possession by this wickedness, and he began to back off into the shadows beyond the fire. Trajano, too, moved away.

Abeguar and slaves who had accompanied Amador sat on the ground. The chants of the dancers quieted and their pace slowed; and then the pagé indicated that Amador and the Tupi should be seated.

Amador had left the stockade with Abeguar and the slaves with the intention of seeking wild pigs, but they had been offered food and drink at these malocas, and while at a longhouse they were joined by the pagé, Creep Foot. In his desperation after the desertion of Cordeiro de Matos, Amador had appealed to Creep Foot:

"What evil keeps me from my treasure? What do your gods see that's hidden from me? O, pagé, tell this old warrior whom you greet as a brother the secrets of bright green stones!"

Creep Foot now addressed Amador, fingering the plug below his lip. "You have told us that these stones we find near our village are weak charms," he said. "Our ancestors knew this. They told of green stones with which a warrior is protected against his greatest enemy and man seed a woman carries is not weakened."

"These are emeralds!" Amador exclaimed. "Green fire of earth, Pagé! My emeralds!"

Amador scrambled to his feet. "*You!*" he said to Creep Foot. He limped along the semicircle of villagers. "All who know the story of the fathers. Tell me everything said about the magic stones." Olímpio remained in the shadows beyond the fire, but Trajano had moved forward. "Heed every word, Trajano," Amador commanded.

The pagé pointed toward the villagers. "Not one of these men has seen such a stone."

"But you, Pagé, what do your gods see?" Amador asked.

"It is said that the stones are at a lake in these mountains."

"Where, Pagé? *Where?*"

"I do not know."

"More, Pagé. What more did the Tupi saints reveal?"

"The magic stones live in this lake. They move below the waters, from one shore to another. They are as difficult to catch as the snake fish."

There was a burst of laughter from Trajano. "Stones that swim!" he cried.

"*Silence!*" Amador shouted hoarsely at his son. "A lake with magical green stones. Emeralds, Trajano. *Emeralds!*"

Trajano looked at him pityingly.

☙

Olímpio accompanied his father on the first foray Amador made into the mountains, but he quickly reverted to his role as camp master, preferring to laze at the stockade rather than exert himself.

Trajano continued to march with Amador, but alone one night with Olímpio and seven Paulistas — five more deserted before a second prospecting trip in December 1678 — Trajano derided his father:

"'Onward! Onward!' he commands. 'There's a valley! A ravine! A lake!' A lake, my good companions, filled with emeralds! I tell my father: 'Six years we've searched and haven't found this lake.' He points to the hills. 'My horse!' he cries. 'Armor! Banner with the Cross of Christ! For the love of St. George! For young Dom Sebastião! Hasten! All Portugal waits!'"

Olímpio reminded him that as sons they owed Amador their loyalty. "We do?" Trajano queried. "When brave men of this bandeira flee from the sight of the bold beggar, our father, dragging himself across these hills?"

Procópio Almeida also remained sympathetic toward Amador, and was not depressed by the huge pile of worthless rock samples outside his hut. "I feel it in my bones, Olímpio," he would say, and laughing, he would slap his wooden leg — carved by himself and adorned with two wide bands of silver filigree. "There are riches here! Your father climbs the highest peaks, but the treasure is down here. Not emeralds. Not silver. *Gold!*"

When the emerald hunters were away, Procópio Almeida prospected for gold in the streams near the camp. Olímpio often went with him, and Procópio taught him how to use a wooden *bateia*, for panning sand and gravel from a riverbed.

On a day in June 1679, when Amador was on his third prospecting trek since the flight of Cordeiro de Matos, Olímpio was dozing in the shade of a jacaranda tree in the stockade when slaves came running with cries that Procópio Almeida was calling for him. Olímpio feared another terrible misfortune to have befallen the luckless Procópio and hurried to his aid.

But Procópio was perfectly safe, and standing in the middle of a stream with his wooden leg rammed into the mud. He was stripped to his waist, the big muscles on his arms and shoulders flexing as he washed the pebbles and soil. When he saw Olímpio approach, he sang out: "Gold! Gold! Gold!"

During the next four weeks, Procópio and Olímpio went on to recover fifty-two *oitavos* — eighths of an ounce — from this stream before the traces of gold dwindled. Procópio, convinced that more would be found, continued to prospect for the metal.

When Amador came back from his latest search at the end of August, they excitedly presented him with their find. But he laughed at the small pile of gold dust. "Emeralds!" he reminded them. "Emeralds!"

೧

September 11, 1679, was a violent stormy night with a downpour that turned the ground within the stockade into a quagmire. Two weeks ago the prospecting column had made its way back to the camp after the third unsuccessful search this past year. Tonight the seven Paulistas with the bandeira met in a shelter that housed the camp's manioc mill. Trajano da Silva had summoned them here.

"Are you with me?" Trajano asked them.

"Yes!" they replied, almost with one voice. "Yes!"

"God sees me as the captain-major's son. The Lord knows that I've supported him for six years. I remind him of the ruin he's brought to these da Silvas. 'No! No! No!' he protests. 'I won't be poor and defeated. I'll have my emeralds!'"

"We're the last group with him," a Paulista said. "When we return to São Paulo, he'll go with us."

"Never," Trajano said. "He'll never forswear his vow."

"With Olímpio Ramalho? And Almeida hopping between these hills?"

"Don't laugh, senhor! Not tonight."

There was sudden solemnity. "What must be done?"

Trajano began to speak, but there was a mighty roll of thunder and flashes of lightning. "May God forgive me," he said when it had passed. "There's but one way. Words won't convince him; nor will reason." His voice trembled. "I . . . will . . . kill him." There was silence, and then one of the Paulistas offered to do the deed himself. Trajano shook his head. "It's an act of mercy. Let it be my hand."

An hour later Trajano headed for the hut he shared with Amador and Olímpio. Great drops of rain splattered the mud as he walked to the entrance of the wattle-and-daub structure. Ten feet away, he drew a long knife and then hastened to the opening.

"Take him!" Amador commanded. "Now!"

Trajano froze with shock as four Carijó disarmed him. Olímpio stood there, too, with a pistol.

"Trajano da Silva!" Amador growled his name. "Did you truly believe that the Lord would forsake me? That He wouldn't send old Abeguar to hear every word at the mill and report to me: 'Your son, my Master, plots to kill you!'" Amador gave a short, hysterical laugh. "Savage! My Tupiniquin bastard!" He turned his back on his son. "Take him, Carijó. Throw him into the stocks. Let him pass this night with God's anger ringing in his ears."

The seven Paulistas who had conspired with Trajano fled the camp, choosing the raging storm and terrors of flight through the mountains. Trajano da Silva lay alone this long night with the rain lashing down on him, his legs thrust through the stocks, his ankles fettered with shackles and chains.

વ્ઝ

Amador got up before daybreak and changed his clothes, selecting the best items left in his leather chest. Everything he put on was frayed and ruined, his war jacket gashed, with the cotton twill hanging out, his last pair of boots cracked and encrusted with dirt. Still, when he went to sit on the bench outside the hut, all who watched and waited were able to discern pride and dignity.

Then he stood up and began to walk to the Carijó and Tupi. As he crossed to the malocas, Amador had to pass the stocks. Trajano raised his shoulders and twisted in his father's direction, but Amador continued walking and Trajano did not call out.

Olímpio and Procópio Almeida watched from the goldsmith's hut and saw Amador speak with Abeguar. Immediately afterward, Abeguar returned to the slaves and began issuing orders. Amador made his way to Olímpio and Procópio.

"You witnessed everything last night," Amador said.

"Yes, senhor, sadly I did," Olímpio replied.

"This bastard of mine whom I accepted so freely came to kill me. I would lie dead at this hour were it not for Abeguar. I must accept that I'm an old man who has had a long life. I see this. But, God knows, Olímpio Ramalho, I've searched my soul and find no cause for such an end."

"By God's grace, you were spared it."

"Yes, I was spared." Amador turned around and faced the stocks, where Abeguar and a group of slaves were releasing Trajano.

Olímpio watched them, too. "Your mercy?"

The slaves unshackled Trajano and dragged him to his feet. Amador turned slowly to Olímpio and Procópio Almeida.

"Quarter? They all cry for quarter," he said. "I have no pity."

"Senhor, you're not above God and the law."

Amador reached out and placed a hand on Olímpio's shoulder, a rare demonstration of affection toward this son. "You're right: I'm not above God. But in the sertão . . . here I am the law."

They followed him until he stopped fifteen feet from Trajano. The slaves had reattached Trajano's leg irons and he stood with difficulty, leaning against the stocks. He was covered with mud and dirt, his hands clenched at his sides, his legs trembling.

Abeguar and five natives who acted as his officers stood ready to rebuke any who misbehaved, but the Carijó and Tupi were quiet and attentive.

"His mother was a daughter of the Tupiniquin to whom I gave my seed. He was a boy when she died and he was taken into a home to be fed with love and kindness. He was led to the table of our Lord." Several natives cried out with praises for Jesus Christ. "He was raised with every hope of salvation. And he was given my name, this warrior: '*My son*,' I declared before all men. 'Trajano da Silva.'"

Trajano listened with bowed head, the only sound from him the rattle of the chain and shackles when he shifted his feet. Olímpio and Procópio Almeida exchanged glances of deep perturbation.

"When the prince regent asked that I lead this bandeira, I rejoiced. My own father longed for the smallest token of thanks but there was no reward for him in the days of the Spaniard. Tenente Bernardo was near his end and blind and yet stormed into the enemy camp . . . a *da Silva!* You bear his name and you would stain it with your bloody treason!"

Trajano had started to speak, but his words were incoherent.

"A defense?" Amador had turned to address Olímpio. "An excuse for his murderous intent?"

"Allow him to speak, senhor."

Trajano had gained control of his voice. "I was wrong," he said weakly.

"You damned yourself in the eyes of your father. And before Almighty God."

"Our Lord of mercy." Trajano tried to approach Amador, but he tripped and fell. A slave near the stocks started toward him, but Amador ordered him back.

"You dare appeal to our Lord of mercy?" Amador said.

"From *you* — forgiveness!" Trajano lifted his arms. "Have mercy!"

Amador looked across at Abeguar. "You have my orders."

The old Tupiniquin nodded and signaled to six slaves.

Olímpio moved next to Amador. "Father?"

"Stand back!"

"Father . . . spare him. You must."

Amador pointed to a jacaranda tree. "Hang him!" he shouted to Abeguar and the slaves.

"No!" Trajano cried. "Oh, God, no!"

Amador went to take up a position thirty feet from the tree. Olímpio and Procópio Almeida — struck dumb by this horrendous spectacle — followed him.

The Carijó and Tupi stood at the place of execution and were silent. But a few were unable to restrain themselves and called out with taunts and jeers for The Enemy of their master.

Trajano wept. He sobbed and screamed for his father's pity.

The jacaranda was a thin-limbed but an agile Tupi climbed up and tied the rope to a strong branch. Others secured Trajano da Silva's neck in a noose and hoisted him onto the back of a horse. Two whips cracked against the animal's flanks. It bolted forward and the rope snapped taut.

"Dear forgiving Jesus," Olímpio moaned, and started to move away.

"Stay!" Amador ordered. "It's not ended."

"For the love of God, what *more* do you demand?"

"This!" Amador shouted, his eyes blazing. "*This!*" He beckoned furiously for Olímpio and Procópio Almeida to follow him as he started toward the Carijó and Tupi.

"Let this be heard by all. I came to this sertão for emeralds." Silver, which Amador also sought, had never assumed the same importance. "The men who joined my bandeira have deserted — all but my slaves, my Tupi." He looked at the figure swinging below the jacaranda. "God has spared Amador Flôres da Silva to continue the search. This will be done!" He glared at Olímpio. "I will make my testament, Olímpio Ramalho. Let all hear! I was spared the assassin's blade, but if I die in the sertão . . . I command you to persist with the journey. You will neither take nor send my remains for burial in a civilized place without first discovering emeralds. You will fulfill my vow, under penalty of my curse!"

☙

The lake was twenty days' journey northeast of the camp at Sumiduoro. It was a mile long and half that distance at its widest section, and lay in a valley eight hundred feet above sea level. Slides of forest clung to a range of knoblike hills to the north, but at the lake the vegetation was sparse. Two streams entered the valley from the southeast, with a sluggish flow that contributed little to the still water. The air at the lake was hot and humid, breeding pestilential fevers.

The northern rim of the lake was swamplike, with a shallow ooze and rotting vegetation, dark and foul.

On a raw, windy morning in May 1681 at this rocky site, Amador cried out: "Mother of God! Mary! Jesus most blessed!" He danced across the stony ground, several times losing his footing and flinging his arms around wildly, but he maintained his balance and bounded along, his silver hair flying, his eyes darting from one place to another.

At this lake, Amador had found his emeralds.

Olímpio stood next to Procópio Almeida, who sat with his wooden leg stretched out in front of him, and they watched as Amador scrambled toward them.

"Again! Again, Procópio Almeida! Again!" Amador yelled out. "Tell me it's not a mirage! Tell me it *is* a lake!"

Procópio threw back his shoulders and looked up, his slightly slanted green eyes narrowed in concentration. "Esmeraldas." He waved his hand above samples of rock that lay in front of him. "Esmeraldas." He picked up a piece of rock with a vein of deep green gems. "*Esmeraldas!*"

His great beard jutted forward, and he cocked his head at a defiant angle. "Fidalgo! Governador! Hero of Portugal!"

Olímpio suddenly leapt toward Amador and grasped him in a wild embrace. "Esmeraldas!" he shouted. "*Esmeraldas!*" They danced around in front of Almeida, laughing and cheering at the top of their voices: "*Viva! Viva! Viva! Vitória!*" When they finally separated, Olímpio pointed at the outcrops of rock. "Here will be a quarry, Father — a mine to rival the wealth of Potosi!"

"Yes!" Amador shouted. "Oh, yes! The mine of Amador Flôres da Silva . . . and Olímpio Ramalho!" He looked down at the goldsmith. "And you, my faithful soldier, Procópio Almeida!"

Trajano had been executed in September 1679, twenty months ago. The camp had been abandoned two days after the hanging, and the bandeira had been on the move ever since, Amador's obsession growing stronger with every day that passed. At night he would rave for hours about emeralds and curse the forces that concealed them from him. Sometimes he would wake trembling from nightmares in which he wrestled with the ghost of Marcos de Azeredo. A few words of doubt, an expression of hopelessness from Procópio Almeida or Olímpio, and Amador would fly into a rage and threaten the punishment he had inflicted on his bastard son.

Amador had shown no remorse over Trajano's death, and if he referred to him, it was with contempt. In contrast, he had wept openly when Abeguar died the previous winter.

Wherever they stopped, Procópio Almeida had prospected for gold, finding more traces but no significant source. He had not wanted to undertake this journey, but he'd had no alternative, for he could not flee back to São Paulo by himself. He rode one of Olímpio's mules, exhausted and downhearted.

Like Procópio, Olímpio had despaired that they would find emeralds. Trajano's death had left him with a lasting fear of Amador, but it was more than this that kept him with the column. Olímpio was dutiful to his father, and accepted that he must stand by him for as long as he was called upon to do so.

They had been moving in a circular route, first west, then north and back toward the southeast, when they entered this valley. Passing along the northwest rim of the lake, they had been forced to swing to the south by the foul vegetation there — to a rocky terrain, where the exposed matrix in which the green gems were embedded indicated a vast deposit of emeralds.

They remained at the lake for two weeks collecting samples of rock. Procópio removed ten fine gems from the richest of these matrices. "I will personally take these emeralds to the infante Pedro," Amador announced. "I'll beg our prince to accept these first jewels of Terra do Brasil for the crown he will come to wear."

When they had enough samples, Amador ordered thirty of the seventy-six Tupi and Carijó who remained with him to set up camp near the lake, until he returned to mine his emeralds.

On June 2, 1681, Amador mounted one of Olímpio's mules to begin the journey home. A deerskin jerkin had replaced his ruined leather jacket, his breeches were cut from a gray blanket, his sandals had been made by the slaves. The appearance of Olímpio and Procópio Almeida was no better, and as he looked at them, Amador gave a burst of laughter. "Come, my beggars! Come! To São Paulo de Piratininga!" He made an effort to straighten his stooped shoulders; he slapped the pouch at his side and gave a triumphant cry. "Raise your eyes! Lift your spirits! When the voyage ends, you'll be princes. And I?" He laughed again. "A king — the king of emeralds!"

&

On June 22, 1681, they headed across a hilly tableland toward the Mantiqueira Mountains.

For several days Olímpio had watched his father with concern. It was as if the full effect of the years in the highlands had suddenly reached him. Amador's excitement had diminished. He complained of exhaustion and begged that they hurry to São Paulo; at times he leaned forward with his head drooping and had difficulty staying on the mule. Olímpio kept close to him and encouraged him along with talk of the grand reception that awaited them. But Amador's responses grew fewer and fewer, and though he urged the column to move hastily, he could not travel for more than a few hours a day.

On June 27, 1681, shortly after noon, Amador called a halt at a stream three days' journey from the Mantiqueira. When he'd been helped to the ground, he immediately dozed off in a feverish sleep. But he awoke toward evening, and for the first time in days he showed improvement and called for food. Olímpio and Procópio Almeida sat with him and expressed relief to see his strength returning.

"How many times have the devils of the sertão tried to carry me off?" Amador asked. "Here in these hills, in the north with Segge Proot . . . wherever I voyaged, they waited. Too late! Too late! The conquest is mine!"

Amador asked that more wood be thrown on the fire, and in the light from the flames, he opened the pouch with the emeralds, rolled some gems into the palm of his hand, and held up the smallest, admiring it. He saw Procópio Almeida staring at him and gave an expressive snort. "This pebble is worth more than that whole bag of dust you carry, Procópio. Not gold . . . not silver in these highlands." His expression grew reverent as he gazed at the stone. "Esmeraldas."

"There is gold, Captain-Major."

"Yes! Yes! Gold of El Dorado. Gold of fools!"

"I've seen many traces."

"All led to nothing. Why dream of gold? Why dream when your very eyes have seen a fortune?"

"True, Captain-Major," Procópio said, and soon afterward, he got up and went to his sleeping place.

It was bitterly cold. In the middle of the night, Olímpio got up and added more logs to the fire. His father was uncovered, and he threw a blanket over him before returning to his own covers.

Before dawn the camp began to stir as slaves prepared for the day's journey. Olímpio saw that Amador was still asleep and did not disturb him but went to attend to his mules. He was with them when Procópio Almeida came to him.

"Your father . . ."

Olímpio turned to look at Amador's still form. Immediately he knew. "Now? Here? So near the end?"

"He had his triumph," Procópio Almeida said quietly.

And so, in his sixty-seventh year, while he lay in a deep and contented sleep, dreaming of the glory to come, with his pouch of emeralds at his side, Amador Flôres da Silva died. In the sertão.

⁊

"For God's sake, what are you doing?" Olímpio asked Procópio Almeida three hours later. Procópio was struggling with a hide bearing rock samples that had been strapped to a mule. Amador's body had been wrapped in hides and tied to one of the other mules, for it was Olímpio's desire that his father be interred by the Benedictines.

"I told the slaves to discard these," Procópio said irritably. "You don't understand, my friend?"

"What?" Olímpio asked urgently. "*What* must I understand?"

"These green stones are tourmalines. Inferior. Flawed. Not worth the trouble to carry back."

"But . . . but you said *emeralds*."

"How else could we end this madness?" Procópio Almeida responded.

⁊

At first, Olímpio Ramalho had been furious at the deception, but then he came to realize that Procópio Almeida had done the right thing. Both, however, were very wrong in thinking that the last bandeira of Amador Flôres da Silva had ended there. It was Ishmael Pinheiro who appreciated the real finale to that tremendous quest — eleven years later.

Ishmael was seventy-eight, and by this time his sons and grandsons conducted the Pinheiro trading venture. Ishmael was mostly to be found on a bench at a tree near his storehouse, where he held court with friends and anyone who would stop for conversation. He was sitting here on a November morning in 1692 when he espied a mule-drawn wagon approaching. He watched it for some minutes and then raised his still corpulent, flabby body and moved slowly toward it.

Olímpio Ramalho walked beside the mules. He hailed Ishmael and went to meet him. Ishmael smiled with pleasure, for Olímpio was not only the son of Amador Flôres, who had been his great friend; he was also Ishmael's son-in-law, having married his daughter Marianna ten years ago. Ishmael called out a greeting and looked past Olímpio to the wagon, which was being brought to a stop by two slaves. He saw that it held another consignment of quince preserve.

Maria Ramalho da Silva! There were few women to compare with old Maria, Ishmael thought. Amador had died leaving his family with enormous debts, and religiously Maria had sent her produce year after year and taken only the barest supplies in return, determined to repay the thousands of cruzados still owed.

"Please, senhor!" Olímpio said excitedly after their greetings. "Come . . . please." He took Ishmael's arm and guided him toward the high-wheeled wagon.

"What is it?" Ishmael asked, but Olímpio simply urged him on. When he was close to the wagon, Ishmael stopped.

"Such a day, senhor, I promise you . . ."

Ishmael looked incredulously at the huge figure of Maria Ramalho enthroned on a pile of animal skins. Almost eighty, wrinkled, toothless, nearly blind in her good eye now, and showing the strain of the thirty-mile trek from the da Silva lands, Maria bent her head toward Ishmael. "My son has told you?"

"What, Dona Maria?" he asked. "Your preserve. A fine harvest. But there was no need for you to come."

Maria laughed, no ordinary laugh but a burst of pure joy. "Tell him, Olímpio," she said. "Tell him!"

Olímpio smiled at his mother's impatience. "Let's go inside, Dona Maria."

This took time, for the slaves had difficulty getting Maria off the wagon. Ishmael fussed and fumed and threatened dire punishment for the slightest discomfort to the grand old mameluco matron. After twenty minutes, they had Maria safely installed in Ishmael's best brocaded chair.

Maria's expression of joy increased. "I'm here," she began, and hesitated, her fleshy chins wobbling. "Ishmael Pinheiro, I've come . . ." Again she hesitated, and moved her hand slowly from side to side. At last she managed to say, "To pay the debt of Amador Flôres!"

Ishmael looked at her with perplexity. Always she had paid with preserve. What he had seen in the wagon would bring a few hundred cruzados — certainly not enough to settle the balance.

Olímpio entered the room carrying a good-sized cask.

"Show him, my son!" Maria cried.

Olímpio banged off the top of the cask. Ishmael swayed forward, frowning deeply.

"Gold!" Olímpio cried. "We've found a river of gold, Procópio Almeida and I."

They had gone back to the highlands a year after Amador's death. They had not committed themselves to one interminable journey but had returned to São Paulo every eighteen months or so. Again and again they had found traces — enough to pay for their expeditions — but it had taken eleven years before they came to a river, two days' journey north of the old camp, where a single day's work with the bateia produced one thousand oitavos! Procópio Almeida was back there now, guarding their precious claim, for many others had become convinced that gold in great quantities was to be found in the highlands of Terra do Brasil.

Ishmael had to steady himself by holding onto Olímpio as he peered into the cask and beheld the golden treasure.

Maria clapped her hands. "The *quinto* for Lisbon. The rest — will it be enough, Ishmael Pinheiro?"

"Dear heaven, yes!"

"There's more," Olímpio said. "More than you ever dreamed possible."

"It was his dream, too," Maria said, a broad smile on her face. "Your father's dream, Olímpio Ramalho. What did it matter that he hunted emeralds? He led the way."

Ishmael crossed slowly to her and took her hands into his own. "Oh, yes, Dona Maria. Amador Flôres da Silva led the way."

BOOK FOUR

Republicans
&
Sinners

XIV

October 1755 – March 1756

*M*arcelino Augusto Arzão da Fonseca was a pale and cherub-faced libertine with the eyes of a saint. These eyes, blue and agleam with innocence, had rescued him from many a scrape with student patrols at the University of Coimbra, and had disarmed countless peasant maidens in the poplar groves along Coimbra's Mondego River. Marcelino Augusto's wenching and an enthusiasm for cockfighting were matched by a quick intelligence and a good memory, and he had been awarded his diploma in law.

On a serene autumn day in October 1755, life could not have been more promising for twenty-three-year-old Marcelino Augusto and two companions whom he had invited to his father's country estate at Sintra, seventeen miles northwest of Lisbon. These young men were also recent graduates of Coimbra, where Marcelino Augusto had befriended them; they were both from Brazil, and were soon to take passage back to Brazil.

Marcelino Augusto was the eldest son of Dom António Pinto da Fonseca — he had served for a decade in Portuguese India and at the Bahia, where he had been an aide to a governor-general before retiring to Portugal in 1729.

After leaving the Bahia, Dom António had devoted himself to increasing his fortune and was now a wealthy man. This preoccupation with commerce had damaged his reputation among envious fidalgos who regarded the merchants with whom Dom António associated as parasitical and suspect of Judaic sympathies grave enough to arouse the Grand Inquisitor. Though rarely seen at court, Dom António remained loyal to his king; twice he had made secret loans to His Majesty. But Dom António was openly contemptuous toward pampered courtiers and worthless sycophants, and he could not abide overzealous ecclesiastics.

Marcelino Augusto had been influenced by his father's ideas, which, though lagging behind the enlightened thinking elsewhere in Europe during these middle years of the eighteenth century, were eminently reasonable. Thus it was that Marcelino Augusto, scion of a wealthy and noble family of Portugal, could, with Dom António's encouragement, associate with two young men upon whom many highborn Portuguese would look down.

Luis Fialho Soares was twenty-five, the oldest of the three, and hailed from the southern captaincies of Brazil. His prominent cheekbones, a slight bronze tinge to his skin, and almond-shaped eyes bespoke a Tupi heritage; he freely admitted a savage princess among his ancestors, a claim so prevalent as to suggest there were no commoners among the pagans of old Santa Cruz. Generations of Luis Fialho's family had followed the bandeirante pursuits of slaving, exploring, and prospecting, until his grandfather, Baltasar Soares, a Paulista, struck gold north of the Mantiqueira Mountains during the rush that followed the initial discoveries. Today, the Soares family had gold washings, and a farm with cattle and pigs; Luis Fialho's father, Floriano Soares, had also prospered as a moneylender. Luis Fialho had been sent to the Jesuit colégio at Rio de Janeiro, and from there to Coimbra to study law, though his ruling passion was poetry of Arcadian simplicity.

The second of Marcelino Augusto's friends had also been born in Brazil, but he differed from Luis Fialho in all other respects. Paulo Benevides Cavalcanti was the first member of his family to be sent from Engenho Santo Tomás to Coimbra, where he, too, had stood in the Sala dos Capelos to receive his law degree. Descended from Dom Fernão Cavalcanti, one of the heroes of the "War of Divine Liberty" against the Dutch, Paulo was the son of Bartolomeu Rodrigues Cavalcanti, the great-grandson of Fernão. Senhor Bartolomeu's first wife, Dona Eglantina Castelo, bore him five girls before her death in 1727; his second wife, Catarina Benevides, the daughter of a planter from Cabo district south of Recife, was the mother of Paulo and two other sons, Graciliano and Geraldo.

Paulo, the oldest son, was twenty-three. He had finely arched eyebrows, thick lashes, and a straight, thin nose. He had the typical Cavalcanti physique, compact and muscular, though taller than average, and exuded an aura of vitality and confidence. He shared his companions' preference for the French fashion, and wore powdered wig, salmon-colored embroidered silk waistcoat, brown breeches, and buckled shoes. A knee-length velvet coat with gold frogging and passementerie completed his outfit, but Paulo had removed the coat and now carried it over his arm, since a short ramble suggested by Marcelino Augusto this afternoon had lengthened into a two-hour assault on a steep hill behind the Fonseca property.

They had climbed along a winding path through shadowy pines and hazelwoods to the summit, where the fortresslike monastery of Pena stood gloomy and silent, its desolation the result of a fire twelve years ago. From these heights, they had a stupendous view of sandy beaches and rocky promontories along the dark blue Atlantic six miles to the west, and in the distance, the mouth of the Tagus River.

Marcelino Augusto sped from one vantage point to another, dramatically describing the scenes below: "Here, my friends, at this very place a lookout spied the first of Dom Vasco da Gama's ships sailing toward the Tagus. 'All India is ours!' cried the fellow, and ran to deliver this news to Dom Manoel the Fortunate. This sanctuary was built by the king in thanks for the passage to the East!"

Marcelino Augusto swung his arm to the north. "And there you see evidence of the gratitude of another king of Portugal!"

He pointed to an immense pile of buildings on the horizon — the towered, domed 880-room Mafra palace, which had been completed fifteen years ago. After three years of childless marriage, Dom João V had vowed that if given an heir, he would erect a monastery on the site of the poorest priory in his kingdom. When his prayers were answered with the birth of a daughter and a son, Dom João had ordered the construction of this colossal building.

Though Dom João had devoted most of his largesse to the court and the church, he had also provided Coimbra's university with a splendid library, a gilded and lacquered extravaganza. And his engineers had given Lisbon several impressive public works, including a nine-mile aqueduct in the valley of Alcantara just outside the capital.

Before coming to Portugal, Paulo Cavalcanti had traveled no farther than Pernambuco, and his visits to the towns of Olinda and Recife had been infrequent. Like earlier generations of Cavalcanti sons, Paulo had been imbued with respect for the motherland, and he admired the fact that the new structures were as splendid as those built when the riches of the Indies had reached Lisbon. The continuity suggested that the genius of the Portuguese remained as bold and inventive as in the days of *As Conquistas.*

Luis Fialho was from the sertão and had been raised among people to whom Portugal had a magical quality, in some ways not unlike Land of the Grandfather. He had been exultant when the ship carrying him from Rio de Janeiro crossed the bar of the Tagus: "Portugal! Home of the heroes!" Through a forest of masts, he had glimpsed the royal palace, the wharves and warehouses, and had rushed to a higher deck for his first sight of Lisbon's seven hills crowned with tower and spire, with every slope and promontory, every valley populated. The Mother City!

Nor had Luis Fialho's wonder diminished at Coimbra, a city that had figured in every phase of Portuguese history since its capture from the Moors in 1064; "I hear the music of the past," Luis Fialho had told his friends, "the immortal song of Lusitania."

Often Luis Fialho's lyrical contemplations had been followed by dark melancholy at the thought of Brazil. He had spoken of America as sensuous and corrupting. It was in Luis Fialho's carefully chosen words, "A hell for blacks, a purgatory for whites."

But, toward his third year in Portugal, Luis Fialho's friends had noticed a change in his attitude. He still praised the glories of old Portugal, and he brooded over the deprivations facing a man of gentility in Brazil, but a new critical note had crept into his conversation:

"This swarm of monks and friars in Portugal, these priests in every office of the kingdom . . . Don't two black robes suffice for four thousand pagans in Brazil? Here, twenty priests are called to minister to the same number of true Christians." The Inquisition had informers everywhere, and Luis Fialho shared such comments only with like-minded friends, but other observations he made freely: "Why is it that the king's officers must labor as servants and coachmen or starve? That no street is without soldiers in rags begging for alms? Dear God in heaven, what has become of proud Portugal?"

What Luis Fialho found so difficult to accept about the poverty and stagnation in Portugal was that the kingdom had been given riches as never before. Great Mafra and all the lavish works from Dom João V's reign, the brilliantly adorned churches and convents — exorbitant as these expenditures had been, they represented only a fraction of the fabulous treasure of gold and gems sent from the captaincies of Brazil.

Olímpio Ramalho da Silva and Procópio Almeida had not been the only Paulistas to discover gold in the early 1690s; three groups of prospectors had made simultaneous strikes beyond the Mantiqueira Mountains in a region that had become known as Minas Gerais ("General Mines"). By 1709, Vila Rica de Ouro Prêto ("Rich Town of Black Gold") and surrounding mining camps had a population of fifty thousand whites, half-breeds, and slaves. In 1718, Paulistas had found gold at Cuiabá, eight hundred miles directly northwest of São Paulo and Minas Gerais. So great was the wealth of the Cuiabá diggings that the first pair of cats transported to the rat-infested camp had been sold for a pound of gold!

And there was more than gold to fill the royal purse. North of the lake where Amador Flôres da Silva had found his "emeralds," gold prospectors had picked up cloudy crystals in the alluvial beds; they considered these worthless and used them as backgammon pieces, until lapidaries in Lisbon identified them as diamonds. Crown officials stepped in to prevent the illegal exploitation of Dom João's fields and eventually proclaimed a "Forbidden District," some 130 miles in circumference, east of the range known as The Spine. A miner caught extracting diamonds without the king's authority could be thrown into jail or banished to Angola; illegal possession by a slave could bring up to four hundred lashes, often after forced ingestion of a purge of Malgueta pepper to flush out any gems he had swallowed.

Luis Fialho stood with his back to the others and was looking at Mafra. "Dear God, what a majestic pile! What would those Paulistas searching for El Dorado say? What could they believe but that here, before their eyes, was the palace of El Dorado!"

Marcelino Augusto laughed. "Every stone paid for with the gold and diamonds of Brazil."

"Exactly. And so the fable becomes reality," Luis Fialho said, turning to them. "They marched through the sertão, our men of the bandeiras, with a vision of a fabulous city of palaces and glittering temples. They couldn't see that it was they who would make this possible, this El Dorado of their dreams, with Mafra and every other grand edifice."

"I know some dreamers," Paulo began. "They —"

"I dream!" Marcelino Augusto broke in.

"Francisca Caetano!" Luis Fialho said. "You and a hundred others, my friend, all with your sleep disturbed by fair Francisca."

Marcelino Augusto had met Francisca at the house of his aunt, who was married to a Neapolitan merchant, a patron of the new Lisbon opera house, where the Caetano girl had recently made a triumphant debut.

"Tell us about your dreamers, Paulo," Luis Fialho said.

"The senhores de engenho who went to the mines. They passed through the sertão with their peças to evade the dragoons." The supply of slaves to Minas Gerais was controlled by Crown quota, but thousands were taken in illegally via the backlands because of the high price they commanded. "After months, if the senhores were not caught by the soldiers, the only gold they saw came from the sale of their blacks."

The Cavalcantis had not been enticed away from Engenho Santo Tomás by the hope of a quick fortune, despite the difficulties Pernambuco's sugar industry faced as English and French plantations prospered in the Antilles, but had extended their control over a valley beyond Santo Tomás. In the sertão, 250 miles west of Recife and north of the Rio São Francisco, the family had also obtained four holdings covering fifty square miles for a stock-breeding fazenda.

"Selling their slaves was a serious mistake," Luis Fialho said in response to Paulo. "A claim is useless without slaves to work it."

"And so, too, a cane field. Some came back from the mines and lived like squatters on their lands; some were seen begging in the streets of Recife. They cursed the day they had the notion of going south to a den of peddlers and marinheiros who robbed and cheated them."

"The rabble of Europe!" Luis Fialho said. "It was a dark day for us when they set their covetous eyes on the highlands of Brazil!"

Paulo and Luis Fialho shared a disdain for Portuguese-born merchants and traders in Brazil, whom they called peddlers and marinheiros, and for Emboabas ("Feather Legs"), a Paulista epithet for foreigners at the mines. It was Luis Fialho's theory that the Tupi word had something to do with the outsiders' fear of dropping their breeches or going barefoot in the jungle.

When Luis Fialho had first spoken to Paulo of the Emboabas, he revealed the rancor toward these outlanders passed on to him by his elders: "The Feather Legs swarmed over the mining camps like vermin. They showed no respect for the Paulistas who had conquered that sertão. 'Savages!' they called men like my grandfather, Baltasar Soares."

The Paulistas had taken up arms against the Emboabas in 1708, when the mining camps controlled by a Paulista superintendent were in a state of anarchy.

"For three years, Grandfather Baltasar fought the damn Feather Legs. If only our people hadn't quarreled among themselves. 'Too many generals! Too many grand *chefes!*' says my grandfather.

"In the end, the king's soldiers came from Rio de Janeiro to restore peace, for the uproar at the diggings was robbing His Majesty, too, by cutting off his supply of gold."

Of course, Paulo knew of the troubles that had erupted at the gold diggings four decades ago, but his disdain for the foreigners stemmed from a cause far closer to home, for in Pernambuco, too, there had been conflict with Portuguese-born rivals between 1709 and 1711. Olinda had never fully recovered from the devastations during the Dutch invasion the previous century, but the senhores de engenho had maintained it as capital of the captaincy and controlled its municipal câmara, which had full political power over Recife, the commercial center with its population of twelve thousand. The merchants and traders had repeatedly appealed to the Crown for their own municipal council, and in 1709 a royal decree elevated Recife to town status and ordered the erection of a new pillory, the symbol of royal and municipal authority.

"The peddlers came from Portugal with rags on their backs and the huge conceit to seek privileges that belonged to the noble families of Pernambuco," Paulo had told Luis Fialho. "But when Bartolomeu Rodrigues Cavalcanti and others hurled down the pillory at Recife, the peddlers cried 'Treason!' and took up arms. The governor supported them and was forced to flee to the Bahia. The war lasted a year, until Lisbon sent a new administrator in October 1711 — My father and other rebels were granted a royal pardon, but Dom João insisted that the pillory be raised."

There had been experiences at Coimbra that had also affected Paulo's feelings toward Portugal, none so disturbing as the prejudice he found toward the mazombos, as the Portuguese disparagingly referred to the Brazilian-born whites.

"Where will the king find subjects more loyal than the great plantation owners of Pernambuco?" Paulo had said angrily. "Nowhere! Is it wrong for a man like my father to long for rank and honor from the court? God in heaven knows how faithfully Bartolomeu Rodrigues has served the kingdom!"

This had not been Paulo's only disillusionment: He had found the atmosphere at Coimbra suffocating. Paulo's early education had come from Padre Eugênio Viana, a priest/tutor at Engenho Santo Tomás.

"What a wonderful teacher we had in Padre Eugênio," Paulo had told Luis Fialho. "Certainly he had his supply of quince switches and a broad leather strap that he soaked in water to increase its sting. But he didn't believe that all young boys were possessed by the devil. If he saw us drowsy and irritable, the padre would throw open the door of our schoolroom and lead us outdoors. 'Come boys,' he would say, 'let's walk! We have as much to learn beneath our Lord's sky as under dusty rafters!'"

After the enlightened guidance of Eugênio Viana, Paulo had found Coimbra medieval and called the ancient seat of learning "the tomb of thought." Whereas other European universities were being swept up in the intellectual ferment of these midyears of the eighteenth century, the pedagogues of the Jesuit-controlled Coimbra adhered to their ancient statutes and were obsessed with technicalities and hairsplitting debates.

Now, on the hill above Sintra, Marcelino Augusto gazed across the plains below them. "Even before Vasco da Gama's day, when we had settled the Atlantic islands, men left Portugal to make a better life for themselves. Your ancestors, Luis, Paulo, they may have set out from these very lands."

Paulo Cavalcanti nodded, though he did not know that Nicolau Gonçalves Cavalcanti had left for Pernambuco from João Cavalcanti's house, just six miles southwest of Sintra.

"True. For generations the Cavalcantis have served Portugal against savages, Norman corsairs, Spaniards. The men of Santo Tomás helped drive the Dutch out of

Brazil. Why must we surrender our patrimony to these latecomers?"

Luis Fialho agreed. "The Paulistas welcomed the Feather Legs with open arms. They fed and sheltered them and protected them against the savages. Then thousands of Feather Legs streamed to the gold camps, and they turned against the Paulistas.

"In the same way the savage was dispossessed in earlier times?"

"Ah, my friend, don't heed everything the Frenchmen and others say. The savage so noble and pure-hearted?" He shook his head. "That's what Rousseau tells the world, but he hasn't seen the true savage."

Luis Fialho's lack of sympathy for the natives was in conflict with current feeling in Portugal. In 1748, Dom João issued an order abolishing slavery of the natives of Brazil and the northern territory of Maranhão and Grão Pará. The decree did not affect in any way the million black and mulatto slaves in Brazil, but from July 13, 1748, the enslavement of the natives was prohibited.

"'Dispossessed,' you say," Luis Fialho went on. "Dear heaven, what glorious dispossession! Wherever the savage has been expelled, there's hope that Brazil will one day be a civilized and Christian nation."

"I've heard different reports from my father," the young Fonseca said, as they moved along a small ridge from where they had a fine view of the distant Tagus. "Don't misunderstand men like Dom António. They speak in defense of the natives because reason now dictates that they should no longer be enslaved like peças."

"And who'll speak for the early settlers?" Luis Fialho said. "Who'll recall the terrors endured before plantations and towns were safe from attack? Who'll remember thousands who gave their lives in the sertão?"

"You, my poet friend. You!" Marcelino Augusto said, slapping a hand on Luis Fialho's shoulder. "First you wept at the misfortune of birth in that land of savages. No place was so grand and noble as Portugal; no terra firma so cruel and unforgiving as Brazil. But then, Luis Fialho, we came to hear you praise that continent, its valleys, its rivers, forests, seas, all surpassing what you saw here. You made a discovery here — you and Paulo. Yes, my friends, across the bar of the Tagus, you discovered Brazil!"

☙

The heavily draped salon of the Fonseca country house was austere. The rugs were old, threadbare in places, and reeked of a musty, unpleasant odor. Two huge mahogany tables with heavy carved legs dominated the room. Tall mirrors reflected objects connected with past Fonsecas: a pair of waist-high Chinese porcelain vases; a teak cabinet with ivory marquetry from Goa; a Persian water pitcher; a four-foot iron statue from West Africa, representing a sixteenth-century Portuguese soldier.

Dom António was not given to brooding over the past. He was a small, sprightly sixty-two-year-old, his expression alert and intelligent. He disliked the shabby room but would not change it, less from respect for earlier Fonsecas than from a reluctance to part with thousands of cruzados.

Dom António sat on a sofa, with Marcelino Augusto next to him. Paulo and Luis Fialho were close by, Paulo on a high-backed ebony chair. Paulo shifted from time to time on the hard seat, but for the most part he was as motionless as if he was sitting for his portrait, his attention riveted on Dom António's visitor.

This man sat sideways at one of the mahogany tables, an elbow resting on the surface, where several maps of Brazil were spread open. His long legs stretched out in front of the chair suggested his height. He was in his fifty-sixth year, well preserved, with a powerful physique, his hands large but with slender fingers. As arresting as his piercingly intelligent hazel eyes were the cleft in his chin, emphasizing his well-shaped mouth, and a white wig that flowed to his shoulders.

He was Sebastião José de Carvalho e Melo, and on this day in October 1755, no man in Portugal save the king was more powerful. What made this the more re-markable was that at his birth in 1699, Carvalho e Melo was the son of a cavalry officer.

Educated at Coimbra, Carvalho e Melo had entered the army and gone to Lisbon to improve his miserable prospects with the help of an uncle who served the patriarchal church. But his uncle's appeals and his own voluntary service with the rowdy aristocrats had failed to bring Carvalho e Melo attention at court. He had pressed his suit with a highborn Lisbon lady, but her family rejected him because of his poor pedigree.

These setbacks had left him with an antipathy toward the clique of nobles who ruled Portugal, and seven years passed before he again felt confident to assault these bastions of Portuguese society. His uncle succeeded in getting him an appointment to the new Academy of History. His assignment: to research the background of the noblest family of Portugal, the ruling Braganças.

Thirty-two at the time and still unmarried, he had again cast around for a wife and found an attentive widow, Teresa de Noronha, the niece of a count — only to be rebuffed once more, by the dona's relatives. He eloped with Dona de Noronha, an event that had caused a sensation in Lisbon.

In 1739, Carvalho e Melo's perseverance had been rewarded with the post of Portuguese minister in London, and six years later he was sent as special envoy to Vienna, his services offered by Dom João V as mediator in a dispute between the Austrian Empire and the Papacy.

Dona Teresa de Noronha had not accompanied her husband on these missions; she had retired to a convent, where, shortly after Carvalho e Melo's assignment to Vienna, she died.

The new widower found solace in the arms of Leonor Ernestina Daun, a lady-in-waiting of the Dowager Empress Christina. Leonor was the daughter of Count Leopold Josef von Daun, a hero of the Austrian War of Succession. Marriage to Leonor Ernestina guaranteed the cavalry officer's son a place among the nobles at Lisbon, where he had returned in 1749, his fiftieth year, to consolidate his gains over the previous decade.

But his outspoken criticism of the priests who enthralled His Most Faithful Majesty and dabbled in matters of state, his enmity toward certain fidalgos whom he blamed for corruption and confusion in Portugal, and his support for the middle-class merchant and entrepreneur had brought Carvalho e Melo enemies who were determined to halt his ambitious progress.

Anticipating a confrontation with these men, he had allied himself with a group loyal to Dom João V's heir, Prince José. On July 31, 1750, Dom João died, and the new king, José I, immediately appointed as prime minister a beloved but nearly blind, decrepit statesman, who rarely left his house and received visitors only after midnight. Ministry of Marine and the Colonies went to another ailing court favorite. The third portfolio, Minister of Foreign Affairs and War, was given to Sebastião José Carvalho e Melo, who, with the indisposition of his two colleagues, was in control of the cabinet.

Once launched on his reign, José I had come to find the pursuit of stag and Italian opera preferable to the burdens of government, and Carvalho e Melo's powers increased far beyond his cabinet influence, though he still faced the intrigues of fidalgos and priests who despised the upstart commoner. However, on this day in October 1755, when he had come to visit his friend Dom António, Carvalho e Melo, better known by his subsequent title, Marquis of Pombal, was well on his way to becoming the first modern European dictator.

The three young men, who had been invited into Dom António's salon upon their return from their walk, found Carvalho e Melo's manner so engaging that they lost some of their initial apprehension in his presence. When the minister asked what they had been doing on the hill, Marcelino Augusto responded: "Excellency, I wanted my friends to see the view from the old monastery. — Sintra, The Tagus, Mafra. The old and the new glories of their motherland."

"Glories?" Carvalho e Melo queried. "Mafra is grand," he agreed.

"Luis Fialho compared Mafra with El Dorado, Excellency," Marcelino Augusto said. "Were the Paulistas who led the bandeiras to see Mafra, they could only think that here was the fabulous palace of El Dorado, which they had sought for so long and so patiently."

"Patience! What patience God gave the Portuguese," Carvalho e Melo responded vehemently. "For a century after our first expedition against the Moors at Cueta in 1415, we tore down forests for ships and we filled fleets with the young men of Portugal. One hundred years and we achieved our goal — the wealth of the Indies! But how soon before we lost most of our possessions to the Dutch? The English? The French?

"At Brazil, a century of patience was rewarded with gold and diamonds. And what of the Hollanders, the French, the English in Brazil? For thirty years the Dutch struggled to capture our American colony. They failed. The French, also. And the English?

"The English dispatched no royal fleet, and not one battle was fought on the soil of Portuguese America," the minister continued. "And yet the greatest profit from our Brazil, the labor of the mines of Brazil — the gold, the diamonds — is not for Lisbon but London!"

Though the wines of Portugal flowed to London and the gallant men of England lay groaning with gout, the value of the great shipments of hogsheads and pipes exported from Oporto was only one-fifth of Portugal's imports of English cloth. Portugal owed a fortune for goods supplied by the English, and in payment of her debts sent half the legally dispatched output of gold and diamonds from Minas Gerais and other mining areas to London.

"Gold and diamonds from Brazil are financing England's manufactories — the very cloth we buy from her, her new public works, her canals, her highways,"

Carvalho e Melo added. "Our treasure is launching the East India ships that sail to build an empire for England. And the city of London? With the gold of Brazil, London has won the crown of commerce from Amsterdam.

"Without the riches of Brazil and the Maranhão to pay its debts, Portugal would collapse in six months," Carvalho e Melo said. "The palaces at Lisbon, the crowded wharves, the ships — English ships — jamming the Tagus . . . these are an illusion. Gold, diamonds, sugar, cotton, the spices of the forest — whatever fills our plate comes from America, and this we happily pass on to England!

"We need manufactories in Portugal, and our own trading companies in Brazil, not a pack of agents whose first interest is the profit of the English merchants they serve." With Dom António and others, Carvalho e Melo had recently launched a company with monopolistic rights in Maranhão and Grão Pará. Now he glanced at the maps on the table, stabbing Brazil on each with his forefinger. "Viable trade policies will protect the riches and products of our colony, but this alone will not secure Brazil . . . People! We must have the people to fill this wilderness. Small Portugal supports two million. There are those who suggest that Brazil can be home to twenty times this number. More. Sixty million, perhaps. A population like that of China."

Paulo, more nervous than his friends in the presence of Carvalho e Melo, had said nothing, but he could not imagine how the minister could even contemplate such figures, and he plucked up the courage to ask a question: "Your Excellency, where would so many come from?"

"We can begin with the tens of thousands held in bondage by the Jesuits. The natives must be freed from that wasteful tutelage. Let them take Portuguese names. Let them forget the savage tongue the Jesuits have encouraged and learn Portuguese. Let them be welcome as equals in our society."

Luis Fialho frowned at Carvalho e Melo's remarks. It was common knowledge that Dom José's minister was heading toward a major confrontation with the "Society" of Jesus, as Ignatius Loyola's Company had come to be known.

"Do you disagree?" Carvalho e Melo asked Luis Fialho.

"No, Excellency. The priests have raised their congregations like children and taught them lies about the colonists."

"Vieira did not lie," the minister said dryly, referring to the Jesuit who had labored along the Rio das Amazonas. "'Two million dead,' Vieira wrote sixty years ago. How many more since Vieira's day?" He shook his head. "No, Vieira did not lie about the butchers at the Amazon," he repeated. "And what would he say if he were alive to see aldeias where hundreds are kept as serfs, where they do forced labor on plantations and roam the forests for products to enrich the Jesuits?"

During his years in London, Carvalho e Melo had listened to denunciations of the Jesuits who had gained notoriety for their alleged roles in past plots against Crown and Parliament. On his return to Lisbon, he had seen the power they exercised as confessors at court, and especially that of Gabriel Malagrida, an Italian Jesuit with thirty years' experience in Brazil, where he had gained a reputation as a miracle worker.

When Dom João V was taken critically ill in 1749, Malagrida immediately set sail for Lisbon, bearing an image of the Virgin which had accompanied him on his missions in Brazil and to which marvelous powers were attributed. Malagrida spent months at the bedside of the ailing João consoling His Most Faithful Majesty in his last days. He was the most powerful Jesuit at court and the confidant of nobles opposed to Carvalho de Melo. But neither Malagrida nor these fidalgos had influence over events in South America, where incidents involving the Jesuits were providing Carvalho e Melo with evidence to convince King José that the black robes were a menace.

In 1750, Portugal and Spain signed the Treaty of Madrid, which at long last acknowledged that the Tordesilhas Line of 1494 no longer reflected a true division of their lands in America. The Treaty of Madrid provided for two border-survey commissions, working from the north and the south.

The early invasions of the province of Guairá and subsequent Paulista incursions south along the Atlantic littoral had led to the establishment of two new Brazilian captaincies: Santa Catarina and Rio Grande de São Pedro. This expansion had been in line with Portuguese ambitions to extend their domain to the Rio de la Plata, where, in 1680, they had set up a fortified enclave, Colónia do Sacramento, opposite Buenos Aires. By the terms of the Treaty of Madrid, Colónia do Sacramento was to be ceded to Spain in exchange for lands that would be incorporated in the southernmost captaincy, Rio Grande de São Pedro.

These fertile lands east of the Rio Uruguay contained seven Jesuit reductions, with a population of thirty thousand Guarani. They were ordered to pack up their movable belongings, abandon their homes, and cross the river to Spanish territory.

Appeals by the mission fathers failed to reverse this decision. Fearing the consequences of a confrontation with either the Portuguese or the Spaniards, the Jesuits had tried desperately to persuade the converts to accept the treaty; but the Guarani refused to move, and had blocked the passage of the Spanish-Portuguese border commissioners. In 1754 the Spanish and the Portuguese separately sent expeditions against the Guarani, both of which had failed.

In the Fonseca salon, Minister Carvalho e Melo referred to the incidents. "The Jesuits are leading thousands of Guarani in the field," he said, quoting a grossly exaggerated report. "Even as we sit here, soldiers of Portugal and Spain again march to destroy this priests' utopia."

Carvalho e Melo then mentioned another area where the Jesuits were interfering with the border commission: the Rio das Amazonas and its tributaries, along which the Society of Jesus had established nineteen aldeias. The minister had a special interest in the region because his brother, Francisco Xavier de Mendonça Furtado, was governor of Maranhão and Grão Pará. Proud, excitable, and as ambitious as Carvalho e Melo, when Mendonça Furtado had arrived at Belém do Pará in 1751, his assignment included the post of chief border commissioner for the north. He had accused the Jesuits of impeding his work by refusing to supply aldeia natives for his canoes and by offering inadequate provisions for his survey party.

Mendonça Furtado's criticisms of the black robes went far beyond the difficulties of his border commission: While he deprecated the settlers' inhumanity toward the natives, he was a keen listener to their reports that the black robes kept the natives as serfs; that there were secret Jesuit mines in the sertão; that males of the aldeias were sent to collect plants and spices in the forest, and in their absence, the fathers consorted with their wives and daughters.

The Jesuits denied these allegations, pointing out that the priests were forbidden to receive anything worth more than one cruzado for themselves, and that all the income had to be applied to support the aldeias. They dismissed with contempt the charges of immorality. But they could not allay Mendonça Furtado's suspicions or the envy of the colonists, few of whom had properties to compare with those of the Jesuits. The black robes controlled seven ranches with thirty thousand cattle. They had vast plantings of cane and cotton. And the spices of the Amazon — cocoa, cloves, sarsaparilla, dyestuffs, and other forest products — realized thousands of cruzados a year.

"The colonists are starving and impoverished because of these rich priests," Mendonça Furtado had reported to his brother. "The natives live in a state of ignorance, without hope for the future."

Carvalho e Melo intended to strike his first blow against the Jesuits, at Maranhão and Grão Pará. A law had been passed in June 1755 removing temporal authority over the aldeias of the north from the Jesuit fathers. They would be allowed to catechize the natives, but the control of the villages would be given to a civilian directory.

Carvalho e Melo did not discuss this law with the Fonsecas and their guests; the text was secret and was to be made public only when Governor Mendonça Furtado was ready to move against the black robes. But, for nearly an hour, the minister spoke of dangers posed by the Jesuits in Paraguay and Maranhão. His audience did not contradict his views. Marcelino Augusto appeared content to let Dom António offer whatever response was called for. Luis Fialho was skeptical about equality for the natives, but he was in agreement with everything else said by the minister. As for Paulo Cavalcanti . . .

Paulo found His Excellency Carvalho e Melo's condemnations most troubling. Fourteen miles directly south of Engenho Santo Tomás there was an aldeia, Nossa Senhora do Rosário, which had been established thirty-five years ago at an abandoned plantation bequeathed to the Society. When Paulo had last seen it, Rosário had had an impoverished population of three hundred, a mixed group of natives, half-breeds, and a few free mulattoes and blacks. Everything Paulo remembered about Nossa Senhora do Rosário conflicted with Carvalho e Melo's criticism of the wealth of the Jesuits.

"There's an aldeia near the Cavalcantis' engenho, Your Excellency," Paulo ventured.

"Yes?"

"The aldeia of Nossa Senhora do Rosário, Excellency. There are three hundred families. Most are caboclos—"

Carvalho e Melo waved a hand, signaling Paulo to stop. "'Caboclo,'" he repeated. "The child of a native and a Portuguese." He gave a deep sigh. "This is derogatory; it is insulting and demeaning, Paulo."

"I realize this, Your Excellency."

"I hope that it won't be long before the colonists stop using such words. It will make it easier for these people to be accepted as equals. Please continue, Paulo."

Paulo was distracted by the offense he'd given the minister, but he nevertheless made the point: "There's nothing at this aldeia that suggests the Jesuits are wealthy."

"The priests at Rosário may have few possessions, but they are not typical. The big aldeias produce more in one season than the majority of colonists will see in a lifetime.

"You are young, Paulo Cavalcanti. Take your time. Make your own observations." Though the words were addressed to Paulo, the minister looked at Luis Fialho and Marcelino Augusto, suggesting that they, too, should heed this advice. "You will come to see that the Jesuit who set out to conquer the pagans of Brazil has lost his way. No longer content with heaping up heavenly rewards, he seeks a Jesuit paradise on earth."

"The Society of Jesus is a mighty force, Excellency," Paulo said quietly. "No other Order has the same power, not in Lisbon, not at Rome. By whom will they be judged?"

Carvalho e Melo appeared to ignore the question. He started to talk about the gold output from Minas Gerais, his words directed toward Luis Fialho. But for an instant his eyes shifted to Paulo, a quick, blazing look, and the young Pernambucan knew that Carvalho e Melo himself would condemn the Society of Jesus.

જ

When, at the end of two days, their visit with the Fonsecas ended, Paulo and Luis Fialho went to Lisbon. A fortnight later they were to board a merchantman, *Estréla do Mar*, bound for Brazil sometime during the second week of November 1755. They took rooms with Dona Clara de Castro, a Bahia-born widow of an officer who had served with a Lisbon regiment in Brazil. Paulo and Luis Fialho and Dona Clara's niece were the only guests at Dona Clara's four-story house on a precipitous street northeast of Rossio Square in the heart of the city. The niece, Manuela, was sixteen and had a newborn infant; no mention was made of a husband, and the young men tactfully did not inquire.

For a week, Paulo and Luis Fialho roamed Lisbon and its environs, with increasing impatience to start the voyage back to their homes.

Minister Carvalho e Melo had asserted that rapacious foreigners were draining off Lisbon's wealth, and that the opulence seen in the capital was illusory. But what an illusion! The palaces of the king and the powerful Corte-Real family dominated the waterfront on the west side of the Terreiro do Paço, the palace square; east of the square was a magnificent quay, and behind it the customs building. Dom José I's love of music had inspired the construction of the marble and gilded opera house. No less impressive were the meat and fish markets, said to be the finest in Europe. From Lisbon's hills, the central district between Rossio and the Terreiro do Paço was seen to be level and low-lying, flanked to the east and west by steep hills and to the north by a long ridge. The city had a medieval, congested appearance, its most striking feature its ninety convents, forty parish churches, and several basilicas.

Many fidalgos had pink-and-white-marble mansions in the capital. Equally suggestive of prosperity were the shops in the rua dos Mercadores and rua de Confeitaria, with stocks of jewelry, plate, silks, and fine wares.

The lively bustle of the city and port reflected a general mood of optimism, with few men sharing Carvalho e Melo's concerns. Tens of thousands of Africans, descendants of slaves transported here since the days of *As Conquistas*, were conscious of a movement toward ending slavery. The merchant class were delighted with Carvalho e Melo, who had shown his esteem by permitting them to wear swords in public, a privilege previously reserved for the nobility. The fidalgos who were not in active opposition to the minister had shrugged off such insults, retreated to their faro or baccarat tables, and assured one another that except for the actions of the irksome Carvalho e Melo, they were living in the best of all possible worlds.

ↄ

A thick fog drifting over the Tagus at dawn was dispersed as the sun rose on November 1, 1755, All Saints' Day, and when the church bells were rung for early Mass, the cloudless sky heightened the joy of those hastening to celebrate the hallowed Saints. Luis Fialho rose early to go to the cathedral, the Basilica de Santa Maria, which was below the Castelo do São Jorge. Paulo planned to attend a later Mass at a church close to Rossio.

Paulo awoke just before 9:30. He sat on the edge of the bed to say a brief prayer. Then, suddenly, he crossed to the window. The jalousies were slightly ajar and he pushed them back, flooding the room with sunlight.

He gazed along the street, as far as a sharp bend to the right where it led down to Rossio Square. He wondered what had made him move to the window; he had a vague notion of hearing a cock crow, but that was unlikely at this hour. Four houses away, an old man whom Paulo knew to be deaf sat on the step of his doorway, smoking a pipe; a family going to Mass greeted him and went on their way; behind them, two servant girls with water pitchers chattered noisily as they headed for the fountain at Rossio.

Paulo glanced along the row of houses opposite. Three and four stories, the facades of a few were decorated with blue and white tiles, but most of the houses that abutted each other were grimy, their roofs dingy with age. Several had small balconies attached to the upper windows, but at this hour most shutters behind the iron railings were closed.

At 9:45, as Paulo started to turn from the window, a tremor shook the house. Paulo gripped the windowsill; the family below and the girls behind them stopped walking; the deaf old man rose unsteadily and reached for the handle of his front door. Momentarily, Paulo associated the movement with coaches passing along a main thoroughfare below the hill, but then there came a noise, distant and deep, like the rumbling of thunder. Paulo threw his head back, his expression puzzled as he scanned the strip of blue sky above the street. Abruptly, the tremor stopped.

"Aieee!" a woman cried. "Aieee Maria!" Their sandals slapping on the cobblestones, the girls caught up with the family; one of the servants gave a shrill, nervous laugh. The old man stood with his back to the street and was having difficulty opening his door.

Paulo looked at the myriad specks of dust dancing before him. He again raised his face, his dark eyes searching the sky for a trail of smoke, for he now reasoned that there had been an explosion, perhaps at the royal arsenal in the lower town or in the magazine of the Castelo do São Jorge.

Ten seconds later, there was a devastating shock. The houses opposite Paulo began to sway; the floor beneath him vibrated so violently that he struggled to keep his balance. Chimneys crumbled, loose tiles fell to the ground, crockery in Dona Clara's house shattered. Screams and the pitiful cries of animals rose. But a thundering in the earth dulled Paulo's perception of these noises. *Terremoto!* The word crashed through Paulo's senses. "Earthquake!"

Paulo was mesmerized by the houses opposite, rocking on their foundations, walls cracking and splitting, upper stories leaning toward the street, chunks of masonry falling. Terror numbed him. He stood frozen at the window, expecting death.

Three houses suddenly burst open and collapsed, burying the family of four and the servant girls. The old man did not cease his struggle to open his front door, even as the convulsions rocked the street; he, too, was entombed by an avalanche of masonry. Paulo looked beyond the opening opposite him: The city was rising and falling in waves as if upon a storm tossed sea; landslides swept down the hillsides hurling houses toward the lower ground; distant steeples and towers whipped about wildly. The thunder of the earth, the sound of breaking timbers, the rain of roof tiles — the inconceivable noises came together in one deafening roar of destruction.

Paulo cursed as a jalousie slammed against his fingers, but he did not release his hold on the windowsill. He swung around as a side wall began to split open in several places. Ceiling beams were shifting, floorboards were snapping upward; furniture was sliding across the tilting, swaying floor. The house lurched sideways and Paulo was thrown backward.

Paulo lay motionless as the debris fell around him. "O Santo Tomás, help me," he sobbed.

Paulo opened his eyes and saw a gaping hole opposite him. He clung to the splintered floorboards, with a terror of being pitched over the edge of the opening.

The shocks stopped. The grinding, crashing noises continued, but from somewhere below him, Paulo heard a cry.

"Clara! Manuela!" he shouted.

The door to the room was torn off its hinges. He started toward it, scuttling like a crab, testing loose boards with his hands before entrusting his weight to them.

A second wave of shocks rose, and again the house began to vibrate.

Paulo kept moving. He reached the door and crawled beyond it to the stairway. It had been shoved sideways, the first flight intact, though at a precarious angle. As he scrambled down the steps, between the second and first floors the stairway collapsed and he fell twenty feet onto a pile of splintered wood and plaster, where he lay silent and stunned.

Three minutes later the tremors stopped and the noise abated. Paulo sat up shakily and moved his limbs, one by one; his shoulder ached and one arm was gashed. The screams were close to him now, and he realized that they had not ceased since he'd first heard them. He started to pick his way through the debris, along a passage that led from the front door.

It was 10:00 A.M.; and in just fifteen minutes one-third of Lisbon had been reduced to rubble.

Paulo found the girl Manuela and her baby under the stairwell.

"The world is ending!" Manuela wailed, over and over.

"For God's sake, girl . . . *quiet!*"

Paulo called out repeatedly for Dona Clara but got no reply. Timbers groaned and broke, masonry continued to crash down.

"Take your child!" he said gruffly. "Out! Out! The house will fall!"

He made his way ten feet to the front door, but, finding that he could open it no more than two inches, went back along the passage for a piece of timber, which he used as a lever to pry an opening large enough for them to squeeze through.

Paulo stepped outside. It was dark as night. The immense ruin of the city was silhouetted against the Stygian gloom. Lamentations filled the false night as tormented souls began to stir among the wreckage.

"To the river!" Paulo said. "We'll be safe on the waterfront."

Manuela did not respond but mumbled pleas to Jesus, Mary, Joseph, and every saint whose name occurred to her. She was a strong girl with a solid build, and kept up with Paulo, clutching her baby to her breast.

Far down the hill, they came to a pile of masonry that rose twenty-five feet and sealed the narrow passage. Paulo told Manuela to wait while he sought a safe way over the rubble. He was climbing near the top when he heard a rending sound.

"*Manuela!*"

A section of the upper story of a house fell with a crash upon the spot where mother and child stood, crushing them.

"Manuela," Paulo said weakly. "Manuela . . . "

He started down the pile, frantic now to reach the open quays and wharves along the Tagus, and thinking of his friend Luis Fialho. He considered trying to reach the area of the basilica but dismissed this; his only thought now that of self-preservation.

Paulo passed a demolished parish church; survivors were attacking the rubble where relatives and friends were buried, a priest in dust-covered vestments weeping as he rallied them. Two hundred feet away, a gang of armed rogues leapt and danced over the cobblestones, waving their loot in the air. Lone men and women frantically probed the edge of mountains of masonry, calling out the names of those they sought.

And there was a new cry now upon the lips of those fleeing the center of the city: "*Fire!*" Dozens of tapers had been lit upon the altars, and votive candles set to burn brightly for the saints. The conflagrations started in the destroyed churches and spread rapidly, the flames fanned by a stiffening northeaster.

Just before eleven, Paulo reached the Terreiro do Paço. The wounded and dying who had been carried here lay on the cobblestones, with priests moving among them to give absolution. Some survivors were almost naked, bleeding from wounds, stumbling along with incoherent exhortations. Four *carpideiras*, professional mourning women, weaved through the crowd, wailing without surcease. Two nobles, their wigs and ribbons in place, their dress immaculate, wandered along with two slaves at their heels, each shouldering a chest with his master's valuables.

Paulo was three-quarters of the way down the Terreiro do Paço when he was pushed up against the side of a coach. Peering through the window above the door, he saw three men sheltering within.

There was an outcry from the waterfront. Paulo swung his head in that direction: A wall of water was rushing toward the Terreiro do Paço.

The force of the earthquake produced monstrous tidal waves that raced into the mouth of the Tagus from the southwest. Ships were torn from their moorings and splintered against wharves and quays. Small craft laden with refugees crossing to the south bank were swallowed up in the whirlpools. Smashing through the anchorage, the waters reached the low-lying areas of Lisbon and roared inland.

As Paulo clung to the coach, beams ripped from a wharf hurtled through the water and smashed into it, flinging it onto its side. Paulo was swept forward in the churning water, toward the shaft and crosspieces. He grabbed the harness straps and held on.

There was a tremendous explosion as the customs building, which had been damaged during the earlier shocks, was battered by the wave. The royal palace and other waterfront structures were swamped.

The wave receded. Paulo gasped then when he leaned forward and peered inside the coach: Trapped by a beam that had rocketed through the thin woodwork, the three occupants had drowned.

"Mother of mercy!" An anguished cry escaped Paulo's lips as he saw a second wave crashing inland. He struggled for air when the water cascaded over him; but this torrent lacked the force of the first wave, and Paulo, sputtering, was soon able to stand upright. Still a greater horror greeted his eyes: Undermined by the earlier shocks, the Cais de Pedra, the magnificent marble-faced quay, and the hundreds who had sought safety there, had been carried away by the first wave.

Paulo started away from the river and joined a crowd that seethed toward Rossio Square. It was less than half a mile from the Terreiro do Paço to Rossio, but it took an hour to cover the distance, with hundreds converging on the upper square as fires spread through blocks to the east and west.

At Rossio, priests and a few soldiers who had not deserted the central area struggled to bring order to the agitated horde. Paulo stood with a group listening to a Jesuit who was already offering an explanation for these tribulations:

"God has made the earth quake, the waters rise; God is the instrument of Divine chastisement." The tall black robe raised his arm to indicate flames leaping from the huge Carmo convent on a hill to the west. "Temples raised in His honor are not spared, so grievous have been the sins of our city.

"Why has God struck our capital?" the Jesuit asked, lowering his arm. "Against the Spaniard, He showed His anger at Lima in distant Peru. Are the sins of the Portuguese so monstrous that Lisbon herself is made a mound of ruins, with thousands of unconfessed a harvest for hell?" The reference had been to an earthquake that had leveled Lima in 1746. "Dear God, be merciful! Spare us! *Grant time for penance!*"

Bystanders prostrated themselves on the cobblestones and sobbed with repeated calls for salvation.

Paulo wandered toward the north end of the square. Seeing smoke rise from the southern slopes of the castle hill, Paulo thought of Luis Fialho. If his friend had survived, what ordeal was he enduring?

Paulo heard an elderly man, for forty-five years a clerk at India House, weep as he told that the headquarters of the Overseas Council was in ruins, its great archives and administrative offices that represented three centuries of conquest and commerce all destroyed. The clerk shuffled after Paulo as he wandered the square. Paulo stopped opposite a tremendous heap of toppled walls and columns. "The work of God?" he queried, gazing at the Inquisition's palace.

The clerk looked puzzled. "Why do you ask?"

"God destroys the house of the most militant defenders of the faith?"

In his sixty-six years, the clerk had witnessed Jews, heretics, and not a few professed witches immolated in Rossio Square. He had never questioned the punishment of enemies of the true faith. He shook his head now, and said with grave perturbation, "Perhaps you should ask if our Grand Inquisitor has been too lenient. Had we burned a thousand Jews and heretics, would the saints have abandoned us this day?"

At this moment, as the India clerk was bemoaning the leniency toward foes of the true faith, a group of survivors at another square near Rossio were giving more practical consideration to the disaster. Minister Carvalho e Melo had just come from a brief audience with Dom José, who had also been unharmed. The nobles and city officials with the minister said little about Divine wrath, as they faced innumerable demands for help: the royal mint survived but, deserted by its garrison, needed to be guarded; prisoners from wrecked jails were looting and murdering. It was obvious that tens of thousands were injured, and God knew how many were dead. Already, there was a fear of plague.

One of the men with the minister, the marquis of Alorna, suggested that they begin by finding the simplest approach to every problem.

"Yes, Marquis," Carvalho e Melo agreed. "We must bury the dead . . . care for the living . . . close the ports."

A fidalgo suggested that they prepare to move the capital to Coimbra or Oporto.

Gazing toward a district where the fires were intense, Carvalho e Melo asked, "When London burned, did the Englishmen abandon it?"

"No, Excellency."

"*I* will rebuild Lisbon," Carvalho e Melo said.

೭෮

Dom António and Marcelino Augusto had been in Oporto and returned to Lisbon two days after the earthquake. The Fonsecas' town house on the rua Século west of Rossio was undamaged, and when Paulo arrived there, they gave him shelter. Paulo had hoped to find Luis Fialho at the Fonsecas', but there was no sign of him. Many times Paulo set out on searches for his friend amid the ash-strewn ruins of Lisbon, where fifteen thousand lay dead and three times that number injured. The *Estréla do Mar* had been destroyed at her anchorage, and Paulo was resigned to staying in Lisbon, there being no immediate prospect of a passage to Pernambuco.

Three weeks after the earthquake, Paulo was at the site of a warehouse owned by Dom António in a district above the Terreiro do Paço. The building had been severely damaged but not burned, and inspection had shown that a considerable portion of its goods was salvageable. Paulo had offered to help superintend the receipt of goods carried from the warehouse to a wooden shed erected on the palace square, which was covered with temporary stores and the huts of small merchants and food sellers. Toward noon that late November day, Paulo left another man in charge and wandered down to a wooden shack near the waterfront. He was carrying a small package, and before he reached the shack, the proprietor saw him and came running to meet him.

"Senhor Paulo! Good day!" he called out. "God's blessing and protection, Senhor Paulo!"

Paulo smiled as he returned the greeting.

"Oh, senhor, today" — the man's eyes widened — "today my Oligarinha's stew! Fish, tomatoes . . . The tastiest dish, Senhor Cavalcanti." His eyes flew to the package, but he made no mention of it.

Next to the shack, a woman labored over an iron pot with the steaming stew. She stepped back, greeted Paulo, and stood expectantly.

"Here, Oligarinha Pintado," Paulo said, and gave her the package.

Her husband, Nestor Pintado, said eagerly, "Open it. Go on!" She started to tear back a corner. "Careful! Careful!" he said. When Nestor saw it was open, he poked a wet finger inside, withdrew it, and stuck it into the corner of his mouth, his expression like that of a delighted child.

Paulo roared with laughter. "Oh, Nestor Pintado, what you would give for a day at Engenho Santo Tomás!"

Nestor was passionately fond of sugar, and with Dom António's permission, Paulo gave him this package in exchange for meals — excellent food, for before November 1, Senhor Nestor Pintado and his wife had kept a popular tavern on the rua Sapateiros. Today, they had nothing but two stout iron pots, tin plates and spoons, and a mighty faith in the future.

As Paulo ate the stew, Nestor sat with a mound of sugar in one hand. Two men were approaching his shack from the direction of the damaged wharves east of the Terreiro do Paço. They were still a distance away when Nestor gestured toward them with his sticky fingers. "There, Senhor Paulo, are two men with faith!" he said. "Their ship was riding broadside to the great wave. It broke her back and sent her to the bottom. The one on the left, he was the master; the other a marinheiro. Down they went and suddenly the bed of the Tagus was dry! When the second wave came, they were lifted up and deposited ashore."

"What ship was she?"

"A Brazil trader — *Estréla do Mar.*"

"Good God! The ship Luis Fialho and I were to take!" He had glanced casually at the two men; now he studied them closely. "Luis Fialho and I went aboard her a week before the earthquake to arrange our passages. I spoke with him, the one on the left, Capitão Alvaro Lacerda." Paulo had told Nestor Pintado of the search for his friend.

"Give thanks, Senhor Paulo, that you weren't aboard this *Estréla.* Today, Capitão Lacerda and his men who walked the *floor* of the Tagus are working on the broken quays." He shrugged. "They have to eat, no?"

"I haven't seen them here before."

"Yesterday they came for the first time."

Nestor greeted Lacerda and the marinheiro and shouted for Oligarinha Pintado to serve them bowls of stew.

"I'm Paulo Cavalcanti," Paulo introduced himself. "Do you remember me, Capitão? My friend and I came to the Estréla."

"Yes, senhor, I remember," Lacerda said. "Your friend was looking for you."

"*Luis? Luis Fialho?*"

"The same. Said he had searched the ruins and feared you were dead."

"I'm alive!" Paulo shouted joyously. "And so is Luis Fialho. *Alive!*"

"When did you see Luis Fialho?"

"Two days after the earthquake. Perhaps three. I met him near the ruin of the customs house. He said if I saw you . . . he was going to the rua Século."

"The house of our friend," Paulo said. "Why, then, didn't he arrive?"

The marinheiro with Lacerda said, "Streets filled with assassins . . . so many dangers. Perhaps your friend was injured on his way."

"I've been to many infirmaries. I didn't find him."

"Is it possible he was taken by the soldiers?" the marinheiro, suggested.

"Why would they take him?"

"The jails are *full*," the marinheiro, said flatly.

With the knowledge that Luis Fialho had survived the terrors of November 1, Paulo renewed his search for his friend, but after a week, he still had not found him. Remembering the marinheiro's words, Paulo wondered whether by some ghastly circumstance Luis Fialho had been arrested. Seeking Dom António's help, he got a pass to enter the prisons, and tramped to two makeshift penitentiaries that had replaced destroyed jails, and to five fortresses, from the mouth of the Tagus to Belém.

The hundreds arrested since the earthquake were starving. Even the rats that swarmed at their feet rejected the slops cast toward them; their bodies crawled with vermin, they groaned and cursed, and not a few wailed about wrongful detention when they saw Paulo, whom they took to be a representative of authority. Few were innocent; the quakes that had leveled Lisbon seemed to have cast up from the depths an assembly of assassins, cutthroats, robbers and thieves.

On December 8, 1755, the sixth day of this grim exercise, Paulo was rowed across to the Tower of Belém on a group of rocks beyond the riverbank at Restelo. The boat carrying Paulo across to the fortress grated against a small quay beside the tower; he stepped out and crossed a drawbridge. His pass was taken inside; after ten minutes, he was to an upper floor where an arrogant-looking officer in a splendid uniform awaited him.

"Governador," Paulo began, after introducing himself.

The officer shook his head. "The commander is on duty in Lisbon." He was Lieutenant Mathias Carneiro, he said, and waving the pass in front of Paulo, he asked, "Why do you seek this thief? Has he stolen something from you, Senhor Cavalcanti?"

"Is Luis Fialho Soares here?"

"I don't know." The lieutenant proceeded to bemoan the fact that common villains had invaded the tower, normally reserved for offenders of good rank. "What do I know of such miscreants?" he asked.

"But a record is kept?"

"The governador has a list. Mustering scum is not my duty."

"Perhaps inquiries could be made."

"What is your interest in this man?"

"Luis Fialho Soares is my friend. He's not a criminal. We were to sail home to Brazil."

A soldier came noisily up the steps and hovered in the doorway.

"Yes, Almeida?"

"There is one, Tenente, gives the name of Soares."

"Merciful God!" Paulo cried. "Luis Fialho Soares?"

Carneiro nodded at the soldier. "Bring him to us."

It *was* Luis Fialho. He had lost weight; his cheekbones were more pronounced, his skin jaundiced. One eye was swollen; his hair was matted and filthy; his clothes were torn and his feet bare, the skin above them raw from the chafing of leg irons.

"Luis!"

Luis Fialho leaned forward unsteadily. "Paulo? How, in God's name, is it possible?"

"It doesn't matter. Tell me — why are you here?"

The lieutenant started to move forward, but Paulo said fiercely, "Let him speak!" Carneiro glared but said nothing. "Luis . . . how did you come to be *arrested?*"

"A thief? A looter? It is *I* who have been robbed, the very shoes off my feet. '*Professor*,' they mocked me when they tore them off. Murderers, thieves. 'A man needs no boots, *Professor*, when he dances below the gibbet!'"

"But how . . . what—"

"The day after the earthquake, and the next, I looked for you," Luis Fialho broke in. "I went down to the river."

"The master of the *Estréla*—"

"Yes. After I saw him, I started for the rua Século, walking toward Carmo hill. It was almost night, with the fires that burned lighting the sky. It was then that I met the conde de Junqueira."

"A strange name."

"Wait, my friend. Hear my story. There was the conde, gray-haired and in every way a fidalgo. There was the conde's brother, in the habit of St. Francis, using a staff to limp along, for he had been injured by a fall of stones; and the conde's wife, Dona Maria Madelena, so help me God; and his mother, whose name I never learned. When I came upon them, they were struggling to move a cart across the dirt.

" 'You're a strong young man,' said the conde. 'Please, for the love of humanity, help us.' And laying a hand on my shoulder, he added, 'My son, I am the conde de Junqueira, and these — my wife, my mother, my brother who serves the Lord.' And he looked at his cart laden to the sky. 'We've lost everything but these few possessions.' He pleaded that I help them move the cart to the riverside, where they had a boat to carry them across the Tagus. 'To my estate beyond Barreiro,' he said.

"I told him it was impossible to get the cart to the Tagus. 'You're wrong, son . . . Brother Egidio has found a passage through the ruins. Will you help us?'

"Maria Madelena began to strain against the cart, and the old matron, too, bent her back to it. What could I do but seize the shaft and drag their possessions along? 'God will reward you, my son,' " said Brother Egidio.

Luis ran a hand through his dirty hair, scratching furiously. "It took two hours to move the cart along the circuitous route found by Brother Egidio. At the river, there was another monk, Zacarias, who stood guard over a longboat. 'Now, if you'll help us load, my son, we'll ask no more of you,' said the conde. Maria Madelena and the old mother were already stepping into the boat.

"Without the slightest warning, the conde and the monks suddenly leapt up and ran for the craft. I was facing the river. I spun around and there, advancing toward us, were His Majesty's soldiers. I stood where I was, having nothing to fear as men dashed past toward the waterfront. Soldiers tore off the sailcloth covering the cart. It was laden with plunder — gold, silver, altarpieces. 'It belongs to the conde de Junqueira,' I said. For this, I received a mighty blow with the butt of a musket."

"The conde or whoever he was — were they pursued by the soldiers?"

"I don't know. They dragged me away and flung me into the wreck of a ship that was aground, where hundreds were kept. I was beaten and robbed. Only when the hulk started to break up were we moved, some to Junqueira's dungeons. I was brought here."

"You were fortunate," Carneiro said. "Had you been caught a few days later, you would have been marched directly to the gallows."

"He's innocent!" Paulo declared angrily.

"Of course," Carneiro said. Then he shook with laughter. "Who would ever dream up a story like this to escape the rope?"

Paulo seized Luis Fialho's hands. "You're alive, thank God! Patience, now, Luis Fialho. I'm going to Dom António for help."

Luis Fialho was released within seventy-two hours. Dom António approached Carvalho e Melo, who had ordered an immediate investigation of the case. Though these two powerful men set in motion an official inquiry that brought Luis Fialho's freedom, what assured his exoneration was the discovery — in the dungeons of Junqueira — of one Orlando Freitas, alias the conde de Junqueira.

XV

———◆———

June 1756 – November 1766

*A*warship had been dispatched from Lisbon to Brazil in January 1756, with an official account of the earthquake, but not until Paulo landed at Recife in May and sent a messenger ahead to Engenho Santo Tomás did the Cavalcantis learn of his survival.

Senhor Bartolomeu Rodrigues Cavalcanti's relief was matched by his pride in his son's achievement at Coimbra, and he arranged a joyous thanksgiving for Paulo's safe homecoming. The festa lasted for five days, with so many relatives and friends — neighboring planters, officials, and merchants — that they had to be accommodated under canvas beside the Casa Grande.

The mansion stood on the high ground that six generations of Cavalcantis had occupied since Nicolau and Helena built that first forlorn and forbidding block-house, with its walls of stone and mud and its gunport-like windows. Even the handsome two-storied dwelling of Fernão Cavalcanti's day could not be compared to the Casa Grande, which had been completed five years ago. The house of Senhor Fernão, Bartolomeu Rodrigues's great-grandfather, had not been demolished; its roof and covered veranda had been removed, and its outer walls formed the central section of the Casa Grande. The chapel and sacristy were in the new wing to the left; to the right was an extension with living and sleeping quarters, and, to the rear, kitchens, laundry, and wine cellar. The two-storied U-shaped building was enclosed by a high wall at the back and contained an ornamental garden.

There were thirty rooms in the house. On the ground floor were a reception hall and guest chambers. A carved staircase led to the second floor, where there were three parlors; a dining room that held a rosewood table eight yards long and capable of seating twenty-four guests; and seven bedrooms for the family. From a small library, access was gained to the upper galleries of the chapel, the choir loft, and the priest's quarters.

A deep verandah extended 115 feet along the front of the house and chapel. Beyond the raised verandah the ground sloped gradually toward a river, beside which were located the sugar works, the distillery, and the *senzala*, the main slave quarters.

It was not only its imposing size that gave the Casa Grande distinction but also the harmony with which it blended into the landscape. It appeared so peaceful and secure between slender tufted palms and spreading tamarinds, its gardens and patios filled with elegant shrubs and scented trees and shaded ponds. Tranquil as it was, there were bursts of color and sound: Caged songsters, brilliant macaws, huge-billed toucans, tens of squawking, warbling pets were distributed not only on the veranda but also in the parlors and corridors. The more daring of a troop of tiny monkeys scooted along the veranda, jabbering fiendishly; sometimes they would invade the reception hall, from where they were swiftly evicted by broom-wielding slaves.

The eleven household slaves and their families lived in quarters next to the Casa Grande, several of them able to count many generations of forebears who had served the Cavalcantis in the same capacity. The intimate relationship between the slaves of the house and the *sinhá* and *sinhazinhas*, as the slaves called Senhora Cavalcanti and her daughters, was sometimes subtle and secretive, with confidences no Cavalcanti male was ever likely to hear.

Senhor Bartolomeu Rodrigues's control of Santo Tomás was firm but benign. He was sixty-eight years old, with dark, hooded eyes, a small nose and mouth, and sparse, near-white beard. His lips were often parted, as if he was on the point of saying something. Bartolomeu Rodrigues had had his war with the peddlers of Recife, but, for the most part, he had led a peaceful life at Engenho Santo Tomás. Nothing exemplified the comfort of his world as much as the sight of the patriarch at ease on his veranda in a simple cotton shirt and breeches, sometimes in stockings, with his boots or slippers next to him, moving gently in his rocking chair as he gazed contentedly in the direction of his sugar works.

Senhor Bartolomeu Rodrigues's five daughters had been raised in seclusion, their father convinced that exposure of a wife or a daughter was a prelude to certain adultery or defloration. Good husbands had been found for three of the girls; the senhor had been unable to find satisfactory beaus for the other two and had provided dowries for their admission to a convent at Salvador.

Of his three sons, Geraldo at nineteen was the youngest — a pleasant, lazy young man with a grand disinterest in most things. Graciliano was twenty-one and quite the opposite of Geraldo. He was physically the largest and strongest of the brothers and had frequently demonstrated this in brawls with them. Restless and impatient, he possessed a violent temper, and had once beaten Paulo senseless for taking more than half of a sweet potato offered to them at the *senzala*; but it was Geraldo he had teased and bullied mercilessly.

The senhor de engenho spent a small fortune on the festa for Paulo, a banquet the Cavalcantis themselves were unlikely to see more than once or twice a year. From the great kitchen — filled with aromas and flavors of Africa — came dishes of spicy *feijoada, vatapá, caruru,* and varieties of sweets and sugared candies that the slaves prepared under the watchful eye of Dona Catarina.

There were entertainments by slave musicians, and a parade by the district militia regiment, which Bartolomeu Rodrigues had commanded for the past twenty-two years. On two successive nights, the slope below the Casa Grande thundered and sparkled with fireworks, and rockets lit the sky above. The 140 slaves who worked in the fields, at the engenho, and in the plantation's workshops were generously supplied with meat and drink; after Mass on the last day of the celebrations, they were mustered in front of the Casa Grande. The senhor de engenho granted two old men their freedom, a gesture he made with a tremor in his voice and tears in his eyes, such was Bartolomeu Rodrigues's gratitude for the Lord's having spared his son at Lisbon.

℘

What a strong face he has, Paulo Cavalcanti thought, as he looked at Padre Eugênio Viana. They were sitting opposite each other at an oval table in the library the night after the last guests had left.

Viana's face was shadowed in the candlelight, but the firm set of his jaw and the steel blue eyes reflected the sense of purpose recognized by Paulo. The priest was thirty-three, broad-shouldered and firm-bodied, similar in build to Paulo and showing the same confidence.

During the past weeks, Paulo had answered endless questions about the earthquake and his meeting with His Excellency Carvalho e Melo, but with Padre Eugênio, his friend and confessor, he could speak more frankly than with others, and as they sat in the library this night, he mentioned his concern regarding the minister's strong prejudices against the Society of Jesus:

"His Excellency is convinced that the Jesuits seek nothing less than a conquest of Brazil and the Maranhão. I told him about Rosário, but he dismissed the aldeia as the exception to the Society's great plantations and properties."

"A conquest?" Viana asked. "Of what? Of the evils the Portuguese have practiced in this land? The immorality? The enslavement of the natives? A conquest of ignorance, Paulo? Does Carvalho e Melo consider the debt owed the Jesuits for educating thousands at the colégios?"

"He spoke of their neglect in teaching the natives to speak Portuguese."

"Dear God in heaven, what makes Minister Carvalho e Melo an expert in instructing the heathen?"

"His Excellency says they must be freed and admitted as equals into Portuguese society."

"Freed? From what? From the sanctuary provided for them by the Jesuits? This will not happen. Minister Carvalho e Melo will come to realize what a tragic error it would be."

"The war in the south continues," Paulo remarked, referring to the Portuguese-Spanish campaign to dislodge the Guarani from the seven missions east of the Rio Uruguay. "Carvalho e Melo expects victory."

"The Jesuits of Brazil aren't implicated in the Guarani rebellion."

"The way the minister sees it, whether in Paraguay, Pernambuco, or Portugal, the Society of Jesus is a threat."

"To whom?" Viana asked. "To those of other Orders who resent their success? To the ambition of Minister Carvalho e Melo?"

Paulo began to talk then of Luis Fialho Soares, telling Viana how his friend had been deceived by the looters."

"Thanks to God you found him. You were very close?"

"Yes and no. He was different. A Paulista. One of the first descendants of mamelucos admitted to Coimbra. And I? Mazombo! It made me miserable to think that Portuguese, our own people, who owe so much to Brazil, think so little of good men like my father. Dear heaven, I look at our new house, the lands, the engenho. How can those Portuguese lords who sit in decaying palaces on their tiny estates believe that they are privileged simply by birth in Portugal?"

"You didn't speak like this before you left for Coimbra."

"But it's true, Padre. I feel it so strongly now that I'm back with my people. The Cavalcantis are a noble family of Pernambuco. They deserve recognition."

"What did your friend, the Paulista, have to say about this?"

"Luis Fialho is a poet. The Portugal of Camões stirred him; the grand monuments of the past were an inspiration; but when he thought of the present, he saw only Brazil. His verse flowed with passion for the great valleys and open spaces."

"I would like to meet this young poet with quill in hand dreaming of the far sertão! And his forbears, Paulo?" Suddenly, Viana pushed back his chair, took a candle from the table, and moved to one side of the room. "*There!*" he said, and laughed. "The young scoundrel, whoever he was!"

Secundus Proot's *Bandeirante* hung on the wall, in all its vulgar glory, stocky Amador festooned with weapons and his Paulista troop blazing away with their muskets, a dead savage at their feet, a second native threatening them with his bow. Viana studied the painting so intensely that Paulo was finally moved to ask:

"What is it that fascinates you so, Padre?"

Padre Eugênio, startled out of his reverie, moved back to his chair and sat down. "I was just thinking. The two of you — one, the son of a senhor de engenho; the other, from the sertão."

"The Soares family is wealthy. They own gold mines, a fazenda, properties at Vila Rica."

"More important, Paulo, is the harmony you and Luis Fialho found at Coimbra. Brazil is so big — there are so many Portugals here — most men live and die in their captaincies without knowing what lies beyond. You must not forget the understanding you found with Luis Fialho in Portugal."

"I could not forget, Padre. Luis Fialho and I shared so much together."

Paulo felt a great love for Padre Eugênio. He sometimes wondered why Viana had accepted the post at Engenho Santo Tomás, for he certainly possessed the talent to serve the Society of Jesus or to attain a high position in the Church. When he'd asked Viana about this, the padre had laughed, saying that he had work enough with the parish of Santo Tomás. Which was true, for there were some eight hundred men, women, and children attached to the Cavalcanti estate.

"We are all subjects of the king of Portugal," Viana said. "Yet, from Maranhão and Grão Pará in the north to Rio Grande in the south, we're torn by envy, greed, dissension. Paulista against Emboaba, planter against peddler, colonist against Jesuit, white man against savage. Minister Carvalho e Melo predicts a great Portuguese nation here. This will never be, Paulo, until we find unity and understanding."

ꞔꙬ

Bending low over his pony's neck, one hand on the single rein, the other gripping an iron-tipped goad that he held at the horizontal, the vaqueiro flew at breakneck speed through the caatinga, his horse's hoofs clattering over the stony ground and tossing up puffs of dust where the surface lay brittle and pink. He swept through a stand of cacti; he flung himself flat on the pony's back to pass below a gnarled branch.

A slender black steer with short horns crashed through the caatinga forty yards ahead of the vaqueiro. The cattleman gave a lusty yell and plunged deeper into tangled growth. But then he gave a curse, too, for the point of his lancelike *guiada* became impaled in a tree trunk, and the goad was wrenched from his hand with a terrible jolt, but the vaqueiro hung on, never taking his eye from the dark shape of his quarry. He saw the steer bolt to the right toward an opening beyond the thick scrub.

The vaqueiro spurred his fiery pony. At full charge, bending low in the saddle, his weight on one stirrup, he held the pony's mane; with his other hand, he seized the steer's tail. A powerful twist, a jerk, and he dumped the animal on its side. With dust swirling around him, the vaqueiro leapt from his mount, grabbing the fetters that hung from his saddle. The steer was thrashing on its side, but before it could recover, the vaqueiro slipped on the restraint, fettering its hind legs.

Twenty minutes later, the steer was on its feet, grazing sullenly, and the vaqueiro was still jeering at it, when Paulo Cavalcanti and Padre Eugênio, who had observed the chase from higher ground, approached the group of cattlemen. Before they reached the vaqueiro, his fellows began to shout praises for his marvelous performance and to offer added ridicule for his adversary.

"Viva, Ribeiro Adorno!" Paulo called out. "Viva! My father is correct: 'The very devil of the sertão!'"

"It was nothing, Senhor Paulo. *Nada!* Black Manuel! Agostinho Pequeno! Teimoso the Headstrong! One of these, my young senhor, and there would have been something to see!"

Estevão Ribeiro Adorno was small and sinewy, his copper-colored features gaunt and parched by the sun. He was forty-nine, dour, suspicious, patient. All his life he had lived in the caatinga, leaving it only for cattle drives to Recife and Salvador.

Dressed to do battle with the caatinga, he wore leather doublet and leather breeches, leather jacket with thongs in place of buttons, leather shoes, leather knee caps and leather gauntlets, and a wide-brimmed hat of stiff leather.

Ribeiro Adorno was head vaqueiro at the Cavalcanti ranch, Fazenda da Jurema, which derived its name from a group of acacia-type trees at the main camp.

The fazenda occupied 130 square miles and was bordered on the north by a creek, Riacho Jurema, an influent of the Rio Pajéu, which flowed to the Rio São Francisco, sixty-five miles to the south. Fazenda da Jurema lay 250 miles west of Recife, a ten-day journey through three regions typical of the northeast:

Along the littoral and extending inland for up to sixty miles was the *zona da mata*, the humid lowlands and valleys between the Borborema Plateau and the Atlantic. Beyond the zona da mata was a transition zone, the *agreste*, rocky soil with some areas as fertile as the coastal region and others dominated by arid spurs of caatinga, the prevailing vegetation of the third and largest region, the sertão. The deep red soil of the zona da mata supported the sugarcane plantations; the agreste was being occupied by cotton growers and small farmers; and the sertão, which covered half the northeast, was predominantly cattle country, with almost one million head spread out over the low scrub-forest.

Estevão Ribeiro Adorno was descended from the great clan of Affonso Ribeiro, whom Nicolau Cavalcanti had reluctantly given sanctuary at Santo Tomás. The vaqueiro's mother was a daughter of a Ribeiro who had left the engenho with his family for Fazenda da Jurema at the end of the previous century. Ribeiro Adorno's father, Constantino Adorno, had been a mameluco from São Paulo, the Paulistas having roamed the sertão of the northeastern captaincies ever since they found the headwaters of the Rio São Francisco. Ribeiro Adorno himself had married a Paulista mameluco, Idalina, whose Tupi features were strongly evident.

The opening of the northeast interior for settlement by the Portuguese and their mixed-breed descendants had been similar to the penetration of the sertão beyond São Paulo. The first initiative to venture west of Olinda and Salvador had come from fortune hunters, advancing up along the rivers that emptied into the Atlantic, in search of silver and emeralds. Others, who placed no faith in finding treasure but sought to ennoble themselves through the possession of vast lands, had followed them. *Os Poderosos do Sertão* ("The Great Men of the Earth") today held power over these backlands. The family of Garcia d'Avila, for example, had been adding to their properties since the mid-sixteenth century, when their ancestor settled just north of Salvador. By the mid-eighteenth century, the family controlled more than one thousand square miles of ranches along the Rio São Francisco. This was the largest cattle empire, but there were many fazendas like that of the Cavalcantis.

As absentee landlords, the Cavalcantis left the management of the fazenda to Ribeiro Adorno, in payment for which he received one-quarter of the new calves born annually. Two decades ago, Ribeiro Adorno had attempted to establish a herd of his own. He had trekked to the captaincy of Ceará, northwest of Fazenda da Jurema, but a drought had decimated his cattle and, worse, he had quarreled with the *poderosos* of the area. He had returned to Pernambuco, and the Cavalcantis had taken him back as head vaqueiro.

Except for those three years in Ceará, Ribeiro Adorno had served the Cavalcantis since his twelfth birthday. Whenever he drove cattle to Recife, he always called at the engenho; but only three times in those thirty-four years had Senhor Bartolomeu Rodrigues come to Fazenda da Jurema. And this was Paulo Cavalcanti's first visit, as part of acquainting himself with the family holdings. It was the end of

July 1756, and Padre Eugênio and Paulo had been at the fazenda for two weeks. This roundup of one hundred cattle from a watering hole north of Riacho Jurema would complete the annual count of the herd, which now numbered 5,500 beasts.

The cattlemen had been resting through the heat of early afternoon when the steer bolted into the caatinga. They now continued their journey to the Riacho Jurema, with one of Ribeiro Adorno's four sons, Jacinto, taking up the lead. A small, wiry man, Jacinto lounged in the short saddle, feet sticking forward, shoulders hunched, the image of indolence, in direct contrast to his father.

Approaching the north bank of the Riacho Jurema toward sunset, Jacinto Adorno called for help in getting the cattle across. A herder rode up to him, dismounted, and removed a pack from his pony. Without saying a word, the man unrolled the hide and took out its contents — the blanched skull of a steer. Jacinto assisted him in fitting this object over his head and then attached the hide, cloaklike, to the man's shoulders.

The herder looked like an officiant at a primitive ritual. He climbed down the riverbank into the water. The lead steers moved forward, urged along by other herders, until they entered the Riacho Jurema and swam after the man with the skull. Within twenty minutes the cattle were on the south bank.

The cattle corral and main camp were located a mile from the confluence of the Riacho Jurema and the Rio Pajéu, along which the fazenda had a one-thousand-yard frontage. From the narrow margin along the Pajéu, the ranch fanned out to the northeast and southeast, encompassing the 130 square miles, most of which was covered with caatinga scrub.

The camp itself was a dusty and odiferous collection of low wattle-and-daub huts, with uneven clay walls, single doors, and small windows. The smell of leather was pervasive: In every hut, the covering on the clay-packed floor, the cots, the storage bags for their possessions and for grain and water, the saddlebags, sword and knife sheaths, whips, litters, bindings, belts, harnesses — all were made of animal hide. From his birth, when the woman who bore him rested on a soft hide, to burial, when death in a far place might bring interment in a rough shroud, the vaqueiro existed in a world of leather.

That night, after the cattle had been driven across the Riacho Jurema, the settlement resounded with songs and laughter as the cattlemen and their families saluted the patrão's son, who was returning to Santo Tomás in the morning. A square of ground near the huts had been swept clean, and tree trunks and stumps placed around it as seats. The food offered this night was the same as had been served at every meal during the fortnight Paulo and Padre Eugênio had been here: manioc and beans from the small fields of Ribeiro Adorno's wife and daughters, and beef and goat meat.

The Ribeiro Adorno females who were responsible for this fare hovered in the background near the grill, with the womenfolk of other vaqueiros. The youngest of Ribeiro Adorno's three daughters, Januária, made no attempt to help her mother but squatted on the ground, staring into the fire. Occasionally she'd pick at the meat with a long knife, prying off tiny pieces, blowing on them, and popping them into her mouth, then wiping her lips on the sleeve of her dress. Januária Ribeiro Adorno was fifteen, small like both her parents, with black silky hair and a round, pretty face, but she was a slovenly, awkward girl, and walked with a swaying slouch. She was rude and ill-tempered, her offensiveness such that she had earned the nickname "Piranha" from her two sisters.

The festa had started soon after sundown. Senhor Bartolomeu Rodrigues had sent a liberal gift of cachaça to his vaqueiros, and the raw-cane brandy rapidly broke down the reserve the community had shown toward Paulo and the padre. Ribeiro Adorno, who was by nature taciturn and introspective, leapt across the hard earth, demonstrating that he was as expert at dancing as at riding his mettlesome pony.

A highlight of the evening came when Jacinto and the second guitarist, a mulatto called Stump Head, engaged in a poetic duel. First, Jacinto strummed his guitar, and in a low, beautiful voice, he sang:

> *"Come hear my challenge, friends,*
> *A ballad of the sertão,*
> *A song beneath God's heavens*
> *Where none can rival me!"*

The mulatto's response began with Jacinto's last line:

> *"Where none can rival me,*
> *I accept the challenge, friend!*
> *Here's a song of Paradise I have,*
> *O sweet joy never to end!"*

This went on for twenty minutes, a simple lyrical dialogue, not unlike the tensons of troubadours of old. Finally, in trying to reply to a verse delivered by Stump Head, Jacinto became tongue-tied. Ribeiro Adorno filled a cow horn with cachaça and drank a toast to Stump Head's melodious victory.

An hour later, Paulo and Eugênio Viana were standing at the entrance to the camp. The opening in the stockade was closed for the night with heavy poles and a thorn barrier, a precaution against jaguars and other wild beasts, as well as against savages, small bands of whom still kept isolated refuges in the white forest.

Viana was gazing over the barrier into the shadows beyond when suddenly he declared, "Oh, what a stony desert!"

The despair surprised Paulo. "The creeks and water holes are full, Padre," he said. "The desert blooms. Ribeiro Adorno and his people rejoice."

"And what lies hidden, Paulo? I am thinking of their souls and their hearts in this stony place."

Paulo didn't quite know how to respond to this. "Ribeiro Adorno's people came here of their own free will," he offered.

"Did they?" Viana asked. "They willingly left a valley like Santo Tomás — that fertile Canaan — and chose this barren, lonely land?"

Paulo was silent.

"Would you, Paulo, exchange your life at Santo Tomás for this miserable existence?"

"No," Paulo adamantly replied.

"But we see a never-ending exodus to these backlands of men who are expelled from our valleys."

"'Expelled' is a strong word, Padre."

"What other? First we expelled – expelled or exterminated — Tupiniquin, Tupinambá, Caeté, the great tribes of the coast. Now we send from Canaan, the weak, the dispossessed, and the landless."

"The caatinga is menacing and unforgiving, Padre, but Ribeiro Adorno and his comrades are bold and uncomplaining. I don't believe they feel banished or degraded here. What I see is an almost mystical relationship with the land. Besides, civilization will come to this sertão. Where there's a cattle trail, tomorrow there will be a road. Then a village. Churches. Schools."

"I wonder," Viana said, and started to walk back toward the area where the vaqueiros were dancing. "By the time civilization advances here, it might come up against a brutal and impetuous race lost in the caatinga and forever locked in battle against nature — and as remote from us as were the first Tupiniquin encountered by the Portuguese."

&

"An educated fool," Graciliano Cavalcanti called Eugénio Viana, though never within earshot of Senhor Bartolomeu Rodrigues or Paulo. "The padre sniffs the incense of the French philosophists and freethinkers. He begs not alms but books from my father. 'Read them,' Viana tells me, 'and learn.' But what have they taught him? To listen to the murmurs of the rabble? To chatter like a parrot about the rights of lowborn men who are by nature lazy?" In conversation with his friends, Graciliano would sometimes add that Eugénio Viana had no keener disciple than Paulo Cavalcanti.

Graciliano had the same dark hair, thick lashes, and blue-green eyes as Paulo, but his face was more oval. He divided his time between Santo Tomás and Recife, where he associated with a group of arrogant young men, most of whom were planters' sons.

When not cardplaying with his friends, Graciliano was at the bordello of Senhora Bárbara Ferreira in São Antônio, a district of Recife across the bridge originally built by Count Maurits. Here Graciliano visited a prostitute, Magdalene, who kept a votive candle burning next to her bed but who was known as The Moor, for she was of Levantine extraction. The Moor whistled through her nostrils when excited by furious copulation, a peculiarity that aroused Graciliano.

Like the brutish nobles who roamed Lisbon at night, Graciliano and his associates sauntered through Recife's streets, with a small slave carrying a whale-oil lamp to light their way, and terrorized innocent citizens afoot in the dark. One night Graciliano had killed a man, a drunk Portuguese farrier who had responded to Graciliano's taunts. The event had so enhanced Graciliano's prestige among his friends that they honored him by paying a silversmith to engrave upon Graciliano's sword the words "Justice Lives!"

In November 1756, three months after Paulo and Viana had returned from the roundup, two slaves ran away from Santo Tomás. Onias, one of the two slaves

Senhor Bartolomeu Rodrigues had manumitted to celebrate Paulo's safe return, had been saying openly that freedom was no gift to a sixty-seven-year-old black with no home or family.

Senhor Bartolomeu Rodrigues was especially aggrieved by this ingratitude and since the laws provided for the revocation of manumission of a former slave who was ungrateful, Senhor Bartolomeu Rodrigues declared publicly that Onias had forfeited his freedom and was once more a peça. After evening muster on November 14, Onias and a young black, Daniel, had fled the valley of Santo Tomás.

Graciliano immediately volunteered to hunt them down. Paulo said that this was a mission best undertaken by one of the overseers, but Graciliano insisted on going, arguing that the action of one of the runaways was a direct insult to their father.

Graciliano rode after them the next morning, with Cipriano Ramos, an overseer, and three trustworthy slaves. With them went four large black dogs trained to sniff out runaways. Initially the dogs had no luck, for the trails they picked up led to the houses of Cavalcanti tenants and cane growers, whose slaves had not seen the fugitives. Graciliano rode on into the next valley, most of which the Cavalcantis owned. Here, a sharecropper had seen the runaway pair crossing a field at dawn. Within an hour, there were reports of two further sightings, and the searchers headed toward a range, a continuation of the ridge that lay south of Santo Tomás.

The dogs picked up the runaways' trail near the mouth of a high-walled ravine. Yelping excitedly, they began to probe the bush along the base of the cleft.

The ravine was thickly forested and blocked with boulders, and the search party dismounted to follow the dogs. Cipriano had just clambered up a huge slab of rock when, pointing furiously toward the side of the ravine, he cried out, "*There*, Senhor Graciliano! Upon the rocks!"

"*How* did they get up there?" Graciliano asked.

"Goats!" Cipriano said. "Peça goats!"

The fugitives were on a narrow ledge about 150 feet above the floor of the ravine. They ignored the overseer's shouts for them to come down and only climbed higher.

It was getting dark, but Graciliano ordered Cipriano and two of the slaves to go after the runaways. The dogs were barking and whining in their frenzy to find a way up the ravine wall; when they saw Cipriano begin to climb, they bounded over to follow him, but were ordered back.

The pursuit had no sooner begun than Cipriano let out a stream of oaths as a shower of stones struck him. Graciliano, who stood clear of the projectiles, saw that one of the fugitives, young Daniel, had lost his footing and was clinging to the roots of a stunted tree that grew on the rock face. Onias went down on one knee and stretched an arm out toward him. The root tore loose. With a scream that echoed in the cleft, Daniel fell to his death.

"Down!" Graciliano shouted to Cipriano and the others. He didn't want to risk the lives of the overseer and two healthy peças. "Come down!"

The dogs, their eyes glowing in the dark, slavered over the broken body of Daniel. One of the hounds dragged its long tongue over the bloodied rib cage.

Graciliano drove them away with a horsewhip. When his men reached him, he ordered them to bury Daniel and then to follow him to the house of a cane grower in the valley. They would continue the search for Onias in the morning, Graciliano said. If he got safely over this ridge, then he'd be in the next valley and headed for the southwest.

Onias kept the search party on the move for the next three days. Finally, they ran him down at the aldeia of Nossa Senhora do Rosário, where he had taken refuge, but the two Jesuits who ran the mission refused to hand him over to Graciliano. He had been found in a manioc field that dawn, so exhausted and ill that he was not expected to live.

Padre Salvador de Meireles and his assistant, Leandro Taques, stood with Graciliano in the mission square. The aldeia was as poor as Paulo had described it when speaking with Carvalho e Melo the previous October. A tall wooden Cross was raised in front of the church. Two rows of shabby houses flanked the square; tracks meandered in every direction from the plaza to an ox-drawn cane mill and work-shops, and to clusters of shacks, the largest group on a knoll behind the church. The mission population was four hundred, mostly Tupi- and Tapuya-speaking natives gathered here from as far as two hundred miles away. The mixed-breed families and the free blacks, some seventy souls in all, had joined the aldeia as artisans and laborers.

"I've asked politely, Padres. Onias belongs to my father." Graciliano's voice rose. "*Give him to me!*"

"Be reasonable, Graciliano," Padre Salvador said. "He will be kept under guard. If God allows that he survives, we will return him to Santo Tomás." Graciliano shook his head furiously. "For the love of Christ, a league along the way and that old man will be dead. Senhor Bartolomeu Rodrigues will not thank you for the return of a dead slave."

"If the old goat dies before I get him to the engenho, Padre Salvador, so be it. You have no right to keep him."

"Senhor Bartolomeu Rodrigues has always been our good friend. He knows that we will do nothing to harm his interests."

"Certainly! And our Padre Viana, as well. But, then, how often do they go to Recife? There's not a ship from the south without news of the rebellion by Jesuit *militia* such as these: the regiments of Guarani who challenge the armies of Portugal and Spain."

Thus far, Leandro Taques had been silent during the confrontation. Now he spoke: "Do not comment on matters you do not understand."

"You're new here, Padre?"

"Yes." Leandro Taques was a tall, slim man, sixty-eight years old. His features were ravaged by the pox, and the pitted flesh beside his right eye twitched spasmodically. "But I have met Senhor Bartolomeu Rodrigues. I respect the senhor and his power. I know of nothing that compels me to accept his son's insolence. Move Onias and you will surely kill him. But you will not do so, Graciliano Cavalcanti. Not while I stand here."

"So help me God, if you didn't wear that black robe —"

"*Please!*" It was Padre Salvador. "I promise, my solemn word: If Onias lives, the day he can be moved, I will personally take him to Santo Tomás."

Graciliano glared at Taques. "It's a mistake to make an enemy of the Cavalcantis."

Padre Leandro spoke calmly: "Go to your father. Tell him that if the slave lives, he will be returned. The senhor will accept this."

Padre Salvador was desperately anxious to divert Graciliano's attention from Taques. And he hit upon the perfect solution. He was aware of a tragedy that had afflicted the thirty thousand Guarani of the seven missions across the Rio Uruguay. A decisive battle had taken place in Paraguay nine months ago, in February 1756. Eighteen hundred Guarani from the seven missions, most of them mounted and with cannon made from leather-bound wooden logs, had gone up against the same number of Portuguese and Spanish with cavalry squadrons, an artillery battery, and a detachment of grenadiers. The Guarani commander had been killed in an early artillery barrage, and his force had retreated into deep gullies, where musketeers shot them down. Fourteen hundred Guarani died, compared with three men from the allied units. By the end of May, the six remaining missions had been invaded.

But Padre Salvador pretended ignorance of this battle, and asked Graciliano what he had heard of events in Paraguay. To the padre's immense relief, Graciliano was eager to share these dismal tidings, and though he continued to give Padre Leandro angry glances as he spoke, the tension between them eased.

Padre Salvador had been at Rosário for fourteen years. He was sallow-faced, with a perpetually harried expression. He did his best to alleviate the poverty of his community, but one year the crops failed, the next there was sickness and apathy among the natives — always something to frustrate Meireles's hopes.

Padre Leandro was twenty years Salvador's senior. Before coming to Rosário a year ago, he had served among the Tapajós at the Rio das Amazonas for thirty-five years. He had left Grão Pará after earning the enmity of Carvalho e Melo's brother, Governor Mendonça Furtado, by refusing to supply men for the canoes of the northern border commission. "The governor accused me of hiding my Tapajós in the forest," Leandro had told Padre Salvador, "but what were they to think at the approach of twenty-eight canoes? Slavers! To a man, they fled into the trees."

Mendonça Furtado had sent a report to the Jesuit vice-principal at Belém do Pará and to Lisbon. The vice-principal had considered it politic to move Taques from his aldeia, and another Jesuit had taken his place. But in January of this year, 1756, the Tapajós mission had become one of the first where temporal power was removed from the Jesuits and given to a civilian director, who was to transform the savage converts into loyal, hard-working Portuguese citizens.

Now, as Graciliano Cavalcanti spoke of the invasion of the seven missions in the south, Padre Salvador commented sadly, "Ever since the Treaty of Madrid was signed, the padres did all they could to get the Guarani to move peacefully."

"And who will believe this today," Taques interjected, "when it is so fashionable to denounce us in every quarter?"

"But, Padre," Graciliano said, "surely you can't expect people to believe that tens of thousands of Guarani — those docile converts of your society — will rebel without strong encouragement?"

"They were ordered to abandon churches, homes, plantations. What further encouragement was needed?"

Graciliano glanced again at the group watching them. "But isn't the savage a wanderer at heart?" he asked. "Why should a nomad who drifts from valley to valley object to a just relocation?"

"The Guarani were settled there for a century," Padre Leandro reminded Graciliano. "Their relocation was as unfair as . . . as if a Cavalcanti were told to abandon Santo Tomás."

Graciliano laughed loudly. "Never, Padre!" He gazed across the square. "I ask once more: Deliver my father's property to me."

Padre Salvador appeared to waver.

"Leave — *now*," Padre Leandro said firmly. "Tell Senhor Bartolomeu Rodrigues that we will do all in our power to save the slave."

"You defy me?" Graciliano said, very softly.

"No, Graciliano Cavalcanti, I defy inhumanity."

Graciliano turned abruptly and strode to where a slave waited with his horse. When he had mounted, he shook a finger at Taques. "I'll remember this meeting!"

"I have no doubt you will." Padre Leandro's face began to twitch convulsively.

"Bastards!" Graciliano dug his silver spurs into his mount's flanks and started toward the natives. All but one man scattered. "Son of a bitch!" Graciliano raised his horsewhip to strike this man but the African stepped smartly out of his way. Graciliano stormed off, rending the air with his curses against all at Nossa Senhora do Rosário.

❧

The man who stood defiantly as Graciliano Cavalcanti charged the group was Pedro Préto, "Black Peter." He was forty years old, lean and dignified in appearance, with a long, narrow face. From the age of fifteen until his twenty-eighth year, he had been a slave in the house of Artemas Cabral de Albuquerque, a resident of Recife.

Senhor Artemas, a bachelor, had owned two slaves, Black Peter and Samuel, and he had treated them like sons. They slept under his roof and ate the same food.

Senhor Artemas was a beggar. Three times a week, his slaves carried him through the streets in a hammock suspended from a long pole, their leisurely progress marked by their master's appeals for alms. Nothing ailed Senhor Artemas but an acute case of laziness!

After years of glorious indolence, Artemas had died peacefully, granting Black Peter and Samuel their freedom.

Artemas's house and four thousand gold cruzados that he had accumulated over the years he bequeathed to the Jesuits. A padre sent to inspect the property had offered Black Peter and Samuel work at the colégio. Trained as a carpenter's helper, Black Peter had been sent to Rosário twelve years ago, and he now lived at the aldeia with a wife and four children.

Black Peter was a great-grandson of Santiago Préto, who had been known among those he commanded as Nhungaza, captain of the royal regiment serving Nganga Dzimba we Bahwe. From his own father, Black Peter had learned about the stronghold of the runaway slaves that had survived for sixty-five years in the Serra do Barriga. Eighteen times troops sent from Recife had marched against Palmares, as the Portuguese called the settlements of the runaways, but not until 1694 did they reach the capital, Shoko, and its twin city, 'Ngola Jango.

"They sent a butcher, Domingos Jorge the Elder, with his Paulistas and hundreds of Carijó. They came with two hundred muskets and six cannon, and still it took them twenty-two days to smash our defenses," Black Peter's father had told him. "Had the great Nganga been alive, and your great-grandfather Nhungaza with him, we would not have been defeated. We were twenty thousand strong, but we failed because our leaders were weak."

Domingos Jorge the Elder had campaigned at Palmares for a year, slaughtering blacks who resisted, capturing others to be returned to slavery, and destroying every vestige of this African kingdom in the Americas.

Of all the stories Black Peter's father had told him about Palmares, the one that had had the deepest effect on him concerned the Place of Stones, which had been built by the Nganga Dzimba we Bahwe in the hills behind the capital.

When Domingos Jorge the Elder had overrun Shoko, and resistance became hopeless, 150 men of the royal regiment made their way to the sacred hill. They climbed to the Place of Stones, where the bones of Ganga Zumba lay. One by one, they flung themselves over the wall of the enclosure into the abyss below.

Four weeks after the confrontation between Graciliano and the Jesuits, Padre Salvador and Black Peter arrived at the engenho with Onias.

Graciliano had come back from Rosário demanding that the district militia his father commanded be sent to fetch the fugitive. The senhor was well aware of Graciliano's hotheadedness and had sent Padre Viana to the aldeia instead. Viana returned with a full account of what had happened, and Bartolomeu Rodrigues had been so incensed, Graciliano was forced to flee Santo Tomás. He had gone to the Cavalcanti town house at Olinda, where the third brother, Geraldo, was in residence. (The unambitious Geraldo possessed a talent for penmanship, and his father had secured him a post with the câmara at Olinda.) Two days before the arrival of Padre Salvador, Graciliano had gone back to Santo Tomás and asked his father's forgiveness, which had been granted, with the warning that he was not to go near Rosário.

Graciliano was with Bartolomeu Rodrigues and Paulo when Padre Salvador rode up to the Casa Grande. Graciliano's greeting to the Jesuit was cold and formal but not overtly hostile.

Senhor Bartolomeu Rodrigues thanked the priest for delivering Onias, then said to the old runaway: "I won't have you whipped or branded, but you'll spend your days and nights in the stocks. When you've served your punishment, you'll work like a young ox to fill the place of the slave who died because of you."

"I understand, my Master." Onias's white-haired head was bowed, his eyes fixed on Bartolomeu Rodrigues's boots.

Onias lay in the stocks for two weeks. When he was released, he was put in charge of a high-wheeled cart and four oxen that lumbered back and forth between the cane fields and the mill. It was December, the fourth month of the cutting season, and for ten days Onias led the oxen along the rutted track between the rows of cane from dawn until dark. On the tenth evening, Onias failed to appear at the slave muster.

Bartolomeu Rodrigues considered the old slave's behavior an unforgivable provocation. Graciliano reminded his father that he had warned him that the old goat was stubborn and troublesome. The senhor was now very sympathetic toward Graciliano, and told him to pursue Onias a second time and trap him before he reached Rosário or another sanctuary.

Before the slave hunters could set out, however, Onias and the missing cart were found in a cane field of Santo Tomás.

After ten days, Onias had lost heart. He had led the oxen into a thick stand of cane, where he had unhitched the beasts and left them to browse among the lush leaves. Then he had sought to end his life in a way known to the 'Ngola of Africa: Sinking to his knees, he had consumed great mouthfuls of rich red soil. A young slave couple seeking privacy for a love tryst had found him unconscious but still alive.

Graciliano took charge of the treatment of Onias, who was forcibly administered a powerful emetic concocted from a Tupi recipe. After three days he recovered.

Onias was led to the blacksmith. Here Onias was fitted with a contraption to prevent him from eating dirt: an iron mask that had apertures for his eyes and nose but not his mouth.

When Onias was locked into the mask, Graciliano ordered him to proceed to the mill to work at clearing the cane trash. "Show us you can be trusted not to harm yourself and the mask will be removed," Graciliano said.

෴

During the first week of January 1756, Bartolomeu Rodrigues received a message from Joaquim Costa Santos, one of three independent cane growers in the second valley controlled by the Cavalcantis.

"Senhor Costa Santos asks that we prepare for thirty *tarefas*. Go and inspect his fields, Paulo. See if his canes stand as high as his hopes for riches." A tarefa was the quantity of cane milled at the engenho in a day.

If Bartolomeu Rodrigues was the equivalent of a lord of the manor, then Joaquim Costa Santos was a squire: He owned eighty acres of land purchased from the Cavalcantis, twenty-four slaves, forty oxen, eight carts, and a seven-room house. Joaquim Costa Santos's cane was, in theory, "free" — he was under no obligation to send his carts to Santo Tomás — but the Cavalcanti engenho was the only mill serving these two valleys, and fifty percent of the sugar produced from the Costa Santos harvest went to the senhor de engenho.

At Santo Tomás, since the days of its founder, Nicolau Cavalcanti, senhores de engenho had regarded the cane growers, the *lavradores de cana*, as retainers who owed not only sugarcane but also allegiance. Today, except for the three independent growers, the lavradores were all tenants or sharecroppers.

At one time, however, there had been nine independent growers in these two valleys, an enterprising middle class between the senhor de engenho and his tenants. The drop in the price paid for Pernambucan sugar after the plantations in the Antilles began to prosper had thinned the ranks of the independent growers. But an even worse calamity for them, and for all who lived in the settled areas of Brazil, had been the discovery of gold.

Until men like Olímpio Ramalho da Silva found the treasures of Minas Gerais, the settlement of Brazil had been slow but orderly, and concentrated around the capital, Salvador, at the Bahia, and at towns like Recife and Rio de Janeiro. The bandeirantes of São Paulo, the vaqueiros, and the missionaries had moved into the sertão, but most settlers had remained in the districts along the littoral.

But, in 1693, when gold was seen glittering in the streams of Minas Gerais, many colonists were swept up in the rush to the diggings, a chaotic dispersal over the massifs of the Serra do Mar and south through the sertão.

At Santo Tomás, of nine independent lavradores de cana before the turn of the century, six had lost their lands — three abandoning them to go to the mines; three bankrupted by the low sugar prices and the exorbitant cost of slaves. These lands had been bought back by the Cavalcantis.

Joaquim Costa Santos was the third generation of his family to supply cane to the Cavalcanti engenho. He was forty-one, a small, energetic man with shiny black hair and a thin face divided by a long, sloping nose. Joaquim had married a senhor de engenho's daughter, Isabel Teixeira, a dark-eyed and attractive woman from a plantation north of Olinda. There were five children, three sons and two daughters.

Joaquim had not expected the senhor de engenho's son himself to come in response to his request for a schedule for grinding his cane, and when Paulo Cavalcanti rode to the Costa Santos lands that January day in 1756, Joaquim and his sons were away.

His wife and a daughter, Ana, were ill from eating unripe fruit. The older girl, Luciana, did not like wild figs, and she was there to greet Paulo.

"My father will be back in the morning," she said. Already early afternoon, it was a four-hour ride back to the engenho. "Senhor, will you stay the night?" She kept her hands clasped together tightly, at arm's length in front of her. She wore a plain dress, light blue and dainty, with a wide frilled neckline, small white shoes, and white ribbons in her hair.

"Yes," Paulo said. "I'll stay."

Luciana Costa Santos was fifteen, of medium height, her figure not yet fully formed. Her face was gentle, with soft, rosy cheeks and a small, well-defined mouth. Her eyes were brown and calm, and there was a reddish tinge to her dark hair, which was pulled back from her forehead.

Isabel Costa Santos called out then, from a bedroom behind the reception area. Luciana excused herself and went to her mother. She was back within a few minutes, offering her mother's apologies for not receiving their guest. "I have food prepared," she said. "May I serve you, senhor?"

As the two household slaves among the twenty-four the Costa Santoses owned were also ill from eating the unripe figs, Luciana brought a plate of food, and Paulo sat down at the trestled table. Luciana was shy and embarrassed in his presence. He tried to engage her in conversation, but she responded very little and stood a few feet away from the table, her hands again clasped together in front of her. After a few minutes, she excused herself and fled to the kitchen. After he finished eating and got up to go to the cane fields, she appeared in the doorway.

He praised the food, and then remarked, "Padre Eugênio comes here every week?"

"Yes, senhor. He's a wonderful teacher!"

"Your brothers like him, then?"

"And me, too, senhor," She looked down at the table. "The neighbors laughed at my father when he let me take lessons from the padre. They say a girl needs to know no more than what she can learn from her mother." She looked up then and their eyes met, but, embarrassed, she quickly looked away.

Paulo laughed softly. "Oh, Luciana Costa Santos, I don't think Padre Eugênio's efforts will be wasted on you."

The blood rushed to her cheeks. "Thank you, senhor," she said. And she backed off into the kitchen.

Paulo found Costa Santos's foreman and went to the fields with him. The lavrador had not exaggerated: His harvest was likely to exceed the thirty tarefas he had estimated. Each tarefa crushed at the water-driven Cavalcanti mill corresponded to forty carts of cane.

As Paulo rode or walked beside the foreman, a tall, loquacious man from the Azores, his thoughts drifted to Luciana Costa Santos. He saw her face, her eyes, her inviting mouth. He recalled the shyness, daintiness, the awkwardness of the girl. The foreman spoke of the merits of different species of cane, and Paulo responded appropriately, but he kept thinking of Luciana.

Since Paulo's return from Portugal, Senhor Bartolomeu Rodrigues had frequently suggested that his son should be thinking of a girl from a family of *sangue limpo*, clean blood, which to the Senhor meant no evidence of Jewish, black, or mixed-race ancestry. Paulo's mother, Catarina Benevides, had made pointed references to the daughters of several senhores de engenho and to two cousins in the house of her brother. A visit to the brother's plantation had been arranged two months ago, but Paulo found the girls dull and unattractive.

When he returned to the Costa Santos house, he was met at the doorway by Senhora Isabel, pale and weak but determined to offer him hospitality. She presided over a second meal, with Luciana at the table. Afterward, she sat with them in a front room, until she announced that it was time to retire. The conversation had been formal and polite, but Paulo had been happy simply to be in the presence of this gentle, modest girl.

༺༻

The next morning the three Costa Santos boys came galloping on their bay ponies along the dirt road toward their house, with the oldest, who was twelve, yelling challenges to the others. Their father rode behind them at a leisurely pace, until he saw the young man standing in the shade of a brazilwood tree in front of his house; suddenly he spurred his horse toward Paulo Cavalcanti. As he dismounted, Joaquim Costa Santos called out a greeting to Paulo, following it with profuse apologies for having been absent.

"Were you fed? Did you rest comfortably beneath my roof?"

"Yes, senhor! Senhora Isabel rose from her bed, God bless her. Your Luciana, senhor . . . " — Paulo laughed heartily — "A wonderful daughter!"

Joaquim raised an eyebrow at this last remark. He asked to be excused then and went in to his wife. Senhora Isabel's cheeks were filled with color this morning; the obvious affection for her daughter shown by the senhor de engenho's son had taken her mind off the unpleasantness of the green figs. She now told her husband what she had witnessed — "such soft, kind words from the senhor, such a look in his eyes" — adding that before she had gone to bed she had knelt at their oratory table and prayed to St. Joseph to strengthen senhor Paulo's ardor.

Costa Santos embraced his wife and rushed to his daughter's room. The eleven-year-old Ana lay in bed, still complaining of stomachache. Never again, she had promised her guardian angel, would she eat wild figs. Costa Santos laughed and patted her head comfortingly. Luciana stood opposite him, on the other side of the bed. Costa Santos said nothing about his wife's report, but he mentioned Paulo Cavalcanti's gratitude.

"Senhor Paulo may wish to thank you personally. Be ready for him, my girl."

Luciana blushed and lowered her eyes.

"Be ready, girl," Costa Santos repeated.

Later, Senhora Isabel and Luciana served the men a meal, the females emerging from the kitchen only to attend to Costa Santos's requests, which were numerous, for he wanted Paulo to leave with a good impression of his household. Costa Santos could scarcely conceal his pleasure when he himself saw how Paulo glanced at his daughter. And after the meal, when Paulo bade farewell to them, Costa Santos had been unable to hide that joy, for the senhor de engenho's son took him aside and asked if he might call on Luciana.

"But certainly, Senhor Paulo. Our house is always open to you."

Before he left, Paulo was alone with Luciana for a few minutes, Costa Santos having gone personally to fetch Paulo's horse from a corral near the house.

"I've asked your father's permission to visit you," Paulo told her.

She raised her eyes just enough to meet his and smiled demurely.

"I'll come back soon, Luciana Costa Santos."

"Please do, Senhor Paulo."

"Very soon," he said. "My sweet Luciana."

ლ

Seven months later, early morning on August 11, 1757, there was a heavy knock on the door of the Costa Santos house. Senhora Isabel was in the front room, with a crowd of relatives and friends. She did not open the door but in a breathless, excited voice asked, "Who goes there?"

"We come in peace."

"For what reason?"

Outside, there was a pause. Voices rose beyond the door. "Silence!" a man demanded. "Silence!" Then he announced: "By the grace of God and the Holy Spirit, we're here to fetch Luciana Costa Santos."

Those in the room cried out with alarm; some uttered long moans and groans. But Senhora Isabel gazed steadily at the dark timbers of the door and said nothing as the speaker outside continued:

"She's the betrothed of our godson, Paulo Benevides Cavalcanti."

Now Isabel Costa Santos said firmly, "You've come to the wrong house. Seek elsewhere and, with God's help, you may find the girl."

"No, senhora! How can I mistake this door?" This was a different voice. "How many times, senhora, by day and by night have I entered it?"

Isabel now nodded at a brother-in-law, who unbolted the door and opened it. "You have the senhora's permission to come into the house. Search every room. You won't find the girl."

Paulo Cavalcanti strode boldly inside. He was strikingly handsome in a silver-brocaded jacket, dark breeches, and short black cloak. In one hand he carried three small cakes. He apologized to Senhora Costa Santos for the demand to enter her house but added, "Luciana Costa Santos was promised to me, senhora. Upon this day, she's to enter the holy order of matrimony. Forgive me, senhora, but I won't leave until I've found her." He gazed around the room. "Is there anyone here who will hinder my search?"

"No, senhor. No!"

The adults stayed in the front room. Ana Costa Santos and her brothers followed Paulo on his quest. They waited silently outside each room as he searched within; when he emerged alone, they shrieked with disappointment. "Luciana is not here, Senhor Paulo!" Ana cried. "Oh, senhor, she's gone away." The boys repeated this, showing amusement at the sight of a grown man engaged in this game of hide-and-seek.

Finally, Paulo reached a room at the back of the house. Holding the three cakes in one hand, he pushed the door open. Senhor Joaquim Costa Santos stood protectively beside Luciana. Her two godmothers sat on the edge of the bed; both cried out as Paulo stepped into the room, and one of them crossed herself and began to mutter a prayer.

Paulo acknowledged them, and to each he gave a nuptial cake. The third he offered to Senhor Costa Santos. "With my soul, I ask God's blessing upon you three," he said. He took Luciana's hand. "With my soul, I pray for them. My heart, Luciana Costa Santos, is for you alone."

She looked at her father. "Oh, father, it's time that I leave this house." She was dressed in a black taffeta gown and wore a lace mantilla made by one of the godmothers.

"Go, my child," Costa Santos said. "Go with my full blessing."

The godmothers were standing now, and Luciana embraced them. Then Paulo led her to the front room, where Senhora Isabel stood waiting for them.

"I ask your permission, senhora, for the girl to go with me now."

"Pledge that you will treat this rose tenderly, Paulo Cavalcanti. None is so precious to me."

"A rose made in heaven, senhora! You have my pledge."

"Take your bride, Senhor Paulo. Go in peace. And may God bless this union."

Paulo's brothers, Graciliano and Geraldo, and his godfathers, who had joined the crowd in the front room, now impatiently ushered the couple out of the house and into an open carriage, which was decorated with flowers and ribbons, its floor covered with fragrant cinnamon leaves. A row of carts made up a processional line, the one immediately behind the couple carrying Luciana's bridal chest. The carts filled rapidly with members of the Costa Santos family and their friends, and at a signal from one of Paulo's godfathers, the procession started off, with a group of musicians offering the first of many languid love songs to be heard this morning along the track that led to Engenho Santo Tomás.

The procession reached Santo Tomás early in the afternoon, and moved along the last half-mile to the Casa Grande like the vanguard of a conquering army. Cavalcanti tenants and their families, engenho workers, slaves, and the invited guests stood beside the road cheering the bride and groom. Salvo after salvo of musket fire interrupted their shouts, and a rocket barrage unleashed by a group impatient to wait until dark exploded in the sky. Paulo and Luciana stood up in the carriage, which passed below three flower-bedecked arches, the last of which was opposite the entrance to the Casa Grande.

When the carriage stopped, Senhor Bartolomeu Rodrigues stepped down from the long veranda to greet the couple, his expression joyous. Like Joaquim Costa Santos, Senhor Bartolomeu Rodrigues had given his blessing to this union; he had hoped for a marriage to one of higher birth than a lavrador de cana's daughter, but he had kept this to himself, for the Costa Santos family were respected, their faith beyond question, and their blood untainted.

Paulo and Luciana were married in the chapel of the Casa Grande at three in the afternoon, making their vows before Padre Eugénio Viana.

Luciana stood in front of Viana in her black dress. The lace mantilla that covered her hair and shoulders was open at the front, and her face had a radiant beauty, her cheeks full and rosy, her brown eyes shining. Paulo's attention was on Viana, but at moments his eyes moved to steal a glance at his bride.

"Paulo Benevides Cavalcanti, wilt thou take Luciana Teixeira Costa Santos here present for thy lawful wife, according to the rite of our Holy Mother the Church?"

"I will." A firm, loud response.

When the question was put to Luciana, she also answered in a steady voice.

When Paulo and Luciana emerged from the chapel, there was a tumultuous ovation from the crowd outside. Again the muskets roared, and rockets streamed into the sky, and the chapel bell was rung over and over — by the slave Onias, who had been released from his iron restraint six months ago and, at Padre Eugênio's suggestion, given light duties on the grounds of the Casa Grande.

As the chapel emptied, Paulo's mother, Catarina Benevides, lingered before the small armless statue of Santo Tomás, which was venerated by the Cavalcantis; she said a prayer for the newlyweds.

In January 1758, five months after Paulo's wedding, Graciliano Cavalcanti disgraced himself in the eyes of Senhor Bartolomeu Rodrigues.

It all began on January 23 with the arrival at Santo Tomás of the vaqueiro Estevão Ribeiro Adorno. Ribeiro Adorno was driving three hundred cattle to Recife, and leaving the herd ten miles north of the engenho, he had come to pay his respects to his patrão. At the Casa Grande, Senhor Bartolomeu Rodrigues, Paulo, and Graciliano greeted him and another cattle drover on the veranda. A third rider stayed some distance away, holding the reins of the vaqueiro's horses.

While his father and Paulo spoke with the cattlemen, Graciliano's attention was on the rider who had not dismounted: Januária Ribeiro Adorno. She met Graciliano's curious glances with an impudent look. Januária was seventeen now, and she had lost some weight, her cheekbones more pronounced and accentuating her Tapuya heritage, as did the silky black hair beneath the leather hat pushed far back on her head.

When Ribeiro Adorno saw Graciliano looking at the girl, he interrupted his conversation with the others. "My daughter, Januária, Senhor Graciliano." He addressed his next words to the senhor de engenho: "I can drive three hundred cows in a straight and orderly line, senhor, but this girl? If I crack a whip, the girl laughs. If I speak kindly, she grows deaf." He shook his head despairingly. "Two other daughters obey me, but not this one. I forbade her to come with us. She asked, but I said no. Three days away from the fazenda, we found her following us. What was I to do? I had no one to lead this stray back to camp."

"Why did you run after them, girl?" Graciliano called.

Januária did not reply.

"*Answer* Senhor Graciliano!" Ribeiro Adorno shouted.

Januária fidgeted with the reins. Still she said nothing.

"I'll tell you why, senhores," Ribeiro Adorno said. "This wild, disobedient thing wanted to see the blue water," she said.

Graciliano burst out laughing. Januária began to laugh, too, and they did not stop when they saw the others staring at them, Senhor Bartolomeu Rodrigues with some irritation, and Ribeiro Adorno with no small anxiety at his daughter's impudence.

But the senhor de engenho turned his attention from the girl and asked about the fazenda and the herd. Ribeiro Adorno answered the many questions to the best of his ability, but this took a long time, and when he was dismissed, it was too late to go back to the other cattlemen. Senhor Bartolomeu Rodrigues gave instructions for them to be accommodated in the house of a Portuguese mill worker who was away at Recife.

After a meal, Ribeiro Adorno and the cattleman left Januária dozing in a hammock and went to talk and drink with a group of mill workers.

An hour later, Graciliano went to Januária for sex, a favor she willingly gave the senhor de engenho's son. She had had intercourse with many men since her first experience at the age of nine with her brother, Jacinto.

Graciliano went to her twice more this night, and she pleased him. "I'll take you to the sea, Januária Ribeiro Adorno!" he promised, when their lovemaking was over.

Though showing no great concern, he asked what her father's reaction was likely to be. Januária snorted: There had been an old vaqueiro, Fructuoso, whose house she had kept for a year.

"When Fructuoso asked for me," she told Graciliano, "Ribeiro Adorno didn't refuse. Fructuoso gave him a musket and powder and a pretty ring, and Ribeiro Adorno took me to the old man's hut. Why would he complain if I went with Senhor Graciliano to look at the sea?"

At first light the next morning, Januária slipped out of her hammock and tip-toed past Ribeiro Adorno, who lay with his mouth wide open and his snores reverberating in the room to which he had been carried back by the mill workers after cachaça had numbed his senses. Januária did not expect to find Graciliano Cavalcanti waiting for her at the stockade where the horses were kept, as he had promised before leaving her last night, but there he was, in the slight chill this dawn, rubbing his hands together and smiling as she walked toward him.

They led their horses to the bottom of the hill, beyond the mill and the senzala, and onto the path through the valley. Januária giggled as Graciliano helped her into the saddle, for she was unaccustomed to such gentlemanly behavior. She flashed him a smile as she pulled the strap of her hat tight below her chin.

"To the sea, Januária! To the sea!" he shouted, and dug in his spurs.

They halted twice to rest the horses, and the second time, toward midday, Graciliano again made love to her. Graciliano knew that Senhor Bartolomeu Rodrigues was going to show unholy anger at this expedition with the vaqueiro's daughter, but he had not known his father to be unforgiving. Though the senhor had discouraged his sons from coupling with disbelievers, half-breeds, and blacks, he realized the futility of expressly forbidding such matings. But he had this to say: "Visit your harlots, but do so in privacy, like a gentleman."

Ribeiro Adorno was not likely to set out after the patrão's son with a long knife to draw blood for a daughter he himself had bartered away. Graciliano rode on to Olinda, with little on his mind but his pleasure with wild Januária, who came from the caatinga and wanted to behold the sea.

They began to catch glimpses of the ocean, and the girl reacted with excitement, hurrying her horse along the road. Late afternoon they crossed the Beberibe River, and Graciliano led her up a narrow path along a thickly wooded slope to the top of one of Olinda's hills.

Januária rose in her stirrups, her eyes widening. She leaned forward and moved her head slowly from left to right. She glanced quickly at Graciliano, who was smiling at her, and then hastily returned her gaze to the Atlantic, which lay spread out before her.

"Santa Maria!" she cried. "The sea! Blue water! White water!" She looked at Graciliano with an expression of purest delight. "Oh, senhor Graciliano, it's beautiful! *The sea!*"

❧

Senhor Bartolomeu Rodrigues grew the nail on the pinkie finger of his left hand three-quarters of an inch long, pale pink and manicured, a distinction favored by the aristocrats of Pernambuco to indicate a hand kept free from manual toil. When he was angry, Senhor Cavalcanti probed his white beard with downward strokes of the long nail, accompanying this gesture with irritable clucking sounds. Both these indications of his wrath were seen with alarming frequency after he learned that his son and the vaqueiro's daughter were missing from the engenho.

Their absence was discovered early that morning, and Bartolomeu Rodrigues immediately summoned Ribeiro Adorno. "My son has run off with the girl," the senhor admitted bluntly. "The slaves saw them go at dawn."

"Senhor Cavalcanti, so help me God, I know nothing of this. All night I was with the mill workers."

The vaqueiro, a daring knight in the caatinga, was out of his depth here. At Fazenda da Jurema, he could call for his sons and others to fetch their sharpest knives, for there was a throat begging to be slit. True, there was no rose of virginity to mourn, but the vaqueiro's own honor was impugned.

But, in the presence of his patrão, here on the veranda of the Casa Grande, Ribeiro Adorno was confused. He watched the senhor's long fingernail roaming through his beard and noted the grave and pensive features. Senhor Bartolomeu Rodrigues's expression clearly suggested that his was the greater dishonor.

"I'm sorry, senhor," Ribeiro Adorno said, holding his hat in his hand. "I should have sent the girl back."

Bartolomeu Rodrigues asked Ribeiro Adorno to stay at the engenho to receive his daughter when she was returned to him. The cattleman who had accompanied him to Santo Tomás was sent back to the herd, with orders to take the animals to Recife.

And the senhor dispatched two trusted men to find the couple, with this message: "Tell my son he'll be forgiven if he rides back immediately with the vaqueiro's daughter."

The men returned three days later, with Bartolomeu Rodrigues's youngest son, Geraldo, who now permanently resided in the Cavalcantis' house at Olinda.

"I thought the girl was a servant, but Graciliano brought the caboclo into our salon," Geraldo told his father. "He laughed at me when I objected. Oh, Father, so help me, I begged him to realize the offense this would give the senhor, but Graciliano ignored me."

Bartolomeu Rodrigues made another attempt to solve the crisis peacefully. "Go to Graciliano, Padre Eugênio. He's headstrong, but surely he won't ignore an appeal from you. Tell him of the shame he brings to my house. And tell him of his mother's sorrow."

At Olinda, Eugênio Viana met only stubborn resistance from Graciliano. "My brother Paulo and Luciana Costa Santos fill the senhor with pride — the heir of Santo Tomás and his princess! Always I'm reminded of the honor Paulo brings to the name 'Cavalcanti.' I'm not a child, Padre. Yes, I may later beg my father's mercy, but I will not give up this girl now."

Viana asked to see Januária. A slave woman who served at the Olinda house had been sent to buy a dress for her; pale green with red trimmings, it was tight-fitting and emphasized her full bosom. She had been given shoes, too, but they pinched her broad feet and she had discarded them. She stood in front of Graciliano and the padre, one hand over her mouth, the other fiddling with the trimming on the side of her dress.

"Ribeiro Adorno is waiting at the engenho," Viana said. "He will not return to the fazenda without his daughter."

Januária took her hand away from her mouth and dropped it to her side; her brow creased deeply. She shook her head.

"You belong there, Januária," the padre said.

"Senhor Graciliano has told me that I must stay, Padre." She bared her large white teeth in a smile and raised her dark eyes to look up at Graciliano. "I won't go back."

When Padre Viana returned alone to the engenho, Bartolomeu Rodrigues listened calmly to his report, and thanked Viana for trying to reason with his son. But within six hours of dismissing the padre, Cavalcanti was on his way to Olinda, with Ribeiro Adorno and six men from the engenho. The senhor rode up front, straight-backed in his saddle, his narrow shoulders erect, his expression impassive. Paulo and Geraldo had asked to go with Bartolomeu Rodrigues but been refused. "I don't want you there," he told them brusquely. "I go to perform a father's duty, as sad as it may be."

The ground floor of the Olinda town house, a former silversmith's works, was now a storeroom. A narrow staircase gave access to the living quarters on the second floor. The senhor told Ribeiro Adorno and the others to wait below, and quietly ascended the stairs to the salon.

Graciliano and Januária were on a sofa, with their backs to the stairwell, and they did not hear Bartolomeu Rodrigues approach.

"Graciliano!"

The young Cavalcanti leapt to his feet.

His father jerked his head in Januária's direction. "Leave the room, girl."

She looked nervously at Graciliano.

"Go to the kitchen." Graciliano grabbed her arm as she stood up and pushed her toward a passage that led to the rear of the house.

"For the love of God, Graciliano Cavalcanti, what possessed you?"

"I intended no disrespect toward the senhor," Graciliano said weakly.

"No disrespect? At Santo Tomás, they're laughing behind my back — 'Senhor Bartolomeu Rodrigues's son and the vaqueiro's caboclo fled to their love nest at Olinda!' Here, Graciliano, in my own house, with this bitch of the sertão. Why, my son? *Why?*"

Graciliano frowned. "I don't understand, senhor . . ."

"What? What's difficult to comprehend?"

"Many others have their slave women and their brown mistresses."

"And leave behind mulattoes, mamelucos, caboclos to inherit the conquests won with the noble blood of Portugal!"

"Father, they helped with the conquest. Eugênio Viana reminds us of this, does he not? The peças and caboclos who fought alongside Fernão Cavalcanti and others?"

"God rest our hero's soul!" Bartolomeu Rodrigues said fervently. "Dom Fernão will cry out in heaven this day at the sight of this caboclo and you." His voice rose. "The girl goes back with Ribeiro Adorno, Graciliano. *Now!*"

Graciliano shook his head slowly.

The senhor swung toward the stairwell. "Ribeiro Adorno!" he called. "Your daughter waits for you!"

Graciliano glared at him contemptuously. "Show us, Ribeiro Adorno, the ring the old man Fructuoso gave you!"

Ribeiro Adorno looked puzzled. "Senhor?"

"In exchange for Januária," Graciliano said coldly.

A flush suffused the vaqueiro's face. "Fructuoso was a good man."

"And I'm not?"

"This is not the fazenda, Senhor Graciliano."

"Take the girl away from my house, Ribeiro Adorno," Bartolomeu Rodrigues said gruffly.

As the vaqueiro stepped nervously past him, Graciliano said, "Ask your daughter if she wants to return to the sertão. Ask her, vaqueiro, if she prefers to stay with her lover, Graciliano Cavalcanti!"

"*Mother of God!*" Bartolomeu Rodrigues cried. "O, Jesus, forgive this insolence!"

But the devil was with Graciliano now, and he burst into laughter.

Trembling, Bartolomeu Rodrigues moved to the railing of the stairs and, in a quavering voice, shouted a command that brought four of the men from the engenho storming up the stairs.

Graciliano gaped disbelievingly at his father. "Father, what —"

Before Graciliano could resist, the men dragged him down the steps and pushed him into the open storage area, where two others waited. For twenty minutes they thrashed Graciliano, until he lay senseless at their feet. Earlier, the senhor de engenho had warned them that this punishment might be necessary to remind a son to honor and obey his father.

They carried Graciliano back to Santo Tomás that night, with Bartolomeu Rodrigues riding up front on the cart bearing his son. For two weeks, Graciliano stayed in bed in the Casa Grande, rejecting the sympathy of Eugênio Viana, Paulo, and others who visited him. Early in the third week, he disappeared with two horses and a mule, making for the Fazenda da Jurema, to which Ribeiro Adorno and his daughter had returned.

Senhor Bartolomeu Rodrigues's first reaction was to go to the chapel to pray for guidance. He considered leading a troop of men to bring Graciliano home again, but as he knelt before the Santo Tomás, he changed his mind. "No blood," he promised the saint. "Let my son's exile in that wilderness be a punishment, until a day he looks the bitch of the sertão in the eye and realizes his terrible mistake."

Graciliano did not return. When Jacinto Ribeiro Adorno, driving cattle to the coast, called at Santo Tomás in May 1759, sixteen months later, the vaqueiro's son spoke enthusiastically about Graciliano Cavalcanti's ability to ride, work cattle, and hunt. Graciliano's forays at night through the streets of Recife had been replaced by a more dangerous pursuit: With the vaqueiro's *guiada*, which he had adapted for close combat with the ferocious animals, he went into the caatinga to hunt jaguars.

On one night alone he had single-handedly slain three of the beasts, said Jacinto, who did not conceal his admiration for Graciliano.

Jacinto had been warned by his father to say nothing about Januária, but another vaqueiro had told Senhor Bartolomeu Rodrigues that Graciliano and the caboclo had been blessed with a son in October 1758. The senhor's acute disappointment was alleviated by his joy at the birth of Paulo and Luciana's first child, a daughter, born two months before Graciliano's bastard.

The senhor de engenho had increasingly given Paulo control of the plantation, and his heir's ability impressed him, though occasionally when he listened to Paulo and Eugênio Viana philosophizing about the rights and duties all men shared, he felt that Paulo was overly concerned with these impractical debates. But he kept silent about his misgivings, for he was confident that when the time came, Paulo would be a strong and just master of Santo Tomás.

During the first half of 1759, Bartolomeu Rodrigues heard many conversations between Paulo and Viana on a topic of deep concern to them and one he himself found perplexing: the problems of the Jesuits. Bartolomeu Rodrigues had long been a friend of the black robes, not only the padres at the aldeia of Nossa Senhora do Rosário, but also those at the colégios in Olinda and Recife. Ever since the uprising of the Guarani in the south, however, the charges against the Jesuits had mounted, until the black robes stood accused of complicity in crimes so heinous that Bartolomeu Rodrigues feared there must be some truth to the reports that this holy brigade had mutinied against God.

In Lisbon, the king's chief minister, Sebastião Jose Carvalho e Melo, had provoked the king, Dom José I, into throwing the Jesuit confessors and tutors to the royal family out of his court. The minister had convinced Dom José that the Jesuits had been responsible for the Guarani uprising, and he had supplied the king with reports from his brother, Mendonça Furtado, who had described the exploitation of the king's native subjects in Maranhão and Grão Pará.

In April 1758, Carvalho e Melo's ambassadors at the Vatican had persuaded Benedict XIV to grant a brief appointing the patriarch of Lisbon to investigate the affairs of the Jesuits. The patriarch, Francisco Saldanha, was an ally of Carvalho e Melo's, and within two weeks he had forbidden all commerce of the black robes in Portugal. Two months later, the patriarch had removed the Jesuits' right to hear confessions or to preach to the citizens of Lisbon.

Then, in Lisbon, on the night of September 3, 1758, at 11:30 under a new moon, masked assassins had ambushed Dom José and a companion, Pedro Teixeira, on their way back to the palace at Belém. The musket shots had blasted through the thin panels of the chaise, striking the king in the shoulder and arm. Teixeira was unhurt.

Carvalho e Melo had urged that the attempted regicide be kept secret. The first official notice of the attempt on Dom José's life had been given to his subjects three months later. Among the plotters incarcerated were members of two of Portugal's most illustrious families: The marchioness of Távora, a favorite at the court of Dom João V, and the duke of Aveiro, hereditary grand marshal of the royal household, were incriminated by letters they had written to relatives in which they revealed the attempted assassination and made further threats against the king.

But Carvalho e Melo's satisfaction over the arrest of these fidalgos was as nothing compared with his sense of triumph at the capture of Gabriel Malagrida and twelve other Jesuits. Malagrida's zeal for prophecy had been his undoing: A letter had been found in which he warned of dark days ahead for José I if His Majesty failed to halt the persecutions of the Society of Jesus.

ᴄ⁊

"*Saúva! Saúva! Saúva!*" Padre Leandro Taques cried out at Nossa Senhora do Rosário on a day in September 1759. His cassock swung wildly as he raised one foot high and then slammed it down on the earth.

Paulo Cavalcanti observed Padre Leandro's agitation as the black robe moved in small circles between rows of manioc plants, his head bent toward the ground.

"*Saúva! O rei do Pernambuco!*" Padre Leandro's furious movements as he stamped the soil, belied his seventy years. "*Saúva! O rei do Pernambuco,*" he shouted.

Saúva, the leaf-cutter ant: truly the king of Brazil! Columns of these insects had invaded this clearing near the mission church, but it was not the destruction of the manioc plants that infuriated Padre Leandro: The manioc was there to provide shade for four rows of small coffee trees that he had planted in this field a few months ago, the first attempt to grow the crop in Pernambuco.

At Belém do Pará coffee had been introduced from the French colony of Cayenne, where the governor had been under strict orders not to permit a single seed to be taken out of the colony, which bordered the northern territory of Maranhao and Grão Pará. In 1727 a Portuguese officer, Francisco Palheta, had been sent to Cayenne to negotiate a border delimitation; the story told at Belém do Pará was that the handsome Palheta had so charmed Madame Claude d'Orvilliers, the governor's wife, in parting she dropped a handful of seeds into Palheta's pocket.

Within seven years back at Belém do Pará, Palheta had grown more than a thousand coffee trees and was appealing to Lisbon for permission to obtain slaves for his enterprise. By the time Leandro Taques had sent for his seeds, coffee-growing at Pará was a promising venture that saw tons of coffee exported to Lisbon annually.

Padre Leandro stopped his assault on the ants and walked over to Paulo. "My poor little trees. Every *foot* of bushes ravaged!" Three or four coffee seedlings were planted in one hole, this cluster called a *pé*, a foot of bushes, which formed the base of the tree. "In one year, blossoms; in three, they should be tall and carrying the first berries. Picked and dried in the sun. Shelled and sorted. *Coffee!*" Padre Leandro shook his head. "*Now* what can I hope for?"

"They may recover."

"Perhaps." The right side of Padre Leandro's pockmarked face twitched. "Perhaps I concern myself unnecessarily, Paulo, and I will be gone from Rosário long before the first blossoms."

Paulo, walking silently beside Taques, frowned.

"I pray I can continue my work here, but I don't know. Some days I stand on the steps of the church and look toward the road from Recife, expecting to see a messenger come riding in with the order that Salvador de Meireles and I abandon Rosário."

An hour after Paulo and Leandro Taques had examined the damage to the coffee trees, they were sitting with Salvador de Meireles in the front room of the padres' house. Paulo was at Rosário to arrange for the processing of hides from Fazenda da Jurema at the aldeia's leatherworks, but most of the conversation this day concerned the difficulties facing the Society of Jesus.

There were compelling reasons for Padre Leandro's fear that he might soon be ordered to leave Rosário. By this time, September 1759, the Jesuit province of Maranhão and Grão Pará, where Padre Leandro had labored among the Tapajós for more than thirty years, was all but extinguished. The voluminous propaganda of Mendonça Furtado had resulted in the expulsion of the Jesuits from the aldeias along the Rio das Amazonas and its tributaries, and in the confiscation of their cattle ranches on the Isle of Marajó at the mouth of the great river.

The regulations removing the black robes' temporal power over their converts in the aldeias along the Rio das Amazonas, and providing for the appointment of civilian directors at the missions, had been extended to Brazil in May 1758. But Rosário and many other aldeias remained in the control of the Jesuits, because the governors of the captaincies were having difficulty finding directors with the integrity and virtues needed to carry out Minister Carvalho e Melo's plan to integrate the natives into Portuguese society.

"When did the fathers of the Society have anything less in mind?" Padre Leandro asked. "Of course, it will be wrong for us to deny the charge that we exercised temporal control over the aldeias in a manner far exceeding our priestly roles. To save the savage! God knows how many more would have been slain or enslaved if we had failed to isolate and protect them at the aldeias!"

He rubbed the side of his face. "Our critics omit nothing from their litany: We foster a rude and savage condition; we teach the Tupi-Guarani lingua geral to keep our converts ignorant; we confine them to our aldeias to deprive them of civilization. Even the gowns that cover their nakedness are cited as an example of Jesuit mistreatment in supplying only the meanest raiment. But what else is there to give them, when our king forbids the making of any cloth but the coarsest weave for the loins of slaves?"

Paulo nodded in agreement. The laws banning manufactories in Brazil were explicit, and the king's officials vigilant against illegal products injurious to Portugal's exports to the colony or to the monopolies exercised by contract with the king.

"There have been bitter controversies before," Paulo said, "but they've been resolved."

Salvador de Meireles nodded energetically. "At São Paulo and Santos, the Jesuits were banished. Your own province in the north, Leandro, has twice before been threatened with extinction. In the Lord's good time, the agitators were calmed."

"My Tapajós stood on the banks of the Rio das Amazonas and wept when I left," Padre Leandro said. "'Courage, my children, courage! Padre Leandro will return!' I called to them." He shook his head. "Never." The others did not speak. "Oh, God, how I fear the same will happen here at Rosário."

c/ɔ

Leandro Taques's pessimism was fully justified.

At this moment, a ship from Lisbon was at sea with orders for the viceroy and the governors of the captaincies of Brazil. On September 3, 1759, the anniversary of the attempt on his life, His Most Faithful Majesty Dom José I had issued a royal edict against the Society of Jesus:

> *These religious being corrupt and deplorably remiss in their holy institute, and incapable of any reform, must be properly and effectually banished, denaturalized, proscribed and expelled from all His Majesty's domains as notorious rebels, traitors, adversaries and aggressors of His Royal person and realm, as well as for the peace and common good of his subjects.*

c/ɔ

Padre Leandro stood outside the house near the church, watching impassively as Salvador de Meireles supervised a group of natives carrying their belongings to a cart. From time to time, Padre Salvador glanced anxiously in his direction, but Padre Leandro did not respond.

It was December 23, 1759. A week ago, a messenger from the superior at Recife had brought the order that the two priests leave Rosário in compliance with the royal edict. Forbidden to say Mass or to instruct the children at the aldeias and colégios, the 629 Jesuits of Portuguese America were to be confined in the colégios until ships were found to carry them away from the captaincies, first to Lisbon and then to exile in the Papal States.

The solemn silence of the natives gathered in the square as the padre's belongings were taken out of the house this December morning was indicative of the worry and confusion within the community. The men who served as aldeia officials stood in front of the crowd. Among them was Black Peter, who only recently had been appointed to the council of elders, the first black to join the group of natives who assisted in the administration of the mission.

Some of the natives could scarcely remember the places they had come from in the sertão, but were talking of returning there; some were praying only to be left in peace at Rosário, where they had been born and from where they had never strayed more than a few miles; some, like the small group of mixed breeds, were confident that the governador at Recife was going to send a kind and just director.

Among the twenty-seven blacks, there was little optimism. Black Peter and the heads of the two other families at Rosário were free men, but never so free as to entirely discard the badge of their former status: "*Trabalho e para cachorro e negro!* " — "Work is for dogs and negroes!" — the Portuguese said, and as far as they were concerned, that went for the "free" African as well. At Rosário, Black Peter had enjoyed a good life with his family, and he was proud of his role as inspector of houses: He dreaded the possibility that this could change when the black robes were gone.

The last of the priests' belongings had been placed in the cart and men began to hitch up four mules. Padre Leandro and Padre Salvador moved along the row of aldeia officials to bid each one farewell.

"Jesus be with you . . . Mary . . . Joseph," Salvador repeated, again and again, his voice filled with emotion. When he came to Black Peter, he stopped and gazed

B R A Z I L

into his eyes. "God bless you, Pedro. Tell them to fix their houses. When the director comes, he must not be disappointed."

"I will tell them, Padre."

"Strong houses, Pedro. Houses that will — " He looked appealingly at Black Peter.

"It will be done, Padre. I promise."

Padre Salvador moved on to the next man.

Leandro Taques came along the row to Black Peter. The pitted flesh beside his eye twitched. "God be with you, Pedro Prêto," he said, "and with your family."

"Thank you, Padre." He looked kindly at the old priest. "Jesus walk with you, Padre Leandro."

Padre Leandro bowed his head and started toward the next man, then suddenly turned to look back at Black Peter.

"Jesus walk with the padre!"

The mules had been harnessed, and two men who were to drive the priests to Recife had climbed up onto the cart.

"Let us go, Leandro," said Salvador.

Padre Leandro didn't move.

"What is wrong, my friend? We must not keep them waiting."

Padre Leandro turned and gently touched Salvador's arm. "You ride ahead. I'll follow."

"Leandro?"

He smiled. "'Jesus walk with the padre,' Black Peter said to me. Ah, sweet Jesus, yes, let me *walk!*" Leandro Taques exclaimed. "Let me tramp this long road to exile!"

All this week Leandro Taques had felt a terrible impotence. For the second time in less than five years, he was being forced to abandon his community. Again, nothing for him to do but meekly acquiesce, be transported into perpetual banishment. But wait!

It was twenty leagues — about seventy miles — and he an old man. But oh, sweet Jesus, what a march it would be! *For you, my Lord, a humble penance from an unworthy servant!*

"Please, Salvador, I mean what I say. Leave me to walk."

Padre Salvador knew how strong-willed his old colleague was. Still, he appealed to him to consider his age, and the weakness of his body after his long service at the Rio das Amazonas.

But Padre Leandro could not be dissuaded. "I will drag these old bones joyfully, Salvador, over the hills and through the great valleys of Pernambuco. Tell our Superior I will be at the door of the colégio in five days . . . seven . . . God will know how long He wants this servant to wander the stony road."

☙

Leandro Taques spent eleven days along the road from Rosário to Recife. He intended no more than atonement for his sins and omissions, but in this last and darkest hour for the Jesuits of Brazil, the long walk of Leandro Taques was a small triumph.

There were hundreds of witnesses to the old priest's march. They saw the lone black-robed figure grasping a rough-hewn bough as a staff and haltingly ascending a long pass through the range of hills southwest of Engenho Santo Tomás. Their eyes followed him as he plodded between tall canes as sheets of rain fell from the sky.

Wives and daughters of cane workers peered from doorways and windows, making the sign of the Cross, some appealing for the Lord's blessing on the wanderer.

Padre Leandro averaged seven miles a day. He could not go far before he was breathless. He wore an old pair of heavy boots, and the leather left blisters that bled. The afternoon before reaching Engenho Santo Tomás, about halfway to Recife, the pain was so excruciating that he cried out, but he did not stop immediately and walked on for a thousand paces more, as he meditated upon Christ's Passion.

Senhor Bartolomeu Rodrigues and his family were aware of Padre Taques's approach, and on December 28 the senhor, Paulo, and Eugênio Viana rode out to meet him, taking a spare mount with them.

"In the letter from my Superior, Senhor Bartolomeu, I read that a man can be put to death for talking to a Jesuit," Padre Leandro said when they sat with him.

"Yes, Padre," said the senhor. "And if that day ever comes, we will be no better than the early savages, with the lips of their enemies dangling like bracelets on their arms."

When the senhor asked Taques to ride up to the Casa Grande, the Jesuit declined. "I thank you, but I must finish this walk."

Bartolomeu Rodrigues held his arm. "God has witnessed your great march. Ten leagues from Rosário! It is enough."

Padre Leandro also declined to rest for a few days with the Cavalcantis. He was under orders from his Superior, he said. But he did consent to eat a meal with them.

Padre Leandro was unable to climb the stairs to the dining room, and Paulo carried him there. Eugênio Viana joined them a few minutes later with a slave carrying a bowl of water and towels. Viana himself gently bathed Padre Leandro's feet and applied a salve to the raw wounds.

The three men accompanied him until it began to grow dark. Then Paulo and his father returned to the Casa Grande, but Eugênio Viana remained at Padre Leandro's side through this night, and through the next day and night, until they reached the end of the valley of Santo Tomás, only six miles along the winding track.

Viana would willingly have gone with him all the way to Recife, but he respected the Jesuit's wish to march alone.

After leaving Santo Tomás, Padre Leandro took five days to cover the remaining twenty-nine miles.

On the afternoon of January 2 he entered São Antônio, the district where Count Maurits had built his capital. His bloody, blistered feet were encased in his old boots. He looked around dazedly, the spasms contorting the side of his face.

He was no longer alone but accompanied by an immense crowd, who urged the old black robe onward with constant words of encouragement. Men as old as he was stepped up to offer him their arm; others begged to be allowed to carry him; mothers pushed their young forward to touch the mud-stained and rumpled cassock of this holy man; many sank to their knees on the cobblestones and prayed aloud for angels in heaven to behold one so worthy.

Padre Leandro was bewildered by the commotion. Again and again he gave thanks for offers of help, but he clung to his staff and hobbled toward the colégio and the Church of Our Lady of Expectations. When he finally stood before the handsome sandstone church, he crossed himself and said a prayer of gratitude for a safe journey. The colégio was next to the church, and after a short appeal to God, Padre Leandro started toward it.

Just then a carriage entered the square, and its driver called for the crowd to let him and his passenger through.

Dom Francisco Xavier Aranha, bishop of Olinda, alighted next to Leandro Taques. Appointed Visitor and Reformer of the Jesuits in Pernambuco and responsible for the investigation of their assets and activities, the bishop had found no evidence to support the charges against the Society. This had been before the royal edict banishing the Jesuits from Brazil, but Dom Francisco Xavier continued to believe that the black robes were innocent, though he was powerless to offer anything but friendship and consolation.

The bishop greeted Padre Leandro, and put his other arm around Padre Leandro's shoulders.

"Come, Leandro Taques. I will help you to the door."

๛

The Jesuits sent from Pernambuco, fifty-three in all, including the fathers from neighboring captaincies, were shipped to Lisbon in a small trader. Huddled below decks like convicts, starving and stricken with thirst, five priests died before the ship entered the Tagus in June 1760.

Padre Leandro Taques's name appeared on a list of black robes who had given special provocation to His Majesty's officials. Padre Leandro was flung into a dungeon in the Junqueira, where on January 10, 1761, he died peacefully in his sleep.

๛

A ceremony at Nossa Senhora do Rosário on April 11, 1760, lasted less than an hour but was of great significance, and except for two Tapuya families and five mixed breeds who had deserted the aldeia, the inhabitants were all assembled in the square, the elders standing together as on the day the Jesuits departed.

Bartolomeu Rodrigues and Paulo Cavalcanti were present, the senhor de engenho in his capacity as colonel of the district militia. Thirty men who had accompanied the Cavalcantis were lined up in two rows to one side of the square wearing dark blue uniforms that had been supplied by the senhor himself.

The man in charge of the ceremony stood with the Cavalcantis. He was Elias Souza Vanderley, the director of the settlement. Vanderley's bright blue eyes, ruddy complexion, and ginger hair at once distinguished him from his companions. He was descended from a Dutchman, Jaspar van der Lei, a gentleman-in-waiting to Johan Maurits of Nassau. Van der Lei had been married to a Portuguese woman and turned traitor against the Dutch, fighting alongside the Pernambucans. When the Hollanders had been expelled, Jaspar settled in the south of the captaincy, where his descendants prospered as planters and ranchers.

Elias Souza Vanderley was in his mid-thirties, large and robust, with an imperious bearing. He had been at Nossa Senhora do Rosário for two months now, having left his wife and three children at Recife, where he had been a petty official at the governor's palace.

"I am here to end the wretched and debased conditions you suffered under the black robes," he announced to the elders upon his arrival at the aldeia, waving a document in front of them: "These instructions from the king's men at Lisbon will be my guide."

The director's regulations went into minute detail: Separate classrooms were to be built for boys and girls, both sexes to be taught to read and write Portuguese. The director was never to use the words "peça" or "Negro" to describe a native. The natives were to be lectured on the effects of strong drink. The director was to encourage whites to join the settlement, but the newcomers must cultivate their own lands as an example to the natives.

One of Director Vanderley's first duties had been to enter the names of males between the ages of thirteen and sixty in two registers, one of which was to be sent to the governor at Recife, the other to a Crown magistrate with jurisdiction over the settlement. "The black robes kept you as children," the director explained to the 140 men and boys whose names were listed in the books. "You are now registered as men." At all times, half of the men were to work in the fields of Rosário, the other half to be wage earners on the lands of colonists. "Those who demonstrate that they are most eager to reform the indolence encouraged by the Jesuits will be preferred when the governor's officials distribute offices and privileges," said Vanderley.

Black Peter had had a brief and unpleasant interview with the director soon after Vanderley's arrival. "I am Black Peter," he had said, introducing himself. "I am inspector of houses."

Vanderley had laughed so uproariously that his pink face had turned crimson. "Inspector? Of these hovels and pigsties?"

"There has been no time to improve them."

"The black robes were here for forty years! That was time enough."

"The padres were pleased with the work I did at my house."

"And I, too, Black Peter, will show gratitude. Tomorrow, Black Peter, come to my house." This was the former quarters of the Jesuits.

"For what, Senhor Director?"

Again the color in Vanderley's face deepened, but he was not laughing. "I don't like your tone, Black Peter."

"No, Senhor Director."

"You were a peça liberated through an act of great Christian charity," the director said. "Be humble and grateful. Show that you can earn a place as a free subject."

Elias Vanderley had given Black Peter the job of remodeling the priests' quarters. He made no mention of payment for the many tasks he set, but hinted that if the alterations were satisfactory, the carpenter might retain his post as inspector of houses.

Black Peter and six helpers had worked on the director's abode for a month, installing wooden floors, a new thatched roof, and a covered porch. Vanderley was particularly pleased with the veranda, where he was able to sit in the shade as he directed the affairs of the community.

As Black Peter labored on Elias Vanderley's house, he had seen the director make frequent visits to a back room where he kept two barrels of cachaça. But cachaça wasn't his only weakness, Black Peter had also observed; the director held a special affection for the daughter of another black family, and as soon as his house was ready, he began to take the girl into his rooms.

On this day of the ceremony, Black Peter and twenty natives stood in the middle of the square, facing the great Cross and the church. With ropes and timber supports, they were ready to raise a sixteen-foot wooden column that had been made by Black Peter according to the director's specifications.

Eighteen inches in diameter, straight and smoothly hewn mahogany, the column was surmounted by a small cross and bore a heraldic shield carved with the arms of the king of Portugal. Two iron bars were driven through the column, two feet from the top and at right angles to each other; the four iron sections each protruded for four feet and ended in a curved hook. The lower third of the column was to be embedded in mortar and stone in a hole that had been dug one hundred feet away from the base of the aldeia Cross, a distance paced out by the director himself.

To the natives who had asked what was the purpose of the column, Director Vanderley, pointing solemnly to the great Cross, had replied, "That is the holy symbol of Christ's suffering and love for His children." They had nodded understandingly, and crossed themselves. "This column represents the authority of the king of Portugal. His Majesty loves his subjects and asks that this symbol be raised in every town and village as a reminder of his affection and authority. It also stands as a warning of the king's terrible anger against any who break his laws." The iron hooks were for suspending felons deserving death; the base of the pillory was to be embraced by malefactors deserving a lashing.

Elias Vanderley saw that all was ready, and he raised a hand to signal to the militia. Two men stepped forward to blow a fanfare; when the trumpet blasts died away, two drummers began to tap out a steady beat.

The director signaled to Black Peter, who ordered his assistants to heave on the ropes attached to the pillory. Vanderley grew animated as the natives pulled the ropes and sang out a cadence in time with the drumbeats. His look of satisfaction increased as the mahogany pillar rose without a hitch and Black Peter and the others propped it up with the supports.

"Witness, senhores, how easy it is to establish a town!" Director Elias Souza Vanderley declared. He laughed happily. "My honored guests, I welcome you to the vila of Rosário!"

❧

As Paulo Cavalcanti stood at an upstairs window overlooking the garden at the rear of the Casa Grande and watched his daughters playing near their mother, he felt an outpouring of love toward Luciana.

Paulo's happiness on this July day in 1766 was owing not only to his love for Luciana but also to his great good fortune at having a son, Carlos Maria. Their oldest child, Lúcia, was eight; the younger girl, Francisca, four; two sons had died, one from lung disease before the end of his first year, the other at birth. But now there was Carlos Maria, who was six months old and strong and healthy.

It was just past 11:00 A.M. and two slaves came for the girls to ready them for the main meal of the day. Paulo and Luciana went to their bedroom, opening the door quietly so as not to disturb Carlos Maria. As they entered, a slave on the floor next to the crib started to get up. This was Rachel, a Yoruba woman who was in her sixties and had nursed Paulo when he was an infant.

Rachel shuffled past Paulo. "Jesus Christ be praised," she whispered.

"Forever," he replied.

Carlos Maria Santos Cavalcanti was asleep in the blue lace-trimmed bassinet, with his head resting on a pillow embroidered with religious motifs. Paulo looked down at his son with tender pride. He touched a small cotton bag tied to the end of the bassinet, then sniffed his fingers. "Sleep . . . sleep, my little one," he whispered. "God and His saints watch over you . . . Ama Rachel, with her weeds and wishes, she protects you, too, Carlos Maria."

The nursemaid Rachel had another gift for Senhor Paulo's child: a string of blue beads, tied to the bag of pungent herbs and roots. And there were offerings Paulo and Luciana had not seen: a sprinkling of ash from the burnt bones of a castrated goat — the blue beads were woven with the sinews of this animal — and, secreted behind an oratory table, three small white shells.

Padre Eugénio had expressed doubts about ama Rachel's charms; they were not innocent superstitions, he said, but were based on pagan practices.

Paulo immediately came to her defense: "Certainly she has faith in her magic roots, but I tell you, when I learned my first prayers, it was from ama Rachel. Again and again, Padre, she recited them to me in Latin. She only means well for Carlos Maria, the simple old thing."

Ama Rachel was a great deal more than a "simple old thing," Paulo knew, though he had no idea what gave her such status among the 160 Africans at the senzala and the slave quarters next to the Casa Grande.

The engenho slaves were still predominantly Bantu-speaking blacks from the regions beyond Luanda and Benguela. However, after the discovery of gold, increasing numbers of slaves had come from West Africa, since they were experienced in gold mining and smelting. Some of these shipments of Yorubas, Geges, Haussas, Fulás, Mandingas, and other tribes had been delivered to Recife, among them Rachel's grandmother, who had been bought there to work at the Casa Grande in the time of Senhor Bartolomeu Rodrigues's father. In those days, there had been four Yoruba slaves at the engenho; today there were thirty, less than one-fifth of the Cavalcanti slaves. But, despite their small number, all at the Cavalcanti senzala held Rachel in veneration for she was a high priestess of the Yoruba, the *yalorixá*.

From her mother, Rachel had learned of the supreme being, Olorun, creator of Oxalá and Orixá, who had a son, Aganjú, and a daughter, Yemanjá. Orungun, the son of Yemanjá, had fallen in love with his mother, an uncontrolled passion that led him to rape her. This union produced eleven great gods, the orixás of the Yoruba, among them Xangô, god of lightning and thunder; Ogun, god of war and iron; Oxossi, god of the hunt; Omulú, god of pestilence; and the twins Ibeji, gods of good fortune. Later, as many as four hundred additional divinities were created, including Exú, the mischievous messenger of the orixás.

Enslaved and duly baptized into the Catholic faith, the Yoruba had not abandoned the gods of their people but had come to liken them to the divinities and saints worshiped by the Portuguese. Thus, they identified Olorun with the Almighty; his son Oxalá, known for his purity, with Jesus Christ; and Yemanjá, whom they had begged to carry them safely across the ocean from Africa, with Our Lady. Xangô, master of the elements, became John the Baptist, for whom the terrors of the wilderness had held no fear. Exú was not entirely deserving of his reputation as mischiefmaker, though he had been known to complicate the fortunes of the Yoruba and so he became the devil.

When ama Rachel sat on the floor next to Carlos Maria's bassinet, her appearance was not impressive. Her eyes were small and deeply sunken. Her body was thin and angular. But when she was in command of a ceremony for the gods, ama Rachel was transformed into a great mother of the saints, superintending the daughters through whom the Yoruba gods were called down to earth.

These eleven women and girls, who had been taught by the yalorixá, were summoned by her to dance to the beat of three sacred drums, their movements observed by other slaves crowded into a large room at the senzala, the men to the left, the women to the right.

The daughters danced with their hands behind their backs, their shoulders thrusting backward and forward, their bodies swaying from the hips upward. Round and round they moved to the pulsating beat until, one by one, they were seized with violent convulsions as their orixá took possession of their bodies.

Besides being priestess of the orixás, Rachel possessed a knowledge of herbs and roots that gave her a reputation as a *curandeira*, who was able to prescribe remedies for many ailments, and charms and amulets of a beneficial nature. She had a rival at the engenho, an 'Ngola woman, who knew nothing about the orixás but was able to read the bones for those who consulted her and to offer concoctions and amulets similar to Rachel's, except that the 'Ngola's divinations and prescriptions were those of the *feiticeira*, a practitioner in black magic. Rachel despised this woman and never permitted her near the rejoicings for the orixás, often remarking that the 'Ngola belonged outside, there along the path behind the senzala where the polished fetish stone of the devil Exú was hidden.

చ౫

At the vila of Rosário on a Friday in the last week of July 1766, the drums rolled in the square to summon the natives to witness the lashing of a thief.

Director Elias Souza Vanderley stood thirty feet from the pillory, with his hands on his hips. Over the past six years, he had grown huge and bloated. His face was puffy and purple.

Two assistants accompanied Vanderley: a magistrate, Sampião, and a priest, Pessoa. Vanderley had approached the Cavalcantis with the suggestion that Bartolomeu Rodrigues or Paulo seek the post at Rosário, but they saw the director as a self-serving and rapacious drunkard and had refused. Instead, Vanderley had found Sampião, a mediocre jurist at Recife, and had supported his application for the position. Similarly, he had encouraged Pessoa to serve as vicar of Rosário. Pessoa was incorrigibly venal, his brown eyes gleaming and alert for profit from the barbarians, as he called the natives.

Rosário's miserable huts and shacks were still grouped along the paths leading from the square and on the hill behind the church. But facing the square were new houses for thirty Portuguese who had settled here, a group who ignored the decree that their industry serve as an example to the natives. The settlers had been allotted small fields upon which to cultivate legumes, and this they did, standing out in the sun for hours as they observed the natives hired from the director tending their holdings.

To the right of the church was the solidly built two-story municipal câmara and jail. Vanderley's zeal in establishing a câmara had brought a commendation from Lisbon, since few aldeias had progressed this far. However, Vanderley's eagerness to have a câmara derived from a desire less to promote the natives' participation in colonial society than to increase his control of the vila. The native elders attended the meetings as observers, with only two actually serving the council as standard-bearer and porter. For most of the time, the council room was unused, and Vanderley directed the affairs of Rosário from his place in the shade on the veranda of his house.

When the natives were assembled and the supervisors had quieted them, Vanderley raised his right hand. He paused, nodding his ginger head slowly at the big mulatto, who stood with his upper body bare. Then Vanderley brought his hand down with a quick motion. The drums banged away. The mulatto swung the chicote. Black Peter, the carpenter, received the first of one hundred lashes.

☙

Black Peter's hands were tied with one end of a long rope that had been flung over an iron bar at the top of the pillory; he had been forced to raise himself on the balls of his feet. His right cheek was pressed against the wood, and he looked at the tall Cross in front of the church.

'Jesus, Jesus, Jesus . . . where is Black Peter who was free?" The knout stung his back. "Jesus, Jesus . . . here I am a peça!" Again the knout. "Sweet Jesus . . . there with Senhor Artemas I was free!" The thongs struck low across his back. The mulatto shifted position. The next blow landed on his right shoulder blade. "I was free with the padres!" Again to the right, closer t o the center of his back. "I stayed here. Why?" Lower now, above the top of his buttocks. "Why did Jesus send the padres away?" The thongs raked his right side, now his left. "I was Black Peter, the inspector —" The tenth blow drew the first blood, opening a cut seven inches long. His head jerked back; his eyes were pressed closed. "*Jesus?*"

Before reason was lost to pain, recollections from the past six years flashed across his mind:

Black Peter remembered Director Vanderley lecturing the council of elders and reminding them that when the Portuguese came to Brazil, they found not men but beasts devouring one another. "And never did God set a more daunting task than to tame them," he said.

Black Peter remembered Director Vanderley hoisting a pudgy thirteen-year-old Tapuya onto a cart. "Work! Work! Work!" The time for long lectures had passed. The church bell rang at dawn for assembly; no morning chants but coarse words from the overseers; no choice for the natives but to tramp to the fields. "Work! Work! Work!" The slow and the lazy to be reformed by hard labor where trees and rocks were to be cleared; malingerers condemned as vagabonds and led to the pelourinho. "Work! Work! Work!" Men and boys on the lands of settlers for six months and longer; some with good masters, but some working like peças and living like pigs.

Some natives had rolled up their hammocks and walked away with their wives and children, but most stayed at Rosário, for they did not know the sertão. They remembered, too, the teachings of the black robes: "Be obedient."

The twenty-fifth blow landed on Black Peter's bloody back.

Vanderley had removed him from the council of elders. "They are natural sons of the land and are accepted as equals of the Portuguese," said the director. "Your presence in the council confuses them. And do not poke around their houses," he had added. "You are not their *inspector*."

Black Peter had avoided the director as much as possible, but the animosity between them from that very first interview remained intense. Black Peter managed to hide his resentments. In one instance, however, he did show his hatred of the director: He forbade his two daughters to go near Vanderley, who had been casting longing glances at the girls. Their avoidance of Vanderley was so obvious as to leave no doubt in his mind that the girls were acting on their father's instructions.

Black Peter now had few coherent memories. But there was one flash, like lightning, as the chicote tore his flesh for the thirty-seventh time: *trees*. Brazilwood trees. A wagonload of logs.

Tapuya had found a stand of brazilwood three days' journey from Rosario upon lands without an owner. Black Peter had been sent to fell and trim the trees. Five loads were delivered to Rosário, and he had been waiting for the wagon to return, when a peddler came by. The peddler's wagon was empty after a journey among the vaqueiros in the sertão. "Fill it, Black Peter! Fill it!" said the peddler, and he offered payment in silver. Seven great dyewood logs from land that did not belong to the director, but when Vanderley learned from a native about the sale of the wood, he had flung Black Peter into jail.

❧

Early in the evening three days after the punishment of Black Peter, Director Vanderley was lazing in his chair on the veranda of his house. His hands rested on his belly, and through the slits of his hooded eyes, he watched the natives drift back from the fields of Rosário.

Little George sat on the ground twenty feet from the director, leaning against a veranda support. Little George supervised the mulattoes and mamelucos who directed the work of the natives. After reporting to Vanderley on progress at a new clearing for cotton, he had gone to sit at the end of the veranda, a place he liked to occupy to remind others of his authority.

Vanderley had lived alone at Rosário these past years. His wife and three children were still at Recife, and he saw them perhaps two or three times a year. He had silenced his wife's complaints about this arrangement, insisting that he was not going to have his children raised among savages. Of course, the absence of Senhora Vanderley facilitated the director's adultery with natives and blacks: He had taken a prodigious number of lovers, and he had fathered at least six children.

Now, as he sat outside at sunset, the director saw Black Peter's daughters coming from the direction of the carpenter's house, which was down a lane on the opposite side of the square. Jovita, the fifteen-year-old, and Vera, the thirteen-year-old, both tall and slender like their father, were carrying water containers and were heading toward the church to reach a path that led to a creek three-quarters of a mile away.

"Little George . . ."

"Yes, senhor Director?" The mulatto turned to look at Vanderley and started to get to his feet.

"Are the thief's daughters without shame?" Vanderley asked. "Black Peter was degraded in public and yet they strut like peacocks across the square."

The mulatto knew that the director's interest in Black Peter's girls went beyond their behavior. "Shall I bring them to the senhor Director . . . to lecture them on their father's disgrace?" he asked, his eyes alight.

The girls reached the church and after a few moments were out of sight. "Yes," Vanderley said. "Yes." But when the mulatto started to go after them, Vanderley beckoned him to wait. "Not here, Little George." He rose from the chair. "There." He pointed in the direction the girls had taken. "At the coffee trees," he said. "Go after them. I'll follow."

Vanderley stood up and strode slowly to the small grove of trees that had been planted by Padre Leandro. The director was not interested in a crop that took from three to five years to produce a profitable yield, but the trees had been cultivated by a native elder and his sons and were now more than six feet high and laden with berries.

Little George was waiting along the path as the girls returned from the creek, the earthen water containers balanced on their heads. At the sight of Little George, Vera grew so alarmed she dropped her water jar, which shattered at her feet. Jovita's hands flew to grasp her own container and she took it off her head, swearing at Little George and then comforting her sister, who had started to cry.

No sooner had Jovita put down her jar than the big mulatto seized them both. Vera shrieked for help; Jovita struggled in Little George's iron grip, and was still resisting when Vanderley came running along the path. Jovita froze and stopped fighting to free herself.

Black Peter's daughters were dragged into the grove of coffee trees. Little George assaulted Vera. Vanderley raped and sodomized Jovita. When it was over, Vanderley stood above Jovita. "Go to the carpenter, my little black one," he said. "Tell him that you have a new lover!"

ତ

Black Peter heard a soft weeping. He was naked and lying face down. His flesh was lacerated from his shoulders to below his thin buttocks, but his wounds had been cleaned and dressed by a Tapuya elder who knew the methods of the pagés. For twenty-four hours after the lashing, Black Peter had been delirious; by this third night, he was deeply exhausted and in constant pain.

He picked up a length of cloth that had been spread over the straw and covered his nakedness. With his first steps, his legs were unsteady.

There was light from an oil lamp. His wife sat in a hammock with Vera, who was crying convulsively, her head buried in her mother's lap. Jovita, her face bruised and swollen, her clothes torn and bloodstained, lay on a blanket on the floor. Black Peter's oldest son, a boy of twelve, sat with his back to the wall; a younger boy was asleep near him. Two men who worked in the woodshop and were Black Peter's closest friends sat at his table: Tobias and João, a father and son. The older man got up as Black Peter entered the room. The son, to whom Jovita had been promised, remained seated.

In that instant, Black Peter knew. "*Van . . . der . . . ley?*" His mouth moved stiffly.

"Father!" It was Jovita. "Oh, my Father!" Black Peter's wife stared at him, her eyes filled with alarm.

"*Van . . . der . . . ley?*"

Tobias left the table and reached out a hand.

Black Peter shook his head dazedly. His eyes were wide and unblinking. He started toward Jovita. "It was Van . . . der . . ." A demented wail escaped his lips as he lurched forward and crashed against the side of the table.

They carried him back to his resting place. When he awoke in the middle of the night, Tobias was sitting near him on the floor, puffing at a thin roll of tabak. Tobias offered him the tabak; mixed with the holy herb smoked by the natives were the leaves and flowers of a plant introduced by slaves from Africa, *maconha*, a variety of hemp. Black Peter moved onto his side, and Tobias held the tabak for him to inhale.

"What did my girls tell their mother?"

"Tomorrow, Pedro. Rest."

"Now, Tobias."

In the glow as he puffed at the tabak, Black Peter's face was impassive, a hardness more alarming to Tobias than his friend's earlier frenzy. Soon Black Peter refused the tabak and dozed.

When he awoke a second time, he was aware of having had a vision: "Follow me, Pedro," he had heard his father say, here in this room at his resting place. "Follow me, my son, to where we are men of men."

And Black Peter had gone with his father to a distant place, the settlement of Nganga Dzimba we Bahwe, where his great-grandfather Santiago Prêto — Nhungaza — had been captain of the royal regiment.

His father had taken him into the Serra do Barriga, high up on the sacred mount of Ganga Zumba. He watched as 150 young men climbed to the Place of Stones and, turning their faces toward Africa, leapt from the heights one by one, to die not like dogs but like men of men.

Black Peter looked at Tobias, asleep on the floor. He thought of Tobias's son, João, and of Jovita. Hatred of Elias Souza Vanderley consumed him. He stood up slowly, not waking Tobias; taking a pair of breeches, he crept from the room.

It was 3:00 A.M. Cold, with a hint of rain in the air. At his workshop, he pulled on his breeches and sat down on a bench. He rolled some maconha and tabak together, his hands shaking violently, ignited a small fire of shavings, lit the roll, and sat puffing it for a while. He grew calm and began his next task: As quietly as possible, with even strokes, he honed an oilstone on the head of a double-bladed ax.

He stopped at the edge of the plaza. His gaze rested on the pelourinho. His eyes moved slowly to the Cross and the church. He suddenly recalled the day the Jesuits left, and his own words to Padre Leandro, who had walked to Recife: "Jesus walk with the padre!"

Sweet Jesus! he thought. *Jesus walk with Black Peter!*

Now he crossed the deserted square, heading directly to the veranda that he had built and that was so pleasing to the senhor director.

೧

Vanderley lay on his back in bed, his barrel chest rising and falling, his snores vibrating through the air.

Black Peter stood motionless in the doorway. He held the ax loosely in front of him. A tremor ran through his body. When it passed, he moved to the bed, gripping the shaft of the ax with both hands and raising it. But instead of striking the sleeping man, he punched Vanderley's ribs with the top of the shaft.

The director's eyes burst open.

"Black Peter, senhor," he calmly announced.

The director was half asleep and befuddled.

"Father of Jovita." He poked Vanderley again. "Father of the child Vera."

Hoarse, phlegm-filled words formed deep in Vanderley's throat: "*Jee-susss . . . salva—*"

Black Peter was silent.

Paralyzed with terror, Vanderley made a weak attempt to raise his huge body.

Black Peter drove the blade into Vanderley's short, fleshy neck, severing the jugular and releasing a torrent of blood. Two more blows silenced the ghastly noises. The rage within Black Peter was not stilled. Again and again he swung the ax.

"*Pedro!* "

Black Peter cursed with pain as he twisted around.

"Tobias," the man in the doorway identified himself.

"Dead!" Black Peter said. "To hell — where he belongs!"

"Not alone," Tobias said.

"No, Pedro Prêto! Here's company for the senhor director!" Young João stepped forward, holding in his right hand the genitals of Little George.

Even before Black Peter had seen his daughters, Tobias and his son had spoken of avenging the rape of the girls. The moment Black Peter left the house, João, who had been awake, roused his father. Together they went to a hut where Little George lived with a native woman, and killed them both in their sleep.

The three men took muskets, powder and lead, and a bag of silver from the director's house. They led their horses from Rosário, without a word to their families and little hope of seeing them again.

A mile from the vila, Black Peter rode leaning forward against his horse's neck, trying to steady himself to lessen the pain of his scourged back. He called out, "Tobias!"

Tobias reined in his horse to ride beside Black Peter. "You are in great pain?"

"The Portuguese will ride after us."

"Yes."

"They will hunt the valleys and climb the hills for three black dogs."

"Yes, Pedro. The soldiers will come."

"They will not find dogs, Tobias." His voice rose. "*Men*, Tobias! Men of men, like those who stood with the great lord Ganga Zumba!"

☙

For three weeks after the slaughter of Elias Souza Vanderley and Little George, militia patrols hunted for the fugitives, extending their searches west and south toward the sertão but finding no trace of them.

In the fourth week, five slaves of a lavrador in the second valley controlled by the Cavalcantis deserted. The next night, a planter's house was attacked, three Portuguese butchered, buildings and fields torched, and four more slaves joined the renegades.

The governor at Recife promised a detachment of troops, but they were not sent immediately. The district patrols continued, and for two weeks there were no incidents, and also no leads to the killers and runaways.

Then there were two more attacks in mid-September, ten miles to the north of the Cavalcantis' valleys. Two settlers, a mulatto, and four slaves who had fought alongside their owners were murdered.

A connection between the fugitives from Rosário and the raiders had been suspected since the first attack in the Cavalcantis' valley, and a slave who had been forced to join their ranks and had fled from them now confirmed this. Their leader was Black Peter, the carpenter, the slave told the militiamen who interrogated him.

At Santo Tomás, the cane harvest had commenced early in September, and Paulo Cavalcanti had ordered that normal routines be followed to maintain calm among the 164 slaves. But he also warned the eleven overseers to be vigilant. The overseers' zeal was encouraged by a report that at one of the plantations, a mulatto had been immersed in a copper cauldron of boiling syrup.

☙

At the beginning of October 1766, for the third time in nine weeks, Paulo Cavalcanti was ready to set out from Santo Tomás with a militia. The twenty-two horsemen were assembled in front of the Casa Grande; some were mounted, others were making final checks of their equipment when Paulo stepped out onto the veranda with Bartolomeu Rodrigues holding onto his arm. The seventy-eight-year-old senhor de engenho retained his post as colonel of the district force and insisted on witnessing its departure. Beyond the chapel were three rows of tents for the sixty regular line troops from Recife. The soldiers were on a four-day sweep north of Santo Tomás.

After prayers, Paulo embraced Bartolomeu Rodrigues. A slave brought his horse to him and he mounted. The patrol moved smartly down the hill toward the senzala and the road beyond, when suddenly a figure darted out from the slave quarters and ran toward Paulo. A rider behind him came up, reaching for a machete in a sheath attached to his saddle.

"No!" Paulo shouted. "No!"

It was the nursemaid, ama Rachel.

Paulo reined in his horse as the old Yoruba ran to him, and he indicated for the militia to go on ahead.

"What is it, ama Rachel?"

"Senhor Paulo" — she paused to catch her breath — "you must not ride with these men!"

Paulo laughed. "*I'm* in command, ama Rachel. I lead them." The small eyes were filled with concern. "Oh, Senhor Paulo—"

"What's wrong, ama Rachel? Has there been talk of Black Peter?"

She spat contemptuously on the ground beside her. "I will spit on his grave."

"Have you heard something?" Paulo asked again.

"Do not ride from Santo Tomás today, senhor. Please, believe ama Rachel: It will not be a good journey."

"Why?" he asked. "Why not?"

"The saints warn of danger and evil."

"True, ama Rachel. And with the help of God and the saints, there'll be an end to the savagery." He started to move forward. "God bless you, ama Rachel. Go now and care for Carlos Maria, my son."

"Do not leave the engenho." Her voice was weak.

Paulo spurred his horse forward to catch up with the patrol.

And ama Rachel, mother of the saints, stood alone and emitted a low, repetitive wail. When the gods had come down to her in the deep of the night, she had seen great sorrow and the eye of the devil, Exú, gleaming brightly in the dark.

෴

The militia rode through the two valleys and over the pass to Rosário, where a sergeant and six soldiers were in control until a new director was appointed. From Rosário, they patrolled to the southeast, and on the fourth day, at a small engenho, an agitated planter reported the theft of two oxen. He added that he had questioned his twenty slaves and was convinced of their innocence.

Paulo divided the patrol into four groups, one of which he led himself. Using the engenho as base, for two days they roamed the district, and on the third morning, one group found the remains of the oxen at a creek seven miles south of the engenho.

It was late afternoon when Paulo received this report, and two of the search parties had not yet returned, but he ordered that the men with him ride south immediately. The others were to follow as soon as they got to the planter's house. At nightfall the advance group reached the creek, which lay below hilly uplands, but as it soon grew dark, they resolved to wait until daybreak. Two hours after they had reached the creek, the rest of the militia rode in.

The proximity of the forested hills beyond the creek encouraged the militia, for it was this kind of terrain where runaways established *quilombos*, as the hideaways were known. So far, Black Peter had kept his band constantly on the move; but ultimately, it was thought, he'd be forced to seek a safe hideaway, and tonight, Paulo's militia was convinced that Black Peter was in these hills.

At daybreak, they were relieved to see that the first line of hills was not precipitous; even so, the thick undergrowth and trees on the slopes required that they go on foot, leaving two men to guard the horses. The militia was divided into three patrols to cover as much ground as possible, and by midmorning they were deep in the hills. Paulo's group was in the center, moving through a marshy depression, when a man from the section to the left hurried through the trees to them:

"Capitão, come quickly!"

"Black Peter?"

"A settlement, Capitão," the man said breathlessly. "Deep in the trees."

Paulo sent a man to fetch the group searching to the right of his party, and led the rest of the men swiftly through the trees. But when they reached the patrol that had sighted the clearing, there was a disappointing report from one who had scouted ahead:

"Gypsies, Capitão! Thirty, forty, perhaps more. Caboclos. Tupi. A white man. A few blacks. I see no gang of peças." There were Gypsies from the great Romany tribes in the captaincy. A few prospered as slave merchants; many were horse dealers in the sertão, and not infrequently horse thieves.

When the third patrol joined them, Paulo ordered the militia to spread out and approach the settlement from several directions. They advanced unchallenged, until they could hear the voices of people in the clearing. With three men beside him and a cocked pistol in each hand, Paulo walked into the open.

A native screamed a warning. Women ran for cover into their huts, dragging their children with them.

"Stay!" Paulo demanded. "We won't harm you!"

A Portuguese came running toward Paulo, crying, "Senhor! Capitão! Lower your pistols. We won't fight." A man in his thirties, dark olive complexion, sharp features, keen black eyes, he carried no weapons.

"We're looking for runaway peças," Paulo said, keeping a steady grip on his pistols.

"Not here, Capitão."

"Gypsies?"

The Portuguese shook his head. "Not Gypsies, either, Capitão." He looked at a group of natives and mixed breeds. Two blacks stood with them. "Free men, Capitão, not runaways. We live peacefully. We disturb no one."

A militiaman growled, "Vagabonds! Renegades, Capitão."

"We seek a gang of peças led by a free black. A murderer of Portuguese. They camped at the creek." He indicated with a pistol in the direction from which they had come. "They must have passed this way."

"No, Capitão, they did not."

But Paulo gave the order: "Search the huts."

"I swear to you, Capitão, no peças hide here."

"Search every place!" Paulo repeated. He stuck one pistol into his belt and held the other loosely.

The Portuguese called out to the natives and caboclos telling them to cooperate, then turned back to Paulo: "I beg you not to alarm them, Capitão."

"How many people live here?"

"Sixty. More, with the children."

"Other whites?"

The man shook his head.

"Where do these people come from?"

The Portuguese shrugged. "Here. There. It's a safe place."

"To hide? From what?"

"We've committed no crimes, Capitão. As God is our witness, we disturb no one beyond these hills."

Paulo asked no further questions but walked toward three huts clustered together. Just beyond them, he saw a long, low structure with a small Cross above the entrance and a larger one on the open ground in front of it.

The Portuguese was a few feet behind him. "I've told you, Capitão, we're not criminals. This is our church. Simple, yes, but adequate."

Several of Paulo's men called out to him, saying there were no peças at the huts they had inspected. Women, children, and the most terrible squalor and poverty, yes, but no runaways.

"Where is your house?" Paulo asked the Portuguese.

As the man gestured toward a palm-frond hut near the church, two militiamen emerged, indicating to Paulo they had found nothing.

"Let us go to your house," Paulo said.

"Your men have searched it, Capitão."

But Paulo started toward the hut. "Where are you from, Portuguese?"

"The south, Capitão. The Algarve."

"Why do you live like this?"

When the man did not answer, Paulo did not press him for a response. He put his second pistol away as he stepped into the small hut. He saw a hammock, a table and two chairs, a chest, two saints' images on a shelf near the hammock.

The Portuguese stood just inside the entrance, with his arms folded, his expression strained as he watched Paulo.

"My name is Paulo Benevides Cavalcanti of Engenho Santo Tomás. What is yours . . . Padre?"

The Portuguese nodded. "You didn't come for peças, did you?"

"How long have you lived here?"

"Four, five years. My name is Antunes Machado."

"I seek a black murderer and those with him, Padre Antunes. Not Jesuits."

"But you'll take me away? A fine catch to throw at the governor's feet!"

"No, Padre, I won't."

"O merciful God!"

The priest had been at an aldeia seventy miles south of these hills and was one of a handful of renegade Jesuits in Brazil and the regions of the Rio das Amazonas who were hiding in the sertão with their native converts. He told Paulo that the hills extended only a mile to the south with the settlement's fields in that direction; they had seen no runaways in that area.

Satisfied that Machado was telling the truth, Paulo left his hut, called the militia together, and led them back toward the creek. By one o'clock they were on the hill overlooking the small stream, with two trackers moving ahead of the force. The trackers were halfway down the hill when they stopped, motioning for those behind them to do likewise. Paulo made his way forward.

"The horses, Capitão! Where are our horses?"

The militia worked their way down to the edge of the trees, and for ten minutes they remained under cover observing the bivouac. There was no sign of the horses or of the two men left behind to guard them.

Paulo ordered three men across the creek, and others to be ready to give them covering fire. The men went a quarter of a mile upstream to where the creek narrowed; they crossed and worked their way back to a stony depression to the right of the camp. Minutes passed before one began to move forward, first crouching low, then slowly standing and walking toward the trees where they had left their supplies.

Those watching from across the creek saw the man grow wildly agitated. Muskets and pistols were raised ready to fire. The man started back toward the creek with an unsteady gait, holding a hand to his head as if in pain. The others who had gone to the camp stood up and waved to indicate that it was safe to cross.

As Paulo splashed through the shallow water, he called to the man, asking what was wrong. In response, the man gestured frantically toward the trees. Paulo hurried past him, but after fifty feet, a sight in the gloomy forest ahead brought him to an abrupt halt. "O Mother of God!"

The men left behind were suspended upside down, naked, between two slender trees, their hands and feet spread-eagled and tied to the trunks. Their torsos had been slit open from abdomen to neck, disemboweling them and leaving pools of blood beneath each corpse.

"Cut them down!" Paulo screamed. "For God's sake, take them down!"

స

The attack at the creek left the militia without mounts and supplies, and with no doubt that Black Peter was responsible for the slaying of their comrades. Paulo decided that, while the rest of the militia marched to Rosário, he would take three men to the engenho that had served as their base for two days and secure mounts to dash ahead to the vila. There, riders could be sent on to Santo Tomás to summon the regular troops and immediate steps taken to reequip the militia.

To accompany him, Paulo chose two mixed breeds, one an expert tracker, and the fifteen-year-old son of a senhor de engenho, a boy riding with the militia for the first time. Paulo had promised the boy's father that he would keep an eye on the lad. They left the creek within an hour of finding the victims, moving with extreme caution through the trees until they reached an area of open scrub and grass. They sighted the engenho's cane fields before five o'clock. The cane fields were laid out in four great blocks, and the planter's house was at the end of a deeply rutted road that ran for eight hundred yards between two of them. When Paulo and those with him turned into the road, they saw slaves cutting canes at the far end of the opening.

As they drew level with the slaves, some called out with greetings for the senhor capitão. A thin plume of smoke rose from a clay oven to the right of the one-storied building.

"Senhor Mariano is at the engenho?" Paulo asked a slave near him.

"Yes, Senhor Capitão!" The slave gestured toward the house with his machete.

There was an open area, 120 feet wide, between the canes and the house. Entering this, Paulo called out, "Senhor Mariano!" Again, twenty feet farther on: "Senhor Mariano!"

"Ca-pi-tão," one of the mixed breeds began uncertainly, "there is—" He stopped in mid-sentence. "Aah! *Jesus!*"

The front door was flung open. Black Peter stood there, tall, thin, in breeches and ragged shirt, a bright blue kerchief tied round his head, a musket in his hands.

"Halt, Portuguese! Halt!"

Paulo's pistols were loaded and ready to fire. He reached for them but stopped when, in every direction, blacks stepped out from behind cover and trained their guns on the small party.

One of the mixed breeds went for his machete. Two musket shots cracked and he fell, mortally wounded. The other mixed breed stood rigidly next to Paulo, a foul odor rising from his soiled breeches, a string of incoherent appeals falling from his lips.

There was a soul-wrenching scream. Paulo turned his head and saw behind him the fifteen-year-old boy he'd promised to keep an eye on: The blacks at the canes were not Senhor Mariano's slaves but part of Black Peter's band and had seized the boy when he tried to flee.

"For love of God!" Paulo shouted, swinging his head toward Black Peter. "Have pity on the boy!"

Black Peter started walking toward Paulo. He did not look in the direction of the senhor de engenho's son, who was crying out and struggling with the men holding him.

Paulo turned his head again. "*Oh, my God!*"

In that instant, one of the runaways slashed the boy's throat with his machete, so deep that the head flopped back, blood spurting from the gaping wound.

"Murderers! God curse you!"

"Yes, Senhor Capitão . . . the butchers of Portuguese dogs!" Black Peter gestured toward Paulo's weapons. "Throw them down!"

The blacks standing near them began to move forward.

"Drop them, Senhor Paulo Cavalcanti." Black Peter knew the captain of Santo Tomás's militia. There was the time he had gone to the engenho with Padre Leandro to return Onias, and he had seen Paulo on his visits to Rosário.

Paulo threw down his weapons. "You'll hang, Black Peter. You'll hang as surely as God witnesses your bloody murders."

Black Peter smiled. "I'm ready to die, Cavalcanti," he said. "I was ready the night I killed Elias Souza Vanderley."

The mixed breed next to Paulo had stopped his appeals. He was dumbfounded with terror, his mouth hanging open as he looked at Black Peter.

Paulo glanced past Black Peter toward the house. "Where are they? Senhor Mariano and his family?"

Black Peter did not answer. Other blacks laughed, and brandished their machetes. One of them cried out, "Why do we wait?"

Black Peter looked at his men. His lean features hardened. "Kill him!" he commanded. "Kill the Portuguese!"

"O holy God!" Paulo cried. "Jesus!"

The runaways began to move forward.

"Wait!" It was Black Peter. His men stopped.

At this point, the mixed breed tried to run off but was quickly seized and hurled to the ground. Six or seven machetes and clubs rose and fell above him. Other blacks guarded Paulo.

"This is a Cavalcanti," Black Peter said, when the mixed breed was silenced. "A noble of the land! Let him die like a dog!"

With Black Peter giving commands, the circle of men closed in. Paulo struck out with his fists, but he was quickly overpowered and stripped naked. A length of rope was tied around his neck.

He was forced to his knees and made to crawl along beside the house, where his captors showed him the bodies of the planter and his family. He was kicked and cursed.

Suddenly one of his captors leapt forward, waving a sharpened length of thick cane. "Let the dog have a tail!" he shouted. Paulo screamed hideously as the cane was driven up his anus.

Half of the planter Mariano's slaves stood with the runaways. Of the other ten, four were dead and six had fled into the fields. But one of the blacks who had joined the renegades was so horrified by the savagery against the senhor capitão that he stormed forward with his machete to drive off Paulo's tormentors. He was swiftly hacked to death.

Black Peter did not take a direct part in the torment of Paulo. He came toward him now, carrying Paulo's own sword.

Paulo was still on his knees, mumbling prayers to God and the saints. To the little *Santo Tomás*, too, the battered image before his eyes. He looked up dazedly.

Black Peter gave a triumphant cry and thrust the blade deep into Paulo's side.

☙

After the slaying of Paulo Cavalcanti and his companions, Black Peter changed his tactics. Until now he had been constantly on the move, evading capture by hiding during the day and passing through the valleys at night. Now he led the fifty men with him to the densely wooded foothills of the Serra do Barriga, almost one hundred miles south of Engenho Santo Tomás.

They reached the Serra do Barriga on October 9, three days after Paulo's death, and almost immediately made a discovery that elated Black Peter. Between the palms and trees, they found the ruins of Palmares.

Black Peter went alone to a hill just to the south of the range. Near the summit, he came to a narrow passage formed by a wall of tightly packed stones that followed the contour of the hill. The wall was sixty feet long and had collapsed in several places, and as Black Peter clambered over piles of stone, he saw that the passage opened into an enclosure littered with broken pottery figurines, old tools, and rusty weapons. A toucan had alighted on the stones to his left.

"I am Black Peter," he addressed the bird. "I have come to the place of Ganga Zumba!"

He gave an exultant cry then, frightening off the bird, but he laughed as it flew down to the trees, for his father had told him that the huge-billed birds always returned to the sanctuary where Nganga Dzimba we Bahwe had worshiped.

℀

In the middle of the night eleven days after Paulo Cavalcanti's body had been carried to Santo Tomás, Padre Eugênio Viana was awakened from a troubled sleep. He climbed out of bed and put on his cassock, then opened the door to his room, stepped outside, and paused, listening to sounds of lamentations coming from below.

The boards of the choir loft creaked as Viana crossed to the right gallery. Three-quarters of the way along the balcony, he stopped and stood with his hands on the railing, glancing down into the chapel, where several candles had been lit.

Bartolomeu Rodrigues was down on his knees, beside Paulo's coffin. His sobbing was interrupted by long silences.

"Hear his weeping, O Lord," Viana whispered. "Console his suffering, I beseech thee."

Through the eleven days since October 10 when Paulo was brought back to the Casa Grande, a constant stream of relatives and friends had come to pay their respects. Joaquim and Isabel Costa Santos were still here to comfort Luciana and the children. Geraldo, who was now married and living at Recife, was here, too, with his wife. Of the close family, only Graciliano Cavalcanti was absent.

Eight years had passed since Graciliano left Santo Tomás for the sertão. Bartolomeu Rodrigues had steadfastly refused to forgive Graciliano. "He must come to my house, dragging his pride with him!"

The senhor had grown deafer to Viana's pleas to make peace with Graciliano, as reports of more bastards Graciliano had fathered reached the engenho: There were now five children. Yet Bartolomeu Rodrigues had not had Graciliano evicted from Fazenda da Jurema. "I should have acted while there was a chance to crush his rebellion," he had told Viana. "I promised the Lord no blood would be shed between father and son. I will keep my promise."

Viana had seen Graciliano several times the past three years on the young Cavalcanti's cattle-drive expeditions with the vaqueiros to the coast. Graciliano was as unyielding as his father: "I was thrashed like a peça until my eyes were bloodied and my sides heaving. It's senhor pai, not me, who must seek peace. Let him call me to his side and offer a few words of regret. I'll listen. Until then, I stay where I am."

Viana had seen a change in Graciliano: He was quieter, introspective, and had developed a passion for the backlands. He spoke with admiration of the poderosos, "the great men of the earth," and made it clear that he saw himself in a similar role. "I can make something of the place," he had said at their first meeting two years after his flight, and he had spoken of lands north of Riacho Jurema that the Cavalcantis could buy, and of other improvements he would make to the property.

"Will you stay forever in that pitiless wilderness?" Viana had asked him.

"What is there for me here? What has there ever been? I'm not the firstborn heir to these valleys."

When Bartolomeu Rodrigues did not evict him and Paulo gave support to his plans for the ranch, Graciliano had gone on to increase the holding by a third and to raise the herd to eight thousand animals. Viana had hoped that this success would encourage the senhor to forgiveness, but it did not.

"He will come to me," Bartolomeu Rodrigues had said resolutely.

Viana was thinking of Graciliano now as he watched the senhor turn away from Paulo's coffin and begin to move across the stone slabs. When he finally reached the marble altar, he pressed his cheek against it and wept aloud.

Viana descended the stairs. When Bartolomeu Rodrigues saw him, his sobs abated.

Then Bartolomeu Rodrigues spoke, in a voice so low that Viana had to lean forward to hear him: "Please, Padre, ride to the sertão. Go, Eugênio Viana, and fetch Graciliano."

"*Thank God!*" Viana said fervently.

"I want my son here," Bartolomeu Rodrigues said. "I will ask his forgiveness."

"Bartolomeu, he *is* sent for."

The senhor did not grasp what Viana had said. "Now, Eugênio. Go yourself."

Viana placed a hand on his shoulder. "The day after Paulo was carried home . . . forgive me, Bartolomeu, I didn't wait for you to ask. Ten days ago I dispatched men to the fazenda."

❧

The thirty-two men galloped up the hill to the Casa Grande of Santo Tomás, their expressions grim, their eyes blazing with murderous intent. Five days and two hundred miles they had ridden, stopping only to rest their heated mounts and ready their spare ponies.

They wore the vaqueiro's suit of leather and low wide-brimmed hats, but some had added embellishments: a flaming red waistcoat, a tattered gray coat with flared pleats and enormous cuffs, purple breeches, a wig with two pigtails tied with bows, a three-cornered felt hat trimmed with gold braid and ostrich fronds, a bright green turban. Two-thirds were vaqueiros from Fazenda da Jurema, a mixed group of small, wiry caboclos, three mulattoes, and two blacks. Ten riders were from neighboring ranches, with whom there had long been an alliance. Armed with muskets and wide-mouthed pistols, and with swords and knives as sharp as razors, to a man they had volunteered to hunt the devil in these valleys to the east.

Graciliano Cavalcanti led this rustic cavalry to the open ground in front of the Casa Grande, reining in his pony at the last moment, so that the lead horses halted at the edge of the long veranda. The vaqueiro Estevão Ribeiro Adorno, fifty-nine now, his skin wrinkled and dry, his hair gray, drew up beside Graciliano and acknowledged the order to have the men dismount and wait.

Graciliano was leaner, and the loss of weight made him seem taller. He wore tanned breeches and high boots, a red silk waistcoat, and a long leather coat that hung below his knees. He carried two knives, one long, one short; a pistol; and the sword with which, twelve years ago at the age of nineteen, he had killed a man at Recife and which was engraved with the words "Justice Lives." His favorite weapon was borne with other equipment on a spare mount — a nine-foot cattle goad fitted with a steel blade.

Eugênio Viana came hurrying along the veranda as Graciliano swung down from his saddle. "Thanks to God you're here, Graciliano!"

"Jesus Christ knows, when they told me, I heard Paulo cry out in that wilderness. I listened in the caatinga to his cry for the last drop of the murderer's blood. What word of the devil's legion?"

"Nothing. Three hundred men search for them. Nothing."

"How is it possible?"

"At first they kept on the move. Now they are said to be in the sertão."

"We'll find them, Viana," he said.

"Your father prayed that you would come."

"I'll go to him now," Graciliano said.

They met in Bartolomeu Rodrigues's bedroom. The senhor de engenho sat on a shabby brocaded sofa in his underclothes and a gown. When Graciliano stepped toward him, Bartolomeu Rodrigues spoke as if a third person was in the room: "This is my son. God in heaven, my son."

"Senhor Pai, I came as soon as I heard." Graciliano was shocked at the frail appearance of his father.

"I asked God to send you back to me. He took my Paulo. An old man who lived his life should have been taken, but no, it was Paulo." His voice faded, then suddenly gained volume: "God broke me. God humbled me. He took one son, I saw. And I, with pride and vanity, lost another. Forgive me, Graciliano. Forgive me."

"Oh, Father, *I* was the one who left Santo Tomás. *I* was responsible!"

Tears streamed down Bartolomeu Rodrigues's sunken cheeks. He clutched the top of the sofa with one hand and started to get to his feet. Graciliano went to help him, and in that moment he embraced his father. "Oh, Senhor Pai . . . why did we wait so long?"

The senhor de engenho pressed his head against the dusty leather of the long coat. "*Meu filho! Meu filho!* My son, it is over," he said. "You are back at Santo Tomás, at last!"

Graciliano broke from the embrace but kept his hands on his father's shoulders. "Lord God in heaven!" he cried. "Hear this son now, Bartolomeu Rodrigues! Upon my most solemn oath, I swear to avenge Paulo. I won't rest until the butchers congregate at the gates of hell!"

"Paulo lies in the chapel," Bartolomeu Rodrigues said. "Go softly, Graciliano. Make your vow to him."

☙

Captain-Major Francisco Andrade da Cruz was in overall command of the troops searching for Black Peter. An additional two hundred men had been sent into the field after Paulo's death, including the Henrique Dias regiment, a unit of black soldiers named for the hero of the wars against the Dutch. Andrade da Cruz had made his headquarters at Rosário and occupied the late director's house.

A small, rotund man, the captain-major stood beneath the covered veranda this morning of October 27 wearing white breeches, blue coat with gold-worked epaulets, scarlet sash, spotless white stockings, and half-boots.

Three vaqueiros at the creek to fetch water this dawn had espied a young black creeping toward the settlement. Alerted by his suspicious behavior, they had captured him and sent for Graciliano, who met them at the creek with a Portuguese settler. This man identified the black as João, the son of Tobias, who was in league with Black Peter. A soldier who had come down to the stream while João was being tortured was chased away, and when he reported the incident to the captain-major, Andrade da Cruz sent men to investigate. But, when they got to the site, they found Graciliano and his men gone, and João with his neck broken. Andrade da Cruz asked that Graciliano share what had been learned from the black. Graciliano refused.

"You forget, senhor" — Andrade da Cruz regarded the roguish leather-clad man opposite him as anything *but* a senhor — "I'm camp master and hold the written orders of our governor."

"And I the brother of Paulo Cavalcanti. I, too, Andrade da Cruz, have a letter of patent, written in my brother's blood."

A huge fly pestered Andrade da Cruz; he gave a slow, majestic swipe in its direction. "In the sertão, senhor, you may make your own laws. Here the king's administrators and judges rule." He slashed at the air with his hand and then hopped off the veranda and walked stiff-leggedly to where Ribeiro Adorno and two other vaqueiros stood glancing sheepishly in his direction as he approached.

A group of soldiers was observing the confrontation. Some Portuguese settlers and mulattoes and a few of the natives were also present. The rest of the vaqueiros and ten men from Santo Tomás who rode with Graciliano sat in their saddles fifty yards away from the soldiers.

Now Andrade da Cruz turned his head toward Graciliano. "I understand your longing for vengeance, but we march with one purpose: to find Black Peter. Share the information!"

Ribeiro Adorno cleared his throat. "Nothing was said, Captain-Major," he responded. "Lies. Stupid things. Nothing important."

"You lie, vaqueiro." Andrade da Cruz raised one of his black half-boots a few inches off the ground, and with the tip of the boot he poked the body of João, crumpled in a heap at the vaqueiro's feet. "Tell me what you learned from him."

João's flesh was punctured with small knife wounds.

"Perhaps, Cavalcanti, a few days in jail with my other guest and you'll tell me what this one said?" Andrade da Cruz's "guest" was the renegade Jesuit Antunes Machado, who had been flushed out of his hiding place by soldiers patrolling those hills. Machado now lay in chains in Rosário's jail awaiting transport to Recife and expulsion from the colony.

"Yes, Captain-Major. Yes." Graciliano gazed pointedly in the direction of the vaqueiros and the men from Santo Tomás. "Shall I walk across to the prison now?"

Andrade da Cruz looked at the riders and his expression soured. "Your assassins can be held for this killing."

Graciliano nodded. "Perhaps my brother would be alive this day if your soldiers had shown the same eagerness."

"The troops are in the saddle day and night."

"And the fourth month approaches with no sign of the runaways. Listen, we won't interfere with your patrols. If the soldiers find them before I do, God grant them a quick victory — and a strong rope!"

"Go, then, damn you! But you'll do no better with these caboclos and cut-throats!"

Graciliano laughed. "We shall see, Captain-Major."

Half an hour later, Graciliano led his men from Rosário.

"Why didn't you tell the captain-major?" asked an engenho worker who was riding beside him. "Wouldn't it be better to ride with a force of hundreds?"

"He's mine! *Mine!*" Graciliano shook a fist in the air. "With this hand upon my brother's cold brow, I swore to kill Black Peter!" Graciliano gave a mighty shout then: "Palmares. Ride for the devils at Palmares!"

Black Peter had made a serious mistake. Secure in the remote Serra do Barriga, and with a growing vision of the restoration of Ganga Zumba's stronghold and himself as "Great Pillager" of the Portuguese, Black Peter had called João to his side: "The Portuguese seek fifty runaways, not one man by himself. Go to Rosário, João, and lead the women and children to Palmares." Captured, João had broken down after the vaqueiros smashed his teeth and punctured his flesh in a dozen places, and had revealed that Black Peter was at the Serra do Barriga.

On November 1, 1766, the forty-two riders reached the Barriga hills. They had stopped the previous day at a settled district to the northeast, where a plantation owner offered as guides two slaves, the descendants of runaways at Palmares. Graciliano and Jacinto Adorno took these men to reconnoiter the area, leaving the force to prepare for battle.

The slaves led them through a forest to the site of Ganga Zumba's capital, Shoko. Beyond the parade ground, they came to a field of wild manioc, a section of which had been recently harvested. Leaving Jacinto and one of the slaves here, Graciliano and the other man scouted ahead to within 150 feet of the former royal enclosure. Graciliano lay behind a clump of ferns. Directly opposite him, a section of the six-foot-high earth embankment had been cleared and a group of blacks were sealing a breach with rocks and sand. Moving to the right, Graciliano got a partial view inside the enclosure through another breach, but observed little activity at the crude shelters that had been erected by the runaways.

Graciliano gestured to the guide, indicating with a circular motion of his hand that they should work their way around the enclosure. This took three-quarters of an hour, for on the north side the tree cover thinned — the blacks kept their horses in a corral here — and they had to fall back to remain unseen.

"I saw no guards posted," Graciliano told Jacinto upon returning. "They probably think that because their lord of the devil, Ganga Zumba, squatted here for decades, they'll do the same." Graciliano said that by following the old thoroughfare, cutting across the open clay area and the manioc field, and striking from the north where the trees were few, they could get through on horseback. "This very night, Jacinto, we attack!"

കെ

Graciliano was wrong about the lookouts: The scouting party had been seen by two men, who reported to Black Peter.

"We must leave!" Tobias said. "Immediately!"

Black Peter disagreed: "Run like dogs, Tobias? Are we not men of men? We will defend the house of our lord, Ganga Zumba!"

At 1:00 A.M. on November 2, under a weak moon in an overcast sky, Graciliano led thirty-nine men from the camp in the forest. Two men were left behind, one half blinded by a thorn that had raked his eye, the other incapacitated by dysentery.

The riders reached the old thoroughfare of Shoko. Graciliano was in front with Ribeiro Adorno and Jacinto. The three lounged in their saddles, keeping the ponies at a steady pace. Beyond the thoroughfare, they moved in single file with Jacinto in the lead, until the ponies' hooves clattered onto the clay at the former kraal of the royal regiment. Firearms were loaded, swords drawn. Graciliano and other vaqueiros left their swords at easy reach beneath their saddle girths and chose for the first charge their iron-tipped goads.

"May God see us this night," Graciliano said, in a muted but hoarse voice. "For His sake, and for Paulo Cavalcanti." He shook his lance furiously. "Ride, vaqueiros! Death to the devil!"

They spurred the ponies through the darkness, faster and faster, crashing through the undergrowth toward the north end of the enclosure. The men were silent; the only sounds the breathing of their ponies, the clatter of hooves, the creak of leather, the jangle of equipment. The trees began to thin out, and the embankment loomed large in the distance. Three or four men gave a suppressed whoop, and others took up the cry. At 150 yards, storming toward their objective, all were screaming for the blood of Black Peter.

Jacinto and two other men had been ordered to stampede the renegades' horses. As the charge began, they broke off to the right. Now Jacinto swung back, racing his mount toward Graciliano. "The horses — "

Suddenly, along the embankment, a semicircle of fire broke out as the muskets of Black Peter's men crackled. A rider and pony up front crashed to the ground. Two men behind were thrown as their mounts slammed into the fallen animal. Elsewhere five men were shot, three struck dead by the hail of bullets. A second volley lacked the ferocity of the first, and the remaining twenty-five cattlemen and seven engenho workers fell like a thunderbolt upon the runaways' camp.

Some riders surged toward two breaches; some charged furiously up the embankment, brandishing their weapons and taking up Graciliano's cry: "Death to the devil!"

The inner embankment was steep and a few ponies stumbled and fell, but most riders were carried safely into the enclosure. Runaways were hammered to death by the thundering hooves; others fell back toward piles of rocks and the hut platforms.

Graciliano stormed beyond a breach in the embankment. A musket ball from runaways at a pile of rocks grazed the side of his neck, raising an angry weal, but he did not slow his charge to the rocks, where he impaled a black with his goad. The other runaways abandoned this position, one trampled by a vaqueiro's pony as he ran, another gunned down by a man beside Graciliano. Riders tore across the 120 yards to the far side of the enclosure, then wheeled their mounts and attacked the blacks at the hut platform. Vaqueiros leapt from their ponies wielding machetes and swords in hand-to-hand combat.

The fight lasted less than ten minutes. When the first slaves threw down their arms and begged for mercy, others quickly followed suit and the resistance collapsed. From every direction, there were cries and groans of agony from men on the blood-soaked ground, seven of Graciliano's horsemen among them.

"*Black Peter!*" Graciliano had dismounted and strode furiously around the enclosure, shouting at the top of his voice. "Where's the devil himself?" he demanded, striking the blacks nearest him with the shaft of his goad.

The runaways swore that their leader was not there.

As Graciliano searched for Black Peter, others of his group fell upon the huts on the raised platforms and set them ablaze.

"That one!" Graciliano suddenly commanded, pointing at a runaway who began to moan with fear. "Bring him!"

The slave was forced to inspect the dead and wounded blacks, first in the enclosure and then, with firebrands to light the way, outside the embankment. Repeatedly the slave shook his head, for neither Black Peter nor Tobias was among the twenty-nine blacks who lay dead.

Graciliano's rage mounted. "Where? Where have they run to, peça?"

Without hesitation, the man blurted out: "The hill."

"What hill?"

"The Place of Stones."

Graciliano grabbed the slave's arm and twisted it violently. "Where?"

"Mercy, Master! I will show you!"

With Jacinto Adorno and one other vaqueiro, Graciliano set out immediately. The moon was obscured by drifting clouds, and in the dark it took two hours to reach the hill.

"This is the Place of Stones," the runaway said, and begged to be left behind. "Black Peter warned against violating — "

"Climb, peça!" Graciliano prodded the man with his lance, making a shallow cut in his side. "*Climb!*"

It took three-quarters of an hour to find the path and, fifteen minutes later, the narrow passage that led to the enclosure. The vaqueiro was behind the slave; then came Jacinto and, at the rear, Graciliano.

They were twenty feet along the passage when two muskets roared. The bullets missed the runaway, but the vaqueiro was hit in the face, and a bullet thudded into Jacinto's shoulder, hurling him against the side of the hill. Graciliano was unhurt.

A cocked pistol in one hand, the goad in the other, Graciliano crept forward, hearing a clatter of stones ahead. Through a break in the cloud cover, he saw a man scrambling over a pile of rocks. He raised his pistol and fired. The man was hit but did not fall. Graciliano flung down his pistol and sprang forward, gripping the goad in both hands. He drove the long blade into the man's back.

Tobias gave a rapid succession of short, sharp, hard sounds and then lay quiet.

Graciliano was fifteen feet from the entrance to the enclosure. Keeping to the right of the passage, close to the stone wall, he continued on.

Black Peter was at the very edge of the enclosure at a spot where a part of the wall had fallen and the stones were but three feet high. He was bare-chested and his right shoulder was bleeding from a bullet wound. He stood unsteadily, swaying back and forth.

"*Devil!*" Graciliano screamed.

Black Peter turned his head slowly. He had no weapon.

Graciliano took a step forward but then stopped, watching Black Peter with the same wariness he showed in stalking a jaguar in the caatinga. "Devil!" he cried again. "I'm a Cavalcanti! Brother of one you butchered!"

Black Peter was staring at the wall next to him. "Ganga Zumba?" he said softly. "Father?"

Graciliano's mocking laughter filled the enclosure.

Black Peter shuddered and cried out: "I am alone!"

"Yes, Pedro Prêto! Alone with Graciliano Cavalcanti!"

Black Peter took a step back from the wall and gave a cry of utter despair. He was here to take the long leap to where the bones of the warriors lay. But he could not bring himself to jump.

"What's wrong, Black Peter? Do you see the devil?" Graciliano stealthily moved forward.

Black Peter's tall, thin body began to shake violently. "Jesus?" he cried out.

The appeal infuriated Graciliano. He lunged forward with the goad and gashed Black Peter's side. "Our Lord will not hear you!" A second thrust penetrated Black Peter's abdomen.

Black Peter sank to the ground, and for the third time, dying, he called out: "Jesus?"

Graciliano leaned against the rock face at the back of the enclosure. Suddenly, there was a noise; he cursed and swung around. But it was only a toucan, disturbed by the cries, rising from its nest in the trees below.

❧

"Senhor Pai!" Graciliano shouted. "Someone! Bring my father to me!" He sat on his horse outside the Casa Grande. Eleven of his men who had died had been buried at a settlement near Palmares; the remainder of the force was assembled on the open ground in front of the house.

Graciliano dismounted but did not greet his father. He took a leather bag that hung from the pommel of his saddle and undid a rope securing it. He stepped onto the veranda and shook out its contents at the feet of Bartolomeu Rodrigues.

"Senhor Pai! Our Paulo is avenged!"

The senhor looked down at the head of Black Peter. "Christ's justice be praised," he said several times. Then he raised his eyes to Graciliano. "Come into the house, my son."

Graciliano took his father's arm and entered the Casa Grande, but in the reception hall he stopped. "Senhor Pai . . ."

"Yes, Graciliano?"

"I'll stay a week. Then I'll return to the fazenda," he said. "If I'm needed, I'll come."

Bartolomeu Rodrigues's voice was unexpectedly strong: "I expected to hear you say this." He paused, his grip on his son's arm tightening. "Go back. Go, Graciliano Cavalcanti, and take my blessing with you."

XVI

April 1788 – April 1792

*B*enedito Bueno da Silva had a reputation for courage equal to that of his ancestor Amador Flôres da Silva, the great bandeirante. And he had a tenacious spirit, too, as firm as that of his own grandfather, Olímpio Ramalho, who had been among the first to find gold at Minas Gerais.

In 1708, Olímpio Ramalho da Silva became embroiled in the conflict between Paulistas and fortune hunters who flocked to Minas Gerais from Portugal and the coastal settlements of Brazil. His defense of his property against a violent band of Emboabas failed, and at the end of 1708, he left the main diggings at Vila Rica de Ouro Prêto, and returned with his immediate family to the da Silva lands beyond São Paulo.

Olímpio Ramalho's years in Minas Gerais had not made him a wealthy man. Not only had he repaid Amador's debts to Ishmael Pinheiro — Ishmael's descendants were merchants at São Paulo and on the coast at Santos — and made good the obligations to others who had financed Amador's last bandeira; he had also been the support of the vast Ramalho-da Silva clan, regularly visiting their lands thirty miles west of São Paulo until Maria Ramalho died in 1700 at the grand age of eighty-seven.

In 1710, savages in Mato Grosso slaughtered two of Olímpio's three sons, who had gone north to prospect for gold. With the memory of Amador and Trajano, both of whom had suffered so greatly on their quest for riches, and the death of his own sons, Olímpio vowed to avoid the accursed pursuit of sudden wealth, and with his surviving son, Antônio — Benedito Bueno's father — he returned to a long-neglected occupation: muleteer. When Olímpio Ramalho died peacefully in

1718, he had left Antônio a good transport business, with pack animals operating between São Paulo and Minas Gerais. Antônio had died in 1753, leaving Benedito Bueno to carry on the tradition.

In the year 1788, Benedito Bueno was sixty-two years old and unusually robust. A noble Tartar, some called him, a description befitting a man who had been the terror of Jesuit, Spaniard, and savage in the contested lands south of São Paulo. But his military exploits had been eclipsed by another activity: his daring convoys to the goldfields of Cuiabá in Mato Grosso.

In both spirit and boldness, these convoys were a continuation of the mighty pathfinding adventures of men like Amador Flôres and Captain-Major Antônio Raposo Tavares. Cuiabá lay eight hundred miles directly to the northwest, but the impenetrable jungle of Mato Grosso, and the danger of attack from savage tribes occupying the region, necessitated a circuitous voyage of 3,500 miles to the mining camps, and whereas the bandeiras of the seventeenth century had mostly advanced on foot or by horse, the Cuiabá convoys were river-borne. This and their seasonal departures gave them the name "monsoons."

From Porto Feliz, a canoe landing about eighty miles north-northwest of São Paulo, the monsoons traveled six hundred miles down the Tietê — the Anhembi, in Amador Flôres's day — a journey of twenty-six days, with waterfalls, rapids, and reefs to navigate constantly, and on to the Tietê's junction with the Paraná. The canoes were then paddled south, for 120 miles, until they came to the mouth of the Rio Pardo on the right bank of the Paraná. The ascent of the Pardo, northwest and for three hundred miles almost to its source, took two months and brought the convoy to the watershed of the Rio Paraguay in the swampy marshes of the Pantanal. Another two months' travel along two thousand miles of the Paraguay and its tributaries and finally the monsoons reached Cuiabá.

The pirogues of these fleets were forty feet long and four feet wide. Up front rode pilot, bowman, and six oarsmen. Nine feet behind them, toward the center of the craft, was the cargo area; each long, slim canoe was capable of carrying from four to six tons of supplies. At the rear was accommodation for up to sixteen passengers. At times, as many as three hundred canoes with three thousand people departed from Porto Feliz or two other embarkation points, but even these great river armadas were no guarantee of preservation from the perils of drowning, pestilence, and starvation or from attack by war parties of Paiaguá and Guaicuru. Some monsoons had been wiped out to a man.

Since 1739, when, as a thirteen-year-old boy, he made his first voyage to Cuiabá, Benedito Bueno had completed thirty journeys with the monsoons. He owned sixteen pirogues manned by natives who, despite the law decreeing their freedom, were in all but name Benedito's slaves. On occasion, his canoes had been commissioned for the official escort of a monsoon, but mostly the pirogues transported men and goods to Cuiabá for the profit of Benedito Bueno. There had been accidents in the tempestuous Tietê and Pardo rivers, and men and cargoes had been lost, but those incidents were rare: The expertise of Benedito Bueno's pilots and bowmen was such that several were able to recite from memory every serious hazard along the nine great rivers en route to Cuiabá.

The river was in Benedito Bueno's blood, and each voyage a renewing of the wanderlust inherited from his bandeirante and Tupi ancestors. Thus, there had been no surprise when on a July morning thirty years ago, returning from a monsoon and a trip to São Paulo, Benedito Bueno announced to his family that they were departing the lands left to him by his father. Two brothers, Agostinho and Vicente, who were muleteers like their grandfather Olímpio, would stay at the old house thirty miles west of São Paulo; his wife and sons, Benedito Bueno said, were going to Itatinga, the Place of White Stones.

Itatinga lay 125 miles north-northwest of São Paulo. Here the Rio Tieté swung sharply east and then looped back toward the northwest; on the inner bank of the great loop were the white stones, a low outcrop of eroded rocks. Within the horseshoe bend of the river the gently sloping hill country was mostly forested, but there were grassy openings, too, ideal for cattle.

Benedito Bueno's original grant from the captain-general of São Paulo had extended three miles along the left bank of the Tieté and inland for three miles, but similar grants subsequently obtained by his sons had enlarged the property to an area four times that size and including most of the land within the loop.

Behind the white rocks and a canoe landing there was a bluff. On this elevation, Benedito Bueno had built a house similar to the one he had left: square and single-storied, with rammed-earth walls, a tiled roof, and twelve rooms. But the construction was poor and the house neglected, and free-roaming pigs, chickens, and dogs contributed to the squalid appearance of the place.

That the settlement at Itatinga represented a regression almost to the days when the first of these da Silvas lived on the lands near São Paulo was indicative of the Paulista frontiersman's priorities. Like his forebears, Benedito Bueno had wanted to be in the sertão, far beyond effective reach of authority, where he could wield absolute power over the fifty-six souls at Itatinga — besides the family members, there were five black slaves and eighteen free Carijó and mixed breeds — and over the men of his pirogues. He had enjoyed this independence for some twenty years; but, with an increasing drift of colonists west and northwest from São Paulo, a settlement had grown up at a cattle halt twelve miles southwest of Itatinga. Tiberica, named after a Carijó chief whose malocas had stood there, was granted town status in 1766, and a dozen years later the district had been elevated to a parish, with the da Silva lands falling within its jurisdiction.

Benedito Bueno's firstborn son, Silvestre Pires da Silva, welcomed these developments. Silvestre realized that with Benedito Bueno, grand admiral of the monsoons, the age of the bandeirantes would come to a close, and he had settled down to develop Itatinga, where he'd planted seventy acres of sugarcane, a crop now cultivated extensively on smallholdings throughout São Paulo captaincy, though not yet on a scale comparable with that of the plantations of Pernambuco. Silvestre had had some education at São Paulo and had served as alderman at Tiberica; he was hoping to become colonel of the local militia and district representative of the captain-general of São Paulo.

Thirty-six years old, Silvestre already had a noticeable paunch. He had been married for fifteen years to Idalina Tavares, who was descended from the family of

Raposo Tavares, and his bride had given him fourteen infants, nine of whom survived. Silvestre was very proud of his large family and ill-disposed to leaving them or the da Silva lands.

On a morning in April 1788, Silvestre was among three men who were witnessing the agony of his father.

Beads of sweat stood out on Benedito Bueno's forehead; his knuckles were white as he clenched his hands.

"Help me, Mother of All Saints! Aaahhh! Jesus! Give me courage!" Benedito Bueno's eyes rolled back, then slowly moved from the face of one witness to the next with a look of frantic appeal.

Benedito Bueno was suffering from a gnawing toothache.

Silvestre showed great sympathy for his father's plight, and now tried to encourage him by talking of Senhor Benedito's bold nature and of the perils he had survived with the monsoons. Benedito Bueno listened silently; a small, brave smile appeared at the corner of his mouth, but his distress was not diminished. Two men present were guests in Benedito Bueno's house. One was a distant relative, André Vaz da Silva, and the other a friend of André's, Joaquim José da Silva Xavier, *alferes*, or second-lieutenant, in the Sixth Company of Dragoons of Minas Gerais.

André was the great-grandson of Trajano da Silva, whom Amador Flôres had executed for treachery during the obsessive search for the mountain of emeralds. When Trajano had marched off into the sertão in 1674, one of his Carijó concubines had been pregnant; Trajano did not live to see the child, Venâncio, who had been raised by the indefatigable Maria Ramalho.

For the family of André Vaz da Silva, the wanderings had stopped long ago. When Olímpio Ramalho left Minas Gerais with his wife and sons, some family members had stayed; among them André Vaz's grandfather Venâncio da Silva. The violence between Emboabas and Paulistas had abated, and for a time Venâncio prospected for gold. But in 1715 he opened a trading shack at Vila Rica de Ouro Prêto, which had thirty thousand miners and their slaves. His son Raimundo, born the year Venâncio set up the trading shack, was now seventy-three and widowed.

The twenty-eight-year-old André Vaz da Silva was the son of Raimundo, and worked in the family business. André was tall, with a straight, sinewy frame. He had thick blue-black hair, a broad, prominent brow, and thin, ascetic lips. His pointy beard emphasized a slightly protruding chin.

The third man in the room with Benedito Bueno, Silva Xavier, had journeyed with André from Vila Rica to São Paulo. Silva Xavier was forty-one and tall like André, straight-backed and square-shouldered. He had penetrating blue eyes and a slightly aquiline nose. His thick black mustache and beard and his long hair were flecked with gray. His long hands and slender fingers suggested sensitivity.

But the very sight of Silva Xavier heightened Benedito Bueno's distress: The hard-riding dragoon was a man of many talents, one of which had earned him the nickname Tiradentes, "Tooth-Puller."

The arrival of Silva Xavier and André a day ago was fortuitous. André's father and grandfather had kept contact with these da Silvas through Benedito Bueno's brothers, the muleteers, who used a smallholding of André's family near Vila Rica as a resting place for their mules. However, André's present journey to São Paulo had nothing to do with the *tropeiros* but rather with collecting a debt owed his father by a Paulista. After seeing the man, who lived on a fazenda near the town of Tiberica, André had come to Itatinga.

Alferes Silva Xavier was on long leave from the dragoons. He had intended to go to Rio de Janeiro — the capital of Brazil since 1763, when the viceroy's seat had been transferred from the Bahia. But when his friend André spoke of a quick visit to São Paulo, Silva Xavier decided to accompany him; he had friends among the military in the captaincy and was keen to visit the Paulista capital, which he had not seen for several years. Silva Xavier always traveled with his dental equipment.

"Courage, Senhor Benedito," André said. He flashed his own white teeth. "Joaquim has attended me. There's little pain."

"O my little Jesus."

"*There!*" Silva Xavier cried triumphantly when it was done. "It is out, senhor!"

Benedito Bueno made a dreadful noise and bent to spit into a silver basin Silvestre held up for him.

೪

Two nights later, the four men were together again in the large front room, the furnishings of which were simple and utilitarian: studded chairs and two armchairs, a jacaranda table, cupboard, strongbox, and bench.

Joaquim José da Silva Xavier was doing most of the talking. "An honor, Senhor Benedito, to be with the family of Amador Flôres, conqueror of the sertão . . . to meet with the descendants of Olímpio Ramalho, who flung open the gates of the treasure-house of Minas Gerais!" Silva Xavier held one hand against his chest. "Ai, Benedito Bueno, an honor, but in my heart, there's sadness, too: Amador Flôres and Olímpio Ramalho gaze down from heaven upon the poor sons of America denied the birthright that was won for them."

André Vaz da Silva had often heard Silva Xavier express such sentiments, and he sympathized with them. Silvestre da Silva was at the card table, a deck spread out in front of him; his face, shadowed in the candlelight, expressed his disagreement, but he said nothing.

"Year after year we sent our treasure to Lisbon," Silva Xavier continued. "Sixty annual fleets sailing from Rio de Janeiro with their timbers groaning beneath the weight of the gold of Minas Gerais. The king asked for a minimum of one hundred *arrobas* a year in lieu of the royal fifth. Ten years the miners met this demand! A thousand arrobas!" This amounted to five hundred thousand ounces. "The rivers were panned, the hills were tunneled, and so long as the gold was there, the obligation was fulfilled by the *Mineiros!*" "Mineiro," a man of Minas Gerais, was the proud regional identity shared now by men like André, the descendant of Paulistas, and by the descendants of the Emboabas.

"But the Mineiros have known for twenty-five years that the gold supply is diminishing. You've seen this, too, Senhor Benedito, at the mines of Cuiabá. But at Lisbon?" He shook his head despairingly. "The Mineiros are liars, scoundrels, *contrabandistas,* they say."

Silvestre laughed and raised his eyes from the cards. "Come now, Joaquim José, be fair," he said. "How many Mineiros have become wealthy as a result of this gold they say does not exist? How many contrabandistas pass through São Paulo carrying gold to the Spaniards at Asunción? You're an officer of the dragoons: How many men do the patrols trap on the road to Rio de Janeiro?"

"I don't deny the smuggling," Silva Xavier said, "but the gold supply is diminishing and the hydraulic works needed to mine it are ever more costly. Lisbon will not acknowledge these facts. 'Settle your great debt, Mineiros, or we will use the *derrama* to extract every cruzado owed to the treasury,'" they say."

When the minimum contribution of one hundred arrôbas had been ordered in 1750, the municipal câmaras of Minas Gerais were made responsible for collecting the gold and were warned that a derrama — a tax on every free man and slave — would be imposed to make up any shortfall.

"The authorities hesitate with the derrama because they know the monopolies, tithes, and taxes are already impoverishing the Mineiro. And what do we get in return for our taxes? Every three years, the captaincies are sent a governor whose instructions are to rule with justice and concern for the well-being of our people. Some have been good men. And then there are others, like His Excellency Luiz da Cunha Meneses . . ."

André had been wondering when Silva Xavier would mention the governor who had been sent to Minas Gerais in 1783. The great majority of Mineiros had detested the pompous martinet, but for Silva Xavier, the loathing had been of a personal nature, deriving from the circumstances of his background.

The son of a first-generation Mineiro of Portuguese ancestry and a Mineiro girl, Silva Xavier was born in 1746 on a fazenda near the town of São João d'El Rei, about one hundred miles southwest of Vila Rica. When he was nine, his mother died. Two years later, his father, a successful miner and municipal alderman, also died. The orphan had gone to live with a godfather, a dentist at São João, from whom he learned his first skills as Tooth-Puller.

Silva Xavier tried his hand at various occupations — muleteer, peddler, prospector — but with little success. In 1775, he enlisted in the paid regiment of the dragoons, with the rank of alferes. He served with distinction, commanding a patrol on the royal road to Rio de Janeiro over the Mantiqueira range. Despite a fine record, however, Silva Xavier was overlooked for promotion on four occasions. When Cunha Meneses came to Minas Gerais, Silva Xavier was removed from his command, which was given to one of His Excellency's favorites.

"Governor Cunha Meneses looks down on every man born in America, rich or poor," Silva Xavier continued. "By God's great mercy, we have notice of his recall and await his successor, the visconde de Barbacena. But how did we protest those years of misrule?" Silva Xavier raised his slender hands in a gesture of despair. " 'Ai! Ai! Ai!' we cried, like so many slaves, and stood around helplessly, awaiting the despot's pleasure."

"Other members of the Cunha Meneses family have served with honor at São Paulo and elsewhere in Brazil," Silvestre said.

"But we got Luiz, strolling through the streets of Vila Rica with his prostitutes swaying beside him. He hung on their every word, but would he listen to our miners' appeals for loans? For modern machinery? For a foundry so that tools needn't be carried halfway around the world to be sold to our miners at exorbitant prices? For new sugar mills? Of course not! 'No iron!' 'No sugar!' 'No enterprise of any kind that takes labor away from the mines!' say the Lisbon authorities. Incredible!" Silva Xavier exclaimed. "I ask you, how long are we to be the stepchildren of Lisbon?"

The present rulers of Portugal were confident that their vast colony could be kept in loyal subjection. On February 24, 1777, Dom José died, and with his royal protector gone, on March 1, Sebastião José Carvalho e Melo offered his resignation to Maria I, Dom José's successor. Carvalho e Melo, who by then enjoyed the title Marquis of Pombal, retired to his country estate north of Lisbon, where he died in 1782, after being served with a royal decree declaring him "a criminal worthy of exemplary punishment." His eighty-three years and ruined health had saved him from corporal chastisement.

Queen Maria I had long been the great hope of the nobles and hierarchy of priests displaced by Carvalho e Melo. She had married her uncle, Dom Pedro, a son of His Most Faithful João V, and Dom Pedro had also surrendered to mystic zeal and doted upon his wife, whom he regarded as a saint.

Queen Maria's accession had also pleased the British government and the merchants of London, who had been frustrated by Carvalho e Melo's successful promotion of local industries in Portugal and Portuguese-owned trading companies in Brazil. The latter were abolished within two years of Maria's enthronement. Equally injurious to British commerce had been the protracted dispute between Portugal and Spain over the territories across the east bank — the Banda Oriental — of the Rio Uruguay. After the fall of Carvalho e Melo, the Portuguese had relinquished their claim to the Rio Plata enclave, Colônia do Sacramento, with the signing of the Treaty of Ildefonso in October 1777. They had accepted a border delimitation much the same as that specified in the earlier Treaty of Madrid, excluding the lands of the seven missions of the Guarani.

Listening to Silva Xavier, Silvestre had grown increasingly irritated, and now he spoke up: "The troubles you detail concern one governor and one captaincy."

"Minas Gerais is not one captaincy; it's the soul of our America! We're still rich in gold, diamonds, iron, fertile lands, and people. More people, Silvestre, than in any other captaincy!"

"One captaincy," Silvestre repeated. "Her Majesty's overseas councilors have to administer all Brazil. With so vast a territory to control, mistakes are unavoidable."

"Is gross stupidity also unavoidable?"

Silvestre looked at his father, but Benedito Bueno's eyes were closed. "Before the discovery of gold and diamonds, Portugal ruled this land for two centuries," Silvestre replied hotly. "Was it stupid to defend a savage and distant domain for a small reward?"

"*Who* defended Brazil against the Spanish, French, Dutch? Against the English pirates? The patriots of Pernambuco and Bahia! Your own Paulistas. White men, black men, brown men, all born in these captaincies — they fought and died to defend this land. A small reward? Forests of brazilwood torn down? Fortunes in sugar transported to Lisbon? Spices of the forest? And what about the great territories conquered by the bandeiras for the Crown?"

Benedito Bueno opened his eyes. "Senhor, does it matter who won what and where?" he asked. "We're all Portuguese."

"Some of us, Senhor Benedito, are more Portuguese than others."

Silvestre ignored the jibe. "Do you agree with Joaquim José?" he asked André.

André did, though he had never been as outspoken as Silva Xavier. He hesitated before replying.

"Do you think Portugal has done nothing for the captaincies?" Silvestre prodded.

"Portugal has been paid ten times and more for her investment in Brazil," André said. "Think about it, Silvestre: With the Indies bankrupt, what would have become of Portugal without the captaincies? God forbid, but the Spaniard himself might have swallowed her up."

"Exactly!" Silva Xavier exclaimed. Then he stood up. "I want to read something to you, Silvestre." He withdrew a book from the leather valise that contained his dental instruments. "My French is poor, but it's enough to understand this." He opened the book and took out a sheet of paper that had been folded in the front. "Here . . . this I've had translated."

"What book is this?" asked Benedito Bueno.

Silva Xavier passed him the volume. "The laws and Constitution of the states of North America, Senhor Benedito," he said.

Benedito Bueno was illiterate, but he appeared to examine the volume studiously. He looked puzzled. "Their laws are in French?"

"No, senhor, only this book, which was published in Philadelphia." Silva Xavier opened the sheet of paper. "This is a translation of the Declaration of Rights by the people of Virginia. Please listen, Silvestre, and tell me if you disagree with these statements."

As Silva Xavier began to read, his voice quickly became charged with emotion:

" 'All men are by nature equally free, and have inherent rights, of which when they enter into a state of society, they cannot, by any compact, deprive or divest their posterity; namely, the enjoyment of life and liberty, with the means of acquiring and possessing property, and pursuing and obtaining happiness and safety . . .' "

Several times, Silva Xavier paused momentarily and looked in Silvestre's direction, waiting for some response, but Silvestre only beckoned for him to continue.

" 'All power is vested in and consequently derived from the people . . .' " Silva Xavier placed emphasis on the next statement: " 'The magistrates are their *trustees* and *servants,* and *at all times amenable to them...*' "

"Yes!" André said. "And what of Governor Cunha Meneses's regard for judges and magistrates? *His* trustees! *His* servants!"

As Silva Xavier read the clauses of the Declaration of Rights proclaimed by the Virginians in June 1776 at Williamsburg, he was interrupted by Benedito Bueno, who sought clarification of certain statements. Silvestre said little, until Silva Xavier came to the end.

"Tiradentes!" — Silvestre spit out the nickname — "what you have just read is a prescription for revolution! We owe allegiance to Her Sovereign Majesty. To think otherwise is to contemplate sedition and turmoil."

"Did I speak of revolution?" Silva Xavier waved the sheet of paper in front of Silvestre. "These truths are the voice of reason *against* turmoil. They were given by men claiming their natural right to reject tyranny." He nodded. *"Tiradentes,"* he said. "Of course, Silvestre, it's far better to save a tooth than to extract it." Then he smiled. "Sometimes, though, the decay is too advanced and there's no choice: The tooth has to be plucked!"

❧

The road over the Mantiqueira range from Rio de Janeiro was patrolled by the dragoons and forbidden to anyone without a Crown passport. North of the Mantiqueira, the crystalline highlands of Brazil, lying three thousand feet above sea level, was a complex of small valley flats, deep-fissured tablelands, and ranges of hills. Some of the slopes were bald and pitted with evidence of the search for gold, but most remained blanketed by virgin forest. Vila Rica de Ouro Prêto was 250 miles from the coast and located at the southern base of the range called The Spine.

Neither royal passport nor mountain barrier deterred the contrabandistas carrying gold or diamonds out of Minas Gerais or bringing in pack mules with goods from Europe and the Orient. Priest, lawyer, miner, shopkeeper, royal official, Portuguese ship captain — all participated in the illegal free trade. From time to time, Crown agents broke up syndicates of smugglers and clandestine smelting works, but the hemorrhage of gold was not staunched. Moreover, by attempting to seal off the region, the Portuguese created the very conditions for the miraculous flowering of genius at Vila Rica.

To best comprehend this miracle, one had only to watch a particular man as he set out to work in Vila Rica on a morning in July 1788. The bastard of a Portuguese architect and a black slave woman, he had been freed at the time of his birth at Vila Rica and was now in his fifties. He moved slowly along the kidney-shaped cobblestones, with a black slave walking beside him and carrying his tools. His short, thick body was wrapped in a black cloak, and his heavy head covered with a huge hat.

Ten years ago, the nerve trunks in the mulatto's arms and legs had thickened; his nails had become hard and clawed; whole fingers and toes had dropped off, reducing his extremities to stumps. The same degenerative leprosy invading his limbs was now affecting the mulatto's face, thickening and deadening the yellow skin and weakening his gums, so that several teeth had loosened and fallen out.

The mulatto and his slave made their way past the jail, slowly down a steep alley, and up again toward a small plaza that was fronted by the Church of St. Francis of Assisi. This building represented a radical departure from the rigid square Portuguese design: The well-proportioned projecting façade was framed by Ionic columns, and to the left and right of these pilasters were graceful cylindrical bell towers, which had no parallel in Christian church architecture. Above the solid wood doors were medallions, devices and whimsical figures, and an ornamentation depicting St. Francis, all of which were intricately carved in soft green soapstone.

The mulatto and his slave stood talking for some time in front of the church doors. Then, with planks, ropes, and ladders brought here the day before, the slave began to assemble a small scaffolding. When he was done, he helped the mulatto up onto the rickety platform, strapping a mallet and a chisel onto his left and right truncated forearms.

Aleijadinho, "The Little Cripple," residents of Vila Rica had begun to call the mulatto since the onset of his affliction. His name was Antônio Francisco Lisboa, and he had designed and built this lovely Church of St. Francis and other churches at Vila Rica and elsewhere in Minas Gerais. His task this morning was to perfect a soapstone cherub above the doorway. Antônio Francisco's leprosy was getting progressively worse, but even as he worked on the small angel with the implements bound to his forearms, his thoughts were on two mighty projects for the future: twelve gigantic Prophets, eight feet tall, sculpted in stone; and a depiction of the Passion of Christ with more than sixty wood-carved figures. "Oh, if God only wills it!" he said aloud.

Antônio Francisco's was not the only original talent at Vila Rica and in the major towns of Minas Gerais. Other master builders, painters, and sculptors, no longer relying solely on Old World models but drawing inspiration from their surroundings, had produced masterpieces of religious art and architecture and had transformed the mining camps into picturesque towns. Vila Rica itself laid out on several steep hills and in the small valleys and gorges between them was a bustling capital with cobbled and stepped streets, an imposing governor's palace and fine churches, and two-storied houses with harmonious white façades, wrought-iron balconies, and red-tiled roofs. There were graceful ornamental water fountains, terraced orchards and gardens, and, along the rua São José, the palatial residences of mining and tax-farming magnates.

The gold supply in general might be diminishing, but not to an extent that affected the eighty thousand people at Vila Rica, who continued to revel in their self-reliant, enterprising society. Keeping pace with the artists and architects, Mineiro musicians composed spontaneous, uncompromising works — there were at one time more symphony orchestras, ensembles, and bands at Vila Rica alone than in all Portugal.

There was also another group of men equally dedicated to developing the culture of Minas Gerais. Among them was Luis Fialho Soares, who was now fifty-eight years old, a prominent Vila Rica lawyer and man of letters. Luis Fialho had two sons, both of whom he had sent to Coimbra University, which the marquis of Pombal had radically reformed by modernizing its archaic curricula. Martinho Soares, thirty-one, taught at the seminary at Mariana six miles away from Vila Rica, where the sons of Mineiros received as good a preparatory education as anywhere in Brazil or Portugal; Fernandes, twenty-eight, was a medical student in France.

Luis Fialho often shared with his sons recollections of his own years at Coimbra and of the Lisbon earthquake. He knew that the friend who had rescued him from the dungeons of the Tower of Belém had died many years ago. Twice after his return to Minas Gerais, Luis Fialho had sent letters to Paulo Cavalcanti, without reply; then, in 1767, a Crown fiscal agent from Recife had been transferred to Vila Rica, and from him, Luis Fialho learned of Paulo's murder.

Among the mementos Luis Fialho shared with his sons were the poems and ballads he had written and sung during his student days.

His friend Cláudio Manuel da Costa, who was also a lawyer and the same age as Luis Fialho, had written *Vila Rica*, a heroic poem telling of the conquest of Minas Gerais. And there was Tomas Antônio Gonzaga, whose erotic and sentimental love poems were the finest in the Portuguese language. Gonzaga also sharpened his quill for political satire, and those close to him knew that under a pseudonym he had written *Cartas Chilenas* ("Letters from Chile"), an attack on His Excellency Cunha Meneses.

At Vila Rica and other Mineiro towns, the poets and intellectuals maintained respectable private libraries with the works of authors whose names were synonymous with the Enlightenment and the teachings of the French Encyclopedists. They had books and pamphlets, too, on the revolution in North America, and such names as Thomas Jefferson, Thomas Paine, and Benjamin Franklin were familiar to the Mineiro elite. They met often — Dr. Cláudio Manuel's house at Vila Rica was a regular venue for their gatherings — to debate subjects as wide-ranging as Jean Jacques Rousseau's *Social Contract*, the Declaration of Independence of the English American colonists, and the works of Abbé Guillaume Thomas François Raynal, particularly *L'Histoire philosophique et politique des etablissements et du commerce des Européens dans les deux Indes*, which criticized the restrictive policies of Portugal.

The meetings at Cláudio Manuel's house were attended by a cross section of influential Mineiros. The poets themselves were powerful men in the community. Cláudio Manuel had served several terms as secretary to the government of the captaincy and was a knight of the Order of Christ; Tomás Gonzaga had been Crown judge at Vila Rica. Judge Gonzaga had recently been appointed to the High Court at the Bahia. The poet Alvarenga Peixoto was a wealthy fazendeiro and colonel of the First Auxiliary Cavalry, with extensive lands and mining interests in the south of the captaincy.

The magnates who kept company with the poets included two men with the distinction of being the greatest Crown debtors in Minas Gerais. João Rodrigo de Macedo had held a royal contract for collecting duties at the customs posts and for the gathering of tithes. His payments to the treasury were now some 750,000 milreis in arrears — an equivalent of no less than 4,800 pounds of gold. The second great debtor, Joaquim Silvério dos Reis, a tax farmer notorious for suborning and bribing the queen's officials, owed 220,000 milreis, or some 1,400 pounds of gold.

Several priests attended the meetings: Luis Vieira da Silva, a fiery and persuasive preacher who was openly admiring of the rebels of North America; Carlos Correia de Toledo e Melo, the wealthy vicar of São José d'El Rei in the south, who shared Vieira da Silva's revolutionary sentiments; and José de Oliveira Rolim, an ecclesiastic preoccupied with legal and illicit diamond and slave deals and with moneylending.

Often after these gatherings, Luis Fialho would head back home long past midnight, with the veil of mist already descending the mountain slopes and the air chill and damp. But, preoccupied with his thoughts, he would not notice the cold. Why, for the love of God, did the Mineiros continue to live in subjection to the Portuguese Crown? Why should governors like Cunha Meneses and the lackeys around him plunder the riches of Minas Gerais, which had been conquered by their fathers and grandfathers? The poets spoke of the winds of freedom blowing between the crags of Minas Gerais and of the breaking of chains; the light of reason and justice dawning. But Luis Fialho sensed that this disparate group needed an inspired leader to give fire to their dreams and dissatisfactions and fan an insurrection against Her Majesty's government at Minas Gerais.

In late 1788, such a man came forward. Many of them knew him personally, for with their gums aflame, they had called for his help: Joaquim José Silva Xavier, the Tooth-Puller.

℮ↄ

Toward the end of September 1788, six months after their trip to São Paulo, André Vaz da Silva and Joaquim José da Silva Xavier rode together from Vila Rica to the fazenda of André's family seven miles northeast of the city. The smallholding was on the road to Cachoeira do Campo, where, six miles beyond the da Silva property, the governor had a country residence close to a barracks of the dragoons. Silva Xavier had reported back to his company a few weeks ago, but had not resumed his full duties and was accompanying André to conclude a business deal that he himself had initiated.

With them was José Álvares Maciel, a young man whom Silva Xavier had interested in buying some horses brought from São Paulo by André's cousins, the muleteers. After inspecting the animals, Maciel chose a gray mare and three piebald Asturiones. Second-Lieutenant Silva Xavier, a keen judge of horses, was impressed with the Asturiones but warned: "Gentle like little girls. Obedient. But in a moment of bad humor . . . *ai!*"

André's only brother, Dionésio, who was twenty years older, lived at the fazenda but was away this day. When the sale was concluded, Dionésio's wife offered the men a meal. It was intolerably hot in the airless mud-walled house, and when they had eaten, they went outside to sit in the shade of a row of jaboticaba trees studded with yellow-white flowers and berries.

José Álvares Maciel was twenty-seven, a year younger than André, the second of three sons of Captain-Major Álvares Maciel, a Vila Rica merchant and landowner. After receiving his doctorate in law, José Álvares Maciel had spent a year traveling in France and England before returning to Brazil this past August.

Silva Xavier knew the Maciel family — no relation to the butchers of Pará, the Parente Maciels — through his commanding officer, Lieutenant-Colonel Francisco Paula Freire de Andrade, who was married to a sister of Álvares Maciel's.

"There's much to be learned from the talk in the coffeehouses and clubs of London, but if you seek a true understanding of the changes taking place in England, you must get out of the capital and go north," Álvares Maciel said. "Birmingham, Nottingham, Manchester, Liverpool — I visited them all." He paused for a moment before asking André, "When an English man-of-war is permitted to enter the bay at Rio de Janeiro, what goes through the minds of those who see the ship?"

André smiled. "Jesus! Maria! Thank God all those gunports are closed!"

"Ah, yes, the very symbol of British power — an invincible fleet. I saw another power, André Vaz. It's going to be greater than anything commanded from the gundecks of George the Third's warships."

"The industries of England?"

"*Exatamente!* Industry and invention! Ironworks, cotton mills, factories for every kind of manufacture. Thousands of people are migrating from the farmlands to the centers of industry. Wherever I went, I was told that what I saw was only the beginning. Every month, the output of their coalmines and iron and steel works increases. Every month a new factory is built. Soon steam-driven engines will replace the water-powered mills. When this happens, no nation on earth will rival the manufactures of the British."

Álvares Maciel spoke of his journeys through the Midlands and the northwest of England. At the works of Boulton and Watt in Birmingham, the Scottish engineer James Watt, whom Álvares Maciel had found humorous and modest, had personally demonstrated his steam engines. At Cromford in Derbyshire, Álvares Maciel had spent three days at the water-driven mill built by Richard Arkwright and his partners. At factories in Manchester and its district, he had seen the results of the trio of great spinning inventions — James Hargreaves's spinning jenny, with its multiple spindles; Richard Arkwright's water frame, which produced yarn suitable for the warp; Samuel Crompton's mule, which improved Arkwright's invention by preventing the constant breaking of thread and producing a finer yarn.

"I saw hundreds of bales of cotton from Pernambuco and Maranhão," Álvares Maciel said. "I examined samples of our product and the best cotton from India. There's no difference!"

"Ah, yes, Dr. José saw the modern wonders of the world," Silva Xavier said, breaking his silence. "And when he returned to Rio de Janeiro filled with enthusiasm for the progress of industry, another marvel awaited him."

"What was this?" André asked.

"The viceroy's agents were dismantling thirteen looms they had found. 'You may be compensated,' the owners were told, 'if you go to Lisbon, where these illegal looms will be shipped and sold.' What a marvel of Portuguese progress!"

Álvares Maciel had spoken with some of the owners. "Not one will sail to Portugal to beg payment for his property. But their losses serve a good purpose. Three months ago, they had no argument with Lisbon. Today, they're thinking what splendid compensation it would be if His Excellency, the viceroy, and his officials were taking the same forced passage."

Álvares Maciel's generation of students at Coimbra University had been the first to benefit fully from the educational reforms instituted a decade ago by the marquis of Pombal. In the freethinking atmosphere, the belief that the captaincies could follow the example of America's English colonies had led students like Álvares Maciel to vow to end Portugal's rule in Brazil. While in England, he had bought every pamphlet and book he found concerning the revolution in North America, and he had openly discussed the idea of a free Brazil with many Englishmen.

"What did they say?" André asked.

"The Englishmen were surprised."

"That we should think of independence here at Minas Gerais?"

"No — that we have waited this long to begin our struggle for liberty."

Silva Xavier gripped the young man's arm. "Your English friends spoke the truth, Dr. José. The struggle begins late, but the result will be the same. Freedom for our rich and beautiful land and all her sons."

Silva Xavier's remarks were inflamed by a personal failure during four months he had been at Rio de Janeiro, after this trip to São Paulo with André. In addition to dentistry, Silva Xavier was also interested in civil engineering. In the past, on visits to the city, Silva Xavier had observed that the water supply for the fifty thousand inhabitants was inadequate. He had come up with a scheme for a canal that would be of particular benefit to the city's water-driven grinding mills.

"How many times I petitioned the viceroy and his officials to support my canal! *Nothing!* 'Go, Tiradentes! Draw teeth! Forget your waterworks!' they said. And how soon, my friends, will a contractor from Portugal be told to build my canal?" Silva Xavier had been striving for years to improve his position, and this latest failure was a bitter disappointment.

"The Portuguese think themselves superior to us in every way," he continued. "Colonel Francisco knows my record." He glanced at Álvares Maciel. "Yet all these years I've remained alferes. Had I been born in Portugal or come from a family with influence . . ." His cold blue eyes narrowed. "Those thirteen whose looms were taken are not the only men to feel anger and impatience. Many others wait only for a signal from Vila Rica. Break the chains that hold the richest captaincy a captive of Portugal and all Brazil can be freed."

"When the first shot is fired here, all Portugal will take up arms against us," André said. "The nobles and merchants of Lisbon will move heaven and earth to crush a rebellion. If they lose Minas Gerais, they lose everything."

"I agree," Silva Xavier said. "*Everything.* But by the time they can float their few ships down the Tagus with men and equipment, Minas Gerais can be ours."

"It will take a year for them to prepare a fleet," Álvares Maciel agreed. "That's time enough for a revolt to spread to Rio de Janeiro. By God's grace, a Portuguese fleet riding into Guanabara Bay — the guns of every fort will be primed by men loyal to our cause." He saw André's skeptical look. "Bold words, yes. But if the patriots of North America had been fainthearted, they would still be taking orders from the minions of George the Third."

"Remember the direct cause of that conflagration, André," Silva Xavier added. "Taxation. It will be the same here in Minas Gerais when the derrama is imposed."

For a while, they spoke of events since July, when the visconde de Barbacena, Dom Luis Antônio Furtado de Mendonça, had taken up his post as governor of Minas Gerais. The ambitious thirty-four-year-old visconde was determined to carry out to the letter the voluminous instructions that had been given to him at Lisbon. At a meeting with local officials a week after arriving at Vila Rica, he had fiercely reprimanded those responsible for the huge sums owed to the royal treasury. He had read them the law of 1750, which provided for the capitation tax, and by September it was generally accepted that he would impose the derrama in February 1789.

The visconde accepted Lisbon's view that the diminishing gold supply was due largely to smuggling and embezzlement. He would help the miners by reducing import taxes on their equipment, but he expected them to cease immediately their thievery, which was robbing the royal purse of its full quota of one hundred arrôbas a year. "And when the captaincy can meet its present obligations to the Crown, I will seek ways of collecting the debts owed on the royal fifth and by the tax contractors whose ill-gotten harvests have deprived the exchequer of millions of reis," he had promised.

Álvares Maciel's father had been treasurer of three tax contracts, an administrative position that made him accountable for monies due to the Crown by the contractor. The tax farmer he represented was heavily in arrears, and as a consequence, the Crown was threatening the Álvares Maciel family with confiscation of its assets.

"We'll be ruined," Álvares Maciel said. "I'll be a poor man."

"It won't happen," Silva Xavier assured him. "Let the visconde de Barbacena threaten Rodrigo de Macedo and others for payment of their great debts. Let him impose the derrama. Every Mineiro, rich or poor, will see only one way to rid himself of these oppressive burdens: independence."

André made few comments as the others discussed the possibilities of support for an independence movement. He was thinking about Silva Xavier, who had been a friend of his family's since his muleteering days. André had been fifteen when Silva Xavier joined the dragoons, and for a time the boy had also wanted to enlist, influenced by the dashing appearance of the alferes. But Senhor Raimundo da Silva had sent him to the seminary at Mariana for three years and had then put him to work in their store, which occupied the ground floor of their house on the rua das Flôres at Vila Rica.

Three years ago, Silva Xavier had introduced André to Constança Oliveira Coutinho, the daughter of a builder Silva Xavier had tried to interest in his canal at Rio de Janeiro. More successful was Silva Xavier's matchmaking: André and Constança had been married two years and were expecting their first child, to whom Silva Xavier was to be godfather.

Sometimes André had found his friend impulsive and impatient. He feared that this fervent preaching of independence could cause trouble for Silva Xavier, and now, during a moment when the others were silent, André admonished him: "You speak too openly, Joaquim. How will the visconde de Barbacena react if his spies tell him that you carry the message of liberty to the streets?"

"I know that I speak very openly of liberty, and I'll continue to do so. I know, too, that this war of words is not enough. There isn't a man in Portugal who will respond 'Here, Mineiro, take your freedom.' How can I fear the visconde's informers when I know that I have to offer much more than words for this struggle? My heart, my soul" — he pressed a hand to his chest and his eyes flashed — "my life, friends, for liberty!"

❧

Two weeks later, on October 11, André was in the shop on the rua das Flôres when Silva Xavier hurried in with a young man whom André had not seen for several years: Fernandes da Rocha Soares, the son of Luis Fialho Soares. When Luis Fialho set up his law practice at Vila Rica after returning from Portugal, Raimundo da Silva had been one of his first clients, and André had continued to consult him since taking responsibility for the business. André and Fernandes had known each other since boyhood, both having attended the seminary at Mariana.

Fernandes had prominent cheekbones, almond-shaped eyes, a slight bronze tinge to his skin, and straight black hair. After obtaining his medical degree in Montpellier, France, he had returned to Minas Gerais, arriving at Vila Rica ten days ago.

Silva Xavier stood by impatiently as the young men plied each other with questions. Finally he interrupted them: "Let Fernandes tell about the students at Montpellier."

Fernandes Soares began by mentioning José de Maia, the son of a stonecutter at Rio de Janeiro. "There was none so committed to our liberation as José de Maia. At Coimbra and Montpellier, he told us that it was our generation's calling to free Brazil from Portugal — to break with the past." Fernandes paused, before adding emotionally, "Oh, God, what a loss! Maia was waiting to sail for Rio de Janeiro when he was struck down — by fever, I think — carried away, with his great dream of independence."

"His dream did not die with him," Silva Xavier interjected. "Minas Gerais *will* be free, and one by one, the other captaincies will follow. Tell André about José de Maia's mission."

Fernandes moved across the room and leaned against a long counter at the back of the store. Though it was only noon, the shop was gloomy, the only light coming from the open doorway.

"It was not us alone who shared Maia's hopes," Fernandes continued. "He was in contact with men at Rio de Janeiro."

"Probably the same men I know. Merchants. Militia officers," Silva Xavier added.

"Two years ago in France," Fernandes said, "Maia began to seek support for our struggle. He had secret connections with some Frenchmen who had fought in North America."

"Thomas Jefferson!" Silva Xavier exclaimed, unable to wait for Fernandes to tell what he wanted André to hear. "Maia spoke with Jefferson himself!"

"I was present," Fernandes said.

André gave a start. "You met Thomas Jefferson?"

Fernandes nodded, eager to continue: "First, Maia wrote to Senhor Jefferson in Paris, where he'd succeeded Dr. Franklin as minister to France." Fernandes laughed. "Maia didn't reveal his identity. 'Vendek,' he signed himself. I think it was the name of a slave in a book he was reading. He said only that he was a foreigner in France with a matter of the utmost importance to communicate to the minister, and asked how they might secretly correspond. Senhor Jefferson responded with an address Maia should use. I saw a draft of his next letter to the minister. He said that he was from Brazil, whose people could no longer endure the slavery imposed upon them by Portugal and were ready to rebel. But, he added, they couldn't do this without the support of the United States. It was not only because they sought to follow the

Americans' example: 'Nature, in making us inhabitants of the same continent, has united us in the bonds of common patriotism!' said Maia."

"What was Jefferson's response?" André asked.

"Maia corresponded with the minister for several months. Senhor Jefferson's replies were guarded and diplomatic, as you might expect from a man in his position. But it was also a difficult period for him personally."

"Why?" Silva Xavier asked. Fernandes had not mentioned this to him earlier.

"I was in Paris in December 1786, staying at the home of a friend from Montpellier. His mother knew the comtesse de Tesse, an aunt of the marquis de Lafayette, and learned from her the cause of Minister Jefferson's distress."

"He was sick?"

"Struck down, great man that he is — by a painful love!"

"Ai! Such bittersweet pain!" Silva Xavier said. "This woman who gave him pain — she was French?"

"English," Fernandes said. "Senhora Maria Cosway. She was in her twenties, a beauty. She sang, she played the harp, she painted, she spoke several languages. And she won Senhor Jefferson's love that summer in Paris. Alas" — Fernandes put a hand to his brow — "Maria was married to an ugly little man, Senhor Richard, a miniaturist of repute. All that summer Senhor Jefferson courted Maria, but when winter came, her husband took her home. Her lover was left behind, with a broken heart and a damaged wrist." He laughed. "The minister was promenading with lovely Maria in the Cours la Reine along the Seine when, out of joy, he leapt over a fence, fell, and cracked his wrist."

"So that's why he went to the mineral waters at Aix," Silva Xavier said, having been told this earlier by Fernandes.

"Yes."

"Ai! The poor thing! I love him for it! This god of liberty, with a heart for sweet romance. And now, Fernandes, tell André of your meeting with the senhor."

"In March, Senhor Jefferson wrote to Maia saying that he was going to Aix and would be visiting Nimes. We met the minister at an inn near the Roman amphitheater at Nimes. I remember how infuriated he was that they were tearing part of it down to pave a road —'"

"His response when you brought up Brazil?" Silva Xavier prodded.

"The man is amazingly knowledgeable about living conditions in Brazil, but he didn't realize how immense our country is. 'Truly a continent by itself.' — those were his exact words. 'In North America, such lands would extend from the Atlantic to the Pacific!' He confessed to having no interest in lands west of the Allegheny or Appalachian ranges. He said that between those mountains and the Atlantic were thousands of square miles, more than adequate for their new nation."

" 'Here, Your Excellency, is a great difference between our early settlements,' Maia said. He made a good point. What do we have just beyond the coast? Serra do Mar, the Mantiqueira, Serra do Geral — mountains rearing up thousands of feet. Here a narrow belt of open land; there a wall of rock standing in the sea. In most areas, the mountains kept our settlers clinging like crabs to strips of land. But there'd been men, who explored the sertão, searching for riches and expanding our frontiers. Every league of land won by them would be liberated from Portuguese tyranny."

"God willing, Fernandes," André said. "But Thomas Jefferson — what did he offer to sustain an insurrection?"

"We told him what we need — cannon, ammunition, ships — and that we'd pay with gold and diamonds from Minas Gerais."

"Yes, Fernandes, it's possible. But Senhor Jefferson — what help did he offer?"

"The meetings were secret," Fernandes said, with some irritation. "Maia put forward our ideas; he did not sign a treaty."

"Fernandes, a rebellion may not be far off. *Did Jefferson offer support?*"

"He wasn't speaking for his government, but he said — and I swear — when the revolution is launched, we'll have hundreds of his countrymen flocking to our shores. Some will come for rewards, but others will have the purest motives. He reminded us that they have many officers with excellent experience in hounding oppressors."

"André, would Senhor Jefferson suggest we recruit their generals if he didn't believe in a free and independent Brazil?" Silva Xavier asked.

"I'm sure he's sympathetic," André said. "But the United States is a new nation, only five or six years away from their own struggle. Why should they become embroiled in our fight with Portugal?"

"Jefferson didn't promise a republican legion from Philadelphia marching over the Mantiqueira a month or two hence," Silva Xavier said. "However, when Minas Gerais openly declares its independence to the world, when our patriots have won their first victories, then I think we can expect help not only from the United States but also from France and England. You heard José Álvares Maciel, André: The English are surprised we haven't yet struck the first blow."

"I've known you for many years, Joaquim, and don't doubt your sincerity, but all this talk — a 'war of words,' you sometimes call it — a declaration of independence! For the love of God, friend, I see no way these dreams can be realized."

Silva Xavier put a hand on André's shoulder. "Promise me something."

"What?"

"When I come to you not with dreams but decisions . . . promise me, André, that you will cease doubting and questioning and join me."

"You have my word," André said solemnly. Then he smiled. "Ah, what a dreamer, Alferes Quixote!"

Silva Xavier himself laughed, but quickly grew serious. "Alferes Quixote, yes. But my fantasy — my dream of an independent republic — this *will* be realized!"

ç∂

Alferes Joaquim José da Silva Xavier proved there was far more to his vision than fanciful dreams. Within three months, his "war of words" brought Minas Gerais to the brink of revolution against Portugal.

In his double role as officer of the Minas dragoons and part-time dentist, Silva Xavier had come to enjoy a wide circle of acquaintances at Vila Rica, among them many of the poets and intellectuals, magistrates and lawyers, contractors and fazendeiros whose loathing for the regime of Cunha Meneses had left them with contempt for Portuguese authority. Now the Tooth-Puller approached these men, offering a prescription for rebellion.

And during Christmas week of 1788, the plans for the uprising were formulated.

The meeting was held at the house of Silva Xavier's commanding officer, Lieutenant-Colonel Francisco Paula Freire de Andrade, whom the alferes had flattered with the suggestion that Providence was offering him a role in his people's liberation, the same as that of General George Washington. Andrade was also responsive to his second-lieutenant's suggestions because of disdain shown toward the Minas dragoons by the new governor. The visconde de Barbacena was proposing a total reform of the cavalry, whom he accused — not without justification — of aiding the contrabandistas.

Also present at the meeting were the young lawyer José Álvares Maciel; the poet Inácio José Alvarenga Peixoto; Padre José de Oliveira Rolim, the diamond dealer and moneylender; and Carlos Correia de Toledo e Melo, vicar as well as mine owner and fazendeiro.

When these men met at Lieutenant-Colonel Andrade's house at Vila Rica, it was taken for granted that in February 1789 the visconde de Barbacena would impose the derrama to make up for an anticipated shortfall in the 3,200 pounds of gold due as payment of the annual royal fifth. Already the rumor of this royal extortion was causing widespread public discontent. For the six plotters, the day the derrama was announced seemed ideally suited for the launching of a rebellion.

Alferes Silva Xavier would lead a group of men to provoke a riot against the derrama in the streets of Vila Rica. Lieutenant-Colonel Andrade and the dragoons from the city barracks would offer no resistance to the rioters or to rebels who would infiltrate the city from surrounding hills. While the rioting spread, Silva Xavier and hand-picked accomplices would dash to the governor's residence at Cachoeira do Campo, where the visconde de Barbacena and his bodyguards would be arrested. Upon Silva Xavier's return to Vila Rica with confirmation that the governor was in custody, Lieutenant-Colonel Andrade would deliver an address to the rioters in Vila Rica's main square. When Andrade asked them to state their demands, Silva Xavier himself would be there to lead the response: *"Viva a Liberdade!"* Andrade would read a declaration of independence and proclaim the Republic of Minas Gerais. The success of these initial actions would be a signal for messengers to ride immediately with orders for rebels waiting to secure the pass across the Mantiqueira and strategic points along the road to São Paulo.

Each man at the meeting was responsible for specific preparations. Silva Xavier was to continue his propaganda; Lieutenant-Colonel Andrade was to secure the support of the dragoons; Alvarenga Peixoto, colonel of the militia in the district of his fazenda, was to have his men ready to hold the Mantiqueira road; Padre Oliveira Rolim, through his connections in the diamond district, would stir up sedition there and provide two hundred men with muskets and ammunition; Padre Carlos Correia would seek support from the Paulistas; and Álvares Maciel was to investigate iron and saltpeter deposits for the manufacture of weapons and munitions.

The conspiracy grew rapidly.

By the second week of January, Judge Tomás Antônio Gonzaga, the poet-lawyer Cláudio Manuel da Costa, the Crown debtors Silvério dos Reis and

Rodrigo de Macedo, and the lawyer Luis Fialho Soares and his son Fernandes were attending the secret meetings.

They expected the war of independence to last three years, during which time Judge Gonzaga would serve as head of state. There was to be a constitution for the new American republic, a supreme parliament, and regional assemblies. Because of its favorable location, São João d'El Rei was designated as capital. The fifth and other royal extortions were to be abolished. Free trade was to be permitted, an iron foundry established, and textile industries set up.

Heated debates arose over the slaves, who comprised half the captaincy's population. Silva Xavier believed that the slaves should be liberated; others argued that this would be disastrous for the economy. A compromise was reached: All slaves born in Minas Gerais were to be given their freedom.

The revolution at Minas Gerais was to be launched independently of actions that might take place at Rio de Janeiro and São Paulo, though like-minded men there were expected to follow quickly the Mineiros' example: A confederation of three states was foreseen. But the immediate objective of the conspirators was the liberation of Minas Gerais, with its gold and diamonds. Deprived of her main plunder from America, Portugal would be hard-pressed to prevent the spread of insurrection throughout Brazil.

Silva Xavier had had several disagreements with Cláudio Manuel da Costa, one of which concerned the flag of the new republic.

"Strike the flags and throw down the arms of Portugal," Silva Xavier said, "but keep the symbol of our faith." Five shields emblazoned the arms of Portugal depicting the five wounds of Christ. "Let us have a triangle upon our banner to represent the Holy Trinity."

"Our crusade is for liberty. It would be better for our patriots to take the field under a flag that proclaims this to the world," said Cláudio Manuel.

"With respect, Dr. Cláudio, the Trinity will also symbolize a restoration of the pious intent behind the discoverer Cabral's naming our land 'Terra de Santa Cruz.'"

"Somewhere among my papers and books, there's a drawing of a flag," Cláudio Manuel said. "It was used by a militia company of the rebels of North America. It depicts a genius breaking chains, and bears the motto *Libertas Aeque Spiritu* — 'Liberty Through Courage.' Let's use the same flag."

Alvarenga Peixoto disagreed. "Dr. Cláudio, this is our revolution. We must devise our own banner."

"Then change the inscription," Cláudio Manuel responded: "*Aut Libertas aut Nihil* — 'Either Liberty or Nothing.'"

The response to this suggestion was negative, and for some time they continued to argue. Finally, Alvarenga Peixoto looked at Silva Xavier and said, "Alferes, you mentioned Terra de Santa Cruz, the paradise Cabral discovered, with Tupiniquin, Tupinambá, and other savage nations in possession. *There* is an original symbol: a Tupiniquin breaking the fetters with which his Portuguese conquerors bound him!"

Cláudio Manuel applauded this idea. "And the motto?"

"For our Tupiniquin, rising triumphantly after centuries of slavery and tyranny?" Alvarenga Peixoto was silent as he thought about this, and the others were quiet, too. Then he said emphatically, "I have a quotation from Virgil: *'Libertas, quae sera tamen!'*"

"'Liberty, even though late,'" Silva Xavier translated. "Liberty celebrating that forgotten Tupiniquin who was there when the great fleet of Cabral hove into sight. Liberty for men who stand and wait in Minas Gerais." His face was radiant. "Yes, Colonel! For every Mineiro who answers the call — *Libertas, quae sera tamen!*"

When Silva Xavier came to him with definite plans for the uprising, André kept his promise and joined the conspiracy. In the third week of January 1789, André, Fernandes Soares, and two slaves traveled to Registro Velho, a customs post south of the Mantiqueira, to collect a supply of gunpowder obtained from Rio de Janeiro.

On January 20, André and Fernandes and the slaves left Registro Velho, known also as the halt of Matias Barbosa, with a wagon carrying the gunpowder concealed in twenty-one vinegar kegs. From the registry to the halt of João Gomes, at the base of the Mantiqueira Mountains, was a journey of thirty-six miles with steep inclines. The road then climbed for four miles to the crest of the range, four thousand feet above sea level, and made a long, winding descent to the edge of the highland plateau, from where it led northwest to the camp of Igreja Nova, New Church. In good weather, a laden wagon could cover the sixty-six miles between Matias Barbosa and Igreja Nova in less than three days, but, as André and the others approached the base of the Mantiqueira range, it started to rain. The downpour lasted an hour and turned the road into a quagmire.

On the third morning, the party was near the top of the Mantiqueira pass, moving through a gloomy tunnel of overhanging foliage, when the sky again darkened.

They led the panic-stricken mules forward foot by foot until they reached a small basin on the heights of the Mantiqueira, where they stopped. But gale-force winds and blasting rain made them press on to descend to the highland plateau, where they could find shelter. This was a mistake. They had gone about a mile when the heavy wagon went off the road at a sharp bend and its left wheels became embedded in a clay-filled ditch. Packing stones around the wheels and using tree limbs as levers, they tried, unsuccessfully, for two hours to free the wagon.

They had not seen another traveler since the storm broke. In late afternoon, with the rain still pelting down, they began to off-load the wagon. Two hours later they finished. The rain had stopped, and they were resting beside a fire, when they heard the approach of horses. The bend where they were stranded was the first of seven along a switchback.

"Dragoons?" Fernandes Soares queried. "Or bandits?"

This section of the Mantiqueira road was notorious for highwaymen. The most recent outrages, which André and Fernandes had been told about at Matias Barbosa, were attributed to a gang of mixed breeds and blacks led by a former vaqueiro known as Dançarino de Corda, "Rope Dancer," for his practice of lassoing victims, stripping them of valuables, and then making them dance at the end of his lariat as he dragged them to the nearest ravine to hurl them to their deaths.

André and Fernandes both had pistols and knives but had put down their weapons. André was first to get up from beside the fire and move to the wagon for his gun, but before he could reach it, six riders were upon them.

"*Olá!* What have we here?" the lead rider cried out, and grinned malevolently. Two of his *camaradas* leveled blunderbusses at the men on the ground, and two others brandished machetes. A sixth rider, obviously in distress, was hunched over his horse.

"See for yourself," André responded.

The leader surveyed the wagon. "Stuck good and fast, eh?"

"Who are you?" Fernandes asked shakily.

The leader did not answer Fernandes but asked his own question: "Who are *you?*"

"I'm Dr. Fernandes Soares of Vila Rica."

"*Doctor?*" The man's laughter rang out as his gaze moved from Fernandes's mud-splattered boots to his torn shirt.

Fernandes looked at the man hunched over his horse. "Of medicine," he added.

"And you — a doctor too?" he asked André.

"No. I'm a Vila Rica merchant. Vaz da Silva. These are my goods."

The leader looked across at the kegs and boxes and the two slaves standing beside them. "Let me see," he said, and dismounted. He was a small brute, with round shoulders and bowed legs and a big, drooping mustache. He introduced himself:

"I'm Rope Dancer."

André took a deep breath. Fernandes stared at his feet and muttered under his breath.

"You! When you're not taking a mud bath, you're a doctor?"

Fernandes looked up fearfully. "Yes."

Rope Dancer jerked his head in the direction of his men, two of whom were assisting their moaning comrade. "Attend him!"

"What's wrong with him?"

"He struggled with a tropeiro over a manioc cake. Son of a bitch put a musket ball in his side."

"I'll look at him," Fernandes said feebly.

Rope Dancer prodded Fernandes's chest with his horsewhip. "Much more, Senhor Doctor. Heal him!"

"Here?" Fernandes shook his head. "I promise nothing."

"Heal him!" Rope Dancer repeated. "My brother, 'Tick,' has smelled the blood of many men, senhor. Help him and your own may be spared."

The two slaves stood close by, observing Rope Dancer with something approximating curiosity. They had heard that the bandit took slaves from their masters and set them loose in the sertão to join other runaways at quilombos in these highlands.

André ordered the slaves to light oil lanterns. A blanket was spread on the ground for Tick, who had bled profusely. He passed out when they laid him down. André stood beside Fernandes as he cut away the bandit's bloodstained shirt; he heard Fernandes mumble that only a miracle could save Tick. This remark did not alarm André as much as the sight of Rope Dancer's men examining the goods off-loaded from the wagon.

But even as André stared helplessly at two bandits prying open a box with their knives, he heard the approach of other horsemen.

"Dragoons!" Rope Dancer said. He bawled commands at his men and then looked at Fernandes. "Give them Tick, Senhor Doctor . . . as there's a God above, you'll not step off this mountain alive." Without another word, he followed the bandits leading their horses into the trees.

"Cover him," Fernandes said.

André had already grabbed a blanket to fling over Tick. "It won't help. They'll want to see him."

"*Variola!*" Fernandes said. "I'll tell them he's got the pox."

André took a lantern and moved toward the road.

Minutes later, eight dragoons rode up. Their officer introduced himself as Alferes Jorge Ferraz. He said they were chasing Rope Dancer and his gang, who had murdered a tropeiro at Igreja Nova.

"We've been stranded all afternoon. No one has ridden past," André said.

The alferes swung his head at a noise from the trees.

"Our mules," André said, adding quickly, "Alferes, if Rope Dancer had been here — Maria! Mother of God! — myself, my friend, the muleteer there, three corpses lying in the mud."

"What's wrong with him?" Ferraz asked, glancing at Tick.

"Fever, Alferes." He looked at Fernandes. "Variola."

The officer showed no alarm and asked to see André's passport. André went to fetch it. The alferes dismounted and walked toward Fernandes and the bandit.

"Sick for two days," Fernandes said. "He may die if we don't get help." He motioned toward the wagon.

The alferes glanced at the wheels embedded in the clay. There was a noise from the trees, and the officer's glance again shot in that direction.

"Abilío!" Fernandes shouted at one of the slaves. "The mules!"

The black hesitated, glancing fearfully toward the dark forest.

"The mules!" Fernandes ordered.

André was walking back to the alferes, but stopped to swear at Abilío and kick the slave's shins: "Move, devil! Quiet the mules!" Abilío stumbled off. André quickly handed the alferes his passport.

Alferes Ferraz gave the document a cursory examination. "You're sure there were no riders?"

"Not one."

Ferraz eyed André suspiciously. "Then, they've gone up the river valley." This was the Rio das Mortes, which lay below the northern slopes of the Mantiqueira. Ferraz looked at the wagon. "My men will help you."

"No, Alferes. Better that you continue the chase."

Ferraz was gazing at the pile of merchandise. "By the time we get below, Rope Dancer will be far away." He gave orders for the cavalrymen to help free the wagon.

The alferes paid no attention to Fernandes, who went to join the dragoons, or to the man he had been told was a muleteer. He asked André for the lantern he was holding and then moved toward the pile of goods. "What's in the boxes?"

"English goods. Clothing. Shirts —"

"What else?" The dragoon placed the lantern on a keg of "vinegar."

"Ai, Jesus!"

"Something wrong" — Ferraz looked at Andre's passport again — "Vaz da Silva?"

"No . . . no, Alferes. I was just thinking how lucky we are Rope Dancer didn't come this way." His eyes never moved from the keg, and now Ferraz showed interest.

"What's in the kegs?" the alferes asked.

"Vinegar," André said immediately, his heart beating wildly.

The officer pointed to the box the bandits had started to pry open. "And this?"

"Let me show you, Alferes." André saw his opportunity: He grabbed the lantern and set it down beside the box. Then he pulled out his knife and slowly began to loosen the lid. He looked across to the dragoons and saw that they were getting ready to lift the wagon with the tree limbs. Finally, he removed the lid, but only to reveal three boxes within. "See, Alferes" — he laughed — "for the senhor of the city of London."

"A hat?"

"Yes! As grand as you'll ever set eyes on." André loosened the strings securing the hatbox and took out an exceptionally tall beaver with a tapering crown. "This is for the man of true fashion, Alferes. Here! Try it on!"

Ferraz grinned as he swept off his regimental bicorne.

"*Maravilhoso!*" André said. "My lord, the gentleman! Take the hat, Alferes. A gift in gratitude for your help."

Fernandes and the cavalrymen shouted that the wagon was beginning to inch forward.

"The hat is yours, Alferes," André said.

"Put it in the box," Ferraz said, handing it back.

"May I suggest some lace, Alferes?"

"Show me."

"Lace! Ribbons!" André took another box from the stack of merchandise. He removed a roll of lace, ribbons, and three bonnets, then emptied one of the hatboxes and filled it with these items. "My pleasure, Alferes. God knows, for the service you give, there's small enough reward."

"Our pay is miserable," the officer said. Just as he was going to say something else, the wagon rolled beyond the ditch and the men cheered.

André shouted his thanks to them and picked up the lantern. "We'll not detain you, Alferes. It's a long ride back to your barracks." He passed one of the hatboxes to Ferraz and, carrying the other, started toward the wagon.

The cavalrymen looked enviously at the boxes, but Alferes Ferraz ordered them to remount immediately. André helped Ferraz tie the boxes to his saddle straps. When the alferes mounted, he belatedly thanked André for his generosity. Then he led his troop away.

"Jesus! Mary! Joseph!" Fernandes exclaimed. "Most merciful guardians!"

André was glancing toward the trees. There was a cracking of branches, but it was the slave Abilío.

"The bandits?" André asked.

"They're not there, Master."

Rope Dancer and his men did not reappear. André and Fernandes helped the slaves with the loading of the boxes and kegs, and within an hour and a half, they had the mules hitched up and were ready to leave. Fernandes had bandaged Tick's wound, but the bandit had not regained consciousness. "He's dying," Fernandes said bluntly. "I can do nothing for him here. We have to get him to a fazenda below, but it will probably be too late."

With André and the slaves walking up front with lanterns and examining the surface of the road before the mules and the wagon were led over it, they made their way along the switchback and down between two great buttresses of the Mantiqueira. Four hours later, they were approaching a crossing at a feeder stream of the Rio das Mortes. There, sitting aside their horses with drawn pistols, were Rope Dancer and his men.

Fernandes moved his head nervously toward the wagon and the motionless figure of Tick: An hour ago, when he had examined the man, he had found no signs of life.

Rope Dancer edged his horse toward the wagon.

"There was nothing I could do," Fernandes said. "We were taking him to a fazenda."

Rope Dancer came alongside the wagon. He raised the edge of the blanket. "Tick?" He nodded and dropped the blanket. "Bury him," he said to Fernandes.

"That's all?"

"What more does he need?"

"Your brother?"

Rope Dancer prodded the corpse with his whip. "They're all my brothers, Senhor Doctor." Rope Dancer dug into a pouch at his side, took out some coins, and handed them to Fernandes. "Find a priest to pray for the soul of Aniceto the Tick."

André walked over to them.

Rope Dancer still held a few coins in his hand. He tossed them onto the blanket. "Those are for the two of you," he said.

"We don't want payment from you," Fernandes said.

"It's for the priest: Have him say a prayer for your good fortune."

"For your mercy, you mean?"

Rope Dancer let out a hoarse laugh and, with his horsewhip, struck the side of the wagon. "The dragoons were dozing in their saddles; otherwise, they'd have found what you hide."

"I'm a merchant — "

"And I, Rope Dancer, am no fool. If there was nothing, you'd have squealed like pigs at the feet of the alferes."

"Take what you want," André said with resignation.

"Nothing," Rope Dancer said. He backed his pony away from the wagon, calling out to his men to ride off. "A good prayer for the soul of Tick. Nothing more." Then he swung his horse away from them and rode after his men.

"Sweet Jesus Savior!" André said, and grabbed hold of Fernandes's arm. "Who would doubt that the angels themselves favor our cause!"

❧

The journey north of the Mantiqueira took a week and passed without incident. André and Fernandes returned to Vila Rica on January 31, and the gunpowder was hidden at the da Silva fazenda on the road between Vila Rica and Cachoeira do Campo. Silva Xavier was elated. With two weeks remaining before the imposition of the derrama, the confidence of the inner circle of plotters could not have been higher.

"How fortunate that His Excellency delights in country airs at Cachoeira do Campo," Silva Xavier said to André and Fernandes. "Those four leagues from Vila Rica might just as well be four hundred, for the little he gleans from the rumors reaching him. Except, of course, when our own messengers go to Cachoeira to enlighten him!"

The bards of Vila Rica and other plotters regularly visited the visconde de Barbacena. They would read their poetry for the governor and also offer their ideas on how best to administer Her Majesty's subjects. Judge Gonzaga, for example, agreed with His Excellency that the Mineiros were incorrigible tax evaders whose rehabilitation could be achieved only with an iron rod: "Don't threaten them with words, Excellency; use the derrama. Don't extract one year's arrears; demand the full debt. Collect every arrôba of gold owing to our sovereign. Tax the Mineiros, Excellency! Tax them till they howl for mercy!"

Luis Fialho Soares was among the visitors who strolled with the visconde in the gardens at Cachoeira, offering false encouragement for acts of despotism that would arouse the Mineiros. Like Gonzaga and Dr. Cláudio Manuel, Luis Fialho became committed to independence as a result of those meetings in the past. His son Fernandes had also been instrumental in convincing him that a revolution could succeed.

Luis Fialho found great pleasure in Fernandes's company. With his other son, Martinho, a professor of Latin at the seminary in Mariana, Luis Fialho had always had a difficult relationship. Martinho was a pedagogue obsessed with cramming young heads with precise Latin, an exercise he accomplished with a leavening of terror.

Three nights after André and Fernandes had returned from their mission, Martinho joined them for dinner with Luis Fialho. Afterward the four were relaxing in an upstairs parlor of Luis Fialho's house when Martinho criticized Alferes Silva Xavier, whose name had come up in the conversation. "I don't doubt the man is besot with the idea of liberty — I've heard the fiery words he throws about — but there are forces this blockhead doesn't grasp."

"A *blockhead*, brother?" Fernandes responded. "If what Silva Xavier says makes him a blockhead, you'd have met many blockheads among the revolutionaries of North America."

Martinho merely shrugged. "The alferes expects the citizens of Vila Rica to take the streets in a popular rising. But actually *who* will stand with Silva Xavier?"

Fernandes looked at his father and André. "There are three in this room."

"Certainly, and others like yourselves, who talk of insurrection. But when the alferes goes his way spreading sedition, who else takes him seriously? The common people? The mulattoes in their tenements? The caboclos? The free blacks? Perhaps I'm wrong and he's made wider contacts than I suspect. But it seems to me that his message doesn't reach the ranks of a revolutionary army."

"A few must take the initiative," André said. "With every hour, others will come forward. The detestation of the derrama is universal."

"True, the people hate the taxes. But how many are timid men with a fear of Portuguese reprisals that surpasses any other feeling?" He turned to his father: "Senhor Pai, men like yourselves — you and Judge Gonzaga and Dr. Cláudio — you have an honest dedication to this cause. But does Silvério dos Reis, with his immense indebtedness to the treasury? Does he seek anything but freedom from those obligations?" Martinho knew that his father loathed this tax contractor, with whom he had been involved in acrimonious litigation several years ago. "And he's hardly the only man rallying to your banner for selfish motives. Would Silvério dos Reis be a supporter if Queen Maria forgave him his great trespasses?"

"Silvério dos Reis's motives may be questionable," Fernandes agreed. "But he openly advocates independence and has contributed money toward the cause. This is enough to guarantee his loyalty."

"With such a crook at the helm, what hope of an honest and free Minas Gerais?" Martinho snorted.

"Men like Judge Gonzaga and Dr. Cláudio Manuel will direct the new government," André pointed out.

Fernandes added, "Yes, Martinho . . . men like your father."

"No one expects independence to immediately extinguish all past wrongs," Luis Fialho said. "The fight against evils like corruption and ignorance will be as great a struggle as any on the battlefield."

"Oh, Senhor Pai, Thomas Jefferson said this, too — that the struggle to build their nation is as demanding as was the war of independence," Fernandes said. "Shortly before we met the minister, a bloody insurrection had been suppressed at Massachusetts. Senhor Jefferson was distressed but by no means disheartened: 'Was it not to be expected that the tree of liberty would be refreshed from time to time with the blood of patriots and tyrants?' he asked."

"And martyrs?" Martinho Soares added, his eyes downcast.

❧

On Sunday, February 8, 1789, after Mass at the Church of St. Francis, André headed back to the rua das Flôres with a feeling of blessed joy. He kept pace with his father, who had difficulty crossing the smooth cobbles. Alferes Silva Xavier walked next to André and Raimundo da Silva, and was handsomely attired in the dress uniform of the dragoons. These three were leading a group of family and friends to the house on the rua das Flôres to celebrate the baptism of André's son, José Inocêncio, to whom Silva Xavier was godfather.

Constança Oliveira was a few feet behind André, with her mother and sisters, carrying José Inocêncio in a white lace shawl. Accompanying the women was the infant's *madrinha* — the godmother — Ana Figueirido, the married daughter of a fazendeiro whose family had been befriended by André's father when they arrived from Portugal thirty years ago.

Constança Oliveira, twenty years old, had lovely deepset eyes, wavy black hair, and a pleasing figure. Extraordinarily large feet were Constança's only unattractive feature; she was conscious of this and pushed her feet into shoes that were several sizes too small. Constança was also painfully shy. During their courtship, André had taken this to be a well-bred daughter's natural reticence; but since their marriage she had grown so quiet that Raimundo da Silva was prompted to ask if his daughter-in-law was sick. André discovered that it was neither illness nor modesty that troubled Constança; quite simply, she had nothing to say. She was a disappointment to him.

A week before the birth of José Inocêncio, André had given her a hint of his involvement with the coming revolution: "Alferes Silva Xavier and others see a day coming when Minas Gerais will be liberated. A land where our child can be free."

Constança had nodded.

"May we be blessed with a son who, when he grows to manhood, will not have to bow to tyrants."

Constança had nodded again.

"He will pay no derrama but taxes decided on by the people."

"Oh, Senhor André," she had wailed suddenly, "our queen in Portugal won't allow this disobedience!"

"The queen won't be able to prevent it."

"God confided power in Dona Maria," Constança had said, a look of acute distress on her normally placid face. "It's our duty to accept her rule."

Senhor Raimundo da Silva shared Constança's opinion. It was his contention that without the protection of Portugal, Brazil would cease to exist; one by one, the captaincies would fall to the Spaniards, who continued to covet the colony. Senhor Raimundo offered an alternative to independence: "An old and exhausted parent deserves nourishment and restoration in his child's house. Mother Portugal is drained by centuries of discovery and conquest and needs the same succor. Brazil must open her house to Dona Maria and the Braganças. Let the court leave Lisbon and establish itself here. With the resources of Brazil, the Portuguese Empire can be restored."

André's response was only to point out that Portuguese royalty would never uproot itself from Europe to settle in remote America among men who were considered barbarians.

It was for old Raimundo's own protection that André had not taken his father into his confidence about the depth of his involvement with the revolutionary plot. Nor had André made any attempt to involve his brother, Dionésio, who lived at the fazenda on the road to Cachoeira do Campo. As far as Dionésio knew, the kegs André and Fernandes had placed in the storeroom there contained vinegar.

Luis Fialho Soares and Fernandes were among the guests at the house during the baptismal celebration, but they exchanged few words about the events anticipated a week from now. Silva Xavier, however, couldn't contain his zeal. At one point during the afternoon, he put his arm around André's shoulders and steered him toward a balcony fronting the second story of the house.

"Oh, my friend, I thank you for this honor," Silva Xavier said, when André and he stood alone on the balcony. "I vow that I won't rest until liberty is assured for my godson."

"God willing, Joaquim José, my son will one day offer you thanks for this precious gift."

"There will be others worthier than I in the struggle for independence."

"Men inspired by you, Joaquim José."

Silva Xavier placed both of his long, slender hands on the balcony railing. He looked in the direction of the governor's town palace, which was on a rise off to the right of the rua das Flôres. "The visconde de Barbacena, too, has a role to play by affixing his seal to the proclamation of the derrama."

"His intention remains firm?"

"I hear nothing to the contrary."

They stayed on the balcony for a while, discussing their plans, until Silva Xavier rejoined the celebration to propose a toast for his godson:

"To the firstborn son of André Vaz da Silva and Constança Oliveira. May God who rules our destinies grant this child a life in which he will enjoy his birthright as a free citizen of our America."

℥

"A derrama!" Silva Xavier struck the top of a table in Luis Fialho's study with the side of his hand. "A derrama, they cry, like so many nervous sheep bleating among themselves. To hell with the derrama! For the love of God, let us take up arms!"

It was March 1, 1789. For two weeks the conspirators had awaited the proclamation of the new tax, but no announcement had come from the visconde's residence at Cachoeira do Campo. Silva Xavier saw the delay weakening the resolve of the plotters, and he was sharing his concern with Luis Fialho, Fernandes, and André, whom he had found together at the lawyer's house this Sunday, three weeks after the baptism of José Inocêncio.

"I don't have the grace or gentility of Dr. Cláudio Manuel. I'm not a man of wealth — or debt — like Silvério dos Reis. I've been told that I'm not fit to command like Colonel Freire de Andrade. I'm the alferes, the Tooth-Puller. Was I wrong to hope that these men would listen to me?"

"Joaquim José, not one of us doubts your word or your dedication," Luis Fialho responded. "I feel the same restlessness, but we must wait."

"If the visconde delays the derrama for six months? A year? We'll see our poets returning to compose their odes, our debtors groveling at the feet of Her Majesty's fiscal agents, our people with heavier chains to drag around."

Silva Xavier continued his argument: "We don't have to wait to launch our rebellion at the whim or pleasure of Her Majesty's servants. Colonel Alvarenga Peixoto's militia are ready in the south. Padre Rolim has his support in the diamond district. At Vila Rica, the ranks of our dragoons seethe with the urge to fight. What more is *needed?*" The others were silent. "My dear comrades, are we truly such slaves that we have to be whipped to the post of liberty?"

∞

Late afternoon, March 9, Senhor Raimundo was dozing on the bench next to the doorway of the shop when Silva Xavier arrived. Silva Xavier spoke with Senhor Raimundo for a few minutes, then went inside to André. "I have to talk with you," he said. He glanced back at André's father. "Not here. Let's walk." They started down the rua das Flôres toward Vila Rica's main square.

The derrama had not been proclaimed. During the past nine days, Silva Xavier had continued to argue that the rebellion should be launched immediately, but to no avail.

"Judge Gonzaga says His Excellency hesitates to impose the derrama because he fears the reaction of the Mineiros," the alferes said. "Could it be that the visconde reads the mood of the Mineiro better than his would be liberators?"

They had reached the square. The governor's town palace was to their left; they turned right, walking toward the city barracks of the dragoons and Vila Rica's jail, which was at the bottom of the square.

"My colonel has retired to his fazenda, where he waits like patient Job," Silva Xavier continued. "While Andrade and the rest wait, their confusion grows. Some now suggest that the visconde de Barbacena himself should be lured to the side of independence. He's young and ambitious and can be tempted by the prospect of leading a new American nation, they say. What nonsense! He's a fidalgo who savors the touch of his lips to Dona Maria's hand. He's as likely to embrace our cause as sup with the devil!"

Approaching the jail, Silva Xavier headed toward the right of the building and an incline upon which stood the Church of Nossa Senhora do Carmo.

"I agree the longer we delay, the more confusion," André said. "But what can we do, Joaquim?"

"That's why I came to see you. I can't wait another day."

"But without the support of Colonel Andrade, of Alvarenga Peixoto —"

"The only man with spirit! Alvarenga Peixoto agrees we must fight. Now! His men are ready to block the road over the Mantiqueira and the approaches from São Paulo. 'Hold the passes!' says Alvarenga Peixoto. 'Establish bases in the mountains. Ten thousand men from Portugal won't dislodge our patriots!'"

"So! Alvarenga Peixoto marches to battle! I'll be ready, Joaquim!" André, Fernandes, and others were responsible for bringing the gunpowder from the da Silva fazenda to Vila Rica to supply the insurgents who would infiltrate the city from the surrounding hills. They were also to participate in fomenting the disturbances in the streets.

Silva Xavier shook his head. "Alvarenga Peixoto's hands are tied by the majority." As they walked up toward the church, they both crossed themselves; then Silva Xavier said quietly, "I'm leaving Vila Rica."

"Leaving? Now?"

"I'm going to Rio de Janeiro to speak with the men there who also hope for liberty. I'll tell them the Mineiro revolution is primed — a flash through the touch-hole and Minas Gerais will explode in rebellion. We need only one incident to provide that flash."

"What incident?"

They were walking slowly along a stone path beside the church. Silva Xavier stopped and seized André's arm. "The month of May," he said, his eyes bright. "The royal fifth will be transported to Rio de Janeiro with this year's extortion of fifty arrôbas. The gold will never leave Minas Gerais. There, on the Mantiqueira road, our patriot militia will seize the royal fifth!"

André was momentarily speechless. Capture the gold convoy? The most heavily guarded transport? Even Rope Dancer, with one hundred bandits at his side, couldn't hope to take Dona Maria's treasure. But if it were possible . . . "What have others said about this?"

"I've told very few. I don't want to be bombarded with excuses. At Rio de Janeiro, I'll find out when the warship sent from Lisbon to collect the royal fifth is expected to arrive. The Mantiqueira I know as well as Rope Dancer himself. I'll think this through carefully. When I have a definite plan, I'll go to Alvarenga Peixoto for the men to carry it out."

They sat on a low wall behind the church for half an hour, talking until the sun went down behind the hills beyond the city.

Silva Xavier told him that in the morning he would go to the visconde de Barbacena's palace to ask for leave from his regiment and apply for a passport to travel to Rio de Janeiro. "I've spread the word that I'm needed at the capital — to attend to my plans for a canal."

They started back toward the square. They were below the Carmo church and walking along next to the jail when Silva Xavier suddenly touched André's arm lightly: The Little Cripple was hobbling across the cobblestones beside his slave.

"God bless him," Silva Xavier said. "He can hardly walk; his fingers are gone, his hands reduced to stumps; his teeth are falling out. If all who long for liberty had the courage of The Little Cripple, this very night you and I would walk the streets of Vila Rica as free citizens of our Republic of Minas Gerais."

❧

The next morning, Silva Xavier went to Cachoeira do Campo and obtained permission to go to Rio de Janeiro. At the governor's palace, he met Colonel Alvarenga Peixoto, who was there to pay his respects to the visconde de Barbacena.

Silva Xavier spoke very briefly with Alvarenga Peixoto: "While we wait for something to happen among these blunderheads, I'll learn who at Rio de Janeiro encouraged José de Maia's contacts with Thomas Jefferson." On an earlier occasion, Silva Xavier had spoken with Alvarenga Peixoto about seizing the royal fifth; now he only remarked, "I'm also going to seek the means for a generous contribution from the Crown itself."

Going back toward Vila Rica, from where he would leave immediately for the south, Silva Xavier met another conspirator riding to Cachoeira do Campo: Senhor Joaquim Silvério dos Reis, the tax contractor, who to this day remained indebted to the royal treasury for the equivalent of almost a ton of gold.

Senhor Silvério dos Reis wore clothes of the finest cut, but as he sat upon his horse with its silver trappings, he groaned, "They'll see me a beggar yet, Alferes. The junta threaten to sequester all my property. They would strip these clothes off my back and auction my breeches if they could."

The past week had been harrowing for the Crown debtor, who had been pressed to meet his obligations by the Junta da Fazenda, the treasury board at Vila Rica.

Silva Xavier knew the tax contractor's unsavory reputation, but believed that Senhor Silvério's difficulties stemmed largely from the repressive administration. Silva Xavier liked to think of himself as a friend of the magnate, for men like Silvério dos Reis and Rodrigo de Macedo, the other great debtor, were certain to prosper when free trade was allowed, and they could assist him with his civil-engineering projects.

They were not together for long. Silvério dos Reis had an appointment with the governor. "I ride like a serf to prostrate myself at the master's feet. I have to beg the visconde for extensions. Debts! Debts! Debts! Mother of Mercy, how weary I am of these battles over debt."

"Courage, Senhor Silvério. Your only battle will be the good fight."

ะ

Joaquim Silvério dos Reis had no intention of waiting for the good fight promised by Alferes Silva Xavier.

"Your Excellency, I have come to settle the debt I owe the royal treasury," he told the visconde de Barbacena later that morning of March 10, 1789.

They were in a parlor overlooking a small quince orchard. The visconde stood, hands clasped behind his back, at a window watching a group of slaves at work beneath the trees. He did not turn around. "What do you propose this time, Senhor Silvério?"

"Excellency, the junta accepts the word of false witnesses and records every lie and accusation made by my enemies. They haven't a good word to say about me, though as God is my witness, you'll find no subject at Vila Rica more loyal or with greater affection for his queen."

The visconde turned slowly, adjusting a high curl at the side of his powdered wig. "You amaze me, Senhor Silvério. For years you fail to submit payments due on contracts generously awarded to you by the Crown. Yet you can stand here proclaiming loyalty to Dona Maria, as if you are one of the most esteemed knights of her realm. Can you give me any reason to disbelieve the findings of my junta?"

"I don't deny that I owe the money. God knows, it's more than two hundred milreis. A fortune, Excellency, but nothing to what I can offer in settlement."

"Let me hear." The visconde plucked at a loose thread on a shirt frill.

"There are influential men who contemplate the ruin of Her Majesty's government at Minas Gerais."

"I'm well aware of this."

The color drained from Silvério dos Reis's face. "Your Excellency knows?"

"Certainly, Senhor Silvério, the air of Minas Gerais is turbulent," the visconde said. "Hotheads everywhere, filled with infatuation for alien ideas. Men moaning about Portugal's unjust and oppressive rule. I knew this before I arrived. I also came with detailed information about an army of gold and diamond thieves, contrabandists, and other men who defraud the royal treasury, Senhor Silvério dos Reis."

"It's much more than idle talk about alien ideas, Excellency." When the visconde looked at him inquiringly, Silvério dos Reis took a deep breath and plunged ahead.

"Your Excellency, you welcome into your palace the very men who plot your destruction."

"What are you suggesting, senhor?"

"Around you, Excellency, there are men — Judge Tómas Antônio Gonzaga and Cláudio Manuel da Costa, whose poems you praise so highly; Alvarenga Peixoto; young José Alvares Maciel, to whom you entrust the tutoring of your children. These and many others plot a revolution to overthrow you and abolish Portugal's rule over this captaincy. They wait only for you to impose the derrama; then they'll launch a rebellion, declare independence, and proclaim a republic."

And so Silvério dos Reis, who had long been regarded as a scoundrel by many, denounced the independence movement to the visconde de Barbacena. For this service to Her Majesty, he asked that the visconde seek a full pardon from the Crown for his debts.

"Tell no one of our discussion, Senhor Silvério, even though they share your horror of this conspiracy," the visconde said when they parted. "When I've decided what action to take, I'll summon you."

The visconde's first official act, after three days of agonizing over Silvério dos Reis's denunciation, was to send a letter to the câmara of Vila Rica on March 14, 1789, informing the aldermen that plans to impose the derrama were suspended indefinitely.

The next day, he summoned Silvério dos Reis to Cachoeira. "You've told no one of our discussion?"

"No, Excellency. I said only that I came to ask for time to pay my debts."

"Time is what I need. The câmara of Vila Rica has been told that the derrama is suspended; a circular letter will be sent to the other councils. The opportunity for revolution is lost, but I won't arrest the traitors until I can be assured of apprehending everyone involved in this treason. Now, Senhor Silvério, tell me all you know, including your own association with these men."

"You agree, Excellency, to ask a pardon for my debts?"

The visconde eyed the informer coldly. "The queen's gratitude is certain to be boundless."

Silvério dos Reis gave a mighty sigh of relief. Then he revealed everything he knew of the plans for the liberation of Minas Gerais.

✑

"André Vaz! André Vaz!"

The call was accompanied by an urgent rapping on the door of the shop in the rua das Flôres. It was past midnight, and a slave sleeping on the floor in front of the counter awoke and quickly opened the door.

"Fetch your master!" Fernandes Soares commanded.

A few minutes later, André came down the steps.

"All is lost!" Fernandes cried. "Joaquim José has been arrested at Rio de Janeiro!"

"Sweet Jesus!"

It was May 17, 1789, nine weeks since Barbacena suspended the derrama. His sudden and unexpected announcement led some of the plotters to believe they had been betrayed. But later, when Judge Gonzaga and others met with the visconde at Cachoeira do Campo, he had given no indication that he was aware of their plans. The alarm had passed, but with the derrama suspended, the plans for an uprising were also postponed indefinitely.

A few of the conspirators argued that they should act immediately. "Either way, if they catch us now, we'll hang on a high royal gallows," said Alvarenga Peixoto.

Such talk increased the anxieties of some who were convinced that a spy among the group was responsible for the suspension of the derrama, and they had begun to look at their fellow conspirators with suspicion. High on their list was Silvério dos Reis because of his past record for dishonesty. His increased visits to Cachoeira do Campo had been noticed, and four weeks ago, he had suddenly announced that he was traveling to Rio de Janeiro "to compliment the viceroy and consult him about my debts." In fact, Silvério dos Reis was carrying a letter of introduction from the visconde de Barbacena to his uncle, Dom Vasconceles e Souza, to whom Silvério dos Reis was to repeat his denunciation.

Silvério dos Reis reached Rio de Janeiro in May, and immediately upon hearing his information, the viceroy, Dom Vasconceles e Souza, had appointed a secret court of inquiry to collect evidence of the conspiracy. He had ordered the arrest of Alferes Joaquim José da Silva Xavier.

Those weeks before his arrest had been frustrating for Silva Xavier, who found himself an increasingly lonely prophet. The group of merchants and intellectuals he thought shared José de Maia's dedication to liberty turned out to be as hesitant toward rebellion as those men he had left behind at Vila Rica.

In late April, friends in the military had warned Silva Xavier that the viceroy was having him watched. Nevertheless, he had boldly presented himself at the viceroy's palace to request permission to return to Vila Rica. Refused a passport, he had gone into hiding in rooms above the workshop of a friend, Domingos da Cruz, whose home was in the rua das Latoeiras, the street of braziers and lathe workers.

Silva Xavier still hoped for the seizure of the royal fifth, which he had spoken of only to his closest friends. He intended to stay in hiding for a few days and then leave the city at night, heading for the road to São Paulo, from where he would travel back to Minas Gerais.

On May 9, the alferes learned that Silvério dos Reis was in the capital. Eager to know about events at Vila Rica, he sent a trusted priest to Senhor Silvério. The turncoat had been evasive, showing more interest in learning Silva Xavier's whereabouts than in giving details of developments in Minas Gerais. The priest, growing suspicious, had left without revealing Silva Xavier's hiding place, but he had been followed.

Twenty-four hours later, soldiers of the viceroy's guard surrounded the brazier's shop.

Silva Xavier had been taken to the Ilha das Cobras in Guanabara Bay. Here he had been locked up in the dungeon of a fortress dominating this rocky Isle of Snakes.

Now, past midnight on May 17, Fernandes was reporting the dreadful news. André was full of questions:

"When did it happen? How did you learn of it?"

"Joaquim was arrested by the viceroy's guard seven days ago. A message was brought to Dr. Cláudio Manuel."

"By whom?"

"All I know is that a rider was sent from Rio de Janeiro to Dr. Cláudio's house. He called my father. He says it's not only Silva Xavier who's been betrayed but all of us. We must go immediately. The gunpowder! We have to get rid of it!"

"Who betrayed us?"

"No traitor was mentioned," Fernandes said. "For the love of God, André, go! Dress! We can talk on the way."

André hesitated. "My cousins, the tropeiros from São Paulo, are at the fazenda."

"The powder is not their concern."

"It will be if we arrive in the middle of the night."

Finally, they decided that in the morning they would go to the fazenda and arrange to conceal the gunpowder in abandoned mine workings in the hills nearby.

The next morning, André and Fernandes Soares went to the fazenda and had no difficulty disposing of the kegs of gunpowder.

When André told Raimundo da Silva that he was leaving Vila Rica immediately with Constança and José Inocêncio, his father surprised him by showing an awareness of his predicament. "Go. Save your bacon, André, while there's time. As old as I am, the Lord has spared my eyes and my ears. All this talk of liberty and independence from the alferes . . . only one man at Vila Rica was not privy to your schemes — the visconde de Barbacena — and only because he chose to live at Cachoeira do Campo."

When André spoke with Constança, she remained silent, until he shook her by the shoulders. "Do you understand me? We must go *now*. If we don't, you'll watch them take me away."

"Damn you!" she said. "Damn you for the shame of José Inocêncio!" Before André could speak, she hurried away to prepare herself and the child for their exile.

They left Vila Rica with the tropeiros on May 19, 1789, heading south on the road to São João d'El Rei. The two muleteers were sons of Agostinho and Vicente, the brothers of Benedito Bueno da Silva of Itatinga. Both Tobias Henrique and Ivo were hard-drinking, taciturn men, who asked few questions about André's request to accompany them, though they suspected it was connected with the excitement at Vila Rica, which was rife with rumors that the visconde was about to round up a gang of contrabandistas.

The road to São João d'El Rei was busy, and on three occasions during the first two days of the journey they were overtaken by cavalry patrols, one of which halted briefly while the officer in charge questioned them. While Tobias Henrique produced his passport and licenses for the mule train, André, who was dressed in shoddy breeches and an old jacket, stayed with the mule drivers. The dragoon found Tobias Henrique's papers to be in order, made a cursory inspection of the mule train without bothering to examine the animals' packs, and then rode off with his men.

Toward evening on May 22, they were twenty miles from São João d'El Rei. Again they saw horsemen bearing down upon them: two white men and four black and mulatto slaves. Slowing their pace beside the mule train, the older of the two white men asked for water. André acknowledged the request and rode over to a mule that carried leather water bags. He untied one and took it to the man.

"Orlando Costa Guedes," the man introduced himself when André passed him the bag. Heavily armed, he carried sword and pistols, and a musket beside his saddle. "My son, Simão," he said, jerking his head toward the younger man.

"Your fazenda is nearby?" André asked.

Guedes did not reply immediately. He drank from the container. "We have a mine ten leagues back," he said, passing the water bag to his son.

André watched Guedes thoughtfully as the man brushed drops of water off his clothes. After some moments, he said softly, "The day of your baptism, senhor?"

Guedes gave a quizzical look in response to what was to have been the watchword for the uprising. "Where are you from?" he asked.

"Vila Rica, senhor. André Vaz da Silva, son of the merchant da Silva. I'm taking my wife and child to São Paulo."

"Then, Vaz da Silva, thank God you left in time."

"What has happened?"

"Judge Gonzaga, Dr. Cláudio Manuel — all have been arrested."

"You were there?"

"My son was. At dawn yesterday the visconde's soldiers arrested them. Simão rode through the night."

André looked at the young man slouched in the saddle. "Luis Fialho Soares? His son, Fernandes?"

Simão Guedes shrugged. "I don't know them. Many were taken away."

"To where do you ride, senhor?"

"São João d'El Rei. There you'll find few houses open to the queen's soldiers. We go to fight for our independence with Alvarenga Peixoto and Padre Carlos Correia."

As Guedes and his son and their slaves rode off, André could not restrain himself, *"Libertas! Libertas, quae sera tamen!"*

He saw Orlando Guedes shake a fist in the air and heard him shout the same words.

For the next hour, André rode beside the mules in deep silence. Many times he looked at Constança, who was carrying José Inocêncio and riding twenty yards ahead of him. He could not get the miner and his son out of his mind and imagined them far along the road spurring their horses to join the fight. *Libertas, quae sera tamen!*

André was torn by indecision. How could he abandon his wife and child at the very edge of the battlefield?

"Stop!" André cried. "Stop the mules, Tobias Henrique!"

"What's wrong?"

"The men who came by, Orlando Guedes and his son, Simão . . ."

"Yes?"

"I have to join them, Tobias Henrique, at São João d'El Rei."

"I won't take my mules there."

"No. You mustn't." He looked across at Constança. "There's a trail that passes north of the town."

"I know it."

"It will be safer for my wife and child. Take them, please, to your uncle, Senhor Benedito Bueno. A few months, God willing, and I'll fetch my family."

                    *

André drove his horse forward toward a gap in the Serra do São José, which rose north of the city of São José d'El Rei. Whatever lay ahead in the weeks and months to come, he would remember this triumphant hour, riding with the knowledge that all their hopes had not been in vain.

A mile from the town, nine cavalrymen burst out of the trees beside the road, four to the left of André, five to the right.

"Halt!"

André spurred his horse to make a run for it. A shot cracked to his left and he was struck in the forearm. As he fought to stay in the saddle, two dragoons swept up beside him, sabres glinting in the moonlight.

"Surrender or die!"

André reined in his horse.

"Ah, Mother!" he cried, when he handed over his pistol a few moments later. "What use was this to me?"

The cavalrymen disarming him laughed. They knew there were others in jail at São José d'El Rei who had said the same, for not one among the traitors arrested this night of May 22, 1789, had fired a shot.

                    *

André was taken to the town jail at São João d'El Rei, where he found Orlando and Simão Guedes, who had been captured in circumstances similar to his own. When André's friendship with Alferes Silva Xavier was discovered, he was transferred, first to Vila Rica's prison, then, in late September 1789, to Rio de Janeiro. There he was put in the dungeons of the fort of Nossa Senhora do Conceição, on the east end of the city above The Valongo, the slave depot and market. He was held incommunicado for thirty months, while a royal tribunal investigated the plot against Her Majesty Dona Maria, which came to be known as the "Inconfidência Mineira."

Alferes Silva Xavier and twenty-eight others suffered the same incarceration. The betrayer Silvério dos Reis had been detained briefly but then released lest unfavorable treatment of the informer deter others willing to testify against the traitors. Absent, too, was Dr. Cláudio Manuel da Costa: On July 4, 1789, his body was found hanging in a closet under the stairwell of the house of the magnate Rodrigo de Macedo, who had also evaded prosecution by collaborating with the visconde de Barbacena. His death was declared a suicide in remorse for an abject confession incriminating his friends.

Luis Fialho Soares and Fernandes had been among the men taken in bonds from Vila Rica to the coast. Luis Fialho had also been imprisoned in Fort Conceição. Luis Fialho's older son, Martinho, had bribed the guards at the fort to allow him to visit his father.

Luis Fialho had ridiculed the idea that Dr. Cláudio Manuel had taken his own life. "Hang himself? That gracious, gentle man? Never!" he had said to Martinho. "He was murdered before he could tell the viceroy's judges the truth about Rodrigo de Macedo and others involved with us. He was killed because of snakes like Silvério dos Reis, who slither around the feet of the visconde de Barbacena. The visconde himself sleeps easier with Dr. Cláudio in his grave. There are many who believe the visconde was listening to Dr. Cláudio and others — listening to the wind and trying to determine which way it would blow."

Luis Fialho had passed his sixty-first birthday in May 1791 in Fort Conceição, with his jailors and the rats and roaches, in a seven-by-five-foot cell. Twenty-two punishing months in this cold, damp place: Luis Fialho died in the first week of June 1791, and was buried by the Franciscans, who cared for the spiritual needs of these infamous men.

André had also been visited by tragedy during this period of imprisonment. He got news of the death of Senhor Raimundo da Silva. And from his cousin, Silvestre da Silva, he had a letter announcing the death of Constança. Unknown to André, she had been in early pregnancy when she undertook the arduous journey to São Paulo. She had miscarried and fallen grievously ill, and despite Senhor Benedito Bueno's sending for not one but two doctors to attend to her, Constança died, on October 11, 1789.

André had been taken before courts of inquiry and the royal tribunal six times to be interrogated about his friendship with Alferes Silva Xavier. He had answered the judges and magistrates truthfully, without mentioning the gunpowder smuggled from Matias Barbosa; he and Fernandes had sworn to keep this secret. He was surprised, at his first interrogation at Vila Rica, that it hadn't come out. But he had no way of knowing that the few conspirators who were aware of active preparations for rebellion were just as anxious as he and Fernandes to conceal these in support of the defense that the Inconfidência Mineira had been no more than talk about independence.

Without this evidence, André, though accused of treason by his association with the leaders of the independence movement, was regarded as having played a lesser role than men such as Gonzaga, Freire de Andrade, and Alvarenga Peixoto, whose lèse-majesté was seen as most horrible because at one time or another they had served in the administration of Minas Gerais and had been among the most respected and influential men in the captaincy.

By October 1791, the royal tribunal had completed its interrogations. Dr. José de Oliveira Fagundes, a lawyer of the Santa Casa de Misericórdia, was appointed counsel for the conspirators.

After a lengthy plea for each man, Dr. Fagundes, while acknowledging that they had met on many occasions to discuss an uprising against the State, pleaded for clemency:

"This disloyalty against Her Majesty and infatuation with republican ideas was no more than a criminal excess of loquaciousness and a pastime of fanciful notions that vanished as soon as the defendants were dispersed.

"They offended only by words and not deeds, and good reason demands a distinction between thought and consummation . . . They humbly ask the forgiveness of Her Majesty for their rashness and foolishness."

The royal tribunal recessed for six months after listening to Dr. Fagundes's appeal to consider the evidence and pleas presented to the three judges. In mid-April 1792, they were ready to deliver their verdict, and on the night of April 17, André Vaz da Silva and the other accused were moved under heavy guard from various dungeons and prisons to the public jail of Rio de Janeiro.

By 8:00 A.M. on April 18, the tribunal was in session. There was no question of the guilt of the majority, and today's proceedings were for their sentencing, but the tribunal's written findings covered every aspect of the Inconfidência. The judgment and sentence took eighteen hours to deliver, from 8:00 A.M. on April 18 till 2:00 A.M., on April 19.

෴

"André Vaz da Silva!"

It was almost midnight. The High Court chamber was illuminated with lamps and candles. When his name was called, André rose and stepped forward groggily, feeling the exhaustion of the past sixteen hours, during which the tribunal had allowed only two short adjournments.

"André Vaz da Silva, your crime of treasonably conspiring to withdraw from the subjugation due to the royal sovereign is proved conclusively. Though the evidence against you indicates that you were not among the leaders of the conspiracy, you attended gatherings where they held their criminal sessions. You had full knowledge of the planned insurrection and failed to denounce it, as is the duty of a loyal and faithful vassal. You rode to São João d'El Rei with every intention of taking up arms against the Crown.

"Wherefore this tribunal condemns the defendant André Vaz da Silva to banishment for ten years to Mozambique, and to the forfeiture of all your goods to the treasury and royal chamber. Should you return to the dominions of America at any time before expiration of your period of exile, you will end your natural life on the gallows."

Fernandes da Rocha Soares was sentenced to ten years' exile in Angola. Ten other accused were also condemned to be transported to Africa, some of them to perpetual banishment, among the latter, Judge Tomás Antônio Gonzaga. Four accused were acquitted for lack of evidence against them.

Alferes Joaquim José da Silva Xavier and ten others, including Colonel Alvarenga Peixoto, Lieutenant-Colonel Freire de Andrade, and Dr. José Alvares Maciel, were condemned to death.

Silva Xavier's plea that he alone be held responsible was rejected.

"The criminal Joaquim José da Silva Xavier, known as the Tooth-Puller, is condemned to be paraded with hangman's noose through the streets of Rio de Janeiro to the gallows, where he will be executed by hanging. When the criminal is dead, his head will be cut off and his body divided into quarters. The head is to be transported to the city of Vila Rica, where it will be fastened to a tall pole in the most public place to remain there until consumed by time. The legs will be attached to poles along the road to Minas Gerais at Varginha and Cebolas; the arms will be exhibited at other places where the criminal sowed the seeds of revolution."

Silva Xavier accepted the sentence with quiet dignity, not the slightest trace of fear in his uncompromising blue eyes.

℃

The men condemned to death were separated from those who were to suffer banishment, and André was taken back to the dungeon of Fort Conceição. He was there, late on April 20, when a guard came shouting the news: "The tribunal has announced that they are to be spared!"

"God be praised!" André shouted.

The guard tramped along the passageway, making this announcement, and as he walked back past André's cell, he added, "All have been granted the queen's mercy, but one. His infamy was too great. The Tooth-Puller will hang."

℃

Since taking up his post as viceroy of Brazil, Dom José de Castro, the conde de Resende, had lived with the disconcerting awareness that on the Ilha das Cobras within sight of his palace were men who had plotted the downfall of fidalgos like himself.

As the conde and his aides had hoped, the announcement that Queen Maria had commuted the sentences of ten conspirators caused a public outpouring of devotion for Her Majesty. Special masses were to be said throughout Rio de Janeiro in gratitude for the sovereign's clemency. And prayers, too, for the queen's health, since Maria was known to be ailing.

Maria's consort and uncle, Pedro, had died in 1786, and just three years later, the queen was smitten by further tragedy: Her first-born son, a daughter, a son-in-law, and a grandson were all carried off by smallpox. Her beloved confessor, the inquisitor-general also died. Dona Maria saw these deaths as heaven's punishment for her subjects' irreligious behavior under the rule of the Marquis of Pombal. She had become locked in a mighty battle with horned demons, swarming in the corridors and chambers of her palace. Those who witnessed her ravings knew that Maria I was incurably insane. Her ministers and nobles pledged their loyalty to her gentle, corpulent son, eighteen-year-old João — "John the Goat," some called him — who himself had a fondness for browsing in the great monastery of Mafra and a good ear for sacred music.

Shortly before 9.00 A.M. on Saturday morning, April 21, 1792, the conde de Resende stood at an upper window of his palace watching a troop of soldiers form up at the top of the Largo de Paço. The conde had left Europe on the eve of the French Revolution and was determined that the punishment of Silva Xavier be an example to others infected with the plague of revolutionary zeal. Much to His Excellency's pleasure, it was a bright, sunny morning, which would encourage a multitude to the field of Santo Domingos, where an outsize scaffold had been erected during the night. Already here in the Largo do Paço a crowd was gathering to see the Tooth-Puller being led out of the public jail behind the palace.

A few minutes after nine, the conde leaned forward at the open window as an agitated murmur rose from the crowd. He saw the condemned man walking toward the waiting soldiers, the escort forming up around him. The officers gave the order to march, and the escort started toward the rua da Cadeia, which led off the square. When they were out of sight, the conde de Resende turned away from the window. He made the sign of the Cross. "Lord have mercy on his soul."

"Lord have mercy on my soul! Jesus, Mary, Joseph — be merciful!"

Silva Xavier wore the garb of a penitent, a plain white robe of coarse cloth that reached his ankles. A length of heavy rope was wound round his neck and tied in a knot above his chest, with the two ends trailing almost to the ground. His hands were bound behind his back. He walked barefooted, having given his boots to a jailer.

Infantrymen with fixed bayonets were posted along the streets of the gallows procession. By order of the tribunal, a crier strode in front of Silva Xavier shouting aloud the crimes of which he was guilty and the sentence he must suffer.

Some who watched the procession laughed at the tall robed prisoner. They taunted him with remarks about his grand canal at Rio de Janeiro and his lost republic at Minas Gerais. "Traitor!" some cried. "Judas!"

But the majority were silent and solemn. On most street corners were posts supporting boxes with holy images revered by those who lived or worked nearby; many turned to these oratories now to offer appeals for the condemned man.

Silva Xavier bore himself with great poise, his shoulders straight. He looked tired as he moved his lips in a ceaseless recitation of prayer. He paid no attention to the taunts and jibes.

Just before ten o'clock, Silva Xavier and his escort reached the field of Santo Domingos. The conde de Resende's son, Dom Luiz de Castro, and his officers had positioned the six regiments and cavalrymen in a great triangle around the high scaffold. The executioner was a black man, and he waited with four valets who were to assist him in dismembering the corpse.

An enormous crowd congregated behind the cordon of troops on the level ground and on the slopes of a nearby hill. Many people had started toward the field of Santo Domingos soon after dawn, and as the hours passed, a holiday atmosphere prevailed. But the sight of the distant white-robed figure standing so calmly on the platform beside a Franciscan friar, with his head bowed and the symbolic rope wound round his neck — this reminded them that death was close now, and thousands raised their faces gloomily toward the scaffold. When lay brothers of the Santa Casa do Misericórdia moved through the throng appealing for donations to pay for Masses for the soul of the sinner, all but the very poor offered alms.

Shortly before eleven o'clock, the hangman took up his place at the gallows. A mulatto valet went to Silva Xavier and gestured that he wanted to remove the rope tied round his neck. He came closer and with trembling hands undid the knot.

"*Calma*," Silva Xavier whispered.

"Joaquim," the Franciscan said, taking one step toward the gallows.

Silva Xavier nodded but did not take his eyes off the great assembly as he crossed over to the hangman.

The Franciscan said gently, "Let us pray."

Together they recited the Creed.

The Franciscan said farewell and stepped back from the gallows.

Then, in that final moment, Joaquim José da Silva Xavier, whom they mocked as the Tooth-Puller, made one last glorious confession:

"I have kept my word. I die for liberty!"

BOOK FIVE

*Sons of
the Empire*

XVII

August 1855 – January 1856

*A*ntônio Paciência, "Patient Anthony," was eight years old on a day in August 1855 when he learned a terrible lesson. Until then, the dark-skinned mulatto boy had known no shame at being naked and often raced bare-bottomed to the Riacho Jurema to swim in the creek.

That August morning, a stranger came to Antônio Paciência, who stood naked with four others, and examined him with the thoroughness the boy had seen with vaqueiros inspecting cattle. His head, shoulders, arms, hands, trunk, legs, and feet were inspected. He was made to open his mouth wide to permit an examination of his teeth. The boy's private parts were searched. When his genitals were touched, Antônio Paciência uttered an involuntary cry, which made the stranger laugh and give the boy's testicles a vicious squeeze.

"As he grows older, senhor, he'll be a good worker."

Antônio Paciência stood with two older boys, a young man, and a girl. They were on the dusty open ground thirty feet away from the main house of Fazenda da Jurema.

After a while, Antônio Paciência raised his head slightly. He saw the senhor capitão sitting on the veranda, fanning himself with his hat. The senhor capitão's son was here, walking with the stranger as he inspected those selected to stand before him. Antônio Paciência's gaze shifted nervously from the senhor capitão to some women gathered off to the left between the house and a storeroom. He looked at the black slave Mãe Mônica — Mother Mônica," the senhor capitão fondly called her — who stood at the front of the group.

"Oh, Senhor Capitão, Antônio Paciência is a good child!" Mãe Mônica pleaded when she saw that her son had been chosen for the stranger. "Antônio will grow to be a man who faithfully serves the senhor capitão. As God sees me, I raise him with nothing but respect for the senhor and his family. Oh, my Master, for the love of Little Jesus of the Children, *please,* I beg for my Antônio!"

But the senhor capitão and the sinhazinha and the senhor capitão's son all ignored her.

Antônio Paciência's gaze moved to a group of vaqueiros in the shade of some trees beyond the storeroom. Several of his playmates were there, including his good friend Chico Tico-Tico, a scrawny, bow-legged caboclo. Tico-Tico, "The Sparrow," was twelve, a devil who led the gang of boys at the fazenda.

Antônio Paciência turned his head stiffly to the right and saw the stranger examining the boy next to him.

The stranger was a Portuguese from São Paulo. He had come to the fazenda late yesterday leading a great caravan through the caatinga. Antônio Paciência and his friends had run to greet them, expecting peddlers or horse dealers. But there were no mules with merchandise or ponies for sale, and instead, the boys of Fazenda da Jurema beheld a sight they had never before seen:

The Portuguese had come riding up front on a black horse. Behind him, strung out for a great distance, a file of people walked across the white-hot sands. Most were as black as Mãe Mônica, but a few were mulattoes and three or four almost white — some so young they were carried on their mothers' backs. Other mounted men rode up and down the column calling for the human beasts to step up their pace.

Antônio Paciência had never seen people as miserable as those shuffling past him. Most unhappy-looking of all were black men whose necks were encircled with iron hoops and who were linked together with chains that swayed and clinked as they trod forward.

"Escravos," Chico Tico-Tico explained.

Antônio Paciência knew they were slaves. Mãe Mônica was a slave in the house of the senhor capitão. There were seven other adult slaves at the fazenda, blacks and mulattoes, and their sixteen children. Though Antônio Paciência belonged to the house of Mãe Mônica, he had not yet come to understand the nature of servitude, since he was accepted as friend and playmate of the vaqueiros' sons and the grandsons of the senhor capitão.

"Where are they taking them?" Antônio Paciência asked Chico TicoTico.

"South to the lands of coffee."

"Beyond those hills?"

Chico Tico-Tico laughed. "Far beyond! They must walk for *months* to reach São Paulo. If they're lucky, they may ride a *balsa* up the Rio São Francisco."

The Portuguese had halted the slave column near the houses and huts and gone alone to the senhor capitão's house. Half an hour later, the slaves had been taken to the jurema trees at the creek, where the column broke up as they rushed forward to the water's edge. Many women and children too spent to cover the last steps to the riacho had lain down at the trees calling for water, but it was a long time before they received any attention.

Hurrying away from the jurema trees, Antônio Paciência had run to Mãe Mônica at the clay ovens behind the fazenda. "Stay away from them, child," she warned. "This Portuguese is a devil who comes to catch little boys like Antônio Paciência!" Mãe Mônica had pulled a face and laughed loudly as she had had no cause for concern then.

ⅇⅺ

Senhor João Montes Ferreira, the senhor capitão's son, who stood with the Portuguese, remembered a night some eight years ago when he had raped Mãe Mônica, there on the hot earth beside the clay ovens at the fazenda. Senhor João Montes knew that the mulatto boy Antônio being inspected by the slaver was his son.

Senhor Capitão Heitor Baptista Ferreira was also aware of the bastard's parentage, but was not moved to compassion for Antônio Paciência. José Montes had five sons: three with his wife, Adelia Veras, and two acknowledged bastards with a vaqueiro's daughter. João Montes had not shown the slightest affection for Mãe Mônica's child and the senhor capitão saw no reason to keep Antônio, especially with the Portuguese offering to pay grandly for healthy purchases.

João Montes had suggested that Mãe Mônica also be sold, a proposal strongly endorsed by his wife. She disliked Mãe Mônica, whom she knew to have given herself to her husband.

But his father would not hear of it. "The bastard can go, since you have no interest in him, but not Mãe Mônica." He had reminded his son of the slave's unmatched skills in the kitchen. "She stays!" Senhor Heitor had said, with a hand pressed to his barrel-like belly.

Heitor Baptista Ferreira's attitude toward the human livestock he was putting up for sale was typical of this poderoso do sertão, a great man of the earth whose grandfather, Militão Cariri Ferreira, a Paulista, had bought the fazenda from the Cavalcantis of Santo Tomás in 1781. Graciliano Cavalcanti had returned to Fazenda da Jurema after slaying Black Peter and avenging Paulo Cavalcanti's murder. But two years later, when his father, Bartolomeu Rodrigues Cavalcanti, died, Graciliano had gone back to oversee the engenho until Paulo's son, Carlos Maria, reached his majority.

When Graciliano left Fazenda da Jurema in 1768, he had deserted Januária Adorno Ribeiro, whom he had never married, and the children he had had with her. After reestablishing himself at Santo Tomás, Graciliano had married the daughter of a judge, fathering three girls with her. He had returned only once to the fazenda in 1779, to witness the effects of a two-year drought during which the forced slaughter or death by starvation of cattle had reduced the herd from eight thousand to less than one thousand animals. At the time, depressed sugar prices had made it impossible for the Cavalcantis to restock the ranch. When Militão Cariri Ferreira, who owned land north of the Riacho Jurema, had offered to buy the fazenda, Graciliano, who had inherited the ranch, had sold him the 180-square-mile property.

Senhor Heitor Baptista Ferreira was the acknowledged chieftain of a vast clan whose lands, encompassing the original Fazenda da Jurema and seven other ranches, amounted to a total of three hundred square miles. The Ferreira clan embraced not only relatives but also vaqueiros, rent-paying tenants, and *agregados*. The agregados, or associates, were permitted to live on Ferreira lands through ties of friendship with Senhor Heitor and other Ferreira elders, service as gunmen in conflicts with Ferreira enemies, and long, uninterrupted squatting during which they had always behaved themselves. Whites, mulattoes, caboclos, freed blacks — the agregados were the majority of occupants of Ferreira lands and were subject to immediate eviction if they offended the fazendeiro.

Fazenda da Jurema had been subdivided since Militão Ferreira's day, and the portion owned by Senhor Heitor covered eighty square miles, including the original settlement at the jurema trees near the confluence of the Riacho Jurema and the Rio Pajéu, an influent of the Rio São Francisco sixty-five miles to the south. Senhor Heitor's house was a big, bare, ugly structure with walls of unplastered rubble and a tiled roof. Nearby stood the slave huts and the vaqueiros' houses, one-storied, one-windowed hovels of wickerwork plastered with mud. A five-foot-high fence of upright stakes thickly interwoven with thin tree limbs and brush marked the perimeter of the settlement. The most striking aspect of the fazenda was how little it had changed since the time Paulo Cavalcanti and Padre Eugênio Viana had visited the ranch in 1756.

On the Ferreira lands, there were several families of Cavalcantes. The slight alteration in the last letter of the name — the "i" to an "e" — had first appeared in the documents of a criminal case involving Quintino Adorno Cavalcante, one of three bastard sons of Graciliano. The change assumed significance in differentiating between these improvident *sertanejos,* men of the sertão, and the senhores de engenho who, in this year 1855, still held fast to the lovely valley of Santo Tomás 220 miles to the east.

The boy Chico Tico-Tico — Francisco Cavalcante — and his father, Modesto Cavalcante, a vaqueiro at Fazenda da Jurema, were direct descendants of Quintino Adorno Cavalcante. Through three generations since Quintino's time, not one family of the Ribeiro-Cavalcante line had obtained possession of a single acre of land. Some Cavalcantes had served as vaqueiros with the Ferreiras and other fazendeiros; some had rented small sites in the district, where they grew subsistence crops; some had become nomadic, wandering far into the sertão in neighboring Ceará and south, too, down the valley of the Rio São Francisco. One family, who had fled the backlands after the 1845 drought, were living in a shack on the outskirts of Recife, with the father and two sons working as harvesters of blue crabs in mud flats near the city.

Among the seventeen families that could be traced to Graciliano and Januária in the year 1855, the highest position achieved by any member was that of an army corporal serving in the far west on the Rio Madeira. The most prosperous Cavalcante was the pilot of a barca on the São Francisco. The most educated was a young man of Chico Tico-Tico's generation who'd had three years at primary school.

If one of Graciliano Cavalcanti's descendants had prospered, as vaqueiros occasionally did, by building up his own herd with his annual share of new calves, he would have had difficulty finding land to purchase. For decades already, most of the 600,000 square miles of the semi-arid northeast sertão had been in the hands of families like the Ferreiras or held by absentee landlords at the coast. With a passion rivaling that that had possessed the lord donatários of Brazil three centuries ago, these poderosos do sertão believed in the splendor and the glory of owning immense territories. Nothing could be more injurious to their estate than to permit the sale of small patches of land where men of the lower classes might plant homesteads. Nothing could be more threatening to their control than to offer tenants contracts to remain permanently on their property.

Chico Tico-Tico's father, Modesto Cavalcante, was the only descendant of Graciliano still working as a vaqueiro at Fazenda da Jurema. Modesto had a wife and seven children, a mud-walled house, a dozen cattle, seven pigs, and a tame parrot. He had made many trips taking cattle to Recife, but his world lay essentially within the boundaries of the Ferreira lands, where he served the patrão with blind loyalty.

This day, when the Portuguese inspected Antônio Paciência and the others, Modesto Cavalcante was with the vaqueiros watching the slaver.

Chico Tico-Tico stood in front of Modesto. "Antônio Paciência is so young," he said, turning to his father. "Why does the senhor want to send him away from the fazenda?"

"He won't be a child forever. A few years and the boy will be big and strong. He'll work with the blacks on the plantations."

"Why can't he work at Jurema?"

"He's the child of a slave. He belongs to Senhor Heitor. It's for the senhor capitão to decide what he wants to do with his property."

"Antônio Paciência will be taken from his mother?"

Modesto looked in the direction of Mãe Mônica but didn't respond.

"Antônio Paciência was born at Jurema," Chico Tico-Tico added. "His family is here. This is his home."

Modesto had difficulty dealing with his son's concern for the child of the slave Mônica. It was common knowledge that Antônio Paciência had been fathered by one of the senhor capitão's five sons. Which one was responsible was of no importance to Modesto; he knew that Mãe Mônica was the mother and she was a slave of unclean stomach. Had she been of clean stomach — *barriga limpa* — she would have delivered a light-skinned mulatto instead of this dark one, this *prêto*. Senhor Heitor might have been less inclined to sell the bastard if Antônio Paciência wasn't quite so black.

Modesto was extremely color- and class-conscious in the feudal-like society to which he belonged. Fazendeiros like Heitor Ferreira and the owners of the engenhos at the coast were the great men of the earth, the rich. Modesto had yet to see one of the *ricos* who was not a *branco,* a white, or a *branco da terra*, a white of the earth — a qualification indicating that though there was evidence of color, the senhor was of sufficient prestige or wealth to be accepted as white.

When Modesto did not respond to Chico Tico-Tico after a long silence between them, his son said, "All the times we played with Antônio Paciência, we never thought of him as a slave."

Modesto replied quickly: "His brother, the prêto with the goats and the other one with the blacksmith — in a few years, you'd have seen Antônio Paciência serving with them. Now he must find his place among the great herd of slaves in the south. But he'll be all right. There, among the coffee groves, he'll forget hard, dry Jurema."

❦

The Portuguese bought Antônio Paciência for three hundred milreis, the equivalent at the time of 150 dollars, a good price for a slave boy in the northeast sertão, though the Portuguese expected to receive double this amount when he sold the boy at São Paulo. The slaver was Saturnino Rabelo, a man in his mid-fifties. Previously involved in the African slave trade, for the past four years Rabelo had been engaged in a lucrative traffic of slaves from north to south Brazil.

Rabelo told one of his slave drivers to take the new purchases to the column at the jurema trees. They were to leave immediately, heading toward the Rio Pajéu and the road to the south; Rabelo would follow when he had eaten the meal the Senhor Capitão offered him.

"Come! Come, little burros!" the driver said, and grinned, showing his dark, decayed teeth. He was known as Tropeiro, for he had been a mule driver before working the slave columns.

"*MãeMônica!*" Antônio Paciência shrieked. "*Mãe Mônica! Help me! Save me!*"

His mother broke away from the other women. Clasping her skirt, she ran to the Senhor Capitão, João Montes, and Rabelo, who were still on the veranda.

"Senhor! Senhor, my child. . . ."

Heitor Ferreira looked sadly at Mãe Mônica but said nothing.

"Antônio Paciência is sold," João Montes announced bluntly.

"Ai! Je — sus! Ai! *Santissima Virgem! No,* Senhor João! *Mercy,* senhor!" She fell to her knees in the dirt and held her head in her hands, moaning loudly.

"The fazendeiros of the south need boys like Antônio Paciência," João Montes explained. "He must go to them. They are good men of great wealth. They'll treat him well."

"My Antônio? Oh, Master João, my obedient Antônio?"

Senhor Heitor was embarrassed by Mãe Mônica's outburst in front of Saturnino Rabelo. He heaved himself out of his chair. "You still have two sons and a daughter at Jurema," he said irritably. "Thank God, Mãe Mônica, that they weren't also sold." Turning to Rabelo, he beckoned that they should enter the house.

João Montes waved to Modesto Cavalcante, who quickly crossed to him, removing his hat as he approached the veranda. "Take Mãe Mônica to the boy and let her bid him farewell."

"Yes, senhor."

Quickly then, João Montes left the veranda.

Isabelinha, Mãe Mônica's daughter, had been standing with her mother during the slaver's inspection and now she went to their hut for Antônio Paciência's clothes. She added to the small pile an old leather hat that belonged to Antônio's stepbrother, the blacksmith's helper, and a new gray blanket that she herself had bartered from the peddler for vegetables from the garden the senhor capitão allowed the slaves to keep.

Antônio Paciência saw Mãe Mônica and Modesto Cavalcante coming toward the jurema trees, where the drivers were assembling the column, snapping their whips and cursing the lazy and listless among the 167 slaves. But the drivers ignored Antônio Paciência when he ran to Mãe Mônica and clung to her legs.

"Oh, my Mother! What did I do?"

Mãe Mônica clasped her son's bony shoulders, rocking her body and sobbing.

"Get dressed, child," Isabelinha said, holding his clothes for him. "You have a long, long way to go."

"Aiieee!" Mãe Mônica wailed. "How can it be? Our Antônio, carried off with these black devils!"

Isabelinha pulled Antônio Paciência away from his mother and hurriedly dressed him. She was putting on his shirt when a slave driver shouted for him to join the column.

The final parting was swift and confused. Antônio Paciência was begging, again and again, to be left at the fazenda. Isabelinha offered prayers aloud to the Virgin for his protection. Mãe Mônica lamented at the jurema trees like a very old woman crying for the dead.

As the column started forward, Isabelinha dashed over to Antônio Paciência. She had forgotten to give him the blanket and the hat, which she jammed on his head. "May God go with you, little brother."

"Isabel —" Suddenly his tears flowed again. A slave behind him swore and shoved him forward.

"Antônio Paciência!"

He saw Chico Tico-Tico wave weakly. He made no attempt to return the greeting, so ashamed that Chico Tico-Tico and other boys of Fazenda da Jurema should see him not as one of them but as a slave child. He lowered his head and the wide-brimmed hat blocked his view, except for the feet of those walking near him.

Dust-covered feet. Feet with open wounds from cuts and gashes. Feet with old scars, calluses, corns, and suppurating blisters. Bare feet of slaves rising and falling, day after day, week after week, as the column marched south through the backlands.

From Antônio Paciência's first night away from Fazenda da Jurema as he lay wrapped in his sister's blanket, weeping, until journey's end three months later, the boy was rarely spared sorrow and fright. Sometimes there would be a dull unreality without fear and he would play with other slave boys when the column rested at night, but it took no more than a sharp word from Tropeiro or another driver to start him crying for Mãe Mônica and the world he had left behind at Jurema.

Many sights on the long march awed Antônio Paciência, none more than the Rio São Francisco, which he first glimpsed from the Pernambucan bank opposite Joazeiro, where the river was 2,500 feet wide with banks rising twenty-five feet above low water. When he saw that they were to cross by ferry, he had shaken with fright, but once on the water, he had enjoyed the crossing. Saturnino Rabelo left the column several times to take a barca or a canoe upstream, but the slaves made the entire journey on foot.

The column marched soon after dawn each day, through storm and rain, cold wind and hot, thick white fogs rising from the river, burning suns. They would rest at noon, the length of this break depending on the mood of the drivers, then on again until sundown. They were given two meals a day of corn porridge and dried beef and beans, a diet varied by occasional finds of wild fruits. Once a week, the men would be given cachaça and a twist of tobacco on the order of Saturnino Rabelo, who promised this generosity so long as all behaved themselves.

Once, the rations of cane brandy and tobacco had been suspended for two weeks after five slaves attempted to flee into the sertão. Caught and returned to the column, these fugitives were flogged, the lashings administered in a way least damaging to their flesh. Instead of one flogging of ninety lashes, which Rabelo determined they deserved, on nine successive days, at each evening's halt, the runaways were given ten lashes.

Seven slaves died from sickness during the march. And twice Antônio Paciência had watched as holes were scratched in the sand beside the road to bury infants born to slave mothers as the column rested at night. But the column was not reduced by these deaths: Saturnino Rabelo acquired seventeen additional purchases from fazendas along their route.

About half the slaves had been born in Africa. They told the boy that they had dreamed of returning to their families, but each day farther out on the ocean, they had realized this would never be. "It is hopeless to long for the past," he was advised. "Forget everything but that you were born to live as a slave in the lands of Dom Pedro Segundo."

Antônio Paciência had heard Mãe Mônica and others talk respectfully of this Dom Pedro Segundo, a poderoso do sertão with power over not merely one fazenda but all Brazil. Hearing more about this powerful patrão served to increase Antônio Paciência's curiosity.

"Are these his soldiers?" he would ask the older slaves at a town or village.

"Every soldier in Brazil serves Pedro Segundo."

"Is this his fazenda?" he asked at a big ranch where Saturnino Rabelo had sought further purchases.

"No. Pedro Segundo has a grander house at Rio de Janeiro. Ask Policarpo to tell you about it."

The slave Policarpo had been bought by Rabelo at a fazenda in the Pernambucan sertão, but several years earlier, he had belonged to a Recife merchant whom he had on occasion accompanied to Rio de Janeiro. Policarpo told Antônio Paciência that he had seen not only the palace but also Dom Pedro Segundo himself, riding along the rua Direita in an open carriage with eight cream-colored horses plumed with green feathers.

"'Long live Dom Pedro Segundo! Long live our emperor of Brazil!' I shouted," said Policarpo, his face radiant.

※

On a bright morning in mid-September 1855 as the slave column marched up the valley of the São Francisco, some 750 miles to the south at Rio de Janeiro, a black man stood for inspection by his master as obediently as had Antônio Paciência at

Fazenda da Jurema. His name was Rafael and he was in his early fifties. He smiled as his master scrutinized him.

"No, Rafael, I do not want you to smile. Relax your face," the master said.

Rafael was standing in the middle of a patio. His master was about ten feet away.

"Fold your arms, Rafael."

Rafael obeyed.

"Good, Rafael. Turn your head slightly to the right . . . Yes!"

Rafael watched his master step over to a brass instrument mounted on a tripod. His master bent his tall body to peer through a peephole at one end.

"Excellent, Rafael. Keep your eyes toward me. Bend your head back ever so slightly . . . Yes! Don't move, Rafael . . . Don't move!"

Rafael heard his master give instructions to an assistant whom Rafael knew to be in a room off to the right, where, bright though the day was, the man worked by candlelight behind black drapes. His master unscrewed the back of the brass instrument, removing a round glass screen. The assistant hurried over to him with a circular wet plate, which was substituted for the screen.

"Steady, Rafael. Steady, now . . ."

Rafael did not blink an eyelid as Dom Pedro, emperor of Brazil, took his photograph.

It seemed to Rafael that no sooner had the emperor told him to be steady than the picture-taking was over and Dom Pedro and his assistant had removed the circular plate and rushed into the workshop with it.

Rafael waited outside the dark room. He heard the two men talking animatedly, and though he understood little of what was being said, he remained attentive. Rafael derived great satisfaction from serving his master, to whom he was devoted. No ruler on earth was wiser and more just than His Majesty, Dom Pedro Segundo of Brazil.

❧

Even today, sixty-three years after the event, there were some older citizens of Rio de Janeiro who vaguely remembered Joaquim José da Silva Xavier as that "madman who had come down from the mountains of Minas Gerais with the crazed notion of making himself king of Brazil." This idea was all the more laughable today, since here, along streets where the Tooth-Puller had taken his last walk to the scaffold and dismemberment; the people often raised their voices exultantly to greet the carriages of true royalty.

For their subjects, nothing was so uplifting as the sight of an emperor and his family, in whose veins flowed the noblest blood of Europe.

Insane Maria I of Portugal had remained queen, with her son, João, carrying out her royal duties as regent. Dom João would have preferred nothing more than the peace of the monastery at Mafra. Instead, he had to make some of the most painful decisions ever thrust upon a prince of Lisbon.

On August 12, 1807, France and her ally, Spain, had demanded that Portugal declare war on England, close her ports to English ships, and imprison English residents and confiscate their property.

Instead of waiting for the inevitable defeat of Portugal's small, ill-equipped army, Dom João and his ministers considered a daring plan: Why not move the court to America? From late September until mid-November 1807, Dom João and his ministers had engaged in a dangerous game of diplomacy. They offered to sign a secret treaty with the British to compensate them if they had to be denied access to the ports of Portugal. In return, England would provide an escort to Brazil for the Braganças if flight became imperative. This treaty had been signed in London on October 22, 1807.

Two days earlier, Dom João had informed the French that Portugal was closing her ports to the British. But Napoleon still demanded the detention of English residents. Dom João and his council had agreed to this, but several days before the proclamation, England's minister at Lisbon, Lord Strangford, was forewarned so that English residents could depart safely.

For a week, with a British squadron off the mouth of the Tagus, Dom João had waited for the French response to his decree against the English residents. Napoleon's answer came on November 23: General Andoche Junot and his army crossed the northern border of Portugal. And from Paris had come news of a pronouncement from Emperor Napoleon himself: "The House of Bragança has ceased to reign in Europe."

The *Principe Real*, carrying Queen Maria, Dom João, and his sons, had made its landfall at the Bay of All Saints on January 17, 1808. Within four days of Dom João's arrival, the prince regent had agreed to open Brazil's major ports to friendly nations and to permit free trade between his vassals and foreigners, thus demolishing the cornerstones of Lisbon's three-hundred-year-old policy of monopolizing and exploiting the wealth of Brazil.

The proclamations aimed at improving conditions in Brazil had not ceased. At Rio de Janeiro, where the House of Bragança had quickly taken root in its lush tropical domain, along with more than twelve thousand refugees, reforms that had been unthinkable at faraway Lisbon were magnanimously granted. Royal edicts abolished all restrictions on manufacturing and industry, and printing presses were permitted; schools of medicine and surgery and academies of higher education were established; a Bank of Brazil was founded; foreigners were welcome.

Within ten months of the Braganças' departure from Portugal, a British force defeated the French. Dom João could've returned, but the French had overrun Spain, and the prince regent thought it wiser to stay in Brazil while the Iberian Peninsula remained a battlefield.

On December 16, 1815, Dom João elevated Brazil from a colony to a kingdom coequal with Portugal. Three months later, Dona Maria died. Dom João became king —João VI of Portugal, João I of Brazil — and still he refused to return to Lisbon.

From his vantage point at Rio de Janeiro, Dom João had observed the beginnings of the disintegration of the Spanish viceroyalties, and deemed it inadvisable to return home until his kingdom of Brazil was safe from contamination by the revolutionary turmoil beyond its borders. Besides, there was a conquest on which His Majesty had set his heart since arriving in America: the Spanish province of the Banda Oriental, east of the Rio Uruguay and extending south to the Rio de la Plata.

Spanish America had witnessed the first rebellion against vice-regal authority in 1810: At Buenos Aires, capital of the extensive viceroyalty of La Plata, a junta had arrested and deported the viceroy. As the Buenos Aires republicans moved closer to a full declaration of independence, they struggled to unite the provinces of La Plata. An early loss to this cause was Paraguay, which had always resented the wealthy and politically powerful *porteños*, those who lived in the port city of Buenos Aires, one thousand miles down the Paraguay and Paraná rivers. Paraguay was declared an independent republic in 1812.

Like the Paraguayans, the sixty thousand inhabitants of the Banda Oriental, led by José Gervasio Artigas, did not want to submit to Buenos Aires and agitated for a loose federation of the La Plata provinces. When, on July 9, 1816, the independent Republic of Argentina — a Latinization of the Spanish "Plata" — was born, José Artigas persisted in his refusal to accept the central authority of the porteños. It had seemed that the Banda Oriental would follow the example of Paraguay, but then Artigas made a fatal error: Bands of his gaucho cavalry violated Brazilian soil, infiltrating into Rio Grande do Sul in 1817.

Dom João sent his forces against Artigas, contemplating a swift campaign to settle the ownership of the Banda Oriental. But bands of gaucho guerrillas continued to harass the Portuguese for three years. By 1820, however, they had been decimated, Artigas had taken refuge in Paraguay, and at last the way had been open for annexation of the Banda Oriental as the Cisplatine Province of Brazil.

Dom João had made his conquest, but his satisfaction had been ruined by events in Portugal. Revolutionaries had convoked the Cortes, the Portuguese parliament, for the first time since its suppression in 1689 and demanded the return of the Braganças and the king's adherence to a proposed constitution.

Among those gathered to bid farewell to the king had been a handsome young man: Crown Prince Pedro. In his son, Dom João had seen hope of preserving intact the Braganças' American estate. "You will maintain our family's presence as my regent," Dom João instructed Pedro. "But should Brazil decide to separate herself from Portugal, let it be under your leadership, my son, not that of an adventurer, since you are bound to respect me."

At the time of the Braganças' flight to Brazil, Prince Pedro had been ten years old. Short and stocky, with a handsome face dominated by large brown eyes, Dom Pedro had thrived in his exotic place of exile. Generous and friendly, Pedro was also impulsive, emotional, and had shown a passion for lovemaking. Week after week, he would hasten from São Cristovão in search of new lovers from all classes and races.

When Pedro was eighteen, Dom João had dispatched a mission to Europe charged with finding a wife for his son. At Vienna, the matchmakers had gained for Pedro the hand of the Archduchess Maria Leopoldina, daughter of Francis I of Austria and great-granddaughter of Maria Theresa. In 1817 the plain, flaxen-haired Leopoldina had sailed for Brazil where she married Pedro, two years her junior.

Pedro had been awed by his wife's superior intellect, particularly her abiding interest in botany and mineralogy. But neither marriage to Leopoldina nor the birth of his first child, Princess Maria da Glória in 1819, had distracted Pedro from his paramours.

When King João sailed for Portugal, the twenty-two-year-old Pedro had been ill-prepared for his duties as prince regent of Brazil. But able advisers from among the Portuguese and mazombo aristocracy had surrounded him, and they guided him through a stormy eighteen months as his regency followed an increasingly divergent path from that sought for it by the Lisbon Cortes.

With King João back on Portuguese soil, the Cortes had insisted — on the pretext that the heir to Lisbon's throne should be given a sound European education — that Pedro and his family also return to Europe. But, at Rio de Janeiro, Prince Pedro had been presented with a petition signed by eight thousand citizens calling on him to resist the Cortes' demand. "For the good of all and the general happiness of the nation, I am ready," Pedro had announced. "I will stay!"

Nine months passed during which Brazil had drifted further from the grasp of the Cortes. Dom Pedro had formed a new ministry, which included a distinguished Paulista intellectual, José Bonifácio de Andrade e Silva, the first Brazilian to hold the key post of minister of the kingdom. And the prince had convened a constituent assembly, with representatives from the provinces, as the former captaincies were known.

The final break with the Cortes — and Portugal — had come on September 7, 1822. Dom Pedro had traveled to São Paulo to unify resistance against the Cortes and was returning to that city after a brief visit to the port of Santos when court messengers from Rio de Janeiro overtook his party at a small stream called Ipiranga. They were carrying dispatches from Minister José Bonifácio, who submitted the Cortes' latest decrees revoking the Brazilian assembly as a rebel body and calling for the dismissal of Dom Pedro's ministers, whom they declared to be traitors.

There was a letter, too, from Dom Pedro's wife, Leopoldina: "Pedro, this is the most important moment of your life. Today, Brazil, which under your guidance will be a great country, wants you as her monarch." Leopoldina and José Bonifácio urged Pedro to declare himself either king or emperor of Brazil.

Dom Pedro had made his decision, beside the stream at Ipiranga: "I proclaim Brazil forever separated from Portugal! From this day hence, our motto is: Independence or Death!"

Emperor Pedro was crowned in the cathedral at Rio de Janeiro on December 1, 1822, commencing a nine-year reign that had been agitated from the start. Even as he sat on his coronation throne, the northern provinces of Bahia, Maranhão, and Grão Pará were still controlled by forces loyal to the Cortes. To expel the Portuguese garrisons, Dom Pedro had sought the assistance of an Englishman, Admiral Thomas Cochrane. With Cochrane commanding a "fleet" of two battle-ready ships and with Brazilian patriots attacking them on land, the last Portuguese garrisons had surrendered by August 1823.

Emperor Pedro had counseled the constituent assembly that the committee responsible for drafting a constitution must produce a document worthy of him and of Brazil. The assembly had considered it their right to present a constitution to which the Crown should adhere no matter what Dom Pedro thought of it. By the time a document was put before the assembly that September of 1823, the debate had grown so acrimonious that Dom Pedro dissolved the assembly and sent several members into exile, including the former minister José Bonifácio de Andrade e Silva.

Emperor Pedro and his Council of State collaborated on a new constitution for the Brazilians, which provided for a moderating power for the emperor: Among his rights were the appointment of one-third of the senators and the appointment and dismissal of ministers of state.

At Pernambuco, following the constitutional crisis, four northeastern provinces declared their independence as the Confederation of the Equator. Six months later, the last republican stronghold had fallen: Fifteen ringleaders had been executed by a firing squad.

Despite this success against the republicans of Pernambuco, Dom Pedro's image had been steadily deteriorating among loyal Brazilians who found his partiality toward the Portuguese infuriating. Dom Pedro also suffered an irremediable blow to his esteem when trouble again arose in the far south, in what was now known as the Cisplatine Province: In 1825 a group of thirty-three guerrillas encouraged by the Buenos Aires government crossed into the territory from Argentina to liberate it from the Brazilians. Within three years, following a war between Brazil and the Argentine confederation, the conquests east of the Rio Uruguay had been lost.

Throughout these years of controversy and conflict, Dom Pedro's private life, too, had left much to be desired, especially among mazombos who were distressed to see the emperor engaged in scandalous pursuit of new loves.

Pedro had taken as favorite concubine Domitila de Castro, a vivacious Paulista in her twenties, and had installed her in a mansion at Rio de Janeiro, where she had given birth to a succession of royal bastards. Domitila had been honored by her lover, first with the title of Viscountess, then with Marchioness of Santos; the firstborn love child had been acknowledged by Dom Pedro and ennobled as the Duchess of Goiás.

The erudite Empress Leopoldina had mostly suffered in silence, while bearing her unfaithful spouse's many children. Besides their firstborn, Maria da Glória, there were three other princesses and three princes, two of whom died in infancy, the third, Pedro de Alcantara, born on December 2, 1825 — Just over a year later, Dona Leopoldina herself died after a miscarriage.

A remorseful Dom Pedro set about reforming his ways. He sacrificed Domitila and sought a new bride. His emissaries succeeded in gaining for Pedro the hand of an enchanting Bavarian princess, Amélie of Leuchtenberg, granddaughter of Napoleon and Josephine Beauharnais.

Dom Pedro celebrated the arrival of his seventeen-year-old bride by creating the Order of the Rose in her honor: Love and Fidelity was its motto.

In the euphoric months after Princess Amélie's arrival, Pedro had been encouraged to set up a moderate cabinet comprised for the first time of Brazilians, but reactionary Portuguese intimates had induced him to dismiss this ministry. Street battles broke out in Rio de Janeiro — "The Night of the Beer Bottles" — between Portuguese absolutists and Brazilians. Members of the assembly petitioned the emperor to reverse his decision. Again he appointed a Brazilian cabinet, without success: Within seventeen days, those ministers had been thrown out of office and a pro-Portuguese cabinet once more installed. On April 6, 1831, thousands of protestors took to the streets; by midnight, the emperor faced a full-blown revolution, with the Rio de Janeiro garrison joining the street mobs.

Dom Pedro agreed to leave Brazil immediately for Europe, abdicating in favor of his son, Dom Pedro de Alcantara, who was then five years old.

છ

In September 1855 Pedro Segundo was twenty-nine, with manners and appearance the very image of imperial dignity. His Majesty was over six feet tall. His countenance was frank and open, aided in this effect by direct blue eyes; his hair and full beard were a light golden brown.

Three years after the abdication, Pedro I died in Portugal. Thus, at the age of eight, Pedro Segundo had been orphaned, and to the regency that ruled Brazil during Pedro's minority, and his governesses and tutors, was given a unique opportunity to instill in him those attributes of justice, wisdom, and honor they deemed most desirable in a benevolent monarch.

As he grew older, the regents and ministers of state had broadened the boy emperor's knowledge of his domain, which, during the nine years of the regency, had often seemed to be on the point of disintegration, through regional violence and sedition.

The boy emperor had been instrumental in preventing the breakup of the empire, for he had been adopted with affection by the Brazilian people and served as a powerful symbol of national unity. In 1840, at a critical period of the regional conflicts and when the assembly itself was shaken by disunity, Pedro was only fourteen — four years short of his majority — but, in response to the wishes of the assembly, he agreed that he was ready to oversee the affairs of his subjects. The assembly proclaimed him sovereign of Brazil, and the following year, he was crowned as emperor.

Dom Pedro, as his mentors had hoped, was adopting a benevolent and paternal attitude in his rule. For example, once a week he would receive members of his Brazilian family at court: exalted nobles, and humble Negroes, and representatives of the few remaining Tupi-Guarani clans.

Yet, for all the respect and esteem shown him, the emperor was prone to a melancholy reflected even in his dress. For official ceremonies, he would appear in full court regalia, but by choice he wore a black suit with frock coat, black cravat, and tall black silk hat, like a man in mourning. His childhood loneliness had not been relieved when a bride was brought for him from Europe: Empress Theresa, whom he married in 1843. Short, slightly lame, brown-eyed, and the essence of plainness, Dona Theresa had been twenty-one when she arrived at Rio de Janeiro.

There had been four children born between 1845 and 1848: Afonso, the firstborn, Pedro, Isabel, and Leopoldina. Within two years of their birth, both sons had died.

Dom Pedro's personal sorrows ran deep, but there was also another cause for his melancholy in the radiant tropical land he had been born to rule: He wore his crown reluctantly, yearning for the retreat of a contemplative and scholarly life and dreading the storms of statesmanship.

"Were I not emperor, I should like to be a teacher," he said on occasion. "What calling is greater or nobler than directing young minds?" Regularly, Pedro would visit schools and academies at the capital, personally inspecting their facilities and encouraging the pupils, for he was greatly distressed by the abysmal lack of education among his subjects, whose numbers had grown since his father's time to some eight million.

At the Corte, as the capital was known, Dom Pedro and his American aristocrats lived with a semblance of European elegance, scrupulously observing court etiquette, worshiping foreign ideas, and devotedly following the latest French fashions. Rio de Janeiro was slowly outgrowing its colonial jumble and squalor. Its bustling streets in the central district contained shops of French merchants and craftsmen who supplied the coveted finery; the countinghouses of English traders; the establishments of the ubiquitous Portuguese shopkeepers; and, of course, the enormous bureaucracy of imperial government, to which thousands swarmed for emoluments.

The city's oil lamps were being replaced by gaslights; unhealthy marshes on the outskirts of the Corte were being filled and drained; and across the bay, from the small port of Mauá, A Baronesa! — the first locomotive in Brazil — shrieked and roared along ten miles of track to the foothills of the Serra da Estrela and the road to Petropolis thirty miles away, the summer retreat of the emperor and his family.

The city was spreading north toward the district of the emperor's palace and south into the shadows of Corcovado and Tijuca. At the small bay of Botafago, with the Sugar Loaf to one side, between thick groves of large-leafed banana trees and stately palms, stood the sparkling white mansions of viscounts, barons, generals. Tropical plants and trees flourished, dense and deeply green, and gaudy blossoms of scarlet, lilac, and blue mixed with the rose and other European imports. In the open valleys behind the city, there was often heard the baying of hounds and bugle blasts as sturdy, pink-cheeked Englishmen thundered after their quarry. In the city itself, at the waterfront public gardens, the scene was more placid, the afternoon sun often slanting down upon a sea of bobbing lace and parasols and gently wafted fans, and high silk hats of black and gray.

But the court, the aristocrats and foreign merchants, the wealthy coffee growers — all these formed only a small upper class at the capital. Much more numerous were the free commoners and droves of wary-eyed provincials come from the sertão to behold the wonders of the Corte.

Half the city's population were black and mulatto slaves: The narrow streets teemed with half-naked men fulfilling the age-old promise that homens bons be spared the curse of manual toil in Brazil. The sun that shone on a sea of bobbing parasols at the Passeio Público elsewhere fell upon 130-pound bags of coffee borne by human transport chains whose leaders shook rattles to keep up an energetic pace; upon grand pianos lifted high and trotted through the streets by sweating Africans; upon water carriers thronging at the fountains to draw from what was still a hopelessly inadequate supply; and upon slaves for hire selling their master's fruit, fish, and poultry or bending over braziers with pots of spicy stew or waiting patiently outside their owner's establishment for those who would come to buy their labor.

Dom Pedro disliked slavery, as much from his moral upbringing as from the offense given by a horde in bondage at a capital that sought to be the Paris of America. The emperor had liberated the slaves he had inherited but dared not exceed this personal magnanimity: Talk of the emancipation of slaves stirred up the wrath of senhores de engenho and fazendeiros, whose plantations provided the empire's greatest wealth. Sugar, cotton, tobacco — all continued to yield good profits, but today's El Dorado was *coffea arabica*.

The coffee groves from those first seeds brought from French Guiana to Pará in 1726 and experimented with elsewhere in the north by growers like Padre Leandro at the aldeia of Nossa Senhora do Rosário had provided seedlings sent to the south before the turn of the century. Today, in the valleys behind Rio de Janeiro and spreading west to the province of São Paulo were tens of millions of coffee trees providing a bountiful export and firmly establishing in the south the same latifundia as existed in the north. And like the independent lavradores who had lost their cane fields to the big engenhos, southern smallholders in the path of coffee's advance were pushed out or absorbed as agregados by the fazendeiros.

From the Corte, Dom Pedro Segundo looked upon the poor and landless, who were the majority of his Brazilian family, with paternal and Christian concern. In a sense, the emperor was the erudite and aloof senhor de engenho of the great estate of Terra de Santa Cruz, with his capital as Casa Grande and an educated and landowning minority there to help him develop his vast plantation. And spread throughout his holdings were millions of vassals who lived as had their ancestors in positions of servility and with little opportunity to possess the smallest part of the patrimony of Senhor Dom Pedro. They had experienced few changes in the years since their country had taken its place among independent nations, and for some of them, things would seem to have grown worse — like the child Antônio Paciência of Fazenda da Jurema, who was torn from his mother and taken a thousand miles and more through the sertão; Antônio Paciência, who had only the vaguest knowledge of this grand patrão and none at all of the freedoms protected by His Majesty.

ひつ

At daybreak on January 28, 1856, Antônio Paciência and seventy male slaves were awakened by their overseer guards in one of three barnlike dormitories on the fazenda of Saturnino Rabelo. The column had reached the fazenda near Sorocaba, sixty miles west of São Paulo, at the beginning of December; since then, the slaves who had come sixteen hundred miles through the northeast sertão and over the highlands of Minas Gerais had found life at Rabelo's barracks surprisingly easy.

Antônio Paciência was now nine, still very much the thin, gangly youth tall for his age, but with a longing, distant look in his big brown eyes. On the long march, he had learned much from the slave Policarpo, and others, all of whom had counseled him to abandon hope of returning to Jurema.

On the last stage of the journey, one theme had dominated the concerns of Policarpo and other slaves: the senhor to whom they would be sold.

Policarpo, from Mozambique, was in his late twenties. He had had two masters in the thirteen years he had been in Brazil — one a Recife merchant, a Portuguese Jew, and the other a cotton grower.

"Why did the Jew sell you?" Antônio Paciência had asked.

"Why?" Policarpo said. "I don't know why. Nothing was said: One morning we got up and were ready for work, but were taken to the slave market instead."

"Your master was angry?"

"He was calm. He took us to the market, with the few things we owned. That was the last we saw of him."

"And the other one? Why did he sell you?"

"Pascoal Sampião? Ai, yes — God *is* merciful."

The cotton grower and his overseers had lashed Policarpo and locked him up in the *tronco,* the stocks, more times than he could remember. "Not the tronco simples," Policarpo added, when Antônio Paciência mentioned that his stepbrother had sometimes sat with his legs in the tronco at Jurema for being filled with cachaça. "The tronco duples!" Policarpo said, holding his wrists up and giving a look of mock terror. "*Tronco diabo!*" The double stocks, where you sat with your body hunched forward, your legs through two lower holes, your arms through two upper holes, for the duration of your punishment, day and night.

"Pray, boy, that the one who buys you is not like the keeper of dogs I knew," Policarpo had said.

"My senhor will be a good master," Antônio Paciência had replied, with blind confidence.

At the fazenda of Saturnino Rabelo, for almost two months now, Antônio Paciência had eagerly awaited the day he would see his new owner. For the first two weeks, there had been no work, just hours lazing beneath the trees outside the dormitories. Morning and night, they were fed copious quantities of food. During the next six weeks, they had worked in Saturnino Rabelo's fields.

"Why doesn't the Portuguese bring our new owners?" the boy asked Policarpo.

"Patience, Antônio *Paciência!* Patience," Policarpo said. "They'll come."

"Why do we wait?"

"Look around you, boy. What do you see?"

Antônio Paciência didn't know what Policarpo was driving at. "Slaves?" he ventured.

"Slaves, yes — slaves who walked sixteen hundred miles. This Saturnino Rabelo sees, too, and he doesn't hurry us to market. Even the smallest calf like Antônio Paciência must be fattened for the better price he will fetch!"

This January morning, when the bell rang and the overseers hollered for all to rise, the slaves knew that the days of fattening were over: At roll call the previous evening, Rabelo had announced that the first group of fazendeiros with whom he dealt were coming to make their selection. Rabelo had exhorted the slaves to do their utmost to gain acceptance by the senhores: "You'll be inspected: Stand straight; keep your eyes bright and lively. You'll be asked questions: Answer immediately — no lies, only the truth."

Antônio Paciência got up off the straw mat where he slept. He walked behind Policarpo as the slaves filed out of the dormitory and streamed toward an open cooking area, where others who had woken earlier stood at cauldrons of porridge and weak coffee.

After the meal, 175 slaves were separated into batches: those in prime condition, who were to be sold individually; a mix of the strong and the weak, to be offered in lots; thirty-eight women and girls to one side; and the *moleques* — little black boys — and three mulatto children, Antônio Paciência among them, kept separately.

When the slaves were settled down and ready for the fazendeiros, Saturnino Rabelo walked among them, showing special satisfaction with the appearance of Policarpo and thirty other males whom he considered his most outstanding stock. Their upper torsos gleamed in the sunlight, a glossy, healthy sheen obtained as the result of Saturnino Rabelo's longstanding instructions that prior to auction, the skin of peças be rubbed with pan grease.

By ten o'clock, Saturnino Rabelo was conducting three parties of prospective buyers on an inspection of the slaves. Rabelo was particularly attentive to one fazendeiro who was seeking no fewer than thirty purchases and whom he knew to have the means for this enormous investment. Rabelo escorted the fazendeiros from one group of slaves to another and was quick to point out desirable features:

"Not a raw savage among them; each one broken in by his owner in the north," Rabelo said to the fazendeiro. "Not one with less than five years' service. I suppose the Englishmen must be thanked for this: Without them, there would have been no need to drive the slave herd from north to south. But damn them anyway! I was a wealthy man, senhor. British cruisers took my ship in the bay of Porto Seguro — my ship and eight hundred slaves! I ask you, Your Honor, was that not plain theft? Was it not an invasion of Brazil's waters?"

Since 1819, the British antislavery movement had been agitating for an end to the slave traffic between Africa and Brazil. An abolition law providing stiff penalties for importing blacks, confiscation of slavers' ships, and liberation of their captives had been passed in 1831. During the next twenty years, despite the law and patrols by British cruisers ordered to enter Brazilian territorial waters in pursuit of illegal slavers, at least 600,000 Africans had been landed in Brazil.

By the month of May 1850, when Saturnino Rabelo had been caught at Porto Seguro, the aggressive stance of the British navy in invading Brazilian territorial waters and threatening a blockade of Brazil's ports had finally led to an effective ban on the African slave traffic by the imperial government at Rio de Janeiro. And by 1853, the illegal imports had dropped to a few hundred. In the three centuries since Nicolau Cavalcanti, the founder of Engenho Santo Tomás, had stood on the beach at Recife to greet the arrival of the first sixty peças shipped from Mpinda at the mouth of the Congo, 3,650,000 blacks had been transported to Brazil, almost ten times the number that had reached English America.

"Eight hundred slaves, senhor," Saturnino Rabelo continued to complain. "I was locked up for a year and fined — it's been five years and I *still* owe others for loans to pay those fines."

"Some fine-looking blacks here, Saturnino Rabelo," the fazendeiro said, observing the group with Policarpo. "You chose well."

"Thank you, Your Honor. I never buy one I haven't personally inspected. When we arrive to buy slaves for the south, their owners will do anything to hide their vices and defects. And the cost? Each journey I make, they ask for more money."

The ban on the slave trade between Africa and Brazil had come at a time when the coffee growers' demand for labor was never greater, with their boom crop already contributing half of the world's supply: Thus this new traffic within Brazil, thousands of slaves being bought and transported annually through the sertão, like Rabelo's column, or huddled together on the decks of ships sailing from northern ports to Rio de Janeiro and Santos. The inter-provincial slave traffic was as barbarous as the African trade had been, but was sanctioned by the imperial government.

The fazendeiro to whom Saturnino Rabelo addressed his remarks was in his late sixties, a man of medium height and dignified bearing, who, despite the heat, wore a frock coat of English broadcloth, black trousers, and a high black silk hat that made him seem taller than he was. His upright carriage was helped, too, by a corset, which, though now out of fashion, the fazendeiro continued to use, suffering the discomfort of tight stays rather than reveal a spreading paunch. He had deep-set eyes, gray-green and flinty, and a broad forehead. His full mustache and whiskers were white and perfectly groomed. He carried a light cane, and about his neck he wore a gold chain reaching to a heavy watch fob in his waistcoat pocket. A sweet and powerful perfume didn't quite mask the unpleasant odor from a body encased in apparel more suited to northern climes.

Walking just behind the fazendeiro was a pale, slender youth, the fazendeiro's grandson. The young man was dressed in similar fashion with frock coat and black hat. He had similar gray-green eyes, with a brightness that contrasted strikingly with his earnest countenance. The youth was a student at the São Paulo school of law, where he should have been in attendance but for his recuperation from a serious stomach ailment.

The fazendeiro carrying himself with all the dignity of an English country gentleman was Ulisses Tavares da Silva, the son of Silvestre Pires da Silva, who had been the first to break from the nomadic ways of his bandeirante ancestors and from the daring canoe convoys of his own father, Benedito Bueno, grand admiral of the seasonal monsoons. Silvestre da Silva had turned his back on the mighty rivers and infinite sertão to devote himself to his nine children and the raising of sugarcane at Itatinga, there within a great bend of the Rio Tietê, 125 miles north-northwest of the city of São Paulo.

Ulisses Tavares had been studying law at Coimbra University in Portugal in 1807 when the Braganças moved to America; but the eighteen-year-old Paulista along with some fellow students, stayed in the beleaguered country and took up arms against the French. In September 1810, seven months before the French were finally expelled from the kingdom, Ulisses Tavares, now lieutenant of the infantry, was wounded at Bussaco, where 51,000 British and Portuguese had defeated 65,000 Frenchmen. When he was fully recovered, he did not complete his studies at Coimbra but, in 1811, returned to Brazil.

In 1816, Ulisses Tavares had again gone to war, this time during the conquest of the Banda Oriental, returning to Itatinga in 1819 with all the honors of a war hero. He had gone into politics, first on the county level at Tiberica, then in provincial government on the eve of Pedro I's call for independence at Ipiranga. His politics were conservative and strongly antirepublican, influenced by Silvestre, who had remained an avowed monarchist and liked to cite the fate of his cousin André Vaz da Silva, a participant in the Inconfidência Mineira. (A report had reached Itatinga six years after André's banishment to Mozambique: The exile had died of fever in September 1798 while exploring Central Africa.)

However, there was one royal personage for whom Ulisses Tavares had only contempt: Emperor Pedro I. As a veteran of the conquest of the Banda Oriental, Ulisses Tavares had been disgusted by the loss of that new Cisplatine Province of Brazil in 1828. He had not served in that second war, for in the year of the insurgency, Silvestre Pires da Silva died and responsibility for Itatinga had passed to Ulisses.

Like others, Ulisses Tavares believed that Brazil's natural southern boundary lay at the Rio de la Plata. *"Uruguay!"* There was always derision in his expression of the new country's name. "We were robbed of our territory by bandits — and by an emperor who surrendered the most vulnerable flank of his realm!"

Ulisses Tavares had continued in provincial politics during the early years of Dom Pedro Segundo's reign, but had become increasingly involved with the development of Itatinga. In the mid-1830s, fazendeiros above the Rio Tietê and northeast of Itatinga had begun to grow coffee. A decade later, Ulisses Tavares decided to undertake a month-long tour of Rio Claro, Campinas, and other districts in this area, and came to the realization that the rolling hills behind the riverine headland at Itatinga were ideal for coffee bushes, since they were rich in *terra roxa*, the purple earth, considered most suitable for this crop. By 1855, the fazendeiro was working 112 slaves at Itatinga and had planted more than 300,000 coffee bushes on one thousand acres of land.

On January 10, 1853, Dom Pedro Segundo, in recognition of the fazendeiro's services to the empire, made Ulisses Tavares da Silva a baron, with his title derived from the great lands he owned: Barão de Itatinga.

Accompanied by his favorite grandson, Firmino Dantas da Silva, the baron strode slowly among the slaves at the barracks of Saturnino Rabelo this January morning, halting often to single one out with his cane and quickly bringing the individual to his feet.

"What is your name?"

"Policarpo, senhor."

"Where do you come from?"

"Mozambique, Master."

Saturnino Rabelo interjected: "In my fields, Your Honor — a strong and uncomplaining worker." There was a belief that blacks from Mozambique and Angola were natural enemies of labor, as opposed to those from the Gold Coast, who had a reputation for diligence.

"Do you want to work for me, Policarpo Mossambe?"

"Yes, senhor. I will work." Policarpo's head was bowed.

"Docile, Barão," Rabelo suggested. "The Pernambucano who owned him was a thorn in the side of slaves, a man not to be disobeyed."

"Nor I, Senhor Rabelo." Ulisses Tavares jabbed the air with his cane. "Turn around," he told Policarpo, and pointed to scars on the slave's back. *"Docile?"*

"The Pernambucano wasn't a patient man, and his overseers were freed blacks who believed the chicote was the only means of teaching right from wrong."

"But did this Mossambe learn?"

"I believe he did."

"How would you know, Rabelo?"

"Policarpo gave no trouble on the journey. When he was rested, I put him among the sugarcanes. A good worker, Your Honor."

Ulisses Tavares's brow contracted. "Why did they beat you, Policarpo Mossambe?"

"It was necessary to learn, Master." Policarpo knew well enough not to challenge the reasons for his lashings, here in front of a senhor who might be his next owner.

"You learned obedience and respect?"

"Yes, senhor . . . I learned."

"I hope so, Policarpo Mossambe." And, to Rabelo: "I'll buy this Mossambe."

"Yes, Your Honor!"

"Jesus Christ be praised!" Policarpo intoned. An illegal import to Brazil, Policarpo bore no royal brand on his breast, but a traveling padre had baptized him at the fazenda of Pascoal Sampião. Not once had Policarpo been inside a church, and the mysteries of the faith were unknown to him, but he had learned that such statements pleased masters.

"Praise Him," Ulisses Tavares responded just above a whisper.

Policarpo stepped over to eleven chosen slaves, who murmured approval of his selection, for he was popular among them.

Ulisses Tavares took almost two hours to pick twenty-five males and five females. The other coffee growers, also from the district of Tiberica, were men with smaller properties and great respect for the barão; they waited until he had made his selection before indicating the sixteen slaves they wanted to buy.

Antônio Paciência sat with the moleques and the two other mulatto boys. He had seen Policarpo taken from the main group and had kept his eyes on Policarpo's new owner, hoping that the fazendeiro would come to him. But the White Beard had not done so, and sitting there in the hot sun, realizing that Policarpo would soon leave him, Antônio Paciência felt again the misery of parting such as he had known that day at Fazenda da Jurema.

An hour passed before the sale was concluded. The overseers the fazendeiros had brought to Rabelo's barracks stepped up to claim their new charges.

Suddenly there was a shout, and a black boy next to Antônio Paciência scrambled to his feet.

"You, too!" one of Rabelo's guards shouted. "All of you! Get up!"

Antônio Paciência was the last to rise.

"Over to the senhores. Quickly! Quickly!"

They were lined up in front of the veranda. The White Beard stepped down to them with Rabelo.

Antônio Paciência felt his limbs trembling, but he tried to stand up straight. He felt fright and shame but a desperate hope, too, that he would go with Policarpo. *Please, Mãe Mônica,* his thoughts appealed. *Policarpo is good to me.*

Ulisses Tavares did not take long to make up his mind. Even as he stepped toward the boys, he had immediately liked the look of the dark-skinned mulatto, with his big eyes and open, honest face.

"What's your name, boy?"

"An — tônio Paciência."

The baron smiled. "Where did you get such a name?"

"From Mãe Mônica . . . senhor."

"Do you want to come with me, Antônio Paciência?"

He looked up, and in his relief, he smiled. "Oh, yes, senhor . . . thank you, senhor!"

ตง

Antônio Paciência and the thirty adult slaves bought for Itatinga were transported from Rabelo's barracks in two mule-drawn wagons that reached Tiberica on January 31, 1856. Ulisses Tavares da Silva and Firmino Dantas had kept ahead of the wagons, spending the two nights at fazendas of relatives along the way; when the slaves arrived at Tiberica, the barão and his grandson were waiting for them.

Late this morning, the wagons were pulled up to one side of the town square in the shade provided by the walls of a pretentiously huge church, the building of which had started thirty-three years ago in the days of Silvestre da Silva. Tiberica was now a busy provincial center with eighteen hundred inhabitants, but the church was still far from complete, though a section had been roofed and consecrated for worship.

The slaves were warned not to wander away from the wagons, which would have been difficult with the overseers watching them from the front of a store where they had gone to quench their thirst, one with doses of cachaça, the two others with warm drafts of Tennant's fine English ale.

Now the senhor barão's grandson came over to the wagons:

"Boy!" Firmino Dantas called to Antônio Paciência. "Come with me!"

Firmino Dantas headed toward the most prosperous store in Tiberica — Silva and Sons — which belonged to José Inocêncio da Silva, Andre Vaz's orphaned son, who had been raised by Silvestre da Silva.

Antônio Paciência hesitated when he saw Firmino Dantas at the entrance to the store.

"Don't be afraid."

Antônio Paciência took a few steps forward but again stopped.

"Come, child. The senhor is waiting."

Firmino Dantas looked at him sympathetically. "This is not a punishment. No one will hurt you."

What does the master want with me, Mãe Mônica? He shuffled forward nervously.

Twenty minutes later, as he stepped out of the store, Antônio Paciência had a partial answer to these questions, which only increased his confusion. Inside the store, he had been treated with amazing kindness. The senhor barão himself had gone across to a tall glass jar, lifted out a ball of pink candy, and popped it into Antônio Paciência's mouth. Never had he tasted such a marvelous sweet! Then the senhor barão had given him a white blouse of soft cotton with a big collar, long gray trousers with thin red stripes down the sides, and, most impressive of all, a pair of bright red braces with which his pants were hitched up. He had not been given shoes, for those were not for slaves, and the senhor barão, amid the satisfaction he showed in having Antônio Paciência dressed so handsomely, had warned that he expected the boy to take great care with these clothes that had cost many reis. "Oh, yes, senhor! My beautiful clothes! Oh, my Master, Antônio Paciência will look after them!"

Outside the store, Antônio Paciência again hesitated momentarily at Firmino Dantas's order to walk ahead. He was afraid that out in the open, sitting on the ground with the other slaves, he might spoil the wonderful new clothes he had been given.

There was no need for Antônio Paciência to worry about spoiling his clothes. Firmino Dantas took him to the barão's open carriage, where he was put beside the driver for the trip to Itatinga. The carriageman was a mulatto slave, a great burly fellow called Cincinnato, who put on a friendly display of mock obeisance to the boy, bowing to him, praising his garments, and helping him up to the carriage seat.

For the first time since leaving Jurema, the boy took a delight in the journey. Six miles north of Tiberica, the carriage entered the da Silva property, the clatter of iron-shod hooves sending flocks of brilliant-feathered birds into the highest branches of the forest. The jungle was alive with sound and color and exotic plants unknown to Antônio Paciência. He gazed about him in awe and a little fear.

Three miles from the main settlement at Itatinga, the forest ended abruptly at the line of advance of the newest clearings. Majestic tree trunks still dotted the hillsides, their columns tall, black, and blasted by the inferno that had raged around them. Half a mile onward and the scene again changed, with the first rows of dark green young coffee plants waving amid a protective growth of other crops. Nearer the settlement, endless rows of older trees up to twelve feet high grew on the hillsides.

Some agregados had built their homes beside the road. Those outside when the baron's carriage approached greeted it respectfully, men removing their hats and pressing them to their chests, women bending their bodies with a motion suggestive of a royal curtsy.

Two hours after leaving Tiberica, the carriage crested a hill beyond which the ground sloped gently to the headland at the great bend of the Rio Tietê, with the Place of White Stones — Itatinga. The old house of Benedito Bueno was still there, an ugly rammed-earth building now used as a coffee store and slave infirmary. Off to the right, amid tufted royal palms and luxuriant bushes and flowers, stood the mansion occupied by the barão de Itatinga and his family. It was a sprawling whitewashed building with two ells extending backward. There were twenty outbuildings, all neat and whitewashed, the largest group of which housed the slaves. One hundred yards in front of the main house was an immense open area of stamped earth, the *terreiro,* where coffee beans were dried.

Cincinnato halted the horses at the front entrance of the mansion, where a flight of stone steps led up to a small open veranda with wrought iron railings. The baron and his grandson got out of the carriage. "You, too, Antônio Paciência,"

Cincinnato said. "Climb down and wait there, at the bottom of the steps." Antônio Paciência did as he was told. "When he wants you, the barão will send for you."

"For what?"

"Be patient, Antônio. You'll find out soon enough."

Antônio Paciência waited for ten minutes. Cincinnato had taken the carriage to a shed near the house, and the boy stood watching him as he unhitched the horses.

Then the senhor barão himself appeared in the doorway: "Come up here, Antônio Paciência."

He climbed the steps quickly, but paused opposite the entrance to the house. The baron stepped across the veranda to him. "Antônio, you must learn to keep your clothes neat." The baron tugged at the tail of the boy's shirt. "Tuck it in!" When Antônio Paciência tried unsuccessfully to comply, Ulisses Tavares helped him. "There!" he said. He straightened the collar of the boy's blouse. "Good," he said, stepping back. "Good!"

At that moment, Antônio Paciência saw the young Senhor Firmino Dantas in the doorway, and with him, a little mistress in a blue dress whom the boy took to be the sister of Senhor Firmino. The sinhazinha was much younger, short and with dimpled cheeks; she moved her pink hands excitedly and kept her fiery black eyes on Antônio Paciência.

"Well?" the barão asked. "What do you think?"

"Oh, yes! Yes, Senhor Barão!" the girl exclaimed.

"He's called Antônio Paciência."

The girl giggled with delight.

Her name was Teodora Rita Mendes da Silva, and in a week's time she would celebrate her thirteenth birthday. She was tempestuous, with the fire seldom absent from her small black eyes and with a sharp tongue, but she was a lively, enchanting creature, especially when others gave her their undivided attention. This she had no difficulty at all commanding, for Teodora Rita Mendes da Silva was the wife of Ulisses Tavares, baron of Itatinga.

Two years ago, the barão, a widower for eleven years, had met the child at the house of her father, Emilio Mendes, a wealthy fazendeiro of Tiberica county and dear friend of Ulisses Tavares. The fresh bloom in Teodora Rita's rosy cheeks and her blazing eyes had warmed the heart of the then sixty-five-year-old baron. Eight months ago, an emboldened hero of Bussaco and the Banda Oriental had strapped himself into his corset and had donned his black suit for a long interview with Senhor Emilio and a request for this little flower to brighten the days of an aging barão. Senhor Emilio, an observant man, had shown no surprise, for Ulisses Tavares's visits to his house had been frequent and his doting upon the girl quite open. Senhor Emilio had no objection to the betrothal of Teodora Rita, though he wondered how long the senhor barão's ardor would last. So had many others, but not Ulisses Tavares, who after these first seven months with his child bride remained as happy and charmed as when he had first set eyes upon his little baronesa.

"Oh, yes, Senhor Barão!" Teodora Rita repeated. "What a lovely little boy!"

Antônio Paciência saw the somber-faced Senhor Firmino Dantas smile for the first time.

The baron of Itatinga's features broke into a broad grin, so pleased was he with his wife's reaction. "Antônio Paciência is yours, my sweet angel," he said. "A gift for your birthday."

XVIII

November 1864 – June 1865

*O*n November 12, 1864,after the midday meal, life aboard the packet *Marquês de Olinda* came to a standstill. The privileged among the passengers and crew retired to bunks and hammocks and wicker chairs; others sought a shaded patch of deck as the *Marquês de Olinda* steamed up the Rio Paraguay at a steady six knots. The first officer and helmsman were alert; the pilot, who they had taken on at Asunción, was gazing forward intently. Engineer's mate Manuel Pacheco was stripped to the waist standing watch over engines and steam gauges. Three firemen worked like automatons as they shoveled coal into the glowing innards of red-hot iron furnaces.

The five-hundred-ton *Marquês de Olinda*, a Brazilian merchantman, made eight round trips a year between Rio de Janeiro and Cuiabá, capital of Mato Grosso province, which remained inaccessible by overland trails.

Two days earlier, the *Marquês de Olinda* had dropped anchor at Asunción to take on coal. In this dry season, the capital of Paraguay lay thick with red dust that swirled up against one-storied houses, mud huts, and lean-tos. But construction gangs were busy at work throughout the city. Presidential palace, opera house, cathedral; shipyard, arsenal, iron foundry, telegraph office, railway — after centuries of colonial slumber, Paraguay was in the midst of an industrial revolution, attracting hundreds of skilled European engineers and craftsmen.

Aboard the *Marquês de Olinda*, as she now puffed along the Rio Paraguay, three passengers, taking their *sesta* in wicker chairs placed beneath an awning toward the ship's stern, spoke of the small republic's progress. They were Pedro Telles Brandão, a miner and rancher from Cuiabá; Coronel Frederico Carneiro de Campos, president-designate of Mato Grosso; and Sabino do Nascimento Pereira de Mendonça, a revenue inspector being sent to survey tax collection in Mato Grosso.

"I don't like it at all," Telles Brandão said. "I first made this passage nine years ago. Beyond Tres Bocas, there was nothing but Guarani and mosquitoes. At Asunción, wharves were sinking into the mud; plazas and houses looked as if they would follow, and good riddance, too. A rusty cannon here and there — not batteries of rifled pieces set to blow intruders to kingdom come! Soldiers were fewer than market women. Today the streets are filled with Guarani in uniform. I don't like the look of it."

"I agree," Mendonça said, his small brown eyes darting about. "War steamers, fortresses, guns . . ." He leaned forward in his chair, peering at Carneiro de Campos. "What for, Coronel?"

"The Paraguayans see enemies everywhere," Carneiro de Campos replied.

"For defense?" Telles Brandão queried, tugging at his full black beard. "Or aggression?"

"Against whom?" Mendonça made an expressive whistling sound. "Brazil?" He gave a short, sharp laugh. "Never! El Presidente will not be foolish enough to ignore the lessons of history: Time and again, the Guarani have been soundly defeated by our armies."

Telles Brandão was staring off to port, where crimson flamingos, rosy spoonbills, dark-colored ibis, and white storks stood motionless on the mud flats as the ship passed them; caiman lay like logs on the sandbars, felled by the heat of early afternoon.

As Telles Brandão looked out toward the riverbank, he thought of a reception he had attended in the French Embassy at Asunción six years ago. He'd met several members of the most powerful family in Paraguay, from whose ranks had come two of three presidents since independence: Don Antonio López, known popularly as "The Citizen," whose dictatorial rule lasted eighteen years; and his son Francisco Solano López, who had taken over the reins in 1862. The young López had been at the reception, a stocky man with an attractive openness about him; but Telles Brandão remembered, he had felt uncomfortable in the presence of the future president.

"Perhaps Solano López has a purpose in building his war machine," Telles Brandão said, thinking aloud.

Mendonça looked up expectantly. Coronel Frederico's eyes were half open.

"Emperor López, the Napoleon of the Plata!" Telles Brandão added, with marked scorn.

"And a crown for his Irish princess?" Mendonça said, a glint in his beady eyes.

Telles Brandão smiled at this reference to Eliza Alicia Lynch, mistress of Solano López. "You jest, Sabino. There's talk at Buenos Aires that López has crown and scepter on order from Europe."

"An old story," interjected Coronel Frederico. "It originated at Rio de Janeiro, not Buenos Aires. López was said to have made an approach to the Braganças for a marriage with one of Pedro Segundo's daughters."

"The gall of it!" Telles Brandão exclaimed. "Europe's noblest sons beg an audience with our princesses!" At Rio de Janeiro, where he'd been on a visit, Telles Brandão had witnessed the celebrations to mark the October wedding of Princess Isabel and Prince Louis Gaston d'Orleans, comte d'Eu, and the marriage planned for December between Princess Leopoldina and Prince Louis Augustus, duke of Saxe-Coburg-Gotha.

"Emperor López and La Lynch!" Mendonça said. "A royal pair on the throne of Paraguay!"

Telles Brandão had met Madame Lynch at the reception in Asunción:

"What a beauty! Her skin is alabaster; her eyes are blue-green. La Lynch is tall, with a seductive figure. When she crosses a room, from her crown of reddish hair to her small feet — a goddess!"

Telles Brandão shared what he knew of Eliza Lynch's background: "She was nine when her father, a poor merchant from County Cork, fled Ireland for France in the great famine of 1845. At fifteen, she was given to Quatrefages, a French officer, who took her to Algiers. There's some question about whether or not they married, but within the year she was back in Paris. Some say she left him for a Russian noble; some, that Quatrefages deserted her. Whatever the truth, when López met her in Paris, Eliza Lynch was nineteen and rid of Quatrefages. La Lynch has given López five sons; but the word is he'll never marry her, not while he's so eager to infuse his line with royal blood."

Coronel Federico looked up suddenly. "My friends, there's more to Paraguay than gossip about El Presidente and La Lynch," he said. "Fourteen thousand Guarani are training at the main camp at Cerro León; tens of thousands more have already been drilled and posted to other bases. Today, El Presidente addresses his barefoot regiments and speaks of defending Paraguayan soil. Tomorrow? He'll tell them no country on this continent is so powerful or has such happy citizens. He'll say, 'If only it weren't for the *macacos . . .*'"

Inspector Mendonça scowled fiercely at Coronel Frederico's use of "monkeys" as an epithet for Brazilians, but he did not interrupt him.

"López lies to them. He says Brazil and Argentina are plotting to destroy Paraguayan independence. It's all nonsense, but if El Presidente orders them to battle, they'll follow him, to the last man and boy." He gazed upriver as if searching for something on the far bank. "Mato Grosso has a few hundred soldiers and some run-down forts along hundreds of miles of borderlands that Asunción and Rio de Janeiro were arguing over when my grandfather was alive. We are at López's mercy."

"Mato Grosso?" Mendonça said in a squeaky voice. "You expect an invasion, Coronel Frederico?"

"With Solano López, I would not discount it."

"A few hundred soldiers?"

"Yes, Sabino." Coronel Frederico saw the inspector's crestfallen look. "We carry a cargo of new weapons," he reminded Mendonça. "Let the Paraguayan devils come! They'll be met with fire!"

"Ai, Jesus, pray not. Our ambassador considers it possible?"

"He doesn't like the mood of the Paraguayans. Since he got to Asunción in August, he's been living on a powder keg."

"Dear God, the news we brought with the *Marquês de Olinda*," Telles Brandão said. "It may be all that's needed to light the powder."

"Exactly what Ambassador Viana de Lima feared most."

The news the *Marquês de Olinda* carried *was* explosive. In mid-October, the Brazilian imperial army had invaded Uruguay, independent ever since Brazil lost control of the old Banda Oriental in 1828. Two parties had dominated Uruguayan politics since independence — Blancos ("Whites") and Colorados ("Reds"). The latest bloodletting had started in April 1863, when a Colorado exile, General Venancio Flores, landed on Uruguayan soil from Argentina in rebellion against a Blanco government in power at the capital, Montevideo.

For a year, as the Uruguayan civil war raged, Dom Pedro Segundo and his ministers at Rio de Janeiro followed a policy of strict neutrality. But there were forty thousand Brazilian citizens in Uruguay, many of them descendants of settlers who'd stayed behind after Brazil surrendered the Banda Oriental. These expatriates had close ties with their countrymen in Rio Grande do Sul. By May 1864, the clamor from Rio Grande do Sul about murders and cattle rustling across its border with Uruguay, and the threat to the lives of Brazilians in Uruguay itself, prompted Rio de Janeiro to send one of its ablest diplomats, José Antônio Saraiva, to seek redress from the Blanco government at Montevideo. Imperial regiments were also concentrated in Rio Grande do Sul and a naval squadron sent to cruise the Rio de la Plata.

The Blancos had rejected Saraiva's ultimatum. In October 1864, advance guards of the imperial army had crossed into Uruguay. The Brazilian naval squadron had been ordered to steam up the Rio Uruguay from the Plata to blockade the Blanco-held port of Paysandu.

As the crisis worsened, however, Francisco Solano López offered his services as mediator between Uruguay's factions, but his offer had been rejected. Thereafter, Asunción's emissaries had warned that Paraguay would regard a threat to the sovereignty of Uruguay as imperiling the stability of all nations of the Plata basin.

Aboard the *Marquês de Olinda*, Telles Brandão took a sanguine view: "How many threats and counterthreats by Paraguay and Brazil have there been in the past? How many times did tempers cool before we came to blows? López's father, Don Carlos Antonio, saw that no argument over the limits of our territories — no patch of jungle or uncharted stream — was worth the sacrifice of their small nation's blood. Solano López will also accept this."

"López gazes far beyond a contested riverbank," Coronel Frederico interjected. "He sees himself as arbiter of the Plata. Peacemaker, he tells the world. But month-by-month his army grows. And so, I believe, does the ambition of Francisco Solano López."

↧

When the *Marquês de Olinda* anchored at Asunción, bringing the news that the Brazilians had invaded Uruguay, President López had been at Cerro León, fifty miles to the southeast at the terminus of the railroad from Asunción. A special messenger had been sent by locomotive to the sprawling complex of thatched barracks and parade grounds where thousands of recruits between the ages of sixteen and sixty were in training.

The messenger had found El Presidente at ease in the camp headquarters, a low whitewashed building with a suite for His Excellency adjoining a conference room whose latticed windows opened upward, giving a view of the main parade ground. López personally had been drilling a platoon of recruits earlier that morning and wore the same uniform as his officers: scarlet military blouse with blue collar and facings, white trousers, and high black boots.

López had turned thirty-eight on July 24. His dark brown eyes were close set, slightly oblique, and rimmed with thick lashes, under prominent eyebrows — characteristic features of the purebred native. Among the Guarani and Guarani-descended mestizos, López spoke with pride of a Guarani great-grandmother, though there were malicious whispers that El Presidente's maternal forebear was from the savage Guaicuru. López's mercurial moods suggested this. The swift change from engaging charm to volcanic rage, from manic optimism to crushing despair, could be terrifying.

Among the officers with López in the conference room at Cerro León were three men of disparate background: Juan Bautista Noguera, better known to his comrades as "Cacambo," a venerable warrior of pure Guarani stock; Lieutenant Hadley B. Tuttle, an Englishman who had been at Asunción since 1859, when he joined the engineers and artisans recruited by J. & A. Blyth, London agents of the Paraguayan government; and Lucas Kruger, a U. S. citizen, who called himself an inventor and was as vague about his background as he was about the experiments he conducted in a shed at the Asunción arsenal.

General Noguera was seventy-seven, small and shriveled, with tiny hands and features ravaged by age. The general was proud of being called Cacambo, after the hero of *O Uruguai,* an epic poem celebrating Guarani resistance to the Portuguese-Spanish campaign against the seven missions. (The author of *O Uruguai* had himself taken "Cacambo" from Voltaire's *Candide.*) For Juan Bautista Noguera, the nickname had special meaning, for he was the grandson of the Guarani commander who had led the mission troops in the very battles celebrated in *O Uruguai,* and the general himself had fought the Brazilians in 1817 when they pillaged the reduction of San Carlos on the west bank of the Rio Uruguay. The Nogueras, who had got their Spanish family name in the distant past as part of the black robes' process of elevating the savages, had been forced to flee to Paraguay, where Juan Bautista had become political leader of seven former mission towns and of the few remaining groups of pure Guarani.

The Englishman, Hadley Baines Tuttle, was also a veteran of a great conflict, but rarely spoke of it. At the Crimea, he had stood at the brink of hell with the devil's laughter ringing in his ears at the stupidity and tragedy of it all, Her Majesty's starving, hollow-eyed troops as ready to fight one another as to do battle with the Russians — and for nothing more than a square of mildewed blanket or a canvas strip to wrap around their frostbitten limbs.

With the coming of winter, the single road between Balaklava and the British main forward camp opposite Sevastopol six miles away had become almost impassable, obstructing the shipment of supplies and the transport of the wounded. This disastrous condition had moved two of England's greatest railroad builders, Morton Pete and his rival Thomas Brassey, to offer to construct a railroad between the base and the camp at no profit. The first party of their voluntary corps had left Liverpool in December 1854, and nineteen-year-old Hadley Tuttle had been with them, along with an older brother, Ainsley.

Hadley had been an engineering apprentice since the age of sixteen, and when Brassey approached his master, Armstrong Hogg, for the work at Balaklava, Hadley — Hogg's brightest and favorite technician — begged to be taken along. Inspired by his younger brother's patriotism, Ainsley also joined the ranks of navvies, gangers, masons, carpenters, blacksmiths, and engineers sailing to do battle with picks and shovels, cranes and pile drivers. The men of the Light Brigade were immortal, but for thousands at the Crimea that Russian winter, the heroes of the day were those who had built the Balaklava line.

In June 1859, Hadley had been contracted by J. & A. Blyth to work as engineer/surveyor on Paraguay's railroads. Tuttle and eight others had made the long voyage together, transferring from the crack steamer that took them to Buenos Aires to an ancient paddle wheeler owned and captained by Angelo Moretti, who swilled brandy and sang day and night as he conned his smoke-belching vessel along the Paraná-Paraguay rivers with a lack of concern that brought nine young Englishmen close to mutiny. The channels he knew by instinct, the ever-changing sandbanks did not confuse him, and neither *aguardiente* nor aria affected his powers of navigation.

Tuttle's five years in Paraguay had passed swiftly, and his initial contract was renewed for an additional one hundred pounds a year. Until May 1864 he had been involved with the construction of the railroad to Cerro León and surveys for branch lines to the north and south of a junction near the military camp. Six months ago, El Presidente had asked him to serve in the Paraguayan army. Lieutenant Hadley B. Tuttle was now an assistant to another Englishman, Colonel George E. Thompson, a former British army officer.

Their services had become essential to López because of the failing health of his chief engineering officer, yet another foreigner, Lieutenant-Colonel Baron von Wisner de Morgenstern, a Hungarian with nineteen years' residence in Paraguay; his pride and joy was the Bateria des Londres, on a level cliff at Humaitá overlooking the Rio Paraguay, twenty-five miles above Tres Bocas. "The Sevastopol of South America," von Wisner called the revetted fortification with its sixteen great guns, a description that troubled Hadley Tuttle, who still recalled the horrors behind the siege lines at the Russian redoubt.

Locks of the twenty-nine-year-old Tuttle's wavy, sand-colored hair fell across his forehead; he had blue eyes that, in their steady gaze, suggested a constancy of character, and a pugnacious jaw. His manner was one of deliberation, not unlike that of his ancestor Will Tuttle, a seventeenth-century seafarer who had finally settled in London, where he had served as a dockmaster in Blackwall. Hadley Tuttle had no

knowledge of his forebear; but London's Hakluyt Society, founded in 1846 for printing accounts of voyages and travels, contained a journal that reported the following:

> *A briefe relation of the voyage of The Hopewell, a ship of London in
> the service of the King of the Portugales against the Dutch at Pernambuco in
> the yeere 1640, wherein divers rare things are truely reported, with certaine
> notes on the towne of Bayha, by Master Will Tuttle.*

Hadley was genial and gregarious, though not involved, like some of the foreign contingent, in endless rounds of parties with their whores and their passion for
Paraguayan cane brandy. The Englishman had developed a genuine feeling for Paraguay, and had given no thought to leaving Asunción as the crisis at the Plata
mounted.

Besides, Hadley Tuttle was in love. Luisa Adelaida was the eighteen-year-old
daughter of John "Scotty" MacPherson, who had come to Asunción at the same time
as Baron von Wisner. MacPherson's wife, Dona Gabriel, was from a family of
upper-class merchants, and she was practically a lady-in-waiting to Eliza Lynch. John
MacPherson, a senior engineer at the arsenal, had befriended Hadley soon after his
arrival. A year ago, Hadley became enamored of Luisa Adelaida, who had her
mother's dark hair and hazel eyes and a complexion as fair and fresh as the loveliest
Highland maid. By this month of November 1864, he was resolved to take the lovely
woman as wife, and had Scotty MacPherson's full blessing.

The other foreigner at Cerro León headquarters when Solano López was
handed the dispatch from Asunción was the mysterious Lucas Kruger. "Luke," as he
was known, was short and dumpy with a big nose, puckering lips, and a permanent
scowl. He alone wore no uniform and was shabbily dressed in dirty cotton trousers,
a frayed shirt, and upon his head, a battered straw hat that he never removed, not
even in El Presidente's presence and, some suggested, not even when he retired.
Luke's age was difficult to discern: He appeared to be in his early forties, but when he
emerged from the shed where he worked, sullen, ill-tempered, and worn-out, he
seemed much older.

"Get Luke" was the call when some piece of machinery had defeated the efforts
of others to fix it. He was respected not only for this ability to repair anything from a
broken watch to the engine of *La Golconda,* Capitán Angelo Moretti's antique paddle
wheeler, but also for his linguistic prowess: Luke spoke seven languages — an eighth,
if his growing mastery of Guarani was included.

Though born in Pittsburgh, Kruger had gone to New York as a youth and
spoke of it as his home. How he had come to Paraguay was a tale even the secretive
Luke could not suppress. At Shanghai, in 1862, Kruger met Silas J. Petrie, formerly
of New Haven, Connecticut. Petrie was on his way from Rangoon to Callao, on the
west coast of South America, with a strange cargo: four elephants, which he intended
to use as the center attraction for a traveling circus in Peru. Luke sailed with Petrie
and his pachyderms. Eighteen months later, the circus venture had failed — in La
Paz, Bolivia, which Kruger and Petrie finally reached after leading the four great
beasts on an epic plod over the Andes. Petrie then went to Lima, with a scheme to

export llamas to Asia; Kruger, hearing that technicians were in demand in Paraguay, traveled south, reaching Asunción in February 1864.

Luke had found work at the arsenal, where his mechanical aptitude was quickly recognized. Six months after his arrival, he had proposed to Baron von Wisner, chief military engineer, that even more effective, as well as less costly, than cannon-borne shells to detain the enemy were water-borne explosive devices. Given the go-ahead to experiment, Kruger had successfully demonstrated a stationary torpedo, the explosion of which was witnessed by President López; but the inventor's main efforts were directed toward developing a self-propelled weapon. López had summoned Kruger to Cerro León to report on his progress. "How much longer?" El Presidente had asked. "As long as it takes," Luke Kruger had replied laconically. "My torpedo will be a weapon against your enemies, General" — Kruger eschewed the grander addresses — "not your friends."

On November 10, 1864, at Cerro León, watched by Kruger, Tuttle, the venerable Cacambo, and other Paraguayan officers, President López had read the dispatch from Asunción with a deliberate calm, sharing aloud confirmation of the Brazilian invasion of Uruguay.

"I tried to keep the peace, God knows," López said. "Every appeal by Asunción has been dismissed with contempt."

"The macacos will not respect Paraguay until we show our teeth!" Cacambo exclaimed.

López responded directly to Cacambo: "And if the voice of Paraguay is not heard now, what nation on earth will respect us?"

"Least of all the Brazilians." The remark came from one of the Paraguayan officers, José Diaz Barbosa Vera, former chief of police of Asunción and now commander of the Fortieth Battalion, a crack unit drawn from the citizens of the capital. "They are in Uruguay for one objective: to extend the empire's influence to the Plata." Then José Diaz said portentously, "Excellency, the future of South America is in your hands."

Cacambo drew his four-foot eleven-inch frame to rigid attention. "El Libertador!" he saluted López. "El Libertador de la Plata!"

El Presidente's voice shook with emotion: "Thank God we foresaw a day of testing, that when the provocation of Brazil became too great to bear, Paraguay would be ready!"

Lieutenant Hadley Tuttle was unmoved by this combative rhetoric. He did not doubt that the Paraguayans could defend their country against attack, but he was skeptical of an offensive. There were 44,000 soldiers, three times the number in the standing Brazilian army, and perhaps sixteen thousand effectives could be added. The Paraguayans were rigorously trained: Colonel George Thompson said he knew of no soldiers subjected to and willing to accept such brutal discipline, and they would make a formidable foe. But what would they fight *with?* Tuttle wondered.

Three elite battalions were equipped with new breech-loading carbines, but thousands carried flintlock Brown Besses and old German muskets. Modern rifled cannon were being cast at the arsenal, but the artillery park consisted mostly of pieces the likes of which, in England, served splendidly as pillars and posts at military barracks. Even Humaitá's revetted batteries, of which Baron von Wisner was justifiably proud, mounted antiquated ordnance alongside new weapons.

Lieutenant Tuttle had inspected most of Paraguay's southern defenses with Colonel Thompson, and his knowledge of the limited and outdated equipment made him fear the consequences of a military adventure by López. Tuttle looked at Lucas Kruger, whom he knew only casually, hoping that Kruger, who had a reputation for bluntness with López, might introduce a cautionary note. But Luke had just stood there, with his straw hat askew and an impatient expression suggesting that he was mainly concerned about returning to his shed and his ideas.

And then came Francisco Solano López's next pronouncement:

"We asked for peace. We have their answer: war!" El Presidente's eyes bulged. "We must seize this moment or we shall have to fight at a less advantageous time in the future. My comrades! Paraguayans! We must strike now!"

❧

At 2:00 P.M. on November 12, 1864, the *Marquês de Olinda* was churning upriver, black smoke pouring from her single stack, water cascading off her side paddle wheels. Engineer's mate Manuel Pacheco came topside for a brief escape from the inferno below. The *Marquês de Olinda* had navigated three bends and was heading toward the fourth, which she now rode, when Manuel Pacheco and a lookout on duty in the bow to watch for snags and sawyers spotted a black plume rising above the low tree cover, but neither they nor others reacted instantaneously: Pacheco's first thought was that the forest was being burnt for a clearing. No other vessel was due to sail north from Asunción for two weeks. But after a few moments Pacheco knew that another vessel was closing in on the *Marquês de Olinda.* "A ship!" he shouted at the top of his lungs. "A ship coming up behind us!"

Coronel Frederico Carneiro de Campos and his companions had ended their speculation about López shortly before Pacheco gave the alarm. The coronel had fallen asleep. Telles Brandão was smoking a thin cigar and looking at the riverbank near them with an expression of utter boredom. Mendonça was dozing lightly, with his mouth hanging open. A sailor resting on the deck at their feet lifted his head at Pacheco's first cry; then he sat up, looking at the three senhores as if they could explain the presence of the other vessel.

"Coronel Frederico?" Telles Brandão stood up. "Coronel?"

Carneiro de Campos was slow to respond.

"What ship?" The question came from Mendonça and was directed at the sailor, who did not answer.

Coronel Frederico stood up groggily. "Where?"

The awning was slung aft, where the first-class accommodation was located. This area was considered safer should one of the ship's boilers explode, a not infrequent disaster, especially on steamers like the *Marquês de Olinda,* which was approaching her twentieth year of service.

As soon as he saw it, Coronel Frederico rushed off in search of the captain, whom he met hurrying up from his quarters. Together they went to the pilothouse, where the talk was swift and urgent: Clearly, the vessel riding their wake was in pursuit of the *Marquês de Olinda.*

"Why?" Mendonça asked, where he stood with Telles Brandão and the sailor.

Telles Brandão's features were fixed in a dark frown. "We'll know soon enough," he said. He looked at the smoke. "One of López's fast gunboats?" The question was addressed to the sailor.

"Yes, senhor."

"Can we outrun her?"

The sailor shook his head gravely. "No, senhor. Not the old *Marquês de Olinda.*"

"Why must we run from the Paraguayan?" Mendonça was indignant.

"Why do they send a warship after us?" Telles Brandão asked in response. "It can only mean trouble."

"But, why?" Mendonça persisted. "If there was an objection to our passage, surely they'd have detained us at Asunción."

They were interrupted by the commands of an officer, moving swiftly along the deck, calling every sailor to duty and demanding that people step away from the port bulwarks: The *Marquês de Olinda* carried more than one hundred passengers, and so many had crowded to one side that the ship was listing. Telles Brandão and Mendonça ignored the order to move back.

The sailor hesitated momentarily, then pointed out the chief engineer and Manuel Pacheco hurrying to the engine-room hatchway. "The captain has ordered more steam, more coal." He sauntered off, muttering an inaudible profanity.

The *Marquês de Olinda* was on a heading almost due west as she came round the fourth bend of the Rio Paraguay to enter a two-mile reach where the river narrowed to five hundred feet, with its main channel close to one bank, and shallows and sandbars lying toward the other. Low hills rising in the distance indicated another bend up ahead to the north. When the *Marquês de Olinda* entered the reach and raced toward the bend to the north, she was doing seven and a half knots. A fire roared in her furnaces, steam hissed from her safety valves, and a shower of burning embers rained on her deck. Still, the telltale smoke now behind the low bank opposite showed that the other vessel was gaining on them.

"Tie down the safety valves!" was the order, as the *Marquês de Olinda* neared the end of the reach. With her steam pressure raised to screaming pitch and her fireboxes overheating, the *Marquês de Olinda* left the narrows and swung north; the Rio Paraguay widened dramatically, its banks soon almost a mile apart, the surface of the river glasslike.

The *Marquês de Olinda* was doing nine knots across the slack water, her maximum speed with her safety valves closed, and standing every risk of a boiler explosion — a catastrophe in itself enough to break her back in the middle of the Rio Paraguay, but likely to be much worse with the munitions she carried.

"O Mother of God!" Mendonça cried. *"There! There! There!"* Three times he jabbed his fingers in the air to indicate the ship coming out of the narrows and speeding toward them.

She was the *Tacuari,* the pride of Francisco Solano López's river-borne navy. Built for peacetime use, the *Tacuari* had nevertheless been designed for rapid conversion to a warship; this had been done some time ago, and she now carried six guns, with a swivel cannon mounted on her poop deck.

"Mother of God!" Mendonça cried again. "What are we to do, Telles Brandão?"

"If they catch us — "

"If? They're upon us!"

"They have no right — "

"Right? Guns! They have guns!"

"Calma, Sabino."

"They can blow us out of the water," Mendonça whimpered.

"They dare not fire upon a Brazilian vessel."

"What if they do?"

"God help them. One shot and they'll have all Brazil to answer!"

The *Marquês de Olinda* was losing headway, with a crack in a pipe carrying water to a boiler. Foot by foot the *Tacuari* began to overtake her quarry, keeping about one hundred yards off to port. Her uniformed crew stood smartly at their stations, with several men gathered at two of the steamer's guns.

On the deck of the *Marquês de Olinda,* all was in chaos. Amid the flying embers and a rain of soot, a few defiant passengers stood shaking their fists and screaming curses at the *Tacuari.* Begrimed sailors emerged from the machine room, staggering up top for air after a stint of helping the *Marquês de Olinda's* firemen feed the blazing furnaces. A few marinheiros hung around at her stern and looked sharp to leap the instant her boilers blew. At her pilothouse, Coronel Frederico and the captain and officers of the *Marquês de Olinda* watched grimly as the *Tacuari* overhauled them, and they hoped for a miracle.

It did not come. The *Tacuari* ran up signal flags ordering them to stop immediately. The *Marquês de Olinda* ignored the command. And then, without warning, there was a roar and a flash, and the cannon on her poop deck threw a shell across the bows of the *Marquês de Olinda.*

Instantaneously, aboard the *Marquês de Olinda,* the order was given to shut off power. Two of her officers stood beside the pilothouse waving frantically at the Tacuari, whose men greeted this act of submission with a resounding cheer.

వ∽

On the first Saturday in February 1865, colored lanterns illuminated the gardens of the Fazenda de Itatinga and the moon silvered the Rio Tietê beyond. From within the mansion came the music of quadrille, waltz, and polka danced by the guests of the baron and baroness of Itatinga.

The seventy-five-year-old Ulisses Tavares da Silva, immaculate in black tailcoat and trousers with white waistcoat, shirt, cravat, and collar, moved through the figures of a quadrille with a lively step and with a twinkle in his eye for the baronesa. Teodora Rita had lost her youthful plumpness. Her slender waistline was pulled in tight above an immense oval-shaped skirt, with her corset rising high under her breasts and lifting them slightly.

The baronesa confounded those who had scoffed at Ulisses Tavares's infatuation with a twelve-year-old, for, growing to womanhood at his side, she had become a faithful, loving wife. And a mother, too; the barão had known a virile renewal with Teodora Rita, and they had been blessed with a son five years ago and a daughter the next year.

When the quadrille ended and Ulisses Tavares bowed gracefully to Teodora Rita, spontaneous applause for the couple filled the ballroom, on this night of a grand ball, to which 140 couples had been invited to celebrate Teodora Rita's twenty-second birthday.

Few celebrations at Itatinga had been as carefully planned as this party for Teodora Rita or so clearly marked the shift of prosperity from the engenhos of the north to the fazendas of the southern coffee growers. At Itatinga, the barão could ride for hours between endless rows of half a million coffee trees, their fragrance as strong and heady as the prospect of the fortune to be collected from branches heavy with small reddish-brown berries.

Ulisses Tavares had seven surviving children from his previous marriage, two of whom lived at Itatinga with their families: a daughter, Adélia, and Eusébio Magalhães, father of Firmino Dantas. (The baron's firstborn son, Silvestre, named for Ulisses Tavares's own father, had drowned when the ship carrying him from Lisbon after five years' study and travel in Europe was lost near the Azores.) Eusébio Magalhães, the second-born son, already in his fiftieth year, was a silent, tense man with pale eyes. He had a prodigious memory and a tendency toward obsequiousness in the presence of Ulisses Tavares. "The Bookkeeper," the baron called this son, intending praise, for Eusébio Magalhães was a wizard with figures and an excellent administrator of Itatinga.

Eusébio Magalhães and his wife, Feliciana, a matronly, mild-mannered woman, had taken a long time to adjust to Teodora Rita, whose early impudence toward Dona Feliciana had moved Ulisses Tavares himself to admonish his child bride to show consideration for his daughter-in-law. But now, as she watched the baron and his young wife pick up again and glide gracefully past her, Dona Feliciana gave them a broad smile, for perplexed as she had been and still was by her father-in-law's romance, she did not begrudge Teodora Rita admiration for the happiness the girl had brought the old man.

Ulisses Tavares and Teodora Rita had been at the top of the line of couples for the quadrille; Firmino Dantas and his partner had been at the bottom. Twenty-five years old, Firmino Dantas da Silva held a law degree from the school at São Paulo and a baccalaureate from the University of Paris. He was scholarly and serious but not pedantic, and his gray-green eyes sometimes held a restless, dreamy look. Of medium build and slender, Firmino Dantas had long, dark lashes, a straight, perfectly shaped nose, sensual lips, and a dimpled chin, which he kept shaved. The eyes of many young ladies drifted toward Firmino Dantas this night, but he was beyond reach of all save one, to whom he had been betrothed this past December.

Firmino Dantas's fiancée was nineteen, a lively, lovable girl, petite and dark-haired, with a strong face and a determined look that said something of her ambition to be Firmino's wife, a cause in which she was now certain of triumph. But then, Carlinda da Cunha Mendes had had powerful support in winning the affections of Dantas da Silva: She was the sister of Teodora Rita.

Carlinda had been a regular visitor to Itatinga before Firmino Dantas left for Paris; but, upon his return eleven months ago, the baronesa energetically set about promoting a match between them, with the support of Ulisses Tavares, whose encouragement often had the ring of command behind it. As a suitor, Firmino Dantas was absentminded and reticent. With Carlinda Mendes, he had been kept on track by the baronesa and Ulisses Tavares, who continued to coax him toward this promising and sensible union. Not that he needed coaxing; he had a genuine affection for Carlinda — and she an intense passion for him.

These past eleven months, Firmino Dantas had spent most of his time at Itatinga, and appeared reluctant to follow the practice of law, for which he had studied so long and diligently. His father, Eusébio Magalhães, had spoken with him about this, urged on by an impatient Ulisses Tavares eager for his grandson to begin a career that offered so much to the bright young men of the empire. Dom Pedro Segundo esteemed cap and gown and frock coat, and regarded the *senhores académicos* as the new pioneers who would spread law and justice through his backward and rustic realm.

"You will be leaving for São Paulo soon?" Eusébio Magalhães had suggested to Firmino one day the previous June.

"I've thought about it, Pai."

"Good." Eusébio Magalhães had looked at his son expectantly. Father and son were not close. Eusébio Magalhães and Dona Feliciana had three daughters, all married. Firmino was their only son. But they had lost him, in a way, even when he was still a boy, for he had been the favorite grandchild of Ulisses Tavares, who had involved himself in every aspect of Firmino Dantas's upbringing. The barão had never said as much, but the attention he gave this grandson was not unrelated to the loss of his own firstborn, Silvestre, for whom he had entertained high hopes.

"The barão himself is anxious to see you established."

"I understand, Pai. I won't disappoint Grandfather."

"Of course — *Doutor* Firmino Dantas." Lawyer, medical doctor, scientist, intellectual — all sons of the empire who had graduated from university earned the respectful address of "Doctor."

Suddenly, Firmino had said, "Pai! Please, come outside!"

The harvesting of mature coffee trees had begun in May, the first of the cool, dry months. From dawn until dark, 220 adult slaves and 190 agregados — tenants, sanctioned squatters, sharecroppers — worked at stripping the branches of 400,000 trees, the harvest of coffee beans expected to reach six hundred tons.

Firmino Dantas had taken his father toward the fazenda's smithy and workshops, past the terreiro, an acre-sized terrace of slate where picked berries were spread out to dry in the sun. When the skins of the fleshy berries were shriveled, hard, almost black, they were ready for processing in a water-driven mill near the terreiro.

Firmino Dantas had stopped at the mill. *"Maravilhoso!"* he had shouted sardonically above the stamp of four huge metal-shod pestles. "We live in the age of steam and invention, and here — a medieval monstrosity!"

They had watched as slave women expertly tossed the pounded berries on screens to separate them from the broken outer covering. The two beans in each berry were still sealed in a double membrane: The pounding process had to be repeated, with hand-driven *ventiladores* blowing away the chaff, and the blasts of fine dust swirling around the coughing, spitting workers.

"Six hundred tons to be fed to this monster!" Firmino Dantas had exclaimed, throwing up his hands. "Father! There has to be a better way!" And he had moved off, beckoning Eusébio Magalhães to follow him as he crossed to the fazenda's workshops.

Eusébio Magalhães and Ulisses Tavares had become aware, from Firmino Dantas's letters from Paris, that the philosophical studies intended to broaden the young lawyer's horizons had taken second place to a fascination with science and technology. They had not expected, however, that upon his return to Itatinga, after a month of brooding over the "monster" the barão regarded as one of the finest mills for a hundred miles, Firmino Dantas would suddenly be seized with the idea of building a machine to shell and clean the harvest. Ulisses Tavares had initially been indulgent, and had even encouraged the scheme by approving the purchase of a small steam engine from Rio de Janeiro, believing that Doutor Firmino Dantas's flirtation with the role of mechanic would pass quickly and was but a healthy diversion after eight long years of study.

But Firmino Dantas had remained dedicated to "The Invention," as the family called it. Repeatedly the contraption had rattled and shaken itself apart, and it lay dismantled in a sad heap, like a cast-off suit of armor. Firmino Dantas had reassembled it patiently, piece by piece, and though his invention continued to break down and spew coffee beans in every direction, he had shown no sign of abandoning the project.

The senhor barão had become impatient and not a little vexed to see his grandson laboring beside tradesmen. On this night of the ball, several times already, Ulisses Tavares had steered his grandson into the company of a district judge and a lawyer — the latter, the present incumbent of the seat Ulisses Tavares had held in the provincial assembly — in the hope that contact with these homems bons would remind Firmino Dantas of the high calling for which he had been trained.

The quadrille had been followed by a long interval during which several couples hovered impatiently beside the dance floor before the orchestra signaled they were ready to play a waltz. Three skilled musicians had been engaged from São Paulo and nine local bandsmen belonging to the Guarda Nacional of Tiberica; four Itatinga slaves, three who played fiddles, one a flute, joined them. This disparate group had been brought into harmony in only two days of practice led by M. Armand Beauchamp, master of music and dance.

Seated at an English grand piano, Professor Beauchamp played a few opening bars to alert the dancers and then paused for some moments, casting a sidelong glance at the couples and smoothing down his thick black mustache. M. Armand took pains with the upkeep of his mustache; he believed that a good mustache improved the tone of the voice, acting as a resonator and helping to conceal any distortion of the mouth in singing.

Firmino Dantas and Carlinda were first on the floor for the waltz, followed by Teodora Rita on the arm of a lieutenant of the Guarda Nacional. Ulisses Tavares stood with a smile at the sight of his bride swept along by the young officer. But after a while the barão said wistfully to a man next to him, "Oh, Clóvis, God grant that I were ten years younger this night."

Clóvis Lima da Silva was the third son of the Tiberica merchant José Inocêncio da Silva and the grandson of André Vaz, who had perished in exile in Africa. Together, Clóvis's dark eyes and slightly coppery skin hinted at his native ancestry: Through the family of André Vaz, the thirty-six-year-old Clóvis was descended from Trajano, the bastard son whom Amador Flôres da Silva had executed on his seven-year odyssey in search of emeralds. At nineteen, Clóvis had gone to the Escola Militar at Rio de Janeiro, where he had trained as an artilleryman. He had served with the army ever since and now held the rank of captain.

Clóvis da Silva knew that Ulisses Tavares's remark had nothing to do with envy of Teodora Rita's dancing partner. "Senhor Barão, in your day few served their king with as much valor," he said.

"I did my duty, Clóvis."

"Much more, Senhor Ulisses. *Much* more. The barão's deeds are remembered."

"Today, Clóvis . . . if only I could ride with the army today! To triumph, as in King João's day, in lands that were ours until Pedro I surrendered them." His voice rose sharply: "How many times, Clóvis, must the cost of that defeat be borne by Brazil — and paid for with the blood of our nation's sons?"

Ulisses Tavares's anguished appeal caused several heads to turn in their direction and seemed out of place in that romantic setting. But half the men waltzing their sweethearts round the ballroom were in the dress uniforms of the imperial army and Guarda Nacional, for amid the music and laughter, there was talk of war — three conflicts, in fact: one drawing to a close, one of uncertain outcome, and one that had begun four months ago and to which the barão de Itatinga but for his age would have marched posthaste.

Reports from North America suggested the imminent collapse of the Confederacy. Brazil had maintained an official policy of neutrality throughout the Civil War, though her recognition of the South's belligerent position had been the cause of acrimonious exchanges between Dom Pedro's officials and envoys of the Lincoln government at Rio de Janeiro, especially when raiders like the *Alabama* and the *Florida* put in for provisions in Brazilian ports.

The second conflict exciting interest among the guests at Itatinga this night was in Mexico, where more than 35,000 soldiers of Napoleon III had secured the Crown for Ferdinand Maximilian, brother of Franz Josef of Austria.

The third conflict involved Brazil on two far-flung fronts. After firing her shot across the bow of the *Marquês de Olinda,* the Paraguayan steamer *Tacuari* had escorted the Brazilian packet back to Asunción, where her cargo of munitions and strongboxes were seized and all Brazilians aboard, including Mato Grosso's president-designate, Carneiro de Campos, interned. Rio de Janeiro's minister at Asunción, Viana de Lima, had been handed his passports and ordered out of Paraguay. When news of these events reached Rio de Janeiro in late November 1864, war fervor had quickly spread.

The bulk of Brazil's sixteen-thousand-man army was already engaged in Uruguay, fighting in support of the Colorado faction against the Blancos in power at Montevideo. The Guarda Nacional was prohibited from foreign service, a law for which numerous colonels and their local militia showed a sudden respect: It was one thing to parade around the local square and maintain the peace of the colonel's district; quite another to go up against the Guarani horde of Paraguay. To meet this contingency, the imperial government had issued a decree for volunteers for battalions of 830 men between the ages of eighteen and fifty.

Response to the call for *voluntários da patria* was brisk, for the decree had immediately followed reports of a Brazilian victory in Uruguay. On January 2, 1865, after a month's blockade and a fifty-two-hour bombardment by ships of the imperial navy, the Blanco port of Paysandu on the Rio Uruguay, one of the Blancos' last strongholds outside Montevideo, had surrendered to the Brazilians and Colorados. But there was much more than this to spur the Brazilians to act against their newer foe, Paraguay.

"Thousands of Paraguayans defiling Brazilian soil! Our brave defenders slaughtered!" Ulisses Tavares said to Clóvis. "Men, women, and children driven into captivity. Others cast into the sertão upon the mercy of savages. Oh, *dear God*, Clóvis: Mato Grosso invaded by López!"

On December 27, 1864, a Paraguayan naval squadron with three thousand troops and a land force of 2,500 cavalry and infantry had attacked Fort Coimbra, southernmost defense works of Mato Grosso, which had surrendered after a thirty-six-hour resistance.

The barão and Captain Clóvis da Silva left the dance floor and went outside, walking slowly across the paving between the two ells.

"What terrors they must be enduring there," Ulisses Tavares said, looking up at the sky. "Beneath these stars."

"López struck where we're weakest, Senhor Ulisses. He — "

"Rejoices!" Ulisses Tavares interrupted. "López pirates our *Marquês de Olinda*. He violates a frontier where the forts are few and falling to pieces. These are his victories over Brazil, this despot who dreams of being emperor and stirs his Guarani regiments with talk of glory."

"The Paraguayan will realize his mistake," Clóvis said, breaking his silence, "but it may take longer than we think to bring him to his senses."

"López?"

"The Guarani soldier, Senhor Ulisses. He's been taught absolute obedience to his dictator."

"They will be matched, Clóvis, man for man, by the voluntários."

Ulisses Tavares was too old for the battlefields of Paraguay, but he was doing all within his power to recruit a company of volunteers to be sent from Tiberica. As he walked with Clóvis da Silva, holding his arm again, he steered him toward an open doorway, through which they saw Firmino Dantas and Carlinda waltzing across the ballroom.

"In two weeks, Lieutenant Firmino Dantas and the voluntários of Tiberica leave for the Plata," Ulisses Tavares said. "Three months, Clóvis, and I believe they'll march into Asunción."

౷

Firmino smiled at Carlinda, but his thoughts were far away. He had no argument with Brazil's cause, especially since the invasion of Mato Grosso, though he recognized López as provocateur and felt no particular hatred toward the Paraguayan people. And he was not without experience of the parade ground, having served with Tiberica's Guarda Nacional. But the prospect of combat sickened him.

The day word of the decree calling for voluntários da patria reached Itatinga, Ulisses Tavares had come to the fazenda's workshop in search of Firmino, whom he found standing on a platform at the second level of bins and ventilators of the coffee engenho. When Firmino waved a greeting to his grandfather, a slave misinterpreted the signal and flung open a valve to power the engine. With a tremendous clatter and grinding, the engenho came alive, making the barão jump back in fright. Shouting for the mill to be shut off, Firmino quickly scrambled down the platform.

One glance at the expression on the baron's face told Firmino that the old man's patience was exhausted, and he understood why: He had only to look at his own hands, ingrained with dirt, his knuckles grazed, his fingers cut and scratched. Ulisses Tavares's generation (and not a few senhores acadêmicos, too) was blinded by love of the past and faithful to ideas compatible with those of the lord donatários who had come to Terra de Santa Cruz in the sixteenth century: Progress was the extent of lands they owned; honor was the degree of royal approval they earned; dignity was the scorn of all useful labor.

Firmino lamented Brazil's backwardness compared with what he had seen in Europe. During those three years, 1860-1863, Firmino had found Paris being rebuilt to the grand designs of Emperor Napoleon III and his master planner, Georges Haussmann. "The broad boulevards, underground sewers, parks — gigantic works giving the city a new face! Glorious open vistas of air and light! Paris is in the midst of a revolution as dramatic a break with the past as the upheaval of 1789!" Firmino had enthused back at Itatinga.

He had also crossed the Channel to England, where he had marveled at the 22.000-ton *Great Eastern:* At Liverpool, he had roamed through the cavernous ship and stood in silent awe before engines capable of eleven thousand horsepower. How could he not consider positively medieval four iron-shod pestles serving to process six hundred tons of coffee beans!

He wondered if his grandfather would ever understand. But that day in the workshop, Ulisses Tavares had said nothing about Firmino's invention.

"Grandfather? There's something you wish me to do?" he had asked as he followed the old man outside.

"Yes, Firmino," Ulisses Tavares had replied gravely. "Francisco Solano López must be taught respect for the empire. A decree from the Corte asks for volunteers to crush the tyrant and his Guarani rabble." And then Ulisses Tavares had seized Firmino's hands: "My son" — his voice broke — "may God grant a swift, bold campaign." His grip on Firmino's hands tightened. "You will lead the voluntários of Tiberica, Firmino Dantas!"

Firmino knew that he would obey Ulisses Tavares, though he wanted nothing more than to continue the work on the coffee engenho. Three years away from Itatinga should have strengthened his independence, but back at the fazenda, he was one of several hundred people, slave and free, over whom the barão exercised absolute control.

In the ballroom at Itatinga, as Firmino danced past the barão and Captain Clóvis da Silva, his smile belied the deep concern he felt over his impending departure for Paraguay. Firmino had not shared his fears with Carlinda — perhaps because it was his mind and not his heart that guided him in accepting his coming marriage with this charming girl. This lack of ardor on her fiancée's part was not something Carlinda hadn't noticed. In fact, she had expressed some concern to her sister.

"My dear, be prudent and patient," Teodora Rita had counseled when Carlinda expressed dismay at Firmino's preoccupation with his invention. "The poor thing doesn't know love. An inventor. Be especially careful, Carlinda. Say not a word against his obsession with this machine. Your love is a prisoner in another shrine — the temple of learning. Show understanding. Keep him in good humor. He will bless the day he chose you!"

Restrained and chaste at the age of twenty-five, Firmino had not given those coaxing him into Carlinda's arms the slightest cause for doubting the success of their mission. Not until this night of the grand ball.

ဢ

As midnight approached, Firmino remained on the dance floor under close scrutiny from his family, and especially Teodora Rita. Her pretty face was placid, but her dark, fiery eyes followed Firmino Dantas and the partner with whom he was dancing. The elation evident on Firmino's face made the baronesa regret having invited this girl and her father, August Laubner.

Laubner was a Swiss, a big, quiet man with drooping whiskers in the English "Piccadilly Weeper" style. He and his family had emigrated to the province of São Paulo from Graubünden, the easternmost canton, nine years ago with a group of two hundred people desperate to escape the hard, cold winters and the harder bite of poverty in the lonely valley of the Prätigau.

August Laubner had been a foundling. An apothecary, Jeremias Laubner, had found the infant in his barn, or so he said; rumor had it that Laubner had agreed to care for the bastard of a member of a family of old nobility who lived beyond Davos. August had been raised by the Laubners, who had one child, Matthäus, five years older than August.

From his fourteenth year, August had worked in the apothecary's shop. The Laubners had treated him kindly, if not with the love they were able to give only their own flesh and blood. Ultimately, he married and had two children. Then, in the winter of 1854, tragedy struck. Jeremias Laubner froze to death in a snowdrift into which he'd been thrown by his horse while riding back to Klosters from neighboring Davos, and six weeks later, Jeremias's wife had died of pneumonia.

Matthäus and his wife, as mean-spirited as her husband and expecting her first child, had given notice to August, who occupied two rooms at the back of the house with his family, demanding that they leave. "Find your own place, August, and find it soon," Matthäus had said, "for my wife's time is near, and there isn't room enough for two families."

At the time Matthäus ordered August to leave the house, recruiting agents for a group of Paulista fazendeiros had been active in the Prätigau valley seeking indentured workers for the coffee plantations, a free-labor alternative prompted by the ending of the slave trade from Africa to Brazil in 1850. At his brother-in-law's house, August had attended a meeting addressed by one of these agents, who offered passage money, transport from Santos to the north of São Paulo province, a subsistence allowance for the first year.

That same night, August Laubner decided to seek a new life for himself and his family in Brazil. A few harvests and his family would be free of debt. As soon as he had the means, he would establish himself as an apothecary.

After the long voyage from Europe and the trek over the Serra do Mar, August had come to a crude wattle-and-daub hut, with holes for windows and a thatched roof. Such was the home offered his family and five others whose contracts had been assigned to Alfredo Pontes, a fazendeiro who could scarcely distinguish between his *colonos*, as the share-wage earners were known, and his sixty slaves.

The colonos discovered that if Senhor Pontes was dissatisfied with their work, he could cancel their contracts and demand immediate payment of all monies due him. Failure to reimburse him resulted in two years in jail with hard labor or the same period at public works.

Senhor Pontes was, of course, only striving to instill in his colonos those virtues of obedience and subservience that fazendeiros expected from their agregados, the associates they permitted to live on their land under varying conditions of tenure. But the Swiss did not understand. After the first harvest, they complained that the prices quoted by their fazendeiros were far below market value for coffee beans at Santos, and many went on strike.

This confrontation had led to an investigation by a Swiss commissioner from the consulate at Rio de Janeiro, and the grievances of the colonos had mostly been confirmed. The imperial government had also sought to mollify the colonos, for the Corte was eager to attract European settlers. Several thousand German colonists were established on Crown lands in Rio Grande do Sul and prospering; the São Paulo indentured labor experiment with Portuguese, Germans, and Swiss was a private venture. Though both sides had calmed down and relations had improved, the effect of the "uprising," as Senhor Pontes and others saw it, was disastrous for Brazil: When the complaints of the colonos became known in Europe, Prussia forbade the recruiting of further migrants, and the Swiss cantons discouraged their poor from leaving for Brazil.

Senhor Alfredo Pontes had sold the contracts of the Laubner family and the others to another coffee grower, whose fazenda was twenty-four miles from Tiberica. This new employer, a Mineiro from Vila Rica, was scrupulously honest. Within three years, August and his family had paid off what they owed for their passage and subsistence allowance; at the beginning of 1862, August had been released from his contract and had come to Tiberica with his wife, Heloise, and two children, a boy and a girl, then aged eleven and fifteen. In March that year, in the front room of a small house, August Laubner had opened his apothecary shop, the first at Tiberica.

The barão de Itatinga himself was a customer of apothecary Laubner, and regularly used his dyspepsia powders for heartburn, and a tonic of beef extract, iron, and sherry as a flesh builder and blood purifier. Ulisses Tavares had heard only good reports about the Swiss and his family. Still, Ulisses Tavares had been disturbed when Teodora Rita told him that she had asked Senhor Laubner, his wife, and daughter to the ball.

"He will be uncomfortable among our friends," the barão had suggested. "They seek his professional help, yes. They value his advice, but they wouldn't want to see him in our ballroom."

"It's true, Senhor Barão," Teodora Rita had agreed.

"Then, why did you invite him?"

"Forgive me, Barão, but there were several who asked."

"What, my girl?"

"The senhor barão, my love, has eyes only for Teodora Rita. He doesn't see that Tiberica's bachelors, young men of our best families, besiege the house of August Laubner."

"Ah, yes, indeed!" the barão said as it dawned on him. "Such a lovely girl!"

"Three hearts" — she had mentioned the names of three young men — "beating with one purpose: Oh, Senhor Barão, could I reject their lovelorn appeals that she be present at our ball?"

Renata Laubner was eighteen, a long-limbed girl with round blue eyes and a crown of blond hair parted in the center and pulled back to side ringlets, the golden tresses on the right adorned with small blue flowers. Renata's dress was a delicate blue, quite plain compared with the elaborate gowns of Teodora Rita and the others, but perfectly suited to her fair features. This girl who was so different from the sultry maidens of the tropics smote the bachelors of Tiberica who saw the flash of gold in her hair and the glorious blue of her eyes.

Firmino Dantas had met Renata Laubner for the first time this night. The apothecary had settled in Tiberica when Firmino was in Paris. After being introduced to August Laubner and Renata, Firmino had listened to the apothecary tell of a recent field trip to contact a group of semi-wild Tupi whose medicines August wanted to investigate.

"Truly, senhorita, you went with them into the sertão?" Firmino declared when August Laubner had finished his account.

"Why ever not, Senhor Firmino?" A smile, with a hint of impudence.

"Renata has a mind of her own, Doutor Firmino," Laubner said, looking fondly at his daughter.

"I wasn't afraid, Senhor Firmino," Renata said. "It was a wonderful journey. Beyond the last fazenda, we spent three days on a trail through the forest. Every step was like walking through Eden. The flowers! The birds! A *paradise,* Senhor Firmino!"

Firmino had a feeling that this senhorita who so daringly walked beside her father on his quest for knowledge would also understand his passion to launch

Itatinga into the present.

But Firmino had shown characteristic restraint, pursuing serious topics of conversation for quite a while before asking permission for a dance. And then, when he'd taken Renata in his arms, he felt an exhilarating nervousness. He had had to wait almost an hour before he could politely approach her for a second dance, and had seen the three young men of Tiberica take turns throwing themselves at the feet of their idol.

When Firmino had been granted another dance, he was unable to hide his pleasure. He clasped Renata tightly round the waist as they glided swiftly along the floor.

When Firmino had escorted Renata back to her seat, Teodora Rita took her future brother-in-law aside. "The Swiss is lively," she said. "Such a fragile beauty blazing through the polka!"

Firmino at first did not sense the baronesa's concern. "Fragile, Teodora Rita?" He laughed. "A girl who spent ten days in the sertão on a journey with her father?"

Teodora Rita looked shocked. "Whatever for?"

"Apothecary Laubner wanted to study the old remedies of the pagés. Senhorita Renata went with him. Wasn't it marvelous?"

"It was silly," Teodora Rita said. "The girl belongs at home with her mother."

"Ah, but, Baronesa, Renata Laubner is different."

"Different?" Teodora Rita raised one eyebrow.

Firmino hesitated, becoming aware of the baronesa's irritation. But then he smiled. "Don't worry, Teodora Rita. Firmino Dantas hasn't lost his head in a Swiss cloud."

"I hope not, Firmino Dantas," the baronesa said, eyes blazing. She saw Ulisses Tavares coming toward them. "The barão, too." She nodded to herself. "He wouldn't like it, Firmino."

☙

Early morning on June 11, 1865, nine Brazilian warships were anchored ten miles below Tres Bocas, the junction of the Paraná and Paraguay rivers, lying along a great bend of the Paraná — six hundred yards wide here — with the Riachuelo, a stream, flowing into it from the east. The squadron had a total firepower of fifty-nine guns, including Whitworth-rifled 120- and 150-pounders. The flagship was the *Amazonas,* a 195-foot, 370-ton wooden frigate, the only paddle wheeler among the nine ships. The others were screw-driven for greater maneuverability in the swift Paraná. Flying the blue naval ensign with stars at her mainmast, the green and gold flag of the empire at her mizzen, the black-hulled *Amazonas* carried a heavy ram at her bows, and strong and lofty nettings stretched above her bulwarks to protect against boarders.

This Sunday morning, the day of the Blessed Trinity, squadron commander Vice-Admiral Francisco Manoel Barroso, his officers, and 2,200 men, including 1,174 infantry of the Ninth Battalion, were turned out in dress uniform for sacred Mass, and their devotions were conducted with little concern for the enemy ashore. But, peaceful as the scene was, with the war steamers riding comfortably at anchor under a cloudless sky and the voices of men raised fervently with sacred song, on the east bank of the Paraná, just beyond range of their position, two thousand Paraguayans were encamped with a battery of twenty-two guns and Congreve rockets.

Clearly the optimism of men like the barão de Itatinga, who had predicted in February 1865 that Asunción would fall within three months, had not been justified. More than six months after the Tacuari lobbed her shot across the bows of the *Marquês de Olinda,* Brazilian soldiers had yet to set foot on Paraguayan soil. Worse, the war had widened: Argentina had joined in a triple alliance against Paraguay with Brazil and the victorious Colorado faction of Uruguay. This had come about after Francisco Solano López asked Buenos Aires to permit his army to cross Argentinian territory between the Upper Paraná and Uruguay rivers so that the Paraguayans could engage the Brazilians in Uruguay and drive eastward to Rio Grande do Sul. When Bartolomé Mitre, president of Argentina, refused this request, President López had gone ahead anyway, sending ten thousand men into the old Misiones district. In mid-March 1865, the Paraguayan congress had declared war against Argentina; on April 14, the Paraguayan navy had landed a force of three thousand men to capture Corrientes, a river port in the Argentine province of the same name. Corrientes had fallen without resistance, and within weeks, 25,000 Paraguayans had invaded the province with the objective of pressing south to Buenos Aires itself.

At the end of May 1865, the Brazilian squadron, under Vice-Admiral Barroso, had steamed up the Paraná carrying four thousand men to assault the Paraguayan occupiers of Corrientes. The attack had been successful, but after twenty-four hours, the Allies had reembarked their force, fearing a counterattack by units of 24,000 Paraguayans deployed within a few days' march of Corrientes. Since then, the Brazilian squadron had taken up position six miles from Corrientes in the river bend near the mouth of the Riachuelo to blockade the Paraná and prevent its navigation by the Paraguayan fleet.

By 9:00 A.M. on June 11, the two chaplains with the Brazilian ships had completed holy services. Less than a fortnight after the squadron had begun its blockade, the men already knew the monotony of a twenty-four-hour watch, day after day, with nothing to challenge but a few small riverboats and canoes, whose crews sometimes came upon the anchorage from backwaters where even the rumor of war was still unheard. Innocently, they would ride the swift current into the great bend, where first they encountered the lead ship *Belmonte,* then the flagship *Amazonas,* the corvettes *Jequitinhonha and Beberibe,* four gunboats — *Parnaíba, Iguatemi, Mearim,* and *Ipiranga* — and finally the rear guardship, the *Aruguari,* a gunboat with 32- and 68-pounders. Most impressive to the startled rivermen was the towering size of the black-hulled *Amazonas,* with her high paddle boxes and great ram, which lay menacingly in the channel between sandbanks and reed-clogged islands.

Aboard the *Mearim* this morning, the bell was rung for 9:00 A.M., the second hour of the forenoon watch. The *Mearim* was astern of the *Belmonte* but anchored so that her lookouts had a good view upriver. The notes of the *Mearim's* bell had no sooner died than there was a call from aloft: "Ship ahead!" And very soon, as a second and third vessel were seen: "Enemy squadron in sight!"

Riding down with the three-knot current were fourteen Paraguayan vessels — eight steamers and six flat-bottomed barges towed by the ships and each mounting an eight-inch gun. The total firepower of the Paraguayans was forty-seven guns, and like the Brazilians, more than one thousand soldiers augmented their crews. The lead vessel was the *Paraguari,* a modern iron-plated warship with eight guns. Rear guard was the *Tacuari,* flagship, with fleet commander Pedro Ignacio Meza. And just ahead of the *Tacuari* rode the *Marquês de Olinda,* her Brazilian colors struck months ago (and made into a floor rug for El Presidente's office at Asunción), her old decks bristling with eight pieces ready to blast the ships of her former owners.

The Brazilians began to clear for action, their engineers and firemen hastening to get steam up, but they had less than fifteen minutes between the alarm given by the *Mearim* and the first cannonade from the Paraguayans as they passed their anchorage. The Paraguayans made their run down a channel close to the west bank. The range between their vessels and the Brazilian warships was too wide to permit an effective bombardment, but the sound and smoke of their guns was invitation enough to combat. On the Brazilians' decks, drummer boys who but an hour ago had served at the altar in cassock and surplice stood boldly at their posts beating the rataplan. Whistles blew as men ran to quarters, with gun crews loading immediately, and soldiers were mustered on their decks in readiness to repel boarders.

Vice-Admiral Barroso had been on the *Parnaíba* and was rowed back to his flagship. Aboard the *Amazonas,* he and his officers soon saw the lead Paraguayan ship start to make her turn. Barroso, sixty-one years old this day, was Portuguese-born but had served in the navy of his country of adoption. He had thinning gray hair and a full white beard, but his eyebrows were dark, and beneath them were eyes as commanding as the rest of his features. To get a better view of the enemy, Barroso had climbed up onto one of the *Amazonas's* paddle boxes. As he stood there, he passed on an order to a midshipman: "Make this signal to the squadron."

Barroso glanced swiftly along the line of his ships. Then he addressed the midshipman with orders for signal flags to be flown with two commands: *"Bater o inimigo que estiver mais próximo!"* and *"O Brasil espera que cada um cumpra o seu dever!"*

The first command was for the ships to engage the enemy at close quarters. The second was inspired by the glory of Admiral Horatio Nelson's triumph at Trafalgar sixty years ago: "Brazil expects that every man will do his duty!"

As the Paraguayan fleet completed its turn and started back upriver, the Brazilian ships maneuvered into position in the channels between the sandbanks and islands and opened fire: One of the Paraguayan steamers, the *Jejuí,* took a shot through her boiler and drifted out of action; the remaining seven and the six barges closed for battle, breaking their squadron line, with groups of ships and gun barges making for specific targets. The Brazilian corvette *Jequitinhonha* was battered by three Paraguayans firing ball and grapeshot and by their musketeers raking the corvette's decks. The gunboat *Parnaíba* also found herself under attack by three ships, including the iron-plated *Tacuari* and *Paraguari,* which fired round after round as they steamed up to the Brazilian with the intention of boarding her.

Within the great bend of the river, as the twenty-one ships and gun barges blazed away at one another, the air rapidly grew thick with the acrid yellow smoke of battle drifting past the fiery mouths of cannon and mingling with the soot and ashes spewed from ships' funnels. The opening stages of the Battle of the Riachuelo went badly for the Brazilians, for no sooner had they given challenge to the Paraguayans than they faced an additional threat: The twenty-two guns and Congreve rockets of the Paraguayan shore battery just north of the mouth of the Riachuelo opened up in support of their squadron.

The small crews of the *chatas,* one-gun barges eighteen feet long, concentrated their fire on the wooden hulls of the Brazilian ships, seeking to blast through planking to pierce a boiler or detonate a magazine. For the crew of one chata, the fervor was short-lived when a shot from a 68-pounder on the *Amazonas* struck the barge, igniting its explosives and blowing it to bits. This did not daunt the Paraguayans as they prepared to board their adversaries.

But here in the rising heat of battle as the *Tacuari, Paraguari,* and the small *Salto* converged on the *Parnaíba,* and the boarding parties made ready to leap upon the foe with cutlass and machete, they made a terrible discovery: Those now waiting at the port of Asunción for news of a great victory had neglected to place aboard the war steamers the only indispensable items for the impending action: grappling irons.

"Damn them! *Oh, damn them!*" a sergeant aboard the *Salto* raged.

His soldier comrades near him, their breath fiery with shots of *cana* swigged before the battle, blazed forth with even greater curses.

"Damn the stupid bastards!" the sergeant screamed again, watching the *Tacuari* attempt to close with the *Parnaíba.* Two men made a desperate leap for the Brazilians' bulwarks, jumping from the *Tacuari's* paddle boxes; but, as the vessels were not grappled, the *Tacuari* could not keep beside the enemy long enough for others to follow. When the *Tacuari* stood off, the pair of boarders leapt back to her deck, lucky to escape the Brazilian rifle fire.

The *Salto* was screw-driven, and her helmsman was able to maneuver her into position and pass slowly alongside the enemy gunboat; in minutes the sergeant and twenty-nine others had boarded the *Parnaíba,* their battle cries drowning the screams of one Paraguayan who lost his footing and was crushed between the two ships.

The hail of bullets from Brazilian riflemen felled four Paraguayans, but the remaining twenty-five stormed across the *Parnaíba's* decks. Supported by small-arms fire from marksmen aloft in the three vessels harassing the *Parnaíba,* the boarding party began to overwhelm those Brazilians on deck. Many Brazilians had already been driven to take refuge below during the repeated bombardments by the Paraguayans.

The Paraguayans won the fight on the decks: Within fifteen minutes they had control of the *Parnaíba,* the first prize taken for El Presidente this day.

The sergeant who had been in the thick of the fight was exultant. He spied the body of a drummer boy on the deck near the *Parnaíba's* funnel, and with his cutlass, he slashed the straps holding the boy's instrument. Jubilantly, he took up the drum and sticks he had pried loose from the boy's fingers and strutted along the deck, raising cheers from his comrades as he beat a triumphant roll.

And then, steaming through the swirl of smoke, riding the swift current, the *Amazonas* came down upon this scene of battle. She held her fire until the last moment, when her starboard guns blazed at the two nearest Paraguayan vessels, *Tacuari* and *Salto*. The port guns of the *Amazonas* were loaded with grape: With a flash and a roar, they raked the deck of the *Parnaíba* with a merciless tornado of shot that instantly downed three out of every four Paraguayans.

For four and a half hours the battle raged along the bend of the Rio Paraná. With their towering size and greater firepower, the Brazilians slowly began to prevail: The *Jejuí* was sunk; the *Salto* was beached; the *Marquês de Olinda*, the very sight of which spurred the Brazilian gunners, also took a shot in her boiler house and ran aground on a sandbank.

The Paraguayans lost three ships and two chatas, but still the battle was undecided, for the Brazilians were also mauled: The *Belmonte* was holed at the waterline and aground; the *Jequitinhonha* was stuck fast on a sandbank; the *Parnaíba*, too, was effectively out of action.

After going to the rescue of the *Parnaíba*, the flagship *Amazonas* steamed slowly up the channel exchanging shots with the enemy, though these cannonades were secondary to another objective of Vice-Admiral Barroso and his men. About a mile upstream, the *Amazonas* turned. Then, full steam ahead, her great paddle wheels churning the water, the *Amazonas* came down before the three-knot current. On and on she rode, belching black smoke from her stack and red flame from the mouths of her cannon, steaming directly for the *Paraguarí*, the newest vessel in President López's fleet.

She struck the *Paraguarí* amidships, her ram buckling iron plates, smashing through the enemy's bulwarks. The *Amazonas*'s steam whistle shrieked, her decks vibrated violently, her engines raced at full power with a mighty force that shoved the Paraguayan steamer sideways through the water and onto a sandbank.

"Viva Dom Pedro Segundo! *Viva Brasil!*" the Amazonas's men cheered, as the frigate backed away from the crippled vessel.

Some Paraguayans had been hurled off the gunboat by the impact; some had abandoned her to swim to the west bank. But a dozen or so shouted back abuse at the macacos and hurried to clear the debris around a 12-pounder. It was a desperate defiance: They were enraged at the destruction of their ship, and afire with the knowledge that generations of Guarani before them had been called to stand fast against this enemy of enemies.

With the grounding of the *Paraguarí* and damage to a fifth gunboat, which was limping along with a hole in her boiler, the Paraguayan flagship, *Tacuari*, signaled: "Break off action!" Aboard the *Tacuari*, the squadron commander, Pedro Ignacio Meza, lay mortally wounded, one of a thousand Paraguayans killed or wounded this day, triple the number of Brazilian casualties. With the *Tacuari* holding their rear, the three remaining vessels steamed off and were pursued for a distance by two Brazilians, until they, too, dropped back, their crews so exhausted and equipment so damaged that they dared not risk a chase to the Rio Paraguay, where they would come under fire from the enemy's river fortresses. For the Brazilians, it was enough to know that with the destruction of Paraguay's fleet, Francisco Solano López was denied access to the Paraná.

But the guns at the Riachuelo were not yet silent, and for one Brazilian warship, the hell that had begun more than four hours ago was not over. The corvette *Jequitinhonha* had run aground on a sandbank within range of the twenty-two guns and the Congreve rockets of the Paraguayan shore battery. The corvette had come under so murderous a fire that of her crew of 138, fifty were killed or grievously wounded.

Twice during this brutal afternoon, two of the *Jequitinhonha's* sister ships came in under the enemy's barrage to attempt to tow her off the sandbank, but they had failed. Respite came almost seven hours after the commencement of battle when, bombarded by the *Amazonas* and other vessels, the Paraguayan shore batteries finally withdrew. With that ceasefire, some of the *Jequitinhonha's* crew sat down on her splintered deck and wept.

Below deck, in a stern section of the *Jequitinhonha*, were two men who had remained at their posts these seven deadly hours with no thought for their own safety. There had been no need for them to go on deck to fix in their minds the awful scene, for it was all around them — the broken arms and legs, the mutilated trunks, the ripped-open faces.

The older of the two men was Manuel Batista Valadão, lieutenant-surgeon of the *Jequitinhonha*. His assistant, twenty-seven years old, was Second-Lieutenant Fábio Alves Cavalcanti, and this was his trial by fire. The suffering around him was beyond his imagination. Four lamps lighted the cabin, their yellow glare increasing the hellishness of the scene visible to men waiting their turn on the operating table; the deck stained darker with blood and the surgeons themselves besmeared. A pungent smell pervaded the cabin, but for this the wounded thanked Almighty God: it was ether, which had not been long in use and would spare them excruciating pain.

At times during those seven bloody hours, Fábio Alves Cavalcanti had been numbed by the horror: He would look at Manuel Valadão, who worked quietly, steadily, and gain the strength to ignore the battle beyond. Sometimes Fábio would be suturing a tear in a man's flesh, part of him far away, at Engenho Santo Tomás, which had belonged to his family for generations. "O God, my Father, allow me to return there," he once prayed aloud, unaware that surgeon Valadão overheard him.

For Fábio Alves Cavalcanti, a grandson of Carlos Maria, the child who had been left fatherless when Paulo Cavalcanti was murdered by Black Peter and his band of runaway slaves, the flashes of memory in this cabin where men looked at him with eyes that craved death were immensely soothing. He saw the Casa Grande where he had spent his childhood; a grand old house built more than a century ago and filled with mystery for him. He associated Santo Tomás with his youth, for he had not lived there permanently for a decade: His father, Guilherme Cavalcanti, spent most of the year at their town house at Olinda, and he himself had attended school there, later matriculating at the medical school at the Bahia, until he had entered the imperial navy eighteen months ago. Now, as he stood in this place steeped with blood and with suffering men all around him, Fábio wondered about that decision and felt a longing for that valley of the Cavalcantis so distant from this carnage.

Fábio Cavalcanti's doubt was short-lived. When the shore battery's bombardment ceased, Lieutenant Valadão told his assistant to go topside and find out if the
battle had truly ended. Fábio started off slowly along a passageway, his shoulders
bent with fatigue.

"Tenente . . ."

The call came from a gunner lying on the mess deck. The man had been one of
the first to be injured. He had been brought to the surgeons with multiple lacerations
and both legs broken by the blast when one of the *Jequitinhonha's* 68-pounders had
been put out of action by a Paraguayan shell.

"What is it, sailor?" Fábio asked, bending down toward the man.

The gunner reached out and with his unbandaged hand gripped the hand of
the young surgeon. "Thank you, my friend."

Fábio Alves Cavalcanti felt his own surge of gratitude for the privilege of being
there — amid the hell that had raged at the Riachuelo, where men as brave as this
broken gunner needed him.

XIX

⟡

April 1866 – March 1870

*I*n late March 1866, the venerable Guarani general, Juan Bautista Noguera –
Cacambo — seventy-nine years old now, small, shrunken, with his hatred of the
Brazilians mightier than ever, took great pleasure in a war trophy delivered to Francisco Solano López at his headquarters across the Upper Paraná: a leather bag filled
with the heads of nine Allied soldiers.

Cacambo waved his tiny hands and danced with glee at the sight of these enemies. Unsheathing his sword, Cacambo cut the air above the trophies and repeated
his vow: "I, Cacambo, will slay the first macaco who dares to leap to our soil!"

An Allied invasion was imminent. The Paraguayan offensive in the Argentine
province of Corrientes had been disastrous: Sixteen thousand Paraguayans perished
in battles and through sickness before the last units crossed the Upper Paraná back
into Paraguay at the end of October 1865.

Paraguayan conscripts had again brought their army up to 25,000 men, most
of whom were deployed in camps above the Upper Paraná. Their main base was at
Paso la Patria, ten miles east of Tres Bocas. Between these two locations, the *carrizal*
— deep lagoons and mud flats that extended inland for one to three miles — broke
the northern banks of the Upper Paraná. At Itapiru, between Tres Bocas and Paso la
Patria, there was a battery revetted with brickwork and mounting seven cannon. At
Paso la Patria, thirty feet above the carrizal, there were thirty field guns; elsewhere in
the jungle along the riverbank, artillery companies were concealed in the woods at
likely enemy landing places.

By March 1866 the Allied army of Brazil, Argentina, and Uruguay was assembled below the Upper Paraná. The Brazilians now had an effective strength of 67,000 men, including 35,000 voluntários da patria. President Bartolomé Mitre, who, in terms of the Triple Alliance Treaty, was commander-in chief of the Allied army during operations on Argentinian territory, headed an Argentinian contingent of 15,000 men. The Uruguayans, led by the Colorado general Venancio Flores, contributed 1,500 men, all they could muster in the aftermath of the civil war with the Blancos.

Dom Pedro Segundo had made a brief journey to the seat of war with his two sons-in-law, Prince Louis Gaston, comte d'Eu, and Prince Louis Augustus, duke of Saxe-Coburg-Gotha. Traveling by horseback through southern Brazil, the royal trio had been present when a column of 4,200 Paraguayans had surrendered at Uruguaiana in September 1865. The thirty-nine-year old Dom Pedro, imposing as ever with his six-foot-three-inch frame and luxurious golden-brown locks and beard, had been unimpressed by the captured Paraguayans. "An enemy not worthy of being defeated," His Majesty had declared in a letter to a friend.

❧

The ninety-two voluntários of Tiberica, led by Firmino Dantas da Silva, had left the town late February 1865, marching first to São Paulo and then down to Santos, where they had taken passage on a ship with other Paulista volunteers for Rio Grande do Sul. There they had been drilled for four months until July 1865, when they were posted to guard a crossing on the Uruguay River. For eight months they sat here without a glimpse of the enemy and with nothing to break the monotony but news of victories won by others, until they received orders to join the Brazilian First Corps at Corrientes.

In April 1866, the main body of the Brazilian army began to move to forward positions on the south bank of the Upper Paraná opposite the Paraguayan battery at Itapiru. On April 5, an advance group of eleven hundred men with La Hitte cannon and mortars occupied and entrenched themselves on a grassy sandbank separated from Itapiru by a narrow channel. Supporting their landing were eight Brazilian warships.

At 4:00 A.M. on April 10, thirteen hundred Paraguayans launched a counterattack by canoe from Itapiru to dislodge the men on the low spit of land opposite the battery. Within a quarter of an hour, immense flashes broke the blackness of predawn as the Brazilian ships opened fire, the booming guns adding to the din of battle rising from the sandbank.

Only sixty of the ninety-two men who had left Tiberica in February 1865 were present to see the first action since departing their town: The rest had contracted dysentery, smallpox, and other diseases, and of these, fourteen had died, eight were in the hospital at Corrientes, and ten had been sent home unfit for service. Firmino Dantas da Silva himself had spent two weeks in the hospital with measles. He was serving as liaison officer between the battalion and the headquarters of General Manuel Luís Osório, commander of the Brazilian First Corps.

Two Tiberica voluntários watching the flashes of cannon and musketry stood together yelling encouragement to the unseen gunners aboard the Brazilian ships. The enemy's cannon blazed in the dark line of jungle opposite, and shells intended for the warships roared through the air above them, but the two men greeted the Paraguayan shot with derisive laughter. When it began to grow light, they climbed the hillside to reach a better vantage point, though they found the sandbank obscured by thick smoke, the gun flashes less distinct as dawn broke.

The early light showed one of these voluntários to be much older: The man had not yet fought a skirmish with the enemy, but he bore a scar so terrible that soldiers thinking of the battles they must soon face were reluctant to gaze upon it. The old wound lay across his skull, from above his left temple to the back of his head. He had gone completely bald after suffering this awful blow.

This voluntário was Policarpo, one of the slaves bought for Itatinga from the trader Saturnino Rabelo by Ulisses Tavares in January 1856. Policarpo, twenty-nine at the time, had assured the senhor barão that he was a Mossambe whom the lash had taught obedience and hard work.

In truth, Policarpo was lazy, and had resented the regimen of the plantation, particularly at harvest time, when the slave bell rang at 5:00 A.M. for assembly and prayers in front of the mansion before work in the coffee groves until dusk. One morning four years ago, when Policarpo did not respond to the bell, an overseer had rushed to the dormitory, but Policarpo was not there. A search had been mounted immediately for the runaway; with the soaring prices for slaves after the abolition of imports from Africa, even idle Policarpo was a valued possession of the senhor barão.

Policarpo had not run from Itatinga. When the search party set out, he had been less than five miles from the senzala, snoring loudly in a patch of forest beside the road from Tiberica. He had collapsed there in the early hours gloriously drunk, a jar of cachaça and a package of the best Bahiana tobacco beside him. Policarpo detested the work of the harvest, but there had been a consolation: He would occasionally steal a sack of coffee beans from where they were stored in the old fazenda, and trade them to the squatter Gonzaga for a supply of cachaça and tabak and trinkets.

Policarpo had still been befuddled when they found him. His captors tied his hands and made him run back toward the fazenda at the end of a length of rope attached to one man's saddle pommel; when the horse had suddenly jerked forward, the rope flew loose and Policarpo sprang away toward a hill covered with coffee trees. Dashing between the trees, he had eluded his mounted pursuers for a few minutes until their shouts alerted the overseers of a slave gang working on the next hillside. An overseer had arrested Policarpo's flight by striking him over the head with a seven-foot iron bar used for driving holes into the earth to plant seedlings. Unconscious and with his skull indented by the blow, Policarpo had not been expected to survive.

But he had recovered, and had been led to Ulisses Tavares, who closely inspected his wound and questioned him at length. (The squatter Gonzaga had fled Itatinga immediately upon hearing what had happened to Policarpo.) Policarpo had been placed in the stocks, the tronco diabo, and had also been flogged with one hundred lashes. Returned to the coffee groves, he had suffered fainting spells and sudden ravings and was unable to meet his daily quota. The overseers had finally confined him to the terreiro to rake the berries as they dried in the sun.

Policarpo had become tractable, and apart from overindulgence in cachaça, gave little trouble at Itatinga. But other slaves working on the terreiro grumbled about him: It seemed to them that whenever the sun blazed down on the drying terrace and it became unbearably hot, Policarpo would have one of his spells, shaking his head and moaning until he was compelled to seek the shade for a recuperative nap.

There were slaves, too, who wondered about Policarpo, the Mozambican: Wasn't it true that after his head had been broken, Policarpo had risen higher than any man in the eyes of the mãe de santo, the mother of the daughters of the saints? When the drums played, wasn't it extraordinary what energy came to Policarpo Mossambe as he danced for the African deities? And when the spirits descended, wasn't it the feebleminded Policarpo whose lips spoke with the greatest strength?

The young man with Policarpo this morning watching the fight for the sandbank near the Paraguayan shore was the mulatto Antônio Paciência. Patient Anthony, nineteen years old now, was tall and lean, with a tough, spare frame and iron muscles. His nose was slightly aquiline; the look in his brown eyes suggested inner strength; his dark-skinned countenance was frank, an expression often misconstrued as insolent. A good worker, slaver Saturnino Rabelo had predicted, and this was correct: Antônio Paciência had given no cause for complaint about the quality of his labor. Still, he had been a thoroughly bad slave.

Antônio Paciência could remember the delight of the *iaiá* — the slaves' corruption of "Sinhazinha" — when he had been given to her. Teodora Rita couldn't wait to show him off when visitors came to Itatinga.

Except for his behavior during inspection by the *iaiá's* relatives and friends, however, Antônio Paciência had seemed incapable of pleasing the baronesa. Teodora Rita's tongue wagged incessantly with complaints about Antônio Paciência and the difficulty she had training him.

There had been the time the iaiá's silver shoehorn disappeared. Iaiá Teodora Rita said she had left it in a boot given to Antônio for cleaning. The iaiá and Dona Feliciana, wife of Eusébio Magalhães, insisted on watching Cincinnato, the carriage driver, cane him, ordering that the punishment continue, until Antônio Paciência had finally admitted stealing the shoehorn: "Oh, iaiá, forgive me! I put it in my pocket . . . Oh, iaiá, I lost it, I do not know where!" (Months after the caning, the iaiá told Antônio to clean a pair of shoes she hadn't worn for a long time, and as he was carrying them to the fazenda's kitchen, something dropped with a clink to the stone floor. His terror was absolute when he saw that it was the silver shoehorn! Pausing just long enough to pick it up, he crept out of the house and buried the shoehorn far down the slope toward the Rio Tietê.)

Two and a half years after arriving at Itatinga, Antônio Paciência had been ordered to the senzala. He was genuinely puzzled, for there had been no recent clash with the iaiá, certainly nothing as grim as the loss of her shoehorn.

"I'm the slave of Iaiá Teodora Rita," Antônio Paciência protested to the overseer who had been sent to fetch him from the fazenda's kitchen. "I work in the big house."

The overseer, a mulatto like Antônio, had grabbed him by the scruff of his neck. "The senhor barão's wife herself gave the order!"

It took a long time for Patient Anthony to understand that Teodora Rita simply had lost interest in her birthday gift from the senhor barão.

The move to the senzala had been almost as traumatic as being sold away from Mãe Mônica. Cast among the mass of Itatinga's 220 slaves, Antônio had experienced a deprivation that went far beyond being stripped of the nice clothes he had worn on parade in front of the iaiá's guests or denied the food from the fazenda's kitchen.

Chigger Man was the first to bring Antônio Paciência close to understanding the loss of dignity.

Chigger Man, who was said to be more than ninety years old and had served the senhor barão's father in the canoes of the monsoons, was expert in prying loose the tiny mites that attacked the slaves' feet, burrowing under the skin to lay their eggs. Chigger Man performed his crude surgery outside one of the slave dormitories, and Antônio himself had submitted to Chigger Man's knife. Watching the old slave probe and scratch for chiggers had left Antônio with a feeling of revulsion and sharpened his sense of loss at leaving the fazenda.

By the time he was fourteen, Antônio Paciência was doing the work of an adult, for which he was praised by the senhor barão himself. "I was not wrong in listening to Rabelo. You are a good worker. God willing, Antônio, when you are older, you may be an overseer at Itatinga."

Seven months later, Antônio Paciência was given fifty lashes for running away from Itatinga. Eighteen months later he was a fugitive for forty-seven days until he was caught at São Paulo.

Antônio's second flight had been planned with two other slaves. He had wanted Policarpo to go with them, but the Mozambican refused: "The risk is too great."

"We'll go to São Paulo; perhaps to Rio de Janeiro. We won't be found among thousands in the cities."

"Perhaps you'll be lucky."

"Come with us, Mossambe!"

"And lead them to you?"

"We won't be caught."

Policarpo had lowered his head, exposing the deep scar. "Like the mark on a beast," he had said. "Any man who sees it will know: 'Mossambe-with-the-broken-head' — the property of the barão de Itatinga. I cannot go with you, Antônio."

The three slaves had fled Itatinga at the onset of winter 1863. One of Antônio's companions died of pneumonia in a crude shelter they had erected in a forest seventy-five miles southwest of Itatinga. The other had been caught at a senzala. Antônio had been waiting in trees on a hill behind the slave quarters of a fazenda thirty miles from São Paulo. He had heard a commotion as the fugitive was seized by those from whom he sought food. Without waiting to learn what happened, Antônio had run from the hill. He was the only one of the three to reach São Paulo, but he had been in the city only three days when he was arrested as a vagrant.

The senhor barão himself had stood on the far side of the senzala to witness the lashes given the young mulatto under the supervision of head overseer Eduardo, whom the slaves called "Setenta" (Seventy) for the number of lashes he most favored: "Neither too many nor too few" were Setenta's sentiments. "I should sell you to another fazendeiro, Antônio Paciência," Ulisses Tavares had said, "but I'm not a man to pass on my mistakes to others. You came to me as a child and your bad ways were learned at Itatinga. However long it takes, here, too, we will teach you to be a good slave."

But Ulisses Tavares had changed his mind about keeping Patient Anthony. One morning in February 1865, Antônio and five others condemned as lazy or rebellious by the overseers had been lined up in front of the mansion to be told by the senhor barão that they were leaving Itatinga.

"You have not served me well," Ulisses Tavares had said. "You've earned more lashes than the rest of the slaves together. May Jesus Christ, who forgives all, help each one of you! Be loyal! Be trustworthy! Be proud of the service for which you are chosen! Above all, slaves — be brave!"

Ulisses Tavares was donating the six slaves to Emperor Dom Pedro's army. Though careful to select a group of malefactors whom he considered incorrigible, the senhor barão had made this gesture out of noblest patriotism. Many other slave owners picked out a few blacks or browns for the war against Paraguay, but only because these were accepted as substitutes in lieu of service by themselves or their sons. The senhor barão had a mighty contempt for cowards unwilling to fight for Brazil, and in this he was justified, for when the ninety-two voluntários of Tiberica had left the town square, his grandson had ridden at the head of the column.

Included in the column, marching three abreast, had been twenty-seven slaves from fazendas in the district. Some had tramped along with bewildered looks, for they feared this service for which their masters had volunteered them; some had stepped forward elatedly as the townsfolk cheered them. Antônio Paciência had been among the latter, and beside him marched Policarpo Mossambe, one of the six chosen from Itatinga as voluntários da patria.

❧

As the sun rose on the Upper Paraná on the morning of April 10, 1866, Antônio and Policarpo had started down the hill toward their camp. They could hear the sounds of battle from the sandbank opposite the Paraguayan battery at Itapiru. Through the thin tree cover, to the left and right of them, were others who had climbed up for a view of the battle. As in the camp below, and wherever the Brazilian army was gathering for the invasion of Paraguay, the scene held a certain incongruity.

This was South America, but here were thousands of Africans massed for battle. The number of African slaves enlisted in Dom Pedro's army by April 1866 was no fewer than ten thousand; mulattoes and other mixed breeds swelled the number of slave soldiers to fifteen thousand. And as popular enthusiasm for the war waned with the dimming prospect of swift victory, another group of voluntários had had to be compelled to serve their emperor: In the sertão of Pernambuco, the Bahia, and other provinces, recruiters were rounding up the landless class, chaining them together and marching them down to the coast for shipment to the Plata.

This morning, shortly after Antônio and Policarpo reached the camp, the guns at Itapiru fell silent. Firmino Dantas was away at the headquarters of First Corps commander General Manuel Luís Osório, and his two camp attendants had the morning to themselves. They had gone to the riverbank above the assembly point of the invasion flotilla when the first news came of the fight on the sandbank.

"The Paraguayans are defeated!" a boatman had shouted. "The island is ours!" *"Viva! Viva! Viva! Viva Dom Pedro Segundo! Viva Brasil!"* A tremendous cheer rose from the men on the bank.

Policarpo seized Patient Anthony in a fierce embrace. "At last, the battle can begin! We can cross the Paraná to drive the Paraguayans to Asunción! We can cross the river, Antônio Paciência, to freedom. *Freedom!"* Policarpo believed the circulating rumors that slaves who fought for the emperor in Paraguay were to be freed.

"It's only a rumor, Policarpo — the hope of all slaves," Antônio Paciência cautioned.

"Remember, Antônio, I have seen the emperor riding in his carriage at Rio de Janeiro. A great monarch! A wise man! When we defeat his enemies, he will say to us, 'From this day, you are free, my Brasileiros.'"

&

On April 15, 1866, ten thousand men of the Brazilian First Corps under Manuel Luís Osório boarded eleven steamers and canoes and floating piers towed by the ships. Another force of seven thousand Allies, mostly Argentinians, was assembled for embarkation immediately news came of a successful landing by the Brazilians. A Brazilian fleet of seventeen ships in three squadrons rode off the Paraguayan banks, along three points from Tres Bocas to a position fifteen miles away, close to the town of Paso la Patria, the headquarters of Marshal López.

The company of Tiberica volunteers were being transported on one of the three floating piers towed by the steamer carrying General Osório. By 7:00 A.M. on April 16, this vessel was heading directly toward a channel between Itapiru and the sandbank where the Brazilians had been victorious five days ago. "Isle of Redemption," the spit of land had been called, though there had been no deliverance for eight hundred men killed there.

Firmino Dantas da Silva was aboard the steamer with Osório and his staff. He stood at the starboard bulwarks with other officers of the voluntários, feeling an intense nervous excitement as explosions from shells fired by the heavy guns of the naval escort tore up the riverbank, knocking trees to splinters and setting the forest ablaze. The Itapiru battery responded with a continuous grumble, the water rising like a geyser when the Paraguayan shot burst in the river.

Firmino had waited fourteen months for this moment, months during which he'd thought often of returning to Itatinga. At the garrison of Bagé, where the company had been trained, Firmino had not impressed the regular army officers, with whom he had little in common. "O Pensador" ("The Thinker"), his fellow officers had nicknamed him.

At last, the company had been sent to the northwest of Rio Grande do Sul, and Firmino had discovered an unoccupied ranch beside a tributary of the Rio Uruguay where they could camp during the bitterly cold, wet winter. Daily patrols scoured the riverbank, as much to look for Paraguayans as to forage for food. Slave soldiers like Antônio Paciência and Policarpo were set to planting corn, manioc, and other crops.

Firmino dispatched regular reports to the Bagé garrison, but, though he received routine acknowledgments, it seemed that the Tiberica company had been forgotten.

Some of the voluntários resented the inactivity and blamed Firmino Dantas, who could have appealed to Bagé to have the company transferred but seemed perfectly content to stay at the old ranch house reading books he had brought with him. O Pensador, thinking, dreaming, waiting for the war to come to him! Inevitably, others had another explanation for Firmino's apparent willingness to sit out the war far from the battlefront: "The barão de Itatinga's grandson is frightened."

Finally ordered south, the company headed for the camp near the port of Corrientes; there Firmino Dantas found his cousin, the artillery captain Clóvis da Silva, at Lagoa Brava. Clóvis, who had already fought against the Paraguayans in Corrientes province, was also critical of Firmino Dantas's inaction since leaving Tiberica.

"The barão didn't encourage you to volunteer for so miserable a post," Clóvis da Silva said that first night as they dined together at the Hotel Riachuelo, one of many establishments flourishing at Corrientes with the influx of thousands of troops and camp followers.

"I'm not a professional soldier, Clóvis."

"Good God, man, that's not the issue. As the grandson of the barão de Itatinga, you can do better than sit in camp for eight months. Ulisses Tavares expects more than this, Firmino Dantas."

After that meeting, Clóvis da Silva had arranged for Firmino to be made liaison officer with Osório's headquarters. The promotion had brought him into contact with the command of the First Corps and offered good prospects for rapid advancement. Still Firmino Dantas had been a reluctant participant, carrying out his orders efficiently but without the show of spirit to win the attention of his superiors.

Firmino dearly longed to be back at Itatinga, where he could continue his experiments with the coffee mill. Where he could see the girl about whom he had dreamed all these months! Since the night of the baronesa's ball, Firmino's passion for the golden-haired Renata had grown. Before marching away, he had gone to August Laubner's shop in Tiberica and asked the apothecary to put together a personal medical kit for his campaign. There he had seen Renata Laubner. Firmino had gazed into those brilliant blue eyes as she talked with him, and had openly revealed his admiration — his adoration! The moment August Laubner went to the back of the shop in search of something, Firmino had suddenly taken hold of Renata's hand and pressed it to his lips.

His commitment to Carlinda troubled him. He knew also that his betrothed's fiery-tempered ally, Teodora Rita, would oppose any breach of promise. But, as the months passed, Firmino had built up hopes of a relationship with the Swiss beauty that went far beyond what could be justified by one touch of his lips to her hand. "Oh, my love, Renata," Firmino would whisper to himself "I'll fight this war and return to Tiberica, where you await me."

Now, as Firmino stood on the deck of the steamer leading the invasion flotilla toward Itapiru, the thunder of war bursting around him, with an ironclad off to starboard, her flame-belching Whitworths unleashing destruction against the enemy, his nervous anticipation gave way to elation.

Firmino glanced toward General Osório, who was fifty-eight years old, gray-haired, with alert, genial eyes, a bona fide officer and gentleman. Osório had been nineteen when he fought in his first battle in the Banda Oriental in 1827, and had gained a legendary reputation as a lancer.

When Firmino first met the general at his headquarters, where he had gone as battalion liaison officer, Osório had remarked that the name of Ulisses Tavares da Silva ranked high among those who had made King João's conquest of the Banda Oriental in 1817. "Show half the spirit of the barão on that campaign, Firmino Dantas, and you'll make the old Paulista a proud man." Firmino Dantas had promised to do his best. Alone, he had felt his deep dread of failure in battle against the Guarani, whom Ulisses Tavares, like His Majesty Dom Pedro, considered a worthless enemy.

But Firmino's apprehension vanished as the invading force rode forward. The Paraguayan gunners were finding their mark now, and scored hits on a nearby ship and a floating pier. But as the range closed, with the steamers still several hundred yards off the Isle of Redemption, the lead ships of the flotilla began to turn to port. One after the other, with the floating piers in tow and the canoes keeping in the lee of the transports, the ships began to move down the Upper Paraná toward Tres Bocas: The landing had been planned not at Itapiru but at a point about half a mile beyond Tres Bocas on the Rio Paraguay itself.

e/3

"Macacos . . . macacos . . . macacos."

General Juan Bautista Noguera intoned the epithet with a deadly calm as he watched the river armada draw near the low-lying banks where the Rio Paraguay fell into the Paraná.

Four thousand soldiers were in position along the banks of the Upper Paraná, the majority between Itapiru and Paso la Patria. An invasion by the Allies had been accepted as inevitable for months, and the Paraguayan High Command had seen little hope of effectively resisting a landing by the enemy's overwhelming numbers. Cacambo had been among the few to protest this; he agreed with Marshal López's English engineers, Colonel George Thompson and Lieutenant Hadley Tuttle, who had argued that Paso la Patria, Itapiru, and other possible landing places should be defended with every gun that could be brought down from Humaitá garrison.

Marshal López had rejected this plan. He accepted the fortification of Humaitá as Paraguay's key defense. The riverside batteries provided tremendous firepower, and almost a year after the victory at Riachuelo; the Brazilian fleet had not yet dared make passage toward Humaitá. But more than the guns of Humaitá awaited an enemy: There were the *esteros*, a natural defense every bit as daunting as the man-made works at Humaitá. The "Place of the Damned," Marshal López called it.

Behind the carrizal, situated between two parallel streams — Bellaco Norte, just below one line of outworks of Humaitá, and Bellaco Sur, about three miles to the south toward the Upper Paraná — lay the esteros. A dense forest of Yatai palms grew on heights thirty to eighty feet above the swamps, which were clogged with rushes and three to six feet deep. For an invading force, few fields of operation could be worse than that toward which the Allied troops were heading this morning of April 16, 1866.

Just past 8:30 A.M., Cacambo and his company were in a palm grove two hundred yards from the Rio Paraguay. Behind them was an extensive morass; in front of them, a narrow strip of open, firm ground, which for the past twenty minutes had been plowed up in a continuous bombardment by the enemy.

"Macacos . . . macacos . . . macacos."

War steamers, transports, flat barges, and canoes as far as the eye could see. And to challenge them, Cacambo with two hundred men and boys, most of them carrying flintlock muskets and machetes. Cacambo had sent three men to a Paraguayan detachment two miles to the east, behind the morass and below Itapiru, but he knew it would take his messengers at least an hour to get through the marshes.

The palm grove stood on low-lying ground and provided the scantiest cover for Cacambo's force. Here and there, men had thrown up small earthworks where they sheltered, but the Brazilian barrage was relentless and deadly. In fifteen minutes, Cacambo's company had lost fifty men, and in the firestorm between the palms, many more were deafened by the blasts. Only a few stood firm as the majority backed off into the morass.

Cacambo saw how bad it was. He did not curse those who fled. The company flag bearer, a boy of eleven, stood near him. Cacambo stared at the red, white, and blue banner of the Republic of Paraguay. "Go!" he said. "Carry our flag to safety."

The boy was a Guarani from Cacambo's town. He shook his head.

"Go! Go!" Cacambo said. "You can do nothing here. Take our colors to Marshal López. Tell him, Cacambo —" A shell whistled into the palm grove, exploding close by. "Go!" he shouted. The young Guarani ran for the morass.

The Brazilian guns stopped firing. In the palm grove, trees cracked and thudded to earth; wounded men cried out; and on the ground beyond, where dust and smoke drifted, silence. But the stillness was soon broken by voices as three floating piers and two canoes of the enemy approached the bank of the Rio Paraguay.

With six men remaining, General Juan Bautista Noguera stormed toward the invaders. His comrades ran ahead of him, for he had not much wind left, this old Guarani who long ago should have taken his rest with those elders who lay in their hammocks. He stumbled a few times, almost losing his footing as he skirted the craters from the enemy cannonade. He had unsheathed his sword and was wielding it with both hands.

The men in the floating piers saw the six front-runners bunched close together, their red blouses offering easy targets. Fusillades from two crowded piers stopped the six Paraguayans in their tracks.

"Macacos . . . macacos . . . macacos."

Cacambo ran on. His gaze was on the lead canoe. He saw a great macaco there, standing insolently in the prow, wearing a white kepi and blue poncho and carrying a silver-plated lance.

Cacambo was twenty yards from the edge of the riverbank when four Minié balls struck him. General Juan Bautista Noguera stumbled forward a few feet and then fell.

"My Guarani . . ." he wept, with his last breath.

The man in the white kepi was the first Brazilian to set foot on Paraguayan soil: General Manuel Luís Osório, who would be honored for this triumphant moment with the title Barão de Herval.

e⁄ɔ

Thirty-eight days after the landings near Tres Bocas, the exhilaration Firmino had experienced during the invasion was gone.

On the push through the carrizal east from the low banks at Tres Bocas toward Paso la Patria, Brazilian troops had skirmished with Paraguayans deployed around the lagoons and morasses. The Tiberica contingent had reached Paso la Patria on April 21 without firing a shot other than rounds spent by nervous voluntários blazing away at noises in the jungle.

Firmino began to pay the price for the months in which he had kept to himself: utter loneliness, no fellowship at all with other officers or the men of his company. Even with Clóvis da Silva, whom he saw often at Paso la Patria — now a sprawling base for the Allied bridgehead — Firmino found it difficult to make conversation. The artilleryman's confidence left Firmino feeling totally inadequate. He recognized the major — Clóvis had been promoted since the landings — as exactly the kind of soldier Ulisses Tavares expected Firmino to be.

To make matters worse, listening to Clóvis and the others, with their boisterous, passionate, jocular talk of combat, only intensified Firmino's feeling of isolation. He looked at dead Paraguayans beside the route of march and imagined himself a corpse; he spoke with survivors of the May 2 attack on the vanguard, which had lost sixteen hundred men, and was certain he would run from such an onslaught. These anxieties grew until he could contemplate little else, not even the command of Ulisses Tavares, who had sent him south to uphold the heroic name of the da Silvas of Itatinga.

e⁄ɔ

On May 24, 1866, thirty-eight days after the landings, the Allies' forward positions were along a three-mile front at Tuyuti, an area of higher ground with palm forests just north of the stream of Bellaco Sur and on the southern fringes of the swamps and morasses. Thirty-five thousand men had moved up here from Paso la Patria, with more than one hundred field guns. The Brazilian divisions held the left flank, the Argentinians the right. There were nine hundred Uruguayans, all that remained of the battalions led by the Colorado general Venancio Flores. The Allies were still under the overall command of the Argentinian president, General Bartolomé Mitre, and General Osório led the Brazilian army.

On May 24 at Tuyuti, General Mitre ordered a reconnaissance in force into the esteros. Firmino Dantas and the Tiberica company were with a division near the rear of the Brazilian left flank. General Antônio Sampião, a veteran infantryman from the northeast province of Ceará, commanded these battalions of Paulista, Carioca, and Cearense voluntários holding positions in support of an artillery regiment — the

Bateria Mallet — with twenty-eight Whitworth and La Hitte cannons. Major Clóvis da Silva served with these batteries, which were led by and bore the name of the French-born Emilio Mallet, who had come to Brazil as a mercenary in the 1820s and had risen to be the best gunner in the imperial army.

Late morning, along the Allied lines, the battalions chosen to reconnoiter the esteros were awaiting orders to penetrate the marshes. The atmosphere was hot and humid, the sky cloudless, and as the reconnaissance forces were mustered, sweat-drenched men cursed impatiently; they didn't expect the probe into the esteros to amount to much.

Firmino Dantas and his men were with other voluntários three hundred yards to the left of the Bateria Mallet. The company's position was on an elevation covered with Yatai palms. Below the slight slope, the ground leveled out toward an open morass extending from the reed-clogged esteros. A wide, deep ditch had been dug in front of the twenty-eight field guns, and the earth that had been removed from this trench spread out in front of and behind it so that from the edge of the esteros the long pitfall would not be visible.

At precisely 11:55 A.M., a Congreve rocket tore into the air and burst above a patch of jungle to the left of the Brazilian positions. Here and there a bugle sounded, a whistle shrilled, as officers quickest to react brought their men to orders.

A few minutes after the rocket explosion, a Brazilian skirmisher came running out of the jungle:

"Camarada! Camarada! Os Paraguaios! Os Paraguaios!"

From the jungle on the left came eight thousand infantry and one thousand cavalrymen, who had had to dismount and lead their horses in single file through the dense undergrowth. Sweeping down on the right toward the Argentinian flank, thundering out of the cover of a palm forest, came seven thousand cavalrymen with two thousand foot soldiers running up behind them. Pouring directly from the estero in a frontal assault on the Bateria Mallet were five thousand infantrymen, with four howitzers. Altogether some 23,000 men, the bulk of Paraguay's army.

By noon of May 24, 1866, five minutes after the Paraguayans' rocket signal to commence the attack, the battle of Tuyuti raging along the whole line of the Allies.

&

The Tiberica company was in position with its battalion between the Yatai palms, firing down the slope toward the enemy at the edge of the esteros seven hundred yards away. The Paraguayans were closely bunched together as their front ranks sploshed through the morass toward the firm ground in front of the Bateria Mallet and in the direction of the heights with the palm forest. Colonel Mallet's twenty-eight guns went into action with a thunderous oration, but the deluge of fire and iron did not break the red-bloused wave rolling toward the Brazilians.

"Fogo!" Clóvis Lima da Silva commanded the men at the four brass La Hittes, with the earth quaking beneath his feet and bullets whistling and singing over his head.

Colonel Emilio Mallet himself moved among his gunners, with only one order for the line: "They shall not enter here!"

"Fogo! Fogo! Fogo!" came the command, and three hundred yards from the roaring guns, Tiberica's voluntários blazed away at the Paraguayans.

Firmino Dantas was thirty feet behind his men, taking cover at the base of a Yatai palm. With the utmost effort, he manipulated hands that trembled, fingers that seemed frozen as he took out cartridges and caps.

Bayonets flashed and gleamed as the Paraguayans advanced resolutely through the morass. Those up front charged the instant they hit firm ground: The rapid fire from the Bateria Mallet cut them down in bunches, but the gaps were quickly filled.

Firmino Dantas's feelings plunged from terror to hopelessness as he glanced around for a safer place and saw none.

No matter. Within seconds, screaming at the top of their lungs, several hundred Guarani horsemen broke through the extreme end of the Brazilian left flank and came thundering toward the Yatai palms.

∾

Antônio Paciência was no less afraid than Firmino Dantas. He and Policarpo Mossambe and seven voluntários had taken up a position behind a group of low rocks that gave far less protection than the men hugging the earth behind them imagined.

"Load, Antônio! Fire, Antônio! Load, damn you!" Policarpo growled when he saw the young mulatto paralyzed behind a big stone. Antônio obeyed. Mechanically, he pointed his weapon and fired at the mass of men at the edge of the esteros. Then he waited motionless again, his mouth open as he stared at the enemy.

"*Baioneta,* Antônio! *Baioneta!*"

Antônio heard Policarpo's command, but he did not obey. Like others, he was transfixed with horror as he saw the Guarani cavalrymen.

Heavy rifle fire from the voluntários brought down the front riders and sent several ponies crashing to the ground. But the voluntários had no time to reload and no place to hide before the thundering, yelling, snorting stampede was upon them, slashing with saber and machete.

With a bloodcurdling yell, a Paraguayan rode at Policarpo, swinging his machete. There was a clash of iron as Policarpo warded off the blow with his bayonet; then he jabbed upward with his weapon, the razor-sharp triangular bayonet biting into the Guarani's cheek, and the man's horse tore away with its screaming stricken burden. A second cavalryman came, and he fell from his saddle as he lunged for Policarpo, who bayoneted him.

But there were few kills like Policarpo's. One hundred voluntários lay dead or wounded beneath the palms; many more had fled toward the Bateria Mallet. The Paraguayans rode on, too, to cover the three hundred yards to the guns, but their ponies stormed into a solid wall of rifle fire from troops massed by General Sampião.

Antônio Paciência looked up shamefacedly at Policarpo. "Oh, Mossambe, I did *nothing!*" When the cavalry struck, Antônio had clung to the earth behind the rocks.

The Mozambican held out his hand to help Antônio to his feet. "It was the first fight," he said.

❧

Firmino Dantas lay at the palm tree. His face was streaked with blood, his jacket stained crimson. He heard the continuing thunder of battle, but it seemed far away; he heard voices of troops coming up to fill the breach in their lines, but made no effort to appeal for help. Firmino looked at his fingers, which he had pressed against his side. He moaned softly.

A Paraguayan cavalryman lay six feet away. Mortally wounded, this enemy had been hurled from his horse, his body smashing into the palm, splattering Firmino Dantas with blood.

❧

On the Allied right flank, detachments of the seven thousand Paraguayan cavalrymen clashed with a mounted Argentinian regiment, cutting them up and scattering them. Four hundred Paraguayan chargers did not stop, for the rout of the enemy horsemen had cleared the way to a twenty-gun battery. They raced for the guns, with canister and grape emptying their saddles at such speed that only half their number reached the canyon, killing or putting to flight the men who had stayed beside their pieces. The Paraguayans were busy turning the field guns in order to drag them over to their own side when Argentinian cavalry reserves suddenly appeared. Numbers of Paraguayans immediately dismounted to maneuver the guns — they refused to abandon their prizes — and to a man, they were slaughtered.

The Argentinian battery was brought back into action, adding to the cannonade all along the three-mile front.

Nowhere along the Allied line was the Paraguayan assault as ferocious and sustained as against the guns of Emilio Mallet and Antônio Sampião's division supporting the artillery. Wave after wave of the five thousand Paraguayans who had crossed the esteros stormed the Brazilians, breaking to the left and right as they made for the battery or the troop positions at the Yatai palms.

For the Twenty-fifth Paraguayan Battalion — new recruits called to rebuild Marshal López's army — the price of valor was high: The rapid fire from Emilio Mallet's guns was devastating. The next company sent forward discovered that the quagmire had been filled in with the bodies of the men of the Twenty-fifth.

But those troops who broke to the right were able to join up with infantry from the column of nine thousand foot and horse soldiers who had come through the jungle east of the Brazilian positions. The combined infantry made three charges against the Brazilians, driving them deeper into the palm forests. Three times the Brazilians rallied and hurled the Paraguayans back toward the esteros. After almost four hours of fighting, Antônio Sampião himself was critically wounded and one thousand of his men, both regulars and voluntários, were dead or injured. By 3:00 P.M., news of the perilous situation of the surviving defenders was carried to the Brazilian army chief, Manuel Luís Osório.

Osório was known to his men as "The Legendary," a title as well deserved as any baronetcy his emperor chose to bestow upon him. Gathering every man he could detach from his post, Osório hurried to assist Sampião's battered division.

The main body of Paraguayans were in the open between the Yatai palms and the esteros, mustering for another assault on the Brazilian positions. When Osório and his force began to advance, the Paraguayans blasted the front ranks with volleys of musket fire that felled men all along the line.

"Avançar, Brasileiros! Avançar!" Osório commanded, his poncho blowing in the wind, his hand gripping the silver-plated lance he favored as weapon even when afoot.

A bugler running next to Osório was shot dead. Out of the corner of his eye, Osório saw a soldier pick up the cornet. "Sound it, voluntário! Blow!" Osório shouted.

The soldier held his rifle in his right hand; with his left, he raised the bugle to his lips and blew what sounded like the advance.

Spurred on by The Legendary, the Brazilians tore into the Paraguayans with an almighty rage. In fifteen minutes, hundreds of Paraguayans were shot down at point-blank range or bayoneted.

Osório's infantry charge smashed the Paraguayans in this sector. By 4:30 P.M., all along the front, the Allied cannons began to fall silent.

When it was over, General Osório saw the man who had picked up the bugle walking back to camp:

"What is your name, voluntário?"

"Policarpo Mossambe, my General, from Tiberica."

"Take note of it," Osório told an aide. Policarpo had lost his forage cap and Osório noticed the deep dent in his skull. "Where did you get that wound, Policarpo Mossambe?"

"It was before the war, my General. I am the slave Policarpo."

"I saw you fight today, Mossambe," Osório said. "Go back to your company. Tell your commander General Osório says you earned your promotion on the battlefield of Tuyuti. You are to be corporal."

ↄ

"Thank God you're alive!" Major Clóvis da Silva found Firmino Dantas sitting at the edge of a field of wounded.

Firmino had been slow to accept that he had been splattered by the blood of the Paraguayan cavalryman and not his own. The survivors of the battalion were being regrouped when Firmino had dragged himself to his feet. General Antônio Sampião himself had been there as Firmino returned dazedly to his men. "I'm not hurt," he had said in response to the general's concern. But, seeing the state he was in, Sampião had ordered him to join a reserve company guarding a munitions dump in the rear of the line.

Clóvis, knowing nothing of this, looked respectfully at Firmino Dantas's bloodstained uniform. "If only Ulisses Tavares could see you now, Firmino!" he said, beaming. "You have done him proud!"

ↄ

Antônio Paciência walked unsteadily beside Corporal Policarpo.

"My Corporal, I was like a worm," Antônio admitted. "I crawled into the earth to escape the enemy. But you saw me, Corporal Policarpo." How he loved the very sound of his friend's new rank. "When they came a second time, I fought."

"Like a young lion, Antônio Paciência!"

It was the day after the battle. Policarpo and Antônio had been drinking cachaça at the wagon of a trader before going back to their encampment.

Antônio saw smoke rising in front of the Allied lines. "What is it?" he asked.

"I don't know," Policarpo replied, frowning.

"I heard no gunfire."

They hurried forward, and saw the cause of the fires.

"Ai, Jesus Christ! How terrible!" Antônio cried. "Some are so small and thin, there's nothing to burn!"

The Paraguayan dead were being heaped up in alternate layers with wood, in piles from fifty to one hundred, and set on fire. Of 23,000 sent into battle, six thousand were dead and seven thousand injured. The Allied losses were four thousand. The Place of the Damned had reaped its first harvest.

❧

The night was incredibly dark as seven canoes glided swiftly down the Rio Paraguay. Four craft were lashed together in pairs and heavily laden, their gunwales four to five inches above the water. One of three dugouts escorting them rode ahead, two to the rear, the shapes of their crews just distinguishable. It was nearing midnight, August 20, 1866.

"Steady, men. Steady. Let her run with the current," said an officer in the lead canoe.

The craft had come down from a marshy inlet near Curupaiti, an advance battery on the east bank of the Rio Paraguay six miles below the fortress of Humaitá, and were headed toward another earthwork, Curuzu. With thirteen guns in a sunken battery and 2,500 men, Curuzu was the first Paraguayan river defense above Tres Bocas.

All eyes were on the officer in the lead canoe. Before the great war, Capitán Angelo Moretti, former master of the paddle wheeler *La Golconda,* had navigated the Paraguay under every condition. *La Golconda* had made her last trip six months ago, with her boilers cold, her machinery irreparable. Towed by the *Tacuari,* one of three war steamers remaining in service, *La Golconda* had ended her days in a channel in sight of Curupaiti battery, where she was sunk to impede the enemy's passage.

With his livelihood sitting on the bottom of the Rio Paraguay, the Italian capitán had offered his services to the navy, joining almost one thousand men of a dozen nationalities serving the forces of Marshal López, the majority paid technicians and artisans working day and night to supply war materiel from Asunción's arsenal.

Besides Moretti, there were three other officers with the forty men in the canoes. One was Ramos, a young Paraguayan who had spent several years in England, where he had trained as a munitions expert. Another was a Pole named Michkoffsky, who had arrived penniless at Asunción before the war and had had the good fortune to marry a cousin of El Presidente.

The fourth officer sat amidships in one of the two pairs of canoes lashed together. Lucas Kruger had given scant attention to the navigation of the river. With a big straw hat pulled down low over his forehead and his shoulders hunched, he mostly dozed as the unwieldy craft shot forward, and looked up only when the sailors warned of a rough stretch of water ahead.

The itinerant tinkerer from Pittsburgh, who had promised Francisco Solano López that he could make the Rio Paraguay a damnable passage for the enemy, had done exactly that. Just four months ago, sixteen wooden-hulled steamers and four ironclads of His Imperial Majesty Pedro's navy had sailed up the Paraguay from Tres Bocas for about ten miles, and there they sat, twenty powerful warships kept at bay by Luke Kruger, master torpedoman of Paraguay.

Luke's torpedoes were of two kinds: explosive devices planted in pattern in the channels between the islands and high sandbars from Humaitá to beyond the battery of Curuzu; and those dropped into the river to be carried down to the enemy's ships by the current. Varying in size from 50-pounders to a monster boiler-plated 1,500-pounder, the stationary weapons were anchored so that they drifted four to five feet below the surface; those sent downstream floated attached to barrels or demijohns.

Since the outbreak of the war, Luke had continued his attempt to devise an accurate self-propelled torpedo, but with no success. Three hundred torpedoes were anchored in the river by May 1866, when the Brazilians had finally entered the Paraguay; thereafter, Luke and his men had made regular trips downriver to release floating charges.

The Brazilian warships were guarded by boats that carried long lines with grappling irons to hook the float of a torpedo, which they then towed ashore. They were on station day and night, the night watches the worst as they rowed across the river with only flickering lanterns to help them spot the menace drifting toward them. Young Ramos had recently confused the Brazilians with a diabolical scheme he himself had proposed: sending countless demijohns and barrels bobbing downriver weighted with leather bags filled with nothing more lethal than stones.

On the night of August 20, the seven canoes racing toward the Brazilians carried ten torpedoes in the dugouts that had been lashed together. About a mile and a half above the enemy's anchorage, four islands divided the waters of the Rio Paraguay, with two high, narrow strips of land near each bank and two islands close to the middle of the river. In the dry season, the inner islands were connected by a marsh, which was now flooded.

This was the first time they had used this approach; previously they had released torpedoes in the channels to the left and right of the inner islands. Repeatedly the canoes came up against a wall of rushes, a solid, impenetrable mass of vegetation. The sailors waded into the rushes, wrenching them out of the mud by their roots, working a passage through them foot by foot. Mosquitoes and flies and a myriad other pests swarmed around the men, biting and stinging; birds nesting in the rushes scattered; larger creatures, possibly capybara, the great water rats, broke noisily into deeper cover.

It took an hour to break through the rushes. Kruger and Michkoffsky themselves had to climb out to help lighten the craft and drag them through the soft mud.

Moretti, who had had the idea of this approach, sat high and dry in his canoe humming to himself as he waited for them.

"Moretti, next time you'll be first over the side," Luke said.

Moretti greeted this with a huge, toothy grin. "I will, Luke?"

"Damn right! With your fancy pants, silver buttons, and all, my lord Admiral!"

Unlike Luke, whose shabby appearance had elicited complaints from none other than Marshal López himself, but who had done nothing to improve it, Moretti wore navy whites and blue jacket adorned with silver buttons bought from a soldier who had stripped the body of an Argentinian colonel killed at Tuyuti.

"I think not," Moretti said. "Our next stop will be opposite the Brazilians."

"Angelo, I hope you're right," Luke said.

Moretti laughed. "Use your paddles quietly now, men," he told his crew. "Not a sound."

Luke gave the same order. His canoe dropped back as Moretti left the open, inundated area for a narrower passage between the rushes.

Fifteen minutes later, Moretti's crew took their paddles out of the water. The dugout rode forward gently, coming to a stop behind a stand of rushes. One after the other, the rest of the squadron came up, drifting slowly near Moretti's canoe.

Through the rushes, the torpedomen could see the lanterns of the boats on guard duty in front of the Brazilian ships.

"Have I ever misled you, Luke?" Moretti asked softly.

Luke Kruger did not reply. He was already directing the off-loading of the first torpedo and float. Before the first pair moved off, other men swam to the opening to check for hazards — a log caught below the surface, for instance, against which a torpedo could strike. After crisscrossing the area several times, the men reported it all clear.

"Easy, boys. Easy now," Luke said. He glanced to the left through the reeds at the distant lanterns flickering like tiny fireflies. "Ramos," he said. "What do you think?"

"Maybe we'll be lucky tonight. Sink one son of a bitch," he said, mimicking Luke.

In the open river behind the rushes, the current was running at three knots, carrying the torpedoes swiftly toward the fleet. A lieutenant with seven oarsmen in a guard boat shouted an alarm when he spotted a float.

A minute later, the lieutenant swung out a line with a heavy grappling hook. The iron claws banged against the side of the barrel float; then the hook plopped into the water. The lieutenant jerked the line; the grappling iron slammed against the torpedo, striking the piston.

A brilliant flash lit up the river behind the rushes.

"Mother of God!" Ramos cried. "Luke!"

"It was a guard boat."

"They work! The torpedoes work, Luke!"

"Sooner or later, Ramos," he said laconically.

༄

On August 27, 1866, one week later, Luke Kruger and young Ramos were prepared for another night raid on the Brazilian fleet. Paraguayan scouts operating in the carrizal below the Curuzu battery and toward Tres Bocas reported numerous transports steaming up behind the fleet — indication of an imminent assault against the defenses at Curuzu and Curupaiti.

Luke's plan of attack was different tonight and involved one boat, eight men, including Luke and Ramos, and one five-hundred-pound torpedo. The boat was a forty-foot steam launch that had been captured during the Paraguayan invasion of Mato Grosso in December 1864. The Paraguayans had called this prize *"Yacaré"* — *"Alligator"* — but Angelo Moretti had his own name for her: *"Lucky Luke."*

Moretti was to have gone on this mission, but he'd been summoned to Asunción.

"What for?" Luke asked.

"Perhaps they want to talk about *La Golconda.*"

Luke saw no chance of Moretti being compensated for the steamer that had been scuttled by the navy. "You're wasting your time, Angelo. They did you a favor taking her off your hands."

"It isn't true."

"I worked on her engines —"

"Then you know: They ran like new."

"No, Angelo. It was a miracle you cleared Asunción Bay, but go to Asunción, Angelo. Go. I'll take Ramos."

Luke Kruger shared Moretti's view that the struggle by 525,000 Paraguayans against three nations with a combined population of twelve million was a battle for the very existence of Paraguay.

"López's enemies say they make war on him alone, but the Paraguayans know this is a lie," Luke had said on one occasion. "Buenos Aires has many a score to settle with Asunción. I can accept this. But Pedro of Brazil, who sends his slave horde into battle claiming it's to free Paraguayans from López? Pedro, whose armies slaughter Guarani by the thousands?

"Pedro knows his own future will be decided on the battlefields of Paraguay. If Paraguay defeats Pedro's armies, the Braganças won't last six months. Six months and Brazilian republicans will follow the example of Juarez in Mexico."

"There will be more than an end to Bragança rule," Moretti had suggested. "Emperor Pedro and his slaveholding barons know that your Civil War has doomed that institution in the Americas. To lose the war in Paraguay will be as devastating to the empire as the Confederate defeat. A republican Brazil will not tolerate the continued enslavement of three million people."

This evening of August 27, Luke was alone in the one-room house he shared with Moretti. He had spent most of the day on the *Yacaré* preparing the steam launch for this night's mission, which he'd modeled on William Cushing's attack on the Confederate iron-plated ram *Albermarle* in October 1864. The *Yacaré* would steam for a Brazilian ship with the torpedo lowered into the water. By means of a cable leading back from the spar, the torpedo would be released to float below the ship's hull; backing off, the *Yacaré's* crew had only to pull a second line to fire the weapon.

As he lay back on his cot, with smoke curling from a cigar, Luke thought of Angelo Moretti on his way to Asunción. He did not believe the Italian's story about being called to discuss compensation for *La Golconda*. Luke laughed to himself. *Truth is, you would rather sail with the devil than set foot in* Lucky Luke *tonight! Can't say I blame you.*

Puffing on his cigar, Luke realized with a jolt that his journey could end here in Paraguay. He had come through many scrapes on his travels, though at no time had he placed himself in as hazardous a position.

A half-hour before he had to leave to join Ramos aboard the launch, Luke got up from his cot and lit a lantern. The yellowish light revealed a sparsely furnished room: two cots, a table, two chairs. All Luke's things were in one trunk at the side of the room. Neatly stacked on top of the trunk were his most treasured possessions — his collection of books. He took up his Bible and carried it to the table. He thumbed through the pages seeking the passage he knew by heart but found more powerful still when read aloud:

"The Lord is my shepherd . . ." He spoke in a strong, resonant tone, and his voice rose as he reached the last verse: ". . . and I will dwell in the house of the Lord forever."

Then Luke Kruger stood up. He took his straw hat from Moretti's bed and stuck it on his head. He blew out the lantern and stepped outside, walking briskly toward the bank of the inlet and the mooring of the *Yacaré*.

The forty-foot launch was painted black to make her less visible to the enemy. Luke heard young Ramos call out that they were ready. Luke waved in acknowledgment, but nearing a plank walkway between the bank and the side of the boat, he glanced toward the *Yacaré*'s prow. Jutting out in front of the launch was a sixteen-foot spar that was hinged to the bow and could be raised or lowered by a windlass; secured near the end of this iron beam was a five-hundred-pound torpedo.

"Cast off, Ramos!" Luke commanded the instant he stepped aboard.

Drifting clouds intermittently obscured a sliver of moon. Ramos conned the launch out of the inlet and into the channel that lay closest to the east bank of the Rio Paraguay on their left. This route passed the batteries of Curupaiti and Curuzu and had not been strewn with anchored torpedoes. If the enemy captains were foolhardy enough to steam up this way, their ships would come under direct fire from the fifty-eight guns at the two earthworks.

Ten minutes after leaving the inlet, the launch was throbbing forward in the lee of Curupaiti battery. Luke stood with Ramos, leaning back against the side of the boat. Ramos had the *Yacaré* heading steadily down the channel, keeping her in midstream. Two sailors were tending her firebox and boiler; the others were sitting on the deck, checking their rifles — new Enfields taken from Allied soldiers killed in battle.

The *Yacaré* was passing below the thirty-foot sand-and-clay cliff at Curupaiti when Ramos, who had been talking incessantly since leaving the inlet, said, "I'm happy Angelo Moretti was summoned to Asunción."

"Why, Ramos?"

"I would've stood there watching you leave with Moretti."

"You may yet change your mind."

"No, Captain Luke! I want to be there when you get your son of a bitch —"

Young Ramos died with the epithet on his lips.

Riding swiftly down the dark channel with the five-hundred-pound torpedo secured to her spar, the Yacari smashed into the wreck of *La Golconda*, her stack submerged by the rise in the river. Angelo Moretti would have known of this deadly hazard.

Six crewmen were blown skyward by the blast.

And what had been just a passing thought for Lucas Kruger a short while ago became reality. His journey did end here on the Rio Paraguay.

e/o

On September 1, sixteen Brazilian ships began to thread their way up the channels of the Paraguay, steaming slowly north toward Curuzu. A smaller squadron provided cover for the transports, which began to land fourteen thousand men on the edge of the carrizal below the Paraguayans' first river defense work. At noon, with most of the fleet within range of Curuzu, an artillery duel commenced between the ships and shore batteries, which lasted seven hours.

At dawn, September 2, the cannonade was resumed. The Brazilians fired more than two hundred shells an hour at the sunken battery of Curuzu, without doing much damage and in return taking only light punishment from the defenders' thirteen guns.

Among the Brazilian ships that had been hit was the *Rio de Janeiro*. Launched in February 1866, the new ironclad, with four-and-a-half-inch plate and six guns, was one of the fleet's most powerful warships; in the vanguard, she had taken a pounding from the guns of Curuzu, losing a 68-pounder and suffering other damage to her decks. But her commander kept her on station, fighting back gallantly.

At 2:00 P.M., the *Rio de Janeiro* blew up. An anchored torpedo had blasted her poop, and a second had blown a gaping hole near her bow. Within minutes she began to sink.

Master torpedoman Luke Kruger had got his ironclad.

e/o

On September 22, the flags of the Allies flew above the earthworks at Curuzu, which had been taken on September 3. With the fall of Curuzu, Curupaiti battery, three thousand yards to the north, was the only obstacle preventing the Allies from attacking the Paraguayan trenches at Humaitá.

For seven hundred men of the Paraguayan Tenth Battalion who had held the trenches on the left of Curuzu, the burden of defeat was terrible. The Tenth had been so outnumbered that they broke rank, leaving only their commander and a few officers, who had been killed. Back at Humaitá, Marshal López had ordered the men of the Tenth to fall in on the parade ground, at attention. When they were assembled, every tenth man in the rank was told to step forward, and the soldiers thus selected were shot in front of their comrades.

At Curuzu, General Bartolomé Mitre ordered an assault on Curupaiti on the morning of September 22. The Allied commander-in-chief's plan of attack involved eighteen thousand men — eleven thousand Brazilians and seven thousand Argentinians —- who would approach Curupaiti from three directions, the bulk of the Brazilian divisions taking the only road between the two positions.

For three days and two nights, torrential downpours had flooded the carrizal, turning the simplest camp duties into feats of endurance. There were guns to be moved up for the attack, and with one hundred men harnessed like beasts to a piece and wallowing up to their knees in mud as they hauled on the drag ropes; there were rearguard trenches to be dug, and companies of sappers worked day and night against tons of earth that slid back into the ditches; there were passages to be slashed through patches of inundated jungle. Just last night, September 21, the rain had finally stopped, and the fleet had been signaled that the attack was on, its preliminary bombardment to commence at 7:00 A.M.

The rolling fire of the guns brought the great army to its feet. The men were tired and hungry and walked stiffly in damp, dirty uniforms, but they reacted quickly enough to the shrieking whistles and bugle blasts. The sun rose; a light breeze carried with it the sweet perfume of the thorny *aromitas*; the sound of guns played in the background.

The slave soldiers Antônio Paciência and Policarpo, two of forty-seven volunteers remaining from the Tiberica contingent, were attached to a battalion consisting mainly of Pernambucans, Bahians, and other men from the northeast provinces, which were contributing a disproportionate number of volunteers, both slaves and free men. The Tiberica volunteers had been in action once since the battle of Tuyuti, when the Paraguayans again attacked the Allied left flank, in July 1866, an indecisive engagement, but the thousands of Allied soldiers either killed or wounded at Potrero Sauce had brought to an end the days of glory that followed the great victory of Tuyuti.

Firmino Dantas da Silva was not with the Tiberica company. Three weeks after Tuyuti, Second-Lieutenant da Silva had been posted behind the lines at Itapiru on the Upper Paraná, where he joined the quartermaster-general's staff. The slaves from the fazenda of Itatinga — three of the six had been killed — had not seen or heard a word about Firmino Dantas since his taking leave of them.

At Curuzu on September 22, Corporal Policarpo's squad was attached to a section under a caboclo sergeant, Mario Bomfim, whose family were vaqueiros in the Pernambucan sertão north of the Rio São Francisco.

Antônio had told Sergeant Bomfim all he could remember about Jurema, which was not much. "Senhor Heitor Batista and his son, João Montes, sold me to a slaver when I was a child."

"Coronel Heitor Baptista Ferreira and his family? I know the Ferreiras, boy," Bomfim, a scraggy, yellow-faced man in his forties, had responded. "If you cross Coronel Heitor Baptista himself or another poderoso of the family, any one of their hundred armed *capangas* will make your throat sing like a violin!"

"I can't forget Mãe Mônica," Antônio had said. "I will go back for her."

"Boy! If you set foot on Ferreira lands, know what you're doing: Coronel Ferreira isn't a man to tamper with!"

"My mother is an old slave with not many years left. Why would Coronel Ferreira want to keep an extra mouth to feed?"

Late this morning of September 22, 1866, Sergeant Bomfim and his section were about halfway along the Brazilian column and had to wait ten minutes after the first battalions had started up the road near the riverbank before they themselves began to move forward.

They had covered three hundred of the three thousand yards to Curupaiti, when a deafening barrage drowned the noise from the guns of the Brazilian ironclads. The Paraguayans had forty-nine guns at Curupaiti, thirteen along a concave cliff facing the river, thirty-six covering the land approaches from the direction of Curuzu.

At fifteen hundred yards, Sergeant Bomfim and his section had not lost a man, but were finding it difficult to advance in close order. They went forward a hundred yards or so, through smoke spreading like fog over the carrizal, with the fearsome sounds around them, until they came to a place in the road where a Paraguayan shell had exploded. They broke to the left and the right to pass the corpses heaped up there, and tramped on resolutely.

At one thousand yards, the order came down to move into the carrizal to the right, the snap and crack of reeds and rushes and the oaths of men indicating that hundreds were already pushing through the water-logged marshes to reach positions opposite the enemy's earthworks.

"Right! Keep to the right! Forward! Forward!" officers moving along the advancing lines shouted into the reeds.

"Oh, my God!" Sergeant Mario Bomfim cried when he got his men to the trees.

Two hundred yards away, beyond a broad stretch of earth cleared of trees, was Curupaiti's first defense lines. The felled trees had been piled up along the front of the Paraguayans' earthworks to make an abatis — a twenty-foot-wide, eight-foot-high mass of thickly entwined tree trunks and boughs, every projecting limb fashioned into a sharp stake. Behind the abatis, the earth sloped toward the thirty-six guns mounted on raised platforms to give them the broadest possible range. Their crews used this to great advantage, raking the Allied columns with canister and grape as they came out of the carrizal.

Two Brazilian battalions had come through the morasses to a narrow strip of forest at the edge of the clearing in front of the abatis. To the left, the clearing was strewn with men who had marched ahead of them and had charged toward the abatis; groups of soldiers who had made it across were pinned down behind the wall of tangled timber. To the right, an Argentinian battalion was advancing across the clearing, its officers on horseback, riding between the infantry and rallying them forward. The voluntários saw the Argentinian commanding officer and his horse hurled to earth when a shell burst next to them. Four men immediately went to the colonel's aid and began to carry him back toward the carrizal.

Another shell exploded, leaving a swirl of smoke and dust and no sight of the wounded officer and his four rescuers.

Fifteen minutes later, a colonel with sword in hand gave the order for the battalion to advance: "Forward, Brasileiros! Forward, voluntários!"

Corporal Policarpo Mossambe broke out of the trees and ran forward, with Antônio Paciência close on his heels. Policarpo dodged between stumps and charred undergrowth, shouting for his squad to follow him.

"Up, Brasileiros! Up!" shouted officers to any who dropped behind stumps to escape the storm. "*Viva Dom Pedro!*" they yelled.

A shell plowed up the earth within thirty feet of Antônio Paciência. The screams of the men caught there mingled with an insane cacophony of shrieks and roars and the hiss and hum of musket balls, the volleys rising in deadly accompaniment to the thunder of the guns.

When Antônio and Policarpo got to the tangled mass of timber, Sergeant Bomfim was already there, with perhaps five hundred others spread out along several hundred yards of the abatis. Some voluntários found places where they could fire at the enemy through the abatis, but a curtain of dust and smoke in front of the trench made it impossible to see the effect of their shots. Some were assaulting the abatis itself with axes, trying to open a passage for a charge against the enemy.

A soldier standing on a log as he swung his ax suddenly dropped the implement: "O Mary, Mother —" He fell back on the ground beside Bomfim, a ball in his chest.

Policarpo Mossambe stepped up to the log. He seized the ax and swung it, sending chips of wood flying like bullets.

"At it, Corporal! At it!" Sergeant Bomfim shouted.

When Policarpo had chopped through a thick limb, Bomfim and the others dragged it away. Policarpo kept swinging at the timbers, tearing off smaller branches with his hand, ignoring the bullets singing over the abatis.

Sergeant Bomfim soon saw how little progress Policarpo was making against the great barrier. "We won't get through this way!" he said. "Set fire to it!"

Policarpo had worked his way about six feet into the abatis. He didn't react immediately to the sergeant's words but continued swinging the ax.

"Policarpo!" Antônio shouted. "Come down! We'll burn it!"

Policarpo had his back to Antônio; he nodded his head affirmatively but raised the ax for one last swing. He froze, with the blade held high.

An instant later, the shell exploded at the front edge of the tangle of trees, hurling Policarpo Mossambe high into the air.

Antônio was stunned by a chunk of flying timber and fell to the ground. "Oh, God!" he gasped, rocking his body, as a shattering pain shot through his head. He opened his eyes: Sergeant Mario Bomfim was lying ten feet away, his brains scooped out and spread on the ground beside him.

"Policarpo?" Antônio mumbled. "Mossambe?"

Policarpo lay at the edge of the abatis, one eye glaring lifelessly, the other mashed in with the flesh and bone of a wound at the side of his face.

A bugler close by was blowing the Retreat. Antônio saw voluntários all along the abatis start back toward the trees. The gunfire from the Paraguayans was intermittent, desultory, but a new sound came from that direction. Maddening to men who had survived the slaughter: the sound of music from Paraguayan bands behind the parapet — saluting the gunners of Curupaiti.

"Fall back!" an officer shouted, running toward Antônio. "Back, voluntário! Save yourself!"

Patient Anthony joined the stampede to the trees and the carrizal beyond.

‹›

The full extent of the Paraguayan victory was not immediately known; they could count only fifty-four casualties among their gunners and infantry. When the routed Brazilians and Argentinians were lost from sight in the carrizal, thousands of Paraguayans left their trench, climbing over the abatis and swarming into the clearing. For hours they worked, bayoneting the wounded enemy, stripping the dead, rejoicing in the gold coin so many macacos carried. When it was over, the Paraguayans left five thousand corpses in the clearing. And two thousand wounded were being carried through the marshes, altogether more than one-third of the Allied army.

‹›

"Tu-*ru*-tu-tu . . . Tu-*ru*-tu-tu . . ."

The ululation of the turututu horns was a response to the ineffectual bombardment from ten Brazilian ironclads that steamed upriver within range of both Curupaiti and Humaitá. After the rout at Curupaiti, the Allied offensive had bogged down beside the esteros, the first major advance coming nine months after the disaster, with an encircling movement of thirty thousand troops to positions north-east of Humaitá.

Hadley Baines Tuttle, the young Londoner, found the sound of the turututus ominous: After three years of hard service, Hadley Tuttle saw no end to the sacrifices that were being asked of the Paraguayan people. Humaitá and the esteros, reeking with the smell of death, increasingly reminded him of that dire winter of 1854/1855 outside Sevastopol.

Tuttle had been promoted to major and had served these past three years under Colonel George Thompson, the former British army officer whom López had made responsible for the defenses of Humaitá. With seven hundred shovel-wielding men in their engineering battalions, Thompson and Tuttle had directed the construction of 75,000 yards of earthworks — altogether forty-two miles of trenches and fortifications. At Humaitá, eight riverside batteries with sixty-eight guns now flanked the brick-and-stone Bateria de Londres. With Curupaiti battery and artillery positions on Humaitá's outer earthworks, the total firepower was 380 guns, mortars, and rocket stands.

For the two armies ground to a halt amid the steaming jungles and swamps just below Capricorn, summer was murderous: Forty-two miles of Paraguayan trenches either baked in the sun or were raked by torrential downpours; cholera raged, a minimum of fifty men a day carted off to the garrison hospital, and on some days, more than fifty carried out of the wards to mass graves at the *cementario*.

Hunger was another problem. The scouring of the countryside for new recruits after the carnage at Tuyuti was stripping Paraguay's small farms of labor. The ordinary soldier was in rags, considering himself lucky if he held onto a tattered poncho. And with the dwindling rations, he was growing emaciated. But his eyes still flashed boldly, and when the turututus sounded, he cheered. No matter how great the privation and sorrow to be endured, so long as the marshal-president lived and commanded, the soldier could believe in the ultimate success of Paraguay's cause.

Hadley Tuttle was present at an affair one evening in late October 1867, during which Francisco Solano López was praising the spirit of his soldiers:

"Listen," López said, holding up a hand for silence from those seated near him. The marshal's face was flushed from the brandy he'd consumed after dinner. "Listen." In the distance, the turututus answered a shell from the Brazilian squadron. "Blow, my brave trumpeters!" he declaimed. "Blow, my sons, like the valorous three hundred of Gideon, champion of farmer warriors. Let the Brazilians hear you! May they tremble out there!"

The group with López this night were gathered in the house of Madame Eliza Lynch, who maintained a separate residence in the garrison at a respectable distance from her lover's quarters. She was seated at a table with three other ladies at the far end of the room playing whist, a game at which she excelled.

As Hadley Tuttle sat with the marshal, Colonel George Thompson, and two other guests, he occasionally glanced toward the card table with a look of adoration at the young woman on Madame Lynch's right — Luisa Adelaida.

Hadley Tuttle had married Luisa Adelaida in May 1865. López and Eliza Lynch were present because of Madame Lynch's fondness for Luisa Adelaida's mother, Dona Gabriel — one of the few to befriend La Lynch when she arrived at Asunción from Paris in 1855, already pregnant with her lover's child. "They are not worth your tears," Dona Gabriel had said once in response to Eliza Lynch's misery at being scorned by the ladies of Asunción. "They reject you because they envy your beauty and intelligence."

After Luisa Adelaida's marriage to Tuttle, Madame Lynch had often invited the couple to her entertainments, for they were a lively and handsome pair. Of course, Major Hadley, like other officers present this night, was beginning to show the strain of three hard years. His uniform was clean but shabby, with a patch on one arm and a tear that had been stitched by Luisa Adelaida; and his face was scorched by the sun and revealed lines of worry and weariness as he listened to the marshal.

Three times already, López had sought peace: On the eve of the battle of Curupaiti, the marshal-president had met with Mitre of Argentina; early in January 1867, López had agreed to accept an offer by the United States to mediate an accord; this past August, a British diplomat from Buenos Aires had found López amenable to a peace settlement. Each attempt had failed, for the Allies' demand was totally unacceptable to López: "We will not discuss peace until Francisco Solano López is off Paraguayan soil."

When he met the British diplomat from Buenos Aires in Humaitá this past August, Tuttle had given him letters for his family in south London: Writing to his brother, Ainsley, who had served with him at the Crimea, he had given his impressions of the situation:

> Since the start of the war, the enemy has said its belligerence is a crusade in the name of humanity to free Paraguay from a tyrant who rules by terror alone. López is a man to be feared. God knows, I have been within earshot of Asunción jail more times than I want to remember, when the secret police were torturing some unfortunate enemy of El Presidente. But the enemies' claim that the destruction of López is

their only objective must be doubted. Their own hands are red with the blood of political opponents they have butchered.

The terms of the treaty signed by Brazil, Argentina, and the Colorados of Uruguay are well known here, including the secret clauses that guarantee Brazil and Argentina thousands of square miles of Paraguayan territory. The Paraguayans believe the enemies' real objective is nothing less than the extermination of their race.

The Paraguayan peasant, unlike his counterpart in Brazil, owns his small parcel of land or rents it from the state at a low price; his children are being educated at schools established in every pueblo; his health is protected with mass campaigns of inoculation against smallpox and with other measures instituted by the English doctors. He sees all this as coming from the despot who rules him and whom he esteems as passionately as his ancestors did the black robes of the reductions. As long as the marshal-president is there, the Paraguayans will continue the struggle, even if their beloved fatherland is left in ashes.

Like his commanding officer, Colonel Thompson, and most of the foreigners paid by López, Hadley Tuttle had chosen to remain in Paraguay, though not without increasing concern for the safety of his wife.

Luisa Adelaida and Dona Gabriel had been at Humaitá for six months, staying with Hadley in a house near Madame Lynch's quarters. Eliza Lynch herself had asked them here to assist in organizing a women's corps. Several hundred mothers and daughters served in the hospital, cleaned the barracks and campgrounds, and cultivated field crops. Madame Lynch was often seen in the uniform of a colonel of the Paraguayan army when she went among the women, who had their own captains and sergeants; they had sent deputations to the marshal-president asking to be drilled as soldiers and allowed to fight, but López had turned down these requests.

At Eliza Lynch's house this October night, Marshal López still believed the enemy could be driven off Paraguayan soil with one more hammer blow like Curupaiti.

López was planning to strike that blow with another attack against Tuyuti, where the Paraguayans had suffered their worst defeat. Tuyuti, now the main supply base for the Allied divisions deployed northeast of Humaitá, could be seen from watchtowers along Humaitá's outer earthworks. López intended to send eight thousand men — sixteen battalions of infantry; six regiments of cavalry — against Tuyuti. "We failed last year because surprise was lost. This time we will cross the esteros at night and be in position before dawn. We will avenge the slaughter at first Tuyuti," López promised.

The guns on the Brazilian ironclads had stopped firing, and the turututus had been laid aside, when the Tuttles left Eliza Lynch's quarters. The silence that followed the bombardment was pierced by the scream of the cicada. Sentinels in the trenches and watchtowers saw the enemy camps and ships frozen in the moonlight, but for most at Humaitá, late night brought a false but welcome peace.

Hadley held Luisa Adelaida tightly on the short walk from Madame Lynch's house to their own place, for they had only a few hours together: In the morning, Luisa Adelaida and Dona Gabriel were returning to Asunción.

Alone in their room, Hadley and Luisa Adelaida spoke in whispers, for the simple interior had makeshift partitions plaited with reeds and thick grass. They made love, knowing that they would have to cherish these moments through months of separation.

The next morning, Hadley escorted Luisa Adelaida and her parents to an embarkation point near Humaitá to board a steamer for the voyage north. A regimental band played as the paddle wheeler that had come down from Asunción arrived at the landing. It was crammed with new recruits. A few were pure Guarani; a few, mulattoes; the majority, of mixed Guarani-Spanish descent. Some were in rags, but most wore their best shirts and trousers or *chiripas,* loose-fitting gear of a square of cloth draped from the waist and between the legs. A few sported red shirts, white trousers, and military caps — uniforms home-sewn or inherited from fathers and brothers who had not returned. What was common to every recruit, from the tall ones who looked older to little fellows having trouble keeping up, was youth: The youngest of these new soldiers was nine years old; the oldest warrior-to-be, thirteen.

&

By the spring of 1867, the Allied generals chose their words carefully when speaking of the foe. "I expect to do a thing or two," said Field Marshal Luís Alves de Lima e Silva, marquês de Caxias, who served Dom Pedro Segundo as minister of war and took command of the Brazilian forces after the disaster at Curupaiti. Caxias was sixty-four years old when he got to Paraguay in November 1866, boasting a reputation as a skillful tactician and organizer who had not lost a battle since graduating from the military academy at Rio de Janeiro at the age of eighteen. With the Brazilian fondness for grandiose sobriquets, the field marshal was called "O Pacificador" in honor of his triumphs, especially in suppressing revolts against the empire. Gray-haired, with a bristly white mustache, slightly hooded eyes, and sharp features; Caxias was endowed with a strong, spare physique and the stamina of a man twenty years younger. The field-marshal had need of all his energy for the tasks he found awaiting him upon landing in Paraguay at the end of 1866.

After Curupaiti, where thousands were slaughtered, the heartsick survivors had slogged back through the carrizal with the wounded. Their demoralization had swiftly spread to every quarter of the Allied front.

Among the fifty thousand men waiting below the miasmal Bellaco esteros were thousands of "voluntários" here against their will, both those who had come as slaves and the wretched of the sertão herded out of the caatinga in irons. Many would have deserted but for the fact that thousands of miles separated them from their hometowns.

There was another sinister aspect to the malaise that was wearing down the Allied army: Brazilians and Argentinians were stationed along different sections of the front, but word of insolence from either group and bloody fights erupted between them, the streets of Paso la Patria not infrequently a battleground for mobs of violent Brazilians and Argentinians.

Above all, there was the loathsome terrain occupied by the Allied army. The river below the morasses, Bellaco Sur, had become a torrent in the rainy season; the water table of the marshes had risen; campsites had been engulfed.

Inevitably, there was sickness. Cholera and typhoid fever became the true enemies. Early in 1867, the daily toll was three hundred. By May, no fewer than thirteen thousand men were in hospitals.

The Allied command was in theory still shared by Bartolomé Mitre, president of Argentina; Venancio Flores, the Uruguayan, who had only a few hundred men left under his command; and, now that he had taken over the Brazilian forces, the marquês de Caxias. In practice, Caxias was virtually supreme commander, for Mitre was suffering most of the recriminations for the losses at Curupaiti, and Venancio Flores was called back to Montevideo to deal with one of the perennial disturbances between Blancos and Colorados.

Field-Marshal Caxias spent six months reorganizing the army, which was now predominantly Brazilian. Base camps like Tuyuti were cleaned up and their fortifications improved; telegraph lines were laid and buried below earth; a serious attempt was made to map the enemy's positions.

Caxias restored discipline and improved morale, and by July 22, 1867, had thirty thousand men ready to move for the encirclement of Humaitá by land. General Manuel Luís Osório, who had led the initial landings in Paraguay, commanded a newly formed Third Corps. For three months, Osório's men slogged northward, cutting almost fifty thousand yards of trenches and establishing batteries all along their twenty-eight-mile route. By late October 1867, they had swung toward the west and were in sight of the Rio Paraguay. On November 2 they captured Tayí, a small riverside post fifteen miles north of Humaitá.

But November 2 was also the night Marshal López chose to send eight thousand men through the esteros to destroy the Allied First Corps at Tuyuti.

✂

November 2 was a Saturday, All Souls' Day. Morning Masses at Tuyuti offered prayers for those in Purgatory, but by nightfall the dead were forgotten amid a carnival atmosphere around the *comércio*, where sutlers plied the ranks with cachaça and other promises of blessed oblivion and escape from the drudgery of duty in the trenches and redoubts.

Tuyuti's High Command kept sedately to their quarters, playing cards or relaxing with their brandies and port. Another group of Brazilian and Argentinian officers, at peace with each other this night, were gathered in an open-sided mess tent at camp headquarters. Young men and old; regular army, Guarda Nacional, and voluntários — this crowd's behavior was anything but sedate, with *garrafas* of liquor passing quickly from one hand to another. Smoke from a battery of thick black cigars lay banked up in the yellowish glare from oil lamps.

Firmino Dantas da Silva — Capitão Firmino Dantas — and his cousin, gunner Clóvis Lima da Silva, were among the officers in the tent. They sat next to each other at a table to the right of a dance area where twin sisters, Sabella and Narcisa, morena girls from the Bahia, were performing. They had wavy brunette hair, ruby lips, green eyes that laughed, teased, invited; their cinnamon flesh was warm as the tropical night. They wore V-necked white lace blouses, which scarcely contained their full breasts; their dark red satin skirts swirled against their swinging hips.

Two black soldiers, their khaki drill uniforms soaked, sat to one side, their hands a blur above the drums they played in accompaniment with three guitarists. A lancer from Rio Grande do Sul rose and joined the morenas in dance.

The girls laughed and exchanged bawdy quips with the lancer as they moved their bodies to the beat of the drums. A procurer of prostitutes at Salvador had transported them here a year ago.

Clóvis's eyes followed the girls across the dance floor. Firmino Dantas melancholy gaze was more reserved.

Firmino had returned to Tuyuti in July 1867, a few weeks before the Second and Third Corps' drive to the north and west. Firmino still served on the staff of the quartermaster-general and had been promoted to captain, for he had done good work at Itapiru's stores.

Firmino had a packet of letters now from his fiancée, Carlinda, and from Ulisses Tavares. "Come back to Itatinga," the barão had written this past April. "You have done your share, Firmino. Come home, to the honors you deserve!" That Ulisses Tavares should make this appeal had come as no surprise to Firmino. His grandfather's expectation of a swift, victorious campaign against a barbarous foe had to seem lunacy now viewed within the slow murderous reality of a conflict claiming thousands of Brazilian lives and costing the empire sixty million dollars a year.

Earlier tonight, Firmino and Clóvis had gone for a walk along the perimeter of the citadel. Major Clóvis had been at the base since May 1866, commanding a battery to the right of Tuyuti's first and second lines of trenches.

Stocky, muscular, his Tupi heritage discernible in his broad face, Clóvis da Silva was imbued with the brazen spirit of his bandeirante ancestors.

"The Guarani still hear the Jesuits preaching about devils from São Paulo. I don't know how long their resistance will last. Whatever it takes, however great our sacrifice, in the end, we will conquer them."

"Conquer, Clóvis? Or exterminate?"

"Either way, cousin . . . either way, Brazil will triumph."

Firmino had not doubted, when Brazilian territory was invaded, the just cause of the war, but talk of exterminating the Paraguayans made him wonder if this conflict was to bring honor or shame to Brazil.

Firmino agonized over such concerns. Yet, his anxieties over a protracted war and his own personal fear of combat had not driven him away from Paraguay. Ulisses Tavares had called him home, but still he remained.

For the first time, Firmino Dantas found himself free of the patriarch who had ruled his life since childhood. Free to daydream about his inventions, to indulge his musings about technology, to fantasize about the Swiss girl, Renata Laubner.

Firmino had even considered confessing to the barão his passion for Renata, but after several attempts at writing to Ulisses Tavares, he had thought better of it and kept his love a secret.

Firmino had been less discreet with Clóvis da Silva. "When I return to Tiberica, she'll be mine," he had said to his cousin.

"Carlinda Mendes will be there, Firmino."

"I'll be honest with Carlinda."

"Dream all you want, Firmino, but when you go back to Itatinga, you'll take Carlinda Mendes in your arms and be happy with your bride."

In the mess tent, as they watched Sabella and Narcisa, Clóvis suddenly turned to Firmino: "Why so sad, cousin? Sick with longing for your princess? Jewels flutter before you, but do you see them? You're blind, Firmino, stricken with the old sickness."

"And what may that be?"

"Ah, such a malady! The sickness that's raged like an epidemic ever since the Portuguese came to Brazil: our craving for El Dorado!"

"But Renata Laubner is *there,* Clóvis. She sleeps this very hour at Tiberica, her crown of golden hair upon a satin pillow."

"Yes — at *Tiberica!* And here, Firmino — tonight? With one of these jewels fluttering between your fingers?"

"One jewel? Compared with the treasure I seek?"

"Ah, dreamer, a drink, then. To your golden princess, cousin Firmino — El Dorado of your heart!"

¢⁄ɔ

At daybreak on November 3, 6,500 Paraguayan infantry and fifteen hundred cavalrymen who had crossed the Bellaco esteros in the dark fell upon Tuyuti base. The first line of trenches, manned by Paraguayan exiles, deserters, and prisoners compelled to serve the Allies, fell to the attacking brigades in minutes. At the second, defended by Argentinians and Brazilians, the few companies who stayed at their posts were slaughtered and the mass of defenders hurled back toward the comércio.

Major Clóvis da Silva was at a redoubt to the right of the trenches to which he had returned the early hours of November 3. The artillerymen were taken by surprise: At the alarm, seven hundred Paraguayan cavalrymen leapt from their ponies and were on the earthworks with swords drawn as the gunners poured out of their tents and shelters in total confusion. At 6:30 A.M., half an hour after the Paraguayans had left the esteros, the redoubt surrendered; twelve officers and 249 men were taken prisoner.

By 7:00 A.M., Tuyuti base lay beneath a pall of smoke from blazing stores and destroyed powder magazines. Hundreds of Allied soldiers fleeing with the horde of camp followers did not stop running until they reached the banks of the Upper Paraná, three miles to the south. Others streamed into the citadel, where they sheltered behind the earthworks, waiting for the next enemy onslaught. The attack did not come immediately, for the Paraguayans had halted at the comércio.

They went berserk there, plundering the wagons and stores, swilling garrafas of liquor, stuffing their mouths with handfuls of sugar, fighting one another for dainties they had not seen before, gnawing at raw artichokes and rock-hard English cheeses.

The rampage cost the Paraguayans dearly, for it gave the battered garrison an opportunity to regroup. At 8:00 A.M., Brazilians and Argentinians counterattacked from the citadel and other positions, engaging the Paraguayans in ferocious hand-to-hand combat.

By 9:00 A.M. the second battle of Tuyuti was over. The Paraguayans streamed back through the esteros, leaving twelve hundred dead and the same number wounded. The Allies claimed victory, but they had lost two thousand men and their garrison was a smoldering ruin. The Paraguayans took fifteen Allied guns back to Humaitá and many captives, including Clóvis da Silva.

❧

Firmino Dantas da Silva relived every agony of his first battle. He rushed like a madman toward those very Yatai palms where he had cowered during the earlier battle. One hundred yards from the trees, he was cut down by Paraguayan soldiers, two bullets buried in his flesh, a machete wound in his shoulder.

Firmino Dantas was carried back into the citadel, among hundreds of wounded, and, miraculously, survived. But his trials in Paraguay were not over.

❧

Four days after the battle, Firmino was moved from a field hospital to the base at Paso la Patria and placed in a tent ward with thirty officers from Tuyuti. He felt immensely guilty among these men, who greeted him as a brave man among brave men. His first night he lay awake listening to others cry for mother, for God, for water.

At daybreak, two orderlies moved from cot to cot dispensing mugs of coffee and checking names against a list prepared for the surgeons. An hour after the orderlies had completed their rounds, Firmino was dozing fitfully; he sensed someone approach his cot and opened his eyes to see one of the surgeons standing beside him.

"Firmino Dantas da Silva?"

He made a slight movement of his head in acknowledgment.

"From Tiberica? The fazenda of Itatinga?"

"Yes."

The surgeon gave him a friendly look. "Relax, Capitão, I'm not here to take you to the operating table."

"You know our vila? The barão?"

"I'm told it's a fine town. You'll soon be back there, Firmino Dantas."

"And your name, Doctor?"

"Cavalcanti," he introduced himself. "Fábio Alves Cavalcanti. I'm from Recife."

"There were ninety-two voluntários in Tiberica's company, Doctor," Firmino said. "Oh, God, so many are dead. . . ." Pain in his arm caused him to wince. "Which one told you about Tiberica, Doctor?"

"Not a voluntário, Firmino Dantas. One of Dona Ana's girls. A perfect angel from your Tiberica — Senhorita Renata Laubner."

"Renata . . . Renata." An inner voice had told him it was Renata Laubner, yet he repeated her name with disbelief.

"The daughter of apothecary Laubner. Golden hair, blue eyes . . . a lovely girl. Surely you remember her, Capitão?"

"Renata . . . in Paraguay?"

"At Corrientes hospital. She's been there for six months, since May," Cavalcanti said. "Senhorita Laubner is a wonder. However foul or tedious her duties, you'll never hear a complaint. Oh, she's brave, that girl! I've seen men reduced to tears of gratitude when she bathes their wounds or wipes their fevered brows. A gentle word from her and their courage is restored. A perfect angel."

"Yes, Doctor. Senhorita Renata is a rare jewel."

"I must go," Fábio Cavalcanti said abruptly. "I have other patients to attend to. I'll be back, Capitão — to remove the enemy's bullets." He looked happily at Firmino. "I want to hear all you know about the senhorita, Capitão."

ᘓ

All that night, Firmino's fever raged. Several times he cried out for Renata. The next morning, he lay motionless, spent. He could just make out the figure of a nurse in black leaning over him. "Oh, Renata . . ." His parched lips formed her name.

"The fever's breaking. Rest quietly."

As the nurse sponged his face, Firmino saw that she was an older woman, with gray hair.

The woman nursing Firmino was "Dona Ana," Ana Néri, the inspiration for Renata and others who had come to nurse the sick and wounded. Dona Ana had been fifty-one years old, living comfortably at her family holding at Cachoeira outside Salvador, Bahia, when she had caused a stir by publicly volunteering to go to Paraguay as a nurse. The city fathers of Salvador lauded her noble gesture, but despite her plea Dona Ana had been turned down with a polite reminder that the Casa Grande, not the battlefield, was the proper place for a lady of her quality. Five days later, Dona Ana took passage for Rio de Janeiro, where she badgered the military authorities until they were happy to see her sail for the Plata. Ana Néri had become a legend, not only for her compassion toward both friend and foe, but also for fearlessness in passing through the very fire of battle to aid the wounded, a mission that had brought her the deepest sorrow a mother can know: Following a skirmish near the esteros, Dona Ana had found one of her own sons dead at the edge of the morass.

Lieutenant Surgeon Fábio Alves Cavalcanti had been here since his first experience of war on the blood-drenched decks of the *Jequitinhonha* at the battle of Riachuelo in June 1865. In early 1867, when thirteen thousand men were stricken with cholera, the army medical corps had appealed to the navy for help, and Lieutenant Cavalcanti was among the surgeons and doctors who had accepted a transfer to the army. He had been at Corrientes hospital until sent up to Paso la Patria four days ago to deal with the hundreds of casualties from Tuyuti.

As he'd promised, Fábio himself removed the bullets from Firmino's right leg and right shoulder and sewed up the machete gash. Firmino's wounds healed slowly, and twice within three weeks he came down with high fevers. Fábio Cavalcanti was responsible for the patients in this tent ward, so that not a day passed without his stopping at Firmino's bedside; besides the routine visits, he came here, too, to talk about Renata Laubner.

Firmino had little to tell Fábio about Renata Laubner: He met her at a ball at Itatinga; he saw her a few times at apothecary Laubner's shop; he remembered her as a lovely girl with a strong, independent spirit. And he loved her dearly, the Renata Laubner of his dreams, but this he did not tell the young doctor.

When Fábio spoke so admiringly of Renata, Firmino listened with envy, yes, but without rancor. He felt a bond in their mutual admiration for the girl.

Firmino and Fabio were almost the same age — Fábio, at twenty-nine, was two years older — and both were sons of old families of Brazil: Fábio Cavalcanti, the Pernambucano, whose forebear Nicolau Gonçalves Cavalcanti had founded Engenho Santo Tomás; Firmino da Silva, the Paulista, a descendant of Amador Flôres da Silva. Pernambucano and Paulista, their families had carved personal empires out of the Brazilian wilderness.

Fábio was the third son of Guilherme Cavalcanti, the present owner of Santo Tomás. One of his brothers was a lawyer; the other lived at the engenho. Fábio himself had stayed mostly at the Cavalcantis' town house since his school days at Olinda. Senhor Guilherme also spent much of the year at Olinda, leaving the plantation in the care of Rodrigo, his eldest son, but neither Guilherme Cavalcanti nor his two sons whose careers had taken them away from Santo Tomás for one moment forgot that the clan's power lay in those green valleys.

Firmino Dantas felt a pang of guilt when he listened to Cavalcanti talk of his family and pictured himself returning to Itatinga, where Ulisses Tavares waited to greet a hero. It would disgust Ulisses Tavares to know that his grandson had quailed before the Guarani.

Firmino left Paso la Patria on December 20, 1867, with other wounded men on a steamer sailing for Buenos Aires, where they would be transferred to a ship bound for Santos. He had been up and walking for a week, and had bade farewell to Fábio Cavalcanti the previous night.

"Thank you, Doctor, for everything."

"I enjoyed talking with you, Firmino Dantas," Fábio said. "There are too many heroes here."

Firmino flushed, wondering if Cavalcanti had somehow learned of Firmino's cowardice.

"Conquistadors!" Fábio added. "They seek a conquest no matter what it costs in blood and suffering."

Relieved, Firmino said, "The war can't go on much longer."

"We were told that when we sailed from Rio de Janeiro three years ago."

On the evening of December 20, the *Aurora*, the steamer in which Firmino sailed, stopped at the port of Corrientes, where her captain announced they were to anchor for two days. Firmino was often at the ship's railing those two days, but he did not set foot ashore.

❧

Two months later at Humaitá, in the early hours of February 19, 1868, at the Bateria de Londres and other gun emplacements, men and boys waited at eighty-four cannon. Some were battle-hardened veterans, the best artillerymen left in López's army, and to them fell the duty of manning the modern rifled pieces. Some stood ready at a seventeenth-century thunderer, *San Gabriel*. Child gunners waited gallantly to serve their elders beside cannon the muzzles of which they could reach only on tiptoe.

Four miles inland, strategic points along the network of trenches were reinforced by the bulk of fifteen thousand defenders remaining at Humaitá. Paraguayan scouts had come back through the marshes and swamps to report battle preparations by units of fifty thousand enemy troops now in siege position beyond Humaitá's earthworks.

Major Hadley Tuttle was with the gunners in the Bateria de Londres. Colonel George Thompson had left him at Humaitá to complete an earthwork west of López's headquarters at Paso Paicú on the outer trenches. Thompson himself was across the Rio Paraguay in the Chaco, setting up a river battery ten miles above Humaitá, a work in itself indicative of the increased awareness of the threat to Humaitá in the three months since Luisa Adelaida Tuttle and her parents had returned to Asunción.

Marshal-President López kept up a defiant stance for the sake of the men and boys in the ranks. Mounted on a white horse, he rode with his aides along Humaitá's trenches, stopping often to chat with soldiers and share their jokes about the macacos bogged down beside the esteros. After second Tuyuti, López had ordered campaign medals struck and distributed them to the survivors, a celebration that some — Hadley Tuttle among them — found farcical, for El Presidente himself had instigated the looting of the enemy's camp, a grave error that had cost the Paraguayans many lives.

Publicly, El Presidente continued to show confidence. On his instructions, the slightest damage to his house by the enemy's shells was repaired instantly, so that the Guarani and mestizo ranks who saw the unmarked whitewashed walls would take this as a sign of the great señor's invincibility. But privately, with his generals and top aides, Marshal López accepted that Humaitá could not hold out indefinitely against the enemy.

López and his generals had no intention of surrendering Humaitá outright. Before the Allies could cut them off completely, however, ten thousand men would be withdrawn across the Rio Paraguay into the Chaco, the only route of escape with Humaitá enclosed by land and the enemy fleet stationed below the fortress.

Just past 3:00 A.M. on February 19, Major Hadley Tuttle was with the commander and other officers at the Bateria de Londres, where Tuttle had been given charge of two 32-pounders this night. Hadley Tuttle felt an anticipation of battle keener than at any other time, for, like the rest of the men, he accepted the hour as critical for Humaitá.

For more than a year, the Brazilian squadron anchored in the channels between Curupaiti and Humaitá had thrown thousands of shells at the two positions, but had made no attempt to force a passage beyond Humaitá's formidable batteries. The bows of every warship were reinforced and fitted with protective overhanging spars; patrol boats constantly searched the river as far up as they dared go. But the loss of master torpedoman Luke Kruger had been a fatal blow to the Paraguayan torpedo unit, for Capitán Angelo Moretti and others had been unwilling to risk further hazardous experiments. The channels of the Rio Paraguay were increasingly free of torpedoes; the enemy still had to run the gauntlet of Humaitá's guns, but otherwise the way to Asunción, 150 miles up the Rio Paraguay, was open.

At the 32-pounders in the Bateria de Londres, Hadley Tuttle's glance moved frequently to the gun embrasures and the dark river beyond, straining for the first sight of the enemy. Tuttle did not have long to wait. At 3:30 A.M., with a distant roar, cannon on nineteen ships began to fire against various positions ashore. When they opened their bombardment, most of the ships were steaming along a sinuous bend of the Rio Paraguay that swung toward Humaitá's cliffs and then looped back to the northwest.

A small battery a mile below the Bateria de Londres was first to return the enemy's fire. Then three positions — Coimbra, Taquari, Maestranca — with a total of twenty guns, opened up, and the darkness along the cliff to the south was broken with flash after flash of cannon fire.

The vanguard of the enemy fleet passed through the storm of plunging shells. Their own gun flashes marked their position for the sixteen heavy cannon of the Bateria de Londres, the first rounds of the battery like a broadside from a man-of-war.

Tuttle's gun crews sprang to reload in the haze of powder smoke swirling in the light from lanterns strung along the roof of the battery. Tuttle stepped up to an embrasure and peered out, seeing the flame of guns on the armor-clad corvettes positioned along the Chaco shore. He discerned in the main channel three new vessels of war — gunships that had joined the Brazilian fleet a week ago.

Constructed at Rio de Janeiro, these ships weren't much to look at: Almost oval in shape, 127 feet long, they lay low in the water like squat black beetles. Each was 340 tons, with iron plates nearly six inches thick, this armor backed by eighteen inches of Brazilian hardwood stouter than oak. *Alagoas, Pará, Rio* Grande — they were named for provinces of the empire. Of a revolutionary design, the first vessel of their kind had steamed to battle and glory on her maiden voyage in 1862 during the U.S. Civil War: the *Monitor,* victor of the clash with the rebel steamer *Virginia.*

The Brazilian monitors each had a single oval-shaped revolving gun turret, the *Alagoas* equipped with a 70-pounder Whitworth, her sister ships with 120-pounders, the guns capable of a 180-degree angle of fire. The monitors had steam up, but were not proceeding under their own power; each was under tow by an ironclad with engines capable of greater knots for the run past Humaitá.

Brazilian shells ignited an ammunition supply and set fire to the brush and trees. A Brazilian corvette close to the cliffs was burning, and an ironclad towing a monitor took a hit amidships, but neither vessel was in danger of sinking.

The guns of the Bateria de Londres kept up a relentless bombardment. The smoke was so dense, Tuttle and his men could scarcely make out gun crews to the far right and left of them. The battery was the prime target of the monitors and ironclads, their shells exploding along its revetment and tearing the earth in the cliff below Londres. One shot passed clean through an embrasure on the right of the battery, where the men at an ancient muzzle-loader had run the gun back on its slides to reload. The blast killed every one of the crew, wounded others close by, and sent a drizzle of blood and brains far up along the line of guns.

The lead ironclad crossed the place where the chain boom lay submerged in the river; it turned to port, steaming toward the north. The ironclad still had to pass two batteries on the northern end of the cliffs, but it was out of range of Londres' guns. The ironclad *Bahia,* towing the monitor *Alagoas,* also rode comfortably over the sunken boom.

Tuttle jerked the lanyard of one of the 32-pounders, stepping aside quickly to avoid the recoil as the gun roared out. The second 32-pounder and two other cannon fired almost simultaneously, their shot also directed against the *Alagoas*. Two shells struck the monitor's stern, with no more effect than before; two projectiles exploded in front of the vessel.

"Damn! Damn! Damn!" Tuttle swore. His uniform was soaked, his jacket clinging to his back. His face was streaked with dust and powder grains.

Minutes later, from off to the right, a man shouted, "The monitor! We've cut the cable, sir!"

Tuttle leapt to the embrasure. In the glow from the blazes along the cliffs, he saw the monitor dropping back rapidly, the third ironclad and her tow passing the small ship. "Hurry, boys! Load!" he shouted. "We can sink her yet!"

For thirty minutes, the *Alagoas* was under a violent cannonade. Shell after shell struck the monitor, including steel-tipped shot that pierced her plates; missiles burst in the water next to her hull, shaking her from stem to stern and deluging her deck; balls from Humaitá's vintage cannon shattered into fragments against her turret. They were drifting back almost helplessly, for when the tow had parted, there had been low pressure in the *Alagoas's* boilers.

At the Bateria de Londres, Tuttle and a gunnery sergeant were trying to extract the stem of a priming tube wedged in the vent of a 32-pounder when they heard someone shout "Cease fire!" Tuttle looked up to see the battery commander standing there.

"*Cease* fire?" Tuttle asked incredulously.

"Stop shooting at the monitor. Watch closely, Major. There are one hundred fifty men out there. They'll storm her decks and take her prize!"

The batteries along the river north of Londres were still shooting at the three ironclads and two monitors, but it was a desultory, futile cannonade. At Londres itself and farther south, the rate of fire also decreased. The sky was beginning to turn a deep gray; the surface of the river no longer flamed with the reflections of battle. Hundreds of eyes stared down at the river now as the flotilla raced to capture the monitor.

One hundred fifty men paddling twelve canoes! *Bogavantes,* they called themselves; but they gave the word — "paddlers" — a whole new meaning. They stood up as they dipped their paddles in the water to drive their craft swiftly toward the enemy. The lead canoe would cut across the monitor's bows, letting the rope catch against her hull so that as she forged ahead.

"Hurry, boys! Hurry, there!" Hadley Tuttle said breathlessly, as if spurring on his gun crews. The monitor was beginning to move upriver again. "Oh, take her, boys! Take her now!"

A canoe shot past the *Alagoas*, the rope linking it to a second craft snared by the monitor's bow. The *Alagoas* surged forward; the two canoes were rapidly drawn up beside her. The first bogavantes made to leap to the enemy's deck as two other canoes raced alongside.

Four canoes managed to put men aboard, but only a handful of bogavantes got within thirty feet of the turret. Two men stormed the pilothouse, striking it with their sabers in frustration at finding it sealed with an iron cover. Other bogavantes fell to their knees at the hatches, tearing at the covers with their hands until bullets from the turret ports riddled them. In less than ten minutes the attack was repulsed, with the *Alagoas*, her decks littered with the bodies of the bogavantes, dragging along the empty canoes.

It was not over. The commander of the *Alagoas* now had his monitor under full steam. It would have been easy for them to drop back with the swift current to protection by the line of corvettes, but they had waited for pressure to build up in their boilers.

The monitor's iron bows shattered the wooden craft; her hull rode over the men spilled into the water. Four canoes of bogavantes perished; four escaped into shallows too hazardous for the monitor to navigate.

The *Alagoas* ended her pursuit and crossed the sunken boom to join the five other ships this gray dawn when the Brazilians forced the passage beyond Humaitá.

e᷉o

Six Brazilian ironclads now operated above Humaitá, and Allied land divisions had been victorious in their simultaneous attack against an outwork two miles north of the garrison. But the Bateria de Londres and the other guns on Humaitá's cliffs still commanded the loop of the river. Across the Rio Paraguay lay the jungle and swamps of the Chaco, which the Allies, once again underestimating their enemy, had failed to secure. During March 1868, López crossed into the Chaco with ten thousand soldiers, taking the best guns from Humaitá and leaving three thousand men, who abandoned Curupaiti battery and withdrew into Humaitá's fifteen thousand yards of inner trenches.

Through the winter of 1868, a cold, miserable four months, the Allies laid siege to Humaitá. The three thousand defenders deceived the Allies into believing their strength to be much greater with such ruses as rows of Quaker guns — leather-bound tree trunks — and a frequent clangor and thud of brass and drums. In July, under fire from Brazilian ships and the Allied guns now higher up on the Chaco bank, the defenders evacuated their wounded and women, for they still had access to the narrow jungle peninsula opposite the fort. On August 5, 1868, Humaitá surrendered to the Allies; it was four days since the men had eaten the last food in the garrison, and two hundred of its thirteen hundred soldiers were unable to rise from the ground, where they had collapsed.

López's new headquarters were at San Fernando, fifty-five miles north of the fortress and about one hundred miles from Asunción. El Presidente had earlier ordered all but essential military personnel to leave the capital; the administration had moved to Luque, nine miles east on the railroad to Cerro León, which had been Paraguay's main military base before the war.

When Paraguayan outposts beyond Humaitá began to fall to the Allies, López and his army left San Fernando and marched sixty-five miles farther north to an area below Asunción, thirty-five miles to the northwest. According to a previous land survey by George Thompson and Hadley Tuttle, it offered the strongest positions for a defensive front. The Paraguayans dug in five miles inland from the small port of Angostura, above the Pykysyry, a narrow river that flowed into the Rio Paraguay.

Beyond the extreme left of their trenches was Itá-Ybate, "The High Rock," an elevated position among the low hills known as Lomas Valentinas, where López set up his headquarters. Some four thousand troops manned the Pykysyry line and Angostura's batteries; five thousand with twelve guns were kept as a mobile reserve to intercept the Allies on their approach to Lomas Valentinas.

In late August 1868, when the Allies finally began to advance north to Asunción, the conduct of the war was in Brazilian hands, with the marques de Caxias commander-in-chief: Bartolomé Mitre was in Buenos Aires; and Venancio Flores was dead, the victim of an assassin's bullet at Montevideo in February 1868.

The Allied commanders decided against a frontal assault on the Pykysyry line, sending their engineers into the Chaco, at a point below Angostura, to forge a passage through the jungle and across the swamps. Seven miles of the road passed through morasses that had to be filled in with the trunks of palm trees laid side by side, but when the engineers were finished in late November, the Allies sent 32,000 men along the route. Ironclads that had run past the guns at Angostura then transferred the soldiers back across to the east bank of the Rio Paraguay, landing them above the Pykysyry line. At the beginning of December 1868, the Allied corps began to move south toward Lomas Valentinas, bent on dealing the death blow to López and his army.

৵

"Here! Antônio Paciência! Here's one! A general? A colonel? A commander-in-chief?" The dim yellow light of a lantern swung low as the man bent down for a closer inspection. "Ai, *caramba!* Spurs of silver! Gold! O Santa Maria! Bless me! A Cross the size of my hand! Hurry over, Antônio! *Hurry!*"

"I'm coming."

The man suddenly straightened up and turned around, held the lantern away from him, and peered into the dark. "Padre?" He got no response. "Where is Padre?"

"Behind us." Antônio Paciência carried his own lantern as he made his way slowly across to the man.

"I don't see him."

"He's down there in those trees." Antônio Paciência reached the place where the man was standing. The light from his lantern fell on a dead Paraguayan.

"Look, Antônio . . . I do not lie!" The man had short arms, and with one furious movement, his lantern swinging wildly as he bent down, he tore the gold Cross from the Paraguayan's neck.

Antônio smiled grimly. "He won't run away."

The man placed his lantern on the ground, went down on one knee, and, pulling out a knife, began to rip open the pockets of the man's uniform. "A bullet here." He touched the tip of his knife to the man's chest. "A lance." He pointed to a slash in the abdomen.

The man continued to speak as he worked, complaining about the paltry treasures from the Paraguayan's pockets: a few religious medallions, some pieces of silver, a broken cigar, some loose cartridges. Antônio loosened the silver spurs, consoling his partner with the fact that here at Avaí the ground was thickly sown with enemy.

But the man responded with another grumble: "Brazilians, too! And tomorrow, when the sun rises like fire in the sky? Aieee! We'll work like slaves!" He stopped talking as he saw a lantern moving toward them. "Padre?"

In reply came a distant "Yes."

The man said to Antônio, "As always, late!"

Like the one he called "Padre," this man had a nickname: "Urubu." None was so adept as he in picking his way across a field after battle to find spoils among the dead.

Urubu, a full-blooded native of Brazil, was one of thirty-four Pancurus enlisted as voluntários da patria from a village in the sertão beside the Rio Moxoto, about twenty miles above the Rio São Francisco. Their village had once been a Jesuit aldeia where their forefathers had found refuge, and long before that, these Pancurus had roamed the surrounding caatinga.

Urubu's real name was Tipoana. He was in his forties, a small, vigorous man with straight, pitch-black hair, sparse eyebrows, and no trace of a beard.

Antônio Paciência had met Tipoana after the storming of Curupaiti, where Policarpo Mossambe had been killed. That battle had so reduced Antônio's battalion that its survivors had been sent to other units; Antônio went to the Fifty-third Battalion, which had been organized at Recife, Pernambuco, and included the company with the Pancurus.

Antonio, Urubu, and the man they called "Padre" were attached to the Second Corps, which, together with the First and Third, had advanced toward Lomas Valentinas at the beginning of December 1868. Five days ago, on December 6, the army had come to a narrow bridge at a stream, the Itororó, defended by five thousand Paraguayans. Three times the bridge was won and lost, until a final assault drove the Paraguayans away.

The combat at Itororó had been a prelude to what occurred earlier this day, December 11. The spot where the silver-spurred Paraguayan lay was at the edge of a narrow plateau three miles inland from the Rio Paraguay. Directly below were two rivers, one of which, the Avaí, gave its name to the battle that had raged today across these heights and in the depressions between them: For four hours in an incessant rainstorm, with heaven's roll above the thunder of the guns and lightning rending the skies, 22,000 men had fought here, 18,000 Allies and 4,000 Paraguayans, with no quarter given. The Paraguayan battalions had been annihilated, 2,600 dead, 1,200 wounded, and 200 left to make their way south to Lomas Valentinas. But 4,200 Brazilians and Argentinians, too, went down, among the wounded the veteran commander of the Third Corps, Manuel Luís Osório.

Almost four years since Antônio Paciência had marched from Tiberica, he had participated in every major campaign since Curupaiti, though his role had changed after his transfer to the Fifty-third Battalion: He had been drafted to serve as stretcher-bearer with the Second Corps field hospital.

It was 2:00 A.M. now, and Urubu, Antônio Paciência, and others were still out searching for wounded. They had been busy for nine hours since the battle ended, wandering across this landscape of horrors. Arms, legs, heads, torsos had been scattered by shell blasts; hundreds of men were strewn haphazardly in unnatural positions, their bodies broken and contorted; as many horses littered the area, huge, stiff, with flies swarming upon their warm carcasses.

Urubu had finished with the dead Paraguayan's pockets, but on the Paraguayan's belt he had found a broken leather strap to which a pouch would have been attached, and he was prowling the darkness, swinging his lantern from side to side, as he searched the ground just beyond the corpse.

Padre was over six feet tall, with bony limbs, sloping shoulders, and a spare, angular frame. He bent his head as he walked, holding his lantern to search the ground he covered.

"*Ola!*" he shrilled. "*Ola!* I have it!" He stooped and picked up an object. "Is this what you seek, Tipoana?" He dangled a pouch in front of Urubu; there was a distinctive clink as he shook it. "Silver? Gold?" Padre grinned, his huge teeth exposed. He had a long, narrow face with a narrow, hooked nose, his eyes were small and set close together.

Urubu squirmed with displeasure. "Open it! Open it!"

"*Calma!*" Padre nodded toward the Paraguayan. "Or you'll wake the dead yet!"

Urubu spoke to Antônio: "See? What did I tell you? He strolls up here, late like a grand senhor. The first thing he sees — *my* pouch!"

"*Your* pouch?"

"I found him."

"And I found the pouch," Padre said.

Urubu sulked. "Go on, then," Urubu said. "Open it."

"Not much here."

"Look at him! The man was no Guarani beggar!" Urubu said. "There *must* be more."

There was some money loosely tied in a small kerchief: ten silver coins.

Urubu was visibly relieved. He dug into one of his pockets and pulled out the Cross. "This is worth much more!" he announced.

"To a pagan like you?"

Urubu laughed. "A beauty, isn't it?"

The three made their way back to camp walking a distance apart, holding up their lanterns to light the ground and undergrowth.

Padre's great loves in life were talking, ale, and women. And since he couldn't enjoy the other two at the moment, he talked.

Padre's loquacious outbursts often led to sermons on whatever theme happened to occupy his mind; thus his sobriquet. He was a mulatto, like Antônio Paciência, though light-skinned, and three years older than Antônio. His name was Henrique Inglez, the same as his father's.

An English actor of no mean talent, Henrique Inglez the elder had been in Brazil for forty years, first at Belém do Pará and later at Pernambuco, where he had found acceptance among the gentry of Recife and Olinda. The loquaciousness of Henrique Inglez the son came from an early start on the stage. His father had made him recite love poems for his audiences at the tender age of four. The precociousness had not matured into real acting skill, and his grotesque teeth and rakish looks were a further hindrance. By his early twenties, Padre was a habitual loafer, whom Henry the Englishman had been delighted to see enlisted with the voluntários.

Padre and Urubu had become close comrades of Antônio Paciência in the eighteen months they'd served together as stretcher-bearers. Before coming to Paraguay, Antônio had known only the company of slaves. The images of that day he had stood like a beast for sale had haunted him since childhood; as he reached manhood, the memory of being inspected by the slaver, while still vivid, was but one of many memories that had aroused a burning hatred of his enslavement.

Freedom! How often he had listened to Policarpo Mossambe talk of his great hope — that he would earn his freedom by fighting for Dom Pedro Segundo. If only Policarpo had lived two months longer, till November 1866, to hear Dom Pedro II's decree that slaves with the imperial army in Paraguay were to be emancipated. The law freed 25,000 black and mulatto slaves then serving with the Brazilian divisions and provided the same freedom for all future recruits for the Paraguayan War.

In truth, freedom had not yet come to mean much to Antônio. Nor, for that matter, to many slave soldiers. When their initial euphoria was tempered by the routines of war, they saw that apart from the promise of freedom, their circumstances were unchanged. When thousands were stricken with cholera and other diseases in the summer of 1867, the slaves were reminded that to earn the reward Dom Pedro II was offering them, they had first to survive the jungles and swamps of Paraguay. Liberty was as distant as ever.

But on that August day at Curupaiti, Patient Anthony had climbed down the face of the earthworks and walked toward the spot where Policarpo had died. He would do as others did who paid personal homage to a dear friend: He would mark this place with a simple wooden Cross bearing the inscription "Corporal Policarpo Mossambe — Brasileiro."

Returning to the tent he shared with Tipoana and Henrique Inglez, Antônio Paciência had told his friends of his plan, and asked if one of them would write the inscription on the Cross.

Over the next three days, when Antônio was off duty, he carved out each letter with a knife.

Never before had Antônio Paciência attempted to write anything more than a scrawled "X" next to his name on lists of voluntários da patria. When he was finished, he heated the blade of his bayonet in a flame and seared the letters.

Henrique Inglez had gone with Antônio to Curupaiti, where Antônio had planted the Cross. "Corporal Policarpo Mossambe — Brasileiro," he had repeated several times as he looked at his handiwork. Just as they were leaving, Antônio stepped up to the Cross and ran his fingers lightly over the crosspiece.

"Never again a slave, Policarpo Mossambe," he whispered. "Never again."

☙

At Itá-Ybate, where Francisco Solano López had his headquarters, first light on Christmas Day 1868 was heralded by a bombardment from forty-six guns and rocket stands deployed in a semicircle opposite the hill. It was the most violent and sustained cannonade of the war, and was answered by six guns remaining in the Paraguayan positions.

Four days ago on December 21 in a blazing 101 degrees, 25,000 Brazilians came down through the Lomas Valentinas from camps near Avaí, reaching positions opposite the trenches below Itá-Ybate at noon. A group had immediately been sent off to destroy the Pykysyry line, which they had done, slaying or capturing nine hundred of the fifteen hundred defenders and forcing the rest to flee toward the Rio Paraguay. At 3:00 P.M. the main attack on Itá-Ybate commenced, with wave after wave of cavalry and infantry charges; the Brazilians took fourteen guns but failed to penetrate López's lines. At six o'clock the assault was called off, with Allied losses at four thousand. But the defenders had been reduced to two thousand men.

The three days from December 22 had seen incessant cannon and rifle fire, but no major moves by either side. On December 24 though, the Allied commanders sent a message inviting President López to surrender, which had been rejected.

The bombardment of Itá-Ybate on December 25 was followed by new attempts to break through the Paraguayan lines. The Brazilians advanced up the hill along two narrow gorges, only to be repulsed again, with heavy casualties.

The next day, seven thousand Argentinians who had come up across the demolished Pykysyry line joined the Brazilians. These fresh troops were to decide the battle of Itá-Ybate.

Again, on the morning of December 27, an artillery barrage thundered against the Paraguayan positions. Then, with the Argentinians in front, the Allied generals sent 25,000 men along the two defiles and up the slopes of the hill. Here and there, a Paraguayan gun, dismounted but propped up on a mound of earth, roared defiantly. Here and there, a lone Paraguayan rose up in the trenches along the hillside, a Guarani war cry upon his lips and his sword raised against an entire battalion running toward him. Here and there, a child of tender years, his body riddled with bullet wounds, lay down to die as silently as he had suffered. By 11:30 A.M., the flags of the Allies flew triumphantly on the shell-splintered flagstaff of Francisco Solano López's headquarters.

స

At first, when the Brazilian officer was still a distance away, Antônio Paciência didn't recognize him, and he thought, too, that he was coming toward them with a child in his arms. Antônio, Padre, and a medical orderly were in a wood a mile behind López's headquarters, where the victorious troops had found a stockade holding prisoners of the Paraguayans. As the officer drew nearer, Antônio saw that he was carrying not a child but a man whose small body was horribly emaciated. The officer himself walked unsteadily, his ragged uniform hanging loosely on his frame.

"Gently, now. Be gentle with him," the officer said, when Antônio and Padre helped him lower the man onto a stretcher. "He's been a prisoner of these dogs for four years."

The dark eyes of the man on the stretcher shifted from one rescuer to the next. Suddenly he grew terrified and uttered an awful cry.

"Calma . . . calma, Sabino," the officer said. He reached down, giving the frightened man a reassuring pat on the shoulder.

It was Sabino do Nascimento Pereira de Mendonça, the revenue inspector who had been a passenger on the *Marquês de Olinda* when the ship was seized by the

Tacuari. Mendonça's traveling companions, Coronel Frederico Carneiro de Campos, president-designate of Mato Grosso, and the Cuiabá miner and farmer Telles Brandão, were dead, the victims of disease. But Mendonça, for whom life had been a living hell from the instant the *Tacuari's* gun blasted his ears, had survived the long internment at an *estancia* north of Humaitá. When López retreated north to Itá-Ybate, Mendonça and other prisoners had been moved to this stockade.

As Antônio Paciência and Padre picked up Sabino, the officer introduced himself to the medical orderly: He was Major Clóvis Lima da Silva. There had been times during the past thirteen months when Clóvis da Silva himself had not expected to survive his incarceration. At San Fernando, after the retreat from Humaitá, he and other captured Allied officers had been penned up with the political opponents of López: Day after day, they had seen men dragged away for trial and execution.

Antônio had seen Firmino Dantas's cousin at Corrientes and Tuyuti, but did not immediately recognize this gaunt-featured man who had been a captive of the Paraguayans for over a year. The five of them moved off, Clóvis da Silva and the orderly walking beside the stretcher.

"I served with Tenente Firmino Dantas," Antônio told Clóvis da Silva when there was a lull in the conversation between the major and the orderly.

"Firmino Dantas is here?"

"I don't know, Major. After the tenente went to the depot at Itapiru, I didn't see him again."

"Firmino Dantas was back at Tuyuti last November."

"I wasn't there, Major."

"God willing, I'll find my cousin alive."

It was three hours since Itá-Ybate had been taken. For Clóvis da Silva, the relief at being liberated was marred by news that López had escaped with a hundred men.

"How could our generals permit it!" he said to the orderly.

"It's all over, Major. With no army, López is finished. He has no guns. No support. No hope. The war is over!"

"The beast is loose. Until they run him down, López will remain a curse on this land," Clóvis da Silva said, prophetically.

❦

On December 29, forty-eight hours after the fall of Itá-Ybate, the Angostura battery was the only point in the battle sector still held by the Paraguayans. Angostura had been under fire from Brazilian ironclads since December 21, and had received a flood of refugees from the Pykysyry line and other positions; 2,400 men and women, eight hundred capable of fighting, were in the earthworks, with provisions for less than ten days. The battery's guns had ninety rounds of ammunition for each weapon, a supply that would last no more than two hours if they were attacked.

By this night, too, Lieutenant-Colonel George Thompson, commander of the battery, accepted Angostura's situation as hopeless. During the day, he had sent a commission of five officers under a flag of truce to Itá-Ybate: They had been allowed to inspect López's headquarters and interview wounded Paraguayans, and had returned with confirmation of the defeat. After a conference with his staff, Thompson had sent a letter to the Allied generals proposing surrender of the garrison by noon on December 30.

Hadley Tuttle had been with the commission that went to Itá-Ybate, and had voted in favor of capitulation. When Thompson dismissed the officers, Tuttle had stayed behind.

"It's the only thing to do," Tuttle said. "They outnumber us twenty to one, with one hundred guns."

"Not from the Paraguayans' point of view. You've heard them, Hadley. They consider it a sacred duty to oppose the Brazilians to the last man."

"All that matters is to *save* lives and begin the work of rebuilding this devastated land."

Thompson had been in Paraguay for eleven years. Throughout the war he had served the country with such unswerving loyalty, López had made him a knight of the Order of Merit, the only foreign officer so honored. "Paraguay won't be rebuilt," he said flatly. "Emperor Pedro and his minister, for all their denials, favor annexation. The threat of a war with Buenos Aires — that's all that may stop them."

Tuttle, too, feared the aftermath of war, above all the danger to his wife, Luisa Adelaida, and her family, who left Asunción when López ordered the capital evacuated.

"I must go to my family, George," he said.

"I see no problem. Our surrender is conditional on our liberty to go where we please."

"How long before the formalities are settled, do you think?"

"A few days?"

Hadley laughed. "More like *weeks,* George."

"Did you forget? The roads to the north are sealed. Perhaps it would be best to wait a bit."

Tuttle shook his head. "No. Tonight, George. I'll go through the Chaco."

Thompson realized he couldn't dissuade Tuttle, and did not order him to stay at Angostura. "You're probably right," he said. "Go to them, Hadley. Get them to safety. God knows, it may not be over yet."

"One drop of blood shed now would be a waste."

"López is making for Cerro León." This was the military base at the railhead fifty miles from Asunción, where several thousand men were in the camp hospital. "The Marshal will get those invalids out onto the parade ground. If the slaughter continues, one man alone will be to blame: Marquês de Caxias. What stops him from ordering the capture of López? Does he want to keep a Brazilian army in occupation and prepare for annexation? Or could it be that the Brazilians want López to escape and reassemble the surviving men of Paraguay?"

Tuttle was genuinely puzzled. "Whatever for?"

Thompson smiled grimly. "Wouldn't it provide, through *civilized* warfare, the opportunity to exterminate the last Guarani?"

From the spires of Asunción's cathedral on the third Sunday of January 1869, the peal of bells rang out over the capital as the marquês de Caxias, his fellow commanders, and a host of Brazilian and Argentinian officers gathered to thank God for victory. Three days earlier, January 14, the marquês issued Order of the Day, Number 272: "The war has come to its end, and the Brazilian army and fleet may take pride in having fought for the most just and holy of all causes."

As the marquês de Caxias and his officers raised their voices to heaven, outside the cathedral the scene was closer to hell. The first Allied troops had entered Asunción on January 1, encountering minimal resistance; a few days later, the bulk of the army started to march in from Lomas Valentinas, until by this Sunday there were thirty thousand men in and around the capital. López had ordered Asunción evacuated months ago. His administration, the remaining foreigners, and the upper-class citizens had gone to towns east of the city; but when the Allied army marched in, there remained several thousand poorer Guarani and mestizos who had not fled or had drifted back to the city from the outskirts seeking food.

And there were the defeated, who watched the macacos stream into a city deserted and neglected, her broad boulevards overflowing with trash and the bloated carcasses of beasts, and stinking like open sewers. Propped up against the wall of the unfinished opera house, leather pads bound to the stumps of his legs, was a gunner who had been at Itapiru resisting the enemy's first approach to Paraguay; in the shade of a tree stood a Guarani lancer who'd ridden for the guns of the Argentinians at first Tuyuti; he'd been blinded by grape, and half his nose was shot away. A mestizo infantryman, the victim of a skirmish in the Chaco, lay on his back, wearing a ragged poncho that failed to conceal his upper legs and genitals, which were reeking and moist with gangrene. "Macacos . . . macacos . . . macacos," the soldier gibbered.

And for every man, there were four or five women and twice that number of small children. The women, emaciated and almost nude, stood silently staring at their conquerors. The children peered out from behind their legs at the giants passing noisily in parade.

The rape of the Mother of Cities by the victors began slowly. A group of camaradas smashed their way into a *pulperia* and made off with the tavern's most expensive supplies. Looters stormed a silversmith's shop. Frustrated booty hunters torched an empty house. Discipline so broke down that even officers were about, pilfering items for shipment back to Brazil.

The ravaging of the city gained momentum with the rumors being spread about the nature and whereabouts of the fortunes of El Presidente and his mistress, La Lynch. Mobs of soldiers prowled the residential barrios on the outskirts of the city searching for booty. Ax-wielding men chopped through the doors of warehouses and attacked the homes of Asunción's elite, ripping them apart. No place was inviolable: The U.S., French, and Italian consulates were devastated. When none of these efforts uncovered the fortunes of López and Madame Lynch, the soldiers looked elsewhere — to the cemeteries, where the best-appointed tombs were burst open for inspection.

Night after night, the sky above Asunción glowed with fires set by the rampaging soldiers. In the light from those flames, men who were either bored with the treasure hunt or satisfied with what they had already stolen from deserted homes turned to other pleasures: Some of the living skeletons who had lined the streets when the Brazilians marched in gave their bodies freely to the soldiers in exchange for food;

other Guarani women and girls had to be held down forcibly, but their cries went either unheeded or unheard.

The sixty-five-year-old marquês de Caxias was well aware that his troops were on a rampage, but two years in Paraguay had left him utterly exhausted and unable to control them. In the cathedral this January 17, during the elaborate thanksgiving, the marquês collapsed in a faint: The following day, Caxias relinquished his command and immediately set sail for Brazil.

ᘛᘚ

Fifty miles to the east of Asunción, Francisco Solano López walked among the wounded at Cerro León base. The half-blind, the crippled, the maimed listened intently as their leader swore that the fight would not be over as long as a single Guarani was able to stand up to the macaco horde.

ᘛᘚ

Fábio Cavalcanti was present at the thanksgiving service in the cathedral. Cavalcanti and other members of the army medical corps had come up from Humaitá, where they had been based since the garrison's surrender in August 1868; they had taken over the barrack hospital outside Asunción to receive hundreds of wounded men from the Lomas Valentinas campaign.

Like every man celebrating the victory Te Deum, Fábio Cavalcanti, who had been in Paraguay for almost four years, had offered heartfelt thanks for an end to the war. And like others in the weeks following the service, he came to be bitterly disappointed as reconnaissance patrols found that López was up to something. At first, there was talk that El Presidente, his concubine, and their sons were dashing for the Bolivian border. But, as the weeks passed, scouts discovered bands of armed Paraguayans moving up along the cordillera and along lower sections of the fifty-mile railroad between Asunción and Cerro León.

When the marquês de Caxias left Asunción, the command of the army passed to a field-marshal, Xavier de Souza. When it dawned on the army that they might yet have to march again to mop up Guarani resistance, morale collapsed. The soldiers intensified their depredations against Asunción; many officers sought and were granted leave to return home for reasons of poor health, though most were simply sick and tired of the war, and some began to talk of the need to offer López terms for an honorable surrender.

A thousand miles away, His Imperial Majesty Dom Pedro thought differently. Supported by his more bellicose ministers, Pedro reaffirmed his belief that Brazilian honor demanded the elimination of Francisco Solano López. What was needed to achieve this, His Majesty decided, was a young commander capable of reinvigorating the imperial army and leading the hunt for López — a bandit upon whose head His Majesty now placed a reward.

The young man whom Emperor Pedro chose for the final conflict was his son-in-law, the twenty-six-year-old Prince Louis Gaston d'Orléans, comte d'Eu, husband of the imperial princess, Isabel. The comte, who had reached Rio de Janeiro on the eve of the war, had been considered too young and inexperienced to go to battle alongside such veterans as Caxias and Osório. There was also some question about the comte's ability to inspire Brazilian troops. In March 1869, however, Dom Pedro and his ministers appointed the young Frenchman marshal in full command of the Brazilian army in Paraguay.

Fábio Cavalcanti was among the hundreds of officers who went down to Asunción Bay on April 14 to greet the comte d'Eu. Prince Louis Gaston set up headquarters at Luque, eleven miles to the east of Asunción, and wasted no time beginning an overhaul of the army. But, on April 28, he reluctantly agreed to a suspension of drills and inspections while the army mounted a review in mass and held a festa to celebrate the twenty-seventh birthday of its new commander-in-chief.

On the night of the comte's birthday, the officers of the medical corps held a dance in their quarters, the villa of an army doctor who had been executed for treason at San Fernando. The rambling single-story house was neglected, its whitewashed walls stained with red dust; its huge garden, though overgrown, carried the scents of magnolia, jasmine, gardenia.

When the bandsmen playing for the officers and their guests were almost ready to end their performance, Fábio was out in the garden, experiencing an odd mixture of joy and guilt: In this dolorous land, where he had witnessed so much pain and suffering, he, Fábio Cavalcanti, now found himself sublimely happy, strolling arm in arm with Renata Laubner.

Fábio had gone back to the main hospital at Corrientes after tending the wounded from second Tuyuti at Paso la Patria. Again, he had watched wonderingly as nurse Laubner cheered up her patients, the majority of them freed slaves and rude sons of the backlands. And this time he had taken every opportunity to show his affection for her, knowing full well he was but one among many who cherished the hope of courting Senhorita Renata. And then came the night when they sat together on a bench on the hospital grounds at Corrientes and Renata laid her golden head against his shoulder and said, "I love you, Fábio."

When Humaitá had been surrendered, Fábio was sent there with other doctors to take over the garrison hospital. Renata had asked her superior, Dona Ana Néri, for a transfer to the fortress, which a sympathetic Dona Ana had granted, there being no secret about the love between Dr. Cavalcanti and nurse Laubner. Early in January they had been so hopeful that the war was finally over and they could go home — first to Tiberica, where Fábio would ask apothecary August Laubner for his daughter's hand, then to Recife, Pernambuco.

Renata knew that Fábio was compassionate and understanding, and loved her dearly, but even as a child she had noted the contempt of the fazendeiros toward the common people, like the Swiss, they hired to pick their coffee. She remembered what her father had said to her the night they went to the ball at Itatinga: "We are here, daughter, because Baronesa Teodora Rita invited you to the fazenda. The barão himself welcomes me, apothecary Laubner, from whom he takes his pills and tonics, but I see he is not happy. It bothers him to have a poor, untitled, unlettered man like August Laubner among his guests." There had been no rancor in his voice.

Oh, how she had danced that night! How she had flashed her eyes and laughed and sighed in the arms of the handsome grandson of the barão de Itatinga!

And he had come to her afterward, treading softly into her father's shop, saying she was the loveliest girl in the world. When her father remarked on his visits, she had said, "Don't worry, Papa. They already plan to marry him off to the baronesa's sister. Besides" — and she'd kissed him on the cheek — "I'd never be comfortable in a house where my father wasn't welcome!"

And now she was apprehensive about the reception she would get from other members of the Cavalcanti family. To waltz around playfully in the arms of Firmino Dantas was one thing, but to walk into the Casa Grande at Santo Tomás the chosen bride of Doutor Fábio — she prayed that she would have the patience and strength of her papa, who had refused to be the slave of the fazendeiros.

Fábio had no such doubts about his family's acceptance of Renata. "Soon, my love, soon we will be walking like this but in the beautiful gardens of Santo Tomás. There the air is sweeter and —"

"Oh, Fábio, how I wish it!" Renata burst out. "I wish the war was over!"

"It won't be long, my dear. Three months, they say. López has at most three thousand men, most of them in bandages." Fábio himself added soberly. Suddenly he quickened his step. "My darling, let's go inside. It's the last waltz!"

☙

Thirty miles beyond the comte d'Eu's headquarters at Luque lay the long valley of Pirayu, with wooded hills rising on either side. On April 30, 1869, forty-eight hours after the celebration of the comte's birthday, in the dead of night, forty enemy raiders entered Pirayu on their way to offer Prince Louis Gaston a different reception in the land he had come to conquer.

The raiders did not travel quietly. They burst into Pirayu from their base camp at Cerro León to the south in a locomotive hurtling past the dark slopes of Mbatovi Mountain at the bottom of the valley, with two tattered red, white, and blue banners of the Republic of Paraguay streaming to each side of the engine's smokebox, its chimney spewing a fiery rain of hot ash and cinders. The raiders rode on two sand-bagged flatcars, one coupled in front of the engine, the other behind the tender, each car carrying a three-inch field gun.

The engine was a rickety piece of equipment, nineteen tons of iron and brass, but her two six-foot-high driving wheels powered her forward at a cracking forty miles an hour: She had been built twenty-five years ago at the great works in Crewe, England, and had served the London and South Western until late 1854, when she had been shipped out to the Crimea. As she chuffed along, the glow above her chimney illuminated the name plate on her boiler: Piccadilly Pride. Standing on her footplate was Major Hadley Baines Tuttle, who knew her well, old Number 11 of the Balaklava line, which he had helped to lay on the hills overlooking Sevastopol in that murderous winter of 1855.

"Say, Hadley, man! We've seen a wee miracle here!" Scotty MacPherson had declared earlier at Cerro León station, when the armored train was ready to depart. Scotty was referring not only to the raiding party with Piccadilly Pride but also to the astonishing fact that four months after Francisco Solano López had fled Itá-Ybate with a handful of officers, he was ready to march again-with an army of thirteen thousand soldiers.

The nucleus of the force comprised fifteen hundred troops who had withdrawn from Asunción on the eve of its occupation by the Allies; among thousands of wounded at Cerro León, as soon as a man had strength to pick up a rifle, he, too, joined the ranks. But the majority responding to López's call came in small groups from every corner of Paraguay: escaped prisoners of the Allies, soldiers who had been scattered across the countryside during the Lomas Valentinas battles; veterans who had laid down their arms welcoming peace but chose war again when they saw what the invaders were doing to their country; tribesmen from the interior of the Chaco, where they had heard talk of the macaco horde, a pest greater than the Spaniards and other interlopers they had resisted for generations.

Guarani had come with their own ancient muskets; with homemade lances and swords hammered out at village smithies; with weapons and ammunition stolen, item by item, from Allied camps. Parties of men scoured the deserted Pykysyry trenches and other battlefields returning with discarded arms and cartloads of cannon balls and shell fragments. The latter, along with every church bell and other useful piece of metal, were delivered to a makeshift arsenal where Scotty MacPherson and other foreigners were employed.

At the arsenal, near López's provisional capital of Piribebuy just north of Cerro León, Scotty and his engineers had by April cast eighteen new field guns and mortars; several hundred thousand shells had been stockpiled. They had also made the light guns for the flatcars coupled to Piccadilly Pride and had bolted high iron plates to the sides of her open engineer's platform to give the men there protection from enemy fire.

Hadley Tuttle had been reunited with Luisa Adelaida and her parents in late January at an estancia outside Piribebuy. They had stayed there since then, Scotty working at the arsenal five miles away, Hadley taking patrols into the cordillera, where he had surveyed the escarpment for trenches and battery positions, putting to good use his experience with Lieutenant-Colonel Thompson, who had left Paraguay after the fall of Angostura.

With Thompson gone, Hadley Tuttle was among López's senior officers. El Presidente had come close to total defeat at Itá-Ybate: He had made his last will and testament on that hill, leaving all his worldly goods to Madame Eliza Lynch. In the four months since Itá-Ybate, as thousands of men and boys rallied to him, and his anger and sorrow rose at reports of the devastation of Asunción, López had found new spirit to combat the enemies of the fatherland.

Among those foes were Paraguayans suspected of plotting to overthrow the dictator. There were still a number of prime suspects under guard at Piribebuy, among them Venancio López, his other brother; two sisters; and, most injurious of all to El Presidente, his mother, the aging Dona Juana.

As Piccadilly Pride shot along the valley, Hadley Tuttle was confident of success. The Piccadilly Pride had a run of twenty-two miles to her objective, an advance Brazilian post near the comte d'Eu's headquarters at Luque. The train had to pass through two stations above the valley of Pirayu, both of which scout patrols had reported deserted. Beyond the first of those stations, the railroad skirted the lake of Ipacaraí, at the tip of which was the village of Aregua, where the Brazilian forward units were camped.

Piccadilly Pride chugged comfortably up through a forested incline at the head of Pirayu valley. Beyond the forest, the engine picked up speed passing Tacuaral twenty minutes later, the station silent and deserted as the scouts had reported. Great Ipacaraí was off to the right now, the railroad skirting the lake. A six-mile run beside Ipacaraí and Piccadilly Pride passed the second unoccupied station, Patiño Cué. Aregua, the Brazilian advance post, lay six miles farther along the track. There was a cutting a mile from Aregua; beyond the cutting was a bend in the tracks, then a straight, level run to Aregua bridge, 138 feet long, supported by a trestled framework of ironhard timber.

Half a mile from the cutting, Hadley eased off the throttle, until Piccadilly Pride was panting along slowly. Entering the cutting, Hadley put the engine in reverse. The big driving wheels bit the iron rails, and Number 11 came to a stop with a shudder and hiss of steam.

When Hadley climbed down from the engine, the soldiers were assembling in front of the train. Five minutes later this group began to move off up along the railbed.

Hadley walked with the Paraguayan sergeant in charge of the company, Julio Nuñez, who had served with Hadley at Angostura. Nuñez was taking eighteen men to deal with a guard post on the north side of the bridge.

"They'll be asleep, Major," Nuñez said, the stub of a fat black cigar jammed in the corner of his mouth.

"I wouldn't count on it."

"At this hour? Macacos sleep, Major!"

Hadley accompanied them as far as the bend beyond the cutting. "If there's trouble, you know what to do," he said to Nuñez.

Hadley glanced at a soldier carrying two signal rockets; in the event of trouble, they would be fired. Tuttle would still make the run with Piccadilly Pride, hoping to force their way across, but it would be far better if the bridge, and their escape route, was secured.

"I promise you, Major Hadley, not one will sound the alarm."

Seven Brazilians had been posted to guard the bridge, but not one was alert. It was almost 2:00 A.M., and Nuñez's confidence was not misplaced, for the macacos were asleep, including one voluntário who had fallen into a deep slumber up on the bridge as he lay on his back between the rails. He did not wake until the instant a Paraguayan crept up to him: The man slit his throat. It was the same with the Brazilians in the tents.

Ten minutes later, Piccadilly Pride puffed out of the bend beyond the cutting and gained speed along the straight, level track to the bridge of Aregua. It rumbled onto the 138-foot span, running smoothly, the noise of her driving and coupled wheels, iron against iron rails, amplified, the flatcars clanking along with a jangle of links and pins. Past the bridge, fifteen hundred yards to go, Piccadilly Pride rolled on almost sedately at low speed to bring her to an easy halt within range of the enemy camp.

The gunners had loaded their pieces with projectiles that would ignite on impact, setting fire to everything within reach. This bombardment would be followed with canister delivering a hail of iron balls.

The small lead gun fired, with a bang and a flash, the first shell exploding to reveal a row of tents ahead and off to the right. A shell from the rear gunners shooting from a difficult angle fell short, but the flames showed men falling out of the tents. The gunners pumped rounds of carcass shot into the camp, the intense flame of these shells making a bonfire of tents and supplies. Hadley himself blazed away at the enemy with a .44 revolver.

But twenty minutes into the attack, the Brazilians began to retaliate effectively. Three of the men on the lead gun car were shot in quick succession.

With a long *toot-toot-toot* on Piccadilly Pride's whistle, Hadley signaled they were pulling out. "Come on, old warrior!" The old engine responded beautifully. Under a small cloud of black smoke, Piccadilly Pride backed up, showering soot on the men up front, where the three-inch gun kept firing to keep the enemy at bay.

Sergeant Julio Nuñez ran along the bridge beside the engine as Hadley backed her up. Nuñez shouted that charges were placed in the trestles; his men were ready to fire the gunpowder.

Brazilian soldiers who had run down the tracks began to shoot at them from positions north of the bridge.

Julio Nuñez himself was a victim of this exchange. Struck by a bullet that ricocheted off the engine's tender, he plunged headlong to the timbers beside the track.

Hadley backed up Piccadilly Pride as fast as he could go, to one hundred yards beyond the bridge. Then the charges blew with a thunderous roar, and flames leapt into the sky. Momentarily nothing was heard but the hiss and pant of Piccadilly Pride; then there was a mighty rending and crash of shattered timbers.

"Good work, men. Good work!" Hadley shouted amid the cheers of others as Aregua bridge came tumbling down.

They stopped to take on water at Patiño Cué. The small town was deserted, with its population moved behind López's lines. While the engine's tank was filled, some soldiers wandered off, smashing their way into a *pulpeira*, where they found a barrel of rum left behind by the owner. There were yells of laughter from another group who found a fat pig trotting down a street near the station: They cornered the terrified beast, slashed its throat, and lugged it back to their flatcar, where despite the protests of the wounded, the porker was hefted aboard.

It was a half-hour before Piccadilly Pride's whistle blew and they were on their way again, with the liquor flowing and the laughter and singing growing louder mile by mile.

Hadley rejoiced with his men. He sent the engine backward smartly, the pile of wood in the tender low enough for him to see the rails behind.

The Brazilians had been bloodied, with one hundred casualties, a third fatal, and their camp a shambles. But out of this debacle rode three hundred horsemen belonging to a superb Rio Grande do Sul cavalry regiment. A mile south of Aregua, they forded the river. They did not sweep directly back to the tracks but thundered along a road that led to the valley of Pirayu.

Piccadilly Pride chugged along beside Ipacaraí Lake and then past deserted Tacuaral, the last station before Pirayu valley. Hadley had her throttle open halfway, for there was no need to race on this last leg home.

"Fool! He'll get himself killed!" Hadley shouted as one of his men leapt from the lead car onto the front of Number 11. The soldier was cheered as he loosened one of the flags next to Piccadilly Pride's smokebox; balancing precariously on the frame, he waved the banner and cheered for Paraguay.

They were two miles from the forest at the head of the Pirayu valley when the Brazilian horse soldiers came thundering toward the tracks. Twenty-five of the cavalrymen had soon detached from the main group to await the train in the valley itself.

"Oh, damn!" Hadley cursed aloud, and flung open the throttle.

There was a scream as the man who had remained perched on Piccadilly Pride's frame lost his footing and fell between the engine and flatcar. There were anguished shouts from the soldiers on both flatcars as they tried frantically to prepare for the onslaught. The prize pig was dumped as the men on that car sought to swing the fieldpiece around.

The cavalrymen did not quite know how to assault the monster, the first armored train to ride the rails in South America. As they stormed the train, Brazilians were killed by their comrades shooting wildly in the melee; others fell to their death after hurling lances that clattered harmlessly against Piccadilly Pride's iron sides. But they were 275, and the men on the train who were not wounded, thirty, and wave after wave swept in, emptying their carbines and revolvers, charging beside the flatcars with lance and saber, raking them with lead and laying open heads and shoulders with their steel-bladed weapons.

Piccadilly Pride had picked up speed as she reached the forest and the decline, now, at the head of the valley. The cavalry were rapidly thinning out as exhausted chargers dropped behind.

Hadley scarcely had time to register his shock at the sight that suddenly loomed ahead of him. The cavalrymen detached from the main body had reached the bottom of the incline ten minutes before the attack and had heaped up logs on the track, throwing the last one on the pile as the train started down the slope.

"God blast them! The bastards!" He could not stop Piccadilly Pride, not a chance.

The rear flatcar rocketed into the logs. The nineteen-ton locomotive jumped the rails, her great driving wheels gouging the earth, plowing up dirt, splintering felled trees like twigs. With a screech of tortured metal and breaking parts, the engine tipped over, hissing and spluttering as water gushed out of her tanks and piles until nothing remained to cool the fire in her iron belly. In a matter of seconds, her overheated boiler blew with a terrific explosion, throwing iron like shrapnel, killing two cavalrymen who stood in the trees watching her die.

And then all was silent around Piccadilly Pride, engine Number 11 of the Balaklava line. Major Hadley Baines Tuttle, who had met her in the Crimean winter of 1855, lay close by, his long fight to help the warriors of Paraguay ended.

ℰℐ

Paraguayan hit-and-run raids continued and the Brazilians retaliated in force, but in the Allied camps, most of May and June was given over to preparing for the final campaign. By the end of June, the Brazilian imperial army had twenty-six thousand battle-tested veterans ready to march. Several thousand Argentinians and a token squad of Uruguayans were on hand, but the last push against López was to be essentially a Brazilian effort, with the army divided into two corps, one of which was commanded by Osório, The Legendary.

At the beginning of July, the long columns of infantry, cavalry, and artillery rolled forward slowly until they reached the valley of Pirayu. North of the valley, the forested heights of the cordillera held the advance positions of the new Paraguayan line; eight miles northeast of the cordillera lay Piribebuy, provisional capital of Marshal-President López.

On August 1, the comte d'Eu gave the order to advance. The plan was a pincer movement to envelop Piribebuy: Argentinians, with heavy artillery support, were to move northeast up the escarpment against the Paraguayan right; the bulk of the twenty-six thousand Brazilians were to march southeast to cross the cordillera and deal with the Paraguayan left.

On August 11, Piribebuy was enveloped, and the next morning, after a devastating artillery barrage, the town was taken.

The army marched on, for Francisco Solano López, the beast who was the prey of this great hunt, remained at large. On August 15, the Brazilians took Caacupé, where the Paraguayans had their arsenal, with little resistance. Among the Europeans taken prisoner was Scotty MacPherson. Luisa Adelaida Tuttle, pale and dressed in widow's black, stood silently between her mother and father as a Brazilian officer offered congratulations for their liberation from the tyrant López.

At dawn on August 16, the sledgehammer was raised again on a plain called Acosta Ñu, sixteen miles north of Piribebuy. The comte d'Eu brought twenty thousand men with him and divided them into four divisions, one on each side of the plain. Facing them in the red earth trenches were 4,300 Paraguayan soldiers, the rearguard and largest surviving contingent of the army López had built the past summer.

Among thousands of Brazilians at Acosta Ñu were three veterans who had been in the war from the start: Colonel Clóvis Lima da Silva; Lieutenant Surgeon Fábio Alves Cavalcanti; voluntário Antônio Paciência. They were all witness to what happened on the plain of Acosta Ñu this southern winter's day in August 1869.

Clóvis da Silva, fully recovered from his incarceration by López and recently promoted to colonel, commanded an eighteen-gun battery on a knoll 2,100 yards west of the Paraguayan trenches. On eminences to the south and east were more howitzers and guns to sweep the enemy positions with a belt of fire. At 7:00 A.M., Colonel da Silva gave the order for two guns on the right of his battery to fire the first rounds.

As the artillery crews came smartly to orders, Clóvis da Silva stood with a telescope glued to his eye. The morning was overcast, a raw chill in the air, with patches of mist hanging over the plain, which was covered with clumps of *macega*, a short, hardy grass. Clóvis saw sections of the Paraguayan earthworks and part of their camp — a long, dark smear in the macega.

"Ready! Fire! *Fire!*"

Clóvis's body stiffened noticeably as the guns roared out. Mentally, he counted off the seconds, waiting for the distant boom. He held the glass steady, watching the shells burst. Immediately, there were other loud reports from the other batteries.

"Another round, Number one and two," Clóvis ordered. "More to the left."

Clóvis cast a practiced eye over the gunners as they loaded charges and ammunition, trained the pieces laterally, adjusted elevation, and stepped to their places to the right and left at the command "Ready!"

"*Fire! Fire!*"

Again, Clóvis counted off the seconds before the shells burst, throwing up earth and dust at the Paraguayan trenches. Again, there were explosions from the Brazilian cannon on their right.

And from the enemy, answering fire, the first shells from six Paraguayan guns facing their position, whistling high over their heads to explode behind them.

"Keep this range," Clóvis ordered. "Battery fire!"

Clóvis da Silva's battery and the artillery to their right hammered the enemy's positions. The Paraguayans returned fire with twenty-three fieldpieces, and where there had been mist, there were patches of drifting white smoke.

By mid-morning, the infantry and cavalry attacks began. The overcast sky livened with battle's fury; the white kepis of thousands of soldiers spread like blossoms in the macega, the steel of their bayonets dull gray as they pressed toward the enemy's trenches. And coming down from the north-still too distant to be more than a dark, indistinguishable mass; still too distant to hear the rumble of the earth — were the first blocks of cavalrymen unleashed from the body of eight thousand waiting to assault the enemy.

The Brazilians attacked from every direction, bullets humming and hissing through the macega. The cavalry sweeping down from the north tore into a band of Paraguayan horses riding out to meet them, sabering to the left and right, making swift work of the slaughter. But the Paraguayans' inner defenses withstood the first onslaught and kept the Brazilians pinned down in the macega and at the overrun advance trenches. There was a lull in the battle. Then the Brazilians launched fresh assaults, hour after hour, slowly but relentlessly cleaning out the Paraguayan trenches.

Lieutenant Surgeon Fábio Alves Cavalcanti was at a field hospital two miles south of Acosta Ñu. There had been a steady trickle of ambulance wagons since early morning, bringing the human wreckage of battle to be pieced together, stitch by stitch.

Mid-afternoon, Fábio was still at the operating table. The orderlies had brought him a screaming Paraguayan, with one foot sliced off and one leg pulped below the knee, a Guarani boy, no more than twelve years old.

In the sixteen days since the start of the campaign across the cordillera, Fábio Cavalcanti had experienced a growing sense of tragedy. The sight of victims like this boy were ever more frequent as the Brazilian columns obliterated the enemy's position and drove in the Paraguayan left. Two days ago, at Piribebuy, Fábio and his fellow surgeons had treated fifty-three of their own wounded. It was more than the carnage at Piribebuy that troubled Fábio: There were reports that the Brazilian troops had massacred women and children fleeing the ruined town. There was a rumor, too, that the infirmary of Piribebuy had been purposefully set alight and those within prevented from fleeing that hideous bonfire.

Fábio had left Asunción in June, with the medical corps, for the cordillera campaign. Renata had remained at the barrack hospital, and Fábio was thankful she was spared the horrors of this final thrust against the enemy — for that it would bring an end to the war, he had no doubt.

In the operating tent, the Guarani boy, sedated with ether, lay naked on the table. Fábio and his helpers staunched the flow of blood where the boy's foot had been severed; the other leg was amputated below the knee.

The boy died while they were stitching the flaps on the stump.

Late afternoon at the plain of Acosta Ñu, the Paraguayan lines were collapsing. For nine hours they had withstood the onslaughts, but on every quarter now, gun positions were overrun; trenches were stormed and taken. Hundreds of prisoners were being driven back behind the Brazilian lines.

"*C'est magnifique!*" said the comte d'Eu at his headquarters near Clóvis da Silva's battery. "*Ce moment de la victoire!*"

The homely Prince Louis Gaston had proved himself a veritable tiger in battle, galloping fearlessly from one position to another exhorting his troops to fight. And now, as the overcast sky darkened, the moment of victory was almost at hand.

There was a wood just south of the plain. In the fading light, and viewed from a distance such as lay between the comte's headquarters and the forest, tiny black dots could be seen emerging from out of the trees, scuttling through the macega toward the Paraguayan lines; they looked like so many squads of small, dark peccaries bolting through the grass. And like wild pigs, they provided excellent sport for cavalrymen who rode them down, sticking them with their lances.

Those tiny figures dashing across the macega were the mothers of boys in the trenches. They had hidden in the woods all day watching the progress of battle and were running to see if their children were dead or alive.

e⁄ɔ

Stubborn Guarani still held patches of macega. So the grass was set on fire. It burned furiously, the flames consuming the wounded who lay there and driving their comrades out into the waiting lines of Brazilian steel.

The battle of Acosta Ñu was over. But once again Francisco Solano López had escaped his pursuers. As night fell, Brazilian scouts rode in to report López and the remnant of his army — a vanguard of two thousand, at most — miles away, moving to the north.

The 4,300 Paraguayans holding the plain at Acosta Ñu all day long had bought precious time for López — at the cost of two thousand lives. Of these, eighteen hundred were boys, and there were children of six and seven here, lying beside flintlock muzzle-loaders.

That night, Antônio Paciência and Henrique Inglez were sitting on the parapet of an earthworks; Tipoana was down in the trench, inspecting the crowded dead with a lantern. Behind them at numerous fires, their comrades were rejoicing.

"Ai, *caramba! Meninos . . . meninos . . . meninos!*" Tipoana complained. Boys! Just boys! No commanders-in-chief with gold crosses and silver spurs; no select pickings for Urubu, king of corpse robbers! He prowled down there all the same, rolling over small, mutilated bodies, poking into pockets, exclaiming hopefully when he came to an old man who had come to battle in a shabby frock coat. But the veteran's pockets offered nothing of value to Tipoana.

"You're wasting your time," Henrique Inglez said. "The bones of Paraguay are picked clean!" He turned to Antônio: "What more does he want?"

They all had their share, Antônio knew. He himself owned a pouch of gold and silver coins.

Urubu came back along the trench. "Meninos!" he whined. "Not one peso among the lot of them!" There was a boy at his feet. Urubu bent down to pluck something from the corpse. Chuckling malevolently, he straightened up, holding the object in the light of his lantern.

Henrique Inglez's long, narrow face contorted with rage, his buckteeth bared. "Savage!" he shouted at Tipoana. "Heartless savage! Dead, brave boys! They deserve respect!"

"Let it be, Tipoana," Antônio Paciência said. "They fought and died like men, did they not?"

The object Tipoana dangled in the lantern light was a crudely fashioned false beard. Every boy in this trench had strapped one of these to his jaw hoping to make the macacos think he was a man.

༄

Francisco Solano López eluded his pursuers for six months. Deeper and deeper he fled into the wilderness, through swamps and jungles where no man before had tread, leaving in his wake the bodies of his followers dead from starvation and victims, too, of final purges of suspected traitors. On March 1, 1870, El Presidente, who had been declared an outlaw by a provisional government at Asunción, was at Cerro Corá, "The Corral," a deep, wooded basin surrounded by hills, 230 miles northeast of Asunción. With him were five hundred emaciated men and boys, the last warriors of Paraguay.

And here, too, in this wild and lonely amphitheater ringed by hills, was Eliza Alicia Lynch: Through the roar of guns at Humaitá, the retreat in the miasmal Chaco, the defeat at Itá-Ybate, the last days at Piribebuy, through it all, Eliza Alicia Lynch had stood by the man she loved. She was here at Cerro Corá, hoping against hope, with her five sons from Francisco beside her.

The Brazilians attacked at 7:00 A.M. They sent a cavalry regiment to punch a hole in the ring of hills; outside The Corral, they had eight thousand soldiers waiting.

"For the love of Christ, Eliza! Go! Go!" El Presidente ordered. "Take our boys! Go!"

Eliza rode off in a carriage with four of her sons. The fifth led her escort: fifteen-year-old Colonel Juan Francisco López.

The Brazilian cavalry swept away the guard post in the hills and poured into the basin. One hundred horsemen crashed through the undergrowth toward Madame Lynch and her sons.

"Halt! Halt!"

The driver of the carriage reined in the jaded animals hauling the vehicle.

"Surrender!"

"Never!" Colonel Juan Francisco López raised his revolver and fired a shot. An instant later a lance driven into his chest mortally wounded him.

The battle at the camp of Cerro Corá raged fifteen minutes. The Brazilians went to work with carbine, saber, and lance, shooting and cutting their way through the ragged lines of four hundred defenders. The enemy drew ever closer to El Presidente on his white steed in the heart of the camp.

A lancer spurred his charger's flanks, and with an iron grip on the shaft of his lance, stormed toward Francisco Solano López. His long blade slashed El Presidente's abdomen, but López stayed on his horse as his assailant burst past him. Several of his staff saw what happened and closed in protectively. With the lines of defenders smashed, this small group made a run for it with their chief, cutting their way through the Brazilians and fleeing into the forest. They got as far as the steep-banked Aquidaban-Niqüí, a mile or two north of the camp.

López was bleeding profusely. His horse splashed through the shallow stream. López could not make it up the high bank. Some of his staff helped him off his horse; some sped in search of an easier crossing.

Brazilians who had given chase found the marshal president there, sitting in the mud next to a small palm.

"Surrender!"

He said nothing. With what strength he had left, he flung his sword at the group of macacos.

A Brazilian stepped forward and shot him at point-blank range.

Francisco Solano López then spoke his last words: *"¡Muero con mi patria!"* ("I die with my country!")

✂

There never was a truer epitaph.

In five years of war, ninety percent of the men and boys of Paraguay were slain. Paraguay, the land of the Guarani, was dead.

✂

At Rio de Janeiro, they counted the cost of the greatest war between nations in the Americas.

The Allies lost 190,000 men, the majority of them Brazilians.

Even so, at Rio de Janeiro, it was the hour of triumph for Pedro de Alcantara, emperor of Brazil. Like his ancestors who had sent their soldados from Lisbon to smite the Infidels in India and subject the savages in Africa and Brazil in the glorious age of *As Conquistas,* Dom Pedro Segundo had made his conquest.

Book Six

The
Brazilians

XX

———— >⠀◦⠀< ————

November 1884 – November 1889

*A*t Recife on a Sunday afternoon in November 1884, a crowd filled the Teatro Santa Isabel and overflowed onto the Campo das Princesas in the city center; those unable to get into the building surged toward its open windows hoping to catch a glimpse of Joaquim Aurélio Nabuco, lawyer and journalist, the man of the hour in Brazil.

"Handsome Jack," his friends called him. He was well over six feet tall. His dark, wavy hair was parted in the center, his mustache luxurious.

Nabuco was nearing the end of a hard-fought battle for election as national deputy in the First District of Recife. He represented the Liberal party against Dr. Manoel Machado Portela, the Conservative candidate, a law professor and veteran politician. The elections had been called after a vote of no confidence toppled a Liberal cabinet that had proposed the liberation of slaves sixty and older. Until this open support for abolition, the two major parties had spoken as one on matters of concern to the rural elite, who were still the power brokers of Brazil. A third political party, the Republicans, had published a manifesto in 1870, advocating the abolition of the monarchy, but had yet to win a seat in the national chamber.

One hundred and twenty thousand were eligible to vote in the coming elections, little more than one percent of the free population of the empire.

Joaquim Nabuco's credentials for office were impeccable. He came from two of the oldest and most distinguished families of the Northeast: His father, Senator José Thomaz Nabuco de Araujo, had been the third generation of Nabucos to serve in the imperial parliament; his mother, Dona Anna Benigna de Sá Barreto, belonged to a family descended from João Paes Barreto, who had settled in Pernambuco in 1557 and founded at Cabo one of the great plantation dynasties.

After his schooling at the Corte, Joaquim Nabuco had attended law school at São Paulo during the time the empire was at war with Paraguay.

He shared those years with a group of idealistic young men, among them Antônio de Castro Alves, a poet who, like the bards of Vila Rica in the eighteenth century, had made "liberty" a watchword.

In 1876, Nabuco accepted a post at the Brazilian legation in New York. He spent eighteen months in the United States before he was transferred to London. In 1878, his father's death brought him back to Brazil. That same year, at the age of twenty-nine, he took his seat in the imperial parliament as a deputy from Rio de Janeiro.

At the Corte, the young Nabuco had lost no time attacking slavery in the Chamber and at public meetings, but the supporters of abolition were still few and the tropical capital itself was trapped between two worlds and deeply rooted in the past. On the eve of the 1880s, Rio de Janeiro had 450,000 inhabitants. Its imperial nobles lived in garden suburbs below Corcovado Mountain, where some of their palatial homes were far grander than the imperial palace at São Cristovão. The majority of the Corte's citizens inhabited the bleak regions of the city, like Swine's Head, where thousands were crowded together, many of them veterans of the Paraguayan War. But the war had also given impetus to industry: Factories rose beside ancient convents, and telegraph lines and railroads extended for hundreds of miles into the interior.

Just as in the past Recife and the Bahia had been the nuclei for the great sugar regions, the Corte was the commercial center for Rio de Janeiro, São Paulo, and Minas Gerais, which produced more than half the world's coffee. The three wealthiest provinces of the empire were also the greatest slaveholding areas, with more than two-thirds of Brazil's 1,500,000 slaves.

Some fazendeiros had again raised the possibility of importing Asians to work in the groves, but the call for "coolies" drew little support. And there had been new attempts to attract peasant laborers from Portugal, Spain, and Italy, but the number of new settlers was still insignificant. In the "Black Triangle," as men like Nabuco referred to the three coffee provinces, the great harvests of red berries continued to depend on slave labor.

Nabuco had introduced a bill in the Chamber in 1880 calling for an end to slavery by 1890, but it had been defeated. That same year, he had joined others in launching the Brazilian Antislavery Society, of which he was the first president. Despite their ceaseless propaganda for abolition, the movement was at a nadir in 1881, when Nabuco and other pro-abolition deputies lost their seats in the Chamber.

One of the most serious obstacles to the cause of total abolition was a law passed in 1871 — the Free-Womb law, which offered conditional liberty to slave children born after September 27, 1871. The ingênuos ("innocents") were to be supported by their mother's owner until the age of eight, at which time they could be released for an indemnity paid by the government or apprenticed to the slave owner until their twenty-first birthday. Obviously, the majority of owners preferred to keep the ingênuos as laborers until they turned twenty-one, and by 1884 only 118 of an estimated 400,000 ingênuos had been freed.

The "free-womb" law had silenced all but a few vociferous abolitionists. Dom Pedro himself had maintained a dignified calm. His Majesty's instincts were against slavery and he was sensitive to petitions for abolition, but since the landowners and slaveocrats opposed to abolition were the strongest supporters of the monarchy, he exercised utmost caution.

Despite these obstacles, the abolitionists scored their first triumph in the northern province of Ceará in March 1884. The Northeast had been devastated by one of the periodic droughts that scourged the interior. Ceará had been worst hit: More than one-third of its population — 300,000 people — were dead from starvation and disease.

Before the drought, there had been thirty thousand slaves in Ceará. Many perished, but several thousand were sold to slave traders from the south. Then in 1881 the coffee provinces had placed high taxes on slave imports. The fazendeiros were afraid that depletion of slaveholdings in the north would foster a climate of abolitionism that could spread to the south. But they acted too late. When traders took a group of slaves down to the beach at Fortaleza, the capital of Ceará, the ferrymen refused to carry the slaves to ships waiting to take them south. The boatmen's strike spurred a wave of abolition sentiment. On March 24, 1884, Ceará declared itself free of slavery.

In the Teatro Santa Isabel at Recife this Sunday afternoon in November, Joaquim Nabuco was inveighing against the foes of abolition:

"Our opponents tell the world that because the womb of the slave is free, slavery is extinct in Brazil. That law is a sham that serves the interests of the slaveocrats and will prolong Brazil's humiliation. Consider the female slave born on September twenty-seventh, 1871, the day before the law came into effect: Her mother's womb was not free, so she remains a slave, who at the age of forty, 1911, may bear a child. Now, if this ingênuo's master refuses the indemnity, the ingênuo can be kept in provisional slavery until the age of twenty-one — 1932. Seventy years after Abraham Lincoln's proclamation, Brazil will have a generation languishing in the senzalas!

"Abolition will ruin and bankrupt Brazil, the slaveocrats cry. Our adversaries in the Black Triangle, where a million slaves are held, propose an alternative: Asiatic emigration. My friends, that would be a fatal error. It would bring millions of yellow slaves to mingle in hovels with black slaves.

"*Free* emigrants we do welcome. Brazil occupies half the South American continent. We can offer a home to many millions from Europe. Every year, one hundred thousand go to Argentina; the United States welcomes three hundred thousand. Brazil? We are fortunate to receive thirty thousand. What emigrant longing for a better life will take ship at Naples or Lisbon to sail to a gloomy prison where slavery flourishes amid agricultural fiefs?

"With all my heart and strength, I denounce slavery. I denounce it as a violation of every article of the penal code, of every commandment in the law of God!"

℘

At Engenho Santo Tomás, the Casa Grande dominated the landscape like a bulwark against change. Five generations of Cavalcantis had controlled the plantation from this grand old mansion built by Bartolomeu Rodrigues Cavalcanti in 1751. The present senhor de engenho, Rodrigo Alves Cavalcanti, a great-great-grandson of Bartolomeu, was progressive enough to have been one of the first Pernambucans to install steam turbines in his mill, but if he saw the slightest threat to his dominion, Rodrigo Cavalcanti would dig in his silver-spurred boots.

Late one January afternoon in 1885, on the deep veranda in front of the Casa Grande, Rodrigo was engaged in conversation with his brother, Fábio Alves, and his own son, Celso, who was nineteen.

Rodrigo was fifty-two, four years older than Fábio, the difference in age accentuated by their appearances. Rodrigo was of middle height, bronzed and athletic-looking, with a round face and alert green eyes; his dark brown hair was thinning, but more than compensated for by bristling side-whiskers, flowing mustache, and a heavy beard.

Dr. Fábio was the same height as his brother but much thinner. He had the same intelligent green eyes, but compassion shone in them. His small beard and modest mustache were in marked contrast to Rodrigo's hirsute splendor. His clothes were the latest London fashion, but he was no dandy and he seemed slightly disheveled. There was an aura of impatience about him, a sense of urgency.

Fábio had been on the platform in the Teatro Santa Isabel that Sunday in November, as a member of Joaquim Nabuco's election committee. A personal friend of Nabuco, who often visited Fábio's home near the Passagem do Madalena — a bridge across the Rio Capibaribe in Boa Vista, a suburb of Recife — Fábio shared Nabuco's belief that Brazil would not take its place among the community of free nations until the day slavery ended.

And, like Nabuco, with whom he had often discussed this subject, Fábio saw abolition as only the beginning of the struggle. To this day, he was haunted by the memory of the Paraguayan boys slaughtered at Acosta Ñu during the great war. And six years ago, here in northeast Brazil, Fábio for the second time in his life witnessed an immense human tragedy: For eight months he worked with other doctors at Fortaleza, Ceará, among the tens of thousands who had fled the drought in the interior. The refugee camps were a hecatomb; 15,390 souls were carried out to trenches during one month alone. The *seca* was a calamity of nature, but the improvidence, ignorance, filth, and abject poverty of the stricken people stampeding to the coast — Fábio saw this as the work of man.

"I could love no place as much as the valley of my family," Fábio had told Joaquim Nabuco. "For generations, the Cavalcantis of Santo Tomás have been on those lands. Of course, the great estate of our forefathers has been subdivided by inheritance, but even now, twenty thousand acres belong to the engenho, three-quarters of which have never been cultivated. For us, a blessing for the future; for Brazil, a curse!"

Guilherme Cavalcanti, the father of Fábio and Rodrigo — a third son had died in 1872 — had himself died in 1874, leaving Fábio one-third of Santo Tomás and property at Recife and Olinda. Today Recife, with its three main districts — Recife or

São Pedro, the old quarter; São Antônio; Boa Vista — separated by salt creeks and the Rio Capibaribe, was, after Rio de Janeiro and the Bahia, the third city of Brazil, with a population of 140,000. At Olinda, there remained fine town houses dating from the days when the senhores de engenho looked down with contempt, from those emerald-green hills, on the peddlers and artisans of Recife. But, though the presence of the cassocked faithful was still marked in the steep streets between ancient monasteries and churches, Olinda, too, was changing. Boardinghouses and music pavilions proliferated beneath the palms near the water's edge, and there were bathing machines for those seeking a curative plunge in the surf.

Fábio's home and medical practice were at Boa Vista, and his life there a total break from the patriarchal regime of the engenho. Fábio saw an evil for Brazil in the vast landholdings that kept hundreds of impoverished families tied to the large estates like serfs. Recife teemed with indigent thousands who flocked from the countryside to find work, unskilled men who would be far better off as small farmers but had no hope of finding good land or the means to buy it. On low-lying, swampy lands below São Antônio district and on hilly parts of the Capibaribe valley, they built rude huts — *mocambos*, from a Bantu word meaning "cave."

Here at Santo Tomás itself, there were 180 families of agregados, many of whom worked for two or three days a week for no compensation except the right to grow food for themselves. Senhor Rodrigo was not without sympathy for the poor. "You know as well as I do, Fábio, there are families who have been with us for generations. This valley is their home as much as it is ours," Rodrigo had said on occasion. "In our father's day, there were two hundred slaves; I must do with eighty-five. The agregados can't provide enough labor; more and more, I have to turn to the idlers and vagabonds who drift in from the sertão for the harvest. Cane trash! I can't walk in the fields without a man to watch out for me."

Now, during this latter part of January, it was the height of the cane harvest and Rodrigo Cavalcanti was indeed escorted by armed capangas when he rode among the gangs of itinerant cane cutters; but from the veranda where the three men were sitting, the scene could not have been more tranquil. At the foot of the gentle slope toward the river, smoke from the chimneys at the mill and distillery rose above the small forest behind the sugar works. To the right of the veranda, past the tall Cross on the chapel patio, a red ribbon of road winding through the palms and tamarinds and other trees marked the edge of the cane fields nearest to the Casa Grande. The rolling hills behind the road were planted with sugarcane, which looked like waving grass in the distance. The crests of some hills close to the mansion were crowned with clumps of trees; the heights far to the north bore dark smudges below the ridges; and elsewhere, too, there were survivors of the great forest that once covered the valley.

With Joaquim Nabuco, Dr. Fábio could talk about the curse of great estates, and indeed his concern for the landless mass of Brazilians was genuine. He was a man of the city, and much about life at the engenho struck him as quaint and old-fashioned — and brutal. But each time he returned to Santo Tomás, he had the feeling of coming home. His mother, Dona Eliodora Alves Cavalcanti, lived here. And in the valley and across the hills south toward the town of Rosário were

Cavalcantis and in-laws and relatives too distant to be more than favored agregados. Rosário was referred to no longer as a vila but as Cidade da Rosário; its status as a city reflected its position as município with a population of 2,300.

Sitting with Rodrigo and Celso, Fábio could hear the laughter of his children, two girls and a boy, who were on the chapel patio, the boy holding the string of a red-and-white kite. Near the children, sitting in the shade of two ancient trees ablaze with yellow blooms, with her back to him, was his wife, Renata.

Dr. Fábio would always remain in Rodrigo's debt for the welcome Rodrigo had given them on their return from Paraguay. His brothers Rodrigo and Leopoldo (who had since died) had both chosen girls from the noblest class of Pernambucan families. One sister, Virginia, had given Guilherme Cavalcanti cause for painful heart-searching when she became enamored of the pale mulatto Cicero de Oliveira. But Senhor Guilherme ultimately consented to the union, for Dr. Cicero had fine features, held a degree from Edinburgh University, spoke several languages, and owned an engenho in Rosário district, all of which elevated the mulatto to the upper class.

From the start, Rodrigo Cavalcanti had been greatly taken with Renata, whom he called his little sister. Rodrigo's wife, Dona Josepha, the mother of Celso and seven others, was a veritable Amazon, who along with Dona Eliodora, ruled the Casa Grande. Beside Josepha, Renata looked like a rosy-cheeked china doll. The mother of two girls, Ana and Amalia, eleven and thirteen, and a son, Emílio, nine, she had lost none of her beauty.

"Joaquim Nabuco fans the fires of slave insurrection," Rodrigo was now declaring. "It will be the ruin of agriculture."

Rodrigo Cavalcanti knew that Fábio and even Celso were both in the camp of the abolitionists, but this didn't deter him from speaking his mind. Fábio and he had always been frank with each other. As for Celso, Senhor Rodrigo welcomed a chance to lecture the young whelp infatuated by ideas that, to his father's way of thinking, verged on anarchism.

"Joaquim Nabuco isn't a firebrand or fanatic," Fábio said in reply to Rodrigo. "He's said on every occasion that emancipation must be handled calmly and without hatred."

"I read the *Diário*, Fábio. What's the reality? Is it the church of São José?"

"São José was a tragedy. What happened there can't be related to the abolition movement." The election for national deputy had been held on December 1. In the ward of São José, when the ballots were counted and showed a victory for Nabuco's Conservative opponent, a Liberal mob rioted, causing the death of two Conservative election officials and the destruction of the ballot papers. A new election was held across the entire First District of Recife on January 9, and Joaquim Nabuco won overwhelmingly.

"Joaquim Nabuco may personally advocate moderation," Rodrigo said. "But those who foment rebellions and encourage slaves to run away to Ceará consider their crime legitimized by the appeals of the son of a great Brazilian statesman."

"No, Rodrigo, it isn't Joaquim Nabuco who destroys slavery; it's the spirit of our time."

"I accept that," Rodrigo said.

"Then, why continue to oppose abolition?"

"With the womb-free and the elderly, I have no argument against freeing them. Slavery *is* doomed. But we've had slavery for three centuries. We can't abolish the system overnight. Let it die gradually, as the law provides. You know, Fábio, there are planters who talk of taking up arms here in Pernambuco. What can we expect in *our* south? The same bloody convulsion that tore apart the United States?"

"The situation is totally different," Fábio said.

"Is it? Ceará is free of slaves. Amazonas. Rio Grande do Sul will be next, and other provinces will follow. The coffee plantations have a million slaves. Without their labor, the fazendeiros will face ruin. Do you honestly expect the Paulistas to surrender their slaves without a fight?"

"The fazendeiros won't go to war and destroy the empire for a cause that's foredoomed," Fábio replied. "It's false to compare our situation with that of the Confederacy in the United States. There's a fundamental difference in our attitude toward the slave." Fábio looked in the direction of the senzala.

"We didn't make a religion of slavery," he continued. "We branded them in Africa, yes, with the mark of the slave, but it was our mark, not God's. We didn't look upon the black as ordained by the Almighty to labor for us. The bigotry needed to sustain a bloody crusade to defend slavery has never taken root in Brazil."

Celso gazed at his uncle with awe. Celso was the youngest of Rodrigo's three sons. The oldest, Duarte, lived at the engenho with his family but was away this day. The second son, Gilberto, was a teacher at a private school in Rio de Janeiro. Celso was slim, almost consumptive-looking, his features grave beyond his years but for his brilliant blue-green eyes. For the past two years, while attending Recife Law School, he had lived with his uncle's family at their house in Boa Vista. Dr. Fábio's home was open to a regular stream of abolitionists and freemasons — Fábio was Grand Master of one of Recife's lodges — from whom the student got many of the ideas that made Senhor Rodrigo fear an incipient anarchist. Rodrigo's concern was groundless, though Celso did harbor a secret passion that would have been just as upsetting to Senhor Rodrigo: Celso wanted to be a priest. Fábio knew this, but the subject had not yet been broached to his brother. Rodrigo maintained the chapel of Santo Tomás and made regular pilgrimages to Mass at Rosário, but he kept a distance between himself and the clergy and was unlikely to greet with enthusiasm Celso's abandoning the toga for a cassock.

When Fábio stopped speaking, Celso said nothing: He might tramp through the streets of Recife with other students singing that Joaquim Aurélio Nabuco was their guiding light, but in the presence of his father, he respectfully curbed his defiance and, unless spoken to, rarely uttered a word.

Rodrigo pursued the topic: "True, Brazil doesn't have the climate of hatred that would set brother against brother over the slavery question, but what about the anarchists" — Rodrigo's favorite catchword – "and subversives who say our monarchy is an anachronism in America?"

"I don't fear a minority of hotheads. The mass of our people love the emperor. How much greater will their respect be if Pedro is our Lincoln?"

Rodrigo grimaced. "What support can *they* offer His Majesty? Flowers strewn in his path? They have no power. They do not vote for parliament. If the slave owners of the south turn against Pedro, republican agitators may seduce them. That virus is spreading, Fábio. We're no longer dealing with a few fools and crackpots or" — he cast a censorious eye over Celso — "student revolutionaries. The Republican party has become a dangerous reality."

"Dom Pedro has held Brazil on course for almost half a century, Rodrigo. The monarchy will survive abolition."

"My brother, I pray to God you're right."

His Majesty was benign toward virulent foes like the Republicans. But almost three years ago, some of these radicals had started a potentially alarming new enterprise: on April 21, 1882, a group of men launched a republican club, the Clube Tiradentes, in honor of the republican martyr Alferes Joaquim José da Silva Xavier, the Toothpuller.

Dom Pedro had made two other powerful enemies. The first was the Church. In 1864, Pope Pius IX had condemned the Masonic Order, which flourished in Brazil among laymen and priests alike. But Dom Pedro, tolerant of other faiths and beliefs, had exercised his authority over the Brazilian church and refused to sanction the encyclical for publication in the empire. In 1872, Dom Vital Maria de Oliveira, bishop of Olinda, challenged the Crown by ordering the lay brotherhoods of the Roman Catholic Church to expel Masons from their ranks. The brotherhoods appealed to Pedro, who in turn asked Dom Vital to rescind his order. The bishop refused, and was arrested, tried for contempt of the Crown, and sentenced to four years' hard labor.

The second group whose enmity Pedro had earned was the army. By this year 1885, its ranks had been allowed to dwindle to thirteen thousand scattered in barracks throughout the country. Officers who had battled their way through the esteros and jungle of Paraguay increasingly grumbled about Pedro's ingratitude to the courageous veterans of his great war.

There was one final and critical problem facing His Majesty: He was fifty-nine, his health impaired by diabetes and malarial attacks, and many of his subjects were giving serious consideration to the question of his successor, the imperial princess, Dona Isabel, who was married to the Frenchman Prince Gaston d'Orléans, comte d'Eu. The comte had returned triumphant from Paraguay, and for a time had enjoyed the affection of the Brazilians, but his quiet domesticity and his French manners had gradually dulled the luster of his battlefield glory. Dona Isabel was charming and intelligent, and generally popular, but it was feared that a third empire with her at the helm would be steered by the hand of the comte.

Outside the Casa Grande, Rodrigo Cavalcanti, for all his talk of the dire consequences of abolition, suddenly turned to his brother and said, "You're right, of course. Slavery must go. Have you heard a dissenting word from me about your plans to free Rosário?"

"No, Rodrigo."

Dr. Fábio had been invited by a group of abolitionist townsmen to be guest of honor at Rosário two days hence for the launching of the Associão Libertadora Rosário. Its objectives were to buy the freedom of slaves in the city or to persuade individual slave owners to voluntarily manumit their slaves, a tactic that had succeeded, town by town, in Ceará.

"Go to Rosário, Fábio. Speak to the citizens. Encourage them to free their slaves. I'll be the first to rejoice in the liberation of our city."

"Your support is crucial."

"You have it. My gift, too: two milreis. Enough, I hope, to buy freedom for three or four."

Young Celso chose this moment to voice an opinion: "God would bless Pai, too, if the slaves of Santo Tomás were freed."

Rodrigo took a long, deep breath. "Celso . . . "

"Yes, Pai?"

"Have you listened to a word?"

"Every word, Pai."

Rodrigo addressed Fábio: "Is this how he attends his professors?"

"Don't blame Celso. He's impatient. Not so, Celso?"

"Yes, Uncle."

"You won't have much of a future, boy, if Brazil is bankrupt, with its plantations a wasteland."

"May I speak, Pai?"

"*Yes,*" Rodrigo grunted.

"I know the cutters who migrate to the valley and the poor labor they give. I've seen the trouble you have getting the agregados into the fields. A day or two of work and they must rest. This won't change, Pai, so long as there's slavery."

"It will *never* change. They're bone-lazy idlers."

"Yes, Pai, they *are* lazy, but it's because they see no dignity in working alongside slaves in the fields."

"Ah! How many times I've heard this. Since the first Tupi was plucked out of the forest in the days of the donatários, no free man has wanted to lift a finger in Brazil. Tell me then, Celso, who built Engenho Santo Tomás?"

"It's not the same, Pai. These are poor peasants. Their fathers didn't have a great valley to colonize."

"So we should give them our land?"

Fábio saw Celso drifting into dangerous waters. "What he's saying, Rodrigo, is that with abolition, the slave won't be there to degrade the value of labor in the eyes of the agregados."

"Exatamente! The slaves will abandon the plantations. Our harvests will be at the mercy of these lazy rascals."

"Give them a chance, Rodrigo. Empty the senzala. Let all who work in our cane fields be free men. In time, the agregados will learn to take pride in their labor."

"Go to Rosário," Rodrigo said flatly. "Convince the citizens of our city to free their slaves." He directed his next words at Celso: "I was told this week that there are one hundred and sixteen registered at Rosário. At the engenhos and on the cane fields of the district, we have twelve hundred. Tell me how to redeem this number, Celso — not one or two house slaves or Negroes for hire in the streets, but twelve hundred slaves?"

Celso looked at his father with that intense, grave expression, but offered no reply.

⌘

"Costa Santos's *extravagância*" — as Rodrigo Cavalcanti sometimes referred to it — lay eight miles from the Casa Grande. Fábio and Rodrigo rode there the next morning, taking the old road to Rosário into the valley beyond Santo Tomás. Seven miles to the northwest at a crossroads, they turned off to the right, a mile to the Jacuribe, which flowed through both valleys. Across a wooden bridge was the extravagância.

The Cavalcanti brothers dismounted at the bridge, leaving their horses with two capangas who had ridden out with them.

The two men walked along the front of a massive building, its zinc roof supported by iron columns. Off to the left was another solid structure, fire-damaged, with a tall brick chimney reaching as high as some of the forest giants behind it. There were numerous smaller structures, too, and near the opening on the north side, abandoned on its meter-wide track, a forlorn-looking little steam engine someone had taken care to cover with palm fronds.

"Costa Santos's extravagância" — the East Pernambucan United Sugar Milling Company — was an engenho central that should have been capable of crushing 100,000 kilograms of cane every twenty-four hours. It stood deserted, its promoter, one Vinicius Costa Santos, gone to his grave, and its shareholders commiserated with one another in their London clubs over its foundering.

Vinicius Costa Santos was descended from the family of Joaquim, the independent cane grower who had so rejoiced when his daughter Luciana became the bride of Paulo Cavalcanti. Though Paulo's murder had left Luciana a widow, the mother of Carlos Maria and great-grandmother of Fábio and Rodrigo had risen to become a power at the Casa Grande. The tough, uncouth Graciliano had been there, returned from the side of the rejected Januária, but by right of primogeniture, which had still been in force, Santo Tomás belonged to the infant, Carlos Maria. Graciliano had been a support to Luciana, though; and so, too, had Padre Eugênio Viana, who had instilled in Carlos Maria many of the ideas that led to his fatal involvement in a Republican revolt in 1824, during Pedro I's reign. Subsequently jailed for five years in a Bahia fortress, Carlos Maria had died soon after his release.

As Joaquim Costa Santos had hoped, the prestige of the Costa Santos family had increased immeasurably, as had their holdings in the second valley. Vinicius Costa Santos, the grandson of one of Luciana's three brothers, had been the most prosperous, and the most ill-starred, for never had there been such a reverse as his in the fortunes of the Costa Santoses.

In London, which Dr. Vinicius frequently visited in the late 1870s to promote his scheme, the East Pernambucan United Sugar Milling Company seemed a tempting investment indeed to those who listened to him: "Two great valleys with endless cane fields and vast lands yet to be cleared for planting. Water in abundance from the Rio Jacuribe. Easy access for a link to the railway planned from Recife to the interior." The English engineers who visited the valley in 1878 returned home with glowing confirmation of all Vinicius Costa Santos had promised: On February 1879, the East Pernambucan United Sugar Milling Company was launched.

On September 27, 1880, at the start of the harvest, Dr. Vinicius had watched proudly as the 40-horsepower engine was started and the mill machinery shook the cavernous building. The first canes went into the long feeder trays to the rollers, crackling and crushing as they passed through the gigantic squeezers, and the first juice poured into the trough to the straining box. Exactly twenty months later, in May 1882, the engenho central was shut down, the company bankrupt.

Costa Santos had made a terrible miscalculation. There were twenty-two engenhos in the two valleys, Engenho Santo Tomás, with five thousand acres of cane fields, by far the largest (and the only engenho powered by steam). Four were in the Costa Santos family, but more than half belonged to relatives and associates of the Cavalcantis and so delivered their crops to Engenho Santo Tomás.

Dr. Vinicius had tirelessly promoted his engenho central among the plantation owners. His relations backed him, and half of the remaining eighteen senhores showed interest in a project that could free them to concentrate on extending their cane fields. Rodrigo Cavalcanti, too, seemed in favor of the proposed mill, but Dr. Vinicius had not been able to get a firm commitment from him. "It's natural that he should hesitate," Costa Santos told the English investors. "The senhores de engenho of Santo Tomás have been in the valley since time immemorial. However, I'm sure when Commendador Rodrigo sees how the other planters are prospering with ever-greater harvests, he'll support our mill." And Dr. Vinicius had given an added assurance to the Englishmen: "Besides, gentlemen, we are practically family, the Cavalcantis and the Costa Santoses."

Rodrigo Cavalcanti had not come around, family ties notwithstanding. Not one stalk of cane from the 1880 harvest at Santo Tomás reached the engenho central, and of fourteen engenhos allied to the Cavalcantis, only two sent canes to the mill, being indebted to Dr. Vinicius for loans he'd made to them in the past. Still, Dr. Vinicius had hopes for the 1881 harvest; he had gone from planter to planter, and he had gone to Santo Tomás. "I'm very sorry, Vinicius," Rodrigo Cavalcanti had said, "but I gave you no promise. I will not send my canes to the Englishmen."

That the major shareholding of the East Pernambucan United Sugar Milling Company had been in foreign hands was only part of the reason for Rodrigo Cavalcanti's refusal to support the engenho central. "To abandon our mill and send our cane to the central will be the ruin of Santo Tomás," Rodrigo had said to Fábio, who was of mixed mind about Dr. Vinicius's scheme. "Our plantation will be hostage to the company. I, Rodrigo Cavalcanti, will be nothing but a *fornecador!*" It was Rodrigo's belief that to be a fornecador — a mere supplier of cane to a mill — was to be stripped of all honor and dignity.

On August 30, 1882, on the eve of the harvest, Vinicius Costa Santos set fire to the engenho central and then hanged himself in the trees behind the steamhouse.

"The poor man, I tried my best to dissuade him," Rodrigo was saying as he and Fábio strolled in the desolate mill yard. "I'm not against English capital, I told Dr. Vinicius. They own the railways, gasworks, ironworks. They want to build factories for textiles and other industries. Brazil needs the English. But here at Santo Tomás?"

"He knew he was right. The district needs an engenho central."

BRAZIL

614

"And I agreed with him, but I warned him, it was wrong to bring in the English. 'Let's put our heads together, Vinicius,' I said. 'We'll work up our own plan and present it to the minister at Rio de Janeiro. I have influence at the Corte. I'll get the loan guarantees we need.' Did he listen?"

Fábio stopped walking. The caretaker had been told in advance of their visit and had opened the massive doors to the main building. The dimly lit interior was more desolate than the scene outside. The mill, with its great horizontal rollers, was gone, and the engines, too, most of the movable equipment sold to a central at the Bahia. The great six-hundred gallon juice tanks, the pans, the network of troughs and pipes, and a jumble of abandoned equipment remained. In the air was the smell of grease mixed with a heavy, sweet pungency.

Fábio stepped inside. "It's a tremendous risk, Rodrigo."

"God knows, Vinicius learned this, but it's not the same, Fábio. Vinicius failed because he went his own way. I'll have every planter behind me."

"No doubt, but still — a million reis!"

Rodrigo was planning — with absolute confidence that it would pose no threat to Santo Tomás — to establish a *usina*, a factory able to process raw cane through every stage until there remained only pure and sparkling crystal grains of sugar. When the London company went bankrupt, Rodrigo, with no particular ambition to start a factory at the time, had bought this site. But in the past six months he had been gathering support for a usina: He was going to Rio de Janeiro in a week's time for consultations with the minister of agriculture.

Rodrigo named four senhores de engenho, two of them Cavalcanti relatives, one his brother-in-law, Dr. Cicero de Oliveira, the mulatto husband of Virginia Cavalcanti. Dr. Cicero, whose engenho was south of Santo Tomás on the new road to Rosário, was to have joined them on this tour of the central but had to cancel, as Virginia Cavalcanti's delivery of their fourth child was imminent. Rodrigo had been disappointed, for his brother-in-law, who had studied engineering at Edinburgh University, was a staunch supporter of the planned venture.

"Dr. Cicero and the others are willing to put up capital," Rodrigo said, as Fábio and he walked through the deserted central. "The government will guarantee the loans we need."

"Why not simply refurbish the central?"

"No!" Rodrigo said emphatically. "We must invest in a modern usina."

Rodrigo's excitement mounted as they wandered around the deserted central. "Usina Jacuribe" — he had already chosen a name for the factory — "Fábio, what an achievement! Not for me or you alone. For every Cavalcanti who lived and fought to preserve our valley. Usina Jacuribe!"

At Rosário, the former Jesuit church of Nossa Senhora do Rosário stood high on the west end of the city. The massive clay-packed walls of the lofty building were marked and weathered with age, but its handsome gabled façade recently had been restored, and the wooden shutters on its windows painted sky blue. The town had spread to the left of the old church and square, along the base of a low hill and on ground that sloped gently to the east. In the center of Rosário at the Praça do Jardim, the main square, was a new church, São Pedro. The town hall and other official buildings were on a street off to the right of the main square, the rua Carlos Maria Cavalcanti — "rua Cavalcanti," to the locals. Other streets leading from the Praça do Jardim were lined with neat rows of one-story houses, most of them white with red tile roofs.

The most inviting aspect of Rosário was the luxuriance of its setting. Tamarind, mangueiro, cashew, wild banana flourished beside cultivated groves of coffee, orange, lemon. Ancient forest giants bearded with moss towered above gardens with roses, carnations, lavender.

On February 1, 1885, the Praça Velho at the Jesuit church was the venue for a grand fair to celebrate the launching of the Associão Libertadora Rosário. At 3:00 P.M. this Sunday afternoon, several hundred citizens were in the old church to hear Dr. Fábio Cavalcanti and other dignitaries call for the freeing of Rosário's slaves. When the formalities concluded at five, the audience streamed out to the Praça Velho to join the crowds at the fair.

The square was lined with flower-bedecked kiosks, several named for prominent figures of the abolitionist movement: Luis Gama, a leader of the São Paulo antislavery crusade years after fleeing his master to join a militia company and gaining freedom with proof of illegal enslavement; José Patricinio, "The Black Marshal," a militant campaigner and editor of the abolitionist *Gazeta da Tarde* at Rio de Janeiro; André Reboucas, a quiet, refined mulatto engineer and a favorite of Dom Pedro and Princess Isabel; the late Castro Alves, the young "poet of the slaves"; and, of course, Nabuco.

At the Nabuco kiosk, there was a brisk trade in "The Emancipator," a hat not unlike a low bowler. "Approved by Senhor Joaquim himself," cried a vendor. "Ah, senhores! Maravilhoso! A crown for every lover of freedom!" There were Nabuco braces, handkerchiefs, cigars, snuff, and for the ladies, the Joaquim Nabuco parasol. At the other kiosks, the scene was similar, all profits intended for the Associão Libertadora.

Fábio and his fellow committee members stopped at the kiosks to encourage participation. Rodrigo Cavalcanti's generous donation had been acknowledged with Vivas for the commendador, but Rodrigo himself was absent. Rodrigo personally supported the freeing of Rosário's town slaves, but as representative of the district planters, he deemed it prudent to keep a distance from the Associão. But Celso Cavalcanti was here, with two student friends, the three of them in dark frock coats, strutting behind the dignitaries with an air of exaggerated importance.

Padre Epitácio Murtinho, the curate of Rosário, was a member of the committee. The town priest, Padre José Machado, was also present as an observer, although his enthusiasm for the Associão was restrained and more typical of the position of the Church, which maintained absolute silence on the question of abolition.

After visiting the kiosks, Fábio and Celso found Renata with a group of women near an improvised bandstand where Rosário's town band was entertaining the crowd. An area to the right of the band was open for dancing, but as yet its only occupants were a group of children, Fábio's son among them, who were chasing one another around, their shrieks drowned by the tremendous din from the *filarmônica*.

"Aunt Renata, I saw you with the widow Escobar," Celso said, when they were sitting in a "garden" near the bandstand, where tables and chairs were set out for the gentry. "I wouldn't have believed Dona Ricardina would be first to free her slaves."

Dona Ricardina was the widow of Manoel Escobar, a merchant who had died a year ago. Among the property Escobar bequeathed to his wife were seven slaves, three of whom were hired out by Dona Ricardina. At the church meeting, Dona Ricardina let it be known that she would voluntarily grant immediate freedom to four of her slaves and free the three laborers, too, on condition they rent their services on her behalf for one more year.

"Dona Ricardina says she wants abolition," Renata said. "Her slaves are too much trouble without Manoel Escobar there to control them. They're not worth the expense of keeping them."

"Well, she's honest enough," Fábio said. "It makes no difference, though. Her slaves will be free — that's what's important."

"And where Madame Ricardina leads, others are sure to follow!"

Fábio laughed. "Dona Ricardina has started something today." He looked across at a table where Ricardina Escobar sat with the wives of some of Rosário's most prominent citizens. "Those with slaves will go home tonight and talk with their husbands. They'll fear Ricardina's house will be closed to them."

The widow Escobar was the daughter of an imperial ambassador and had traveled widely in Europe before marrying Manoel Escobar. It was thirty years since Dona Ricardina had been in the Paris of Louis Napoleon and Empress Eugénie, but at Rosário, where she had lived for twenty-six years, Madame Escobar, a large matron with a friendly face, kept the local senhoras in awe with tales of the French court, where she had been a belle.

"Dona Ricardina's offer is wonderful," Celso agreed. "And freedom for nine more will be bought by the Associão. But one hundred slaves remain. How long must they wait?"

"Sixteen free, Celso. The Associão Libertadora Rosário is not one day old. Look around you: Do you think Rosário's citizens would be here in their hundreds if they weren't moved by the spirit of abolition?"

"Certainly it's heartening here, Uncle Fábio, but in the fields just beyond Rosário?"

"Be patient, Celso. You weren't born when the struggle for abolition began. Victory will come slowly, step by step."

"It will take *decades*."

"Yes, it may, but it will be achieved peacefully. This is preferable to the alternatives."

Both Fábio and Celso knew the alternatives, but they did not speak of them now: In Ceará, a Brazilian underground railway was beginning to function; and at Recife, secret abolitionist societies were being created to aid runaway slaves.

As night fell, the Praça Velho was jammed with people. In the light from blazing bonfires, the more humble of Rosário's citizens danced the sensuous *batuque*, while in the garden of the gentry, under gently swaying colored lanterns, the senhores and their womenfolk took turns at the waltz, the polka, and the tango.

Toward nine the indefatigable filarmônica left the bandstand to prepare for the highlight of the fair. Dr. Fábio and the committee members took their places on the platform to await the signal that would herald the climax to the celebrations. It came just after nine. The thirty men of the filarmônica struck up a Sousa march. The groups of musicians playing for the dancers at the bonfires took up the march. The church bell of Nossa Senhora do Rosário began to peal, and then a barrage of fireworks exploded, rocket after rocket bursting in the heavens above the city.

Twenty yards behind the band was a small cart decorated with flowers and drawn by a pony; standing in the cart in a white cotton robe was "Liberty" — a Tupi maiden. The girl chosen for this tableau was a pretty black-haired caboclo; the last Tupi in Rosário district had died long, long ago.

"Liberty" was followed by a crowd, mostly young men, whites, mulattoes, blacks, the sons of senhores like Rodrigo Cavalcanti — Celso was in the middle of this group — and the sons of freed black men like José Carvalho, one of Rosário's three farriers. They were vying for the honor of moving a big cart.

Riding in the cart were thirteen slaves, eight men and five women. Four were the property of Dona Ricardina Escobar, who had been invited onto the platform by the officers of the Associão Libertadora; nine were town slaves whose masters had agreed earlier this day to the immediate purchase of their freedom for a total of 4,400 milreis.

A deafening cheer rose as the young men dragged the cart toward the platform. The joy of the crowd was nothing compared with that of the thirteen men and women in the cart. They sang. They clapped their hands. They praised Jesus Christ and Liberty. When the cart stopped at the platform and the slaves climbed down, the band began to play the national anthem. The church bell was rung with new vigor, and the sky was blasted with a fresh barrage of rockets.

One by one, the thirteen slaves stepped up to the platform, where Dr. Fábio Alves Cavalcanti presented them with their certificates of freedom.

It was a glorious moment at Rosário, and what made it even more so was the sight of the old pelourinho erected by Elias Souza Vanderley, a column sixteen feet high, with its iron hanging hooks rusting, its ancient mahogany surface scratched and pitted. It was still here, one hundred yards from the platform, dark and gaunt in the light from the bonfires.

☙

On a night eight months later, seven men met in absolute secrecy in one of the narrow Dutch-style houses on the rua da Cruz, the principal street in the old quarter of Recife. They were members of the Clube do Cupim, which took its name from the *cupim,* the termite, and its motto, too: Destroy Without Noise.

During the past six months, this branch of the citywide club had helped ninety-seven runaway slaves, most of them from plantations beyond Recife. The club members sent agents posing as itinerant workers into the countryside to incite slaves to flee the senzalas. They provided hideaways for fugitives and guides to the coast, where the slaves were transported north by sailing barge to the free province of Ceará.

The men in the house on the rua da Cruz this night of October 2, 1885, were irate. Four days ago at Rio de Janeiro, Dom Pedro had sanctioned a new law for the liberation of elderly slaves: Those who had reached sixty, instead of being unconditionally free, were to compensate their masters with three years' unpaid labor. Those older than sixty but not yet sixty-five were to work for free until their sixty-fifth birthday, at which time they were to be liberated. One provision in particular incensed the members of the Termite Club: aiding and abetting a runaway slave now was to be considered a felony.

"If the police catch us, gentlemen, we're to be treated like common criminals," the chairman declared. "We can be sent to jail for two years. I will go willingly to the Casa do Detenção, with my head held high."

This statement was met with noisy, unanimous agreement from the others. The members of this branch of the Termite Club ranged in age from twenty to fifty-seven. Their occupations varied, too, from student to elderly bookkeeper of the Casas Pernambucanas, a dry-goods chain, to a leading actor at the Teatro Santa Isabel — the chairman himself.

The chairman had put his dramatic flair to full use as he spoke; gesturing flamboyantly with his long, thin arms. He was in his early forties, over six feet tall, exceedingly thin, with a narrow face and small chin and two enormous front incisors.

Known in the theater as Agamemnon de Andrade Melo, he was none other than the mulatto Henrique Inglez the younger, who had prowled the battlefields of Paraguay as "Padre," robbing Guarani corpses with his compatriots, Antônio Paciência and Tipoana.

Henrique had quickly squandered the gold and silver he had brought from Paraguay upon his return in 1870. He had been reunited with his father, Henry the Englishman, who had still been eking out a living with his Teatro Grande at Itamaracá, twenty-five miles north of Recife. For a while, Henrique had regressed to his youthful dissipation, but Henry the Englishman would have none of this: "I'll be damned if I give a penny, Henrique Inglez, for your philandering. If you want money, you'll earn it."

And earn it he did, on the boards of the little theater Teatro Grande, revealing a marvelous innate acting ability, especially in French farces, where he excelled in roles as a consummate fop.

After the death of his father in 1873, Henrique abandoned the Teatro Grande and made his way to Rio de Janeiro, where he had eventually surfaced as "Agamemnon de Andrade Melo," playing on several occasions to no less a personage than His Imperial Majesty. In 1880, Henrique had returned to Recife, where his reputation as a comedy actor made him a favorite with audiences at the Teatro Santa Isabel. Henrique had been married five years ago to Joaquina, the daughter of a court official. They had two children, both boys, both distinguished by huge sloping teeth like those of their father, whom they were taught to call Senhor Agamemnon.

Though he was a master of comedy, Henrique — or Agamemnon, as his fellows in the Termite Club called him — was deadly serious about the abolitionist cause. He was personally acquainted with many of the movement's leaders, including Nabuco and José Patricinio, The Black Marshal, who was an advocate of revolutionary liberation methods such as were used by the Termite Club.

Now, in the house on the rua da Cruz, when the members quieted down, Henrique Inglez said, "There is a greater danger, gentlemen, than the threat to our own liberty. The slave owners held up the ingênuos for the world to see: 'Slavery is extinct in Brazil!' For ten years, the voices crying for abolition were muted. Today, the slave owners praise The Monster. They hope this perverted legislation will extinguish the flame of freedom." Several shouted "No!" "I hear you," Henrique called back. "So do the slaves who need our help. Gentlemen: what is the threat of two years in jail compared with a lifetime of bondage? The work of the club goes on. When the call comes, be ready."

"Bravo, Senhor Agamemnon! Bravo! We're with you, Agamemnon, to a man."

It was Celso Cavalcanti, as famished-looking as Henrique, his eyes afire. Celso had met Henrique at his uncle's house, and had been drawn into the Termite Club by Henrique himself, despite Fábio's attempts to dissuade his nephew from membership in the club, believing the abolitionist movement better served by legal means.

During the past three months, Celso had assisted the club by raising funds among the students at the law school. He had also, on one occasion, accompanied a guide leading four slaves to the island of Itamaracá; the old Teatro Grande, now in disuse but still owned by Henrique Inglez, was used as a hiding place for runaways prior to their being taken to the north shore for embarkation to Fortaleza in Ceará.

Later that night in the house on the rua da Cruz that belonged to Henrique, the actor spoke with Celso about Senhor Rodrigo Cavalcanti.

"When do you expect your father to return?"

"I can't say, Senhor Agamemnon. He sent a cable last week saying he was going to London."

Rodrigo Cavalcanti had sailed to France the past July to visit the works of the Compagnie de Fives-Lille, manufacturers of sugar works and distilleries, who had supplied plant and machinery for several Brazilian factories.

"Would to God that your father could see the senzala for what it is — a blight upon your valley, beside the modern usina he will build."

"I think he realizes that," Celso said.

"If Senhor Rodrigo takes the lead in Rosário district, the other planters will follow."

Celso knew this. The liberation of the city of Rosário itself, despite the excitement of the launching of the Associão Libertadora, had not yet been accomplished. One-third of the town's 116 slaves had not been freed, and hundreds of slaves continued to serve on plantations in the município. Though Celso had just that afternoon helped runaways from a plantation near Recife, it was difficult for him even to contemplate any activity that might bring direct conflict with his father or his older brother, Duarte, who lived at Santo Tomás and was there now, taking charge of the harvest in their father's absence.

Henrique put a hand on Celso's shoulder: "I know it's difficult for you, Celso, a Cavalcanti of Santo Tomás, but think of the day this rotten institution ceases to exist in Brazil — the hour when men like your father are free, too. The chains of slavery bind them no less than those they hold in bondage."

ᐒᐱ

Two weeks later, Henrique Inglez sent a small black boy, the son of a freed slave woman in his employ, to the law school with a message that he urgently wanted to speak with Celso. They met at the Trapiche, the busiest section of the city, and strolled across the square in front of the warehouses as they spoke. Slave bearers of sugar sacks and cotton bales moved like ants between the warehouses and lighters moored beside the quay, while mule drivers and horsemen who had journeyed from the far west of Pernambuco streamed onto the broad quay with new deliveries from the engenhos and cotton fields. An endless parade of peddlers offered goods as varied as brilliant macaws, bundles of firewood, cakes, oranges, remedies for the pox.

Henrique told Celso that he had received a report that forty "pineapples" — the code word for fugitive slaves — were ready to run from the district of Rosário. Jorge, a caboclo laborer and agent of the Termite Club, had sent word that the slaves were preparing to desert several engenhos in two days' time and needed guides to escort them to the coast. Jorge had given a rendezvous point along the old road to Rosário.

"Five men are being sent to escort the slaves to Itamaracá. I believe they can get there safely, but your presence would be a great help," Henrique continued. "You know both these valleys. No one will blame you if you refuse to help, Celso. If you say no, I'll understand."

Celso looked at a group of beggars who bestirred themselves to besiege a prosperously attired senhor alighting from a chaise with his ocean-bound luggage. "I can't," Celso said, without turning to Henrique. "God help me, I can't say no."

⟡

Celso tramped impatiently to and fro across the open ground between rows of luxuriant canes. It was past midnight, two nights later, and he was at the runaways' assembly point a mile below the Paso do Natal, on the old road to Rosário. Why it was called "Christmas Pass," no one could say; the memory of the aged Jesuit Leandro Taques, who had spent Christmas Eve 1759 on the pass during his walk to Recife and exile was long forgotten.

Twenty yards behind Celso, sitting on the ground deep inside the dark walls of cane, were eighteen slaves who had fled two engenhos in this valley. The main group of twenty-two were expected at any moment. They were coming from Engenho Santo Tomás.

Celso had known intuitively the instant Henrique said forty "pineapples" were to be escorted from these valleys that the Cavalcanti engenho would be involved.

"Why wasn't I told that the club had an agent at Santo Tomás? Did you think you couldn't trust me because I was a Cavalcanti?" Celso had asked.

"If I didn't trust you, would I appeal for your help now? You still have time to alert your family. I knew that Jorge Chinela was with the cane workers at Santo Tomás, but I didn't expect a message so soon."

Celso was direly apprehensive. That Senhor Rodrigo Cavalcanti was half a world away in London scarcely alleviated his fear of being caught on this mission. I *shouldn't be here,* he told himself repeatedly, even as he had ridden from Recife with two of the five men who were to escort the slaves. They were big, brawny, silent fellows, heavily bearded, and their fearsome countenances had increased the uneasiness of Celso, who was so pale and slender and who seemed almost comical in a pair of black trousers, shabby plaid jacket, and old silk hat. His leather riding boots were new, however, a gift from Uncle Fábio for his twentieth birthday a week ago. Celso had left the house in Boa Vista at noon, when his uncle was visiting a patient at the Hospital Portuguez, and Aunt Renata was gone to the girls' school where she gave lectures on nursing once a week. He had written a note saying only he would be away several days and they were not to worry, though he knew Fábio Cavalcanti would realize what this meant.

As much as Celso felt that he shouldn't be here, as he'd told Henrique, he was incapable of refusing his help. He had been with Joaquim Nabuco's guard of honor. He had marched through the streets singing the anthems of abolition. He had given his pledge. He could not betray the cause, or himself. More than this, there was his longing to serve the Church: If he turned a deaf ear to the call for help from the slaves, could he ever hope to hear the summons of the Lord?

The safe delivery of forty "pineapples" seventy-five miles along a roundabout route northeast to Itamaracá Island wouldn't be easy. There was a march of fourteen miles from the point below Paso do Natal out of this valley beyond Santo Tomás. Then north across the tracks of the Great Western Railway to an engenho owned by an abolitionist lawyer at Recife and staffed by a manager under orders to provide shelter for fugitives. And finally, the trek to a second hideaway at a stone quarry, from where, if all went well, the last group would cross to Itamaracá Island late on the fourth night.

Suddenly Celso stopped and spun around.

"Olá, senhor." The speaker was a man who had crept up on him with amazing stealth.

"Jorge Chinela?"

"I am Chinela."

"Where the blazes did you come from?"

"Across there, senhor." He pointed toward some trees.

"I didn't hear you approach."

"None do, senhor." He grinned. "None hear Jorge Chinela."

He was tall, well knit, sinewy. He wore cotton trousers and shirt, but his vest and an odd helmetlike hat were leather, hinting at a connection with the tawny knights of the caatingas. He wore soft leather shoes; these, and his manner of treading ever so lightly, had earned him his nickname, "Slipper George."

"Senhor Agamemnon got a message to me to expect a senhor who knew the valley."

"I am a Cavalcanti."

"The son of a senhor in the district?"

"The son of Rodrigo Cavalcanti."

Slipper George just whistled.

"I'm with the Termite Club, Jorge Chinela. Our objective is to help slaves to safety."

"Yes, senhor, but . . . "

"What?"

"The slaves from Santo Tomás will know you."

"Does it make a difference?"

"Not if we get them north without trouble."

"Then let's start, Jorge Chinela. The sooner we're away from these valleys, the better."

"Yes, senhor. Yes." Slipper George padded along beside him. "Yes," Jorge said a third time, glancing sideways at the young Cavalcanti. *Louco*, he thought. A crazy young man. The saints help him if the brother, Duarte Cavalcanti, comes after them. Six weeks ago, Jorge had got work as a cart driver at Santo Tomás. They had better be far away when the bell rang at the senzala for roll call, Jorge thought, if this pale young thing beside him was to be spared the rage of Senhor Duarte.

Slipper George had brought thirty-two slaves, ten more than the number expected. Among the fugitives were nine children. Celso Cavalcanti stood to one side as Jorge and the five escorts divided the runaways into six groups. When the blacks from Santo Tomás recognized the senhor de engenho's son, they expressed alarm, but Slipper George silenced them with the assurance that the *nhonhô* – the slaves' word for "senhorzinho" ("little master") — was their ally. Three of Santo Tomás's slaves were included in the seven blacks who would go with him and Celso. The slave Verna had worked in the Casa Grande when Celso was a child.

Verna approached Celso with one hand covering her mouth. "Ai, it is my little master," she said through her fingers. "Nhonhô, why are you here? Your place is not with these Negroes."

"I came to help, ama. Verna."

Verna shifted her hand from her mouth to the side of her scarf-covered head. "Leave, nhonhô. Go home."

"No, ama Verna. I'm taking you to Itamaracá. You will reach free Ceará."

Slipper George interrupted them: "We're ready, Senhor Celso."

"Come, ama, it's a long walk."

"Ai, Jesus Christ," she said, as she fell in behind her husband, Isaac. "My nhonhô . . . my nhonhô." They moved off.

With Slipper George's group in the lead, at 12:30 A.M. the runaways began to walk in a northerly direction, keeping to the rugged track of the old road from Rosário. At 3:00 A.M., Slipper George and Celso had led their group off the road and were moving up the side of one of the low tree-covered hills dotting the two valleys when, from the east, along the road, came the sound of horsemen riding furiously.

There were noises, too, in the underbrush below them as other groups climbed the hill. Celso and Slipper George moved through the trees to a point overlooking the road, but they could make out little in the dark. The sound of approaching hooves grew louder.

"From Santo Tomás, do you think?" Celso whispered.

"Perhaps."

"From where else? So many riders?"

"I led them away quietly, senhor, one by one to the trees behind the senzala. None saw."

"Six hours ago, Jorge Chinela. Plenty of time for this."

"Perhaps one of the other slaves? A capanga hungry for his black *puta*?"

"No matter. My brother knows. We're in trouble, Jorge Chinela."

"Much trouble, senhor." Then he vanished, moving noiselessly back down the hill to check on the groups making their way up toward them.

But the rear groups of fugitives were well off the road, undetected by the riders who came racing along in the direction of the Paso do Natal.

"They'll be back this way, senhor," Slipper George said. He had hurried the rear groups up the hill and returned to Celso's side. "And they'll alert all the engenhos and call out the guarda."

"What do you suggest?"

"Three hours, perhaps four to the railway. Damn it, senhor, it will soon be daylight. It's too risky with the capangas riding all over the valley. We must hide the slaves. When it's night, we can move again."

Celso agreed. "I know just the place, Jorge Chinela."

They were half a mile from the abandoned engenho central. Rodrigo Cavalcanti and his partners had already put men to work on the usina project, but only to restore the railroad from the mill yard to its junction with the Great Western, twelve miles away. Celso, Slipper George, the slave Isaac, and two of the guides approached the wooden bridge at the Rio Jacuribe. The rest of the slaves and their escorts hid in the trees behind the riverbank. Across the bridge, the massive iron building stood darkly beyond the deserted mill yard. Off to the right, at the caretaker's compound, a dog barked.

Slipper George beckoned Isaac and one of the guides. "We'll pay a visit to the caretaker. Wait for our signal." He drew a long, thin knife.

"There's no need to kill him."

"Senhor?"

"Don't harm the caretaker."

"No, Senhor Celso."

But, as Slipper George crossed to the caretaker's house, he whispered to the men with him, "If he does as he's told, all right. If not — the young senhor is too kind." Slipper George had been amazed to discover, when they started the march, that Celso Cavalcanti was unarmed. No revolver, no knife, nothing! The ama, Verna, was right, Slipper George thought: Her nhonhô didn't belong here.

The mongrel at the caretaker's compound stopped barking and came over to greet the intruders, wagging its tail enthusiastically. Two minutes later the dog was whining impatiently outside its master's shack as Slipper George held the blade of his knife against the caretaker's throat. "Listen, friend, to every word, if you want to see the dawn."

Minutes later from the bridge, Celso Cavalcanti saw several shadowy figures emerge from the house. He heard Slipper George whistle. "Get them across," Celso said to the man beside him. "Quick! Hurry them over!" As the first slaves came down to the bridge, Celso joined them, running to meet Slipper George in the mill yard. Celso and Slipper George sent the slaves, along with the caretaker's wife and children, into the cavernous building, and took up position here also for the long wait until the next night. A mulatto guide stayed with the caretaker in case searchers came this way. Slipper George, afraid the caretaker's dog would betray their hiding place, slit its throat.

At 9:00 A.M., as the sun began to bake the iron roof of the engenho central, and with the wall of forest behind the clearing hissing with the sibilance of insects, the capangas came, twenty of them, riding over the small bridge into the mill yard.

The caretaker stood outside his compound. The mulatto, keeping an eye on him, sauntered closer to the leading horsemen as they reined in their mounts beside the caretaker.

"*Bom dia,* Gomes Cabral," the caretaker said to a horseman bristling with arms. Gomes Cabral was head capanga at Santo Tomás.

"We're looking for slaves," he said, without returning the greeting.

"From Santo Tomás?"

"From there. From Engenho Formoso. From Tucuma. Fifty runaways."

"Not here," the caretaker said. "Not this way."

"Who is he?"

"Him?" the caretaker said, looking at the mulatto.

" Yes."

"A cousin. Diego."

The capanga gave the mulatto a long, hard look, but then he glanced away, across the mill yard. "No slaves?"

"I saw none, Gomes Cabral."

The capanga laughed derisively. "João Cunha," he said, addressing the caretaker by name, "they could pass under your nose and you wouldn't see or smell them." "Lazy-Boy" Cunha had been sent from Santo Tomás two years ago to watch over the engenho central, after the overseers had given up trying to break his slothful habits.

To his men, Gomes Cabral said, "Search the place." He himself, with another rider, wheeled away from Lazy-Boy and Diego and rode into the main building. The animals' hooves clattered across the concrete floor as the riders moved slowly among the jumble of equipment. They stopped, letting it grow quiet, until the only sound was the water dripping from a broken pipe. Cabral started forward again, deeper into the building, his horse snorting nervously. He passed beside the troughs and tanks. "Nothing!" he shouted, his voice resounding beneath the iron roof. "Nothing here!" The two men rode back through the clutter and out into the yard.

Ten minutes later, after searching every building and skirting the forest around the clearing, Gomes Cabral and his men rode back across the Rio Jacuribe.

Celso Cavalcanti, Slipper George, and the slaves emerged from where they had been hiding. Some had been crammed into spaces beneath the enormous measuring tanks. Some had crawled into a long ground-level trough filled with six inches of fetid water and covered along most of its length with planks on which parts of machinery and piping had been stacked. Some had climbed to an upper gallery, thirty feet above the place where the mill had stood, and hid atop a straining tank.

The day became blazing hot, and the atmosphere in the central was stifling. The fugitives had plenty of water, though, and food the escorts had brought from

Recife. Hour by hour they waited, ready at a moment's notice to crawl back into their places of concealment.

"How did you get involved with the Termites?" Celso asked Slipper George later that morning.

"Me, senhor?" Slipper George's round face creased into a smile. "It's a long story."

"We have hours, Jorge."

"I'm from Ceará. I was there when the struggle for abolition began." He wasn't smiling now. "I suppose it was the great drought that changed my life."

Slipper George had been in the interior of Ceará province when the seca ravaged the sertão of northeast Brazil. His family had been cotton growers in the district of Pedra Branca, 150 miles from the coast. The drought had wiped out their small plantation, driving them to the town of Pedra Branca to seek sustenance. But in the first months of 1878, the second year without rain, Slipper George had buried his mother and father, dead from starvation, and in May 1878, his wife and three children, dead from disease and exhaustion on the flight to Fortaleza, to which they had been heading, along with 400,000 other famine-stricken sertanejos.

"I don't know why God spared me," Slipper George said. "I passed through lands, Senhor Celso, that were silent. Nothing lived there. No insects. No birds — they dropped off the branches of dead trees as you passed. No animals. No man or woman. No child. The roadside littered with corpses. Houses filled with the dead. Horrible, senhor. Vampires in those huts, sucking for blood. It was a kindness to set fire to the shacks.

"For those of us who got to the capital, there was no relief. The government sent food, but there were men, senhor, who stole much of the supplies. The people went hungry. The camps were pestholes, where refugees died like flies. There was a woman in our camp: She took a knife to her little brother, carved him up, and ate the flesh. Ai, Jesus Savior, like a savage at the Tupinambás' boucan!

"The government provided ships to take the Cearenses to the Amazon," Slipper George said, after describing the disaster. "Thousands sailed from Fortaleza. The agents of the rubber companies promised Paradise. I didn't go. Enter that green hell? After surviving the seca? I wasn't louco. Besides, I'd got a job working with the port laborers. And I saw slaves who had come through the same hell, but their suffering was only beginning. They were driven to the coast for sale in the hundreds, living skeletons. This was too much: slaves who had survived the seca, punished for living! I knew nothing of slaves, Senhor Celso — at Pedra Branca, we were too poor to own any — but my heart went out to those poor things standing on the sandy beach."

"That's how you joined the abolitionists?"

"Ah, my young senhor, you should have seen us, the men of the sea on the beach at Fortaleza: 'From the port of Ceará, no more slaves will be embarked!'"

This had been the battle cry of the "Dragon of the Sea," Francisco do Nascimento, a boatman who piloted the great jangadas in Fortaleza Bay carrying out cargo to ships in the roadstead. The Dragon and another raftsman, João Napoleao, both of them ex-slaves, had refused to ferry out to ships a group of slaves who had been sold and were to be transported to the south of Brazil.

"The slavers tried everything to break our strike," Slipper George continued. "Threats. Bribes. Police. Not one jangada set sail! Not one slave left the port!"

This action had touched off a wave of abolitionist sentiment that had spread through the province, leading to its abolition of slavery in March 1884.

Toward late afternoon, put at ease by the long, uneventful hours since the visit of the capangas, Celso and Slipper George went outside. The other guides and the fugitives stayed confined in the building. Crossing the mill yard, Slipper George shouted a greeting to Diego, who was sitting outside Lazy-Boy Cunha's house keeping an eye on the caretaker, snoozing beside him.

They had just reached the bridge when Slipper George suddenly cried "Silence!" Then: "Horses!"

Celso heard them too, still far in the distance where the road was hidden by trees.

"Under the bridge!" Slipper George shouted. "Pronto!"

They hurled themselves off the timbers into the Rio Jacuribe, six feet deep here, and in moments they were clinging to reeds and grass against the bank nearest the mill yard, with the bridge above them. They were safe, with only seconds to spare.

"Capangas?" Celso queried in a fierce whisper, as the very bank they clung to shook from the hooves pounding above, and dust and debris rained down on them.

When the horsemen had passed over into the mill yard, Celso and Slipper George cautiously moved up behind the thick brush that grew on the riverbank beside the end of the bridge. They saw a dozen or so men in the yard. The riders were not capangas but a detachment of the Guarda Nacional of Rosário district.

"Our Lady!" Celso Cavalcanti appealed. "Heaven help us now."

Duarte Cavalcanti led the troop.

"The slaves," Slipper George said, looking toward the main building. "They'll know to hide."

Celso watched his brother pace his horse toward Lazy-Boy Cunha and Diego. Celso prayed as he had never prayed before.

Duarte Cavalcanti was far more like their father in appearance. Ten years older than Celso, he was robust and broad-chested, and, like Senhor Rodrigo, sported glorious whiskers.

"*Boas tardes,* Senhor Duarte," Lazy-Boy Cunha said, with his hat in his hands and his eyes meeting those of Senhor Duarte's horse.

"Boas tardes . . . tardes senhor! Boas tardes, my Capitão! Boas . . . boas tardes, João!"

It was Diego, portraying the drunkest man in the world. He came lurching toward Duarte Cavalcanti, swaying, almost tripping, a look of stupefaction on his face, a toothy grin. As if struggling to keep his balance, he flung his arm around Lazy-Boy's shoulders.

"I'm Diego!" the mulatto announced. "Cousin Diego of João Cunha!"

Duarte Cavalcanti looked down at him disdainfully.

Lazy-Boy Cunha studied the horse's eyes.

"*Escravos!*" Duarte Cavalcanti said. "Any sign of them?"

Lazy-Boy shook his head.

Diego stopped smiling. He still clung to Lazy-Boy, but his expression changed radically. Now it was the look of a drunk at a wake, trying desperately to appear mournful. A performance that would have done Senhor Agamemnon proud!

"Aieee, senhor! The capangas came, too. Nothing, senhor. We look. We watch. All day. Nada!" Two fingers of the hand on Lazy-Boy's shoulder bored into Cunha's flesh.

"Nada," Lazy-Boy croaked.

"Bah!" Cavalcanti said, with a snort that ruffled his mustaches. "Go back to your cachaça." Then he ordered his men to leave.

As the riders started back to the bridge, Duarte himself cantered toward the main building, peering inside as he passed the open doors. On he rode to the steam house and other buildings; then he came back to Lazy-Boy and Diego.

"Close those doors!" he demanded.

"Yes, senhor," João Cunha said.

"*Immediatemente, patrão!*" Diego said, giving Lazy-Boy a shove that sent him on his way, and starting off behind him with long, unsteady steps.

Duarte Cavalcanti rode after his men, who were already across the bridge.

"Thank you, God," Celso Cavalcanti whispered below the bridge.

Slipper George smiled broadly and, reaching out, squeezed the young senhor's arm fiercely.

They left the engenho central at 10:00 P.M. They took Lazy-Boy Cunha and his family with them. Lazy-Boy came willingly; he was terrified that Senhor Duarte Cavalcanti would discover his complicity, forced though it had been. On the march north to the tracks of the Great Western, they kept to the forest, avoiding the strip that had been cleared for the railway to the engenho central, for somewhere along there was the camp of the men repairing the private line's railbed. At 5:00 A.M. they reached the Recife lawyer's engenho, where they sheltered through the next day.

The following night, on the march to the stone quarry, the rear group, led by the inimitable Diego and trailing a quarter-mile behind the others, stumbled into an army officer and four men who were out searching for a horse thief. When the officer had satisfied himself that they had no connection with the thief, he let them pass — affronted by what it perceived as the imperial government's neglect of the army by keeping it undermanned, and with its ranks including many freed slaves, the army was showing an increasing reluctance to pursue runaways.

On the fourth night, confident of success now, Celso and Slipper George led the final dash to Itamaracá Island. At 3:00 A.M., they stood with all fifty slaves on the bank of the broad river separating Itamaracá Island from the mainland. They were ferried to Itamaracá ten at a time on a jangada that had been left at this designated crossing point by other members of the Termite Club.

On the outskirts of the island village of Pilar, Celso and Slipper George left the slaves hiding in a patch of jungle and went ahead to the Teatro Grande, which stood at the end of a long lane overgrown with weeds and bushes. They approached the building cautiously, keeping to the trees beside the path.

The double doors were slightly open. Treading softly, Slipper George entered first. The benches were piled up to one side. In a moment, Slipper George cried,

"Senhor Celso! Come in! There's no one here."

But, as Celso entered, another voice called out: "Welcome! Welcome, my brave young fellows!"

Senhor Agamemnon de Andrade Melo swept out of a dark corner on the stage. A thin shaft of moonlight from a hole in the roof showed him to be attired in black, a great cloak over his shoulders. He leapt down to the floor and hurried over to embrace Celso.

"Oh, my boy, what a lovely thing you've done!"

"We brought fifty slaves, Agamemnon!"

"No, Celso —"

"Yes, Agamemnon. *Fifty!*"

"Not slaves, Celso. They are free!"

In the front parlor of his house the next afternoon, Dr. Fábio Cavalcanti was staring down at the fine leather boots he had given Celso for his twentieth birthday. The boots were ruined.

"Thirty-two slaves stolen from Santo Tomás." Fábio had learned of the flight of runaways from the engenho two days ago, informed by a telegram from Rosário. Celso had come home, Fábio had been questioning him, and Celso had now confessed his part. "Why did you do it?" Fábio asked.

"I'm with the Termites. I *had* to go."

"God help you, Celso, if your father learns you were there."

"Please, Uncle, you won't tell him?"

Fábio moved his eyes from the battered boots to his nephew's face.

"No, Celso. If he finds out, it won't be from me." There was in Fábio's expression just the hint of admiration.

The procession started forty-five minutes late, the delay caused by Rodrigo Cavalcanti's insistence on a final inspection of the usina. At 11:45 A.M., the director of the Rosário filharmônica raised his baton for the national anthem. When the anthem ended, there was a short pause, and then the filharmônica began to play the religious march "Santa Cecilia." Six altar boys in lace-adorned surplices led off the procession across the mill yard, followed by Rosário's priests, José Machado and Epitacio Murtinho. Immediately behind them, Rodrigo Cavalcanti and his sons led the group of planters who had invested in the usina. Behind the owners came a body of dignitaries and rural magnates, then the usina manager and foremen, and other guests invited to partake in the ceremony blessing the grand enterprise.

It was September 11, 1886, the day for the inauguration of Usina Jacuribe. The procession moved past five hillocks of cane in the yard, the towering lots from Santo Tomás, and four other plantations. Crowds of spectators stood behind whitewashed lines painted on the ground to the left and right of the entrance to the main building, where capangas were stationed to curb any excessive enthusiasm.

With the filharmônica's bold, brassy music swelling, and the first firecrackers snapping, the procession entered the cavernous iron building and moved beside a long feeder tray to the massive Fives-Lille mill. Padre José said a prayer and asked the

Lord's blessing on this great piece of machinery and sprinkled holy water in its direction. He repeated the appeal as he moved slowly through the maze of equipment — engines, measuring tanks, sedimentary troughs, clarifiers, boilers, centrifuges.

The procession emerged from the building to a tumultuous cheer from those outside and the first mighty barrage of rocket fire.

A Guarda Nacional detachment presented arms as the dignitaries exited, and stood by smartly as the procession passed on its way to the blessing of other sections of the usina: the boiler house; the sheds for *bagasse,* the cane trash for fuel; the laboratory; and other outbuildings. Padre José made only a perfunctory gesture toward the distillery and its eight hundred-gallon vats and casks, for he held strong views regarding the abuse of cachaça.

It took more than half an hour of slow marching, with the filharmônica now in tow, for the procession to circuit the usina grounds and return to the main building. At this moment, a small, energetic man sought Rodrigo's attention.

"Senhor Barão?" (Rodrigo Alves Cavalcanti, for "services in the Province of Pernambuco for the good of the Empire and national honor," as the decree of four weeks ago read, had been granted a baronetcy by Dom Pedro Segundo: Barão de Jacuribe.) The man addressing the barão was M. Alain de Lamartine, the mill manager. "Everything is ready."

There were calls for silence from the guests, as the barão wanted to say a few words:

"I cannot greet this bright new dawn without humbly giving thanks to our Lord God for the old planters who came before us. From the day of Nicolau Gonçalves Cavalcanti, the first of our family to reach this promised land, our forebears persevered at Santo Tomás and in this valley of the Jacuribe.

"And now, in this golden moment, I raise my eyes to a new horizon. Senhores, for a long time the engenhos of Pernambuco have struggled against competition from many quarters — from the sugar-beet producers of Europe to the cane growers of the West Indies. The usina will be our salvation!"

Then, guided by a smiling M. Alain, with Vivas rising from two hundred throats even before he reached for the valves and levers, the barão started the 60-horsepower steam engine. On the platform, the mill workers fed canes to the first set of rollers, and the first juice poured into a trough down below.

After the inauguration of the mill, the senhor barão delivered another round of speeches, this time to the mass of agregados and seasonal laborers. His promises of progress and order were no less grand than those made to the senhores.

When the speechmaking ended, the senhor barão directed the crowd's attention to the more immediate benefits of the day: three oxen roasting nearby, six pigs, a mountain of sweet cakes, a wagonful of casks of Santo Tomás cachaça. "*Viva! Viva! Viva!*" the people roared.

As eager as they were for the festa, some agregados had misgivings about the coming of the usina. A few months ago, three families of agregados who had squatted at Santo Tomás had been ordered to move out of the valley. They were gone now, their shacks demolished and the rich red earth far around their place planted with cuttings of cane.

After leaving the agregados, Rodrigo Cavalcanti mingled with the guests who were being entertained by the filharmônica as they sipped champagne and enjoyed a light meal served at a marquee. There had been no ladies at the usina; the donas and their daughters were at the Casa Grande of Santo Tomás, where they were getting ready for a banquet to which eighty guests were invited.

Throughout the ceremonies, Celso Cavalcanti had kept close to Fábio. Celso's role in the flight of the fifty runaways from these valleys had not been revealed, a mercy for which he continued to thank God. Although proud that he'd led the slaves of Santo Tomás to Itamaracá, he wished he had the courage to tell his father.

During this difficult time for Celso, there had been one joyous event: On July 23, 1886, Rosário had declared itself free of slavery. The owners of the last seventeen slaves in the city had finally agreed to accept generous compensation for them. Rodrigo had attended the Associão Libertadora's celebration and put his name to a telegram sent to His Majesty, but still regarded the abolition of plantation slavery as a separate problem.

Toward three o'clock in the mill yard, the guests invited to the banquet at the Casa Grande began to leave for Santo Tomás. Rodrigo rode in a carriage with Fábio, his son Duarte, and Dr. Cicero de Oliveira on the old Rosário road, which had been repaired and widened. On the left of the road lay the tracks for the small locomotive and cars of the usina railway, which had three branches: this one to Engenho Santo Tomás; one to the north and a siding beside the Great Western; and a third into the valley where the usina had been built. The third line passed two engenhos belonging to relatives of Vinicius Costa Santos, the ill-fated promoter of the East Pernambucan United Sugar Milling Company's engenho central. One of the Costa Santoses had attended the inauguration, but the other would have no part of it and was one of four owners who refused to send their canes to the mill.

"Give them a few seasons and they'll come to the usina," Rodrigo said as they passed the plantation of one who declined to do business with the Cavalcantis.

Fábio remarked, "And if they value their independence, even above the prospect of greater harvests?" He had not forgotten his brother's past declaration that to surrender one's engenho and become a fornecador of cane to a central mill ultimately could lead to the loss of one's lands.

"I promised we'd break with fatal routines of the past, and we will, with our modern usina. But the men of Santo Tomás have always preserved the unity of these valleys —"

"We have a covenant with them, Pai!" Duarte Cavalcanti interjected.

The barão de Jacuribe gave his son a look of the greatest affection. "Yes, Duarte!" he said passionately. *"Forever!"*

☙

It was almost time for the banquet to begin at the Casa Grande. Rodrigo Cavalcanti moved among his guests, graciously accepting their congratulations. As five o'clock approached, he was in one of the big reception rooms just off the entrance to the Casa Grande, and showed no hurry to have the guests ushered to the upstairs parlors for the banquet.

While Rodrigo spoke with a group of planters — dressed almost to a man in dark frock coats, black vests, and silk cravats — his glance roved the room. There was Fábio, off in a corner with Dr. Cicero; his brother, for whom he had deep admiration despite their differences. Across the room, Renata Cavalcanti was as lovely as ever in a mauve evening dress with her waist drawn in like an hourglass. Renata stood beside a love seat occupied by Dona Eliodora Cavalcanti and Rodrigo's wife, Dona Josepha, now the baronesa. None had been so pleased as Dona Eliodora at Dom Pedro's award: She sat here now with all the airs of a grand duchess, beaming with pride as she took gentle puffs of one of the dainty little cheroots to which she was addicted. Glancing around the room, Rodrigo was looking for one of his sons in particular. Duarte was here, Gilberto, the teacher, too, who had traveled from Rio de Janeiro for the occasion. But Celso, whom Rodrigo sought, was not in the room. After a few minutes' conversation with the planters, Rodrigo excused himself and went in search of this son. He had a good idea where to find him.

The chapel doors stood open. Rodrigo stepped forward softly and stood framed in the doorway. Though it was many years since the engenho had had a resident priest, the small sanctuary was well maintained; its woodwork varnished, the walls immaculately white, and the altar gilded. There had been two padres after Eugênio Viana, but the last one had left in 1847 and not been replaced. From time to time, a priest from Rosário officiated at the engenho chapel.

Celso was kneeling at the first row of benches in front of the altar, his head bowed.

Rodrigo saw Celso look up at the crucifix on the altar, and he started to walk toward him.

"Celso . . ."

It seemed as if Celso had known all along that his father was there. He showed no surprise at hearing his name, but rose calmly to his feet.

"I came to give thanks to our Lord for this day, Senhor Pai."

"I thank God, too, for His blessings." He stood opposite Celso now, and there was a change in the tone of his voice. "I know everything, Celso. Fábio told me."

Celso blanched. "O my Jesus."

But Rodrigo said calmly, "Yes, my son. Fábio told me how you have agonized over approaching me. You know my bitterness toward the Church and why I feel this way. I opposed the bishop because we have only one ruler in this land — our emperor. But it's not for me, Celso, to oppose the will of God."

"Oh, Pai . . . Pai," Celso said, breathless with relief that his father knew nothing about the runaways.

With tears in his eyes, Celso embraced Rodrigo, and as he held his father, his gaze fell on an image in a niche just behind Rodrigo Cavalcanti.

The little Santo Tomás had been beautifully restored by the same mulatto responsible for the portrait of Dom Pedro Segundo in the entrance hall of the house. The image's cheeks had been delicately painted with a faint blush. The saint's cassock was gold with a red floral design, its girdle brown with gold knots; the sandal straps, too, were carefully painted across the small feet. But the stumps of the arms, which had been hacked off by a Dutch soldier in 1645, remained jagged, the wood dark and encrusted with age.

"May God bless you, my son, as He has blessed your father this day."

They walked from the chapel and out to the long veranda in front of the Casa Grande. Near the front door, they paused silently, father and son, gazing out across the lands below the hill, green and gold in the setting sun. Neither said a word. Arm in arm, they entered the Casa Grande.

કે૭

In July 1886, at Paraíba do Sul, a town in a coffee-growing valley below the Mantiqueira Mountains ninety miles north of Rio de Janeiro, a jury sentenced four slaves guilty of assaulting an overseer to three hundred lashes each. Two of the four died from the beatings.

Joaquim Nabuco revealed the details in a column he wrote for *O Pais*, a liberal daily newspaper at the Corte. By October, the outcry it provoked led to the passing of legislation prohibiting the whipping of slaves by public authorities.

With the abolition of the public lash, desertions from the coffee fazendas began to increase. In the city of São Paulo, a secret group of militant abolitionists calling themselves "*caiphazes*," after the Jewish high priest Caiaphas, aided runaways. Their leader, Antônio Bento de Souza e Castro, who belonged to a planter family, rallied them with Caiaphas's adjuration to the Sanhedrin: "It is expedient for you that one man should die for the people, and that the whole nation should not perish." Runaways who made for São Paulo came alone or in small groups, which could be sheltered by the caiphazes; those who fled into the countryside hid in quilombos deep in the forests.

In the first half of 1887, from district after district, reports of desertions and rumors of mass slave uprisings reached the Paulista capital. By July 1887, with two thousand runaways squatting in a camp outside Santos below the Serra do Mar, where no capanga dared enter, and an unknown number scattered in quilombos in the backlands, the provincial authorities appealed to Rio de Janeiro for help: A warship was dispatched with a small landing force; troops were sent overland.

The 1887 coffee harvest had been under way since April, and the Paulista planters were confident that this season's berries would reach their drying terraces. But, with the mounting crisis, many fazendeiros were worried, not only about the next harvest, but also about the planting season that was to begin in October.

Resolutions passed by district agricultural clubs — the planters' response to groups such as the caiphazes — condemned the urban anarchists' assistance to runaways, but increasingly accepted the inevitability of an end to slavery. A resolution adopted by fazendeiros of the município of Tiberica at a meeting on July 9, 1887, suggested five years as the absolute minimum required to prepare for a free labor system.

કે૭

The meeting of Tiberica's fazendeiros had been stormy.

One old fazendeiro spoke of bringing Chinese to harvest the coffee, but was shouted down with cries that the importation of Asians would mongrelize the population. Another speaker reminded the meeting that the provincial assembly had approved funding of full-fare subsidies for European immigrants in 1886. The agents of the São Paulo-based Sociedade Promotora de Imigracão were already actively recruiting the peasantry of Italy. A few of the planters felt that the employment of masses of Italians was fraught with the danger of strikes.

In the end, the fazendeiros of Tiberica could agree only on the need to slow the pace of emancipation to five years.

When the meeting broke up, some of the planters stood talking in small groups outside the câmara on the east end of Tiberica's central praça. The câmara was diagonally opposite the parish church, the bell tower of which was still incomplete. A new market stood on the south end of the square, the big store of Silva & Sons on the west, flanked by smaller shops and several tabernas. The praça had been planted with trees and a patchwork of gardens between circular stone-paved paths, a favorite place for "footing," the evening promenade of the town gentry and their young.

Finally, two of the planters started across the Praça in the direction of Silva & Sons. The older of the two walked with a slight limp and carried a slender cane, which many of the taberna customers knew to be topped with a diamond worth a small fortune and set in gold. The fazendeiro was not yet fifty, but had thick silver-gray hair. His small mustache was dark, his chin clean-shaven. The young man was striking-looking, with jet-black hair, deep-set brown eyes, and a high forehead. He was of medium height and slightly stocky, but had a light, easy step. He had returned to Tiberica two years ago after many years' absence in Europe, and had amazed the locals with a contraption he'd brought from England, "The Rover," the first bicycle seen in Tiberica.

The older man was Firmino Dantas da Silva, walking with a limp from his leg wound at the battle of second Tuyuti. Firmino had returned to Fazenda da Itatinga in January 1868, a month short of three years after marching off with Tiberica's voluntários, and deeply ashamed of his lack of courage. Ulisses Tavares had died in 1871, believing his grandson had served with honor in Paraguay.

Firmino Dantas and Carlinda Mendes, the sister of Baronesa Teodora Rita, had been married in 1868, the year of his return. Apothecary August Laubner and his wife had attended the wedding with no idea that the extreme friendliness shown them by the barão's grandson was a reflection of his secret passion for their daughter, Renata. August Laubner had prospered, and the profits from his pharmacy had enabled him to buy a coffee fazenda, which was run by his son, Maurits — "Mauricio," among his fellow planters.

Firmino and Carlinda Mendes had three children — Evaristo, Delfina, and João. It had not been a happy marriage. Carlinda was loving and attentive to him, but they had little in common. Carlinda had become plump, domestic, and deeply superstitious. She rarely left the mansion overlooking the Rio Tietê, where she lived like a grand dona of the past, reclined on lace-edged satin cushions, attended by her slaves. Her special delight was sticky cakes, which were baked daily. And she was obsessed by the Catholic saints, and by the saints of the senzala. Carlinda Mendes lived in terror of the evil eye of Exú. With the aid of a sorcerer, a free black woman whose husband was a mulatto overseer at the fazenda, she had resorted to black magic. From *bábá* Epifânia — *"bábá,"* like *"ama,"* was an affectionate address for a woman who served as nursemaid — Carlinda Mendes obtained a constant supply of toad parts, feathers, herbs, and candles to ward off malady and misfortune.

Firmino Dantas knew that his wife dabbled in superstitious practices — he often detected strange aromas floating in the rooms of the mansion, and he had found tiny feathers and crushed herbs in his pockets — but he had no idea of the intensity of Carlinda's obsession. What was important to Firmino was that she left him free to pursue his own interests.

Ulisses Tavares had died in 1871 and Eusébio Magalhães, Firmino's father, just four years later, leaving Firmino Dantas in control of the plantation. Firmino had completed his experimental coffee mill, which had gone into operation in 1872, but it rarely functioned for long without breaking down. But in 1876, Firmino Dantas da Silva accompanied a delegation of Paulistas representing the province at the Centennial Exhibition at Philadelphia and stayed on for eight months in the United States, buying machinery that turned the fazenda into one of the most modern in the province.

Thousands of acres had now been cleared on those twelve square miles within the great bend of the Rio Tietê. The coffee groves now held 750,000 trees, 500,000 of which were fully matured. There were pasturelands with herds of white-humped cattle, a crossbreed between zebus from India and local animals; a sugarcane mill, sawmill, and countless workshops; stores to supply the needs of 500 agregados, and slave quarters for 370 blacks and mulattoes.

Two years after the barão's death, Teodora Rita had gone to live in Paris, where the forty-four-year-old baronesa was a vivacious belle among a small colony of Brazilians, many of them nobles, sheltering in cool luxury away from the tropics.

The young man crossing the praça with Firmino Dantas was Aristides Tavares da Silva, the son of Ulisses Tavares and Teodora Rita. Aristides had studied the humanities at the Sorbonne. He had traveled widely in Europe, particularly Italy and Greece, and had lived in London for a year.

In London, Aristides had met Joaquim Nabuco at a banquet at the Brazilian legation in Grosvenor Gardens. The young da Silva was awed in the presence of Ambassador Francisco Moreira's guests, among them Baron Alfred de Rothschild, whose family were official bankers of Brazil and who himself was a personal friend of Nabuco's.

Nabuco, known in London as a Brazilian abolitionist leader, had taken Aristides under his wing at the banquet, introducing him to Baron Alfred. Subsequently, Aristides had been invited with Nabuco to Exbury, the bachelor Rothschild's country estate, where Aristides had beheld the amazing spectacle of Baron Alfred wielding a jeweled baton to direct his private symphony orchestra.

"Where is your home, Aristides? Is it Paris? Is it London?" Nabuco had asked that night, not waiting for an answer. "I love London above all cities I've visited, but my heart is in Brazil. You must choose, Aristides, and choose soon. You can spend years loitering in Europe or you can go home, back to a land that is one of these days going to be free. *Home*, Aristides, to Brazil, where you belong."

A year passed before Aristides Tavares da Silva sailed for Brazil. Baronesa Teodora Rita had delayed him in Paris through the winter, for she had her eye on a wife for him, nineteen-year-old Anna Pinto de Sousa, daughter of a Portuguese viscount who preferred Paris to old Lisbon, a city glorying in the past. Aristides fell madly in love with the girl. He had feared Anna Pinto would dread the thought of living in Brazil, but when he told her of his decision, she had said, "I would follow you to the end of the earth, my love." They were married in Paris on June 10, 1885. Eight days later, they had sailed for Rio de Janeiro and Santos.

Firmino Dantas and Aristides had got on well from the start, strange though their relationship was. Firmino, the forty-seven-year-old, was the grandson of Ulisses Tavares; Aristides, the twenty-seven-year-old, was the son of the old barão and his child bride, Teodora Rita.

It had pleased Firmino Dantas to discover that Aristides shared many of his interests, including mechanics. Aristides had spent months mastering every aspect of the enormous da Silva enterprise, loathing only the contacts with the slave quarters but accepting the continuation of slavery as a temporary evil. He knew Firmino Dantas would have released many more slaves than the elderly but for certain considerations, one being the mortgage held by the fazenda's bankers, for which 147 slaves were security.

On this July evening in 1887, as Firmino Dantas and Aristides strolled across the praça at Tiberica, they spoke of one particular subject debated at the meeting: Italian immigration.

"There's no hope in Italy for the peasants," Aristides said. "When I toured the country I saw the depth of poverty. God only knows, but the families who land at Santos can hope for a life better than they've ever known."

"I still think we should wait until we're better prepared to receive them."

"Twenty families, Senhor Firmino — they'll use the old coffee store as a dormitory. It will only be for a month or two."

Firmino paused beside a fountain that he had donated to the town in memory of the barão, and poked with the end of his cane at some weeds growing up against the base. "When will you leave?"

"I'd prefer to leave tomorrow. Senhor Martinho Prado expects me in the capital on Wednesday. We'll go together to Santos." Prado was an organizer of the Sociedade Promotora de Imigração. "He'll help me select our workers."

Firmino started walking again. "I rely on you to make the best choice, Ari."

Aristides laughed. "Clear eyes! Good muscles! Strong hands! Like an old slaveocrat inspecting his stock?"

Firmino ignored this remark. "What happens with the colonos at Itatinga will influence others in the district."

"I understand, senhor. I'll bring only those who show a willingness to settle down and work hard."

"The work *is* hard, but they'll be treated fairly at Itatinga. You can promise them this."

They had walked beyond the stone paths and trees and did not cross the road in the direction of Silva & Sons but kept going up the street past the tabernas. They reached the end of the square and passed alongside the church; a short distance down a side street, they stopped at a stable where they had left their horses.

"You'll want an early start tomorrow," Firmino said. "Ride straight to the train. Don't bother to stop here."

"Not unless I think of something I must speak to you about."

They exchanged farewells then and Firmino continued down the street, his light cane rapping the stones. As Aristides waited for his horse to be saddled, he stood at the stable doors, watching Firmino disappear around a corner.

He knew exactly where Senhor Firmino was headed, and it pleased him to think of the joy the unhappily married man now found with his great love, Jolanta.

❧

The twenty-nine-year-old Jolanta Pinheiro dos Santos was the daughter of Américo dos Santos, a white teacher and poet from Salvador, and Adelia Pinheiro, whose family were prosperous mulattoes at the Bahia.

Firmino Dantas had first met Jolanta in 1877 at Rio de Janeiro on his way back from the United States. He had stayed at the Corte for a few weeks with Colonel Clóvis Lima da Silva and his family at their home in Flamengo. Clóvis continued to serve in the army as artillery specialist, and like other veterans, he deeply resented Dom Pedro's neglect of the military. During Clóvis's five-year absence in Paraguay, his wife, Maria Luisa, and two sons, Eduardo and Honório and his daughters had stayed with his brothers, the owners of Silva & Sons. After the war, Clóvis had returned with his family to Rio de Janeiro, but Eduardo da Silva was married and back at Tiberica now, filling the post of district chief of police.

While visiting Clóvis, Firmino had attended a dinner at the house of Américo dos Santos, where he met Jolanta. She was nineteen at the time, a natural beauty with her auburn hair, hazel eyes, and statuesque body. She had captivated Firmino.

When Américo dos Santos moved to São Paulo at the end of 1878, Firmino had renewed his acquaintance with the family, visiting their home whenever he traveled from Tiberica to the Paulista capital. Firmino Dantas was in love with the poet's daughter, and Jolanta dos Santos adored him. In November 1880, Firmino Dantas went to Dr. Américo and openly announced that he had bought a house at Tiberica for Jolanta. "I have nothing against you," dos Santos said. "And I also realize that my daughter is a woman, not a child. But I beg you to reconsider, for her sake. Jolanta needs a man who can offer her marriage and a home, not humiliation."

Firmino Dantas had been sympathetic to dos Santos's appeal: "I will wait six months, Américo dos Santos. I will not visit your home or see Jolanta. At the end of that time, I will come back. If Jolanta still feels the same way, I will take her to Tiberica."

Three weeks later, Jolanta had run away to Tiberica. Firmino had gone immediately to São Paulo. "Jolanta is as precious to me as she is to you," he had told her father. "I swear to God, Américo dos Santos, I will not humiliate or hurt her." Firmino Dantas had kept his promise through the past six and a half years, fulfilling his duties as husband to Dona Carlinda Mendes at Itatinga but openly and unashamedly worshiping Jolanta.

Thanks to Dr. Américo, Jolanta was well educated, an avid reader in Portuguese and French, a lover of music, a lively, forthcoming companion. Given the openness about such affairs in Brazil, the house on Tiberica's rua Riachuelo was a venue for regular soirees attended by Firmino's friends. At Itatinga, Dona Carlinda said nothing. Although she regarded Firmino's carnal pleasures with the mulatta as no threat to her own position as wife and mother, intermittently she sought aid from bábá Epifánia in casting spells against the enchantress.

At the house in Tiberica this July night, Jolanta dos Santos found Firmino tense and disturbed after the planters' meeting. They dined together, waited upon by three liveried servants, all former slaves manumitted by Firmino Dantas at Jolanta's request. The poet Américo dos Santos, an abolitionist, had raised his daughter to share this sentiment; today, Dr. Américo was associated with the militant caiphazes of Antônio Bento at São Paulo.

Fábio told her that he had sensed a growing panic among the planters. "Tiberica has been spared mass action by the slaves. It won't last, though, if the slaves get wind of the disarray in our own ranks, which they surely will. They'll begin to desert, no matter how reasonable we've tried to be."

Firmino had little to say about the 370 slaves at Fazenda da Itatinga itself. Since the beginning of the year, there had been nine runaways, two of whom had been caught by the police chief, Eduardo da Silva, who had returned them after a savage flogging. Firmino found his cousin an ill-tempered young man, as brutish in nature as in appearance, and totally the opposite of his father, Clóvis Lima.

"By God's mercy, Itatinga will survive this storm," he said to Jolanta.

"Yes, 'Nhor. Dr. Américo says five years from now, slavery will be a bad memory."

"Perhaps. We need time, Jolanta — the owners *and* the slaves. Freedom is more than a pair of shoes and a new hat. It will be a new way of life. The slaves must be prepared for it."

"Yes, 'Nhor."

"Enough." His expression brightened. "Play, my little mulatta," he said affectionately.

Jolanta laughed as she stood up. "What does 'Nhor want to hear?"

"Anything, my dear girl."

The poet's daughter had a rare talent Dr. Américo had encouraged ever since he found her, at a tender age, playing in his library with a simple bamboo flute.

For Firmino, it was bewitching. A medley of sensitive improvisations, now taking him far, far back, deep into a green and enchanted glade of the primeval forest, deep into the sertão of the past; now rising evocatively with the rhythms of the Bahia, a city with its heart close to Africa.

When Jolanta stopped playing, Firmino remained sitting, his own eyes closed. He did not open them when he heard the rustle of her dress as she crossed the room. "'Nhor?" she said softly. He reached out and drew her to him.

%

Bábá Epifánia, a big, square-faced woman in her early fifties, had come to Brazil from the lands of the BaKongo in 1847, transported illegally after the abolition of the slave trade. Bought by Ulisses Tavares, Epifánia had served as wet nurse at Itatinga, suckling numerous da Silva infants, Aristides and his sister, Carmen, among them. When the barão died, bábá Epifánia had been among ten favorite slaves manumitted according to the terms of Ulisses Tavares's will. That same year, bábá

Epifánia had set up house with Basilio Pedrosa, a mulatto potter in charge of Itatinga's kilns. She had also developed her practice in the arts of magic.

Bábá Epifánia professed to be a curandeira, a specialist in herbal cures, always invoking "God and Christ" to bless her patients. But Itatinga's community, including Dona Carlinda Mendes, well knew that bábá Epifánia also practiced black magic. Bábá Epifánia could cure the bite of any serpent or she could kill with the vipers that were said to obey her commands, the deadly long-fanged jararaca.

From time to time, bábá Epifánia disappeared from Itatinga. Her absences gave rise to speculation that she was off consulting with her mentor, Lucifer, but in fact her journeys were to a settlement eighty miles northwest of Tiberica inhabited by semi-wild Tupi, caboclos, and descendants of runaway slaves. "Taman-duatei-mirim," the place was called — "Little River of the Tamanduá," the anteater. Bábá Epifánia regarded the tamanduá as a helper sent her by the spirits, for where it tore up the earth for insects, there it also turned up magical roots Epifánia used for her potions and remedies.

In the first week of October 1887, Epifánia journeyed to Tamanduatei-mirim, with two young boys as her escorts.

On this trip, bábá Epifánia's mission was not only to procure supplies but also to plot the flight of more than one hundred slaves from Fazenda da Itatinga. Since the beginning of the year, Tamanduatei-mirim had become a refuge for runaways and the operating base of a nest of caiphazes. A messenger from the caiphazes had contacted bábá Epifánia at Itatinga, where he had worked during the coffee harvest. At first, Epifánia had been reluctant to betray the trust of the da Silvas, particularly that of her client, Dona Carlinda, but the persuasive caiphaze, who was called "Nô," had reminded her of her own slavery and had convinced her to use the great prestige she enjoyed among the slaves to get them to flee Itatinga.

When the bábá arrived at Tamanduatei-mirim, a crowd was there to greet her. Bábá Epifánia responded with all the majesty of a visiting regent, promising audiences at her convenience. She sat on a chair in front of the most substantial mud-and-wattle hovel in the settlement, with her long skirt crimped between her legs, one of the boys holding the parasol against the fierce sun. She armed herself with a two-foot flywhisk — made from the long hairs of a cow's tail — which she used to thrash the insects pestering her, but this was also bábá Epifánia's wand protecting her and possessing power to ward off evil influences. The crowd was dispersed except for six men, the caiphaze, Nô Gonzaga among them.

"What's the news, bábá Epifánia?" asked Nô, a middle-aged mulatto who had been with Antônio Bento's caiphazes from the start of their campaign.

"It is good."

"Yes?"

Bábá Epifánia was in no hurry to reveal her information. Slashing the air with her wand, pausing to make the boy shift position with the parasol, gazing off myste-riously toward the forest, she first launched into a long account of contacts with Itatinga's slaves, naming many, often remarking on an evil afflicting the particular individual and her course of treatment.

This took time, but Nô Gonzaga knew better than to interrupt the bábá.

At last, bábá Epifánia declared, "I have them ready. Name the day, Nô Gonzaga, and they will vanish from Itatinga."

Nô laughed. "Like magic, bábá Epifánia?"

She glared at him. Her silver charms rattled as she shook the flywhisk angrily. "It was a great risk. If one of them told the senhor . . . "

"Sorry, bábá." Nô watched the path of the fly whisk nervously. Since recruiting the former slave to help the caiphazes, he had had many meetings with her, at each of which she demonstrated an increasing tendency to assume command of the dangerous enterprise.

She confirmed this now: "I expect one hundred forty to desert. Do you think they would follow you, Nô Gonzaga?" She answered the question herself, with a derisive snort: "Never!"

"No, bábá Epifánia. You have *the* power."

She breathed heavily, and triumphantly surveyed those around her.

Nô scratched his bullet-shaped head. "We'll come in two weeks. First I must go to São Paulo to fix the train." The caiphazes had collaborators working on the railway. "Itatinga's slaves must go directly to Santos. The night of October eighteenth."

Bábá Epifánia shook her head.

"It's too soon?"

"Not at night," she said. "They must leave by day."

"Impossible, bábá."

She gave him a withering look. "The slaves are locked up every night. The overseers have doubled the guards since reports of many runaways in other municípios. There are men and dogs everywhere from dusk till dawn. If a slave sticks his head out of a window, the dogs are there howling at him. To run at night is impossible."

"But in broad daylight?"

"The slaves who will desert are clearing the forest five miles from the mansion. When they are served their meal on the eighteenth Nô Gonzaga, be there with your men. There are ten overseers. They all carry guns."

Another man said, "Perhaps we should go to another fazenda?"

"The slaves are not expected back at the fazenda until sunset," bábá Epifánia said, ignoring the speaker. "In six hours, they can be at the railway. They will have all night to get away."

"But the overseers, bábá?" Nô Gonzaga asked worriedly.

"Ai, Jeesssuus!" Bábá Epifánia said, exasperated. "Are you a man or an insect?" Bábá Epifánia towered above him. "Insect!" she called him. "The overseers stop work at eleven, for their coffee and cachaça, not so?"

"Yes, bábá."

She gave a hearty laugh. "I'll prepare a potion for them, Nô Gonzaga. A most powerful remedy!"

❧

Nô Gonzaga and eleven men entered the da Silva fazenda after midnight on October 17, 1887. At dawn, they were concealed in the trees on a hill less than a mile from where the jungle was being cleared. The slave gangs began to arrive at 7:00 A.M.

An advance gang moving up along a hillside with axes and machetes struck at the virgin forest, slashing the undergrowth. Behind this area lay a tract of black, smoldering earth where the forest had gone up in a conflagration a week ago. The slaves moved among the charred trunks, using hoes and digging sticks to turn over the ash-strewn dirt, probing for the rich purple earth, preparing it for the coffee seedlings.

Nô Gonzaga used a small brass telescope to observe the slaves and their overseers. Gonzaga had been to São Paulo, where Antônio Bento himself had assisted him in planning the flight of Itatinga's slaves. Gonzaga was to lead the fugitives along back trails through the forests to a point six miles beyond Tiberica.

Just before eleven, Gonzaga saw the slaves in the burnt clearing start toward a clump of trees where slave women had their cooking pots. The first slave gang had no sooner started to drift toward the trees than other gangs began to follow them, with mounted overseers riding among them.

"Now we'll see if the bábá's medicine works," Nô Gonzaga said to a black man beside him, a runaway slave, Anselmo, who had served with the caiphazes since being given sanctuary by Antônio Bento. Bento had paraded Anselmo through São Paulo's streets exhibiting his wounds; his palms still bore deep scars from the knife blade driven through them by an overseer.

"We should move forward, Nô?" Anselmo was sitting on the ground with his legs crossed, a rifle in his lap.

Gonzaga looked around at the other caiphazes. "Camaradas," he called to them, "start down between the trees. Slowly. Keep out of sight."

With Nô and Anselmo leading, the caiphazes began to work their way between the trees, passing noisily through the undergrowth until they were about a quarter-mile from the scorched clearing. Nô signaled for the men behind to stop; he moved forward to the edge of the forest with Anselmo.

The overseers had got their food and drink and were sitting in the shade of some trees, from where they could keep an eye on the slaves. Two had finished eating and were lying on their backs; one of them got up and turned in the direction of Nô and Anselmo, looking directly at the spot where they were as he urinated.

"That dog seems lively enough," Anselmo whispered.

Nô looked at the other overseer, lying flat on his back, his mouth wide open. "Not *that* one!"

The man facing them buttoned up his pants; he turned and started back toward the others.

"See how he walks!" Nô said in a fierce whisper. Like a man roaming in his sleep." The overseer got to the shade, where the other man lay, and shouted something, but got no response. Then he too lay down, pushing his hat over his face.

Suddenly a third overseer collapsed. Another overseer, Cesar, a son of the notorious Setenta, stood up, showing no sign of drowsiness. He shouted for the two men already on their backs to get up and gave one of them a kick in the ribs, with no effect.

In the trees, Nô Gonzaga signaled his men to move forward. "Now! Take them!" he commanded. He himself leapt from the trees, with Anselmo at his side.

"Caiphazes!" the overseer Cesar shouted. "Up! Up!" he screamed at the others. Four got to their feet.

"Throw down your weapons!" Nô Gonzaga hollered. "You won't be harmed."

But Cesar fired, two shots in rapid succession. Anselmo was struck in the arm; he cursed, and fired back, a blast from an old Enfield that caught Cesar in the shoulder.

"Give up!" Nô shouted. "Surrender!"

There were 128 slaves out here this day, all of them prepared to flee, but only the ringleaders had been told of bábá Epifánia's scheme to drug the overseers. When the slaves saw Nô Gonzaga and his men rushing from the trees, many of them leapt to their feet, advancing toward the overseers with axes and machetes.

"Mercy! Mary Mother, mercy!" Cesar cried. He had dropped his rifle and was clutching his shoulder. He glanced wildly from side to side, first at the caiphazes, then at the slaves. "Mercy . . ."

Another overseer was clinging groggily to a branch jutting from a charred tree trunk. Slowly he began to sink to the ground, succumbing to Epifánia's potion.

"Halt!" Nô Gonzaga ordered, gesticulating at the slaves. "Stop there!"

The front row of slaves continued to edge forward. Others shouted for the blood of the overseers.

"We kill only if we have to," Nô said. "It's a long way to Santos. If we leave a trail of dead men, we'll be hunted by an army of capangas out to avenge them."

Gonzaga's men stood guard over Cesar and the other overseers.

"Bastards!" Cesar said. "You'll be caught before you're a mile from Itatinga."

Nô ignored him. "Collect your things," he told the slaves. "We march immediately. When they come seeking us, we'll be far from Itatinga. . . . You?" He looked at Cesar. He laughed. "Take your rest, overseer. There'll be no peace for you when you return to your master, da Silva." Nô gestured toward the slaves. "Some of you help us carry these sleeping beauties into the trees. My men will show you what to do with them."

Twenty minutes later, the slaves began to move off. Many were laughing now, and admiring the weapons and clothes acquired by ten of their fellows: The overseers had been stripped naked, gagged, and roped securely to trees. Cesar and two men were still fighting the effects of the potion and making incoherent noises as fire ants swarmed over their flesh.

੭੭

It was after 4:00 P.M. outside the mansion at Itatinga. Firmino Dantas's customary poise vanished as he stepped back from the overseer, Cesar, who was lying on the ground beside the horse of an agregado, who'd been sent to the clearing to inspect the hardwood set aside for the fazenda's carpenters; he had found the overseers and released them, riding back immediately with Cesar. The head overseer was moaning with pain from his shoulder wound and innumerable insect bites. He had scarcely been able to whisper a report to the senhor.

Aristides was standing behind Firmino on the steps up to the fazenda's main entrance. "How many runaways?" he asked.

"Every slave at the clearing."

"How, for the love of God, did they get away?"

"Others came to help them."

Workers were streaming toward them from the outbuildings as word spread of the flight of the slaves.

"Were you blind?" Aristides demanded harshly of the man on the ground.

Cesar was silent, but Firmino responded: "He said the slave women put poison in their food."

Running from an outbuilding was a lean, angular agregado, Ulisses Ramos, whose family had served the da Silvas as far back as the time of the monsoon canoe convoys. He was head capanga. His voice trembling with anticipation, he asked: "Your orders, please, Senhor Firmino."

"Send men out for the other overseers and slave gangs. Get the slaves back to the barracks. Lock them up."

"Yes, senhor. The runaways?"

"Have two men ride immediately to Capitão Eduardo. When the slaves have been brought in, assemble your men here."

When Ramos left, another man stepped forward: "We will help, too, Senhor da Silva."

"Thank you, Patrizio. You can guard the barracks."

Patrizio Telleni was one of twenty Italian men and their families whom Aristides had brought from Santos in late July. The colonos, as the immigrant community of ninety were known, were now settled in huts two miles from the mansion.

After the flurry of commands, Cesar was carried off to the infirmary. Firmino Dantas limped slowly up the steps. "Antônio Bento's caiphazes are responsible. They seek to spread insurrection throughout Tiberica."

Aristides shouted to old Cincinnato, who was standing with some of the household slaves: "Saddle my horse quickly!"

Firmino Dantas continued to talk about the runaways: "They are too many to hide at the quilombo at Tamanduá; they'll try to reach Santos."

"I'm going to Tiberica, Senhor Firmino."

"Slave hunting is not your business, Aristides."

"I agree, Senhor Firmino. It is only that I fear what Eduardo da Silva may do to them. We want them returned alive, not flogged half dead or full of shot."

"Go, then, but for God's sake, be careful. Take no risks." Firmino Dantas lowered his eyes. "Go, Ari," he said. "My leg . . . if I could stay in the saddle for long . . ."

"No, senhor, there is no need for you to go. I will ride for you, Firmino Dantas."

✧

"The train!" Eduardo da Silva said emphatically. Just after 6:00 P.M., he was sitting on the edge of a table at Tiberica's police barracks, putting on his boots. Aristides Tavares had arrived ten minutes ago. "The runaways know if they hide in the forest I'll root them out. The train is their only way of escape."

The thirty-one-year-old son of Colonel Clóvis Lima da Silva was a heavy, thickset man with cold black eyes beneath wiry brows. Eduardo had spent two years at the Escola Militar at Rio de Janeiro, where his record had been dismal. He had joined the Rio de Janeiro police, where he had won a reputation for ruthlessness: "Cockroach Killer," his colleagues had nicknamed him. Seven years ago, Eduardo's relatives at Tiberica, the family who owned Silva & Sons, had recommended him for chief of police, a position he had accepted and carried out with vigor, especially where slaves were concerned.

There was a third man in Capitão Eduardo's office — tall, slender, with hollow cheeks and a tuft of beard — known to his fellow policemen as "Tex." Cadmus Rawlings was his name, and he was not from Texas but Alabama. Rawlings had come to Brazil after the Civil War, along with several hundred families of Confederate exiles now scattered from the banks of the Tapajós to the coffee lands of São Paulo. Some of these émigrés struggling in ramshackle dwellings in the jungle of the Tapajós were demoralized but others were making a go of it in their new homeland, especially a group of farmers at Santa Barbara, eighty miles north of São Paulo, who had achieved particular success growing a succulent watermelon, the "Georgia Rattlesnake." A few, like Cadmus Rawlings, had abandoned farming for other pursuits. Rawlings, who was forty-four and had buried his first wife at Santa Barbara, lived in Tiberica with a mulatta and their three dark-skinned children. Rawlings had no trouble reconciling his domestic situation with his abhorrence of Negroes.

"The train was due to leave at 6:00 P.M.," Aristides said.

"Yes, Aristides. And when did the São Paulo train *ever* leave on time?" Eduardo finished putting on his boots and stood up. "They'll be there, cousin, waiting for their precious consignment."

Rawlings's Portuguese was poor: "I hope you're right, Capitay. Jesus, I hope so."

"Sergeant Tex has his own ideas on how to handle the runaway problem," Eduardo da Silva said. He knew his cousin favored abolition. "He thinks we're too soft on them."

"Day by day, your people are retreating from these black cowards," said Cadmus Rawlings. "As there's a God above, the free nigger will be the ruin of your land. Just as it was with us."

"Let's ride for the train," Aristides said. "I hear your men outside."

Rawlings stepped toward the door with his arms laden with cartons of shells to distribute to the twelve men in the police unit. "I've told the capitay: Hang a few of the bastards. String 'em up along the Tiberica road. That'll put God's fear into the rest!" He strode past Aristides, used one boot to pull open the door that stood ajar, and stepped outside.

"You have your fancy French ideas, Aristides," Eduardo remarked. "There are others — Brasileiros, my cousin — who think Tex Rawlings is right."

"And you're one of them?"

Eduardo da Silva didn't answer this. "Perhaps, Aristides, it's better for you to stay here, no?"

"I'm going with you."

"Mmmmp! . . . " Suddenly he grinned. "Ride with my sergeant, then, Aristides!"

"Are you trying to goad me?"

"No, cousin. I'm only thinking Sergeant Tex will be there to save your skin if there's a fight." He laughed loudly, and did not hear Aristides swear at him.

They reached the railhead in the dark an hour later, and learned from a railway worker that the train had left twenty minutes ago. He swore no runaways had got aboard.

"Ride on!" Eduardo da Silva ordered, galloping alongside the tracks. "The swine are sure to be waiting up ahead."

Half an hour later they saw the train stopped on a straight section of track. The capitão raced at the head of his men toward the locomotive, ignoring the possibility of attack from caiphazes and runaways if they were already aboard.

"You, there!" Eduardo da Silva cried, with a long-barreled revolver leveled at two men gaping at him from the cab of the engine. "Get down!"

The two men obeyed. Da Silva and three of his men dismounted.

"Now, you bastards: Why are you stopped here?"

"Broken valve," the engineer said. He made a sound suggesting escaping steam.

Da Silva struck him a crushing blow to the side of his head with his revolver. "Why are you stopped here?"

Two policemen were interrogating the fireman, slamming him against the side of the tender, beating him with their fists.

"All right! All right! I'll tell you," the engineer said.

"Speak!"

"We were waiting for a few slaves."

"Liar!" Eduardo da Silva looked for Aristides, but didn't see him. "Their owner is here. More than a hundred ran from Itatinga."

"O good Jesus! Mercy!"

Da Silva threw the man to the ground and kicked him until he lay silent.

Bábá Epifánia and her family were in the third of five coaches. She saw the front riders storm past the windows; moments later, there were orders for everyone to get off the train.

Basilio Pedrosa, bábá Epifánia's husband, was a little soft in the head. He had been capable of molding clay for tens of thousands of seedling pots at Itatinga, but not much else. At Itatinga he had often been pushed into another room when bábá Epifánia was consulted by slaves and men like Nô Gonzaga, who had been there for the harvest, but Basilio had had sense enough to realize his mate was offering them more than her magical medicines. When she told him a day ago that they were leaving for Santos, he had surprised her by asking if they were marching with the slaves. Epifánia had got very angry at first, raising her big hands to strike him, but he promised he had told no one.

"Bábá, what will we do?" he asked now.

"Listen to me, Basilio. Why are we here?"

"Why, bábá?"

"We're going to São Paulo" — she thought a moment — "to visit your brother."

"I have no brother, bábá."

"Basilio!"

"Yes, bábá. My brother . . ." He looked puzzled.

"Get out!" A policeman stood in the doorway at the end of the coach.

Bábá Epifánia dragged Basilio to his feet. She ushered the children forward, too. "Why must we get off?" she asked belligerently.

"Shut up! Get your fat backside off the train!"

The bábá gave the policeman a malignant scowl, but as she stepped off behind Basilio and the children, her defiance wavered: Aristides da Silva sat on his horse ten feet away.

He recognized her in the light of a lantern held by one of the dismounted policemen. "What are you doing here, bábá Epifánia?" And then he saw the potter trying to creep behind his wife's immense body. "Pedrosa!"

Basilio appeared to leap six feet into the air at mention of his name.

"Why are you here?" Aristides repeated.

"*Answer* the senhor, nigger!" Tex Rawlings had ridden up beside Aristides when he saw him talking to the big black woman and the mulatto.

Bábá Epifánia's chest heaved as she struggled to be calm. "To Pedrosa's brother at São Paulo, senhorzinho," she said awkwardly.

"What the hell is she talking about?" Rawlings asked.

"I'll find out," Aristides said. "Pedrosa!"

Basilio was next to Epifánia now, staring down at the ground, swinging his head from side to side.

"When did you leave Itatinga, Pedrosa?"

Basilio mumbled an unintelligible reply.

"This morning, senhorzinho," the bábá said.

Rawlings stepped his horse up to Basilio. "The senhor spoke to you!"

"Oh, bábá! Bábá!" Basilio bawled.

Rawlings's boot was out of the stirrup. He slammed it into Basilio's back, sending the mulatto stumbling toward Aristides. The daughter of Pedrosa and Epifánia began to cry at the top of her lungs.

"Answer me, Pedrosa, or it will only be worse," Aristides said.

"I'll kill the bastard," Rawlings threatened.

"Bábá said we must leave."

"Because of the runaways?"

Basilio repeated what he'd just said.

"Is it true, bábá Epifánia?" Aristides asked, turning to his old wet nurse.

The bábá's daughter had moved to her side and was clinging to her skirt. Epifánia held a protective arm around the girl. The boy, too, was near her. She raised her big, square face to look at Aristides Tavares, the little master whom she had once held lovingly to her breast. "Yes, Senhorzinho Aristides, it's true. Bábá Epifánia did what she had to do for her people."

"Nigger bitch!" Rawlings yelled, slashing at Epifánia with his riding whip.

"Rawlings!" Aristides shouted. "Stop! Stop!" He had just started forward when suddenly Nô Gonzaga and his men and the ten armed slaves showed themselves, standing up on the roofs of the coaches, stepping across the rails at the front and back of the train. Another body of slaves, armed with axes and other weapons, rose up in the long grass behind the police and passengers. The caiphazes and slaves had been half a mile from the train when they saw the mounted police racing beside the railbed. While Eduardo da Silva had been interrogating the train crew and other police were inspecting the passengers, Nô Gonzaga and his men had circled around to the opposite side of the train, climbing up silently to the positions they now held.

Nô Gonzaga wanted to avoid a battle. At his orders, the guns of the caiphazes and runaways roared with a volley fired into the air above the heads of the police.

"There are many more of us," Nô called down.

Eduardo da Silva fired first, killing a slave at the front of the locomotive.

Tex Rawlings yanked the reins of his horse, wheeling away from the side of the train, and opened fire on the men above him. "Kill the bastards!" he shouted.

Nô Gonzaga's men began to fire back at the police. There was pandemonium among the passengers standing beside the train: Some ran wildly toward the slaves advancing in the grass; others, including bábá Epifánia and her children, dove under the coaches for protection; and a few, like Basilio, dashed blindly into the night.

The battle lasted only as long as it took Tex Rawlings to empty his six-shooter. Abruptly, Tiberica's policemen were dumping their weapons and running away — all but their capitão, Eduardo da Silva, the Cockroach Killer, who lay dead on the ground with a bullet in his heart.

"Cowards! Come back!" Rawlings shouted, but he was alone. Then he noticed Aristides Tavares crumpled over the neck of his horse. "Da Silva?" Rawlings grabbed the reins of Aristides's horse.

Aristides was shot in the shoulder. "I'll be all right," he said.

All along the top of the train, Nô Gonzaga and his men held their fire.

"*Bastards!*" Rawlings shook his empty revolver at them.

"We wanted no bloodshed," Gonzaga said. "Your men fired first. Now take your wounded." His gun was on Rawlings. "*Leave!*"

As Cadmus Rawlings, veteran of the Twentieth Alabama Infantry and Union prisoner after Vicksburg, rode off with Aristides Tavares, a cheer rose from Nô Gonzaga and his irregular troop.

Aristides was taken to the house of Jolanta dos Santos, where Tiberica's doctor came to treat his wound. August Laubner also went to the house as soon as he heard what had happened. Firmino Dantas was summoned by a messenger sent to Itatinga and arrived at Tiberica in the early hours of the morning. He found Jolanta watching over Aristides, who was weak from a loss of blood but, August Laubner assured him, in no danger. Aristides was awake when Firmino got to the house.

"Thank God, Ari, you're safe."

"Eduardo da Silva —"

"I heard."

"We were trapped, senhor. Outnumbered. We couldn't stop them."

"You're not to worry about it, Ari. We can only thank God you were spared."

"São Paulo has been told?"

"São Paulo has been asked to send a detachment of troops to Tiberica, for what that may be worth." Many army units were known to be close to mutinying against service as slave hunters.

Jolanta, who had gone out of the room while they spoke, returned with a damp towel to wipe Aristides's brow.

"Senhor Firmino . . ."

"Yes, Ari?"

"Eduardo da Silva gave his life for a hopeless cause. God help us all if we fail to see this."

やり

On October 19, the São Paulo authorities dispatched fifty troops to block the roads and trails down the Serra do Mar, with orders to bring in the Tiberica runaways dead or alive. Twenty-three slaves, including two men wounded in the brief skirmish outside Tiberica, were caught and taken to São Paulo in irons. But, one by one, the rest of the groups began to reach sanctuary at Santos.

On October 24, 4,500 runaways now living in Jabaquará witnessed a unique procession through the narrow streets of the quilombo. First came a company of thirty drummers, some thumping war drums. Behind the drummers were musicians with the *berimbau* and *xaque-xaque.* A troop of agile young men pivoted and cart-wheeled as they played *capoeira,* the slaves' now-dreaded form of unarmed combat, and groups of gaily dressed women sang and danced joyously.

Highlight of the procession was a huge cart decorated with colored paper and flowers and drawn by two oxen.

Solemnly seated in the cart, under a canopy of royal blue cloth, wearing a massive crown fashioned of cardboard and silver paper, a bright yellow dress, and long train of crimson cloth was the "Queen of Liberty," weighed down with brace-lets, rings, and necklaces given to her by admirers.

"*Viva! Viva! Viva Regina!*" the crowd saluted her.

It was bábá Epifánia, beaming from cheek to cheek, thrashing the air with her fly whisk to bestow a blessing on her free subjects, reveling in her hour of glory.

やり

On the same day, Eduardo da Silva was buried at Tiberica. Colonel Clóvis Lima da Silva and his second son, Honôrio, had traveled from Rio de Janeiro for the funeral. After the service, Clóvis and Honôrio rode out to Itatinga with the family of Firmino Dantas, who had invited them to stay at the fazenda.

The morning after the funeral, Clóvis and Firmino Dantas were strolling on the paths behind the mansion. At fifty-eight, Clóvis Lima still walked ramrod straight, an alert look in his eyes, an undiminished sharpness, the same as when he had directed the guns at Acosta Ñu and a dozen barrages before that final battle in Paraguay.

"I saw the expressions on the faces of some at the funeral," Clóvis said. "'Eduardo da Silva would be alive if the army had been there to help his men,'"they said. It's probably true. I find this difficult to say, Firmino, but I wouldn't want to have been responsible for sending men to catch your slaves. And even if they had all been caught, what good would it do? If the army were to stand against abolition, what could we do, I ask you: twelve thousand men to suppress six hundred thousand who remain in the senzalas? Our ranks are depleted; our requests for equipment are denied. Good God, do they believe that we're no better than capangas? That we can best serve our nation by rusticating in the sertão? Do they consider us duty-bound to accept every insult in silence?"

After the war in Paraguay, veterans had returned to Brazil with battlefield honors and promotions, expecting continued recognition. Instead, they found themselves neglected and humiliated. But just this past June a group of officers had founded the Clube Militar, electing as its first president Marshal Deodoro da Fonseca, who had served the duration of the war as an artilleryman. Clóvis, a member of the club, told Firmino of a forthcoming meeting at which members would vote on a petition Marshal Deodora was to present to the Crown asking that the army be relieved from slave-hunting duties.

"It's well known: The emperor is not a military-minded man," Clóvis said "But he's the only ruler of Brazil. The army respects this."

"The mass of our people love Pedro Segundo, but they don't understand him. He stands head and shoulders above them. Pedro's light shines dimly at the Corte, and beyond Rio de Janeiro, it's hardly seen at all."

"Are you a Paulista Republican now?" Clóvis asked, laughing, for he knew Firmino Dantas was a monarchist, convinced that even a bad monarchy was better for Brazil than the alternatives proposed by the Republicans.

"Not yet."

"But you're flirting with the ideas of those dreamers?"

'No, Clóvis. It's young Ari down there, who assaults my ears at every opportunity."

They had reached the edge of the high bluff. Aristides Tavares and Honório da Silva were below, at the white rocks that gave Itatinga its name. Aristides waved when he saw them.

Clóvis laughed again. "My Honório, too, tries to infect me with his ideas. Abolition? A third empire? A republic? Federation? These questions will be answered sooner than we think, cousin. And these young men will have to live with the consequences."

❧

Aristides Tavares often came down to the white rocks. He remembered Ulisses Tavares clutching his hand fiercely as he led him down here, and his thrill as the barão told him stories of his own grandfather, Benedito Bueno da Silva, whose canoes had traveled a thousand leagues to Cuiabá.

Hônorio Azevedo da Silva had been almost six years old when Clóvis Lima returned from Paraguay. The joy he gave his father had deepened the rift between Clóvis and Eduardo; Honório, quite the opposite of his older brother, had excelled at the Escola Militar in Rio de Janeiro, the twenty-two-year-old student officer today ranking among the top ten in his class. Honório was clearly of da Silva ancestry but for his nose, which had a pronounced ridge where it had been broken in a gunnery accident.

As the talk of their elders confirmed, both Aristides and Honório favored a republic. But Honório was also a believer in the positivist philosophy of Auguste Comte, who emphasized the progress of society by scientific method and observation. At Rio de Janeiro, Comte's positivism had an ardent apostle in Major Benjamin

Constant Botelho de Magalhães, professor of mathematics at the Escola Militar, who inspired his cadets with visions of a new society organized along meticulously rational lines. Positivism's motto — Order and Progress — appealed to young men like Honório da Silva, who had no qualms that a scientific-minded elite directing a positivist paradise would in effect be heading a strict dictatorship.

"The monarchy has been ailing for years, Ari, and not only with the failing health of our emperor. There are thousands of civil servants at the Corte, but they're too weak to cope with the administration of a land as vast as Brazil. We need a federal system to allow each province to progress."

"Why do you think your Positivists will be more effective than others who've sought change in Brazil? Will they be any more successful than our poets who wanted a republic at Minas a century ago?"

"André Vaz da Silva was with them!" Honório da Silva was the great-grandson of André Vaz.

"He died in exile in Africa. Others involved in the Inconfidência lived to see Pedro the First declare the independence of Brazil."

"Independence from Portugal, but not from the past — and not without a royal seal of approval! At the Clube Tiradentes at Rio de Janeiro, we honor our Brazilian martyr, Silva Xavier, whom the Portuguese butchered, and André Vaz and others, whom they sent to perish in exile. The cry of Tiradentes rings down through those one hundred years."

" '*Libertas, quae sera tamen!*' " Aristides responded.

"I believe we'll soon answer that call — 'Liberty, even though late!'"

℘

The two and a half months between the flight of Itatinga's slaves in mid-October 1887 and the end of the year were critical for the abolition movement, not only in Tiberica district, but also throughout the Black Triangle of São Paulo, Minas Gerais, and Rio de Janeiro. Violent confrontations like that at Tiberica railhead multiplied. There were direct attacks against town jails by freedmen and runaways seeking to release captured fugitives. Fazendas reported sieges of owners' houses by slaves demanding freedom.

By early December 1887 in São Paulo province, the quilombo outside Santos had ten thousand fugitives; there was no estimate for the number of slaves hiding in the forests and backlands of São Paulo.

Firmino Dantas and Aristides Tavares attended a mass meeting of fazendeiros at the city of São Paulo on December 15. It was agreed that to save the 1888 harvest, the planters should offer their slaves a small wage and term contracts until December 31, 1890, after which date the slaves were to be freed.

On Christmas Day, Firmino Dantas ordered the remaining slaves at Itatinga to be assembled in front of the mansion. The twenty-three runaways recaptured in October were back at the fazenda, but there had been desertions by two smaller groups and the mandatory liberation of twenty elderly blacks and mulattoes, leaving 203 slaves from a total of 370 six months ago.

Firmino Dantas's address to the slaves was brief and to the point: From New Year's Day 1888, the slaves were to be given work contracts and paid a wage, the exact amount to be announced early in January. The slaves greeted the news with a joyous ovation before going to their quarters to celebrate the holiday and the promise of freedom.

By the end of the Christmas week, all but thirty-three slaves had abandoned Fazenda da Itatinga.

∾

Late morning on a cold, dry April day the following year, Firmino Dantas and August Laubner were on the veranda outside Tiberica Station. Laubner was sixty-three, his hair and drooping whiskers snow white. A resident of Tiberica for twenty-five years now, apothecary Laubner had served several terms with the town câmara. His son, Mauricio, was wedded to the daughter of a branch of the Mendes family, which, after the da Silvas of Itatinga, was the second most powerful clan in the district.

With the collapse of slavery imminent, more and more Paulista planters saw immigrant labor as the alternative. The work contracts being offered the predominantly Italian arrivals were immeasurably more liberal than those offered to the Swiss in the 1850s. During 1887, some thirty thousand Italians had arrived in São Paulo province; within the first three months of 1888 alone, another thirty thousand had landed at Santos and ten thousand more were at sea or ready to embark for the voyage to Brazil. The São Paulo-based Sociedade Promotora de Imigracão was confident of reaching a goal of 100,000 migrants in 1888.

August Laubner had not forgotten the harshness of his early years in Brazil as a contract worker. He took a personal interest in the welfare of the new immigrants, serving as Tiberica representative of the Sociedade Promotora de Imigracão. On this morning of April 21, 1888, Firmino Dantas and Laubner were waiting for the São Paulo train, which had among its passengers a second group of Italians for Itatinga, 115 souls in all, whom Aristides Tavares had gone to the capital to recruit.

August Laubner had recently traveled in neighboring areas of Rio de Janeiro trying to interest planters in the work of the Sociedade. As Firmino Dantas and he waited for the train, Laubner spoke of this mission: "I remember particularly one old fazendeiro, Ivo Tupinambá Texeira. 'I have nothing against immigrants,' Ivo Tupinambá said. But our scheme to bring the beggars of Italy to Brazil? He called it a Paulista fad — a disreputable experiment that would bankrupt the province's coffers. The Italians would pick coffee for a harvest or two, then be gone — down to Uruguay or the Argentine or back to Italy and their lives of indolence. Senhor Ivo Tupinambá said it was a big mistake — as big a mistake as trying to make steady laborers of the lazy Brazilians who squat on our lands."

As Firmino listened to August Laubner, he could see Patrizio Telleni, who had emerged as leader of the first twenty Italian families at Itatinga, standing at the wagons that had been brought to transport the new arrivals to the fazenda. He gestured with his head toward the slender, dark-featured, dark-haired man. "They worked well through the planting season, disrupted as it was. With the others Aristides is bringing, we can make something of this harvest, and God knows we need it. But I'm interested in Ivo Tupinambá's observation about lazy Brazilians."

"He was exaggerating."

"Many agregados at Itatinga do an honest day's work," Firmino said, "and many don't lift a finger. Don't misunderstand me either, old friend: I'm all for the migration of the Italians; we need them. But what about the mass of our people?"

"With abolition, there will be greater opportunities for all."

"So the optimists say."

"And you're a pessimist?"

"Perhaps 'realistic' is closer to the truth. Those 'lazy Brazilians' Ivo Tupinambá refers to? Daily their number increases as former slaves who haven't yet found work join their ranks. Those who talk of a paradise after abolition don't know what they're saying. *Abolition* is bringing us to the edge of the cataract."

August Laubner's eyes widened in surprise. "You *are* a pessimist, Firmino. You see this change in the country in the worst possible light."

"Let us just say 'in the light,'" Firmino replied, warming to the discussion. "Slavery hasn't yet been abolished, but already they're talking about a rural democracy, about 'redistributing existing estates.'"

"From what I've read, the idea is to open public lands to the poor and the former slaves."

"Dumping-grounds for 'lazy Brazilians!'" Firmino responded. "I know of no fazendeiro who'll sit by and let his property be carved into little parcels to be handed out to the first takers."

"It's only talk, Firmino."

"Our reformers are dazzled by the rapid advance of abolition. They don't see old Ivo Tupinambá on his veranda with his shotgun. They may overcome his resistance to slavery with speeches and flowers, but just let them try to take one inch of his coffee groves."

"No politician in his right mind would threaten the landowners. Emperor Pedro understands the feelings of the fazendeiros."

"True enough. But will his successor show the same sympathy?"

"I see no reason to doubt this."

"The princess imperial opens the Assembly on May third. I guarantee you, August, slavery will be abolished within the month. But the government can't afford to go one step further. Most fazendeiros have had their patience tested to the limit."

They stood up then, for they could hear the train on the outskirts of Tiberica.

"For now, my friend, there is only your Italians to welcome," Laubner said. "One hundred fifteen men, women, and boys coming for the harvest at Itatinga."

The locomotive steamed into town hauling eight coaches; Aristides Tavares stood on the small platform at the front of the first coach. The Italians were in the three rear coaches, many at the open windows. They were silent as the train came to a halt, but soon began a cheery exchange with Patrizio Telleni and other compatriots from Itatinga.

Aristides called out a greeting to Firmino Dantas and August Laubner as he descended the steps. "Not one hundred fifteen," he said moments later. "One hundred *seventeen,* Senhor Firmino. Two more than you bargained for — twins born during the night!"

"Where?" Laubner asked, immediately concerned.

"The last coach, Senhor Laubner."

When August was gone, Firmino asked, "Did you have a good journey?"

"Excellent, senhor." Aristides had been away for three weeks. "The capital is in a festive mood. Everyone accepts that abolition is here." The city of São Paulo had abolished slavery in February.

"August Laubner and I were just talking about this before you arrived."

"It will be Brazil's greatest hour, senhor! At last we can feel welcome among the community of respectable nations."

"Yes, Ari, we can."

They started walking beside the coaches. Patrizio Telleni saw them approach and shouted for the Italians to make way for the signor of Itatinga. The air was permeated with the stench of unwashed bodies.

Firmino Dantas discerned a glance of embarrassment from an old silver-haired man; an embittered stare from one much younger; a strong, protective expression on the face of a woman with her big peasant hands wrapped around a small girl; a dreamy look in the eyes of a barefoot boy.

At the last coach, August Laubner hailed them from one of the windows: "The mother should rest at my house before traveling to Itatinga."

"Certainly, August. The infants?"

"Boys!" Laubner cried. "Two giants!" He pointed to a man standing on the train platform: "The father."

Patrizio Telleni was standing close by and summoned the man. The Italian was huge, over six feet tall. "Pietro Angelucci," he said, when Telleni asked his name. He took off his misshapen felt hat. "Good day, signors," he greeted the two da Silvas.

"Welcome to Tiberica, Pietro Angelucci," Firmino said. "There will be a good home for you at Itatinga."

"God bless you, signor."

"You are the one who has His greatest blessing this day. Two boys — Brazilians — blessed to be born on the eve of our liberation!"

*

On May 13, 1888, ten days after the opening of Parliament by Princess Isabel acting as regent for Dom Pedro, who was still in Europe, an Act abolishing slavery in Brazil completed its passage through both Houses.

The news of "The Golden Law" was flashed by telegraph from one end of the country to the other, from Rosário in Pernambuco to Tiberica in São Paulo.

*

Clóvis Lima da Silva cursed to himself as gusts of driving rain lashed him, streaming down his rubber poncho, splattering the mud around his boots. His flesh was covered with insect bites; one arm ached from rheumatic pain; he had not had a decent meal in days. After three weeks on the march through Mato Grosso in August 1889, Colonel Clóvis Lima's column had every appearance of a force in retreat, an impression heightened as their commander stood observing a section of wagons and guns mired down along a jungle trail.

In January 1889, Paraguay and Bolivia had appeared to be on the brink of war over a territorial dispute involving part of the Chaco region, and Marshal Manuel Deodoro da Fonseca and several Rio de Janeiro units, Clóvis Lima's among them, were ordered to the garrison town of Corumbá to reinforce the post and act as observers. Almost one thousand miles northwest of Rio de Janeiro, Corumbá overlooked the Rio Paraguay, which formed the border between Bolivia and Brazil. On this occasion, Paraguayan and Bolivian tempers had cooled. For the soldiers of Rio de Janeiro, though, eight months in Mato Grosso had raised a fever against the Frock Coats responsible for sending them to the far west.

When the recall came three weeks ago, Clóvis Lima's column had been sent back overland toward São Paulo, following trails that often ran beside or crossed rivers along which Benedito Bueno da Silva had made his marvelous voyages to Cuiabá. But there was nothing glorious in this trek back to the Corte through what the soldiers called simply, "inferno." For several hundred miles beyond Corumbá, at the edge of the Pantanal, the column had slogged through swampland infested with caiman and vipers, then struggled across patches of bone-shaking stony countryside, through palm forests, and into thick jungle like that in which the column was now bogged down, not far from the border between Mato Grosso and São Paulo province.

Embittered by these privations, one of Clóvis Lima's officers had remarked during the previous night's halt, "I can see them now, those damn Frock Coats taking the air along the rua do Ouvidor. 'Go, brave patriots! Serve Brazil with honor,' the bastards said, knowing we were bound by oath to obey."

"There are going to be a few scores to settle at the Corte," Clóvis Lima had responded.

"Right, Colonel! This time our smart politicians have gone too far."

The fifteen months since the freeing of the slaves had been a period of mounting uncertainty throughout the country. Denied compensation by the government, several former slave owners joined the ranks of the Republicans, but the majority simply withdrew their support from the monarchy. Thousands of slaves returned to their plantation barracks, accepting whatever wage was offered them, and even more joined the ranks of millions of indigent Brazilians, finding themselves with even fewer rights than were theirs before abolition.

The emperor had returned to Rio de Janeiro from Europe in August 1888. His health had improved, but not to the extent that he could take rigorous control of a deteriorating situation around him. There was now little question in the minds of his subjects that Pedro was approaching the end of his reign.

Republican propagandists alarmed the populace with tales that Isabel's husband, the comte d'Eu was scheming to be the power behind the Brazilian throne.

There were now some 250 Republican clubs — the most influential, Clube Tiradentes among them, in the southern coffee provinces — and more than seventy inflammatory Republican newspapers and pamphlets. But, for all the fervor they generated, the Republicans still fared hopelessly in elections.

A section of the Republican party and press had been wooing the army since the beginning of the "military question," as the various clashes between army and government were known. These Republicans, aware of their impotence at the polls, were coming to a consensus with their military friends that only a revolution could oust the decaying monarchy.

The overwhelming feeling was that the ailing Pedro Segundo should be allowed to end his reign peacefully, and only then should the nation decide on the fate of Princess Isabel and her spouse.

At Corumbá, Colonel Clóvis Lima had had months to brood over these questions. But, however angry he got, Clóvis remained loyal to the Crown. When he said there were scores to be settled at the Corte, he was thinking only of revenge against the politicians responsible for the continuing insults to the military. He was aware that his son Honório, who was at Rio de Janeiro, belonged to the clique of Positivist-minded officers who favored radical solutions. They could debate with their Republican friends until they were blue in the face, but without the support of Marshal Deodoro and older officers like himself, there would be no revolution.

✧

At Tiberica, Senhor Firmino Dantas da Silva could not have found life more comfortable or promising. In the months from May to July, more than 600,000 mature coffee trees at Itatinga, had been stripped of their red-to-brown cherries, the richest harvest seen at the fazenda. By August, the harvested trees showed the first flowering of white rosettes, blossoms of triumph for coffee, the real master of man and land in southern Brazil.

Paulista fazendeiros like Firmino Dantas who had abandoned slave labor before abolition had naturally been better prepared for the consequences than planters who waited until May 13.

At Itatinga, Firmino Dantas and Aristides had divided the 207 Italians into two colonies, where they had their mud-walled houses and small plots for their own use. At the end of the contract year, an Italian could pack up and leave for another plantation or with the hope of bettering himself in town. At Itatinga, there had been but one departure, the family of a bootmaker who had got work in Tiberica.

The Italians were subject to fines for various misdemeanors, including tardiness, inebriation, failure to keep their livestock from wandering into forbidden pastures, and excessive wife-beating. Firmino Dantas carefully reviewed all cases brought to him by an administrator appointed to handle the affairs of the colonos.

The tenants and squatters, into whose lower ranks the liberated slaves had drifted, were treated less patiently. Vagabonds or troublemakers were swiftly expelled from the fazenda. The head overseer, Cesar, now controlled a work gang of camaradas, free agregados, and former slaves, and still administered the occasional clout to the blacks when aroused beyond endurance.

Thus, with an evolving regime that showed promise of preserving intact the vast fiefs of the great landowners, and with two bumper harvests to boot, Firmino Dantas had every reason to find life so agreeable.

His oldest son, Evaristo, a pale, thin nineteen-year-old, was enrolled at São Paulo Law School, just as his father had been at that age. João, the youngest child, was also in the capital, at boarding school. Delfina, the eighteen-year-old daughter, was a handsome girl, if too plump from years of sharing her mother's delight in sticky cakes. Dona Carlinda herself was growing stouter, with a shadow of down on her upper lip.

Senhor Firmino spent ever more time with Jolanta dos Santos at the house on rua Riachuelo, where he made love with a passion he had once believed would be denied him forever.

On the evening of August 23, 1889, Jolanta's thirty-first birthday, Firmino Dantas marked the occasion with a gift he did not reveal until late that night.

"How many years have you been mine, Jolanta?"

"Forever, 'Nhor. A thousand, thousand years!"

"Yes, but exactly how long?"

"Oh, my!" she said, with mock alarm. "'Nhor is tired of Jolanta?"

"No . . . never."

"December 1880," he confirmed. "Nine years ago you left Dr. Américo's house."

"I've been happy, 'Nhor." Her voice grew very soft. "Oh, so happy."

"Open it, Jolanta," he said, placing a velvet-covered box on her lap.

"Oh, Senhor Firmino, what a treasure —" she said in wonderment.

The necklace sparkled, nine emeralds set in diamonds, blazing like green fire, the finest gems from deep in the sertão of Minas Gerais.

❧

"The institutions of our nation are run-down and bankrupt. The longer we delay the fulfillment of Brazil's true destiny, the more it will cost us in the end," Aristides Tavares declared, and waited for a response from Firmino Dantas and Clóvis Lima da Silva.

The three men were sitting in one of the upstairs parlors at Itatinga. Two days ago, September 7, 1889, Clóvis Lima's column had reached the railhead, now sixty miles west of Tiberica. The colonel's men had gone straight on to São Paulo, but Clóvis had stopped off and come out to the fazenda, where he spent much of the day venting his anger over the "banishment" to Corumbá and the long march through Mato Grosso. It was early evening now, after dinner, and Clóvis was puffing a superior Havana, the rapid bursts of smoke suggesting he was still far from calm.

Clóvis finally replied to Aristides: "The price will be just as high, my young friend, if we're swept away by illusory ideals."

"With respect, Colonel, the United States of Brazil is not a vision of Utopians."

"And what about the Sauls converted by abolition, the thousands of slaveocrats flocking to the Republicans for revenge? Until May thirteenth, they were the emperor's best friends. What vision do these men have beyond self-interest? Will they stand by you if your republic doesn't work out as planned?"

"The nation is at heart Republican."

"Rubbish!"

Firmino Dantas supported Clóvis. "Two Republican seats in Parliament, Ari — that's not very convincing." Liberals and Conservatives had swept to victory in an election held in August 1889.

"It was a massive vote of sympathy for the emperor," Aristides suggested.

Clóvis blew out a small cloud of smoke. "It was more than that. The nation isn't ready for a republic. Can you *imagine* what it would be like if there were a successful revolt against the monarchy? We have a mass of illiterates out there who would be thrown into total confusion."

"Exactly! Most of our people are semi-barbaric. They vegetate and die without contributing to the nation. This is the legacy of our empire."

"We've had forty years of internal peace," Firmino objected.

"Yes, senhor — and a bloody war waged, for which the patriots who served got no thanks."

"Would you rather have seen Brazil dismembered? Half a dozen squabbling republics?"

"I have more faith in our people, senhor."

Clóvis interjected: "You have faith that our 'semi-barbarians,' as you just called them, would have continued to dwell together peacefully in Brazil, advancing toward the 'Order and Progress' my Honôrio is so fond of prattling about?"

"Yes, Colonel, I have the utmost faith in a united Brazil. We are one people — by language, race, religion. Our patriots fought the French, the Dutch, the Spaniards, and by the time of Tiradentes, we were ready to take on the Portuguese themselves."

"André Vaz da Silva *thought* we were ready," Clóvis remarked. "Like your Republicans and others who think it's time now to overthrow the monarchy. 'Liberty, even though late!' the Tooth-Puller promised. The sad truth was, no one was there to listen. Ask the mass of our people what they understand by 'liberty' or 'democracy.' You'll get a thousand different answers, and not one will make much sense. I agree our politicians are making a mess of things, but I'll say this: Without Dom Pedro to keep them in check, it would be a damn sight worse."

"Dom Pedro can't last forever, Colonel."

"That *is* a problem," Clóvis Lima said, smoke clouding the air as he exhaled deeply. "A great problem," he added.

"Things are coming fast," Firmino Dantas added. "A few wrong steps and we could wake to a nightmare in this land."

"I seem to have heard the same concern, Senhor Firmino, from others, before abolition," Aristides said. "The future of our nation is in the balance. We must have the courage to act."

"And to face the consequences," Clóvis Lima said heavily.

Aristides was not dissuaded: "We must do whatever is necessary, not for ourselves — for the future of Brazil."

༄

The night of November 9 was partly overcast, the thin clouds drifting eerily past the moon. The granite sentinel Sugar Loaf and the low hill of Urca lay outlined in the distance; other peaks were clustered darkly behind the gaslit streets and houses of Rio de Janeiro. From the quay at Praça de D. Pedro II, formerly the Praça Palácio, and from other embarkation points dozens of launches plied back and forth between the quay and Ilha Fiscal, an island offshore from the old praça, the boat lanterns bobbing like so many fireflies above the waters of Guanabara Bay. Approaching the island, the launches were dwarfed by three battle cruisers — *Riachuelo, Aquidaba,* and *Almirante Cochrane* —anchored off Ilha Fiscal, their superstructures a blaze of light.

Beyond a landing where the ferryboats were disembarking their passengers, the illuminations blazed even brighter along a broad stone walk and from the windows of a palatial ballroom. Barons, viscounts, marquises, knights were coming ashore in droves, the cream of Brazilian aristocracy pouring onto the Ilha Fiscal to mingle with members of the city's upper crust.

A swarm of liveried attendants waited upon the four thousand guests, who that night consumed 500 turkeys, 1,300 chickens, 64 pheasants, 1,600 pounds of shrimp, 20,000 sandwiches, 1,400 sorbets, 2,900 platters of confections, 10,000 liters of beer, 304 cases of wine and assorted libations. Several orchestras provided uninterrupted entertainment, the strains of their music drifting out over Guanabara Bay.

The host for the gargantuan affair was His Imperial Majesty, Dom Pedro Segundo, who was giving the ball to honor the commander and officers of the *Almirante Cochrane,* a Chilean warship. The Chileans and their counterparts in the imperial navy were conspicuous in their dress uniform. The army was represented, too, some forty-five officers in all, fewer than would have been invited had there been less bad blood between them and the Frock Coats who were here en masse.

It was fantastic, Aristides Tavares thought: the aristocracy of a tottering empire sharing pleasantries as they waited to welcome their emperor and empress, behaving as if a thousand nights were left to them. He looked at Anna Pinto dressed like a princess in a pale-pink off-the-shoulder Paris gown with tiny puff sleeves. *Oh, Anna Pinto, how lovely you are,* he thought. *So real, amid this grand illusion!*

೧೨

Aristides and Anna Pinto were staying at Clóvis Lima's house in the suburb of Flamengo. The colonel himself was still with those officers loyal to the emperor, but from the incendiary declarations of Honório da Silva — "I am ready to fight and die in the public praças for the honor of the nation!" — Aristides Tavares knew that were it not for the hesitancy of older men such as Clóvis Lima and Marshal Deodoro da Fonseca, the army would be in open rebellion.

This very day, Lieutenant Honório da Silva had been present when 150 officers met at the Clube Militar to consider the latest affront to their dignity. Lieutenant-Colonel Benjamin Constant Botelho de Magalhães, the Positivist professor with Republican leanings, was at the center of a storm that had blown up over antigovernment statements he'd made during an address to the visiting Chileans on October 25. A group of cadets and officers had been censured for applauding the colonel; then came an announcement that the Twenty-second Battalion was to be packed off to Amazonas on November 10. At the Clube Militar meeting, Lieutenant-Colonel Benjamin Constant was empowered, once and for all, to seek satisfaction from the Frock Coats — in effect, to organize a revolution.

In the fairy-tale setting on Ilha Fiscal, most nobles and Frock Coats, secure in the knowledge that the empire had survived previous outbreaks of republicanism and other manifestations of discontent, were confident that the monarchy would ride out this storm.

A few minutes before 10:00 P.M., the vast crowd grew animated as word passed that the royal barge was approaching. At precisely ten, the schoolteacher/emperor and his suite landed on Ilha Fiscal amid a spontaneous uproar of Vivas for Their Majesties. Dom Pedro walked with a slight stoop. His thin hair was white; his great beard, too, the perfection of his image as a father figure.

Aristides and Anna were a few yards away from the royal party as they came up the steps to the ballroom. Da Silva's eyes followed His Majesty as he walked into the big room. Suddenly, he saw Dom Pedro stumble at the edge of the long red carpet laid from the doorway. Several people rushed to help His Majesty regain his equilibrium, and Aristides, for all his criticism of the monarchy, couldn't help feeling a deep sadness.

ℰↃ

The barão de Jacuribe, Rodrigo Alves Cavalcanti, was one of the men who reached out to help Pedro. When Cavalcanti grabbed his arm, the emperor light-heartedly said, "The monarchy slipped, Barão, but did not fall," and resumed his passage into the ballroom. The barão smiled and stepped back to his party, which included the Baronesa Josepha and their son Gilberto.

It had been three years since Senhor Rodrigo and his partners launched Usina Jacuribe. The sugar factory was a success from the start, crushing the canes of Engenho Santo Tomás and, by this year's harvest, which was now in progress, the canes of every engenho in the two valleys.

Despite continued appeals from his brother, Dr. Fábio, Rodrigo had maintained the senzala at Engenho Santo Tomás until the morning of May 14, 1888, when a telegram reached Rosário with news of The Golden Law.

The barão was in Rio de Janeiro to renew loans for the usina, for, though the factory operated successfully, low sugar prices kept its profits to a minimum. The older Cavalcantis were staying with Gilberto and his wife, Nadina. Senhor Rodrigo was proud of his middle son's achievements as a professor, though he was fonder of Duarte, whom he considered a pillar of strength and tradition and saw as the next *usineiro* — the modern version of "senhor de engenho." On the voyage from Recife to the Corte, the barão and his wife had stopped at the Bahia to see young Celso, who was in a seminary at Salvador.

Senhor Rodrigo found the air at the Corte unsettling. "Why does the government hesitate?" he had asked Gilberto, who was as much a diehard monarchist as his father. "Ouro Prêto should round up these anarchists before it's too late." The visconde de Ouro Prêto, Afonso Celso de Assis Figueiredo, was the prime minister heading the Liberal cabinet.

"The minister has to tread warily to avoid touching off a powder keg," Gilberto Cavalcanti said. "Benjamin Constant carries a torch wherever he goes."

"Ouro Prêto can use the Guarda Nacional."

"It won't come to that, senhor."

"Long ago, the Guarda should have been strengthened. A few batteries of Krupp guns would make our Benjamin Constant think twice before opening his mouth."

"It will blow over," Gilberto had predicted. "The generals are loyal to the emperor."

On Ilha Fiscal, the barão de Jacuribe remained reasonably confident that Gilberto was correct. Even his brother, Dr. Fábio, who followed these developments more closely than he, believed that the army placed the interests of the nation above all considerations and realized that the empire *was* Brazil. Dr. Fábio had also set Rodrigo's mind at rest about the Republicans, who were infiltrating at least the merchant class of Recife: The monarchy could, if it acted decisively, accommodate most of the reforms proposed by the Republicans, even the granting of greater autonomy to the provinces, Fábio maintained. Rodrigo was relieved: *Anything* was preferable to a republic, especially one dominated by the Paulistas and Mineiros, who were at the forefront of the agitation.

?

Late Thursday afternoon, November 14, 1889, Aristides Tavares saw both his cousins briefly at Clóvis Lima's house.

For the twenty-four-year-old Honório da Silva, there was only one option: rebellion. The young lieutenant was attached to the Eleventh Artillery Regiment, which had sworn a "blood pact" Monday night to carry out whatever order came from Lieutenant-Colonel Benjamin Constant. The lieutenant-colonel himself and the officers around him had since engaged in an offensive to win over their superiors still loyal to the Crown. Together with the small group of republican politicians who supported an armed uprising, Benjamin Constant and his followers continued to spread rumors that various regiments were to be posted from the Corte. They embellished these with stories ranging from Dom Pedro's having decided to abdicate in favor of Princess Isabel on his next birthday, to a warning that Prime Minister Ouro Prêto was about to order the arrest of Marshal Manuel Deodoro da Fonseca. Honório da Silva had taken Aristides aside just yesterday and placed a Smith & Wesson pistol in his hand. "Keep it with you," he had said. "The Corte may look asleep to you, and maybe it is, but a few days and the Cariocas will wake. Ai, Jesus, yes! All Brazil will wake from the long sleep of royal oppression."

As the days passed, with meeting after meeting at Marshal Deodoro da Fonseca's house, Clóvis Lima had moved to join the mutineers, though, like Marshal Deodoro himself, with a less final objective in mind. He stressed this to the two younger men when they met on the veranda briefly this Thursday afternoon, before Clóvis and his son went off to join their units.

"Honório da Silva, for the sake of the nation, you're being asked to perform one of a soldier's saddest duties."

"I understand perfectly, senhor," Honório said.

"I wonder whether either of you understands this sacrifice. I hope you do. Marshal Deodoro has agreed to a show of force against Ouro Prêto. Ouro Prêto and his Frock Coats must go. Nothing more. The marshal will not countenance disloyalty toward His Majesty."

"Yes, Colonel!" Honório said stiffly.

"We seek a government that will restore dignity to the army — the imperial army, Honório, there to serve Dom Pedro. That's all Marshal Deodoro wants: to defend our military institutions, not destroy them." Then Clóvis turned to Aristides: "Your republic will come one day, but not this time."

"Yes, Colonel," Ari acknowledged simply.

On the veranda, Honôrio said to Aristides, "I honor and respect my father. I don't doubt what he says is true, but tell me, Ari, do you believe that it will stop with a show of force?"

"Perhaps, but not likely. One step beyond your barracks, the mutiny is irrevocable."

"A week ago, Marshal Deodoro and my father would have nothing to do with us. Today, with Ouro Prêto threatening to arrest the marshal and call out the Guarda to confine us to the barracks, they agree there's no choice: Ouro Prêto must go. Tomorrow?"

"It's in the hands of the gods."

"The gods, yes — and Benjamin Constant."

☙

The Revolution of November 15, as it came to be known, was in many ways a remarkable affair. With a single shot fired in protest, the decaying Bragança dynasty was swept away.

On Thursday night, Honôrio left to join his unit. Colonel Clóvis went to Marshal Deodoro's house, into which a stream of dissident officers poured through the night as regiments of the Corte armed themselves for mutiny.

The emperor and empress were at their summer residence in the mountains at Petropolis, forty miles away from the capital. At 4:00 A.M. on November 15, His Majesty received a telegram from Prime Minister Ouro Prêto warning that sections of the army were in a state of imminent insurgency. Dom Pedro saw no real danger from what he perceived as a tiny dissident faction. His Majesty proceeded to take his customary cold bath at dawn and prepare himself for early Mass.

At 8:00 A.M., Deodoro da Fonseca, who was suffering a raging fever, a recurrence of attacks that had plagued him since his stay in Corumbá, led six hundred men to the quarters-general at the Campo de Santana. The marshal was diminutive in stature and had the look of a terrier about him, a broad jutting beard complementing the image. True to his word, he carried the sword of rebellion under the imperial flag and with Vivas for His Majesty as he marched with Clóvis Lima and other officers to the quarters-general, where the visconde de Ouro Prêto and several of his ministers had taken shelter.

"Storm them!" Ouro Prêto demanded repeatedly of Adjutant-General Floriano Peixoto, the commander of the garrison in the quarters-general. "Capture their artillery!"

Floriano Peixoto refused to obey. "The guns I faced in Paraguay were those of the enemy. The cannon I see before me, Minister, are Brazilian."

It was during this impasse that the minister of the navy arrived at army headquarters. The navy itself supported the rebellion, but the minister, the barão de Ladário, José da Costa Azevedo, was taken by surprise. As he stepped down from his carriage outside the barracks, he was told he was under arrest. The barão pulled out a revolver and fired at the rebel officers, who shot back, wounding him.

After this single exchange, Floriano Peixoto threw open the gates of the quarters-general, allowing Marshal Deodoro and his officers to enter amid more

Vivas and cheers for His Majesty. After demanding the resignation of Ouro Prêto and his cabinet, and guaranteeing to respect the will of the emperor, Marshal Deodoro marched his men through the city to the marine arsenal, where they were greeted with more Vivas by the navy officers and marines actively participating in the uprising. By late morning, Marshal Deodoro returned to his house to nurse his fever. As far as he was concerned, the revolution was over.

At 1:00 P.M., Emperor Pedro and Dona Theresa arrived in the city from Petropolis. Dom Pedro went to the city palace near the waterfront, where the viceroys of Brazil had stayed in colonial days. At 3:00 P.M., Princess Isabel and the comte d'Eu joined him at the old palace, and Dom Pedro began to listen to urgent advice from many quarters; one idea was that he should return to Petropolis or move farther into the interior to establish a government around which his loyal subjects could rally. But it was as if the old palace of the viceroys had become a world unto itself, for beyond those musty corridors, a small but delirious crowd was celebrating.

At 3:00 P.M., at the city hall, a group of Republicans prevailed on the municipal câmara to pass a motion calling for a federal republic: Estados Unidos do Brasil, the United States of Brazil.

❧

Aristides had been outside the city hall when the republic was proclaimed. The news had been greeted with a tumultuous new cry: *"Viva a Republica!"* and spontaneously from several thousand throats rose a chorus of the Marseillaise.

Aristides was swept along with the crowd when word passed that the victorious Republican delegation was going to Deodoro da Fonseca's house to offer the marshal the post of chief of the provisional government. Outside Fonseca's house, Aristides kept watch for Clóvis da Silva but did not see him, though he recognized several of the visitors, among them Lieutenant-Colonel Benjamin Constant and the Bahian politician and journalist Rui Barbosa. Without question the most brilliant of the men contributing to the overthrow of the monarchy, Rui Barbosa had gone over to the Republicans a few days ago, a decision now bringing him the portfolios of minister of finance and acting minister of justice. At 7:00 P.M., the scene outside the city hall was repeated when it was announced that Marshal Deodoro had agreed to head the provisional government.

Despite the jubilation of the crowd near the Campo de Santana, elsewhere in the city the mood of the Cariocas swung between indifference and confusion. Not a few nobles, however, heard the strains of the Marseillaise and feared the worst, locking themselves up in their palaces. Among the mass of black and brown citizens, too, not all stood dumbfounded: They heard the Marseillaise and were reminded of their own newly found freedom, for which they thanked Princess Isabel. The freedmen received the rumor that the emperor and his family were to be banished forever from Brazil with consternation: Here and there, the boldest spoke of rising in support of their beloved Redemptress.

Aristides roamed the city with others until midnight, hoping to run into either of his cousins, but to no avail. It was almost 1:00 A.M. when he returned to Flamengo. As he climbed the steps to the veranda, he smiled at the reminder of the Smith & Wesson, heavy in his pocket, which he'd not had the slightest thought of using. He was about to enter the house when he saw a curl of smoke in the dark. Clóvis Lima da Silva was sitting in one of the many rattan chairs on the veranda.

"Colonel?"

"Yes, Aristides. It's me."

Aristides approached him slowly, surprised to find him there.

"I suspected for some days that Deodoro would agree," Clóvis said. "I prayed he wouldn't give in, but he did. I don't doubt that he acts with the purest motives for the safety of the nation. Benjamin Constant, Rui Barbosa — they both swear by God that it's so. I don't question their patriotism, but I can't celebrate with them. A festa! How will it be tomorrow, when Brazil struggles with the reality of your republic?"

"I believe that the events of today were inevitable, Colonel."

"We should have waited, as Deodoro himself said a few days ago. We needed more time to prepare for a transition."

Aristides knew that Marshal Deodoro and the men around him had had no choice. *For our Brazil*, he thought passionately, and felt a strong urge to share his exhilaration with the colonel, but heard Clóvis Lima say, "Leave me now, Aristides."

"Good night, Colonel. I promise you our patria will prosper."

"I would dearly like to believe that, Ari."

Honório da Silva, ebullient, victorious, shared none of his father's doubts, and demonstrated this to Aristides when they were together two days later in the early hours of the morning on the old palace square. The previous day, the emperor had been served with an order of banishment that gave him and his family twenty-four hours to leave Brazilian soil. Two o'clock this Sunday afternoon had been set as the time for their departure, but at 1:30 A.M., fearing that a daylight procession by the royal family could ignite a popular demonstration, army officers had demanded that they leave forthwith. At first Dom Pedro had refused: "I am not a runaway slave. I will not embark at this hour." But the officers had insisted.

Honório was with a section of his unit posted at a praça not far from the old palace. Cavalrymen had cordoned off the palace square since early on November 16. Honório knew one of the officers in charge, and he and Aristides had no difficulty getting through their lines.

At last, just before 3:00 A.M., the first members of the royal household, Princess Isabel and the comte d'Eu among them, emerged from the palace and were escorted across the Praça to the quayside. Soon afterward, the emperor and empress made their short journey in a carriage. It was drizzling, but from where Honório and Aristides stood, they had a good view of Their Majesties in the gaslight of lamps at the boat landing.

"Oh, dear God, how sad that it should end like this," Aristides said, watching one of the ladies-in-waiting help the Empress Theresa as she bent down to put her lips to the ground.

"To hell with them!" Honório grabbed his cousin's arm fiercely. "Gaze upon this dark, wet square, Aristides. From this very spot, Brazil's martyr of liberty started his walk to the gallows. What compassion did Queen Maria show Tiradentes?"

Aristides felt an involuntary shiver, for what Honório da Silva said was true. "Perhaps Alferes Silva Xavier is watching . . ."

Honório gave a short, tense laugh. "God knows, he is. Tiradentes lit the torch a hundred years ago. This dark night it blazes brightly all over our United States of Brazil!"

Ͼᴓ

On November 24, the packet Alagoas carrying the Braganças to exile in Europe rode slowly past the island of Fernando do Noronha, about two hundred miles off the coast, the last Brazilian territory they were to see. As the island began to drop astern, Pedro's fourteen-year-old grandson suggested that one of the carrier pigeons aboard the Alagoas be dispatched with a final message to the patria.

His Majesty stood on the deck, the breeze ruffling his white hair. *"Saudade,"* he said, thinking aloud. . . . Saudade, an expression of profound melancholy.

"Saudades do Brasil," Pedro wrote on a slip of paper, which was signed by all the family.

The pigeon was released with the message tied to its leg. Within sight of the exiles, it dropped into the sea and vanished.

XXI

---◆◇◆---

June 1897 – December 1906

The creak of saddle leather and clack of iron-shod hooves upon stony ground scarcely intruded upon the silence as Clóvis Lima da Silva walked his horse toward the soldiers. The men moved to either side of a majestic mandacuru cactus that dominated the surrounding caatinga. They looked curiously at the colonel, wondering how he would react to their find.

The dead soldier's back was propped up against the spiny base of the mandacuru. Patches of his uniform were deep blue, the rest discolored, and down the side of each trouser leg was a broken red stripe. Protruding above the fastened top button of his jacket was a dark, uneven stump. The decapitated head lay off to one side, the face pressed down in the dirt.

Clóvis da Silva halted ten feet away. He gave the corpse a cursory glance before turning to the men who'd found it. "Back to your lines," was all he said. Clóvis did not follow them, but lowered his eyes once more to the body: The dark foreboding he had experienced the night of the revolution returned strongly here, deep in the sertão of northeastern Brazil, on a day in late June 1897.

Almost eight years since the proclamation of the republic, Clóvis da Silva's pessimism that day had been justified. Political quarrels, military uprisings, and a civil war had convulsed Brazil following Marshal Deodoro da Fonseca's election, in February 1891, as first president of the new republic. Nine months after taking office, the marshal dissolved Congress and declared a state of siege. Faced with a rebellion, Deodoro had resigned in favor of his vice-president, Marshal Floriano

Peixoto, who restored Congress but did not relax the army's iron grip on the nation. There had been a rebellion by the navy and an uprising in Rio Grande do Sul. The naval revolt had been put down, but the fratricidal conflict in Rio Grande do Sul was still raging in March 1894 when São Paulo, the wealthiest state in the republic, exercised its political power to back the election of the first civilian president, a Paulista, Prudente de Morais. By August 1895, the Rio Grande insurrection had been suppressed. It seemed that the United States of Brazil was beyond its baptism by blood and fire.

Twenty-two months later, on June 27, 1897, Clóvis da Silva was with five thousand men marching to crush an uprising in the backlands of Bahia, 250 miles northwest of Salvador. The beheaded soldier at the mandacuru was not the only evidence of disaster the First Column had found since leaving its base camp eight days ago. Other men lay dead in the caatinga, and all along the route was the awful debris of defeat — smashed equipment, a discarded boot, a kepi trodden into the dirt.

The force to which Clóvis was attached was the fourth expedition to march this way. The previous November, 104 men sent from Salvador had had a quarter of their number killed or wounded before retreating from the village of Uauá. In January 1897, 557 men and officers, with two Krupp cannon and two Nordenfeldt machine guns, had been sent from the state capital; after a two-day engagement in which several hundred fell, they retreated. The third expedition set out a month later with 1,300 men commanded by the fiery Antônio Moreira César, renowned for his decisive action against the Rio Grande do Sul insurgents. Colonel Moreira César and his second-in-command, Colonel Pedro Nunes Tamarindo, were killed, along with three hundred men; the survivors fled, abandoning all their equipment, four Krupp guns included, in the caatinga.

Clóvis's foreboding was compounded by unanswered questions about the rebels, who were variously described as bandits, fanatics, and monarchists. After the defeat of Moreira César, newspapers at Rio de Janeiro had reflected a hysterical public's belief that the uprising in the sertão was the vanguard of a movement to restore the Braganças. Dom Pedro had died in exile in Paris in 1891, and the empress two years before that, but Princess Isabel and her sons were still there to claim the throne. There were rumors of royalist sympathizers flocking to join the Bahia rebels, along with French and Austrian tacticians recruited in Europe.

Clóvis accepted "bandits" and "fanatics" as more likely descriptions of the rebels. And one thing was clear: The instigator of the uprising was a madman. Antônio Conselheiro, he was called — "The Counselor." Church authorities had had trouble with the man as long ago as the early 1870s, when he first began to disturb the spiritual peace of the sertanejos. Time and again the archbishop of the Bahia had received complaints from priests that The Counselor had invaded their parishes and disturbed the god-fearing sertanejos.

Reports had it that The Counselor was originally from the town of Quixeramobim, in the province of Ceará, where he was born in 1828 as Antônio Vicente Mendes Maciel, a member of the vast Maciel clan, long prominent in Ceará and other far northeastern states. His father wanted him to be a priest, but Antônio Vicente preferred the cashier's bench in his father's dry-goods store, eventually becoming a clerk and working for his father until he was twenty-nine. In 1857 the elder Maciel died deeply in debt, forcing the closure of the store; that same year, Antônio Vicente married and took up bookkeeping at various fazendas in the district. Pursued by his father's creditors, he moved to a town south of Quixeramobim, where, it was rumored, he sustained a blow that deranged him, when his wife deserted him for a police sergeant.

The distraught Antônio Vicente fled farther south, through Pernambuco to Bahia, where he settled at Itapicurú, 120 miles directly north of Salvador. By 1876, he had become known as The Counselor and was attracting a wide following of peasants to his "Camp of the Good Jesus." Soon the Itapicurú police delegate was appealing to Salvador for help in suppressing the "excesses of the fanatics against good nature and authority." The Counselor himself had prevented an open confrontation: Like the prophets of old, with a small band of pilgrims he entered the wilderness.

For sixteen years, Antônio Conselheiro had roamed the sertão, passing through the caatinga from fazenda to fazenda, vila to vila. Finally, in 1893, The Counselor, sixty-five years old, found a permanent refuge: Canudos. The chosen ground lay 250 miles northwest of Salvador, on a great plain between rugged hills that, because of the low-lying caatinga surrounding them, appeared deceptively precipitous. Along the southern edge of the plain flowed the Vasa-Barris, which came down from the east and looped around to the northwest, and The Counselor elected to build his New Jerusalem beyond the banks north of that bend.

Antônio Conselheiro and his followers were not the first to settle here. As far back as the eighteenth century, a settlement called Tapiranga by the natives had been the refuge of runaway slaves from the coastal plantations. The quilombo had survived for generations, its inhabitants and their descendants known in the district for their ironwork. From time to time, backlands bandits seeking a hideaway from the law had joined them. There had been periodic fairs at Canudos, where the ironworkers sold their wares and others offered long-stemmed smoking pipes made from the reeds — *canudos* — that grew beside the river.

Clóvis had heard several descriptions of Antônio Conselheiro from sertanejos serving with his column. They spoke of The Counselor as a man of medium height with a body wasted by fasting and privation. His features were suggestive of the caboclo mix of white and native. He had dark, piercing eyes, and his shoulder-length hair and heavy beard were both mottled with gray. His daily garb was a blue robe with a black leather belt from which a wooden crucifix on a leather thong was suspended. He wore sandals and, on his head, a small blue skullcap; his hand clasped a great staff. He carried with him, too, wherever he went, *A Missão Abbreviado,* an ancient liturgical work, and a copy of *Horas Marianas,* a book of devotions.

Clóvis's belief that Antônio Conselheiro was a madman was strengthened by what the sertanejos had told him about The Counselor's sermons.

"'Lift up your eyes to the East,' The Counselor tells the people," said one of these informants. "'The day is approaching when Dom Sebastião will march out of the surf to expel the Antichrist from Brazil.'"

The belief in a resurrection of the ill-fated king of Portugal, who marched against the Infidels at Alcacer-Quibir in 1578 and fell with fifty thousand, was not new. In Portugal over the centuries, there had been sporadic revivals of Sebastianism, which had become a cult.

"The Counselor predicts the end of the world in 1899. There will be a rain of fiery stars, then darkness, followed by pestilence and famine. The new millennia will dawn only for the elect of the Company of People at New Jerusalem. They alone will be there to greet the victorious Dom Sebastião," the sertanejo told Clóvis.

The Counselor had not confined himself to mystical pronouncements: since 1889, as he tramped the sertão, he had increasingly come to identify the republic as the regime of the Antichrist.

"I was there, Colonel, at the weekly fair at Bom Conselho. I saw Antônio Conselheiro tear down the new tax notices at the vila. 'Death to the Republicans!' he shouted."

Clóvis da Silva himself had looked darkly upon the advent of the republic, but when it was proclaimed, he felt it his duty to support it. Gradually, though, Clóvis's initial misgivings had increased as he observed the Machiavellian maneuverings for power of Marshal Peixoto and the generals around him, and he went into semiretirement, taking a desk job at a barracks in Rio de Janeiro.

The presidential election in March 1894 had found the army divided, with men like Clóvis adamant that civilian rule be restored, and others hoping to force another term for Floriano Peixoto; but Prudente de Morais had been elected and was inaugurated in November that year without incident. Clóvis had returned to active duty, intending to serve in Rio Grande do Sul, where the civil insurrection was still dragging on, but he'd not been posted there. Three months ago, Minister of War Carlos Machado de Bittencourt, long an opponent of military rule, had personally asked Clóvis to command an artillery division against the fanatics. The minister had promised, too, that Clóvis's promotion to general, which would have come years ago but for his attitude toward the militarists, would soon be announced.

Clóvis had sailed from Rio de Janeiro for the Bahia in April in the same ship with his son Honório da Silva. Hônorio was a major now, but had left the artillery for a cavalry regiment. He was attached to the Second Column, which was marching for Canudos through the caatinga directly to the east.

At the Bahia, Clóvis's regiment had immediately entrained for the sertão on the Central Railway, which operated between Salvador and Juazeiro, three hundred miles away on the banks of the Rio São Francisco. They got off at Queimadas, about ninety miles directly south of Canudos, and marched forty-five miles to the vila of Monte Santo, which had been the base camp for the previous expeditions.

Clóvis had been at Monte Santo for five weeks before the commander of the First Column, General Artur Oscar de Andrade Guimarães, gave the order for the three thousand men to advance on June 19.

The more Clóvis saw of this blistered land, so frequently scourged by droughts, the more he understood how this place could raise the fires of hell in a man's soul. The base camp itself lay below the slopes of Monte Santo, for centuries a holy place with a winding path to the top of the mountain, along which pilgrims halted to pray at stations of the Cross. Clóvis himself made the ascent, with a sense of reverence mixed with apprehension, gazing across the caatinga toward the hills in the direction of Canudos, and wondering if the Devil himself had gone that way.

The same question was in his thoughts as he stared at the decapitated soldier. There had been scenes much worse in Paraguay, and he remembered this, too, with despair: He had hated the Guarani, but, misled as they were by López, they had fought honorably. Here was no honor, only pure savagery — barbarians hammering at the foundations of society.

Clóvis felt a sudden wave of fatigue. He was, after all, sixty-eight, a veteran of many campaigns. His face was fuller; his hair and beard silvered. Many of his old Paraguayan comrades were dead, Deodoro da Fonseca among them — Floriano Peixoto, too, was gone — and he felt alone. Momentarily, he thought of Hônorio da Silva riding with General Cláudio do Amaral Savaget's Second Column. They were to meet up in twenty-four hours to assault the lair of bandits now only seven miles ahead. He looked forward to seeing Hônorio, in whom, for all their disagreements, he took uncommon pride.

Silently, he asked God's mercy for the nameless soldier. Then he turned his horse and rode after his men.

&

The light was fading as advance units crawled up a steep incline a mile from Canudos. Lieutenant-Colonel Siqueira Menezes and his engineering corps were at the front of the column, a position they'd held for eight days as they cleared the road and bridged the riachos for the artillery and supply train. The Twenty-fifth Battalion marched with them, providing cover as the engineers worked their way through the caatinga. Half a mile behind the battalion, Colonel Clóvis Lima da Silva was bringing up four Krupp 7-pounders and two machine guns.

It was six hours since they'd found the soldier at the mandacuru. The mules drawing the gun carriages had been unhitched; the guns were being manhandled up the slope. The gunners put their backs into it with frantic energy, for they were frightened. Momentarily, they would swing their heads to the left and right, searching the gray-green scrub wall, the outcrops of rocks. Twice this afternoon, farther back along the lines, musket fire had blazed out of the caatinga; men had fallen; bullets had raked the bush in response. Then, silence. No sight of the enemy. Nothing.

Clóvis rode with the flap of his revolver holster loosened. Siqueira Menezes had sent a messenger back to report that after cresting the hill, the road sloped down a long depression on the summit and then climbed again to a ridge. The hill was called Monte Favela; beyond its northern slope lay several smaller hills, and four thousand feet away — Canudos.

Clóvis wanted his guns on the northern ridge before nightfall. He, too, kept glancing into the caatinga. Not once since leaving Monte Santo had he caught sight of a rebel. The column was strung out for six miles. General Artur Oscar was two miles away. Somewhere behind him was the rest of the artillery, lumbering along with a Whitworth siege gun hauled by twenty oxen. "God's Thunderer," men were calling it — a 32-pounder to silence the voice of the false prophet. Far behind the Whitworth, at the rear of the column, was the supply train, with more than 150 mules carrying food and ammunition.

Clóvis told a major — Lauro Correia, who had been with the colonel on the march back from Corumbá, Mato Grosso, in August 1889 — to keep the guns moving smartly up the hill. Clóvis went on ahead, up to where the Twenty-fifth had outlying pickets on both sides of the road. Spurring his horse on, Clóvis rode quickly down the hilltop road, passing more men of the Twenty-fifth; at one or two places, he saw the white kepis of skirmishers fanning out between the low scrub. He glanced toward other hills, to the east and west; the sun was low now, the hillsides shadowed. His eyes narrowed warily as he studied a long, dark line far off to the left where the rocks were piled up, not unlike a parapet. Elsewhere, too, he glimpsed unnatural circular rock formations, but saw no movement there.

Ten minutes later, he had dismounted and was standing on the northern ridge, his eyes upon Canudos.

Beside him, Lieutenant-Colonel Siqueira Menezes, himself a northeasterner, said, "The Paradise of the sertanejo! From a hundred miles away and farther he came. Sold his worldly goods, abandoned his fields . . . for *this*."

Clóvis was silent. A vast, uneven plain rose behind the Vasa-Barris. Near the river stood a massive unfinished church with two huge towers; to its right, in an open area, was a dilapidated chapel. Behind the church were several substantial buildings. What made the greatest impression, though, was the vast number of dwellings behind these buildings and in barrios spreading across the Vasa-Barris, most of them mud-walled and thatch-roofed, though a few rough-baked tile roofs could be seen; five thousand homes built in no particular order, with a labyrinth of streets and alleys winding among them.

"How many?" Clóvis asked, thinking aloud.

"Fifteen, twenty thousand. Perhaps more."

"Where do they come from?"

"From wherever their counselor spread his poison."

"Why was this great assembly allowed? Surely the authorities knew no good could come of it?"

"Not all felt that way. Some district chiefs saw value in an alliance with Antônio Conselheiro." Siqueira Menezes explained that certain poderosos involved in fierce political contests as they strove to assert themselves in the new republican order, had considered the legions of faithful as potential allies. "They soon realized their mistake. As Canudos grew, their own sertanejos deserted them. And, while Conselheiro and his saints preached their mad gospel, killer thieves rode from Canudos to pillage the land for miles around. What we've seen on our way here were once thriving fazendas."

The light was fading rapidly now, but he could just discern people streaming toward the chapel. "It's more like a fort," he suggested, looking at the new church to the left.

"Yes, Colonel. And if it were lighter, you would see evidence of war preparations. There are trenches all over the place."

"The guns?" Clóvis was referring to the Krupp cannon abandoned by the second expedition.

"I haven't seen them."

"What do you think, Lieutenant-Colonel? Have they got help?"

"I don't know. I just don't know."

Clóvis was still looking at the chapel. "They must know we're here."

Siqueira Menezes laughed thinly. "They've watched us day and night along every mile of the road from Monte Santo."

"I see no panic down there."

"They've repulsed three expeditions already," Siqueira Menezes said, offering an unneeded reminder. "Besides, why should they panic? Their counselor prepares them for the end of the world."

Hour after hour, the government troops kept coming up the long incline and down into the depression on top of Favela. At 9:00 P.M., the Whitworth, drawn by the oxen and with teams of men hanging onto guide ropes, was dragged up the long slope; then the cannon moved slowly down through the basin. Bone-weary soldiers cheered as God's Thunderer passed them: "Well done, camaradas, well done! Wake the sons of bitches! Blast them to kingdom come!"

General Artur Oscar was camped near the Krupp and Nordenfeldt battery on the northern ridge. By 10:00 P.M., two thousand men were on Monte Favela and bivouacked all along the road through the basin; the rest of the column and supply train were miles behind and stopped for the night. Pickets had been thrown out, and before the moon was risen, some rockets had been fired above nearby hills. But there'd been no contact with or even sight of an armed fanatic this night of June 27, 1897. An artillery barrage against Canudos was set for dawn. General Savaget and the Second Column were expected by midday June 28; then the combined force of five thousand expeditionaries would make a general advance.

Sometime after 11.00 P.M., Clóvis da Silva had left a staff meeting with General Artur Oscar and was preparing to bed down near his guns.

Clóvis shared a canvas shelter with Lauro Correia. Before turning in, he went over to the major at one of the Krupp guns. Others expected a miracle with the Whitworth, but Clóvis knew that if the fanatics' defenses were strong, the 32-pounder would have to punch a thousand holes in the crude citadel before it could be stormed. For a while, Clóvis discussed this possibility with Lauro Correia: They agreed that as soon as feasible in the morning, the guns should be moved to one of the hills below, closer to the Vasa-Barris.

"It's too damn quiet," Clóvis said, as he was about to leave the major. "It makes me think of Tuyuti."

"They know what's going to hit them in the morning. They're saving their strength."

"Perhaps," Clóvis said.

"Get some sleep, Colonel. We're not in Paraguay now."

"It's too damn quiet," Clóvis said again.

"Let them sleep, these fanatics with their visions of Paradise." He laughed again. "We've a rude awakening for them. A *rude* awakening."

But the fanatics were not asleep.

Clóvis was walking back to the shelter when he heard the shrill of a whistle far off to his right. And even as Clóvis swung back to Lauro Correia, the column came under fire from positions all over Favela and on hills to the east and west.

"Too *damn* quiet!" Clóvis exclaimed as he ran back to the major.

Lauro Correia stood there dumbfounded.

"For the love of Christ, man! Ready the guns!"

Clóvis himself shouted orders to gunners tumbling out of their blankets. He sent the first men on their feet running to site the Nordenfeldts; as others came up, he ordered them to get the Krupps turned toward the fanatics' positions.

There were at least three thousand. They emerged from behind rows of rocks; they rose from hidden circular pits; they crept forward on their bellies through the caatinga.

The Nordenfeldts came into action, sending six hundred rounds a minute into the caatinga. The 7-pounders, too, were not long in answering the fanatics; Major Lauro Correia had recovered from his shock and brought the guns to rapid fire.

General Artur Oscar, a master of the classic campaign, appeared along the line, hatless, disheveled, his jacket loose, but still rather magnificent, for he was on his horse, and with an old soldier's supreme confidence, he rode along the basin ignoring bullets whizzing past him as he tried to bring order to his troops. Many companies were beginning to return fire, peppering the caatinga with shots. But far too many soldiers were dashing around half naked, panic-stricken. Some poor fools bolted blindly into the caatinga, where a dozen arms reached out eagerly to receive them.

The battle raged for an hour. Four of Clóvis's gunners were struck by bullets, two of them fatally. One of the 7-pounders jammed, but the others kept firing; the Nordenfeldts, too, continued their fusillade.

Then, almost as abruptly as it began, the attack ended. Not more than a hundred yards away from where Clóvis stood, the caatinga was on fire, the flames reaching toward one of the many pits where rebels had been concealed. When a number of figures rose up, a gunner cranked the handle of the Nordenfeldt for a burst in that direction. Several ran, but one lone figure lingered fearlessly on the rocks.

Colonel Clóvis da Silva had heard the cry before, and it sent a chill down his spine.

"Macacos! Macacos! Macacos!" the fanatic screamed. Then he was gone, vanished into the caatinga.

℘

The man who had mocked the gunners moved swiftly through the caatinga, passing others headed back to Canudos. He hurried along, the stones clattering under his boots as he slid down the side of a defile. He followed this for five hundred yards. Then he swung farther left in the direction of a stream, the Umburana, which flowed into the Vasa-Barris.

At the Vasa-Barris, he shouldered his Mannlicher and helped carry a wounded man across the river, where dozens lay waiting to be taken by cart to an infirmary on the west end of town. The man moved on past the new church and across an open area to a low building, the headquarters of the troops of Antônio Conselheiro. As he approached a group of men warming themselves at a fire in front of the building, several shouted an enthusiastic welcome. He joined them, offering a rapid account of the action near the guns.

Standing in the shadows, listening raptly, was a young boy who suddenly darted toward the man. "Father!" he shouted.

The boy's father laughed. "Well," he said, looking at the others, "shall we hear his report?"

The response was unanimous: "Yes!"

"Yes, boy?"

The lad stiffened. He almost dropped the old blunderbuss he was holding loosely, its butt just touching the ground. He opened his mouth, but no words came.

"I'm waiting, son."

"I think, Father—"

"*Yes?*"

"I think I . . . shot one."

"Eleven years old! His first macaco!" The man briefly embraced the boy. "Not his last!"

There was a flurry of praises from the commanders.

"Go home, boy! Sleep! You've work tomorrow!"

Still smiling, the boy stepped away smartly.

His father watched him go. Then he gave all his attention to the commander-in-chief, who began to talk of plans for the next assault against the government soldiers.

The light from the fire showed the man to be past middle age. He was tall and slim, with a tough, spare frame. His face was narrow, his nose aquiline; his brown eyes were hard, though when he'd looked at the boy they seemed to soften. He wore a leather waistcoat, opened at the chest; his trousers, too, were leather. Unlike several of his fellow commanders who were barefoot, he wore boots — a fine pair pulled off the legs of one of Moreira César's officers. On his head he wore a big leather hat, its turned-up front brim decorated with small silver stars in the center of which was the Cross of Christ. A bright red kerchief at his neck added a jaunty look to his earth-colored leather battle dress. He carried three cartridge belts, one around his waist, two slung over his lean shoulders and crossed over his chest.

Like several others at the fire, the curse he'd just yelled at the enemy had been the very epithet hurled against him more than twenty-five years ago when he served his emperor in the jungles and esteros of Paraguay.

And there was much, much more Antônio Paciência, son of Mãe Mônica, slave at Fazenda da Jurema, remembered about those days long before he had come to take up arms for the Good Jesus and The Counselor who spoke for Him.

♥

Patient Anthony still recalled vividly his return to Fazenda da Jurema in 1870. That year the arid land of the caatinga bloomed. The first week of February, the sertanejos had raised their sun-baked faces to the heavens: Thick banks of cloud were rolling in on the northeaster. The first raindrops struck the parched ground, raising tiny puffs of red dust. In minutes, a torrential downpour filled the cracks in the earth, swirling over sandy depressions, flooding rock-hard creeks and riverbeds. The people of the sertão had witnessed a miracle. As far as the eye could see, a million blossoms colored the caatinga, from tiny mauve buttons underfoot to trees and cacti adorned with a riot of flame red, violet, and yellow flowers.

Antônio reached the fazenda of Coronel Heitor Batista Ferreira four weeks after departing Recife, to which he had sailed from Paraguay with the Fifty-third Battalion of voluntários, together with his friends Henrique Inglez and Tipoana. Parting with Henrique, Antônio had traveled to the sertão with Tipoana and six other Pancurus from their village near the Rio Moxoto, journeying alone to Jurema on his quest to find Mãe Mônica. Half scared, half defiant, he had reached the fazenda on April 18, 1870, and had gone directly to the main house, where one of the fazenda's capangas ordered him to wait outside while his presence was reported to the senhor coronel.

Antônio waited for what seemed an interminable time before Coronel Heitor Batista Ferreira appeared in the doorway, a mountain of flesh in a sweat-stained undershirt and cotton trousers that barely contained his massive thighs. Then in his late sixties, the senhor coronel was so burdened by his obesity, he had difficulty walking even a dozen paces.

"You're Mãe Mônica's son?" Batista Ferreira asked.

"By your leave, Senhor Coronel," Antônio replied, seeking permission to speak in the presence of the poderoso and receiving a nod. "I am Antônio Paciência."

"A *liberto* of Paraguay?"

"I was given my freedom, yes, Senhor Coronel. I came back to Jurema to find Mãe Mônica. She—"

"After so many years?"

"I did not forget my mother, Senhor Coronel."

Batista Ferreira frowned heavily, his bloated jowls moving furiously as he expelled a jet of dark tobacco juice.

"Mãe Mônica, Senhor Coronel?" Antônio persisted.

"Your mother's here."

"Jesus Christ *bless* Senhor Coronel!" Antônio Paciência cried joyously. "I was freed in Paraguay. I came back hoping to get the same freedom for my mother."

"The slave Mônica is free."

At first, Antônio did not grasp Batista Ferreira's words. "Yes, Senhor Coronel. I hope for this."

"I liberated her two years ago, Antônio Paciência. She lives with Isabelinha, there by the jurema trees."

"Blessed Christ! Mãe Mônica alive and free! Oh, Senhor Coronel, God *bless* you!"

Heitor Batista Ferreira smiled momentarily, but his frown just as quickly returned. "My son is away. He'll want to see you," Batista Ferreira said suddenly.

"I will be here when Senhor João Montes calls for me."

Batista Ferreira then spoke to the capanga, standing a few feet away: "Take the mulatto to his mother."

The caboclo had taken Antônio along a path beyond the main cluster of buildings, stopping within sight of a mud-walled, thatch-roofed house one hundred feet away at the juremas. As Antônio ran toward the house, it crossed his mind that perhaps it was exactly here that the sad herd had been led away by Saturnino Rabelo.

"Mãe Mônica! Mãe Mônica," Antônio called out, even before he reached the front door, which was closed. "Mãe Mônica?"

"Who is it?"

"Antônio . . . Antônio Paciência," he said breathlessly.

There was no immediate response. The house had two small windows with wooden shutters; one of these to the right of Antônio had creaked open a few inches.

"Isabelinha?" he asked, when he saw a youngish woman at the window. He had only a vague recollection of his half-sister. "I am Antônio Paciência."

"It's not possible. The boy was sold by Senhor Coronel."

"Yes . . . yes, Isabelinha. I *was* sold. And I was with the slaves fighting in Paraguay. I was *liberated.*"

The window was opened another inch. "The child Antônio left Jurema years ago."

"They took me to São Paulo. I worked in the coffee groves. Five years ago, I went to war with the voluntários. Oh, open the door, Isabelinha. You'll see it's me — Antônio."

The instant Isabelinha opened the door, Antônio Paciência saw his mother sitting at a table in the front room. His heart had been so full, it was almost too much for him to say her name:

"Mãe . . . Mônica . . . Mother."

Slowly she raised her old face to him, the light from the doorway upon her short gray hair. There was fright in her eyes, and she looked for answers — not to him; to Isabelinha — but her daughter only smiled.

"Oh, Mãe Mônica!" Antônio had gone to her and was kneeling at her feet. "It's Antônio. *Your boy, Antônio Paciência,*" he cried, grasping her arms.

Mãe Mônica's hands began to tremble. "An—tônio?"

With tears on his cheeks, Antônio embraced his mother, all the while pouring out words to convince her he was the child torn from her side so many years ago.

When she finally believed, Mãe Mônica, too, wept and cried out with thanks to God: "Isabelinha! Our little Antônio . . . my son! He's come home!"

In the days that followed, there had been other happy reunions, such as that between Antônio and his boyhood friend Francisco Cavalcante — Chico Tico-Tico. "The Sparrow," twenty-eight at the time, was a vaqueiro at Jurema and also served as gunman for the Ferreiras, who had remained the district chieftains in the município of Jurema. Depending on the locality where they operated, the landowners' gunmen were known as *jagunços,* meaning simply "ruffian," or *cangaçeiros,* from "*canga,*" a yoke for oxen. Utterly ruthless, brave, impetuous, many of the gunmen were former vaqueiros with an intimate knowledge of the sertão.

It had been Chico Tico-Tico who — over a jug of cachaça two nights after Antônio Paciência returned — had shocked Antônio with a revelation delivered quite innocently. Antônio had already learned that his half-sister Isabelinha was the mother of two bastards by João Montes Ferreira, but he did not know that twenty-four years ago, Senhor João had raped Mãe Mônica at the clay oven behind the fazenda. "We all felt so sorry for Mãe Mônica," Chico Tico-Tico said, referring to the time Antônio had been sold. "She was heartbroken when you were taken from her, and then, when Isabelinha lay with your father —"

"My *father!*" Antônio's face had contorted with agony.

"You didn't *know*, Antônio?" Chico Tico-Tico gasped.

"João Montes Ferreira . . . my father . . . sold me. His *son!*"

Antônio spent the night on the bank of the Riacho Jurema, fueling his hatred for Ferreira. Chico Tico-Tico found him at daybreak. "Friend, I understand your misery," he said, sitting down beside Antônio, "but you wouldn't do anything . . . foolish, would you?"

That afternoon, João Montes Ferreira returned and summoned Antônio to come to the main house in the evening. Chico Tico-Tico accompanied Antônio, who donned his uniform and kepi for the meeting.

Ferreira met them at the door. In his fifties then, he lacked the proportions of his father, but the resemblance was there in the puffy cheeks and developing paunch. Like his father, too, João Montes was a coronel in the Guarda Nacional. His eyes had roved from Antônio's kepi to his boots. "So you earned your freedom, eh?" He had looked at his son admiringly. "And fought in the great battles against López?"

"Tuyuti, Curupaiti, Humaitá — others, too, Coronel," Antônio replied calmly.

"I lost two sons with the Guarda Nacional."

"And what of the other son you lost? The one you sold to the slavers?"

No one moved or said a word.

It was Ferreira himself who defused the explosive atmosphere: "Ai, Jesus knows, I'm not a cruel man, Antônio Paciência. I have other sons at Jurema. I look after them. Ask Isabelinha: I'm good to the boys. I'll do the same for you. Stay at the fazenda, Antônio Paciência. I'll help you."

Antônio *had* stayed — for seven years — riding with Chico Tico-Tico and the vaqueiros of Fazenda da Jurema. Mãe Mônica died peacefully in 1875, the same year that saw the birth of the second of two daughters Antônio had had with Carolina Cavalcante, a cousin of Chico Tico-Tico's. In 1877, the great drought descended on the land: At Fazenda da Jurema, the Ferreiras' gunmen, Antônio Paciência included, fought with squatters who had resisted eviction from the banks of the upper Riacho Jurema. They had eventually been driven out, but to little purpose, for the creek soon dried up and the Ferreiras' herds had to be taken far up Rio Pajeú.

For Antônio, the seca had brought personal sorrow: Carolina Cavalcante, with whom he'd lived for eight years, died from disease; and a year after the drought, Chico Tico-Tico was knifed by one of the squatters they had expelled from the fazenda. Chico Tico-Tico's murder had had serious consequences for Antônio. Chico's oldest son, eighteen-year-old José — "Zé" — wanted revenge for the stabbing of his father. The squatter who had killed Chico Tico-Tico had fled the district, but he had a brother who was with the police in the town of Jurema, north of the fazenda. When this trooper attempted to arrest Zé for disobeying a town rule against carrying weapons in the street, Zé shot him dead. Antônio had witnessed the killing, and left town with Zé, but four troopers soon apprehended them. Shots were exchanged and a trooper was wounded.

Years later, Antônio would recall that day with bitterness: "Zé Cavalcante rode away like the devil was on his tail and didn't stop until he'd crossed the São Francisco into Bahia. Zé had warned me to flee, too, but I, like a fool, went to the fazenda and told João Montes Ferreira everything, just as it had happened. I was with him when the sergeant and his men came to the house. 'The law must be obeyed,' was all he said. 'Go peacefully, Antônio.' Ai, good Jesus, I didn't want to believe it, but it was true! He gave me to them, telling me not to worry: He would put in a good word for me at my trial. Oh, the son of a bitch! For ten years I'd done his dirty work for him, and this is how he repaid me! I told the bastard, my father, I'd eat cow shit before I opened my mouth to beg his help. I paid for it, though. The sergeant and his men knocked me senseless in front of him. Then they got the cow shit and wiped my face with it."

In August 1882, Antônio Paciência had been sentenced at Jurema to eight years' hard labor. One night eleven months later, he had escaped, fleeing south to the sertão of Bahia. He had crossed the São Francisco in the canoe of a fisherman fifteen miles below Juazeiro. A mile below the south bank where he disembarked was a tributary, the Rio Salitre, which flowed from deep within the caatinga. It was along the Salitre, two weeks after escaping the chain gang, that Patient Anthony found the sanctuary that was to be his home for the next ten years.

He had followed the Salitre south for two days. Toward sunset the second day, he had come to a riacho flowing into the Salitre: On the opposite bank of the creek stood the ancient ruin of an immense church. He had crossed over to it, intending to spend the night there, and was gazing up at the vine-choked pillars, the tangle of cactus that all but hid the altar, when he heard:

"Yes, mulatto, say your prayers. There's not much time left to you."

Antônio swung around at this calmly voiced threat, coming face to face with a dark, gloomy-looking man in a chimney-pot hat, aiming a bell-mouthed blunderbuss at him.

This was Antônio's introduction to Vivaldo Maria Marques. Then in his forties, Vivaldo was the son of a Portuguese who had immigrated from Setúbal, south of Lisbon, in the time of Pedro the First, with the hope of making a royal fortune. Instead, he — and later his son — had followed a trade the family had been carrying on for generations in the estuary of Setúbal: They were *salineiros*, harvesters of salt.

When Antônio finally convinced Vivaldo that he had no intention of invading his property, the salineiro took him to a settlement half a mile up the Rio Salitre, where some forty people lived in a cluster of hovels behind the riverbank. Dwellings, people, cattle, mules, dogs — all were covered with a layer of clay dirt, the substance from which Vivaldo Maria Marques and his family extracted a living.

That night, Vivaldo had seen the scars left by Antônio's leg irons, but he asked no questions about Antônio's past and plied him with meat, beans, and manioc.

For months Antônio dug clay, until the wet season came and the river rose. Then the dirt-encrusted community rejoiced as the rains washed off the clay and salt that clung to everything.

Often during those first months, as Antônio lay in a hammock too tired even to attempt to remove the clay coating his body, he had thought of moving on. But

Vivaldo had treated Antônio well. And besides, there was Rosalina.

Rosalina Marques, a big, strong girl with surprisingly delicate features, had been sixteen when Antônio met her in that year, 1882. She and Antônio became lovers during the first rainy season. Vivaldo had enthusiastically welcomed the match, for it made it less likely that the thirty-seven-year-old Antônio would desert him.

Vivaldo had been proven right: Antônio stayed, and by the late 1880's, he no longer dug clay but traveled with Vivaldo to sell salt at Juazeiro and in numerous small towns in the sertão east of Lagoa Grande. On one of these journeys in November 1890, a year after proclamation of the republic, Antônio and Vivaldo first saw The Counselor at Chorrocho, a town east of Juazeiro.

The gaunt anchorite had been with a small band of devoted followers as worn by fasting as he himself. In his blue robe, with his gnarled staff in one hand, prayer book in the other, he stood in the shade of a giant acacia.

Antônio and Vivaldo had listened to The Counselor's sermon that day, his terrible warning of a Final Judgment, with the army of Dom Sebastião risen to put to sword every sinner in Brazil. The prophecies profoundly moved them, so that afterward they stayed on and joined a group of men who sat talking with The Counselor. The backlands had been stricken by drought that year — a sign of God's displeasure with the republic, Conselheiro said. But, he promised, a day would come when Brazil would be cleansed of evil; the caatinga would become like a fertile garden!

Eleven months after their first encounter with him, Conselheiro had come to a fazenda thirty miles east of the Rio Salitre, and stayed three weeks. Antônio Paciência and Vivaldo's family, including the fervent Idalinas Marques, went to listen to him, for by then The Counselor's fame had spread throughout the region.

In fact, a profound religiousness existed in the sertão. Not a dwelling, however humble, lacked the image of a favorite saint chosen to watch over its inhabitants. The poorest pilgrims prayed to travel at least once in their lifetime to places like Monte Santo, just south of Canudos, and the grotto of Bom Jesus da Lapa. Above all, there was the awesome caatinga itself, where sons and fathers and their fathers before them had seen the rivers disappear and the earth die, a scorched temple where God scourged the unholy.

In 1893, when Conselheiro went to Canudos to build his New Jerusalem, hundreds of peasants who had heard him preach began to migrate to the holy city.

Early that year, Vivaldo and Antônio had crossed the caatinga to Canudos to sell salt. The Counselor had personally invited them to move to Canudos — for their salvation. When they decided to do this some months later, their move had been prompted by material as well as spiritual considerations. Year after year the salt clay at Lagoa Grande had been diminishing, until finally one morning in August 1893 Vivaldo, kicking over six tripods, announced, "We're finished here. We'll go to Canudos."

Having lived with Vivaldo Maria Marques and his family for ten years, Antônio Paciência accepted Vivaldo's decision without question. He was forty-seven years old, and where else was he to go with his family? Besides, he too had been impressed by The Counselor's prophecies. There were nights when he would lie awake wondering whether the world would end soon — whether men like João Montes

Ferreira, who had abandoned him like a dog, would be consumed in the fires of hell while he and those with him enjoyed everlasting peace at New Jerusalem.

That very month, they left for Canudos — Vivaldo and Idalinas and their two unmarried daughters, and Antônio and Rosalina and their two surviving children. Rosalina had had five, but three had died in infancy. Eleven-year-old Teotónio was the boy who had come to Antônio at the fire where he stood with the commanders of the army of Canudos. The last-born, also a boy, was but four months old in August 1893.

When they arrived at Canudos early in September 1893, one thousand people were living in the town. Over the next two years, the population had grown at a dizzying rate, the town spreading north of the Vasa-Barris and also east and west in barrios on the lands of an abandoned fazenda below Monte Favela. Antônio Conselheiro was supreme leader, with a council of four, responsible for military, civil, economic, and religious affairs. All lands, herds, and flocks were held in common, the head of each family allowed to keep only what was necessary for his table. The sale of cachaça was forbidden; unrepentant prostitutes were expelled; crimes committed in Canudos itself were severely punished.

One of the keenest advocates of these measures and a close advisor of The Counselor was a Spaniard, Xever Ribas, who had been judged an incompetent novitiate by the Society of Jesus. Xever Ribas had arrived in Brazil in 1888 and had roamed the backlands of the northeast as an itinerant scribe, earning his keep by writing letters for the illiterate. The frustrated black robe had been at Canudos since the beginning of the settlement, seeing in it a triumphant return to the days of the Jesuit aldeias.

The growing community had developed contacts with neighboring villages, selling their produce at the weekly fairs in Uauá and in other towns. With the Church, too, there had initially been peace, for Conselheiro made no attempt to perform holy offices, leaving this to an elderly curate who regularly visited Canudos from the nearby parish of Cumbe. But the larger Canudos grew, the less indulgent the Church authorities became, and in 1895 the archbishop at the Bahia sent two Capuchin friars to Canudos to order Conselheiro to disperse his flock. He had refused, and the Capuchins had returned to the Bahia with the report of an insurrection in the making.

Inevitably, Antônio Conselheiro's preaching against the changes brought by the republic had led him into conflict with the backlands chieftains. Bahia in the early years of the republic was in a state of political chaos as men who had wielded absolute power under the empire fought to assert themselves in the republican regime. In this tumultuous climate, opponents of the state governor, Luis Viana, were quick to point to his lack of interest in persecuting the fanatics at Canudos as an intolerable weakness; further, they accused him of harboring secret monarchist sympathies.

Politics aside, Governor Viana had received increasing complaints that Canudos was a nest of bandits, among them Zé Cavalcante, the son of Chico Tico-Tico. After fleeing Jurema município in 1882, Zé had joined a band of jagunço outlaws operating below the São Francisco, attacking remote vilas and robbing unwary travelers. Zé had reached Canudos a year later than Antônio Paciência, riding in with eight bandits of whom he was undisputed leader.

The outlaws at Canudos numbered several hundred, but by late 1896, an estimated twenty thousand souls were gathered on the plain, the majority of them sertanejos whose most serious offense had been to turn their backs on the poderosos de sertão. They were vaqueiros, squatters, agregados, the poor from dozens of fazendas and towns, not only here amid the caatingas but also from the green valleys of Pernambuco and Bahia. All had heard the voice of Hope calling them to the New Jerusalem.

☙

Gathered around the fire with the rebel leaders on June 27, 1897, Antônio Paciência listened as João Abade, the commander-in-chief, spoke about the next assault against the government forces: The camp on Monte Favela was to be stormed again at daybreak.

Antônio had emerged as one of the community's military leaders when the second and third expeditions had been sent against Canudos. Respected for his courage and his modesty, he had repeatedly proven himself in battle, often riding with Zé Cavalcante to ambush the government columns. Equally important, though, he had brought to the conflict his experience from the Paraguayan War. Several hundred veterans now served in the army of Canudos. They had directed the construction of a maze of trenches and dugouts along the perimeter of the town; the half-constructed church had been converted to a fortress.

Except for two black men, the group of commanders were caboclos and mulattoes. There were a handful of foreigners at Canudos, mostly poor Portuguese, but also a few Syrians, a family of Bolivian Gypsies, and the Spaniard Xever Ribas. The majority were sertanejos from Bahia and Pernambuco.

Like Antônio Paciência, several commanders were fugitives from justice. The general, as they addressed João Abade, was from a good family in the município of Bom Conselho, where Antônio Conselheiro had torn down the new republic's tax notices. He had served many years as a capanga for a priest landowner in Pernambuco, brutally enforcing his patrão's rights until even the normally inactive district police could not ignore João Abade's crimes. And there was "Pajeú," who had deserted from the Pernambucan police after slaying a fellow trooper; and João Grande, a black commander, fast as lightning with a knife, who was rumored to have slit the throats of six men; and old Quimquim, a jagunço-turned-bandit, with features strongly reminiscent of his warrior-Tapuya ancestors.

Over the months, the commanders had become consummate guerrilla fighters, for whom the caatinga provided an impenetrable shield. Around Canudos itself, thousands of rebel foot soldiers manned the trenches and dugouts, many of them interconnected, but in the field, the bands of rustic leather-clad cavalry, with the steel of their cattle goads honed razor sharp, had lacerated the earlier assault columns in lightning attacks. Whether longtime bandits like Zé Cavalcante or simple, honest vaqueiros who had left their ranches for the better life promised at Canudos, mounted on their fiery ponies they stormed through the caatinga seeing a hundred passages where their enemies were hopelessly lost. As quickly as they rode upon the soldiers they were gone, their war cries fading as the caatinga closed behind them.

Discussing their plans for the next day, General João Abade, a short, bow-legged man in his late forties, proposed that Antônio Paciência and two other com-manders lead one of these hit-and-run attacks: While the main assault was launched against the camp on Favela, they were to take two hundred men to the south to am-bush the First Column's supply train.

"We can't stop the Second Column," João Abade said, referring to the soldiers approaching Canudos through the sertão from the east. "We've cut them up badly, but they'll get through to Favela. Grab the supplies, Antônio. Artur Oscar will sit sweating up there, with five thousand starving men."

"We'll do it, General."

"What you can't bring back, burn."

"Everything, my General, except *our* ammunition."

The commanders laughed. The rout of Moreira César's expedition had sup-plied the rebels with several hundred thousand rounds. Two Krupp guns they had captured were in working order, but with only thirty-seven shells: The pieces were mounted to defend the most likely crossing point of the Vasa-Barris, to the left of the new church.

The meeting broke up. Walking up a steep street in the center of the town, Antônio glanced off to the left. Facing the open area behind the new church and headquarters building stood the house of Antônio Conselheiro. It was in darkness, but six women kept vigil outside. They were part of a small contingent of pious women — including Idalinas Marques — chosen as *beatas*. Complementing these "saints" was a male brotherhood, the Santa Companhia, comprised of eight hundred members who had taken a vow of poverty and guided the community's religious observances.

"God keep you, Counselor," Antônio Paciência murmured as he passed the women, an appeal for the health of the sixty-nine-year-old Antônio Conselheiro, who was ailing. With the escalation of the conflict to a full-blown rebellion, The Counselor had left the military operations to João Abade and the other commanders, meeting with them often but devoting himself to preparing the faithful of New Jerusalem for the apocalyptic battle that lay ahead — when Dom Sebastião and heaven's legions came to combat the army of the Antichrist.

As Antônio Paciência approached his house on an alley in the upper town, he saw Teotônio sitting outside the doorway, his back against the wall, his cheek pressed against the blunderbuss in his hands. He was fast asleep. Antônio stepped past him to the half-open front door and entered the larger of the two modest rooms. As he did, he heard a small voice: "Papai?" Antônio Paciência crossed to the hammock. "Yes, Juraci."

Juraci Cristiano was now almost four and a half years old. "I heard the guns, Papai."

He ruffled his son's hair. "You were frightened?"

The child did not answer the question. "Papai killed the macacos?" he asked, and before Antônio could respond, he added, "Teotônio says *he* killed one."

"We saw many macacos fall."

"I *was* scared, Papai."

Antônio held the boy close to him, his mind teeming with memories of the rage of these same macacos, his fellow Brasileiros, there at Curupaití where Policarpo had died.

⁊

The surprise attack had struck General Artur Oscar's men on Monte Favela like a shock wave, leaving 109 dead or wounded. What had been cocky regiments marching into the basin behind triumphal drum and bugle just hours before had been reduced to small groups huddled in terror wherever they could find cover. When, after an hour, it was accepted that the fanatics had withdrawn, an irate Artur Oscar had ordered his troops into immediate battle formation.

At 5:30 A.M., Clóvis da Silva was on a low hill to the right of Favela. The night cold having numbed his rheumatic pain and, at the same time, kept him alert since the 11:00 P.M. attack. With companies of the Third Brigade to protect them, the Krupps had been taken down the north slope of Favela to this hill a thousand yards closer to the Vasa-Barris. To the right of their position, on another eminence, was a second battery, with the Whitworth.

Clóvis stood behind his guns, holding a mug of steaming coffee with both hands; as he sipped the scalding liquid, he watched Major Lauro Correia prepare for action. His gaze moved beyond the Krupps, down past two other hills, and across the Vasa-Barris. A bank of mist along the river and the gray light above Canudos heightened the menace of the place. Clóvis studied the two towers of the half-built church: he could feel the eyes of lookouts upon him.

To the left of the Krupps was a defile with a stream, and opposite, a tabletop hill. Clóvis's eyes roved it, from south to north, searching every crevice, every outcrop that could hide a sharpshooter. As on the previous afternoon, he detected no movement. He looked down the slope of the hill where his guns were emplaced: Toward the defile, it was steep and rocky; toward the north, it sloped gently, with thick patches of thorny brush. Just visible below their position was the ruin of the fazenda, which an advance company had gone to secure.

Before moving his guns down here, Clóvis had had a private conversation with General Artur Oscar, who'd served in Paraguay for five years:

"For a time, there, I thought I was back in Paraguay," the general said.

"I heard them screaming at us like the Guarani," Clóvis replied.

"They have their mad dictator, too, who prepares them for sacrifice. Clóvis, we must bring a swift end to this insanity. Fanatics, monarchists, bandits, whatever they are, we must strike them hard and fast. It's not only a question of the army's honor; they challenge the very soul of the nation."

"I've long feared this, General. The republic I accepted, and gave Marshal Deodoro my full support. But the very night of November fifteenth, I stared into the gulf that separates us from millions of illiterate serfs and former slaves who understand nothing but orders from their master. In this godforsaken region, those orders come from Antônio Conselheiro."

"Most of our poor are honest and god-fearing; in time, the republic will pull them up. What we have, here, Clóvis, are degenerates. They want to drag Brazil back into the dark ages. They must be eradicated without mercy."

At precisely 6:00 A.M., June 28, General Artur Oscar gave the order for the eradication to begin.

In quick sequence, the guns of Clóvis's battery commenced firing, the first shells plowing up the ground beyond the new church. The battery on the right opened up, the roar of the guns becoming continuous, the cross fire reaching deep into the rebel citadel. After fifteen minutes' bombardment, when the dust and debris cleared, it was seen that the damage was negligible. Some mud houses were demolished; a few shacks blazed.

"What the hell are they shooting at?" Clóvis complained to Lauro Correia. "The praça at Uauá?"

The Whitworth's shells were exploding in the caatinga beyond the northwest bank of the Vasa-Barris.

At 6:30 A.M., the defenders of Canudos counterattacked — from the hills opposite the Krupp batteries; from out of the defile; from the direction of the old fazenda, where the advance platoons were overwhelmed.

The Nordenfeldts on the battery's left poured a stream of bullets into the defile. The Krupps' range was shortened to blast the fanatics advancing below. Men of the Third Brigade protecting the battery fought back, but their positions were exposed to a lethal fire from the hill to the west.

Major Lauro Correia was shot dead minutes into the attack, dropping instantly with his neck torn open.

Clóvis saw the gunners near Correia's body glance back in alarm toward the slopes of Favela. All around them, soldiers were falling back in that direction. The Nordenfeldts were holding back the advance from the direction of the defile, but the 7-pounders did little against the sertanejos swarming over the lower hills.

"So help me God, I've a bullet for the first man who runs!" Clóvis shouted.

To his right, the Whitworth stopped firing. Two Krupps were also out of action. But the support for those guns held a stronger position, with a line of communication open to the rear along a spur of Favela.

Twelve minutes later, Clóvis's guns began to fall silent.

"God help us," he said calmly, as a young lieutenant at the third Krupp gun fired their last shell. There was no hope of resupply, as the battery's ammunition was miles away with the mule train.

"Viva Bom Jesus! Viva Conselheiro!"

The cries rose from the foot of the hill occupied by Clóvis's guns.

Clóvis had had one of the Nordenfeldts moved in front of the Krupps. The machine gun, too, had little remaining ammunition. All along the battery now the gunners were firing down the slope with their rifles.

From the top of Favela and a dozen places below the northern ridge, where men of the Third Brigade had been regrouped, there was a continuous barrage against the rebels. But on the hill below Favela, Clóvis and his gunners were virtually isolated.

"Viva Bom Jesus! Viva Conselheiro!"

"Wait, boys! Wait till you hear the bastards breathing," Clóvis ordered the men at the Nordenfeldt.

Not one gunner had run away. What had kept them there was not the revolver in Clóvis's hand but the sight of their commander standing straight and unflinching as the bullets sang around him.

"Viva Bom Jesus! Viva Conselheiro!"

The Nordenfeldt mowed down the front-runners. The riflemen picked off others — left, right, and center. Still they came storming up the hill, screaming their holy appeals, cursing the macaco weaklings, hurling themselves at the thin line of gunners. The artillerymen on the extreme left of the battery took the brunt of the assault — trampled on, bayoneted, hacked to death with machetes. Jubilantly, the sertanejos began to drag away the 7-pounder.

Clóvis had emptied his revolver and fought with sword in hand, holding the ground in front of the first and second Krupps with sixteen men. Out of the corner of his eye he saw the rebels dragging off number 4. He did not hesitate. With a cry of rage, he broke from the fight and ran across the ground behind the other guns, shouting for others to follow. Nine men took up the charge with him; first to reach the enemy was a black sergeant from Santa Catarina wielding a double-bladed ax he had snatched from a rebel. He was shot in the thigh before he reached the Krupp, but this didn't stop him: With his first blow, he severed the lower arm of a caboclo clinging tenaciously to the Krupp.

The hand-to-hand combat at number 4 was ferocious. Clóvis swore at the top of his lungs that the rebels would not move the gun another inch. He was right. Minutes into the bloody clash, there was a tumultuous cry from behind them: Men of the Third Brigade who had fallen back toward Favela had seen the struggle and were advancing to help the gunners.

A bayonet charge by two companies of Bahianos carried them into the midst of the men fighting around the Krupp. The rebels were thrown back, those with a hope of saving themselves plunging down toward the defile.

Clóvis stood with one hand on the gun's wheel rim. A cadet gunner, a stripling of barely eighteen, knelt a few feet away, his hands trembling as he pulled cartridges from a belt across a dead rebel's chest and reloaded his own weapon. The cadet looked around as Clóvis said something inaudible to him, and was shocked when he saw the dark stain at Clóvis's abdomen. The colonel's sword hand, too, was red with blood from an arm wound.

"Oh my God, Colonel Clóvis — "

"Shoot, son! Shoot the devils!"

Five minutes later, several hundred soldiers of the Third Brigade were streaming toward the guns. Some men of the Third Brigade cheered the valiant artillerymen; others rained curses on the field of dead below.

The soldiers found Clóvis Lima da Silva on the ground next to number 4. Here he breathed his last:

"*Brasil . . . oh, Brasil . . .* "

Then, like his bandeirante ancestor Amador Flôres da Silva, the old gunner died. In the sertão.

Five miles to the south, Zé Cavalcante let fly with insults as his pony clattered down a breakneck slope charging toward General Artur Oscar's supply train. Antônio Paciência was close by, the two of them leading two hundred men whose fanaticism differed from the pious terror preached by their supreme commander.

Soldiers who stood their ground fought bravely but hopelessly. Many tropeiros, themselves sertanejos, took off into the caatinga, abandoning the broken line of mules. A third of the animals bolted and were lost to both sides. After fifteen minutes, the soldiers still alive made a run for it, back in the direction of Monte Santo. Behind them, Zé Cavalcante, Antônio Paciência, and others yelled triumphantly as they began to round up as many mules as they could find.

The sertanejos were still there at 9:00 A.M., an hour after the attack. Forty mules laden with supplies were ready to be led back to Canudos. Most carried ammunition, including a team hauling a cart with Krupp shells.

"Take the supplies to Conselheiro, Antônio," Zé Cavalcante said. "I'll be there later."

"I'll go with you."

"I need no voluntários!" Zé joked. "My men know how to handle this."

Antônio laughed. "I'm sure they do."

Zé rode with eleven men to a fazenda two miles to the south. Before burning down the ranch house, they executed the owner and his son. It was a punishment for having permitted the supply train to halt overnight on their property.

అ

On the night of June 30, forty-eight hours after the first battle, the army was trapped on Monte Favela, a huge beast run to earth in the caatinga, breathless, flanks quivering, ears straining. On the dark hills beyond, a deadly silence enveloped the slopes.

It was quiet on Favela, too, as soldiers began to settle in for the night. Except to the south, where a mournful wail rose from 817 wounded. A short distance from the field hospital, the caatinga had been burned and cleared for the graves of Colonel Clóvis Lima da Silva and 108 men.

At 8:00 P.M., a priest who had been called to a dying soldier emerged from a canvas shelter on the extreme right of the field hospital. He walked thirty yards and then stopped, looking in the direction of the fresh graves. After a time, he continued toward a tent he shared with two army chaplains, but stopped again. He changed direction and began to walk quickly to the north and the main encampment.

It was Celso Cavalcanti, thirty-one years old, looking plump now beneath his worn, stained cassock. Exhaustion marked his features; but his blue-green eyes burned with their characteristic fervor. Eleven years since the day he received Rodrigo Alves Cavalcanti's blessing to enter the priesthood, Celso had been attached to the archbishopric at Salvador. His superiors saw great things in store for Padre Celso, provided he curb his impatience and modify his questioning nature.

The archbishop himself had sent Celso to observe events at Canudos, a duty to be combined with helping the chaplains of General Cláudio do Amaral Savaget's Second Column, with whom Celso had marched from the coast. On June 25, Savaget had been eight miles from Canudos. Over the next three days, three hundred men fell along those eight miles as the column battled past ambuscades and through deep gorges where the fanatics waited to crush man and beast with huge boulders they had dislodged and sent against them. But the greater blow had been to reach Monte Favela and find the First Column battered and its supply train taken. With the three trails to the base camp fifty miles away equally perilous, the army sent to conquer Canudos was besieged.

At the main encampment, Celso Cavalcanti asked where the officers of a Second Column cavalry squadron were billeted, and was directed to a tent close to the headquarters of Artur Oscar and Savaget. As he walked there, Celso thought of what he would say to Hônorio Azevedo da Silva, whose father he had buried earlier in the day.

They had met soon after the column left the port of Aracaju, Sergipe. Major Hônorio was a stocky, powerful lancer, his military bearing leaving no doubt the profession of arms had been his first and only choice. It was his outspoken belief that civilian rule notwithstanding, the army had to keep Brazil on course: "It's simple, Padre Celso: the army must exercise the moderating power, just as Emperor Pedro did. Until the nation grows up, the army must be its guardian, as much to prevent the excesses of Frock Coats as to punish the rabble in these backlands."

Celso had taken issue with these views, but their arguments had been friendly; the major welcomed Celso's opinions, especially on the sertanejos, about whom Hônorio knew little. In all these years since his work with agents of the Termite Club, aiding runaway slaves, Celso had not lost his concern for the oppressed: He supported the Church's fight against the rash of fanaticism among the sertanejos, but was not without awareness of the intolerable conditions that drove the poor to accept the promises of false prophets such as Antônio Conselheiro.

On the march from the coast, Hônorio had mentioned that his father belonged to the da Silva family of Tiberica, São Paulo, and Celso asked if he happened to know his Aunt Renata's father, August Laubner. Only slightly, Hônorio had replied, but told Celso that his cousin Aristides Tavares da Silva had been instrumental in getting August's son, Mauricio Laubner, elected to the São Paulo legislature.

When Celso reached Hônorio da Silva's tent, greetings were exchanged, and two men with Hônorio got up and left. The major's batman, a former slave, had knocked together a table with pieces of ammunition boxes. An oil lamp hung from a tent pole, throwing a dim light on the major's face and accentuating his black mood.

For a while, with Celso sitting opposite him on the edge of a tin trunk, Hônorio reminisced about his father.

"The colonel and I had our disagreements," he admitted at one point. "He was a professional of the old school; he wanted the army out of politics. It wasn't easy for him, after Marshal Deodoro was gone. He took a desk job, convinced it was only a matter of time before they pushed him out of the army. But he acted with absolute dignity; he never said a word in public against his superiors. And then, suddenly, he was back in the field."

Abruptly, Hônorio lost his composure: "Damn these fanatics! The colonel stood for everything just and honorable in Brazil. *Damn* them!"

Celso reached out a comforting hand.

"Earlier today . . . there was a group on the Geremoabo road coming to join Conselheiro. We killed them." Celso started to speak, but Hônorio interrupted him: "Don't waste your breath, Padre. They were as guilty as the rest. They deserted the fazendas of men who try to keep order in these backlands. They came to live — and die — like savages."

"It's not so simple, Hônorio."

"No, Padre, it's not! The savages in our past were simple brutes of the forest. They ate each other and danced for the Devil in their isolation."

"The sertanejo, too, lives in isolation. But of a different kind. Spiritual."

"They're criminals, these sertanejos! They butcher innocent families, destroy fazendas, terrorize villages."

"Hônorio, we *abandoned* them in these backlands. Church, empire, state, the authorities at the coast . . . we turned our backs on this barbaric region. And because we did, our coastal civilization is impotent here. The sertanejo knows only two masters: the poderoso and the drought."

The rickety table shook as Hônorio rapped it. "Listen to me, Padre. I may not know the north, but I do know that the sertão is crisscrossed with cattle trails from fazenda to village, from the interior to the coast. The Rio São Francisco flows more than a thousand miles through the backlands. The Central Railway runs through the heart of the caatinga. How can you say the sertanejo is abandoned?"

"You can't imagine, Major, the vastness of this sertão," Celso began.

"Isn't it true that for centuries there's been movement here? Cowboys, priests, peddlers, slave traders, army recruiters — I could go on. The jungle of Amazonas is the place to look for a lost tribe, not here in Bahia."

"You don't know these backlands," Celso said flatly.

"I know the plight of the poor in Brazil, Padre. I stand for Order and Progress, remember — a total break from a past in which, rich or poor, we were pawns of the Braganças. I want a new society in Brazil based on reality, not the deranged vision of Antônio Conselheiro."

"We *all* want this, Major — a land free of the ignorance and impenitence that has allowed Conselheiro to take advantage of the sertanejos."

"No one took advantage of them. No one forced them to pack up and head for Canudos. They came because they wanted to be part of this nest of bandits, *isolated* in these hills, and thank God for it! Thank God this corrupt element in our society, these lunatics, *are* isolated in one place. And I will destroy them — the prophet Antônio and every one of his accursed tribe!"

ᘓᕲ

"Where's Teotônio?"

"I don't know." Rosalina, sitting on the ground with her mother, Idalinas, and one of her unmarried sisters, Maria, did not look up at Antônio Paciência as she rasped a manioc tuber.

Juraci Cristiano was playing near the women. Upon becoming a man, Teotônio had given his little brother his bag of glass marbles.

"He didn't come here?"

"No. Perhaps he's with my father?"

"I was there. Vivaldo hasn't seen him, either." Thus far, the battle-shy Vivaldo had managed to avoid the fighting by working in the town armory.

Rosalina turned her head sideways to look at her husband. "It's not the first time he's been missing."

"True." Antônio was worried all the same.

It was July 24, 1897. The mounted bands of Zé Cavalcante and others still rode far out across the caatinga; and paths to trenches and dugouts in the surrounding hills remained open. But the major effort was the defense of Canudos itself. For sixteen days following the attack on June 28, the sertanejos had kept the macacos pinned down around Favela, with enemy supply lines cut off. On July 14, the first substantial mule trains had got through from Monte Santo: Four days later, Artur Oscar and Savaget had launched a massive assault across the Vasa-Barris to the barrios southeast of the main town. After forty-eight hours of furious combat, the soldiers had been driven back with heavy losses, but they were on the hills below Favela now and had dug in near the ruins of the outlying settlements. In eleven days since July 18, Canudos had come under fire from nineteen guns, God's Thunderer now sited to shoot its 32-pound shells deep into the town.

The lower part of Canudos was in ruin. Entire rows of huts had been blasted apart. A large section of the headquarters building was demolished, and one wall of the old chapel was down. The new church had been pounded: One tower was damaged and half its south wall battered. The two Krupps had been moved here; the rebel gunners had used up most of their shot against the main assault on the barrios, and weren't eager to spend their last rounds.

The people of Canudos did not count their dead. Among the living, there had been several hundred desertions, whole families heading for the Cannabrava hills. The majority stayed, though many who still had homes in the lower town left to join others living like beasts in the open plain above Canudos.

The houses of Antônio Paciência and Vivaldo were in a section of the upper town that had taken little damage, though even here piles of rubble were growing. When the guns opened up, women and children would flee to the open ground above the town; if they were lucky, they would have homes to return to when the shelling stopped.

"I have to go back," Antônio said. He commanded the trenches opposite the barrios east of Canudos.

"If the boy comes here, I'll send him to you," his wife said.

"No — send him back to his post."

"If he comes . . . " she murmured with resignation.

❧

Teotônio had been at his post at noon when a dozen men led by a young jagunço arrived. They had received General João Abade's approval for a special mission against the enemy. When they left the guard post to cross the Vasa-Barris, Teotônio slipped into the reeds behind them. A quarter-mile beyond the river the sertanejos found him at their rear, but did not send him back.

The squad spent the afternoon working its way through the dry scrub toward one of the hills below Favela, where they waited hours for nightfall.

In the middle of the night, they started up the hill. They crept over the stony ground on their bellies, skirting a sentry post. They were 150 yards from their objective when their jagunço leader gave the order to charge: thirteen men and a boy rising up from the caatinga to hurl themselves forward against God's Thunderer, standing dark and silent in the distance.

Thin-legged and scrawny, Teotônio shot forward at the heels of the leaders. The jagunço and three other men carried spluttering grenades, but they threw them too soon, and the missiles exploded in front of the Whitworth.

The gunners asleep behind the 32-pounder leapt to arms. Elsewhere in the camp, scores of soldiers jarred awake by the blasts grabbed pistol and sword and closed in on the raiding party.

Teotônio was shot down, three bullets striking him in his chest and back. Twelve men fell with him. One sertanejo fled back into the caatinga, badly cut up but able to return to Canudos. He gave his report to João Abade, telling him his comrades were dead. Since he hadn't spoken to the boy Teotônio, he said nothing about him to the general.

ల

As he had for the past two nights, Antônio Paciência made his way to the makeshift infirmary to check among the wounded for his son. Vivaldo accompanied him. It was still unspoken between Antônio and Rosalina, but both strongly believed Teotônio had fallen into the hands of the enemy. Just moments ago, Antônio was told that a boy had been brought to the infirmary. Despite himself, he felt a surge of hope.

Of the two men in charge there, one was a curandeiro who specialized in native medicine, the other a man from Ceará who had worked in a hospital years ago. The Cearense, a caboclo known simply as Simão Medico, "Simon Medic," hailed Antônio Paciência as soon as he saw him and Vivaldo approaching. He was holding a lantern above a young mulatto with a stomach wound swathed in strips of rag. It wasn't Teotônio. "Better for your son, Antônio Paciência, if the end came swiftly."

Simão Medico's callous remarks reflected a prolonged resignation to suffering. Nineteen years ago, when he was twenty, he had fled the great Ceará drought of 1877-79 and gone up to Belém do Pará to join thousands recruited to work among the rubber trees of Amazonas. But, at Belém, Simão and five hundred other Cearense got jobs that promised far greater rewards than latex gathering: They were contracted as laborers for a railway being built in the jungle along the Madeira and Mamoré rivers. P. & T. Collins, of Philadelphia, U.S.A., had got a contract to build a 320-kilometer railroad to bypass the great rapids and allow landlocked Bolivia access to the passage of the Amazon. At Santo Antônio, the base camp, Simão Medico had worked in the infirmary: never a day passed without a third of the railroad builders hospitalized. After eighteen months, the project was abandoned with only seven kilometers completed, the firm of P. & T. Collins bankrupt. Of the five hundred Cearense laborers, three hundred died.

Simão Medico had stayed thirteen years in Amazonas. In 1891, he had returned to Ceará, finding the sertão just as he had left it in 1878 — in the midst of a devastating drought. "And I thanked Almighty God to be back. I wanted to fall on my knees to kiss this *dry* earth. I'm one of the lucky ones, Antônio. You think slavery has ended in Brazil? Go to Amazonas and see the life of the sertanejos of Ceará."

Simão Medico had arrived at Canudos soon after its occupation by Antônio Conselheiro. He was one of The Counselor's most ardent followers. Though perfectly lucid most times, he had been seen on his knees beside men who were already dead, beseeching them to utter revelations about Dom Sebastião and others they were embracing in Heaven.

When they left Simão Medico, Antônio and Vivaldo walked in silence for a while. Until Teotônio's disappearance, Vivaldo had rarely expressed his doubts about the rebellion, but in the past two days, he had become despondent.

"Antônio Conselheiro looks very weak," Vivaldo said, almost in a whisper. "If The Counselor goes, what's left, Antônio?"

"Others will continue the struggle."

"And in the end? When not a stone at Canudos is left unturned?"

Antônio continued to stare straight ahead. "Are you thinking of running, Vivaldo?"

"No, Antônio! Never! The Counselor promises a thousand years of peace on earth when the battle ends, isn't that so?"

"For those who keep the faith, Vivaldo."

Vivaldo stole a sideways glance at his son-in-law. *Perhaps*, he thought, *for those who believe in miracles.*

☙

Three nights later Vivaldo Maria Marques vanished, leaving behind his wife and two daughters. No one believed that the salineiro was a victim of the enemy. A distraught Idalinas submitted to the flails of her sister beatas and put herself on a fast that brought her close to death. It was atonement, she said, for the coward who had deserted Bom Jesus.

☙

Following the burial of Hônorio's da Silva's father on June 30, week by week, as they campaigned at Canudos, the major and his men underwent a transformation.

At first, the change was hardly noticeable: one cavalryman in a leather waistcoat; one with a pair of gauntlets; one wearing a leather apron; one covering his horse's quarters with a hide reaching almost to the animal's hocks. Each sortie beyond Monte Favela saw more men riding out in the armor of the vaqueiros, until by early September, nine weeks after the first major battle, Honório da Silva and his men were indistinguishable from their enemies. The similarity went deeper than the reddish leather carapaces they had donned: Most of the lancers were gauchos, the cowboys of Rio Grande do Sul, accustomed to racing across the grassy plains of the south. To a man, they found the caatinga loathsome, but they did not fear it. Repeatedly through July and August, they thundered between the walls of thorn and cacti: On some days, they were after wild steers, their rawhide lassoes snaking through the air; on others, they chased the sertanejos, riding far across the caatinga in search of rebel horsemen, the clashes with the vaqueiros of the dry lands taking on all the elements of a deadly personal duel between brothers.

The fourth expedition had come very close to repeating the earlier disasters. Half starving and short of water, the army had depended on the sertanejos serving in its ranks for the fruits and tubers of the caatinga; these and the wild cattle driven in by the cavalrymen were all they had had to subsist on for weeks until the supply trains began to get through from Monte Santo. During August, three thousand reinforcements had arrived, coming to replace two thousand men wounded or exhausted by sickness. In August, too, word came that Marshal Carlos Machado de Bittencourt, minister of war, was to take personal charge of the campaign.

೧

Late morning September 10, Hônorio da Silva and his fifty-four cavalrymen rode up to a fazenda in the Serra Vermelha east of Canudos. The owner and his vaqueiros, all armed to the teeth, were waiting for them. The fazendeiro gave Honôrio, a surly greeting, Hônorio asked if the jagunços had been there. "Yes, Major. Last night. The Devil himself winking at me."

"How many bandits?"

The fazendeiro, Luis Teixeira, gestured with his rifle toward the horses trampling the ground in front of his house. "Forty, fifty . . . as many as your men."

"You fed them? Watered their ponies?"

"I'm alive, no?"

"Careful, Senhor Luis."

"Major?"

"Your neighbors tell a different story."

"My neighbors?" Teixeira rolled his eyes. "God preserve me! Great liars, Major. Goat stealers."

"Which way did the jagunços ride?"

"I heard one mention the Geremoabo road."

"To Canudos?"

"No, Major. To the north."

Hônorio swung away from the fazendeiro and ordered his men to leave.

The cavalry troop had been scouring the caatinga west of Monte Favela for two days, in advance of battalions pushing north toward the Cannabrava hills to establish siege lines around Canudos. A similar operation was taking place to the west.

With a point of six riders galloping ahead as scouts, the main section reached the Geremoabo road two hours later and followed it east. Eight miles up the road, they were met by a scout who reported fresh tracks of a large body of horse on a cattle path leading north.

Strung out in single file, the leather-clad cavalrymen entered caatinga so thick it was impossible to deploy flankers. Each man searched the maze of thorn and cactus until his eyes ached.

Twenty minutes later, Hônorio's troops were forced to slow their pace, the cattle path narrowing to a five-foot passage between the walls of thorn.

Suddenly there was a crash of rifle fire behind Hônorio. The first volleys knocked down six cavalrymen.

The soldiers began to break into the caatinga on both sides of the path. Hônorio and five men, firing as they advanced, plunged toward a group of jagunços on their right. A man next to Hônorio was shot in the face. Another trooper screamed as bullets struck his chest. Hônorio and the others got through the thorn barrier unscathed: In a small opening, they fell upon the four jagunços they found there. Hônorio had emptied his revolver, but with his saber he killed one bandit swiftly and half-severed the arm of another.

Soon the jagunços, whose tactics were to hit and run, had had enough. Those still on their ponies scattered into the caatinga, leaving more than half their number dead or wounded.

Zé Cavalcante had already been shot in the chest when his pony fell. Thrown to the ground, he broke his leg, but managed to grab his rifle and drag himself into a thick patch of thornbush, where he was hiding when the fighting stopped. He could hear the talk of cavalrymen, and the single shots as wounded jagunços were executed.

An hour and a half after the clash, the soldiers rode off in the direction of the Geremoabo road. Zé Cavalcante left his hiding place at nightfall, moving painfully over the stones to the cattle path. He wanted to reach a water pit at the deserted fazenda four miles away.

Two days later, a party of his men who had fled into the caatinga found him just beyond the fazenda. The urubu had started on the face of Zé, leaving hollow sockets beneath his wiry black brows.

&

Canudos came under daily bombardment as the siege lines advanced east and west of the plain in mid-September. The towers of the new church were leveled to the ground, the walls blasted apart, the guns moved here smashed. One hundred sixty-seven rebels died at the church under the repeated cannonading, but others still went willingly to defend the huge pile of rubble where Antônio Conselheiro himself had labored to build the temple of New Jerusalem.

Concurrent with the incessant bombardment and the march to isolate the insurrectionists, government battalions assaulted the rustic citadel. Marshal Bittencourt was a cool, methodical strategist who set out to conquer Canudos house by house. By mid-September, they had overrun the eastern barrios. There the advance was halted within sight of the main praça and the ruins of the new church, which the sertanejos continued to hold as a fortress. The rebels had several trenches on two sides of the church, some facing the praça, others above the Vasa-Barris.

But, as the siege lines closed around them, the defenders also lost ground in other outlying areas: Government patrols destroyed groups of houses on the upper plain, driving survivors down into an ever-decreasing area.

João Abade and several officers were killed in these attacks. Overall military command passed to João Grande. Big John was quick on his feet, an expert at capoeira, the lightning-fast mock combat the slaves had often turned to deadly purpose.

Antônio Paciência, who had ridden with Zé Cavalcante in the past, had not left Canudos for a month. He was now in command of 570 men and boys in the trenches at the church.

&

As night fell on September 22, hundreds of women began to make their way to the open ground near The Counselor's temporary sanctuary on the west of Canudos.

Most walked silently along the narrow lanes, but some could not restrain their laments.

Antônio Conselheiro was dying.

Day by day, as he witnessed the destruction of his holy city, he had grown weaker, his skin jaundiced, his frame racked by coughing and vomiting. Plagued by dysentery, too, he had been confined to his cot a week ago, with Simão Medico and the curandeiro vying with each other to nurse him.

The crowd of women gathering outside The Counselor's house was radically diminished from two months ago. Numberless women and their daughters had died in the bombardments and in the trenches, where they loaded rifles and carried ammunition. The incidence of sickness, too, already widespread, was increasing as food supplies dwindled.

At the meeting ground, most women sat down or squatted, motionless, their eyes turned toward the small house where The Counselor lay.

Rosalina sat with her mother, Idalinas Marques, and Juraci Cristiano, whom Rosalina had not let out of her sight since the presumed death of Teotônio. She looked ten years older than her thirty-one years. Her long black hair had become infested with lice and was shorn close to her scalp; her face was puffy, exaggerating sunken eyes that revealed all the terrors that haunted her mind.

The beata Idalinas, barefoot, in a grubby chemise, sat praying out loud and rocking back and forth. For Idalinas, her husband's desertion had been compounded by the flight of one of her unmarried daughters with a group that managed to get through the encroaching siege lines; the other daughter, Maria, was gone, too — killed during an attack.

Juraci Cristiano sat pressed up against his mother, shivering in the cold night air. He looked at Grandmother Idalinas's wild eyes, her blue lips and black teeth: Her cries terrified him. She had told him that Jesus was going to throw the stars at the macacos; the end of the world was at hand. Juraci Cristiano stared up fearfully at the heavens.

No women were permitted inside The Counselor's house, where Xever Ribas was keeping vigil. He was joined by men of the Santa Companhia, three or four of them at a time coming to pray at a long table, where tall candles threw a wavering light on the images of the community's most cherished saints.

Antônio Conselheiro lay on a cot against the wall on the right of the room. A stench rose from his soiled robe; his beard was streaked with vomit; his hands were drawn up on his chest, his fingers clutching the crucifix he had worn at his belt.

Toward nine, The Counselor suddenly opened his eyes. "My brothers . . . my company," he said, in a quavering voice. His lips were dry and cracked. "Good Jesus sees our struggle." He turned his head toward the open door, listening to the women. "Why do they cry, Xever?"

"They're frightened, Counselor."

"No! Jesus loves them! Tell them, Xever!"

Xever Ribas looked as emaciated as the dying prophet. He only nodded — out of exhaustion and out of profound disappointment: His vision of the New Jerusalem as the restoration of a great Jesuit aldeia was shattered.

A spasm of coughing left Antônio Conselheiro gasping for air. Then he grew calm, and spoke once more:

"I wanted to help the poor, Xever Ribas. Wherever I went in these backlands, I saw them suffering from hunger — in body and soul. Who was there to counsel them? The poderosos who cared more for a stray beast than for these lost souls? The priests who turned their backs? The colonels who needed them for their private armies?"

The Counselor, interrupted by another coughing fit, continued with a rambling diatribe against the republic — "It extinguished the light of Rome! It brought the Antichrist!" — interspersed with his prophecies about the end of the world. Momentarily, he would stop talking, struggling for breath. Xever Ribas and the men of the Santa Companhia saw that death was imminent.

"The Antichrist has not vanquished Canudos," The Counselor said in a hoarse whisper. "In Heaven, ten times ten thousand swords are raised to help us . . . A brilliant host . . . our Santo Antônio carrying the sword of truth . . . our little Dom Sebastião in shining armor, coming to restore Eden . . . Oh, Xever! The trees bloom. Creeks are filled. Beasts are fed. Men thirst no more!"

Antônio Vicente Mendes Maciel, saint of the sertanejos, died with Paradise before his eyes, his vision of El Dorado promised to the poor of New Jerusalem.

&

Idalinas Marques joined other beatas moving breathlessly through the streets of the upper town. The saints had a message for every person they encountered:

"Praise Good Jesus! Antônio Conselheiro has gone to fetch Dom Sebastião. The Counselor is coming back with the infante. Santo Antônio is coming to save us!"

&

The investment of Canudos was completed on the morning of September 24. That afternoon, regiments of lancers began to clear the upper plain, a wave of men and beasts rolling down from the base of the Cannabrava hills. Major Hônorio da Silva and his company, galloping forward on the east, were on the extreme left of the long line of horse.

Hônorio's veterans tore through caatinga that daunted other troopers. They passed isolated houses destroyed by patrols that had earlier been detached from the siege lines. They covered a mile before they met the first resistance, from a band of sertanejos dug in below a small hill.

Instantaneously, the cavalrymen opened ranks, many beginning to fire from the saddle.

"The charge, bugler!" Hônorio commanded.

At the first note, the troop sped forward, screaming battle cries. But Hônorio remained tight-lipped, his dark eyes upon the blazing rifles ahead. A bullet ripped through his leather trousers, grazing him. His eye flashed to his leg, then back to the enemy fifty yards ahead. At the very last moment, Hônorio let fly with a mighty shout: "Viva Patria!"

The earthworks were heaped up four feet high, a useless defense against the murderous line of steel and fire. Hônorio and a dozen front riders clattered quickly over the sand and stones.

The sertanejos were outnumbered three to one. As the cavalrymen fell upon them, rebels who evaded the lance thrusts rallied. Small men they were, but they fought like giants. The rifles they had emptied against the chargers they used as clubs. The very stones of their earthworks they seized as missiles. Some leapt up bare-handed to unseat cavalrymen. Not one sertanejo attempted to flee. Not one survived.

The cavalrymen regrouped, counting six of their own dead, eleven wounded.

Hônorio da Silva rode slowly through the broken, blood-spattered bodies randomly strewn on the ground. "My God, what an enemy!" he exclaimed. "What an enemy!"

ↂ

At the army hospital behind Monte Favela, south of the hill where Hônorio's company clashed with the rebels, Celso Cavalcanti rose from the side of a soldier to whom he had given the last blessings.

Celso Cavalcanti had approached friend and foe with compassion during his three months in this unhappy place. He heard the confessions of the dying and prayed with them for Christ's redemption. Daily he visited the wounded and sick, even the captured sertanejos in the stockade, doing all he could to comfort them.

As the battles raged on against the rebels, the heat, the superstition that plagued men's minds in this isolation, Celso continued to agonize over what he regarded as a broader national tragedy — something he had once tried to communicate to Hônorio da Silva.

"Another sacrifice on the altar of madness."

Celso swung around at the sound of the voice. He knew the man by sight, but had not been introduced to him since his arrival ten days ago.

"Euclides da Cunha," the *Estado de* São *Paulo* correspondent introduced himself. "Padre Celso Cavalcanti?"

Celso nodded. Euclides da Cunha appeared to be close to his own age. The correspondent of the *Estado de São Paulo* wore a dark suit with two jacket buttons dangling by a thread; his pin-striped trousers were baggy-kneed and covered with dust; his bow tie had obviously been hastily stuffed under his collar flaps. He had high, pronounced cheekbones, a strong jaw, and unruly black hair, in keeping with his untidy dress.

"Who was he?" da Cunha asked, looking at the young volunteer.

Celso told him what little he knew: The soldier, a bank clerk in Rio de Janeiro, had been shot the night before during a rebel raid on the siege line east of Canudos.

"A year ago he had never heard of Canudos," Euclides da Cunha said.

"A sacrifice to madness, you said?"

"What else, Padre?" He smiled faintly. "I was told you would understand. 'Go see Padre Cavalcanti,' my informant said. 'He has some queer ideas about the jagunço devils.'"

"Major Hônorio da Silva?"

"It wasn't the major. It's not important. I want to hear your ideas." He looked at Celso keenly. "They taught me the science of war at the Escola Militar. This campaign defies military logic, but I daresay when it's over there'll be answers. I'm more interested in the human aspect — What caused Antônio Conselheiro and his twenty thousand fanatics to raise the banner of the Dark Ages on the soil of Brazil."

"Ai, Euclides da Cunha, my friend . . . I thought I was the only one who asked such questions."

They left the tent and strolled down toward a river that was now a mere trickle between walls of sand. There was a rush of words between them as each sought to learn the other's views. Born in Rio de Janeiro province, Euclides had spent some childhood years in the Bahia, his father's birthplace. About his military career, he said only that he had resigned from the army a year ago to work as a civil engineer for the state of São Paulo. "I'm not a pacifist," Euclides said at one point. "I took up arms to defend the republic once and I would do so again, but I abhor war."

When Celso offered his views on the rebellion, da Cunha, his face taut with concentration, nodded emphatic agreement several times.

"I agree they're an oppressed class, but is it their anger or their *abandonment* that led to the rebellion?"

"The two go together, I believe. Abandonment in this hell heightened their sense of deprivation."

"When I left Salvador, I thought I had a good idea what to expect. I was wrong. The farther away from the coast, the more I felt that not only was I entering a foreign land; I was journeying into the *past*. If the sertanejo is a pariah owing to his poverty and ignorance, it's because for three centuries we concerned ourselves with building up our civilization at the coast, abandoning a third, perhaps more, of our nation in these backlands."

Celso slapped his thigh. "Just what I told Hônorio da Silva! The sertão was left behind, ignored. The major didn't agree. The paths of the bandeirante and the Jesuit, the trails to the cattle markets, the Rio São Francisco — he insisted that all these provided access for the influence of civilization."

"Then how does he account for this barbaric rebellion?"

"He shares the common view: Canudos is a nest of criminals representing the worst element in our society."

"If we left Canudos believing this, ours would be the greater crime." Euclides da Cunha resumed his pacing. "It's interesting he should mention the bandeirantes."

"But not surprising," Celso said, smiling. "Hônorio belongs to the family of the old devil himself, Amador Flôres da Silva, the emerald hunter."

"These *criminals,* as the major calls them, are mostly the descendants of the bandeirantes. More than this, I see them as the very core of our nationality. The men of the backlands are the bedrock of our race, and yet . . . they're as alien to us as the Tupi were to the Portuguese discoverers. That young soldier's sacrifice will be worthless if our cannon fail to open the way for a new conquest of the sertão — a relentless campaign to draw the sertanejos into our national life."

❧

Late that night in the rebel-held section of Canudos, Antônio Paciência climbed out of the trench opposite the praça and went to sit alone thirty yards away, leaning against an undamaged part of the rear wall of the new church. He had a blanket around his shoulders, for the temperature had dropped greatly from the blazing heat of day. He heard gunfire in the distance — a party of Big John's raiders on a night attack against the macacos.

Patient Anthony looked at the Southern Cross blazing brilliantly above. Others were searching the skies for a sign of the return of The Counselor, but Antônio expected no miracle at Canudos.

Day after day, he had seen more people killed; more wounded carried to Simão Medico, who waited with strips of rag, sharp knives, and pots of salve from wild plants. The survivors stayed put, worn out by hunger and fear.

Antônio expected the final battle to come any day. In the trenches, he saw men who faced this prospect with joy, singing psalms and calling upon The Counselor for help. Jagunços as brutal as the late Zé Cavalcante prayed with love for Christ the Redeemer as they sharpened machetes and stuffed bullets into cartridge belts. There were boys of twelve and younger, as confused by the references to Dom Sebastião as they were by their elders' talk of Dom Pedro Segundo, in whose time, they were told, things had been better in Brazil. There were venerable sertanejos, too, who carried a rosary in one hand and a gun in the other; they listened respectfully as others spoke of Canaan here at Canudos, but their eyes revealed their skepticism.

At 5:30 A.M. Antônio was with his men in the trench when the cannonade began from a Krupp battery on a hill half a mile away. Twenty minutes later, in the wake of the barrage, fires were raging along several congested lanes.

Antônio left the trench and started home just before eleven. There had been only a brief exchange of shots with government soldiers in the ruins of the eastern barrios, but a mile from the trench, the smoldering ruins of shacks set afire this morning made him quicken his step.

He found Rosalina outside the house, squatting at an iron pot, adding edible wild plants to a gray mush. Idalinas was sitting at a table inside; the door was open, and a shaft of sunlight illuminated an unframed picture of the Virgin Mary on the wall next to her.

Juraci Cristiano was at a house at the top of the narrow lane. He saw his father and came running toward him. He was pitifully thin beneath his rags. Idalinas had pinned two religious medals onto his shirt, and told him not to fear the guns of the macacos, for if he died, he would be a little angel at the feet of Jesus. But Juraci was terrified all the same.

The house Juraci Cristiano had been visiting belonged to an aged caboclo, Plácido de Paula. Plácido himself did not know exactly how old he was, but he had been born in the time of King João of Portugal. Feeble, half blind, Plácido did not fight the macacos. However, his failing eyesight did not prevent "Woodcutter," as he was known to all, from working on an immense carving he called *"Gabriel,"* an eight-foot-high angel, which had begun to look remarkably like The Counselor.

Plácido had been a wood-carver all his life, specializing in figures for the prows of barchas on the Rio São Francisco, but *Gabriel* was his most ambitious project.

Juraci spent many hours with Woodcutter. Juraci would sit ten feet away, watching the old man work with his chisels and gouges. Sometimes Woodcutter stared at him, and it seemed as though he was about to say something, but he never did.

When Juraci Cristiano ran up to his father, Antônio Paciência gave a forced smile. He asked after Woodcutter.

"He worked all morning, Pai."

"Good. It's time he finished great *Gabriel*," he said. "Old Woodcutter is as brave as any man in the trenches," he said. "He hears the guns. He sees the explosions. Nothing takes him from his work."

"Where will we put *Gabriel?* We have no church."

Antônio saw Rosalina look up at them. "There will be a new church —"

"When the macacos go!"

"Yes, son. A church of Santo Antônio, bigger than the one they destroyed,"

"Ai, Nossa Senhora! Pray for this," Rosalina said suddenly. "Haven't we suffered enough?"

Antônio knew how much Rosalina feared the coming battle. "We've beaten the macacos before, Rosalina. We can do so again."

Juraci chanted, "Beat the macacos! Beat the macacos! Chase them, Pai!"

Antônio put a hand on Juraci's shoulder. "There's going to be a big fight, boy. Stay close to your mother and Grandmother."

"I'll be brave, Pai. Like Teotônio."

Antônio gripped the boy's shoulder so fiercely that Juraci winced. "Pai? What is it, Pai?"

Almost to himself Antônio said, "I will give my life. I will give anything you ask, Good Jesus. But spare the son of Antônio Paciência."

℘

As it began to grow light on October 1, 1897, the government guns boomed, every cannon emplaced on a mile-wide arc facing Canudos, twenty-one pieces in all.

The rain of shells screaming over the caatinga, blowing apart the remaining houses held by the fanatics, lasted almost an hour.

℘

Simão Medico saw a wall of fire race through the tinder-dry brush where two hundred wounded lay. The flames shot along hide shelters, trapping the incapacitated men below them; they leapt to the rags on the backs of men trying to outrun the fire on broken, rotting limbs. Some of the wounded tried to help their friends, frantically pulling at arms or legs, only a few with the strength to carry others beyond the inferno.

Deranged by the sight of his infirmary ablaze, Simão Medico, who in fits of religious mania had implored the dying to tell of Paradise, now stood at the edge of the flames, screaming incoherently at the victims. It was not heaven-bound saints he saw but devils scorched by the flames of hell. When a horribly burned patient ran up to him crying for help, he fled toward the caatinga.

Simão Medico escaped the flames, only to be shot minutes later by a government scout.

℘

Xever Ribas, though denied entrance into the Society of Jesus, was with the black robes in spirit and liked to think of himself as a Padre Mola defying the Paulista slave raiders at the missions of Guiará. But, during the past week, the Spaniard had grown weak and dispirited: The night before, he had decided to make a run for it. He had reached the bank of the Vasa-Barris without meeting an army patrol, and was just stepping gingerly through the low, muddy water when he stopped.

"O Good Jesus. . . . O Counselor!"

Xever Ribas saw Antônio Conselheiro standing on the opposite bank, the light of Heaven emanating from his blue robe.

The remorseful Spaniard had turned around, hurrying back to help the faithful.

Xever Ribas had safely reached the sanctuary that housed the community's saints, where he fell on his knees to beg The Counselor's forgiveness for having considered desertion.

He was still in this position minutes later, head bowed, lips moving in silent prayer, when he was buried under a pile of rubble two perfectly aimed shells had made of the small building.

✧

Idalinas Marques sat huddled in a pool of her own urine in a comer of the one-room shack, talking to Good Jesus and the saints. Rosalina was on the opposite side of the room, her arms around Juraci Cristiano, both mother and child struck dumb with terror.

No bombardment in the past had been as violent. Explosions rocked the ground and sent blasts of dust and smoke through cracks in the mud-and-reed walls and swirling around the hide cover that served as a door.

Idalinas's beseeching was cut short as she struggled for air in the rank and suffocating atmosphere.

It was the beata's last prayer. With a deafening noise, a Whitworth shell burst next to the house, demolishing the corner where Idalinas had been sitting. In that blinding instant, as tree-limb rafters gave way, the walls caved in and a shell splinter fatally pierced Rosalina's brain. The blast tore Juraci Cristiano from his mother's grasp.

✧

Under rapid fire from Krupp guns just across the Vasa-Barris, Antônio Paciência and his men and boys scrambled out of their trench, following other rebels who disappeared into the ruins of houses.

Antônio Paciência mounted a broken wall and climbed to the highest point. To his left, the upper ridges of Favela and other hills lay golden in the rising sun. To his right, it was pitch dark beneath the black smoke, except where sheets of flame leapt between the houses, the fires fanned by a stiffening northeaster.

His senses were numbed by the devastation and by the noise, the cries and shrieks rising from the stricken town blending into one hideous howl of agony.

"What do you see, Antônio? What?" The question was shouted from below him.

Antônio replied in a low, agitated voice only he could hear: "The end of the world. O Jesus, yes, as The Counselor warned . . . the end of the world."

✧

"Viva Bom Jesus! Viva Conselheiro!"

Here and there, the old battle cries rose hopefully, but mostly the rebels waited in silence.

There were perhaps 500 in the trenches and at the church, another 500 in the crackling, smoldering hell behind them. One thousand survivors from 20,000 at New Jerusalem three months ago.

Behind the praça to the east and across the Vasa-Barris to the south, 2,500 soldiers waited for the order to wipe out the last rebel positions. Another 3,000 stood in reserve. Most men in the ranks differed little from their enemies: They were poor, uneducated, untroubled by questions such as those in the minds of Celso Cavalcanti and Euclides da Cunha. For them, Canudos was a blistering, fearful Hades where 5,000 comrades had fallen.

The machine gunners opened the action. For fifteen minutes, they cranked the Nordenfeldts until their wrists ached, pumping three streams of lead across the Vasa-Barris.

"Advance, men! Advance!"

Whistles shrilled. Bugles blew.

"*Viva a Republica! Viva Brasil!*"

Fifteen hundred bayonets weaved between the scrub as companies ran down toward the Vasa-Barris. Simultaneously, one thousand soldiers streamed from the eastern barrios toward the praça.

From the rebel positions, a few shouts, a few cries from men hit by machine-gun bullets. Not much else, as dirt-ingrained fingers tightened around triggers.

"Hold your fire, men," Antônio Paciência said.

Every rebel leader gave the same order. Here, at the praça, Antônio and his men wanted the macacos to run deep into the square before the fusillade began. Closer and closer they came — 500, 450, 350 feet away — and still Antônio had not given the order.

"Fire! Fire! Fire!" Antônio shouted in that instant.

The fanatics had pulled sixty men out of the trenches and sent them to the ruins north of the square, where, immediately firing, they dropped thirty soldiers. Now the men in the square were exposed to a murderous cross fire.

The soldiers at the Vasa-Barris fared no better. They were easy targets for rebels in the long trench at the river, as well as for dozens perched on the broken wall of the church.

At his headquarters, Marshal Bittencourt remained outwardly calm, but warned his generals: "Three months ago the army promised victory. Brazil has been patient with us. If we fail today, we will be totally disgraced."

It was impossible to call on their artillery, because of the danger of decimating their own ranks. But there was an alternative they now employed: dynamite bombs.

Six bombs thrown from the canudos reeds blasted the trench at the river. Charging through the smoke and dust, a second massive assault wave hit the north bank of the Vasa-Barris and overran the defenders.

Antônio Paciência's trench was under heavy fire from the soldiers at the old chapel. Twice, soldiers had run forward with spluttering bombs, only to be shot down, the explosions of the devices they carried killing them and many of their wounded comrades nearby.

It was approaching nine o'clock. Antônio had lost a quarter of his men. To the north, the blasts were coming very close now, with rebels visible as they ran back between the houses. Antônio fired across the praça until his rifle was empty. He reloaded, but said to a caboclo next to him, "They want their victory? Good! Let them have it!"

Antônio gave a succession of sharp blasts on his whistle. Quickly and without fuss, for they had been expecting the order, the sertanejos began to withdraw. At the church, too, as the first dynamite blasts shook the south wall, the defenders began to leave.

At 9:15 A.M., soldiers swarmed across the praça and up from the Vasa-Barris. Ten minutes later, two thousand men gave a jubilant cheer as a soldier unfurled the green-and-gold banner of Brazil above the battered ramparts of the temple of New Jerusalem.

At 9:30 A.M., the Vivas were silenced. Three men of the first squad to probe the gutted houses behind the church were shot dead.

"For the love of Christ, can't the lunatics see it's over?" declared a general who had led the men at the praça. "Do we have to burn them out house by house?"

An answer came from out of the ruins:

"Viva Bom Jesus! Viva Conselheiro!"

The general sat down on a rock in Antônio Conselheiro's sanctuary as men were sent to fetch more dynamite bombs and cans of kerosene.

৩

It was hours before a break in the fighting allowed Antônio Paciência to check on the fires in the direction of his house. Three streets away from his shack, he found Plácido de Paula and Juraci Cristiano, who ran sobbing to him.

"Pai! Pai! Pai!" His small, narrow face was contorted with agony, tears streaming down cheeks streaked with dirt and soot.

Antônio knew immediately. He picked up Juraci and went over to Woodcutter, who was leaning against a wall.

"My house?"

"Yes."

"Rosalina? Idalinas?"

"Yes."

"Ai, Good Jesus." He felt Juraci's tears on his own check. "My boy? He was with you?"

Woodcutter, who had found Juraci lying outside the shack, gave no answer.

"Pai! Oh, Pai Antônio!"

"It's all right, Juraci. Pai's here. It's all right."

Woodcutter began to walk away.

"Old man" — Woodcutter did not turn around — "thank you."

Woodcutter moved slowly back toward their street, his gray head bent as his weak eyes searched the ground for obstacles.

Antônio put his son down and, squatting beside him, gently reminded the boy of what Grandmother Idalinas had told him — there was a place with Jesus for those who died at Canudos — but Juraci was inconsolable. After a few minutes, Antônio took the boy's hand and started up a street to the home of Bettina, a friend of Rosalina's, who had been widowed early in the war. Antônio hoped he would find her alive and be able to leave Juraci with her for the time being.

To reach Bettina's house, they had to go up a street parallel to theirs. So many shacks had been flattened in the area that Antônio could see his own, where his wife and her mother lay. And he could see Woodcutter, whose shack also had burned to the ground. The old man stood staring at what looked like a huge fire-blackened tree stump: great angel *Gabriel.*

Wading through the debris with Juraci following him, Antônio went over to Plácido: "I'm sorry, old man. It was so much work."

Woodcutter said nothing.

"God will punish them, Plácido."

"Yes."

Juraci stared with wide, wet eyes at the angel. The carving was smoldering, with wisps of smoke rising from it.

Antônio said that Plácido de Paula should come with them.

"Where?"

He told him about Bettina.

Woodcutter shook his head and, kicking ashes aside, started to make a place for himself to sit down.

Antônio and his son left quietly.

"Is *Gabriel* dead, too?" Juraci asked.

Antônio did not answer.

&

Twenty-four hours after the capture of the praça, Celso Cavalcanti sat resting, his head in his hands, in a tent at a field hospital half a mile south of Bittencourt's headquarters. Celso had been up all night with the dying and wounded, the last offensive having thus far cost five hundred casualties. At dawn this October 2, Canudos had again been bombarded, but the battle was at a virtual standstill. Soldiers were moving forward yard by yard, where each remaining house was a small mud-packed fortress, each lane barricaded with rubble and whatever the defenders could drag from shacks that had not been destroyed.

As Celso sat on the edge of a canvas cot in the ferocious afternoon heat, despite his utter exhaustion, unable to rest, he heard a commotion beyond the tent:

"They've given up! The fanatics have surrendered!"

Celso Cavalcanti pressed his knuckles against his forehead. "Thank God," he said fervently. He began to close the small buttons at the top of his cassock, his hands shaking with his sudden and immense relief.

But Celso was again bitterly disappointed, for when he went to general head-quarters, he learned that there was no surrender, only a three-hour cease-fire granted by Marshal Bittencourt at the request of the rebels.

"They're sending us their women and children," an officer told Celso.

&

Antônio Paciência and other rebels were escorting several hundred of their people toward the praça, where they were to be handed over to the government soldiers. Some children were naked; some women wore only a cloth around their privates, their breasts encrusted with dirt. Some walked silently; some wept; some begged water; some cried aloud for Antônio Conselheiro, that he should see them and carry them to Heaven.

They had known the situation was hopeless. No food. No water. And for those still able to fight, perhaps two hundred rounds per man.

As they had sat around their fire last night, the leaders had spoken about giving up. For some, surrender was unthinkable; they remained unswerving in their belief that they were fighting the Antichrist in a preliminary battle to Armageddon. For others, Antônio Paciência included, the best they could expect if they capitulated would be their return to a chain gang; the worst, which they considered more likely, a firing squad. And there were some, like João Grande, who contemplated flight. "Not one of us, if he took his chances in the caatinga, could ever be called a coward," he said.

For the women and children and those too old to do battle, the fight was over. Fourteen women wouldn't go, most because their men were still here, five because they refused to abandon the holy ground. Several old men, too, had chosen to remain rather than be taken prisoner by the macacos. One of these grandfathers approached the rebel chiefs as the refugees were about to be led out of the ruins:

"I won't go." It was Woodcutter, poor of sight and feeble in body. He had spent the night alone at the ruin of his house.

"You're a brave one, old fellow, but go. Get some peace in the time that's left you."

"I had my peace here," he said.

Joao Grande shouted "Old man!"

Woodcutter stopped in his tracks.

"If it's your wish — stay! Fight the devils!"

Woodcutter did not say a word but raised one of his big hands, with which he had worked so painstakingly on *Gabriel,* balling it into a fist and shaking it as furiously as was possible for him.

The moment the cease-fire had gone into effect, at 1:00 P.M., Antônio left his forward post and went to Juraci:

"Pai?"

Juraci could just see the praça and the soldiers.

"Don't be frightened," Antônio said, squeezing his shoulder.

"Macacos!"

"They won't hurt you."

"But, Pai . . . oh, *Pai—*"

"Go!" Antônio said fiercely. Bettina took the child's hand. *"Go!"*

Juraci burst into tears as Bettina pulled him away. Antônio stood in front of the men at the trench, his eyes fixed on his son. He shouted for Juraci to be good, to be brave, but the boy didn't hear him.

Then, as the rear of the column passed deep into the square, Juraci Cristiano broke away from Bettina. As fast as his thin legs could carry him, he ran between the macacos, dashing back toward his father. A soldier tried to grab him but missed.

"Juraci!" He grabbed him roughly by the shoulders. "Listen to me, boy! I know what's best. Bettina will see that the macacos don't hurt you."

"Pai . . . oh, *please,* Pai!" Juraci pleaded, sobs shaking his body.

"Stop it!" Antônio shouted. "For the love of God, child, *listen* to your father!"

Antônio was still struggling with Juraci and did not see the priest walking quickly in their direction until he was almost upon them.

"Let me take the child," Celso Cavalcanti said.

Antônio stared into those blue-green eyes. For an instant, he held the padre's gaze. What was there? Compassion? Agony? Sorrow for him? A *macaco priest!* he thought savagely, and looked away.

"I will see that no harm comes to him," Celso said gently.

Despite himself, Antônio sensed that this padre could be trusted.

"You hear the padre, boy?"

Juraci dug his head deeper into the stiff leather.

"Your son?"

"Yes."

"The boy's name?"

"He is Juraci Cristiano."

"Come, Juraci. I won't hurt you."

Antônio pushed Juraci away from him but still held his shoulders. "Haven't you always been brave? Like our Teotônio?" Juraci managed to nod. "Go with the padre to Bettina."

"His mother?"

"Dead." He showed no emotion. "Bettina is a friend."

For the last time, as Celso took a step toward the boy, Antônio told Juraci to go quietly. "Pai will find you, son."

"Stay with him," Celso said suddenly.

"It's too late."

"Merciful God, what hope do you have back there?"

"Take the boy!" Antônio said gruffly. "For the love of Jesus, yes — take my son! One day he'll understand."

"Pai . . ."

But Antônio was walking away furiously toward the other rebels, who were already moving back into the ruins. At the bomb-shattered hovels, Antônio turned his head. As he watched the priest walking toward the great crowd of women and children with his son, he gasped in horror:

"Oh, my God. *My God!*"

It was not Juraci Cristiano he saw there but Antônio Paciência, son of Mãe Monica, being led to join the sad herd of slaves waiting in the sun at the jurema trees.

❧

There were fewer than three hundred rebels, many of whom were wounded. João Grande and sixteen men crept away into the caatinga. The rest stayed, carrying on the battle lane by lane until they were driven back into the cordoned-off area with the last one hundred houses. Three days later, at 2:25 P.M. on October 5, the government soldiers stormed a trench, killing the last defenders, among them a mulatto and a venerable caboclo. They died side by side, these two fanatics who had answered the call of Antônio Conselheiro.

One was Plácido de Paula, Woodcutter, who had come late to the fight in silent anger after he had seen great angel *Gabriel* go up in flames.

The other was Patient Anthony, who had asked little of the great men of the earth and had got nothing. Antônio Paciência — Brasileiro!

c/s

New Jerusalem was razed. For two days and two nights, fires burned across the plain; before the earth cooled, the sky to the east was black with a legion on wing, the first flock of urubu coming to perch upon the ruins of Canudos.

In the interests of science, Antônio Conselheiro's body was dug up and his head cut off and dispatched to the Bahia, where it was to be probed for indications of madness.

c/s

Ten days after the battle, Padre Celso Cavalcanti was on his way back to the coast, jammed into the rear coach of a packed train with Hônorio da Silva and the correspondent of the *Estado de São Paulo,* Euclides da Cunha. Sitting on the floor in the space between the seats was another passenger drowsy in the stifling atmosphere: Juraci Cristiano.

After the conquest of Canudos, Celso had gone to inspect the rebel citadel with Bittencourt and his staff. When they reached the trench where the last defenders had fought, Celso saw Antônio Paciência among the dead.

The women and children were in a camp not far from the infirmary at Favela. Celso had gone there to tell Bettina about Antônio Paciência and to ask what would become of the boy.

"I said I would take him, Padre."

"Where will you go?"

"I don't know. My brother is on a fazenda at Bom Conselho, and I have an uncle at Uauá."

The boy wanted to know when Pai Antônio was coming to fetch him.

As gently as he could, Celso told him about his father's death.

Celso had told Bettina there was a church-run home for orphans at the Bahia, where he would find a place for Juraci.

"It's best, Padre," she had responded.

As the train clattered over the rails, Juraci Cristiano would occasionally open his big brown eyes and gaze on the dusty boots and shoes of the men on the benches. Padre Celso had been kind to him: He had given him a shirt and trousers at Monte Santo. Still Juraci was frightened and wouldn't look the macacos in the eye.

During the six hours since the train left, Celso and his two companions had lapsed into long periods of silence. For the past ten minutes, Euclides da Cunha had been staring out of the window, while Hônorio sat with his arms folded, a look of boredom on his face.

The train passed through an enormous tract of eroded land, and Euclides turned to the others: "Was it always like this? Entirely barren?"

"I can't imagine its ever being fertile," Celso said.

"It doesn't take much to deplete such soils," Euclides said. "The good grass cover and better trees deteriorate. The thirst plants conquer the land yard by yard, like an unwelcome invader."

Hônorio's heavy eyebrows shot up expressively.

"The caatinga, Major, not *human* invaders," Euclides added evenly.

Still, Hônorio retorted, "We did *not* invade; we came to restore peace."

"When it was too late."

"Too late?"

"Yes. As with past generations, we sat by complacently while behind our backs a maniac roamed the sertão. When we turned around to see what was happening in the heart of our country, it was too late: We were forced to meet barbarity with barbarity."

"Really?" The muscles on Hônorio's face went rigid.

Celso attempted to ease the tension: "Canudos shocked the nation. We can only pray it delivers us from age-old vices—"

"Yes, Padre! Pray it makes us focus on the reality of Brazil," Euclides said.

"What reality?" Hônorio asked tightly.

"Let's stop deceiving ourselves with foreign ideas. We're wasting our time considering theories and solutions that simply won't work for Brazil."

"Now you're saying something, Euclides da Cunha!"

Hônorio took this to be an indirect attack on the affectations of the Frenchified monarchists. "Europe loved our Pedro Segundo, they remind us. The most civilized man in the Americas! Does it matter that the Corte was Pedro's oasis, his little elitist haven? And the rest of Brazil — a desert. So! The republic ended that tyranny. What we have is a total break with the past!"

"Antônio Conselheiro and the sertanejos failed to realize this," Euclides said.

"Look, you two. I saw their poverty and ignorance. The plight of the sertanejos is a disgrace. But both of you — excuse me, Padre — are preaching to a man who's glimpsed a better future."

Euclides laughed softly. "Haven't we had enough visions, Major?"

"Not a vision, Euclides. I'm thinking of my cousin, Aristides Tavares da Silva. I tell you, when he's around, the air crackles with electricity. He and his uncle Firmino Dantas already made a fortune with coffee. It wasn't enough. Aristides is pouring millions into a textile mill . . . footwear . . .a road-building company."

Aristides da Silva's name was well known far beyond São Paulo, where he was playing a prominent role in the Paulistas' drive to modernize their state, already the richest and most powerful in the nation.

"Every time I see Aristides, he has a new scheme, with the Italians in his factories and workshops. I tell you, the Paulistas and their immigrants — one hundred thousand a year — they're going to make Brazil's motto a reality: Progress and Order!"

"Progress is essential, my friend," Euclides agreed. "But we must be careful that it doesn't carry us even farther away from the sertão."

"Agreed," Hônorio replied, "but those factories and industries will give us the means to educate our masses. Besides, the European immigrants who aren't afraid of getting their hands dirty set an example for our degenerate horde!"

Contempt for those of mixed race was common in Brazil at the time. Even Euclides, who defended the sertanejos as the bedrock of the Brazilian people, took a dismal view of miscegenation. "But can we hope to uplift the mestizo?" he asked. "He is unstable, restless, inconstant. He lacks the strength of his savage ancestors, the intellect of the superior race."

"My friends, you're contradicting yourselves," Celso Cavalcanti interjected.

"How so?" Hônorio asked defensively.

"You just said we've been too ready to accept foreign ideas and methods; yet you turn away from the very *reality* of Brazil you say you seek to address. And that reality is that the races have intermingled here for four centuries. What purpose does it serve to concern ourselves with the theories of Gobineau and other intellectually superior Europeans? If I stand in the Praça de Sé at the Bahia, I see around me men of every shade: blacks; whites; mulattoes; morenos; caboclos. This is the reality of Brazil: a new race is evolving here in the tropics, not a pale imitation of the Europeans."

Hônorio persisted. "What prospects are there for the future of this new race?"

"The future?" Euclides da Cunha queried. He looked down at Juraci Cristiano and said simply, "Perhaps he will know the answer."

✧

The three men had parted at Salvador in October 1897, Hônorio and Euclides da Cunha traveling on to the south, Celso returning to his duties at the archbishopric. Celso's detailed report of the rebellion had received the praise of the Church authorities. There had been much talk of steering the sertanejos back to orthodoxy, but in the end, Celso's report had been allowed to gather dust: With one priest for every fifteen thousand souls in Brazil, the Church was hard-pressed to minister to its town congregations, let alone reach out to the population of the sertão.

Celso had found a place for Juraci Cristiano at a Salvador orphanage, where the sisters were at first skeptical about training this barbarian waif who bore the name "Christian." But Juraci turned out to be a patient, obedient child, if withdrawn and melancholy, possessing a natural intelligence and ability.

Celso never forgot the remark Euclides da Cunha had made about Juraci. In January 1903 he wrote to da Cunha having just read *Os Sertões:*

"My dear Euclides, I thank God a thousand times over that there was one among us with the courage to tell the truth."

Da Cunha's masterpiece, written over a five-year period and published in December 1902, was a detailed account of the Canudos campaign, evoking the full horror of the conflict. Euclides depicted the stark reality of the caatinga and the lives of those who dwelled in the backlands. *Os Sertões* was a powerful plea for unity between seaboard and sertão; between the privileged class and the poor. With his pen, this soldier/engineer who had thrown down his sword achieved what no Brazilian before him had been able to do: He brought a generation face to face with the sertanejos, their own people who had been total strangers to them. And in so doing, he stirred the conscience of the nation and made it search its soul. It was the beginning of true Brazilian nationality.

ट⁄つ

"Padre Celso, look out of the window, please. What do you see?"

"Boys playing," Celso replied, beginning to smile.

"Yes!" The man made a sound with his lips, mimicking a spluttering engine. Celso laughed as the sound rose, filling the room. Abruptly the other man stopped making the noise. "They're possessed, I tell you. It's been like this for weeks." He pointed to a dark corner of his office. "*There* is the evidence — the handiwork of the young devils."

There were bits of wood and tin, pieces of cardboard, and what looked like a broken box kite.

"I tried reasoning with them. I threatened. I thrashed the worst offenders. Nothing calms their fever," the man continued to complain. "Morning, noon, and night it rages. I see them in class with their eyes glued to the blackboard. Their minds? Miles away! Up in the sky! Heaven knows, it's not the angels they see there! Senhor Santos Dumont may think he's done a grand thing hurling himself through the air of France!"

It was a morning in December 1906. The speaker, Brother Rodolphe, who himself came from France, was Latin master at a school of the Marists in Olinda. For weeks now, he and his fellow teachers had had to deal with an aviation craze among their pupils that reached its peak when two boys tried to glide off the roof of a dormitory on a contraption with wings of papier-mâché. The aviators had plunged downward into a mango tree, unhurt but with Brother Rodolphe below proclaiming a twenty-four-hour fast, the time to be spent on the earthbound task of writing out five hundred lines of Virgil.

Celso had returned to Recife from the Bahia in July 1903 and was an assistant of the bishop of Pernambuco. His visit to the Marists' school this December morning, the start of the boys' Christmas break, was personal: He was here to fetch Juraci Cristiano, who had been at the school the past year.

"Your boys are not alone, Brother Rodolphe. Alberto Santos Dumont has set all Brazil awhirl."

"It's unnatural. It's dangerous—"

"And it's grand! Your own France, all Europe, the *world* salutes Santos Dumont!"

Brazilian national pride had soared in the five weeks since Alberto Santos Dumont made the first recognized flight in Europe, covering 722 feet in his aérodromo, as he called his 50-horse-powered machine.

"And Juraci Cristiano?" Celso asked, wanting to know how the boy had behaved.

Rodolphe gave an immense sigh, whether of relief or heightened exasperation Celso couldn't tell.

"He gave you trouble?"

"Our Juraci? Oh, no, Padre, Juraci Cristiano didn't lose his head. He's a worker. Reads well. Writes well. His Latin . . . I'm satisfied."

Before they reached a dormitory at the end of the passage, they heard the excitement of thirty boys who were packing up their belongings. The instant Brother

Rodolphe opened the door, a wave of silence swept the big room.

"Juraci Cristiano?"

He was thirteen years old, tall for his age, thin, with his father's narrow-shaped face, deep brown eyes, and aquiline nose, and a light brown complexion from his mother, Rosalina Marques. Shy and sensitive, he greeted Padre Celso in a soft voice, while glancing apprehensively at Brother Rodolphe.

"Have you packed your things?" Celso asked after greeting him.

"Yes, Padre Celso."

"Then come, Juraci. We've a long way to go today."

Two hours later, Celso and Juraci Cristiano were riding the Great Western from Recife to the station at Jacuribe Norte on their way to Engenho Santo Tomás, where Juraci Cristiano was to spend the Christmas holiday, his first visit to the lands of the Cavalcantis.

The boy spoke only when addressed by Celso and sat gazing out of the window as the train passed through Recife's outer suburbs in the Capibaribe valley. Houses were encroaching on lands formerly occupied by sugar engenhos; some casas grandes still dominated small stands of canes, but in many places only the buildings remained, their upper stories visible behind high stone walls. Between the mansions, clustered among wild banana and other trees, were vast conglomerations of shanties. Beyond Caxanga, the tropeiros' halt where muleteers coming in from districts not served by the Great Western and branch lines still congregated, the countryside gradually took on a traditional appearance with ever-vast fields of cane and patches of forest, most of the latter secondary growth.

The train was pulling out of a station fourteen miles outside Recife when Celso put down a book he was reading. "Brother Rodolphe tells me he's pleased with you, Juraci."

Juraci Cristiano straightened his back against the wooden bench. His look became guarded.

"He was happy to see you attend your studies when the other boys went crazy over Santos Dumont's aérodromo."

Juraci Cristiano clenched his hands and anxiously bit his lower lip.

"Dr. Fábio and Aunt Renata will also be glad to have Brother Rodolphe's report."

But Juraci suddenly looked miserable. His eyes averted, he said, "Padre Celso must know the truth. I was with them, Padre."

"Really?"

"Luís and I—"

"Luís?"

"Luis Cardoso, the grain seller's son. Luis is my friend." He stopped, having great difficulty with this confession to Padre Celso, whom he loved more than anyone else. Often at night there were memories of Canudos: Pai Antônio; fire and smoke; great angel *Gabriel*. But the past was confused, a nightmare, the one sharp image Pai Antônio shouting that he must be a good boy. Then he had been in a train with Padre Celso, leaving for the Bahia. . . .

"What did you do?" Celso asked.

"Luis and I made the drawings, Padre."

"And where did you learn this, my little genius?"

"We saw it in a book, Padre." He looked at Celso's face with desperate anxiety as he awaited the rebuke. The great kite Luis and he had "invented" had been the same that had dumped two other boys in the mango tree. Their accomplices had not revealed their part in the disaster.

Celso Cavalcanti quickly picked up the book he had been reading. "You must explain to me, Juraci, how these things work," he said, holding the book up to hide his smile.

"I will, Padre Celso, I promise." Juraci looked out of the window again. Several times he thanked his patron saint, Antônio, for Padre Celso's lack of anger.

And Celso thanked God for this child who had come to mean so much to him. In the nine years since the Canudos rebellion, Celso for the most part had kept his charity toward the boy private; only with his Uncle Fábio and a few others did Celso share his joy as Juraci progressed further and further from the hopelessness of his past.

Celso Cavalcanti was one of the Church's few and foremost advocates of active charity — not to one orphan alone but to the masses of Brazil's underprivileged. To many, Celso was becoming, in the classic sense, a meddlesome priest. His conservative foes of the cloth were distressed that a priest of superior intelligence and from one of the noblest families of Pernambuco should lose himself among the mocambos and other hovels of the lower classes.

On this December afternoon as he rode the Great Western with Juraci, Celso's thoughts were not on the problems of his ministry but on his family, who were coming together at Santo Tomás for the Christmas season. Since his transfer to Recife from the Bahia, Celso had attended several such gatherings, the great clan of Cavalcantis traveling from afar to the valley where seventy-three-year-old Rodrigo Alves Cavalcanti presided over the Casa Grande. Rodrigo was an unrepentant monarchist who ordered black drapes hung around the huge painting of Dom Pedro Segundo on each anniversary of the emperor's death. Rodrigo regarded the republic as a farce created for the amusement of common people, and he showed acute displeasure when anyone forgot to address him as "Barão." This despite the fact that his oldest son, Duarte, who ran Usina Jacuribe, was one of those who had quickly gone over to the republicans. Now forty-nine, Duarte was a national deputy, a fact the barão accepted as a mere convenience until sanity triumphed and the Crown was restored.

Dr. Fábio Cavalcanti still had a thriving practice in Boa Vista. He was also a director of Recife's public health services, which, after making advances thirty years ago, had again deteriorated; epidemics broke out intermittently, especially among the fetid mocambos, where half the city's residents lived.

Celso was grateful to Fábio and to his Aunt Renata for their interest in Juraci Cristiano, whom they had first learned about from Celso on his occasional visits to Recife before his transfer to the diocese. One night almost a year ago, when he had gone to their house near the Passagem do Madalena, he'd met a visitor who showed great interest when Celso talked about Juraci and his father, Antônio Paciência, a mulatto killed at Canudos.

"Antônio Paciência? A tall man? Dark-skinned, almost like a prêto?" the visitor had asked.

"That's how I saw him."

"Oh, my dear Jesus! I knew him, Celso. We fought together, Antônio Paciência and I, in Paraguay."

It was Henrique Inglez, alias Agamemnon Andrade de Melo, still occasionally seen on the boards of the Teatro Santa Isabela. Henrique Inglez, with whom Celso had served in the Termite Club, helping runaway slaves. Senhor "Agamemnon Andrade de Melo" was a widower now, and there had been other changes in his life: Turning his back on Recife's thirty thousand prostitutes, he was enjoying a discreet affair with the son of a prominent senhor de engenho.

"Killed with the fanatics at Canudos? I can't believe it."

"It's true, Henrique."

Henrique had studied the elaborate rings on his fingers as he told Antônio Paciência's story, remembering how he and his comrades had plucked rings and other loot from the dead in Paraguay but saying nothing of this. "We came back together with the Fifty-third Voluntários. I never saw him again, after he went to find his mother. Ai, the poor man was so proud of the freedom he'd won. It wasn't fair — to die like an unwanted dog in the sertão!"

That night after Henrique left, Fábio had offered whatever help Juraci Cristiano needed. Later, at Celso's suggestion, Fábio had paid for Juraci's admission to the Marists' school. They had both worried about how the boy would fit in at the school, which was attended mostly by the sons of the rich. The past year had been difficult for Juraci. Brother Rodolphe had once contacted Celso, deeply disturbed by a lie the boy had been telling that his father, Pai Antônio, had been the chief of a town in the sertão, a powerful coronel whom everyone had to obey. Brother Rodolphe had wanted Celso himself to suggest a suitable punishment. "Do nothing," Celso had said. "The boy is telling the truth." Brother Rodolphe, who had come to Brazil after the rebellion, reminded Celso that Canudos had been the mecca of dangerous fanatics. "They were also Brazilians," Celso had said, walking away from him.

At 2:00 P.M., the train from Recife reached Jacuribe Norte. Celso and the boy were met by a carriage sent from Santo Tomás, and took the road into the two valleys following the narrow-gauge railway to Usina Jacuribe. Long before they reached the factory, the air reeked of sugarcane. Twenty years after the inauguration of the usina, a small village had grown up around it, with houses for the mill workers and their families and barracks for itinerant cane cutters.

As they rode in the open carriage, passing between the usina buildings, Celso explained the mill operation to Juraci, making the driver stop at the main building and taking the boy inside to show him the huge crushers. Juraci stood there open-mouthed, keeping close to the padre, for the noise in the cavernous building frightened him.

"Well, my inventor of aêrodromos, what do you think of this machine?" Celso asked when they stepped outside.

Juraci looked at the hillocks of cane in the mill yard. "All this will be crushed?"

"Everything you see and many, many tons more."

"There will be a *mountain* of sugar!"

"More sugar, Juraci, than you could ever imagine. Mountains of it, yes!"

They left the usina, the carriage rattling over the wooden bridge across the Rio Jacuribe. Celso could not pass this way without remembering how Slipper George and he had hidden below the bridge when Duarte Cavalcanti came looking for the runaways from Santo Tomás. Duarte had subsequently learned of Celso's involvement with the Termite Club, but had not said a word to their father; Celso himself had not confessed his part in the flight of the slaves, for even though so many years had passed, Rodrigo Cavalcanti would still be unforgiving.

Across the bridge on a hillside a mile from the river, a new house was being built for Duarte and Joaquina Nogueira, whom he had married six years ago after his first wife died. Duarte wanted to be closer to the usina, the Casa Grande being eight miles away; and besides, the mansion that had been home to six generations of this Cavalcanti clan over more than a century and a half was showing its age, with ever more effort needed to maintain it.

Across the Rio Jacuribe, the carriage road lay between endless blocks of cane. The Cavalcantis now possessed more fields than ever before; the usina had enabled them to consolidate their holdings at Santo Tomás and in this adjoining valley and to dominate areas beyond, forcing other senhores de engenho to sell up or become furnishers of cane to the factory. The old paternal relationship with the agregados was also breaking down; many squatters were gone from the valley, their houses demolished, their land given over to cane.

Several times, the carriage driver pulled aside to allow carts hauling cane to the usina railway to pass. Drawn by teams of white Zebu, these were not the only reminder of the past: Armed capangas sat half asleep in their saddles while overseeing the gangs of cane cutters. Reaching the valley of Santo Tomás, the carriage rattled past the old senzala, now occupied by former slaves and migrant workers with their families. Both here and at the engenho, which had been adapted for milling manioc, groups of women called out a blessing for the padre.

At last the Casa Grande came into view on the hill, flanked by royal palms and tamarinds. Dark shades softened the deteriorating whitewash and cast long shadows across the veranda and the patio in front of the chapel of Santo Tomás. Celso felt a surge of emotion. No matter where they went — Celso to the hell of Canudos, Fábio to Paraguay, Rodrigo to France — always they returned, even if only for a family gathering, with a sense of reverence for this old house, noble and triumphant amid a sea of green and gold.

Fábio and Renata were outside to welcome the carriage. White-haired, thin and stoop-shouldered, and wearing spectacles, Fábio looked all of his sixty-nine years. To this day, he labored long hours at his Boa Vista clinic and with the health authorities of Recife. His beloved Renata, sixty now, was even more beautiful, a look of strength, of independence, enhancing her lovely features.

As Celso embraced his uncle, Juraci Cristiano stood by the carriage, his hands clenched in front of him. "Juraci, say hello to Dr. Fábio and Aunt Renata."

Juraci came forward nervously. "Boa tarde, Senhor Doutor."

Fábio ruffled Juraci's hair. "Welcome to Santo Tomás, my boy."

Juraci greeted the senhora. Then he looked down, concentrating on his dusty shoes as Dr. Fábio and the padre began mounting the steps to the veranda.

Rodrigo Cavalcanti came to the front door then, and Celso raced up the remaining steps to hug his father. They spoke for a few moments before Rodrigo called out, "Boy! Come here! Let me see you!" Rodrigo knew about the orphan Celso had been taking care of, but this was his first meeting with Juraci Cristiano.

Juraci approached Rodrigo Cavalcanti on weak legs. The senhor barão was old, with huge silver whiskers and thinning hair on the top of his head. He was much bigger than Dr. Fábio, his brother.

"Padre Celso has brought you to stay over Christmas."

"Yes, Senhor Barão. Thank you Senhor Barão." Juraci twisted his fingers together.

"The padre tells me you're a good boy."

Again, Juraci gazed down at his shoes. "I'll be good, Senhor Barão. I promise."

Rodrigo put a hand on the boy's shoulder. "Come, Juraci Cristiano, let's go into the house."

Celso Cavalcanti hung back as the others entered, watching his father lead Juraci across the threshold of the Casa Grande. Celso saw the senhor barão come to a halt in front of the painting of Emperor Pedro, with his hand still on the boy's shoulder, the two of them gazing up at His Majesty.

Dear God, to think of this boy so nearly lost in the ruins of Canudos!

How often Celso had heard others speak of a better tomorrow — of Brazil, a land of the future. *My God in Heaven, our Brazil is a* blessed *land,* he thought. Pedro Álvares Cabral had sailed off course in 1500 and found a paradise, with a bounty to offer mankind. And yet, after all these centuries, the greatest resource, the real wealth, of the nation remained neglected: her people.

Celso knew that this was only one child, but he took great joy in imagining that others like Juraci Cristiano, now and in times to come, would find the opportunity to flourish in Brazil. The land of the future. Their land.

EPILOGUE

The Candangos

XXII

———⟡———

April 1956 – April 1960

*A*mílcar Pinto da Silva watched the twin-engine Beechcraft approach the Rio
Tietê from the southeast. The plane banked and turned as it crossed the river, passing
directly over the Place of White Stones, heading for Itatinga's landing field.

Amílcar da Silva, sixty-six, was a son of Aristides Tavares. A big, sallow-faced
man with deep-set eyes and a receding hairline, he gave off a relaxed, confident air,
which his clothes reflected: loose-fitting beige shirt and khaki trousers, beige cardigan
sweater with elbow patches, and an old pair of black shoes. Just visible at his open
collar — and suggesting his enormous wealth — was an elaborate antique chain supporting a four-inch-long gold Cross.

It was April 19, 1956, and Senhor Amílcar was in the gardens behind the
house. As he started back to the mansion, his eye caught a flash of scarlet and he
changed direction.

"Pedro! Paulina!" he called out to two great macaws basking in the morning
sun.

Pedro nodded his head and blushed with excitement — a characteristic of the
male of the species that amused Amílcar — while Paulina ignored him. He had
bought them at a São Paulo pet store a while back; but Dona Cora da Silva, disturbed
by their screechings and their scattering of seeds and excrement across the veranda of
the da Silvas' town house on the Avenida Paulista in the capital, had banished the
birds to Itatinga.

Senhor Amílcar and Dona Cora, his second wife — a handsome woman of thirty-five — spent two months every year at the fazenda, usually arriving at the beginning of the harvest in April. Four million trees now flourished in the terra roxa of the hill country behind the Rio Tietê. More than 2,500 people lived here in seven colonies, each a small village in itself. The majority of Itatinga's laborers were native-born peasants, many of whom had fled the dust devils of the Northeast; but the work force also included second- and third-generation Italians and a small number of Japanese.

Senhor Amílcar left the macaws and entered the mansion through the French doors to the main reception room. Here were possessions that had been in the da Silva family for generations, among them a two-centuries-old jacaranda table; a love seat that belonged to Baronesa Teodora Rita; a four-foot-high candelabra said to have come down from Benedito Bueno himself, a reward to the captain of the monsoons from a Portuguese fidalgo grateful for being transported safely to Cuiabá.

Of the portraits on the walls, most arresting were those of the white-haired Ulisses Tavares in the blue-and-gold uniform of the first empire; handsome Firmino Dantas, wearing a melancholy expression; Aristides Tavares in middle age, the set of his mouth revealing the aggressiveness with which he had expanded the family fortune.

Twenty minutes after the arrival of the plane, Senhor Amílcar greeted his son Roberto, thirty-six, and Raul Andracchio, who worked at the headquarters of the da Silva enterprises and frequently copiloted the Beechcraft with Roberto. Besides the coffee fazenda, the da Silvas either fully owned or held a major interest in twenty-four São Paulo-based companies, including textile and clothing factories, an iron foundry, and a construction firm. Three cattle ranches in Mato Grosso also belonged to the da Silvas, as did a small shipping fleet.

"So, Pai, Juscelino has done it!" Roberto da Silva exclaimed, moments after embracing his father. "He's gone and told Congress Brazil is to have a new capital."

Amílcar shook his head. "I heard it on the radio last night," he said. "There was talk, too, of a new pharaoh in Brazil."

Roberto laughed. Like his father, he had a tawny cast to his skin, dark eyes, and a robust, rugged physique, in the manner of so many of his bandeirante ancestors. The similarity ended at his jet black hair combed straight back, accentuating a high, broad forehead, and his small, thin mustache.

"A capital in the sertão?" Amílcar snorted. "Utter nonsense! Always has been." At his son's puzzled expression, Amílcar explained, "Listen, my son, Kubitschek is not the first to come up with this crazy idea."

As far back as 1822, the year Brazil made her break with Portugal, the empire's founders had talked of moving the capital from Rio de Janeiro inland, "Brasília" being one of the names suggested for the new city. In 1891, the year Antônio Conselheiro led the faithful to the New Jerusalem at Canudos, a small government expedition marched into Goiás seeking a site for the capital, and the area recommended in their commission's report lay within the location finally chosen six decades later.

In 1955, following the most honest and orderly election since the establishment of the republic, commitment to the "cause" of a new capital was voiced by

Brazil's new president, Juscelino Kubitschek: "Someone must dare to start this enterprise," Kubitschek had declared during his campaign. "I'll do it!" — This turned out to be no idle promise. The poor boy from Diamantina, who had put himself through medical school and completed the arduous if unlikely journey from surgeon to presidential nominee, was now embarked upon his most visionary project.

Amílcar, Roberto, and Raul were still discussing it over lunch: "Dreamers, all of them!" Amílcar declared. "A city built on nothing, rising out of nothing . . ."

The day before at Anapolis, five hundred miles north of São Paulo, Dr. Juscelino Kubitschek de Oliveira had signed a proposal to build a new capital within a federal district comprising 5,814 square kilometers in Goiás, on the high central plateau of Brazil.

"You're right, Pai, Brasília has long been a dream — "

"Another El Dorado," Amílcar interjected.

"No, Pai — a new beacon for Brazil," Roberto responded fervently.

"What a grand slogan!" Amílcar said, winking at Raul and Dona Cora, who had joined them at the table. "Juscelino couldn't do better. If our Roberto here ever tires of building things, as Brazil was *built*, not *dreamed,* I see a promising career for him in politics."

Roberto was undaunted: "Yes — a beacon, Pai." He picked up a saltcellar and dramatically placed it in front of him on the table. "Brasília!" he announced. He drew a line from it across the cloth with a fingernail. "Rio, six hundred miles southeast." Then he drew five more lines radiating from the saltcellar in different directions, and cited the approximate distances to outlying cities and frontier towns he had designated with pieces of cutlery: Salvador, Belém do Pará, Boa Vista, Rio Branco, Porto Alegre.

Amílcar studied his first-born son with pride, though they sometimes disagreed, as on just such issues as this one of Brasília. His other son, Lourimar, a lawyer, also worked for the family corporation, but he had neither the intensity of involvement nor the reckless daring of Roberto, who, trained as a civil engineer both in São Paulo and at Cornell University in the United States, today headed the da Silvas' construction company.

There had been a time, though, when Senhor Amílcar worried about the boy's ever settling down, for Roberto had been and still was obsessed with flying. As a very young child, he had been as fascinated with airborne machines as little Juraci Cristiano with Santos Dumont's aêrodromos. Roberto was only fifteen when he first took off alone from a dirt strip outside Tiberica. In February 1944, after his return from the United States, he had volunteered for the Brazilian Air Force. In October of that year, Roberto and four hundred men of the First Pursuit Group sailed for Europe, where they joined the U.S. 350th Fighter Group.

On missions in northern Italy, Roberto's squadron flew in support of a Brazilian land force of 25,000 men attached to Mark Clark's Fifth Army and deployed along the "Gothic Line." Hitler had predicted that the Brazilians would be ready to take the field against him the day Brazil's snakes took to smoking pipes; consequently, the Brazilian soldiers called themselves "the Smoking Cobras." The only South

American soldiers to go to war alongside the Allies, the Smoking Cobras — caboclo, sertanejos, black Bahianos, brown and white boys from Rio — triumphantly accepted the unconditional surrender of the first German division to lay down arms in Italy.

When Roberto da Silva returned home in late 1945, he had — to his father's surprise and immense relief — immediately concerned himself with the da Silva enterprises, notably the construction firm, which was into the business of building roads.

"Roads," Roberto said now, continuing to scratch intersecting lines across the tablecloth. "From north to south, east to west. Roads to unite the country, to draw our people together." The new capital, he declared passionately, would alter the colonial mentality, put an end to the inertia that kept Brazilians clinging to lands near the coast. Compared with countries like Peru and Chile, Brazil was vast indeed, but her settled areas were very little greater than those countries combined: There had been no Pacific to beckon the pioneers of Brazil west, as in the United States — only the massifs of the cordillera.

"In *this* sense, Pai, Brasília will be a beacon: Whether a man thinks of it as El Dorado or not, it will invite him to a new conquest."

"And instill in him new hope," Raul Andracchio added. Andracchio was in his forties, the descendant of an Italian family who had emigrated to Brazil in the 1890s. "There's a tidal wave of the poor swarming into Rio from the sertão. Half a million in the favelas." Taken from "Monte Favela," the word now described the squatter-shack settlements clinging to the hills and in the swampy lowlands of Rio de Janeiro. "We see the same thing developing in São Paulo. Open the door to the interior, provide land for these people, and we'll turn the tide."

Senhor Amílcar shrugged. "The Nordestino may want to make something better for his family out there, but tell me honestly, what Carioca is going to plant himself in the jungle?" He looked at his wife, whose family was from Rio de Janeiro. "Can you see your brother and his wife leaving the capital?"

Dona Cora, who had been shaking her head during most of this conversation, said that her brother Luis, an official with the Ministry of Education, would quit his post and go back to teaching. And her sister-in-law? "Ana would consider it Purgatory — worse than Siberia!"

"Yes!" Senhor Amílcar agreed. "A place of banishment."

"Perhaps that's what's needed," Roberto said mischievously. "With all due respect to Senhor Luis, life in Rio is too easy. There are too many temptations. A man needs incredible willpower to pass Copacabana and lock himself in a government building on a sunny day. The officials may feel banished, but at least they'll get some work done in Brasília."

"A bush capital," Senhor Amílcar retorted in English. "That's what the world will see. I repeat: It's madness. It's a luxury Brazil can't afford."

"Perhaps, Pai, it's just the opposite: It's a chance we can't afford to pass up. Kubitschek has said as much, and I agree with him: If we can do this — if we can build Brasília — we can do anything!"

Senhor Amílcar frowned. "Pharaoh Juscelino may just leave us with a mirage in the desert."

❧

Two years after the first bulldozers went to work on the dry red soil of Goiás at the site of the future capital, a group of peasants in the valley of Santo Tomás made their own bid to break with the past.

The man who came to be identified as their leader was a fifty-nine-year old cane cutter, Anacleto Pacheco, though it was in fact his son Raimundo who was the primary instigator of the agitation at Usina Jacuribe in the latter half of 1958.

Anacleto Pacheco had cut cane for forty-four years, stalk by stalk, twelve stalks to a bundle, between one and two hundred bundles a day depending on his health and humor. His recall of the past was invariably linked to some major event at Santo Tomás: the Flood (1927); the Burst Boiler (1935); the Pestilence (1947), when the cane fields were invaded by hordes of a small rodent, the *irara*. He had started cutting cane in Senhor Duarte Cavalcanti's time, then served Senhor Alvaro, the son of Duarte, until Alvaro's death in 1950, and now worked for Alvaro's sons, Senhor Durval and Senhor José.

Anacleto's family occupied two and a half acres of land in the southern region of the valley of Santo Tomás, for which they paid rent to the Cavalcantis. Anacleto regularly attended the weekly fair in Rosário, but he could count on one hand the times he had traveled farther than the town.

Pacheco's face bore a look of stolid patience. The caboclo had fathered twenty-three children with three wives, two of whom were dead; the third, Maria, a Bahiana mulatta, he had met at the Rosário fair eight years ago. Twelve of his offspring, too, had died, most of them in infancy. Raimundo, twenty-three, was the only one of his grown sons working on the plantation; four others had left the cane fields for the city.

On the first Saturday in September 1958, Anacleto Pacheco and his friend Bald Valdemar were sitting under the large mango tree in front of the cane cutter's house. The sun had not yet begun to dip behind the hills and already there was a fire in their bellies from cachaça. From time to time, Maria would come to the door of the mud-walled abode to eye them sourly. The short, chubby mulatta was fuming because Anacleto had come back from the usina store having forgotten the batteries for the radio. Three young boys, two of whom were sons of Anacleto and Maria, played outside in the dirt, kicking a soccer ball. *Futebol* was an obsession with them, as it was with the team from Usina Jacuribe, who battled opponents from other sugar factories with as much gusto as if they were members of the national team that had just this year captured the World Cup. As far as Anacleto was concerned, it was a bad day for Brazil when people went around chanting "Pelé! Pelé! Pelé!" like the name of a blessed saint.

It was getting dark when Raimundo Pacheco, who had spent the day in Rosário, came home. He joined the two men at the tree, where the conversation turned to the latest juicy topic at the usina: Senhor Durval had dismissed a book-keeper under what seemed to the workers mysterious circumstances. Some were speculating that the man had stolen money; others, that he had grabbed the breasts of the social worker, Senhora Xeniá Freitas de Melo.

Here, too, was an innovation Anacleto Pacheco did not take to: the "social worker." Maria Pacheco had attended a meeting at which the senhora told the wives and daughters of the usina workers that things would go better for the poor if they learned to help themselves. Senhora Xeniá was going to teach them how to keep their houses clean, and to sew their own clothes, and to weave tapestries they could sell at the Rosário fair. It was all nonsense, Maria said. Didn't she sweep the floor every day? Take the boys to the clinic for injections? And where was she supposed to find the time to make tapestries? But anyway, she added snidely, everyone knew that the social worker's mind was on more than the poor: Senhora Xeniá was weaving a "tapestry" of her own — a net to catch Senhor Durval's son.

Mention of the social worker prompted a remark by Raimundo: "There was a young white from Recife in Senhor Nilton's bar today. He says the senhora is wasting her time with a sewing school: The women have other, more important lessons to learn."

"Uh-*huh!*" said Bald Valdemar, making an obscene gesture with his fingers.

"Who was he?" Anacleto asked.

"A man named Eduardo Corrêa. He's with the League."

"Coming to Santo Tomás, eh?" Anacleto said, reaching for the bottle of cachaça. "They'll cut his balls off."

Anacleto had been present when Senhor Durval denounced the Ligas Camponêsas as nests of Communists who wanted to tear the very soul from a man. Three months ago, speaking to the workers at Santo Tomás on the occasion of the feast day of St. John, the senhor had warned that anyone attempting to spread the Red poison in these valleys would be thrown off the land in no time flat and with just the clothes on his back. Some peasants and migrant workers arriving for the cane harvest this September in other districts had had contact with the Ligas Camponêsas, but so far no member of the organization was known to have set foot on Cavalcanti property.

The Ligas Camponêsas had their origin in a mutual-benefit society founded four years earlier by 140 tenant families on a plantation forty miles from the coast — Engenho Galiléia — owned by one Senhor Oscar Beltrão. In late 1954 these tenants, with the help of a local judge, founded the Agricultural and Stock-Raising Society of the Planters of Pernambuco. Among its aims was the formation of a cooperative to buy seeds and implements, the building of a chapel, the hiring of a schoolteacher, and the purchase of coffins to spare its members the ultimate indignity of being buried as paupers.

Old Oscar Beltrão welcomed his tenants' initiative and consented to being honorary president of the society, which was launched with a festa at Galiléia. The senhor also gave permission for some trees to be felled for the construction of the chapel. But the first timbers had no sooner been hewn than Beltrão changed his mind: He withdrew as honorary president and, moreover, demanded the tenants immediately disband their society or face eviction from Galiléia.

Senhor Beltrão had been influenced in this abrupt decision by his family and by neighboring senhores de engenho who managed to convince him that the society was the vanguard of Communist subversion, which, if allowed to flourish at Galiléia, would spread an epidemic of sedition throughout the district.

The tenants refused to comply with Beltrão's order, and following repeated attempts by private enforcers to remove them from Galiléia, in January 1955 the society's officers took their case to Francisco Julião, one of the few Recife lawyers willing to represent the peasant and small farmer. Julião was also by this time a prominent political figure, having been elected a Pernambucan state deputy in 1954.

The forty-three-year-old firebrand saw in the society a grass-roots movement among the landless. As legal adviser to the organization, he promoted it in the state assembly and at meetings throughout the cane-growing region. Called simply "the League" by members of the society, in the mouths of its opponents it became "the Peasant League," evoking memories of a failed attempt by the Brazilian Communists to start a peasant movement a decade before.

The new Peasant Leagues, with their main platform of agrarian reform, spread rapidly until, by late 1958, they could claim to represent some fifty thousand peasants in Pernambuco and neighboring states. At Galiléia, the tenants were still on Senhor Beltrão's land and within sight of victory: Besides waging the protracted battle to prevent their eviction, Julião was pressing in the assembly for state expropriation of Engenho Galiléia with compensation to the Beltrão family, the plantation thereafter to be farmed as a cooperative.

As his father poured himself another drink, Raimundo talked more of his encounter with Eduardo Corrêa in Senhor Nilton's bar: "He says too that the League has much to offer the women, if only they'd listen. It's all here in this notice." He had dug into his trouser pocket and was unfolding a large sheet of paper.

Anacleto went into the house for a moment and returned with a lantern, which he handed to his son. "Well? And what does it say, this notice?"

Raimundo alone of Anacleto's grown sons had at least rudimentary reading skill. He cleared his throat and, scanning the sheet quickly, began to paraphrase:

"It says that when we got the republic, things were better for a lot of people, but not for the peasants. For them it was worse. We're no better than *slaves*, Pai – *that's* what this says! We work and work and work for the great senhores and still we have nothing."

"We have *this!*" Bald Valdemar cried, taking a long swig from the bottle.

"And our land, don't forget," Anacleto added.

"But it isn't ours, Pai. We don't own it; we rent it!"

"It gives us food — "

"Which we have to give to the patrão," Raimundo shot back.

"So! What would the League *have* us do?" Anacleto said.

"They would have us break with the system, Pai. How much would you say we owe the usina store by now, for instance?"

Anacleto shrugged.

"And we work ten, twelve hours a day, when we should be working eight, nine at most."

"You're talking crazy now, Raimundo," Anacleto said, shaking his head.

"I'm talking democracy, Pai."

"Democracy!" Anacleto suddenly smiled. "The man who gave you this — "

"Eduardo Corrêa."

"He's big? Strong?"

"For what?"

"Joazinho!"

Bald Valdemar guffawed. There wasn't a man within the district, he said, stupid enough to cross Joazinho Villa Nova, head capanga for the Cavalcantis. He, Valdemar Pires Fonseca, thanked God that in all these years as cart driver he had had no trouble with Joazinho. What the Leagues said was true: Life was tough. It would be tougher — *much* tougher — if one got on Joazinho's bad side.

"That's right," Anacleto said, his words beginning to slur together. "Senhor Eduardo can take his *democracy* somewhere else. We don't want trouble at Santo Tomás."

"He didn't say he was coming here," Raimundo said.

"Good! Throw away that paper and forget about him. Leave us in peace."

"To work for *free?*" Raimundo responded. He was referring to the *cambão* — the "yoke" — whereby one day a month they were obliged to labor for the Cavalcantis without pay as partial recompense for the use of the land.

"What's got into you?" Anacleto asked, peering into his son's flushed face.

"Oh, Pai, don't you see? The Leagues are right."

"This Senhor Eduardo — he's poor?"

"He has a car," Raimundo said. "But that — "

"Then what does he know about the poor? Has he cut cane? Has he fought with the Portuguese at the usina store? What does *he* know?"

"He says we're being cheated," Raimundo persisted.

"All gone!" Bald Valdemar announced, waving the empty cachaça bottle in the air.

"Help my friend," Anacleto said to Raimundo, glad to have an excuse to end this depressing discussion.

❧

The next morning when Anacleto Pacheco moved leadenly to the mango tree, where he wanted to sit very quietly and let his body come to life again, he saw the crumpled Ligas Camponêsas notice on the ground where Raimundo had probably dropped it. Probably. Anacleto was having difficulty remembering just what occurred last night. With a trembling hand, he picked up the paper. Unconsciously, he folded it and tucked it into his shirt pocket. He would think about it.

For three weeks, Anacleto Pacheco thought about the cambão. And Raimundo, too, brought it up, especially on the Friday when they rendered the yoke, cutting several hundred bundles, from sunrise to sunset. Raimundo stood between the rows of cane, wielding his machete and singing a song he'd made up about the present they were giving Senhor Durval — little drops of sweat that turned to pearls in the hand of the patrão.

Anacleto Pacheco began to understand. But when Raimundo even hinted at refusing the cambão, Anacleto shook his head:

"Santo Tomás is my place. I'm not stupid. I don't want trouble with Senhor Durval or Senhor José. I don't want Joazinho standing on my neck."

Now, almost a month after Raimundo's first mention of the League man in Senhor Nilton's bar, and his going on and on about the cambão, Anacleto decided to discuss the problem with a man he trusted above all others.

On the morning of October 4, also a Saturday, he borrowed Bald Valdemar's mule and rode to the clinic, several miles away. He waited in the shade next to the old engenho of Santo Tomás for an hour and more until the sick had got their medicine, and only then entered the building, pulling off his hat as he did so.

"Doutor?" he called softly.

There was a sound of a cabinet being closed and then the doctor stepped out from the surgery, into the front room. "Bom dia, Anacleto," he said, smiling and extending his hand.

"Bom dia, Doutor," Anacleto replied, quickly adding that he was in excellent health.

"Well, then, what can I do for you, my friend?"

In a rush, Anacleto began to tell the doctor about Raimundo's meeting with the man from the Leagues, Senhor Eduardo Corrêa.

Juraci Cristiano leaned against the edge of a table as he listened to Anacleto Pacheco, certain worries the old man expressed stirring up memories of his own concerns at different periods in his life. It was more than half a century — Juraci turned sixty-five in March 1958 — since Celso Cavalcanti had taken him from the praça at Canudos. Few beyond his family and most intimate friends knew that he had been there, the child of a fanatic called Antônio Paciência, for even now, trying to comprehend the tragedy of that place caused him almost unbearable anguish and he rarely spoke of it.

Monsignor Celso Caetano Cavalcanti, without whom Juraci's life would have been so different, had died in 1918, at only fifty-two, during the great flu epidemic. Already honored by Rome, Celso was nevertheless ready to descend into the fetid mocambos, where he labored among stricken thousands until the hour he himself was dying.

Twenty-five at the time, Juraci — supported and encouraged by Celso and Fábio — was in his final year of medical school in Salvador, and upon qualifying, he returned to Recife, where he worked for many years at the Hospital Português and at a Church-sponsored clinic for the destitute of São Antônio district. In 1923 he married the daughter of an impoverished senhor de engenho from Pernambuco, with whom he had four children, all but the last-born, Antônio, now married.

Juraci had always felt a part of the Cavalcanti family — that is, until Celso died and, soon after, both Dr. Fábio and Dona Renata, within a year of each other. He felt their absence all the more keenly when his increasingly radical views were cause for a nearly permanent rift between him and the archconservative Alvaro Cavalcanti.

In 1934 Juraci became an organizer of the Communist-backed Alianca Nacional Libertadora (ANL), which, with its motto Bread, Land, and Liberty, campaigned for cancellation of Brazil's foreign debts, nationalization of foreign enterprises, universal suffrage, and agrarian reform. When President Getúlio Vargas outlawed the ANL the following year, the militant wing of the Communist party staged bloody revolutions in Recife, Natal, and Rio de Janeiro, all of which were suppressed, but with great loss of life.

Juraci Cristiano, opposed to armed rebellion in principle, had been vehemently opposed to the insurrection. In the aftermath, however, he was arrested, along with the instigators, and imprisoned for ten days until Fábio's grandson Edson, a lawyer, secured his release.

Alvaro Cavalcanti had been outraged and wanted nothing more to do with Juraci, but eventually, with his own strong sense of loyalty to family members — in this instance, to Celso and Fábio, who had assumed responsibility for the orphan waif from Canudos — he relented.

Both of Alvaro's sons shared this commitment to family ties. Senhor Durval himself several years ago had asked Juraci to take charge of Santo Tomás's two clinics, and ever since, "the old Communist," as Durval privately called him, had been driving out to the usina from Recife each Wednesday and Saturday without fail.

Dr. Juraci, almost a carbon copy of his father, Antônio Paciência, stood patiently, arms folded across his chest, as Anacleto finished his story and held out the notice he'd carried around for weeks.

"What the Leagues say — is it true, Dr. Juraci?"

He glanced quickly at the sheet of paper. "Yes, Anacleto," he replied evenly, "it's true. These facts are well known."

Anacleto gave a small, nervous laugh. "'What does he know, the man in Senhor Nilton's bar?' I said to Raimundo. A rich man who drives a car — what would he know about the life of a poor man, Doctor?"

"No, Anacleto, it is true," Juraci repeated.

"My Raimundo, he goes on and on about the cambão. I tell him we don't want trouble at Santo Tomás."

"No one does, my friend. But your son is right: The cambão is a curse." He glanced toward the open window, beneath which he could hear someone sweeping the ground. "Since Rodrigo Cavalcanti's time," he added, thinking aloud. "They say the cambão is for the benefit of all — to fix the roads, clean the Jacuribe, repair dams — "

"Cut cane!" Anacleto offered.

Juraci straightened up. "Senhor Durval means what he says, Anacleto," he said, almost harshly. "He will not tolerate a League in these valleys. It would be a serious mistake to challenge him now. Change is bound to come, but it will be slow. Tell your son he mustn't do anything foolish."

Anacleto nodded, and waited for Dr. Juraci to say something more. When he didn't, Pacheco trudged out of the building and headed slowly toward the river, where he had left Bald Valdemar's mule. Had he glanced back, he would have seen Dr. Juraci at the window of the clinic, watching him until he was out of sight.

❧

Half an hour later, Juraci Cristiano was behind the wheel of his old Packard, climbing along the narrow rutted lane between cane fields as far as the eye could see. When he reached the large open area he was seeking, he parked, removing from his trunk the sandwiches his wife had made, a battered hat, which he stuck on his head, a three-legged stool, a portable easel, and a canvas. He'd come to this place many Saturday afternoons, sometimes staying till the shadows lay dark and heavy on the deserted Casa Grande of Santo Tomás.

After Duarte Cavalcanti moved to the new house near the usina, the Cavalcantis had opened up the mansion to accommodate relatives and guests gathered for some special occasion, but Christmas 1940 was the last time anyone had stayed here.

Juraci Cristiano had painted for a hobby as long as he could remember. His views of the Casa Grande were unique for their focus. Never had Juraci attempted to depict the mansion as a whole, convinced that what would be revealed was nothing more than a decaying, sad ruin. Rather, he trained his eye on intimate aspects — a section of façade mottled with shadows; a bench on the verandah, its blue tiles shot through with hair-thin cracks; the chapel patio, clumps of weeds growing between the stones and around the base of the Cross; the padlocked front doors.

He would sit there in the blessed silence, the air reeking of cane and, every so often, a drift of perfume from what remained of the untended gardens. He would look at those sealed doors and remember the day they opened for him.

Sometimes he would put down his palette, overwhelmed by the memories. He had so much to thank God for. And to his dying day, he would owe a debt of gratitude to the Cavalcantis.

Juraci could scarcely contemplate what his life would have been had he been left behind after the war of Canudos. But there were rare occasions when it entered his mind — when he felt a distance between himself and the family who had adopted him. Sometimes he would sit with them when they were together en masse at the usina: Senhor Durval, himself, and the older males in the sitting room, most of the women in another room, the younger people outside on the verandah with a few guitars. And there would be a fleeting moment in which he felt he did not belong.

As he sat down at his easel today, he experienced that feeling of alienation from the people of the Casa Grande. This time, it was thinking about Anacleto Pacheco that aroused it. The man had come to him for help and what had he said?

"Change is bound to come, but it will be slow."

How slow? he wondered. *A century from now? When Raimundo Pacheco and his sons are in their graves, with their callused hands crossed on their chests?*

Juraci Cristiano was suffering from a feeling of absolute frustration. Fifty years ago, he had listened to Celso Cavalcanti talk of hope, of change. Dear God in heaven, *when?* This was 1958, and in this valley it was still the same: the cambão; the capanga fitting bullets into his gun; the older peasant barely eking out a living and still not able to read. Even in the caatinga it was the same. There had been no rain this year, not a drop, the worst drought in decades. A quarter of a million *flagelados* — the desperate, the hopeless — were fleeing the seca and jamming the streets of Recife, and the same old remedies were being prescribed: more surveys, more dams, more hydraulic works. Relief for the scorched earth, yes; but the pain of those who lived there went ignored, undiagnosed.

క్య

Long before dawn on Friday, October 24, Anacleto Pacheco set out with Raimundo and five other tenants for Usina Jacuribe to set before Senhor Durval Cavalcanti their decision regarding the cambão.

Since his meeting with Dr. Juraci three weeks ago, whenever Anacleto sat under his mango tree with friends, there was some talk of the cambão.

Raimundo had again spoken with Senhor Eduardo Corrêa, who gave him a card with a telephone number in Recife where he could be reached in the event of trouble. The Ligas Camponêsas would take Senhor Durval before the magistrate in Rosário, Corrêa had assured Raimundo; they would use the law against Cavalcanti. Still, Anacleto had balked at the idea. What finally convinced him to approach the senhor was the return, on October 20, of José Cavalcanti.

It was well known among the peasants that Senhor José and his wife, Dona Clara, had sympathy for the poor. Dona Clara, a teacher before marrying Senhor José, had not only improved the two schools in the valley; it was she who had brought the social worker, Senhora Xeniá Freitas de Melo. And Senhor José, who had organized the usina's soccer team, was said to be planning a recreation hall for the workers.

On the way to the usina, the *"delegacão,"* as Raimundo boldly called it, was in high spirits. They joked about Bald Valdemar, who had climbed up on a bench last night proclaiming he was the patrão and informing them that the cambão was finished. Bald Valdemar had every intention of going with the delegacão, but when one of the tenants stopped by his house earlier, he found the cart driver curled up in a ball on the floor of his front room, snoring loud enough to bring down the roof.

◦◦

Coffee cup in hand, Durval Meneses Cavalcanti awaited them at the top of the short flight of steps leading to his veranda. He had come out here the moment one of his servants told him some men were walking up the driveway. Though not quite fifty, Durval Cavalcanti had an almost imperious air, as might be expected of one who held sway over the lives of 2,800 people.

At the bottom of the steps, the delegacão offered the traditional greetings and blessings. Senhor Durval responded in kind, then asked brusquely:

"What's the trouble?"

Momentarily, the peasants were struck dumb.

There was a sound behind Senhor Durval as José Cavalcanti joined his brother on the veranda.

At sight of him, the peasants broke their silence with a flurry of greetings. In their eyes, he was "softer" by nature than his older brother, whom they saw as *the* patrão.

As manager of the usina's financial affairs, which frequently involved him in protracted negotiations, primarily for loans, Senhor José was often called away from Santo Tomás. And when they were not gone on business, he and Dona Clara divided their time between their house in Recife, their apartment in Rio de Janeiro (to which they migrated annually at Carnival), and occasional trips to Europe.

Senhor José, who was still in his dressing gown, warmly acknowledged the delegacão but grew silent as his brother took a step toward the men.

"Well, Anacleto?" Senhor Durval asked, singling out the one he knew best.

"Yes, senhor. We came to see the patrão" — he paused, and his son nudged him in the ribs —"about the cambão."

"What about it?" Durval asked, with great calm.

Anacleto clenched his jaws and glanced sideways at Raimundo, who nodded encouragement. "The others, myself . . . we want to work for pay. If the patrão wants more rent, we will give it. But" — again he paused; again Raimundo nodded — "we will not work like slaves." This last word was barely audible, and Anacleto looked down at his feet.

"What is that you say, Anacleto? *Slaves? Who* is a slave?"

Speaking into his chest, Anacleto replied, "A man who works without pay."

Senhor Durval no longer looked calm. "You were *told* to come here. Who sent you?"

"We came by ourselves," Anacleto said, looking down again.

"You're lying, Pacheco."

"No, senhor. Ask them — they will say the same," he said, gesturing toward the others.

Durval turned to his brother: "The bastards have come here."

José Cavalcanti asked Anacleto directly if he had joined the Ligas Camponêsas. "No, Senhor José!" Anacleto replied instantly. "I swear it!"

"I tell you he's lying," Durval said to José while keeping his eyes on Anacleto. "How many others are in this?"

"No others, senhor. Just us. We — "

Durval Cavalcanti began to pace back and forth on the veranda. "How long have you lived at Santo Tomás, Anacleto?" he finally asked.

"*Me,* senhor? The patrão knows. I was *born* here."

"Which means you've always worked the cambão, isn't that so?"

"Yes, senhor."

"And suddenly it's slavery?"

Anacleto didn't answer.

Durval addressed his brother again: "I've warned them time and again: I don't want those Reds here. Not them. Not their priest friends, either. *This* is what their interference brings." He turned back to Anacleto: "Where did you meet the bastards? When did they come?"

"They *didn't,* Senhor Durval — God's truth!"

Durval shook his fist in the air: "I won't have a League here! Not on *my* land!"

Before Durval could say another word, Raimundo stepped out in front of the delegacão, and between gritted teeth he said, enunciating every syllable, "There is no League at Santo Tomás . . . *senhor.*"

Durval raised an eyebrow as he studied the brawny young man.

"There was a man in Senhor Nilton's bar," Raimundo continued. "Eduardo Corrêa, of the Ligas Camponêsas. He spoke to us. About the cambão. And about other things. He — "

"You see?" Durval said to José. "I *knew* they were lying!"

"No, Senhor Durval, you don't understand. By 'us' I mean us in the bar. My father and the others weren't there. Just me."

But Durval Cavalcanti had begun pacing again. "We've got to put a stop to this," he said. "Christ only knows how far it's spread already. Jesus, José! We *worked* for this land, every acre, and now these bastards demand that we give it away. Five thousand useless little plots. Two, three acres."

"It won't happen," José began.

"You're damn right!" Durval shouted. "They'll do it over my dead body!" Suddenly he stopped pacing and faced Anacleto and Raimundo. "You can leave now. Go back to the fields."

The peasants didn't move. "The senhor — "

"*Go!*" Durval ordered.

Without a word, the peasants started down the asphalt driveway, their hats in their hands.

"The Pachecos are finished here," Durval mumbled. "I'll send Joazinho to clear them out."

In the past, José's had often been the voice of reason that prevailed when tempers — most often Durval's — flared at the usina. What was less obvious to the workers was that despite Durval's quickness to anger, he was eager to bring reform to the valley, even if he didn't go along with all of José's "liberal" ideas. José knew it wasn't the loss of a free day's labor each month that so incensed Durval; it was the thought of giving up one inch of what he believed rightfully and forever belonged to the Cavalcantis.

Durval stormed back into the house and José followed him, keeping up a quiet but steady patter: "It could very well be true, Durval, just as the son said. You know Anacleto. He gets carried away sometimes. It could even be the cachaça talking —"

Durval suddenly wheeled around to face his brother squarely. "No!" he barked, his face bright red. "This time he's gone too far. They go!"

೪೨

Just after 10:00 the next morning, when Juraci Cristiano arrived at the main clinic at Usina Jacuribe, one of the Cavalcantis' capangas was among the patients waiting to see him. The man had a deep cut on his forearm. "What was it this time, Felipe?" Juraci asked, as he applied bandages to the wound. The man was forever getting into brawls.

"Pacheco's Bahiana bitch cut me."

Juraci's head snapped up. Be careful — that's all he'd been able to say: *Be careful, Anacleto.* Juraci just stared at the capanga, afraid to ask what had happened. He didn't have to.

"The patrão sent us to throw them out."

"Anacleto? But why?"

"The old fool said he wasn't going to give the cambão anymore."

"Oh, sweet Jesus . . ."

"Don't worry, Dr. Juraci. They're gone." Felipe then went on to recount how the head capanga, Joazinho, and eight men had raided Anacleto's house yesterday afternoon, taking all their belongings, forcing the family into a truck, and dumping them on the Rosário road, with just the clothes on their backs, "like the patrão said."

೪೨

An hour later, even though the waiting room still held a few patients, Juraci Cristiano climbed into the Packard and drove to the Cavalcantis' house. Senhor Durval was in Rosário, talking to their cousin, the chief of police, about the man in Senhor Nilton's bar. But Senhor José was there. He was reluctant to talk about the eviction of the Pachecos.

"It was my brother's decision," he said.

"Pacheco cut cane here all his life," Juraci responded, his face grim. "His father and grandfather, too."

José Cavalcanti sighed deeply. "I know life is hard for them. I've always tried to help where I could."

Juraci's expression softened somewhat. "But Anacleto asked too much?"

José nodded slowly. "Durval says if he gives in and abolishes the cambão. . . . What will the peasants demand next time?"

"No more than they've always wanted," Juraci answered. "To be treated with a little dignity."

José averted his eyes. "I tried, Juraci," he said in a muted voice. "Truly I did."

"Yes, José, I believe you did. If I find Anacleto, I'll be sure to tell him."

☙

The door of the house stood open. Inside, the dirt floors were littered with debris: parts of a broken chair; a deflated soccer ball, a burst bag of manioc flour. There were patches on the grimy walls where pictures had hung. A row of batteries was neatly arrayed on a shelf teeming with black ants collecting scattered grains of sugar.

Juraci Cristiano walked out of the house and went over to the lush mango tree, where he sat down on Anacleto's bench. As he looked back at the desolate sítio and the field of beans and manioc off to the right, he found himself thinking of the Casa Grande.

For centuries, the mansion had symbolized the conquest of these lands, and the senzala and the shanty the conquest of man. Today, the Casa Grande and the home of Anacleto Pacheco, worlds apart and yet inseparable, were both empty and deserted. But God knew, the way of life they both represented hadn't changed. True, José Cavalcanti wanted to improve the peasants' lot, and so too did Durval, hard-headed as he was, but within bounds determined four hundred years ago, when Nicolau Gonçalves Cavalcanti came to this valley. Anacleto Pacheco had thought it was time to throw off the yoke. Others told him he was wrong.

"Senhor Doutor?"

Juraci hadn't heard Bald Valdemar stepping cautiously toward him. "You were here, Valdemar?"

The cart driver's eyes misted over. "I saw it all."

Juraci put a hand on Valdemar's shoulder. "Did Anacleto say where they were going?"

Valdemar hastily wiped his eyes with his sleeve. "Raimundo thinks — "

"*Raimundo?*" Juraci's fingers tightened on Valdemar's shoulder. "He's here?"

"At my house," Valdemar said. "I was starting for the clinic. I saw the doctor's car coming. Raimundo, he's bleeding, Doctor."

Without another word, Juraci got up and quickly followed Bald Valdemar to his house, about a quarter-mile away. Raimundo Pacheco was sitting outside, his back against the wall. The right side of his face was lacerated, and his right trouser leg was torn and bloodstained.

"Good God, boy, what did they do to you!" Juraci exclaimed.

"I jumped. . . . From the truck."

"And your father, Maria — "

"No — I wasn't with them." Raimundo grimaced in pain, and Juraci sent Valdemar into his house to fetch hot water and clean rags.

"Go on," Juraci urged, when he'd determined that the young man's injuries looked worse than they were.

Raimundo told him that after leaving the Cavalcantis' house yesterday morning, the delegação had returned to Santo Tomás, at Anacleto's insistence, to cut cane for the cambão. They were in the field when a friend of Maria's, a servant in Senhor Durval's house, came to warn them that Joazinho and his men were about to force them off the land. Raimundo had raced to the house of Carlos Mota, one of the few cane growers in the area who allowed the peasants the use of his phone for emergencies. Not knowing how to work the instrument, Raimundo had given him Eduardo Corrêa's card and asked him to ring the number printed there. Mota said he'd have to wait, someone was on the line, but as soon as he could, he'd call.

It was while Raimundo was sitting on Senhor Mota's front porch, waiting to be called to the telephone, that a truck drove up with two capangas from Usina Jacuribe. As they were dragging him to the truck, Senhor Mota suddenly appeared, hands on hips, face dark with fury. Who did Raimundo think he, Carlos Mota, was — an idiot? As if he'd *ever* call the Ligas Camponêsas!

Bald Valdemar returned, and Juraci cleaned Raimundo's abrasions superficially, then, with Valdemar's help, loaded him into the Packard and drove him back to the clinic at the old engenho.

"Where will your family go?" he asked, when he'd stitched up the gash on Raimundo's cheek.

"To my half-brother Pedro's place near Jeremoaba, I'm pretty sure. He keeps goats in the caatinga."

Juraci had just started on Raimundo's leg wound when they came — three capangas in a jeep, among them Joazinho Villa Nova. The head enforcer's flabby cheeks, bulbous nose, and thick, round spectacles belied his viciousness. He had never actually killed a man, though the peasants spoke of at least ten sent to their graves by Joazinho, a reputation the capanga did nothing to discourage. He had murdered no one, but not a few had wished they were dead before he was through hammering them for some offense — cheekiness to their overseer, perhaps, or purloining sugar from the usina store. Durval Cavalcanti set strict guidelines for his capangas' behavior, but behind his back, they swaggered around and struck out brutally at will.

"Bom dia, Dr. Juraci," Joazinho said cheerfully from the doorway of the clinic.

Juraci Cristiano was in the surgery behind the front room, but he'd heard the jeep arrive and the capangas laughing.

"O Mother of Mercy, Santo Antônio!" Raimundo gasped, his body going rigid with fright. Juraci told him to stay calm.

"Senhor Doutor?" Joazinho called, heading for the surgery.

Juraci cut him off in the front room. "He's in my care," he said icily, offering the capanga no greeting.

In a soft voice, Joazinho replied, "Dr. Juraci must understand, the patrão wishes to talk with him."

"He stays here."

Joazinho's eyes flashed behind his thick lenses. "The doctor is making it difficult."

Juraci involuntarily raised a fist. "For the love of God, man, what more do you want! The Pachecos are gone! Forty-four years cutting cane in this valley and all the old man has to show for it are the bruises one of your brutes gave his wife!"

"She cut Felipe," Joazinho said defensively.

Juraci lowered his voice to a whisper, but his eyes had narrowed and he was trembling with rage. "Get out, damn you!"

"Very well," Joazinho said, backing out of the room. "Very well, Senhor Doutor."

The capanga didn't intend to give up this easily. He dared not put a finger on the doctor — there'd be hell to pay from Senhor Durval — but he *wanted* Pacheco. His men had become laughingstocks after Raimundo's escape.

As Joazinho stood at the jeep, talking over the problem with his cohorts, he espied Senhor Durval Cavalcanti's car coming down the road that led into the valley from Rosário, and turning off toward the old engenho. "Aha!" he exclaimed, with a jubilant grin. "Now we have him!"

Minutes later, Durval Cavalcanti walked into the surgery.

"Where did you find him?" he asked Juraci.

"Does it matter?"

Raimundo Pacheco was sitting on the edge of an iron bed. His head was bowed, his eyes on the floor.

Durval looked at him with genuine sympathy. "Is he badly hurt?" he asked.

"It could have been worse."

"You see now, Raimundo, the trouble the Leagues bring. Your father has lost everything."

"Yes, Senhor Durval," Raimundo said, his head still bowed.

"Bastards!" Durval said. "Old Anacleto was a good man."

"Yes, Durval," Juraci Cristiano said. "And he would have continued to be, here at Santo Tomás."

"I know what you think of the eviction. I was saying to myself as I drove back from Rosário: Dr. Juraci wouldn't be unhappy to see the Ligas Camponêsas haul me before the court in Rosário on charges of persecuting my peasants. Well, I don't see it that way. I have a right to protect my property."

"I can't speak for the Ligas, Durval."

"What about the party, then, Juraci? Your old comrades have their hands full, trying to fill the peasants' heads with Bolshevik theory. We're not going to sit with folded arms while a swarm of *pamphliteiros* invades the countryside spreading propaganda to turn the peasants against us."

"These people don't need to be told by outsiders that they're suffering."

"When they find their voice, I'll listen."

"Like you listened to Anacleto Pacheco?"

For a moment, Durval Cavalcanti seemed about to explode. He exhaled noisily through his nostrils. Then, unexpectedly, he relaxed. There was even a faint smile on his lips. "Ai, Juraci . . . you have your views, I have mine." He tapped Raimundo on the shoulder, catching the young man's eye. "I'm sorry it was your family. I can think of a few others I'd much rather have seen go. . . . No, Juraci, don't say anything; you won't change my mind. Let them keep opening up the west. There's land enough there to accommodate the landless a thousand times over. But I tell you God saw fit to give the Cavalcantis these valleys, and I intend to keep them, my friend."

This was Durval Cavalcanti's last word on the matter. When Juraci Cristiano walked him to his car a few minutes later, Joazinho Villa Nova scrambled forward like an eager terrier.

"You can go home, Joazinho," Durval told him. "Dr. Juraci is taking care of him."

"As the patrão says," Joazinho responded stiffly.

☙

Half an hour later, Juraci was guiding the old Packard between the hills on the south end of the valley. Raimundo had accepted his offer of a room in his house in Recife until his leg was better and he could catch up with his family.

"It's not much of a place, the caatinga where your half-brother keeps his goats," Juraci said lightly, hoping to convince the young Pacheco to remain in Recife.

"Oh, I won't stay there. I just want to see my family before I go."

Juraci looked at him quickly. "Go?"

"With the *pau-de-arara*." In the "parrot's perch," roosted in the back of a truck, a man could ride for a thousand miles and more to areas where there was work — and hope.

"To São Paulo?" Juraci asked.

"No, Dr. Juraci. Brasília! That's where the jobs are."

The Packard reached the top of the incline. Raimundo Pacheco turned his head sideways, wincing with pain, to look for the last time at the valley where he had been born. He gazed across those rolling green acres, with the clumps of forest, the small groups of laborers' houses, the Casa Grande.

Juraci Cristiano, who had come from a place far from this lovely valley, saw Raimundo glancing back at Santo Tomás.

"Yes, son," he said softly. "For the Cavalcantis, this is Canaan."

☙

Late afternoon on March 27, 1959, a thousand miles west of Santo Tomás at a construction camp deep in the rain forest, Roberto da Silva listened to a foreman explain why work had stopped on a 232-kilometer section of the Brasília-Belém highway the company had won a contract to build sixteen months ago:

"We had no warning, Senhor Roberto. It wasn't like before, with the others who showed up at Kilometer 96. Those were *pacified* savages; they begged for gifts. Not these devils, senhor. We never set eyes on them. I had seven men with two Caterpillars working at the head of the road. The savages peppered them with arrows." Suddenly he laughed, pointing to one of the workers. "Vasco there took one in the buttocks! Another boy, too, was hit. Senhor Roberto's orders are not to shoot back. We don't shoot back. Fine! So! When the men calmed down, I told them to go back to work. I went myself, senhor. I put presents close to the trees. The devils didn't come for them. They let us alone for an hour or two. Then . . . " He began to make sounds approximating flying arrows.

The incident had been reported to Roberto thirty hours earlier via the short-wave radio with which his São Paulo office kept in contact with the camps. Roberto had immediately arranged to fly up to an airstrip at Kilometer 189, a camp near the area where construction had been halted. He had landed at Brasília the previous night with his copilot, Raul Andracchio, and a passenger, Bruno Ramos Salgado, an officer of the Serviço de Proteção dos Indios (SPI); at first light this morning, Salgado and Roberto had continued in a single-engine plane to the advance camp, five hundred miles north of Brasília.

Roberto frequently flew up to the campsites, following the new road across the cerrado, with its thickets of scrub forest. Far to the north, the vegetation became denser as the road reached the southern spurs of the great forests, until only a red vein of earth penetrated the endless green. This sight more than any other brought home to Roberto the challenge of building a thirteen-hundred-mile highway across these virgin lands. Sometimes, as the small plane drifted high above the forest canopy, it seemed almost laughable; this thin line of road — one surge of the green wave and it would disappear.

This past January, almost two years after initial surveys for the highway, teams hacking a trail through the jungle from the north and south had met up one hundred miles beyond the da Silvas' advance camp. In the rain forest during the wet season from October to April, the torrential downpours brought work to a standstill, and stranded road builders had to be supplied by parachute drops of food and medicine. Across the cerrado, a sea of mud also slowed down construction, but wherever work could continue it did, the struggle to clear the forest the same as in ages past, inch by inch. The trailblazers were followed by six-man gangs with machetes and saws, slashing through the undergrowth, cutting loose cablelike lianas, felling tree after tree, selecting the best wood for lumber and leaving the rest for the fires, the smoke from the conflagrations visible for miles behind. Where the destruction was complete, bulldozers and Caterpillars lurched forward to shove aside charred timbers and uproot blackened stumps. Only then could the engineers and laborers begin preparing the roadbed for the gravel-surfaced highway that would link Brasília with the mouth of the Rio das Amazonas.

The roadworkers and those employed on the construction of the new capital itself were known as *candangos*. Among the Kimbundu taken as slaves in Africa, the word had been used pejoratively of their Portuguese captors; in Brazil, it came to be applied to the humble laborer who struggled to earn his keep. To the sixty thousand

Brazilians striving to meet President Juscelino Kubitschek's April 1960 deadline for the completion of Brasília, "candango" had become a badge of honor: It meant, simply, a man who worked hard.

As Roberto listened to the foreman's report, he glanced at Salgado, who, was standing nearby talking with several of the workers. The SPI's usual procedure, where there was a likelihood of encountering hostile savages, was to send in its experts in advance of the construction crews, placate the natives with gifts, and arrange for their transfer to a sanctuary where they could be prepared for assimilation with their fellow Brazilians. These arrow-shooters who refused to show themselves had been entirely unexpected.

"The gifts haven't been touched, Senhor Roberto," the foreman concluded.

"Shavante," Salgado announced, raising a bamboo arrow that had been passed to him by one of the workers.

Bruno Ramos Salgado was thirty-nine, almost six feet tall, muscular, with a mane of coarse black hair and dark, almond-shaped eyes, like those of his mother, from the Paresí tribe. Salgado's family was originally from Ceará; his grandparents had been part of the great exodus of drought victims to Amazonas in 1878. Murilo, the grandfather, had gone there to collect latex in the forests, but never once tapped a rubber tree. Instead, he worked for three brothers of Manaus, keeping order among their gatherers and taming the savages in their territory. Sewn on his deerskin belt were the ears of Muras, Mundurucu, and other enemies of "Mad Murilo."

Bruno's father, Izaias Ramos Salgado, was 19 years old in 1907 when a U.S. firm began construction of a 364-kilometer railroad through the jungle to bypass the rapids on the Madeira River and facilitate the export of Bolivia's rubber via the Amazon basin. Izaias worked on the Madeira-Mamoré railroad for five years, serving beside men of twenty-five nationalities. Three times, he was carted off to the company hospital at Candelária with various ailments, but he was one of the fortunate who survived; six thousand men died during the construction. Izaias had been in the crowd at the station of Guajará Mirim, the end of the line, on April 30, 1912, when a gold spike was driven home and the work completed. Just one year later, the rubber boom collapsed, the exports from the plantations of the Far East surpassing those of the Amazon Basin. Within a decade, the railroad was abandoned.

Izaias had shown signs of emulating the excesses of Mad Murilo in his zeal to punish Caripuna, Pacaas Novas, and other natives who attacked the railroad workers, poisoned streams near their camps, and tried to tear up with their bare hands the rails laid down on their lands. Izaias took his first pair of ears off a Caripuna he'd shot at a poisoned pool.

In 1912, when his job on the railroad ended, Izaias found work with the Telegraphic Commission, which was cutting a trail for its line through the jungle to link Santo Antônio on the Madeira, with Cuiabá, the old gold mining capital of Mato Grosso, nine hundred miles to the southeast. The head of the commission, Colonel Cândido Mariano Rondon, an army engineer and explorer, absolutely forbade the slaying of the tribes whose villages lay along the route of the line. "Die if necessary, but never kill," Rondon, himself half native, told his men. Rondon inspired the authorities at Rio de Janeiro to establish the Serviço de Proteção dos Indios. He began a lifelong battle against those who saw the survivors of the great native tribes as bestial and deserving of extinction, especially if they occupied lands where there was rumor of gold and diamonds or where the forest could be destroyed to make way for cattle.

While working on the Rondon line, Izaias was himself pacified. In 1916, as a result of his exemplary behavior, he was put in charge of a telegraph station three hundred miles down the line — a miserable place with five huts next to a river, where Izaias also maintained a raft. Ten yards upstream from the ferry point, a huge boulder that rose in the middle of the river had long been a source of mystery to the rare travelers braving the jungle trail. As a youngster, Bruno Salgado — the son of Izaias and the second of his three "wives" — had ferried these adventurers across to the rock so that they might examine its "hieroglyphics"; the more hopeful fancied that the worn inscription was a clue to a hidden treasure trove:

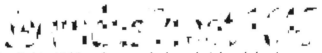

Izaias died in 1946, and no one had yet deciphered the time-worn name of Secundus Proot or the date carved there.

By the time Bruno turned fourteen, three Jesuit priests had established a mission four miles from the station. Bruno went to school there, and afterwards at a colégio in Cuiabá, where, a bright, eager pupil, his devotions had given the fathers reason to think he might be destined for holy orders. But, at twenty-four, Bruno had found another mission — the Servíço de Proteção dos Indios — one even better suited to expiating Mad Murilo's sins.

Roberto and Salgado had a brief consultation and agreed that it was too late to investigate. They spent the night in a trailer at the camp and were awake before dawn, leaving ahead of the trucks taking construction workers to "safe" sections along the seven kilometers. Salgado expected to make contact with the Shavante, but he didn't expect to find them waiting for him beside the road; therefore he suggested that Roberto and the two men who'd volunteered to go with them — scrawny Fernandes Estevam, known as "Dried Meat," and a giant of a man who rarely spoke, Garcia da Silveira — be prepared for at least a day and a night in the forest. They took supplies, gifts for the Shavante, and weapons. Salgado himself carried a .38 Smith & Wesson, which he had fired only once, in the line of duty — to defend himself against a mob of diamond hunters who had invaded the lands of a Paresí clan not far from the old telegraph station where he'd been born.

In some places beside the roadway, where a wide swath of jungle had been cleared, fire-scorched hulks of trees rose from gray fields. The rainy season was not yet over, and along stretches, the brown-to-mauve-to-red earth was churned into a quagmire by the short, furious tropical downpours. Heavy equipment — immense Caterpillars, galvanized iron culverts, gasoline drums, piles of shovels and pickaxes — stood like machines of war, primed for this day's battle against the enemy: the Forest.

Fernandes, at the wheel of the Jeep, drove maniacally, his foot jammed down on the accelerator, swerving from side to side to avoid deep ruts, roaring at full speed along the side of a cutting. No, Senhor Roberto, he had assured the man sitting rigid beside him, eyes focused straight ahead, not to worry; he, Fernandes Estevam, was the son of a great *motorista* who had driven a bus in the sertão of Bahia!

When they stopped at the end of the roadworks, Bruno Salgado and Roberto got out and approached the trees cautiously; Fernandes and Silveira were told to wait at the jeep. To wile away the time, Fernandes entertained the laconic Silveira with grisly tales he'd heard about the savages, beginning with Kayapo hordes who, in 1950, on the Araguaia – a river about ninety miles west of their section of the road — had killed or injured one hundred settlers. And the Shavante? "Nossa Senhora, pre-serve us!" said Dried Meat, crossing himself.

There were grounds for Dried Meat's trepidation: Not until the early fifties had peaceful contact been made with bands of the semi-nomadic Shavante, inhabit-ants of the cerrado and the forests of northern Mato Grosso since time immemorial. For three centuries explorers, adventurers, madmen had ventured into this sertão, the incursions increasing as groups of land-hungry pioneers began to take their chances near the appropriately named Rio das Mortes, along which the Shavante held sway. The river flowed into the Araguaia at a point some two hundred miles south-south-west of the da Silvas' advance camp.

As recently as 1934, the Shavante had slain Padres Sacilotti and Fuchs, two Salesians who had gone up the Rio das Mortes to befriend them. Seven years later, they butchered an entire SPI expedition. The Shavante were also believed responsible for the disappearance of the British engineer and explorer Percy H. Fawcett and two companions, who had marched in the direction of the Rio das Mortes in 1925 seek-ing a fabled lost city.

Despite the tragic setbacks, the SPI and the Salesian fathers had persevered, and in 1953, largely due to Bruno Salgado's involvement, the first community of Shavante were settled at a post the SPI had established beside the Rio das Mortes. By 1958, there were seven Shavante settlements along the river, where, with varying degrees of success, the savages were being assimilated.

Bruno Salgado had spent the past two years going from one to another of these settlements, living among the Shavante, learning their dialect and customs. It was during this period that he first met Roberto da Silva, and at meetings between SPI officials and representatives of the road-construction companies, Salgado had found Roberto to be one of the strongest advocates of peaceful relations with natives along the roadworks.

Assigned to the SPI's São Paulo office the first week in February, Salgado had immediately got in touch with his new friend Roberto, and when, two days ago, da Silva told him of the trouble at Kilometer 96, Salgado had instantly offered his ser-vices.

The gifts the foreman said they'd left at the edge of the forest were now gone. There had been a thunderstorm since they were originally placed there, but human footprints were still discernible. Salgado walked slowly from one side of the clearing to the other, then back to the trees on their left. He picked up three arrows at the abandoned Caterpillar and confirmed his suspicion that they were crafted by the Shavante. After fifteen minutes' more scouting, he told Roberto he was also certain the Shavante had not crossed the roadway but had turned back to the west.

They entered the forest, Bruno Salgado in the lead and Fernandes bringing up the rear.

Salgado was an expert tracker and moved quickly and stealthily through the undergrowth, his eyes darting in all directions searching for clues to the route the Shavante had taken. Nervous excitement compelled Dried Meat to joke about the terrors — the one-legged Caipora and other demons — waiting to greet them. To Roberto da Silva, the forest was far less alien: On visits to the Mato Grosso cattle ranches, he had often joined his vaqueiros hunting the wildcats that were a menace to the herds.

As they plunged deeper into the humid twilight world, the eerie stillness, broken only by the hissing concert of insects and a few shrill bird calls, gave way to a riot of sound that closed round them like a solid net as monkeys screeched in the branches above and wild beasts crashed through the brush at the men's approach.

Two hours after leaving the road, they discovered the remains of a Shavante camp: three low shelters of saplings and palm fronds; the ashes of the nomads' fire; the feathers of a macaw; the bones of a slaughtered peccary; discarded bits of plant and tuber. The shelters suggested a band of a dozen or so natives, Salgado said. They had probably made camp here on their march in the direction of the road, but if they were retracing their steps now, he reasoned, they hadn't stopped here again; the rotting animal bones were several days old.

It didn't take Salgado long to pick up the Shavantes' trail. The forest began to give way in places to more open terrain, dotted with shrubs and tall grasses. Forty minutes later they came to a river, a yellowish flood swollen from the great rains. The broken reeds at a canebrake showed that the Shavante, too, had come this way.

Salgado headed directly into the canebrake, heading straight for more than a mile before turning off to the left toward firmer ground above the riverbank.

"Silêncio!" Salgado hissed suddenly. Roberto and the other men froze. "Wait there!" Salgado ordered.

"Has he found the savages?" Fernandes whispered, but neither Roberto nor Silveiro said a word and instead shushed him with their hands.

Salgado went farther, up a steep slope, and then halted, looking down toward the river. He turned his head quickly as a cane snapped behind him: Roberto was coming up as quietly as he could.

"Shavante?" da Silva asked softly, from the edge of the canes.

With a slight motion of his arm, Salgado beckoned Roberto forward.

A lone Shavante stood on the opposite bank, motionless, his eyes turned toward them. A young warrior in the prime of manhood. His naked body was streaked with urucu dye. One hand held a long bow; the other, a war club.

From the high ground, the men watching him could see a narrow bend in the river half a mile away, strewn with rocks that afforded a safe crossing. No other Shavante were in sight, either along the bank or at the edge of the trees behind the warrior.

"Stay here, Roberto," Salgado said. "I'm going down." He handed da Silva his Smith & Wesson.

"Alone? Unarmed?"

"It will be all right," Salgado said calmly. "At least for now. He's just as curious about us. His friends, too, wherever they're hidden. Later, after a meeting, things can change." He didn't elaborate, but was adamant that Roberto stay where he was and make certain the others kept out of sight. Then, Salgado started off toward the riverbank.

"Maluco!" Fernandes exclaimed, when he caught sight of Salgado. "The man's crazy!"

The Shavante was already at the crossing-point. Salgado raised his hands in a gesture of friendship, indicating, too, that he had no weapon. The Shavante stood absolutely still for several minutes. Suddenly he lifted an arm and pointed upstream.

Salgado began to cross the river. Four Shavante armed with bows stepped out of the trees behind the lone warrior.

Unconsciously, Roberto put his hand on the holster at his side. But just at that moment big Bruno Salgado, his mane of black hair flying, leapt along the riverbank, pounding the earth in a short, impromptu dance. Two Shavante offered a similar demonstration, running along beside him.

Half an hour later, Salgado signaled his party to come down to the river. The rest of the band of Shavante, nineteen in all, had emerged from the forest and stood or sat on the open ground beyond the crossing. Like the young warrior, the six other adult males were naked but for penis sheaths; their heads were closely shorn and their eyebrows plucked; in their earlobes, they wore ceremonial plugs. The five women all bore large baskets with the possessions the group had taken with them on this trek from their village.

When Roberto and the others reached the river, Salgado shouted that only one of them should cross over with a pack of gifts Silveira was carrying.

"Hand me the pack, Garcia," Roberto said.

"I'll go," the taciturn Silveira offered.

"Yes," Dried Meat quickly agreed. "The danger to the senhor . . ."

Roberto just stared at him, and the caboclo added lamely, "I wouldn't want to see the senhor harmed."

"Oh? Well, then, *you* can go, Fernandes."

"*Me,* senhor?" Dried Meat gasped, blanching.

Roberto, laughing, took the gifts from Silveira and crossed over to Bruno Salgado.

"For a while there, my friend, it didn't look good," he said. "Until you began to dance like a savage!"

Bruno grinned. "It wasn't a dance. I was telling them I know the Shavante are great runners. I've seen their log races."

"Where is their village?"

"Far west of here. They say they've been on trek for weeks. The scleria plant flourishes around here." Seeing the look of total confusion on Roberto's face, Salgado explained, "The seeds are what they're after. See that one's necklace? The tiny beads are made from the scleria seeds. Sacred regalia."

The Shavante stood a dozen feet away, behind the elder and the young warrior. They fell silent as Roberto opened the pack. Salgado removed a pair of scissors, an assortment of mirrors, fishhooks, bandannas, cheap jewelry, and other trinkets — all hastily purchased by a secretary at Roberto's office. Salgado delighted the Shavante by snipping off a long strand of his hair. The elder's hand immediately shot out to indicate that he, as leader of the band, merited this prize. Salgado gave him the scissors. The old man cautiously began to work them, studying the shears intently as they opened and closed.

Other Shavante began to demand their presents, and Roberto quickly obliged them, doling out fishhooks and mirrors.

When the gift-giving was over, Salgado spoke for a while with the elder and then went back to Roberto. "We'll go now," he said, "to our side of the river." Roberto gave him a puzzled look. "The Shavante will camp here, and discuss my offer to settle them at one of our posts. In the morning, we'll talk again."

They returned to the high ground above the canebrake, where they prepared to spend the night. Dried Meat worked feverishly collecting wood for a fire, alarmed by a remark from Salgado that the friendly mood of the Shavante could change in a matter of hours, as suggested by the massacre of the SPI expedition in the forties. It was known that those men had been carrying gifts for the savages, too; bits of broken mirror were found on the ground beside their bodies.

Darkness came, deep and intimate, with clouds obscuring the moon. Imperceptibly at first, the night chorus rose, until the very air seemed to vibrate. Every once in a while, there would be a sharp, jarring sound above the drone of insects. Dried Meat stirred uneasily in his sleep at these noises, but Silveira dozed soundly nearby; they were to keep watch after midnight.

Gazing across the canes and the river to the flicker of light from the Shavantes' fire, Roberto asked, "What will happen to them?"

Bruno stared into the embers of their own fire. "They will be civilized."

"The way you say it, it sounds like a curse."

"I'm not sure it isn't. Sorry to sound morbid, but I've seen it happen too often."

"What?"

"Within a year, a quarter will be dead," Bruno said flatly. "Disease. Dejection, I suppose. We ask too much of them. We take a stone ax out of their hands, give them a shirt and trousers, and expect them to step into our world just like that. But the Vilas Boases know what they're talking about when they say it takes fifty or sixty years for a tribe to adapt its way of life."

The three Vilas Boas brothers had founded the Xingu Indian Reservation along the river of that name in northern Mato Grosso. They had first entered the region in the early forties with a government expedition Getúlio Vargas had proclaimed as "Brazil's march to the West." The brothers had contacted a dozen small tribes in an area of more than 10,000 square miles, living with them and gaining their respect — and beginning a struggle not yet ended to have the region declared a federal reservation protected from encroachment by land grabbers and prospectors. In this fight, they had earned the disapproval of missionaries keen to work with the Xingu natives but who were forbidden entry to their villages by the Vilas Boases. They were acting in opposition to the official goal of quickly assimilating the 200,000 or so natives remaining in Brazil; but the brothers argued that it was destructive to throw the survivors into the melting pot when there was no place for them yet in the structure of Brazilian society.

"We at the SPI feel pity and want to help them," Bruno added. "Too often things go wrong. And yet we continue to drive them off their land in our march to the North and the West. Today it's the road to Belém. Next year, Cuiabá to Porto Velho — there's talk of that already."

"I pity them, too, Bruno. But we have to open the interior for development."

"Development? Or ransacking?"

"Development," Roberto said firmly. "The new roads will open areas of settlement for millions."

"I hope so."

"Why so pessimistic?"

"Two reasons, my friend: One" — he scuffed the earth beneath his boot — "the forest soils are poor. That's why these Shavante and other tribes are nomads, planting a clearing for a season or two and then moving on."

"And your second reason?"

"Settle millions out here? The landless masses? What do we see happening? Speculators running to buy up millions of hectares. Brazilians. Foreigners. There's a wild fever to get a stake on this last great frontier."

"Yes, Bruno — this is the last great frontier. And there's room for all who come to settle the sertão."

*

The next morning before sunrise, with Fernandes Estevam striding up front, the four of them made their way down past the canebrake. Mist lay banked up along the river, so thick it obscured the view of the opposite bank. Bruno crossed over alone. A few minutes later, he had returned.

"They've gone," he said simply.

"You want to go after them?" Roberto asked.

"I'll write a report at my office. In time, the SPI will locate their village."

The look in his dark eyes told Roberto da Silva that Bruno Salgado hoped it would not be soon.

*

"I agree, Grandpapa, it's a terrific expense," the girl said, "but why *shouldn't* we have it?"

Mariette Monteiro da Silva posed the question as if she was considering an extravagant purchase. The oldest of four children of Roberto and Sylvia Monteiro, she was nineteen, dark-haired and dark-eyed, with an oval face and full red lips. Senhor Amílcar would sometimes glance at Mariette and at the painting of his own grandmother, Teodora Rita, and note the strong resemblance of these two strong-willed, vivacious women.

Mariette, a second-year law student at the University of São Paulo, was sitting in the Jeep next to her father, who was driving. Senhor Amílcar sat behind them. It was the afternoon of April 19, 1960. Earlier that day, Roberto had fetched the two of them from Brasília airport, along with Dona Cora and Roberto's wife, Sylvia, a small, attractive woman of thirty-seven, only three years younger than Dona Cora. Cora and Sylvia were at an apartment in one of the new blocks where Roberto had arranged for all of them to stay during the inauguration celebrations at Brasília.

"The Turks have Ankara. Le Corbusier is building Chandigarh in the Punjab," Mariette said, when her grandfather remained silent. "Why shouldn't Brazil have *her* new capital?"

"Because, my dear girl, we can't afford it," Amílcar said, as he'd been saying for four years. "Five hundred million dollars already, and that won't be the end of it!"

"But don't you agree, Grandpapa, it's so magnificent! So absolutely grand!"

Amílcar da Silva made a sweeping movement with his hand, embracing the entire vista to the right of where Roberto had just parked the jeep. "Who on earth could deny that!"

Roberto had pulled up along a six-lane ramped boulevard that crossed an 820-foot-wide civic mall flanked by identical ten-story ministry buildings. At the top of the mall, the Plaza of the Three Powers was dominated by a pair of slender, twenty-eight-story skyscrapers, at the base of which were two gleaming white domes, one of them inverted, the roofs of the Congress and Senate chambers. In the distance, behind the concrete, glass, and marble, the sun caught the waters of Paranôa, a fifteen-square-mile artificial lake.

Workmen were clearing up the site where for the past year battalions of candangos had labored twenty-four hours a day to meet the deadline set by President Juscelino Kubitschek and Novacap — Companhia Urbanizadora de Nova Capital — the government body with overall responsibility for construction. "We've got five years to build Brasília," Dr. Israel Pinheiro, one of Novacap's directors, had said at the outset. "If we take longer, the jungle will overrun what we've won." Dr. Pinheiro, a Mineiro like Kubitschek, was talking figuratively, there being no great forests in the cerrado, but his meaning was clear. It was now exactly thirty-seven months since Novacap had approved the pilot plan for a city of 500,000.

This was Mariette da Silva's first visit to Brasília, and she was enthralled by Oscar Niemeyer's supremely graceful structures and by his mentor Lucío Costa's winning design. (No fewer than twenty-six Brazilian architectural firms had submitted proposals in an internationally judged competition.) To Mariette, the outline of the capital resembled a mammoth airplane with swept-back wings; where they came together was the commercial district, and within their span, sweeping north and south, were one hundred superblocks of housing, each eight hundred feet square; at the top of the "fuselage" was the Plaza of the Three Powers.

Cora and Sylvia, too, were making their first trip here. Cora had turned down Roberto's offer to go sight-seeing: She had no intention of leaving this comfortable apartment that belonged to the da Silvas' bankers until it was time to hear the president's excuses for throwing away so much money. Besides, she needed time to decide which dress to wear for the inaugural ball, which was to be held — most appropriately, in Cora's opinion — in the cavernous bus station. From the moment she stepped onto the plane at São Paulo, Dona Cora had made it clear that she was coming only to keep Senhor Amílcar company, her husband being part of a São Paulo state delegation.

Senhor Amílcar was of the same mind as his wife. For most of the year, they lived in their town mansion at São Paulo, in the heart of the Paulista capital, a city of 3.5 million now, greatest metropolis in South America.

Senhor Amílcar did not forget that he had said Juscelino Kubitschek's vision of Brasília might turn out to be a mirage in the desert. Brasília was real enough, but planted out here in the sertão, where was this dream city to find its power and energy? It would never grow like São Paulo, not in a hundred years!

Senhor Amílcar himself had made several trips up to Brasília, the last only two months ago, when he and Roberto had been present as four convoys that had set out simultaneously from Porto Alegre, Rio de Janeiro, Cuiabá, and Belém converged on the new capital, a symbolic caravan of national integration. With the major work on the Brasília-Belém highway complete, the da Silvas still had several smaller contracts in the federal district itself, Amílcar da Silva having no objection to profiting from Juscelino Kubitschek's mirage.

And, for all his misgivings, Senhor Amílcar could not hide a sense of pride in what was being achieved here in so short a time. Just four years ago, there had been only a modest ranch house, the Fazenda do Gama, near two streams that had been dammed up in the lake, and beyond the fazenda, the open cerrado, with the rhea and the jaguar. It was pure Brazilian madness, this gleaming city in the middle of nowhere. But perhaps men like his two sons might just work a miracle and make it a success.

And Mariette, too, he thought, as he listened to his granddaughter's bubbling enthusiasm in the jeep. "Who knows, my dear girl," he said. "Perhaps when you've got your law degree, you can come and use it out here in the sertão."

"Oh, Grandpapa, I wouldn't mind that at all," she exclaimed breathlessly. "Not at all!"

⁊

Back at the apartment, Roberto announced that he was taking them to dinner at the best restaurant in Brasília.

"The Brasília Palace by the lake?" Cora asked expectantly.

"No, I'm sorry, Dona Cora, but the Palace is under siege. Perhaps General Marcelo could find a place for us, but you wouldn't enjoy it, not with hundreds jammed in there."

General Marcelo Araujo da Silva, the son of Honório da Silva, was the third generation of that branch of the family to follow a military career. Senhor Amílcar had known Honório well, but General Marcelo, who had distinguished himself with the Smoking Cobras in Italy, had gone to Minas Gerais after the war and become distant from the Tiberica da Silvas. But there was talk enough among the family to know that the general was a rising power in the military who remained ever vigilant against the Communists and other agitators among the masses, especially in the troubled Northeast.

"Then where *are* we going?" Cora asked, petulantly.

"Chez Maximilian. Your old friend Max's place."

"In that *favela?*" Cora said, recoiling.

Max Grosskopf, from an old German immigrant family, had sold a restaurant he owned in São Paulo and moved up here, where he'd opened Chez Maximilian in

Cidade Livre, a settlement seven miles outside Brasília. Intended as a temporary nucleus for workers and their families not housed in construction camps, Cidade Livre was home to tens of thousands, its neon-lit, unpaved streets crowded with restaurants, banks, shops — a gaudy and unruly antidote to the precise order of Brasília.

Despite Dona Cora's initial anxiety about visiting Cidade Livre, once they were in the restaurant, with Max himself fussing over them, she became more spirited; it comforted her, too, that Chez Maximilian was filled with other members of high society also seeking an alternative to the rush on the Brasília Palace.

"Poor Max! What a mistake he's made," Cora said over her schnitzel. "He had such a lovely place in São Paulo."

"He'll move to Brasília one of these days, Dona Cora," Mariette said. "Make a fortune, too; you'll see. And he'll be proud to have been one of the pioneers."

"A candango?" Cora said, with a derisive laugh.

"Exactly!" Roberto said vehemently, clapping Dona Cora on the shoulder as if she'd said something terribly clever.

ও

Late morning April 21, Senhor Amílcar stood with the Paulista delegation watching one of the numerous ceremonies honoring Brasília's official replacement of Rio de Janeiro as capital.

An endless parade was inching along the mall toward the Plaza of the Three Powers. Ten thousand men, led by a dozen bands. Between their ranks, huge machines rolled forward ponderously, monolithic pieces of earth-moving equipment bedecked with buntings and flags. The men wore boots, jeans, straw hats. They were the men who had built Brasília: the candangos.

Roberto da Silva was among them, walking beside one of his company's Caterpillars, which was being guided by Fernandes Estevam, son of a great motorista from the Bahia. Dried Meat cheered wildly as they approached President Juscelino Kubitschek and other dignitaries on the reviewing stand.

Amílcar da Silva was just behind the president's party and waved in response to an exuberant gesture from Roberto. One of the da Silvas' workers who saw Senhor Amílcar wave came to an exaggerated halt and saluted smartly. Senhor Amílcar laughed and returned the salute.

The caboclo went on his way, limping slightly, the result of an old wound. But that was all past now, the trouble Raimundo Pacheco had known in far-off Pernambuco. Two years ago he'd come to Brasília in the parrot's perch and he'd made a go of it here, working alongside thousands of others who'd migrated from the Northeast.

The celebrations lasted for hours, and of course there were speeches, the one that drew the most emotional response by Juscelino Kubitschek himself.

"Some of you have come from Minas Gerais, some from other neighboring states, the majority from the Northeast. You came because you heard the message that a new star was to be added to the other twenty-one on our flag. Brasília is here only because of you, candangos, to whose ranks I am honored to belong . . .

"On this day, April twenty-first, in honor of Lieutenant Joaquim José da Silva Xavier, at the one hundred thirty-eighth year of independence and the seventy-first of republic, I, under the protection of God, do hereby declare the city of Brasília, capital of the United States of Brazil, inaugurated."

❧

That evening, Amílcar da Silva stood alone at a window on the twentieth floor of one of the twin skyscrapers. The room behind him was filled with guests attending a reception given by a group of Paulista legislators. Roberto had gone to fetch Cora, Sylvia, and Mariette, who'd returned to the apartment early in the afternoon to get ready for the ball at the Rodoviária. Amílcar gazed out, not at the gleaming city below, but far off into the distance, to where the cerrado was darkening.

This vast sertão, not only over the next hill or across the next river, but deep within the soul. A call to Paradise or to Hell for our forefathers. Were they out there now, Amador Flôres da Silva and Benedito Bueno — all who had opened the way for this conquest? Were the old bandeirantes gazing back in awe at this city — this El Dorado they had sought for so long?

AFTERWORD

March – April 2000

TÔNINHO

*P*adre Tôninho told no one where he was going on a morning in October 1996. He wrote a note for his housekeeper, Maria Pedra, saying he was leaving on a short journey and would return in three days. Maria was not to worry about him. At 4:00 A.M., Tôninho climbed into his VW Beetle, driving through the empty streets of Magdalena parish in Rosário, Pernambuco and taking the road to the interior. That afternoon, he was in Petrolândia on the Rio São Francisco, and stayed the night at a hotel by the river.

Tôninho crossed the São Francisco the next morning, ten miles below Petrolândia. He stopped to consult a map before turning onto a dirt road that led southwest into the *sertão* of Bahia. The land grew desolate. Barren hills studded with stunted vegetation, eroded gullies scored by violent rains of the past, fields turned to powder. Vilas lay ashen in the sun. Beasts were pitifully thin. Humans fared no better, groups of men in dusty clothes stood idly in the shade, eyes turning slowly as the VW clattered past them. The rains had not come and the *sertanejos* were again at the mercy of a cruel, dry earth.

Five miles from his destination, Tôninho stopped for directions. An old vaqueiro with time on his hands offered to ride with him. He thanked the man but said he wanted to visit the place alone. Fifteen minutes later, he stopped the car at the side of the road in the heart of the caatinga, as melancholy a landscape as any seen that morning.

He got out and picked his way between dusty-gray entanglements, here and there a solitary spiky sentinel thrusting twenty feet above the arid underbrush. Suddenly, the caatinga vanished and he stood at edge of a vast depression with low hills, resembling a great rolling plain. In places, the ground was cracked and bare; elsewhere a covering of tough grasses and tiny bromeliads had appeared almost magically.

He was not alone. As he walked across the open ground toward a small rise on which stood a ruin, he didn't see the young woman working in a long cutting off to his right.

"Olá!" she hailed him. *"Bom dia."*

He greeted her. "You're not from these parts."

"With this accent?" she said laughing. Her name was Jennifer Coleman and she was from Stonington, Connecticut. A student at the University of Miami Center for Latin American Studies, Coleman was in Brazil doing fieldwork for her MA dissertation. "And what brings you to Canudos . . . ?"

"Tôninho," he introduced himself. His eyes swept the ruins on the hill. "Dr. Juraci Cristiano, my grandfather, was born in Canudos."

ↄↄ

Padre Antônio Paciência — "Tôninho" — is thirty-five, tall and lean, and with a spare frame. He has the same aquiline nose, brown eyes and dark-skinned countenance as his ancestor, Antônio Paciência, who was born a slave and died a rebel in the service of the Counselor, Antônio Conselheiro. When Tôninho made his pilgrimage to Canudos in October 1996, it was ninety-nine years since Brazilian government troops killed 20,000 men, women and children at the New Jerusalem in this valley watered by the Vasa-Barris River.

For forty years, Canudos lay below Cocorobó barrage, built by a government that flooded the blood-soaked basin to erase evidence of the sertanejo rebellion. Nothing was visible except a grassy island, where goats and sheep grazed, rowed over by a local herdsman. The year 1996 brought one of the worst droughts in memory. Week after week, the waters of Cocorobó fell, lower and lower, until the ruins of Canudos began to emerge under the red, hot sun.

Most prominent were the remains of the Counselor's church, standing on one of the knolls. Two heavy arches and supporting walls of the huge rectangular sanctuary had survived cannonades from the Whitworth batteries and "God's Thunder," a 32-pounder dragged up from Salvador to demolish the lair of the Anti-Christ. Below the church lay the trench where Antônio Paciência stood with the handful who fought until the end of their world.

Dr. Juraci Cristiano, Antônio Paciência's only surviving child, lived at Canudos until just before his fifth birthday. Dr. Juraci had researched the uprising for *The Biography of a Patient Man*, which he was writing at the time of his death in 1981. — His grandson recently found the manuscript about the life and times of his namesake and planned to finish it for publication.

Padre Tôninho felt a deep, personal connection to the people of Canudos, so that when he read about the "resurrection" of the Counselor's city, he immediately went to visit the site. He wanted to make the pilgrimage alone, but afterwards wasn't sorry that the young American student was there. Jennifer Coleman was spending a semester with a University of Bahia archaeological team, given a unique opportunity to revisit the past when Cocorobó dried up. Tôninho found her intelligent and sensitive, with a fine grasp of her subject — Coleman's dissertation deals with the Rebellion of Canudos — and genuine sympathy for the Brazilian masses.

She took him on a tour of the ruins, across rubble-strewn ground where 5,200 habitations had stood. Patches of hardened clay indicated the foundations of houses; here and there, a section of broken wall; an outdoor oven that had collapsed into a pile of stones. There was a burial ground 100 yards from the fortress-temple. When the army razed Canudos, they burned most of the dead. In the trench, where the last defenders fell, rusted weapons and spent cartridges were unearthed alongside the bones of the faithful.

They sat beneath the arches of the big church, talking about Antônio Conselheiro and his followers. Historians published the Counselor's sermons in 1974: These revealed a devout man who advocated social justice, diligence and love among human beings. It was now recognized that the 20,000 who died were not a bandit rabble but landless peasants scourged by drought and abandoned by their government. Most were black people and mulattos scorned by racist elites of the day, who favored a "whitening" of Brazil and weren't against exterminating a barbarian race in the backlands.

Padre Tôninho looked at the trench, where his forebear perished. "A hundred years since the last shot was fired," he said. "And still the battle goes on."

c/s

Antonio "Tôninho" Paciência was born in Recife, Pernambuco in 1965, the only child of Juraci Cristiano's third son, Alberto, and his wife, Elena. When Tôninho was three, his father died in a car accident and the boy and his mother went to live in his grandfather's house.

Dr. Juraci had been taken from the battlefield of Canudos as a child by Celso Cavalcanti, from the Cavalcanti family of Engenho Santo Tomás. Padre Celso, later Monsignor Cavalcanti, and his family generously supported Juraci's education that saw him graduate as a doctor. In the 1930s, Juraci's radical politics led to his imprisonment following a failed communist-led revolution in Recife.

With rare exception, the senhores de engenhos of Santo Tomás, who have been in Pernambuco since the founding of the captaincy in the sixteenth century, have been pillars of the landed oligarchy. Dr. Juraci's close ties to the family prevented a total break and he gradually restored his relationship with them. Disillusioned when the "Bread, Land and Liberty" movement in which he was involved collapsed in 1934, he rarely took an active role in party politics. This did not lessen his commitment to helping the masses living under a merciless system.

When Tôninho was a boy, Dr. Juraci was in his eighties but remained in charge of the clinic at Santo Tomás. On Wednesdays and Saturdays, Tôninho went to the engenho with his grandfather, riding in Juraci's ancient Packard. Everyone was petrified of driving with Dr. Juraci, but he was destined to die peacefully in his sleep just two weeks short of his eighty-eighth birthday. Only days earlier he had steered the Packard out to the valley of the Cavalcantis to attend his patients.

Tôninho was sixteen when his grandfather died and had been making the trips to the plantation with him on and off for ten years. "I've memories of Dr. Juraci at the wheel of the Packard with a big truck hurtling toward us. Grandpa sat like a rock. He said he'd nothing to fear because the archangel Gabriel protected him." — When asked why he chose Gabriel as his guardian, Dr. Juraci told his grandson that the archangel had watched over him at Canudos.

Tôninho remembers his grandfather talking to him about how things worked in Brazil. He would discuss anything from the peasants' struggle for land to the church. — "All these politicians only look to the next election. The Church has until Judgment Day to carry out its work."

"There was much I didn't understand, but one thing I know is that Dr. Juraci taught me what was right and wrong in our land. One time I recall vividly, he took me to an old hand-fed sugar-cane mill. He demonstrated how overseers chopped off a slave's arm caught in the rollers. 'Slaves were treated worse than beasts in Brazil,' he said. Sometimes, it would be a simple lesson, as on a day a woman brought her child to the clinic. He let me watch him examine the little thing. 'Do you remember what you had for dinner last night?' he asked me. I told him. 'This baby hasn't eaten for three days,' Dr. Juraci said."

The influence of the 'old communist,' as the Cavalcantis called Dr. Juraci, not without some affection, led to Tôninho's decision to become a priest. He began his service with the church in Recife's slums, where he worked until 1994 when he went to the parish of Magdalena in Rosário.

𝒞𝓈

Padre Tôninho had just finished lunch on March 31, 2000, when Maria Pedra came to tell him that three young men wanted to see him. She didn't know them, but they said they were from *Sem Terra* — "Without Land," the Portuguese nickname for the Landless Rural Workers Movement (MST.)

With 500,000 members, the MST is the largest, strongest and best-organized grassroots movement in Brazil. Since 1985, the movement has led the struggle for agrarian reform by invading and occupying idle lands and getting the government to expropriate them for the new settlers.

Padre Tôninho's visitors were recruiting members for the MST in Rosário. They asked if they could use the church hall that night. Tôninho supported their campaign and had no objection.

Magdalena is the poorest parish in Rosário, a sleepy rural town in the *zona da mata*, still called the "forest zone" of Pernambuco, though where once there were trees, there has long been green waves of sugarcane. Most residents of Magdalena, if they can find jobs, labor for a pittance as field workers; *bóia fria*, they're called, literally "cold meal," for they head off at five in the morning, eat a cold lunch beside the canes, and return around seven in the evening. By the time they get home, their supper of rice, beans and manioc is cold. Everyone in the parish has some tie to the land, from families who've been farmhands for generations to others who've worked in the sugar mills or tried to make a go of it as sharecroppers. Not one owns a piece of land.

The MST organizers told a packed hall about the movement's successes: 250,000 families had acquired land in 2,600 settlements nationwide. The MST set up 400 cooperatives and developed 96 small to medium plants that produced fruit and vegetables, meat and dairy products, grains and sweets. The most profitable coop, Novo Sarandi in Rio Grande do Sul, was grossing $12 million a year, bringing its families an income ten times greater than the $75 a month on which most country people have to survive.

"The struggle isn't only for land and bread," said organizer Milton Soares. "It is for the minds of our children." He told his audience about the settlements' schools, where 95,000 children from first to fourth grade receive a basic education. Older children and adults attend classes to learn to read and write. "Wherever there is a camp of the landless, you will find teachers dedicated to planting the seeds for this priceless harvest."

Luiz Alves de Sá, a sharecropper working a plot seven miles outside Rosário, was one of several people who stood up and spoke. He is a tall, scrawny mulatto, with thinning gray hair.

"I've been working ever since I was nine, and now at fifty-six I still can't scrape together enough to buy a bicycle. I never went to school. I went into sharecropping slavery with my father. It's like selling yourself to the devil. You never get out of debt. A landowner can come and pay what you owe and take you to his farm. They buy you and sell you over and over. You are degraded from people down to merchandise."

Before the meeting ended, Luiz Alves de Sá and twenty-nine others declared their families ready to march with the Landless Army.

❧

The invasion of Engenho Santo Tomás took place ten days later on April 9, 2000. The MST organizer, Milton Soares, and Padre Tôninho led the thirty families involved, including ninety-two adults and sixty-eight children. Tôninho was on good terms with the senhor de engenho, Clodomir Cavalcanti, and wanted to be present in case of a confrontation.

The Cavalcantis possess 25,000 acres in the valley occupied by Nicolau Gonçalves Cavalcanti in March 1545. The habit of dividing inheritances and lands among the heirs of senhores de engenho reduced the original holding three times that size. The Cavalcantis are major shareholders in the giant Usina Jacuribe refinery owned by a Dutch multinational group. Allied to this enterprise, Engenho Santo Tomás has 15,000 acres of cane under cultivation, producing one million bags of sugar annually.

The MST shock troops set their eyes on a 900-acre parcel a mile from the Casa Grande. This land, which abuts the old road between the engenho and Rosário, has a wild, deserted appearance like a small, overgrown jungle.

When Nicolau Cavalcanti first came to the valley, a Tobajara clan's malocas stood here. Afterwards, the place became the stamping ground of the degredado, Affonso Ribeiro, and his numerous descendants. The old reprobate held court under some ancient trees, rejoicing in a Garden of Eden, where no free man needed to work. Generations of Affonso Ribeiro's tribe squatted on this land, doing precious little until the last one drifted off. A thick matted plantation extends in every direction. Here, the Cavalcantis never grew one stalk of cane.

❧

The church hall at Magdalena served as assembly point for the 160 insurgents. They gathered in the early hours of Sunday morning, April 9, bringing bundles of bedding and clothes, bags of food, pots and pans, farm implements, even small animals and crates of chickens. Three buses and four trucks stood ready to transport them to Engenho Santo Tomás.

The atmosphere was festive, with bold talk, laughter and camaraderie. Once they took the decision to invade, the MST organizers acted swiftly. They wanted to be on the march before word of their plans spread. When the opposition came, as inevitably it would, they planned to be on the ground and ready to resist.

At 2:00 A.M., Milton Soares told the families to board the buses and trucks. A handful of friends were present to bid them farewell. The engenho was only thirty-five miles from Rosário on the old road, but the journey they were embarking on could take them immeasurably farther than they'd ever been.

Padre Tôninho's VW roared into life. Soares climbed in beside him. They rattled over to the head of the column. A defiant blast from the VW's horn and they were off.

It took three hours to cover the thirty-five miles. The old road was in poor condition. As they crawled up the heights south of the valley, one of the trucks slid into a ditch. The men and boys struggled for an hour to free it. The mishap didn't dampen their spirits. Excitement rose as they drove on, singing MST songs and shouting slogans.

"Agrarian reform! When do we want it? Now!"

"Land! When do we want it? Now!"

At 5:00 A.M., the column drew up on the road next to the Cavalcantis' property. The bus doors flew open and men, women and children poured out. Others jumped off the trucks, carrying sickles and machetes. They streamed across the road onto the vacant land.

Tôninho was at Soares' side, as he led the occupation. In no time at all, men and boys were hacking away at the brush to make a clearing for the settlement. Women and children carried their possessions from the trucks and buses. The sense of urgency was real, for every minute counted.

The sharecropper, Luiz Alves de Sá, helped Soares cut down a long, thin tree, for a flagpole. They stripped its branches and planted it in a hole. Soares took out the MST flag and hoisted it to the top of the pole.

A cheer rose from all who lifted their eyes to the red banner floating against the sky.

Tôninho bade them join in a prayer of thanks and to ask for God's protection.

When the worship ended, Luiz Alves de Sá said what was on everyone's mind: "Nothing will get me off this land — *my land!*"

ɔ∕ɔ

Tôninho was alone in the Casa Grande's reception hall, waiting below the carved staircase. In the past, when he came to the engenho with Dr. Juraci, the Cavalcanti mansion had been locked up. A few times, he climbed inside and crept through the dusty rooms, amazed at their number and size. He'd gone into the chapel, where he'd seen a saint's image revered by the family, a little *Santo Tomâs* with only stumps for arms. Later he learned that a Dutch soldier had committed this sacrilege in 1645, when the Cavalcantis resisted the Hollanders who ruled Pernambuco.

In the 1980s, after years of neglect, Clodomir Cavalcanti's wife, Xeniá Freitas de Melo, restored the Casa Grande. Senora Xeniá came to Santo Tomás as a social worker in 1958, employed by Clodomir's father, Durval Cavalcanti, to uplift the lives of the plantation workers. In 1960, Senora Xeniá triumphantly bettered her own fortune by marrying the senhor de engenho's first-born son.

Since becoming a parish priest at Rosário, Tôninho had come to the Casa Grande several times to say mass in the private chapel. The previous November, he celebrated the wedding of Clodomir and Xeniá's third son, Darcy. — On this day in April 2000, when Clodomir Cavalcanti came to greet him, Tôninho's reception was less cordial.

"Is this doing God's will? Do you think it is right to disrespect the laws of Brazil?" Cavalcanti fumed. "This isn't land reform. It is theft, plain and simple. It's chaos and madness."

"It is against God's will to deny hope to the poor. For centuries, Brazil heard the Cry for Land. Until *Sem Terra*, nobody listened," Tôninho said.

Clodomir Cavalcanti is president of the local Brazilian Farmers' Association. The MST's decision to invade Engenho Santo Tomás was a calculated one: Cavalcanti is an outspoken opponent of *Sem Terra's* methods, but strongly condemns landowners who take the law into their own hands. In the past decade, 1,000 peasants have died in land conflicts, the majority killed by hired guns in the service of landowners. Rogue police enforcers have slain MST members, as happened in 1996 when nineteen landless citizens were butchered in a stand-off on a road at Eldorado de Carajás in the state of Pará: The attackers hacked peasants to death with their own farm implements, and executed seven victims in cold blood.

"I'm not against land reform. The government has seized land for 300,000 families. I've no problem with this. I'm against people who think they're above the law," said Cavalcanti.

He would go to court to get the thieves kicked off Engenho Santo Tomás. "I can't guarantee what others will do," he added. He warned the young priest that other members of the Farmers' Association might take action against the squatters to forestall further invasions.

❧

On Wednesday afternoon, Padre Tôninho received word of an imminent assault against "Affonso Ribeiro," the name given the new settlement by its founders. A Magdalena parishioner overheard men in a bar talking about a raid that night.

Tôninho left immediately to warn the families. He took the main highway to Engenho Santo Tomás, which was half the distance; two miles from the plantation, an intersection led to the old road. He reached Affonso Ribeiro in less than thirty minutes.

There'd been three days of furious activity. Each family raised a single-roomed structure of branches covered with black plastic sheeting. Two thatched shelters housed a dispensary and schoolroom, where the children had attended their first classes that morning. Work had started on a communal vegetable garden, as well as the heavy labor of clearing the jungle for fields.

Milton Soares was away in Recife and had left Luiz de Sá in charge of security. There was no panic at the padre's news. Luiz reminded everybody that at any sign of trouble, he would ring a bell to assemble around the flagpole. They'd stand together, men, women and children, to defend *their* land.

Tôninho was staying, too. He took a machete and helped cut tree branches and sticks to make a fence on the side of the encampment facing the road.

At 3:30 A.M., lookouts saw the lights of a car. Luiz ran to the bell and rang it. People began streaming to the flagpole. Those with children to wake took longer, picking up their smallest ones and running with them. Men, women, and teenagers held machetes and sickles. A few carried clubs made from tree limbs.

One after the other, five vehicles rolled to a stop and switched off their lights.

Tôninho had had his head down at a table in the schoolroom. He ran over to Luiz and together they did what they could to calm the people around them.

The siege of terror lasted three hours. Almost immediately, the hired intimidators started firing their shotguns into the air, blast after blast that tore into the night. In moments of silence, their voices carried to the camp, cursing the "communists" and the "red priest." They exploded dynamite bombs beside the stick fence and set a section alight. There was the sound of breaking glass, from bottles of cachaça they emptied.

Just as it was getting light, a pick-up with six men in the back, stormed the gap blasted open in the fence and headed for the shelters. A seething crowd, brandishing farm implements and shouting defiantly, quickly surrounded the truck.

Only the pleas of Padre Tôninho averted a bloody confrontation. Both sides backed off, the men in the pick-up reversing out of the camp, half-drunk and vowing never to abandon their campaign for "justice."

For another hour, the *justiceiros* stood around, talking and smoking, and continuing to hurl threats and insults across the fence. The defenders shook their fists and shouted back. Suddenly, the groups standing in the road broke up and swaggered over to their vehicles. A few more shots in the air and they roared off.

The defenders of Affonso Ribeiro gave a mighty shout. Husbands hugged their wives. Parents grabbed children and hoisted them on their shoulders for a victory march through the camp. It was not over, they knew, but they'd won the first battle. The soil they trod was a step closer to being their own.

❧

Too late, Tôninho caught the glimmer of sun on the pick-up. The hitmen had pulled off the Rosário road, concealed the vehicle behind bushes and lain in wait for him. They fired five shots at the VW, shattering the windshield and blowing out its tires. The last Tôninho knew he was fighting for control, as the car spun off the road, hit a tree stump and overturned.

Clodomir Cavalcanti came down the highway ten minutes later and found him. He jumped out of his Mercedes and ran over to the wreck. Tôninho had cuts and bruises, but miraculously was otherwise unhurt. His rescuer used a tire lever to jimmy open the door and free him.

Twenty minutes later, Tôninho was in the Casa Grande at Santo Tomás, where Clodomir Cavalcanti insisted he rest, until the engenho's doctor came to check him over. They were alone in the big house, Clodomir's wife away on a trip.

Tôninho accepted Cavalcanti's word that he had no part in the attempted assassination nor had he sent armed men to harass the squatters.

While they waited for the doctor, Clodomir remembered the priest's grandfather. "Dr. Juraci tried to make a revolution that could've got him killed. It didn't work. Instead, he came to serve the poor the best way he knew. They revere his name at Santo Tomás still."

"That revolution didn't begin with Dr. Juraci," Tôninho said. "My grandfather, Antônio Paciência, died fighting in the same struggle at Canudos, and countless others, too, in every corner of Brazil where men and women dream of a better life. They are only asking what has been denied them for centuries: justice."

Clodomir Cavalcanti stood silently at a window of the Casa Grande overlooking the valley of his ancestors. In the distance, he could see the patch of jungle with the settlement of Affonso Ribeiro and the people who came to seek a new country. Not for the great men of the earth alone but all Brazilians.

MARIETTE DA SILVA PRADO

*O*n a night in March 2000, the mother of fifteen-year-old Carminha Nascimento reported to the police at Tiberica in São Paulo state that her daughter had been missing for sixteen hours. "She's probably sleeping with some man," a policeman told her. Another advised her to return to the police station in six hours if she had not found her child by then.

Irene Nascimento walked five miles in the rain to a house on the north of the city to seek help. She got there at 2:30 A.M. Despite the hour, Dona Mariette invited her in.

Mariette da Silva Prado listened to the woman's story, and even before she finished, picked up the phone to the police. She let fly with a barrage of words, denouncing them and demanding that they look for Carminha, and keep looking until they found something.

Irene Nascimento was shivering with cold. Dona Mariette made her put on dry clothes, which came from her own wardrobe.

The two women kept a vigil for six hours. Irene often saw Dona Mariette in Riachuelo, the biggest of Tiberica's *favelas* or shantytowns, but never spoke personally with her. Now she sat in her kitchen and talked about Carminha, who worked hard like her mother. Her daughter did washing for families in Pinellas, not far from

Dona Mariette's house. Carminha had a steady boyfriend, Ernesto Leal, a gas station attendant who was saving money for the couple's wedding.

The vigil ended tragically at 9:15 A.M., when the police called to report that they'd found the young woman's body at the Rio Ipê. She'd been raped and stabbed multiple times.

Mariette da Silva Prado was at Irene Nascimento's side when she identified her child in the Tiberica morgue. Afterwards she sped across the city to the meeting of a human rights group, juggling a cell phone as she tore through the streets. Lunch followed with members of the powerful *Clube das Monções*, where the name of Dona Mariette had been anathema. The *Clube* still didn't like her, but were respectful, like old dogs with wounds to remember.

At 3:00 P.M. she swept into the Casa dos Meninos, the House of Children, in the center of Riachuelo. The crowd of kids playing outside rushed to greet her, small hands grasping to touch her dress. She stayed in her office until 8:30 P.M., when she left for the Teatro Machado de Assis to see *Pelago*, a new play about a crooked union boss in São Paulo.

"Living is *necessary*," Dona Mariette says, remarking on her staying power. "A great part of our lives, we need to work for food, for politics, for solidarity. Working like a machine, I'm tremendously tired. Even super-tired I'm Brazilian. I find time just to enjoy living."

❧

Mariette da Silva Prado shares the zest for life of her bandeirante ancestors, pathfinders like the fearless captain of river convoys, Benedito Bueno da Silva, whose statue dominates the entrance to the *Clube das Monções*. — A great hero of the old dogs who bristle at the *entrada* of women like Dona Mariette. — She is bold and tough, and has patience and perseverance. Her tirelessness in pursuing her goals approaches a religious fervor, but she is not a demagogue. She can be warm and funny, and for all her toughness, she has a tender heart.

Co-workers at the Casa dos Meninos, founded by Dona Mariette in 1994, see her at the end of a day setting out with a carload of "her" children. The shelter regularly cares for 200 boys and girls, from toddlers to young adults. Moving among them, Dona Mariette appears to know every one by name. On nights when she drives a group to their homes, she rarely stops work before 10:00 P.M., taking time to chat with parents and others along the way.

There are people, Dona Mariette's neighbors in Pinellas, for example, who've never put a foot in Riachuelo. They glimpse the red and brown canker when they take off or land at Tiberica Airport. They read stories in the *Tribuna de Tiberica* about drugs, shooting wars, blood and abject misery in the favelas. Sporadically, Tiberica's military police put on a fierce show of storming the shantytown, but are as impotent as the Brazilian army that bogged down at the great fort of Riachuelo in Paraguay in the nineteenth century.

Her neighbors find it incredible that she risks her life going to the favela by day, let alone driving around in the dark. "I admire what she's doing but one night she'll be assassinated," said a neighbor. "It will be one of her kids who pulls the trigger and ends her good work."

Dona Mariette has no place for such cynicism. She accepts the perils of traveling in a combat zone, where things can go terribly wrong without the slightest warning. She sees the danger of ignoring the poor as far greater. "A starving child doesn't know what is right or wrong, only that hunger hurts. Really hurts physically. If we won't give the poor a crust of bread, we will lose them. We will have a second Brazil populated by a desperate anarchic people."

Her reputation provides a measure of protection in the favela. — She personally avoids the word "favela" and refers to Riachuelo as a community. — She also makes accommodations with the shadow government: the drug bosses and gang leaders who rule the streets. Residents recall a famous meeting between Dona Mariette and crime boss, Café Carvalho. They sat together at the Seven Steps, a notorious boteco, drinking Antarctica and talking over matters. Which was more than any policemen ever did, unless he had his hand out under the table. Dona Mariette won't accept a penny from Café Carvalho for the Casa dos Meninos.

☙

The meeting with Carvalho in July 1995 was not the first time this courageous woman came face to face with corruption. Seven years earlier, Mariette da Silva Prado was the first woman elected mayor of Tiberica. She was the candidate for the Partido dos Trabalhadores, the Workers' Party, which was in itself a revelation among the upper-class citizens of Tiberica. They were more startled when she trounced Oscar Amaral Dutra, who held the office for twenty-four years with the backing of the Clube das Monções, the richest and most respectable *homen bons* of the city.

Oscar Amaral Dutra was hailed for the "miracle" of Tiberica in the 1970s that saw the município advance from a provincial backwater to a bustling manufacturing center of 190,000. Every Friday, Dutra took lunch with members of the Clube; not grand meals but simple, genial affairs with a discreet word dropped here and there about impediments to progress. Dutra made careful note of everything said by his confederates to figure out how to help them. Sometimes, when his birthday was on the horizon, the old chefe gave a hint of gifts that would be welcome; one year he was collecting saints' images; another time it was seventeenth century silver spoons.

Dona Mariette served two terms combating the Dutra miracle that manifested itself in waste and corruption from the highest municipal offices to subterranean levels of society. The very sewers of Tiberica were a cesspool of bribery. Factories and chemical industries that sprouted along the banks of the Rio Ipê spewed a toxic rainbow into the waterway. The lower reaches of the fetid river snaked through the favelas. City inspectors issued hundreds of summonses over the years. A trickle of fines reached the municipal coffers from small businessmen who didn't know how to handle their affairs judiciously.

The município was a gold mine for fraudsters aided and abetted by employees who never did a day's work in their lives, for the simple reason that they never existed except on the rolls of street cleaners, health officials and other essential workers. As a source of graft, the phantoms were rivaled by ghost projects like the Benedito Bueno da Silva Highway, south of the airport. To show what she was up against, Tiberica's mayor took visitors for a drive on this pot-holed strip that led nowhere. Corrupt officials siphoned off funds for the road and an industrial park that was never built.

Dona Mariette's initial term as mayor was during the presidency of Fernando Collor de Melo, the first democratically elected leader of Brazil since 1960. Collor took the sash with a vow for moral reform and a promise to rein in the *marajás* of Brasília, high civil servants who held the jewels of big government. Collor's presidency ended in disgrace, with his resignation in December 1992 on the eve of his impeachment in a corruption scandal involving $50 million in payoffs and kickbacks. Collor's wife, Rosane, was accused of embezzling funds from the Legion of Welfare, which she headed for the public good. While attending to the wants of needy Brazilians, the First Lady was reportedly spending $20,000 a month on jewelry and clothing.

"The country came alive," says Dona Mariette. "Millions of people wore black and protested in the streets. It was dangerous and it was difficult, for we remember what happened before. The military didn't make a move. The people got Collor out."

Democracy triumphed and for the first time, Brazil resolved a major political crisis by constitutional means and not armed soldiers. However, Dona Mariette is quick to point out that in Brasília, the *marajás* breathed a sigh of relief and went back to business as usual.

"The same power and patronage that you find in a city like Tiberica," she says. "Only here, it can be worse. The farther you get from Brasília, the fewer watchdogs. The pickings may not be so grand, but the cake is still big. There is a piece for everybody."

కీర్తి

Mariette Monteiro da Silva began her life fifty-nine years ago in the manor house at Fazenda Itatinga, which her family has owned since 1758. In that year, Benedito Bueno da Silva ran his great canoes up on the bank of the Rio Tietê at the Place of White Stones, 125 miles north west of São Paulo, ending the mighty journeys through the Brazilian wilderness that began with his forebear, Amador Flôres da Silva. Benedito Bueno's grandson, Ulisses Tavares da Silva, a baron in the Brazilian Empire, planted the first coffee bushes on these lands in the mid-nineteenth century. Today Fazenda Itatinga is still one of the finest and richest coffee plantations in the world.

Itatinga lies barely twenty miles from Tiberica, but they are worlds apart, the whitewashed mansion on the headland overlooking the great bend of the Rio Tietê and the favela of Riachuelo. Dona Mariette moves effortlessly between the two, from a humble shack, where later that week she attended Carminha Nascimento's wake, to the magnificent fazenda with its polished hardwood floors gleaming like mirrors and rooms filled with treasures. She is proud of the family she comes from and can point to this or that item and tell a story associated with one or other of the da Silvas of Itatinga, from Amador Flôres, the "King of Emeralds," to her own father, Roberto da Silva, who has retired to the fazenda.

She spends time with Roberto every week, no matter how busy she is. He is eighty and very active, a fine old Brazilian gentleman who will sometimes greet his daughter in immaculate, well-tailored riding gear, the two going out together on the fazenda. Mariette is still a handsome woman, her hair slightly graying, her dark eyes with a kind, open expression. Seeing them ride side-by-side, father and daughter, offers a glimpse of the intimate bond between them.

Roberto da Silva belongs to the Clube das Moncões, practically an institution of Itatinga's men. Unlike other members, he wasn't surprised when his daughter took up the banner of the Worker's Party. When she was in her twenties, Mariette da Silva Prado was with the right, an organizer of the "March of the Family with God for Liberty" in São Paulo on March 19, 1964. Several hundred thousand upper and middle class women protested the reform government of João Goulart. Twelve days later, the army launched a lightning coup d'etat that overthrew Goulart, extinguished democracy and instituted a military dictatorship that ruled Brazil for twenty-one years.

Mariette was working as a lawyer at the São Paulo headquarters of the family's vast enterprises. When the generals took over — General Marcelo Araujo da Silva of the Minas Gerais branch of the family was one of the coup leaders — she believed, as did most citizens, that they stepped in to save Brazil from a Red revolution.

Roberto also saw no reason to oppose the military. "Goulart was a gaucho from Rio Grande do Sul. What he forgot was that you have to prepare the hoof and the shoe to make a good fit," he says, a reference to Goulart's lack of political tact. The military's first order of day was to build up the country teetering on economic collapse. The da Silva construction company landed multi-million dollar contracts for roads and dams in the north.

In the summer of 1965, Mariette was traveling in Europe, when she met Gilson Prado, the son of a retired São Paulo judge studying in England at the London School of Economics. They were married in 1966 and set up home in São Paulo, where Prado was a lecturer at the University of São Paulo. By 1971, the couple was living with their two young sons, José and Sergio, in an apartment on Avenida Paulista.

Prado was on his way home from the university one day in March 1973, when the São Paulo DOPS picked him up. — The Department for Political and Social Order. — Eleven days after Prado's abduction by the political police, they turned his body over to his widow. Two doctors, Rudolfo Lopes and Hector Saito, signed an autopsy done at São Paulo's Forensic Medical Institute on March 26, 1973. The report registered "HISTORY: According to what was told to us, he died by hanging in his cell, where he was detained."

Gilson Prado's final hours were more truthfully recorded by a fellow detainee, Ana Leite Barreto, twenty-three, testifying at her own trial in the 2nd Military Court at São Paulo in 1974:

> That she was taken to an interrogation room where she witnessed the torture of a prisoner, and that his name was Gilson Prado; . . . that he was naked and had been strapped into in a contraption known as the dragon's chair, made of heavy wood covered with strips of corrugated iron; that they connected electric wires to his ears, teeth, tongue, and fingers and sexual organs, and began administering the shocks; that the magneto produced sparks that burned the skin. A strip of wood at the base of the chair forced the prisoner's legs backwards, so that with each spasm his legs slammed against the bar tearing his flesh. There was a ra-

dio in the room and they turned up the volume when he began to scream; . . . Prado was perversely tortured and tormented for three days. On the morning of the fourth day, I saw his corpse dragged out of his cell, spreading blood over the entire corridor.

Gilson Prado was involved with Popular Action, a Catholic group with a strong following among university students and peasants. After his detention, his wife's family and his father, Judge José Prado, did everything possible to gain his release. Roberto da Silva went to Brasília to see his cousin, Marcello Araujo da Silva, who made some calls and confirmed Gilson was in custody in São Paulo, but his source would not say where they were holding him. Marcello da Silva was a fervent anti-communist who steadfastly believed that the "revolution" was a victory for freedom, no matter how loud the blows from the secret houses of torture.

Mariette came under suspicion. The DOPS raided her apartment and removed books and papers. Roberto wanted his daughter and grandsons to leave the country. She refused to go. "The only crime I committed was to open my eyes," she recalls. "I marched in the streets in support of the military. I never expected them to go to war against our own people. They killed my husband and hundreds more; others were 'disappeared' and never seen again. No one knows how many perished in the terror. None of the culprits has ever had to say they're sorry. They took off their uniforms and put on gray suits. The blood was still on their hands."

☙

It was the gray hour in Riachuelo, when mist from the Rio Ipê blankets the favela. Children began to stir in makeshift beds in the two largest rooms at the Casa dos Meninos. Forty boys and girls from three to seventeen years old spent the night here, with no homes to go to.

By 7:00 A.M. on April 12, 2000, the plaza flanked by the shelter's three buildings was crowded. Parents brought some of the children to the Casa. Most came by themselves, even the smallest ones who walked a mile or more. Their families — often a single working mother — have no option but to leave them alone during the day. They are called children *on* the street, *meninos na rua*, to distinguish them from those whose family ties are broken and live on the streets day and night, children *of* the streets, *meninos da rua*.

"The army of the streets is constantly on the lookout for recruits. It takes them at any age and moves them rapidly through the ranks. In no time at all, the kids are in the front lines fighting to stay alive," says Dona Mariette.

Tiberica's 3,000 street children represent a national problem in microcosm. A lack of childcare facilities and inadequate schooling compound the poverty and horrible family conditions that drive them onto the streets. Half of the street children do not make it past the second grade. Half of them are black or mulatto kids occupying the most perilous ranks of the street army. "With blacks you shoot first and ask later," said a military policeman, when asked why he didn't try to stop and question a sixteen-year-old boy who ran away from him. He put three bullets in the teenager, who bolted because he was embarrassed to be caught looking at a *Playboy* magazine.

Many of Tiberica's street kids are involved in crime, from petty theft to drug dealing and child prostitution. Many admit to substance abuse. Many are not criminals and work the old praça and other downtown locations; they sell lottery tickets, "guard" people's cars, do cartwheels and other drills for a few coins. — Like *voluntários da patria* of the past, the Tiberica youths are reluctant to join Brazil's army of the streets, but have no choice.

Tiberica's police periodically launch operations to "clean things up," storming the praça and scattering the street kids squatting in the shade of the acacia trees. In August 1993, a night raid left three children shot execution-style in an alley behind the square. Off-duty policemen were suspected of carrying out this cleansing, paid for by local businessmen who sought the pest control.

Mariette da Silva pressed for a police investigation that turned up nothing beyond an allegation that drug dealers from São Paulo had the boys murdered. *Tribuna de Tiberica* journalist, Rafael Santos, who investigated the deaths of thirty minors, all under eighteen years of age, concluded that the police killed 30 percent. Professional assassins were responsible for 50 percent of the deaths. The remaining 20 percent were attributed to revenge, gang rivalries or unknown motives. "A code of silence protects the death squads and the police. It is the same secrecy that granted impunity to the security organisms of the military regime," wrote Santos.

☙

By 9:00 A.M., 200 children had settled into the day's activities at the Casa. The center has a staff of eighteen, including ten mothers whose own children attend. The women originally volunteered to work, but are now paid a small wage. Dona Mariette's aim is to motivate Riachuelo's poor to take the initiative for themselves. The Casa's teachers and social workers are young and dedicated to breaking the cycle of violence and distrust that traps the children.

In her office, Dona Mariette received word that a boy had been hanging around the plaza all morning. New kids often come to the Casa when they are frightened and starving or just plain weary of the streets. In each case, a social worker will interview the boy or girl and make an evaluation. The center will not provide sanctuary for genuine criminals and is vigilant against drug peddlers given the vulnerability of its young charges.

Dona Mariette knew the boy, Marcos Gonzaga, a fourteen-year-old who shines shoes in the street outside the five-star Hotel Paraupava in the city center. Marcos' parents migrated from the interior of Bahia to find work at Tiberica; his father moved to São Paulo ten years ago and vanished. At the age of five, Marcos became a "child of clay," going to labor at the brick furnaces outside the city. He put in ten hours a day for the equivalent of US $13 a week, carrying clay, shaping it and piling up bricks for the miracle of Tiberica. In 1997, a pile of bricks toppled over and crushed Marcos' leg. No longer employable in heavy industry, Marcos bought a shoeshine box and went into business next to the gleaming Paraupava.

A year ago, Marcos's sister Rosalia, thirteen, ran away to São Paulo and was given up for lost like their father. Then two days ago, Rosalia was seen at the Tiberica bus station with Teresa Dominguez, the daughter of Pedro Dominguez, king of

Tiberica's garbage dump. Marcos was frightened to go alone to Pedro Rei — "King Peter." He came to ask Dona Mariette for help.

The Tiberica landfill teems with men, women and children who mine the mound like *garimpeiros* looking for gold. Late morning, trucks roll in from the suburbs of the rich. Agile prospectors leap onto vehicles for first grabs at the refuse. Others swarm around the trash that boils and cascades from the trucks. Children burrow into the steaming piles at their parents' feet. Dogs snarl and fight for possession of a meaty bone. Growling trucks, shrill cries of carrion birds, human shouts, howls of savagely beaten mongrels — worse than the din is the stench that permeates this field of treasure.

Pedro Rei knew Dona Mariette from her days as mayor, when she fought to break his monopoly on the landfill. Dominguez engineered a strike by garbage men at the height of summer that forced her to back down. A huge, rude man in his sixties, Pedro Rei controls his malodorous empire from a corrugated iron building packed with his followers from the favelas.

"A great honor to greet the *prefeito!*" he saluted her, when she arrived with Marcos. He offered the "mayor" a seat but she remained standing as she inquired about Rosalia.

Pedro Rei said that Teresa Dominguez had brought Rosalia to his house two days ago. He hadn't seen them since and couldn't say where they'd gone. Did someone in his Court know where the girls were? One man suggested that the pair had gone to Ipêlandia, a suburb next to Tiberica's factories known for its bars and brothels. Pedro Rei agreed this was possible. "My daughter is trash, worth nothing to me," he said.

Driving from the dump, Dona Mariette opened the car windows so that she and the boy could breathe more easily. While some neighbors in Pinellas admire her commitment, others express disgust that a woman from Tiberica's first family crawls over garbage dumps and talks with people like Pedro Rei.

"Some people refuse to accept the reality of Brazil," she says. "They know Orlando and Miami better than their own country. They go shopping on Fifth Avenue, New York. They come back and cry to their servants about how expensive life is in Brazil."

At the dawn of the twenty-first century, Mariette da Silva is in the vanguard of a new revolution. It required no force or visions of El Dorado but began with one man, who changed the conscience of Brazil.

In 1993, Herbert "Betinho" de Souza opened the nation's eyes to the misery around them, when he launched Citizen Action Against Poverty and For Life. What was different from earlier campaigns was that Betinho, a world-renowned sociologist, called on every Brazilian to help the poor. He galvanized 3,000,000 people from all walks of life to go out and assist their neighbors. Millions more dug into their pockets to give money or supplies spurred by a media barrage that laid the truth before them: 32,000,000 Brazilians suffer from chronic hunger, some of the poor consuming no more than 500 calories a day.

Betinho was no stranger to suffering. A hemophiliac who tested positive to the HIV virus in 1985, he lost two brothers to the disease. — Betinho was the first Brazilian to publicly declare that he had AIDS and campaigned to educate people about the epidemic, until his own death in 1999. — Forced to flee the country during the dictatorship, he spent ten years in exile and returned to Brazil in 1979. He launched a grassroots campaign for "adjective-less" democracy involving every citizen in building a new society, not with words but actions.

"Betinho gave a face to millions of Brazilians who were pariahs in their own land. No one expects poverty to end tomorrow. The rich are getting richer and the poor poorer than ever, but they are no longer faceless. When the weakest and littlest one gives up life for lack of food, we cannot say we didn't know," says Dona Mariette.

In Ipêlandia, Dona Mariette and Marcos learned that the girls were outside the Goodyear factory earlier in the morning. They found a street kid who knew Teresa Dominguez and volunteered to show them where she took the men who paid her for sex. He led them to a vacant lot a block from the tire factory, with an abandoned bus sitting just off the road. As they drove up, two men climbed out of the bus, joking with each other as they headed back to work after their lunch break.

Marcos' sister, Rosalia, was resting on an old mattress in the filth-strewn bordello. The thirteen-year-old was obviously pregnant. At first, she was aggressive toward Dona Mariette, adding her voice to Teresa's demands that they be left alone. Then her bravado faltered and she let Marcos take her hand and lead her outside. Teresa refused help and left them, swinging her hips derisively as she sauntered back to the streets.

Somewhere in Tiberica in four months' time, Rosalia's child will be born in the favelas. It will give its first cry in an unjust country. Brazilians like Mariette da Silva Prado hear that cry.

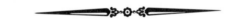

BRUNO RAMOS SALGADO

*T*ajira sat cross-legged in the canoe, bow and arrow ready, as the craft drifted downstream with the engine shut off. He was in the bow, his almond-shaped eyes narrowing as he swept the water. A ripple of green falling to earth in the forest caught his eye. Like the great hunter he was, the boy didn't let the movement distract him.

The Old Devil was taking a siesta in the back of the canoe. To his enemies, Bruno Ramos Salgado was a terror of the Serra dos Paresís in southern Rondonia, where he made his home the past twenty-five years. Plunderers penetrating the wilds to cut down mahogany or dig for gold avoided the green hell and the Old Devil's fire. There was a story of three loggers caught by Salgado and immolated on a pyre built from timber they were hauling away. It was false, but the alleged perpetrator encouraged and embellished the tale to warn off trespassers.

To those who loved him, the eighty-year-old was a living hero who risked his life to save the forest people of Rondonia. Salgado worked for thirty years with the

SPI, the Indian Protection Service, and the National Foundation for the Indigenous (FUNAI), which replaced the SPI in 1967. He belonged to a group of agents dedicated to the credo of Colonel Cândido Rondon, the SPI's founder: "Die if necessary, but never kill." In 1975, Salgado resigned when no action was taken against an SPI man accused of accepting pay-offs from a cattle rancher: The rancher's henchmen poisoned two families of Pacaas Novas with arsenic. Between 1950 and 1968, the Pacaas Novas declined from 4,500 to 400 people, their extinction accelerated by the building of the Cuiabá-Porto Velho road that brought a multitude of colonizers to the Far West.

Bruno was fifty-five when he left FUNAI and went to live at Kaimari in the Serra dos Paresís. His father, Izaias Salgado, had maintained a telegraph station at this spot on the Apidiá River. Bruno was born here, the son of Izaias and Iara, a Paresí woman; he spent his childhood at the station and ferry point. The place never grew beyond a small village, becoming more isolated when the road from Cuiabá passed sixty miles to the north.

Bruno never married, and when he returned to Kaimari in 1975, he was alone in the world. He settled down to lead a simple life among the twenty families in the village. From time to time, interlopers who threatened the peace of the forest interrupted his retirement. The Old Devil would awake to put the fear of God into them.

He wasn't responsible for the slaying of three loggers in the Serra dos Paresís in March 1990, but tracked and confronted them before they were murdered. He despised the timber cutters for destroying the rainforest: Where they took a single mahogany tree, they toppled or uprooted twenty-eight other trees. To get the mahogany out, the loggers used bulldozers to tear passages through the jungle; the logging roads opened the way for ranchers and colonists to take possession of the land.

He'd gone to warn the loggers that they'd be expelled if they invaded the forest at Kaimari. — Three nights after his visit, a rival band of loggers attacked and killed the men.

Bruno was first on the scene, early the next morning. The raiders had destroyed the camp and removed everything of value. Bruno sent two villagers with him to fetch the police at Pimenta Bueno, the nearest town on the Cuiabá road. He started back to Kaimari, walking through the forest.

A mile beyond the camp, a cry stopped him in his tracks. He found a small child hiding in the trees, terrified and weeping.

Bruno had seen the four-year-old the previous day. His father was one of the slain loggers: Edson Monteiro, a Pataxó from the state of Bahia, whose Indian name was Apuriná. Bruno asked him why he brought the child on such hazardous work. The boy's mother had died at Porto Velho where they lived, and there'd been no one to care for him.

It was ten years since Bruno found Tajira in the forest and took him to Kaimari. He sent letters to friends at FUNAI asking their help in tracing the boy's relatives. After eighteen months without success, he gave up and accepted that the child was staying with him.

Tajira spotted a good-sized catfish in the shallows. He gripped the bow and arrow, keeping perfect balance as he straightened his body. He took a deep breath and held it, bracing himself as he drew back the bowstring. His eye followed the catfish, judging the right moment. The bowstring hummed, the arrow flew straight and true, cutting the water and striking home.

"Aiiee!" Tajira cried in triumph.

The Old Devil opened one eye. "You woke me!"

"Sorry, senhor Bruno," Tajira said. He pointed excitedly at his catch. "A *big* one!"

"Bah!" Bruno growled. Then the deep lines on his face broke into a smile. "Bravo, my little *Indio*."

Tajira beamed with pride.

ᘓ

Late one morning in April 2000, a month after Tajira caught the catfish, Bruno was sitting on a chair outside his house. He was waiting for the boy to come home from a mission school, four miles up the Apidiá River.

Kaimari village stood on the riverbank, its thirty wattle and daub dwellings facing three sides of a small plaza that fronted the water. Two houses doubled up as a shop and a boteco. Broken boat engines littered one property, the place of senhor Evaristo, an itinerant mechanic who landed here many years ago. Most of Kaimari's residents tended fields outside the village or fished and hunted for their needs.

Five families, thirty souls in all, were Paresí Indians; other villagers like Bruno Salgado were part Paresí. In the past, Bruno used his FUNAI connections, attempting to have Kaimari and the lands around the village demarcated as a Paresí area. FUNAI has successfully registered half the territory claimed by Brazil's 350,000 Indians, from 210 indigenous peoples: The Indian lands represent 11 percent of the national territory, about 360,000 square miles, most in the Amazon region where half the Indians live. The Paresís failed to satisfy the Ministry of Justice that Kaimari was their traditional domain, Bruno's father having founded the village.

The Paresís never doubted that their ancestors visited this forest. The name Izaias Salgado chose in the 1920s honored a legendary seventeenth century elder and shaman of the Paresí, Kaimari, chief of eighteen villages two days' journey to the south. Paresí hunters who ventured to these woods had come face to face with the Great Spirit: the anaconda. Very occasionally, a Paresí would still find one of the great serpents, which by legend helped men steal the secrets of women. The sacred houses and the huge trumpets that represented the snakes no longer exist. But the modern hunters still flee from the anaconda, like the worms men were when warrior women ruled the earth.

Around noon, Bruno saw Tajira's canoe approach the landing. Four children from the village went to school three mornings a week, taking lessons from the wife of a Baptist missionary. Bill and Nancy Proffitt came from Fort Worth, Texas and wanted to plant their church at Kaimari, but the Old Devil worked against them. It wasn't a question of religion, for he hadn't been inside a church in twenty years. Like other strangers who penetrated the forest, the Proffitts' incursion brought colonization closer. The family and their three boys had spent a year at Manaus, learning the Portuguese language and preparing for their crusade in the jungle, part of a stream of evangelicals coming from North America to convert the Brazilians to Protestantism.

The Proffitts settled at the site of an abandoned Jesuit mission, where they lived the past eighteen months, their struggle against the inferno of pests as mighty as the battle for the hearts and souls of the people of Kaimari and two other villages in the forest. The pastor and his wife found great reward in nine children who came to the one-room school. Their own boys sat on the same benches. The young Proffitts though already filled with grace often fell victim to the demons of the forest.

"They're becoming as wild as their playmates," Bill Proffitt wrote in *Green Pastures*, the missionary family's Internet newsletter. He posted photos of his little savages and their friends, including Tajira half-naked in a ragged pair of khaki pants, playing soccer with the boys from Texas.

Bruno visited the mission a few times, including the previous July 4, when the Proffitts invited him to celebrate their Independence Day, a brave affair with hot dogs and apple pie baked by the missionary's wife. Evaristo the Mechanic became indignant, seeing the Stars and Stripes fluttering next to the Brazilian flag. "The Americans want to steal Brazil," Evaristo protested.

"Not these Americans," Bruno said. "They're looking for the Garden of Eden. I hope they won't be disappointed like so many who came to make their conquest of Brazil."

∾

Tajira beached the canoe and bounded across the plaza, shouting a greeting as he ran. The past years could have been an ordeal for an Old Devil, with his world turned upside down by a rambunctious youngster, but it was not so. Instead, he knew only joy, and sometimes a tinge of regret that he not had a son of his own.

Now he felt sadness, too, for he'd made a decision that must lead to their separation.

"What did senhora Nancy teach you today?" he asked.

Tajira said the senhora told the class about Americans who went to the moon. He didn't believe the story until the teacher showed them a book with pictures of the astronauts.

"It's true," Bruno said. "The Americans are everywhere. Right here in our jungle, senhor Proffitt and his tribe. In this sertão so far from their home, they might as well be on the moon."

"Daniel says when he is big, he is going to live on Mars." — Daniel is the Proffitt's ten-year-old son. — "I told him I'm happy to stay in Brazil with senhor Bruno."

"When I am gone, who will be there for you?"

"Senhor Bruno is going away?"

"I'm eighty years, Tajira. I have not much time left."

"Senhor Bruno is *not* sick. You are *very* old, but strong like . . . an Old Devil!" Tajira heard people call senhor Bruno this, especially when they wanted him to fix their troubles.

Bruno laughed. "So! While this old devil has strength left, I want us to leave Kaimari and take the bus from Pimenta Bueno. It will be a long, hard journey."

"Where are we going?" Tajira asked.

"To find your father's people."

☙

Bruno Salgado still cut a formidable figure, over six feet tall with a wild mane of gray hair and piercing dark eyes. His trousers were shabby, his shirt collar frayed and discolored. He had no jacket but wore an ancient Shetland jersey given to him by a Glasgow professor studying the Nambikwara people at his last FUNAI post in Mato Grosso. The jersey was a ruin, elbow patches paper thin, cuffs trailing threads of green wool, but still cherished after thirty years of wear and tear in the jungle.

Bruno and Tajira left Kaimari in a canoe with two villagers, who took them up the Apidiá to a landing below the Porto Velho-Cuiabá road. They hitched a ride with a truck to Pimenta Bueno, where they caught the Cuiabá bus at midnight.

Bruno fell asleep almost immediately they roared off into the dark. Tajira remained awake, his face pressed against the window, staring at the swath of light next to the bus. The forest rose darkly beside the road, here and there a small clearing with a one-or-two roomed house standing in darkness. Then suddenly, the trees were gone and the land lay open, mile after mile cleared for cattle ranching. Along one stretch across the Mato Grosso border, the bus drove through banks of smoke from smoldering fires, tree stumps aglow from the inferno.

They made frequent stops on the way to Cuiabá. Every three or four hours, the *motorista* rolled up to a "restaurant," often no more than an ugly concrete block that represented the dream of a new life on the frontier. Every month since the road opened, thousands of dirt-poor farmers came to clear the forest, cutting down trees one by one, selling the valuable wood and torching the rest. They planted a crop of manioc, then some beans, rice, and squash; within a few seasons, the poor quality soil was exhausted.

Some pioneers moved on to new land, where they repeated the debilitating cycle. Some sought work in towns like Pimenta Bueno, crowding into favelas as squalid as shantytowns they fled in São Paulo and other cities. Some gave up the fight against the forest and retreated to their roadside habitations, where they hung a hand-painted sign, "Restaurant Formosa," and began to make their fortune.

The ride to Cuiabá lasted twenty-two hours. Bruno climbed stiffly off the bus, his big shoulders sagging. Tajira was also tired, as much from excitement as weariness. Bruno wanted to get a room across the street from the terminal and rest before tackling the next leg of the journey, 600 miles to Brasília. He stopped to inquire about the Brasília bus: There were two cancellations on an express leaving within the hour. Somehow, the Old Devil mustered the energy to get back on the road.

They reached Brasília the next afternoon, arriving at the Rodoviária toward sunset. The futuristic capital built in 1,000 days in the late 1950s has 2,000,000 inhabitants in its super quadrants and satellite cities. The Candangos are fiercely proud of the white marble palácios and towers rising on the savannah. At no time is the vision of Utopia more striking than at sunset when the cerrado sky lights the Plaza of the Three Powers and turns the Lago do Paranoá into molten gold.

Bruno called an old friend, Corinne Nery Mangoni, who worked for FUNAI. Corinne picked them up at the bus station and took them to her house on the shore of Paranoá, where she lived with her husband, Jorge, a secretary in the foreign ministry. She was a young anthropologist at FUNAI in 1975, when Salgado left the agency, but kept in contact with him over the years. She helped him when he originally tried to find Tajira's relatives.

They stayed with the Mangonis for three days. The rigors of busing across half the country exhausted Bruno. He spent hours sprawled in a chair at the poolside, while Tajira swam and played in the water. For a boy from the forest of Kaimari, visiting Brasília was like being on the moon or Mars even; everything was a wonder to him.

Corinne Mangoni drove Tajira around Brasília, stopping in at her office, where functionários of FUNAI met the boy and wished him luck in finding his Pataxó family.

When Corinne was showing Tajira the city, she pointed out a monument in Compromisso Square, which the people of Brasília erected in 1997 to pay homage to Galdino, a hero of the Pataxós. Tajira stood respectfully in front of the sculpture symbolizing Justice and Freedom.

Corinne spared the boy details of how Galdino Jesus dos Santos, a Pataxó Indian had come to be honored. On April 20, 1997, the forty-four-year-old Galdino was in Brasília, where he arrived as a member of a delegation pressing a land claim. Early that Sunday morning, locked out of the building where he was staying, he slept on a bench in Compromisso Square. Five youths aged sixteen to nineteen, from well-to-do families poured gasoline over Galdino and set him alight. "It was a joke. We thought he was a beggar," they said when arrested and confronted with the atrocity. Only hours before, Galdino took part in observances for the "Day of the Indian."

&

A week after leaving Kaimari, Bruno and Tajira resumed their journey, taking a bus traveling from Brasília to the south of Bahia. Their destination was Santa Cruz Cabrália, on the coast fifteen miles north of Porto Seguro, where a group of Pataxó Indians lived. — On April 23, 1500, the Portuguese captain, Pedro Álvares Cabral dropped anchor off the islet of Coroa Vermelha in Santa Cruz Cabrália and claimed the land for Portugal. Five hundred years later, Brazil planned to celebrate the event in the shadow of a Cross that marked the spot where the first mass was held at Coroa Vermelha. From every corner of the country, too, surviving Indians traveled to Bahia to remember their ancestors who paid a mortal price for their "discovery."

Bruno and Tajira broke the 1,000-mile trip from Brasília at Montes Claros in the mist-shrouded Serra do Espinhaço, the highlands of Minas Gerais, where seventeenth century bandeirantes like Amador Flôres da Silva clawed their way along the jagged slopes in search of emeralds and gold. Bruno and Tajira spent the night in a small hotel three blocks from the bus station. They were up at 4.30 in the morning to catch the bus to Porto Seguro.

The passengers included a class from a high school at Montes Claros, going to the 500-year celebrations with their history teacher, who sat across the aisle from Bruno. The teacher, Carlos Alberto Texeira, was a Portuguese who immigrated to Brazil from Mozambique in 1974, after the African colony became independent.

Teixeira was a strong defender of Portugal's role in the conquest of the Tupiniquin, Tupinambá and other Indians. He quoted from the letter of Pero Vaz da Caminha, who sailed with Cabral's fleet: "This people is good and of pure simplicity,

and there can easily be stamped upon them whatever belief we wish to give them."
The Portuguese greeted the natives as innocents, who would soon be model Christians. "They were dealing with cannibals, who butchered each other," said Teixeira.
"They had to pacify and civilize the savages and win this land inch by inch."

"Few Indians were cannibals," Bruno said. There were as many as five million
Indians when Cabral landed. "The colonists made war on the Indians, and killed or
enslaved them. Diseases from Europe decimated those who were left."

Teixeira argued that many Portuguese perished in the conquest, including
Brazil's first bishop, Pedro Sardinha, shipwrecked and eaten with one hundred other
survivors who landed in the jaws of the Caeté. Thousands of *marinheiros* were lost at
sea before reaching Brazil's shores. Thousands of colonists sacrificed their lives in
Indian attacks on settlements and against bandeiras that marched into the jungle.

"The Portuguese were not brutes without reason. They were brave men and
women, who came to build a country in this wilderness. Without them, Brazil would
not exist."

It was a long way to Porto Seguro and the argument went back and forth.
Bruno remained imbued with the spirit of Rondon and the belief that Brazil owed a
debt to the Indians. This meant not only redressing past wrongs but respecting the
forest peoples' traditions.

Teixeira said he believed in teaching respect for the Indians. "But I can't agree
with people who say that the Stone Age life of a Yanomami is superior to anything
that modern civilization can offer." It would be as unjust to deny the Indians a place
in twenty-first century Brazil, as any wrongs of the past half millennium or to pretend that it was possible to halt civilization and progress. Was it preservation or exploitation to keep Indians isolated in a human zoo, where anthropologists and journalists from New York and Berlin came to study them?

Bruno had agonized over similar questions. In the past, Brazilian government
policy had been toward assimilation of the Indians, a process Indianists believed
could take forty to sixty years. Since 1988, the idea of integrating the indigenous
people was dropped in favor of recognition of the rights of the Indian nations and
their traditional territories. It was one thing to decree that 10 percent of Brazil's national soil belonged to the Indians, but something else to guarantee peaceful occupation and enjoyment of those lands.

Bruno's last FUNAI post had been with the Nambikwara in Mato Grosso. He
was there when the government began forcibly to remove groups of Nambikwara to
make way for BR364, the Cuiabá-Porto Velho highway. Driven from their ancient
wandering grounds and dumped in strange places, the little nomads died in great
numbers from epidemics — and from the sickness of despair. Bruno was no longer in
FUNAI, when the Nambikwara received a grant of the 67,000-hectare Sarare reserve
in the 1980s.

When the area was finally registered in 1990, 6,000 illegal placer miners were
active in Sarare. The government expelled the miners in 1992, by which time they
had ravaged thousands of hectares of land and polluted Sarare's river and streams.
Four years later, miners and loggers continued to trespass in the reserve. Nambikwara
resistance was met by violent attacks against their villages and property.

"It is impossible to bring back the past or isolate the Indians from the future," Bruno said, responding to Teixeira. He looked at the boy next to him. "Change is inevitable. Who will be there for them: The destroyers or the builders of civilization?"

☙

Bruno and Tajira arrived at Porto Seguro on April 25, three days after the official start of festivities. Sixty thousand people jammed the seaside resort and neighboring town of Santa Cruz de Cabrália. There was a massive show of force by 5,000 military police deployed to maintain order. On the opening day, police used clubs and tear gas to stop a march of 2,000 Indians and Afro-Brazilians on the road from Cabrália to Porto Seguro. They took 140 protestors to jail, including thirty Catholic priests and lay workers. Peace was preserved. Then the sky opened up and a torrential rain drowned out the celebrations.

At Porto Seguro, Bruno and the boy caught a mini-bus to Cabrália. Ten miles down the highway, the bus stopped at a roadblock. They were with eight other passengers, all ordered off by the police.

"What are you doing here, old man?" a sergeant asked Bruno.

"That's my business," he said.

"You've come to make trouble?"

"No, sergeant . . . Brazil is still a free country, isn't it?"

The policeman glared at Bruno, but didn't press him further.

When the mini-bus started off, a man next to Bruno laughed. "You're lucky the sergeant didn't break your balls, old fellow."

"What are they frightened of? A few hundred Indians aren't going to drive them back into the sea."

"They want us to put on paint and feathers and dance, as our forefathers did when Cabral landed. They will listen to our songs and chants. They don't want to hear the noise of democracy!"

Vitorino Francisco Fonseca was a Pataxó from Monte Pascoal, which lay 120 miles to the south. Pitiacú, his people called him. In August 1999, Pitiacú and other Pataxó occupied the 58,750-acre Monte Pascoal National Park and declared it theirs. Monte Pascoal was the first landmark sighted by Cabral and his men, as their ships approached *Terra de Santa Cruz*. The park was one of several disputed areas claimed by the Pataxó in Bahia.

Vitorino listened to Bruno's story about the journey to find Tajira's relatives.

"Ticua Mattos knows all the Pataxó families around here," said Vitorino. He offered to take Bruno and Tajira to the woman's house.

It was the eve of the commemorative mass at Coroa Vermelha, where Cabral and his men knelt on April 26, 1500 to give thanks to God. The tiny seaside town swarmed with outsiders, the most colorful of whom strode the streets in their traditional dress. Delegates from 186 indigenous groups had been at Cabrália the past week taking part in a national conference dedicated to '500 Years of Resistance.'

"We are not like our ancestors, who picked up war clubs and fought with each other," said Vitorino. "Today, we see how few we are in Brazil. We have to stand together to survive."

Ticua Mattos' lived on the Patoxó reservation at Coroa Vermelha, a community that had been ignored for decades, eking out a living by selling trinkets to tourists who made the pilgrimage to the Cross on the beach. The anniversary celebrations brought a swarm of government officials to negotiate with the Pataxó for the building of a Discovery Park on their land housing a museum and handicrafts mall.

Ticua was in her eighties, a grand old dame of the Pataxó, who looked suspiciously at the *vagabundo* brought to her door by Vitorino Fonseca.

"Who is this old beggar, Pitiacú?" she asked.

"Not a beggar, senhora Ticua, but a friend." Vitorino introduced Bruno Salgado. "He has come all the way from Rondonia to look for the boy's family." Tajira was standing behind them. "The boy's parents were Pataxós from Bahia. They both died and left the boy behind. Senhor Bruno found him in the forest and cared for him."

Ticua stood in her doorway. She shuffled forward into the light. "Come here, boy, let me look at you."

Tajira smiled as the old woman studied his face.

"He is the son of Apurinã," she said without hesitation. "He went to cut wood in Mato Grosso ten years ago and never came back."

℘

The Old Devil stood at the edge of the huge crowd at Coroa Vermelha. The April morning was overcast, a blustery wind bending the palms at the altar in front of the towering Cross. The papal legate, Cardinal Angelo Sodano, presided over the mass attended by 300 bishops and fellow clerics, celebrating the hour in which Friar Henrique of Coimbra prayed with Cabral's men and the Tupiniquin who rejoiced with the Long Hairs.

After identifying Tajira, Ticua Mattos had sent for Apurinã's brother, Obajara, a Pataxó elder, who came immediately to her house, astounded by the news about his nephew. There was sadness at the realization that the boy's parents were dead, but joy nonetheless that he was back with his people. And gratitude to Bruno Salgado, who had brought Tajira to them, many coming to thank him as word spread about the boy.

Tajira had stayed close to his old protector, not a little shy and overwhelmed by all the attention. He had almost no memory of his mother and father, but senhor Bruno always reminded him he was a Pataxó, a people who lived close to the sea. — He saw the ocean for the first time at Porto Seguro. "O, senhor Bruno, the sea is so big!" he cried, and then added. "A good place to fish!" He was going to take a canoe out onto the blue water and catch the biggest fish in the world for senhor Bruno.

It was close to midnight before people stopped coming to the house. Ticua Mattos made a place for the pair to sleep on makeshift beds.

"Thank you, senhor Bruno, for bringing me here," Tajira said. "I am happy to see my family."

"I'm glad, Tajira."

"I will be very sad, when you go." Over the past week, Bruno took time to explain why it was better for the boy to live with the Pataxó, and not at Kaimari where he'd have no family when Bruno was gone.

"It is best for you," he said in a gruff voice.

Now, as Bruno stood in the crowd gathered for the commemoration mass, his gaze moved across to the group of Pataxós near the altar. The elder Obajara was with his three sons. Uxarra, the oldest, was the same age as Tajira.

The two boys met the day before, quickly finding that they had one thing especially in common: Uxarra was also an avid fisherman, riding the waves out to the bar in the bay of Cabrália, for the big ones.

Early that morning, Uxarra came to fetch Tajira and take him to his house, where Araci, Obajara's wife, gave the boy a Pataxó skirt to wear. Araci painted Tajira's face with lines of red urucu dye. Then she helped him put on a headdress crowned with the brilliant red and blue feathers of Macaw.

Bruno Salgado caught sight of the boy, standing next to Uxarra. "Tajira Pataxó!" he whispered and smiled to himself. "Go safely, my little *Indio!*"

Then the smile vanished from the Old Devil's face, as he heard the voice of the Most Reverend Jayme Chemello, president of the Brazilian National Bishop's Conference, rise with a solemn declaration:

"We ask God to forgive the sins committed against the human rights and dignity of the Indians, the first inhabitants of this land, and the blacks who were brought to this country as slaves."

Pataxo, Shavante, Nambikwara, Yanonami and Indians from all over Brazil listened solemnly by the sands of Coroa Vermelha, as descendants of the discoverers asked forgiveness for the sins and errors of five centuries.

There was no Tupiniquin to hear the apologia.

Aruanã watched as they came closer. The sun was gone behind the trees, and he found it difficult to discern the craft, but he stood rooted a while longer before he realized that he must hasten to the village and tell what he had seen. This made him gaze at the horizon again, to be absolutely certain, for it was a fantastic discovery for a man who had gone to seek no more than shells. They were there, darkening images now, these canoes that had come from the end of the earth.

GLOSSARY

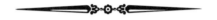

agregado	'associate'; agricultural labor on large estate; in colonial times, one of the retainers or "men" of the master of the Casa Grande
aldeia	a village, particularly mission village
alferes	second lieutenant
armador	'supplier'; person who finances and outfits expeditions
arroba	measure of weight, about 15 kilograms
azulejos	glazed tiles
bábá	priestess of Afro-Brazilian religion; nursemaid
bagaço	baggase; refuse material of crushed sugarcane; 'cane trash'
bandeira	armed adventurers, particularly from São Paulo, who marched into the backlands in search of Indians and gold, or in exploration
bandeirante	a member of a bandeira
bateque	Afro-Brazilian dance
beata	devout woman
berimbau	stringed musical instrument
bogavante	paddler
boucan	grill for meat
branco	white
caatinga	'white forest'; Indian name for stunted forest and scrub in drought-prone northeastern Brazil
caboclo	'copper-colored'; first applied to a 'civilized' Indian; a person of mixed Indian and white ancestry; a rural person or hillbilly
cachaça	a rum made from the juice of sugar cane
caipora	traditional Indian mythological being; goblin or malevolent spirit
câmara	chamber; town council
cambão	'yoke'; labor owed to a landowner for use of land
cana	(sugar)cane
capanga	personal bodyguard; henchman
capitão	captain
Carioca	resident of Rio de Janeiro

carpideira	hired mourner
casa grande	big house or mansion of sugar plantation
cerrado	savannah
chefe	boss, leader
colégio	in colonial times, school kept by Jesuits; present day, a private school
colono	colonist; a small farmer
compadre	godfather; sponsor; friend
conde	count
conquista	conquest
conselheiro	counselor, adviser, wise person
coronel	colonel; a political boss in a *município*
Cristão-Novo	a converted Jew or new Christian in the colonial era
curandeiro(a)	medicine man or woman, who practices the healing arts
degregado	'degraded one'; criminal exiled to colonial Brazil to serve out sentence
devassa	official inspection or inquiry
dona de casa	female head of household
donatário	recipient of hereditary land grant in sixteenth century
doutor	doctor; person with university degree; honorary form of address
emboaba	'feather legs'; pejorative term for an outsider, especially Portuguese newcomers to Brazil in eighteenth century
engenho	sugar plantation; sugar-mill
entrada	expedition into interior of Brazil by band of explorers
escravo	slave
estância	ranch or country estate
estero	marsh
Exú	divine messenger and tutelary spirit of Afro-Brazilian religion
favela	shantytown
fazenda	estate; ranch or plantation
fazendeiro	owner of a large landed estate
fidalgo	Portuguese nobleman, gentleman
fogo	fire
futebol	football
gaucho	cattleman from southern Brazil or Argentina
genipapo	black dye or body paint, from the genip tree
governador	governor
homem bom	'a good man'; member of upper class of Brazilian colonial society; *homen bons* (pl.)
iaiá	in colonial times, familiar term in addressing girls and young women
Inconfidência	a conspiracy for independence; particularly 1789 *Inconfidência Mineira* plot in Minas Gerais
Indio	Indian
infante	crown prince

jangada	raft
lavrador	small landholder
liberto	freed slave
lingua geral	'general language'; language derived by Jesuits from various Indian dialects
macaco	monkey
maconha	marijuana
maloca	large Indian dwelling occupied by several families
marinheiro	seaman
mãe	mother
mãe de santo	female sacerdote of Afro-Brazilian religion
mameluco	offspring of Indian and white
mazombo	derogatory epithet for one born in America of Portuguese parents
menino	young child
mestizo	a person of mixed blood
município	administrative division, roughly a county
orixás	generic name for Yoruba deities
oitava	'an eighth'; an ancient weight for gold and precious gems
padre	priest
pagé	shaman; medicine man; witch doctor
pai	father
Paulista	inhabitant of or referring to the state of São Paulo
pé	foot
peça	'piece'; a slave
pelourinho	pillory
posseiros	peasant squatters
praça	town square or plaza
prêto	black; Afro-Brazilian
pulperia	bar
puta	whore
quilombo	fugitive slave colony
ratazana	rat
reduction	Spanish Jesuit mission village
reis	royal; old Brazilian currency
roça	forest clearing
riacho	creek or stream
rua	street
samba	Brazilian dance of African origin
sangue	blood
seca	drought
senhor de engenho	owner of a sugar estate
senzala	slave quarters on a plantation
serra	mountains
sertanejo	frontiersman; inhabitant of the *sertão*
sertão	the interior, backlands, wilderness, especially northeastern Brazil

sinhá	a young lady of the Casa Grande
sinhazinha	term of endearment used by slaves in addressing their mistress's daughter
tenente	lieutenant
terreiro	area for drying coffee beans; also Afro-Brazilian religious center
terremoto	earthquake
tropeiro	a driver of pack animals
urubu	common black vulture
urucú	dye-yielding shrub, used by Indians for orange-red body-paint
usina	modern sugar refinery and plantation
vaqueiro	cowboy of northeastern Brazil
vila	small town
voluntário	volunteer, particularly during Paraguayan War
Xangô	deity of Afro-Brazilian religion, god of lightning and thunder